THE BROTHERHOOD OMNIBUS

THE BROTHERHOOD OMNIBUS

David Morrell

HEADLINE

First published in this omnibus edition in 1993
by HEADLINE BOOK PUBLISHING PLC

This omnibus edition was originally published in three separate volumes.
The Brotherhood of the Rose was published in 1985 by New English Library;
The Fraternity of the Stone was published in 1986 by New English Library;
The League of Night and Fog was published in 1987 by New English Library;
Subsequently all three volumes have been published in hardcover
and paperback
by HEADLINE BOOK PUBLISHING PLC

10 9 8 7 6 5 4 3 2 1

British Library Cataloguing in Publication Data

Morrell, David
    Brotherhood Omnibus: 'Brotherhood of the
    Rose', 'Fraternity of the Stone',
    'League of Night and Fog'
    I. Title
    813.54 [F]

ISBN 0–7472–0864–6

Typeset by Keyboard Services, Luton

Printed and bound in Great Britain by
Clays Ltd, St Ives PLC

HEADLINE BOOK PUBLISHING PLC
Headline House
79 Great Titchfield Street
London W1P 7FN

CONTENTS

THE
BROTHERHOOD
OF THE ROSE

for Donna
The years go faster, my love grows stronger.

Teach them politics and war so their sons
may study medicine and mathematics in order
to give their children a right to study
painting, poetry, music, and architecture

– John Adams

CONTENTS

PROLOGUE

THE ABELARD SANCTION

REFUGE

Paris. September 1118.
Peter Abelard, handsome canon of the church of Notre Dame, seduced his attractive student, Heloise. Fulbert, her uncle, enraged by her pregnancy, craved revenge. In the early hours of a Sunday morning, three assassins hired by Fulbert attacked Abelard on his way to mass, castrated him, and left him to die from his wounds. He lived but, fearing further reprisals, sought protection. First, he ran to the monastery of Saint Denis near Paris. There, while recovering from his injuries, he learned that political elements desperate for Fulbert's approval were conspiring once more against him. For a second time, he took flight – to Quincey, near Nogent, where he founded a safe house that he named 'The Paraclete,' the Comforter, in honor of the Holy Ghost.

And finally found sanctuary.

SAFE HOUSES/
GROUND RULES

Paris. September 1938.
On Sunday, the twenty-eighth, Edouard Daladier, minister of defense
for France, broadcast the following radio announcement to the French
people:

> Early this afternoon I received an invitation from the German
> government to meet with Chancellor Hitler, Mr Mussolini, and Mr
> Neville Chamberlain in Munich. I have accepted the invitation.

The next afternoon, while the Munich meeting was taking place, a
pharmacist in the service of the Gestapo recorded in his logbook that
the last of the five black 1938 Mercedes had passed the checkpoint at
his corner drugstore and had arrived before the innocuous-looking
stone facade of 36 Bergener Strasse in Berlin. In each case, a powerfully built plain-clothed driver stepped out of the car, surveyed the
pedestrians on the busy street without seeming to do so, and opened
a passenger door from which the only occupant, a well-dressed elderly
man, emerged. As soon as the driver had escorted his passenger safely
through the thick wooden door of the three-story residence, he proceeded to a warehouse three blocks away to wait for further
instructions.

The last gentleman to arrive left his hat and overcoat with a sentry
behind an enclosed metal desk in an alcove to the right of the door.
For reasons of tact, he wasn't searched, but he was asked to surrender
his briefcase. He wouldn't need it, after all. No notes would be permitted.

The sentry examined the man's credentials, then pushed a button
beside the Luger beneath his desk. At once, a second Gestapo agent
appeared from an office behind the visitor to escort him to a room at
the end of the hall. The visitor entered. Remaining behind, the agent
shut the door.

The visitor's name was John 'Tex' Auton. He was fifty-five, tall,
ruggedly handsome, with a salt-and-pepper mustache. Prepared for
the business at hand, he sat in the one remaining empty captain's
chair and nodded to the four men who'd arrived before him. He did
not need to be introduced; he knew them already. Their names were
Wilhelm Smeltzer, Anton Girard, Percival Landish, and Vladimir

Lazensokov. They were the directors of espionage for Germany, France, England, and the Soviet Union. Auton himself represented America's State Department.

Except for the captain's chairs and the ashtray beneath each of them, the room was totally barren. No other furniture, no paintings, no bookshelves, no drapes, no rug, no chandelier. The starkness of the room had been arranged by Smeltzer to assure these men that no microphones had been hidden.

'Gentlemen,' Smeltzer said, 'the adjacent rooms are empty.'

'Munich,' Landish said.

Smeltzer laughed. 'For an Englishman, you come to the point abruptly.'

'Why do you laugh?' Girard asked Smeltzer. 'We all know that at this moment Hitler is demanding that my country and England no longer guarantee the protection of Czechoslovakia, Poland, and Austria.' He spoke English for the benefit of the American.

Avoiding the question, Smeltzer lit a cigarette.

'Does Hitler intend to invade Czechoslovakia?' Lazensokov asked.

Smeltzer shrugged, exhaling smoke. 'I've asked you here so that, as members of the same professional community, we can prepare for any contingency.'

Tex Auton frowned.

Smeltzer continued. 'We don't respect each other's ideologies, but in one way we're all alike. We enjoy the complexities of our profession.'

They nodded.

'You have a new complication to propose?' the Russian asked.

'Why don't you boys say what the hell you're thinking?' Tex Auton drawled.

The other chuckled.

'Directness would ruin half the enjoyment,' Girard told Auton. He turned to Smeltzer, waiting.

'No matter what the outcome of the impending war,' Smeltzer said, 'we must guarantee to each other that our representatives will have the opportunity for protection.'

'Impossible,' the Russian said.

'What kind of protection?' the Frenchman asked.

'Do you mean money?' the Texan added.

'Unstable. It has to be gold or diamonds,' the Englishman said.

The German nodded. 'And more precisely, secure places in which to keep them. The proven banks in Geneva, Lisbon, and Mexico City, for example.'

'Gold.' The Russian sneered. 'And what do you propose we do with this capitalist commodity?'

'Establish a system of safe houses,' Smeltzer replied.

'But what's so new about that? We already have 'em,' Tex Auton said.

The others ignored him.

'And rest homes as well, I presume?' Girard told Smeltzer.

5

'I take that for granted,' the German said. 'For the benefit of my American friend, let me explain. Each of our networks already has its own safe houses, that is true. Secure locations where its operatives can go for protection, say, or debriefing or to interrogate an informer. But while each network tries to keep these locations a secret, eventually the other networks find out where they are, so the places aren't truly safe. Though armed men guard them, a larger opposing force could seize any house and kill whoever had sought protection there.'

Tex Auton shrugged. 'The risk is unavoidable.'

'I wonder,' the German continued. 'What I propose is something new – an extension of the concept, a refinement of it. Under extreme circumstances, any operative from any of our networks would be given a chance for asylum in carefully chosen cities around the world. I suggest Buenos Aires, Potsdam, Lisbon, and Oslo. We all have business there.'

'Alexandria,' the Englishman suggested.

'That's acceptable.'

'Montreal,' the Frenchman said. 'If the war doesn't turn out to my benefit, I might be living there.'

'Now wait a minute,' Tex Auton said. 'Do you expect me to believe that, if a war is goin' on, one of *your* boys won't kill one of *my* boys in these places?'

'As long as the opposing operatives remain inside,' the German said. 'In our profession, we all know the dangers and the pressures. I'll admit that even Germans sometimes need to rest.'

'And calm the nerves and heal the wounds,' the Frenchman said.

'We owe it to ourselves,' the Englishman said. 'And if an operative wants to retire from his network completely, he'd have the chance to go from a safe house to a rest home and enjoy the same immunity for the rest of his life. With a portion of the gold or the diamonds as a retirement fund.'

'As a reward for faithful service,' the German said. 'And an enticement to new recruits.'

'If events proceed as I foresee,' the Frenchman said, 'we may all need enticements.'

'And if events proceed as I expect,' the German said, 'I'll have all the enticements I need. Nonetheless I'm a prudent man. Are we all agreed?'

'What guarantees do we have that our men won't be killed in these safe houses?' the Englishman said.

'The word of fellow professionals.'

'And the penalties?'

'Absolute.'

'Agreed,' the Englishman said.

The American and the Russian were silent.

'Do I sense reluctance from our newer nations?' the German said.

'I agree in principle, and I'll attempt to appropriate funds,' the Russian said, 'but I can't promise Stalin's cooperation. He'd never submit to shielding foreign operatives on Soviet soil.'

6

'But you promise never to harm an enemy operative as long as he's in a designated safe house.'

Reluctantly the Russian nodded.

'And Mr Auton?'

'Well, I'll go along. I'll kick in some money, but I don't want any of these places on American territory.'

'Then with these compromises, we agree?'

The others nodded.

'We'll need a code word for this arrangement,' Landish said.

'I recommend *hospice*,' Smeltzer said.

'Unthinkable,' the Englishman replied. 'Half of our hospitals are called hospices.'

'Then I recommend this alternative,' the Frenchman said. 'We are all learned men. I'm sure you recall the story of my countryman from the Dark Ages: Peter Abelard.'

'*Who*?' Tex Auton said.

Girard explained.

'So he went to a church and was given protection?' Auton said.

'Sanctuary.'

'We'll call it a sanction,' Smeltzer said. 'The Abelard sanction.'

Two days later, Wednesday, October 1, Daladier, France's minister of defense, flew back from the meeting with Hitler in Munich to his home in Paris.

His plane landed at Le Bourget Airport. As he stepped outside, he was greeted by surging crowds who shouted, 'Long live France! Long live England! Long live peace!'

Waving flags and flowers, the crowds broke through the sturdy police barricades. Reporters rushed up the aluminum gangplank to greet the returning minister of defense.

Daladier stood dumfounded.

Turning to Foucault of the Reuters News Service, he muttered, 'Long live peace? Don't they understand what Hitler plans to do? The stupid bastards.'

Paris. 5 P.M., Sunday, September 3, 1939.

An announcer had just come on the radio, interrupting the Michelin Theater to say, 'France is officially at war with Germany.'

The radio went silent.

In Buenos Aires, Potsdam, Lisbon, Oslo, Alexandria, and Montreal, the international safe houses of the world's great espionage networks were established. By 1941, these networks would include Japan, and by 1953, mainland China.

And sanctuary was formed.

7

BOOK ONE
SANCTUARY

A MAN OF HABIT

1

Vail, Colorado.

The snow fell harder, blinding Saul. He skied through deepening powder, veering sharply back and forth down the slope. Everything – the sky, the air, and the ground – turned white. His vision shortened till he saw no more than a swirl before his face. He swooped through chaos.

He might hit an unseen tree or plummet off a hidden cliff. He didn't care. He felt exhilarated. As wind raged at his cheeks, he grinned. He christied left, then right. Sensing the slope ease off, he streaked across a straightaway.

The next slope would be steeper. In the white-out, he pushed at his poles to gain more speed. His stomach burned. He loved it. Vacuum. Nothing to his back or front. Past and future had no meaning. Only now – and it was wonderful.

A dark shape loomed before him.

Jerking sideways, Saul dug in the edge of his skis to stop himself. His pulse roared in his head. The shape zoomed past from right to left in front of him, vanishing in the snow.

Saul gaped through his goggles, hearing a scream despite the wind. He snowplowed frowning toward it.

Shadows gathered in the storm. A line of trees.

A moan.

He found the skier sprawled against a tree trunk. There were bloodstains in the snow. Beneath his mask, Saul bit his lip. He crouched and saw the crimson seeping from the skier's forehead, and the grotesque angle of one leg.

A man. Thick beard. Large chest.

Saul couldn't go for help – in the chaos of the storm, he might not be able to find this place again. Worse, even if he did manage to bring back help, the man might freeze to death by then.

One chance. He didn't bother attending to the head wound or the broken leg. No use, no time. He took off his skis, removed the skis from the injured man, rushed toward a pine tree, and snapped off a thickly needled bough.

Spreading the bough beside the man, he eased him onto it, careful to let the good leg cushion the broken one. He gripped the end of the

11

bough and stooped, walking backwards, pulling. The snow stung harder, cold gnawing through his ski gloves. He kept tugging, inching down.

The man groaned as Saul shifted him over a bump, the snow enshrouding them. The man writhed, almost slipping off the bough.

Saul hurried to reposition him, tensing when he suddenly felt a hand behind him clutch his shoulder.

Whirling, he stared at a looming figure, 'Ski Patrol' stenciled in black across a yellow parka.

'Down the slope! A hundred yards! A shed!' the man yelled, helping Saul.

They eased the skier down the hill. Saul bumped against the shed before he saw it, feeling corrugated metal behind him. He yanked the unlocked door open and stumbled in. The wind's shriek diminished. He felt stillness.

Turning from the empty shed, he helped the man from the Ski Patrol drag in the bleeding skier.

'You okay?' the man asked Saul, who nodded. 'Stay with him while I get help,' the man continued. 'I'll come back with snowmobiles in fifteen minutes.'

Saul nodded again.

'What you did,' the man told Saul. 'You're something else. Hang on. We'll get you warm.'

The man stepped out and closed the door. Saul slumped against the wall and sank to the ground. He stared at the groaning skier, whose eyelids flickered. Saul breathed deeply. 'Keep your leg still.'

The man winced, nodding. 'Thanks.'

Saul shrugged.

Scrunching his eyes in pain, the man said, 'Massive foul-up.'

'It can happen.'

'No. A simple job.'

Saul didn't understand. The man was babbling.

'Didn't figure on the storm.' The man scowled, his temples pulsing. 'Dumb.'

Saul listened to the storm, soon hearing the far-off roar of snow-mobiles. 'They're coming.'

'Did you ever ski in Argentina?'

Saul's throat constricted. Babbling? Hardly. 'Once. I got a nose-bleed.'

'Aspirin . . .'

'. . . cures headaches,' Saul replied, the code completed.

'Ten o'clock tonight.' The man groaned. 'Goddamn storm. Who figured it'd screw things up?'

The roar grew louder as the snowmobiles stopped outside the shed. The door jerked open. Three men from the Ski Patrol stepped in.

'You still okay?' the one man asked Saul.

'I'm fine. But this guy's babbling.'

12

Maintain a pattern. Every day, Saul kept the same routine, appearing at scheduled places at established times. Eight-thirty: breakfast at the coffee shop in his hotel. A half hour's walk, the route unchanging. Twenty minutes' browsing in a book store. Eleven o'clock: the slopes, again his route consistent.

For two reasons. First – in case somebody needed to get in touch with him, the courier would know where he was at any time and be able to intercept him, though it had just been demonstrated how an accident could jeopardize procedure. Second – if Saul was being watched, his schedule was so predictable it might bore his shadow into making mistakes.

Today, more than usual, he had to avoid suspicion. He helped take the injured man down to the ambulance. At the lodge, he chatted with the Ski Patrol in their office, waiting for his chance to slip away. He went to his room and changed from his ski suit to jeans and a sweater. He reached his customary bar exactly when he always did, sitting in the smoke-filled conversation pit, watching cartoons on the giant television screen, sipping a Coke.

At seven, he went to dinner, as always at the dining room in his hotel. At eight, he went to a Burt Reynolds car-chase movie. He'd seen the feature before and knew it ended at quarter to ten. He'd chosen the theater for its pay phone in the men's room. Making sure the stalls were empty, he put the proper change in the phone and dialed a memorized number precisely at ten o'clock as the man on the slope had instructed him.

A gruff male voice announced basketball scores. Saul didn't pay attention to the names of the teams. He cared only about the numbers, ten in all, a long-distance telephone number, mentally repeating them.

He left the men's room and, without being obvious, checked the lobby to see if he was being watched.

No indication of surveillance, though an expert shadow wouldn't let himself be noticed.

He stepped from the theater, pleased that the storm had persisted. Through the dark and confusion, he slipped down a side street, then another side street, waiting in an alley to make sure he wasn't being followed. With sight so restricted in the storm, a tail would have to follow him closely past this alley to keep up with him.

But no one did.

He crossed the street and chose a pay phone in an unfamiliar bar two blocks away. Near the din of electronic games, he dialed the numbers he'd been given.

A woman's sexy voice said, 'Triple A Answering Service.'

'Romulus,' he said.

'You've got an appointment. Tuesday. 9 A.M. Denver. 48 Cody Road.'

He set the phone back on its cradle. Leaving the bar, he walked through the cover of the storm to arrive at his hotel precisely when he would have if, after seeing the movie, he'd taken his usual thirty-minute walk.

He asked the desk clerk, 'Any messages for Grisman? Room 211.'

'Sorry, sir.'

'No problem.'

Avoiding the elevator, he walked upstairs to his room. The strand of hair at the bottom of his door remained exactly where he'd placed it when he'd gone out, assuring him no one had entered in his absence. One more routine day.

With two exceptions.

3

Follow standard procedure. In the morning, Saul bought his ticket at the last possible moment. When the driver started the engine, Saul got on the bus. He sat in back and watched for anyone boarding after him.

But no one did.

As the bus pulled from the station, he eased back, nodding with satisfaction, staring at the condominiums of Vail and the far-off dots of skiers on the snow-covered mountains.

He liked buses. He could see out the back if he was being followed. He could buy a ticket without getting logged in a computer, the reason he didn't fly or rent a car – he didn't want to leave a paper trail. What's more, a bus made several stops along its route. He could get off at any of them without attracting attention.

Though his ticket was for Salt Lake City, he never intended to go there. He left the bus at Placer Springs an hour west of Vail. After waiting to see if anyone else got off, he bought a ticket for Denver, boarded the next bus heading east, and slumped in the back seat. Analyzing what he'd done, he decided he'd make no errors. Certainly if someone had been watching him, his shadow would be puzzled now, soon nervous, making urgent phone calls. Saul didn't care. He'd gained his freedom.

He was ready to do his work.

4

Tuesday, 9 A.M. The Denver wind brought tears to his eyes. Gray clouds hulking over the mountains made the morning seem like dusk. Despite his down-filled coat, he shivered, standing on a suburban corner, squinting toward a building in the middle of the block.

Long, low, and drab. Counting from the address on the corner, Saul guessed the building was 48 Cody Road. He walked through slush to reach it. Though he'd used local buses to get here, transferring often, he nonetheless glanced behind him, just in case. He saw few cars and none that looked familiar.

Turning forward, he stopped in surprise, gaping at a Star of David above the door. A synagogue? Himself a Jew, he wondered if he'd misheard his instructions. Granted, he was used to meetings in uncommon places.

But a synagogue? His spine felt numb.

Uneasily he entered. He faced a shadowy vestibule. His nostrils flared from the smell of dust. As he shut the door, its rumble echoed.

Stillness settled over him. He chose a yarmulke from a box on a table, put the small black cap on the back of his head, and, lips taut, pulled another door.

The temple. He felt a pressure. The air seemed heavy and dense. It seemed to squeeze him. He stepped forward.

In a front seat, an old man stared at the white curtain that hid the Ark, his skullcap shiny from years of worship. The old man lowered his eyes toward his prayer book.

Saul held his breath. Except for the old man at the front, the temple was deserted. Something was wrong.

The old man turned to him. Saul tensed.

'*Shalom*,' the old man said.

Impossible. The man was –

5

Eliot.

He stood. As always, he wore a black suit and vest. A matching overcoat and homburg hat lay on the seat beside him. A gentile, he was sixty-seven, tall and gaunt, gray-skinned, dark-eyed, his shoulders stooped, his face pinched with sorrow.

Smiling warmly, Saul replied, '*Shalom*.' His throat hurt as he approached.

They hugged each other. Feeling the wrinkled kiss on his cheek, Saul kissed the old man in return. They studied one another.

'You look well,' Saul said.

'A lie, but I'll accept it. *You* look well, though.'

'Exercise.'

'Your wounds?'

'No complications.'

'In the stomach.' Eliot shook his head. 'When I heard what happened, I wanted to visit you.'

'But you couldn't. I understand.'

'You received good care?'

'You know I did. You sent the best.'

'The best deserves the best.'

Saul felt embarrassed. A year ago, he *had* been the best. But now? 'A lie,' he said. 'I don't deserve it.'

'You're alive.'

'By luck.'

'By skill. A lesser man could not have escaped.'

15

'I shouldn't have needed to escape,' Saul said. 'I planned the operation. I thought I'd allowed for every factor. I was wrong. A cleaning lady, for God's sake. She should have been on another floor. She never checked that room that early.'

Eliot spread his hands. 'Exactly my point. Random chance. You can't control it.'

'You know better,' Saul replied. 'You used to say the word *accident* had been invented by weak people to excuse their mistakes. You told us to strive for perfection.'

'Yes. But –' Eliot frowned '– perfection can never be attained.'

'I almost had it. A year ago. I don't understand what happened.' He suspected, though. He was six feet tall, two hundred pounds of bone and muscle. But he was also thirty-seven. I'm getting old, he thought. 'I ought to quit. It's not just *this* job. Two others went bad before it.'

'Random chance again,' Eliot said. 'I read the reports. You weren't to blame.'

'You're making allowances.'

'Because of our relationship?' Eliot shook his head. 'Not true. I've never let it sway me. But sometimes failure can have a beneficial effect. It can make us try much harder.' He took two slips of paper from the inner pocket of his suitcoat.

Saul read the neat handprinting on the first one. A telephone number. He memorized it, nodding. Eliot showed him the second sheet. Instructions, six names, a date, and an address. Again, Saul nodded.

Eliot took back the papers. Picking up his hat and overcoat, he left the temple to cross the vestibule toward the men's room. Thirty seconds later, Saul heard flushing. He took for granted Eliot had burned the pages and disposed of the ashes. If the temple had been bugged, their conversation alone would not have revealed the subject of the notes.

Eliot returned, putting on his overcoat. 'I'll use the exit in the rear.'

'No, wait. So soon? I hoped we could talk.'

'We will. When the job's completed.'

'How are your flowers?'

'Not just flowers. Roses.' Eliot shook a finger at him in mock chastisement. 'After all these years, you still enjoy baiting me by calling them flowers.'

Saul grinned.

'Actually,' Eliot said, 'I've developed an interesting variation. Blue. No rose has ever been that color before. When you come to visit, I'll show it to you.'

'I look forward to it.'

Warmly they embraced.

'If it matters,' Eliot said, 'the job you'll be doing is designed to protect all this.' He gestured toward the temple. 'One more thing.' He reached into his overcoat, pulling out a candy bar.

16

Saul's chest tightened as he took it. A Baby Ruth. 'You still remember.'

'Always.' Eliot's eyes looked sad.

Saul swallowed painfully, watching Eliot leave through the back, listening to the echo of the door snicking shut. In accordance with procedure, he himself would wait ten minutes and go out the front. Eliot's cryptic remark about the purpose of this assignment troubled him, but he knew only something important would have caused Eliot to deliver the instructions in person.

He squeezed his fists, determined. This time he wouldn't fail. He couldn't allow himself to disappoint the only father he, an orphan, had ever known.

6

The man with a mustache munched a taco. Saul explained the assignment to him. They used no names, of course. Saul hadn't seen him before and wouldn't again. The man wore a jogging suit. He had a cleft in his chin. He wiped his mustache with a napkin.

Baltimore. Three days later, 2 P.M. The Mexican restaurant was almost deserted. Even so, they sat at the remotest corner table.

The man lit a cigarette, studying Saul. 'We'll need a lot of backup.'

'Maybe not,' Saul said.

'You know the protocol.'

Saul nodded. Established method. A team of fourteen men, the bulk of them working on surveillance, the others obtaining equipment, relaying messages, providing alibis, each of them knowing as little as possible about the others, all of them dropping out of sight an hour before the specialists stepped in. Efficient. Safe.

'All right,' the man told Saul. 'But this is *six* jobs. Times fourteen backup men. That's eighty-four. We might as well hold a convention, advertise, sell tickets.'

'Maybe not,' Saul said.

'So humor me.'

'The key is all together – at one time, one place.'

'Who knows when that'll be? We could wait all year.'

'Three weeks from today.'

The man stared down at his cigarette. Saul told him where. The man stubbed out his cigarette. 'Go on,' he said.

'We can keep surveillance to a minimum, simply making sure all six of them show up for the meeting.'

'Possibly. We'd still need communications. Someone else to get the stuff.'

'That's you.'

'No argument. But getting the stuff in the building won't be easy.'

'Not your worry.'

'Fine with me. It's flaky. I don't like it. But if that's the way you want it, we can do the job with twenty men.'

17

'You're right,' Saul said. 'That's how I want it.'

'What's the matter?'

'Let's just say I had a few assignments with people who let me down. I'm losing my faith in human nature.'

'That's a laugh.'

'For this job, as much as I can, I want to depend on myself.'

'And me, of course. You'll have to depend on me.'

Saul studied him. The waitress brought the check.

'My treat,' Saul said.

7

The estate spread across the valley – a three-story mansion, swimming pool, tennis courts, stables, a lush green pasture, riding trails through a parklike forest, ducks on a lake. He lay in tall grass on a wooded bluff a half mile away, the warm spring sun on his back, its angle such that it wouldn't reflect off the lens of his telescope and warn the bodyguards in front of the house that someone was watching them. He studied a dust cloud on a gravel road, a limousine approaching the house, four other limousines already parked in front of a six-stall garage to the left. The car stopped at the house, a bodyguard stepping forward as a man got out.

'He ought to be there by now,' a voice said from a walkie-talkie next to Saul, the raspy tone of the man he'd talked to in Baltimore. The walkie-talkie had been adjusted to a seldom-used frequency. Even so, there was always a chance of someone accidentally overhearing the conversation, so the walkie-talkie had been equipped with a scrambler. Only someone with another scrambler tuned to the same uncommon frequency could receive a clear transmission. 'That's the last of them,' the voice continued. 'Eyeball ID. Counting the guy who lives there, all six targets are in the zone.'

Saul pressed the 'send' button on the walkie-talkie. 'I'll take it from here. Head home.' He stared through the telescope at the house. The visitor had gone inside, the limousine joining the others in front of the garage.

He checked his watch. Everything on schedule. Though the mansion was closely guarded now, its security force had been minimal a week ago, just a man at the gate, another patrolling the grounds, a third in charge of the house. With a Starlite nightscope, he'd studied the estate three nights in a row, learning the guards' routine, when they were relieved and when they were careless, choosing four A.M. as the best time to infiltrate the grounds. In the dark, he'd crept through the forest toward the back. Precisely at four, two members of his team had created a diversion on the road that ran past the gate by pretending to be kids revving loud jalopies in a drag race. While the guards were distracted, Saul had picked the lock on a storm door, entering the basement. He hadn't worried about a warning system since he'd noticed that the guard in charge of the house never took

18

precautions to shut off an alarm when he entered. In the basement, he used a shielded penlight, hiding plastique explosive in a furnace duct, attaching a radio-activated detonator. Taking his equipment, he locked the door and disappeared into the forest, hearing the roar of the jalopies finishing the race.

Two days later, a full security force had sealed off the estate. When they searched the house, they might have found the explosive, but from his vantage, he'd seen no commotion. The guards had seemed concerned only with watching the perimeter of the house.

He'd soon learn if the explosive remained. Glancing at his watch again, he saw that twenty minutes had passed. Time enough for the man with the cleft in his chin to have got away. Putting the walkie-talkie and the telescope in his knapsack, he concentrated on a single blade of grass, focusing on it, narrowing his vision till the grass absorbed his mind. Free of emotion, achieving a stillness, he picked up a radio transmitter and pressed a button.

The mansion blew apart, from the basement upward, outward, its walls disintegrating, rubble flying, spewing in all directions. The roof lifted, toppling, shrouded with dust, engulfed with flames. The shock wave hit him. Ignoring it, he shoved the radio transmitter in his knapsack. Hearing a rumble, he ignored it also, running from the bluff, approaching a car in a weed-covered lane.

Eight years old. The team member responsible for transportation had bought it cheap, using cash and an alias, from a man who'd advertised in the Baltimore want ads. No one could trace it here.

He obeyed the speed limit, calm, allowing no satisfaction, even though he'd achieved what his father had asked.

8

EXPLOSION KILLS SIX

COSTIGAN, VIRGINIA (AP) – An unexplained explosion Thursday evening destroyed the secluded mansion of Andrew Sage, controversial oil magnate and energy adviser to the president. The powerful blast killed Sage and five unidentified guests who, highly placed sources speculate, were representatives from various large American corporations, members of the Paradigm Foundation, which Sage had recently founded.

'Mr Sage's family is too distraught to talk about it,' an FBI official announced at a press conference. 'As much as we can determine, Mr Sage had convened a kind of industrial summit meeting in an attempt to solve the nation's economic crisis. The president, of course, is deeply shocked. He lost not only a trusted adviser but a cherished friend.'

Sage's family was not present on his country estate at the time of the explosion. Several members of his security staff were injured by flying rubble. Investigators continue to search the wreckage for a clue to the cause of the blast.

9

Saul reread the front-page story, folded the newspaper, and leaned back in his chair. A cocktail waitress, breasts and hips bulging from her costume, passed his table. He glanced from the piano player in the lounge, across the noisy casino, toward the blackjack tables, watching a pit boss study the crowd.

He felt uneasy. Frowning, he tried to understand why. The job had gone smoothly. His getaway had been uneventful. After leaving the car at a Washington shopping mall, he'd taken a bus to Atlantic City. He'd made sure no one followed him.

Then why was he worried? As slot machines rang, he continued frowning.

Eliot had insisted on explosives. But Saul knew the job could easily have been done in a less dramatic way. Prior to the meeting, the six men could have died from apparent natural causes at different times in widely separate parts of the country: heart attack, stroke, suicide, traffic accident, a variety of other ways. The inner circle would have noticed the pattern, understanding what it meant, but there'd have been no publicity. Saul had to conclude, then, that publicity was the reason for the job. But why? Saul's instincts nagged him. Publicity violated the logic of his training. Eliot had always insisted on subtlety. Then why now had Eliot suddenly changed?

Another thing bothered him – his present location, Atlantic City. After a job, he always went to a predetermined neutral site – in this case, a locker at a Washington gym – finding money and instructions on where to disappear. Eliot knew the locations Saul preferred – the mountains, Wyoming and Colorado in particular – and as a favor, Eliot always agreed to them. So why the hell was I sent to Atlantic City? he thought. He'd never been here. He didn't like crowds. He tolerated them only as a necessary evil when he gratified his need to ski. Here, people swarmed around him like scavenging insects.

Something was wrong. The orders to use explosives, to go to Atlantic City – they were blatant violations of routine. As roulette wheels clattered, Saul's hands itched with apprehension.

He left the cocktail lounge, approaching the blackjack tables. He hated crowds, but in the locker at the gym, he'd found two thousand dollars and orders to play blackjack.

Accepting his cover, he found an empty chair and bought five hundred dollars' worth of chips. After betting a twenty-five dollar chip, he received a king and a queen.

The dealer won with blackjack.

'*Goddamned bastards,*' the president said. He punched a fist against the palm of his hand. He hadn't slept. The news had aged him shockingly, much more than the recent assassination attempt. Fatigue made him tremble. Grief and anger pinched his face. 'I want the man who killed my friend. I want those sonsofbitches –' Abruptly the president stopped. Unlike his predecessors, he understood the wisdom of silence. What he didn't say couldn't be used against him.

Eliot wondered if the president knew the tapes of his Oval Office conversations were being duplicated.

The director of the CIA sat next to Eliot. 'The KGB got in touch with us at once. They flatly deny they had anything to do with it.'

'Of course they deny it,' the president said.

'But I believe them,' the director said. 'The job was too sensational. It's not their style.'

'That's what they want us to think. They've changed their tactics to confuse us.'

'With respect, Mr President, I don't think so,' the director said. 'I'll grant you, the Soviets don't like the shift in our mideast policy – away from the Jews toward the Arabs. The Soviets have always counted on our pro-Israeli stance. They've used it to turn the Arabs against us. Now we do what they've been doing. They're upset.'

'So it makes sense for them to interfere,' the president said. 'Our deal with the Arabs is simple. If we turn our back on Israel, the Arabs will sell us cheaper oil. The Paradigm Foundation was established to hide our negotiations with the Arabs – businessmen dealing with other businessmen instead of government with government. Destroy the Paradigm Foundation – you destroy the negotiations. You also warn us not to reopen them.'

'Sure, it makes sense,' the director said. 'Too much sense. The Russians know we'd blame them. If they wanted to interfere, they'd hide their tracks. They'd be more clever.'

'Who the hell did it then? The FBI found Andrew's arm a half a mile away from the wreckage. I want to get even with someone. Tell me who. Qaddafi? Castro?'

'I don't think so,' the director said.

'We did,' Eliot said. He'd been silent, waiting for the proper moment.

The president swung toward Eliot, stunned. '*We what?*'

'Indirectly at least. One of our men did. Naturally it wasn't authorized.'

'I hope to God not!'

'We found out by accident,' Eliot said.

The director, who was also Eliot's superior, stared at him indignantly. 'You didn't tell *me*.'

'I didn't have a chance. I learned about it just before this meeting. We've been watching the man for several months. He's ruined several assignments. His behaviour's erratic. We've been thinking of letting him go. Three weeks before the explosion, he dropped out of sight. Today he resurfaced. We managed to retrace his movements. We can put him in the area at the time of the blast.'

The president's face turned pale. 'Go on.'

'He's under surveillance in Atlantic City. He seems to have a lot of money. He's losing at blackjack.'

'Where'd he get the bankroll?' the president said, eyes narrowed.

'He's Jewish. The Mossad helped us train him. He fought in their October War in seventy-three. He's got expensive tastes, which he can't maintain if we let him go. We think the Israelis paid him to turn.'

'That *does* make sense,' the director said grudgingly.

The president clenched a fist. But can you prove it? Can you give me something to raise hell with Tel Aviv?'

'I'll speak to him. There are ways to stimulate conversation.'

'After that, do we have procedures for dealing with double agents?'

The president's evasive language made Eliot wonder again if he knew the Oval Office tapes were being duplicated.

Tactfully Eliot nodded.

'I suggest you implement them,' the president said. 'It doesn't make a difference, but for my satisfaction, what's his name?'

11

As he left the casino's restaurant, Saul saw a man in the crowd who suddenly turned to walk the other way. A man with a cleft chin and a mustache. *No, it couldn't be.* From the back, the man had the same narrow build. The color and style of his hair were the same. The man Saul had spoken to in Baltimore. The man who'd helped on the job.

Saul's muscles hardened. He had to be wrong. When a team disbanded after a job, the agency never sent two men to disappear in the same place. For the sake of caution, the team wasn't supposed to see each other again or be connected in any way. Then what was this man doing here?

Relax, Saul told himself . You've made a mistake. Go after the guy and take another look. Satisfy your mind.

The man had blended with the crowd, moving along a corridor, going through a door. Saul slipped around two women, passing a row of clattering slot machines. He recalled the moment when he'd seen the man – the sudden turn to walk the other way, as if the man had forgotten something. Maybe. Or had the man turned because he didn't want Saul to recognize him?

Grabbing the door, Saul pulled it open and saw a theater, dimly lit, deserted. The entertainment wouldn't start for several hours. Empty tables. A curtain hid the stage.

The right edge of the curtain trembled.

Saul ran down plush stairs. He reached the lowest tables and vaulted to the edge of the stage, creeping toward the right edge of the curtain, silently cursing himself because he'd left his automatic in his room. There'd been no choice. In Atlantic City, the quickest way to draw attention was to carry a handgun, no matter how well concealed.

The curtain stopped trembling. He stiffened as a door banged open – to his right, below the stage, past the tables, beneath an Exit light. A waiter came in, carrying a pile of tablecloths.

The waiter squinted at Saul and braced his shoulders. 'You're not supposed to be here.'

Random chance again. Another version of the cleaning lady coming in the room when she wasn't supposed to. Christ.

Saul made his choice, dropping to the floor, rolling beneath the heavy curtain.

'Hey!'

He heard the waiter's muffled shout beyond the curtain. He ignored it, continuing to roll, springing to a crouch beside a grand piano. Dim light from the wings cast shadows on the stage. Drums, guitars, microphones, musicians' stands. His eyes adjusted to the shadows. He crept toward the right wing of the stage. A space between angled partitions led him to a table, a chair, a rack of costumes, a wall of levers and switches.

No one.

'He went through there!' the waiter shouted beyond the curtain.

Saul stepped toward a fire door. He'd trained himself to ignore distractions, staying alive this long because of his concentration. Again, it saved him. As he touched the knob on the door, he paid no attention to the quick steps on the stage beyond the curtain. He was preoccupied by something else – the whisper of cloth behind him. He dodged. A knife rebounded, clattering off the metal door. A shadow lunged from behind a crate, the only corner Saul had deliberately failed to check. Don't go to your enemy. Make him come to you.

As adrenaline quickened his instincts, Saul crouched, bending his knees for balance, ready to meet the attack. The man struck, surprising Saul by using the heel of his palm as a weapon, his fingers upright, thrusting straight ahead. Trained to defend himself against this form of combat, Saul blocked the hand. He used the heel of his own palm, slamming the man's ribcage, aiming at his heart.

Bones cracked. Groaning, the man lurched back. Saul spun him, grabbed from behind, and pushed the fire door, dragging him out.

Five seconds had passed. As he closed the door, he glimpsed two waiters on the stage. He spun toward a hall of doors. At its end, a guard had his back turned, making a phone call.

Saul tugged the injured man in the opposite direction, shoving open a door marked Stairs but not going through, instead rushing farther down to a door with a large red star. He turned the knob. It wasn't locked. He went into a dressing room, dropped the man, and shut the door. Flicking the lock, he swung to protect himself. The room was deserted.

He held his breath, listening at the door.

'Hey!' a waiter shouted. 'Anyone pass you down there?'

Saul didn't hear the guard's response.

'The door to the stairs!' a second waiter shouted.

Saul heard them running. The sound of their footfalls receded.

He stared at the man on the floor. Unconscious, the man breathed shallowly, expelling red foam from his nostrils and mouth. The splintered bones from the shattered ribcage caused extensive internal bleeding. Death from lung and heart congestion would occur in minutes.

A man with a mustache. The man Saul had talked to in Baltimore. No doubt about it. He must have followed him here, Saul thought.

But how? He'd been confident he wasn't shadowed. Conclusion – the man was good at his work.

Too much so. When the man had turned abruptly outside the restaurant, his motive hadn't been to keep Saul from recognizing him. Exactly the opposite. The man had wanted to confuse Saul into following him – to lead Saul to a quiet place and . . .

Kill me. *Why?*

Something else disturbed him. Method. The knife would have done the job if I hadn't been alert. But the way he came at me, lunging straight ahead with the heel of his palm, aiming toward my ribcage. It's unique. Only someone trained in Israel knows how to do it.

The Mossad. The Israeli intelligence network. The best in the world. Saul had been taught by them. So had the man on the floor.

But why would they –?

No professional assassin works alone. Somewhere close, other members of the death team waited.

He stepped from the dressing room, glancing along the hall. The guard was gone. Wiping his fingerprints off the doors, he left the way he'd come – past the stage and its curtain, through the empty theater.

In the casino, the noises from the crowd swept over him. Slot machines jangled. He glanced at his watch. A voice crackled from the public address system, asking Princess Fatima to pick up a service phone. Translated, the announcement meant the casino had an emergency. All security personnel were ordered to contact the office at once.

He tried not to hurry as he left the casino's glitter and reached the boardwalk, his eyes not used to twilight. Tourists leaned against a rail, a cool breeze tugging their clothes as they gazed past the beach toward whitecaps. Passing them, his footsteps rumbling on the boardwalk, he glanced at his watch again.

The man would be dead by now.

12

The lights of the greenhouse reflected off its glass, concealing the night. Pacing the aisles, Eliot tried to distract himself with his roses, savoring their fragrance. Different varieties – myriad sizes and colors. Complicated, delicate, they required perfect care and cultivation.

Like the men he controlled, he thought. Indeed he'd always

believed that his men were as sensitive as his roses and as beautiful. With thorns.

But sometimes even the best of his creations had to be culled.

He paused to study a rose so red it was crimson. It seemed to have been dipped in blood. Exquisite.

He concentrated on the rose he'd mentioned to Saul in Denver. Blue.

Frowning, he glanced at his watch. Near midnight. Outside, the April night was chilly and dry. But the greenhouse was warm and humid. Though he sweated, he wore his black vest and suitcoat.

He pursed his lips. His wizened forehead narrowed. Something was wrong. An hour ago, he'd been told of the mission's failure. Saul had survived. The death team had removed the assassin's body, but not before an Atlantic City security guard had found it. That sloppy detail had to be taken care of. To quell his nervousness, Eliot amused himself by imagining the startled look on the Atlantic City headliner's face if he'd entered the dressing room and found a corpse on the floor. After the many gangster movies the superstar singer had appeared in, real life might have been an education for him. But how would *that* sloppy detail have been taken care of?

His amusement died when he heard the phone. The special phone – green, appropriate for a greenhouse, next to the black phone on the potting table. Only a handful of people knew its number. He hoped one man in particular would be calling.

Though he'd waited anxiously, he forced himself to let the phone ring two more times. Clearing his throat, he picked it up. 'Hello?'

'Romulus,' the strained voice said. 'Black flag.' The man sounded out of breath. Eliot took for granted the greenhouse and its phones were bugged. He and his men used prearranged codes. Romulus was Saul. Black flag meant an emergency – specifically that his cover had been blown and someone was dead.

Eliot answered, 'Give me a number. I'll call you back in fifteen minutes.'

'No,' Saul blurted.

Eliot bit his lip. 'Then tell me how you want to do it.'

'I've got to keep moving. You give *me* a number.'

'Wait ten seconds.' Eliot reached in his suitcoat, pulling out a pen and note pad. He wrote down a number he knew Saul had memorized.

967–876–9988

Below it, he wrote the number of a pay phone he knew was safe.

703–338–9022

He subtracted the bottom from the top.

264–538–0966

He read Saul the remainder.

25

Saul in turn would subtract that number from the one he'd memorized.

$$967–876–9988$$
$$–264–538–0966$$
$$703–338–9022$$

He'd then have the number of the pay phone Eliot planned to use.

'In thirty minutes,' Saul said abruptly.

Eliot heard a click as Saul hung up. He set the phone down. Tense, he forced himself to wait till he had control. Saul's insistence that he call Eliot, not the other way around, was unexpected but not disastrous. He'd have needed to leave here and reach a safe phone, no matter what. But if Saul had given him a number, he could have used it to locate the phone Saul was calling from. He could then have sent a team to that location.

Now he had to think of another way. He concentrated on his roses, nodding as the solution came to him.

He checked his watch, surprised that ten minutes had elapsed since Saul had hung up. But he still had time to drive to the phone he planned to use outside a local supermarket – after midnight, no one would be in the area – and make a hurried call to set up the trap. A minute to explain instructions. Then he'd wait for Saul to get in touch with him again.

All the same, as he turned off the lights in the greenhouse, he felt a moment's hesitation. Standing in the dark, he thought that Saul was so superior he regretted having to terminate him. But then again, Eliot had many superior men. One less wouldn't matter, given the stakes.

But something else troubled him. The way Saul had avoided the trap in Atlantic City. What if Saul was even better than Eliot thought?

13

The bowling alley rumbled from strikes and gutterballs. Only a third of the lanes had players. Ricky's Auto Parts was beating First-rate Mufflers.

Saul sat with his swivel chair turned so his back was to the luncheon counter. He tried to look preoccupied by the games, but actually he studied the entrance to the bowling alley.

Stay off the streets – too great a risk of being seen. Choose a public place – the cops won't bother you. Pick a spot that isn't crowded – you've got to have room to maneuver. And an exit – the service door behind the counter.

'Refill?' the waitress said behind him.

He turned to the tired woman in the wrinkled uniform. She held a pot of coffee. 'No, thanks. I guess my friend won't be coming.'

'Closing time.' She glanced at the clock above the milk dispenser. 'In five minutes.'

'What do I owe you?'

'Eighty cents.'

He gave her a dollar. 'Keep the change. I'd better call and find out what happened to him.'

'Over there.' She pointed to a pay phone near a glassed-in display of bowling balls for sale.

Distressed, he hoped his smile looked convincing as he walked to the phone. He'd told Eliot he'd call back in thirty minutes. On schedule, he shoved a coin in the slot and pressed the button for the operator. He told her the number Eliot had given him. A Virginia area code. The corresponding pay phone would have to be near Falls Church, where Eliot lived. Eliot didn't have time to drive far.

The operator told Saul the charges for three minutes. He inserted the coins, listened to the different tones as they dropped through the slots, and heard a buzz.

Eliot answered quickly. 'Yes?'

Though these phones weren't tapped, the operator might overhear the conversation. Saul used indirect references, quickly explaining what had happened. 'Our friends from Israel,' he concluded. 'I recognized their style. They don't want me working for the magazine. Why?'

'I'll ask the editor. Their accounting office must be confused.'

'It's something to do with the last article I wrote. One of my researchers wanted to stop me from writing another one.'

'Maybe he thought you were working for a rival magazine.'

'Or maybe *he* was.'

'Possibly. It's a competitive business,' Eliot said.

'It's cutthroat. I need job security.'

'And health benefits. I agree. I know where you can go to relax. An executive retreat.'

'Not far, I hope. It's late. On foot, I might get mugged.'

'There's a hotel in your neighborhood.' Using code, Eliot told Saul the address. 'I'll make a reservation for you. Naturally I'm upset. You have my sympathy. I'll find out why they're angry.'

'Please. I knew I could count on you.'

'That's what fathers are for.'

Saul put the phone back on its hook. He'd been watching the entrance to the bowling alley. He heard the rumble of another gutterball. An opposing player laughed. Beyond an open door marked Office, a bald man flicked some switches on a wall. The lights went dim.

'Closing time!' the waitress said.

Saul glanced through the glass door toward the parking lot. Arc lights gleamed. Behind them, shadows loomed. No other choice. Skin prickling, he crossed the lot.

From the dark at the end of the deserted block, he saw his destination. A hotel. Eliot had said he'd make a reservation, but Saul hadn't guessed he was being literal. A kind of joke. Saul almost smiled.

The only light on the street was the glowing neon sign above the dirty concrete steps leading up to the dilapidated wooden structure.

AYFARE HOTEL

Saul decided the burnt-out letter on the sign was either an M or a W. Mayfare. Wayfare. It didn't matter which. The important thing was one of the letters was missing, a signal to him that all was ready, the place secure. If every letter had been working, he'd have been warned to stay away.

He scanned the neighborhood. Seeing no one, he started down the street. The district was a slum. Broken windows. Garbage. The tenements looked deserted. Perfect. Alone, at three o'clock in the morning, he wouldn't draw attention here. No police cars would bother patrolling this district, stopping to ask where he was going and why he was out so late. The local residents would mind their own business.

His footsteps echoed. Unwilling to risk getting trapped in a taxi, he'd been walking for several hours, his legs stiff, shoulders aching. He'd backtracked, often going around a block, to check if he was being followed. He hadn't seen a tail. That didn't mean there wasn't one.

But soon it wouldn't matter. He was almost home.

The neon sign grew larger as he neared it. Though the night was cool, sweat trickled down his chest beneath his turtleneck sweater and the bulletproof vest he always wore for a few days after a job. His hands felt numb. He subdued the urge to hurry.

Again, he glanced behind him. No one.

He approached the hotel from the opposite side of the street, tempted to go around the block, to scout the neighborhood, to reassure himself everything was as it should be. But since no opponent could have known he was coming here, he didn't see the need for further evasive tactics. All he wanted was to rest, to clear his mind, to learn why he was being hunted.

Eliot would care for him.

He stepped from the curb to cross the street. The dingy hotel, its windows darkened, waited for him. Past the door, a rescue team would have food and drink and comfort ready. They'd protect him.

Though his heart raced, he walked steadily, seeing the warped cracks on the wooden door.

But he felt uneasy. Procedure. Eliot had always said, no matter what, don't violate procedure. It's the only thing that guarantees survival. Always circle your objective. Check the territory. Make extra sure.

Obeying the impulse, he pivoted, shifting abruptly toward the sidewalk he'd just left. If in spite of his caution he'd been followed this final unexpected change in direction might confuse a tail and make him show himself.

The blow jerked him sideways, its impact stunning, unanticipated, high on his left side near his heart against his bulletproof vest. He didn't know what had happened. Then he realized. He'd been shot. A silencer. He gasped, the wind knocked out of him.

His vision blurred. He fell to the street, absorbing the jolt as he rolled to the gutter. The bullet had come from above him, from a building opposite the hotel. But the vest should have stopped it. Why was he bleeding?

Confused, he groped to his feet, bent over, stumbling across the littered sidewalk. His chest felt on fire. He lurched down an alley, pressing himself against its wall, peering through the dark. Shadowy objects hulked before him. At the far end, he saw another street.

But he couldn't go down there. If he'd been followed, it wouldn't have been by just one man. There'd be backup – other members of the death team watching the nearby streets. When he came to the end of the alley, he'd be shot again, maybe in the head or the throat. He'd trapped himself.

He staggered past a fire escape and the stench of overflowing garbage cans. Behind him, silhouetted by the hotel's neon sign, a man approached the alley, his footsteps echoing in the eerie quiet. The man walked with his knees bent, stooped, aiming a small automatic with the tube of a silencer projecting from its barrel.

The Mossad, Saul thought again. The characteristic, flat-footed, seemingly awkward crouch that insured an assassin could keep his balance, even if wounded. He himself had been trained to maintain that posture.

The assassin entered the alley, pressing himself against the dark of the wall, inching forward, blending with the night.

He's being careful, Saul thought. He doesn't know I left my handgun behind. He'll come slowly.

Whirling, Saul stared toward the other end of the alley. A second figure entered. No way out.

But there had to be. The fire escape? No good – as he struggled up, he'd attract their fire. He sensed them pressing closer.

The door beneath the fire escape? He lunged, twisting the knob, but it was locked. Using an elbow, he smashed a window next to the door, knowing the crash would alert his hunters, rushing, feeling the glass lance through his jacket. Blood soaked his arms. His shoes scraped as he thrust himself through the window, wincing from pressure on his chest, tilting, falling.

He struck a floor. Darkness surrounded him. Soon, he thought. The men in the hotel. They'll charge out to help me. Stay alive till they get here.

He scrambled forward, bumping against an unseen bannister, jarring his chest. Sweat slicked his face. Feeling around, he touched two stairways, one up, one down. Stifling a groan, he staggered up. The hall stank from urine. He sprawled on a landing, squirmed ahead, and cracked his skull against the spoked wheels of a baby carriage.

He touched its greasy side. As blood dripped off his arms, he shoved the carriage toward the top of the stairs. The wheels creaked. He froze. Don't make a sound. Outside the window, a shadow crept near.

He sensed what his hunter felt. The only entrance to this building was the broken window. But the window might be a trap.

The shadow paused.

But Saul had been shot. He was on the run. The shadow might feel confident.

He did. With amazing speed, the shadow dove through the window, thudding on the floor, rolling quickly, stopping in the dark.

The assassin would find the two sets of stairs. But up or down? Which way had Saul gone? The rule was up. The high ground was easier to defend.

The problem was, had Saul remained consistent, obeying the rule, or had he gone to the basement, hoping to fool his enemy? A mental toss of a coin.

The tenement was silent. All at once, the gunman charged the stairs. Pushing the baby carriage, Saul struck him in the face, hearing the carriage clatter as the gunman toppled. Lunging down, Saul kicked, feeling the jaw give way.

He heard a moan and grabbed the gunman's sweater. Jerking it down with one hand, he rammed his other arm up toward the throat. The larynx snapped. The gunman fell, convulsing, suffocating. His pistol thumped.

Saul bent in pain to find it. The feel was familiar, palm-sized. He'd used the weapon often – a Beretta, this one equipped with a barrel long enough to accommodate a silencer. A customized .22, so precisely remachined that what it lacked in power it gained in accuracy. The handgun preferred by the Mossad – another of their calling cards.

He peered through the shattered window. Down the alley, the second gunman stalked through the shadows. Saul squeezed the trigger, jerking from repeated spits, continuing to shoot as the gunman fell and heaved.

He leaned against the wall, trying to keep his balance. There'd be other hunters. He had to assume it. His survival depended on assumptions. Get away. He hurried up the stairs.

A baby cried in an apartment. He reached the top of the stairs, pushed a metal door, and came out crouching on the roof, his pistol aimed at air vents, clotheslines, pipes, TV aerials. No one. Move. He crept through shadows, biting his lip from pain as he eased to a lower level. Stars glinted coldly.

Abruptly he faced the edge. The next building was too far away for him to reach with a jump. Glancing around, he saw a rectangular structure projecting from the roof, opened its door, and stared toward the black of a stairwell. Dear God, the pain!

One floor, then another, then another. At last on the bottom, he peered toward an exit. Someone might be waiting, but he had to take the risk. The street was dark. He eased out. Holding his breath, he reached the sidewalk. No shots. No figures lunging at him.

He'd made it. But where could he go? He didn't know how badly he was hurt. He couldn't show himself much longer or they'd find him.

He thought of the hotel. The gunmen had intercepted him, trying to stop him from reaching it. He didn't understand why help wasn't here. The gunmen had used silencers. Maybe the rescue team didn't know he'd been shot.

But he'd been hit on the street outside the hotel. Surely the rescue team had been watching. Why had they failed to rush out, to help him?

Because they didn't know where he'd gone. They didn't want to jeopardize the integrity of the hotel. They were keeping their position in hope that he'd reach them. Get there.

He saw a rusty Plymouth Duster parked at the curb, its battered shape the only car on the shadowy block. If it wasn't locked. If it would start.

If.

He pulled the door. It opened. The keys weren't in the ignition switch. Chest aching, he bent down, fumbling beneath the dash, finding what he needed. He joined two wires. The Duster started.

Clutching the wheel, he stomped the accelerator. The Duster roared from the curb. He screeched around a corner. Buildings blurred. The street seemed to shrink as he squealed around another corner.

Ahead, he saw the hotel and veered toward the curb. In the light from the neon sign, his hunters couldn't use a nightscope. Its lens would magnify the light so much a gunman would be blinded.

He jerked from the impact as the Duster hit the curb and shuddered across the sidewalk. Skidding to a stop before the grimy concrete steps, he shouldered open his door. The car was positioned so it gave him cover. He charged up the steps, hitting the entrance, slamming through. At once he dropped to the floor and spun to aim his handgun toward the street.

He'd reached the hotel. He was safe.

The silence stunned him. The rescue team? Where were they?

Peering behind him, he saw only darkness. 'Romulus!' he shouted, heard an echo, but received no answer.

He crawled around, smelling dust and mildew. Where the hell –? The place was empty. Confused, he searched the murky lobby. No one. He checked the office and the rooms along the hall, darting glances toward the entrance, straining to listen for anyone coming.

Completely deserted. Nothing had been prepared for his arrival. Not a secure location. Christ, this hotel had been the bait to lure him into a trap! They'd never expected him to get inside!

31

He understood now that the men who'd waited here had indeed come out. But not to rescue him. Instead to track him down and kill him. They were out there searching for him. And the car outside would tell them where he was.

He ran toward the door. Hurrying down the steps, he saw a gunman appear at the corner, aiming a short-barreled submachine gun, unmistakably an Uzi.

Saul shot as he ran, seeing the gunman grab his arm and jerk behind the corner.

He hadn't bothered to waste time reaching for the wires beneath the dash to turn off the Duster's engine. The driver's door hung open. He yanked the gearshift. Squealing, the car jolted off the sidewalk, fishtailing, roaring down the street. A volley of bullets shattered the rear windshield. Glass exploded over him. Slumping, he steered, trying to hide himself.

On the corner ahead, another gunman stepped out. Saul swung the steering wheel in his direction, pressing the accelerator, racing toward him. Thirty feet, twenty. The gunman aimed a pistol. Ten feet. Suddenly the gunman broke his stance, diving in panic toward a doorway.

Saul veered, avoiding a fire hydrant, speeding past the gunman, screeching down a side street. A cluster of bullets whacked the Duster.

He skidded through an intersection, listing, racing down another side street. Checking his rearview mirror, glancing ahead, he saw no other gunman.

He was safe. But blood streamed down his chest where he'd been shot, and from his elbows where he'd cut himself breaking the window. Safe. But for how long?

Despite his urgency, he eased his foot off the accelerator. Don't run traffic lights. Obey the speed limit. Bleeding, in a stolen car with a shattered rear window and bullet holes in the body, he didn't dare get stopped by the police. He had to ditch this car.

And do it fast.

15

He drove past a truck stop, squinting at the bright lights of a gas station and a restaurant. Two pickup trucks, three semis. Heading a quarter mile farther, he turned toward a trailer court. Four-thirty. No lights were on in the trailers. He parked between two cars on a strip of gravel, shut his headlights off, and disconnected the ignition wires beneath the dash.

Pain made him wince. After glancing around to make sure he hadn't attracted attention, he wiped the clammy sweat from his brow. Straining to take off his jacket, he lifted his turtleneck sweater, touched the Velcro straps on his bulletproof vest, and tugged them, pulling the vest off.

Eliot had always insisted, never violate procedure. After a job, take precautions. Wear your vest. In case of complications from the job. Established methods keep you alive.

The vest was somewhat bulky. A quarter-inch thick, weighing a pound and a half, it was made from seven layers of Kevlar, a synthetic nylonlike fiber five times stronger than steel. But Saul was big-boned, rugged, and the extra girth made him seem merely overweight. At the casino, though he hadn't risked carrying a gun, he'd felt confident the vest would be unobtrusive. Once again, a habit had saved his life.

But the bullet should only have stunned him. It shouldn't have gone through the vest. It shouldn't have wounded him. Frowning, he fingered the blood on his chest, probing for the bullet hole. Instead he touched the bullet itself, embedded a quarter-inch into his chest, sticking out between two ribs, its impact slowed by the vest.

He gritted his teeth and pulled it free, exhaling, stifling the urge to vomit. For a moment in the dark, the car seemed to swirl. Then the spinning stopped, and he swallowed bile.

He wiped the bullet, troubled. Nothing made sense. It shouldn't have gone through the vest. The bullet was slim and pointed, but its tip should have been blunted by its impact against the vest.

He took a chance and opened the car door, using the interior light to study the bullet, more troubled by what he saw.

The bullet was green. Teflon streamlined its shape, making it capable of piercing the vest. A special item favored by elite intelligence networks. Including the Mossad.

He studied the silencer on the Beretta. Possession of one was as illegal as having a machine gun or a rocket launcher. Rather than risk getting caught with one or trying to buy one on the black market, operatives assembled their own, using parts easy to obtain and innocent-looking if distributed in a toolkit. In this case, the gunman had bought a plastic tube, wide enough to fit over the Beretta's muzzle. The tube had been filled with an alternating series of metal and glass-wool washers, the holes in the washers wide enough to allow for the passage of a bullet. The tube had a hole in the end, small enough to prevent the washers from falling out, large enough to let the bullet escape. Three holes had been drilled a quarter-inch down from the tube's open mouth. Set screws through these holes braced the silencer over the pistol's barrel. Quickly assembled, it was effective for seven shots before the glass wool lost its muffling power. It could then be swiftly taken apart, its components thrown away with no sign of what they'd been used for. Simple. The method preferred by the Mossad.

What the hell was going on? How had his opponents known he was going to that hotel? He himself had known only a few hours before. It wasn't a question of his having been followed. The assassins had anticipated his movements. They'd been *waiting* for him.

Eliot had made the arrangements. Eliot must have done something wrong. Perhaps he'd used an unsecured phone.

But Eliot didn't make mistakes.

Then Eliot must have been followed, his conversations picked up by a directional microphone.

But Eliot knew better. He always carried a jamming device that interfered with microphones.

Maybe one of Eliot's men was a double agent. But for whom? The Mossad?

Saul shut the door. The light went off. He used a handkerchief to wipe the blood from his chest. In the night, he felt tired and cold.

He didn't like coincidences. Eliot had sent him to Atlantic City, a location that seemed unusual, where a member of the disbanded team had tried to . . . Saul began to shiver. Eliot had also sent him to the abandoned hotel, where again Saul had almost been killed.

The common denominator. Eliot.

The implication was unthinkable. Eliot – Saul's foster father – had put out a contract on him?

No!

Saul pulled down his turtleneck sweater and stepped from the car, tugging on his sportcoat. Five o'clock – the eastern sky was turning gray.

He left the trailer court, walking in pain along the highway. At the truck stop, he waited in the shadow of a semi till its driver left the restaurant.

The driver stiffened when he saw him.

'Fifty bucks for a ride,' Saul said.

'Against the rules. You see that sign? No passengers. I'd lose my job.'

'A hundred.'

'So you mug me when you get the chance. Or your buddies hijack the truck.'

'Two hundred.'

The driver pointed. 'Blood on your clothes. You've been in a fight, or you're wanted by the cops.'

'I cut myself shaving. Three.'

'No way. I've got a wife and kids.'

'Four. That's my limit.'

'Not enough.'

'I'll wait for another driver.' Saul walked toward a different truck.

'Hey, buddy.'

Saul turned.

'That kind of money, you must really need to get out of town.'

'My father's sick.'

The driver laughed. 'And so's my bank account. I hoped you'd offer five.'

'Don't have it.'

'Ever seen Atlanta?'

'No,' Saul lied.

'You're going to.' The driver held out his hand. 'The money?'

'Half now.'

'Fair enough. In case you get any funny ideas, I'd better warn you. I was in the marines. I know karate.'

'Really,' Saul said.

'Assume the position while I search you. I'd better not find a gun or a knife.'

Saul had thrown away the silencer and put the small Beretta in his underwear, against his crotch. The gun felt uncomfortable, but he knew only naked body searches were accurate. The driver would frisk the contours of Saul's body – the arms, up the legs, and along the spine. But Saul was doubtful the driver would feel his privates or reach inside his underwear. If the driver did . . .

'All you'll find is four hundred dollars,' Saul told him. 'In Atlanta, if the cops come looking for me, I'll know who to blame. I'll phone your boss and tell him about our arrangement. It'll be a comfort to me to know you lost your job.'

'Is that any way to talk to a pal?' The driver grinned. As Saul expected, the frisk was amateurish.

Through the gleaming day, as the truck roared down the highway, he pretended to sleep as he brooded over what had happened. Eliot, he kept thinking. Something was horribly wrong. But he couldn't keep running. He couldn't hide forever.

Why does Eliot want to kill me? Why the Mossad?

This much was sure – he needed help. But who to trust?

The sun glared through the windshield.

Clutching his chest, he sweated, feverish, thinking of Chris.

His foster brother.

Remus.

CHURCH OF THE MOON

1

Among the surge of Orientals on noisy, acrid Silom Road, the tall
Caucasian somehow avoided attention. He moved with purpose,
smoothly, steadily, blending with the rhythm of the crowd. As soon
as someone sensed him, the man was already gone. An untrained
observer could not have guessed his nationality. French perhaps, or
English. Maybe German. His hair was brown, but whether dark or
light was hard to say. His eyes were brown, yet blue and green. His
face was oval yet rectangular. He wasn't thin but wasn't heavy either.
Ordinary jacket; shirt and pants of neutral color. In his thirties, maybe
older, maybe younger. Without scars or facial hair. Unusual in only
one respect – he seemed to be invisible.

In fact, he was an American. Though he traveled under many identities, his real name was Chris Kilmoonie. He was thirty-six. His scars
had been disguised by plastic surgery. Indeed, his face had been
reconstructed several times. He'd cut the labels from his clothes. He'd
stitched the equivalent of five thousand dollars in large bills of various
currencies beneath the lining of his jacket. The rest of his fifteen-
thousand-dollar emergency fund had been converted into gold and
gems – an eighteen-karat Rolex watch, for example, and a precious
necklace – which he wore out of sight. He had to be able to move
from country to country as quickly as possible, freed from dependence
on banks. He didn't worry that a thief who suspected his wealth would
try to take it from him. Beneath his jacket, behind the belt at his
spine, he carried a Mauser HSc, 7.65–mm automatic pistol. But more
than the weapon, Chris's eyes discouraged confrontation. Deep within
them, past their shifting colors, lurked a warning confidence that
made a stranger want to keep his distance.

Halfway down the street. Chris paused among bamboo-awninged
stalls where vendors shouted to be heard above one another, waving
elaborate kites, silk scarves, and teak statuettes. Ignoring a pushcart
salesman who offered him a piece of roasted monkey, he glanced
beyond the cacophonous rush of bicycles and mopeds toward a thin,
peaked, two-story church, enmeshed with vines, between the Oriental
Hotel and a mission. From this angle, he saw the rectory, a two-story
bungalow attached to the rear of the church. Beyond it, he saw the
graveyard and the pepper garden that sloped down to the muddy,

36

crocodile-infested river. In the distance, rice paddies merged with the jungle. What interested him most, though, was the six-foot stained glass window beneath the church's peak. He knew that years before, a one-foot slice of glass had been broken during a storm. Because this Parish in Sawang Kaniwat, old town, Bangkok, was poor, the slice – which resembled a crescent moon – had been replaced by a cheap piece of galvanized steel. The crescent, stark beneath the peak, accounted for the nickname: Church of the Moon.

Chris also knew that, at the request of the Russian KGB, the church had been converted into an Abelard-sanctioned safe house in 1959, available for use by operatives from any agency, no matter their differences in politics. As he waited for a break in traffic, then crossed the street, he took for granted that agents from various intelligence networks watched from nearby buildings. They didn't matter. Within the church and the surrounding area, he was guaranteed immunity.

He opened a listing wooden gate and walked along a soggy gravel path beside the church. In back, the blare of the street was muffled. He tugged his shirt away from his sweaty chest, the temperature ninety-five, the humidity smothering. Though the rains weren't due for another month, thick black clouds loomed over the jungle.

He walked up the creaky unpainted steps and knocked on the rectory door. An Oriental servant answered. Speaking Thai, Chris asked to see the priest. A minute passed. The old priest came and studied him.

Phonetically, Chris said, 'Eye ba.'

In Thai, this phrase is an expletive, referring to a dirty or large monkey. It can also mean guerrilla. It was all Chris had to say to gain asylum here.

The priest stepped back and nodded.

Chris went in, squinting while his eyes adjusted to the shadows in the hallway. He smelled pepper.

'You speak –?'

'English,' Chris replied.

'Are you familiar with our arrangements?'

'Yes, I've been here once before.'

'I don't recall.'

'In 1965.'

'I still don't –'

'I looked different then. My face was crushed.'

The old priest hesitated. 'Ruptured appendix? Fractured spine?'

Chris nodded.

'I remember now,' the old priest said. 'Your agency should be complimented. Its surgeons were meticulous.'

Chris waited.

'But you're not here to recall old times,' the priest continued. 'My office is more convenient for conversation.' Turning left, he entered a room.

Chris followed him. He'd read the old man's file and knew that Father Gabriel Janin was seventy-two. His white whisker stubble matched the bristle of his close-cropped hair. Emaciated, stooped and wrinkled, the priest wore muddy canvas shoes and dingy pants below a shapeless mildewed surplice. Both his age and slovenly appearance were misleading. From 1929 to 1934, he'd been a member of the French Foreign Legion. Bored by the challenge he'd met and exceeded, he'd entered the Cistercian Order of monks at Citeaux in 1935. Four years later, he'd left the order and, during the war years, trained to become a missionary priest. After the war, he'd been transferred to Saigon. In 1954, he'd been transferred again, this time to Bangkok. In 1959, he'd been blackmailed by the KGB, because of his preference for young Thai girls, to be the housekeeper for this internationally sanctioned safe house. Chris was well aware that, to protect his guests, the priest would kill.

The office was narrow, cluttered, musty. The priest shut the door. 'Would you like some refreshment? Tea perhaps, or –?'

Chris shook his head.

The priest spread his hands. He sat with a desk between them. A bird sang in the pepper garden.

'How may I help you?'

'Father –' Chris's voice was hushed as if he were going to confession, '– I need you to tell me the name of a dentist who'll extract teeth and stay quiet about it.'

Father Janin looked troubled.

'What's the matter?'

'Your fine organization should not need this information,' the old priest said. 'It has dentists of its own.'

'I need the name of yours.'

The priest leaned forward, frowning. 'Why does this concern you? Why come here? Forgive my bluntness. Has this dentist wronged someone or destroyed the cover of someone? Are you returning a favor by removing him?'

'No favor,' Chris assured him. 'My employers worry about information leaks in our network. Sometimes we have to go outside our sources.'

Father Janin considered. He kept frowning as he nodded. 'Understandable. But all the same . . .' He tapped his fingers on his desk.

'When you make inquiries, my cryptonym is Remus.'

The priest stopped tapping his fingers. 'In that case, if you'll stay the night, I'll try to have your answer by the morning.'

That's not soon enough, Chris thought.

2

In the dining room, he sat at a table eating chicken and noodles laced with hot peppers, as the Thais preferred it. His eyes watered; his nostrils flared. He drank warm Coke, glancing out the window toward the back. The clouds had reached the city, rain falling densely, like molten lead. He couldn't see the crosses in the graveyard.

38

Father Janin's reluctance disturbed him. He was sure that at this moment the priest was making phone calls, investigating his background. The phone, of course, would not be bugged. Neither would the safe house. The place was neutral territory. Anyone who violated its sanctity would be exiled from his network, hunted by the world's intelligence community, and executed.

All the same, Chris felt troubled. As soon as the agency learned he was here, the local bureau chief would wonder why. He'd contact his superior. Since cryptonyms gained their significance from their first two letters – AM, for example, referred to Cuba; thus AMALGAM would be the cryptonym for an operation in that country – the bureau chief's superior would check the first two letters in Chris's cryptonym REMUS and learn that RE meant Chris was answerable only to headquarters in Langley, Virginia, and in particular to Eliot. Soon Eliot would be informed that Chris had arrived unexpectedly at the Bangkok safe house. Eliot, of course, would be puzzled since he hadn't directed Chris to come here.

That was the problem. Chris didn't want Eliot to follow his movements. Given what Chris intended to do, he didn't want Eliot to know the consequences, didn't want Eliot to grieve or feel embarrassed.

He tried not to show impatience. At the earliest opportunity, he'd go to the priest and get the dentist's name.

Preoccupied, he turned from the dismal rain beyond the window. Wiping his sweat-blurred eyes, he gaped in disbelief at a man whom he had last seen seventeen years ago.

The man, a Chinese, had entered the dining room. Slender, round-faced, genteel, he wore an impeccable khaki suit, the jacket of which was buttoned to his collar in the Mao style. His youthful face and his thick black hair belied his sixty-two years.

The man's name was Chin Ken Chan. IQ: one hundred and eighty. Multilingual in Russian, French, and English in addition to Chinese. Chris knew his background. Chan had received his formal education from Dame Sahara Day-Wisdom, OBE, at Merton College, Oxford University, from 1939 till the war had ended. During that time, he'd been influenced by the Communist members of clubs at both Oxford and Cambridge, easily recruited by the mole Guy Burgess to help Mao after the war. Because Chan was a homosexual, he'd never risen higher than the rank of colonel in the intelligence arena of China. But he was a valuable idealist in the Maoist cause and, despite his effete appearance, one of its finest killers, particularly with the garotte.

Chan glanced dismissively at Chris and walked toward another table. He sat primly, reaching between the buttons of his jacket to pull out his own set of chopsticks.

Chris chewed and swallowed, hiding his surprise. 'The Snow Leopard.'

Chan raised his head.

'Does the Snow Leopard miss Deep Snow?'

Chan nodded impassively. 'It's been thirteen years since we've had Deep Snow in the Orient.'

'I was thinking of *seventeen* years ago. I believe it snowed then in Laos.'

Chan smiled politely. 'There were only two Americans in the snow that year. I recall they were brothers – but not by birth.'

'And this one is eternally grateful to you.'

'Chris?' Chan said.

Chris nodded, throat tight. 'Good to see you, Chan.'

His heart raced as he grinned and stood. They crossed the room and embraced.

3

Father Janin felt apprehensive. As soon as a servant had taken the American to the dining room, he grabbed the phone on his desk and dialed quickly.

'Remus,' he said.

He hung up, gulped a glass of brandy, frowned, and waited.

Coincidences bothered him. Two days ago, he'd given sanctuary to a Russian, Joseph Malenov, the director of the KGB's opium traffic into Southeast Asia. Malenov had stayed in his room, where, by agreement, the priest supplied him daily with 300 milligrams of the suppressant Dilantin to try to calm his outbursts of rage and hypertension. The treatment was working.

Yesterday, the priest had given sanctuary to a Chinese Communist operative, Col. Chin Ken Chan. Informants had told the priest that Chan was here to meet the Russian and perhaps become a double agent for the KGB. Such arrangements were not unusual. In an Abelard safe house, opposing operatives frequently took advantage of neutral territory to transact business, sometimes defecting. But the priest was not convinced of Chan's motivation. He knew that the Chinese Communists opposed Russia's opium smuggling into South-east Asia, partly because they resented Soviet interference in the region, partly as well because they felt that opium undermined the character of the area. It made no sense that Chan, who for years had been sabotaging Russia's opium shipments, would defect to the very man who directed the smuggling.

Now, today, the American had arrived. His request for a dentist who would extract teeth and stay quiet about it could have only one purpose – to prevent someone's body from being identified. But whose? The Russian's?

His thoughts were interrupted when the phone rang.

The priest picked up the receiver and listened.

In a minute, he set it down, twice as puzzled.

REMUS, he'd learned, was the cryptonym for Christopher Patrick Kilmoonie, one-time lieutenant in the American Special Forces, who in 1965 had worked in conjunction with the CIA in an operation called Deep Snow, the purpose of which was to destroy the flow of Russian opium. In 1966, Kilmoonie had resigned from the military and joined the CIA. In 1976, he'd entered a Cistercian monastery. In 1982, he'd rejoined the CIA. The combination of religion and politics seemed unusual, but Father Janin could empathize since he himself had combined them. Still, what troubled him was that all three men were connected in different ways with the opium traffic.

And one other connection. When the American had mentioned that in 1965 he'd come here with a crushed face, ruptured appendix, and fractured spine, the priest had remembered the American's escort – the same Chinese now in this building – Chin Ken Chan.

Coincidences bothered him.

4

Chris stood on the rectory's porch as rain drummed on the corrugated metal roof. He still couldn't see the graveyard. Next to him, Chan leaned on the railing, facing outward. Though the safe house wasn't bugged, they used the noise from the rain to prevent their conversation from being overheard. They'd chosen a windowless corner.

'Two things,' Chan said.

Chris waited.

'You must leave here quickly. Joseph Malenov is in a room upstairs,' Chan said.

Chris understood. In their profession, what was said was seldom what was meant. Discretion was the rule. For Chan to speak even this directly was unusual. Chris quickly made the connection, filling the gaps between Chan's statements.

He was shocked. The basis of their way of life was adherence to strict codes, the most extreme of which was the sanctity of an Abelard safe house.

Chan intended to commit the cardinal sin.

'It's never been done,' Chris said.

'Not true. While you were in the monastery –'

'You've been keeping tabs on me.'

'I saved your life. I'm responsible for you. During your stay in the monastery, the code was broken twice. In Ferlach, Austria. Then again in Montreal.'

Chris felt a chill.

Chan's gaze never wavered.

'Then the world's gone crazy,' Chris said.

'Isn't that why you left it? Because the monastery offered a code with honor?'

'No. Back then, the profession still had rules. I left because I failed the profession. Not the other way around.'

'I don't understand.'

'I can't explain. I don't want to talk about it. If the sanction's lost its meaning, how can we depend on anything else?' He shook his head in dismay. 'Nothing's sacred.'

41

'Everything gets worse,' Chan said. 'Six years ago, what I plan would have been unthinkable.'

'And now?' Chris asked.

'Since precedent has been established, I feel free from obligation. Malenov is mentally diseased. These past few months, he's increased the opium traffic beyond tolerance. He has to be stopped.'

'Then kill him outside,' Chris insisted.

'He's too well guarded then.'

'But you'll be hunted.'

'By them all.' Chan nodded. 'Everyone. The Snow Leopard has his tricks.'

'The odds,' Chris said. 'If everyone's against you . . . Ferlach, and then Montreal? What happened?'

'To the violators? They were found, and they were killed. And so will I be killed. In time. But I will stretch the time.'

'I ask you not to do this.'

'Why?'

'Because I feel responsible to *you*.'

'The debt is mine. I interfered with what you understand as fate. But I must face my own. As I grow old, I must prepare to die with what you Westerners call dignity, what I call honor. I must face my destiny. Too many years I've waited for this chance. The opium is wrong. It has to be stopped.'

'But the KGB will only send another man to replace him.'

Chan clutched the rail. 'Not Malenov. The man is evil.' Sweat drenched his face. 'He has to die.'

Chris felt distressed by Chan's directness. 'In the morning, I will leave.'

'But I can't wait that long. The Russian leaves tomorrow.'

'I need important information from the priest.'

'Then get it soon. When I act, our friendship won't be overlooked. The coincidence of our meeting after all these years will seem suspicious. Fate, my friend. I didn't save your life so long ago to have you lose it due to me now. Get out of here. I beg you.'

The rain fell harder.

5

Something wakened Chris. He lay in his room in the dark, squinting at the luminous dial on his watch. Three-thirty. Puzzled, he kept still and concentrated. The storm had passed. Occasional drops of water trickled off the eaves. As moonlight glimmered through his open window, he smelled the sordid odor of the river and the fertilized soil of the garden below. He listened to the songs of the birds beginning to stir.

For a moment, he thought he'd wakened from habit and nothing more. His six years in the monastery had trained him to use the hours before dawn for meditation. Normally he would have wakened shortly anyhow.

But then he glanced toward the hall light filtering through the crack below his door. A shadow passed. Whoever it was, he thought, the person knew how to walk like an animal, carrying the weight of his body along the outsides of his feet. He imagined a cat stalking silently toward its prey.

It might have been a servant patrolling the hall. Or Chan. Or someone after Chan. Or after me, Chris thought, because of my friendship with Chan.

He grabbed the Mauser by his side and threw off his sheet, lunging naked in the dark toward the protection of a chair. His testicles shrank. He held his breath and waited, cautious, aiming toward the door.

Beyond it, he heard a noise like a fist slamming into a pillow. Muffled, it nonetheless carried a great deal of force.

As someone groaned, an object thudded to the floor out there.

Chris left the cover of the chair, creeping toward the wall beside his door. With his ear to the wall, he listened to the rattle of a latch as a door came open in the hall.

Someone spoke, alarmed, in Russian. '*What have you done?*'

Chris heard the old priest answer, also in Russian. 'He was going in your room. You see his garotte. He meant to strangle you. I had no choice. I had to kill him.'

Chris opened the door. If he didn't, if he stayed in his room, the priest might wonder why the noise hadn't wakened him. Suspicious, the priest might decide Chris was somehow involved in this.

Chris squinted from his open door toward the light in the hall.

The priest swung toward the sound he'd made, aiming a Russian Tokarev automatic pistol with a silencer.

Chris froze. He raised his hands, the Mauser high above his head. 'Your voices woke me.' He shrugged. 'I can see this is none of my business.'

Waiting for a nod of dismissal from the priest, Chris stepped back in his room and closed the door.

He stared at the dark. He'd seen a man in another doorway. Middle sixties. Shrunken, pale. Dark circles under his eyes. Rumpled hair. Nervous twitches. Wearing sweat-stained silk pajamas. Joseph Malenov, Chris thought. He'd never met the man, but he'd seen photographs of him and knew that Malenov was addicted to the opium he smuggled.

On the floor, between the priest and Malenov, Chris had seen Chan's body, the base of his skull shattered by the Russian pistol's 7.62–mm bullet. The floor had been dark with blood and urine. There'd been no point in checking to see if Chan was alive.

Chris seethed. Other shadows blocked the light at the base of the door. He recognized the sound of someone unfolding a blanket. He heard men, more than two, quietly, but not as quiet as Chan had been, lift the body, wrap it, and carry it away. He smelled acrid sandalwood, then the resin odor of pine. Someone must have lit a pot of incense and thrown sawdust on the floor to absorb the body's fluids.

Chris stepped toward the window, careful not to show himself. The birds erupted from the trees, alarmed by intruders. Silhouetted by the moonlight, two Oriental servants left the rectory's porch, hunched over, carrying a heavy object wrapped in a blanket between them. A third servant led the way, flashing a light toward the path through the crosses in the graveyard and the pepper plants in the garden.

They went down the slope toward the river – to feed Chan to the crocodiles, or else to boat him across to the jungle.

Friend, Chris thought. His throat felt tight.

He clutched his Mauser.

6

Father Janin made the sign of the cross. In the church, he'd been kneeling at the altar rail, reciting his daily prayers. He stared at the votive candles he'd lit, enveloped by the fragrance of beeswax and frankincense. They flickered in the dark.

5 A.M. The church was quiet.

Sanctuary.

Pushing from the altar rail, the old priest stood and genuflected to the tabernacle. He had prayed for God's forgiveness. Having vowed to guard this safe house, he believed he'd lose his soul if he didn't fulfill his obligations. Though the KGB had recruited him, he felt allegiance to every network. Every operative in the world was his parishioner. Their differences in politics – or religion, or lack of it – didn't matter. Even atheists had souls. Cold, tired men came here for refuge. As a priest, he had to offer them the corporal works of mercy. If he had to kill to protect the sanctity of this safe house, then he prayed for God to understand. What justification could be more compelling? In the dark, the candles flickered in commemoration of the dead.

The old priest turned from the altar, stiffening as he saw a shadow move.

From the dark of the nearest pew, a man stood, walking toward him.

The American.

The priest reached through the slit in the side of his surplice, pulling the pistol from his belt, aiming it under the loose folds of his garment.

The American stopped at a careful distance.

'I didn't hear you come down the aisle,' the priest said.

'I tried to be quiet, to respect your prayers.'

'You came to pray as well?'

'The habit dies hard. You must have been told by now that I too was a Cistercian.'

'And your friend? You feel no need for retribution?'

'He did what he had to. So did you. We know the rules.'

44

Nodding, the priest clutched the pistol beneath his surplice.

'Did you get the name of the dentist?' the American said.

'Not long ago. I have it written down for you.'

The priest set his prayer book in a pew. With his free hand, he reached through the other slit in his surplice, pulling out a piece of paper. After setting it on the prayer book, he stepped carefully back.

The church was still. The American smiled and picked up the message. In the dark, he didn't try to read it.

'The man you seek lives far away,' the old priest said.

'So much the better.' The American smiled again.

'What makes you say that?'

But the American didn't answer. Turning, he walked silently toward the back of the church, his shadow disappearing. Father Janin heard the creak of a door being opened. He saw the gray of early dawn outside. The American's figure blocked the gray. The door abruptly closed, its rumble eerie in the stillness.

He'd been holding his breath. Exhaling, he put the pistol back in his belt, his forehead slick with sweat. Frowning, he glanced at the stained glass window beneath the peak at the back of the church. Pale light filtered through, emphasizing the silhouette of the galvanized steel sickle moon.

7

The Russian, Chris thought.

He didn't blame the priest. What he'd told the priest was true. The priest had only been obeying the rules. More than authorized, the priest was *obligated* to insure the safety of a guest, even if he had to kill another guest who attempted to violate the sanction.

The Russian, though. As Chris left the church, skirting the pools of water in the morning twilight, heading toward the rectory in back, he thought about him, seething without showing it. From habit, he seemed more relaxed the more determined he became. His pace appeared leisurely, a stroll at dawn to appreciate the stillness, admiring the birds.

The Russian, he kept thinking.

He reached the back, pausing in half light, pretending to enjoy the view of the river, debating. For years, Chan had fought against the Russian, becoming so obsessed he sacrificed his life for this chance to kill him. Back in '65, Chris as well had fought the Russian, joining forces with Chan in a combined CIA-Communist Chinese operation to stop the flow of opium from Laos into South Vietnam. Following a failed attack on a Pathet Lao camp, while Chris was being tortured for information (face crushed, appendix ruptured, spine fractured), Chan had led a rescue mission, saving Chris's life. Chan had brought Chris to this safe house, caring for him, never leaving his side till the American surgeons arrived.

Now Chan was dead.

In the same place Chan had nursed Chris back to life.

Because of the opium.

The Russian had to die.

He knew the danger. He'd be an outcast, hunted by everyone. Regardless of his skill, they'd find him eventually. He'd soon be dead.

It didn't matter. Given his reason for wanting the dentist, given what he intended to do, he'd soon be dead regardless. What difference did it make? But this way, without losing anything he wasn't already prepared to lose, he could return a favor to his friend. That was paramount, more than the sanction, more than anything. Loyalty, friendship. Chan had saved his life. Obeying honor, Chris was obligated to repay his debt. If not, he'd be in disgrace.

And since the sanction had been violated twice already, the only meaning that remained was in his private code.

He squinted from the river to the graveyard. Mindful of the paper the priest had given him, he pulled it out, reading the dentist's name and address. His eyes hardened. Nodding grimly, he walked up the porch steps, entering the rectory.

In his room, he packed his small overnight bag. From a leather pouch, he removed a hypodermic and a vial of liquid. Carrying his bag, he left the room.

The hall was quiet. He knocked on the Russian's door.

The voice was tense behind it. 'What?'

Chris answered in Russian. 'You have to get out of here. The Chinese had a backup man.'

He heard the urgent rattle of the lock. The door came open, Malenov sweating, holding a pistol, so drugged his eyes were glazed.

He never saw the web of skin between Chris's thumb and first finger streak toward him, striking his larynx, crushing his vocal cords.

The Russian wheezed, falling back.

Chris stepped in, closing the door. As Malenov lay on the floor, unable to speak, struggling frantically to breathe, his body convulsed, his feet turning inward, his arms twisting toward his chest.

Chris filled the hypodermic from the vial of liquid. Pulling down the Russian's pajama pants, he injected 155 international milliunits of potassium chloride into the distal vein of the Russian's penis. The potassium would travel to the brain, the chloride to the urinary tract, causing the body's electrolytes to depolarize, resulting in a massive stroke.

Already the Russian's face was blue, turning gray, about to turn yellow.

Chris put the hypodermic and the vial inside his overnight bag. Picking up the trembling body, he leaned it against a chair so the Russian's neck was in line with the chair's wooden arm. He tilted the chair so it fell across the Russian, making the injury to his neck seem the consequence of a fall.

For Chan, he thought.

He picked up his bag and left the room.

The hall was empty. Using the Russian's key to lock the door, he went downstairs, across the rectory's porch, toward the graveyard.

In the gray of dawn, he knew if he went out the front toward the street he'd be followed as a matter of course by agents from various intelligence networks, so he went down the slope toward the river. Smelling its stench, he found a boat that seemed less leaky than two others. Paddling from shore, he ignored the gaping jaws of a crocodile.

8

Two hours later, the priest (after knocking repeatedly on the Russian's door) instructed his servants to break it down. They stumbled in and found the body sprawled beneath the overturned chair. The priest gasped. As the guardian of this safe house, he was accountable to his guests' superiors. He could justify killing Chan, but now the Russian had died as well. Too much was happening at once.

If the KGB decides I failed . . .

Appalled, the priest inspected the body, praying the death was natural. He found no sign of violence, except for the bruise on the throat, but that could be explained by a fall against the chair.

He quickly calculated. Malenov had come here, distraught, in need of a rest, requesting drugs to treat his rage and hypertension. He'd nearly been assassinated. Possibly the added strain, combined with the drugs, had caused a heart attack.

But now the American had disappeared.

Too much was happening.

The priest rushed to a phone. He called the local KGB. The Bangkok bureau chief called his superior. An unexplained death in an Abelard safe house qualified as an emergency, requiring immediate investigation.

One hour after the priest's discovery of the body, a Soviet IL–18 cargo plane took off from Hanoi, North Vietnam, battling a headwind to fly the 600 miles to Thailand in slightly under two hours. The KGB's investigating officer, in tandem with a team of expert physicians, studied the position of the body, taking photographs. They rushed it to the cargo plane and took off for Hanoi, this time helped by a tailwind, returning in ninety minutes.

The autopsy lasted seven hours. Though the Russian's heart had not occluded, his brain had hemorrhaged. Cause of death: a stroke. But why? No embolisms. Blood tests showed the presence of Dilantin, which the Russian had been taking; also opium, which Malenov had been addicted to. No other unusual chemicals. After a microscopic examination of the body, the coroner discovered the needle mark in the distal vein of the Russian's penis. Though he couldn't prove it, he suspected murder. He'd seen a handful of cases like this before. Potassium chloride. The separation of the chemical into its two component parts would cause a stroke. A body normally contained potassium and chloride, so the evidence was hidden. He reported his suspicion to the investigating officer.

An hour after that, the KGB bureau chief of Bangkok was sent to the Church of the Moon. He questioned the priest at length. The priest admitted that an American, a friend of Chan, had been staying at the rectory.

'His name and particulars?' the bureau chief asked.

Afraid, the old priest answered.

'What did the American want?' the bureau chief asked.

The old priest told him.

'Where does this dentist live?'

When the bureau chief heard the reply, he studied the priest across the desk. 'So far away? Our coroner in Hanoi has established the time of death as 6 A.M.' The bureau chief gestured toward the night beyond the office window. He pointed at his watch. 'That's fifteen hours ago. Why didn't you tell us about the American right away?'

The priest poured another glass of brandy, drinking it all at once. Drops rolled down his whisker-stubbled chin. 'Because I was afraid. This morning, I couldn't be sure the American was involved. If I'd killed him for precaution's sake, I'd have been forced to explain myself to the CIA. But I didn't have any evidence against him.'

'So you preferred to explain yourself to us?'

'I admit I made a mistake. I should have kept closer watch on him. But he convinced me he had no intentions toward your operative. When I found the body, I hoped the cause of death was natural. What point was there in admitting my mistake if I didn't have to? You can understand my problem.'

'Certainly.'

The bureau chief picked up the phone. After dialing and waiting for an answer, he spoke to his superior. 'The Abelard sanction has been violated. Repeat: violated. Christopher Patrick Kilmoonie. Cryptonym: Remus. CIA.' The bureau chief repeated the description the priest had given him. 'He's on his way to Guatemala.' The bureau chief gave the address. 'At least, he claimed he was going there, but given what's happened, I don't think he'll do the expected. Yes, I know – he's fifteen hours ahead of us.'

After listening for a minute, the bureau chief set down the phone.

He turned to the priest and shot him.

9

'Are you sure?' the CIA director blurted into the phone.

'Completely,' the KGB director answered on the emergency long-distance line. He spoke in English since his counterpart did not speak Russian. 'Understand – I didn't call to ask permission. Since the rogue is yours, I'm merely following protocol by informing you of my intention.'

'I guarantee he wasn't acting on my orders.'

'Even if he were, it wouldn't matter. I've already sent the cables. At this moment, your communications room should be receiving yours.

Under the terms of the Abelard sanction, I've alerted every network. I'll read the last three sentences. "Find Remus. Universal contract. Terminate at your discretion." I assume since your agency has been embarrassed, you'll go after him more zealously than all the other networks.'

'Yes . . . you have my word.' The CIA director swallowed, setting down the phone.

He pressed a button on his intercom, demanding the file on Christopher Patrick Kilmoonie.

Thirty minutes later, he learned that Kilmoonie was assigned to the paramilitary branch of Covert Operations, a GS–13, among the highest-ranking operatives in the agency.

The director groaned. It was bad enough to be embarrassed by a rogue, but worse when the rogue turned out to be a world-class killer. Protocol – and prudence – required that to execute this man the director would have to use a team of other GS–13s.

The file on Remus told the director something else. He stood in anger, stalking from his office.

Eliot was Remus's control.

10

'I don't know anything about it,' Eliot said.

'Well, you're responsible for him! You find him!' the director said, completing the argument, storming from Eliot's office.

Eliot smiled at the open door. He lit a cigarette, discovered ashes on his black suit, and brushed them off. His ancient eyes gleamed with delight that the director had come to him instead of demanding that Eliot go to the director. The angry visit was one more sign of the director's weakness, of the power Eliot enjoyed.

He swung his chair toward the window, letting sunlight warm his face. Below, a massive parking lot stretched to the fence and the trees that buffered the agency from the highway at Langley, Virginia. From his perspective, he saw just a portion of the ten thousand cars surrounding the huge, tall, H-shaped building.

His smile dissolved. Already preoccupied by the hunt for Saul, he'd been troubled yesterday when told that Chris, Saul's foster brother, had arrived at the Abelard safe house in Bangkok. Eliot hadn't instructed him to go there. For the past several weeks, since Chris had abandoned his station in Rome, he hadn't been reporting in. Assumption: Chris had been killed.

But now he'd suddenly reappeared. Had he been on the run for all that time, finally able to reach asylum? Surely he could have found a way to contact Eliot before then, or at least have got in touch with him when he arrived at the Church of the Moon. It didn't make sense. To ask for a dentist not affiliated with the agency. To violate the sanction by killing the Russian. What the hell was going on? Chris knew the rule. The best assassins from every network would be hunting him. Why had he been so foolish?

Eliot pursed his wrinkled lips.

Two surrogate brothers, both on the run. The symmetry appealed to him. As sunlight glared off the cars in the lot, his smile returned. He found the answer to his problem.

Saul and Chris. Saul had to be killed before he guessed the reason he was being hunted. So who knew where he would hide better than his counterpart?

But the dentist . . . Eliot shivered. Something troubled him about that detail. Why, before he killed the Russian, would Chris have wanted the name of a dentist?

Eliot's spine felt cold.

11

'Mexico City,' Chris said. 'The soonest flight.'

Behind the airline's ticket counter, the Hawaiian woman tapped on a computer keyboard. 'Sir, how many?'

'One,' he answered.

'First class or coach?'

'It doesn't matter.'

The woman studied the screen on the console.

Voices droned from speakers in the noisy crowded terminal. Behind him, Chris felt other customers waiting.

'Sir, Flight 211 has room in coach. It leaves in fifteen minutes. If we hurry, we can get you aboard. Your name?'

Chris told her the false name on his passport, paying cash when she asked for his credit card, avoiding a paper trail as much as possible.

'Any luggage?'

'Just this carry-on.'

'I'll phone the boarding attendant and ask him to hold the flight. Enjoy your trip, sir.'

'Thank you.'

Though he smiled as he turned to hurry through the terminal, his muscles hardened. Carefully he scanned the crowd for anyone watching him. He reached the metal detector, a Sky Policeman studying him, but Chris had dropped his Mauser down a Bangkok sewer, knowing he'd be caught trying to carry the pistol on board a plane. He could have put it in a suitcase and arranged for the case to be stored beneath the plane. That luggage wasn't searched. But he couldn't risk waiting for it to be returned. He had to keep moving. He grabbed his overnight bag after it came through the scanning machine and rushed down the corridor toward the boarding dock.

A stewardess watched from the plane's open door as he ran down the passenger tunnel. His footsteps echoed.

'Thanks for waiting,' he told her.

'No problem. They're late getting food on board.' She took his ticket.

He passed the first-class passengers, going through the bulkhead toward the seats in back. Several were empty. The boarding attendant had asked him if he wanted smoking or nonsmoking. Chris didn't smoke, but since the smokers' section was in the rear, he'd chosen the seat that was farthest back. He needed to watch as many passengers as he could, the aisle, and especially the door.

His seat was between an overweight man and an elderly woman, near the washrooms. Squeezing past the man, he sat in the middle, smiling to the woman, sliding his compact bag beneath the forward seat. He buckled himself in and, looking bored, peered along the aisle.

He had to assume the worst – that the needle hole in Malenov's body had been discovered and a universal contract issued against him. Though his intention remained the same – to find a dentist – he couldn't go to the one the priest had recommended. The address the priest had given him was in Guatemala, but the priest would have told the KGB's investigators where he was going. In turn, the investigators would have radioed their people in Guatemala to watch for him. He had to choose another country, one he knew well, in which he could disappear and use his own resources to find a trustworthy dentist. Mexico appealed to him. But leaving Bangkok and then Singapore, he hadn't been able to get on flights as quickly as he needed them. The plane to Honolulu had landed forty minutes behind schedule. He'd missed the next flight to Mexico City and been forced to wait for this one. At the start, he'd hoped for a twelve-hour lead, but it was now sixteen hours since he'd killed the Russian.

He waited tensely. In Bangkok, it would be night, but eight thousand miles to the east, it was morning in Honolulu. The sun glared through the windows, making him sweat as he listened to the hiss of the cabin's air conditioning. He felt the vibration of the idling engines through the fuselage. A hatch thumped beneath him, probably last-minute baggage being stowed. Through the window, he watched two loading carts drive away.

He peered along the aisle. A stewardess pulled the passenger door shut, reaching to secure the locking bolt. In a minute, the jet would taxi toward the runway.

Breathing out, he relaxed. Abruptly his stomach burned; he stiffened. The stewardess opened the door. Two men stepped in. As she locked the door, the men came down the aisle.

He studied them. Midtwenties. Muscular yet lithe. Shirts and pants of muted colors. They seemed determined not to glance at the other passengers, concentrating on their ticket folders, then the numbers and letters above the rows of seats. They split up, ten rows apart, ahead of Chris.

He'd waited as long as he could before he'd bought his ticket, hoping to be the last passenger to board the plane. From the back, he'd been watching for anyone who hurried to get on even later than he had.

51

As they turned to take their seats, he leaned across the man beside him, staring down the aisle. Their shoes. He wasn't looking for extra-thick soles or reinforced caps that would make the shoes a weapon. Despite the myth of karate, an operative seldom struck with his feet. A kick was too slow. He looked for a more important characteristic. These men wore high-backed shoes snug above their ankles. Preferred by operatives, the high fit supplied the primary function of preventing them from slipping off in a chase or a fight. Chris wore the same design.

He'd been spotted, no way to tell by whom – the Russians, the English, the French, maybe even his own people. At this moment, someone was making urgent calls to Mexico City. When he landed, a team of assassins – maybe several teams – would be waiting for him.

The jet moved, backing from the dock. It turned, its engines roaring louder as it taxied past the terminal.

A bell rang in the cabin. A stewardess came along the aisle, checking that everyone's seatbelt was fastened.

He gripped the arms of his seat, swallowing hard, turning to the woman beside him. 'Excuse me. Do you have any Kleenex?'

She seemed annoyed. Groping in her purse, she handed him several pieces.

'Thanks.' He tore the Kleenex, shoving wads of it in his ears. The woman blinked in astonishment.

The sounds in the cabin were muffled. Across the aisle, he saw two men talking to each other, their lips moving, words indistinct.

The jet stopped. Through the window, he saw the take-off strip. A plane streaked out of sight. Another plane took its place. There were only two more planes in front of this one.

He shut his eyes, feeling the plane's vibrations. His chest tightened.

The jet moved forward again. When he opened his eyes, he saw only one plane between this jet and the runway.

Suddenly he yanked his seatbelt. He jerked up, squeezing past the man next to him toward the aisle. A stewardess lunged to grab him. 'Sir! You have to stay in your seat! Fasten your belt!'

He pushed her away. Passengers turned, startled. He heard a muffled scream.

The two men stared back, surprised. One scrambled to stand.

Chris grabbed the handle of the emergency door across from him, pulling.

The door flew open. Wind rushed in. He felt the deeper rumble of the jets.

The plane approached the runway. As the stewardess lunged again, he clutched the lower edge of the door frame, swinging out into space. He dangled, peering toward the cabin, the frantic passengers, the killer who darted toward him.

Chris let go of the moving plane. He hit the tarmac, rolling, his knees bent, his elbows tucked, the way he'd learned in jump school. Despite the Kleenex in his ears, he winced from the shriek of the engines. Exhaust roared over him, heat smothering. Another jet loomed close to him.

He ran.

12

The room was massive, antiseptic, temperature-controlled. Computer terminals lined the walls. Fluorescent lights hummed, glaring.

Eliot's wizened forehead narrowed in concentration. 'Airline passengers,' he told a clerk.

'Which city?'

'Bangkok. Departures. The last sixteen hours.'

The agency clerk nodded, tapping on a keyboard.

Eliot lit another cigarette, listening to the clatter of print-outs. The problem stimulated him. There was always the chance that Chris had stayed in Thailand, hiding somewhere. Eliot doubted it, however. He'd trained his operatives to leave the danger zone as soon as possible. Before the Russian's body was discovered, Chris would have wanted a good head start. He'd have used a cover name, possibly an independently acquired passport. Probably not, though. Freelance forgers were a security risk. More likely, Chris would have used a passport Eliot had supplied to him, hoping to go to ground before his trail was spotted.

When the clerk came back with several sheets of paper, Eliot leaned across the counter, drawing his bony finger down the list. He straightened excitedly when he found one of Chris's cover names on a United flight out of Bangkok to Singapore. He told the clerk, 'Departures from Singapore. The last thirteen hours.' Again he waited.

When the clerk brought the second list, Eliot lit another cigarette and concentrated. Chris would have used the same passport. After all, he couldn't risk a customs agent's discovery of other passports with different names in his luggage. He exhaled sharply. There – the same alias on a Trans World flight from Singapore to Honolulu. 'Departures from Honolulu,' he told the clerk. 'The last five hours.'

As the clerk brought the third list of names, Eliot heard the computer room's door hiss shut. Turning, he saw his assistant walking toward him.

The assistant was a Yale man, class of '70 – button-down collar, club ring and tie, a black suit and vest in imitation of Eliot. His eyes crinkled with amusement. 'MI-6 just called. They think they found Remus. The Honolulu airport.'

Eliot turned to the new list of names. He found the alias on a Hawaiian Airlines flight. 'He's on his way to Mexico City.'

'Not anymore,' the assistant said. 'He must have noticed his baby-sitters on the plane. A half minute before takeoff, he popped an emergency door and jumped.'

'On the runway?'

The assistant nodded.

53

'My, my, my.'

'Surveillance couldn't catch him.'

'I'd be surprised if they had. He's one of the best. After all, I trained him.' Eliot smiled. 'So he's on the run in Honolulu. The question is, what would I do if I were Remus? An island's a poor place to hide. I think I'd want to get out of there. Fast.'

'But how? And to where? At least we know where he won't go. He'd be crazy to try for Gautemala or Mexico. He has to figure we'll be waiting for him there.'

'Or maybe he'll figure we won't be waiting since those countries are so damned obvious,' Eliot said. 'It's check and countercheck. A fascinating problem. In Chris's place, how would I get out of Hawaii? A teacher ought to be able to outguess his student.'

His smile died as he thought, then why haven't I outguessed Saul?

13

In Atlanta, the azaleas were in bloom, though the only view Saul had of them was from glaring headlights as the truck zoomed past a park, heading into the city. Their pink flowers, mixed with the white of dogwood, seemed like eyes along the road. His bleeding had stopped, though his chest still throbbed from the bullet wound. His fever remained.

'As far as you go,' the driver said, stopping beneath an overpass, the semi's air brakes hissing. 'My depot's a mile away. I can't let 'em see you. Like I said, taking riders I'd lose my job.'

'This is far enough.' Saul opened his door. 'And thanks.'

The driver shook his head. 'Not good enough. You're forgetting something.'

Saul frowned as he stepped to the road. 'No, I don't think so.'

'Think again. The money. Remember? Half at the start, and half when we got here. You owe me another two hundred bucks.'

Saul nodded. Preoccupied with the problem of why his father was hunting him, he'd forgotten his deal with the driver. It hadn't seemed important.

The driver slid his hand beneath the seat.

Relax, Saul told him. He needed all his money. But the driver had kept his bargain. Shrugging, Saul gave it to him.

'For a minute there.' The driver brought his hand from under the seat.

'You've been on the road too long. Your nerves are shot.'

'It's the speed limit.'

'Buy your wife a fur coat.'

'Sure. And go to McDonald's with the change.' The driver grinned, putting the money in his pocket.

The air brakes hissed. The semi pulled from the curb. In the dark beneath the overpass, Saul watched the tailights disappear. Hearing traffic roar above him, he started along the shadowy road.

54

The last time he'd been to Atlanta, he'd checked on several hotels in case he ever needed them. His wound required attention. He wanted a bath. A change of clothes. He couldn't risk a place where they cared about the quality of the guests, as long as the bill was paid in advance. It had to be far from the luxury of Peachtree Street. He knew exactly where to go.

A train wailed in the distance. Old buildings flanked him. He hunched, easing the pressure in his wound, sensing them converge. Four, if his fever hadn't weakened his hearing.

Just after he crossed a river bridge. The current whispered below him. Past a burnt-out building, at a vacant lot, he braced himself. With blood on his clothes, hunched the way he was, he must have looked like an easy mark.

They came from the dark, surrounding him. For a moment, they reminded him of a gang who'd beaten Chris and himself outside the orphanage years ago.

'I'm not in the mood,' he said.

The tallest kid grinned.

'I'm telling you,' Saul said.

'Hey, all we want is your money. We won't hurt you. That's a promise.'

The others giggled.

'Really,' Saul said. 'Back off.'

They crowded him and snickered.

'But we need,' the tall kid said.

'Try someone else.'

'But who? There's nobody else. You see someone else around? The tall kid flicked open a switchblade.

'You need lessons. You're holding it wrong.'

The tall kid frowned. For a moment, he seemed to suspect. Then he glanced at the others. Pride made him lunge with the knife.

Saul broke their extremities.

'Like I said, a mistake.'

He almost walked away. On impulse, he searched them.

Seventy dollars.

14

'That seat's reserved,' the square-jawed man growled, pointing at the glass of beer on the counter before the bar stool.

Chris shrugged and sat, tapping his fingers to *The Gambler* by Kenny Rogers. 'Your friend won't need it while he's in the men's room.'

On a stage in back, a stripper did a slow grind to the rhythm of the country-western tune. 'She'll hurt herself,' Chris said.

The burly man scowled. 'She's not the only one. You a masochist? That your problem?'

'Not me. I discriminate. I have sex only with women.'

'I get it.' The man wore a flowered shirt hanging loose over his faded jeans. He stubbed out his cigarette, stood, and glared down at Chris. 'You want that stool so bad you want me to shove it up –'

'You tried to do that in Saigon once. It didn't work.'

'But this is Honolulu. I could take you now.'

'I don't have time for you to try.' Chris turned to the barman. 'Another beer for my friend. I'll have a Coke.'

'Not drinking?' the man in the flowered shirt asked.

'Not today.'

'Bad action?'

'It's not good. You look ridiculous in that shirt.'

'A change from the uniform. On R and R, I go nuts for color. You'd be surprised. It attracts the women.'

'Tell them you're a major. That'll impress them more than the shirt.'

'Uncool.'

Chris paid for the drinks.

The husky man sipped his beer. 'You've been making the rounds of Special Forces bars?'

Chris nodded.

'Checking for friends?'

Chris nodded.

'Who owe you favors?'

Shrugging, Chris glanced at the doorway. 'You've got a suspicious nature.'

'And you've got the knee ripped out of your pants.'

'I had to leave a place in a hurry. I haven't had time to buy another pair.'

'You're safe in here. Nobody's going to bother you with several A-teams to back you up.'

'But when I step outside . . . In fact, I'd like to take a trip. Off the islands.'

'Any special place?'

'I hoped you'd be my travel agent. As long as it's not the mainland.'

The thick-necked man glanced toward the naked stripper. 'We fly out of here tomorrow.'

'Military transport?'

'The Canal Zone.' The man glanced back at Chris. 'Okay?'

'You can get me aboard?'

'No problem. A couple guys owe me favors.'

'I owe *you* one now.'

'Hey, who keeps score?'

Chris laughed.

'I got another problem, though,' the major said.

'What is it?'

'The guy I'm with who was sitting there. He should've been back by now. He's so damned drunk he must've fallen in or passed out in the men's room.'

A Waylon Jennings record started blaring. The stripper put her clothes back on.

15

Chris sweated, throwing more dirt to the side. He leaned on his shovel, squinting at the semitropical forest around him – sweet-smelling cedars, thorny laurel trees. Bright-colored birds, having adjusted to his presence, fluttered and sang in the boughs. Mosquitoes hovered, never settling on him. He didn't worry about fever since the major, en route here to Panama, had supplied him with the necessary suppositories. Standard equipment for Special Forces, their chemical was absorbed by the capillaries in his lower intestines, causing his body to emit a subtle, mosquito-repelling odor. Chris had known the chemical was working when his urine turned green.

In the humid sun, he resumed his work, shoveling more dirt to the side, enlarging the hole. He'd borrowed the idea from the 'man traps' the Viet Cong had dug in the jungle during the war. A deep pit covered by a sheet of metal, with earth and ferns placed on the sheet to disguise it. Carefully balanced, the sheet would tilt down when an unwitting soldier stepped on it, impaling his body on the *pungi* stakes arranged below. Though Chris would not use stakes, the pit retained its deadly purpose.

He'd been digging throughout the morning. The pit was now seven feet long, three feet wide, and four feet deep. It resembled a grave. 'Two more feet down,' he told himself, wiping sweat from his forehead, continuing to shovel.

When he finished, he walked from the clearing to the forest, searching among ferns till he found four solid sticks, each four feet in length. He wiped his sweaty forehead again, walked back to the clearing, and eased down into the pit. In contrast with the sun, the pit felt cool. He reached for the sheet of plywood he'd set to the side. The sheet measured seven feet by three, a half-inch thick. He'd struggled through the forest to carry it here. Few people lived in this region. He'd made sure he wasn't followed.

Using the sticks, he supported each corner of the plywood so it covered the pit. Then he crawled from the dark through a burrow he'd dug. In light, he gently covered the plywood with dirt from the hole, dug up ferns, and planted them above the sheet.

Stepping back, he studied the camouflage. The freshly-turned earth was dark, in contrast with the light brown surface ground. By tomorrow, there'd be no difference. Satisfied, he placed a rock across the entrance to the burrow.

He was almost ready. Only one more thing to do. He'd have gone to the dentist first, but in his subsequent groggy condition, he wasn't sure he'd have had the strength to carry the plywood here and dig the hole. He had to arrange things properly. As soon as he came back

from the dentist in Panama City, he wouldn't need the suppositories
the major had given him. Malaria wouldn't matter.

16

'Mr Bartholomew?' the nurse asked Chris. She was Panamanian,
attractive, her dark skin stark against her white uniform. 'The doctor's last appointment took longer than he expected. You'll have to
wait a few more minutes.'

Nodding, Chris thanked her. Panama was bilingual: Spanish and
English. Chris spoke Spanish in addition to three other languages.
Even so, he'd found it easier to use English when he'd come to the
dentist two days ago, explaining what he wanted.

'But there's no reason to do it,' the dentist had said.

'You don't need a reason. All you need is this.' Chris had taken off
his eighteen-karat gold Rolex watch, giving it to the dentist. 'It's
worth four thousand dollars. There'll be money too, of course. And
this.' Chris had shown him the precious necklace. 'When you're
finished.'

The dentist's eyes had glinted avariciously. He suddenly frowned.
'I won't be part of anything illegal.'

'What's illegal for a dentist to take out teeth?'

The dentist shrugged.

'I'm eccentric. Humor me,' Chris had said. 'I'll come back in two
days. You'll keep no record of my visit. You won't take X rays.'

'Without X rays, I can't guarantee my work. There might be complications.'

'It won't matter.'

The dentist had frowned.

Now Chris sat in the waiting room, staring at cheap wooden chairs
and a cracked plastic-covered sofa. There weren't any other patients.
A fluorescent light sputtered. He glanced toward the magazines
printed in Spanish. Instead of picking one up, he closed his eyes and
concentrated.

Soon, he thought. Tonight, before returning to the forest, he'd
come back here and destroy the office. After all, despite the dentist's
promise, there was always the chance he'd make records and take X
rays while Chris was unconscious from the anesthetic. It was important there be no evidence.

He'd return to the forest clearing and begin his fast. Sixty days
would probably be how long it took, though once the mosquitoes
began to attack him he'd no doubt get malaria, and that would speed
the process. Thirty days maybe. Sixty at the most.

He would meditate, praying to God to forgive his sins – the countless people he'd killed, not like the Russian whose death had been
justified because of the opium, because of Chan, but those whose
crime had merely been that they existed. In anguish, he recalled their
names, their faces, how most of them had begged for mercy. He'd

beg now for mercy toward himself. He'd try to purify himself from shame, the sickness in his soul, the accusation of his emotions.

He would fast till his mind was filled with rapture. As his flesh shrank to his body, he'd hallucinate, his mind floating. For his final conscious act, while ecstasy transported him, he'd crawl down the burrow to his grave. In the dark, he'd kick and pull the sticks that supported the sheet of plywood. It would fall, the earth above it sinking, smothering.

His body would be hidden. Either it would decompose, or else scavenging animals would dig it up. They'd scatter his bones. Probably only his skull would remain intact, but without his teeth, the authorities wouldn't be able to identify him.

That was important. He had to die namelessly. For the sake of Saul and Eliot. They'd no doubt be shocked that he'd violated the sanction. But their embarrassment would be tempered by admiration that he'd never been caught. Of course, they'd wonder where he'd gone. They'd always be puzzled. But puzzlement was better than their grief and shame if they learned he'd committed suicide. He wanted to do this cleanly. He didn't want to be a burden to the two men he was closest to – surrogate brother, surrogate father.

Fasting is the only method of suicide permitted by the Catholic Church. All other ways imply despair, a distrust of God's wisdom, an unwillingness to bear the hardships with which God tests his children. An absolute sin, suicide's punishment is eternal damnation in the fires of Hell. But fasting is undertaken for the purpose of penance, meditation, and spiritual ecstasy. It purifies the spirit by denying the body. It brings a soul closer to God.

Considering his sins, it was the only way Chris could think of to go to Heaven.

'Mr Bartholomew, the doctor will see you now,' the nurse told Chris.

He nodded, standing, walking through an open door to a room with a dentist's chair. He didn't see the doctor, but behind a closed door, he heard water trickling in a sink.

'I'm qualified to administer the anesthetic,' the nurse explained.

He sat in the chair. She prepared a hypodermic.

'What is it?' Chris said.

'Atropine and Vistaril.'

He nodded. He'd been concerned that the anesthetic would be Sodium Amytal, the so-called truth serum that reduced a person to an unconscious, almost hypnotized condition in which his will was so impaired he'd answer the most forbidden of questions.

'Count backward, please,' the nurse said.

When Chris reached ninety-five, his vision began to spin. He thought of the monastery, his six mute years with the Cistercians in which the only communication had been by means of sign language, in which each day had been blessedly the same – meditation and work. He thought of the white robe he'd worn, a white like the swirling in his mind.

59

If he hadn't been asked to leave, if he weren't thirty-six, one year beyond the age when he could apply for readmission, he could still find solace and redemption there.

Now, with the secular life unacceptable to him and the religious life unavailable to him, he had only one choice remaining – the fast of death, of purification, the journey toward ultimate perfection.

But the swirling in his mind intensified. His mouth felt dry. He struggled to breathe. 'It isn't atropine,' he murmured. 'It's something else.'

He fought to escape the dentist's chair. The nurse fought back, hands massive. 'No,' he mumbled, frantic.

But the swirling whiteness became another kind of whiteness. In the spinning blur, a door came open. A figure in white approached him, floating ghostlike.

'No.'

The face loomed close – old, wrinkled, gray.

Chris gaped. The dentist. It couldn't be.

He thrashed. As his mind sank into blackness, it flashed a final lucid thought.

Impossible. The dentist was Eliot.

BOOK TWO

SEARCH AND DESTROY

'MY BLACK PRINCES'

1

Eliot brooded, his wrinkles deepening as he checked Chris's pulse. Finally nodding, he turned to the nurse. 'The doctor's in a bar around the corner.' His voice rasped. 'I suggest you join him.'

Wide-eyed, she backed to the door.

'One other thing.' She froze as he reached beneath the dentist's coat, pulling out an envelope. 'Your money. Lock the other door as you go out.'

She swallowed, leaving the dentist's office, crossing the waiting room, fleeing.

Eliot listened to the click of the lock. He shut the door between the waiting room and his office, staring at a tray of dental instruments.

Chris slumped in the chair, breathing shallowly, unconscious from Sodium Amytal. The drug repressed inhibitions, allowing an interrogator to obtain information from an unwilling subject. For the subject to answer, though, he couldn't be totally unconscious, rather in a controlled half sleep, unaware of his surroundings but not oblivious to what he was asked. Since the nurse had been ordered to subdue Chris completely, Eliot had to wait for some of the drug to wear off.

He inserted a needle-tipped tube in a vein in Chris's arm, then opened a drawer, removing two full hypodermics next to the ampule in which the Amytal had been stored. Since it came as a powder, 500 milligrams of the drug had been mixed with 20 milliliters of sterile water. He inserted one hypodermic in the tube extending from Chris's arm. When he pressed the hypodermic's plunger, the flow of the solution could be controlled by a valve in the tube. He set the second hypodermic near him in case he needed it, though if the session took longer than thirty minutes he'd have to mix a new solution since Amytal decomposed quickly in liquid form.

Five minutes later, as Eliot expected, Chris's eyelids began to flutter. Eliot opened the valve in the tube, allowing a portion of the drug to enter the vein. When Chris's speech became garbled, Eliot would have to close the valve till Chris showed signs of becoming too awake, then open the valve again to subdue him. The procedure required care.

It was best to start simply. 'Do you know who I am?' Receiving no answer, Eliot repeated the question.

63

'Eliot,' Chris whispered.

'Very good. That's right. I'm Eliot.' He studied Chris, for a moment reminded of the first time he'd seen him – thirty-one years ago. He recalled the boy clearly, five years old, dirty, thin, in rags, his father dead, his mother a prostitute who'd abandoned him. The row house in the slum in Philadelphia had been filled with tables. On each table, the boy had neatly arranged piles of flies he'd killed with a rubber band. 'You remember,' Eliot said. 'I took care of you. I'm as close to you as a father. You're as close to me as a son. Repeat it.'

'Father. Son,' Chris murmured.

'You love me.'

'Love you,' Chris said tonelessly.

'You trust me. No one else has ever been as kind to you. You're safe. You've nothing to fear.'

Chris sighed.

'Do you want to make me happy?'

Chris nodded.

Eliot smiled. 'Of course you do. You love me. Listen carefully. I want you to answer some questions. Tell me the truth.' He was suddenly conscious of the smell of peppermint in the dentist's office. 'Have you heard from Saul?'

Chris took so long to answer Eliot thought he wouldn't. He breathed when Chris said, 'No.'

'Do you know where he is?'

Chris whispered, 'No.'

'I'm going to give you a sentence. What does it mean?' Four days ago, the message had been cabled from Atlanta to Rome, in care of Chris at the Mediterranean Flower Shop, the agency's office there. Till his disappearance, Chris had been the assistant bureau chief, on probation while Eliot studied the possible bad effects of the monastery on Chris's work. The message had not been signed, but that was not unusual. All the same, its arrival coincided with Saul's disappearance. Assuming Saul would try to contact Chris, Eliot had learned that this message – in contrast with many others Chris had been sent – bore no relation to agency codes.

'"There's an egg in the basket,"' Eliot said.

'A message from Saul,' Chris answered, eyes closed groggy.

'Go on.'

'He's in trouble. He needs my help.'

'That's all it means?'

'A safety-deposit box.'

Eliot leaned closer. 'Where?'

'A bank.'

'*Where?*'

'Santa Fe. We both have keys. We hid them. In the box, I'll find a message.'

'Coded?' Eliot's bony fingers clutched the dentist's chair.

Chris nodded.

'Would I recognize the code?'

'Private.'

'Teach it to me.'

'Several.'

Eliot straightened, his chest tight from frustration. He could ask Chris to explain the several codes, but there was always the chance that, by failing to ask a crucial question, he might not learn all the information he required. No doubt Chris had taken precautions to stop an enemy from posing as himself and gaining access to the safety-deposit box. Where was the key, for example? Was there a password? Those questions were obvious. What troubled Eliot were the questions he *couldn't* imagine. Chris and Saul had been friends since they'd met in the orphanage thirty-one years ago. They must have hundreds of subtle private signals. All Eliot had to do was fail to learn one of them, and he'd miss this chance to trap Saul. Of course, the agency's computers could decipher the private code, but how long might the process take?

Eliot had to move *now*.

He rubbed his wrinkled chin, abruptly thinking of another question. 'Why did you want your teeth removed?'

Chris answered.

Eliot shivered. He'd thought nothing could shock him.

But *this*?

2

Chris swelled with affection as he cradled the candy bar. 'A Baby Ruth. You still remember.'

'Always.' Eliot's eyes looked sad.

'But how did you find me?' Chris's tongue felt thick from the Amytal.

'Trade secret.' Eliot grinned, his lips taut as if on a shrunken skull.

Chris glanced out the jet's window, hearing the muffled roar of the engines as he squinted from the sun and studied the snowlike clouds spread out below him. 'Tell me.' He sounded hoarse, staring back at his foster father.

Eliot shrugged. 'You know what I've always said. To guess an opponent's next move, we have to think as *he* would think. I trained you, remember. I know everything about you.'

'Not quite.'

'We'll discuss that in a moment. The point is I pretended I was you. Knowing everything about you, I became you.'

'And?'

'Who owed you favors? Who could you depend on for your life? Who *had* you depended on? As soon as I knew what questions to ask, I calculated the answers. One of them was to have men watch the Special Forces bars in Honolulu.'

'Clever.'

'So were you.'

65

'Not enough – since I was spotted in the bar. And followed, I assume.'

'You have to remember you were playing against your teacher. I doubt anyone else could have guessed what you intended.'

'Why didn't you order me picked up in Honolulu? I violated the sanction, after all. The other networks are hunting me. You'd have earned some points with them, especially the Russians, if you brought me in.'

'I wasn't sure you'd let us take you alive.'

Chris stared at him. Eliot's assistant, wearing a Yale ring and tie, brought a tray of Perrier, ice, and glasses, setting it on the table between them in this lounge section of the plane.

Eliot didn't speak till the assistant left. 'Besides –' he seemed to choose his words, pouring Perrier in two glasses, 'I was curious. I wondered why you wanted a dentist.'

'Personal.'

'Not anymore.' Eliot handed him a glass. 'While you were unconscious in the dentist's chair, I asked you some questions.' He paused. 'I know you intended to kill yourself.'

'Past tense?'

'For my sake, I hope so. Why did you want to do it? You know your death would hurt me. Your suicide would hurt even worse.'

'That's why I wanted my teeth removed. If my body was ever found, it couldn't be identified.'

'But why ask the priest? Why go to the safe house?'

'I wanted a dentist who was used to working with operatives, who wouldn't ask questions.'

Eliot shook his head.

'What's wrong?'

'That isn't true. With a little trouble you found a dentist on your own. You didn't need someone familiar with our profession. All you needed was sufficient money to bribe a man into silence. No, you had a different reason for asking the priest.'

'Since you know all the answers . . .'

'You went to the priest because you knew he'd make inquiries before he gave you the information. I'd learn where you were. I'd be puzzled about your request and intercept you.'

'What good would that have done? I didn't *want* to be stopped.'

'No?' Eliot squinted at him. 'Your request to the priest was the same as a cry for help. A suicide note before the fact. You wanted to tell me how much pain you were in.'

Chris shook his head.

'Unconsciously? What is it?' Frowning, Eliot leaned forward. 'What's wrong? I don't understand.'

'I'm not sure I can explain it. Let's just say . . .' Chris debated in anguish. 'I'm sick. Of everything.'

'The monastery changed you.'

'No. The sickness came before the monastery.'

'Drink the Perrier. Your mouth will be dry from the Amytal.'

66

Automatically Chris obeyed.

Eliot nodded. 'What kind of sickness?'

'I'm ashamed.'

'Because of what you do?'

'Because of what I feel. The guilt. I see faces, I hear voices. Dead men. I can't shut them out. You taught me discipline, but the lesson isn't working anymore. I can't stand the shame of –'

'Listen to me,' Eliot said.

Chris rubbed his forehead.

'You're a member of a high-risk profession. I don't mean just the physical danger. As you've discovered, there's also a spiritual danger. The things we have to do can sometimes force us to be inhuman.'

'Then why do we have to do them?'

'You're not naive. You know the answer as well as I. Because we're fighting to protect the way of life we believe in. We sacrifice ourselves so others can have normal lives. Don't blame yourself for what you've needed to do. Blame the other side. What about the monastery? If your need was spiritual, why couldn't the Cistercians help you? Why did they force you out? The vow of silence? After six years, was it too much for you?'

'It was wonderful. Six years of peace.' Chris frowned. 'Too much peace.'

'I don't understand.'

'Because of the strictness of the Order, a psychiatrist came to test us every six months. He checked for signs – tiny clues of unproductive behavior. The Cistercians believe in work, after all. We supported ourselves by farming. Anyone who couldn't do his share couldn't be allowed to live off the sweat of others.'

Eliot nodded, waiting.

'Catatonic schizophrenia.' Chris breathed deeply. 'That's what the psychiatrist tested us for. Preoccupations. Trances. He asked us questions. He watched for our reactions to various sounds and colors. He studied our daily behavior. One day when he found me sitting motionless in a garden, staring at a rock – for an hour – he reported to my superior. The rock was fascinating. I can still remember it.' Chris narrowed his eyes. 'But I'd failed the test. The next time somebody found me paralyzed like that – catatonic – I was out. Peace. My sin was I wanted too much peace.'

On the tray, beside the Perrier bottles, a long-stemmed crimson rose stood in a vase. Eliot picked it up. 'You had your rock. I have my roses. In our business, we need beauty.' He sniffed the rose and handed it to Chris. 'Did you ever wonder why I chose roses?'

Chris shrugged. 'I assumed you liked flowers.'

'Roses, though. Why roses?'

Chris shook his head.

'They're the emblem of our profession. I enjoy the double meaning. In Greek mythology, the god of love once offered a rose to the god of silence, as a bribe, to keep that god from disclosing the weaknesses of the other gods. In time, the rose became the symbol for silence and

67

secrecy. In the Middle Ages, a rose was customarily suspended from the ceiling of a council chamber. The members of the council pledged themselves not to reveal what they discussed in the room, *sub rosa*, under the rose.'

'You've always liked playing with words,' Chris said, returning the rose. 'My trouble is, I can't believe in them anymore.'

'Let me finish. Part of my delight in roses comes from the different varieties. The various colors and shapes. I have my favorites – Lady X and Angel Face. I used those names as cryptonyms for two of my female operatives. My ladies.' Eliot smiled. 'The names of other varieties appeal to me. The American Pillar. The Gloria Mundi. But the goal of every rose enthusiast is to create a new variety. We cut and layer and graft, or we cross-pollinate seed. The ripe seed is kept in sand till spring, when it's sown in pans. The first year produces only color. After that comes the full bloom and the merit. The new variety is a hybrid. Only a large, well-formed, singly grown blossom standing higher than the rest will do. To enhance the quality of the bloom, the side growth must be removed by a process called disbudding. You and Saul – you're my hybrids. Raised without families, in the orphanage, you had no side growth – you didn't need to be disbudded. Nature had already done that. Your bloom was developed through rigorous training and discipline. To give your characters substance, certain feelings had to be cut from you. Patriotism was layered onto your character. Military experience and, of course, the war were grafted onto you. My hybrids – you stand higher than all the rest. If your conditioning failed and you now feel, it shouldn't be guilt you feel but pride. You're beautiful. I could have given you a new name for a new species. Instead I think of you in terms of the particular rose I'm holding, so dark crimson it's almost black. It's called the Black Prince. That's how I think of you and Saul. As my Black Princes.'

'But Saul didn't fail. He . . .' Chris's eyes changed. 'Wait a minute. You're not telling me all this just for . . .'

Eliot spread his hands. 'So you guessed.'

'What's wrong? What's happened to Saul?'

Eliot studied him. 'Because of your brother, I'm asking you not to try again to kill yourself.'

'What is it?' Chris sat forward, tensing. '*What about Saul?*'

'Five days ago, he did a job for me. After, a member of the team tried to kill him. He got in touch with me. I arranged for him to go to a secure location. When he got there, he discovered the location had been compromised. Another team tried to kill him. He's on the run.'

'Then, Jesus, bring him in!'

'I can't. He's afraid to get in touch with me.'

'With *you?*'

'The mole. I've always said there was one. From the agency's beginning. Someone who infiltrated us at the start, who's been compromising us ever since. Someone close to me is using what Saul tells me, using it to try to get at Saul.'

'But why?'

'I don't know why he's so important he has to be killed. What he's discovered, or whom he threatens. I *won't* know till I catch the mole. It isn't easy. I've been looking since 1947. I have to find Saul, though. I have to insure his safety.'

'How? If he won't get in touch with you, if he's afraid the mole will intercept his message.'

Eliot set the rose down. '"There's an egg in the basket."'

Chris felt the jet lurch.

Eliot said, 'That message arrived in Rome four days ago. Addressed to you. I think from Saul.'

Chris nodded.

'I don't know what it means,' Eliot said. 'For God's sake, don't tell me. Even this rose might have ears. But if it's from Saul and it tells you where to find him, use it. Go. Be careful. Bring him in.'

'One Black Prince to rescue another?'

'Exactly. Your surrogate father is asking you to save your surrogate brother. If you're looking for a reason not to kill yourself, you've found it.'

Chris turned to the window, eyes narrowed, more than just from the sun. He brooded – all thought of suicide canceled by concern for his brother. His heart quickened. Saul needed help. Beside that, nothing else mattered. His brother needed him. He'd found the only reason that could make him want to live.

He turned to Eliot, his voice grim. 'Count on it.'

'Ironic,' Eliot said. 'A hit team's chasing Saul, and everyone else is chasing you.'

'You'll appreciate the complexity.'

'I'll appreciate it more when Saul is safe. What country should I tell the pilot to fly to?'

'Home.'

'What city?'

Chris considered. The safety-deposit box was in Santa Fe, but he couldn't go there directly. He had to land close to it, yet far enough away to lose a tail. He had to be evasive in case this conversation was being monitored. 'Albuquerque.'

Eliot straightened, his ancient eyes bright, signaling he recognized deception and approved.

'Has it occurred to you?' Chris said.

Eliot frowned. 'I don't understand.'

'That hybrids are usually sterile.'

The jet descended through the clouds.

The Sangre de Cristo mountains loomed in the distance. Snow still capped the peaks, the slopes dark with oak and fir. Despite the blazing sun, the air felt dry.

Chris walked along the narrow street, passing flat-roofed adobe houses with red slate trim and walls around gardens. Through a gate, he saw a bubbling fountain. Piñon trees provided shade, the green of their needles contrasting with the earth tones of the houses.

Pausing at the end of the block, he glanced back down the street. He'd chosen this expensive residential section of Santa Fe because he knew it would be quiet – little traffic, few pedestrians. The isolation made it easy for him to check on anyone following him. He took for granted that, if the KGB or MI–6 or any of the other networks hunting him had spotted him, they'd never have let him wander the streets this long. They'd simply have killed him right away. He had to conclude, then, that they weren't close.

For Saul, though, he'd been willing to take the risk. His eyes gleamed. For his brother, he'd take *any* risk. He'd gladly make himself a target to draw out someone besides his hunters.

The mole. Whoever was intercepting Eliot's messages to Saul. Whoever wanted Saul dead. The questions nagged him. What had Saul done, or what did he know? This much was clear. Since Chris was not supposed to report to Eliot for fear of a leak, the only way the mole could get his hands on Saul was by following Chris. But so far Chris had seen no evidence of surveillance.

Glancing behind him again, he passed a house with a courtyard and veranda partly concealed by junipers. He peered toward the mountains, crossed a street, and approached a Spanish cathedral. Climbing the high stone steps, pulling the iron ring on a huge oak door, he entered a dark cool vestibule. The last time he'd been here was in 1973. In honor of its hundredth anniversary, the church had been extensively restored that year. Since then, as he'd hoped, it hadn't changed. The vaulted ceiling, the stained glass windows, the Spanish design around the stations of the cross remained as they had been. He walked to the marble holy water fountain, dipping his hand in, genuflecting toward the distant golden tabernacle on the altar. Crossing himself, he went to the row of confessionals on his left, beneath the choir loft, at the back of the church, his footsteps echoing on the smooth stone floor.

The confessional in the corner drew him. Nobody sat in the nearby pews. He heard no muffled voices from inside, so he opened the ornate door, stepped in, and closed it behind him.

The church had been shadowy, but the narrow penitent's cubicle was totally dark, its musty smell stifling. Out of habit, he silently recited, 'Bless me, Father, for I have sinned. My last confession was . . .' He recalled the monastery, his sins, his plan to kill himself, and stopped. His jaw hardened. He couldn't be distracted. Saul alone mattered. Instead of kneeling to face the screen behind which a priest would normally be hidden, he quickly turned and reached toward the top right corner. In the dark, his fingers searched. All these years. He sweated, wondering if he'd been foolish. What if a carpenter, repairing the confessional, had discovered . . . ? He pulled the loose molding from the seam where the wall met the ceiling and grinned as he touched the key he'd wedged into the niche years before.

4

The bank had been designed to look like a pueblo: flat-roofed, square, with support beams projecting from the top of the imitation-sandstone walls. Two yucca plants flanked the entrance. Traffic blared. In a restaurant across the street, a businessman sat at a middle table, facing the window and the bank. He paid for his lunch and left, ignoring another businessman who came in and sat at the same middle table, facing the window and the bank. All along the street, other members of the surveillance team seemed a part of the normal pattern. A young man handed out advertisements. A truck driver carried boxes into a building. A woman browsed through a record store, close to a window. Lingering as long as seemed normal, they left the area, replaced by others.

In the restaurant, the businessman lit a cigarette. He heard a short muffled beep from the two-way radio in his pocket, no more obtrusive than a doctor's paging device, the signal that Remus had been sighted along the street. Peering through the heat haze toward the entrance to the bank, he saw a woman come out, her hand raised to shield her eyes from the sun. A man wearing tan clothes passed her, going in. As a waitress brought a menu, the businessman reached in his pocket, pressing the radio's transmitter button twice.

Remus was in the bank.

5

Chris passed the security guard and a row of cages with signs for Deposits and Mortgages, descending the stairs at the back. Indian sand paintings hung on the walls. He reached a counter, gave his key to a clerk, and wrote *John Higgins* on a bank form. He and Saul had opened an account here in 1973, depositing a thousand dollars, leaving instructions that the rent for the safety-deposit box should be deducted from the account. Chris hadn't been back here since, though he knew Saul contacted the bank each year to make sure the account and the box hadn't been put on inactive status. The clerk stamped the date on the bank form, initialed it, and pulled out a list of renters, comparing signatures.

'Mr Higgins, I'm supposed to ask for a password.'

'Camelot,' Chris said.

Nodding, the clerk marked an X beside the name on the list. He opened the counter's gate and led Chris through the vault's massive door to a long high wall of safety-deposit boxes. Lights glared. As the clerk used both the bank's key and Chris's key to unlock a box, Chris glanced to the end of the hall toward a floor-to-ceiling mirror. He didn't like mirrors. Often they were also windows. Turning his back to it, he took the closed tray the clerk gave him and went to a booth.

As soon as he'd shut the door behind him, he checked the ceiling for a hidden camera. Satisfied, he opened the tray. The hand-written message was coded. Translated, it told him, *Santa Fe phone booth. Sherman and Grant.* He memorized a number. Shredding the message, putting it back in the box, he took a Mauser from the tray and tucked it beneath his jacket behind his belt at his spine. He pocketed the two thousand dollars he'd left here for an emergency.

6

While the businessman ate his salad, he stared through the window toward the bank. The blue cheese dressing tasted stale. A Ford van stopped before him at the curb, blocking his vision. Sunlight glinted off the windshield.

The businessman swallowed nervously. Come on. Hurry up. Get that damned thing moving.

Standing, he peered beyond the van, reached in his pocket, and pressed the transmitter button three times.

Remus was leaving the bank.

7

Chris put the Santa Fe map in his pocket as he stepped in the phone booth at the intersection of Sherman and Grant streets. Cars rushed by. Shoppers paused at the windows of trendy boutiques. He shut the door and muffled traffic noises. Though he didn't smile, he felt amused, assuming this location with its combination of street names – Civil War generals – had been chosen by Saul as a joke. We'll soon be together again, he thought. His chest swelled, but he couldn't allow his eagerness to distract him. Putting coins in the slot, he dialed the number he'd memorized. A recorded voice told him the time was 2:46. If an enemy had subdued Chris and forced him to reveal the message in the safety-deposit box, the man would have been baffled by the significance of hearing the time. Unless he'd kept Chris alive to question him further, he couldn't have learned that the specific time meant nothing. Any hour would have been important, the announcement a signal to Chris to study the walls of the phone booth. Among the graffiti, he found a message to Roy Palatsky, a boy he and Saul had known at the orphanage. He glanced away at once. In case, despite his precautions, he was being watched, he didn't want to betray his fascination with the graffiti. In code, the obscene message told him where to find Saul.

8

'He made a call,' the businessman said on the scrambler-protected long-distance line. 'He must have received directions. We could pick him up now.'

'Don't. A call's too obvious.' Eliot's voice sounded thin and brittle from his Falls Church, Virginia, greenhouse. 'These two men have private codes dating back to when they were five years old. That call was likely a bluff to tempt you to show yourselves. What if all he learned was directions to go to another spot where he'd learn still other directions? Don't interfere with him. The only way to capture Romulus is to follow Remus. For God's sake, don't let him see you.'

9

Chris flew higher, skirting a cloud bank, watching the mountains below him. Snow-capped peaks, connected by saddlelike ridges, stretched as far as he could see. Ravines splayed down in all directions. He put the rented Cessna on automatic pilot while he studied a topographical map, comparing its contour lines with the rugged terrain below him. Valleys alternated with mountains. Streams cascaded.

On the wall of the phone booth, the coded message had given him numbers for longitude and latitude, as well as instructions how to get there. He'd gone to the Santa Fe library, where he'd learned that the coordinates referred to a section of mountain wilderness to the north, in Colorado. Renting this plane at the Santa Fe airport had been easy. He'd used the alias on his pilot's license, had paid a deposit and bought insurance. He'd filed a flight plan to Denver, indicating he'd return in three days. But once in the air, he'd gradually veered from his flight plan, northwest, toward the coordinates in the wilderness.

The sky was brilliant. He felt good. The cockpit muffled the engine's drone. He compared a deep long valley to a similar pattern on the map and glanced ahead toward another valley, oval, with a lake. His coordinates met near the lake. He'd almost reached his destination. Checking the sky around him, pleased that he saw no aircraft, he smiled and thought of Saul.

At once he attended to business, slipping on his bulky parachute. The plane soared closer to the valley. Aiming toward a mountain beyond the lake, he locked his controls on target, opened his door, heard the roar of the engine, and felt the surge of the wind. He had to struggle to brace the door against its force.

Pressing his shoes against the lower section of the plane, he leapt out past the wing struts, twisting, buffeted. His stomach rose. Gusts of air pressed his goggles against his face. He couldn't hear the plane now. All he heard was the hiss as he fell – and a roar in his ears. His helmet squeezed against his skull. Clothes flapping, arms and legs stretched out for balance, he fell horizontally, facing the abrupt enlargement of the landscape. The lake grew. But he quickly achieved a sense of stasis, blissful, almost anesthetizing. If he closed his eyes, he no longer had the sense of falling. Rather he felt suspended, floating, relaxed. In jump school, his instructors had warned him about this deceptive, dangerous sensation. Hypnotized by the almost sexual massage of the wind, some jumpers waited too long before they pulled their ripcord.

Chris understood the attraction. He'd been apprehensive before his first jump, but from then on, he'd looked forward to the pleasure of the others. Now his pleasure was moderated by his need to be with Saul. Eagerly he pulled the ripcord, waited, felt the chute unfold from his back and the lurch as the nylon blossomed, supporting him. He hadn't worried about the chute. Last night, after buying it from the local jumpers' club, he'd spread it out, arranging the lines before he packed it. He'd never have trusted someone to do that for him any more than he'd have let someone clean a weapon and load it for him. Swaying in the wind, he glanced toward the peak beyond the lake and saw the tiny outline of his plane – on automatic pilot – approaching the mountain he'd aimed it toward. He gripped the parachute lines and leaned to the right, angling away from the lake, veering toward a meadow. He saw a cabin above a slope of pines, braced in the V between two cliffs.

The meadow enlarged abruptly. As he settled down, it seemed to swoop toward him. With a jolt, he hit, the impact shuddering through him as he bent his knees and toppled sideways, absorbing the shock along his hip, his side, and his shoulder. The chute billowed in the wind, dragging him across the meadow. He surged to his feet, tugging the chute lines, pulling them toward him while he rushed to meet the nylon hood and compact the chute, restraining the wind's resistance.

'You're out of practice,' a husky voice said from the shelter of the pines.

Recognizing it, Chris turned, feigning irritation. 'What the hell? You think you can do it better?'

'I sure can. I've never seen a crummier landing.'

'The wind was against me.'

'Excuses,' the voice said. 'The sign of an amateur.'

'And criticism's the sign of an ungrateful sonofabitch. If you didn't have so much to say, you'd come out here to help me.'

'Definitely not the tough guy I used to know.'

'Tough or not, I'm the closest thing to a brother you've got.'

'No argument. Even with your faults, I love you.'

Chris's throat ached with affection. 'If you're so damned sentimental, why don't you show yourself?'

'Because I can't resist making an entrance.'

A husky dark-haired man stepped slowly from the forest. Six feet tall, solidly muscled, with chiseled chin and cheek and forehead, the man grinned, his dark eyes glinting. He wore high laced boots, faded jeans, and a green wool shirt that matched the pines. He carried a bolt-action Springfield rifle. 'Eight years, Chris. God, what's the matter with us? We never should have separated.'

'Business,' Chris said.

'Business?' Saul answered, the word tinged with disgust. 'We let it ruin us.'

Eager, Chris hurried toward him, clutching his folded parachute. So much to know, to say. 'What's happened? Why are they trying to kill you?'

'Business,' Saul said again. 'He turned against me.'

'Who?' Chris had almost reached him.

'Can't you guess? The man we figured never would.'

'But that's impossible!'

'I'll prove it to you.'

But suddenly only one thing had significance. Chris dropped the parachute, staring at Saul's rugged handsome face. Hardly able to breathe, he opened his arms and hugged him. Straining, they seemed to want to crush each other's chest and back and muscles, to absorb each other's life.

He almost wept.

Their embrace was interrupted. Turning, they peered through a cleft in the pine trees toward the explosion that echoed through the valley as the plane Chris had flown disintegrated on the mountain.

10

'No, you're wrong! He's not against you!' Chris held his parachute, helmet and goggles, running up the game trail through the pines. 'He asked me to find you!'

'Why?'

'To help you! To bring you in!'

'Why?' Saul asked again.

'It's obvious. The mole kept intercepting Eliot's instructions to you.'

'Mole,' Saul scoffed. 'Is that what Eliot told you?'

'He said the only way to bring you in safely was for me to act alone.'

'He couldn't find me, but he knew I'd try to get in touch with you. He set you up to lead him to me.'

From the shadowy woods, Chris saw the cabin brilliant in the sun, small, its long walls chinked with mud, its roof slanting up toward the merging V of the cliffs behind it. 'How'd you find this place?'

'I built it. You chose the monastery. I prefer this cabin.'

'But it must have taken you –'

'Months. Off and on. After every assignment, when Eliot sent me to Wyoming or Colorado, I slipped away and came back here. I guess you could say it's home.'

Chris followed across the scrub-grass clearing. 'You're sure no one knows about this place?'

'I'm positive.'

'But how?'

'Because I'm still alive.' Saul glanced toward the valley's far horizon. 'Hurry. We don't have much time.'

'For what? You're not making sense.' Puzzled, Chris left the sun's glare, entering the musty shadows of the cabin. He had no chance to appreciate the simple handmade furniture. Saul led him past the sleeping bag on the floor toward the back wall, opening a roughly planed door. Chris felt the cool dank air of a tunnel.

'It's a mine shaft.' Saul pointed toward the dark. 'That's why I built the cabin here. A den ought to have two holes.' He turned to the fireplace. Striking a match, he lit the kindling beneath the logs in the hearth. The kindling was dry, but the logs were wet with sap. The flames spread, sending thick smoke up the chimney. 'I probably don't need the smoke. No harm in being sure, though. Leave your chute,' he told Chris. 'Here's a flashlight.' Saul led him into the tunnel.

In the flashlight's beam, Chris saw his frosty breath. Timbers supported the roof of the tunnel. An old pick and shovel lay against the wall to the left. A rusted wheelbarrow leaned on its side. Saul touched a dull glint of metal in the moist cold stone. 'Silver. Not much left.'

The flashlight showed the end of the tunnel. 'Here. We have to climb.' Saul squeezed through a niche in the rock. He reached up, wedged his boot in a crack, and scrambled out of sight.

Chris followed, scraping his back in the narrow cleft. The stone felt slimy. He had to put the flashlight in his pocket. Then he realized he didn't need it. Above, a narrow beam of light attracted him in the dark – a long way up. Saul leaned toward an outcrop above him, blocking the light. When Saul shifted, Chris could see the light again. 'You think I was followed?'

'Of course.'

Chris reached for a rock. 'I'm sure I wasn't.'

'The surveillance team would have been the best.'

The rock broke from Chris's hand, rumbling down the niche. He froze. 'But nobody knew I was looking for you.'

'Eliot did.'

'You keep blaming Eliot. Next to you, he's the only man I trust.'

'Exactly. Your mistake. Mine too.' Saul's voice was bitter. His silhouette disappeared beyond the narrow shaft of light.

Chris scrambled higher. The beam of light became larger, brighter. Sweating, he squirmed from the niche and lay on a funnel of weathered rock, its smooth slope warmed by the sun. He peered toward Saul, who crouched above him, shielded by sagebrush, concentrating on the valley. 'But I saw no other planes.'

'Around you,' Saul said. 'Sure. But above you? A spotter plane at forty thousand feet? The pursuit team would have held back, flying slowly, out of sight. Till they got instructions.'

Chris crawled to him, hunching beneath the sagebrush. 'You set me up,' he blurted angrily. 'You could have met me anywhere.'

'That's right. But here, with elaborate precautions, you'd be convinced. I had to prove it to you.'

'Prove what?'

'I think you know.'

Chris heard a far-off drone – then another and still others, louder, amplified by the echo of the towering cliffs. Through a distant pass, he saw glinting specks swoop nearer. Choppers. Hueys. Four of them. He flashed back to Nam and muttered, 'Jesus.'

Below him, smoke swirled from the cabin's chimney. Across the valley, the Hueys roared closer, assuming attack formation. The lead chopper fired a rocket. Exhaust whooshing, the missile streaked down, exploding in the clearing before the cabin. Earth flew, blast stunning. The other choppers soared nearer, releasing rockets.

Above their rush, Chris heard the repeated cracks of fifty-caliber machine guns. The cabin blew apart. Concussions thundered through the valley. The choppers swooped closer, strafing the crater where the cabin had stood. Even on the bluff, Chris's ears throbbed.

'Two failed attempts against me. This time they've got to make sure.' Saul clenched his teeth.

The choppers pivoted from the flaming wreckage, skimming the tips of the pine trees, hurrying toward the meadow beside the lake. Blades glinting, they hovered twenty feet above the meadow. A rope flipped from each, dangling toward the grass. A man wearing pale outdoor clothes, an automatic rifle slung across his back, appeared at an open hatch. He gripped the rope, rappelling to the ground. Other men, like spiders from dragonflies, slipped down from other ropes. In the meadow, they unslung their rifles, spreading in a semi-circle, their backs to the lake. 'By the book,' Chris said.

'They're not sure we were in the cabin. They have to assume we're still a threat. How many?'

'Sixteen.'

'Check.' Saul pointed. Chris saw a man in one chopper lower a dog in a sling. A German shepherd. A second dog descended from another chopper. On the ground, two men stopped aiming their rifles and squirmed back to free the harnesses from the dogs. Relieved of their cargo, the choppers retreated to the far end of the valley.

Every elite corps preferred a different breed. The Navy Seals used hunting poodles. The Rangers liked Dobermans. 'German shepherds. Special Forces.' Chris's throat felt dry.

The dogs ran with the two men toward the trees. The other men aimed, ready to provide covering fire. A group of four darted toward the trees, then five and another five.

Chris scanned the trees, waiting for the men to appear. 'We don't have a chance. All I've got is this Mauser. You've got just that bolt-action Springfield. Even if we were properly armed –'

'We won't have to fight.'

'But those dogs'll track us into the tunnel.' Chris turned toward the basin behind him, watching the niche from which he'd climbed. 'The men'll find where we went. They'll order the choppers to strafe this bluff. Then they'll climb up here and finish the job.'

'Believe me, we're covered.'

Chris opened his mouth to object, then froze as Saul gestured abruptly toward the trees. A man stepped out, presumably inviting shots so the other men would have a target. As the decoy approached the smoking wreckage, a second man showed himself, then a third. 'They're feeling confident. The dogs must have followed our scent directly to the cabin.' Saul watched the lead man point toward the wall of rock behind the shattered logs. 'He's found the tunnel.'

'We have to get out of here.'

'Not yet.'

'For Christ's sake –'

Five men joined the first man. Cautious, they came near the cliff. From the top, Chris couldn't see them now. Droning, the choppers continued hovering in the safety of the far end of the valley. Saul squirmed back, pausing at the smooth rock funnel that sloped down to the niche. Careful not to show himself, he listened. Chris frowned, puzzled.

Saul abruptly grinned and pointed toward sounds from the niche. Chris didn't understand why Saul seemed pleased. Then he did as Saul pulled a radio transmitter from his pocket, pushing a button.

Bracing himself, Chris felt the earth shake. A roar burst up from the tunnel. Spinning, he peered toward the cabin's wreckage below the cliff. Chunks of rock flew across the clearing. Dust swirled.

'Six down, ten to go,' Saul said.

'You rigged explosives in the tunnel.'

'Eliot always said make sure you protect your escape route. Now I'm turning his rules against him. Have I convinced you he wants to kill me?'

Chris nodded sickly, staring toward the trees below him. The other men ran from the pines toward the rumble of falling rock in the tunnel. 'No one else knew I was looking for you. He used me.' The implications made his stomach feel like ice. 'He tried to kill me too. Goddamn it, why? He's like –'

'I know. He's the closest we have to a father.'

In the clearing, a man blurted instructions into a field radio. The choppers suddenly left their safe position at the far end of the valley and rushed toward the clearing, their roar growing louder. Chris saw the German shepherds on guard at the rim of the trees.

'All right,' Saul said. 'Those men are close enough to the tunnel. Let's get out of here.' He scrambled back. Chris followed, watching Saul push the radio transmitter again. 'Another surprise.' Chris barely heard him in the sudden explosion from the cliff behind him. The shockwave pushed him forward, pressing his ears. A rumble came next, a swelling crash of rocks and earth as the cliff fell toward the men in the clearing. He heard their screams.

'That ought to take care of the rest of them,' Saul said. Running, he dropped the transmitter.

'What about the choppers?'

'Trust me.'

They raced through sagebrush. Chris tasted dust, squinting from the sun. In the rapidly approaching roar of the choppers, he wondered if the other side of the bluff would end at another cliff. Instead Saul led him down a wooded slope toward a different valley. In the shadowy cover of trees, Chris felt the sweat cool on his forehead.

'The choppers'll take a minute to work out their strategy,' Saul said, breathing quickly. 'One'll probably land to look for survivors.'

'That leaves three.' The fallen pine needles muffled Chris's steps.

'They'll have to guess we were on that bluff. They'll head for this valley.'

'On foot, we can't get away before they bring in reinforcements. They'll use other dogs to track us.'

'Absolutely right.' Saul reached the bottom, splashing through a stream, charging up its bank. Chris followed, his wet pants clinging cold to his legs. Ahead, Saul stopped in a thick stretch of timber. He tugged at fallen logs and tangled underbrush. 'Quick. Help.'

Chris heaved the logs. 'But why?' Then he understood. He pulled a rotten stump away and saw a sheet of plastic wrapped around a bulky object. Before he could ask what it was, Saul unwrapped the sheet.

Chris almost laughed. A trail bike – thick wide tires and heavy suspension. 'But how'd you –?'

'I use it to get in and out of here. I don't take chances by leaving it around the cabin.' Saul raised it, guiding it past the deadwood they'd pulled away. He pointed through the trees. 'Over there. A game trail cuts across the valley.' He glanced toward the increasing roar of the choppers. 'They'll separate to search different sectors of the valley.'

Chris helped him. 'But the noise from their engines'll stop them from hearing the bike. They'll never spot us if we stay beneath the trees.'

'Get on.' Saul turned the key and kicked the throttle. The bike coughed. He kicked the throttle again, and the bike droned smoothly. 'Here, take the rifle.'

'It's no help against a chopper.'

Saul didn't answer. He flicked the clutch, toed the gearstick, and twisted the accelerator. The bike lurched forward, jolting on the bumpy ground. Chris crowded against him, grinning as they swerved through a maze of trees. Shadows flickered. At the game trail, Saul drove faster. Feeling the rush of wind on his face, reminded of when they were kids, Chris almost laughed.

He froze when he heard a thunderous roar directly above him. Glancing up, he saw a grotesque shadow swoop past a break in the trees. The game trail sloped up. At the top, as Saul raced through a tiny clearing, Chris stared back across the valley. He saw two choppers

79

diverging to search the far and middle sectors. At this other end, the chopper that had just surged past had apparently failed to see them.

The game trail angled down now. Steering, Saul followed the twists and turns. Chris heard the chopper again. 'It's doubling back, rechecking something!'

The game trail reached a swath of grass that stretched from one side of the valley to the other.

Saul stopped the bike. 'They'll see us if we try to cross. But we can't stay here. If we wait till night, they'll have time to bring in another team with dogs.'

Overhead, the wind from the chopper rustled the nearby trees. Chris braced himself for the impact of fifty-caliber machine gun bullets.

Saul took the Springfield from him. 'I wasn't sure how they'd come for me. On foot or with choppers.' He pulled the Springfield's bolt, catching the round he ejected, replacing it with a round he took from his pocket. He shoved the bolt in place again.

Then he revved the accelerator, urging the bike from the trees, racing across the meadow. Glancing back, Chris saw the chopper pivot, darting in their direction. 'They've seen us!'

Saul twisted the handlebars, veering back toward the trees. Machine gun bullets tore at the ground. The chopper swept over them, its obscene silhouette blotting out the sun. At once, the glare came back. Saul raced the bike into the forest. Jumping off, he aimed through branches toward the chopper as it twisted sharply above the meadow.

Chris said, 'A Springfield can't shoot that chopper down.'

'This one can.'

Belly exposed, the chopper began a strafing approach to the trees, zooming larger. Saul pulled the Springfield's trigger, absorbing the recoil. In wonder, Chris saw the chopper's gas tank explode. He leapt for cover, shielding his eyes. Chunks of fuselage and canopy, of struts and blades erupted amid a roaring fireball in every direction across the meadow. The bulk of the fuselage hung perversely. It suddenly crashed.

'I drilled the core from the bullet, filled it with phosphorus, and put a plug in to keep the air from setting it off,' Saul said.

'The other choppers . . .'

'They'll head this way. They'll search this end of the valley. We'll go back the other way. Where they've already searched.'

Saul grabbed the bike. Chris quickly got on. They rushed back along the game trail. Twenty seconds later, the remaining choppers roared past toward the flaming wreckage in the meadow.

Eliot clutched the greenhouse phone, his tall gaunt body stooped, his forehead aching. 'I understand,' he said impatiently. 'No, I don't want excuses. You weren't successful. That's what matters, not why you failed. Clean up the mess you made. Use other teams. Keep after them.' He still wore his black suit and vest, a chest-high apron draped over them. 'Of course, but I assumed your team was equally good. It seems my judgment was wrong. Believe me, I'm sorry too.'

Setting down the phone, he leaned against a potting table, so tired he thought his knees would buckle.

Everything was going wrong. The hit on the Paradigm Foundation should have been simple, one man to blame, a man who couldn't say he was following orders if he was killed when he tried to fight off his captors. Simple, Eliot thought. Meticulously planned. He'd chosen Saul because he was Jewish, because the hit had to be blamed on someone other than Eliot, so why not the Israelis? He'd arranged for Saul's previous jobs to go badly – a cleaning lady coming into a room when she shouldn't have, for example – to make Saul seem as if he was out of control. Sending Saul to gamble in Atlantic City had been another way of compromising him. Saul had to fit the behavior of an agent who'd gone bad, a rogue beyond salvage. A brilliant, careful plan.

Then why had it gone wrong? After a career of avoiding mistakes, have I finally started to make them? he thought. Have I finally gotten too old? Did I delude myself into thinking that, because I sabotaged Saul's three previous jobs, he was in fact no longer resourceful?

For whatever reason, the plan was almost a disaster now. Saul's escape had jeopardized everything, creating new problems, drawing more attention to the Paradigm hit. An hour ago, the White House had called – not an aide but the president himself, enraged that his best friend's murder was still not avenged. If everything had gone as planned, if Saul had been silenced, the president would have been satisfied, turning his attention to the Israelis, blaming them for engineering the assassination. Now, instead of getting the answers he wanted, the president was asking more questions, digging, probing. If he ever learned who'd actually ordered the hit . . .

An irony struck him. Chris, by violating the sanction, had committed the cardinal sin. But Saul – though he didn't know it – had committed an even greater sin.

Its secret had to be maintained. He picked up the phone and dialed his assistant at Langley. 'Put this on the wire. Every network. KGB, MI–6, all of them. "Subject: Abelard sanction. Reference: Church of the Moon, Bangkok. Violator Remus sighted by CIA in Colorado, USA."' Eliot told his assistant the coordinates. '"Remus has evaded execution. Request assistance. Remus helped by rogue CIA operative Saul Grisman, cryptonym Romulus. Agency requests Romulus be terminated with Remus."'

'Perfect,' his assistant said.

But hanging up, Eliot wondered if it was. Cursing the news from Colorado, he felt threatened, apprehensive. Not only had Saul escaped. Worse, Chris was with him. Eliot blanched. Since no one else had known what Chris was doing, they'll suspect me, he thought. They'll want to know why I turned against them.

They'll come after me.

His hand shook as he dialed again. The phone buzzed so often he feared he'd get no answer. The buzzing stopped, a husky voice responding.

'Castor,' Eliot said. 'Bring Pollux. Come to the greenhouse.' He swallowed thickly. 'Your father needs you.'

12

When the moon came out, they left the ravine where they'd buried the trail bike under rocks and earth and fallen branches. They wouldn't need it anymore. As twilight turned to dark, they hadn't been able to steer it safely through the trees. Of course, another hit team using dogs would find the bike, but Saul and Chris would be far away by then. In the moonlight, they worked their way across a meadow, staying low to hide their furtive silhouettes. They reached the upward draw they'd chosen at dusk when, studying Chris's terrain map, they'd planned their route. They climbed the rocky chasm, never speaking, never glancing behind them, always listening for uncharacteristic sounds from the valley below them. Since the attack on Saul's cabin, they'd traveled twenty miles through three connecting valleys. Chris's spine ached from the shock of the trail bike's wheels on bumps and branches. He enjoyed the exertion of climbing, the release of tension in his muscles.

At the top, they rested, sprawling out of sight in a rocky basin, the moon illuminating their sweaty faces.

'If this were Nam, we wouldn't have a chance.' Saul kept his voice low, catching his breath. 'They'd send a surveillance plane with a heat sensor.'

Chris understood – the trouble with a heat sensor was it picked up animal as well as human body temperature. In Nam, the only way to make a sensor practical had been to spray poison from planes and kill all the wildlife in the jungle. That way, if a sensor registered a blip, the heat source had to be human. Chris recalled the unnatural silence of a jungle without animals. But here there was too much wildlife for a heat sensor to be useful. The forest sounds were constant, reassuring, the brush of leaves, the whisper of branches. Deer grazed. Porcupines and badgers scavenged. But if the noises ever stopped, he'd know something had spooked them.

'They'll bring in other teams,' Chris said.

'But only to flush us out. The real trap's in the foothills. They'll watch every ranger station, every road and town around here. Sooner or later we have to come down.'

'They can't surround the entire mountain range. They'll have to be selective. The nearest foothills are south and west of here.'

'So we'll go north.'

'How far?'

'As far as we have to. We're at home up here. If we don't like the way things look, we'll just keep moving farther north.'

'We can't use the rifle to hunt. The shot would attract attention. But we can fish. And there'll be plants – stonecrop, mountain sorrel, spring beauties.'

Saul grimaced. 'Spring beauties. Well, I needed to lose weight anyhow. At least the dogs can't track us up sheer cliffs.'

'You're sure you're in condition for this?' Chris grinned.

'Hey, what about you? That monastery didn't make you soft, I hope.'

'The Cistercians?' Chris laughed. 'Make me soft? They're the toughest order in the Catholic Church.'

'They really don't talk?'

'Not only that. They believe in brutal daily work. I might as well have spent another six years in Special Forces.'

Saul shook his head. 'The communal life. Did you ever think about the pattern? First the orphanage, then the military, next the agency and the monastery. There's a common denominator.'

'What?'

'Segregrated disciplined cadres. You're addicted.'

'Both of us. The only difference is you never took the extra step. You were never tempted to enter a Jewish monastic order.'

'Didn't those Cistercians teach you anything? There's no such thing as a Jewish monastic order. We don't believe in retreating from the world.'

'That's probably why you stayed in the agency. It's the nearest thing to monasticism you could find.'

'The quest for perfection.' Saul frowned in disgust. 'We'd better get moving.' He pulled a compass from his pocket, studying its luminous dial.

'Why does Eliot want to kill you?'

Even in the night, Chris saw the angry glow on his brother's face. 'Don't you think I keep asking myself? He's the only kind of father I've got, and now the bastard's turned against me. Everything started after a job I did for him. But why?'

'He'll make sure he's protected. We can't just go to him and ask.'

Saul clenched his teeth. 'Then we'll go around him.'

'How?'

They swung toward a sudden far-off rumble. 'Sounds like something blew up,' Saul murmured.

'Dummy.' Chris laughed.

Saul turned to him, confused.

'That's thunder.'

Thirty minutes later, as they climbed to the bottom of a jagged ridge, the stormclouds scudded overhead, obscuring the moon. In a

83

sudden stinging wind, Saul found a protective lip of rock. Chris squirmed beneath it as the rain hit.

'Go around him? How?'

But Saul's reply was drowned by more thunder.

CASTOR AND POLLUX

1

Saul tensed. Crouching on a roof, concealed by the dark, he stared toward the street below him. Cars flanked the curbs; lamps glowed behind curtains in apartments. He watched a door come open in a building across the street. A woman stepped out: midthirties, tall, trim, elegant, with long dark hair, wearing navy slacks, a burgundy blouse, and a brown suede jacket. Saul studied her features in the light above the door. Her skin was smooth and tanned, her high strong cheeks accentuated by a beautiful chin, an exquisite forehead, a sensual neck. She'd often been mistaken for a model.

Saul knew better, though. He crawled back from the waist-high wall at the edge of the roof, then stood and opened the maintenance door that led to a ladder and finally stairs. For an instant, he recalled his escape from the tenement in Atlantic City, racing from the roof down the stairs to the street where he'd stolen the Duster. This time, after he hurried unnoticed down the stairs of this attractive apartment building, he glanced both ways along the street and passed the parked cars to follow the woman.

She walked to his left, reached a streetlight, and turned the corner. Saul heard the echo of her high-heeled shoes as he crossed the street and went around the corner after her. A cruising taxi made him nervous. An old man walking a dog aroused his suspicion.

Halfway down the block, the woman entered a doorway. Saul came nearer, glancing through a window toward red-checked tablecloths in the booths of a small Italian restaurant. He paused as if to study the menu on the wall beside the entrance. He could wait close by for her to come out, he thought, but he saw no acceptable hiding places. All the buildings on this street were businesses. If he stayed in an alley or jimmied a lock to get up on another roof, the police might find him. As well, he didn't want to confront her on the street. Too dangerous. In a way, by going in the restaurant, she'd solved a problem for him.

When he entered, he heard an accordion. Candlelight glowed off polished oak. Silverware clinked amid muted conversations. He scanned the busy room, smelling garlic and butter. Peering past a waiter carrying a tray, he concentrated on the corners in the rear. As he expected, she sat with her back to a wall, facing the front but near an exit through the kitchen. Her waiter had taken the other place settings. Good, Saul thought, she planned to eat alone.

The maître d' came over. 'Do you have a reservation, sir?'

'I'm with Miss Bernstein. In that corner.' Smiling, Saul passed him, crossing the room. His smile dissolved as he stopped before the table. 'Erika.'

She glanced up, confused. Abruptly her brow contorted in alarm.

He pulled out a chair and sat beside her. 'It isn't polite to stare. Keep your fingers on the edge of the table. Away from the knife and fork, please.'

'You!'

'And please don't raise your voice.'

'Are you crazy coming here? Everybody's hunting you.'

'That's what I want to talk to you about.' Saul studied her face – the smooth dark cheeks, the deep brown eyes and full lips. He fought the urge to draw his finger across her skin. 'You keep getting lovelier.'

Erika shook her head, incredulous. 'How long has it been? Ten years? Now out of nowhere you suddenly show up – in the worst kind of trouble – and that's all you can say?'

'You'd prefer to hear you're getting uglier?'

'For Christ's sake –'

'That's no way for a nice Jewish girl to talk.'

She raised a hand in dismay.

He stiffened. 'Please keep your fingers on the edge of the table,' he repeated.

She obeyed, breathing deeply. 'This can't be coincidence. You didn't just happen to choose this place.'

'I followed you from your apartment.'

'Why? You could have come up.'

'To find a roommate or someone waiting in case I tried to get in touch with you?' He shook his head. 'I figured neutral ground was better. Why are they after me?'

She frowned in surprise. 'You actually don't know? Because of Bangkok. Chris violated the sanction.' Her voice was low but tense. The noises from the nearby kitchen kept the other customers from hearing her.

'But Bangkok was after. What's that got to do with me?'

'After *what*? You don't make sense.'

'Just tell me.'

'Chris killed a Russian. The KGB issued a contract against him. Because of the rules of the sanction, the other networks have to help.'

'I know all that. But what's it got to do with *me*? Atlantic City happened *before* Bangkok.'

'What are you talking about? Five days ago, we received a message from your agency – a revision of the contract. Chris had been seen in Colorado. You were helping him, the message said. The CIA declared you a rogue and asked for you to be killed with Chris.'

Saul murmured, 'Eliot.'

'For God's sake, would you tell me what –?' Nervous, she glanced at sudden stares from nearby customers. 'We can't talk here.'

'Then where?'

2

In the dark, Saul gazed through the window toward the distant lights of the Washington Monument. 'Nice location.'

'Ten blocks from our embassy,' Erika said behind him.

He didn't give a damn about the view. His reason for staring out the window was to test her. On guard, he waited for her to try to kill him. When she didn't, he closed the draperies and turned on a corner lamp, angling it so he and Erika would cast no shadows on the drapes.

He nodded in approval of the living room, its furniture simple, carefully chosen, elegant. He'd already searched the bedroom, the kitchen and the bathroom. As she'd promised, he'd found no room-mate, no one waiting for him. 'Microphones?'

'I checked this morning.'

'This is tonight.' He turned on the television, not because he wanted its noise to muffle their conversation, instead because he needed a constant sound for a test. He'd seen a portable radio in the kitchen. Now he got it and turned it on, switching to the FM band. He divided the room into quadrants, checking each section for bugs by slowly moving the radio's dial. A hidden microphone was normally tuned to an FM number not used by a station in the area. All an eavesdropper had to do was wait in a nearby safe location, adjust a radio to the FM number he'd chosen, and listen to whatever was said near the mike he'd planted. Similarly, Saul could use a radio to pick up the same transmission. As he moved the dial, if he heard the noise from the television come from the radio – often as squawky feedback – he'd know the room was bugged. In this case, no matter which FM station he tried, he didn't pick up the laugh track from the sit com. He scanned the ceiling, the walls, the furniture, the floor. Satisfied, he turned the TV and radio off. The room seemed unnaturally still.

'The sanction?' he said as if their conversation in the restaurant hadn't been interrupted. 'That's the only reason your people are after me? Because I'm helping Chris?'

'What other reason could there be?' Erika raised her eyebrows, troubled. 'We hate to help the Russians, but the sanction has to be maintained. Abelard's the cardinal rule. If it's destroyed, we sink toward chaos.'

'Then if you had the chance, you'd kill me? A fellow Jew, a former lover?'

Erika didn't answer. She took off her jacket. The two top buttons of her blouse were open, spread by the swell of her breasts. 'You gave me the chance a few minutes ago when you looked out the window. I didn't take it.'

'Because you knew I did it deliberately – to see how you'd react.'

She grinned.

The gleam of amusement in her eyes made him grin in return. He felt as attracted to her as he'd been ten years ago, wanting to ask how she was, what had happened to her since he'd last seen her.

But he had to deny himself. He couldn't trust anyone except his brother. 'For what it's worth, Chris is out there. If you killed me . . .'

'I assumed you'd have backup. He'd come after me to get revenge. I'd be foolish to try unless I had you both together.'

'On the other hand, maybe you'd feel lucky. I don't have time for this. I need answers. Eliot's hunting me, but not because of Chris. That's merely Eliot's excuse. Hell, he asked Chris to find me – *after Chris had already violated the sanction.*'

'That's insane.'

'Of course.' Saul gestured with frustration. 'If the Russians knew Eliot had asked Chris for help instead of killing him, they'd put out another contract. Eliot risked his life to try to find me.'

'Why?'

'To kill me.'

'You expect me to believe this? Eliot's like a father to you.'

Saul rubbed his aching forehead. 'Something's more important than his relationship with me, more important than the sanction, so important he has to get rid of me. But dammit, I don't know what. That's why I came to you.'

'How would I –?'

'Atlantic City. *Before* Chris violated the sanction. Even then, the Mossad came after me. I have to assume your people were helping Eliot.'

'Impossible!'

'It's not! It happened!'

Erika's eyes flashed. 'If we helped Eliot, I'd know about it. A lot of things have changed since the last time I saw you. I'm supposed to be a clerk in our embassy, but I'm a colonel in the Mossad now. I control our intelligence teams on the eastern seaboard. Unless I approved it, none of our people would have tried to kill you.'

'Then whoever ordered it lied to you and covered it up. Someone in the Mossad works for Eliot.'

Erika continued glaring. 'I can't accept it! If what you say is true –' She shuddered, raising her hands. 'Just wait a minute. This is senseless. I'm arguing with you when I don't even know the details. Tell me about it. Exactly what happened.'

Saul slumped in a chair. 'Ten days ago, Eliot asked me to do a job. The Paradigm Foundation.'

Erika's eyes widened. 'Andrew Sage's group. The president's friend. That was you? The president's blaming *us.*'

'But why?'

'The Paradigm Foundation worked for the president. A group of American billionaires who negotiated with the Arabs to get cheaper oil if the State Department abandoned its loyalty to Israel. The president thinks we protected our interests by destroying the foundation.'

'And stopping the negotiations,' Saul said. 'For once, the president's being logical.'

'Go on. What happened?'

'You mean I've finally got your attention? You see the point? If you help me, you'll be helping yourselves.'

'You mentioned Atlantic City.'

'After the job, Eliot sent me there to drop out of sight.'

'Absurd. That's no place to hide.'

'Damn right it isn't. But I always do what Eliot tells me. I don't argue. Someone from the Mossad tried to kill me in a casino. I called Eliot for protection. He sent me to a hotel where a Mossad team set up another trap. Only Eliot knew where I was going. The team must have worked for Eliot.'

'I tell you it's impossible!'

'Because you didn't know about it? You're being naive.'

'Because of something else. Whoever helped Eliot was also helping whoever wanted Sage's group destroyed. We'd never be stupid enough to kill the president's friend, no matter how badly we wanted those negotiations stopped. We'd be the first country the president accused, exactly what's happened. The hit didn't help us – it hurt us! What Mossad team would turn against Israel?'

'Maybe they didn't know why Eliot wanted me killed. Maybe they didn't know the connection between me and the hit.'

'I still don't understand what makes you sure they were Mossad.'

'You figure it out. They used the heels of their palms in hand-to-hand combat. They used Berettas and Uzis. They walked with that flat-footed, half-crouched stance for balance. No one else is taught to do that. They even made silencers the way your people do.'

She stared in disbelief.

3

Chris crept up the stairs, his rubber-soled shoes touching the concrete softly. Close to the wall, out of sight from anyone peering past the railing down the stairwell, he approached each landing. Fluorescent lights hummed as he listened for other sounds above him. Checking all five levels, he found no one, then came down one level to open a fire door, studying the fourth floor hall. Numbered apartments flanked both sides. Directly to his right, he saw an elevator, pushed its button, and waited. A light above its door showed 5, then 4. A bell rang as the door slid open. With his hand on the Mauser beneath his jacket, he discovered no one.

Good, he thought. As much as possible, the building was secure, though he didn't like the flimsy locks on the outside doors or the absence of a guard in the lobby. He debated whether he should have continued to watch the building from the street. The problem had been that from his vantage he couldn't see the back, nor could he determine if someone entering the building belonged here or was hunting Saul. Besides, he couldn't know if trouble was already inside. He had to assume that agents from various networks – especially from Eliot – were watching the people he and Saul would likely ask for help, and Erika certainly qualified as their friend, though they hadn't seen her since '73. It was possible no one knew how close the friendship was, but since they needed her help, Chris believed in being thorough. Now that he'd checked the building, he felt more confident, knowing that Erika's apartment – on the left, halfway down the hall – was protected. A hunter couldn't reach the fourth floor, by either the elevator or the stairs, without his knowing it. He went back to the stairwell, left its door slightly open, and listened for the elevator's bell or footsteps below him.

Earlier, he'd smiled from a roof near Saul, recognizing Erika's figure as she left her apartment to walk down the street, enjoying the memory of the first time he'd met her, when he and Saul had gone for special training to Israel in 1966. Then as now her elegance deceived. A veteran of the Israeli Six-Day War in '67 and the October War in '73, she was as capable – indeed as deadly – as any man. Ironic, he thought. In America strong women were considered threats whereas in Israel they were treasured, since their nation's survival left no room for sexual prejudice.

The creak of a door coming open below him troubled him. He turned to the rail, seeing shadows at the bottom of the stairs. As the door snicked shut down there, he took advantage of its echo to shift to the level above him, drawing his Mauser, easing to his stomach on the chilly concrete.

The shadows might belong to people who lived in the building and preferred climbing the stairs for exercise instead of using the elevator. If they came all the way up, they'd panic at the sight of his Mauser. He'd have to run.

The lights hummed, almost obscuring the gentle brush of footsteps climbing higher.

Second floor, he thought. No, third. They're stopping. He almost relaxed, then corrected his guess.

The fourth, directly below him. The footsteps paused. He clutched the Mauser, staring at the distorted silhouettes projecting up.

He aimed. Were they tenants? They seemed to inch higher. In a moment, he'd see their faces. He pressed his finger on the trigger, braced for an instant's judgment.

The shadows stopped. The door creaked open down there, then shut.

He rose to a crouch and pointed the Mauser down the stairs. Seeing no one, he hurried down. Cautious, he opened the door and squinted out.

Two men stood halfway down the hall, facing left toward Erika's apartment. One man held a submachine gun, short-stocked, stubby-barreled, unmistakably an Uzi, while the other man tugged a pin from a grenade.

Chris saw them too late. The first man fired. In a continuous deafening roar, the Uzi's bullets splintered the door to Erika's apartment. Ejected casings flew through the air, clinking against each other on the carpet. The acrid stench of cordite filled the hall. The gunman shifted his aim, continuing to squeeze the Uzi's trigger, spraying the wall beside the door. The second man released the lever on his grenade and kicked the door's shattered lock, preparing to throw as the door burst in.

Chris fired twice. The second man spun from the impact to his skull and shoulder, dropping the grenade. The first man pivoted, shooting at Chris. Despite the noise, Chris heard a bell. He ducked to the stairwell. Footsteps charged from the elevator. The gunman kept shooting. Amid a roar of bullets, people screamed, their bodies ripped, falling.

The grenade exploded, amplified by the hall, shrapnel zinging. The stench of cordite flared Chris's nostrils. He fought to overcome the ringing in his ears, to listen for sounds in the corridor.

On guard, he peered from the stairwell. To his right, in front of the elevator, two men with Uzis lay motionless in a pool of blood.

Of course. Two pairs covering both routes to this floor. But their timing was off. The elevator arrived too late. The second pair heard the shots and charged out but got killed by the man they wanted to help.

He turned to his left. The gunman who'd shot at Erika's apartment sprawled beside his dead companion, his face blown off.

Hearing panicked voices in apartments, Chris raced down the hall. Erika's door was shattered. Dangling open, it showed the living room. The Uzi's spray of bullets had mangled the furniture, blowing apart the television. Drapes hung in tatters.

'*Saul?*' But he saw no bodies.

Where the hell were they?

4

As the first roar of bullets had erupted through the door, Saul dropped to the rug, hearing Erika do the same. His impulse had been to crawl to the kitchen or the bedroom. But then the bullets burst through the wall instead of the door, beginning at waist level, angling down. The rug across which he'd have to crawl toward either room heaved from their impact. Chunks of carpet flew in a systematic pattern, marching back and forth from the far end of the room toward the middle where he lay. He and Erika had to roll in the opposite direction, away from the bullets toward the wall beside the door. He felt it shudder above him. Fragments of plaster pelted him. The rug heaved closer. If the gunman dropped his aim much lower . . .

91

The door crashed in. Saul aimed his Beretta, hearing two pistol shots, a body falling, screams, an explosion, silence.

Close to the wall, he rose to his feet, sensing Erika do the same. He heard shouting out there and aimed toward a shadow in the doorway.

'Saul!' someone yelled. The shadow entered.

Saul eased his finger off the trigger.

Chris turned, peering anxiously along the wall. 'Are you hit?'

Saul shook his head. 'What happened?'

'No time. We have to get out of here.'

Doors opened along the hall. A woman screamed. A man yelled, 'Call the police!'

Chris froze, staring past Saul toward something in the room.

'What's wrong?'

Saul spun toward Erika, afraid she'd been hit. She faced the two of them, backing away from a chair beneath which she'd drawn a hidden pistol, another Beretta.

'No!'

She aimed at Chris. Saul remembered what she'd told him earlier. She'd be foolish to try to kill Saul unless she also had a chance at . . .

'No!'

Too late. She fired. Saul heard the sickening whack of a bullet hitting flesh. A groan. He whirled. Beyond Chris, a man with a pistol lurched back against the corridor's wall, his throat spurting blood.

Chris clutched the side of his head. 'Jesus!'

'I missed you,' Erika said.

'By a quarter-inch! The bullet singed my hair!'

'You'd prefer I let him kill you?'

Past the shattered windows, sirens wailed in the night.

Erika hurried toward the door. Saul quickly followed. 'Where did that guy come from?'

As he reached the corridor, rushing past the bodies on the floor, he saw his answer. Down the hall, from the apartment next to Erika's, a man aimed an Uzi. Erika fired. Saul and Chris shot one second afterward. The man wailed, doubling over, his finger still pressed on the trigger, spraying the floor. The Uzi jerked from his hands.

Erika ran toward the elevator.

'No,' Saul told her. 'We'll be trapped in there.'

'Don't argue, dammit!' Avoiding the pool of blood around the bodies, she pressed the elevator button. The door slid open. She pushed Saul and Chris inside, touched number 5, and the door slid shut.

Saul's stomach sank as the elevator rose.

'We can't go down,' she said. 'God knows who's in the lobby. The police or –' Reaching up, she tugged a panel from the elevator's roof.

Saul straightened when he saw the trapdoor beyond the panel. 'Emergency exit.'

'I checked the day I rented the apartment,' she said. 'In case I needed a private escape route.'

Saul pushed the trapdoor to raise it. The elevator stopped. As his stomach settled, he saw Chris press the button that kept the door closed. Jumping up, Saul grabbed the trapdoor's edge and climbed through the narrow exit, kneeling in the dark. He reached down for Erika's hands, smelling the grease on the elevator cables beside him.

'They didn't need to bug my apartment or watch the building from outside.' She climbed up next to him. 'You saw. They had two men in the apartment next to mine. As soon as you arrived, they sent for help.'

From the elevator, Chris handed them the panel. Squirming up, he leaned down, sliding the panel back in place. He shut the trapdoor. 'Now what? God Almighty, the dust. I can hardly breathe.'

'Above us. On the roof, there's a superstructure for the elevator. It's the housing for the gears.' Erika's voice echoed in the dark shaft. She climbed, her shoes scraping against the concrete wall.

Saul reached up, touching a metal bar. The moment his shoes left the elevator's roof, he heard a rumble. No! The elevator was going down! He dangled. 'Chris!'

'Beside you!'

Saul's fingers almost slipped from the greasy bar. If he fell, if the elevator went all the way to the bottom . . . He imagined his body crashing through the elevator's roof and squirmed to get a better grip on the bar. Erika's hand tightened on his wrist. He scrambled up.

'Keep your head low,' she ordered. 'The gears are directly above you.'

Saul felt the speeding cables, the rush of air from the whirring gears. He hunched on a concrete ledge.

'My jacket,' Chris said. 'It's caught in the gears.'

Their rumble was magnified by the echo in the shaft. Saul spun to him, useless, blind. The rumble stopped. The cables trembled in place. The silence smothered him.

He heard the rip of cloth. 'My sleeve,' Chris said. 'I have to get it out before –'

The rumble began again, muffling Chris's words. Saul reached for him, almost losing his balance, straining not to fall.

'I did it,' Chris said. 'My jacket's out.'

The elevator stopped below them. As silence returned, Saul heard the door slide open. A sickened voice moaned, someone gagging. 'It's worse than they told us! A goddamn slaughterhouse! Call the station! On the double! We need help!' Footsteps rushed from the elevator. The door slid shut. The rumble began once more as the elevator descended.

'They'll seal off the building,' Erika said.

'Then let's get out of here.'

'I'm trying. There's a maintenance door to the roof. But it's locked.' Saul heard a rattle as she tugged at a latch. 'We're stuck in here?' The elevator stopped. He heard the scrape of metal.

'The hinge pins. One of them's loose.' Erika kept her voice low. Saul heard more scraping. 'There. I've got it out.'

'What about the other one? Use my knife.'

93

'It's moving. Okay, I've got it.' She pulled the hatch. Through a crack. Saul welcomed the glow from the city. He leaned close, gasping fresh air.

'They'll check the roof,' Erika said. 'We'll have to wait till they've finished.' Despite Saul's eagerness to leave, he knew she was right; he didn't argue. 'I can see the door to the roof,' she added. 'If it opens, I'll have time to shut the hatch and slide the pins back in.'

The elevator rumbled again, rising. A male voice drifted up, muffled. 'The coroner's on the way. We're searching the building. Who lives in that apartment?'

'A woman. Erika Bernstein.'

'Where the hell is she? I searched the apartment. I didn't see any bodies.'

'If she's still in the building, we'll find her.'

Ten minutes later, two policeman came through the door to the roof, aiming revolvers and flashlights. Erika shut the maintenance hatch, silently replacing the pins in the hinges. Saul heard footsteps and voices.

'Nobody up here.'

'What about the hatch to the elevator?'

A flashlight glared through the grill in the hatch. Saul pressed back with Chris and Erika, deep in the shadows.

'There's a lock.'

'Better check it. Maybe it's been jimmied.'

The footsteps came closer.

'Be careful. I'll stay back and cover you.'

Saul heard a rattle as the lock was jerked.

'You satisfied?'

'The captain said to be thorough.'

'What difference does it make? He always double-checks everything himself. Then he sends us back to *triple*-check.'

The footsteps drifted away. The door to the roof creaked shut.

Saul breathed out sharply. Sweat stung his eyes. Double-check and triple-check? he thought, dismayed. We're trapped in here.

5

All night, the elevator kept going up and down, raising dust that smeared their faces and clogged their nostrils, making them gag. After Erika reopened the maintenance hatch, they took turns straining for fresh air through the gap. Saul kept checking the luminous hands on his watch. Shortly after six, he began to see Chris and Erika, their haggard features becoming more distinct as the morning sun filtered through the grill.

At first he welcomed the light, but as he sweated more intensely he realized the shaft was getting warmer, baked by the sun's glare on the elevator's superstructure. He felt suffocated. Taking off his jacket, he pried his gritty shirt away from his chest. By eleven o'clock, he'd removed his shirt as well. They slumped in a stupor, wearing only their underwear. Erika's flesh-toned bra clung to her breasts, sweat forming rivulets between them. Saul studied the exhaustion on her face, worrying for her, at last concluding she was tougher than Chris and he. She'd probably outlast both of them.

By noon, the elevator went up and down less often. The ambulance crew and the forensic squad had come and gone. In the night, the bodies had been taken away. From muffled conversations in the elevator, Saul learned that two policemen were watching Erika's apartment, two others watching the lobby. Still it wasn't safe to leave. Grimy, they'd attract attention if they showed themselves in daylight. So they continued to wait, struggling to breathe. When the sun went down, Saul's vision was blurred. His arms felt heavy. His stomach cramped from dehydration. They finally reached the limit they'd agreed on – twenty-four hours from the attack.

Crawling wearily from the narrow hatch, they stumbled to stand on the roof. Fingers slack, they put on their clothes, gulping the cool night air, swallowing dryly. Dizzy, they stared toward the far-off gleam of the Capitol building.

'So much to do,' Chris said.

Saul knew what he meant. They needed transportation, water, food, a place for them to bathe and find clean clothes and rest. Above all, sleep.

And after sleep, the answers.

'I can get us a car.' Erika pushed her long dark hair behind her shoulders.

'Your own or from the embassy?' Chris didn't wait for an answer. He shook his head. 'Too risky. The police know who you are. Since they didn't find your body, they have to figure you're involved. They'll watch your parking spot beneath the building. They'll find out where you work and watch the embassy.'

'I've got a backup car.' Her breasts arched as she put on her blouse. She buttoned the sleeves. 'I used a different name to buy it. I paid cash – a slush fund from the embassy. The car can't be traced to me. I keep it in a garage on the other side of town.'

'That still leaves us with the other problem – a place to go,' Chris said. 'The police have our descriptions from the neighbors who saw us outside your apartment. We can't risk going to a hotel. Two men and a woman – we'd be obvious.'

'And whoever's hunting us will check your friends,' Saul added.

'No hotel. No friends,' she said.

'Then what?'

'Stop frowning. Don't you like surprises?'

95

The captain of homicide clutched the phone in his office, staring bleakly at the half-eaten Quarter-Pounder on his cluttered desk. As he listened to the imperious voice on the phone, he suddenly lost his appetite. His ulcer began to burn. Past the screen of the open window, sirens wailed in the Washington night. 'Of course.' The captain sighed. 'Sir, I'll take care of it. I guarantee no problem.'

Curling his lips in disgust, he set the phone down, wiping his sweaty hand as if the phone had contaminated him. A man appeared in the doorway. Glancing across his desk, the captain saw his lean-faced lieutenant – jacket off, tie loosened, wrinkled shirtsleeves rolled up – light a cigarette.

Beyond the lieutenant, phones rang; typewriters clattered. Weary detectives searched files and questioned prisoners.

'That scowl on your face,' the lieutenant said. 'You look like you just heard the department's forcing you on another exercise program.'

'Shoveling shit.' The captain sagged in his creaky chair.

'What's wrong?'

'That bloodbath last night. Six men with enough weapons to invade a small country, blown away in an apparently ordinary apartment building.'

'You ran out of leads?'

'You could say that. It never happened.'

The lieutenant choked on his cigarette smoke. 'What the hell are you talking about?' He stalked past filing cabinets into the room.

'The call I just got.' The captain gestured with contempt toward the phone. 'It came from high up, I mean so high I'm not even allowed to tell you who. It makes me sick to think about it. If I don't handle this thing right, I'll be back in a squad car.' Wincing, the captain pressed his burning stomach. 'This damn town – sometimes I think it's the ass-end of the universe.'

'For Christ's sake, tell me.'

'The men who got killed. The government's impounded their bodies.' The captain didn't need to explain what 'government' meant. Both he and his lieutenant had worked in Washington long enough to recognize the synonym for covert activities. 'For security reasons, those corpses won't be identified. Official business. No publicity. The government's handling almost everything.'

'Almost?' The lieutenant jabbed his cigarette in an overflowing ashtray. 'You're not making sense.'

'Two men and a woman. We've got the woman's name – Erika Bernstein. We've got detailed descriptions. If we find them, I've got a number to call. But we can't let them know they've been seen, and we can't pick them up.'

'That's crazy. They shot six men, but we can't arrest them?'

'How the hell can we? I told you the government impounded the bodies. Those corpses don't exist. What we're looking for are three nonkillers for a mass murder that never happened.'

Erika left the building first. One at a time, Chris and Saul followed shortly afterwards, using different exits, scanning the dark before they retreated along shadowy streets. Making sure they weren't pursued, they each hailed a taxi as soon as they were out of the neighborhood, giving the drivers instructions to take them to separate districts on the other side of Washington. While Erika went to the parking garage to get her car, Chris waited at a pizza parlor they'd agreed on. Saul in turn went to a video-game arcade where he played Guided Missile while he glanced through the window toward the street they'd chosen.

Just before the arcade closed at midnight, he saw a blue Camaro stop at the curb, its engine idling. Recognizing Erika behind the wheel, he went out, automatically scanning the street as he opened the passenger door.

'I hope the two of you won't feel cramped in back.'

He wondered what she meant. Then he noticed Chris hunched down out of sight behind the driver's seat. 'The elevator shaft, now this?' Groaning, he climbed in back. As Erika pulled from the curb, he hunkered on the floor near Chris.

'You don't have to be chummy too long,' she said.

Saul noticed the periodic glow of streetlights as she drove. 'How long exactly?'

'An hour.'

He groaned again, shoving Chris. 'Hey, move your big feet.'

She laughed. 'The cops want two men and a woman. If they saw us together, they might pull us over, just on a hunch.'

'I'm not so sure,' Chris said.

'But why take chances?'

'That's not what I mean. While I waited at the pizza parlor, I got a look at a newspaper. The killings weren't mentioned.'

'It must have been yesterday's paper,' Erika said.

'No, today's. Six men dead. Your apartment shot up. I expected a front-page story, description of us, the works. I checked some other papers. I found nothing.'

'Maybe they got the story too late to run it.'

'The shooting happened at quarter after ten last night. There was plenty of time.'

She turned a corner. Headlights flicked past the Camaro. 'Someone must have convinced the papers not to run it.'

'Eliot,' Saul said. 'He could've impounded the bodies and asked the police to stay quiet for the sake of national security. The papers would never have known what happened.'

'But why?' Chris said. 'He's hunting us. He could have our pictures on every front page in the country. With so many people searching for us, he'd have a better chance to catch us.'

'Unless he doesn't want publicity. Whatever this is all about, he wants to keep it private.'

'What, though?' Chris clenched a fist. 'What's so damned important?'

8

Saul felt the Camaro turn. In the night, the smooth highway suddenly changed to a bumpy side road. On the back floor, he gripped the seat. 'Don't you have any shocks in this thing?'

Erika grinned. 'We're almost there. It's safe to sit up now.'

Grateful, Saul raised himself to the seat. Easing back, stretching his cramped legs, he peered through the windshield. The Camaro's headlights showed dense bushes on both sides of a narrow dirt lane. 'Where are we?'

'South of Washington. Near Mount Vernon.'

Saul tapped Chris's shoulder, pointing toward a grove of trees. Beyond them, moonlight glimmered on an impressive red brick mansion.

'Colonial?' Chris said.

'A little later. It was built in eighteen hundred.' Erika stopped the car where the lane curved from the trees toward the lawn before the extensive porch. She aimed her headlights toward the forest beyond.

'You know who lives here?' Chris said. 'We agreed we couldn't risk going to friends.'

'He's not a friend.'

'Then who?'

'This man's a Jew. I fought beside his son in Israel. I've been here only once – when I came to tell him his son died bravely.' She swallowed. 'I gave him a photograph of the grave. I gave him the medal his son never lived to receive. He told me if I ever needed help . . .' Her voice sounded hoarse.

Saul felt what she hadn't said. 'You knew the son well?'

'I wanted to. If he'd lived, I might have stayed in Israel with him.'

Saul put a comforting hand on her shoulder.

The house stayed dark. 'Either he's asleep,' Chris said, 'or he isn't home.'

'He's cautious. Unexpected visitors this late – he wouldn't turn the lights on.'

'Sounds like us,' Chris said.

'He survived Dachau. He remembers. Right now he's probably staring out here, wondering who the hell we are.'

'Better not keep him waiting.'

She stepped out, walking past the headlights toward the house. From the car's back seat, Saul watched her disappear behind a flowering dogwood, absorbed by the night. He waited five minutes. Suddenly nervous, he reached for the door.

Her tall slim figure emerged from shadows. She got back in the car. Saul felt relieved. 'He's home? He'll help us?'

She nodded, driving past the front of the house. A lane curved

98

toward the murky forest in back. 'I told him some friends and I needed a place to stay. I said it was better if he didn't know why. He asked no questions. He understood.' The Camaro bumped along the lane.

Saul turned around. 'But we're leaving the house.'

'We won't be staying there.' Her headlights glared through the trees.

With the windows open, Saul heard the predawn songs of birds. Mist swirled. He hugged his arms against the dampness.

'I hear frogs,' Chris said.

'The Potomac's up ahead.' She reached a clearing and an old stone cottage, partly covered with vines. 'He says it's his guest house. There's power and water.' Stopping, she got out, studied the cottage, and nodded approvingly.

As she went in with Saul, Chris walked around the back, instinctively checking the perimeter. Wooden steps angled down a steep slope to the misty river. In the dark, he heard waves lap the bank. Something splashed. He smelled decay.

A light came on behind him from a window in the cottage. Turning, he watched Saul and Erika open cupboards in a rustic kitchen. With the window closed, he couldn't hear what they said, but he was struck by their ease with one another – even though they hadn't been lovers in ten years. He'd never experienced that kind of relationship. His inhibitions nagged at him. His throat felt tight as Saul leaned close to Erika, gently kissing her. Ashamed to be watching, he turned away.

He made a warning noise when he entered. The living room was spacious, paneled, with a wooden floor and beams across the peaked ceiling. He noticed a table to his left and a sofa before a fireplace to his right, the furniture covered with sheets. Across from him, he saw two doors and the entrance to the kitchen. He smelled dust.

'We'd better open the windows,' Erika said as she and Saul came into the living room. She took the sheets off the furniture. Dust swirled. 'There's some cans of food in the cupboards.'

Chris felt ravenous. He lifted a window, breathing fresh air, then checked the doors across from him. 'A bedroom. A shower. Tell you what. I'll cook. You can have the bathroom first.'

'You won't get an argument.' She touched her hair, already unbuttoning her blouse as she stepped in, closing the door behind her.

They heard the sound of the shower and went to the kitchen, where they cooked three cans of beef stew. The steam made Chris's stomach growl.

The water soon stopped. When Erika came back, she wore a towel around her hair and a robe she'd found in the bathroom closet.

'You look beautiful,' Saul said.

Mocking, she curtsied. 'And you look like you need a bath.'

Saul rubbed the dirt on his face and laughed. But nothing was funny. While they ate their first few spoonfuls, no one spoke. Finally Saul set down his spoon.

'Those men in the apartment next to yours would have known it was me, not Chris, who came home with you. Even so, they sent for a hit team. Sure, I'm helping Chris, but he's the one who violated the sanction. He should have been the primary target, but he wasn't. *I* was. Why?'

'And Colorado had nothing to do with the sanction either,' Chris said. 'Whatever their reason, they didn't attack till I found you. It wasn't me they wanted. It was *you*.'

Saul nodded, troubled. 'Atlantic City. The Mossad.'

'Those men at my apartment weren't Mossad,' Erika insisted. 'I'd have been told about the hit. They'd have made sure I was safe before they tried to kill you.'

'But they handled themselves like Israelis.'

'Just because they used Uzis and Berettas?' she said.

'All right, I grant you. Even the Russians sometimes use those weapons. But the other things. The heel of the palm in hand-to-hand combat.'

'And the way they made silencers, and their flat-footed crouch for balance when they stalked you. I know,' Erika said. 'You told me. Those tactics don't prove a thing.'

Saul's face turned red with impatience. 'What are you talking about? Nobody else is trained like that.'

'Not true.'

They stared at her.

'Who else?' Chris said.

They waited.

'You said they seemed to be cooperating with Eliot,' she continued, 'but trained by the Mossad.'

They nodded.

'Think about it,' she said.

'My God,' Chris said, 'you just described *us*.'

9

The implications kept Chris awake. He lay on the sofa and stared toward dawn beyond the window. Past the closed bedroom door, he heard a muted gasp – Saul and Erika making love. He closed his eyes, struggling to ignore what he heard, forcing himself to remember.

1966. After he and Saul had finished their tour in Nam and their stint in Special Forces, Eliot had wanted them to receive extra training, 'final polish' he'd called it. Flying separately to Heathrow Airport outside London, they'd rendezvoused at the baggage area. With keys they'd been given, they'd opened lockers and taken out expensive luggage filled with French clothing. Each suitcase had also contained a yarmulke.

During the flight to Tel Aviv, they'd changed clothes in the washroom. A stewardess put their discarded outfits in shopping bags and stuffed them in an empty food container at the rear of the plane. At the airport, once past customs, they were greeted by a heavy middle-aged woman who called them affectionate nicknames. In their skullcaps and French clothing, they looked like typical Parisian Jews embarking on their first kibbutz experience, and so it would have seemed when they boarded a bus designated for travel outside the city.

A few hours later, they were given rooms in a gymnasium-residence complex similar to a YMCA in America. Instructed to go at once to the main hall, they and twenty other students were met by an old man who introduced himself as Andre Rothberg. His casual appearance belied the deadly legend he'd created for himself. Bald and wrinkled, dressed in white shoes, white trousers and a white shirt, he resembled a genteel sportsman. But his history told of a very different man. His father, the fencing instructor for the last Russian czar, had taught Andre the quickness and coordination of hand and eye that had propelled him through the sports activities of Cambridge in the thirties, British naval intelligence during the Second World War, and finally the Israeli intelligence community after the '48 truce. Though Jewish, he'd remained a British citizen and thus had never been given access to the inner circles of power in Israel. Undaunted, he'd made his own valuable contribution by devising a system of self-defense training unequaled for its precision. Rothberg called it 'killer-instinct training,' and the performance Chris and Saul witnessed that day stunned them.

Using a trolley suspended by a chain from the ceiling of the vast room, an assistant pushed in the naked cadaver of a male, six feet tall, robust, recently deceased, in his twenties. Before the corpse had been harnessed and hooked in an upright position, it must have been stored on its back, where blood had settled, for the posterior side was blue-black while the front was yellow. It hung in a standing posture, feet on the floor, next to Rothberg. He took a large scalpel and made a ten-inch slash on each side of the chest, then across the bottom. With additional strokes, he separated the subcutaneous tissue from the rib cage and lifted the flap to expose the bones. He waited while his students inspected his work, drawing their attention to the undamaged ribs. He put the flap back in place and sealed the incisions with surgical tape.

Chris never forgot. Rothberg turned so his back was to the corpse. He stood flat-footed, legs spread apart, holding his arms out, palms down, parallel to the floor. His assistant placed a coin on the back of each hand. The assistant counted to three. In a blur, Rothberg flipped his hands over and caught the coins. But at the same time the corpse jerked back, its harness snapping against the hook that suspended it. Rothberg showed the coins he'd caught. He put them in his pocket and turned to the corpse, stripping the surgical tape, raising the skin flap. The ribs on both sides had been shattered. Not only had Rothberg flipped his hands to catch the coins with eyeblink speed. At the same instant, he'd also rammed his elbows back to strike the corpse, a movement so swift it was undetectable. The agility would have been remarkable in anyone, let alone a man in his sixties. As the other students murmured their surprise, Chris glanced around him, for the first time noticing Erika.

'So you see,' Rothberg explained, 'if our friend were still alive, his shattered ribs would have punctured his lungs. He'd have died from asphyxiation due to foam produced by the blood and air in his lungs. Cyanotic in three minutes, dead in sixteen – plenty of time to inject a drug if called for. But most important, an irreparable wound that results in little damage to your own ability to defend yourself against others. For the three major weapons your body offers you, which do not lose their ability to function even under the most serious impact, are the tip of your elbow, the web of skin between your thumb and first finger, and the heel of your palm. In the future, you will learn to use these weapons with speed, coordination, and the proper stance for balance. But for now we'll adjourn to dinner. Tonight I shall demonstrate the proper use of the garotte and the knife. For the next few days, it's all show and tell.'

A 'few days' turned out to be seven weeks. From dawn till sunset, every day except for the Jewish Sabbath, Chris and Saul went through the most intensive training they'd ever received, Special Forces included. Demonstrations were followed by practice sessions and then by grueling exercise. They learned fencing and ballet.

'For agility,' Rothberg explained. 'You must understand the need for refinement. Endurance doesn't matter, nor does strength. It makes no difference how huge and sturdy your opponent may be in comparison to yourself. A well-placed blow to the proper spot will kill him. Reflex – that's the most important factor, hence the fencing and the ballet. You must learn to control your body, to feel at home with it, to make your mind and muscle one. Thoughts must be transmitted instantly into action. Hesitation, faulty timing, and misplaced blows allow your opponent the chance to kill you. Speed, coordination, and reflex – these are your weapons as much as your body. Practice till you're too exhausted to move, till your prior training – as brutal as it was – seems like a holiday. Then practice more.'

When not in the classrooms or the gym, Chris and Saul spent hours in their room, developing their skills. In imitation of Rothberg, Chris held out his arms, palms down. Saul put a coin on the back of each hand. Chris jerked his hands away and tried to turn his palms to catch the falling coins. Then it was Saul's turn to try. For the first week, they thought the trick was impossible. The coins would strike the floor, or Chris and Saul would catch the coins too low and awkwardly. 'You just got killed,' they'd tell each other. By the end of the second week, their reflexes had improved sufficiently for them to catch the coins in one smooth blur. The coins seemed suspended in the air, captured before they began to fall.

But the coins were merely a device, not the final purpose. Once the skill of catching them had been mastered, another difficulty was added. As Rothberg explained, they had to learn not only how to deliver blows backward, with their elbows, instantly – but also how to do it forward, with the heels of the palms, equally fast. Practicing this second method of attack, Chris and Saul put pencils on a table. When they jerked their hands from the coins, they had to jab the pencils off the table before they caught the coins. Again the trick seemed impossible. They failed to catch the coins or they missed the pencils, or they moved so clumsily that again they told each other, 'You just got killed.'

Miraculously, by the end of the third week, they could manage both tricks at once. But jabbing the pencils wasn't the final purpose either. To their speed and coordination, they now added accuracy, spreading ink on the palm of each hand, then dropping the coins and striking at a circle on a sheet of paper tacked to the wall. At first they either failed to leave an inky palmprint in the circle or else failed to catch the coins, but by the beginning of the fifth week, they could study the well-placed ink stains, glance down at the coins in their hands, and congratulate themselves. 'The other guy got killed.' Eventually Rothberg judged them skilled enough to practice on cadavers. But the last week he insisted on the final test. 'Put the coins in your pocket. Slip on these padded vests,' he told them. 'Practice on yourselves.'

Chris lay on the sofa in the cottage, watching sunlight glint off the window. The Potomac whispered along its bank. A breeze nudged branches. Birds sang. He remembered, on that kibbutz in Israel there'd been no birds. Only heat and sand and seven weeks of sweat and concentration and pain. But when his killer-instinct training had been completed, he'd been as close as he would ever come to the goal of perfection Eliot constantly recommended – among the chosen few, the best, the most disciplined, capable, deadly, a world-class operative about to begin his career. In 1966, he thought. When I was young.

Now after successes, defeats, and betrayals, Chris mused on the years that had intervened. The agency, the monastery, the agency again, his probation in Rome, the Church of the Moon, the grave he'd dug in Panama. The pattern seemed predetermined. At the age of thirty-six, he considered everything he'd learned. He analyzed those seven weeks in Israel, recalling what Erika had said – that the description of the men who'd hunted Saul in Atlantic City also matched Saul and himself – men affiliated with Eliot but trained by the Mossad. Still, as hard as Chris tried, he couldn't remember any other Americans at Rothberg's school. The implication made his stomach sink. Had Eliot lied about that as well? Had he sent others to Rothberg at different times, even though he'd promised Chris and Saul they were unique? Why would Eliot lie about that?

Chris remembered something else. As Erika moaned in sexual climax beyond the closed door of the bedroom, he relived the moment sixteen years ago in Israel when he'd first seen her. Shortly afterward, Saul had been taken from Chris's group and put with Erika's. Despite the intensive schedule, they'd somehow found the time to become lovers. Chris felt a weight on his chest. In those days, his need to please Eliot had been so great he'd denied all emotion except loyalty to his father and his brother. He'd purged himself of any wish for gratification and fulfillment – unless his father permitted it. Sex was allowed for therapeutic purposes. But a love affair was unthinkable. 'It compromises you,' Eliot had said. 'Emotion's a liability. It prevents you from concentrating. In a mission, it gets you killed. Besides, a lover might turn against you. Or an enemy might hold her hostage to force you to turn against the agency. No, the only people you can love and trust and depend on are myself and Saul.' The weight pressed harder on his chest. Bitterness scalded him. For despite his conditioning, Chris had eventually experienced emotion – not love for a woman, but guilt for the things he'd done, and shame for having failed his father. Confusion tore at him. He'd sacrificed what he now realized were basic human needs in order to please his father. Now his father had turned against him. Among his deceptions, had Eliot lied about love as well? Chris seethed with regret for the life he might have known, a life his shame and guilt would not allow him now. If not for his need to help Saul, he'd have killed himself to stop the agony of self-disgust. The things Eliot made me do, he thought. He clenched his fists. And the normalcy I was never granted. Incapable of anger toward Saul, he nonetheless felt envious, for Saul had managed to stay true to Eliot and yet find self-fulfilment. He felt capable of rage toward Eliot, though. He shuddered, squeezing his eyes shut, wincing with regret. If things had been different, he wondered, rigidly shaking his head, if he and not Saul had been put in Erika's group in Israel – his throat clamped shut – would *he* not be the one to hold her as she shuddered?

10

Erika studied herself in the dressing room's mirror. Through the louvers in the door, she heard two saleswomen talking. She'd arrived at ten, as the department store opened. Few customers had been waiting to get in, so her grimy skirt and blouse hadn't attracted much attention. Walking quickly through the women's department, she'd chosen bras and panties, a corduroy jacket, a paisley blouse, jeans, and high leather boots. She changed in the dressing room.

Clutching her discarded clothes, she opened the door and peered out cautiously, seeing no other customers. The saleswomen turned as she approached.

'Don't ever try to change a flat tire in a brand new outfit,' Erika said. 'I should have called Triple A.'

'Or your boyfriend,' the younger woman said, apparently noticing Erika didn't wear a wedding ring.

'I just broke up with him. To tell the truth, he was useless.'

The saleswomen laughed.

'I know what you mean,' the younger one said. 'My boyfriend's useless too. Except for –'

They laughed again.

'I wish I had your figure,' the older one said. 'Those clothes fit you perfectly.'

'After the flat tire, something had to go right. Would you mind taking care of these?' She held up the grimy slacks and blouse.

'I've got just the place.' The younger woman dropped them in a wastecan behind the counter. While the older woman cut off the tags on the new clothes, Erika paid for them, smiling to herself at the name on the receipt she was given. Goldbloom's. Might as well stay kosher, she thought.

In the men's department, she glanced at the paper on which Saul and Chris had written their sizes, choosing poplin slacks, a tennis shirt, and a lightweight windbreaker for Saul, a tan oxford shirt and pale blue summer suit for Chris. Her timing was perfect. At precisely ten-thirty, she paused at the pay phone near the lost-and-found counter by the exit. She told the Alexandria operator the Washington number, inserted the proper coins, and listened as the phone buzzed once before a woman's voice replied, 'Good morning, Israeli embassy.'

'*Ma echpat li?*'

11

In English, the phrase meant, 'I should care?' It corresponded with the Hebrew lettering on a poster of a Jewish washerwoman with her arms raised in either surrender or disgust that hung on the wall directly above the switchboard in the embassy's communications center. The operator knew at once to relay the call to an emergency switchboard in the basement.

Misha Pletz, a harried man of thirty-five with a mustache and a receding hairline – chief of logistics for the Mossad on the United States eastern seaboard – plugged in his jack. 'One moment please.' He turned on a meter next to his desk and watched a dial. The device measured the electrical current on the phone line. If the line had been tapped, the drain of electricity would have caused the dial to veer from its normal position. The needle showed a normal current. '*Shalom*,' Pletz said.

A woman's attractive husky voice spoke slowly to him. 'Don't take any outside calls. Fourteen-thirty.'

A bell rang abruptly, indicating the line had been disconnected.

Pletz unplugged his jack. He drew his finger down the index on the wall to the left of his switchboard. Pulling out this day's card, he stared at a list of numbers. The call had come through at ten-thirty. Beside that number, he found the name of the operative assigned that time for checking in during emergencies. BERNSTEIN, ERIKA.

Pletz frowned. For the past thirty-six hours – since the attempted assassination at her apartment – no one at the embassy had known where Erika was or if she was still alive. The police had come to the embassy early yesterday morning, explaining what had happened, wanting information about her. They'd been greeted by the personnel

105

director, who expressed dismay at the killings and offered to help in every way. His help amounted to showing the police the embassy's file on Erika, a carefully edited document that established her cover as a clerk and completely obscured her actual function as a colonel in the Mossad. She kept to herself, the personnel director explained. She had few friends. He provided the names. Having learned a lot but in effect nothing, the detectives left, dissatisfied. Pletz assumed they'd watch the embassy in case Erika showed up, though his informants had told him last night that the investigation had inexplicably been terminated. Since then, Pletz had waited. Because she should have called him as soon as possible, her thirty-six hours of silence suggested she was dead.

But now she'd made contact. Pletz's relief changed quickly to alarm. She'd told him, 'Don't take any outside calls,' a code phrase instructing him to abandon all collaboration with any foreign intelligence service, even the United States. She'd mentioned 'fourteen-thirty,' military time for 2:30 P.M., the signal for when she'd call back, presumably from a safer phone. Four hours from now. Pletz hated waiting.

What the hell was going on?

12

'They'll stay together,' Eliot said. 'Both of them with the woman.'

'Agreed,' his assistant said. 'Together they'd have a better chance to protect themselves.'

'And use her contacts.' For security reasons, Eliot avoided his office as much as possible. Using his greenhouse as a distraction, he studied the hint of blight on an American Beauty rose. 'We have to assume she'll call her embassy. Its scrambler system's too sophisticated for us to intercept her conversations.'

His assistant glanced toward the square-faced muscular sentry at each entrance to the greenhouse. Eliot could have had his pick of regular agency personnel to guard him. Instead he'd chosen a pair the assistant had never heard of, introducing them only as Castor and Pollux, unfamiliar cryptonyms. The house, the grounds, and the street were also being guarded, but those teams had been chosen by the assistant himself. The sanctum, though – Eliot apparently trusted only these men to guard him here. The assistant was puzzled.

'But we can guess what she says to her embassy.' Eliot's hand trembled slightly as he treated the rose's blight with a chemical. 'In her place, I'd need money and identification – passports, drivers' licenses, credit cards, presumably under several different names. The Israelis don't trust outside help. They do that kind of job in their embassy.'

The assistant handed Eliot a cloth to wipe his hands. 'So they'll have to deliver a package to her.'

Eliot studied him with uncustomary approval. 'Good. You see my point. Arrange to have anyone who leaves the embassy followed.'

'We'll need a lot of people.'

'Use the sanction as your excuse. Tell the KGB and the other networks that the courier might lead them to Remus. Tell them we're close to finding the violator.'

Now it was the assistant's turn to say, 'Good.'

'Amazing, the way things get out of control. If Romulus had been killed in Atlantic City, none of the other problems would have happened.'

'Remus would still have violated the sanction.'

'He doesn't matter. Romulus does. The Paradigm Foundation had to be destroyed. The president had to be convinced the Israelis did it.' Eliot winced; the blight had spread to another rose. 'But after Colorado, once we assumed which friends they'd ask for help, we shouldn't have failed at the woman's apartment. We're a step behind them, but we shouldn't be. I chose Saul because he's past the age of maximum ability, like an athlete on the decline. I never dreamed he'd –'

'– make a comeback?'

Eliot shrugged. 'The same with Chris. I was sure he'd use his special knowledge of Saul to find him. But after the monastery, and particularly after what happened in Bangkok, I never dreamed he'd stay alive this long. It's going bad.' Eliot frowned. 'If they learn the truth . . .'

'How could they?'

'Two weeks ago, I'd have said they couldn't. But with the luck they've been having . . .' Eliot's face seemed pinched. 'Or maybe it's more than luck.'

13

'I can have you in Israel by tomorrow,' Pletz told Erika from the scrambler-protected phone in his office. 'You'd be secure while we sort this out.'

'I can't.' Erika's husky voice was worried. 'I have to stay with Chris and Saul.'

'We can't protect your friends. If the other agencies found out we were helping someone who violated the sanction –'

'That's not the issue. Yes, they're friends, but they're involved in something besides the sanction, something important enough that to kill them it didn't matter if I got killed as well. I want to find out what. I can tell you this. It's related to the Mossad.'

Pletz stiffened. 'How? You know we didn't try to kill you.'

'Someone wants to make it look as if you did.'

'But that's crazy. Why?'

'That's what I want to find out. I can't talk longer. I've got to assume this call is being traced. Get me the identification papers I asked for – the drivers' licenses, the credit cards. And something else.'

107

'I know. The money.'
'Something more important.'
Pletz asked, 'What?' He gasped when he heard the reply.

14

As the well-dressed man stepped from the embassy, squinting from the sun, carrying a briefcase, he took for granted he was being watched. All day, the embassy's security team had been noticing an unusual amount of surveillance. Anyone leaving the premises, no matter if on foot or in a vehicle, was being followed. In turn the security team, cooperating with Pletz, had arranged for an unusual number of couriers to leave the building. Given the intense activity, this particular courier had a good chance of completing his mission.

He stopped at a bookstore first and bought Stephen King's new novel. He walked another block and stepped in Silverstein's Kosher Market, buying matzos and chicken-liver pâté. Next he went to a liquor store and chose white wine. In another block, he arrived at his apartment building, soon to be greeted by his girlfriend.

He'd substituted his briefcase for an identical one in the kosher market. Already the grocer had hidden the original after removing a package from it. Wrapped in butcher's paper, labeled 'smoked salmon,' the package lay now at the bottom of a large cardboard box, covered by kosher meats and gourmet canned goods. While the grocer's wife watched the store, Silverstein carried the box to his delivery truck in the alley. He loaded several other boxes in front of the first one and drove across town to the Marren Gold Catering Service.

The following morning, Gold's Catering delivered the boxes to the Georgetown home of Dr Benjamin Schatner, where guests soon arrived from the synagogue to congratulate Schatner's son on a brilliantly performed Bar Mitzvah. After the reception, one of the guests, Bernie Keltz, decided to drive his family down to George Washington's estate at Mount Vernon. The mansion was only twenty miles away, Keltz's children had never seen it, and the flowers would be in bloom.

Keltz parked the car in the visitors' lot. He walked with his wife and two young daughters along a path till they stopped at a gate. Smiling in the pleasant breeze, they gazed along a sweeping lawn toward the mansion at the far end of the grounds. As they strolled beneath soaring trees past glorious gardens, Keltz explained to his daughters about the smaller buildings: the spinninghouse, the smokehouse, the warehouse. 'The estate was like a village. Completely self-sufficient.' His daughters played a jumping game on the weathered brick path.

At half-past three, Keltz's wife set her large burlap purse on the floor in front of a display case in the Washington's Home Is Your Home gift shop. Next to her, Erika studied a rack of colorful slides. While Keltz bought a cast-metal replica of the Washington Monu-

108

ment, insisting it be gift-wrapped, Erika picked up the purse and left the estate.

15

Beside the drivers' licenses and credit cards, the computer printout stretched across the dining table in the cottage near the Potomac. As the river whispered beyond the sunset-tinted screen of an open window, Saul, Chris, and Erika stared down at the paper. It showed a list of names – all Americans who, though not affiliated with the Mossad, had nonetheless received killer-instinct training at Andre Rothberg's school in Israel. Though Erika's request had puzzled him, Misha Pletz had gathered the information from the embassy's computers.

1965 Sgt First Class Kevin McElroy, USA, SF
      Sgt First Class Thomas Conlin, USA, SF
1966 Lt Saul Grisman, USA, SF
      Lt Christopher Kilmoonie, USA, SF
1967 Staff Sgt Neil Pratt, USA, Rangers
      Staff Sgt Bernard Halliday, USA, Rangers
1968 Lt Timothy Drew, USA, SF
      Lt Andrew Hicks, USA, SF
1969 Gunnery Sgt James Thomas, USMC, Recon
      Gunnery Sgt William Fletcher, USMC, Recon
1970 Petty Officer Arnold Hackett, USN, Seals
      Petty Officer David Pews, USN, Seals

The list continued – nine years, eighteen names.

Chris said, 'I don't believe it.'

Erika glanced at him. 'You thought you were unique?'

'Eliot told us we were. He said he wanted to make us special. The only operatives in the world with our particular combination of skills.'

She shrugged. 'Maybe he thought you turned out so well he decided to repeat the idea.'

Saul shook his head. 'But we went to Israel in '66. This list shows two other men went there before us. Eliot lied when he said we were the only ones.'

'Even later,' Chris said. 'In the seventies. After the rest of those men had killer-instinct training, he still kept telling us we were the only two of our kind.'

Erika glanced back toward the list. 'Maybe he wanted you to feel unique.'

'My ego isn't tender,' Chris said. 'I wouldn't have cared how many other men were trained the same as I was. All I wanted was to do my job well.'

'And please Eliot,' Saul said.

Chris nodded. 'That's why we wanted to do our jobs well. Why the hell would he lie about these other men?'

'We're not sure Eliot's the one who arranged for these other men to study with Rothberg,' Erika said.

'We have to assume he did.'

'Not yet we don't,' she answered. 'We can't afford assumptions. Maybe somebody else had the same idea Eliot did. For now, we know just what's on the list. So what does it tell us?'

'Patterns,' Saul said. 'The men were sent in pairs.'

'Like us,' Chris said.

'Each member of a pair had the same rank. In '65, McElroy and Conlin were sergeants. In '66, Saul and I were lieutenants. In '67, Pratt and Halliday were staffsergeants.' Saul drew a finger down the list, noting other paired ranks: gunnery sergeants and petty officers.

'Each member of a pair came from the same military branch,' Chris said. 'McElroy and Conlin belonged to Special Forces.'

'Like us,' Saul said, echoing Chris's remark.

'Pratt and Halliday were in the Rangers. Thomas and Fletcher were from Marine Reconnaissance. Hackett and Pews were Navy Seals.'

'But the pattern isn't consistent,' Erika said. 'In that respect, the pairs are different from each other. Four different military units – Special Forces, Rangers, Recon, Seals.'

'They're different, but they're the same,' Chris said.

Erika frowned in confusion.

Saul explained. 'They're elite. Those units are the best-trained cadres we've got.'

'Of course,' she said.

Saul didn't need to elaborate. She knew as well as he did that the US military was structured like a pyramid. The better the training, the fewer soldiers received it. Near the top were the army's Rangers and the Marine Corps' Recon unit – small, extremely well prepared. But the army's Special Forces stood above them, even smaller and better prepared. At the summit, the smallest, best-prepared group was the navy's Seals. This hierarchy was part of a system of checks and balances that the US government imposed on the military. If the Rangers or Recon attempted a coup, Special Forces would be called in to stop them. In turn, if Special Forces attempted a coup, the Seals would be brought in to stop them. The question remained – who would stop the Seals if *they* tried a coup?

'It doesn't matter if those units are different from one another,' Chris said. 'Compared to conventional military forces, they're in a class by themselves. The best.'

'Okay, it makes sense,' Erika said. 'Take soldiers from exclusive American cadres. Give them even more sophisticated training in Israel. But why?'

'And why those particular men?' Saul asked. 'And why so few of them? What's the principle of selection?'

Erika frowned. 'I know I said we shouldn't make assumptions, but I'm going to make one anyhow. Those men were sent to Israel from

110

1965 to 1973. Do you suppose –?' She studied their faces. 'Maybe they distinguished themselves in combat.'

'Where? In Nam?' Chris said. 'Like us?'

'The years fit. By '65, America was deeply involved in the fighting. By '73, America had left. Maybe those men were war heroes. The best of the best. Once they proved their ability under fire, how much better could they get? Only killer-instinct training would be higher.'

'You're describing men who'd eventually be better prepared than the Seals.'

'I'm describing yourselves,' she said.

Chris and Saul stared at each other.

'Something's missing,' Chris said. 'I can feel it. Something important. We've got to find out more about these men.'

16

Sam Parker left the glass and chrome structure, enjoying the sweet smogless Sunday breeze. As senior computer programmer for the National Defense Agency, he spent most of his days in windowless, temperature-controlled, antiseptic rooms. Not that he minded. After all, the computer had to be protected. But despite the intellectual stimulation of his work, he did mind coming here on Sunday. The trouble with being an expert was that underlings kept passing their mistakes to him.

He glanced from DC across the river toward Virginia and the Pentagon. Its parking lot, like the defense agency's, was almost deserted. Sure, they're at home drinking martinis, grilling steaks the same as I should be, he thought as he walked toward his drab brown, fuel-efficient, made-in-America car. Martinis? In truth, Parker didn't drink, though he didn't object if others did, in moderation. Even on Sunday, he wore a jacket and tie to go to work. He admired propriety and was constantly embarrassed by the way his freckles and red hair made him stand out in a crowd. At fifty-five, he hoped the red would soon turn diplomatic gray.

Driving from the parking lot, he didn't notice the Pinto that began to follow him. Nor five minutes later did he notice the other car, a Toyota, till it weaved from the passing lane, scraping his left front fender, cutting him off. Sunday drivers, he raged. Probably a tourist. He pulled to the side of the road. His fury cooled as he shut off his engine and saw the Toyota's driver get out. An absolutely gorgeous woman, tall and lithe, with long dark hair, wearing jeans and boots. She approached him, smiling. Well, he thought, if he had to have an accident, he might as well enjoy it.

He stepped out, trying his best to look stern. 'Young lady, I hope you've got insurance.'

She touched his shoulder. 'I'm so scared. I don't know how it happened.' She embraced him. As he felt her breasts against his chest, he heard a car stop. Two men suddenly flanked him, a muscular Jew and, Jesus, the other guy looked like an Irishman.

'Anybody hurt?' the Irishman said.

The Jew leaned close. Parker flinched, feeling something sting his arm.

His vision blurred.

17

They did it quickly. Saul leaned Parker's limp body back in his car, then slid beside him and drove toward a break in traffic before any curious motorists had a chance to stop. Erika followed in the Toyota, Chris in the Pinto. They soon split up, each taking a different exit. Making sure no one followed them, they headed south and rendez-voused at the cottage.

Parker was alert by then. He struggled as Saul tied him to a chair in the living room.

'I've seen your faces,' Parker said foolishly. 'I saw some of the roads you used to get here. Kidnapping's a federal offense. You'll go to jail for this.'

Saul squinted at him.

'Oh,' Parker said, his eyes bleak with understanding. 'Please, don't kill me. I promise I won't say a word.'

Chris approached him.

'My wife's expecting me home at four,' Parker warned. 'When I'm late she'll call Security.'

'She already has. It's *after* four. But how can they find you?'

'Oh,' Parker moaned again. He strained at the ropes around him. 'What do you want?'

'It's obvious, isn't it? Information.'

'Promise you won't hurt me. I'll tell you anything.'

'You'll tell us lies.'

'No, I'll cooperate.'

'We know you will.' Chris rolled up Parker's sleeve. Parker gaped as Chris rubbed his arm with alcohol, then filled a hypodermic from a vial. 'It feels like Valium,' Chris said. 'Since you've got no choice, you might as well stop fighting and enjoy it.' He slid the needle in Parker's arm.

The interrogation lasted thirty minutes. The Israeli embassy had supplied all the information it could. Chris needed another source. Because the men he was interested in had all been in the US military, he knew he'd find the background he wanted in the National Defense Agency's computers. The trick was to gain access to the computers, and the first step was to learn the codes that would make the computers responsive to questions. The wrong codes would trigger an alarm, alerting the NDA's security force that someone without clearance was trying to infiltrate the data-bank.

Torture was an obsolete method of interrogation. It took too long, and even when a subject seemed to have been broken, he sometimes lied convincingly or told only part of the truth. But Sodium Amytal – the same drug Eliot had used on Chris in the dentist's office in Panama – was quick and reliable.

Voice slurred, Parker told Chris everything he wanted to know. The codes were changed weekly. There were three of them: a numerical sequence, an alphabetical sequence, and a password. The numerical sequence was a joke of sorts, a variation on Parker's social security number. Satisfied they could communicate with the computers, Chris drove Parker back to Washington.

En route, Parker wakened, complaining that his mouth felt dry. 'Here, sip this Coke,' Chris told him.

Parker said it helped. He sounded groggy. 'You're letting me go?' 'Why not? You did your part. We've got what we wanted.'

The Coke had been mixed with scopolamine. By the time they arrived in Washington, Parker had become hysterical, flailing at hallucinations of spiders that tried to smother him. Chris let him out in a porno district where prostitutes backed away from Parker's wails and insane gesticulations.

The scopolamine would wear off by the next day. Parker would find himself in a psychiatric ward. Though his hallucinations would have disappeared, another effect of the drug would persist. His memory of the last two days would have been erased. He wouldn't recall being kidnapped. He wouldn't recall his interrogation or the cottage or Chris, Saul, and Erika. The authorities, having been warned by Parker's wife about his disappearance, would feel relieved to have found him. They'd conclude he wasn't the saint he pretended to be. A porno district. Sure, the hypocrite had gotten more fun than he bargained for. By the time the authorities investigated further, Saul and Erika would have finished the job.

18

The Haven Motel was half hidden behind a steak house, a movie theater, and a bar on the outskirts of Washington. 'All the comforts,' Saul said as he parked near the office. He and Erika had chosen the place because it looked sleazy enough so a clerk wouldn't question why they'd rent a room for just a few hours. But it wasn't sleazy enough that the police would make a habit of rousing it.

While she waited in the car, Saul went in the office. The soft drink machine had an Out of Order sign. The Naugahyde sofa was cracked. The plastic plants were dusty. Behind the counter, a woman barely turned from a Clint Eastwood movie on television. Saul registered as Mr and Mrs Harold Cain. The only time the woman looked interested was when she took his money.

Back in the car, Saul drove to the unit assigned to him. He turned the Pinto around, noting a driveway that led to a side street. Checking the room, they found a black and white television, a bureau with glass stains, a bed with wrinkled sheets. The faucet dripped in the bathtub.

They carried several boxes in. Using one of the credit cards Misha Pletz had suppled, they'd gone to a Radio Shack and bought a computer, printer, and telephone modem. Working quickly, they unpacked the components, integrated, and tested them. Saul went outside, chose a concealed vantage behind a garbage bin, and studied the entrances to the motel's parking area. If he saw trouble approaching, he could warn Erika, using a small walkie-talkie he'd also bought from Radio Shack.

In the room, Erika picked up the phone and touched a sequence of numbers Parker had mentioned. The sequence put her in contact with the NDA. She heard a beep from the phone. The computer had answered its number, awaiting instructions. She touched an alphabetical sequence – SUNSHINE, the name of Parker's cocker spaniel – and heard another beep; the computer was primed to gather information. This method of dealing with the computer had been designed to allow the efficient exchange of data over long distance. Parker's equivalent in San Diego, for example, didn't have to come to Washington to use the NDA's computer, nor did he have to contact Parker and explain what he needed. All he had to do was phone the computer directly. The method was simple and secure, but to make it work, you had to know the codes.

Erika set the phone in the modem, a small receptacle for the ear and mouth-piece, linked to the computer. She sat at the keyboard, typing instructions. The message passed through the modem and the phone to the NDA's databank. Parker had explained that his computer wouldn't release information unless it received the code word FETCH. She typed this now. The printer next to her began to clatter, translating the electronic signals received through the phone. She waited, hoping the NDA's security force wouldn't trace the phone call.

The printer stopped. Nodding, she typed GOOD DOG, the sign-off code Parker had given her, turned the computer off, put the phone on its cradle, and grabbed the printouts.

19

Chris slumped discouraged on the sofa. The night's rain added to his gloom, drumming on the cottage's roof. Drops trickled down the chimney, landing on the burnt wood in the fireplace, raising the bitter smell of ashes. He felt damp. 'If there's another pattern, I don't see it.'

Saul and Erika frowned at the printouts on the table. She'd asked only for essential data: place and date of birth, religious affiliation, education, special skills, commanding officers, battle commendations.

'None of them was born at the same time or place,' she said. 'They're a mixture of religions. They're each specialists in different things. They had different commanding officers and served in differ-

114

ent areas of Southeast Asia. What's the connection? Unless we're wrong, there has to be *something* that links them together.'

Chris stood wearily, crossing the room toward the table. He paused beside Erika, reading the printouts again. 'There.' He pointed down the left side of the page. 'Each pair was educated in the same city, but the cities are different from each other. Omaha, Philadelphia, Johnstown, Akron. It doesn't make sense. And over here.' He pointed to the right. 'They each had cryptonyms, but I don't see any other pattern. Butes and Erectheus. What the hell does *that* mean?'

He ignored the data he'd already eliminated, focusing on the information that puzzled him.

Omaha, Neb. Kevin McElroy. Castor.
Omaha, Neb. Thomas Conlin. Pollux.

Philadelphia, Pa. Saul Grisman. Romulus.
Philadelphia, Pa. Christopher Kilmoonie. Remus.

Johnstown, Pa. Neil Pratt. Cadmus.
Johnstown, Pa. Bernard Halliday. Cilix.

Akron, Ohio. Timothy Drew. Amphion.
Akron, Ohio. Andrew Wilks. Zethus.

Shade Gap, Pa. James Thomas. Butes.
Shade Gap, Pa. William Fletcher. Erectheus.

Gary, Ind. Arnold Hackett. Atlas.
Gary, Ind. David Pews. Prometheus.

The list continued – nine pairs, eighteen names.

'Pennsylvania's mentioned often,' Saul said.

'But what's it got to do with Nebraska, Ohio, and Indiana?'

'Let's try the cryptonyms,' Erika said. 'The names are foreign. Greek and Roman, right? From myth.'

'The category's too general. That's like saying Omaha and Philadelphia are in the United States,' Chris said. 'We've got to find a more specific connection. Cadmus and Cilix? Amphion and Zethus? I don't know who they were or what they did, let alone what they've got to do with each other.'

'Then start with the pair you do know,' Erika said. 'Yourselves. Romulus and Remus.'

'Common knowledge. They're the brothers who founded Rome,' Saul said.

'But we never founded anything, and we're not brothers,' Chris said.

'We might as well be.' Saul turned to Erika. 'Castor and Pollux. They sound familiar. Something to do with the sky. A constellation.'

Erika nodded. 'When I learned night navigation, my instructor said to let the ancient warriors guide me. Castor and Pollux. They're called the Gemini – the morning and evening stars.'

'Gemini,' Chris said. 'Twins.'

'What other names look familiar?' Saul asked. 'Here – at the bottom. Atlas.'

'The strong man who holds the sky above the earth.'

'Prometheus.'

'He stole fire from the gods and gave it to humans.'

'But there's no connection between them.'

'Maybe,' Erika said.

Chris and Saul looked at her.

'What we need is an index to myth,' she told them. 'I think I know the pattern now, but I have to find out who Cadmus and Cilix and the others were.'

'There's a dictionary over here,' Chris said, checking several shelves of books beside the fireplace. 'A lot of old paperbacks. Here. A desk encyclopedia.' Two volumes. He picked up the first, turning its dog-eared pages. 'Atlas,' he said and started reading. He glanced up abruptly. 'Shit.'

'What is it?' Saul looked startled.

'What's the other cryptonym that begins with A?'

Saul quickly scanned the printout. 'Amphion. He's paired with Zethus.'

Chris urgently flipped pages, reading. 'Jesus, I don't believe it. Tell me the other names.'

'Alphabetically? Butes is paired with Erectheus, and Cadmus is paired with Cilix.'

Chris kept flipping pages, reading anxiously. 'I know the pattern. I know how they're related.'

The room was still. 'They're related in the most basic way there is,' Erika said.

'You figured it out.'

'I wasn't really sure till I saw the look on your face.'

'Atlas and Prometheus were brothers. Amphion and Zethus were twins.'

'Like Castor and Pollux,' Saul said.

'Butes and Erectheus? *Brothers*. Cadmus and Cilix? *Brothers*. Romulus and Remus . . .'

'But where's the parallel?' Saul spun to the printouts. 'Castor and Pollux were twins, but the men assigned those cryptonyms are McElroy and Conlin. They sure as hell don't sound like twins.'

'That's true,' Erika said. 'And here, farther down, Pratt and Halliday don't sound related, but they've been given cryptonyms that refer to brothers. It's the same with all the other names. Drew and Wilks, Thomas and Fletcher, Hackett and Pews – if they're not related, why give them cryptonyms that refer to brothers?'

'Maybe they came from broken homes,' Chris said. 'If their parents got divorced and married someone else, McElroy and Conlin could have different names but still be related.'

116

'Maybe in one case,' Erika said. 'But all of them from broken homes with parents remarried?'

'I know. It's stretching,' Chris agreed.

'Besides, you and Saul don't come from a broken home. As you said, you're not related.' Suddenly her eyes became wary. She turned to Saul. 'Then *you* said something else. You said, "We might as well be." Why did you say that?'

Saul shrugged. 'We've known each other almost as long as if we'd been brothers. Since we were five. Right, Chris?'

Chris smiled. 'You're the best friend I've got.'

'But why?' Erika said, her voice strained with confusion. 'I don't mean why you're friends. I mean why you've known each other so long. Did you grow up in the same neighborhood?'

'In a way. We met at the school,' Saul said.

'*What* school?' Erika frowned.

'The Franklin School for Boys in Philadelphia. Where we were raised. We didn't come from a broken home. Hell, we didn't come from any home at all. We're orphans.'

Chris stared toward the rain beyond the window.

'That's the other puzzling detail in the pattern,' Erika said. 'Each pair of men was educated in the same city. McElroy and Conlin in Omaha. You and Chris in Philadelphia. The others in Akron and Shade Gap and so on. Since all their cryptonyms form a pattern, you'd think those cities would form a pattern as well.'

'They do,' Chris said. In anger, he turned from the rain at the window. 'Boys' Home.'

'What?' Saul stared in dismay.

'It's in Akron.' Trembling with rage, Chris walked toward Saul and Erika. 'The Haven for Boys is in Omaha. Pennsylvania has the Johnstown Boys' Academy and the Shade Gap Boys' Institute, not to mention our own Franklin School for Boys in Philadelphia. The cities on these printouts read like the top ten boys' schools in the country. But don't let the titles fool you,' Chris told Erika bitterly. 'Haven for Boys, or School for Boys, or Boys' Institute. They all mean the same damn thing: orphanage.' He clenched his teeth. 'The men on this list all share one thing in common with Saul and me. They're orphans. Each pair was raised in the same institution. That's why their cryptonyms suggest they're brothers, even though their last names are different.' Chris breathed painfully. 'Because when each member of a pair met the other, their loneliness forced them into a bond. They formed so strong a friendship they became the emotional equivalent of bloodbrothers. Goddamn him, Saul! Do you understand what he did to us?'

Saul nodded. 'Eliot lied to us in the most fundamental way I can think of. He never loved us. All along – from the start – he used us.'

Erika clutched Saul and Chris strongly by the arms. 'Would one of you mind telling me what in God's name you're talking about?'

'It takes a lifetime,' Chris said. He slumped on the sofa and moaned.

117

The rain fell harder, making the morning seem like dusk. Eliot stood at his office window, brooding, unaware of the stormy Virginia landscape. His skin looked as gray as the rain. Behind him. someone knocked on his door. He didn't turn to see who entered.

'Something strange, sir. I don't know what to make of it, but I thought I'd better let you know.' The voice belonged to Eliot's assistant.

'It's not good news, I gather,' Eliot said.

'They had a security leak over at the National Defense Agency. Yesterday their chief programmer was found in a porno district. Hallucinations, fits. The police thought he was high on something, so they put him in the psychiatric ward to dry out. Well, this morning he's all right, but he can't remember going to the porno district, and he doesn't remember taking any drugs. Of course, he could be lying, but –'

'Scopolamine,' Eliot said and turned to him. 'Get to the point.'

'Last night, while he was in the psych ward, someone used his code to get in the NDA's computer bank. They've got a system over there to find out who asked for what information. That's where we come in. Whoever used that programmer's code didn't want classified information. All he wanted was the major statistics on eighteen men. Since you supervised their training, the NDA thought you ought to know about the leak. The thing is, sir, two of the names were Romulus and Remus.'

Eliot sat wearily behind his desk. 'And Castor and Pollux, and Cadmus and Cilix.'

'Yes, sir, that's right.' The assistant sounded puzzled. 'How did you know?'

Eliot thought about Castor and Pollux standing guard outside his office door. Then he thought about Saul and Chris. 'They're getting closer. Now that they've guessed what to look for, they won't take long to figure the whole thing out.'

Mournfully he swung toward the rain streaking down the window. 'God help me when they do.'

He silently added, *God help* us all.

BOOK THREE

BETRAYAL

THE FORMAL
EDUCATION
OF AN OPERATIVE

1

At 1700 hours on December 23, 1948, United States military intelligence at Nome, Alaska, picked up the evening weather forecast from the Russian ports of Vladivostok, Okhotsk, and Magadan. The air force used these reports in conjunction with forecasts from Japanese ports to schedule night testing flights for its B–50s. The Russian forecast told of unseasonably warm weather. Nothing to worry about.

Seven minutes later, all frequencies were jammed by an amplified signal from the Russian naval base at Vladivostok to one of its submarines at sea. Coded and exceedingly lengthy for a Soviet communique, the message was sufficiently unusual for American military intelligence at Shepherds Field in Nome to concentrate on deciphering it rather than pay attention to the Japanese weather reports. They routinely cleared four B–50s for a high-altitude flight to test de-icing systems.

At 1900 hours, all four planes were hit by a Siberian cold front with wind gusts of over seventy knots. All de-icing systems failed. None of the planes returned to base. The lead plane, *Suite Lady*, had been piloted by Major Gerald Kilmoonie. When news of his loss arrived at the Eighth Air Force base (SAC) in Tucson, Arizona, General Maxwell Lepage called Roman Catholic chaplain Hugh Collins in Philadelphia to deliver the news to Mrs Dorothy Kilmoonie and her three-year-old son, Chris. He told the chaplain to tell Gerry's wife that the country had lost the finest skeet shooter he'd ever known.

2

Two years later – 1950. On Galcanlin Street in Philadelphia stood thirty rowhouses. It was a miserable place for a child to play. The street was dark and narrow. The coal ashes and sandlots held concealed traps of rusty nails, broken glass, and rat droppings. The weed-choked cracks in the sidewalk widened to crevasses at the curb and craters in the road. Toward the middle of the block, at its darkest, stood the dilapidated home of Dorothy Kilmoonie.

The house overflowed with tables: a card table with mother-of-pearl inlay; end tables; three-legged parlor tables; a coffee table with cigarette burns all over its top; a high tea table wedged against the Maytag wringer-washer in the bathroom; a dining table; a kitchen table with a chrome border and a Formica top supporting a plastic bowl of wax fruit. There were piles of dead flies beside the imitation fruit. There were similar piles on every table in the house. Also on every table, next to the flies, were pieces of dry bologna, curled like shavings of cedar wood.

The first thing Chris had done that hot August morning was slide the screen from the parlor window and place a fat headless oily sardine on the window sill. When his mother had left him alone in the house in July while she went to spend the summer in Atlantic City, she'd put a roll of bologna in the icebox as well as several cans of soup and sardines and boxes of crackers in the cupboard. She'd given money to the neighbors, telling them to look after Chris, but by the end of July, the neighbors had spent the money on themselves and left Chris to survive alone with the food he had. He hated bologna. He'd used it for days to lure the flies into the house. But their distaste for bologna was equal to his. And the rat droppings from the street, though the flies enjoyed them, dried even faster than the meat. The sardines worked perfectly, however. By nine that morning, he could nod with pride at a new heap of flies on the coffee table, killed with a long rubber band from one of his mother's garters.

At the most exciting moment of the hunt, as he perched fighting for balance on an end table, aiming his rubber band toward a clever fly that always took off a moment before he shot at it, he sensed an unfamiliar movement in the street and glanced out the window toward a large ominous black car parked in front of his house. At the age of five, he prided himself on knowing the difference between Hudson Hornets and Wasps, Studebakers and Willys and Kaiser-Frazers. This was a 1949 Packard, and its bulk took up most of the width of the street. From the driver's seat, a heavy man in a military uniform with a body like a punching bag seemed almost to roll from the car to the road. He straightened and, while surveying the cluttered neighborhood, smoothed the rear of his pants. With his shoulders hunched and his body stooped slightly forward, he rounded the back fenders of the Packard and opened the front passenger door. A tall slim gray-faced man in a badly wrinkled trenchcoat slowly got out. The man had slender cheeks, thin lips, a downward bend in his nose.

Chris didn't hear what they said to each other, but the way they stared at this house made him nervous. He crept from the table near the window. As the men left the car, walking up the crumbly sidewalk, he turned in panic, running. He dodged past a tea table and the kitchen table toward the listing door to the cellar. It creaked when he closed it leaving a finger-wide gap that allowed him to see through the kitchen to the parlor. In the dark, on the cellar steps that smelled like

122

rotten potatoes, he felt that the strangers would know where to catch him because they could hear the drumming of his heart.

The front door rattled as they knocked. He held his breath and reached for the rope that stretched from the parlor through the kitchen to these stairs. There hadn't been time for him to lock the front door, but he had other ways to protect himself. He clutched the rope. The front door scraped open. A man's deep voice asked, 'Anybody home?' Heavy footsteps rumbled, coming down the hall. 'I saw the boy at the window.' Their shadows entered the parlor. 'What's with all these tables? My God, the flies.'

Chris hunched on the stairs, peering through the crack in the door across the dirty linoleum toward the net on the parlor floor. When not killing flies, he'd been making the net since his mother had left, taking kite string from Kensington Park, cord from vacant lots, rope and shoelaces from trash cans, wool and thread from neighbors' bureau drawers, twine from the mill down the street, and clotheslines from nearby yards. He'd tied them all together – long pieces, short pieces, thick and thin – to form a huge intersecting pattern. His mother had promised to come back. She'd said she'd bring saltwater taffy and seashells and photographs, lots of photographs. And the day she did come back, he'd capture her in the net and keep her trapped till she promised never to go away again. His eyes stung as he watched the two men enter the parlor, standing on the net. If it could trap his mother . . .

'And what's with all this twine and stuff on the floor?'

Chris yanked the rope. He'd attached it to chairs perched on tables in the parlor. When they fell, they pulled twine through the chain in the ceiling light and raised the corners of the net.

As the chairs clattered the two men shouted 'What the –? Jesus!'

Chris puffed his chest, wanting to cheer, then suddenly scowled. The men were laughing, doubled over. Through the crack in the door, he saw the one in the uniform grab the net and rip the knots apart, breaking the string, stepping out of the twine.

Tears burning his cheeks. Furious, he scrambled down the cellar steps, swallowed by darkness. His hands shook from rage. He'd make them sorry. He'd get even with them for laughing.

The cellar door creaked open. Light struggled to reach the bottom of the stairs. Through a knothole in the wall of the coalbin, he watched their shadows come down. Their laughter continued. Someone must have told them everything about him, he thought – how he'd stolen the clothesline, the thread, and the twine; even where he'd hide. The cellar's light switch didn't work, but they seemed to know that also, for they had a flashlight, aiming it around the musty basement, stalking him.

He crept back toward the deepest corner of the coalbin. It was empty in summer. Even so, grit scraped beneath his sneakers. The flashlight swung his way. Dodging it, he stepped on a chunk of coal. His ankle twisted. Losing balance, he banged against a wall.

The flashlight came closer. Footsteps scurried. No! He slipped from a hand, but as he scrambled from the bin, another caught his shoulder. No! Weeping, he kicked, but he touched only air, flailing as the hands spun and lifted him.

'Let's get you up in the light.'

He struggled frantically, but the hands pinned his arms and legs, allowing him only to squirm and bang his head against a chest as the men took him up the cellar stairs. After the dark, he blinked from the sunlight through the kitchen window, crying.

'Take it easy,' the heavy man in the uniform said, puffing from his exertion.

The one in the trenchcoat frowned at Chris's tar-coated sneakers, filthy pants, and grimy hair. He took out a handkerchief, wiping the tears and coal dust from Chris's face.

Chris pushed the arm away, trying to seem as tall and strong as his tiny frame would allow. 'Not funny!'

'What?'

Chris glared at the net in the parlor.

'Oh, I see,' the civilian said. Despite his cold eyes and sickly face, his voice sounded friendly. 'You heard us laughing.'

'Not funny!' Chris said louder.

'No, of course not,' the man in the uniform said. 'You've got us all wrong. We weren't laughing at you. Why, the net seemed a good idea. Course you could've used some better material and a few lessons in design and camouflage. But the idea . . . Well, that's why we laughed. Not at you but *with* you. Sort of in admiration. You've got spunk, boy. Even if you didn't look like him, I could tell from the way you handle yourself – you're Gerry's son.'

Chris didn't understand a lot of the words. He frowned as if the man in the uniform was trying to trick him. A long time ago, he vaguely recalled, someone had told him he'd once had a father, but he'd never heard of anybody named Gerry.

'I can tell you don't trust me,' the man said. Spreading his legs, he put his hands on his hips, like a cop. 'I'd better introduce myself. I'm Maxwell Lepage.'

Like 'Gerry,' this name meant nothing. Chris stared suspiciously.

The man seemed puzzled. '*General* Maxwell Lepage. You know. Your dad's best friend.'

Chris stared even harder.

'You mean you never heard of me?' The man was astonished. He turned to the tall gray-faced civilian. 'I'm no good at this. Maybe you can get him to –' He gestured helplessly.

The civilian nodded. Stepping ahead, he smiled. 'Son, I'm Ted Eliot. But you can call me just Eliot. All my friends do.'

Chris glared with mistrust.

The man called Eliot pulled something from his trenchcoat. 'I figure every boy likes chocolate. Especially Baby Ruths. I want to be your friend.' Eliot put his hand out.

Fidgeting, Chris pretended not to care, refusing to look at the candy bars.

'Go on,' the man said. 'I ate one already. They're good.'

Chris didn't know what to do. The only advice his mother had ever given him was not to take candy from strangers. He didn't trust these men. But he'd eaten nothing except stale crackers all week. His head felt light. The growling in his stomach persisted. Before he knew it, he grabbed the candy bars.

The man called Eliot smiled.

'We've come to help,' Lepage said. 'We know your mother left.'

'She's coming back!'

'We're here to take care of you.' Lepage glanced at the flies in disgust.

Chris didn't understand why Eliot closed the windows. Was it going to rain? As Lepage gripped Chris's arm, he realized he'd dropped his weapon, the slimy rubber band. They took him to the porch, Lepage holding him while Eliot locked the door. He noticed Mrs Kelly squinting from her window next door, then suddenly ducking away. She'd never done that before, he realized – and suddenly felt afraid.

3

He sat in the front seat of the car between the two men and stared first at Lepage's heavy shoes, next at Eliot's gray-striped tie, and finally at the door handle. The thought of escape passed quickly once the car began to move and he became fascinated watching Lepage shift gears. He'd never ridden in a car before. The indicators on the dashboard, the movement of people and vehicles outside held him enthralled till, before he could anticipate their arrival anywhere, Lepage parked in front of a huge building with pillars that reminded Chris of the post office. Directed by Lepage's firm grip on his shoulders, Chris walked between the two men through marble halls lined with benches. Men and women dressed as if to go to church went by, carrying stacks of paper and what looked like small suitcases.

Behind a frosted glass door, a young woman sat at a desk. She spoke to a box beside a phone, then opened another door where Chris and the two men went through. In the inner office, an old man with white hair and a pencil-thin mustache sat at another desk, but this one was larger, before an American flag and a wall lined with thick leather-covered books.

As Chris stopped before the desk, the man looked up. He searched through some papers. 'Let's see now. Yes.' He cleared his throat. 'Christopher Patrick Kilmoonie.'

Afraid, Chris didn't answer. Lepage and Eliot both said, 'Yes.' Chris frowned in confusion.

The man studied Chris, then spoke to Lepage and Eliot. 'His mother abandoned him . . .' He ran his finger down a sheet, his voice astonished, disapproving. 'Fifty-one days ago?'

'That's right,' Eliot said. 'His mother went away with a male companion for the Fourth of July weekend. She hasn't been back.'

125

Chris kept turning his head from one man to another, waiting for what they'd say next.

The man glanced at a calendar, scratching his cheek. 'Soon be Labor Day. Has he got any older brothers or sisters, any relatives who'd take care of him?'

'No,' Eliot said.

'For the whole summer? How'd he survive?'

'He ate sardines and bologna and killed flies.'

The man looked stunned. 'Killed . . . ? His mother? Is she employed?'

'She's a prostitute, your honor.'

It was yet another word Chris didn't understand. Curiosity overcame him. For the first time in the office, he spoke. 'What's a prostitute?'

They turned away and didn't answer.

'What about his father?' the man said.

'He died two years ago,' Lepage replied. 'It's all in his file. You can understand why the Welfare Department recommends he become a ward of the city.'

The man tapped his fingers on his glass-topped desk. 'But I'm the one who has to make the decision, and I don't understand why the Welfare Department sent you to this hearing instead of its own representative. What's the government's interest in this matter?'

Lepage answered. 'His father was a major in the Air Force. He died in the line of duty. He was my friend. Mr Eliot and myself, we've sort of – well, we've unofficially adopted the boy, you might say. Discounting his mother, we're the nearest thing to a family he's got. Since our work prevents us from raising him ourselves, we want to make sure someone else does it properly.'

The man nodded. 'You know where he'll be sent.'

'We do,' Eliot said, 'and we approve.'

The man studied Chris and sighed. 'Very well.' He signed a piece of paper, put it in a folder with a lot of other papers, and handed the folder to Lepage. 'Chris . . .' The man struggled, unable to choose his words.

'I'll explain it to him,' Eliot said. 'When we get there.'

'Explain what?' Chris began to tremble.

'Thank you,' Lepage told the man.

Before Chris knew what was happening, Lepage turned him to the door. Confused, Chris was taken out again into the hall past the green glass doors that reminded him of the bank and the telegraph office around the corner from the five-and-dime. But where was that now? he thought. And where was he going?

The metal gate was high and wide and black. Its bars looked as thick as Chris's wrist, the space between them so narrow he knew he could never squeeze through. To the left, a large iron plaque said,

BENJAMIN FRANKLIN SCHOOL FOR BOYS

To the right, another plaque said,

TEACH THEM POLITICS AND WAR
SO THEIR SONS MAY STUDY MEDICINE AND MATHEMATICS.
JOHN ADAMS

Beneath this plaque, built into the high stone wall that seemed to stretch forever in both directions, a heavy door led to a sentrylike room filled with stacks of newspapers, mail sacks, and packages. A man in a sweater vest tipped a conductor's cap, smiled, and continued sorting the packages. Lepage and Eliot didn't say a word but, with Chris in hand, went directly through the room, out into the sun, across a lawn toward a huge brick building.

'That'll be your high school some day,' Lepage told Chris. 'But for now it's only where we'll sign you up.'

Carved in stone, above the entrance to the building, were the words:

WISDOM THROUGH OBEDIENCE,
PERFECTION THROUGH HUMILITY.

It was only half-past noon, so they waited on an old refectory bench, its oak thickly varnished and waxed. The bench felt hard, and the contour of its seat made Chris slide back while his feet dangled over the floor. Uneasy, he stared at the clock on the wall, tensing every time the second hand jerked forward. Its dull snick seemed to grow louder; it reminded him of the sound in a butcher shop.

A woman arrived at one. She wore low heels, a plain skirt and sweater. Unlike his mother, she didn't use lipstick, and her hair instead of being curly was combed straight back in a bun. She barely glanced at Chris before she went with Lepage to her office.

Eliot stayed on the bench with him. 'I bet those two hamburgers we bought you didn't begin to fill you up.' He smiled. 'Eat those Baby Ruths I gave you.'

Chris hunched his shoulders, staring stubbornly at the wall across from him.

'I know,' Eliot said. 'You figure it's smarter to save them for when you get hungry again. But you'll be fed here – three times a day. And as for the candy bars, the next time I see you I'll bring you some more. Do you like any other kinds?'

Chris slowly turned, bewildered by this tall thin man with gray skin and sad-looking eyes.

'I can't promise I'll visit you often,' Eliot said. 'But I want you to know I'm your friend. I want you to think of me as . . . let's call me a substitute father, someone you can count on if you get in trouble, someone who likes you and wants what's best for you. Some things are hard to explain. Trust me. One day you'll understand.'

Chris's eyes felt hot. 'How long will I be here?'

'Quite a while.'

'Till my mother comes to get me?'

'I don't think . . .' Eliot pursed his lips. 'Your mother's decided to let the city take care of you.'

Now Chris's eyes felt swollen. 'Where is she?'

'We don't know.'

'She's dead?' Chris was so desperate to hear the answer he took a moment to realize he was crying again.

Eliot put an arm around him. 'No. But you won't be seeing her anymore. As far as we know, she's alive, but you'll have to get used to thinking of her as dead.'

Chris wept harder, choking.

'But you're not alone.' Eliot hugged him. 'I care for you. I'll always be close to you. We'll see each other often. I'm the only family you've got.'

Chris jerked from Eliot's arms as the door came open. Lepage stepped out of the office, shaking hands with the woman, who now wore glasses and held Chris's folder. 'We appreciate your help.' He turned to Eliot. 'Everything's taken care of.' He looked at Chris. 'We're going to leave you with Miss Halahan now. She's very nice, and I'm sure you'll like her.' He shook Chris's hand. Chris winced from the pressure. 'Obey your superiors. Make your dad proud of you.'

Eliot bent down, touching Chris's shoulders. 'More important, make *me* proud of you.' His voice was soft.

As the two men walked down the hall, Chris blinked in confusion through his tears, feeling the security of the candy bars in his pocket.

5

Too much to sort out. The forty-eight acres of the school were divided by a solitary road. To get to the dormitory from the high school building, Miss Halahan told Chris they had to walk quite a way. He had trouble keeping up. The road was completely empty, as if a parade were about to begin, but there were no barricades along the route, no spectators, only the immense trees on either side, like umbrellas shielding Chris from the sun.

Despite her explanations, he felt disoriented. Across from the high school was a cluster of buildings that made up the 'residence halls and refectory,' she said. To the left was the immense stone 'chapel,' and across the road from it, the 'infirmary.' The wind had been light, broken by the mass of buildings, but as he followed Miss Halahan past the 'gymnasium' at the center of campus, he was suddenly struck by a fierce hot gust that surged across playgrounds on either side of the road. He saw goalposts and track hurdles and baseball backstops, but what surprised him was the lack of earth. Everything around him was a huge expanse of concrete.

The sun now blazed as Chris passed the 'armory' and the 'energy plant' with its smokestacks and hills of coal. His legs ached when he finally reached the end of the road. Staring at the bleak gray building she called the 'dormitory,' he became apprehensive. She had to tug his resisting hand, leading him down an echoing stairwell, taking him to a large basement auditorium that smelled of wax, where he peered uneasily at a dozen other boys, some older, some younger, all wearing dingy clothes as he was.

'You arrived just in time,' Miss Halahan said. 'For the weekly initiation. Otherwise we'd have to do it all over again just for you.'

Chris didn't understand. 'Initiation' was yet another word he'd never come across. He didn't like its sound. Nervous, he sat in a creaky seat and realized that all the other boys had followed his instincts, staying apart from each other. The auditorium was unnaturally quiet.

An old man dressed in khaki pants and shirt with an olive drab tie marched to the center of the stage. He stood before a podium, and again Chris noticed an American flag. The old man held a baton beneath one arm and introduced himself as Colonel Douglas Dolty, director of admissions and headmaster of the dormitory. He began his speech with animal and sports jokes. A few boys laughed. The colonel ventured to guess that many heroes of the sports world knew about the school and on occasion would visit the boys. Though anxious, Chris was surprised to find himself interested. His cheeks felt tight from his now-dried tears. The colonel told a story (incomprehensible to Chris) about a place called ancient Greece and three hundred soldiers called Spartans who died heroically trying to hold off an army of Persians at a pass called Thermopylae. 'Gentlemen,' he concluded, 'I'm going to show you what this school is all about.'

He formed the boys in two lines and led them outside, down the road to the vocational arts building. There, the *newbies*, as they learned they were called, were shown the foundry, where boys filled cast-iron molds. In the print shop, other boys were setting type for the next issue of the school's paper. Chris saw the carpentry and machine and auto mechanics shops. He went to the tailor shop, the shoe shop, and the laundry. Even there, his group was impressed by the noise and activity and the importance of children like themselves doing the work. They wanted to try out the machines.

But the colonel saved the best for last. With a smile of pride, he took them to the armory, showing Chris and the others the 1917 Enfield rifles, polished to a gleam, that they soon would carry, as well as the sabers, the dress uniforms of gun-metal gray, and the snap-on white collars they would wear in their student platoons. Here especially Chris was awestruck. No boy spoke up or clowned around. Chris inhaled the sharp sweet smell of gun oil, Brasso, and bore cleaner. The respect he and the other boys gave this old man was the same respect they would show him on the day in their senior year when they signed up for Army Airborne or the Second Marine Division. Respect indeed would turn to love. Nurtured in a male system, in the Spartan atmosphere of Franklin, love would turn to patriotism and pride. Fear, through prolonged punishment, would soon become commonplace and would finally be unknown. The glitter of saber scabbards, the charisma of rifles, insignias, and chevrons would create excitement, fusing all the needed alloys of heroism and loyalty to produce the men Franklin passed on to the outside world.

'We can't have you looking the way you do now, can we?' the colonel said. Continuing to reassure them with his smile, he took them to another building where he gave each boy two pairs of lace-up high-cut black shoes, similar to combat boots. He handed each a white dress shirt and three plain shirts of various colors, four pairs of pants, socks and underwear, four handkerchiefs – all wrapped in a tight bundle by a long bilious cotton nightshirt. With their shoes tied around their necks and their bundle of clothes clutched to their chests, they looked like miniature airborne troops as they ventured out into the dry hot wind again and trotted at double time back along the road to the dormitory.

6

The barber was waiting. When he finished, two inches of scalp showed above Chris's ears. With the back of his head shaved bare, he looked like a boot camp recruit. He felt nervous and shy, but as he studied the other boys and they studied him, he straightened, glancing at himself in a mirror, seeing his newly acquired rugged features, feeling unexpectedly athletic, strangely confident.

But the showers were next: a small tiled room with fixtures that had no handles, the flow of water controlled by a governess who peered through a window and manipulated dials. A male attendant told them to take off their clothes and stuff them in a large canvas bag at the end of the room. Chris felt ashamed. He'd never been naked in front of any person except his mother. His eyes felt swollen again as he remembered her. He tried to cover himself with his hands and saw other boys do the same. But it puzzled him that the male attendant and the governess didn't seem to notice they were naked.

Herded into the small shower, they tried hard not to touch each other, an impossible task as they struggled with bars of soap and cringed beneath the powerful steaming nozzles. The spray was so thick Chris barely saw the other boys. The water abruptly stopped. Disconcerted, Chris left the shower room with the others. They dripped on the tile of a locker room, huddling, feeling cold now. The attendant handed each of them a towel and pointed toward a large metal pail filled with something gooey and sweet-smelling he called cold cream, telling them to rub it on their faces, their arms and legs, and any spots that were red and raw. Chris suddenly noticed that the large canvas sack where he and the others had stuffed their clothes was gone. He never saw his tar-stained sneakers and grimy shirt again.

Or his candy bars.

He wanted to moan, feeling tricked and betrayed. Eating them had been all he'd had to look forward to.

But there wasn't time for self-pity. The attendant took their towels and led them shivering, naked, from the locker room up the stairwell to a huge room where bunk beds lined the walls. Each bed had two shelves and a storage locker. The windows were barred. Demoralized, Chris put on his gray wool socks and pants and shirt. But though uncomfortable in the itchy new clothes, he glanced at the other boys in amazement. Except for their differences in hair color and complexion, all looked alike. He didn't know why, but somehow that reassured him.

The attendant explained their schedule. Wake-up at 6, breakfast at 7, school from 8 to 12, lunch till 12:30, rest till 1, school till 5, play till 6, then supper and study hall, in bed by 8. 'Any discomfort, itchiness, bloody gums, or illness of any kind report it to me at once. Tomorrow I'll teach you how to make your bed so I can bounce a quarter off it. The first few weeks, you'll sleep with a rubber sheet – in case.'

The attendant marched them from the dormitory to the mess hall, where they were joined by hundreds of other children, all sizes, all ages, all dressed in gray with their hair cut severely. They'd been in classes till now, but despite the crowd, the room was oddly silent as the boys filed past the counters with their trays to receive their food.

Chris gagged when he saw the first meal he would eat here. One boy had mentioned tuna casserole. Another had grumbled about brussels sprouts. Chris had never heard of that before. All he knew was that this green stuff was covered by white guck and the whole thing smelled like spit-up. He sat with his group at a plastic-covered table, staring at the salt shaker, refusing to eat, when he felt a shadow loom over him. 'Everybody eats, or everybody's punished,' a deep voice growled. Chris had to think about what the man had said. He gradually understood. He saw the other boys staring at him and realized that, if he didn't eat, the other boys would be blamed because of him. He debated with himself, stifling the pressure in his throat. Slowly he picked up his fork. He stared at the creamy white stuff. He didn't breathe as he chewed and swallowed, and somehow not breathing seemed to help.

They were told after supper they'd get a treat. A movie. Just as Chris had never had a car ride before, he'd never seen a movie. As he crowded with the other boys, his eyes expanded with delight. The black and white images flickered magically on the screen. He watched an actor named John Wayne – the rest of the boys seemed to know who he was and applauded with delight – in a war story called *The*

Fighting Seabees. His chest pounded. Shooting and explosions. The other kids cheered. He loved it.

That night, as he lay in his bottom bunk in the dark of the dormitory, he wondered where his mother was. He tried to understand what he was doing here. He recalled what Lepage had said about his father dying in something called the line of duty. Frightened and puzzled, he heard a boy across from him begin to sob. Chris felt his own tears hot and bitter at the corners of his eyes as an older boy yelled, 'Quit yer cryin'! I wanna sleep!'

Chris stiffened, embarrassed. When he realized the older boy had been yelling at the new boy across from him, he swallowed his sorrow, squeezing his eyes shut, determined to avoid attention, to be one of those who didn't cry. But he wished he'd made Lepage tell him why his mother was called a prostitute, and he wished with all his heart that his mother would return from Atlantic City and take him away from here. Grief strangled him. But in his dream, he saw Eliot handing him a Baby Ruth candy bar.

7

'I root for the Phillies,' a boy to Chris's right said.

Chris knelt with his group at the back of the first-grade room, putting puzzles together – mostly maps of the United States with cartoons of corn and apples, factories, mines, and oil wells drawn on various sections, though sometimes the maps were of countries Chris had never heard of, China, Korea, and Russia, for example. The puzzles were brightly colored, and he quickly learned how to put them together. He'd never been to school before, but despite the complaints he'd heard from the older boys, he thought he was going to like it. For a little while, at least. Despite what Eliot had told him, Chris was sure his mother would come to take him home.

The boy who'd said he rooted for the Phillies looked even thinner than Chris, his face so lean his eyes bulged. When the boy smiled, waiting for approval from the others, Chris noticed he had several missing teeth. But when the boy got no response, his smile quickly vanished, replaced by humiliation.

Another boy spoke. To Chris's left. Though the same age as the other boys in the group, he was bigger – not just taller but heavier – than the rest. He had the darkest hair, the tannest skin, the squarest face, the deepest voice. His name was Saul Grisman, and last night in the dorm, Chris had heard an older boy whisper that Grisman was a Jew. Chris hadn't known what he meant. 'What's the matter with ya?' the other boy had said. 'Where ya been? A Jew.' Chris still hadn't known what he meant. Aw, for Pete's sake, the other boy had said, 'I didn't know Micks could be so dumb.' When Chris had asked what a Mick was, the older boy had walked away in disgust.

Now Saul said, 'I root for *all* the teams! And I got the baseball cards

132

to prove it!' He reached beneath his shirt and pulled out two handfuls of them.

The other boys blinked, astonished. They stopped putting together the puzzles and quickly glanced toward the governess, who sat at the front desk, reading a book. Assured, they leaned forward guiltily, staring in awe at the baseball cards. Saul showed the cards one at a time: pictures of men in uniform swinging bats or running or catching balls, Yogi Berra, Joe DiMaggio, Jackie Robinson, names Chris had never heard of, with their life story on the back of each card, how many home runs they'd hit or outs they'd made. Saul enjoyed watching the other boys admire his treasures, but he wouldn't let them handle one card, which he raised with reverence. 'He played before those other guys, and he was better,' Saul said.

Chris squinted at the heavy man in the picture, then down at the name – Babe Ruth. Feeling nervous because he didn't know anything about these players, he tried to think of something to say that would make the other kids accept him. 'Sure,' he nodded wisely. 'They named a candy bar after him.' For an instant, he thought of the gray-faced man named Eliot.

Saul frowned. 'A what?'

'A candy bar. Babe Ruth.'

'That's *Baby* Ruth.'

'That's what I said.'

'It's not the same. It's *Babe*. Not Baby.'

'So what?'

'The candy bar's named after some guy's baby named Ruth.'

Chris blushed. The other boys sneered at him as if they'd known the secret all along. The governess glanced up from her book, sending a shock through the room. Saul fumbled to put the cards beneath his shirt while the other boys ducked quickly down to put more puzzles together. The governess stood, walked ominously over to them. She towered, making Chris nervous as she watched for a long time before she returned to her desk.

'How'd you get to keep the cards?' one boy asked Saul as the class walked in double file to lunch. The other boys strained to hear Saul's answer. Not only did Saul have something none of the rest of them had but he'd actually managed to smuggle the cards into school. Chris remembered that everything the boys had brought here with them had been taken from them the first day, including (he recalled bitterly) his candy bars, which he wished he'd eaten right away instead of saving. So how had Saul kept the baseball cards?

'Yeah, how'd you get to keep them?' another boy asked.

Instead of answering, Saul only smiled.

'Can I sit next to you at lunch?' a third boy asked.

'Me too. Can I sit next to you? Can I look at the cards again?' another boy asked. Though they had to walk in ranks, they nonetheless seemed to crowd around Saul as they entered the refectory for lunch.

When Chris carried his tray of weiners and beans to their table, he found that the only empty seat was the farthest from Saul. The other boys sat proudly next to Saul or across from him, a few even daring to whisper more questions about the cards till a supervisor stopped and glared them all into silence.

Outside the refectory, they were allowed to speak as they went to their room for rest period, but Chris couldn't get a word in. All anybody wanted to talk about was where Saul had gotten the cards and how he'd managed to keep them. Because of Chris's disastrous remark about Babe Ruth and the candy bar, the other boys treated him as the dummy of the group, and Chris wished harder for his mother to come and rescue him. He decided he didn't like school after all.

He disliked it even more when, late in the afternoon, the governess marched them to the swimming pool in the basement of the gymnasium. An instructor told them to strip and shower, and again Chris felt ashamed to be naked in front of other people. His shame soon turned to fear when the instructor ordered them to jump into the pool. Chris had never seen so much water. He was afraid of his head going under and choking as he had one time when his mother was giving him a bath. But the instructor nudged him toward the pool, and Chris finally jumped in willingly because the water would hide his nakedness. Splashing down through the cold sharp-smelling water, he landed abruptly, surprised the water came up only to his waist. The other boys entered as reluctantly as Chris, except for Saul, who considered the pool a thrilling challenge and even sank down so his head was under water.

'You!' The instructor pointed. 'What's your name?'

'Saul Grisman, sir.' The 'sir' was an absolute rule. They'd learned whenever a boy spoke to a grownup he had to say 'sir' or 'ma'am,' depending.

'You look like you've gone swimming before.'

Saul answered, 'No, sir.'

'Never had lessons?'

'No, sir.'

The instructor rubbed his chin, impressed. 'Maybe you're a natural.'

With their admiration of Saul reinforced by the instructor's approval, the boys competed with each other to get close to Saul as they held the edge of the pool and the instructor showed them how to kick their legs.

'That's right. Watch Grisman,' the instructor said. 'He's got the idea.'

At the farthest place from Saul, sputtering, struggling to keep his head above water, kicking awkwardly, Chris had never felt so lonely. Back on Calcanlin Street, he'd spent the summer alone waiting for his mother, but in the familiar house in the familiar neighborhood with friends to play with, he hadn't felt alone. In fact, that hadn't been the first time his mother had left him alone; he was almost used to living by himself, though he always missed his mother when she was gone.

134

But now in these strange surroundings, shivering in the water, excluded by the other children, envying Saul, he felt the bitter ache of loneliness and decided he hated this place.

The only time he mustered interest was the next night, Saturday, when after a day of practice making his bed, learning to lace, tie, and polish his shoes, to knot and adjust his tie to the proper length, he went with every boy in the school to see another movie. Chris eagerly recalled the first one he'd seen here, *The Fighting Seabees*. This one was called *Battleground*. Everyone cheered as it began, and again the action was exciting, lots of shooting and explosions. Chris loved the plot about a group of American soldiers fighting as a team in war. The music – blaring trumpets, pounding drums – made his stomach feel warm.

But after, none of his group cared what he thought about the movie. Everybody wanted to know what *Saul* thought. Chris almost broke the rule by crying himself to sleep. Instead he clenched his teeth in the darkness, planning to run away.

8

The sudden glare of the overhead light woke him at six. Someone said it was Sunday. Blinking sleepily, he shuffled with the other boys to the washroom, where with his toothbrush in his left hand he held out his right hand for the supervisor to pour him some tooth powder. As he cleaned his teeth, making sure he reached all the way to the back the way the supervisor had shown him, the peppermint taste of the Colgate made him feel slightly sick. He listened to the flushing of urinals and toilets and tried not to look at the boys getting off the seats. The toilets were in the open – no walls or doors – and his shyness prevented him from relieving himself till he absolutely had to. He surprised himself by sitting, not caring who watched him, his need too great. In fact, no one seemed to care. And the relief he felt afterward, combined with the confidence he'd acquired by overcoming this further taboo of shyness, made him anticipate the day with unexpected optimism. He even enjoyed the milky scrambled eggs he washed down with orange juice, and he felt a little like the soldiers in their uniforms in *Battleground* when he put on his stiff dress shirt and his cadet clothes before the supervisor marched his group to chapel.

It had colored windows, but no crosses or other religious symbols could be seen anywhere. As every boy sat at his assigned place in the pews, the chaplain, Mr Applegate, stepped up to a podium and led the boys in song – first 'The Star-Spangled Banner,' then 'God Bless America.' Next the chaplain pulled out a dollar bill (which gained Chris's interest right away) and read the words on the back of Washington's picture. 'The United States of America!' he said loud enough to be heard at the back of the chapel. 'In God We Trust! Remember those two statements! We trust in God! He trusts in us! That's why this country is the greatest, richest, most powerful on earth! Because

135

God trusts us! We must always be willing to be His soldiers, to fight His enemies, to preserve our God-ordained way of life! I can think of no greater honor than to fight for our country, for its greatness and glory! God bless America!' The chaplain held up his hands, demanding a response. The boys shouted it back to him. 'God bless America!' he repeated. Again they shouted it back. As the chapel gradually became quiet, Chris felt the echo of the shouts linger in his ears. He felt excited in a frightened way, not understanding what the chaplain meant but responding to the emotion in his words.

'The Biblical text this morning,' the chaplain said, 'is from the Book of Exodus. Moses, leading God's chosen people, is pursued by the Pharaoh's soldiers. Helped by God, Moses parts the Red Sea, allowing His People through, but when the Pharaoh's men attempt to cross, God returns the Red Sea and drowns them.' The chaplain opened the Bible, drawing a breath to read. Then he hesitated. 'Considering today's politics, I suppose the Red Sea is not the most apt image for drawing a parallel with our country against the Communists. Perhaps Red-White-and-Blue Sea would be more appropriate.' Chris didn't know what he meant, but the instructors sitting in the front row laughed discreetly, mindful they were in chapel. The chaplain pushed his glasses back on his nose and read. The service concluded with 'God Bless America' again, then 'The Battle Hymn of the Republic,' and finally another chorus of 'The Star-Spangled Banner.'

Hoping for a chance to play, Chris was dismayed to learn that at the close of what was called the nondenominational service all the boys had to divide into their own religious groups, Lutheran with Lutheran, Anglican with Anglican, Presbyterian with Presbyterian, for further worship. He was confused, not knowing where to go because he didn't know if he had a religion or what it was. Glancing uneasily around him as he left the chapel with the other boys, he felt a hand on his shoulder and whirled to a red-haired freckled supervisor who looked as if he had a sunburn. 'Kilmoonie, you come with me.' The supervisor's voice had a lilt. He said his name was Mr O'Hara. 'Yes, Kilmoonie, I'm Irish like you. We're both RCs.' When Chris frowned, the supervisor explained, and that was the day Chris learned he was something called a Roman Catholic. That was also the day he learned a little about what it meant to be Jewish. As the different religious groups walked toward separate buses that would take them to various churches, Chris glanced across the concrete that led toward the dormitory and saw a boy walking all alone. Without thinking, he blurted, 'But why doesn't Saul have to come?'

The supervisor apparently didn't notice Chris hadn't said *sir*. 'What? Oh, that's Grisman. He's Jewish. His Sunday's on Saturday.'

Chris frowned as he boarded the bus. Sunday on Saturday? What sense did that make? He thought about it as the bus drove past the big iron gates at the entrance to the school. He'd been here only a few days, but already he'd lost track, and though as recently as the night before he'd fallen asleep making plans to run away, now the outside world seemed foreign and scary. His eyes widened nervously at the crowded sidewalks and the busy streets. The sun hurt his eyes. Car horns blared. The boys were under strict orders not to say a word while they were on the bus and especially not to make faces or do anything else that would attract the attention of people on the street. In the strange silence of the bus (except for the muffled roar of its engine), Chris stared ahead as did the other boys and felt unsettled, incomplete, eager to get back to the school and its routine.

The bus stopped in front of a church whose towers made it look like a castle. A cross loomed over it. Bells droned. A lot of people wearing suits and dresses were going in. Mr O'Hara lined the boys up two by two and marched them in. The church was dark and felt cool. As Mr O'Hara led the boys down a side aisle, Chris heard a woman whisper, 'Don't they look cute in their uniforms? Look at that young one. Isn't he sweet?' Chris wasn't sure if the woman meant him, but he felt self-conscious. All he wanted was to be invisible within the group.

The church made him feel even smaller than he was. He stared at the peaked roof (the highest he'd ever seen) with its crisscrossed beams and hanging lights. He peered at the front where a red light flickered above the altar. Candles glowed. The altar was covered with a stiff white cloth. A small shiny golden door on the altar looked as if it held a secret.

But beyond the altar hung the most disturbing sight of all. His chest shrank, suffocating him. Kneeling, he had to grip the seat ahead of him tightly to control his trembling hands. He'd never felt so scared. Beyond the altar hung a statue – a lean, twisted, agonized man whose hands and feet were nailed to a cross, whose head was pierced by what looked like spikes, whose side had been cut open, blood streaming down.

He glanced around in panic. Why didn't the other boys seem shocked by the statue? Or the other people (the 'outsiders,' as he'd begun to think of them) – why weren't *they* gaping in horror? What kind of place *was* this? Subduing himself, trying to understand, he heard Mr O'Hara snap his fingers twice, and at once the older boys stopped kneeling. They sat in the pews. Chris followed their lead. He felt even more afraid when an organ began to blare, its eerie chords filling the church. A choir began singing, but the language was foreign, and he didn't understand. Then a priest wearing a long color-ful robe came to the altar, followed by two boys in white cloaks. They faced the small gold door, their backs to the people, speaking to the statue. Chris hoped for an explanation – he wanted someone to tell him why the man was nailed up there.

But he couldn't understand what the priest was saying. The words seemed gibberish. They made no sense. '*Confiteor Deo omnipotenti . . .*'

All the way back to school, Chris felt confused. The priest had spoken briefly to the people in English, talking about Jesus Christ, who apparently was the man nailed above the altar, but Chris hadn't learned who Jesus was. Mr O'Hara had mentioned that next week

137

Chris would be starting something called Sunday school – maybe, Chris thought, I'll find out then. In the meantime, he sighed as the bus returned through the open gates of Franklin School, heading up the single road toward the dormitories. After the disturbing experience of being on the outside, in the scary church with the awful statue, he welcomed being back. He recognized some of the boys. He looked forward to sitting on his bunk. Knowing what he was supposed to do and when he was supposed to do it, he felt secure, pleased not to be confused. And lunch was served exactly on time. Hungry, he swallowed huge mouthfuls of hamburger and potato chips, drinking glass after glass of milk. It was good to be back home, he thought, then abruptly stopped chewing as he realized the word that had flashed through his head. Home? But what about the house on Calcanlin Street? And what about his mother? Confused again, he understood – without knowing why – that he was going to be living here for a long time. Peering along the table toward Saul in his honored center place, he told himself if this was going to be his home he'd better learn how to get along. He needed friends. He wanted to be Saul's friend. But how, when Saul was bigger and stronger and faster, and above all had the baseball cards?

9

The answer came to him the next day in swimming class. By now, he was less ashamed of being naked in front of the other boys. As the instructor told the class to kick their legs the way Saul was, Chris felt his heart race with satisfaction. I'm doing it! he thought. I'm really doing it!

'That's right, Kilmoonie,' the instructor said. 'Keep those legs out straight. Kick strong and steady. Just the way Grisman does.'

The other boys looked astonished at Chris as if they hadn't known he existed till the instructor said something good to him. Chris blushed, kicking harder, his chest filled with pride. He glanced down the line and noticed Saul turn his way as if curious to see who Kilmoonie was and whether he kicked as well as the instructor said. For a moment, while the other boys splashed, Chris and Saul stared into each other's eyes. Chris might have been wrong, but Saul seemed to grin as if the two of them shared a secret.

After class, they all hurried shivering to the dressing room, where their gray shirts and pants hung on pegs. Chris hugged himself, hopping from one bare foot to the other on the cold tile floor as he grabbed a towel from a pile in the corner, drying himself. An angry voice startled him.

'*Where's my cards?*'

Chris turned, bewildered, seeing Saul paw frantically through his clothes. The other boys gaped.

'They're gone!' Saul swung accusingly toward the group. 'Who stole my –?'

'No talking,' the instructor warned.

'But my cards! They were in my pocket! Somebody must have –'

'Grisman, I said no talking.'

But Saul's anger made him lose control. 'I want my cards back!'

The instructor stalked toward him, stopping with his feet spread apart, his hands placed threateningly on his hips. 'I want my cards back, *sir*!'

Distraught, Saul opened and closed his mouth, no sound coming out.

'Go on and say it, Grisman. *Sir*!'

Saul blinked toward the floor, confused, angry. 'Sir!'

'That's better. What cards are you talking about?'

'My baseball cards.' Saul quickly added, 'Sir. They were in my –'

'Baseball cards?' The instructor curled his lip. 'We don't issue baseball cards. Where'd you get them?'

Saul's eyes looked swollen and misty. 'I brought them to school with me.' He swallowed. 'Sir. I had them in my pants pocket and –'

'You weren't supposed to keep anything you brought here. You don't have toys here, Grisman. You don't *own* things. All you're supposed to have is what you're *told* you can have.'

Chris felt a snake uncoil in his stomach, embarrassed for Saul, who nodded, staring toward the floor, beginning to cry. The other boys gasped.

'Besides, Grisman, what makes you so sure one of your classmates stole these precious baseball cards? *Illegal* baseball cards. How do you know it wasn't me?'

Tears streaming down his cheeks, Saul peered up, sniffling, struggling to speak. 'Did you, sir?'

The silence made Chris squirm.

'I ought to claim I did, just to keep peace around here,' the instructor said at last. 'But I didn't. If I had these ridiculous cards, I certainly wouldn't give them back to you. It was one of your friends.'

Eyes red, squinting, Saul turned to the other boys, face tense with hate. Though Chris hadn't taken the cards, he nonetheless felt guilty when Saul's gaze stabbed him before continuing to the next boy and the next. Saul's lips shook.

'A lot of rules have been broken,' the instructor growled. 'You shouldn't have had the cards. But since you did, you should've kept another rule – if you've got a secret, make sure no one else knows it. There's an even more important rule, and this one's for everybody. You never steal from a teammate. If you can't trust each other, who *can* you trust?' His voice became low and hard. 'One of you is a thief. *I intend to find out who*. All of you,' he snapped, 'line up.'

They trembled. He scowled as he searched their clothes.

But he didn't find the cards. 'Where are they, Grisman? Nobody's got them. You made trouble for nothing. You must have lost them outside.'

Saul couldn't stop weeping. 'But I know they were in my pants.'

'Say *sir*.' Saul jumped. 'And if I ever see those cards or hear about them again, you'll be the sorriest wretch in this school. What's the matter with the rest of you? Move it! Finish dressing!'

The boys scrambled to do what they were told. Chris pulled on his pants, watching Saul stare angrily at everyone as he buttoned his shirt. Chris guessed what Saul was doing – looking for bulges in somebody's clothes – as if he didn't think the instructor had searched hard enough. While the instructor locked the door to the swimming pool, Saul moved next to a boy and studied a lump in his shirt pocket. The boy pulled a handkerchief from that pocket and blew his nose.

The instructor turned from locking the door, shouting, 'Aren't you dressed yet, Grisman?'

Saul hurried, tugging on his pants, tying his shoes. Tears dripped on his shirt.

'Fall in,' the instructor said.

The boys lined up, two by two. Fastening his belt, Saul ran to his place. As they marched to the dormitory, the world seemed to change. A few boys were sympathetic. 'Gee, that's too bad. What a dirty trick. Who'd be mean enough to steal your cards?' But the group didn't have the same eagerness to be close to Saul and get his attention.

Saul, for his part, didn't want to be close to them either. He stayed to himself in the dormitory. At supper, he gave up his honored central place, preferring to sit at the end of the table, not talking to anyone. Chris understood. If they were excluding Saul, *he* was excluding them. Though only one boy had stolen the cards, Saul couldn't tell which one. As a consequence, Saul was blaming everybody. The boys in turn had discovered Saul was vulnerable. He'd even cried, and that made him just another kid in the group. His cards had made him special. Without them, he'd still be taller and stronger and faster – but he had no power. Worse, by breaking down, he'd embarrassed them.

Soon the class had other heroes of the moment. In swimming class, a few kids even managed to equal Saul's performance, possibly because he showed no enthusiasm. He'd lost his joy. But Chris never went to the pool without feeling troubled by what had happened in the locker room that day. Who'd stolen the cards? he wondered, noticing the angry flare in Saul's eyes each time the group dressed, as if Saul relived his loss and humiliation.

Another question equally troubled Chris. How had the cards been stolen? The instructor had searched each boy's clothes. So how had the cards disappeared? He felt excited as a sudden thought occurred to him.

Eager, he couldn't wait to tell Saul, but then he remembered what had happened when he confused Babe Ruth with the candy bar, and he stopped himself, afraid of being laughed at if he was wrong. He waited for his chance to prove what he suspected, and the next day when his class walked from the school building to the dormitory, he hung back. Out of sight, he hurried to the changing room in the basement of the gym. After searching beneath the benches and behind the equipment locker, he found the cards wedged between a pipe and the wall beneath the sink. He shook as he held them. Whoever had stolen the cards must have been afraid the class would be searched. To protect himself, the boy had hidden them in the changing room, planning to come back when it was safe. Chris shoved the cards in his pocket, breathless as he ran from the gym to the dormitory to give them to Saul. He imagined how delighted Saul would be. Now Saul would be his friend.

Unlike the group, Chris had never stopped wanting to be close to him. From the start, he'd felt attracted as he would to a brother, and he'd never forgotten that afternoon in swimming class when the instructor had praised him for kicking as well as Saul did and Saul had turned to him grinning as if they shared a bond. But Saul now had built a wall around himself, and without the gift of the cards, Chris didn't know how to break through.

As he reached the dormitory, though, Chris suddenly felt uncertain. The cards had been stolen a week ago. Why hadn't the boy who hid them come back to get them? Pausing on the stairs, Chris knew the answer. Because the boy realized he couldn't show them to anyone or play with them except in secret. Otherwise word would get around – Saul would find out, and there'd be trouble. The bulge of the cards in Chris's pocket made him worried. Though he hadn't stolen the cards, it would seem as if he had. Saul would blame him. After all, how else would Chris have known where they were?

Panicked, Chris had to get rid of them. In the dormitory's basement washroom, he thought of hiding them under a sink as the thief had done. But what if a janitor cleaned beneath the sinks and found them, or what if a boy dropped his comb and happened to glance beneath the sink as he picked the comb up? No, he needed somewhere out of reach. Glancing above him, he noticed the steam pipes covered with grimy asbestos liners suspended along the ceiling. Climbing on the shoeshine stands, then across the cast-iron towel racks attached to the wall, he wedged the cards above a steam pipe. Nervous, he climbed back down, sighing in relief that he hadn't been caught. Now all he had to do was figure out how to return the cards to Saul without being blamed for stealing them.

He couldn't sleep all night, thinking about it. There had to be a way.

The next day, Saul was still sulking when Chris came over to him outside the refectory after lunch. 'I know who stole your cards.'

Saul angrily demanded, 'Who?'

'The swimming instructor.'

'He said he didn't take them.'

'He lied. I saw him give them to our teacher. I know where she put them.'

'Where?'

A supervisor came over. 'You guys are supposed to be in your room for rest period.' He followed them into the dormitory.

'I'll tell you later,' Chris whispered to Saul when the supervisor wasn't looking.

After school, Saul hurried to Chris. 'So tell me where.'

In the school building, Chris told Saul to watch the corridor while he snuck back in the classroom. 'She put them in her desk.'

'But her desk is locked,' Saul said.

'I know a way to open it.' Chris left Saul in the corridor. He'd seen their teacher go outside, so he guessed it was safe to be in the classroom. He didn't try to open the desk, but he waited long enough to make it seem he had. Finally he joined Saul in the corridor.

'Did you get them?' Saul asked anxiously.

Instead of answering, Chris made Saul follow him down the stairs. With no one around, he quickly reached beneath the front of his pants, pulling the cards out. Earlier he'd retrieved them from the pipe in the dormitory's basement washroom.

Saul looked delighted. Then his brow contorted, mystified. 'But how'd you get in her desk?'

'I'll show you sometime. You got your cards back. I'm the one who found them. Just remember who helped you – that's all.' Chris started toward the exit.

Behind him, Saul said, 'Thanks.'

Chris shrugged. 'It was nothing.'

'Wait a minute.'

Chris turned. Coming toward him, Saul frowned as if trying to decide on something. Pained, he fumbled among his cards and handed Chris one. 'Here.'

'But –'

'Take it.'

Chris looked at the card. Babe Ruth. His knees felt weak.

'Why'd you help me?' Saul asked.

'Because.' The magic word said everything. He didn't need to add, 'I want to be your friend.'

Saul glanced self-consciously at the floor. 'I guess I could show you a better way to do that kick in swimming class if you want.'

Heart pounding, Chris nodded. Then it was his turn to frown. He groped in a pocket. 'Here.' He handed Saul a candy bar. Baby Ruth.

Saul's eyes widened in amazement. 'Candy's not allowed. Where'd you get this?'

'How'd you bring the cards into school without getting caught?'

'A secret.'

'Same with me and the candy bar.' Chris scuffled his feet. 'But I'll tell *you* if you tell *me*.'

They stared at each other and started grinning.

10

Chris had a secret all right. Earlier that day, when the governess had taken Chris out of class and marched him to the administration building, he'd been afraid he was going to be punished for something. His legs shaky, he entered an office. At first it looked empty. Then in confusion he noticed a man by a window, peering out. The man was tall and thin. He wore a black suit, and when he turned, Chris blinked in surprise, recognizing the gray face of the man who'd brought him here.

'Hello, Chris.' The man's voice was soft. He smiled. 'It's good to see you again.'

Behind him, Chris heard the door shut as the governess left the office. He tensed, gazing up at the man, who continued to smile.

'You do remember me, don't you? Eliot?'

Chris nodded.

'Of course you do. I came to find out how you're getting along.' Eliot approached him. 'I know the school must seem strange to you, but you'll get used to it.' He chuckled. 'At least the food must agree with you. You look as if you've put on a couple of pounds.' Still chuckling, he crouched so Chris didn't have to strain to look up at him. 'I had another reason for coming here.' He peered directly into Chris's eyes.

Chris shifted from one leg to the other.

'I told you I'd come back to see you.' Eliot put his hands on Chris's shoulders. 'I want you to know I keep my promises.' He reached in a pocket. 'And I promised to bring you more of these.' He held out two Baby Ruth candy bars.

Chris's heart beat fast. By now, he knew how valuable candy was in the school. The only way to get it was by smuggling it in. He studied them eagerly.

Slowly, formally, Eliot gave them to Chris. 'I promise something else. I'll bring them every time I come to see you. Count on that. I want you to know you've got a friend. More than a friend. I'm like your father. Trust me. Depend on me.'

Chris put one of the bars in his pocket, vaguely sensing a way to use it, uncertain how. He glanced from the other bar toward Eliot, who smiled again. 'Oh, by all means, eat it. Enjoy it.' Eliot's eyes twinkled.

Tearing off the wrapper, his mouth watering as he bit into the chocolate, Chris suddenly felt hollow. His chest ached. Unable to stop himself, he threw his arms around Eliot, sobbing convulsively.

11

Eliot sometimes visited twice in a week. Other times he was gone for half a year. But true to his promise, he always brought Baby Ruth candy bars. Chris learned that no matter how stern the school could be there was one adult whose kindness and interest he could always depend on. Eliot arranged to take Chris from school to see boxing and tennis. They went to Howard Johnson's for chocolate sundaes. Eliot taught Chris how to play chess. He took Chris to his large home in Falls Church, Virginia, where Chris marveled at the huge chairs and sofas, the enormous dining room, and the spacious bedrooms. Eliot showed him the brilliant roses in the greenhouse. Intrigued by the suburb's name – Falls Church – Chris smelled the roses, reminded of the fragrance of Easter service, feeling as if the greenhouse indeed were a church.

As his relationship with Eliot grew, so did his friendship with Saul. The two boys seemed inseparable. Chris shared his Baby Ruths with Saul, and Saul for his part shared his physical skills, teaching Chris the secrets of baseball and football and basketball. But Saul, the natural athlete, had trouble with mathematics and languages, so Chris, the natural scholar, helped Saul to study and pass his exams. They complemented each other. What the one couldn't do, the other could, together unbeatable. Saul again became the envy of his group. But so did Chris.

Only one thing was lacking to make it all perfect.

Eliot's next visit was the first weekend in July. 'Tomorrow's the Fourth, Chris. Tell you what. Why don't I take you to the big fireworks show downtown?'

Chris got excited.

But Eliot seemed troubled. 'I've been wondering. Now tell me the truth. You won't hurt my feelings.'

Chris didn't know what he meant.

'These trips we go on.'

Chris felt afraid. 'You're going to stop them?'

'No. Good Heavens, they mean too much to me.' Eliot laughed and mussed Chris's hair. 'But I've been thinking. I bet it must get boring for you with only a grownup to talk to. You must get tired of seeing the same old face. What I've been wondering – well, would you like to share these trips with someone else? Have you got a friend, a *special* friend, you'd like to bring along? Someone you're really close to, who's almost family? I won't mind.'

Chris couldn't believe his luck – the chance to be with the two most important people in his world at once. He'd always felt bad, not being able to share his fortune with Saul. In turn, he felt so proud of being friends with Saul he wanted Eliot to know him. His eyes beamed, excited. 'You bet!'

'Then what are you waiting for?' Eliot grinned.

'You won't go away?'

'I'll stay right here.'

Bursting with anticipation, Chris ran from the bench near the armory where they'd been sitting. 'Saul! Guess what?' Behind him, he heard Eliot chuckle.

Therefore Saul was always included. Chris felt overjoyed at Eliot's approval of his friend. 'You're right. He's special, Chris. You made an excellent choice. I'm proud of you.' Eliot brought candy bars for both of them now. He took them for Thanksgiving to his home. He let them go on a plane ride. 'Chris, there's one thing that bothers me. I hope you're not jealous when I give Saul candy bars or show him attention. I wouldn't want you to think I was ignoring you or treating him with more importance than you. You're like a son to me. I love you. We'll always be close. If I make Saul feel good, it's because I want to make *you* feel good – because he's your friend, because he's family.'

'Gosh, I couldn't be jealous of Saul.'

'Then you understand. I knew you would. You trust me.'

Every Saturday night, in the many years to come, the school showed a different movie, but in one way, they were all the same. *Battle Cry, The Sands of Iwo Jima, Guadalcanal Diary, Francis Goes to West Point, Francis in the Navy.* 'That talking mule sure makes the military seem a lot of fun,' the boys said. *The Frogmen, Back to Bataan, Combat Squad, Beachhead, Battle Zone, Battleground, Battle Stations.* In ancient history, they learned about Alexander's conquests and Caesar's Gallic wars. In American history, they learned about the War for Independence, the War of 1812, the Civil War. In literature classes, they read *The Red Badge of Courage, For Whom the Bell Tolls, The Thin Red Line.* They didn't mind the repeated theme, for the books were filled with heroics and action, always exciting. As well, the boys liked rifle practice, tactical maneuvers, precision marching, and the other training they received in the school's militia. They enjoyed the war games. In class as well as in sports, they were encouraged to compete against the other boys, to see who was smarter, stronger, faster, better. And they couldn't help noticing the strangers who often appeared silently at the back of the gym or the football field or the classroom, sometimes in uniform, sometimes not. With dark narrowed eyes, the strangers watched, comparing, judging.

12

Candy. Because of it, Saul saved Chris's life in 1959. The boys were fourteen – though they didn't know, they were about to end one set of adventures and begin another. With money Eliot had given them, they'd gone into business, smuggling candy into school in exchange for kitchen detail and similar nuisance jobs the other boys did for them. On December 10, after lights out, they snuck from the dormitory across the snowy grounds to a secluded section of the high stone wall. Saul stood on Chris's shoulders and climbed. Chris grabbed his arm, squirming up after him. In starlight, they saw their frosty breath escape from their mouths as they lay on top and studied the dark street below them.

Seeing no one, they eased over. Dangling, Saul let go first, but Chris suddenly heard him groan and peered down, startled. Saul had landed on his back, sliding in a blur to the street.

Chris didn't understand. He quickly jumped to help, bending his knees to absorb the impact, but the moment he landed, he realized something was wrong. Like Saul, his legs shot out from under him. Falling, he cracked his head on the sidewalk and slid out into the street. Dimly he became aware that the snow had melted during the day but now at night had frozen to a slick sheet of ice. Frantic, he failed to stop himself as he continued skidding toward Saul. His boots struck Saul where he lay and knocked him farther into the street.

The sudden clanging paralyzed him. A streetcar swung around a corner, approaching them, its headlight glaring. Its wheels scraped on the icy tracks. Chris saw the driver shouting behind the windshield, tugging the rope that rang the bell, and yanking a lever. The brakes squealed, but the wheels continued sliding ahead. Chris tried to stand. Dizzy from his injured skull, he lost his balance, falling again. The streetcar's headlights blinded him.

Saul dove across him, grabbed his coat, and dragged him toward the curb. The streetcar's shadow passed with a wind that made Chris shiver. 'You damn crazy kids!' the driver shouted from his window. The bell kept clanging as the streetcar rumbled down the street.

Chris sat on the icy curb, breathing deeply, his head between his knees. Saul checked his skull.

'Too much blood. We've got to get you back to the dorm.'

Chris almost didn't manage the return climb over the wall. A supervisor nearly caught them as they crept up a stairwell. In a shadowy washroom, Saul cleaned Chris's wound as best as he could, and the next day when a teacher asked about the scab on Chris's head, Chris explained he'd tripped down some stairs. That should have been the end of the matter, except because Saul had saved Chris's life, their bond was closer. But neither boy anticipated repercussions or realized what else had almost happened to them.

Ten days later when they next went over the wall, a gang confronted them as they headed toward the stores on the other side of Fairmont Park.

The biggest kid demanded their money, grabbing at Chris's pockets.

Angry, Chris pushed him and never saw the fist that struck his stomach. Through blurry eyes, he saw two other kids grab Saul's arms from behind. A fourth kid punched Saul's face. Blood spattered.

Unable to breathe, Chris tried to help Saul. A fist split his lips. As he fell, a boot cracked his shoulder. Other boots rammed his chest, his side, his back.

He rolled from their impact, writhing. Muffled punches threw Saul on him.

Mercifully, the beating stopped. The gang took the money. On bloody snow, Chris peered through a swirl as they ran away. Delirious, he nonetheless felt mystified about . . .

He wasn't sure what – something about . . .

He sorted it out only after a police car found them staggering back to school and took them first to the emergency ward at the hospital, then to the infirmary at school.

The gang had looked more like adults then kids, their hair too short and neat, their boots and jeans and leather jackets strangely new. They'd driven away in an expensive car.

Why had they been so sure we had money? Chris thought. He remembered the last time he and Saul had gone over the wall – when

Saul had pulled him away from the streetcar – and wondered if the gang had been waiting then.

His thoughts were interrupted. In the infirmary bed, aching, he smiled through swollen lips when he saw Eliot hurry in.

'I came as soon as I could.' Eliot sounded out of breath, tugging off his black topcoat and homburg hat, snowflakes melting on them. 'I wasn't told till – oh, dear God, your faces!' He glanced appalled from Chris to Saul. 'You look like they beat you with clubs. It's a miracle you weren't both killed.' He studied them, sickened.

'They used just their fists,' Saul answered, weak, his face bruised and puffy. 'And their boots. They didn't need clubs.'

'Your eyes. You'll have shiners for weeks.' Eliot winced. 'You can't know how sorry I am.' His voice became stern. 'In a way, I suppose, you invited it, though. The headmaster told me what he discovered you'd been up to – sneaking from school, buying candy. Is that what you do with the money I give you?'

Chris felt embarrassed.

'Never mind. It's not the time to raise the subject. Right now, you need sympathy – not a lecture. As long as it happened, I hope you gave them some lumps in return.'

'We never touched them,' Saul murmured.

Eliot looked surprised. 'But I thought the school gave you boxing class. You guys are tough. I've seen you on the football field. You mean you didn't land even one punch?'

Chris shook his head, stiffening from the pain. 'They hit me before I knew what was going on. Boxing? I never had a chance to raise a fist. They were all over us.'

'They moved too quick for me,' Saul added. 'Boxing's a joke. They were better than that. They were –' He struggled for the proper word.

'Experts?'

Aching, Saul nodded.

Eliot studied them and frowned. Lips pursed, he seemed to consider something. 'I assume you've learned not to sneak out of school anymore.' He didn't wait for an answer. 'Even so, you ought to be prepared for an emergency. You should be able to defend yourselves. I certainly don't like seeing those handsome faces of yours turned into ground beef.' He nodded thoughtfully as if making an important decision.

Chris wondered what.

13

Saul's fifteenth birthday occurred on January 20, 1960. On that occasion, Eliot drove up from Washington to take the boys out on the town. They went first to a Horn and Hardart automat for baked beans and coleslaw, then to an Elvis Presley movie, *GI Blues*. When Eliot returned them to the school, he gave them a set of books filled with stop-action photographs of men in white uniforms throwing or kicking

147

each other. At that time, the only thing Americans knew about martial arts came from stories about Japanese soldiers in World War Two. The boys thought the pictures showed a form of professional wrestling. The next week when Eliot came to see them, they'd had a chance to study the books. He spoke of patriotism and courage and offered them the opportunity to forfeit all high school sports, instead to train privately for three hours a day, seven days a week till their graduation.

Both boys jumped at the chance. For one thing, it was a wonderful way of escaping the routine at Franklin. For another, more important, they still showed signs of the beating they'd received, and they were determined not to suffer like that again. Neither boy realized how extreme their determination would become.

The second weekend in February, Eliot took them to meet their instructors. The boys had known for some time that Eliot worked for the government, so they weren't surprised when he told them that seven years earlier, in 1953, the CIA had recruited Yukio Ishiguro, a former Japanese world judo champion, and Major Soo Koo Lee, a one-time senior karate instructor for the South Korean army. Both Orientals had been brought to the United States to train operatives in what, prior to killer-instinct training, were the finest forms of hand-to-hand combat. The base of operations consisted of a large gym, called a *dojo*, located on the fifth floor of a warehouse in downtown Philadelphia, about a mile from the orphanage.

The elevator to the fifth floor looked like a rusty shower stall. It barely accommodated the three passengers and stank of urine and sweat. Graffiti covered the walls. The *dojo* itself was a larger loft with steel girders in the ceiling and rows of harsh floodlights. Most of the floor was covered by green three-inch-thick *tatami* mats. Beyond them, a border of oak gleamed before mirrors on all the walls.

When Chris and Saul entered with Eliot, they noticed several gaming tables between the dressing room and mat area. At one of these tables, they found Lee and Ishiguro using black and white stones to play an oriental game that Eliot explained was called Go. Both instructors wore suits, Ishiguro's made of blue silk, Lee's of gray sharkskin. Both men were shoeless. Their socks were clean and white, their shirts heavily starched, their striped ties carefully knotted and pressed.

With no hair on his head and his belly protruding, Ishiguro looked like an oversized Buddha. But when he stood, his six-foot-three-inch height and two hundred and ninety pounds presented an awesome figure. In contrast, Lee stood five foot four inches tall on a small frame and still had his shiny ebony hair as well as a black thin mustache. His musculature suggested springy steel.

The game stopped at once. The two orientals gave short bows of respect to Eliot, then shook hands with the boys.

'I do hope our mutual friend, Mr Eliot, has explained that we are not here to teach you a sport,' Ishiguro said in flawless English. 'Sensei Lee and I hope you will accept our service. If you do, we promise you will learn to perceive rapid movement as if it were slow. That much alone will place you above most men. Here, everything you learn will become second nature, as it must, for you will not have time to think if death approaches – instead you will have only a moment to prove that you should live. You may tell your school friends what you learn, but you will soon discover they don't understand. What you must never do is *show* them. Since you can't predict a future enemy, isn't it better if no one else has the knowledge you do?'

Lee said nothing, neither smiled nor frowned. While Ishiguro went to boil water for tea, Eliot broke the silence by asking Lee about the game of Go. Lee immediately came to attention.

'Appearance is deception,' he said with a smile. 'As you see, the board is made up of half-inch squares. The spaces are not important. The lines mean everything. By placing a stone on the board and building a pattern from there, I hope to enclose as much territory as possible. The object is simple – to offset my opponent with the suspicion that I'm establishing a network to entrap him. Which of course I am.' Lee laughed. He demonstrated how to handle a stone using two fingers like a claw. Ishiguro returned with the tea, and eventually the meeting concluded with the orientals admonishing the boys to consider the proposition and decide in private.

It was all too brief. Puzzled, they listened to Eliot's explanation as the creaky elevator descended.

'When you were little, you were interested in sports. As you got older, you idolized heroes in war movies. You've just met two middle-aged men in a sleazy Philadelphia warehouse. Two men who are recognized as great, as having superior skill, by over two-thirds of the world. Perhaps humility is the only visible sign of wisdom. I don't know. But they've accepted the responsibility of training men in specific areas of security for our government. Both are paid well, but I don't think they're interested in money. I believe their interest involves the opportunity to teach young men to become the best fighters in the world. Today was just an introduction, a chance for you to see what's involved. If you decide to participate, the program must be carried out to its conclusion. Never break a promise. They accept you as men. They won't appreciate little kids who stand around with their mouths open in wonderment or who give up. So make your choice wisely and call me collect before next Sunday. Oh, and by the way, if you do decide to join, there'll be no more evening meals at Franklin. But don't expect to be eating hoagies and steak sandwiches. They've got a special diet for you: flank steak, heart, fish for protein, rice to fill you up, tea occasionally, grapefruit juice always. No more Baby Ruths for a while, I'm afraid. Keep to their menu, it'll do you good. But if you tire of the food, you mustn't stop drinking the juice. Lee and Ishiguro swear by it. They say it takes all the cramps and stiffness away. This isn't the Marine Corps – you're gonna have to work your ass off for these guys.'

When the boys phoned Eliot to say they wanted to join, he told them he'd pick them up on Sunday. 'Dress up, wear clean underwear, be prepared for a ceremony. Think along the lines of a Bar Mitzvah or a confirmation.'

149

On their second visit to the *dojo*, Chris and Saul were initiated into manhood through a ritual called *gempuku*. Instead of the traditional short sword and long sword, they were given a judo *gi* and a karate *gi*. The uniforms caught their attention. The first was heavily woven cotton, the second lightweight serge. Called *haori*, the coats reached down to the knees. The pants were *hakama*, and the purpose of their wide flaring sides was to give no suggestion of the build of the wearer.

Ishiguro noticed the boys' curiosity. 'Mr Lee and I have decided to accept you as *shizoku*, which means descendants of samurai. It has special meaning to us and to your friend Mr Eliot. It places the added responsibility on you to protect yourself against humiliation. If you accept that duty, you may need to dispose of yourself some day. That is why this ceremony of manhood tells you how to use the sword. True manhood is challenged when a decision of this type is needed. I must tell you of *jijin*, the proper use of the sword to end one's life.'

Ishiguro sat down on the floor with his legs crossed before him. He took the small sword whose blade was only fourteen inches long and moved it from right to left horizontally across his abdomen.

'The pain will be intense. Your final act will be to rise above the pain by remaining still with your head bowed. Your assistant will finish the procedure.'

Standing beside him, Lee took a sword whose blade was forty inches long and dramatized the final act of beheading. 'Be careful not to cut completely through the neck but instead to leave a flap so the head will remain attached to the body.'

Ishiguro looked up and smiled. 'That is *seppuku*, and it means disembowelment – death with honor. Anything by other means is *jisai* or mere self-disposal. It is all a part of an honorable tradition, the initiation into a divine way of manhood we no longer have in this century. The instruction you receive will have no mystery, no glamor. It will train you to kill or, if you fail, to die with honor.'

The boys were stunned.

'There is no longer time in your life to idolize others,' Ishiguro continued. 'Now there is only the self – without the approval of others. That is important, for to fascinate others with your skill places your personality in their stereotype of you, a stereotype at one time accepted, at another time unaccepted, depending on current fashion. You will rise above this. When you are through with us, your black belt will tell everyone only that you are a serious student. You will never officially pass beyond *shodan* or the first degree, though you'll go far beyond that. To reveal the true extent of your training would expose you to national and international competition. But the way of the samurai makes you more than a mere technician of swordplay or a specialist with the knife for the amusement of others. Your destiny is profound.'

The boys learned how to sit properly, to bow, to show respect, and to release an opponent in distress. Ishiguro took Chris aside; Lee worked with Saul. The next day, the instructors switched partners. The first two weeks were devoted to learning proper falls, the *katas* or dance steps, and the means to unbalance an opponent. Once these basics were understood, the boys began the advanced training commonly reserved for black belts. They learned to choke an opponent, to lock his arms, to break his extremities.

'For men with instincts as quick as your own,' Lee explained, 'you will see a kick coming as if it were suspended. All you must do is step back or to the side and watch your assailant lose his balance. Never allow yourself to be cornered. Instead keep moving forward to corner your man. At the same time, wait for him to attack. Defend yourself so surely that your one and only blow serves its purpose. Never square off with him within the length of his legs. Never allow him to grab you from the front. To do so is merely to wrestle with him, to create a sport with him. I will show you how to protect yourself against an attacker who grabs you from the rear, who clutches your neck, your arms. You will learn to bend at the knee, to use the fulcrum of your hip. These tactics must be automatic.'

They came to understand profoundly that the ability to overpower an opponent did not belong to the young or the athletic but to those with secret knowledge. The skills they learned gave them the confidence to relax and recognize danger. Their power made them humble.

Lee told them stories. 'I went to missionary school. I learned your Bible – both books. I will tell you something that has always interested me. In the old book, Isaiah, your God said, "I created day; I created night. I created good; I created evil. I, the Lord, did all these things." I have always wondered how a Westerner can judge evil as wrong when his own God created it and permitted Lucifer to protect it. Strange how the warrior who has seen death and miracles either remains in the military or else joins a monastery – for the sake of the discipline. Meanwhile, those safe at home, who know nothing, talk of the bad, the wrong, the sinful. How wonderful that the history of the warrior does not allow the contemplation of good and evil but only of duty, honor, and loyalty.'

Ishiguro allowed the boys to make a game of *shinigurai*. In Japanese, the word meant being crazy to die. He hoped that someday this horseplay would allow the boys to leap into the jaws of death with no hesitation. The game involved jumping over each other and objects, falling from heights and landing flatly on their chests.

Lee said, 'There is nothing more exciting than to know that a friend is somewhere in the dark facing death. Such exhilaration!'

Ishiguro said, 'I will read to you from the *Hugakure*. The title means hidden among leaves. It explains the classic code of ethics for the samurai. The way of the samurai is death. In a fifty-fifty life-or-death crisis, simply approach the crisis, prepared to die if necessary. There is nothing complicated about it. Merely brace yourself and proceed. One who fails in a mission and chooses to continue living will be despised as a coward and a bungler. To be a perfect samurai, you must prepare yourself for death morning and evening, day in, day out. Hell is to live in uneventful times when you have no choice except to wait for valor.'

151

On the day they finished their training, Ishiguro gave them their final lesson. 'For many years in Japanese history, a commander held respect from his people. He was called a shogun, something like your president. Beneath him were his masters of skill, such as your Pentagon and CIA. Under the care and command of these masters were the *hatamoto*, who as samurai served their masters in the shogun's camp. The masters were intermediaries – they guaranteed honor to the chief and justice to the men. In turn, the samurai promised gratitude, bravery and obligation. Their responsibility was known as *giri*. If a samurai developed a monastic conviction or sustained a crippling blow, he was dismissed from the service of the shogun. When a master died, the shogun released the master's samurai from service. These samurai would travel the country alone – they showed no allegiance to a wife – but because their skills were so precise and deadly, they were often hunted, certainly challenged often. Many formed teams. A few became bandits, but most became monks. Isn't it strange how the power to kill often makes a warrior monastic? But in your case, the shogun is not your president. Such a man passes in and out of favor by the whim of popular opinion. No, your shogun is Eliot. He may retire you, or he may die. But without him, you are only wanderers.'

14

The rain kept drumming on the cabin's roof. Outside, the morning was as bleak as dusk.

Erika blinked in dismay. Taking turns, Chris and Saul had explained. 'How long did you say you received instruction?' she asked.

'Three years,' Saul answered. 'Three hours every day.'

She inhaled. 'But you were only kids.'

'You mean we were young,' Chris said. 'The way we were raised, I'm not sure we were ever kids.'

'We enjoyed those classes. We liked making Eliot proud of us,' Saul said. 'All we wanted was his approval.'

Chris pointed to the computer printouts on the table. 'Given the other parallels, my guess is the men on this list grew up in the same kind of atmosphere we did.'

'Conditioned,' Erika said.

Saul's eyes were grim. 'It worked. The spring we graduated from high school, Special Forces and the 82nd Airborne each sent recruiters to the school. They spent a week competing to convince our class which unit had more to offer.' His voice became bitter. 'The same way IBM and Xerox recruit at a college. The boys in our class chose one military unit or the other, but as a group, they enlisted one hundred percent. In doing so, they continued a tradition. No boy ever graduated from Franklin without joining the military. They wanted to prove their courage so much that six years later, in '68, by the time

152

of the Tet offensive in Nam, eighty percent of our class had been killed in combat.'

'Jesus,' Erika said.

'But for us, the process still wasn't finished,' Chris continued. 'Eliot called it layering. After the school and the *dojo*, after Special Forces and Nam, we went through Rothberg's killer-instinct training. Then we went to the agency's farm in Virginia. Eliot had long since recruited us. In a sense, our training had begun when we were five. But after the farm, we were finally ready to work for him.'

'He made you the best.'

'He made us. Yes.' Chris pursed his lips in anger. 'And these other men as well. He programmed us to be absolutely dedicated to him.'

'Never to question anything. Like the Paradigm job,' Saul said. 'I never dreamed of asking him why he wanted it done. If he ordered something, that was good enough.'

'We were so naive he must have been tempted to laugh. When we snuck from school that night and the gang beat us up . . .' Chris glared. 'I only now realized. Something about them always bothered me. They looked too neat. Their leather jackets were new. They drove an expensive car.' He shivered. 'They must have been operatives. He sent them to work us over, to make us angry so we'd grab the chance to learn at the *dojo*. God knows how many other ways he manipulated us.'

'Those Baby Ruth candy bars. He gave me one in Denver when he set me up to be killed.'

'The same when he asked me to hunt for you,' Chris added. 'We're Pavlov's dogs. Those candy bars are the symbol of his relationship with us. He used them to make us love him. It was easy. No one else ever showed us kindness. An old man giving candy to kids.'

The rain drummed harder on the roof.

'And now we find out everything he said was wrong. A trick. A lie,' Saul said. 'He never loved us. He used us.'

'Not only us.' Chris seethed. 'These other men must have felt he loved them too. He lied to everyone. We were all just part of a group. I could almost forgive his lies – the things he made me do! – if I thought we were special to him. But we're not.' He listened to the storm, his words like thunder. 'And for that I'll see him die.'

NEMESIS

1

Two minutes after the bootlegger opened, Hardy stepped back on the street, clutching two bottles of Jim Beam in a paper sack. He prided himself on his choice of brand. His government pension allowed him few frills, but he'd never debased himself by drinking unaged, bottom-of-the-price-list whiskey. Nor had he ever been tempted to try the cheap pop wines or the sick-sweet fruity rum concoctions preferred by the other drunks in his building. He had standards. He ate once a day, whether hungry or not. He washed and shaved daily and wore fresh clothes. He had to. In the Miami humidity, he sweated constantly, the alcohol oozing from his pores as fast as he tossed it down. Even now, at five after eight in the morning, the heat was obscene. His sunglasses shielded the glare and hid his bloodshot eyes. His flower-patterned shirt stuck to him, soaking the paper bag he held against his chest. He glanced toward his stomach, appalled by the pale puffy skin protruding from an open button on his shirt. With dignity, he closed it. Soon, in two more blocks, he'd be back in the dark security of his room, the blinds shut, the fan on, watching the last half-hour of 'Good Morning, America,' toasting David Hartman.

The thought of the day's first drink made him shake. He glanced around in case a cop was watching, then veered toward an alley, feeling sheltered beneath a fire escape. As traffic roared past the entrance, he reached in the paper bag, twisted the cap off one of the bottles, and pulled the neck out, raising it to his lips. He closed his eyes, luxuriating in the warmth of the bourbon trickling down his throat. His body relaxed. His tremors stopped.

Abruptly he stiffened, hearing the blare of music throbbing, coming closer. Puzzled, he opened his eyes and gaped at the tallest Cuban he'd ever seen, wearing a shiny purple shirt and mirrored glasses, gyrating to the raucous beat of the ghetto box strapped around his shoulders. Husky, cruel-lipped, the Cuban crowded him against the wall beneath the fire escape.

Hardy shook again – from fear this time. 'Please. I've got ten bucks in my wallet. Just don't hurt me. Don't take the whiskey.'

The Cuban only frowned. 'What're you talking about? A dude said to give you this.' He stuffed an envelope in the paper bag and walked away.

154

'What? Hey, wait a minute. Who? What'd he look like?'

The Cuban shrugged. 'Just a dude. What difference does it make? You all look alike. He gave me twenty bucks. That's all I cared about.'

As Hardy blinked, the Cuban disappeared from the alley, the music from his ghetto box fading. Hardy licked his lips and tasted a residue of bourbon. Nervous, he reached for the envelope in the bag. He felt a long thin object sealed inside. Awkwardly tearing the envelope, he dumped a key in the palm of his hand.

It looked like the key to a safety-deposit box. It had a number: 113. And letters: USPS. Groggy, he tried to concentrate, finally guessing what the letters referred to. United States Postal Service. A mail drop.

Like the old days. The notion disturbed him. He hadn't worked for Intelligence since 1973, when Watergate had resulted in a massive house-cleaning of the agency. Despite his drinking, he'd still been valuable enough that he'd hoped to cling to his job as director of South American operations till he reached the age for retirement. But the political scandals after the break-in had required scapegoats, and a boozer made a good one. At sixty-two, he'd been forced to resign – at least he'd received his full pension – and with an alcoholic's hatred of cold, he'd headed toward Miami.

Now he thought, Hell, I'm too old for games. A mail drop. What a crock. First they kick me out. Then they figure they can snap their fingers and I'll work for them again. He stuffed the key in the paper bag and stepped from the alley. Well, they'd better figure one more time.

He walked half a block before he questioned his assumption. Maybe the key didn't come from the agency. He frowned and paused. It might be from the other side. His head ached. Which other side, though? More important, why? Who needs a boozer? Even if I was sober, I'm out of practice. After nine years, I don't know anything about the agency's operations. What the hell?

The fierce sun stabbed through his tinted glasses, making him squint. His spine itched with the sense he was being watched. He glanced around him. Stupid, he thought. Pal, you're not kidding you're out of practice. An obvious move like that could have got you killed in the old days.

Not that it mattered anymore. Whatever game was being offered, he didn't intend to play. Someone had wasted time and twenty bucks. All he wanted was to get back home, turn the fan on, and drink his toast to David Hartman. Drink a lot of toasts. And have a few more when his good old pal Phil Donahue came on.

He soon saw the entrance to his apartment building. The owner called it a condominium, but a tenement would have been more accurate. The wreck was fifteen stories high – the concrete so substandard it crumbled from the salty air, the glass so thin it shuddered from the noisy traffic. The halls smelled of cabbage. The plumbing knocked. Through the thin walls, Hardy heard every time his neighbor took a leak. Retirement Villa, the sign said. Premature burial, Hardy thought.

He reached the building and stared at the seagull dung mixed with feathers on the sidewalk before the cracked glass door. His stomach soured as he analyzed the pattern of his days – the bourbon, the game shows, the soaps, at last the news if he could keep himself awake that long, the midnight nightmares, the 3 A.M. sweats. Hell, David Hartman can wait, he thought and turned from the entrance, continuing down the block. He admitted to being a fool. The trouble was, in spite of his bitterness toward the agency and his premonition of trouble, he couldn't stifle his curiosity. He hadn't felt this interested since he'd watched last season's hurricane.

Which postal station? Since he had to start somewhere, he chose the nearest one, stopping in alleys along the way to strengthen his courage with bourbon. The station was glass and chrome, long and low, flanked by palm trees that seemed to stoop from the heat. He walked through the hissing automatic door and smelled the pungent industrial cleaner the janitor used on the concrete floor. The postal boxes lined both sides of a corridor. He found 113 on an oversized door on the right-hand bottom row. Of course, every postal station in the city probably had a box numbered 113. The key might not fit, but when he drew it from the paper bag, he found the key turned smoothly in the lock. The box was so low that when he opened it he had to kneel to look inside. Because of the box's size, he'd expected a package. But he found nothing. Hollow with disappointment, angry at being fooled, he almost stood before his instincts warned him. Why a bottom box? Because, even kneeling, you can't see the top. To see the whole inside, you have to bend down toward the floor. If something's attached to the top, the clerk inserting mail from the other side can't see it. Not unless the clerk bent down to the floor, as Hardy did, and there it was, a small flat plastic container with a magnet sticking it to the top of the box.

His face red from bending over, Hardy pried the magnet free. Unsteadily, he got up. He glanced along the corridor of boxes. No one in sight. Instead of going to a safer location, he took a chance and yanked the flap on the container.

He frowned at another key What the –?

Not a postal box key. It did have a number: 36.

He turned it over. Atlantic Hotel.

2

Saul tensed when he heard the key scraping in the lock. He crouched behind a chair, clutching his hidden Beretta, staring toward the gradually opening door.

He'd made sure the room was dark, tugging the drapes shut. The light from the hall streamed narrowly across the floor, then widened. A shadow obscured the light. An overweight man stepped slowly in, nervous, clutching something in a paper bag.

'Shut the door and lock it,' Saul said.

The man obeyed. In the dark, Saul switched on a swivel-necked desk lamp, aiming it toward him. There wasn't any question now. From behind the lamp, shielded from its glare, he recognized Hardy. The man took off his tinted glasses, raising a hand to protect his eyes. Saul hadn't seen him in thirteen years. Hardy had looked bad then. Now, at the age of seventy-two, he looked worse – puffy fishbelly skin, red blotches on his wrinkled cheeks, a distended abdomen from his swollen liver and the fluid an alcoholic's body retains. His hair was gray, dull, lifeless. But at least it was combed. He'd shaved. He gave off no odor, except from bourbon. His clothes – a hideous flower-patterned shirt and electric-blue polyester pants – looked clean and pressed. His white shoes were freshly polished.

Hell, Saul thought, if I was a lush, I doubt I'd pay as much attention to my appearance. 'Hardy, it's good to see you. The light switch is to your left.'

'Who –?' Hardy's voice trembled as he groped for the switch. Two lamps – on a bureau and over the bed – came on. Hardy squinted, frowning.

'You don't recognize me? I'm insulted.'

Hardy continued frowning. 'Saul?' He blinked in confusion.

Still keeping the Beretta hidden, Saul grinned and reached across the chair to shake hands with him. 'How are you? What's in the bag?'

'Oh . . .' Hardy shrugged, embarrassed. 'Just a few things. I had an early errand.'

'Booze?'

'Well, yeah . . .' Hardy wiped his mouth self-consciously. 'I'm having some friends over. I didn't realize the liquor cabinet was empty.'

'Looks awful heavy. Set it on the dresser. Give your arm a rest.'

Bewildered, Hardy did what he was told. 'I . . . what's this all about?'

Saul raised his shoulders. 'A reunion I guess you could say.'

The phone rang. Hardy flinched and stared. It rang again. 'Aren't you going to answer it?' But Saul didn't move. The phone stopped ringing. 'For Christ's sake,' Hardy said, 'what's going on? That Cuban –'

'Impressive, wasn't he? I had to look for quite a while before I found him. Just the right sneer.'

'But why?'

'We'll get to that. Are you armed?'

'You're kidding. With all these Cuban refugees?'

Saul nodded. Hardy was legendary for never going anywhere without a handgun, including to the bathroom. Once, to the dismay of the Secret Service, he'd worn a revolver to a White House conference with the president. Another time, during a prestigious dinner party, he'd fallen asleep from overdrinking, slumping in his chair till his handgun slipped from his shoulder holster, thumping on the floor in front of two congressmen and three senators. 'Put it next to the booze on the dresser.'

'Why?'

Saul raised the Beretta from behind the chair. 'Just do it.'

'Hey, come on.' Hardy's eyes widened. He tried to laugh as if convincing himself this was a joke. 'You don't need that.'

Saul didn't laugh, though.

Hardy pursed his lips. Nervous, he stooped to lift his right pantleg, showing a snub-nosed Colt.38 in an ankle holster.

'Still like the revolvers, huh?'

'You know what they used to call me.'

'Wyatt Earp.' Saul tensed. 'Use just two fingers.'

'You don't have to tell me.' Hardy sounded indignant. 'I still remember the drill.' He set the handgun on the dresser. 'You satisfied?'

'Not quite.' Saul picked it up. 'I have to search you.'

'Oh, for Christ's sake.'

'I won't tickle.' After frisking him, Saul showed particular interest in Hardy's buttons.

Hardy blanched. 'Is *that* what this is all about? A microphone? You thought I was wired? Why should I –?'

'The same reason we used the Cuban. We're not sure if you're being watched.'

'Watched? But why would anybody want to –? Wait a minute. We? Did you say we?'

'Chris is working with me.'

'Kilmoonie?' Hardy sounded confused.

'Good. The booze hasn't ruined your memory.'

'How could I forget what you guys did for me in Chile? Where –?'

'That phone call was him from the lobby. Two rings meant he doubts you were followed. If he spots any trouble, he'll phone again – one ring – to warn me.'

'But I could've told you I wasn't followed.' He noticed Saul avoid his stare. 'I get it.' He nodded grimly. 'You figure I'm in no condition to spot a tail.'

'Out of action, a person's skills get blunted.'

'Especially if he's a lush.'

'I didn't say that.'

'Hell, you didn't have to.' Hardy glared. 'What made you sure I'd even come?'

'We weren't. When the Cuban gave you the key, you could've dropped it down a sewer.'

'And?'

'We'd have left you alone. You had to prove you were ready to get involved – not just with us but with anything. You had to show you wanted some action.'

'No.'

'I'm not sure what –'

'You had another reason.'

Saul shook his head.

'The Cuban,' Hardy said. 'I can see why you needed him. The key makes sense.'

'Well, then –?'

'But the postal box and the second key?'

'Added precautions.'

'No, you wanted to give me plenty of time in case I had to slip away and make a phone call. Chris would have seen me do it. He'd have called and warned you to run.' Hardy seethed. 'So who the hell did you think I'd be working for?'

Saul debated. It was possible Hardy had been approached. On the other hand, Saul didn't know where else to turn. He weighed the possibilities.

And told him.

Hardy looked stunned. For a moment, he didn't seem to understand. Abruptly his face turned red. The veins in his neck bulged. '*What?*' His voice cracked. '*Eliot?* You thought I'd cooperate with that sonofabitch? After what he did to me, you figured I'd help him?'

'We weren't sure. It's been a lot of years. Maybe you'd changed. Sometimes a person forgets to be angry.'

'Forgets? Never! That bastard got me fired! I'd like to get my hands around his throat and –'

'Care to prove it?'

Hardy laughed.

3

Saul finished explaining. Hardy listened, eyes harsh, face even redder, feverish with hate. At last he nodded. 'Sure. He turned against you too. I'm not surprised. He turned against everybody else. The wonder is he took so long.'

'Keep talking.'

'I don't know what –'

'Eliot always said if you want to learn a man's secrets, ask someone who hates him.'

'You know more about him than anybody does.'

'I thought I did. I was wrong. But you were his rival. You investigated him.'

'You heard about that?'

Saul didn't answer.

Hardy turned to the paper bag on the dresser. Yanking out a half-empty bourbon bottle, he twisted off the cap and raised it to his lips. He suddenly stopped, glancing self-consciously. 'I don't suppose you've got a glass.'

'In the bathroom.' Saul took the bottle from him. 'But I've got something else for you to drink.'

'What is it?'

'Get the glass.'

Suspicious, Hardy obeyed. When he came back from the bathroom, his fingers tightened on the glass. He gaped at the bottles Saul had taken from a drawer and swallowed sickly. 'No.'

159

'I need you sober. If you have to drink –'

'Vermouth? Is this a joke?'

'Am I laughing?'

'That's disgusting.'

'Maybe you won't drink so much. In case you get tempted, though . . .' Saul took the whiskey bottles into the bathroom and emptied them down the sink.

Hardy moaned. 'Sixteen bucks they cost me!'

'Here's a twenty. Keep the change.'

'Sadist!'

'Think of it this way. The sooner we're finished, the sooner you can buy more bourbon.' Saul went to the dresser and opened both kinds of vermouth – red and white – pouring them in Hardy's glass. 'In case your stomach's stronger than I thought.'

Hardy scowled at the pink concoction. He reached, drew back his hand, then reached again – and drained the glass in three swallows. Gasping, he clutched the dresser. 'Jesus.'

'You okay?'

'It tastes like Kool-Aid.' Hardy shuddered. 'I'll never forgive you for this.' But he poured another glassful. 'All right, I've got to know. So how'd you find out I investigated him?'

'I didn't.'

'But you said –'

'I had a hunch – given the way you felt about him. But I wasn't sure. I figured if I asked, you might get scared and deny it. So I claimed I already knew, hoping you'd agree.'

'I *have* been down here too long.' Hardy sighed. 'Okay, it's true. But you had me scared for a minute. Nobody should have known. Believe me, I was careful. A job like that, I didn't trust anybody for help. A little digging here, a little there. No obvious pattern. No time I couldn't account for.' Hardy scowled. 'Just my luck, Watergate came along. I wasn't involved in the break-in. But Eliot and I had been rivals quite a while. He convinced the director to dump me. As an example. I can see the logic. Hell, I was – still am – a lush. But I can't shake the feeling he saw it as a chance for a final victory.'

'You think he knew you were investigating him?'

'Obviously not.'

'What makes you sure?'

'He'd have had me killed.'

Saul stared. 'You learned that much?'

'I was close. There was something. I could feel it. Some days I thought all I needed was one more fact. Just one more –' Hardy shrugged. 'But he won. Outside, with no way to continue the investigation, I let the booze control me.' He held up his glass. 'This is really awful.'

'Maybe you'd like some coffee?'

'God, no, that's worse than the vermouth. Retirement.' Hardy brooded. 'You get lazy down here. How was I supposed to finish what I started? I couldn't get at the computers.'

'You wanted to stay alive.'

'Or I deserved to be fired. If I'd had any balls, I'd still have kept after him.' His forehead broke out in sweat. 'It's awful hot.'

Saul crossed the room, turning on the air conditioner beside the drapes. It rattled, sending a musty breeze through the room. 'What made you want to investigate him?'

Hardy sipped in disgust. 'Kim Philby.'

4

Back in 1951, Kim Philby had been a high-ranking member of Britain's foreign intelligence network, MI–6. Earlier, during the Second World War, he'd helped to train the inexperienced recruits of America's fledgling espionage network, the OSS. He'd offered advice when the OSS became the CIA in 1947. He'd come to Washington in 1949 to help the FBI investigate Soviet spy rings, and indeed he'd been responsible for proving that a well-respected British diplomat, Donald Maclean, was a Communist agent. Before Maclean could be arrested, however, Maclean had been alerted by another British diplomat, Guy Burgess, himself an unsuspected Communist agent, who fled with Maclean to Russia.

The revelation of such deep Soviet infiltration shocked the Western intelligence community. Equally disturbing was the mystery of how Burgess had known Maclean was under suspicion. Preoccupied by that question, Hardy, then a junior officer in the CIA, had sat in his car in a Washington parking lot, waiting for a sudden rainstorm to end so he could run to his favorite bar for lunch, when a startling thought occurred to him. Foregoing his thirst, he quickly drove back to his office in one of the Quonset buildings that had crowded the Washington Mall since the war. Throwing his rain-drenched topcoat over a chair in his cubicle, he searched through several files, scribbling notes to document the pattern he suspected.

Burgess had warned Maclean. Burgess knew Philby, the man who accused Maclean. Indeed Burgess had once been a guest in Philby's home. Had Philby made an inadvertent slip, letting Burgess know Maclean was in trouble?

That explanation made no sense. Philby had too much experience to reveal sensitive information to a friend of the man he planned to accuse.

Then what was the connection? Burgess, Maclean, and Philby. Hardy made a drastic leap in logic. What if Philby too was a Communist agent? What if Philby had accused Maclean but first had sent Burgess to warn him?

Why, though? Why would Philby accuse a fellow Communist agent? Hardy could think of only one reason – to protect a more important Communist agent who was close to being uncovered. But who'd be more important than Maclean? Hardy's breathing quickened. Philby himself? By accusing Maclean, Philby would raise

161

himself above suspicion. Perhaps, in his work with the FBI, Philby had discovered he was close to being identified as a spy.

Assumptions, Hardy thought. But where's the proof? He suddenly recalled a Communist defector named Krivitsky who, years before, had warned about three Soviet agents in the British diplomatic corps. Krivitsky had identified one man by his last name, King (subsequently arrested), but Krivitsky had been vague about the other two: a Scotsman attracted to Communism in the thirties, and a British journalist in the Spanish Civil War. The Scotsman had now been identified as Maclean. But who was the British journalist?

Hardy studied the small details in Philby's dossier, almost laughing when he found what he wanted: Philby had once been a journalist – in the Spanish Civil War. Abruptly everything fit. Philby and Burgess had known each other as students at Cambridge. Maclean had also gone to Cambridge. In the thirties, each of them had been sympathetic to communism but then had undergone a drastic change, all at once preferring capitalism, joining the British diplomatic service.

Of course, Hardy thought. They'd been approached by the Russians and agreed to become deep-cover Soviet agents.

5

'That made my reputation,' Hardy said. The sour vermouth tainted his breath. 'People forget I'm the man who unmasked Philby.'

'Some of us know who the legends are,' Saul said.

'Me and Eliot.' Hardy drank. 'The golden boys. Eliot scored his points by using ex-Nazis and ex-Fascists who rebuilt their intelligence networks after the war, this time working for us. It seemed we couldn't do anything wrong.'

'What's his background?'

'He didn't tell you even that much? Boston. His family was in the social register. His father went to Yale, then worked for the State Department. Shortly after Eliot was born in 1915, his father died when the Germans sank the *Lusitania*. His mother died in the 1918 flu epidemic. You understand what I'm saying?'

'Eliot's an orphan?' Saul felt a chill.

'Like you and Chris. Maybe that explains his interest in the two of you.'

'He went to an orphanage?'

'No. He didn't have any grandparents or uncles and aunts. There were some distant relatives who might have taken him in. His inheritance was large enough that supporting him wouldn't have been a problem. But a friend of his father offered to raise him – a man with influence in the State Department. Eliot's relatives agreed. After all, this man could train Eliot as his father would have wanted. The man had wealth and power.'

'Who?'

'Tex Auton.'

Saul's eyes widened.

'That's right,' Hardy said. 'One of the designers of the Abelard sanction. Eliot got his training from Auton, who helped to establish the ground rules for modern espionage. You could say Eliot was there at the start of everything. Of course, before the war, America had no separate intelligence network. The military and the State Department did it all. But after Pearl Harbor, the OSS was formed, and Auton encouraged Eliot to join. Eliot went to England to receive his training. He ran some effective operations in France. He liked the work, so after the war he made the shift when the OSS became the CIA. Auton had retired by then, but Eliot often went to him for advice, and the most important thing Auton told him was not to try for the top positions in the agency.'

'But for an ambitious man, that advice makes no sense.'

'It does if you think about it. How many directors and deputy directors has the agency had over the years? So many I can't remember them. Those positions are political appointments. They change with whoever's in the White House. The real power in the agency – by which I mean the consistent power – lies just below the deputy director and his subordinate: the number four position, nonpolitical, nonappointed, based on merit, on experience within the agency.'

'So Eliot took Auton's advice.'

Hardy nodded. 'He rose as high as he dared. Hell, one president even offered him the directorship, but Eliot turned it down. He wanted to keep his job secure. But he also wanted more power, so he broadened his base, arranging for more and more agents to be responsible to him, spreading his influence into operations in every hemisphere. Chief of counterintelligence. He got that title in 1955, but he had considerable clout even in the forties. Senators, congressmen, presidents, they depend on elections. Eventually they have to leave office. But Eliot never had to worry about elections. Year after year, regardless of whether the Democrats or the Republicans ran the country, Eliot kept the number four slot in the agency. Only one other man ever managed the trick of holding power so long.'

'J. Edgar Hoover.'

'Right. But Hoover's dead now, so it's no exaggeration to say that Eliot's been the most consistent influence in American government since the forties. Mind you, Eliot always faced the danger of another ambitious man coming along to bump him out of his number four position. To give himself an edge, he investigated anyone who might be a threat to him. Presidents, cabinet members, the various directors of the agency, it didn't matter who. Maybe he learned that tactic from Hoover, or maybe Auton taught it to him. But he put together the best-documented collection of scandals you can imagine. Sex, booze, drugs – you name a vice, he found out about it. Tax evasion, conflict of interest, kickbacks, bribery. If someone threatened to take away Eliot's power, Eliot simply showed that person his file, and all threats stopped. That's why he's still in the agency even though he's past the age for retirement. Because of those files.'

163

'Where are they?'

'Anybody's guess. Maybe a bank vault in Geneva. Maybe a locker at the local Y. Impossible to tell. Believe me, people have tried to find them. He's been followed, but he always loses a tail.'

'You still haven't told me why you investigated him.'

Hardy thought about it. 'Another hunch. You remember how Eliot always insisted there were other Communist agents, not just Philby, Burgess, and Maclean, but a lot more, hidden here and in Britain, high in the government? In particular, he felt sure we had a Russian spy in the agency. He used this theory to explain the U-2 incident, the Bay of Pigs disaster, the JFK assassination. Whenever we started a new operation, the Russians seemed to know about it beforehand. Eliot's theory had seemed paranoid. Now it sounded convincing. Everybody in the agency started checking on everybody else. We got so busy looking behind our backs, suspecting each other, no work got done. We never found the spy. It didn't matter. Eliot's theory did as much damage as any spy could have done. In effect, he paralyzed the agency, and that's what started me thinking. Maybe Eliot protested too much. Maybe Eliot himself was the spy, cleverly disrupting the agency by insisting there was a spy. That was Kim Philby's tactic. Accuse someone else, and no one suspects the accuser.'

'You suspected, though.'

Hardy shrugged. 'Let's say I was jealous. We started our careers together. At first, we were equally brilliant. But over the years, he had more successes. He rose higher while I stayed where I was. If things had been different, maybe I could have equaled him.' He raised his glass. 'I guess I wanted to bring him down and in the process pull myself up. I kept remembering my first big success. Maybe I could repeat it – exactly the same. I told you Eliot went to England for his OSS training during the war. We didn't know much about espionage, but the British did. The man in MI-6 who taught him. You'll never guess who he was.'

Saul waited.

Hardy drained his glass. 'Kim Philby.'

6

Saul stopped breathing. '*Eliot's a mole?*'

'I didn't say that.'

'Why the hell mention Philby if you're not accusing –?'

'It's only what I thought. I can make assumptions, but they're meaningless without proof.'

'And you don't have the proof.'

'I told you I never got that far. When Eliot had me sacked, my office was sealed. My apartment, my car, my safety-deposit box were searched. Every scrap of paper even vaguely related to the agency was taken from me.'

'Including your research?'

'I never wrote it down, thank God. If Eliot had seen a file on him, if he thought I was dangerous . . . well, he wouldn't trust a drunk. I'd have had a sudden heart attack or fallen off a building.'

'You remember what you learned?'

Hardy straightened indignantly. 'Of course. I'm not – look, he's a man of habit, so I have to become suspicious when I find variations in his routine. In 1954 – his travel vouchers tell an interesting story – he made several unexplained trips to Europe. For a week in August, he dropped completely out of sight.'

'Vacation?'

'Without leaving an address or a phone number where the agency could reach him in an emergency?'

'I see your point.'

'I can trace him to Belgium. After that . . .' Hardy lit a cigarette, exhaling smoke.

'And no one questioned his disappearance?'

'Not only wasn't it questioned, the next year he got promoted. For all I know, he'd been sent on a mission, and his promotion was a reward for success. All the same, that missing week . . .'

'If he's a mole, he could have been meeting with his KGB control.'

'That suspicion occurred to me. But it's sloppy tradecraft. I can think of too many other less mysterious ways for the KGB to get in touch with him. Why invite attention by having him disappear like that? Whatever the reason for his disappearance, it was obviously necessary – something that couldn't be done any other way.'

Saul frowned. As the air conditioner rattled, he shivered but not from the chill.

'Something else,' Hardy said. 'In 1973, he disappeared again – this time for the last three days in June.'

'To Belgium again?'

'Japan.'

'So what's the connection?'

Hardy shrugged. 'I've no idea what he did on those trips. But I keep going back to my first assumption. Let's say during the war, when he went to England, he joined Philby, Burgess, and Maclean in becoming a Soviet double agent.'

'Or a triple agent.'

'Could be.' Hardy scratched his chin. 'I never thought of that. He could have pretended to go along with Philby, planning to use his relationship with the Soviets to the advantage of the United States. He always liked complexity, and being a triple agent's the most complex role of all. The difference is the same. Whether a double or a triple agent, he'd have been in contact with the KGB. Someone had to pass messages to him, someone so much a part of his routine no one would question if they regularly got in touch with each other, someone with freedom of movement, preferably with European connections.'

'And you found him?'

'Roses.'

'What?'

'As much as complexity, Eliot loves roses. He structures his day around them. He exchanges letters with other enthusiasts. He sends and receives rare varieties.'

Saul felt a jolt. 'And goes to flower shows.'

'In Europe. Particularly a show in London every July. He hasn't missed that show since the first one in '46, right after the war. A perfect meeting place. He always stays with a friend who owns an estate near London . . . Percival Landish Junior.'

Saul inhaled sharply.

'So you recognize the name?' Hardy asked.

'His father represented England's intelligence network at the Abelard meeting in '38.'

'An interesting pattern, don't you think? Auton, who was also at that meeting, became friends with Landish Senior. Eliot – Auton's foster son – became friends with Landish's son. By the way, the senior Landish was Philby's supervisor.'

'Jesus,' Saul repeated.

'So I have to wonder,' Hardy said. 'Was Landish Senior a mole as well? The trouble with believing in a conspiracy is that after a while you can make anything fit your theory. Have I got too much imagination? Let's put it this way. If Eliot works for the Soviets, Landish Junior would be my candidate for the courier passing messages. He's perfect. He occupies the same position in MI-6 that Eliot does in the CIA. Like Eliot, he's been insisting there's a mole in MI-6. If Landish Senior worked for the Soviets, maybe Landish Junior continued the job after his father died.'

'The question is how to prove it.'

7

Erika stopped halfway down the aisle and leaned toward a passenger in a window seat. 'Sir, fasten your seatbelt, please.' She wore an attractive El Al stewardess uniform. Because of the hurried arrangements, she'd been given a limited choice of women for whom she could substitute. Her height, hair color, and facial structure had been similar to a scheduled member of the flight crew. But the woman whom Erika had replaced and who was now driving south from Miami toward Key West on a sudden all-expenses-paid vacation was a bit smaller than Erika, so the uniform fit tightly, emphasizing the contour of her breasts. The males on board looked pleased instead of puzzled.

Continuing down the aisle, she made sure everyone else's seatbelt was fastened. After asking a woman to slide her bulky purse into the space beneath the forward seat, she scanned the passengers. No one was smoking. The seats were locked in their upright position, the food trays folded up and secured. She nodded to another stewardess and walked toward the front, where she turned to survey the passengers again. As much as she could determine, none of them reacted

166

strangely to her. No eyes tensed when she looked at them. No passenger avoided her gaze. Of course, a well-trained operative wouldn't have made those mistakes. All the same, she went through the formality – to fail to do it would have been her own mistake.

She knocked on the cockpit door and opened it. 'Anybody up here want some coffee?'

The pilot turned. 'No, thanks. The ground crew loaded the baggage. We're cleared to taxi.'

'How's the weather look?'

'Couldn't be better. Blue skies all the way,' Saul answered beside her. He and Chris – looking handsome in their pilots' uniforms – carried documents authorizing them to be supervisors on this flight. They sat at the rear of the cockpit, watching the crew, who had no reason to doubt they were what they claimed. With Erika, they'd boarded early, via the private stairs to the service entrance in the passenger tunnel, avoiding surveillance in the terminal. Their credentials had been beautifully forged. Again the Israeli embassy's Misha Pletz had worked his magic.

As the jet backed from the boarding platform, Erika returned to the passengers, double-checking for signs of recognition in anyone's eyes. A man seemed captivated by her figure. A woman looked apprehensive about the takeoff. Passing them, she decided they were nothing to worry about, though now that the jet was in motion it didn't matter if a hit team had come on board. El Al excelled in security precautions. Three of the passengers – at the front, the middle, and rear – were plainclothes airline guards. Beyond the windows, two heavy cars abruptly appeared, flanking the jet as it left the terminal toward the runway. In the cars, she noticed large grim men licensed to carry the automatic weapons they held out of sight – standard protection for this airline so often victimized by terrorists. When the plane touched down in London, two more cars would appear and escort the jet to the terminal. Inside the airport, the El Al section would be discreetly but effectively guarded. Under these conditions, a hit team foolish enough to move against Erika, Saul, and Chris would have to be suicidal.

Her sense of relief passed quickly. As she made sure the food lockers in back were securely locked, she remembered with dismay that she'd have to pass out cocktails and meals, mothering the passengers through the flight.

The senior attendant picked up a microphone. 'Good evening.' Static crackled. 'Welcome to El Al's Flight 755 to –'

8

London. Despite the blue sky forecast, gray drizzly clouds hung over the city. Though burdened by her duties during the flight, Erika had nonetheless found time to consider the implications of what she'd learned.

The story Chris and Saul had told her about the Franklin School for Boys disturbed her. She herself had been raised on an Israeli kibbutz and as a consequence had been conditioned as well. But though like them she was skilled as a soldier and an operative, she sensed a difference.

Granted, she'd been separated from her mother and father and raised by foster parents. Still, the entire community had given her love. Every Israeli was a member of her family. In a country so often attacked that many children lost both their natural and foster parents, grief became bearable if the nation as a whole was the ultimate parent.

But Saul and Chris had been shown no love except by Eliot, a love that had been a lie. Instead of the healthy atmosphere of a kibbutz, they'd endured an austere youth of rigid discipline and deprivation – not for the sake of their country, but instead for the secret motives of the man who claimed to be their benefactor. What kind of mind could have imagined such a plan?

Twisted. Perverted.

Like Saul and Chris, she'd been trained to kill. But she did it for her country, for the survival of her people, and with sadness, grieving for her enemy, whereas Saul and Chris had been purged of distracting emotion, denied their dignity, made into robots at Eliot's command. No noble principle justified what had been done to them.

Now their conditioning had failed. Though Erika enjoyed being reunited with them – especially Saul, for whom an affection she'd thought was dead had been revived as strongly as ever – her principal objective had to be idealistic: to help her country, to repair the damage Eliot had done to Israel when he'd made it seem responsible for killing the president's friend. Saul and Chris, though, had a different motive. Personal, and under the circumstances ironic, because emotional. They'd reached the limit of a lifetime's abuse. They'd been betrayed.

Now they wanted revenge.

9

At the London airport, the three of them passed through a private customs area set aside for airline personnel. The escorts Pletz had arranged to meet them waited inconspicuously on the other side. Avoiding the busy passenger section of the terminal, they left through a rear exit reserved for airport employees, their escorts first checking outside, then forming a phalanx through which Erika, Chris, and Saul stepped out to a bulletproof car. They drove past an airport guard at an open metal gate, then merged with the noisy London-bound traffic.

Chris set his watch for the English time zone. The morning sky was bleak. As dampness crept over him, he glanced out the back and frowned. 'We're being followed.'

'That blue car a hundred yards back?' the driver asked. He studied

168

his rearview mirror, seeing Chris nod. 'It's one of ours. But there's something else bothers me.'

'What's that?'

'The orders we got. From Misha in Washington.'

'What's the problem?'

'I don't get it. We're supposed to make sure you arrive okay, but then we're supposed to scram. It makes no sense. Whatever you're up to, even you three have to need backup. There's got to be a mistake.'

'No, that's what we asked for.'

'But –'

'That's how we want it,' Saul said.

The driver shrugged. 'You're the customer. I was told to get you a flat that's safe. The equipment you wanted's in the trunk. They call that a boot over here. I'll never get used to the way these people talk.'

10

Pretending to settle in, they stopped unpacking their bags the moment the escorts left. Saul glanced at Chris. On signal, they scanned the room. The place was small, more homey than rented rooms in America – doilies, lace curtains, flowers in a vase. Like the car, it smelled of dampness. Though the escorts had vouched for the safety of the place, Saul didn't know if he could trust them. On the one hand, he saw no reason not to. On the other, too many people had become involved, too many chances for further betrayal.

As if they heard his suspicions, Chris and Erika nodded. Since the room might be bugged, they didn't say a word but quickly changed from their uniforms. The men paid no more attention to Erika's nakedness than she did to theirs. In nondescript street clothes, they took apart, tested, and reassembled the weapons the escorts had given them. The other equipment they'd requested functioned perfectly. Leaving nothing behind, they crept down the musty back stairs of the rooming house. In the rear, they crossed a mews toward a maze of alleys, using complex evasion procedures to lose a tail in the London rain. Not even Misha Pletz knew why they'd come to England. Now on their own, they'd become invisible again, their destination undetectable.

Except, Saul thought uneasily. One other person knew – the man who'd supplied the address and description of their target. Strict security would have required silencing Hardy to protect themselves. But how could I justify it? Saul asked himself. Hardy helped. I like the sonofabitch too much.

All the same, he kept repeating. Loose ends bothered him.

They were waiting, and he hadn't thought to take even such an elementary precaution as avoiding his apartment. Of course he'd been drinking heavily, the familiar excuse. Not only had it clouded his judgment. It also had stunned his reflexes, so when he staggered into his apartment and turned to lock the door, he didn't move fast enough from the footsteps charging toward him. Maybe sober he could have yanked the door back open and rushed down the hall, but as adrenaline hit the alcohol in his stomach and made him want to throw up, the man who'd been hiding in the closet twisted his arm, slamming him hard against the wall, spreading his legs in a frisk position.

The second man, darting from the bathroom, pawed along his body, checking his buttocks and privates. 'Snub-nosed thirty-eight. Right ankle,' he told his partner, pocketing the weapon.

'Sofa,' the partner told Hardy.

'Lawn chair,' Hardy told him.

'What the –?'

'You guys practice hard enough, you'll soon get up to verbs.'

'Just do what the hell you're told.'

Hardy's forehead throbbed from its impact against the wall. He sat. His heart skipped a beat, but his mind stayed surprisingly calm, no doubt the effect of a day spent at the corner bar. Indeed since Saul had left, he'd been drinking harder than ever. Despite his determination never to let his drunkenness make him undignified, he'd let his pants become wrinkled, his shoes scuffed. Though he'd begged to go along, Saul had refused. 'You've helped enough.' But Hardy had understood. He thinks I'm too old. He figures he can't depend on a . . .

Lush? Hardy had stupefied himself to forget that Saul now did what he himself – if he'd had any guts – should have done years ago.

The two men were in their early thirties. Hardy smelled their sick-sweet aftershave. He glanced at their all-American anonymous features. Short neat hair and Brooks Brothers suits. He recognized them. Not that he'd seen them before, but in his prime he'd often used their counterparts.

GS–7s. The agency's drones. Their rank made him angry, aggravated by his drunkenness, telling him he wasn't considered dangerous enough for a shakedown by a first-class team. They represented contempt.

He seethed but didn't show it, bourbon making him brave. 'Well, now that we're nice and comfy –'

'Shut your fucking mouth,' the first man said.

'I told you.'

'What?'

'You'd get up to verbs.'

The two drones glanced at each other. 'Make the call,' the first one said. The second picked up the phone, and even through a blur, Hardy noticed he touched eleven digits.

'What? Long distance? I hope to God it's collect.'

'I'm gonna love this,' the second one said and spoke to the phone. 'We've got him. No, it was easy. Sure.' He stared at Hardy. 'Guess what?' He grinned. 'It's for you.'

Reluctant, Hardy took the phone. Though he knew what was coming, he pretended he didn't. 'Hello?'

The voice from the other end was as dry as chalk, as crisp as dead leaves – brittle, ancient, without a soul. 'I trust my associates treated you well.'

'Who –?'

'Come now.' Phlegm obscured the voice. 'No need for games.'

'I said –'

'Very well. I feel like being amused. I'll play along.'

Hardy fumed when he heard the name. 'I hoped I'd never hear from you again, you bloodsucker.'

'Name-calling?' Eliot clicked his tongue. 'What happened to your manners?'

'I lost them with my job, you jack-off.'

'Not at my age.' Eliot laughed. 'I believe you may have had some visitors.'

'You mean apart from Tweedledum and Tweedledee here? Visitors? Who the hell would want to visit me?'

'Two very naughty children.'

'The son and the daughter I'll admit to won't even talk to me.'

'I'm referring to Saul and Chris, of course.'

'Refer all you want. Whatever this is about, I haven't seen them. Even if I had, I'd never tell you.'

'That's the problem, isn't it?'

'No, something else is. What's gone wrong?'

'That's very good. Answer a question with a question. It helps to avoid mistakes.'

'It gives me a pain. I'm hanging up.'

'No, wait. I'm not sure what they told you. They're in trouble.'

'They told me nothing. They weren't here. For God sake, I'm trying to enjoy my retirement. Take your drones. Stay out of my life.'

'You don't understand. It's Chris. He violated the sanction. Saul's helping him escape.'

'So the first thing they do is come to me? Oh, sure. For what? A lot of good I'd be. Against the Russians? Bullshit.' Hardy winced.

'Perhaps you're right. May I speak to one of my associates, please?'

Hardy felt too sick to answer. He handed the phone to number one.

'What is it? Yes, sir, I understand.' He gave the phone back to Hardy.

'You made a mistake,' Eliot said.

'Don't rub it in. I know.'

'I have to admit you were doing quite well before that. Especially considering you're out of practice.'

'Instinct.'

171

'Habit's more reliable. Really, the Russians. Why did you have to mention them? I hoped you'd be a better opponent.'

'Sorry to disappoint you.'

'You wouldn't have mentioned the Russians unless you knew they claimed the violation. Apart from our differences, I was right to have you fired. Sloppy tradecraft. When you're interrogated, you ought to know you never volunteer information, no matter how seemingly irrelevant.'

'I don't need a lecture, for Christ's sake. How'd you know they'd come to me?'

'I didn't. Actually – no offense – I thought of you only this morning. After I'd tried all their other contacts. You were my last resort.'

That insult may have been why Hardy made his choice.

Number two put a briefcase on the coffee table. Opening it, he took out a hypodermic and a vial of liquid.

'I'm surprised they didn't use the chemicals sooner,' Hardy said.

'I wanted to talk to you first. To reminisce.'

'To gloat, you mean.'

'I don't have time for this. It's my turn now. Hang up.'

'No, wait. There's something I want you to hear.' Hardy turned to number one. 'In that cabinet.' It was plastic-coated plywood, from the K-Mart. 'Excuse the expression. There's a shot left in a fifth of Jim Beam. Would you bring it to me?'

The drone looked uncertain.

'For God's sake, I'm thirsty.'

'Lush.' Lips curled, the drone opened the cabinet and gave him the bottle.

Hardy stared at it. As if caressing a woman he loved, he slowly turned the cap. He swallowed the inch of liquid, savoring its wonder. On balance, it was the only thing he'd miss. 'Still listening?'

'What was that about?'

'Hang on.'

I'm seventy-two, he thought. My liver's a miracle. It should have killed me long ago, I'm a goddamn remnant, a fossil. Thirty minutes after the chemicals had been administered, he knew he'd have told the drones everything Eliot wanted. Saul and Chris would be killed. Eliot would have won again.

The sonofabitch kept winning.

Not anymore.

A lush? Saul wouldn't take me along because he couldn't depend on me. Eliot sent two drones because he didn't respect me.

'I've got a confession to make,' Hardy said.

'We'll still use the chemicals.'

'It doesn't matter. You're right. Saul came to see me. He asked questions. I gave answers. I know where he is. I want you to understand that.'

'Why so direct? You know I won't make a deal.'

'You'll have me killed?'

'I'll make it as pleasant as possible. Alcohol poisoning. I doubt you'll mind.'

'Keep listening.'

He set the phone on the coffee table and glanced beyond the drones toward the window. He weighed 220 pounds. In his youth, he'd been a tackle on Yale's football team. With a wail, he surged from the sofa, ramming past them, charging toward the window. For an instant, he feared the closed blinds would hold him back, but he should have expected they were as cheap as everything else in this goddamn cracker-box.

His head struck the window, shattering the glass. But his girth jammed in the window frame, his stomach sinking on jagged shards. He moaned, but not from pain, instead because the drones were grabbing his feet, straining to pull him back. He kicked, struggling, hearing the blinds rattle as the shards rammed deeper into his stomach. Desperately, tilting forward, he wrenched his feet away and suddenly hurtled bleeding into space. More glass went with him, glinting from the sun. He saw it vividly, feeling suspended. Gravity insisted. Plummeting, he left the splinters above.

Objects fall at an equal rate, provided their mass is the same. But Hardy had a great deal of mass. Faster than the shards of glass, he swooped toward the sidewalk, praying he wouldn't land on someone. Fifteen stories. The drop made his stomach swell. Toward his testicles. After all, he was upside down. Before he hit, he blacked out. But a witness later said his body exhaled on impact.

Almost as if he laughed.

12

The estate was huge. Saul crouched in the dark on a wooded bluff, peering down a murky slope toward the lights of the English manor house below him. Three stories high, its rectangular shape made it seem even higher. Long and narrow, it had a large middle section flanked by smaller wings to the right and left. Its clean straight lines were broken only by the row of dormer windows projecting from the slight slope in the roof and by the confusing array of protruding chimneys, stark against the rising moon.

Saul aimed a nightscope toward the wall enclosing the estate. In its earliest form, a nightscope had been based on the principle of projecting an infrared beam to illuminate the dark. This beam, invisible to the unaided eye, could be easily detected through special lenses in the scope. The device worked well, though the objects it revealed were necessarily tinted red. Nonetheless it did have a crucial drawback. After all, an enemy using the same kind of scope could detect the infrared beam from your own. In effect, you'd advertised yourself as a target.

A better principle was obviously needed, and during the late sixties, in response to the escalated fighting in Vietnam, an undetectable nightscope was finally invented. Known by the trade name Starlite, it illuminated the dark by magnifying whatever minuscule light source, such as the stars, was available. Since it projected no beam, it couldn't draw attention to the person using it. In the seventies, the scope had become commercially available, mostly in sporting goods stores. There'd been no difficulty in obtaining this one.

Saul didn't use it to study the manor, however, because the lights from the windows would have been so magnified they'd stab his eyes. But the wall was in darkness, and he saw it clearly. It seemed to be twelve feet high. He focused on its weathered rocks, its vivid chinks of ancient mortar.

But something about it troubled him. He felt as if he'd knelt here before and studied the wall. Struggling with recollection, he finally understood. The estate in Virginia. Andrew Sage and the Paradigm group. The beginning of the nightmare. At once he corrected himself, for the wall down there reminded him of someplace else, the orphanage, and that was where the nightmare had really started. With eerie vividness, he imagined Chris and himself sneaking over the wall. In particular, he recalled the night . . .

The screech of crickets stopped. The forest became unnervingly quiet. As his skin prickled, he sank to the ground, drawing his knife, his dark clothes blending with the gloom. Controlling his breath, he kept his face down, straining to listen.

A bird sang, paused, then repeated its cadence. Exhaling, Saul rose to a crouch. Still cautious, he huddled against an oak, pursed his lips, and mimicked the song of the bird.

Directly, Chris stepped from the dark. A second figure emerged like the rustle of wind through bushes. Erika. She glanced back down the slope, then crouched beside Saul and Chris.

'The security's primitive.' Chris kept his voice low.

'I agree,' Erika added. She and Chris had separated down the slope, checking the estate's perimeter. 'The wall's not high enough. There ought to be closed-circuit cameras. There's no electrified fence at the top.'

'You sound like that disappoints you,' Saul said.

'It bothers me,' she answered. 'England's in a recession. Its lower class resents its upper class. I'd be frantic for security if I were Landish. Given his position in MI-6, he ought to know how to protect his estate.'

'Unless he wants to make it seem there's nothing to protect,' Chris said.

'Or hide,' she added.

'You think the security's not as primitive as it seems?'

'I don't know what to think. And you?' She turned to Saul.

'I scanned the grounds,' he said. 'I saw no guards, though there must be some in the mansion. We were right, though.'

'Dogs?'

Saul nodded. 'Three of them. Maybe others I didn't see. They're roaming freely.'

174

'Breed?'

'All Dobermans.'

'The marines would feel at home,' Chris said. 'Thank God, it isn't shepherds or standard poodles.'

'You want to forget about it?'

'Hell, no,' Erika said.

The two men smiled.

'Then let's do it. We were worried about timing – how to get our hands on him. He might have solved the problem for us. Take a look.' Saul pointed toward the rear of the manor. 'See the greenhouse?'

'The lights are on.'

The long glass structure glinted in the night.

'Like Eliot, he worships roses. Would he let a servant in there? Or a guard? In his holy of holies? I don't think so. Only the high priest enters the sanctum.'

'Maybe he's showing his roses to guests,' Chris said.

'And maybe not. Just one way to tell.'

Again the two men smiled at each other.

13

They crept down the slope through the mist and bracken toward the rear of the estate. Clouds drifted across the moon. The night was chilly and damp. Chris braced his hands against the wall and bent a knee so Erika could climb to his shoulders, grip the top of the wall, and pull herself up. Saul went up next, climbing to Chris's shoulders, but when he clutched the top, he dangled, allowing Chris to use his body as a ladder. At the top, Chris and Erika helped Saul squirm beside them.

Flat, they scanned the estate. Lights gleamed. Below them, dark objects loomed.

Chris raised a tiny cylinder to his lips and blew. Though the night stayed quiet, Saul imagined the ultrasonic tone. The dogs would hear it, though. But what if they'd been trained to ignore its appeal?

They weren't. The massive Dobermans came with such deceptive softness Saul would never have heard them if he hadn't been prepared. Their paws didn't seem to touch the grass. Their dark shapes streaked through the night, abruptly materializing at the bottom of the wall. Even then, Saul wasn't sure he saw them till their white teeth suddenly glinted, flashing savagely. Despite their obscene sneers, they didn't growl.

They couldn't, Saul realized. Their vocal cords had been cut. A dog that barked was useless for protection. Growls alerted an intruder and gave him a chance to defend himself. These Dobermans weren't intended to be a burglar alarm. They served one purpose only – to surprise an intruder.

And kill him.

Erika reached in a knapsack. Pulling out a fist-sized canister, she twisted its top and dropped it among the dogs.

The canister hissed. The dogs attacked it. Suddenly backing off, they blinked in confusion, then slumped unconscious.

Saul held his breath as he squirmed off the wall and dropped to the grass, rolling in a parachutist's pose. Retreating from the fumes toward the cover of a hedge, he waited for Chris and Erika. In the moonlight, he studied the lawn before the house. Shrubs had been trimmed to form geometric shapes: pyramids, globes, and cubes, their shadows grotesque. 'Over there.' Saul pointed.

Chris nodded at a tree, whispering, 'I see the glow. An electric eye.'

'There'll be others.'

'But the dogs had the run of the grounds,' Chris whispered. 'They'd have passed through the lights and triggered the alarms.'

'The lights must be higher than the dogs.'

Saul sank to his stomach on the dew-wet grass, crawling forward, squeezing beneath the almost invisible beam of the electric eye.

The greenhouse gleamed before him, gemlike. More spectacular were the roses, their various sizes, their brilliant colors. He watched a lean, stooped, white-coated figure walk among them, recognizing Landish from Hardy's description, especially the shrunken face. 'He looks mummified,' Hardy had said. 'It's like he's dead, but his hair's long as if it kept growing.'

Saul crept to the greenhouse, waiting while Chris and Erika slipped behind bushes, one on each side of the path between the manor and the greenhouse, on guard for anyone coming. He stood and walked inside.

14

The lights hurt his eyes.

The roses smelled oversweet, cloying.

Landish stood at a table, his back to Saul, mixing seed in trays of sand. He heard the door and turned, but he must have guessed it was a servant because his movement was calm. Only when he saw who'd entered did he react, stepping back against the table, his mouth open in surprise.

Saul was ten feet away. That close, Landish looked ill, his pinched skin waxy, jaundiced. Even so, as his shock diminished, his sunken eyes gleamed. 'I wasn't expecting company.' His voice sounded frail, but his British accent made it seem urbane.

Saul aimed his pistol. 'Don't move. Keep your hands and feet where I can see them.'

'You're surely not frightened of an old man harming you.'

'I'm more concerned about this.' Saul pointed toward a wire leading up beneath a grafting table. He stepped across, took pliers from his pocket, and snipped the wire. Feeling under the table, he yanked an alarm button free.

'My compliments.' Landish bowed slightly. 'If you're a burglar, I have to tell you I carry no money. Of course, you'll find silverware and crystal in the house.'

Saul shook his head.

'You intend to kidnap me for ransom?'

'No.'

'Since you don't have the lunatic's glare of a terrorist, I confess to –'

'Information. I don't have time. I'll ask you once.'

'Who are you?'

Saul ignored the question. 'We debated using chemicals.'

'*We?*'

'But you're too old. The strain. We thought you might die.'

'Considerate.'

'We discussed torture. The problem's the same. You could die before you told us what we want.'

'Why go to such extremes? Perhaps I'll tell you freely.'

'Hardly. Anyway, we wouldn't know if you told the truth.' Saul lifted a pair of shears from a bench. 'We finally agreed on the way to persuade you.' He crossed to a bed of roses, glanced at their first-prize ribbons, and snipped the stem off an exquisite dwarf Yellow Princess.

Landish groaned, swaying off balance. 'That rose was –'

'Priceless. Sure. But not irreplaceable. You've still got four others. On the other hand, this scarlet Tear Drop over here is rarer.'

'No!'

Saul clipped it, watching the bloom fall on a plaque it had won.

Landish clutched a table. 'Have you lost your mind? Don't you realize what –?'

'I'm killing your children. This pink Aphrodite here. Beautiful. Truly. How long does it take to grow it to perfection? Two years? Five?' Saul hacked the bloom in half, its petals tumbling over a trophy.

Landish clutched his chest. His eyes bulged in horror.

'I told you I'd ask only once. Eliot.'

Landish gaped at the ruined petals, swallowing tears. 'What about him?'

'He works for the Soviets.'

'*What are you talking about?*'

Saul slashed at a Gift from God, its purple theoretically impossible. Landish shrieked. 'No more!'

'He's a mole, and you're their courier.'

'No! Yes! I don't know!'

'What the hell does *that* mean?'

'I delivered messages. It's true. But that was ten years ago. I'm not sure he was a mole.'

'Then why did the KGB get in touch with him?'

'I haven't any –'

Saul stepped toward the masterpiece of Landish's collection. A Harbinger of Joy. Incredibly it was blue. 'Eliot was wrong. When I saw him in Denver, he told me no rose has ever been blue.'

177

'Don't!'

Saul raised the snips, pausing with the stem between the blades. The lights glinted off their edges. 'If he wasn't a mole, what was he? What was in the messages?'

'I didn't read them.'

Saul squeezed the blades against the stem.

'It's the truth!'

'Since when is MI–6 the delivery boy for the CIA?'

'I did it as a favor to Eliot!' Landish glanced back and forth from the mutilated roses to Saul, swallowing nervously. 'I swear! He asked me to mediate!'

'Keep your voice down.'

Landish shuddered. 'Listen to me. Eliot said the messages identified a spy in the agency.' His voice was strained. 'But the informant was nervous and insisted on a courier he trusted. Since I knew the courier, I was the logical choice to act as relay.'

'You believed this?'

'He's my friend.' Landish gestured frantically. 'Our networks often cooperate. If you want to know what was in the messages, ask the man who gave them to me.'

'Sure. Just hop on a plane to Moscow.'

'No. Much closer.'

'Where?'

'In Paris. He works for the Soviet embassy there.'

'You're lying.' Saul clipped a leaf.

'I'm not! Don't you understand how delicate that rose is? Even injuring a leaf can –!'

'Then you'd better convince me you're telling the truth because I'm about to cut off another one.'

'It's the only rose like that in the world.'

Saul poised the shears.

'Victor Petrovich Kochubey.'

'A name means nothing.'

'He's their cultural attaché. He arranges tours for Soviet orchestras and dance troupes throughout France. He's also a master violinist. Sometimes he plays at the concerts. Sometimes he goes on tours by himself.'

'But of course he's KGB.'

Landish spread his hands. 'He disclaims them. Fifteen years ago he was captured attempting to defect to the West. It was clear he'd try again. As a compromise, the Soviets allowed him to live in Paris, provided he used his talents for the good of the Motherland. They reminded him his children would stay in Moscow, where their excellent jobs and living conditions depended on his cooperation.'

'That doesn't answer my question. Is he KGB?'

'Of course. His attempt to defect was a sham. But it served his purpose. His cover's excellent.'

'And I'll bet you attend a lot of concerts.'

'Not so much anymore.' Landish shrugged but still glanced nervously at his roses. 'Ten years ago, however . . . it wasn't difficult to meet privately with him. While discussing the fine points of Russian music, he passed me messages. On occasion, I gave him one. But they were sealed. I never read them. If you want to know what was in them, you'll have to speak with Kochubey.'

Aiming the shears at the pale blue rose, Saul studied him.

'I've told you all I know.' Landish sounded sad. 'I realize you have to kill me to stop me from warning him. But I beg you not to destroy another rose.'

'Suppose you're lying? What if your information's worthless?'

'How can I offer guarantees?'

'You can't, and if you're dead, I can't get revenge. What use would destroying more roses be? A corpse wouldn't care.'

'Then we've reached an impasse.'

'No. You're coming with me. If I find out you've lied, you'll see what gasoline and a match can do to this greenhouse. Think about it as we go. In case you want to change your story.'

'You'll never get me past the guards at the gate.'

'I won't have to. We'll leave the way I came in. Over the wall.'

Landish scoffed. 'Do I look like an athlete?'

'Then we'll lift you.'

'I'm too brittle. My arms and legs would break.'

'All right, no lifting.'

'How then? It's impossible.'

Saul pointed toward the rear of the greenhouse. 'Simple.'

'What?'

'We'll use that ladder.'

15

Curtains billowed at the open window. Chris squinted toward the bullet-gray sky, his nostrils flaring from the salty air, his shoulders hunched from the damp. An angry wind chased waves across the Channel. He sounded troubled. 'I'll take your place.'

'I told you no,' Saul said. 'We agreed. One of us has to stay here with Landish while the other two get Kochubey. We cut cards to decide who took the risk. You won with the lowest card. You stay.'

'But I don't want to.'

'All of a sudden you feel like being a hero?'

'No. Of course not.'

'Then what is it? I can't believe it's just because you want to go with Erika.' Saul turned to where she had tied Landish to a chair. 'No offense. You've got a wonderful sense of humor.'

She stuck out her tongue.

He turned back to Chris. 'What's wrong?'

'It's crazy.' Chris shook his head, confused. 'It's this feeling I've got. I know it means nothing. The trouble is I can't get rid of it.'

'What's it about?'

179

Chris walked from the window. 'You. I've got this sense, this . . . call it a premonition. Something's going to happen to you.'

Saul studied him. Neither he nor Chris was superstitious. They couldn't afford to be. Otherwise they'd look for omens everywhere and as a consequence become paralyzed. Logic and skill were what they depended on. Even so, they'd each had experiences in Nam that made them respect 'funny' feelings – buddies due to be sent back home who wrote letters to wives or girlfriends or mothers and gave them to teammates, saying, 'Make sure she gets this. I won't make it.' And the day before they left, they got a bullet through the head. Or other teammates due to go out on a routine surveillance mission, a piece of cake, they'd done it a hundred times, but this time they said, 'I won't be seeing you.' And they stepped on a mine.

Saul thought a moment. 'When did it start?'

'At Landish's estate.'

'When you saw the wall?'

Chris nodded. 'How did you know?'

'Because I had a similar feeling.'

'*What?*'

'I was sure I'd been there before. It took me a while, but I figured it out. The wall. Don't you get it? The same kind of wall we had at Franklin. Remember how we used to sneak over to bring in candy? The night we got beat up? Or the night I slipped on the ice, and you jumped down to help me, but you cracked your head? The streetcar? Remember?'

'You pulled me away and saved my life.'

'That explains it. Both of us must have been reminded of that night. At Landish's estate, I got worried about you. I started thinking you were in trouble and I'd have to save you. The same thought happened to you, except reversed. Maybe you've always wanted to save *my* life.'

'I have.' Chris grinned. 'A couple of times.'

'But the wall made you want to do it again. Relax. Something's going to happen for sure. I'm going to Paris with Erika and get my hands on Kochubey. That's what'll happen.'

'I want to believe that.'

'Think of it this way. If I got in trouble, what could you do that Erika couldn't?'

She came over. 'Be careful how you answer.'

'And think about this,' Saul said. 'Suppose I let you go instead of me. Suppose something happened to you. I'd blame myself as much as *you* would if something happened to me. This second-guessing is useless. We made a bargain. You drew the lowest card. You got the easy job. You stay.'

Chris hesitated.

'And as for your premonition, it and a load of manure'll fertilize a garden.' Saul turned to Erika. 'Ready?'

'Paris with a handsome escort? You've got to be kidding.'

Chris wasn't satisfied. 'It's almost ten. You ought to be in Paris this evening. Phone me at six and every four hours after that. Don't pick

180

up Kochubey till you talk with me. As Landish thinks more about his roses, he might decide he gave the wrong information.'

'I told the truth,' Landish insisted from the chair.

'Just keep your mind on the only blue rose in the world.'

The moment arrived. Unable to put it off, they shook hands and grinned self-consciously.

Saul picked up his bag. 'Don't worry. I'll be careful. I want to make sure I'm around to pay back –' His eyes flashed.

'And I'll take care of your brother for you,' Erika said. 'For both of us.' She kissed Chris on the cheek.

His heart felt swollen. He meant what he said. 'Good luck.'

Uncertainly they parted. Troubled, Chris watched from the open door, his throat tight as they got in the rented Austin, his brother and sister, and drove down the weed-covered lane, disappearing past the hedge-lined road.

When he couldn't hear the Austin's motor any longer, he stared at the rocks in the pasture, at last stepped in and closed the door.

'They'll be looking for me,' Landish said.

'But they won't know where to hunt. We're sixty miles from your estate. But London's between, and that's where they'll guess we've gone.'

Landish cocked his head. 'This cottage must be on a cliff. I hear surf below us.'

'Dover. I rented this place for a week, I told the realtor I needed a quiet vacation. This was perfect, he said. The nearest cottage is a half mile away. If you scream, no one'll hear you.'

'Does my voice sound as if I'm strong enough to scream?'

'I'll try to make you comfortable. So you don't get bored, we'll talk about roses.' Chris clenched his teeth. 'If anything happens to Saul . . .'

16

They'd chosen Dover because it provided easy access by water to France. In a busy terminal that reminded Saul of an airport, he and Erika bought tickets separately and boarded the Hovercraft several minutes apart.

Uneasy, he went to a lounge in the stern, hoping to blend with the crowd. He knew that MI-6 and other intelligence agencies kept the Hovercraft under surveillance the same as they did major airports and railway stations. Of course, in theory no enemies knew he'd left the United States. With the hunt against him concentrated in America, he had a good chance of not being recognized.

All the same, he didn't feel reassured. If someone spotted him, there wasn't room on board to run or hide. He'd have to fight, but even if he survived, he'd surely be killed by backup teams waiting for him to arrive in France. With no other choice, he'd have to yank open an emergency hatch and leap out into the Channel. If the undertow didn't suck him to his death, the cold rough water would soon exhaust him, draining his heat till he died from exposure.

It never came to that. The Hovercraft roared above the waves, crossing to Calais in twenty-two minutes. He felt it tilt as it rose from the water up a concrete ramp to the terminal. Stepping off, he merged with the other passengers. Though he hadn't spoken French in years, he understood most of what he read and heard. No one seemed to be watching for him. Customs was uneventful. But he'd left his handgun with Chris so he could get through customs, and he wouldn't relax till he replaced it.

He joined Erika at a seaside café they'd agreed on. They went at once to a black market munitions dealer Saul had worked with in '74, where they were overcharged a mere 200 percent for the equipment they needed. 'A favor,' the dealer said. 'For a friend.' Renting a car, they began the southeast drive to Paris 130 miles away.

17

'No,' Chris said into the phone. 'We've talked about roses till the thought of them makes me sick, but Landish still claims it's the truth.'

'Then we'll grab Kochubey tonight.' Saul's voice was distorted by long-distance static.

'You've got it set up?'

'With help from Erika's connections.'

'Hang on.' Chris stared at Landish tied to the chair. 'Last chance. If anything goes wrong, you know the price.'

'How many times do I have to tell you? He gave me the messages.'

'All right,' Chris told Saul. 'Pick him up. But phone me as soon as you've gone to ground with him.'

'Near dawn.'

'Don't worry about waking me. Till you're safe, I won't be able to sleep.'

'Still got that feeling?'

'Worse than ever.'

'It's a walk-through. He'll be easy.'

'For God's sake, don't get overconfident.'

'I'm only trying to reassure you. Hold it. Erika wants to tell you something.'

Interference crackled. Erika teased him. 'We're having a wonderful time. The food's unbelievable.'

'Spare me the gory details. I just had a peanut butter sandwich.'

'How's your roommate?'

'Swell. When we're not talking about his stupid roses, I deal solitaire for him. His arms are tied, so he has to tell me which cards to turn over.'

'Does he cheat?'

'No, I do.'

She laughed. 'I'd better run. What I wanted to say was not to worry.

Everything's going smoothly. I'll take care of Saul. Depend on it.'

'And don't forget yourself, huh.'

'Never. See you tomorrow.'

Aching with affection for both of them, he heard the click as she broke the connection. The doorstep creaked as he set down the phone.

18

He froze.

He'd locked the doors. The shutters were closed. No light showed to attract a stranger all the way here from the road in the dark. If someone who knew the cottage had come to welcome him, he'd have knocked instead of sneaking up.

They'd found him. He didn't know how. He couldn't think. No time. Grabbing the radio transmitter off the table, he dove to the floor and pressed a button.

Shockwaves made him wince. Explosions roared around the cottage, shaking its walls. He'd planted the charges at strategic spots of cover where someone creeping up would be likely to hide. He'd made sure the bombs were good and dirty, lots of noise and shrapnel, plenty of smoke and flames. Arranging them had been a force of habit, an obedience to Eliot's rule – no matter how safe you think you are, there's always something more you can do to protect yourself.

He drew his Mauser. A projectile blew a hole in the door. A tear gas canister thumped on the carpet, rolling, hissing. He coughed from the thick white fumes, shooting at the door, knowing what would happen next. As soon as the gas filled the room, the door would be shattered, men would burst in.

He swung to a window, freed its lock, and raised it, pushing the shutter. The night was filled with smoke and flames. A man thrashed on the ground, screaming from the agony of his burning clothes. Another man saw the movement of the shutter. As he turned to aim, Chris shot him twice in the chest.

The front door blew apart.

Chris spun toward Landish, aiming, unable to see him in the white gas filling the room. He heard a heavy thump as if Landish had toppled his chair, seeking cover. Footsteps charged up the outside steps. Again no time. He leapt from the window, running as he struck the ground. Angry voices filled the cottage. Charging through the dark, along the cliff top, away from the flames, he imagined the hit team in gas masks searching the cottage, discovering the open window. But by then he'd be far away. In the dark, they wouldn't know which way he'd gone. They'd never find him.

He raced harder, clutching the Mauser, blinking from sweat. Away from the flames, he felt released, sprinting wildly through the night.

Landish'll tell where Saul is. Got to warn him.

Then he heard it. Behind him.

Closer, faster, louder.

Footsteps. Someone was chasing him.

19

'Untie my hands,' Landish blurted. The tear gas made him cough.

A grim-lipped man in black applied a treated cloth to Landish's eyes. Another tugged at the ropes.

The windows had been opened, the shutters unlatched. A sea-breeze wafted the gas from the room.

Landish stumbled to a table, grabbing the phone. He dialed impatiently. Crucial seconds passed. He told the operator the number in Falls Church, Virginia. Trembling he clutched the table for balance, unconsciously fingering the five-inch strip of aluminum attached to the back of his belt. The strip was magnetically coded. As soon as his guards had discovered his disappearance, they'd have activated an emergency procedure, using electronic sensors to trace the code on the metal strip. On land, the sensors worked only for a limited distance, blocked by obstacles and the curve of the earth. But from a satellite or a surveillance plane – both of which MI-6 had in readiness – they were as effective as any other high-altitude scanning device. Twelve hours after Landish had been abducted, his security force would have known where his captors held him prisoner. The rest of the time would then have been devoted to setting up the rescue.

Landish felt the room swirl, hyperventilating. The phone buzzed. It kept buzzing, making him cringe. But someone finally answered.

'Eliot,' Landish demanded, fearing he might not be available. 'Seventeen plus three.'

The man's gruff voice became alert. 'I'll put you through.'

In seconds that seemed like minutes, Eliot answered.

'I've found your Black Princes,' Landish said.

'Where?'

'They were at my home.'

'Dear God.'

'A woman's with them.'

'Yes, I know. What happened?'

'They abducted me.' Landish told him everything. 'Remus escaped. We're hunting him. Romulus and the woman have gone to Paris.'

'Why?'

Landish told him.

'Kochubey? But he's KGB.'

'That worries you.'

'The opposite. Remus killed a Russian at the Abelard house in Bangkok. They put out a contract on him. We don't have to get involved. They'll owe me a favor for telling them how to get the man who helped him.'

184

Chris's opponent gained on him. The rocks along the top of the cliff made running difficult. In the dark, Chris couldn't see where he was going. He felt tempted to spin and shoot, but the night would obscure his target. Worse, his muzzle flash would make him a target, and the noise from the shot would attract the others.

His chest burned. His heart pounded. But the fierce, steady, urgent breath of his pursuer surged even closer. He strained his legs to their maximum, muscles aching. Sweat soaked his clothes. The rapidly approaching footfalls warned of imminent contact.

Through blurry vision, he noticed a patch of white ahead. It sloped to his right toward the cliff. A darker spot in its middle became a trough. The white was chalk.

A niche.

He dove to it, rolling, absorbing the impact along his shoulders and hips. Scuttling down, he grabbed outcrops, scrambling. The trough became steeper. Instead of sloping, it veered straight down, an indentation like a three-sided airshaft, its craggy sides providing hand-and-footholds.

Clambering, he heard the scrape of his hunter's shoes on the rocks above him. Shards of chalk cascaded over him, cracking his shoulders and scalp. His hands bled as he scurried lower.

If I can reach the bottom, he prayed. Wind tugged his hair. The surf on the beach roared louder as he neared it.

Slipping, he almost fell, but he wedged his shoes against a ridge. Squirming over it, he reached a slope, stumbling down to the stony beach. A five-foot slab of chalk provided cover. Fumbling in his pocket, he grabbed the silencer for the Mauser, screwing it on the barrel. Spreading his legs for balance, he aimed his right arm stiffly, raising his left hand to support it.

There. A shadow moved down the niche. He shot. The pounding surf obscured both the silencer's spit and the bullet's impact. He couldn't be sure he'd struck the shadow. In the dark, he couldn't aim properly, couldn't line up his front and rear sights. He shot above and below where he'd seen the shadow.

Move. If he stayed behind this chalk slab any longer, he'd give his hunter time to calculate his position. Hunched, he ran to another slab, then another, rushing farther along the beach away from the cottage. Behind him, the night glowed from the flames on top of the cliff. The thundering surf made it useless for him to listen to anyone racing toward him. He turned, moving backward, studying the now distant niche.

Unable to see it anymore, he assumed his hunter couldn't see him either. Swinging forward, he ran again. The beach was like a tunnel, whitecaps crashing on the right, the chalk cliff stretching on the left. But far ahead, at the tunnel's end, he saw the pinpoint lights of a village. He raced harder.

If he could steal a car . . .

The cliff angled lower, sometimes an incline more than a precipice. When the bullet singed his hair, he dove in surprise to the rocks. The shot had come from the dark ahead of him, a silencer muffling both the sound and the muzzle flash, aided by the surf and the gloom.

He silently cursed. His hunter had never climbed all the way down the niche back there. Realizing the trap Chris would prepare, the man had crawled back up to run along the cliff top. Knowing Chris would eventually hurry along the beach away from the cottage, he'd hoped to find another way down, get ahead of Chris, and intercept him.

Trapped.

I can't go back. They must be searching that end of the beach now. They'll split up, heading both ways along the top and bottom of the cliff. Eventually they'll get this far.

Outflanked.

The sea and the cliff on either side. Ahead and behind him . . .

Something moved. In front of him to the left against the cliff, its pale white Chris's only advantage, providing a screenlike background against which a shadow scurried.

Flat on the rocks, he swung his aim with the shadow, tracking it. The moment he shot, he rolled. A bullet struck the rocks beside him, so close even the surf couldn't obscure its brittle crack as it ricocheted toward the sea.

He rolled again, frantic to keep his gaze toward the cliff, and this time when a bullet whacked the rocks, splinters slicing his thigh – the sharp hot pain irrelevant – he saw his target clearly, a hunkered figure sprinting closer, dropping to one knee, aiming.

Chris fired sooner, excited as the shadow lurched off balance. Despite the surf, he thought he heard a wail. He couldn't stay down here, stalking and dodging till the others found him. Now, in the few seconds given to him, he had to take his chance, charging to his feet, sprinting across the stones. He saw the man – in black, his left arm wounded, fumbling for something among the rocks.

Chris stopped and aimed. He pulled the trigger.

Nothing happened. The Mauser held eight rounds.

He'd shot them all.

His stomach scalding, he rushed ahead, dropping the Mauser, drawing his knife from the sheath up the left sleeve of his jacket.

The man saw him coming, gave up groping for his handgun, rose, and drew his own knife.

21

Amateurs hold a knife with the blade pointed down from the bottom of the fist, the thumb curled around the top of the handle. In that position, the knife must be raised to shoulder level, the blow delivered downward. That takes time. It's awkward.

Street gangs hold a knife with the blade protruding from the top of the fist, above the thumb. This position permits a variety of blows delivered from waist level, angled up or down or to each side. The common stance is similar to a fencer's – one arm held sideways for balance while the other arm slashes and parries. The tactic is graceful, dancelike, dependent on rapid lunges, quick retreats, and speedy footwork. It's effective against an amateur or a member of another street gang. Against a world-class killer, though, it's laughable.

Professionals hold a knife as street gangs do – the blade at the top of the fist – but there the similarity ends. Instead of dancing, they stand flatfooted, legs spread apart for balance, knees bent slightly, body crouched. They raise their free arm, bending it at the elbow, extending it across the chest, as if holding an invisible shield. The arm itself is the shield, however, the wrist turned inward to protect its major arteries. The other arm, holding the knife, doesn't slash straight ahead or sideways. It jabs up on an angle, ignoring the opponent's stomach and chest – a stomach wound might not be lethal; ribs protect the heart – aiming toward the eyes and the throat.

Chris braced himself in the position, startled when his enemy did the same. He'd learned to fight this way at Andre Rothberg's killer-instinct school in Israel. The method was unique. The only way his opponent could have learned it was by going to that school.

The implication filled him with dismay. Had Landish too sent private warriors to Rothberg? Why? How else were Landish and Eliot connected? What else were they involved in?

He jabbed with his knife. His enemy blocked the blow with his arm, sustaining a wound, ignoring it, jabbing toward Chris, who felt the blow pierce the back of his wrist. The sharp blade stung, blood spurting. If there'd been time, Chris would have wrapped his jacket around his defensive arm, but since he hadn't been able to, he was fully prepared to accept extensive damage. A mangled arm meant nothing compared to survival.

Again he jabbed. Again his opponent used his arm to block the thrust, taking another cut. The arm was crimson, its sliced tissue parting. In turn, Chris blocked a jab, the blade so keen he hardly felt the shredding impact on his arm.

A stand-off, each man's reflexes equal to the other's. Flat-footed, crouched, Chris began to circle his enemy, cautious, slow, searching for weakness. His enemy pivoted to continue facing him. Chris hoped to force the man to stay in the middle of the circle. On the perimeter's wide loop, Chris wouldn't get dizzy as fast as the man who turned constantly at the center.

But the man understood what Chris intended. Matching Chris's tactic, he began his own wide circle, their orbits intersecting, almost a figure eight.

Another stalemate, both men equally matched. When Chris had received his martial arts training, Ishiguro had said, 'The way of the samurai is death. In a fifty-fifty life-or-death crisis, simply approach the crisis, prepared to die if necessary. There is nothing complicated about it. Merely brace yourself and proceed.'

Chris did so now. Rejecting self-concern, he concentrated solely on the ritual. Jab and block, continue to circle. Once more. Then again. His arm throbbed, bloody, shredded.

But his perceptions were undistracted, heightened, totally pure, his nervous system tingling. Jab, block, and circle. Years ago Lee, his karate instructor, had said, 'There is nothing more exhilarating than to fight in the dark, facing death.' At killer-instinct school, Rothberg had said, 'If both opponents have equal knowledge and skill, the younger man with the greater stamina shall be the victor.' Chris, who was thirty-six, judged his opponent to be twenty-nine.

The cardinal rule in a knife fight is don't allow your opponent to back you into a corner.

Slowly, relentlessly, Chris's hunter forced him against the cliff. Chris found himself wedged between ridges of chalk. He jabbed in a frenzy. His hunter ducked, then lunged beneath Chris's arm.

The blade plunged in to its hilt.

Chris gagged. His larynx snapped. An artery burst. His mind went blank as he choked on his blood.

22

'You're sure?' Eliot sounded hoarse as he clutched the phone in his greenhouse. 'There's no mistake? No chance of error?'

'None. The kill was verified. I examined the body myself,' Landish said on the scrambler-protected long distance line. 'The man who helped destroy my roses – Remus – is dead.'

Eliot's chest felt cold. In desperation, he distracted himself by thinking of business. 'You cleaned the area?'

'Of course. We burned the cottage to destroy their fingerprints. We left before the authorities arrived. They'll never know who was there.'

'And the body?' Eliot had trouble swallowing.

'It's been taken to my private plane. The pilot will truss it with weights and drop it at sea, too far out for the tide to bring it in.'

'I see.' He frowned. 'You seem to have thought of everything.'

'What's wrong? Your voice sounds strange.'

'I didn't realize I – Nothing.'

'What?'

'It's not important.'

'We've still got to deal with Romulus and the woman.'

He struggled to pay attention. 'I've already made arrangements. The moment I have word, I'll call you.'

Eliot's arm felt numb as he set down the phone. He didn't understand what was happening in him. For the past three weeks, since the Paradigm hit, his single purpose had been to find Saul and eliminate him before he could reveal who'd ordered the job. The president could never be allowed to learn why his friend had been killed. In the process, Chris had become a danger too, but now that problem was solved. With one of them dead and the other located, he'd almost achieved his goal, had almost protected himself. Then why, as he'd tried to tell Landish, did he feel remorse?

He remembered the first time he'd taken Chris and Saul camping – Labor Day, 1952. The boys had been seven then, two years under his influence. He vividly recalled their innocent excited faces, their desperate need for affection, their eagerness to please him. More than any of his foster children, they'd been his favorites. Strangely, his throat aching, he felt gratified that Chris, though doomed to fail, had postponed his death so well. Yes, he admitted he had no right, but after all he'd taught the boy, and he couldn't help feeling proud of him. Godspeed, he thought.

Thirty years? Could so long a time have gone so fast? Did he mourn for Chris, he wondered . . . or for himself?

Soon Saul would be dead as well. The KGB had been warned. If they acted quickly, they'd spring their trap. The crisis at last would be over, the secret safe. Only two more foster children would remain, Castor and Pollux, now guarding the house. The others had died in faithful service.

I might outlive all my sons, he thought, sadly wishing Saul could be reprieved.

But that was impossible.

He suddenly felt uneasy. What if Saul escaped? *Unthinkable.*

But what if he did? He'd learn Chris was dead.

And come for me.

He'd never give up.

I truly think nothing could stop him.

BOOK FOUR
RETRIBUTION

FURIES

1

Saul stared through the windshield toward a misty streetlight, his rented Citroën parked in the middle of a line of cars along a residential block. He sat close to Erika, his arm around her, apparently just another couple in the City of Lovers. But he didn't allow himself to enjoy being near her. He couldn't become distracted. Too much depended on this mission.

'If Landish told the truth, we'll soon have some answers,' Erika said.

Her Mossad informants had learned that Victor Petrovich Kochubey would be at the Soviet embassy tonight, performing Tchaikovsky's Violin Concerto at a reception in honor of the new Franco-Soviet alliance. 'But you can't grab him there,' the informants had said. 'Various intelligence networks have set up surveillance cameras around the clock to watch all the entrances. If anyone looks suspicious, the police'll arrest them. No one's supposed to embarrass relations with the Soviets. France and Russia are getting along too well these days. Your best bet's to grab him later when he returns to his apartment on the Rue de la Paix.'

'But won't he be guarded?' Saul had asked.

'A violinist? Why would he need protection?'

At eight minutes after one, Kochubey drove past in his Peugeot, its headlights flashing. Erika got out and walked along the street. Kochubey – in his fifties, tall, with sensitive but heavy features – locked his car, carefully holding his violin case. He wore a tuxedo. Erika approached him as he reached the stoop to his apartment house. The street was deserted.

He spoke first. 'This late at night, a lady shouldn't be out alone. Unless, of course, you have a proposition –'

'Victor, shut up. In my purse, I've a very large pistol aimed at your crotch. Please go to the curb and wait for a car to pull up.'

He stared but did so. Saul stopped the car, climbing from the driver's seat into the back where he searched Kochubey and took the violin case.

'Gently! It's a Stradivari!'

'It'll be safe.'

'As long as you cooperate.' Erika drove.

'Cooperate!' Kochubey's mouth opened and shut nervously. '*How?*
I don't even know what you want!'

'The messages.'

'*What?*'

'The ones you gave to Landish.'

'You remember,' Erika said. 'To pass to Eliot.'

'*Are the two of you insane? What are you talking about?*'

Saul shook his head, rolled down his window, and balanced the
violin case on the rim.

'I said be careful!'

'The messages. What was in them?' Saul tilted the case out the
window.

'A Stradivari can't be repaired!'

'Then buy another one.'

'Are you crazy? Where would I find –?'

Saul shook his hands from the case. It started falling.

Kochubey wailed and grabbed for it.

Saul pushed him away and snatched back the case. 'The messages.'

'I never knew what was in them! I was a courier, nothing more!
You think I'd risk execution by breaking the seal?'

'Who gave them to you?' Saul held the case out the window.

'A KGB bureau chief!'

'Who?'

'Alexei Golitsin! Please!' Kochubey's hands trembled to grab the
case.

'I don't believe you. Golitsin was shot for treason in '73.'

'That's when he gave me the messages!'

'In '73?'

Saul frowned. Hardy had said Eliot disappeared in '54, then again
in '73. What did a KGB officer shot for treason have to do with Eliot's
disappearance? What had happened in '73?

'It's the truth!' Kochubey said.

'Perhaps.'

'The Stradivari! Please!'

Saul balanced it out the window. Headlights flashed by. He thought
about it, shrugging. 'This is pointless. If I dropped the case, what
reason would you have to change your story? With Amytal, we'll soon
learn what you really know.' He set the case on the floor.

'Thank God.'

'Thank me.'

2

They drove from Paris.

'Who do you work for?'

'No one.'

'Where are you taking me?'

'Vonnas.'

194

'Ah.'

Kochubey's sudden mood shift bothered Saul. 'You know it?'

The musician nodded, strangely pleased by the thought of visiting the small town fifty kilometers north of Lyon. 'Perhaps you'll allow me the pleasure of eating at Le Cheval Blanc.'

'It's not on the expense account.'

Kochubey abruptly scowled. 'You Americans are skinflints. Truth serum leaves such a bad aftertaste – like liver without butter or bacon. Very well.' He squinted angrily. 'We've a good three hours of driving ahead of us. Since you won't discuss your credentials, I'll talk about mine.'

Saul groaned, sensing what was coming, and wished he could sedate him, but that would interfere with the Amytal.

Kochubey leaned back, smiling perversely, his large head framed by long, prematurely white hair in the style of composers and musicians from the previous century. He loosened his tie and rested his hands on the cummerbund of his tuxedo. 'I don't suppose you attended my performance.'

'We weren't on the guest list, I'm afraid.'

'A pity. You'd have been given a lesson in Soviet idealism. You see, Tchaikovsky was like Lenin, and the similarity shows itself in the violin concerto, for the great composer had a theme in mind, as did Lenin. To arrive at his goal, he wove in transitional phrases, just as we in the Soviet Union have an ideal, and we move toward it, not in constant revolution, but in transitional phrases due to adjustments we've had to make because of the war and our economy. I won't say we've reached our finale, but we've come a long way in sixty-five years, have we not?'

'I'll admit you're well organized.'

'An understatement. But I was talking about the great composer. The concerto opens simply, and you think the obvious strains contain the message. But underneath, other strains lie hidden, half-heard, half-guessed, as if the master were saying, "I've a secret to tell you – but not a word to others." It's like a whispered code to a member of our espionage network, or a sign of brotherhood among the people.'

Saul grew tired quickly, fighting off sleep as Kochubey went on and Erika raced along the Autoroute du Sud toward Lyon. Forty minutes before reaching the city, she turned on the gravel access road that would in the next year become the Geneva–Macon spur of the expressway. Along the route, heavy road equipment had been parked for the night. The sharp crack of gravel pelting the underside of the car made Saul apprehensive.

He peered past the Citroën's headlights toward a heavy tanker trunk that rumbled in his direction. Frowning, he watched it suddenly veer.

It blocked the road.

Vans streaked from behind the heavy equipment, flanking the Citroën. Arc lights blazed from the dark.

'My eyes!' Hand up to shield them, Erika swerved to miss the truck, stamping the brakes. The Citroën skidded, jolting against a

195

bulldozer, throwing her forward. Her head whacked the steering wheel, spewing blood.

The impact knocked Saul down. Scrambling up from the floor, he stared at her, moaning unconscious. He couldn't carry her and get away, he realized. His frantic hope was to force the occupants of the vans to chase him, lose them, double back for her. He grabbed at Kochubey's lapel as he opened the door, but the fabric tore away.

On his own, he leapt out, dodged the bulldozer, and raced to avoid the spotlights. Doors banged open on the vans. He heard a car skidding to a stop on the road. Men shouted. Footsteps crunched on the gravel. The spotlights tracked him, throwing his urgent shadow across the muddy field. He stumbled in a rut, flailing his arms for balance, charging forward, desperate to reach the murky trees beyond the spotlights. Metal scraped. He tensed his shoulders, anticipating the wallop of a high-powered bullet, feeling a sting instead. In his neck: a dart. A second dart stung his hip. He flinched from an excruciating jolt. His vision failed. He fell to the mud, his knees jerking up to his chest, his arms twisting inward, convulsing. And that was all.

3

When he wakened, he knew enough to keep his eyes shut and listen. Groggy, he lay on a wooden floor. The pain in his left forearm must have been a puncture wound from a hypodermic. With enough Brevital in him, he could have been out for hours, only to be wakened by Kochubey's urgent shouts to someone else in the room. The handcuffs at his wrists behind his back were cold, not yet warmed by his body. Whoever was in the room must have recently brought him here and cuffed him.

Kochubey kept shouting. 'What are they after? Why haven't you protected me better? You obviously knew I was in danger!'

Saul heard a different voice, deep and smooth. 'Comrade, if you play a scale with your left hand and a contradictory scale with your right . . .'

'It's impossible to tell if the mode is major or minor! Any school boy – but what's that got to do with –?'

'The left and right hands had to be incompatible. If you'd known my intention, you wouldn't have been convincing to Romulus, whose faulty interpretation was essential to the trap. Now please stop shouting, or perhaps you'd enjoy practicing your music in the port of Hodéida in Yemen.'

Saul peered through barely open lids in time to see Kochubey's face go pale.

'Relax, Victor,' the voice said. 'I'll supply you with a nice warm overcoat and send you on the high-speed train back to Paris.'

While the man addressed Kochubey, Saul was able to recognize the ferretlike face between a black leather Tyrol hat and the high collar of a green loden coat. Boris Zlatogor Orlik, GRU colonel and Paris

196

section chief for the KGB. Orlik prided himself on never having directly killed or stolen secrets or passed disinformation. Instead he was a theorist, a methodical planner whose exploits rivaled those of Richard Sorge, the master Soviet operative against Japan in the Second World War. It was Orlik who'd proven that GRU Lieutenant Colonel Yuri Popov was a spy for the CIA from '52 to '58 and that GRU Colonel Oleg Penkovsky was a spy for MI–6 in '62.

As Kochubey left, Saul didn't close his eyes fast enough.

'Ah, Romulus, I see you're awake. Forgive me for raising my voice, but sometimes with men like Kochubey it's necessary.'

Saul didn't bother pretending he was still asleep. Squirming to sit up, he studied the room – a den with paneled walls, rustic paintings, a fireplace. 'Where am I?'

'Near Lyon. A modest château I sometimes use for interrogation.'

'Where's Erika?'

'Down the hall. But you needn't worry. A doctor's with her. She's fine, though she's got a nasty headache.'

So did Saul. He slumped against a chair. His thoughts spun. 'How did you find us?'

'The international language.'

'I don't –'

'Music. Besides the Stradivari, the violin case contained a microphone and a homing device.'

Saul groaned in disgust. 'Kochubey was so convincing I didn't think to check it.'

'But you almost dropped it out a window. I'll admit you had me nervous for a moment.'

'That still doesn't answer my question. How'd you know we'd grab Kochubey?'

'Your agency told us.'

'That's impossible.'

'The information was specific. Since it was our man Remus killed in Bangkok, your people offered us the courtesy of letting us eliminate you.'

'Eliot.' Saul sounded as if he cursed.

'So it seemed to me as well.'

'But how did –?'

'We'll get to that. First let me set the stage.' Orlik gestured toward a window. 'Dawn is breaking. If you think of escape, that's natural. But listen to what you're up against. You're on the edge of the Pilat Regional Park. There's a town to the south called Véranne, another to the north called Péllusin. No doubt you anticipate we have dogs, so you'd take to the wooded high ground – toward Véranne. But there you'd have to avoid the village. By night, you'd be stuck in the soft earth of the graveyard or the open fields. Wherever, we'd catch up with you. Our darts would give you another headache, and we'd have to start all over. Granted, a confrontation in a graveyard would be romantic. But the reality is it's dawn and we need to talk. I'm sorry I can't offer you a Baby Ruth.'

Saul narrowed his eyes.

'You're well informed.'

'Depend on it. Would you like some breakfast? Please don't think I've laced the croissants or coffee with anything. It never works properly.'

Despite himself, Saul laughed.

'Good, let's be friendly.' Orlik removed the handcuffs.

Puzzled, Saul rubbed his wrists, waiting till Orlik poured and drank the coffee. At last he had to ask. 'Then you know about Eliot's orphans?'

'I'm sure it's occurred to you the Latin word for patriotism comes from the same root as father. *Pater. Patriae amor.* You saw your father as an extension of your country. Trained to defend it, you did everything he told you, unaware you were loyal to him – but not your government. His scheme was so brilliant the others adopted it.'

Saul stopped drinking. 'Others?'

Orlik studied him. 'You must have known. Why else would you pick up Landish?'

'Others?'

Orlik frowned. 'You really don't –? I assumed you'd reached the same conclusion I had. 1938.'

'Make sense. Eliot wasn't even in government then. '54 is when he disappeared.'

'And again in '73.'

'But that time one of your men, Golitsin –'

'Not mine, but he did work for the KGB.'

'– was involved, except your people shot him for treason.'

'Then you have made progress.'

'For Christ's sake!'

'Please, you'll have to be patient. I thought you could tell me some things. I never guessed I'd be telling *you*.'

'Then tell me, dammit! What's going on?'

'1938. What does that mean to you?'

'It could mean Hitler and Munich . . . or the Abelard sanction.'

'Good. Then that's where we'll begin.'

4

When Hitler met with Chamberlain and Daladier in Munich, a different meeting took place that same day in Berlin. Hitler – with Mussolini next to him – demanded that England and France renege on agreements they'd made with Czechoslovakia, Austria, and Poland to protect those countries against invasion. Hitler's intentions were obvious, but England and France did nothing to stop him, hoping he'd be satisfied if he expanded Germany's territory into those adjacent countries. The men at the other meeting, the one in Berlin, knew better, however. After all, they directed espionage for Germany, England, France, the Soviet Union and the United States, and they

198

understood that Hitler's invasion of those other countries wouldn't be the end of his need for power but only the start. A war was coming, so vast and destructive it would dwarf all others before it. Though heads of state chose to ignore the implications, the directors of intelligence could not, for they realized the role they would play in the coming war, and they had to make preparations. Since the First World War, their community had dwindled. Conditions had changed. Traditions had been forgotten. With a new conflict about to begin, it was time to reorganize, to agree on principles and establish rules, one of which was the Abelard sanction.

'I've always admired the imagination of the men who created it,' Orlik said. 'Such a brilliant refinement, so clever a variation. But there were other consequences of that meeting in Berlin, the most important of which was the recognition of the bond shared by those men. Because of their profession, they realized they formed a group larger than politics, transcending differences between their nations. One year countries might be friends, the next year enemies, the year after friends again. Such instability was senseless, based on the whim of politicians. It allowed the intelligence community to practice its skills, to enjoy the risks, but the men in Berlin understood that at heart they were closer to each other than to their governments. As well, they suspected the risks were becoming too huge. While they realized the need for rules, the leaders of their governments seemed to recognize no rules at all. How could the world survive if politicians refused to agree on limits? Someone had to act responsibly. Of course, before the war, they couldn't have predicted how serious this question would become. But even before atomic weapons, the issue of responsibility aggravated the intelligence community. Hitler's excesses became intolerable. We know some German intelligence officers collaborated with the English. These same German operatives attempted to assassinate Hitler. The bomb failed to kill him, and of course they were executed.'

'You're suggesting a pattern?'

'What I've told you is fact. What follow are my suppositions. The men at the Abelard meeting agreed unofficially to act as – what shall we call them? – watchdogs on their governments, to see that international rivalry remained within acceptable bounds. A certain amount of conflict was necessary, of course, for the intelligence community to justify itself, but beyond a certain point, every nation stood an equal chance of losing, so the plan was set in motion. Stalin, remember, had begun his purges. My countryman, Vladimir Lazensokov, was executed a few months after he came back from the Abelard meeting. Did Stalin learn about that meeting and what Lazensokov had agreed to? Who can say? But his execution, in tandem with Hitler's reprisals for his attempted assassination, made the watchdogs in the intelligence community much more circumspect. They delegated their responsibility to carefully chosen protégés. Tex Auton, America's representative at that meeting, chose his adopted son Eliot, for example. Percival Landish chose his own son. The French and German representatives did the same. Lazensokov, I believe, foresaw his execution and made arrangements beforehand.'

'You're talking about Golitsin?'

'Then you follow my logic. Golitsin, who was executed for treason in '73, had secret business with Landish and Eliot, and two other men in French and German intelligence. No doubt you'd soon have learned about them. The parallels are remarkable. The five men at the Abelard meeting trained surrogates who refused – despite their ambition – to achieve the highest positions in their networks. Instead they secured jobs just below the upper echelon where they wouldn't be threatened by the whim of politicians. To keep those jobs secure, they each compiled a secret collection of documented scandals, which they used as leverage against anyone foolish enough to try to remove them from power. These men have retained their positions since after the war and thus have been consistent influences on their governments. They've sabotaged operations. Your U-2 incident and Bay of Pigs, for example. To moderate the less enlightened members of their agencies, they've insisted an enemy spy had infiltrated them. As a consequence, each network has been so busy investigating itself only a moderate level of espionage had been maintained, and thus a form of control has been established. Acting responsibly – or so they imagine – these men ensure an international status quo.'

'Eliot's disappearances in '54 and '73?'

'Meetings. To cement their relationship, to reaffirm their intentions. They needed to coordinate their efforts. They met as seldom as they could but as often as they had to.'

'One problem with your theory.'

'Oh?'

'Each man couldn't do all that on his own. They'd have needed personnel and financing.'

'True. But in your case the CIA has an unlimited unrecorded budget. No one knows exactly how much money it receives or where that money goes. If accounts were kept, secrecy would be impaired. Appropriating funds for a private operation wouldn't be difficult. The same rule applies to the other networks.'

'Eliot and the others would still have needed help. They'd have had to delegate authority. Eventually someone would have talked.'

'Not necessarily. Think about it.'

Saul felt his stomach sink.

'You and Remus didn't talk. Or Eliot's other orphans. I suspect the idea came from Auton; it functioned brilliantly. For years, you and the others have been working for Eliot in his attempt to comply with the implications of the Abelard meeting, to obey his foster father's directive.'

'The Paradigm job he asked me to do.'

'Apparently he thought it was necessary. We were blamed for it. So was Israel. Neither of us wants the Arabs to align themselves with the United States. The question is what did he hope to achieve.'

200

'That's wrong. The question is why did he ask me to do it and then try to kill me afterward.'

'You'll have to ask him.'

'If I don't kill the bastard first.' His bowels contracted. 'They all had orphans.'

'The final parallel. Landish, Golitsin, and the others – each recruited foster sons in orphanages, guaranteeing loyalty without question, sacrificing their children when they had to.'

'It keeps getting slicker.' Saul raised his hands. 'If I could –'

'That's why you're still alive.'

Saul squinted, raging. 'Get to the point.'

'Like Lazensokov before him, Golitsin too foresaw his execution and chose a surrogate. I've discovered who, but I fear my efforts have been discovered. My opponent is clever and powerful. If I become too dangerous to him, he'd easily destroy me. As a consequence, I've concentrated on the men in the other networks who inherited the legacy.'

'But why? If they sabotage their networks, they're helping you.'

'Not if they act in accord, Golitsin's replacement along with the others. They're interfering with the natural order. I'm a Marxist, my friend. I believe in Soviet domination. There are evils in our system, but they're insignificant compared to –'

'What?'

'The utter obscenity of your own. I want to destroy these men. I want to let the dialectic take its course, upset the status quo, and complete the Revolution.' Orlik smiled. 'When I received the directive to intercept and kill you, I couldn't believe my fortune.'

'And that's it? You want me to go after these men? So you can protect yourself?'

Orlik nodded.

'My fight's with Eliot. To get out of here, I'll have to compromise. I see that. But to help, I'll need a lot more compromise from you.'

'No, I've got Erika. You wouldn't let her die. But there's something else.'

Saul frowned.

'You claim your fight's with Eliot? You're wrong. It's at least with another.'

'Who?'

'You wondered how Eliot knew you'd come to Paris?'

'Say it!'

'Chris is dead. Landish killed him.'

5

Erika choked.

The bedroom had no windows. Saul wanted to scream, to smash the walls. Rage overwhelmed him, so intense he thought he'd burst.

201

Grief wracked his muscles, shaking him till he ached. 'It should have been me.'

She moaned.

'He wanted to take my place – to go to Paris with you and grab Kochubey while I watched Landish.' Saul fought to breathe. 'Because he had a feeling I'd be killed. But I wouldn't do it!'

'Don't.'

'I wouldn't listen!'

'No, it wasn't your fault. The lowest card stayed. If you'd taken his place –'

'I'd have died instead of him! To bring him back, I'd gladly die!'

'That isn't what he wanted!' Erika stood, unsteadily raising a hand to the bandage around her head. 'He didn't ask to change places with you so he could save his life. He thought he'd be saving *yours*. It wasn't your fault. For God's sake, accept what he gave you.' She shook, starting to weep. 'Poor Chris. So fucked up. He never knew any . . .'

'Peace?' Saul nodded, understanding. He and Chris had been trained to cancel all emotion except dependence on each other and love for Eliot. In Saul's case, it had worked. He'd never been bothered by the things Eliot asked him to do – because he couldn't bear to disappoint his father.

But Chris . . .

Saul's throat ached . . . Chris had been different. His conditioning had failed. The killing at last had tormented him. He must have gone through hell trying to satisfy Eliot and deny his conscience. Even the monastery couldn't save him.

Tears streamed down Saul's face, their unaccustomed warmth shocking. His eyes stung, swollen. He hadn't cried since he'd been a five-year-old at Franklin. He clung to Erika, weeping.

At last his own conditioning failed. Anger aggravated sorrow, grief fed rage till something broke in him, a lifetime's restraint letting loose so grim a resolve its power frightened him. He'd never experienced anything like it, a surging need that for all its pain promised utter satisfaction.

'You bastard.' He gritted his teeth. 'For those candy bars, you'll pay.' The hate in his voice astonished him.

'That's right.' Erika's voice shook. 'Put the blame where it belongs. Not on you. On Eliot. He caused it. He and Landish and those other sonsofbitches.'

Nodding, Saul raged. In fury, he understood. He had to get revenge for Chris.

The sharp knock startled him. A key scraped in the lock. He swung to the opening door as Orlik's ferret face appeared with a guard. 'Our agreement was fifteen minutes.'

'I'm ready.' Saul seethed, impatient. 'Set it up.'

'I already have. You leave right now, though Erika remains, of course. As my insurance.'

'If she's harmed.'

'Please.' Orlik looked offended. 'I'm a gentleman as much as a professional.'

'Insurance?' Erika frowned.

'If you prefer, an added incentive.'

'What you don't understand,' Saul said, 'is I've got all the incentive I need.'

'To do it your way,' Orlik said. 'But I want you to do it mine. When my enemy looks for someone to blame, it has to be you, not me.' His eyes gleamed. 'I hope you've recovered from the sedative.'

'Why?'

'You're about to accomplish an amazing escape.'

6

Saul scrambled to the top of the ridge, catching his breath as he scanned the twilit landscape. Behind him, mist filled the valley. Ahead, thick fir trees beckoned. Smelling their resin, he charged among them, hearing the bay of dogs on his trail. They'd been louder since he'd crossed the meadow back there. He'd tried to find a stream and race along it, hiding his scent, but luck had failed. Sweat stuck his shirt to his chest.

The dogs sounded louder.

Orlik had predicted correctly. Against the dogs, Saul's best choice was north toward the wooded high ground. He hoped to find a cliff the dogs couldn't climb, a chasm they couldn't jump across. But again his luck had failed him.

Evening made the forest damp. His sweat felt slick as he scrambled through the undergrowth. The dogs barked closer. Passing an open swath to his right, he saw the dots of lights in a town, but he couldn't risk heading there. Orders would have been received, sentinels posted. His best route was farther north, through the territory he liked best – the high hills and the forest. He loved the smell of the loam he raced across.

Thick brambles tore his clothes. Dense branches raked his skin. Despite the swelling stings, he felt exhilarated. Adrenaline spurred his senses. As if he'd struggled through a maze, he rejoiced in release. He triumphed.

Except for the dogs. They crashed through the bushes, relentless, closer. Leaping a deadfall, he charged up a shadowy slope, hearing forest animals skitter away as if they sensed an imminent kill. He chose a game trail to his left, rounding a boulder, scrambling toward a plain.

And found himself in the graveyard Orlik had predicted. Headstones jutted before him, silhouetted against the gloaming. Marble angels spread their wings. Cherubs mourned. Against the dying sunset, mist created halos. Everything seemed preordained. He darted among the graves. A wreath and then a single blossom caught his attention. He heard the scratch of claws behind him. He turned to face the undergrowth and reached in his pocket. Orlik had told him not to use it till necessary.

Now it was. He screwed off the cap and poured the pungent cloying chemical on a newly filled-in mound. At once he darted past a hedge and disappeared in the gathering night. The flowers smelled of funerals.

But not for him, he thought. And not for the guards he'd slammed with the heel of his palm at Orlik's chateau, holding back. Though his enemies, they'd live. And Orlik would get what he wanted, a convincing escape without the sacrifice of his men.

Behind, he heard the anguished howl of the dogs, their nostrils tortured, useless. They'd scrape at their faces till the smell of blood obscured the chemical. But they wouldn't chase him any longer.

There'd be a funeral all right. Not his, but soon, he thought, anticipating. He was too much in love with hate to squander it.

7

The car was hidden where Orlik had said it would be – in the shadows behind a boarded-up service station on a secondary road outside Lyon. A three-year-old Renault, its gray inconspicuous, blending with the night. Saul approached it warily, checking the road and the trees around the station before he crept from bushes toward the side away from the road. He'd taken a French MAB 9-mm pistol from one of the guards at Orlik's château. Aiming it, he peered through the window toward the back floor. Seeing no one, he opened the car and found – as Orlik had promised – keys beneath the front mat. He checked to make sure the car had not been booby-trapped, using matches he found on the dash, scanning the engine, then crawling underneath to inspect the suspension. He opened the trunk, where he found the clothes and equipment Orlik had guaranteed he'd supply. Though Saul had other sources, money and identification he'd hidden years before in various countries, he was reassured by Orlik's adherence to their bargain. For certain he intended to made good on his own.

Even so, he was bothered that Orlik hadn't released Erika, though he understood the logic. Orlik had put himself under suspicion by allowing Saul to escape. It would be more believable if Erika hadn't escaped as well. She'd be a way of forcing Saul to do things as Orlik wanted. But he couldn't subdue the suspicion Orlik had another motive. What if when this was over Orlik planned to use her to lure Saul back, then kill them both and present them as trophies, absolving himself from responsibility for what Saul had done?

The complexities were quicksand, sucking him deep. But this he knew – Orlik wouldn't betray them till his purpose was achieved. In the meantime, Saul's direction was clear before him, extremely simple.

Chris was dead. There would be hell to pay.

He started the Renault. It idled easily, sounding recently tuned, its gas tank full.

He drove to the road, his headlights gleaming through the dark. He chose a lane, then another, watching for pursuit lights in his mirror. Seeing none, he turned onto the next main road and, obeying the limit, headed west.

Orlik had chosen his targets, five, the descendants of the original Abelard group. But Orlik hadn't stipulated who came first.

He planned to abandon this car as quickly as he could. Despite his search, he might have missed a transmitter beeping his location to a surveillance team staying far enough back to hide their lights. They didn't matter.

Nothing did.

Except revenge. It gave him pleasure to think the skills his father had taught him would be the weapons he'd use to destroy him.

Hey, old man, I'm coming.

He clenched the steering wheel so hard his knuckles ached.

And sometime in the night, Chris sat beside him, face gaunt eyes dead, grinning as if they were kids again, about to start another adventure.

The best kind. Getting even.

8

'What? Excuse me? I didn't hear what you said.' Eliot slowly roused himself. He sat at the desk in his study, peering up as if he'd been concentrating on important papers, though there were none and the lamps were off and the drapes were closed. He squinted at the open door, at a husky man outlined by the light from the hall.

The man had his legs spread, his arms slightly away from his sides. He was tall, his face square.

Eliot frowned. For an instant he didn't recognize the man – or rather he feared he did. It looked like Chris.

Had Chris survived and come for him? Impossible. Landish had guaranteed Chris was . . .

Dark against the light, the shape looked . . .

Dead? Impossible. Then was it Saul who, having slipped past the guards around the house, was now confronting him?

Not yet. Too soon. But the explanation disturbed him, for he realized the figure reminded him not only of Chris and Saul, but all the others, nine pairs, eighteen orphans, all his foster sons. He told himself he'd loved them. Didn't his throat ache when he thought of them? Wasn't his grief a proof he hadn't acted callously? His pain in sacrificing them had made his mission more heroic.

Fifteen now were dead, though – maybe another if Saul became too eager. Saul wasn't likely to, however. The pattern seemed predetermined. I've never believed in luck, he thought. Or fate. I put my faith in skill. But as he studied the figure in the doorway, he experienced

205

a momentary hallucination, all his dead children superimposed on one another. He shivered. He'd chosen their cryptonyms from Greek and Roman mythology, indulging his love of complexity, but now he recalled something else from that mythology – the Furies. The avenging Shades.

He cleared his throat, repeating. 'I didn't hear what you said.'

'Are you all right?' Pollux stepped forward.

'What makes you think I wouldn't be?'

'I heard you talking in here.'

Troubled, Eliot didn't remember having done so.

Pollux continued, 'I couldn't figure who you'd be talking to. For sure, nobody got past me. Then I thought of the phone, but where I stood in the hall I could see it was still on the hook.'

'I'm fine. I must be . . . thinking out loud, I suppose. No need to worry.'

'Can I bring you anything?'

'No, I guess not.'

'I could heat up some cocoa.'

Nostalgic, Eliot smiled. 'When you and Castor were young and you came to visit, I used to bring cocoa to you. Remember? Just before you went to sleep.'

'How could I forget?'

'Our positions have been reversed it seems. And do you plan to take care of your father in his old age?'

'For you? You know I'd do anything.'

Eliot nodded, in pain from emotion. Fifteen others had given everything. 'I know. I'm fine. I just need time to myself. I love you. Have you eaten?'

'Soon.'

'Make sure you do. And your brother?'

'He's down the hall, watching the back.'

'I'll join you shortly. We'll talk about the old days.'

Pollux departed. Leaning back exhausted, Eliot fondly remembered the summer of '54 when he had taken Castor and Pollux to . . . was it Yellowstone Park? Too many years had passed too quickly. His recollection sometimes failed him. Perhaps it had been the Grand Canyon. No. That had been in '56. Castor had –

With a shudder, he realized how horribly wrong he was. His mind recoiled with dismay. Not Castor and Pollux. No, dear God, it had been another pair, and he almost wept because he couldn't remember who. Chris and Saul perhaps. His Furies crowded closer. His mouth filled with bile.

He'd left the office in midafternoon as soon as his assistant had brought the news.

'Romulus escaped? But everything was arranged, the trap confirmed! The KGB claimed they had him!'

'And the woman. Yes.' The assistant spoke reluctantly. 'But he got away.'

'How?'

'They caught him near Lyon. He broke from a château where he'd been taken to be executed.'

'They were supposed to kill him on the spot!'

'It seems they wanted to interrogate him first.'

'That wasn't the agreement! How much damage did he do? How many guards did he kill?'

'None. The escape was clean.'

It troubled him. 'But they killed the woman?'

'No, they're questioning her to find out where he went.'

He shook his head. 'It's wrong.'

'But they claim –'

'It's wrong. They lie. It's a trick.'

'But why?'

'Someone let him go.'

'I don't see what the motive would be.'

'Isn't it obvious? To come for me.'

The assistant narrowed his eyes.

And that was when Eliot, realizing his assistant thought he was paranoid, had left the building, taking Castor and Pollux with him. Since then, he'd been sitting in his shadowy den, protected for now by guards around the house and his two remaining faithful sons in here.

But he couldn't continue like this forever. He couldn't merely wait. Despite the Shades that haunted him, he didn't believe in fate. I've always depended on skill, he thought. And wile.

I taught him. I can outguess him. What would I do if I were Saul?

The moment he knew what question to ask, the answer came all at once. Thrilling, it gave him another chance. But only if he acted quickly.

He had to get through to Landish.

Saul would savor revenge, making stops along the way, increasing the terror.

Landish'll be his first target. We can set up a trap.

9

Again he felt he'd been here before, seeming to see not only Franklin but the walls of Andrew Sage's estate as well. Everything was coming together. Eliot had used the school to pervert him. One of the consequences was the Paradigm job. Understanding, he grimly delighted in his sense of heading back to where it all began. When he'd blown up Sage's estate, he'd felt nothing. There'd been a job to do. He'd done it for Eliot. But everything was different now. For the first time, he looked forward to a kill. Comparing the walls of Sage's estate with Landish's estate, he realized the change in himself. He *wanted* to kill, and it pleased him that the method he'd chosen was the method he'd used to kill Sage. He savored the irony, using Eliot's tactics against him. I told you, Landish, how I'd punish you if you lied. Dammit, my brother's dead. Imagining the walls of Franklin School, he felt his eyes burn, swollen with tears.

He turned to his weapon. He could have chosen a rifle and simply have shot Landish from a distance. But that wouldn't have satisfied him, wouldn't have been complete enough, a fulfillment of his threat. Landish had to die in a certain way.

But his determination created a problem. Landish either was more cautious or else had learned of Saul's escape, for security on the estate had tripled. Guards patrolled in abundance. Visitors were asked for credentials and then were searched. The walls had now been equipped with closed-circuit cameras. It wasn't possible to infiltrate the grounds as he had before. Then how could he plant the explosives? How could he blow up not just Landish but – I told you what I'd do; they represent everything I hate – those fucking roses?

It was the largest remote-controlled model plane he could buy. He'd gone to half a dozen of the largest hobby shops in London before he found it. A miniature Spitfire with a three-foot wingspan and a half-mile range. His own guided missile. He wiped his misted eyes while he made adjustments, smiling. A toy. If Chris had been here, he'd have laughed. The corrupted child had chosen a plaything to get back at his father.

The model was fueled. He'd tested it earlier at another location. He had no trouble making it work. It responded to radio signals, maneuvered through the sky by a stick on a transmitter. It climbed and banked and dove precisely as he wished. But the plane had cargo: five pounds of stolen explosive, evenly distributed along the fuselage and taped in place. The added weight affected the model's performance, retarding its takeoff, making it sluggish in the air. But not enough to matter. The weapon would do its job. He'd gone to an electronics store and bought the parts he needed for a detonator, anchoring it to the undercarriage, controlled by its own transmitter. He'd taken care that the plane and the detonator were linked to different frequencies. Otherwise the explosive would have gone off when he activated the transmitter for the plane.

He waited. Dawn came slowly, bringing no warmth. Though he shivered, hate burned his soul.

He knew his target wouldn't have hidden somewhere else. The roses were too important. Landish would fear for them and be unable to stay away.

He thought of Chris, enjoying the wait, imagining the satisfaction he soon would know. At seven, he tensed as a white-haired figure, flanked by guards, left a rear door of the mansion, approaching the greenhouse. He feared it was someone else disguised as Landish, but through binoculars, he recognized the old man. No mistake. His gardening coat looked somewhat bulky. He was wearing a bulletproof vest.

It won't do you any good, you bastard.

As soon as Landish and the guards went into the greenhouse, Saul crept back through the trees. He carried the plane, along with the transmitters, in a knapsack on his shoulder, crossing a meadow, its grass too wet with dew to be a takeoff strip. A country road worked perfectly. Seeing no cars, he started the plane and guided it faster till it left the ground and struggled for altitude. Its engine droned. When it was high enough to clear the trees, he returned through the meadow, keeping the plane in sight above him as he shifted through the woods to reach the bluff overlooking Landish's estate. Because of the dew, his pants clung cold to his legs, but even that felt pleasant. Birds sang. The early morning air smelled fresh. He pretended to be the child he never was. Had never been allowed to be.

His toy. His drying tears made his cheeks feel stiff as he smiled. He worked the controls, raising the plane to its limit – a speck against the pale blue sky – aiming it toward the estate. The guards turned, puzzled by its drone. A few cocked their heads. A man with a dog pointed up. Though they couldn't see him from this distance, he crouched behind bushes, manipulating the controls. His pulse thumped louder as the plane veered over the grounds.

The guards seemed paralyzed, then abruptly snapped into motion, urgent, nervous, appearing to sense a threat but not knowing what it was. He urged the plane to its maximum height, then forced it into a dive. As the plane streaked toward the greenhouse, its shape enlarging, its drone increasing, a few men ran toward the greenhouse. Others shouted. Several raised rifles. He heard the crack of shots, seeing the guards jerk from the recoil. Twisting the control stick, he began evasive maneuvers, tilting the plane to the right, then the left, veering, spinning, diving. Other guards began shooting. He studied the greenhouse. Through its glass, he saw a small white-coated figure turn to face the commotion. Only Landish had worn white. He stood among roses, a third of the way along a row. Saul aimed the plane directly at him. So many shots cracked they became a rattle. The plane responded sluggishly. For a terrible instant, he feared it had been hit, but then he realized the weight of the bomb affected the dive. He compensated, moving the plane less abruptly. When it struck the glass, he imagined Landish gasping. He pressed the second transmitter. The greenhouse disintegrated. Shards of glass arced, glinting. Guards dove for cover, obscured by smoke and flames. As a rumble drifted across the valley, he fled, imagining specks of rose petals drifting on, soaking up Landish's blood.

10

The phone rang, making Eliot flinch. He stared, forcing himself to wait while it shrilled again before he had control enough to pick it up.

'Hello?' He sounded cautious, expecting to hear Saul curse in triumph, threatening. He had to convince Saul to meet with him, to lure Saul into a trap.

What he heard was his assistant. 'Sir, I'm afraid we've got bad news. An emergency cable from MI–6.'

'Landish? Something's happened to him?'

'Yes, sir, how did you know?'

'Just tell me.'

'Somebody blew him up. In his greenhouse. He was heavily guarded. But –'

'Dear God.' When Eliot learned how the bomb was delivered, his heart felt numb. Landish hadn't stopped him.

It was Saul all right. He wants to let me know how clever he is. He's telling me he can get at me no matter where I am or how well I protect myself. Eliot shook his head in dismay.

Why should I be surprised? I taught him.

Murmuring 'Thanks,' he hung up. In the dark, he fought to calm himself, to clear his mind, to analyze his options.

Feverish, he shivered, struck by the thought that he hadn't been in danger since he'd worked undercover in France in the war. Since then, he'd risen so high his only risk had been political. No ranking intelligence officer had ever been executed for treason. Only operatives in the field ever faced death. At the worst, he'd have received a prison sentence, probably not even that – to avoid publicity, high-level traitors were often merely dismissed, their capacity to do damage ended. With his collection of scandals to use as blackmail, he might even have claimed his pension.

No, his only fear had been discovery. Because of pride and his determination not to fail.

But the fear he now suffered was fierce. Not intellectual. Instinctive. Reflexive terror. He hadn't felt this way since a night in a drainage ditch in France when a German sentry had thrust at him with –

His heart almost burst from the strain. His paper-thin lungs, brittle from years of cigarettes, heaved heroically.

I won't give up. I've always been a winner. After nearly forty years, he faced again the ultimate. And didn't intend to fail.

A father against his son? A teacher against his student?

All right, then, come for me. I'm sorry Chris is dead, but I won't let you beat me. I'm still better than you.

He nodded. The rules. Don't go to your enemy. Make him come to you. Force him to fight on your own territory. Make him face you on your own terms.

He knew a way. Saul was wrong if he thought he could get at him no matter where he was or how well guarded. There was a place. It offered absolute protection. And the best part was it followed the rules.

Standing quickly, he walked to the hall. Pollux straightened, attentive. Eliot smiled.

'Bring your brother. We need to pack.' He paused at the stairs. 'It's been too long since we went on a trip.'

In London, Saul ignored the rain at the window. He'd closed the draperies. Even so, he turned on the lights only long enough to see the numbers he dialed on the phone. Again in darkness, he lay on the bed, waiting for an answer. In a while, he'd shower and change his clothes, then eat the fish and chips he'd brought here with him. After that, he'd pay for this room, having used it for just an hour, and head for his next destination. He could sleep en route. There was much to do.

The phone stopped buzzing. 'Yes?'

It sounded like Orlik, but he had to be sure. 'Baby Ruth.'

'And roses.'

Orlik. The Russian had given him numbers – pay phones where he could be reached on certain days at certain times for information and instructions.

'I assume you've heard the terrible news about our English friend,' Saul said.

'Indeed. Sudden, but not unexpected. And not without consequences,' Orlik said. 'There's been considerable activity among his associates. It seems they fear additional sudden news about themselves.'

'Have they taken precautions?'

'Why? Would that disturb you?'

'Not as long as I knew where to find them.'

'Travel's good for the soul, I understand.'

'Can you recommend some places?'

'Several. I know of a winery in France's Bordeaux district, for example. And a mountain retreat in Germany's Black Forest. If the Soviet Union's to your liking, I suggest a dacha near the mouth of the Volga on the Caspian.'

'Only three? I expected four.'

'If you went directly to the fourth, you might lose interest in the others,' Orlik said.

'On the other hand, I'm so looking forward to seeing the fourth I might not be able to concentrate on the others.'

'I've a friend of yours who's anxious for you to finish your travels so you can get back to her. We agreed you'd follow directions. If you don't do what I want, what point is there in my helping you? I had in mind you'd pay your next visit to my disruptive colleague in the Soviet Union.'

'And take the pressure off you? Think again. You're helping me only so I'll take care of him. Then you'll blame me and be in the clear.'

'I've never pretended otherwise,' Orlik said.

'But once you're safe, you might decide you can deal with the others by yourself. You'll arrange for me to be killed and come out a winner all the way around.'

'Your suspicion hurts my feelings.'

'I'm in this for one reason only – Eliot. I'll deal with the others later. There's no guarantee I can do them all. Maybe I'll make a mistake and die before I get to the others. If I take them in the order you want, maybe I'll never reach Eliot.'

'All the more reason to be cautious.'

'No. Listen carefully. I have a question. If I hear the wrong answer, I'm hanging up. I'll get to Eliot on my own. If Erika's harmed, I'll come for you the way I did for Eliot.'

'You call this being cooperative?'

'The question. I assume he knows I've escaped and what happened to Landish. He'll have to figure I'm coming. He'll make arrangements. In his place, I wouldn't stay at home. I'd want the best protection I could find, the safest location. *Where do I find him?*'

Rain rattled against the window. In the dark, he clutched the phone, braced for Orlik's response.

'I don't like being threatened.'

'Wrong answer.'

'Wait! What's the matter with –? Give me a chance! Eliot now? Then the others in exchange for Erika?'

'Unless I feel you're using her as a trap.'

'You have my word.'

'*The answer.*'

Orlik sighed, then told him. Saul hung up.

His heart raced. The location Orlik had told him was brilliant. What did you expect? he thought. Despite his hate, he admitted Eliot's genius.

The best, the most controlled of arenas. Chris would have understood.

12

A large black van stood outside the farmhouse. Approaching it, Orlik frowned. His tires crunched on the gravel lane as he parked his Citroën well away from the unfamiliar vehicle, making sure he was pointed back down the lane. He shut off his lights and motor but left the key in the switch. Cautious, he got out, scanning the night.

If he'd seen the van from a distance, he'd have stopped and circled the farmhouse, investigating. But the van had been placed so he wouldn't notice it till he reached the end of the lane. He couldn't have retreated without alerting his visitors. Assuming the night hid guards in addition to his own, he had no choice except to go inside apparently unconcerned.

Lamps glowed from several windows. There. As he neared the house, he noticed a shadow to the right at the corner. Positioned just beyond the spill of light, the figure evidently intended Orlik to glimpse him.

To the left, the screech of crickets abruptly stopped. So that side had someone too. But again the warning could so easily have been prevented by avoiding movement that Orlik had to guess the hidden sentries were letting Orlik know they were there.

To watch my reaction. If I've done nothing wrong, I shouldn't look nervous. If I did what they suspect, though, maybe I'd prove it by trying to run.

He had no doubt who they were. After Saul's 'escape' from the château outside Lyon, Orlik had taken Erika south to this farm near Avignon, wanting to hide her – in case Saul attempted to rescue her instead of completing his bargain. Saul could never have found this place. The French authorities didn't know what was going on. So who did that leave? Who else was involved and had ways of tracking him here?

Two conclusions. A member of his staff, suspicious about Saul's escape, had informed against him. The second: Orlik's superiors were here to interrogate him.

'You,' Orlik said in Russian. 'To the right. Be careful stepping back. There's a cistern behind you. Its cover won't hold your weight.'

He heard no response. Smiling, he continued forward – but not to the main door, instead to an entrance near the right side.

He went in, smelling veal and mushrooms for supper. A narrow hall went left past the kitchen toward the lights in the living room. A muscular guard stood outside a padlocked door.

'Open it,' Orlik said. 'I have to question her.'

The guard looked sullen. 'They won't like that.'

Orlik raised his eyebrows.

'You're expected.' The guard pointed down the hall.

I know who informed against me, Orlik thought. He's in the right place. He'll get what he deserves. 'They'll have to wait. I told you to open it.'

The guard frowned. 'But –'

'Are you deaf?'

Squinting with anger, the guard pulled out a key and freed the lock. Orlik stepped in.

The room had been stripped of furniture Erika could have used as a weapon. She'd been allowed jeans and a flannel shirt, but her shoes had been taken in case she broke free and tried to run. Her belt, a potential weapon, had been taken as well. She glared up from where she sat on the floor in a corner.

'Good. You're awake,' Orlik said.

'How can I sleep with these lights?'

'I need information.' Turning, Orlik nodded to the guard and closed the door.

He crossed the room. Grim, he pulled a Soviet Makarov 9-mm pistol from behind his suitcoat.

She didn't flinch.

He studied her, brooding, deciding.

'So it's time then?' Her eyes were as dark as coal.

He rehearsed the scene he anticipated in the living room and nodded. 'Yes, it's time.' He handed her the pistol.

Her pupils widened.

Leaning close, he smelled the fragrance of her hair.

He whispered. Finished, he straightened. 'My one consolation is that though you don't want to, you'll be helping me.'

Needing the friendly contact of flesh, he stooped and kissed her. On the cheek. As he would a sister. Considering what awaited him.

He turned and left the room. The guard seemed impatient.

'I know,' Orlik said. 'They want me.'

He walked along the hall. The living room grew brighter as he neared it. Plain, sparse, drab. A sooted fireplace. A threadbare sofa. A creaky rocking chair.

On which a gaunt joyless man surveyed him.

Orlik concealed his surprise. He'd expected his immediate superior or at worst the European director. But the man confronting him, more thin-cheeked and ferretlike than even himself, was the quarry he'd hunted, the Russian descendant of the Abelard group, the Soviet equivalent of Eliot.

A man named Kovshuk. Wearing black. He halted in the rocker, voice clipped, speaking Russian. Stern guards flanked him.

'I'll be plain. You had instructions to kill the American. You disobeyed. You arranged his escape. I assume you intend him to kill me.'

Orlik shook his head. 'I don't know what . . .' He sputtered. 'Naturally I'm honored to see you. But I don't understand. I can't be held responsible for inferior assistants. If they're so clumsy –'

'No. I don't have time for theatrics.' Kovshuk turned to a guard. 'Bring the woman. Use whatever method you like. Make her admit what she knows. Document their crimes. Then kill them together.'

'Listen.'

'Interfere, I'll kill you right now. I want to know where the American is.' Kovshuk turned to the guard again. 'I told you, bring her.'

Orlik watched the guard disappear. 'You're mistaken. I want the American as much as –'

'Don't insult me.'

Orlik's senses quickened. He carried a second gun. With no other choice, he drew it. If he killed the remaining guard before –

But Kovshuk had anticipated, already drawing his own gun, shooting.

Orlik took the bullet in his chest.

The impact jolted him. He lurched back, eyes wide, toppling. Despite the blood spewing from his mouth, he managed a grin.

He'd lost.

But won. Because from the hall he heard sharp pistol cracks, recognizing the Makarov's sound, confident both his disloyal assistant and Kovshuk's bodyguard were dead. The woman was as skilled as she was erotic.

A door banged open.

His senses faded. Nontheless he heard the Makarov bark again.

He'd warned her about the guards outside and where they were positioned.

He imagined her running through the night.

He grinned at Kovshuk. Heard the Citroën roar. The Makarov barked again.

And he died.

13

Erika's bare feet were slick with blood. She'd gashed them on the gravel lane as she raced from the house toward Orlik's Citroën. The key had been in the ignition as Orlik had promised. Her bloody feet slipped off the clutch and accelerator. Angry, she applied more pressure, switching gears, roaring faster down the lane, the rear wheels fishtailing, the night like a wall before her. She didn't dare flick on her headlights. Though she might skid off an unseen curve, she had to avoid the risk of making the lights a target.

As it was, the roar of the engine made a sufficient target. The rear window imploded. She heard repeated staccato bursts from automatic weapons, a sequence of wallops jolting the car. In the mirror, she saw strobelike muzzle flashes, recognizing the distinctive crack of the sub-machine guns.

Uzis. She'd had too much experience with them to be wrong. Suddenly understanding what Saul had felt like in Atlantic City, she skidded around a bend in the road she barely spotted in time.

Her thoughts intruded on her instincts. Why would Russians prefer Israeli weapons?

No time. Bleeding on the clutch, she jerked the gearshift higher. The dark was thicker away from the house. The Citroën scraped against a tree. She couldn't postpone it any longer, turned on her lights, and stared at a massive shadow crashing from the underbrush.

A van. She jerked the steering wheel to the left and floored the blood-slick accelerator. The Citroën veered past the front of the van, sliding sideways, its rear end whacking against a stump. The taillight shattered, but the wheels churned gravel, gaining traction, rocketing forward. She surged past the roadblock, seeing a tunnel of trees and bushes – at the end of which a country road beckoned.

Other Uzis rattled. The second taillight shattered. Good, it distracted their aim. She geared down, skidding from gravel to tar, aiming left on the country road. On a straightaway, she switched to high gear and watched the speedometer climb past 120 kilometers, urging it to the top.

She knew she'd be chased. The Citroën shuddered as if from structural damage. She had to run with it till it fell apart. Or she found a better car.

But the open road was before her, and her purpose was vivid. Orlik's whispered warning had been explicit, the interrogation before

215

him, the threat they both faced, the reprieve he was granting her. Prepared, she'd shot the man who came for her – and the guard in the hall. She'd killed the sentries who flanked the house. Though her bare feet stung from gravel, specks of which were embedded in her soles, she felt exhilarated, free and with a goal.

Saul needed her. Orlik had told her where he was.

But racing through the night, seeing headlights in her rearview mirror, resting her hand on the pistol beside her, she couldn't avoid the thought that earlier had occurred to her. The Uzis. Why would Russians prefer Israeli weapons?

The answer troubled her. Because the man who waited for Orlik at the house had been the Russian equivalent of Eliot. His guards, like Eliot's, had received killer-instinct training as their final preparation. They'd been taught to act like Israelis, and the consequences would be blamed on . . .

Erika clenched her teeth. On Israel.

She raged past farms and orchards. If the headlights gained on her, she'd stop and take her chances, blocking the road, blowing her pursuers to hell.

But despite the Citroën's shudders, she kept her distance, roaring through the dark.

Orlik's final whisper repeated itself in her mind. 'Saul's headed for Eliot. The old man chose the perfect sanctuary. It's a trap.'

But for whom? For Saul or Eliot?

She knew this much. Orlik had told her. A province. A city, a mountain valley.

Canada.

And she would get there.

REST HOMES/
GOING TO GROUND

1

The highway became so steep Saul switched from second gear to first, hearing the strain on the Eagle's engine, forcing the station wagon higher. He'd chosen this model because, while it looked conventional, it had four-wheel-drive capability. On the one hand, he didn't want to seem conspicuous. On the other, he didn't know how rugged the terrain would get before he reached his destination.

The terrain looked imposing enough already. An over-packed car with out-of-province license plates was stalled on the shoulder, its hood up, its radiator steaming. The driver – a harried man with his hands spread attempting to reassure his frightened wife and children – had evidently not been familiar with techniques of driving in the mountains. Probably he'd used too high a gear or worse, an automatic transmission, either of which would put too great a stress on the motor. Going back down, the driver would likely use his brakes instead of his gears to control his speed and end up burning the shoes and drums out.

Driving was complicated by more than just the steepness of the road. That slowed a car, but so did the long procession of laboring traffic above, retarded by an exhaust-belching semitruck at the head of the line. In frustration, Saul felt he crawled at a rate of millimeters instead of kilometers. The sharp switchbacks made driving worse. Angled left, Saul would suddenly reach a hairpin turn and try to keep the Eagle from stalling as he swung the steering wheel hard to the right, squeezing past downward traffic.

Above, beyond 10,000 feet, swollen mountains obscured the sky, snowcaps glinting. Granite ridges, studded with fir trees, zoomed down, furrowed as if a giant's fingers had gouged at them. The Canadian Rockies, though strictly speaking this section was known as the Coast Mountains, but Saul thought of them as an extension of the Rockies farther inland. Together, these British Columbia ranges were so huge and rugged they dwarfed the Colorado mountains he was familiar with, overwhelming him.

Below, the plain he'd left had a different splendor. Wooded slopes dipped to grassland, then to the sprawling expanse of Vancouver, its

217

expensive highrises contrasting with underground shopping centers, sleek subdivisions, and landscaped homes. The impressive Lions Gate suspension bridge stretched across Burrard Inlet, linking districts.

Paradise in the sun. A sea breeze dispelled the heat. To the west, sails gleamed in the sound. Beyond, Vancouver Island's mighty hills protected the city from ocean storms while the sheltered strait of Juan de Fuca admitted the warm Pacific current.

A perfect combination of climate and scenery. Saul squinted with hate. A perfect locale for a 'rest home.' Eliot – God damn him – had chosen his battlefield well.

He bristled, aggravated by the slow-moving traffic, anxious to reach the easier road at the top. To get there.

And pay back his father.

Mercifully, the road leveled off. Between slopes of pine, the belching semitruck squeezed toward the crushed rock shoulder, allowing traffic to go around. Saul put the Eagle in second gear, increasing speed, watching the heat gauge dangerously near the top creep lower as the motor worked less hard. He felt a breeze through his open window.

A speed limit sign said 80 kilometers. He stayed below the limit, noticing another sign – in French as well as in English – that warned about sharp curves. The slopes formed a V through which he focused on a towering peak as if he aimed through the notches on a rifle sight. Determined, he steered through corkscrews, mustering patience.

Soon now. Take your time. Eliot's counting on you to be so anxious you make mistakes.

He veered down a winding road to a wooded valley. To the left, he saw a glacial lake as blue as a diamond. To the right, a campground crammed with mobile homes advertised horseback riding and nature walks. The air was dry and warm.

These mountains were pocked with similar valleys. He quickly glanced at his terrain map as he drove. Orlik's instructions had been precise till now, bringing him thirty miles northeast of Vancouver. But from here, he had to rely on half-remembered rumors. After all, when he'd been younger, why would he have guessed he'd ever need a rest home? A safe house maybe, but . . .

There. He saw it on his map. Two ridges over. Cloister Valley. 'Remember that,' Eliot had said. 'If you're ever desperate enough to need a rest home, think of being cloistered. Go to that valley. Look for a sign. The Hermitage.'

Saul fought the urge to speed. He passed a fisherman on a bridge who paused in his angling to sip a bottle of beer. Labatt's. If this had been Cloister Valley, Saul would have taken for granted the fisherman was a sentry. But for now, the scenery was innocent. The sun glared directly overhead, its reflection making him put on Polaroids. With the claustrophobic peaks, though, sunset would come much sooner than he was used to. Though he couldn't rush, he couldn't dawdle. Timing was everything. He had to get there before dusk.

The map was precise. He reached a T intersection, turned right, and passed a log cabin motel. The road flanked a tumbling stream. He heard its splash. As he angled up a ridge, pines blotted the sun. He cursed.

His brother would never again feel cooling shadows.

2

Safe houses, rest homes. The designers of the Abelard sanction had been wise, understanding short-term as opposed to long-term goals. An operative, threatened, on the run, needed hope. Without it, what was the point of belonging to the craft? A neutral zone, a respite – even at Franklin, 'home free' had been the goal of games – was paramount. An operative required the chance to scuff the ground and say, 'All right, you beat me, but dammit all, I'm still alive. And dammit worse, you've got to let me back in play, I got here, see. I'm neutralized.' A guaranteed sanctuary, inviolable, where any attempt to kill meant instant reprisal.

But a safe house was temporary, designed for operatives and hired hands. What if you'd risen so high and made so many enemies you could never dare leave the safe house? What if your hunters hated you so much they'd never stop waiting for you to come out? It wouldn't matter how many guards you had to protect you as you left – you'd still be killed.

Clearly something better was needed than just the protection of what amounted to a motel. How many paces of your room could you tolerate – how many records could you listen to, how much television could you watch – before the wall squeezed in on you? The constantly repeated daily pattern eventually made a safe house a prison. Boredom became unbearable. You started to think about sneaking away, risking your hunters. Or maybe you saved them the trouble, sticking a gun in your mouth. A week of safety? Wonderful. Maybe a month. But what about a year? Or ten years? In a place like the Church of the Moon, even safety became damnation.

Something better, more ultimate, was needed, and the Abelard designers in their wisdom had imagined further. *Rest homes*. Permanent sanctuaries. Complete environments. Absolute satisfaction.

For a price. Faced with death, an outcast would gladly pay the limit for guaranteed immunity and every comfort. Not a safe house. A rest home. Always and forever. Desperation rewarded.

There were seven Abelard safe houses.

Rest homes, though, were complicated. Sweeping, huge, complete. Only three of them. And because their clients tended to be elderly, climate was a factor. Not too hot and not too cold. Not moist but not obscenely dry. A paradise in paradise. Because of the need for long-term security, the rest homes had been situated in traditional neutral countries, their politics stable – Hong Kong, Switzerland, and Canada.

The Cloister Valley. British Columbia. Canada.

The Hermitage.

Eliot had sought retirement, hoping to lure Saul into a trap.

But as Saul urged the Eagle higher, reaching the treeline, passing snow, about to descend to another valley, thinking of Chris, he murmured through his teeth, 'What's good for the goose is good for the fucking gander.'

Traps could be turned around.

3

He reached a crossroads, pausing to study his map. If he headed right again, he'd veer up a slope, go through a narrow pass, and, angling down, reach Cloister Valley. He assumed he'd find a weatherbeaten sign – nothing blatant certainly – for the Hermitage. An unaware traveler wouldn't know if it meant a lodge or someone's cottage. Trees would hide the property. No doubt a padlocked gate and a potholed lane would discourage curiosity.

He also assumed there'd be sentries down the lane to turn back unwelcome visitors. Every entrance to the valley would be watched. A country store would be a surveillance post, a gas station would be staffed with guards, a fisherman sipping Labatt's would this time have a walkie-talkie in his knapsack. From the moment Saul reached the pass, his every movement would be reported.

In themselves, these precautions didn't bother him. After all, a rest home needed security. Its administration would be professional, using first-rate tradecraft. What did bother him was that some of the sentries along the road would belong to Eliot, not the rest home.

That's the way he'd do it, Saul thought. Distribute a hit team through the valley, wait till I was spotted, and kill me before I ever got on the grounds. The rules forbid interference once I'm on neutral territory, but nothing says he can't kill me on the way. The entire valley isn't protected, only the land owned by the rest home. I'd be foolish to drive through the valley.

But he knew another way. Instead of turning right and heading up the pass, he went straight ahead. Three elk grazed in a meadow beyond a stream. A pheasant flew across the road. He studied a line of aspen to his right, glanced at his map, then back at the trees. What he looked for shouldn't be far. Wind fluttered the leaves, their silver undersides turning up, glinting in the sun. That made him conscious of the sun's lower angle. Three o'clock. At the latest, to take advantage of the remaining light, he had to be ready by five.

A half-kilometer farther on, he saw it. There, to the right through the trees, a lane so obscured by undergrowth he wouldn't have noticed if he hadn't been warned by the map. No cars ahead. None in his rearview mirror. Stopping, he flicked a switch on the left side of the steering column and converted the Eagle into four-wheel drive. He entered, snapping bushes.

The lane was narrow, bumpy, arched with trees. A hundred yards along, he braked. Getting out, swatting mosquitos in the forest's stillness, he walked back to the road. The bushes had been broken too severely to spring up and hide where he'd entered the lane. All the same, in theory no one in this valley ought to care.

In theory.

He dragged a fallen limb across the mouth of the lane, using it to prop the branches so they stood as if they hadn't been broken. Someone looking closely would see the cracks along their stems, but a passing motorist wouldn't notice. Several days from now, the bushes would lose their leaves, but by then it wouldn't matter if anyone guessed this lane had been used. His concern was for tonight and tomorrow. He propped up a second row of bushes, studied his work, and decided they looked as natural as he could expect.

He continued driving up the lane. Branches scratched the Eagle. Bushes scraped its bottom. Furrows jostled him. He reached a fallen limb too large for him to drive across. Getting out, he shifted it, then drove ahead and for precaution walked back, placing it across the lane again. Farther up, he bumped across a stream, hoping the water wouldn't soften his brakes, frowning as a boulder whacked his muffler.

But the Eagle had a high suspension, and the four-wheel drive worked perfectly, surviving its torture, gaining traction on a brutal hill. The map didn't show any buildings ahead. That puzzled him. He wondered who'd built the lane and why. Loggers? Hydro crews needing access to pylons through the mountains? Someone who owned this section and used it for hunting?

He hoped he wouldn't find out.

4

Disappointingly, the lane disappeared in the knee-high grass of an upper meadow.

End of the line. He couldn't risk driving through the grass. His tracks would be obvious from the air. He had to assume the Hermitage used surveillance choppers. Strictly speaking, the rest home's guards wouldn't have much reason to check this bordering valley, but Eliot's people would. Since they knew Saul was coming, they'd be extra cautious.

He glanced at his watch – four-thirty – then at the sun behind him, dipping toward the mountains. Dusk soon.

Move. He parked the Eagle off the lane, hidden by bushes from the ground and by trees from the air. Raising the hatch, he took out his equipment.

He'd arranged it skillfully in a Kelty pack: beef jerky, peanuts, dried fruit (protein and carbohydrates he wouldn't have to cook), extra clothes, all wool (in case of a storm, the hollow fibers of wool dried fast without needing a fire), a sleeping bag filled with Dacron (like the wool, it dried fast), fifty yards of nylon rope, a knife, first-aid kit, and canteen, already filled, though when he got higher he'd trust the streams. He wore thick-soled mountain boots, designed to help his feet support the weight of the pack.

Hefting its metal frame to his shoulders, he tightened the straps and cinched the waist belt. In a moment, he'd adjusted his balance to the extra bulk. He eased his pistol along his side where the pack wouldn't pinch it against his skin, then locked the car and started up.

Around the meadow, not across it. He still couldn't leave a trail. Skirting mountain flowers, he reached the other edge, hiking steadily through the foothills, climbing steeper, harder. Sweat soaked his shirt, forming rivulets between his shoulder blades beneath his pack. At first, he judged his direction by sight alone, knowing the ridge he wanted, but as deadfalls blocked his way, as trees hid his view and draws meandered, he checked his map repeatedly, comparing its contour lines to features around him, aligning it with his compass. Sometimes he found a sparsely wooded slope that seemed an easy climb in the direction he needed to go, but the map warned otherwise. Or else he chose a gully so thick with boulders he wouldn't have considered it if the map hadn't shown it soon became a gentle rise. Forewarned of a cliff beyond the next hill, he veered a quarter-mile out of his way to reach a stream he followed up a steep but climbable gorge.

He stopped to swallow rock salt, drinking. At high altitude, the body worked harder than normal, sweating abundantly. But the dry air evaporated sweat so quickly a climber might not realize the risk of dehydration. Lethargy could lead to coma. Water alone wouldn't help, though. Salt was needed for the body to retain the water. But Saul didn't taste the salt, a sure sign he needed it. Shoving his canteen back in his knapsack, he studied the gorge he'd climbed, hearing the roar of the falling stream, then turned to the bluffs above.

Their shadows lengthened. The forest became deep green, like a jungle or clouds before a tornado. Emotions stormed inside him. His steps were relentless, fierce. The thought of jungle had reminded him of missions with Chris in Nam, of a war they'd fought because Eliot wanted them to experience combat. He remembered escaping with Chris from the choppers in the mountains of Colorado because their father had betrayed them.

Chris, he wanted to scream. Remember the summer Eliot took us camping in Maine? The best week of my life. Why couldn't things have turned out differently?

The spongy loam of the forest led higher. Through a break in the trees, he saw the pass he aimed for, a saddlelike ridge between two peaks. He climbed past slabs of granite, the last rays of sunset glinting through the pass, a beacon through the dusk. He reached the entrance, more determined now. Too excited to feel the weight of his pack, he hurried to a sheltered bluff from which he gazed at the valley below.

It wasn't much different from the valley behind him. The peaks, the forest, were similar. A river, the Pitt, ran through it. The map said the next valley over was Golden Ears Provincial Park. But as he

222

stared at alpenglow from the dying sunset, he saw all the difference that mattered.

The valley was bisected by a road, roughly east to west. Another road cut across it, heading toward the park beyond. But the northwest sector . . . there . . . A sizable area was clear of trees. He guessed its lawn filled a hundred acres. Through binoculars, he identified stables, a swimming pool, a jogging track, a golf course.

In the midst of it all, a massive lodge reminded him of a place at Yellowstone where Eliot once had taken him and Chris.

Rest home. Haven.

Death trap.

5

In the night, it rained. Among his equipment, he had a sheet of waterproof nylon. Stretching it across two boulders, anchoring the sides, he made a shelter. Hunched beneath it, wearing his thick wool clothes, his sleeping bag around him, he ate, barely tasting the peanuts and jerky, peering at the dark. Rain pelted the nylon, dripping off the front. His cheeks felt damp. He shivered, unable to sleep, thinking of Chris.

At dawn, the drizzle changed to mist. He crawled from his sleeping bag and relieved his bladder among some rocks. He washed in a nearby stream, shaved, and scrubbed his hair. Hygiene was mandatory up here – he couldn't risk getting sick. Equally crucial, he had to preserve his self-respect. If he fouled his body with dirt and odor, his mind would soon be affected. Feeling sloppy, he'd start to think that way, and Eliot would catch him making mistakes. With yesterday's sweat rinsed off, his bare skin tingling, scoured to a glow, he regained energy, welcoming the goosebumps raised by the chill. Resolve became sharper. Rage surged through him. He was ready.

His clothes felt damp only a moment. His body warmed their hollow wool fiber, causing vapor to rise like steam. Assembling his equipment, he hefted the backpack to his shoulders and started grimly down the mountain.

This far from the Hermitage, he didn't worry about sentries. The terrain was too wild. With several passes leading into the valley, it would take too many men to watch every approach. The main thing was he'd avoided surveillance – and probably snipers – on the road. As he got closer, though, he expected guards, especially near the rest home's site in the valley's northwest corner. Despite his eagerness, he descended carefully, knowing how easy it was to injure an ankle under the stress of going down.

The sun came out at noon, adding to the heat of exertion. A cliff stretched so far in both directions he had to loop his rope around his pack, lower it, pull up one end of the rope to free it, then rappel. At last, by midafternoon, he reached the basin.

Calculating.

223

If snipers watched the road, they'd want a clear wide line of fire. That suggested they wouldn't hide in the trees, where all they'd have was a brief glimpse of a car. More likely, they'd prefer an elevated position, a bluff above the trees with a view for miles.

Concealed by a boulder, he peered from a ridge toward lower ridges, slowly shifting his gaze from left to right, inspecting details.

It took an hour. He finally saw them, two, a half-mile apart, watching both ends of the road. Each lay in tall grass on a bluff, wearing brown and green to match the terrain, a telescopic-sighted rifle in position. He wouldn't have noticed them if each hadn't moved slightly, one to reach for a walkie-talkie, the other a minute later to drink from his canteen. Across the road, a gate in a fence was equidistant between them, no doubt the entrance to the rest home.

The protocol was important. Outside the rest home, the valley was fair to use as a killing ground – there'd be no punishment to the snipers; they wouldn't have broken a rule.

But what about directly in front of the gate? What if someone demanding sanctuary was shot as he reached the fence? A rest home was meaningless if no one could get inside. Logic suggested a buffer zone around the place, a small ambiguous strip – no more than a hundred yards perhaps – that wasn't protected but wasn't un-protected either. A gray area, requiring prudence. An assassin might not risk execution by killing outside a rest home, but he'd face inquiries. There'd be an investigation before he was absolved.

The ambiguity could work to Saul's advantage. I have to show myself to reach the fence, he thought. A mile down the road, I'd be dead the instant they spotted me. But what about directly outside the gate? Would they hesitate, pondering the rule?

In their place, I'd shoot.

But I'm not them.

He crept back from the boulder, entering bushes, working lower. His map protected him. In the crowded trees, he couldn't see the bluffs the snipers lay on. Without a chart and a compass, he could easily wander into their sights. But having marked their positions on the map, he studied contour lines, carefully choosing a middle course through rugged terrain toward the gate. His progress was slow. This close, he had to scan the undergrowth ahead of him in case another sniper watched the gate.

He stopped, not needing to see the gate – his map showed he was in a trough fifty yards from the road, separated by thick shrubs and trees. All he had to do was . . .

Nothing.

Yet. The sun was still too high. It would make him too vivid a target. The best time to move was at dusk, when there'd be just enough light for him to see up close but not enough for them to aim at a distance.

He took off his backpack, eased it to the ground, and rubbed his shoulders. His stomach cramped. Till now, he'd controlled impatience. His goal had been distant. There'd been much to do. But with the rest home fifty yards away, with Eliot almost in his grasp, he ached from tension.

Waiting was agony. To keep his mind alert, he studied his surroundings.

A squirrel run along a branch.

A woodpecker tapped a tree.

The woodpecker stopped.

The squirrel threw up its tail, barked once, and froze.

6

His skin crawled.

Drawing his pistol, Saul crouched and swung to stare around him, quickly attaching a silencer. Alone, the woodpecker's sudden quiet meant nothing. In tandem with the squirrel's behaviour, it became significant. Something – someone else? – was out here.

His position was risky. Three hundred and sixty degrees of space to defend, and no suspicion of where the threat would come from.

If there was a threat.

He had to assume it. Think. If there's a sniper, he isn't behind you. Otherwise you'd have passed him. He'd have made his move by now.

Then he's ahead or on your flank. Trusting his instinct, Saul ignored his back and concentrated on the trees above this trough along the road. He heard me coming and waited for a target. When I stopped, he started to wonder if he was wrong. Maybe he isn't used to the forest and he thinks the noise was an animal.

But he can't take the chance. He'll have to find out.

Or maybe I'm the one who's wrong. Maybe it's me who spooked the squirrel. He shook his head. No, the squirrel kept running after it saw me. Something else made it freeze.

Sweat trickled past his eyes. *Where?*

A patch of green shifted slowly to his left.

His backpack stood upright beside him. Saul toppled it to the left – as a distraction, to make it seem he was diving to the ground. At the same time he pivoted to the right, coming up behind a bush, aiming at the patch of green.

A man in camouflage sighted a rifle where the backpack had fallen. Shooting, Saul heard three spits from his silencer as his bullets struck the man in the face and throat.

But he hadn't been quick enough. The man squeezed off a shot just before he lurched, unable to scream because of blood gushing from his throat. The crack of the rifle echoed through the forest, the bullet walloping the backpack.

Saul didn't bother getting his gear. He didn't pause to see if the man was dead. He didn't have time. He charged up the rim of the trough, scrambling through the undergrowth, not checking to see if someone else was ahead of him. It didn't matter. The shot would have warned them all. They'd turn, glaring at the forest, aiming their

225

weapons. When they couldn't raise their partner on his walkie-talkie . . .

They'll know I'm here. They'll radio for help and . . .

Now or never. Branches lashed his face. He scraped past a stump. But he kept sprinting, bursting from the trees, abruptly facing the road.

The fence was tall.

Barbed wire.

Shit. Not breaking stride, he veered toward the gate. At least, it was lower.

Something cracked on the asphalt behind him, a shot rumbling from a bluff. He zigzagged, a second bullet whacking the pavement ahead of him. He hit the fence, barbs tearing his clothes, ripping his hands. A third bullet snapped the strand of wire he reached for, whipping it forward, then back at his face. His cheek stung, bleeding. Clambering, he grabbed the top, swung over, and jumped.

Bending his knees as he hit the ground, he rolled.

But something stopped him.

Boots and bluejeans. An angry man pointed a magnum revolver at his chest.

Another man flanked him, wearing a brown checked hunting shirt, aiming a rifle toward the hills.

At once, the shooting quit. Of course. He'd reached the rest home. They didn't dare kill him now.

'You'd better have a damn good reason –'

Saul dropped the Mauser, raising his hands. 'It's my only weapon. Search me. I won't need it now.'

'– for coming here.'

'The best.' Blood dripped from his upheld palms, but he almost laughed. 'Abelard.'

It was all he had to say to gain asylum here.

7

They forced him back to the cover of trees and did indeed search him, totally, making him strip.

His scrotum shrank. 'I told you the Mauser's all I have.'

They checked his clothes.

'What's this packet taped to the inside of your shirt?' Instead of waiting for an answer, one guard tore the seal, opening the plastic, scowling. 'Papers.' He threw the pouch dismissively on the pile of Saul's clothes. 'Get dressed.'

'Who shot at you?' the other guard said.

'I thought they were sentries.'

'Cute. We don't shoot at guests. We protect –'

'But I wasn't a guest yet. Maybe some of your people thought I meant to attack.'

'Sure. One man. Attack. Quit being cute. Who was it?'

226

'I wouldn't have come here if everybody liked me.'

Engines roared, approaching.

'We'll find out.'

At once two vans appeared through the trees, swerving around a curve in the lane. They skidded, brakes squealing. Before they stopped, men jumped from the sides, dressed in outdoor clothes the same as these guards, burly, square-faced, cold-eyed, some holding rifles, others handguns, walkie-talkies dangling from their shoulders.

'The shots came from over there.' The first guard pointed up at bluffs to the right and left across the road.

The men scrambled forward as the second guard freed the gate.

'They've got five minutes on you,' the first guard said.

'The roads are blocked.' A man with a brushcut hurried through, his walkie-talkie slapping his side.

Two others with anxious silent Dobermans rushed by.

'One man's across the road,' Saul said. 'Fifty yards through the trees.'

'By now, he'll be gone,' a heavy man snapped.

'I doubt it. He's dead.'

They turned as they ran and squinted at him.

In twenty seconds, they'd disappeared.

The guard in the hunting shirt locked the gate. The other glared at Saul. 'You come with us.'

Saul gestured toward the fence. 'Who'll watch the store?'

The drivers of the vans came over, drawing pistols.

'Good,' Saul said and meant it. If the rest home's security was first rate, the guards who'd found him ought to be his escorts. They knew little about him. Even so, it was more than the others did.

They took him down the lane. He expected a Jeep or another van. Instead he saw a Pontiac with high suspension and oversized wheels, capable of crashing through the forest and ramming out of mud.

He nodded in approval, getting in back. A stout metal grill separated him from the front.

The driver pulled a lever near the emergency brake, locking Saul's doors. As the car surged from the trees, the second guard studied him through the grill, his handgun propped on the seat.

'If I wanted a concentration camp . . .'

'You'll get your retirement. First you have to qualify.'

'With what? A blood test?'

'If we let you in like this was a tourist trap, how safe would you feel? Relax. When you're registered, I'll even buy you a drink.'

'Did you say "buy"? You mean they're not free?'

'This isn't welfare, you know.'

'It's sure not paradise either.'

'Buddy, that's where you're wrong.'

The Pontiac lurched down the lane. Saul gripped the seat, glancing out, seeing metal boxes attached to trees. 'Electric eyes?'

'And sound detectors.'

227

'Quiet,' the driver told his partner. 'You want to give him a fucking guided tour?'

The second guard's eyes narrowed, dark at Saul.

They burst from the forest.

Seeing the estate, he understood. Lawn stretched forever. To the left of what was now a paved road, golfers avoided a sandtrap, heading toward a pond. To the right, guests strolled along a white stone path near flower gardens, benches, and fountains.

A country club. A park.

The road led up to the lodge, the peaks in the background reminding him again of Yellowstone. A helicopter took off.

But he didn't allow distraction. Concentrating on the resort, he prepared himself for . . .

What? He didn't know.

The Pontiac braked in front. Unlocking Saul's door, the driver got out, then the other guard, then Saul.

They flanked him, climbing concrete stairs to a porch that stretched the width of the building. It was made from sweet-smelling cedar, solid beneath his boots. Along one side, he glimpsed the edge of a tennis court, hearing the pock of balls. An unseen player laughed in triumph. With dusk approaching, they'd soon have to quit, he thought.

Then he noticed the arc lights rimming the court.

Sentries? He studied a gardener on a riding mower, a man in a white coat running with towels to the tennis court, a repairman caulking the edge of a window. But they seemed less interested in their duties than in Saul.

Okay then.

The guards took him in through large double doors. A tobacco and magazine counter to the left, a sports shop to the right. He passed a clothing store, a record shop, a druggist, reaching a lobby, spacious and high with wagon-wheel chandeliers and a gleaming hardwood floor. A counter with mail and key slots in the wall behind it reminded him of a hotel.

A clerk spoke urgently from behind a desk. 'He's waiting for you. Go right in.' He pointed quickly at a door marked Private.

The guards made Saul walk ahead – through the door, down a narrow hall, to a second door, this one unmarked. Before the guard in the hunting shirt had a chance to knock, a buzzer unlocked the door. Saul glanced behind him, seeing a closed-circuit camera above the first door he'd come through.

Shrugging, he went inside. The office was larger than he'd anticipated, richly decorated, faddish, leather, chrome, and glass. The wall across from his was a floor-to-ceiling window with a view of a swimming pool – people splashing – and a café. But directly ahead of him, beyond plush carpet, a man sat at a desk, scribbling to the side of a densely typed sheet of paper.

'Come,' the man said, too busy writing to look up.

Saul stepped across. The guards walked in behind him.

'No.' The man glanced up. 'Just him. Wait outside, though. I might need you.'

They eased back, closing the door.

Saul studied him. The man was in his early forties, his round face somewhat heavy, his hair cut modishly so it covered the tops of his ears. He had a bulky chest which, when he stood, became an equally bulky stomach. He wore a red blazer and navy pants, both polyester. When he came around the desk, Saul noticed his white shoes. When he held out his hand, Saul noticed his multibuttoned digital watch. But if the man looked like a high-pressure salesman or a Chamber of Commerce booster, his eyes were sharply alert.

He's dressing a part, Saul thought. Not a salesman. A recreation director. So garish he won't seem threatening to the guests.

'We weren't expecting a new arrival.' The man's smile dissolved as he glanced at blood on his palm from where he'd shaken hands with Saul.

'I had a little trouble' – Saul shrugged – 'getting in.'

'But no one said you'd been hurt.' The director's voice was alarmed. 'And your cheek. I'll have a doctor take a look. Believe me, I'm sorry. It shouldn't have happened.'

'It wasn't your fault.'

'But I'm accountable for what happens here. Don't you see? You're my responsibility. Sit down and relax. Would you like a drink?'

'No alcohol.'

'How about some Perrier?'

Saul nodded.

The man seemed delighted, as if his every wish was to serve. He opened a bookcase, then the door to a small refrigerator, twisting the cap off a bottle, filling a glass with ice, and pouring it full. He gave it to Saul, along with a napkin.

Drinking, Saul hadn't realized how thirsty he was.

The man looked pleased. Rubbing his hands, he sat behind his desk again. 'Food?'

'Not now.'

'Whenever you're ready.' He tilted back in his chair, scratching his eyebrow. 'I understand you came in the hard way, over the mountains.'

He's starting, Saul thought. It's slick, but it's still an interrogation. 'I like the woods.'

'Apparently someone else did. There was shooting.'

'Hunters.'

'Yes. But what were they hunting?'

Saul shrugged like a youngster caught in a lie.

'But why were they hunting you?'

'I'd rather not say.'

'Because you think we wouldn't accept you? That's not true. No matter what you've done, we're obligated to protect you.'

'I prefer to keep my secrets.'

'Understandable. But look at it our way. If we knew who wanted to kill you, we could protect you better.'

'And if word got around, maybe I wouldn't be welcomed.'

'By the other guests, you mean?'

Saul nodded.

'I grant your point. But I'm like a priest. I never repeat what I hear.'

'What about whoever's listening?'

'There's no bug.'

Saul simply stared.

'I admit there's interoffice communication. In case I have trouble.' He reached inside a drawer and flicked a switch. 'It's off.'

'Maybe I made a mistake.' Saul rose from the chair.

The man leaned forward. 'No. I don't mean to pressure you. All I want to do is help.'

Saul understood. If someone rejected the protection of a rest home, the director would have to explain to his superiors why the rest home had not been acceptable.

He sat back down and finished the Perrier.

'There's no protocol to be obeyed, though,' the man said.

'Naturally.'

'I forgot to introduce myself. I'm Don.'

You're also good, Saul thought. Now it's supposed to be my turn. 'Saul.'

'You gave the guards the password?'

'Naturally.'

'What is it?'

'Abelard.'

'Mind you, even a common gangster could have found that out. The password hasn't changed since 1938. Information gets around. You understand only operatives are allowed protection here.'

'I wouldn't have it any other way.' Saul reached beneath his shirt and peeled off the waterproof pouch. Sorting through several documents, he handed Don his passport. 'My legal name. I assume you'll check.'

'Of course.' Don opened the passport, frowning. 'And your cryptonym?'

'Romulus.'

Don slammed down the passport. 'What the fuck do you think you're –?'

Saul clicked his tongue. 'At least you're real. For a minute there, I wondered if you'd try to sell me a life insurance policy.'

'That's exactly what you need. You figure you can trick your way in here and –'

'Trick? Hey, somebody shot at me.'

'Hired help.'

'Not mine. I nearly got killed. You think I'd trust even an expert to shoot at me long distance and make it close enough to be convinc-

230

ing? Look at my hands. Ask your men outside how close the bullets came. I'm qualified. I gave the password. I want asylum.'

'Why?'

'You keep . . . because the president put out a contract on me. The Paradigm hit. I killed his closest friend.'

Don held his breath and shook. 'Your father?'

'What?'

'Or your foster father or whatever you want to call him. I suppose you don't know he's here.'

'What difference does it make? If my father's here . . .'

'He told me you want to kill him!'

'Then whoever he is, he can't be my father. Kill him? Insane. Where is this man? I want to –'

Don slammed his desk. 'That's bullshit!'

The door banged open. The guards came in.

'Get out of here!' Don said.

'But we thought there was –'

'Shut the goddamn door!'

They did.

Dusk thickened through the window. Arc lights suddenly gleamed, reflecting off the pool.

Don pressed his hands on the desk. 'Don't kid a kidder. He told me enough to convince me you want to kill him.'

'That's not the point.'

'What is?'

'The contract on me. It's legitimate. If I leave, I'm dead. Imagine how your reputation would suffer. The only director of a rest home to deny protection to a qualified candidate. The inquiry – and your execution – would entertain me. Except I'd be dead.'

'You've forgotten.'

'What?'

'You didn't win a contest. This place costs.'

'I figured.'

'Did you? It's a private club.'

'Initiation fee?'

'You guessed it. Two hundred thousand.'

'Steep.'

'Our clientele's exclusive. They pay to keep out the riffraff.'

'I prefer it that way. I've got standards too.' Glancing in his packet again, Saul drew out three papers, handing them across.

'What the –?'

'Gold certificates. Actually, it's more than two hundred thousand. Naturally you'll give me credit.'

'How the hell –?'

'The same way the others did.'

Saul didn't need to explain.

By skimming. The CIA had unlimited funds. For security reasons, no records were kept. It was common practice for an administrator to hide ten percent of an operation's cost as an unacknowledged fee, a bonus for deposit in Swiss accounts, the best insurance policy. If mistakes were made or politics became too risky, the administrator used the account for his protection. If his life was at stake, he entered a rest home.

Saul had learned the trick from Eliot, saving a portion of every mission's budget. Again, he'd used his father's tactics against him.

'Bastard. There's more. That's just the initiation fee. Those shops you passed. The tennis courts. The swimming pool. The golf course.'

'Never tried it.'

'The movies. You've got to eat. Quick chicken and burgers, or gourmet. It costs. You like television? We've got satellite reception. Bullfights. Pamplona. You can watch. It isn't free. We offer anything you want – from books to records to sex. If we don't have it, we'll send for it. Paradise. But friend, does it cost. And if you can't pay your way, that's the only time I can kick you out.'

'Sounds like I ought to buy stock.'

'Quit jerking –'

Saul pulled out two further slips of paper. 'Here's fifty thousand. Even a burger can't be that expensive. Rumor has it I can live six months here on that – and even go to the movies.'

Don shook worse. 'You –'

'Temper. Live with it. I qualify.'

Don seethed. 'Make one wrong move.'

'I know. I'm dead. Just tell that to my father. The same should apply to him.'

'Then you admit –?'

'I don't know what you mean. But I expect the same protection my father gets.'

'Shit.'

Saul shrugged. 'It's a problem for you. I sympathize.'

'You'll be watched.'

'Paradise. I hope those burgers are worth a quarter million dollars.' Standing, he walked to the door. 'And now that I think about it . . .'

'What?'

'I'm Jewish. Maybe I'll get religious again. I hope those burgers are kosher.'

8

Passing the guards, he heard Don call them angrily into the office. He grinned – but only till they disappeared.

His eyes smoldered. Leaving the hall, he approached the desk. 'I'm checking in.' His voice cracked with emotion.

He filled out a registration form. The two guards came back and stood in a corner, watching. Guests in tennis outfits walked by, glancing at him. Others in evening dress came out of a restaurant across the lobby, frowning back as they climbed a polished staircase.

Saul imagined what they thought. What was his background? His

232

bloody ragged clothes contrasted with their wardrobes. Friends, the riffraff's here.

He saw few women – the upper echelon of the profession had traditionally formed an aristocratic men's club, the old boy network. Many indeed looked old enough for retirement. Some he recognized: an American section chief who'd been stationed in Iran when the Shah was overthrown; a Soviet who'd attracted Brezhnev's disfavor by underestimating guerilla resistance during the Afghanistan invasion; an Argentine military intelligence director who'd been blamed for his country's loss of the Falklands war.

One pattern struck him. With few exceptions, no members of the same service associated with each other.

The clerk seemed surprised he'd been admitted. 'Here's your key.' He sounded puzzled. 'You'll find a list of services on the table by your bed. The hospital's downstairs in –'

'I'll treat the cuts myself.'

He went to the clothing store and the druggist. The two guards lingered in the background. As he went upstairs, they followed. They reached a muffled corridor, waiting outside his third-floor room.

He locked his door, impressed. The rest home's clients got the protection they paid for. His unit was equally impressive, twice the size of a normal room, a bookshelf separating the sleeping area from the living quarters. He found a tape deck and stereo, a large-screen television, a personal computer, and a modem that allowed, instructions said, a link by telephone with an information service called The Source. Everything from *The New York Times* to the Dow Jones averages could be summoned instantly on the computer's screen. Saul imagined the Wall Street news was paramount. The prices here no doubt forced a lot of clients to check their investments often. If their bills came due and they couldn't pay . . .

The furnishings were too luxurious for anyone's taste to be offended. In the oversized bathroom, he found a television, whirlpool, telephone, and sunlamp in addition to a separate tub and shower. Everything a fugitive could want.

With one exception. Freedom.

He stripped and soaked his cuts in the whirlpool, feeling the surge of water knead his muscles. Sensual, the massage reminded him of Erika, making him more determined to survive. He couldn't allow distraction. Chris. He had to concentrate on his mission. He had to avenge his brother's death. Eliot. Amid the powerful swirl of water, he shut out all enjoyment. Seething, he stepped from the tub.

His shots were up to date, so he wasn't afraid of tetanus. All the same, his barbed wire gashes needed disinfecting. The peroxide he'd bought from the druggist stung them. Bandaging the worst of them, he put on the new underwear, slacks, and turtleneck he'd bought. Their luxury embittered him.

With the lights turned off, he opened the draperies and stared down at the tennis courts. Though illuminated, they weren't in use. A

233

solitary jogger skirted them. Saul glanced beyond toward darkness hiding the mountains.

Paradise. The word kept coming back.

He'd been successful.

Getting here wasn't the point, though. Eliot was, and despite his cavalier act with Don, he knew he'd accomplished little.

So you're in. So what? Don wasn't joking. Those guards outside will watch you. Did you figure all you had to do was simply break into the old man's room and kill him? The odds are you'd be shot before you got that far. Even if you succeeded, you'd never make it out of here alive.

That isn't good enough, he thought. I've got to kill the bastard and live.

9

'He's *what*?' Alarmed, Eliot sat up rigid in bed. 'You're telling me he's here? He's actually in the building?'

'More than that. He applied for asylum,' Castor said. 'He registered and went to his room.'

'Applied for –?' Eliot blinked, astonished. 'That's impossible. The manager knows I came here because of Saul. He should have killed him. Why in God's name did he let Saul in?'

'Because of the contract against him.'

'What?'

'The president's after him. The manager can't refuse admission to an operative in danger.'

Eliot fumed. It wasn't supposed to be like this. The snipers outside should have killed Saul when he reached the valley. If Saul got around them, the rules of the rest home were supposed to take effect. Anyone threatening a guest faced execution. That was the law.

I wouldn't have chosen this place if I thought he could get inside.

The irony dismayed him. The Paradigm job, which had started everything, had resulted in his seeking protection here. Saul, the reason he needed protection, had used the aftermath of that job to force the manager to let him in as well.

I counted on the sanction to be my weapon. I never dreamed he'd use it against me.

'Pollux is out in the hall,' Castor said. 'He's guarding the door.'

'But Saul won't be that obvious. He'll attack in a way we don't expect.'

'Unless he never gets the chance.'

'I'm not sure what –'

'If I kill him first,' Castor said.

'And be killed yourself for breaking the rule?'

'I'd have an escape prepared.'

'They'd hunt you forever. What would it solve? They know you're

234

my escort. They'd assume I ordered you to kill him. I'd be blamed.
And killed as well.'

'Then what do we do?'

Eliot shook his head, distraught. The problem seemed insoluble.
Under the circumstances, given the rules, neither side could attack,
yet both sides had to defend themselves. For a moment, he reluctantly
admired Saul for being more clever than he'd expected. They were
here as equals, caught in a stalemate, the pressure increasing.

Who'd act first? Who'd make the first mistake?

Despite his fear, Eliot surprised himself. He was fascinated. 'Do?
Why, nothing, of course.'

Castor frowned.

'We let the system do it for us.'

10

Don knocked twice, then twice again. A guard, having studied him
through the peephole, opened the door. Don glanced both ways along
the hall – it remained deserted, he hadn't been noticed – and stepped
into the crowded room. He faced two guards, three nurses, a doctor,
and a maid. Squinting past them, he didn't see what he'd come for.

'In the bathroom,' the guard at the door said.

Nodding with detachment, Don subdued an unprofessional groan,
thinking, Jesus, another bleeder. As he walked to the bathroom, he
heard the guard lock the door.

But the body wasn't in the tub. Instead it lay on turquoise tile, face
up, grotesque, wearing pajamas, a bathrobe, both of which had been
opened. A slipper had fallen off.

Thank God I was wrong, Don thought. No blood.

The top of the skull was angled in his direction, so he saw the face
upside down and didn't recognize it till he stepped into the bathroom
and turned. Even so, he knew from the number outside the door,
cross-checked with his files, which guest had been assigned this room.

An Egyptian. The intelligence officer in charge of President Sadat's
security the day he was assassinated.

But the face was so distorted that without the benefit of knowing
who was supposed to be here Don wasn't sure he could have identified
the man the instant he saw him directly.

The cheeks were twisted in an awful grimace. The skin, though
swarthy, was also blue.

'His color,' Don said to the doctor. 'Cyanide?'

Lean and pasty, the doctor shrugged. 'Likely. It stops the cells
from getting oxygen. That would account for his skin being blue.
Hard to know for sure till the autopsy's finished.'

Don scowled in dismay. 'But the pain on his face. Isn't cyanide
supposed to be –?'

'Peaceful?'

'Yeah.' Don sounded confused. 'Like going to sleep.'

'Maybe he had a nightmare,' a guard said at the door.

Don turned, almost angry, uncertain if the guard was making a joke. But the guard seemed genuinely fascinated by the effects of poison.

'Actually,' the doctor said, 'it made him sick. He managed to reach the bowl, threw up, and fell on his face. We turned him over. He's been dead for several hours. The pressure of his cheek against the floor accounts for the way it's twisted. Maybe he didn't die from the poison so much as cracking his head. Or maybe he choked on his vomit. Either way, you're right – it wasn't peaceful.'

'Several hours ago?'

'More or less. We obeyed the protocol and tried to revive him. Adrenaline. Electroshocks to his heart. You can see the circular marks the pads left on his chest.'

'You pumped out his stomach?'

'We went through the motions, but there wasn't much point.' The doctor gestured toward the people in the living room. 'You'll have plenty of witnesses for the inquest. The only debatable issue is why didn't I rush him downstairs to the clinic. My professional response is he was so far gone I couldn't waste time moving him. Off the record, we couldn't rush him down and still maintain secrecy. You know the effect this sort of thing has on the other guests. Believe me, it wouldn't have mattered. He was dead.'

'Who found him?'

'I did.' The maid was trim, attractive, wearing an aproned uniform.

Don checked his watch. 'At eleven at night? Since when do rooms get cleaned –?'

'We had no arrangement if that's what you mean.'

'It wouldn't have mattered. There's no rule against it. But they'll ask at the inquest.'

Nervous, she tried to order her thoughts. 'The last few days he seemed depressed. I don't know – something about a letter from his wife.' She frowned. 'This morning he had the Do Not Disturb sign on his door. He wants to sleep late, I thought, so I came back after lunch, but the sign was still there. Then things got busy, and I forgot about him till a while ago. On impulse, I decided to check his door again, and when I still saw the sign, I got worried. I knocked several times. No answer. So I let myself in with the passkey.'

'Found him and called security.'

She nodded.

'You could have called security before you went in.'

'And embarrassed him if I was wrong.'

Don thought about it. 'You did fine. Tell the investigators just the way you told me. You won't have any trouble.' He glanced at the others. 'Any weak parts we ought to be clear on?'

No one spoke.

'Okay then. Wait. There is one thing. Where'd he get the poison?'

The doctor sounded exasperated. 'Where do any of them get it? These people are walking pharmacopeias. Never mind the drugs we supply. Most of them bring in their own. They know a thousand ways to kill themselves. If they don't use one way, it's another.'

'You took photographs?'

'Every angle.'

'Swell.' Don shook his head. 'A wonderful assignment, huh?'

'Eleven months since I came. Thank God, my tour's almost finished.'

'Lucky.' Don pursed his lips. 'Wait till after midnight to move him. The halls are usually quiet then. You two,' he told the guards. 'Make sure the elevator's empty before –' He glanced at the body. 'You know how it's done. I'll handle the arrangements. Since you're working late, you don't need to report till noon. But I'll want signed statements from you by then. Also' – he suddenly needed to get out of the bathroom – 'this kind of job, you'll get the bonus we agreed on. Use the customary explanation. He made an urgent choice to leave the rest home tonight. No one knows where he's gone.' Speaking quickly, he passed the doctor. 'I want the autopsy done tonight.'

'The tests take longer.'

'Noon tomorrow. The investigators'll be here soon. We have to prove the sanction wasn't violated. We have to be sure it was suicide.'

11

In his office, Don leaned against the door. His forehead broke out in sweat. He'd managed to stay in control all the way down here. He'd even been able to endure a conversation with several guests in the lobby, acting believably, as if nothing was wrong. Now, at last in private, his nerves collapsed.

He poured two fingers of bourbon, drinking them in one swallow. Soaking a towel in the sink of his wet bar, he pressed it cold against his face.

Eleven months? Is that what the doctor had said? Just one more month and the man'd be out of here? Don envied him. His own assignment had begun only six months ago. Another half-year, and sometimes he wondered if he'd make it.

When he'd first drawn this duty, he'd been delighted. A year in paradise, his only regret it'd be only a year. Anything he wanted, free – in addition to his hundred-thousand-dollar salary. Sure, he'd suspected you don't get benefits like that unless the job's a bitch. But he'd worked in intelligence for twenty years, organizing some of the biggest operations. System, that's what he was good at. So a rest home was complicated, fine. It required delicacy, no problem. He was a specialist in public relations.

But no one had told him about the mood here. No one had warned him there'd be so much death.

Of course not. Only a handful of people knew what really happened here – former managers and the investigating board – and they were forbidden to talk. Because if word got out, who'd be crazy enough to want to come? Without the concept of a rest home, who'd want to dedicate his life to the profession? Everyone eventually made mistakes. Everyone needed a heaven.

But this was hell.

He wasn't a field operative. He'd never belonged to the covert section, the dark side, the wet crew, whatever slang applied. He was front office, white collar. Before he'd come here, he'd seen only three bodies ever, and they'd been a friend and two relatives, dead from natural causes, lying in state at a mortuary. They'd given him the creeps.

Before. But now? He shuddered.

He should have guessed. A rest home was designed for ambitious people who were losers. Anything a person wanted. For a price. With guaranteed safety. That was the promise. A hundred acres of paradise. But no one guaranteed happiness. Don, who had to stay only a year, already coveted a trip to a burger joint where he'd stopped on his drive here from Vancouver. Late at night, he dreamed of walking through a crowded mall. A hundred acres. And sometimes he felt he knew every inch. The others – those who'd been here for years and had to stay forever – felt the claustrophobia even worse. To compensate, they indulged themselves. Drugs, alcohol, and sex. Gourmet meals. But how much could you shoot up or drink or screw or eat before it didn't satisfy? A hundred acres, getting smaller every second. Every day like the one before. With subtle variations.

When you used up all the variations, though?

He wasn't contemplative. Nonetheless, he'd noticed that only the losers who disdained the physical became satisfied here. Checking the library, he'd discovered their preference for spiritual topics. Saint Augustine. The teachings of Buddha. Boethius and the wheel of fortune. It intrigued him that the survivors of a life of action became meditative and monastic.

And the rest, who couldn't adjust? They poisoned themselves, OD'd, slit their wrists, or blew their brains out. Maybe they offered suggestions to each other, for lately several had sat in the sauna till they fainted and died from dehydration, or else they drank wine in their hot tubs till their skin was smothered and they died from oxygen starvation. But often when they lost consciousness, they sank and drowned.

12

Saul ignored his guards as he stepped from his room. There were two of them – the same as when he'd arrived last night. A different two, however. Don hadn't been kidding. 'You'll be watched.' No doubt another two would take over shortly. Around the clock in shifts. Two hundred thousand bought a hell of a lot of protection.

Followed, he went downstairs. It wouldn't be difficult, he assumed, to learn the number of Eliot's room. But what would be the point?

He couldn't go near it without alarming his guards. He could try to lose them, but that would cause a greater alarm. Besides, he still hadn't solved the problem of how to escape. The more he thought about it, the more he wondered if his goal was even possible. To avenge his brother, he had to kill his father, and yet – to keep himself alive – he couldn't kill him. The contradiction squeezed his brain.

There had to be a way. Deciding he didn't know enough, he began the hunt, studying the rest home, wandering through the lobby, its stores and restaurants, the medical clinic, then outside, inspecting the exercise areas, the gardens, the grounds. The guards stayed close to him. But the guests, sensing trouble, kept their distance. Their wary glances made him wonder how he could use their nervousness to his advantage.

He checked the swimming pool and the golf course. Eliot must have been told by now I'm here, he thought. So what'll he do? The logical choice would be to stay in his room – he knows I'd never risk going there. How long could he bear confinement, though? He knows I'm not about to leave. He'll refuse to hide forever. Instead of reacting to me, he'll want to force me to react to him.

But how?

Whatever, it would happen soon. Since he was to show himself eventually, he won't bother waiting. He'll accept the inevitable and break the stalemate right away.

But where? The old man's too brittle for bowling and tennis. All the same, he still needs recreation. What would he –?

It couldn't be anything else. Nodding with satisfaction, Saul came to the greenhouse under construction near the jogging track at the rear of the lodge.

He enjoyed imagining ways to use it.

But where would the old man go till it was finished?

13

'I didn't know you liked fishing.'

Hearing the voice behind him, Eliot turned from the river, wide and swift, with trees and bushes crowding the banks, though here a grassy slope led down to an inlet, still and clear. The water smelled sweet, but now and then the wind brought the hint of rancid vegetation – death and decay.

The man on top of the bank had the sun behind him. The glare stabbed Eliot's eyes. He raised a hand to shield them, nodding in recognition. 'You don't remember our fishing trips? I like it. But I seldom had time to indulge myself. Now that I've retired, though . . .' He smiled, reeled in his line, and set the pole on the bank.

'Oh, I remember those fishing trips, all right.' Saul's voice was hoarse with rage. The sinews in his throat tightened, choking him. 'Just you and me.' He stalked down the bank. 'And Chris.' He glared at Eliot's straw hat, red checked shirt, stiff new jeans, and rubber boots. He growled, 'No black suit and vest?'

'To go fishing?' Eliot laughed. 'I don't wear business clothes all the time. You've forgotten how I dressed when you and Chris and I took those camping trips.'

'We keep coming back to Chris.' Livid, Saul clenched his fists, stepping closer.

Bending, Eliot ignored him, reaching into his tackle box.

Saul pointed as if he had a gun. 'That better not be a fucking candy bar.'

'No Baby Ruths, I'm afraid. Sorry. Though I wish I'd thought of one. For old time's sake. I'm only changing bait.'

A foot-long trout rose. Snatching a bug off the surface, it left a widening circle.

'See what I missed. I've been using a lure when it ought to be a fly.'

'Bait.' Saul's nostrils flared. 'I asked around. You've got two body-guards.'

'Companions. That's right. Castor and Pollux.'

'McElroy and Conlin, you mean.'

'Very good.' Eliot nodded. 'I'd have been disappointed if you hadn't done your homework.'

'Other orphans you lied to.' Furious, Saul glanced around. 'So where the hell are they?'

'Playing tennis, I believe.' Eliot picked up a second pole. 'They don't go everywhere with me.'

'That doesn't make you nervous – being out here alone?'

'In a rest home? Why should I feel nervous? I'm protected.'

Saul stepped even closer. 'Wrong.'

'No, *you* are.' Eliot angrily threw down the pole. 'You've lost. Admit it. If you kill me here, you die as well. After all these years, I know how you think. You wouldn't be satisfied unless you got away with it. You can't, though.'

'Maybe.'

'*That's not good enough. You'd want to be certain.*' Eliot's chest heaved. 'That's why I'm out here alone today. I could have hidden in my room, but I'm too old to waste my time. This place is bad enough as it is. You must have sensed the mood. The guests are dead already. They just don't know enough to lie down.'

'You made your grave.'

'Not me,' Eliot raised his chin, proud. 'I'll soon have my roses again. I've got this.' He gestured fiercely at the pole. 'So here I am, the best chance you'll get. Kill me now, and escape across the river. Who knows? You might even get away. Otherwise, either make peace with me, or dammit, leave me alone.' He stared at the river, swallowing, his outburst having weakened him. 'I'd rather, though, we got along.'

'It won't be that easy.' Saul tasted something bitter. 'One thing you owe me.'

'What?'

'An explanation.'

'Why? Would it make a difference? If you know about Castor and Pollux, you must have learned about –'

'There were five of you.' Saul spoke rapidly, spitting his words. 'The descendants of the original Abelard group. Each of you had orphans, sons, fanatically loyal. Just like Chris and me. You used us to sabotage operations you thought were wrong.' He gestured, impatient. *'Get on with it.'*

'You learned all that?' Eliot blinked, astonished.

'You taught me.'

Studying Saul with new awareness, Eliot slowly sat on the bank. His wrinkles deepened. His skin turned a darker gray. 'An explanation?' He struggled with his thoughts. For a moment, he didn't move or even seem to breathe.

He sighed. 'All right, I guess you deserve . . .' He squinted at Saul. 'When I was young' – he shook his head as if he couldn't remember ever being young – 'just getting started in the profession . . . I used to wonder why so many foolish decisions were made. Not merely foolish – disastrous. Cruel. At a cost of so many lives. I asked my foster father.'

'Auton.'

'You know that too?'

Saul only glared.

'He said in his day he'd wondered the same. He'd been told the decisions only *seemed* disastrous. Underlings like himself didn't have the big picture. There was a room with maps and strategy boards. High-level politicians went there to get the big picture, and sometimes they had to make decisions that might look stupid from a narrow point of view but actually were smart if every factor was considered. He said he believed this for many years till he rose so high he was one of the men in that room, and what he discovered was that the decisions were exactly as stupid as they appeared. Those men had no big picture. They were as confused, as petty as anyone else. Eventually my promotions allowed me in that room, and I discovered what he meant. I've seen the secretary of state refuse to talk to the secretary of defense – I mean he literally turned his back on the group and sat in his chair facing a corner. I've seen men arguing about who was allowed to sit next to whom – like school kids – all the while they committed billions of dollars to interfere with foreign governments in the name of our national security, but actually because big business felt threatened by socialist factions in those countries. They endorsed dictatorships or fascist coups or –' Eliot jerked in disgust. 'What we did in Ecuador, Brazil, Zaire, Indonesia, and Somalia alone makes me sick. All told, millions of people have been killed because of our interference. And the rank deception. Skilled operatives dismissed when they send in accurate reports that aren't in line with current political thinking. Then someone in the front office rewrites those reports to make them what the administration wants to read. We don't gather truth. We

241

disseminate lies. When Auton asked me to take over for him as a descendant of the Abelard group, I grabbed the chance. Someone had to act responsibly, to try for balance and sanity.'

'The Paradigm job,' Saul said.

'All right, let's get to it. We've got an energy problem. So what do we do? We make an agreement with the Arabs to buy cheaper oil, provided we stop our commitments to Israel. All unofficial, of course, the negotiations conducted by American billionaires – but with the tacit agreement of our government. The ultimate result? We get to drive big cars while Israel disappears. I'm not denying the claims of Arab factions. The Mideast situation's complicated. But dammit, Israel exists. We're talking about destroying a nation.'

'So you had me kill the negotiators.'

'A few men as opposed to a nation. The message was clear – don't try it again.'

'But after, you tried to kill *me*.'

'The president wanted to get even for his best friend's death. With that kind of power behind the investigation, you'd have been found.'

'You know how I felt about you. I wouldn't have talked.'

'Not willingly. But under chemicals, you'd have sent them to me. And under chemicals, I'd have sent them to the rest of the group. It had to be protected.'

'That isn't logical.'

'Why?'

'Because the nation you wanted to protect – Israel – was the nation blamed.'

'Temporarily. Once you were killed, I planned to show you worked on your own initiative. A Jew, determined to protect your spiritual country. I'd already insured the failure of your last few jobs – to prove you were unstable. Israel would be exonerated.'

'Sure. And I'd be dead. Is that what you call love?'

'You think I did it easily?' Eliot's voice cracked. 'The nightmares. The guilt. Isn't my grief the proof I didn't want to do it?'

Saul shook with contempt. 'Words. Castor and Pollux and me. What the hell happened to the rest? Not counting Chris, fourteen other orphans.'

'Dead.'

'On similar missions?'

Eliot's throat heaved. 'I didn't order it. They were casualties.'

'That's supposed to make it all right?'

'You'd prefer they died for the men in that room? They were soldiers.'

'Robots.'

'But working for someone whose values are more substantial than their government's.'

'Values? You want to talk about . . . ?' Saul's chest constricted. 'Here's one you never heard of. You don't betray someone you love!' He trembled, burning. 'We trusted you. What else made the shit you put us through bearable? We wanted your high opinion. Love? You're so damned arrogant you think it's your right. You want to save the world? When we're all dead, there'll still be assholes in that room. And none of us will have mattered. Except for the comfort we gave each other.'

'You've missed the point. Because of sons like you and operations I had you sabotage, I've saved who knows how many thousands of innocent lives.'

'But Chris is dead. As far as I'm concerned, it's a damn poor trade. Hey, I don't know those other people. I'm not even sure I'd like them.' Glaring, barely able to restrain himself, Saul shook his head with disgust and walked up the bank.

'Wait! Don't turn your back on me! I haven't finished yet!'

Saul didn't stop.

'Come back! Where do you think you're going? I didn't say you could leave!'

Saul swung at the top. 'I'm through obeying. A son ought to comfort his aging father. Me? I'll make your last days hell.'

'Not here! If you kill me, you die and lose!'

'A son gets big enough –'

'What?'

'And smart enough to crush his father. What you didn't count on was I loved Chris more than you.' With a final glare, of utter contempt, Saul pivoted sharply. Stalking away, he disappeared beyond the bank.

14

The river hissed. Eliot tried to stand, but his strength gave out. Legs buckling, he slumped on the bank. Throughout the argument, he'd made sure not to glance at the wooded bluff across the river.

But now he did. In confusion.

Castor and Pollux were over there. Along with the rest home's manager, an investigator who'd come with a team to conduct an inquest on a suicide, and most important, a sniper.

He'd calculated every detail. Saul had two options. To listen to reason. Wasn't the argument – thousands of lives – persuasive? Wasn't one man's life, even Chris's, worth the sacrifice?

Or else to try to kill me.

If Saul had chosen the first, I could've lived my last days in peace, perhaps returned to my mission, and saved more lives.

If Saul had chosen the second? Trying to kill me, he would have been shot. With witnesses, I'd have been absolved. The end would have been the same.

But – Eliot frowned – something was wrong. Saul had done the unexpected, choosing neither. He hadn't been convinced, but he didn't try to kill me. Nothing was changed.

Except.

He seemed too sure. He balanced his actions carefully, never coming too close.

Had he guessed? Is it possible I taught him better than I knew? Can he read my thoughts?

It couldn't be.

15

'You were with them.' Squinting, Saul sat at the top of the lodge steps, waiting.

'What?' Don stopped in surprise, putting a muddy white shoe on the bottom tier.

'You ought to do something about your wardrobe.'

Don peered down at the knee ripped out of his red polyester slacks. Reflexively he picked burrs from his navy blazer. 'I went for a walk.'

'In the woods. I know. With them.' Saul pointed past the tennis courts toward Castor and Pollux, an investigator who'd arrived by helicopter this morning, and a narrow-eyed man who carried a long slim case that might have contained a billiard cue. Or a sniper's rifle.

Approaching from the river, Eliot clutched his fishpoles and tackle box.

'My, my, he didn't catch a fish.'

'What do you mean I went with them?' Don said.

'When I came here, the first thing you did was accuse me of planning to kill a guest. You slapped two guards on me. Then all of a sudden the guards disappeared, so I followed the old man to the river where he offered me the chance to kill him. Since I never intended to kill him to begin with, I didn't know what he was talking about. He's my father, after all. Naturally I felt like seeing him. But he started talking crazy, so I walked away, and you'll never guess what happened next. All of a sudden my guards c̲‗‗‗‗‗‗ ointed at two men on lawn chairs near him. 'What would *you* think?'

'I –'

'It looks to me like that old man set me up. If I laid a hand on him, I'd be dead, and there'd be witnesses to make it legal. Don, tsk, tsk. You're not exactly watching over my interests.'

The manager puffed his chest as if to argue. It deflated like an inner tube. He gave up the effort. 'I had to go along. The old man insisted you'd kill him.'

'And without proof, you believed him.'

'Hey, he went to the investigating team. If I argued, they'd think I wasn't doing my job. A test. That's all it was. If you meant no harm, you wouldn't be hurt. If you tried to kill him –'

'But I didn't. I paid a lot for protection, and what I'm getting for it is threats. Everything's reversed. The old man just proved he wants to kill *me*. I deserve – hell, demand – equal treatment.'

'What are you talking about? You're already guarded.'

'House arrest. They're not protecting me. They're watching me. In the meantime, Eliot can do whatever he wants. It isn't right. He ought to be guarded as well. And not by those clones he brought with him. Your own men. He's paranoid enough to try something foolish.'

'Absurd.'

'If it happens, you'll wish to God you'd listened. The investigators'll ream you out. I'm telling you he's crazy. I also want those thugs of his under surveillance.'

'I don't have the staff!'

'Just six more guards?'

'In shifts of three? In addition to the men I've got on you? That's twenty-four!' Don sputtered. 'I need those men other places. And that's just for now! What happens when the other guests catch on? They'll want protection too! A lot of them were enemies before they retired! The only reason they're able to sleep at night is their confidence in a rest home! If they thought its neutrality could be violated . . . guests being followed everywhere? Bodyguards scrambling all over each other? A rest home's supposed to be quiet and peaceful!'

'You think the others haven't noticed you've got men watching me? When I went for breakfast this morning, everybody in the restaurant took a look at my guards and couldn't wait to get out of there.'

'You've been here only two days and –'

'What?'

'Threatened forty years of tradition.'

'Not me. Eliot. And you. I didn't ask for those watchdogs. What goes for me should go for him. If I'm being tailed, then dammit, so should he.'

Don gestured. 'I won't put guards on him. This madness can't be allowed to escalate.'

'Logically you've got only one other choice.'

'What is it?' Don looked hopeful.

'Do it the other way around. De-escalate. Call off your watchdogs.'

16

Flanked by Castor and Pollux, Eliot tensed as he entered the greenhouse.

He'd been anxiously waiting for its completion. Eager as a lover, he came to his roses.

But someone else was in here. At the other end, a man straightened from under a table and ducked out the back.

Eliot frowned. 'Wait a minute! What were you –?' Rushing to the door, Eliot threw it open, watching Saul cross the jogging track toward the lodge. 'Come back here!'

Saul broke into a run.

'What was he –?' Eliot swung to Castor and Pollux. 'Check under that table.'

Puzzled, Castor knelt. He groped and murmured, 'Wires.'

'What?' Startled, Eliot crouched, peering under. Two wires, red and black, dangled from a hole in the table leading up to a rose bed.

'Jesus.'

'Not a bomb. Not here,' Pollux said.

'The way he killed Landish.' Eliot's eyes gleamed. 'What are you waiting for? Call security. Have him stopped if he tries to leave the grounds.' Eliot lurched to his feet and almost cheered. 'Now I've got him. I can prove he wants to kill me.'

Castor rushed to the phone.

'He figures he's a match for – wasn't even fast enough to finish before I got here.' Eliot laughed. 'I've beaten him.' Turning, he shouted to Castor on the phone. 'Tell that manager to get out here!'

'Where would he get explosives?' Pollux asked.

'The same place you would! Look around! Fertilizer! Peat moss! He could go to the druggist and mix a cocktail! All he'd need was batteries and –!' Eliot shoved his hands in the rose bed. 'Help me find it!'

Pollux watched, dismayed.

17

When Don arrived, he opened his mouth. No sound came out. The greenhouse had been built to Eliot's specifications. State-of-the-art equipment. Rare varieties. All of it was ruined. Eliot had started with the bed beneath which wires dangled. Tracing the wires through soil and roses, he'd yanked and dug, tearing, throwing, lunging from one bed to the next till he was covered with dirt, and roses lay around him.

'Where? Dammit, I know it's here! He planted a bomb! I've got to find it!'

Flinging earth, he staggered against a glass wall, almost crashing through it.

Castor and Pollux rushed to help.

'Where'd he put it?'

Pushing his sons away, Eliot heaved on the wires, lurching back as they pulled free. He stared at two bare-stripped ends. 'Oh, Jesus, no. The bastard . . . ! There wasn't any . . . !' Sobbing, the old man sank to the floor.

18

I've had it, Don thought. A stunt like that. He's made as much trouble as he's going to.

It had taken an hour for him to deal with the disturbing aftermath of what had happened at the greenhouse – medical attendants examining Eliot before they escorted him back to the lodge; bomb specialists verifying the absence of explosives. But at last he'd been able to get away. Raging into the gym at the lodge, he faced the attendant. 'Grisman's supposed to be here.'

246

'He left a minute ago.'

Don slammed back through the door. Too furious to wait for the elevator, he pounded up the stairs. Grisman'll want to change his clothes.

Sweating, telling himself he had to get back in shape, he reached the third floor, pivoting in time to see Grisman go in his room. 'Hey, stop right there! I want to talk with you!'

But Grisman didn't hear. Already in his room, he shut the door.

Don stormed down the hall. 'You bastard.'

Two rooms away, the blast jerked him off his feet. Concussed, his ears rang as the door blew off Grisman's room.

'No!' Stunned, Don crawled to the door. Guests jerked open other doors. He didn't pay attention.

'Grisman!' Smelling sulphur, Don squirmed in.

The room was destroyed, the stereo, television, and computer shattered, the walls charred. Embers smoldered on the bed. The smoke alarm shrieked.

'Grisman!'

Coughing, he lurched to the bathroom.

There! On the floor! Thank God, he was breathing!

19

'You can't be serious! You think I –!'

'Either you or them.' Don pointed at Castor and Pollux.

'He made the bomb himself!' Eliot said.

'And set it off? Ridiculous. It almost killed him.'

'Almost? You think this is fucking horseshoes! Isn't it obvious? He took cover in the bathroom before he set it off!'

'But why would he –?'

'To blame it on me, for Christ's sake! He pulled that stunt with the wires to make it seem I was angry enough to pay him back!'

'Or maybe you rigged the wires yourself. To blame it on him. To make it seem he was playing with bombs and one went off.'

'You dumb . . . You think if I rigged a bomb it wouldn't have killed him?'

'I think the bylaws say if a guest keeps causing trouble I can give him a refund. I'm requesting a hearing. What I'd dearly like – I don't know who's at fault, so I'll pick both of you – is for you and your son to settle your problems somewhere else.'

20

Saul lingered in the lobby, glancing toward the elevator and the stairs. His flashburns hurt, but he felt too excited to care. Pretending interest in a window display of jogging shoes, he studied the reflection of the entrance to the restaurant.

At seven, his patience rewarded, Eliot – flanked by Castor and Pollux – came down the stairs. They went in the restaurant. Waiting a minute, Saul followed.

The guests reacted at once, setting down forks, swallowing thickly, glancing from Saul to Eliot, then back again. Feeling the tension, several demanded checks. Others, coming in, took one quick look and retreated to the lobby. The room became nervously quiet.

Though Eliot faced the entrance, he studied the menu, spoke to Castor and Pollux, and deliberately avoided noticing Saul.

'I'd like that table over there,' Saul told the maître d'.

'May I suggest the one over here, sir – in the corner?'

'No, the one across from the old man suits me fine.'

He didn't give the maître d' a chance to argue. Walking across, he sat so he stared directly at Eliot six feet away.

Eliot tried to ignore him. Other guests got up and left. Surrounded by empty tables, Saul kept staring.

Eliot sipped water.

Saul did, too.

Eliot broke off a piece of garlic bread.

Saul did the same.

They chewed in unison.

Eliot wiped his mouth with a napkin.

Saul reciprocated, keeping his eyes on Eliot's. It gave him pleasure to know he was using one of Chris's tricks against their father. Chris had told him about the monastery. 'Some of us were desperate to stay. A few, though, wanted to leave. They didn't have the courage to say so. What they did was make a nuisance of themselves. The best way? To mock a companion at dinner. Sit across from him and mimic every action. There's no defense. Your opponent gets trapped in your repetition. You follow him, but he follows you. He can't break the pattern. It drives him crazy. Eventually he complains. The irony is the monastery's director can't tell if you're making trouble or the other guy's just imagining things.'

Saul mimicked Eliot's every movement.

A hand to the chin.

A scratch on the eyebrow.

An exasperated sigh.

It took ten minutes. Eliot suddenly threw down his napkin, stalking toward the lobby, followed by Castor and Pollux.

'Was it something he ate?' Saul asked the empty room.

21

He came down to the lobby, puzzled, having been informed that he had a visitor. The rest home permitted them, provided credentials were in order and a search revealed no weapons. But he couldn't imagine who would want to see him. Eliot, he suspected, was retaliating.

When he saw who it was, however, he felt his stomach shrink. He stopped, amazed. 'Erika? How did –?'

Wearing a tan skirt and yellow tanktop, she crossed the lobby, smiling, hugging him. 'Thank God, you're alive.'

Her arms around him, he had trouble breathing. Time stopped. 'I can't believe you're here,' he said. Trembling, confused, he leaned back. 'Orlik . . . How . . . ?'

'He's dead.' She looked disturbed. 'Before he was killed, he let me escape. He told me where you'd gone. I'll explain later.' She frowned at his face, her voice concerned. 'What's happened to you?'

'These flashburns?' He gingerly touched his cheeks, then glanced around the lobby, echoing her words. 'I'll explain it later.' He smiled in anticipation of describing what he'd done.

But she shook her head, frowning harder. 'Not just the burns.'

'Then what?'

'Your eyes. I don't know how to describe . . . They're . . .'

'Go on. Say it.'

'Old.'

He flinched, feeling as if he'd touched an electric current. Disturbed, he had a sudden need to change the topic. 'Let's go.' He tried to sound casual. 'I'll show you the grounds.'

The sun was powerful. His head throbbed as they walked on a white stone path beside a fountain, the mountains encircling them.

But he couldn't forget what she'd said. 'I haven't been sleeping well.'

She faced him abruptly, worried. 'Your cheeks. They're –'

'What about them?'

'Haggard. Look at you. You've lost weight. You're pale. Are you feeling all right?'

'I've –'

'What?'

'Almost beaten him. I've nearly won.' His eyes flashed, and yet were black.

She stared at him, appalled.

'There's a hearing tomorrow,' he said. 'To decide if we should be told to leave. As soon as he's off the grounds –'

She interrupted emphatically. 'It isn't worth what it's doing to you. You've changed. For God's sake, leave. I've got a car. We could –'

'Not when it's almost over.'

'It'll never be over. Listen to me. I know I told you to get revenge. But I was wrong.'

'You couldn't be if it feels this good.'

'But you'll lose.'

'Not if I stay alive.'

'No matter what. This isn't professional anymore. It's personal. You're not emotionally equipped for that. You'll suffer the rest of your life.'

'For avenging my brother?'

'For killing your father. Your conditioning's too strong.'

249

'That's what he's counting on. But I'm beating him.' His voice had the sharp edge of hate.

And Erika suddenly knew she had to get out of here. The place felt like death. It was wrong. She'd never felt such revulsion.

Her only hope was to tempt him to go with her. She'd planned to stay the night, but she sensed she had only the afternoon.

They told each other what had happened since they'd been together last. They returned to the lodge, went up to Saul's room, and slowly undressed each other. She didn't care about the sex. She wanted to lure him, to save his soul.

But even as they embraced, covering each other with nakedness, Saul shuddered in alarm. He knew it wasn't possible, but it seemed Chris lay beside him, dead eyes reproving him.

Guilt wracked his mind. I shouldn't be here. I have to be hunting Eliot.

But loneliness insisted. Joining with Erika, he suddenly realized not two but three of them thrashed on the bed. Not only he and Erika, but Chris as well.

'Love you!' he exclaimed. 'Oh, God!'

And Erika, knowing something terrible had happened, also knew she'd lost him.

22

'You won't even stay for dinner?'

She glanced at the lodge, revolted. 'I have to go.'

'I hoped you could –'

'Help you? No, it's wrong. This place is – Come with me.'

He shook his head. 'I haven't finished.'

'It doesn't matter if you kill him. Don't you see? He's already won. He's destroyed you.' Tears rolled down her cheeks. She kissed him. 'I lost you ten years ago. Now I've lost you again.' She shook her head sadly. 'I'll miss you.'

'In a week, I'll have what I want. I can join you.'

'No.'

'You're telling me not to come?'

'I want you to. But you won't.'

'I don't understand.'

'I know.' She kissed him again. 'That's the trouble.' Getting in her car, she rubbed her tear-swollen eyes. 'In case I'm wrong, the embassy can tell you where to find me.'

'There's a place I know in Greece,' he said. 'The sea's so blue –'

Her throat made an anguished noise. 'I bet. And the waves roll in, and the swimming's – Don't I wish. Guess what?' She raised her chin; it trembled. 'I've been thinking about resigning. See you, love. Take care.' She started the car and drove down the lane.

23

Unsettled, he watched till her car disappeared in the trees, heading toward the valley road. Something felt empty in him. His brain reeled, disoriented, as if an outside influence had intruded on a perfect closed system. What's happening to me?

Confused, he turned to walk up the steps to the lodge, suddenly understanding what she'd tried to tell him. I stayed. Till the old man's punished, I'll never join her.

But by then it'll be too late. She offered herself, and instead I chose my father.

How can she accept me after that?

Remembering his uneasy feeling about the rest home, he suddenly wondered if he'd damned himself. He almost leapt from the steps to run to a car and . . .

What? Chase after her? Tell her I'm going with her?

Thoughts of Eliot intruded. Paralyzed on the steps, he peered again toward the road between the trees. Pressure built in him. Anguish tore his soul. His will tilted one way, then the other. What to do? Whom to choose? Chris seemed to stand before him, his sad eyes narrowed in accusation.

Paralysis changed to resolve.

<h2 style="text-align:center">24</h2>

Don paced, gesturing angrily toward the swimming pool beyond the wall-sized window in his office. Though the day was hot and bright, the pool was empty. 'All the stunts you've been pulling, you've made the guests so nervous they don't want to leave their rooms. The restaurant's deserted. The grounds – hell, I could send out naked dancing girls, and nobody'd be there to notice. Rumors of your . . . disagreement, shall we say? have got around. The smart money outside says stay away from here, pick the rest home in Hong Kong or Switzerland. Talk about trouble. The bunch of you are it.'

The trouble he referred to was composed of Eliot, Castor, Pollux, and Saul. They sat – Eliot and his escorts separated from Saul, watched by guards – as Don continued. 'So here's the situation. The rules of the sanction force a rest home to accept an operative in need, provided he pays the necessary fees. But the rules don't force a director to put up with disruptive guests. I've contacted my superior and explained the problems here. I've been in touch with the supervising board. I've requested a hearing and received a judgment. The Abelard rules say if a director has sufficient cause – and Christ, do I have sufficient cause! – he can instruct a guest to pack his bags.' Don pointed at the door. 'And leave.'

Eliot straightened angrily. 'And have this man try to kill me the instant I leave the grounds?'

'Did I say I'd let him try to kill you? We're not animals. The board's prepared to compromise. You paid for services you didn't receive, so here's the check refunding the balance of your fees. It's only fair. You devoted your life to the profession. You deserve a chance. So what we're giving you is twenty-four hours. That's plenty of time for a man of your experience. You could disappear forever, given your contacts. Take all night. Relax. Tomorrow morning, though, at eight o'clock – that's checkout time. I want you out of here. And one day later, Grisman has to leave as well. Maybe then the other guests can enjoy themselves again.'

Twisting in his chair, Eliot fumed at Saul.

Who merely grinned and shrugged.

25

The sun dipped relentlessly toward the mountains, casting a ruddy glow through the window of Eliot's room.

'It doesn't make a difference,' Eliot blurted hoarsely into his phone. 'I don't care how many men it takes or what it costs. I want this valley bottled up tomorrow. I want him killed as soon as he leaves the rest home. No, you're not listening. Not the team who tried to stop him from getting in here. What's the matter with you? I'm sick of losers. I said I want the best.' His knuckles ached from his tight grip on the phone. He scowled. 'What do you mean there's nobody better than Grisman? I am. Do what you're told.'

Eliot slammed down the phone and turned to Castor. Pollux was out in the hall, where guards sent by Don kept Eliot and his escorts under house arrest. 'You confirmed the reservations?'

Castor nodded. 'Air Canada out of Vancouver bound for Australia. Seven o'clock tomorrow evening.'

'That ought to give us plenty of time.'

Castor raised his shoulders. 'Maybe not. Romulus knows he'll never be able to find you if he's twenty-four hours behind. The chances are he'll try to break out of here before then.'

'Certainly he will. I'm counting on it. He'll want to chase me as soon as possible . . . and that's my advantage.'

Castor frowned. 'I don't see how.'

'What I told that idiot on the phone is true. Nobody's better than Romulus. Except myself. And the two of you. I supervised his training. I can outguess him. The mistake I made from the start was delegating other men to do my work.'

'But you ordered a team to seal off the valley.'

Eliot nodded. 'Romulus expects me to do that. If I didn't provide a distraction, he'd sense the greater trap. Of course, the team might get lucky and kill him.' He pursed his wrinkled lips, musing. 'I doubt it, though. The wilderness is his home. If he leaves the way he came in, even a thousand men couldn't watch every outlet through the mountains.'

Castor brightened. 'In that case, though, we'd be protected. Going

252

through the mountains takes time. He'd still be far behind us. He couldn't catch up.'

'And that's why he'll choose another way.'

Castor's bright look darkened, his frown returning. 'But what way is that? And how can we stop him?'

'Pretend you're him. It's not too hard to predict what he'll do. Logically he's got only one choice.'

'It might be logical to you, but –'

Eliot explained, and Castor nodded, confident again, impressed.

26

The sun was three-quarters down. Shadows lengthened across the valley, at first almost purple, then gray, soon black tinged with mist.

Saul didn't notice. He kept his room dark, sitting cross-legged on the floor, clearing his mind, preparing himself. He knew the door to his room was being watched by guards outside to prevent him from making a move against Eliot while the old man was still inside the rest home. He assumed that Eliot and his escorts were under surveillance as well.

It didn't matter. Despite his need, he couldn't risk killing Eliot in here. Since arriving, his primary intention had been to achieve revenge and yet survive to enjoy the satisfaction of knowing he'd repaid his debt of honor to Chris.

His brother. Anger flashed inside him. He concentrated to subdue it. Now that his goal was close, he had to purge himself of distraction, to reach the purity of a samurai, to prove himself the professional Eliot had taught him to be.

As he meditated, arriving at a core of perfect resolution and stillness, consolidating his thoughts, instincts and skills, he silently repeated a mantra, over and over.

Again and again. He sensed his brother's spirit merging with him.

Chris. Chris.

Chris. Chris.

Chris.

27

The morning was bleak. Clouds hung low, the air damp and chilly with the threat of rain. A dark blue Chevy station wagon – no chrome, no whitewalls, nothing to draw attention to it – waited on the gravel driveway before the lodge.

Two servants filled the back with suitcases and garment bags, then shut the hatch and waited at a distance.

Precisely at eight, the door to the lodge came open. Eliot, Castor, and Pollux, flanked by guards, stepped out on the porch. Don walked directly behind them.

Eliot wore his uniform – his black suit and vest, his homburg. He paused when he saw the car, then turned to the right, squinting sullenly at Saul, who stood at the end of the porch, flanked by other guards.

A gloomy mist began to fall. Eliot's nostrils widened with contempt. The tense moment lengthened.

Turning abruptly, the old man gripped the rail and eased himself down the steps. Castor opened a back door for him, closed it as soon as his father was settled, then got in the front with Pollux and turned the ignition key. The motor engaged at once, sounding like a large V–8.

The station wagon pulled away, its tires crunching on the gravel. Saul narrowed his vision till all he saw was the window of the Chevy's hatch. Intense, he focused on the back of Eliot's head, on the silhouette of the homburg.

But the old man never looked back at him.

The Chevy moved faster, shrinking, its roar diminishing. Soon its dark blue merged with the green of the forest.

Watching it disappear, Saul bristled, his heartbeat thunderous.

Haughty, Don came over. 'Long time to wait, huh? Twenty-four hours. Bet you're tempted to run to the motor pool and steal a car to chase after him.'

Saul stared at the road between the trees.

'Or the chopper in back,' Don said. 'Bet you can barely hold back from making a try for it, huh? It sure is tempting isn't it?'

Saul's eyes were black as he turned to Don.

'Go on and try,' Don said. 'That's why I let you out of your room this morning. So you could watch the old man drive away and maybe lose your cool. Do it. Fall apart. Make a break and try to chase him. You've been a pain in my ass since you got here. I'd love to see you shot to pieces for disobeying the board's directive.'

Still Saul didn't answer but instead slipped past him, calmly heading toward the door to the lodge.

'No?' Don asked behind him. 'Don't feel like making trouble today? My, my. Well, that's a change.'

The guards flanked Saul as he opened the door.

'In that case, pal, go back to your room and stay there.' Don's voice snapped. 'Twenty-four hours. That's the agreement. Tomorrow morning, you can chase him all you want.' He rose to his fullest height. 'Provided you can find him.'

Saul glanced indifferently at him and walked inside.

He'd thought it through with care last night, analyzing various plans . . .

When everything was considered, there'd really been only one choice.

28

Don rubbed his eyes. It had to be he was seeing things. This couldn't be happening. With eyeblink speed, Grisman did something with his elbows as he walked inside. At once the guards behind him tumbled back, collapsing against each each other, toppling. As they did, the door to the lodge slammed shut. The lock shot home.

'What the –? Jesus!' Pushing away from each other, scrambling to their feet, the guards cursed, rushing to the door, jerking at it, pounding angrily.

Don in turn felt frozen, disbelieving, dismayed. It wasn't possible. He'd felt so confident when he taunted Grisman he'd have bet his bonus that the goddamn troublemaker had finally been put in his place.

Oh, fuck, no. It couldn't be. Grisman was actually doing it, making a break.

'The motor pool!' Don shouted. 'The chopper pad! Stop pounding at that goddamn door, you assholes! Head him off!'

Already Don was racing down the steps. He twisted hysterically to the left and lunged toward the side of the lodge.

29

It hadn't been complicated. Once Saul had decided on the only logical tactic, he'd simply imagined various scenarios, looked ahead, and predicted when he'd have the best opportunity to implement his plan. At the first likely moment, he acted. On the porch, in the open, in the presence of Don and many guards, with Eliot barely off the grounds, who'd have expected Saul to make trouble that soon? Certainly not Don and the guards. Their confidence had been his advantage.

By the time the guards had recovered enough to lunge at the bolted door, Saul was sprinting through the lobby. No guests were in view, but several staff members froze open-mouthed in surprise. To the left, at the fuzzy corner of his vision, Saul detected a hurried gesture as the desk clerk lunged for a phone. Behind him, Saul heard muffled pounding as the guards tried to break through the door. He raced toward a hallway beside the staircase, sensing motion to his right: a guard coming out of the restaurant, seeing Saul, hearing the shouts, understanding, and drawing a pistol.

The roar of shots was amplified by the polished walls of the lobby. Bullets walloped against the banister on the staircase, flinging splinters. But already Saul had reached the protection of the corridor. Charging harder, he veered toward a door at the end, in an alcove behind the staircase, yanking it open just as a guard on the other side reached for the knob. The man must have heard the shots and hurried to investigate. But he wasn't prepared for the heel of Saul's palm slamming against his rib cage. As the man groaned, falling, Saul tugged an Uzi from his grasp and swung to spray the hallway behind him. The guard out there dove frantically for cover.

Saul didn't wait. No time. He leapt across the man he'd dropped, then raced down a short set of stairs, yanking at a ceiling-high metal case with towels, soap, and toilet paper on shelves. The unit crashed behind him, objects cascading forming a barricade in the narrow corridor.

A puzzled maid appeared at an open door to the right, understood quickly what was happening, and ducked back, frightened. Again Saul spun with the Uzi, fired a warning volley at the guard in pursuit, and charged out a door in back.

When he'd first arrived at the rest home, he'd automatically obeyed one of Eliot's rules and scouted his hunting ground, familiarizing himself with the layout. Now as he burst outside, he faced the short flight of concrete steps he'd expected. He took them three at a time and rushed ahead.

The clouds hung lower, gray and dismal. The bleak grounds stretched before him, the mist-enshrouded motor pool to his right, the chopper pad to his left.

As drizzle dampened his cheeks, chilly in contrast with his burning sweat, he knew exactly where to go and what to do.

30

Out of breath, stumbling frantically along the side toward the back of the lodge, Don yelled to the guards before him, 'Dammit' – he puffed – 'split up! Head him off!' He stopped and panted, wiping drizzle off his face. 'The chopper pad! The motor pool!' The guards obeyed.

Straining to breathe, mustering strength, Don lurched into motion once again, swerving around to the back of the lodge as a guard crept out, his pistol trained.

'Where is he?' Don shouted.

'He came through this door.' The guard kept his voice low, crouching beneath the concrete steps, warning, 'Get down before he shoots you.'

'He's not armed.'

'He grabbed an Uzi off Ray.'

'That was *Grisman* shooting in there?' A tingle ran up Don's spine and made him shiver. 'I thought it was . . . Jesus!' He dove to the lawn, his shivering worse as the wet grass soaked his checkered pants and burgundy sport coat. 'Where the hell is he?'

Hunkered, the guard kept switching his aim to different sections of the grounds.

Don struggled with paralyzing fear and surprised himself by rolling toward the guard, scrambling down the concrete steps, and hunching near the door. 'Your walkie-talkie. Give it to me.'

Not shifting his gaze from the grounds, the guard pulled the radio from its holster on his belt and handed it over.

Don pressed the send button, alarmed by the croaking sound his voice made. 'This is the director. Motor pool, check in.'

He released the button. Static crackled.

'No sign of him,' a voice said. 'We're still searching.'

'Chopper pad,' Don blurted into the radio.

'Negative,' a voice said. 'We've established a perimeter around the bird. With this many guns against him, he'd be nuts to make a try for it.'

Don flinched as the door came open behind him, another guard creeping out.

'I just left Ray,' the new guard said. 'A doctor's with him.'

Don took a moment before he realized the implication. Again his spine tingled. 'You mean he's alive?'

'Grisman slammed his chest. Broke some ribs. The doctor says Ray's gonna live, though.'

'I don't understand. Grisman's too good to make a mistake like that. I can't believe he slipped up.'

'Unless it wasn't a mistake.'

'You're telling me Grisman deliberately didn't kill him?'

'If Grisman had wanted to, he would have. All he'd have needed was a little more force behind the blow.'

'Then why the hell didn't he? What's he thinking of?'

'Who knows?' The guard made a sound that might have been a chuckle. 'Maybe he didn't want to piss us off.'

Abruptly the walkie-talkie crackled. 'There! I see him!'

'Where?' Don yelled, his voice unsteady as he held the radio near his mouth. 'The motor pool? The –?'

'Not even close! The stupid bastard's way the hell past the jogging track and the greenhouse!'

'*What?*'

'He's running across the grounds! The river! He's headed toward the river!'

Don leapt up, lost his balance and nearly fell, then started running toward the drizzle-enshrouded greenhouse. The two guards sprinted past him. Other guards converged out of nowhere.

31

Saul gripped the Uzi and raced through the increasing drizzle, his legs like pistons, his chest like a bellows. He heard murky shouts behind him. At once the shouts seemed louder. He ran faster, legs pounding, adrenaline fueling him.

A shadow seemed beside him. On his left. Glancing quickly that way, he knew he had to be imagining things. Even so, he would have sworn he saw Chris. They seemed to pace each other. Then Chris gained distance on him. You never used to be faster than me, Saul thought. Excitement almost made him grin. You were smarter, but I was stronger. Think you can get there ahead of me, huh?

Well, brother, you're wrong.

As a rifle cracked, echoing behind him, Saul forced himself to the limit, stretching his legs, gaining on Chris. An Uzi rattled in the distance. Saul came abreast of Chris. He urged his legs to work harder.

The shouts became close.

Chris disappeared, and through the drizzle, Saul faced the river, pounding toward a bank near the spot where he'd argued with Eliot. He crashed through shrubs down a slope. Reached a rocky outcrop.

And dove.

The cold water numbed him instantly. The force of his dive took him down into blackness. The surge of an undercurrent swept him along. He twisted beneath the water, struggling to level off and fight to the top. His overworked lungs rebelled, demanding air, threatening to inhale. As a roar began behind his ears, he surged and kicked and strained, breaking the surface, gasping, hearing gunshots, diving back down as bullets peppered the river.

The strength of the current amazed him. Where he'd argued with Eliot, the water had seemed almost placid. But that had been a kind of cove, away from the river's flow. Here powerful hands seemed to twist and tug at him. Desperate for air, he fought to the surface once more, and as soon as he caught a breath, he ducked back down, too quick to hear further shots but not too quick for him to realize how far the current had already taken him.

He'd left the guards behind, he understood with relief. Now all he had to do was fight the river. Get to the other side, he kept thinking. Dismayed, he realized he didn't have the Uzi anymore.

But he was alive. The first step in his plan had been accomplished. Raising his head above the surface, breathing deeply, he kicked and stroked and aimed himself toward a tree dipping into the water a hundred yards down on the opposite shore.

32

Staring despondently toward the river, Don brushed rain-soaked strands of hair from his forehead, sickened by the frantic pounding of his heart. That fucking Grisman, he silently cursed. Chasing after him nearly gave me a heart attack. 'Any sign of him?'

A guard shook his head. 'The other team hasn't checked in yet, though.'

Don nodded. As soon as he'd understood what Grisman intended to do, he'd radioed to other guards, telling them to post themselves farther down along the river. 'Sooner or later he's got to come up for air. The water's too cold for him to stay in it long.'

The guards continued scanning the river.

'You never know,' Don said, pulling his rain-drenched slacks away from his thighs. 'Maybe we'll get lucky. Maybe the bastard drowned.'

258

Two guards turned to him, their brows furrowed skeptically.

'All right, all right,' Don said. 'I don't believe it either.'

Static crackled on the radio. 'We just missed him,' a voice said.

Don jerked up from the rock on which he'd been sitting. 'Say again. Repeat,' he told the radio.

'We missed him. About a quarter mile down from your position. Just as we got here, he crawled up on the other side and disappeared in some bushes.'

'But I didn't hear shots.'

'We didn't have time. You want us to swim across and continue after him?'

Don watched as the guards around him turned to study his reaction. Pausing, he glanced at the angry gray sky. 'Just a second,' he told the radio. He asked his guards. 'So what would *you* do?'

'He didn't kill Ray,' a guard reminded him. 'He could have, but he didn't.'

'So you're saying let him go?'

'I'm saying he didn't kill Ray.'

Don thought about it, finally nodding. He pressed the send button on the radio. 'Cancel. Return to the lodge.'

'Repeat,' the voice said. 'Request confirmation.'

'He's off the grounds. Out of our jurisdiction. Go back to the lodge.'

'Roger. Affirmative.'

Don set down the radio. The guards continued studying him. 'Besides,' he said, deciding to let them feel confided in, 'I've got a hunch that the old man sent for teams to watch the exits from here – in case Grisman tried this kind of stunt. He'll be running into snipers shortly. I'd just as soon none of you got caught in their fire.'

'Suits me,' a guard said. 'I wasn't thrilled with the notion of hunting Grisman on his turf. Hit and run in the forest. That's his specialty.'

'Well, it's Eliot's problem now,' Don said. Though angry, he nonetheless began to feel buoyant now that the crisis was over. 'We did the best we could. I suppose Grisman left a car out there somewhere when he came in, but those woods are so thick it'll take him hours to reach it. By then, Eliot'll be out of the country. The difference is the same – whether Grisman stayed here for twenty-four hours or wandered around the forest. Either way, the old man got his head start.' He turned, his legs weary as he started back to the lodge. Rain trickled down his neck. Even so, he suddenly felt amused. 'It's a hell of a thing,' he told a guard walking beside him. 'Sometimes an operative tries to break into a rest home. But breaking *out*? Especially if you haven't killed here? That's a new one.'

33

There were arrangements to be made, of course. For one thing, Don had to contact his superior and explain what had happened. He considered this task so important he didn't even wait to put on dry clothes

259

before he made the call. Back at the lodge, dripping on the carpet in his office, he spoke into the phone while he peered through the wall-sized window at the rain making dots on the swimming pool. He sneezed once. His voice shivered a couple of times from the chill of his wet clothes soaking into his bones, but by and large he managed to sound professional and calm. 'I agree, sir. The board will want a detailed report. I'm preparing one now. The point I want to emphasize is this. Sure, Grisman got away. I accept the blame for that. It shouldn't have happened. No excuses. But we promised the old man time, and practically speaking he still has it. No real harm's been done.'

The conversation ended with Don's superior cautiously telling him to wait for the board's decision. In the meanwhile, Don assured him, things were finally back to normal.

Hoping there wouldn't be repercussions, Don set down the phone, gulped a shot of bourbon, and went to his room, where he soaked himself for half an hour in an almost scalding tub. His emotions pulled him in different directions. On the one hand, he still felt angry. Grisman had been such a nuisance, had caused so much trouble that Don had looked forward to taunting him. And now that Grisman had escaped, the sonofabitch had caused even more trouble. Dammit, I wish we could have caught him before he reached the river. I'd have shot the bastard myself.

On the other hand, Grisman was finally gone. The crisis was over. The rest home, as Don had told his superior, was back to normal, if anything about this awful place could ever be described as normal.

On balance, Don felt relieved.

He put on freshly pressed green slacks, a crisp yellow shirt, a brand-new beige checkered sport coat. Tossing down another shot of bourbon – his limit for the day – he stretched his arms, at last relaxed. He went downstairs to his office, rested his white shoes on his desk, turned on his dictation machine to begin his report, and frowned as the roar of an engine passed so close it shook the window behind him.

Now what? He thought in disgust.

His heart plummeted. A terrible premonition squeezed his stomach, making him fear he'd throw up the bourbon.

He grabbed the phone, pressing three buttons to contact –

But it wasn't necessary. A fist pounded on the door. Before Don had a chance to say 'come in,' the captain of guards threw open the door.

'That goddamn Grisman!'

'Say it.'

'All that shit about swimming the river, escaping into the forest!'

'*Tell me.*'

'He was jerking us around! He didn't want to go through a forest! A feint! That's all it was! To put us off balance! As soon as we relaxed surveillance on the chopper, he came back! That's him up there! He stole the goddamn bird!'

Oh, fuck, Don thought and, thinking of the board's reaction, wondered if he could come out of this alive.

34

Saul shivered in his soaked wool clothes and wanted to cheer in triumph. The two men guarding the chopper had been so relaxed after Saul's escape that they hadn't seen him crawl to the greenhouse, then across the jogging track to the fountain, finally to the flower garden, the bench, themselves.

Again, he'd made sure to disable them without killing. That was important. If he killed within the confines of a rest home, he'd be pursued by the fullest might of the profession. He'd likely never catch Eliot, and for sure he'd never survive to enjoy his revenge. Hell, if necessary, the world's intelligence community would hunt him with missiles, anything to guarantee his punishment for violating the sanctity of a rest home.

This way, however, the worst crimes he'd committed were roughing up personnel and stealing a chopper. Compared to violating the sanction, what he'd done was roughly analogous to getting in a fight and stealing a car. The decision makers would understand the control he'd exercised. They'd know he wasn't attacking the system but instead only getting even with Eliot. This wasn't political; it was personal. And understanding the duel in progress, perhaps they'd make allowances.

He hoped.

But his principles made sense at least, and more to the point, Saul took delight in sensing Chris would have approved. Indeed it seemed that Chris sat next to him, grinning, urging him on. Saul grinned in response. He hadn't flown a chopper in seven years, but Eliot had trained him well, and he needed only a minute to feel confident at the controls. He lifted off the pad, swooped past the rest home, and soared up over the trees along the perimeter. On the seat beside him, he had a jacket he'd taken from one of the guards and two Uzis plus several loaded magazines. His heart soared along with the chopper. Eliot logically had only one choice. Oh, sure, he could pretend to leave but actually stay in the area, hoping Saul would pass him. But considering the head start Eliot had been guaranteed, it was smarter for him to drive as fast as he could, reach Vancouver, and catch a flight to the farthest corner of the world, where, Saul admitted to himself, he had no chance to find him. Naturally Eliot would have hired men to watch the rest home, killing Saul when he was allowed to leave. The chopper – and less ideally a car – had been his only practical options.

This, more than anything, was to Saul's advantage. The area was wilderness. Few roads went through the region. Saul remembered the route he'd used to reach the rest home. Nothing complicated. Calculating in the reverse, he knew he couldn't go wrong if he chose whatever road headed southwest toward Vancouver. Eliot had a two-

hour lead. But that was on a zigzagging road whose route was controlled by the complex topography of the mountains, while Saul could
chase him as the crow flew. What was more, the chopper was faster
than the station wagon. Much, much faster.

Forty minutes, Saul guessed. Everything'll be finished then.

He imagined Chris would have cheered.

35

The drizzle thickened, falling harder. When Saul had taken off, the
weather hadn't been a problem. Now, however, the rain was dense
enough to reduce visibility and make the chopper's controls feel
unstable. Studying the meandering road below him, Saul began to
worry about crashing into an unseen barrier, a tree, a cliff, a hydro
pylon obscured by low-hanging clouds. He had to watch for sudden
changes in the terrain.

His sole consolation was that the gloom had discouraged travelers.
The traffic below him was sparse, most of it vans and motor homes.
The few cars he saw were easy to identify and dismiss. A Ford LTD.
A VW Sirocco. A Pontiac Firebird.

But no Chevy station wagon.

In the first minutes of the hunt, he hadn't been concerned. After
all, Eliot should have passed through several valleys already. Though
it never hurt to be thorough, Saul really didn't expect to see the station
wagon yet.

But the minutes accumulated. Thirty. Thirty-five. Forty. As the
rain fell harder and the roaring helicopter became less responsive to
commands, Saul feared he'd miscalculated. Had Eliot anticipated
Saul's response and headed inland instead of to the coast? Had Eliot
gone to ground somewhere, hoping Saul would lose the trail by running past him to Vancouver? Check and countercheck. The possible
variations were like a dizzying maze whose exit could never be found.

He forced distraction from his mind. He couldn't allow himself to
doubt the course he'd chosen. He didn't dare lose patience. Committed to this plan, he had to follow through. There wasn't any other
way now.

Five minutes later, his determination received its reward. Below,
not far in front of him, he saw the reduced shape of a dark blue Chevy
station wagon veer around a wooded curve, heading southwest.

His chest expanded.

But at once he subdued his excitement. The color and model were
the same. Still, coincidence wasn't impossible.

He urged the chopper down for a closer look. No chrome, no
whitewalls. Getting better, he thought. Roaring nearer, he saw the
outlines of three passengers, two in the front, one in the back. It
puzzled him that they didn't turn back to investigate the commotion
behind them. They seemed to be men, though, and the passenger in
the rear wore a hat. Even better. Then Saul was close enough to see

the license plate through binoculars. The same as the one on the car at the lodge.

He raged, swooping faster, closer. Ahead, to the right, a semicircle of trees had been cleared. A rain-soaked gravel parking area was rimmed by picnic tables. The place was deserted.

In a fifty-fifty life-or-death crisis, simply approach the crisis, prepared to die if necessary. There is nothing complicated about it. Merely brace yourself and proceed. So Ishiguro, Saul's judo instructor, had taught him years before in the *dojo*. Saul braced himself and proceeded now, making an instantaneous decision, though he didn't intend to die.

He zoomed above the road, roaring closer. Breasting it on the left, he shifted his controls to the right and veered toward the station wagon.

A great deal happened at once. Saul briefly saw Castor's alarmed face behind the steering wheel. If Castor had stayed on course down the road, if the chopper's landing struts had touched the station wagon, the chopper would have lost its equilibrium and flipped against the Chevy, consuming both in a massive blast of flame. Granted, Eliot would have been destroyed, but Saul had no intention of dying with him.

Castor reacted as Saul expected, twisting sharply on the steering wheel, veering in the only unobstructed direction, toward the parking area, the picnic tables, the trees.

Saul did the same, speeding parallel to the Chevy, forcing Castor not to stop, instead compelling him to keep rushing toward the trees. At the final moment, just before the chopper would have disintegrated on impact with the forest, Saul jerked the controls and swooped up, clearing the treetops. Enclosed in the chopper's plexiglass, his hearing tortured by the roaring flap of the blades, he knew he must have imagined the sound of a crash behind him.

Imagination or not, it gave him satisfaction. Abruptly turning, he swooped back toward the parking area, seeing the Chevy's front end crushed against a boulder between two trees. Setting the chopper down hurriedly, he left the rotors on idle, grabbed the two Uzis and their full magazines, and jumped to the soggy gravel. Rain lashed his face. Even as he stooped to keep from being decapitated by the revolving blades, he began to fire, lunging at the wrecked station wagon, noticing steamy antifreeze gushing from its radiator, riddling the car with bullets.

But something was wrong. The Chevy's windows didn't break. Its doors weren't torn apart by his barrage.

He scowled. The station wagon was armored. Its glass was bullet-proof. He charged through puddles toward it, firing another volley. The bullets walloped fenders and doors but still did little damage.

No one moved inside. Cautious as he hurried forward, peering through a rain-spattered window, he saw Castor slumped across the broken steering wheel, blood gushing from his forehead. Next to him, Pollux was . . .

A mannequin. A dummy dressed in the denim jacket Pollux had worn.

And Eliot? In the back seat, a second mannequin lay on its side, wearing a black suit, a homburg fallen to the floor. That was why they hadn't turned toward the roar of the chopper.

He spotted the two-way radio built under the dashboard and realized at once the terrible danger he was in. Reflexes spurred him. Racing past the station wagon toward the trees, he felt a bullet from behind him sear his arm. Another bullet tore bark from a pine tree. The bark stung his jaw.

He didn't stop to whirl behind a tree and return the fire. He didn't wonder who was shooting at him or how the mannequins had come to be in the car. He just kept charging through the trees, gaining distance, desperate for time to think.

Because the two-way radio said it all. Dammit. Saul thought, why the hell didn't I realize? How could I have been so stupid? From the moment Eliot left the rest home, he must have kept in touch with the lodge. He'd have known I stole the chopper. Jesus, he probably counted on it. The mannequins must have been hidden in the station wagon when he left. The old man outguessed me all the way.

And the sniper shooting at Saul? It had to be Pollux, who'd followed Castor in another car. If Saul hadn't seen the mannequins and the two-way radio, if he hadn't darted toward the trees the instant he sensed the trap, Pollux would have killed him. Eliot would have been the victor.

No! Saul inwardly screamed. No, I won't let him beat me! I've got to get even for Chris!

He scurried deeper through the trees and rain, shifting direction when he knew Pollux couldn't see him. The road, Saul thought. I've got to get back to the road.

Pollux, of course, would be stalking him, aiming toward the sound of rustling bushes and snapping branches, and for that reason, Saul intended to make all the noises he could. He meant to lure Pollux into here. And as soon as Pollux was far from the road, Saul planned to use silence, creeping instead of racing, confusing Pollux, gaining a chance to retreat to the road.

For Pollux didn't matter. Eliot did. And the thickening rain made Saul shiver with understanding. Would an old man expose himself to such terrible weather if he didn't have to? Eliot's plan had been to use Castor as a decoy while Pollux came in from the rear and caught Saul by surprise. But Eliot must have considered the possibility that there'd be a fight. Would Eliot wait unprotected in the second car? Would he hide in the rain in the woods? Not likely. The old man would prefer a place warm and safe.

Dear God, the old man's somewhere along the road I followed. He's holed up, probably in a cabin, a motel, a tourist lodge. He'd never wait at the airport for his plane – if he intended to take a plane at all.

But Saul had flown over several motels. With sufficient time, he could retrace his route and check them all. But that was the point.

264

There *wasn't* time. Pollux would continue hunting him. The provincial police would soon be here to investigate the accident. *I have to get away*, he thought.

In twenty minutes, sweating despite the cold, intensifying rain, Saul reached a bend in the road a half mile away from the picnic area. Despite his silence and care, he felt a persistent prickly spot between his shoulder blades, where Pollux's bullet might strike him.

Have to find Eliot. Have to –

Hearing a motor approach around the bend, he waited to make sure it wasn't a police car. Seeing a battered van, he lurched from the trees and waved to make the driver stop. When the long-haired kid behind the steering wheel tried to veer around him. Saul aimed the Uzi. The kid blanched, slammed on screechy brakes, and got out, holding up shaky hands. 'Don't shoot me.' He backed up and started to run.

Saul scrambled into the van. Its gears whined as he tugged the shift into first. With a lurch, it started forward. Speeding along the road, he passed the picnic area, where the helicopter's blades continued to turn.

The driver's door on the station wagon hung open. Castor –

Wasn't dead. Holding his stomach, he stumbled from the wreck. But Castor heard the rattle of the van and glanced toward the road in time to notice Saul behind the wheel.

Blinking, Castor shook his head as if he doubted what he saw.

Abruptly he straightened with a wince. Blood streaming from his forehead, he lurched toward the trees, no doubt for Pollux.

That was all right, Saul thought, disappearing from the picnic area. In fact, it was fine. It couldn't be better.

He soon saw a dark green Ford parked along the road, probably the car Pollux had used to follow Castor. Determined to be thorough, Saul stopped and got out of the van, aiming, checking the Ford, but it was empty. The mud on the far side revealed no footsteps where an old man might have gone to take cover in the forest.

Saul nodded, more confident of his suspicion.

He whirled to peer through the rain down the road toward the picnic area. Pollux was sprinting in his direction, Castor hobbling behind him. Pollux halted when he spotted Saul, but as he raised his pistol, Saul rushed to get into the van. A bullet whacked the rear hatch. Saul felt elated, pulling away. It wouldn't be long now.

Two bends down the road, certain his pursuers couldn't see him, he turned left down a gravel lane and soon turned left again, shielding the van in a thick grove of trees. He jumped down to scramble, hunched in the rain, toward the edge of the road, and hid behind dense bushes, watching, waiting.

A minute passed. He swelled with satisfaction, seeing what he wanted. His ruse had worked.

The green car raced past. Pollux looking desperate as he drove. Next to him, Castor stared through the windshield, no doubt straining for a sight of the van.

Saul knew he could have shot them as they went by, assuming the car wasn't armored as the Chevy had been. But what would that have gained? They weren't Saul's objective. Eliot was, and Saul was hoping Castor and Pollux would rush to protect their father.

Lead me to him.

Soon now, he thought, running back to the van. The end was close. He felt it intensely. Very soon.

36

But he couldn't let them know they were being followed; he had to stay back out of sight. In their place, he'd have periodically checked his rearview mirror, out of habit, just as he did now – to make sure he himself wasn't being followed, by a police car, for example. Such a precaution had its drawbacks, though. If he couldn't let Castor and Pollux see him, he couldn't allow himself a glimpse of *them*. As a consequence, he had to hide the van near every motel and lodge he came to, sneaking up in search of their car.

The process was tedious, frustrating. After the fourth lodge he checked, he began to fear he'd overlooked the Ford. The police must have reached the scene of the accident by now. The long-haired kid must have told them his van had been stolen. They had to be searching for him.

And what about the guards from the rest home? They'd be hunting him as well. They'd have sent for help. The only good thing was that the rest home didn't have another chopper. They'd have to pursue him in cars. But eventually they'd be coming down this road.

His need to retain his freedom fought to overcome his need to punish Eliot. Give up the hunt, a dark voice warned him. You'll never find the old man before the cops or the guards arrive. You tried, but circumstances worked against you. There'll be other chances.

No, he told himself. If I let him slip away, he'll run so far and burrow so deep I'll never find him. He won't leave a trail. It has to be now. There won't be another chance.

Thirty minutes later, at the seventh place he checked, two parallel rows of cabins with parking spaces in the middle, he found the dark green Ford.

A neon sign in front of the office said Rocky Mountain Inn. The sign was illuminated in the gloomy rain. The Ford had been parked with its back end toward a middle unit on the left, the trunk left open.

Hiding the van down the road, Saul climbed through the rain-swept trees to a bushy ridge that gave him a view of the cabin behind the Ford. He watched from cover as the cabin door cracked slowly open. Pollux glanced out, then quickly put a suitcase in the trunk and closed the lid, ducking back inside.

Saul squinted. All right, then. He gritted his teeth. I got here just in time. They're about to leave.

He quickly calculated. The Uzi wasn't accurate from this distance.

If he positioned himself behind a cabin across from the Ford, he could shoot when Eliot came out to the car.

But he had to get down there fast. He found a sheltered draw that sloped to the cabins and scrambled down over deadfalls, choosing a spot behind a middle cabin in the row opposite the Ford.

The rain came thicker, darker, colder. As he waited, not showing himself, listening for the sound of the heavy engine starting over there, he began to have misgivings.

It's too easy, he thought.

It felt like a setup. Eliot wouldn't allow his escorts to park their car directly in front of his cabin. They sense I'm around. They're using the car as a decoy.

Still Saul remained convinced that Eliot was here.

Which cabin, though?

He remembered what he'd seen from the ridge above these units. Twenty of them, ten on each side. Because of the rain, the tourists had apparently decided not to go out sight-seeing today. How else explain the vehicles in front of fourteen cabins? Of the six empty slots, two flanked the cabin in front of the Ford. A third empty slot was down near the office. A fourth was on that side but at the opposite end, to the right, in back, almost into the forest. The remaining two were over here on *this* side.

Heart aching, Saul remembered a game he and Chris had liked to play when they were at the orphanage. The game had been introduced to them by Eliot. He'd called it the shell game. 'Con men trick suckers with it at carnivals,' he'd said. 'It works like this. Three empty shells. Set them in a row. Put a pea under one. Then rearrange the order of the shells – several times – as fast as possible. Like this. Now tell me. Which shell hides the pea?' Neither Saul nor Chris chose correctly. 'Which goes to prove,' Eliot said, 'the hand is quicker than the eye. Except I want you to practice this game till you always know which shell hides the pea. I want your eyes to be quicker than anyone's hand.'

The shell game. Remembering, Saul fumed. But now instead of three shells, there were six. Which cabin held the pea?

He had to reduce his choices. Would Eliot pick a cabin near the office and the road? Not likely. He'd prefer to hide where the cover was best – in the middle. But then again maybe not. What about the cabin on the opposite end over there – the one closest to the forest?

Saul shook his head. Too far from the road if he had to get away from here fast.

Still its isolation would be an advantage in a fight; few people would hear the commotion.

Again he felt stymied.

What about the cabin on each side of the one where the Ford was parked? They were obvious possibilities. Accordingly Saul discounted them.

But what if Eliot had chosen to hide behind the obvious? The complexity continued to baffle him.

267

A stalemate. Eliot wouldn't show himself till he felt safe. Saul in turn refused to act till he knew he wouldn't be facing a trap. But Eliot knew, just as Saul did, that the police would investigate the accident and come looking for the stolen van. The cops'd be here soon.

And so would the rest home's guards.

Something had to happen to break the stalemate.

Someone had to move first.

He made a decision. It was arbitrary. But deep in his soul, it felt right. *Where would I hide if I were Eliot? Away from Pollux in the cabin over there. I'd want to see what happened. Safely away from the Ford. I'd stay in a cabin over here.*

The possibilities reduced, at least in theory, he shifted through the rain toward the supposedly empty cabins, both of them on his left.

'So you guessed.'

The ancient voice was startling.

Saul twisted sharply, aiming at the space between two cabins.

And found himself staring in shock at Eliot. The old man had been standing out of sight in front of an empty cabin. Now he showed himself, drenched by the rain.

More exhausted and wizened than Saul had ever seen him. the old man shrugged. 'Well, what are you waiting for? Go on and shoot.'

Saul wanted to, with all his heart, amazed at himself – because no matter how much his rage compelled him, he couldn't force himself to pull the trigger.

'What's the matter?' his father said. 'Isn't this what you wanted? My compliments. You've won.'

Saul wanted to scream, but his throat squeezed shut till he couldn't breathe. His chest contracted till he thought his lungs would be crushed.

'You figured it out,' his father said. 'God damn, I taught you well. I always said, pretend you're the enemy you're hunting. And you guessed. You sensed I'd be in a cabin on this side.'

The rain fell so hard Saul couldn't be sure if his cheeks were wet from raindrops or from tears. 'You bastard.'

'No more than yourself. Go on,' his father said. 'I've admitted you've beaten me. So pull the trigger.'

Again Saul had trouble speaking. 'Why?' he murmured hoarsely.

'Isn't it obvious? I'm old. I'm tired.'

'You still had a chance.'

'For what? To die? Or see another of my children die? I'm sick of it. I've got too many ghosts. Furies. On the riverbank, when you came to me while I was fishing, I tried to explain why I'd done the things you blame me for.'

'I can't forgive you for killing Chris.'

'I was wrong to ask you. Shoot me.' Rain slicked Eliot's thin gray hair to his forehead. 'Why hesitate? Your attitude's not professional.' Eliot's black suit clung pathetically to him, utterly soaked. 'Your father's telling you to kill him.'

'No.' Saul shook his head. 'If you want it, then it's too damned easy.'

'True. I understand. Revenge isn't satisfying if the man you hate won't resist. Very well. If that's the way it's to be, then by default you've made a choice.'

Saul and Eliot stared at each other.

'I don't suggest a reconciliation,' Eliot said. 'But I wonder if a grudging acceptance might be possible. I'm your father. No matter how much you hate me, we still share a bond. As a favor, in memory of when you loved me, let me live my last few years in peace.'

Saul almost shot him then, tempted by the thought of denying Eliot what he wanted.

But he realized he'd been talking with Eliot long enough for Castor or Pollux to have killed him where he hesitated in the open. Eliot had truly surrendered.

No, not here, not now, he thought. He couldn't shoot. Not face to face – if his father refused to fight back.

'After everything you taught me. I failed.'

His father raised his eyebrows sadly, quizzically.

'Or you didn't teach me well enough,' Saul continued. He lowered the Uzi. 'And maybe that's all to the good. I'm finished. I'm resigning. Fuck the agency. Fuck you. There's a lady I know. Instead of playing games with you, I should have gone away with her.'

His father brooded. 'I never told you. Back in '51. Perhaps you wondered why I never married. See, I had to make a choice. The agency or . . . Well, I'm not sure my choice was the right one.' Thunder rumbled. The old man peered at black rolling clouds. 'I always wondered what became of her.' His eyes narrowed, nostalgic. Then his mood broke, and he tugged at his suit. 'You and I, we're ridiculous.' He sounded amused. 'Standing in the rain. A young man like you, you don't seem to mind getting wet. But these old bones . . .' He chuckled in self-derision. 'Thank God, this is over.' He held out his hand; it shook. 'I've got some Wild Turkey in my suitcase. A farewell drink might be in order. To chase the cold away.'

'You told us never to drink. You said it dulls the mind and the senses.'

'I didn't expect you to share it with me. But now that you've retired, what difference does it make?'

'Old habits die hard.'

'I know. Forgive me. No matter how hard you try, you'll never be normal. That's something else to haunt me.'

Eliot turned wearily, stepping up on the cabin's porch, shielded from the rain by an awning. He gestured across to the cabin behind the Ford. Pollux stood nervously in the open doorway over there, but seeing the signal from Eliot, he relaxed his shoulders. In a moment, he went back in the cabin, shutting the door.

Saul approached his father.

'Inasmuch as we'll probably never see each other again,' Eliot said, 'I want to share a secret with you.'

'What?'

'About Chris and the monastery. Something that happened to him there. It helps, I think, if you know about it.' The old man went in his cabin, rummaging through a suitcase, finally raising a fifth of Wild Turkey. 'There ought to be a glass around here. Good.' He poured a small amount of whiskey into it. 'Sure you won't join me?'

Saul neared him impatiently. 'What about Chris? What happened in the monastery?'

Behind him, the slight creak of the open door was his only warning. He automatically leaned ahead, stooping to protect his renal artery. It happened swiftly, the brush of cloth, the rush of air. But not a knife, instead a glint of piano wire flashing from above him, streaking past his eyes toward his throat.

A garotte. The weapon was usually hidden under a collar. Two wooden handles, pulled from a shirt pocket, snapped into hooks on each end of the wire, prevented an assassin from cutting his fingers while he controlled the strangulation.

Saul jerked up his hands to protect his throat, the gesture instinctive, also a mistake.

Andre Rothberg: *Use only one hand to protect your throat. Keep your other hand free so you can fight. If the wire traps both hands, you're dead.*

Saul corrected his impulse, wrenching his left hand free. His right hand, shielding his larynx, was caught by the wire. Behind him, Castor, who'd been hiding behind the open door, applied more pressure.

Saul dimly heard Eliot say, 'I'm sorry. But you know I can't trust you. What if you woke up tomorrow and decided you wanted to kill me anyhow?' He shut the door. 'This way's better. There'll be no shooting. No frightened tourists. No calls to the police. We'll have time to get away. I regret having tricked you, though. If it makes any difference, I love you.'

A garotte kills in two ways: by strangling the victim, by cutting his throat. In its simplest form, it's nothing more than a strand of piano wire. But the better type uses several strands, twisted under pressure, with industrial diamonds embedded among them. As a consequence, if a victim manages to raise a hand to stop the garotte from touching his throat, the assailant can use the edge of the diamonds to cut through the victim's fingers.

That began to happen now.

Saul struggled, feeling the diamond-studded wires saw back and forth across the fingers he gripped protectively over his voice box. The diamonds gnawed his flesh and ground his bones. Blood streamed down his arm. Even with his hand as a buffer, he felt the pressure of the garotte squeezing off his air. He gagged.

The door came open. Pollux stepped in, briefly distracting Castor.

It gave Saul time. Though his mind swirled from lack of oxygen, he drew his free arm forward, making a fist, bending the elbow, ramming it back as hard as he could. The blow struck Castor's chest.

Andre Rothberg had taught Saul well. The elbow smashed Castor's rib cage. Bones cracked, impaling a lung.

Groaning, Castor released his grip and staggered back.

Saul didn't waste time removing the garotte. As Castor sagged, Saul swung, feeling a sharp pain in his elbow, realizing he'd fractured it, but that didn't matter. Rothberg's training was based on the theory that a few parts of the body could still function as weapons, even though injured. The elbow was one of those parts.

Saul straightened his arm, ignoring the pain, continuing to swing. The side of his rigid hand caught Castor's brother, Pollux, in the throat. The damage was lethal. Pollux dropped uncontrollably, convulsing.

Incredibly, despite the massive trauma to his chest, Castor had still not fallen. A palm thrust to his shattered ribs jerked him back. He trembled in death throes, collapsing.

Saul tore the garotte from his throat and whirled toward Eliot. 'I meant it. At the last, I couldn't do it. I wouldn't have killed you.'

Eliot blanched. 'No. Please.'

Saul picked up the Uzi he'd dropped in the scuffle. 'No,' he demanded fiercely. Stepping ahead, he embraced his father. Clutching him with his injured arm, he used the other to raise the Uzi to almost point-blank range.

Eliot squirmed.

Hugging him, Saul pulled the trigger. He kept it pressed back. The Uzi rattled, ejecting empty casings, making a noise like a sewing machine.

And stitched out his father's heart.

'You never had one anyhow.' Saul dripped with blood as his father's shuddering body slid from his grasp. 'For Chris,' Saul moaned.

And realized he'd begun to cry.

He wrapped a handkerchief around his bleeding fingers. The bones, though gnawed by the garotte, would heal. The pain was intense, but he ignored it, hurriedly taking off his bloody wet clothes, putting on Pollux's dry jeans and denim shirt.

There was much to do. The guards and the police would soon be here. He didn't dare return to the stolen van, so he'd have to take the Ford, though tourists alarmed by the shots would see him drive away in it. He'd found its keys on Pollux. To be safe, he'd soon abandon it. If he could reach Vancouver, he'd be able to disappear.

And then? The police would have no leads.

But what about the profession? Would he still be hunted? Till he knew he was free, he couldn't join Erika.

Rain gusted in as he opened the cabin's door. He glanced back at Eliot's body. For Chris, he'd said. Now his voice cracked.

'And for me.'

EPILOGUE

THE SANCTION'S AFTERMATH

ABELARD AND HELOISE

France, 1138.

Peter Abelard, onetime canon of the church of Notre Dame, formerly revered as the greatest teacher of his day, had fallen from eminence for love of his beautiful student, Heloise. Castrated by her angry uncle because of her pregnancy, pursued by jealous enemies eager to take advantage of his disgrace, he founded a safe house, the Paraclete, and invited Heloise, now a nun, to be in charge of a convent there. His emasculation prevented them from joining in love, but profoundly devoted to one another as brother and sister, they composed the documents – Abelard's history of his calamities, Heloise's letters – that became the basis for the legend of their tragic passion. After repeated attempts to regain his former glory, Abelard died, dejected, weary, some say of a broken heart. Disinterred from the priory of Saint Marcel, his body was secretly delivered to Heloise at the Paraclete, where after more than twenty years of mourning she died and lay in the ground beside him. Their remains were moved several times during centuries to come but were finally put to rest in the tomb that bears their name in the cemetery of Père-Lachaise in Paris.

Where they found eternal sanctuary.

UNDER THE ROSE

FALLS CHURCH VIRGINIA (AP) – A powerful explosion last night destroyed a greenhouse behind the home of Edward Franciscus Eliot, former Chief of Counterespionage for the Central Intelligence Agency. Eliot, a rose enthusiast, was murdered six days ago while on vacation in British Columbia, Canada. His funeral in Washington, Tuesday, showed a rare accord between Democrat and Republican legislators, who as one mourned the loss of a great American. 'He served his country selflessly for more than forty years,' the president said. 'He'll be sorely missed.'

Last night's explosion, investigators said, was caused by a massive thermite bomb. 'The heat was incredible,' a Fire Department official announced at a press conference. 'What it didn't burn to ashes, it melted. We couldn't get near the greenhouse for several hours. I can't imagine why anybody would want to destroy it. I'm told those roses were gorgeous, some of them extremely rare, one of a kind. It's senseless.'

The mystery deepened when firefighters clearing the wreckage discovered a locked steel vault beneath the greenhouse. CIA personnel, in cooperation with the FBI, sealed off the area.

'We worked all night to open it,' a spokesman said. 'The heat from the thermite bomb fused the locks. We finally had to cut it open. The vault had been used to store documents, that much we know. But what the documents contained is impossible to determine. The heat soaked through the walls of the vault. The documents were seared into dust.'

REDEMPTION

Enjoying the heft of the shovel in his hand, Saul threw dirt along the bank of the ditch. He'd been working for several hours, enjoying the strain on his muscles, the trickle of honest sweat. For a time, Erika had dug beside him, helping to extend the ditch, but then the baby had started to cry in the house, and she'd gone inside to nurse him. Afterward, she'd braid and bake the challah dough for their Sabbath bread. Watching her walk to the house, made from concrete blocks painted white, the same as the other dwellings in this settlement, he'd smiled in admiration at her strength and dignity and grace.

The sky was turquoise, the sun molten white. He wiped his brow and got back to work. When his network of irrigation trenches was completed, he'd put in vegetable seeds and grapevines. Then he'd wait to see if God would do His own part and send the rain.

He and Erika had come to this settlement – north of Beersheba and the desert region – six months ago, just before the baby was due. They'd wanted to help extend the nation's frontier, but disillusioned with international rivalry, they stayed away from land contested by the Arabs, preferring to develop the nation inward rather than out. But borders were never far. An unexpected attack was always possible, so he took care to have a weapon with him everywhere. A high-powered rifle lay near the ditch.

As far as the sanction was concerned, he thought he'd protected himself. In theory, the intelligence community had still been after him, so after punishing Eliot he'd contacted his network along with representatives from MI-6 and the KGB. His revelation of the con-spiracy involving descendants of the original Abelard group had gone a long way to put him back in their good graces. They'd felt bitter pleasure in knowing that their suspicions about internal sabotage of their operations had been justified. Taking steps to undo the damage Eliot and his group had caused by interfering, they let global tensions assume their natural course.

Saul's own network required a further gesture of good faith before they'd absolve him of blame, however. The documents, Saul had said. Eliot's collection of scandals. The blackmail that had kept him in power. 'But no one knows where those documents are,' the agency had said. 'No, I do,' Saul had said. He'd been thinking about those documents since Hardy had first explained about them. Where would Eliot have hidden them? Pretend you're him. In Eliot's place, where

277

would I have hidden them? A man obsessed by verbal games. Whose life had been based on *sub rosa*. Under the rose? The old man couldn't have chosen any other hiding place. Refusing to hand over the documents lest someone else take advantage of them, Saul had suggested a compromise, blown up the greenhouse, and destroyed them. The president, despite his public praise of Eliot in death, had felt immensely relieved.

But the rules of the sanction were supposed to be absolute. Saul received only unofficial immunity. 'What we're agreeing to do is look the other way,' a senior intelligence officer told him. 'If you hide well enough and don't raise your head, we promise not to come looking for you.'

And that was good enough for Saul. Like Candide in his garden, he retreated from the world, enjoying the pleasant exhaustion of manual labor, digging his irrigation ditch. He reflected on the grave Chris had dug in Panama. Now life instead of death would come from turning the ground. Old habits fade hard, however, and when not engaged in establishing a home for Erika, their son, and himself, he taught the youth of the village how to defend themselves if the settlement was ever attacked. He was foremost a warrior, after all, and though he'd disowned the profession, his talents could be put to constructive use. It struck him as ironic that many of the boys he trained had been adopted by the village: orphans. This time around, the process seemed justified. But as he tossed more dirt from the ditch, he remembered that Eliot too had felt justified.

He'd expected revenge to be satisfying. Instead it filled him with misgivings, haunting him. A lifetime of love, no matter how misguided, couldn't be dismissed, any more than his love for Chris could be dismissed. Or his love for Erika. If things had somehow been different. In somber moments, Saul debated with himself. Perhaps what he'd really wanted was the tension of the rest home to last forever. Punishment prolonged. Eliot and himself eternally trapped there. Bound by hate.

And love.

But then Saul's mood would lighten. Glancing at the broad warm sky, smelling the hint of rain in the air, he'd listen to Erika talking to their baby in their house, their home. He'd swell with affection, wholesome, unlike the perverted affection Eliot had created in him, and realize that his father had been wrong. 'No matter how hard you try, you'll never be normal': one of the last things his father had said to him. You bastard, you were wrong. And Saul, who in a special sense had always been an orphan, delighted in the thought of being a father to his son.

He set down his shovel, thirsty, retreating from the highest heat of the sun, picking up his rifle, walking toward his home. Entering its shadows, he sniffed the fragrance of tomorrow's challah, walked to Erika, and kissed her. She smelled wonderfully of sugar, flour, and salt, and yeast. Her strong arms, capable of killing in an instant, held him tight. His throat ached.

Drinking water from a cool clay pot, he wiped his mouth and crossed the room to peer down at his son in a blanket in his cradle. Friends from the settlement had remarked at first about his name.

'What's wrong with it?' Saul had asked. 'I think it's a good name.'

'Christopher Eliot Bernstein-Grisman?'

'So?'

'Half Christian, half Jewish?'

'Chris was a friend of mine. In fact, you could say he was my brother.'

'Sure. Chris Grisman. They'll love it when he goes to school. And what about Eliot?'

'I used to think he was my father. Now I'm not sure what he was. No matter. I'm what he made me.'

The friends didn't understand. But sick in his heart, Saul didn't either.

Even more than the name for the boy, the friends from the settlement drew attention to something unique outside the Bernstein-Grisman home. It seemed a miracle, they said.

A sign from God that the settlement had been given a blessing. How else could it be explained?

A man (with a past, it was rumored in the settlement, and not without respect) who'd never grown anything in his life? And in such brittle ground?

A large black rose.

THE FRATERNITY OF THE STONE

With love
to my mother, Beatrice

In some respects, the intelligence profession resembles monastic life with the disciplines and personal sacrifices reminiscent of medieval orders.

– The U.S. Senate's Church Committee
Report on Intelligence Activities, 1976

CONTENTS

PROLOGUE
WARRIORS OF
GOD

THE DESERT FATHERS

Egypt, 381.
The Roman Empire, dangerously fragmented, made a desperate bid for unity by choosing Christianity as its sole official religion. A few Christian fanatics, disillusioned by this contamination of politics into their religion, retreated from society, venturing into the desert of Egypt, where they lived in caves to seek a mystical conjunction with their God. As word about these spiritual hermits spread, other disillusioned Christians soon joined them, establishing an austere religious community based on fasting, prayer, and physical mortification. By 529, the severe traditions of what some called these 'holy madmen' had begun to drift northward through Europe.

And Christian monasticism was born.

THE OLD MAN OF THE MOUNTAIN

Persia, 1090.

Hassan ibn al-Sabbah, leader of a fanatical sect of Muslims, adopted murder as a sacred duty in his fight to wrest control of his country from Turkish invaders and their ally, the Egyptian caliph. His secret organization of religious killers soon spread west to Syria, where his successors each acquired the title 'The Old Man of the Mountain.' In 1096, the European crusaders invaded the Mideast, commencing their papally authorized Holy War against the Muslims to regain the Holy Sepulchre. These intruders naturally attracted the attention of 'The Old Man' and his followers, who were known as *hashishi* because of the hashish they allegedly smoked to achieve religious ecstasy and promote the frenzy with which they prepared themselves to face possible martyrdom.

But *hashishi* was mispronounced by the crusaders.

They carried a different name back to Europe – Assassins.

HOLY TERROR

Palestine, 1192.

Though the sun had begun to set, the desert sand had not yet given up its heat. Surrounded by guards, the voluminous tent – made from heavy sailcloth – billowed slightly from a searing breeze. Exhausted horses, slick with sweat, raised dustclouds as the knights who rode them approached from opposite camps. Flagbearers preceded each column, their respective banners depicting three golden lions above each other upon a field of red – the English – and a gold fleur-de-lis upon a field of blue – the French. Though united in a holy cause, they nonetheless disagreed profoundly about politics between their countries, for the French contested land owned by the English in their territory. Due to these strained relations, neither column was willing to tolerate arriving first and thus being made to suffer the indignity of waiting for the other. Scouts on nearby dunes had signaled the progress of each group, ensuring that both delegations would converge on the tent simultaneously.

The columns met: four emissaries in each, along with their retainers. They peered toward a barren mountain in the distance where armies swarmed amid the smoking ruin of a minareted castle. The siege had been brutal, costly in lives, lasting for almost three months; but at last the Muslims here at Acre had been defeated.

For a moment, political differences between French and English were forgotten. Weary but resolute, they praised each other's valor, congratulating themselves on victory. First bodyguards dismounted, then valets who assisted their lords. In contrast with the pride that had made each group determined not to wait for the other, their courtly manners now required them to offer their rivals the privilege of being the first to enter the tent. Practicality solved the dilemma. Whichever lord was closest agreed to leave his servants behind and step ahead.

Inside, the flap of the tent secured, the knights stripped off their weapons, helmets, and chain-mail armor. The air was stifling. After the blaze of the desert sun, their eyes adjusted slowly to the murky light. Shadows from the guards outside darkened the walls of the tent.

The knights assessed each other. On this, the Third Crusade to the Holy Land, the lessons of the earlier Crusades had taught them to wear long gowns to preserve their body moisture and prevent the deadly sun

5

from burning their skin. The gowns were pale, attracting less heat than the brilliant colors that they favored in their homeland. The only concession to color was the large red image of a cross that adorned the front of their gowns – along with the coppery splotches of dried heathen blood.

The men had beards. Even so, their cheeks looked gaunt and dehydrated. Raising hoods to cover their matted hair, they drank wine from cups prepared for them. Given the purpose of this meeting, water would have been preferable. Clear heads, after all, were necessary. But the logistics of the Crusade, the massive territory involved, had resulted in insecure supply lines, and wine – which they had saved for a celebration – was the only liquid available. Though thirsty, they drank it sparingly. For now.

The tallest, most muscular man, an English lord known for his skill with a battleax, spoke first, using the accepted diplomatic language, French. His name was Roger of Sussex. 'I recommend that we complete our business first before . . .' He gestured toward the bread, olives, and dried spicy meat laid out for them.

'Agreed,' said the leader of the French contingent, Jacques de Wisant. 'Your King Richard will not be joining us?'

'We thought it prudent not to inform him about this meeting. And your King Philip?'

'There are certain matters best discussed in private. Should it prove necessary, he will be told what we decide.'

Each knew what the other meant. Though they had guards, they themselves were guards as well, of a higher order. Their function was to arrange protection for their respective kings. Such protection required a network of informers who reported even the vaguest rumors about subversive plots. But seldom were these rumors passed on to Richard or Philip. What a king didn't know would not alarm him or make him suspect that his security staff was not what it should be. Dismissal might take the form of an ax to one's neck.

'Very well, then,' an Englishman, William of Gloucester, said, 'I suggest we begin.'

The nature of the group changed abruptly. Whereas before the knights had been conscious of their French or English allegiance, now their national rivalries disappeared. They shared a common bond, an exclusive code, comrades in the fraternity of the Greek god, Harpocrates.

Silence. Secrecy.

The Englishman, Roger of Sussex, held a Bible that the monks of his land had copied for him, bound with leather and gilded with gold. He opened it. 'The Book of Daniel,' he explained. 'The passage in which Daniel keeps control of his tongue despite the threat of being eaten by lions. It seemed appropriate.'

The ritual began. The eight knights formed a circle. As one, they solemnly placed their right hand upon the Bible and swore themselves to secrecy.

In imitation of their enemies – and due to the difficulty of transporting furniture – they sat on an ornate rug that their armies had liberated from the defeated Muslim castle. They leaned back on pillows, swirled the wine in their cups, and listened to Pierre de l'Étang.

'As the man responsible for arranging the conditions of this meeting,'

6

he said, 'I remind you that the guards outside stand well away from the walls of the tent. Provided that your voices remain at a normal level, you won't be heard.'

'So my assistants informed me,' an Englishman, Baldwin of Kent, replied.

The Frenchman nodded his compliments. 'Yes, my own assistants apprised me that they were watched.'

Baldwin nodded his compliments in return. 'But *my* assistants informed me of something else. Your king intends to divorce his army from Richard's Crusade.'

'Indeed?'

Baldwin narrowed his eyes. 'Indeed.'

'As Frenchmen, we weren't aware that this Crusade belonged to Richard.'

'It does if Philip returns to France.'

'Ah, yes, I grant the point.' Pierre sipped his wine. 'Your assistants have excellent sources. And did they tell you when our king intends to lead his army home?'

'Within a fortnight. Philip plans to take advantage of Richard's absence from court. In exchange for the territory that our country owns in France, your king has promised to support Richard's brother in his bid to take over the English throne.'

The Frenchman shrugged. 'And what do you propose to do with this information, assuming that it's true?'

Baldwin did not answer.

'I respect your tact.' Pierre set down his cup. 'It does seem that relations between our countries will soon worsen. Consider this, however. Without rivalry, our skills would not be of use.'

'And life would not have interest. Which brings us to our reason for requesting this meeting,' Jacques de Wisant interrupted.

The Englishmen sat straighter.

'Assuming that your sources are correct,' Jacques said, 'if indeed we leave the Crusade within a fortnight, we regret that we'll also leave a particularly fascinating unsolved problem. As a parting gesture of the fraternity we share, we'd like to assist you in finding an answer.'

Baldwin studied him. 'You're referring, of course–'

'To the recent murder of your countryman – Conrad of Montferrat.'

'Forgive me for being surprised that an Englishman's death, no matter how shocking, distresses you.'

'Almost as much as the previous identically shocking murder of our own countryman – Raymond de Chatillon.'

No further explanation was necessary. Six years earlier, a truce between the crusaders and the forces of Saladin had been broken when Raymond de Chatillon attacked the caravan of Saladin's sister. For this violation, there was no peaceful redress, so the great Muslim counter-crusade, the *jihad*, had begun. One year later during the siege of Jerusalem, Raymond's head had been found on the altar of the Shrine of the Holy Sepulchre. A curved knife lay beside it.

Since then, dozens of identical assassinations had taken place, achieving their intended purpose, teaching fear of the night to the crusading lords. Yesterday, after the fall of the Muslim castle here at Acre, Conrad of

Montferrat's head had been found on the altar set up for the victory mass. A curved knife lay beside it, a knife that the crusaders had now learned to identify with The Old Man of the Mountain and his cult of fanatics.

'Assassins.' Roger made a face as if intending to spit out his wine. 'Cowards. Thieves plundering lives in the dark. The proper way for a lord to die is in daylight in battle, bravely matching his skills with those of his enemy, even if the enemy is heathen. These sneaks have no regard for honor, for dignity, for the pride of the warrior. They're despicable.'

'But nonetheless they exist,' Pierre de l'Étang pointed out. 'More important, they're effective. I confess to morbid suspicions that my own head might be next on the altar.'

The others nodded, admitting fears about themselves.

'Still there's nothing we can do, except to gather more bodyguards around us while we sleep,' William of Gloucester said. 'And even then, these assassins slip past our best defenses. It's as if they can make themselves invisible.'

'Don't credit them with mystery,' Jacques said. 'They're human like ourselves. But highly trained.'

'In barbarous tactics. There's no way to fight them,' William said.

'I wonder.'

The group regarded Jacques intensely.

'You have a suggestion?' Roger asked.

'Perhaps.'

'What is it, then?'

'Fight fire with fire.'

'I won't consider it,' William fumed. 'Use their obscene methods against them? Become as cowardly as they are, creeping upon their leaders while they sleep? It's unconscionable.'

'But only because it's never been done.'

William stood in distress. *'Because it goes against the warrior's code.'*

'But these sneaks are heathen. Uncivilized,' Jacques said. 'If they're too primitive to understand honor and dignity, we're not bound to respect them by adhering to the code.'

His remark had force. The tent became silent as the group considered the implications.

William nodded. 'I confess to wanting Conrad avenged.'

'And Raymond,' a Frenchman reminded him.

'I'd spear a mad dog regardless of whether he was or wasn't facing me,' another Frenchman said, and made a fist.

'But the scheme isn't practical,' Baldwin interrupted. 'The Muslims would recognize any of us who tried to infiltrate among them. Even the night wouldn't hide the purity of our skin.'

'And bear this in mind,' Roger added. 'No matter if we darkened our skin with substances, we don't understand their language or their ways. If one of them spoke to us while we went among them in disguise, or if we made a wrong gesture . . .'

'I wasn't proposing that we try to infiltrate,' Jacques said.

'Then?'

'Not ourselves. We send in one of their own.'

'Impossible. They hate us. Where would we find such a–?'

'One who saw the error of his heathen ways, who converted to the one true God, a Muslim who became a Christian.'

The English were shocked.

'You're suggesting that you know of such a man?' Roger asked.

Jacques nodded. 'In the Benedictine monastery at Monte Cassino in Italy.'

The name was resonant. Monte Cassino had been founded in 529, one of the earliest Christian monasteries, when the austere zeal of the desert fathers spread northward from Egypt through Europe.

'I accepted his order's hospitality for a night on my way here to the Holy Land,' Jacques said. 'I was given permission to spend an hour with him, and he was given permission to speak. His Christian zeal is remarkable. He'd do anything for the Lord.'

'A monk?'

'Indeed.'

'That's blasphemy,' William said. 'To ask a monk to kill?'

'For a sacred cause. The liberation of Christ's Holy Land. Remember that the Pope himself has absolved us of any sins we might commit in this divinely inspired Crusade. I've made inquiries among the priests who came here with us. They feel confident that the monk I have in mind would receive a papal dispensation. Indeed, by becoming a warrior of God, he'd be saving his soul. If it's true that my countrymen and I return to France within a fortnight, I could arrange to stop again at Monte Cassino. I'm sure that he'd be responsive. Rome – and papal encouragement – would not be far away.'

The knights peered down at their wine cups.

Baldwin raised his eyes. 'But he isn't trained.'

'He's familiar with stories he heard about the assassins,' Jacques said. 'And rumors about their techniques. Mind you, I have technical suggestions of my own.'

'How long to prepare him?'

'For what I have in mind? Three months.'

'I needed a lifetime to learn my craft,' William said. 'We have to consider the strong chance that he'll be killed.'

'In the attempt,' Jacques said. 'But don't you see? The attempt is what matters. Once the heathen understand that we – and even one who formerly was their own – are prepared to die for the one true God . . .'

'They'll sleep as restlessly as we do.'

Baldwin squinted. 'Fight terror with terror?'

'With a difference,' Jacques said. 'For our fight is holy.'

PART ONE
ATONEMENT

THE HOUSE OF THE DEAD

1

It was north of Quentin, Vermont. You could see it partly hidden by fir trees, a quarter mile off the two-lane blacktop, to the right on the crest of a hill. Beyond it loomed a higher hill, thick with maple trees, brilliant now in the autumn, vivid orange and yellow and red. A high wire fence ran parallel to the blacktop, the sides veering off at right angles, disappearing back into the forest. You'd have trouble calculating, since you couldn't see how far back the fences went, but you wouldn't be wrong to guess that the property covered at least a hundred acres. The nearest building – apart from the one on the hill – was a boarded-up service station quite a ways behind you, out of sight, on the other side of the corkscrew turn that led to this straightaway. And you wouldn't get to the maple syrup factory up ahead for more than a mile.

Remote. Secluded.

Peaceful.

Glancing toward the pine tree-studded hill, you might suspect that the partly hidden structure, with its gleaming wood, was a millionaire's retreat, a forest hideaway where the pressures of business could be relieved by who could imagine what distractions.

Or possibly the building was a ski resort, closed till the snow fell. Or . . .

But from just driving by, of course, you could never know. There was neither a mailbox nor a sign at the gate, and the gate itself had a thick chain holding it in place – an even thicker lock. The lane on the other side was weedgrown, squeezed by bushes and drooping pines. To be sure, you could always ask at the maple syrup factory if your curiosity lasted till then, but you'd only feel more frustrated as a result. The workers there, true New Englanders, were willing to talk to strangers about the weather but not about their own or their neighbor's business. It wouldn't have mattered, anyhow. They didn't know, either, though there were rumors.

2

From the air, the structure on the hill was larger than the view from the road suggested. Indeed, an elevated vantage point revealed that the building wasn't alone. Smaller buildings – otherwise hidden by pine trees – formed three sides of a square, the fourth of which was the lodge itself. Enclosed by the square was a lawn. Two white-stone walkways intersected at its middle, bordered by flower gardens, trees, and shrubs. The effect was one of balance and order, symmetry, proportion. Soothing. Even the smaller buildings, though joined like rows of townhouses, had small peaked roofs in imitation of the larger peaked roof on the lodge.

Despite the expanse of the estate, however, remarkably few people showed themselves down there. The tiny figure of a groundskeeper tended the lawn. Two miniature workmen harvested apples from an orchard outside one line of buildings. A wisp of smoke rose from a bonfire in a considerable vegetable garden flanking the opposite line of buildings. With so sizable a commitment to agriculture, the estate presumably had many residents, yet except for those few signs of life, the place seemed deserted. If there were guests, it hardly seemed natural for them to ignore the pleasure of this bright crisp autumn day. To remain indoors, they must surely have an important reason.

But then the seclusion of the inhabitants was part of the mystery about this place. Since 1951, when teams of construction workers had arrived from somewhere – not from the local town, though whoever was funding the project at least had the goodness to buy a decent amount of supplies from there – the citizens of Quentin had wondered what was happening on that hill. When the workers put up the gate and departed, the local busybodies noted a fascinating pattern. They recalled stories they'd recently read about the development of the atomic bomb in New Mexico at the end of the war. The government had built a small town in the desert there, it was said. The local communities had therefore hoped for an increase in business; but they'd waited in vain, for the strange thing was that people went into that desert town, but – as with the estate on this hill – they didn't come out.

3

The unit, one of twenty in the complex, each the same, consisted of two levels. On the bottom, a workroom contained whatever equipment its occupant had chosen to use to pass his leisure time. In other parts of the complex, some perhaps painted or sculpted or wove, possibly worked with wood and carpentry tools. Or, since each unit had a small private garden enclosed by a wall, adjacent to the workroom, some might practice horticulture, perhaps growing roses.

In the present case, the occupant had chosen exercise and composition. He knew that he couldn't concentrate if his body was not in condition.

14

Indeed, in his former life he'd been intensely devoted to the principles of Zen, aware that exercise itself was spiritual. Each day for an hour he lifted weights, skipped rope, performed calisthenics, and rehearsed the *katas* or dance steps of the Oriental martial arts. He did all this with humility, taking no satisfaction in the perfection of his physique, for he realized that his body was but an instrument of his soul. In fact, the effect of his daily workouts had little obvious results. His torso was lean, ascetic, low on the protein his muscles required to replace the tissue his exercise wore down. He ate no meat. On Friday, he took only bread and water. Some days, he ate nothing. But his discipline gave him strength.

His compositions fulfilled another purpose. During his early months here, he'd been tempted to write about his motive for coming, to purge himself, to vent his anguish. But his need to forget was greater. To relieve the pressure of his urge for self-expression, he'd written haikus first, an understandable choice given his sympathy with Zen. He selected topics with no relevance to what disturbed him – the song of a bird, the breath of the wind. But the nature of a haiku, its complicated tension based on purity and brevity, led him to greater attempts at compression and refinement until no statement at all seemed the perfect haiku, and he stared past his pen toward the vacuum of a barren page. Compulsively, he'd switched to the sonnet form, alternating between Shakespearean and Petrarchan, each with a different rhyme scheme, both demanding a perfect organization of fourteen lines. The problem of that intricate puzzle was enough to occupy him. More interested in how he wrote than what he wrote, he expressed himself about minuscule matters and was able to forget the troubling great ones. He wrote as best he could, not out of pride, but out of respect for the puzzle. Even so, he knew that eloquence eluded him. Perhaps in another unit of this complex, an occupant had – like himself – become engaged with poetry. Perhaps that other occupant had produced such perfectly beautiful sonnets that they rivaled those of Shakespeare and Petrarch themselves.

It wouldn't have mattered. Nothing any occupant devised – paintings, statues, tapestries, or furniture – had any value. All were insignificant. When the men who fashioned them died, they were placed on a board and buried in an unmarked grave, and the objects they left behind, their clothes, their few belongings, their sonnets, even a skipping rope, were destroyed. It would be as if they had never existed.

4

The psychiatrist, as expected, had been a priest. He'd worn the traditional black suit and white collar, his face somewhat wrinkled, bullet-gray, as he lit a cigarette and peered at Drew from across his desk.

'You understand the gravity of your request.'

'I've considered it carefully.'

'You made your decision – when?'

'Three months ago.'

'And you waited . . . ?'

15

'Till now. To analyze the implications. Naturally I had to be sure.'

The priest inhaled from his cigarette, thoughtful, studying Drew. His name was Father Hafer. He was in his late forties, his short hair the same bullet-gray color as his face. Exhaling smoke, he made an offhanded gesture with the cigarette. 'Naturally. The other side of the issue is, how can we be sure? Of your commitment? Of your determination and resolve?'

'You can't.'

'Well, there it is then.'

'But I can, and that's what matters. This is what I need. I've resigned myself.'

'To what?'

'Not "to".'

'I beg your pardon?'

'From.' Drew nodded toward the clamorous Boston street beyond the first-floor window of this rectory office.

'Everything? The world?'

Drew didn't respond.

'Of course, that's what the eremitical life is all about. Withdrawal,' Father Hafer said and shrugged. 'Still, a negative attitude isn't sufficient. Your motive has to be positive as well. Seeking, not merely fleeing.'

'Oh, I'm seeking all right.'

'Indeed?' The priest raised his eyebrows. 'For what?'

'Salvation.'

Father Hafer considered him, exhaling smoke. 'An admirable answer.' He brushed an ash from his cigarette into a metal tray. 'So quick to the lips, so readily given. Have you been religious long?'

'For the past three months.'

'And before?'

Again Drew didn't respond.

'You *are* a Roman Catholic?'

'I was baptized into the faith. My parents were quite religious.' Suddenly remembering how they'd died, he felt his throat ache. 'We went to church often. Mass. The Stations of the Cross. I received the sacraments up through confirmation, and you know what they say about confirmation. It made me a soldier of Christ.' Drew bitterly smiled. 'Oh, I believed.'

'And after that?'

'The term is "lapsed".'

'Have you made your Easter duty?'

'Not in thirteen years.'

'You understand what that means?'

'By not going to confession and communion before Easter, I in effect resigned from the faith. I've been unofficially excommunicated.'

'And put your soul in immortal peril.'

'That's why I've come to you. To save myself.'

'You mean your soul,' Father Hafer said.

'That's right. That's what I meant.'

They studied each other. The priest leaned forward, placing his elbows on the desk, his eyes somewhat brighter with interest. 'Of course . . . Let's review the information you provided on this form. You say that your name is Andrew MacLane.'

16

'It's sometimes shortened to "Drew".'

'But if we agree to accept your application, that name will be taken from you. Like everything else you own – a car, for example, or a house – your identity will have to be abandoned. In effect, you'll be no one. You're aware of that?'

Drew raised his shoulders. 'So what's in a name?' He allowed the bitter smile to appear now. 'A rose by any other name . . .'

'Or by none,' the priest said, 'would smell as sweet. But to the nose of God . . .'

'We don't exactly smell like roses. I don't, anyhow. That's why I applied. To purify myself.'

'You're thirty-one?'

'Correct.' Drew hadn't lied. All the information he'd provided on the form was verifiable, as he knew the priest would take pains to discover. What mattered was what he *hadn't* put down on the form.

'The prime of life,' Father Hafer said. 'Indeed, even a few years before it if we use thirty-three as the appropriate age for coming into one's own. You're dismissing the possibilities of the road ahead of you. Throwing away your potential, as it were.'

'No, I don't think of it that way.'

'Then . . .?'

'I've already discovered my potential.'

'And?'

'I didn't like it.'

'I don't suppose you'd care to elaborate.'

Drew glanced at the floor.

'Eventually you'll have to.' Father Hafer seemed troubled. 'But never mind. For now, we have other matters to discuss. Our applicants are usually past their maturity, to use a delicate phrase, when they make their request.' He shrugged. 'Of course, very few request, and even fewer . . .'

'Are chosen. Less than five hundred worldwide. And here in the United States, only twenty, I believe.'

'Good, I see that you've done your homework. The point is – to use a less delicate term – most of those men are old.' Father Hafer stubbed out his cigarette. 'They've pursued their ambitions. They've accomplished, and sometimes haven't, their worldly aims. Now they're ready to spend their dwindling years in retirement. Their decision, though extreme, can be viewed as natural. But you – so young, so robust. Women no doubt find you attractive. Have you considered the implications of giving up female companionship?'

With a stab of longing, he remembered Arlene. '*You* gave it up.'

'I gave up sexual relations.' Father Hafer sat straighter. 'Not female companionship. I encounter women many times a day. A waitress in a restaurant. A clerk at the medical library. A secretary of one of my lay colleagues. All perfectly innocent. The sight of women, rather than tempting me, makes my vow of chastity seem less severe. But if we accede to your request, you'll never see a woman again, and very few men, and even then rarely. I emphasize. For the rest of your life, what you're asking to be is a hermit.'

17

5

The unit's second level, reached by crude pine stairs consisted of three sections. First the oratory, otherwise known as the 'Ave Maria' room, where a simple wooden pew, its kneeler an unpadded board, faced an austere altar with a crucifix on the wall. Beyond it was the study – sacred texts, a table and chair – and then the sleeping quarters – a wood stove, but no bed, just an inch-thick woven-hemp pallet.

The pallet was six feet long and three feet wide. It could easily have been rolled up and placed downstairs in a corner of the workroom, spread out when he needed to rest. But the point was to segregate his various activities. To go from his workroom up to his sleeping quarters, or from his sleeping quarters down to his workroom, he had to pass through the oratory, and the rule required him to stop there each time and pray.

6

'If it's simply a life of devotion that appeals to you,' Father Hafer said, 'consider a less strict order. The missionary fathers, perhaps?'

Drew shook his head.

'Or possibly the Congregation of the Resurrectionists. They do good work – teaching, for example.'

Drew told him, 'No.'

'Then what about this suggestion? Earlier you mentioned how the sacrament of confirmation had made you a soldier of Christ. I'm sure you're aware that the Jesuits have intensified that concept. They're much more rigorous than the Resurrectionists. Their training takes fifteen years, ample reason for their nickname – the commandos of the Church.'

'It's not what I had in mind.'

'Because they confront the world?' Father Hafer hurried on. 'But during a considerable part of the training period, you'd be cloistered. It's only toward the end that you'd be nudged from the nest, and perhaps by then you'd appreciate the push. And even earlier, at various stages, you'd have a chance to reconsider your priorities, to change your direction if you cared to.'

'I don't think so.'

Father Hafer sounded more distressed. 'There's even another option. The Cistercians. The second most demanding order in the Church. You live in a monastery cut off from the world. Your days are filled with exhausting work, farming, for instance, something that contributes to the order. You never speak. But at least you labor – and pray – in a group. And if you find the life too difficult, you can leave and reapply at a later time, though not beyond the age of thirty-six. The advantage is that there's a system of checks and balances that allows you to change your mind.'

Drew waited.

'Good heavens, man, why must you be so determined?' Father Hafer lit

18

another cigarette, flicking his butane lighter. 'I'm trying to make you understand. In the fullness of your youth, you're asking to be admitted into the most severe form of worship in the Church. The Carthusians. There's nothing more extreme. It's the total denial of a human being as a social animal. The eremitic way. For the rest of your life, you'd live alone in a cell. Except for an hour of leisure, you'd do nothing but pray. It's complete deprivation. Solitude.'

7

He wore a coarse hair shirt, designed to irritate his skin. At times, its aggravating sensation became a pleasure since at least it was an experience, something intense. When that temptation aroused him, he fought to distract himself, praying harder, sometimes flagellating himself with his skipping rope, stifling his groans.

You're not here to enjoy yourself. You came to do penance. To be left alone.

Over the hair shirt, he wore a white robe, and above that a white biblike scapular, and then a white hood. On the limited occasions when he was forced to endure communal rituals such as choir, perverse requirements designed to test his fortitude, he wore a drooping white cowl that hid his face and allowed him to feel invisible.

8

'There's no need for us to be this intense,' Father Hafer said, forcing a smile. 'Why don't we relax for a moment? Debate may be good for the mind, after all, but not for the constitution. May I offer refreshment?' Stabbing his cigarette into the ashtray, he approached a cabinet, opened it, and removed a carafe of glinting emerald liquid. 'A glass of Chartreuse, perhaps?'

'No, thanks.'

'Its taste does not appeal to you?'

'I've never . . .'

'Now you have the opportunity.'

'No, I don't drink.'

Father Hafer narrowed his eyes. 'Indeed? A weakness that you guard against?'

'I've never indulged. In my line of work, I couldn't afford poor judgment.'

'And what was that? Your line of work?'

Drew didn't answer.

Father Hafer considered him, swirling the emerald liquid. 'Yet another topic for later discussion. I wonder if you realize how appropriate this substance is.'

'Chartreuse.' Drew spread his hands. 'The liqueur is reputed to be the finest. Its distinctive flavor – something I wouldn't know about – is due to angelica root. And, of course, one hundred and fifteen different herbs. It's the principal source of income for the Carthusians. Manufactured at the fatherhouse at La Grande Chartreuse in the Alps of France. The name of the liqueur comes from the place where it's made. Chartreuse. The green type you're holding has an alcohol content of fifty-five percent while the yellow type has forty-three percent. Its recipe was concocted in the early sixteen hundreds, I believe, by a layman who donated its formula to the Carthusians. A century later, a chemical genius in the order perfected it. A bogus version appeared on the market, but those who discriminate know which label to look for.'

Father Hafer blinked. 'Remarkable.'

'In more ways than one. An order of hermits maintains its independence because of the income generated from a liquid designed to produce conviviality. Of course, the liqueur is manufactured by a lay fraternity. Even so, I ignore the contradiction.'

9

His needs were attended to by non-eremitic brothers, whose quarters were in the lodge, which also contained the chapel, the refectory, the kitchen, and a guest room. His spartan meals were given to him through a serving hatch beside a door in his workroom. On Sundays and major feasts, however, the rule required him to leave his cell, which was never locked, and eat with the other hermits in the refectory at the lodge. On those occasions, subdued conversation was permitted, but he never indulged. He was also required to leave his cell and join the other monks in the lodge's chapel at midnight for matins, at 8 A.M. for mass, and at 6 P.M. for vespers. He disliked these interruptions, preferring to worship in the isolation of his cell.

His only distraction was the mouse.

10

'*The vows,*' Father Hafer said, distressed. 'Have you truly considered their gravity? Not only those of poverty, chastity, and obedience, arduous enough on their own. But add to them the oath of fealty to the principles of the Carthusians. I have to be brutally direct. When the committee meets to judge applicants, we customarily reject young men as a matter of course. Their immaturity makes us question their ability to keep their vows of solitude. The consequence of disobedience is unthinkable.'

'If I broke my vows, I'd be damning myself.'

'That's right. And even confession could not return your soul to a state of grace. Your only alternative would be to request a dispensation. So serious a request takes months to be considered. In the meantime, if you should die . . .'

'It wouldn't matter.'

'I don't . . .'

'I'm already damned.'

Father Hafer flinched and raised his voice. 'Because you failed to make your Easter duty for thirteen years? By comparison with violating sacred vows, that other sin is minor. I could reinstate you now by hearing your confession and giving you communion. But even confession could not return your soul to a state of grace if you had no dispensation and you continued to violate the vows. You surely understand why the committee would turn down your request to join the order. If we accepted you but doubted your ability to endure the Carthusian way of life, we ourselves would be scorning the vows you would take. To a great degree, we'd be helping you to damn yourself, and that would make us culpable. We'd be threatening the state of our *own* souls.'

'But if . . .'

'Yes? Go on.'

'If you don't admit me, you'd be culpable anyhow.'

'For what?'

'For what I'd be driven to do. I said I felt damned. I didn't mean because of my failure to make my Easter duty.'

'Then what?'

'I want to kill myself.'

11

During his fifth year at the monastery, after the first chill of autumn had colored the maples, he sensed a movement to his right as he knelt on the hardwood floor of his workroom, praying for his soul. The movement was minuscule, a subtle blur that might have been due to eye strain, the result of his anguished concentration. Sweat beaded his brow. Ashamed that he'd allowed himself to be distracted, he meditated with greater fervor, desperate to shut out the horrid images from his past.

But the movement continued, barely perceptible, nonetheless there. For a moment, he wondered if he'd reached the stage of experiencing hallucinations – other monks, after intense devotion, were rumored to have witnessed presences – but skepticism as well as humility discouraged him, and besides, the movement was on the floor at the base of a wall. What sort of religious vision would be appropriate there?

Deciding that his fortitude was being tested, he resolved not to look; but again the blur caught the corner of his gaze, and in a moment of weakness that eventually saved his life, he turned his head to the right, toward the floor at the base of the wall, and saw a small gray mouse.

It froze.

Drew was taken by surprise.

But so, apparently, was the mouse. Each watched the other for quite a while. As if losing patience, the mouse twitched its whiskers. Unconsciously, Drew scratched the side of his nose. Alarmed, with amazing abruptness, the mouse sped toward a hole in the wall.

21

Drew astonished himself by almost laughing. As the mouse disappeared, however, he frowned at the implications. The hole had not been in his workroom wall when he went to the vespers service last night. He focused on the freshly gnawed wood and wondered what to do. Tonight, while he was again away at the vespers service, he could ask a custodian brother to obtain a trap or possibly poison. After slipping one or the other into the hole, the brother could use his carpentry tools to plug up the hole.

But why? Drew asked himself. In the chill of autumn, the mouse had come to the monastery for refuge, as he himself had wanted refuge. In a sense, they were two of a kind.

The thought was comic to him. Sure, me and the mouse. He did consider the danger of chewed electrical wires, of mice reproducing behind the wall till the monastery was vermin-ridden. Common sense suggested that to tolerate the mouse would be impractical.

But the mouse intrigued him. Something about its daring. And yet its . . .

Helplessness, he thought. I could easily kill it.

But not anymore. Not even a mouse.

He decided to let it stay. On probation. As long as you don't raise hell. As long as you're celibate, he allowed himself to joke.

12

Father Hafer turned pale. 'You admit . . . ?'

'I truly believe,' Drew said, 'that retreat from the world is my only chance to be saved. Otherwise . . .'

'If I deny your application, I'd be responsible for your suicide? For your unforgivable sin of despair? For your going to Hell? Absurd.'

'It's the logic you used a moment ago. You said that you'd be culpable if you let me in despite your misgivings and I later damned myself by breaking my vows.'

'So now I'd be culpable if I *didn't* let you in and you later damned yourself by committing suicide? Ridiculous,' Father Hafer said. 'What's going on here? Who do you think you're talking to? I'm a man of God. I've tried to treat your extreme request with respect, and now you want to blame me for. . . It's all I can do to keep from telling you to get out of here.'

'But you *are* a man of God. So you won't turn your back on me.'

Father Hafer seemed not to have heard. 'And this application.' He pointed angrily at his desk. 'I suspected there was something wrong. You claim that your parents died when you were ten.'

'That's true.' Drew felt his throat swell shut.

'But there's little indication of what happened to you after that. You do say you were educated in an industrial school in Colorado, but you've obviously had training in the arts – logic, history, literature. Next to "occupation" you say you're unemployed. As what? The natural inclination is to state your occupation, whether you're unemployed or not. I asked you a while ago, but you wouldn't tell me. Unmarried. Never have been. No children. Thirty-one years old' – the priest rapped the form on his desk – 'and you're a shadow.'

Drew bitterly smiled. 'Then it ought to be easy for me to erase the evidence of my former life.'

'*Since it seems to have been erased already.*' Father Hafer glared. 'Are you in trouble with the law, is that your motive? You think the Carthusians would make a good hideout? Perverting the Church to –'

'No. In fact, what I used to do was encouraged by the law. At the highest level.'

'That's it. I've lost my patience. This interview is finished right now if you don't –'

'In confession.'

'What?'

'I'll tell you in confession.'

13

The mouse turned out to be as reclusive as himself. He didn't see it for the next few days and began to think that it had gone away. But on a cold drizzly afternoon when the clouds hung low and the sodden maple leaves fell dismally to the ground, he sensed the blur of movement again as he knelt in meditation, and peering across his workroom, he saw just a nose and some whiskers poking from the hole.

He remained as still as possible and watched. The mouse strained its head from the hole, its nostrils twitching, testing for danger. Determined not to scare it, curious about what it planned to do, Drew tried not even to blink.

The mouse took a tentative step, its shoulders appearing. Another step, and now Drew saw its side, its tiny chest heaving, its eyes darting this way and that. Another step, and it left the hole.

But it didn't seem the same. Though gray as before, its fur looked duller, its body thinner, making Drew wonder if this was a different mouse. His previous concern about not just one mouse but a nest of them made him question his refusal to tell a custodian brother to deal with the problem. Instead of amusement, he now watched the mouse with uneasiness.

It inched along the baseboard, sniffing. But it seemed off-balance, listing as if it had injured a leg or was dizzy. Or sick? Drew wondered. No way of telling what diseases it carried or if they could be communicated to humans. Perhaps even rabies, he realized with alarm.

He almost stood to scare the mouse back into its hole, but as it reached a corner and veered from one baseboard to another, continuing to sniff, he guessed what it might be doing – searching for food. That would explain its apparent dizziness. It could be trembling from hunger.

But shouldn't there be plenty of food around? he wondered. Then he realized that the rain outside had almost turned to sleet. The mouse would have to risk freezing to death and overcome difficult obstacles to travel what for it would be a considerable distance to the few ungathered apples in the orchard or the remnants of vegetables in the garden outside the cloister. There was food, of course, in the monastery's kitchen and cellar, but the mouse had made the mistake of choosing this cell in a wing that was far from the lodge. Obviously it hadn't figured out where the kitchen was; otherwise it would have nested there.

You really screwed up, mouse. Your survival instincts are pathetic.

As the mouse reached another corner, wobbling along the next baseboard, it faced in Drew's direction. Its eyes abruptly widened – its nose jerked. It suddenly bolted, streaking across the workroom, shooting out of sight inside the hole.

Drew exhaled what was nearly a laugh. He watched the hole for a moment longer, then turned as he heard the rattle of a latch being lifted. In the hallway outside, unseen hands swung open the serving hatch beside his door. With a scrape and thump, his evening meal was placed on a shelf. The hatch was closed.

He stood and went over, removing a cup and bowl from the shelf. He didn't have a watch or a calendar. His only ways of measuring time were the monastery's bell, the passage of the seasons, and the types of meals he was served. Thus today must be Friday, he concluded, glancing at the contents of his cup and bowl, for that was when he received only bread and water.

He set the spartan meal on his workbench and glanced toward the dreary rain beyond his window. Possibly because of the chill and the damp, he felt uncommonly tempted by hunger today, and as a consequence, for added discipline, he forced himself not to eat all the bread.

He later wondered if all along he'd had another motive for partially fasting, but it nonetheless surprised him when on impulse, as the chapel bell beckoned him to leave his cell for the vespers service, he set a small chunk of bread in front of the mouse's hole.

When he returned, the bread was gone, and he allowed himself to smile.

14

'Abuse the sacrament?' Father Hafer was shocked. 'If you're worried about guaranteeing my silence, there's no need for confession. Don't forget, I'm also a psychiatrist. My professional ethics force me to keep this conversation strictly private. I'd never discuss it in a court or with the police.'

'But I prefer to depend on your ethics as a priest. You put great emphasis on sacred vows. You'd damn your self if you revealed what you heard in confession.'

'I told you I won't abuse the sacrament! I don't know what trick you're trying to get away with, but –'

'*For God's sake, I'm begging you!*'

The priest blinked, startled.

Drew swallowed, his voice pained. 'Then you'll know why I have to be allowed to join the order.'

15

It became a ritual. Every evening, he left a portion of his meal – a piece of carrot, a leaf of lettuce, a section of apple – in front of the hole. His offering was never refused. But as if suspicious of Drew's generosity, the mouse stayed in its hole.

Of course, Drew thought, why bother coming out when your meals are delivered?

The motive that he attributed to the mouse amused him, though he didn't allow his amusement to interfere with his resolve. His purpose was worship, his days taken up with prayer and penance, for the honor and glory of God and the atonement of his heinous sins.

The gusting snow of his fifth winter here piled huge drifts outside his window. He persisted, purging his awful emotions, subduing the guilt that tortured his soul. But sometimes during his prayers, the mouse now ventured out. It looked fatter, its eyes more alert. It went no farther than a yard from its hole, but its pace was steady. Its fur had a healthy sheen.

Then spring came, and the mouse had sufficient confidence to show itself when Drew was exercising. It sat outside its hole, its front feet raised, contemplating what must have seemed odd behavior.

Each balmy day, Drew expected that the mouse would leave. It's time for you to play, he thought. Taste the sweet new buds, and meet some pals. I'll even absolve you of chastity. Go on, kiddo. Raise a family. The world needs fieldmice, too.

But the mouse appeared more often. It came farther from its hole.

When the season grew so hot that sweat rippled down Drew's chest beneath his coarse hair shirt and his heavy robe, he felt a tiny movement against his leg as he sat at his workbench, eating. Glancing down, he saw the mouse sniffing at his robe, and he realized that the animal was here to stay.

A fellow hermit. He didn't know its sex. But given their cloistered circumstances, he preferred to think that it was male, and recalling a mouse that he'd read about long ago in a book by E. B. White, he gave it a name.

Stuart Little.

When I was innocent, he thought.

16

'I don't have my vestments with me.'

'Where?' Drew asked.

'In my room here at the rectory.'

'Then I'll go with you while you get them. We'll have to leave, anyhow – to use a confessional in the church across the street.'

'It isn't necessary.' Father Hafer said. 'The rules have been relaxed. We can perform the sacrament here in the open, in my office, face to face. It's known as "public confession".'

Drew shook his head.

'What's wrong?'

'Let's say I'm old-fashioned.'

They crossed the congested street toward the church. Inside the cool dim loftiness, their footsteps echoed as they each went into a bleak compartment of a confessional. Drew knelt in its musty darkness. Behind a partition, the priest slid a panel to one side. Drew whispered to the shadow behind the grill.

'Bless me, father, for I have sinned. My last confession was thirteen years ago. These are my sins.' He told.

And told, not even stopping when he described the photographs in his pocket and the priest began to gasp.

17

It was autumn again, October, his sixth year in the monastery. The ruddy glow of sunset tinted the brilliant maples on the hill. He heard the rattle of the serving hatch, then the familiar scrape and thump of a cup and bowl being set on the shelf beside his door.

He lowered his ax, the blunt end of which he'd been striking against a metal wedge to split logs for his wood stove, and glanced toward the tiny hole at the base of the workroom wall where Stuart Little suddenly appeared. The mouse sat on his haunches, raising its forearms to brush his whiskers.

All you need is a knife, fork, and bib, Drew silently joked, amused at how the rattle of the serving hatch had become Stuart Little's dinner bell.

The mouse scurried over as Drew brought the meal to the workbench. Bread and water; another fast-day. His stomach rumbling, he noticed Stuart trying to climb up his robe, and with a sigh of feigned disgust, he tore off a piece of bread, tossing it down to the mouse. He sat at the bench and bowed his head, pressing his hands together, praying.

You know, Stuart, he thought as he finished you're getting greedy. I ought to make you wait to eat till grace is finished. A little religion wouldn't hurt you. How would you feel about that, huh?

He glanced toward the mouse on the floor.

And frowned. The mouse lay on its side, unmoving.

Drew stared in surprise, not moving either. His chest tensed. Shocked, he held his breath, then blinked and, inhaling slowly, bent down to touch Stuart's side.

It remained inert.

Drew gently nudged it, feeling the soft sleek fur, but got no response. His throat seemed lined with sand. As he swallowed painfully, he picked Stuart up. The mouse lay still in his palm. It weighed almost nothing, but the weight was dead.

Drew's stomach felt cold. In dismay, he shook his head, baffled. A minute ago, the mouse had practically been dancing for its supper.

Was it old age, he wondered. A heart attack or a stroke? He didn't know

26

much about mice, but he vaguely recalled having read somewhere that they didn't live long. A year or two.

But that was in the wild, exposed to predators, diseases, and cold. What about here in the cell? He strained to think, telling himself that even with warmth and good care, Stuart Little had been bound to die. There wasn't any way to know how old it had been when it showed up last autumn, but in human terms, by now it might have been ninety.

I shouldn't be surprised. By feeding it, I merely postponed . . . If it hadn't died today . . .

Tomorrow.

He bit his lip, grieving as he set the small corpse back on the floor. And felt guilty because he grieved. A Carthusian was supposed to shut out all worldly distractions. God alone mattered. The mouse had been a temptation that he should have resisted. Now God was punishing him, teaching him why he shouldn't become infatuated with transitory creatures.

Death.

Drew shuddered. No. I wouldn't change anything. The mouse was fun to have around. I'm glad I took care of it.

His eyes stung, making him blink repeatedly as he stared down at his lifeless friend. Terrible thoughts occurred to him. What should he do with the body? For sure, he wasn't going to have a custodian brother dispose of it, perhaps even dump it in the trash. The mouse deserved better. The dignity of burial.

But where? Through misted vision, he glanced toward his workroom window. Sunset had turned to dusk, casting his garden wall into shadow.

A cedar bush grew in a corner of the wall. Yes, Drew thought. He'd bury Stuart Little beneath the shrub. An evergreen, it lived all year. Even in winter, it's color would be a reminder.

His throat felt swollen, aching each time he swallowed. Thirsty, he reached for his cup of water, raised it toward his lips, glanced past it toward the thick slab of bread in his bowl.

And paused.

His spine began to tingle.

He peered down at the bread on the floor, the chunk he'd thrown to Stuart Little. He stared at the water in the cup he held. And slowly, cautiously, making sure that no liquid spilled over the top, he eased the container back down on the table. Reflexively he wiped his hands on the front of his robe.

No, he thought. It couldn't be.

But what if you're not imagining?

His suspicion filled him with shame. In his sixth stern year of penance, did he still retain the habit of thinking as he had in his former life? Had his training been that effective? Were his instincts that resistant to change?

But just supposing. You know, for the sake of argument. What kind might it be? Did it kill on contact?

Tensing, he stared at his hands. No, he'd touched the mouse. And the bread. Just a minute ago. But the mouse had died quickly. In the time Drew had taken to close his eyes and say grace. If it's poison and it kills on contact, even with my greater size, I ought to be dead now, too.

He breathed.

27

All right, then, it has to be ingested.

(You've got to stop thinking this way.)

And it's powerful. Almost instantaneous.

Assuming it's poison.

Of course, just assuming. After all, it's still quite possible that Stuart Little died from natural causes.

(But what would you have thought six years ago?)

He struggled to repress his terrible memories. No. God's testing me again. He's using this death to learn if I've truly purged myself. A man of detachment would never think like this.

(But in the old days . . .

Yes?

You thought this way all the time.)

He narrowed his vision till all he saw was the unmoving mouse on the floor. Slowly, frowning so hard he felt the beginnings of a headache, he raised his eyes toward the serving hatch beside his door.

The hatch was closed. But beyond it was a corridor.

(No. It makes no sense. Not *here*, not *now!* Who? Why?)

Besides, he was merely guessing. The only way to know for sure if the bread had been poisoned was to . . .

Taste it? Hardly.

Have it tested? That would take too long.

But there *was* another way. He could investigate the monastery. He stiffened with doubt. The notion repelled him.

But under the circumstances . . .

He stared at the door. In the six years he'd been here, he'd left his quarters seldom, only to convene with the other monks for mandatory communal rituals. Those ventures outside had been keenly disturbing to him, nerve-racking intrusions on his peace of mind. But under the circumstances . . .

He wiped his sweaty lip. His years of disciplined regimen told him to wait a short while longer until he normally left for vespers. Yes. The decision calmed him. Avoiding extremes, it appealed to his common sense.

Dusk deepened, shifting to dark. A misty drizzle beaded on his window. He shivered, grieving, too preoccupied to force himself to turn on a light.

The vespers bell stayed silent, but in rhythm with his daily cycle, he knew that it should have struck by now. He told himself that the mouse's death had disturbed his judgment. Time was passing with exaggerated slowness, that was all. He didn't have a clock in the cell, so how could he be sure when vespers was supposed to occur?

He counted to one hundred. Waited. Started to count again. And stopped.

With a painful sigh, he repressed his inhibitions, broke six years of habit, and opened the door.

18

A light glowed overhead. The hallway was bare, no paintings, no carpeting. Soundless, deserted.

That wasn't unusual. True, when the bell tolled, he on occasion met other monks leaving their cells to go to the chapel. But equally often, he went earlier or later than the others and walked alone down the corridor

He did so now. Still determined to obey the ritual, he reached the end, turned left, and passed beneath another light to enter the lodge. In shadow, the chapel door was fifty paces ahead of him, to the right.

His misgivings increased, his instincts alarming him. Instead of continuing toward the chapel, he made an abrupt decision and turned sharply right, descending the stairs to the monastery's refectory. As he expected, at this time of night (and except on Sunday) it wasn't occupied. But thinking of the bread he'd been given, he stared toward a light in the rear where the kitchen was. Passing empty tables with barren tops, he took a deep breath, pushed through the swinging door, and studied the massive stove, the vaultlike door to the freezer, the extensive counters and cupboards. And the two dead men on the floor.

Though custodian brothers, not hermits, they nonetheless wore the white gown, scapular, and hood of the true Carthusian. The chest of each gown was stained with blood, each hood stained red at the temple.

Drew surprised himself. Perhaps because he'd unconsciously expected something like this, or because his instincts had not been as neutralized as he'd hoped, his heart stayed perfectly calm.

But his stomach felt scorched.

The shots would have been silenced to keep the monastery from being alerted, he thought. Two assassins at least. Each brother had fallen in roughly the same position, suggesting that they'd been caught by surprise. No sign of panic, of either brother trying to escape, which meant that they'd been shot in the chest simultaneously. Drew nodded. Yes, two assassins at least.

And experienced. A wound in the chest was sometimes not fatal. The protocol required a follow-up – just to be sure. And to minimize suffering. The required coup de grâce. A shot to each temple. Professional. Indeed.

Drew controlled the pressure swelling in him, turned, and left the kitchen. Outside the refectory, he nodded in anguish, knowing what he had to do now, what he'd considered doing when he left his room. But he'd put it off as long as possible, until he had no other choice. It would be the absolute violation of the Carthusian rule. As severe as leaving his room at any other time except for the required rituals.

The thought was repulsive to him. But it had to be acted upon.

Going up the stairs, he went back the way he'd come. He reached the end of the corridor in the lodge and angled right to enter his wing of cells. There he paused at the first door he came to. Studied the knob.

And opened the door. An overhead light glowed in the workroom. The monk who occupied it must have switched it on as sunset deepened. The man lay sprawled on the floor. The chair before his workbench was overturned. A wedge of bread was clutched in his hand. A pool of urine spread from his gown.

Drew hardened his jaw and shut the door. Repressing the bile that rose to his mouth, he went down to the next door and opened it. In this case the workroom light had not been turned on. But the light from the hallway was sufficient for Drew to see the monk slumped across his table, the bowl of bread pinned beneath one arm.

He went on like that, opening and closing each door, proceeding to the next one, and the next. A light was sometimes on and sometimes not. The body was sometimes on the table, sometimes on the floor. Sometimes the monk in dying had brushed against his cup of water, spilling it, so that water and urine were indistinguishable.

All of them – the nineteen other monks who'd secluded themselves in this refuge – had been poisoned by the bread. Or by the water, Drew thought. It was logical that the water had been poisoned as well. No sense in not being thorough. Professional.

Too many questions intruded. But the foremost of all was why.

He now understood his motive when, as dusk had thickened, he hadn't turned on his light. He'd assumed that his grief over Stuart Little had robbed him of even the resolve to cross his workroom and flick on the light switch. But now he knew better, his subconscious having warned him. Whoever had poisoned the food would have posted someone outside, probably in the courtyard, to watch the monastery for signs of life. A light that came on when it shouldn't have would have drawn the assassins to his cell.

More questions. Why use poison? Why not shoot each monk as the kitchen staff had been shot? Why wait this long to come in and verify the kill?

Why kill everyone? And where was the death team?

With each door that he opened, with each corpse that he found, he increasingly reverted to his former state of mind. Six years ago, on the run from Scalpel, he'd have naturally assumed that he was the target. But he'd been careful. Scalpel didn't know he'd entered the monastery. Scalpel thought he was dead.

Then who else could be hunting him? Possibly he wasn't the target at all. Maybe one of the other monks had been the target. But why? No, it wasn't likely. And why had *every* monk been killed? The tactic didn't make sense.

In a moment it did, however, and the back of his neck felt cold. The death team couldn't have known which cell was whose. The monks were all anonymous, the doors unmarked. There wasn't any way to determine who secluded himself in which unit. The team couldn't very well have checked each room – so complicated an operation would have been too risky, leaving too many chances for mistakes. It was one thing to confront the kitchen staff on the lower level where no one was likely to hear a commotion. That risk was acceptable. But on the main floor where the monks lived close together – that was quite another matter. Entering each cell, even with silencers to muffle the shots, the team would still have been concerned about an unpredictable scream from a startled monk, a shout that might have alerted the other monks and – if I'm right, Drew thought – one monk in particular, the man the team had come for.

30

Me.

His forehead knotted in torment. Because of my sins? Is that why everybody had to die? Dear God, what have I done by coming here?

The logic of using poison was clear to him now. A way of taking out the entire monastery (with the exception of the already executed kitchen staff) at once. Equally important, it was death from a distance. By remote control.

Because the team respected the skills of the man they'd come to assassinate, because they didn't know if six years of seclusion had been enough to blunt his talents, they'd chosen not to come at him directly. An added precaution. To make extra sure.

But everyone else had to die.

Drew's throat made a terrible choking sound.

He suddenly realized that wherever the assassins were hiding, they'd soon come out. When sufficient time had passed for them to feel confident, they'd inspect the monastery. They'd search each cell. They'd want to verify the kill, *to guarantee that one man in particular had been killed.*

His shoulders tensed as he glanced in both directions along the corridor.

The vespers bell began to toll.

19

It sounded unnatural in the otherwise deathly silence, echoing down the hallway, through the courtyard. Mournful, as if announcing a funeral.

His sinews compacted. He crouched, strong habits insisting, making him understand how a moth must feel when attracted to a flame. Every day for the past six years, that bell had beckoned him, so much a part of his daily schedule that even now as he recognized the threat, he still felt compelled to obey its call. As would any surviving monk who by virtue of extra discipline had decided to refuse even the minimum meal of bread and water. Drawn to the chapel for vespers, the monk would open the door.

And be shot by a silenced handgun that accomplished what the poisoned food had failed to do. No witnesses, no interruptions, refinement upon refinement.

It made Drew quiver with rage.

But this was obvious. When the bell had rung sufficiently, when the team was satisfied that no fasting monk could have possibly refused its call, the search would begin. He had to hide.

But where? He couldn't risk leaving the monastery. He had to assume that its perimeter was being watched. All right then, he had to stay inside.

Again the question, *where?* When the team didn't find his body, they'd check every room and cranny in the cloister. Even if he hadn't been the specific target, their intention had clearly been to kill everyone. He had to assume that they wouldn't be satisfied until they accounted for every corpse. True, he had the advantage of knowing the layout better than they did. Even so, they'd be methodical, determined. The odds were against him.

Unless. Desperation primed his thoughts. If he could manage to convince them that . . .

Each stroke of the bell seemed louder, stronger. He hurried to return to his cell. From custom, he'd closed its door as he left his workroom to go to vespers. But that had been a mistake, he concluded, and now left the door open after stepping back inside. The dead mouse beside the chunk of bread on the floor would show the team that he'd learned about the poison. The absence of his body, the significance of his door – and *only* his door – being open, would make the team think he'd fled. They'd focus their search in other parts of the monastery, more likely outside, alerting the guards on the perimeter that he was trying to get through the woods. They'd feel urgent, impatient.

He hoped. Rushing soundlessly up his dark stairs, he reached his oratory, and for once in six years, he didn't stop to pray. He darted through it to the blackness of his study, and then to his sleeping quarters, where he veered toward the small, murky bathroom.

In the ceiling above the sink, a trapdoor led to the insulation beneath the roof. He removed his shoes so he wouldn't leave marks on the porcelain and, holding them, climbed upon the sink, hearing it creak beneath his weight. He groped above him, exhaled when he felt the rim of the trapdoor, pushed it up, and lifted himself into the musty, cold, yet sweat-producing closeness After sliding the trapdoor back into place, he crawled across the irritating glass wool insulation toward a far corner, where he lay as flat as he could, hiding behind joists and upright support beams. He tried to keep his mind still but couldn't.

Breathing dust, he brooded. About his fellow monks.

And Stuart Little.

20

The bell stopped tolling, its muteness eerie. He went rigid, straining to listen, knowing that his hunters would be leaving the chapel now. The drizzle that had earlier beaded on his window increased to a steady rain that drummed on the slanted roof above him. Shivering from the chill and the damp, he pressed himself harder against the insulation. Despite its bulk, he felt the sharp-edged two-by-sixes that formed the skeleton of the floor beneath him. He waited.

And waited.

On occasion, he thought that he heard far-off muffled sounds. No voices, of course – the team would follow established procedures and communicate with gestures. But other noises were unavoidable, doors being opened, footsteps on hard bare floors. Indeed, with an ear against the insulation, he suspected that several indistinct creaks he heard below him were due to someone creeping through his oratory, study, and sleeping quarters. These sounds could easily have been imagined. Nonetheless he concentrated his attention across the dark attic toward the unseen trapdoor, listening apprehensively for the scrape that it would make if someone pushed it up. He licked his dry lips.

And waited.

The night passed slowly. Despite his tension, the stifling air made him groggy. He blinked at the dark through heavy eyelids, woke with a jerk, and fought not to drowse again. The next time he woke, disoriented, quickly on guard, he noticed a hint of light through the cracks in a ceiling vent that allowed the build-up of heat to escape during summer. Morning. He no longer heard the drumming of the rain on the roof. Indeed, except for the dry controlled hiss of his breath, he heard nothing.

All the same, he waited. In his former life, he'd once been hunted for five days through a jungle. He'd eaten almost nothing, only non-toxic leaves that gave his brain the potassium and lithium it needed to remain alert. Unable to trust the bacteria-ridden water, he'd depended on rainfall to give him moisture. By comparison with that jungle, this attic presented few problems. He was sedentary, after all, and accustomed to fasting. If the month had been August instead of October, the swelter up here (even with the heat vents) would have been unendurable. But given his circumstances, chilly but not dangerously cold, he could remain here for three full days. That was the limit for surviving without water. Perhaps he could last even longer, but he'd be delirious.

He brooded throughout the morning, feeling death below him. The corpses would have passed beyond rigor mortis now, entering the stage of livor mortis, beginning to swell from body gases, stinking. The same would be happening to Stuart Little.

His forehead ached from frowning. In 1979, he recalled, he'd been in such despair that he'd wanted to kill himself. The monastery had provided his only alternative, a way to punish himself and try to save his soul.

Then why now was he so desperate to avoid whoever was hunting him? Why did he feel compelled to stop them from doing what he'd almost done to himself? If the assassins killed him, it wouldn't be suicide, after all. He wouldn't be damning himself.

Because it was one thing to be martyred, quite another to invite being martyred. Presumption was as damning a sin as despair. He couldn't dare count on God to save him merely because he'd been killed for his sins. He had to fight for salvation. He had to use every device In his power, every trick he could think of, to avoid his executioners.

I want to be punished. Yes. For my former life. For the monks who died because of me

But . . .

Yes?

I'm also under an obligation

Oh? To do what?

To punish others, those who killed them.

But you didn't even know those monks. They were hermits like yourself. Personally, they meant nothing to you.

It doesn't matter. They were human beings, and they were cheated. They deserved the chance to pursue their holiness.

Maybe they're in Heaven now.

There's no guarantee. That's presumption again.

So in its place, you prefer revenge? Is that a proper Carthusian motive? An eye for an eye as opposed to turning one's cheek?

He didn't have an answer. Unfamiliar disturbing emotions, dormant for six years, welled up in him. The world had intruded, corrupting him.

33

21

The next night, late, it stormed again. Lightning flashed, dimly visible through the slots in the air vents. Thunder shook the roof. He decided to take advantage of the weather and crawled toward the trapdoor, shifting it as silently as possible, easing down to the darkness that hid the sink. As the storm raged outside he crept to his murky sleeping quarters, pausing, sensing. An assassin would have to be terribly determined, not to mention patient, to wait here two nights in a row on the slim chance that Drew was hiding in the attic. More likely, the team would have sent someone up there after him or at least have used tear gas to force Drew down. Besides, once the team had suspected that Drew was out of the building, they'd have felt compromised, afraid that if he escaped he'd alert the police. When their harried search had failed to reveal him, they'd have been forced to pull out.

Or so Drew hoped. Nothing was sure. But here in the night he had an advantage. One of his principal skills, the result of concentrated special training, was hand-to-hand combat in total darkness. Even after six years of inactivity, he hadn't forgotten how it was done. For an instant, he felt transported back to that oppressive black room in the abandoned airplane hangar in Colorado. Now motionless, breathing slowly, listening intently, he neither smelled nor heard a lurking assailant.

Of course, the drumming of the rain would obscure other sounds. At a certain point, he had to act on faith, crossing his sleeping quarters, on guard against a brush of cloth, a sudden rush in his direction. It didn't occur. He glanced back. As rain lashed his window, lightning streaked beyond it, illuminating the room, giving him a hurried chance to reassure himself that no one was there.

Darkness returned as thunder rumbled, and he realized that staring at the lightning had been a mistake. His pupils had contracted to protect themselves against the sudden brilliance; now in the dark they were slow to dilate again. His night vision had been impaired. He had to wait, unsettled, temporarily blind. With agonizing slowness, he began to see murky outlines in the dark. He bit his lip. All right, he'd made a mistake. He admitted it. But the mistake had been a useful one. He'd learned from it. His skills were returning. Already he was calculating a way to turn the lightning to his advantage.

Keeping his back to the window, he left his sleeping quarters, then passed through the deeper blackness of the study and the oratory, again still feeling and ignoring the tug of habit to stop there and pray. On the stairs that led down to his workroom, he saw his open door, the light that glowed from the hall. He smelled a too-familiar, stomach-turning stench. When he reached the bottom, he cautiously surveyed the room. His cup and bowl remained on the workbench. Stuart Little was in the same position on the floor. But as he'd anticipated, the mouse was now bloated, filled with gas.

Drew swallowed, not in disgust but in pity. Because he needed the body, he lovingly picked up the corpse by the tail and gently wrapped it in a handkerchief that he'd left on his woodpile. He tied the handkerchief to his skipping rope and tied the rope around the waist of his habit.

From a drawer in his workroom bench, he removed four photographs, the only items he'd brought with him from his former life. Six years ago, he'd shown these photographs to Father Hafer after the priest, gasping, had heard his confession. The photographs had verified what Drew had said, convincing the priest to relent, to recommend Drew's acceptance by the Carthusians. The photographs showed a man and woman consumed by flames, a young boy screaming in horror. In the monastery, Drew had studied these images every day, reminding himself of what he'd been, of his need for penance. He couldn't bring himself to leave now without them.

Shoving them into a pocket in his robe, he glanced around. What else? He needed a weapon. The ax from his woodpile.

The storm became more violent. Even with his back to the window, he saw another blaze of lightning fill the room. He approached his open door, peered both ways along the empty corridor, glanced back with longing toward the place that had been his home for the past six years, then hefted his ax and crept down the hall toward the rear of the monastery.

He made one stop – to examine another cell. The sharp, nauseating stench as he budged the door open told him everything. But he pushed the door farther and stared at the grotesquely misshapen body of a monk.

So the team had left the monastery as they'd found it, closing each door on the ultimate secret, not bothering to dispose of the dead – no time to do so – but at least perversely respectful of their victims.

That too didn't matter. Regardless of their peculiar ethics – Drew himself had once been faithful to such ethics – there would be hell to pay.

22

At the rear of the monastery, he faced the exit that led to the vegetable garden. Thunder shuddered through the thick wooden door.

He reconsidered his decisions. The obvious way to leave the monastery was out the front of the lodge, then down the dirt road through the forest to the paved country road at the bottom of this hill. Granted, he'd seen the approach to the monastery only for a brief time six years ago when he'd been driven here. But he remembered that country road and the town – what had its name been? Quentin? – ten miles or so to the south. Still, if leaving through the front toward the road was the obvious route, precisely for that reason he had to take a different direction. Because, although the team had apparently fled from the area, there was a chance – a strong one – that a man had been left behind to watch the monastery from a distance, in case Drew was still on the premises. Their suspicion would be that Drew had escaped and alerted the police. But what if the police didn't arrive? The death team would have to conclude that Drew had *not* escaped. They'd risk returning for one more search. All the more reason for Drew to get out of here.

But not out the front, not by a route that a spotter would pay close attention to. Okay, out the back. Even so, given the quality of the team's professional conduct, Drew had to make other assumptions.

First, the spotter would not ignore the other exits from the cloister. He'd stay a careful distance away, choosing a location that gave him a confident view of the entire complex. Only one location allowed for such a vantage point: in back of the cloister, on the wooded hill that rose above this one.

Second assumption. The spotter would be equipped for night surveillance, using either an infrared scope which projected an invisible beam, or a Starlite scope which magnified whatever minuscule light was available. Because this storm would obscure the stars, an infrared scope was the better choice.

Drew studied his robe. Usually white, it was now a dingy gray from the cobwebs, dust, and insulation in the attic. But even if the robe were caked with coal dust he knew that it could still be seen through a night scope. *Unless*, Drew thought, and remembered the lightning.

He glanced above him, toward the bulb that glowed in the corridor's ceiling. The moment he opened the door, the spotter would be attracted by the new illumination. There wasn't any light switch in the hallway – Drew assumed that the switch was on a master panel in a custodial room he'd never been shown – so he reached up, tall enough to wrap his scapular around the bulb and unscrew it. As an added precaution, he went farther along the corridor and unscrewed two other bulbs, surrounding himself in darkness. Because the hallway had no windows, a spotter couldn't know what had happened.

He returned to the door, took a long breath, exhaled, and twisted the latch. He pulled the door open slowly, trying to avoid an obvious change in this section of the cloister. As he pulled, he stood out of sight behind it.

At last it was fully open. He waited, flexing his shoulders. Timing was everything now, because both infrared and Starlite scopes had a common weakness: sudden illumination blinded the observer. The temporary sightlessness that Drew had experienced in his sleeping quarters when he used the lightning to help him scan the room would be drastically intensified through a night scope. The normal instinct would have been for Drew to run from the cloister during the intervals of blackness between glaring flashes of lightning. Drew realized, however, that his only chance to get out unseen was to do the opposite – to prime himself, to alert every reflex, to race outside for cover as soon as a new fork of lightning blazed.

In darkness, he shifted from behind the door, studying the garden. With breath-held caution, he peered toward the rain-enshrouded night. He closed his eyes and glanced away as lightning struck a tree beyond the garden. A branch crashed. Night resumed abruptly. But he knew where he had to go now. Thunder. Soon the streaks of lightning came closer together. Drew imagined the agony that a spotter would be enduring.

Well, what are you waiting for? he asked himself. You want to hang around, go to mass?

The instant the next bolt flashed, Drew charged from the open doorway. At once rain lashed his face. Keeping his ax away from him, he dove to the oozing mud behind a sculpted cedar bush. The rain drenched his robe, soaking frigid through to his skin. Almost instantaneously thunder shook the sodden earth beneath him. Despite the assault on his senses, a portion of his consciousness registered the unfamiliar sweetness of the air, the forgotten sting of the wind – feelings formerly ordinary to him, now powerfully sensual after long seclusion. But he didn't have time to savor them or to realise how much he'd missed them. He pawed at his mud-splattered eyes, studying his next destination. When lightning flashed once more, he'd already braced himself, skittering through slippery puddles, thudding behind a compost heap. Its fetid odor made him gag, yet it too was unexpectedly welcome.

Though the rain was cold, he started to sweat. Where next? His ultimate destination was the brooding forest beyond the garden, but he had to approach it in a zigzag fashion – to a narrow equipment shed, then a watery furrow between rows of harvested corn, their wilted stubble helping to shield him. His heart pounded sickeningly. But he couldn't sprint more than ten feet during any blaze of lightning. He didn't dare remain in motion when the spotter was able to see through the night scope again. Another flash. He darted from the corn rows, sprawling in mud behind a straw-covered mound where potatoes had been grown. He quickly scrunched his eyes shut, protecting them against a fierce new blaze of lightning. When thunder roared, he opened them again. The interval between lightning and thunder was lessening, only two seconds apart, the center of the storm coming closer. Good. He needed all the distraction that it could possibly give to the spotter.

He studied the dark. Blinking through the cold heavy rain, he chose his next cover, a waist-high stretch of raspberry bushes. Lightning gleamed, and he lunged but slipped on ooze and lost his balance, landing on his face, water spewing up his nostrils, cramming his mouth. He coughed, unable to breathe, rolling toward the raspberry bushes. Darkness enveloped him. He snorted, desperate to clear his nose and mouth.

Had he reached the bushes in time? Had the spotter seen him? Adrenaline spurted into his stomach, his lungs heaved. He shook, exhausted, as if he'd been sprinting for several miles. With his face to the sky, he let the rain wash his eyes, his nose, his lips. He swirled water around in his mouth, released it, then let the rain fill his mouth again and swallowed, tasting its sweetness, luxuriating in the relief to his swollen throat.

He had to keep moving! First to a row of grapevines along a wooden frame.

And after that . . .

At last he burst through the undergrowth, gaining the protection of the forest. Gobs of mud sagged from his scalp, his face, and his robe. Chunks slid down his arms, collecting on his fingers, plopping onto the dead leaves at his feet.

But he'd been successful. He hadn't been seen by the spotter.

By definition. If the spotter had seen him, he'd be dead by now.

He struggled to catch his breath. *I'm out. I'm free.* Now all that remained was to push through the forest, to use its cover and get away.

Where to? For a moment, the question stunned him. In his former life, he'd have automatically sought refuge with his network, Scalpel. But Scalpel in the end had become his enemy. To survive, he'd made Scalpel believe he was dead.

Then where else could he turn? A sudden spark of long and forcefully subdued affection told him to get to Arlene. She would help him, he knew. They'd once been lovers. Despite the separation of years, he was willing to

37

risk that because of what they'd shared, he could count on her. And reaching her, he'd also reach Jake, her brother. Jake, his friend.

Yet reluctantly he had to dismiss them. If in the old days his obligation would have been to contact his network, that obligation still existed, but not to Scalpel; instead, to his present network, the Catholic Church. He had to warn the Church about the hit on the monastery. He had to let the Church decide how to deal with the crisis. The Church would protect him.

But with a goal now in mind, he still didn't use the cover of the forest to get away. Instead, he faced the hill behind the monastery, its looming wooded shape made visible by another blaze of lightning. While darkness cloaked him again, he didn't understand his hesitation. Escape was before him – his chance to get away and warn the Church. Then why did he feel compelled . . . ?

He stared with greater fierceness toward the hill, realizing what he had to do, a strenuous priority insisting. The spotter. Yes, he had to get his hands on the spotter, to make him talk. The man would logically have chosen a vantage point where the trees would not impede his view. That suggested he'd hide with a clearing before him. But after years of living in its shadow, Drew was quite familiar with the contour of that hill. Even in the darkness and the storm, he could pinpoint the three major clearings at the top of the slope, the three most likely vantage points.

If indeed there was a spotter. He had no proof; he was still assuming.

But there was one way to know for sure.

And one way to learn why the death team had been sent here – to find out who was to blame.

23

The storm intensified. Ignoring the stunning impact of the rain, he stalked through the forest, veering past stumps and deadfalls, aiming toward the greater blackness of that hill.

He clutched his ax so hard that his knuckles ached, reached the base of the hill, and walked in a semicircle around it. At its back, he climbed. Trees thrashed him, their branches bent by the wind. He grabbed at saplings, branches, bushes, anything to pull himself up through the mire.

At the summit, he didn't worry about making noise; the din of the storm was louder than any sound he could have made, even an angry scream. He began to creep, using the shelter of bushes and dangling limbs.

From a careful vantage point, he decided that the trees behind the first clearing weren't being used as a hiding place. He stepped back into the woods and approached the second clearing. Below the hill, despite the shroud of rain, specks of light were visible from the monastery. It probably looked the same as on any other night. Except that it wasn't a monastery any longer. Someone had made it a house of death.

He studied the cover behind the second clearing, decided that it too wasn't occupied, and turned to approach the third, when an unnatural ripple among the trees attracted his attention back toward the second clearing. His nerve ends quickened. Squinting from a flash of lightning, he saw a dark nylon sheet supported at head level like a makeshift tent, its sides and back tilted halfway to the ground to prevent rain from slanting under it. Its four ends were tied to the base of trees, the ropes tugged viciously by the wind. A tall upright stick held up its flapping middle. Of course. A spotter wouldn't have wanted the trouble of carrying even a compact tent up here. But in case of bad weather, a nylon sheet would have taken little room in a knapsack. Not as comfortable as a tent, but comfort wasn't the point.

He had to wait for the next bolt of lightning. The effect was like glimpsing sporadic images caught by a strobe light. Under the nylon sheet, through the space between the low sides and the ground, he saw a man's legs and hips – hiking boots, jeans, a sheathed knife on a belt.

Darkness. Drew crouched to peer up beneath the back of the sheet at the rest of him.

Lightning, and he saw the man's upper torso. Tall and muscular, wearing a knitted watchman's cap, a padded nylon vest, and a heavy outdoor shirt, the colors dull to blend in with the forest. The man peered down the slope toward the monastery. He used an infrared scope – its long, wide outline easily recognizable – mounted upon a bolt-action sniper's rifle attached to a swiveling tripod. With the next flash of lightning, the man turned away from the scope, rubbed his eyes, and drank from a Thermos that he'd propped along with a knapsack in the crook of a tree.

Drew backed off, rain streaking across his face. He glanced at the ax in his hand and decided that he couldn't attack by rushing beneath the tilted back of the nylon sheet. That posture would be too awkward. There was too much risk of his slipping in the mud or nudging the sheet and warning the man.

No, Drew thought, there had to be a better way.

He watched the nylon sheet being buffeted by the wind and nodded, creeping toward the right, toward the rope that attached one corner of the sheet to a tree. He felt the knot and recognized its shape. A slip knot. Strong and dependable, it could nonetheless be easily released by a quick tug on the free end of the rope.

He did so now. His plan was to trap the man inside the sheet and knock him unconscious with a blow from the blunt end of the ax. But instead of collapsing, the sheet was caught by the wind and driven upward, exposing the man to the storm. As lightning shattered a nearby tree, the man whirled in surprise and noticed Drew.

The ax was useless now. Too heavy, too slow. Drew dropped it, lunging, but surprise was still in his favor, for the man seemed startled not only by the upraised sheet but as well by what confronted him – the righteous eyes of a raging monk, his ascetic face an image of terror, his robe so dripping with mud that he might have been a nightmare sprung from the earth.

The hit on the monastery had shown that the team was professional, but even so, the spotter screamed reflexively, and at that moment, Drew screamed as well the traditional Zen outcry, intended to distract his opponent while helping Drew to focus the strength he released along with the air from his lungs. He hadn't engaged in hand-to-hand combat for years, but his daily exercises, in part involving the dance steps of martial arts, had kept his reflexes tuned. Those dance steps had been practiced for spiritual reasons. But some things apparently could never be forgotten. His prior instincts returned with alarming precision.

To an untrained observer, what happened next would have seemed even quicker than the thirteen seconds it took to occur. Blurred movements would have been confusing, almost impossible to distinguish from each other.

But to Drew – and no doubt to his opponent – the passage of time became amazingly extended. As a champion tennis player paradoxically sees the ball approach across the net with the bulk and lethargy of a beach ball, so these men confronted each other as if they were giants in slow motion.

Drew struck the heel of his palm against his opponent's chest, directly above the heart. The blow should have shattered his enemy's ribcage, thrusting bone splinters inward to impale both heart and lungs.

It didn't happen. Through the heel of his palm, Drew felt at once what was wrong. His opponent's padded nylon vest was so filled with down, or more likely quick-drying Thinsulate, that it had absorbed the force of the blow. A grunt from the man indicated that damage had been done, but not enough to incapacitate him.

Drew's opponent had already braced himself, bending his knees, supporting his back against a tree. Drew had to thrust with the heel of his other palm, this time toward the throat. But his opponent responded. As lightning blinded Drew (but presumably his opponent as well), he sightlessly sought to deflect the blow that he knew would be aimed at his heart.

He'd used his right hand first. So now he thrust his left palm upward, tilting it slightly inward, anticipating that his opponent – having been struck at the heart – would have to respond from the opposite half of his body.

Drew's left palm struck his opponent's lunging right arm at the elbow, dislocating it. The force of the impact caused them both to reel off-balance in the mud. Drew heard the man's groan. His enemy slipped, colliding with him, entangling his dislocated arm in the bib of Drew's muddy robe. The bib was large enough that it could have been used as a sling.

As darkness returned, they found themselves locked together, chest to chest. Drew smelled the garlicky sausage that the man had eaten. The unfamiliar stench of meat was nauseating.

He pushed, then braced himself, his enemy pushing back. They skittered one way, then another, sliding across the mud, their breathing strident.

Drew felt his opponent reaching backward, groping for something on his hip.

He remembered.

The knife sheathed on his opponent's belt.

Prepared to grab for the hand that would hold the knife, Drew frantically changed his mind. He had to strike sooner. He needed a weapon.

The weapon was close at hand. Oblivious to the significance he grabbed the crucifix that dangled on a chain around his neck. He clutched Christ's head and rammed the long slender base of the crucifix up his opponent's widened right nostril.

The storm unleashed its full fury. As if condemning what Drew had done, the sky blazed with so many jagged bolts of lightning that Heaven itself seemed fractured.

The man wasn't dead. Drew hadn't expected him to be. But such an invasion to a bodily orifice would produce shock. Predictably, the man straightened in agony, wailing, beginning to shake. Amazingly, his survival mechanisms continued to function, his free hand lunging with the knife.

Still locked against the shuddering body, Drew parried the knife, its blade slicing through the sleeve of his robe, and jabbed the web of skin between his thumb and first finger up hard against the man's throat, hearing the windpipe crack.

Lightning struck beside him, disintegrating the nearest tree. The roaring brilliance stunned him, lifting him off his feet. While splinters lanced him, he and the man were thrown from the forest. They tumbled into the clearing, rolling down the slope, twisting over each other, now Drew on top, now the man, thumping to a stop against a boulder. Drew gasped from the impact. Straining to disengage the man's arm from his robe, he peered down at the gloom-obscured face, touched the vein on the side of the neck, and realized that the man was dead.

Drew gagged. The crack of the lightning still reverberated in his ears. Dizzy, he shook his head and squinted through double vision toward the top of the clearing, toward the glowing smoke that rose from the shattered base of a tree ten feet from the now shredded nylon sheet. The smell of ozone drifted heavily around him. Lightning formed a rictus in the sky.

He shuddered, again peering down toward the man he'd killed. When he'd entered the monastery, he'd sworn that the killing had come to an end. And now?

He could have justified killing the man in anger – for the monks, if not for Stuart Little. Anger was a natural human fault, an innate weakness. The legacy of Cain. But he hadn't killed in anger. He'd passed far from anger, descending into an even more basic motive, survival. And the years had made no difference. He still retained the instinct, and his training had been so effective that even now he was capable of unleashing death automatically – as a knee will jerk when the hammer taps.

If I'd killed him by chance, I wouldn't care. But I did it reflexively. Because I was better at it.

Oh, Jesus. He prayed, recalling with horror what he'd done with the crucifix. Have mercy on this sinner. I didn't want to become what I am. It was forced upon me. But I should have had more control.

While rain streaked down his face, mingling with tears, he bowed his head toward the man he'd killed and struck his breast. Through my fault. Through my most grievous fault.

He wanted to vomit.

Still, he had no choice. He had to keep himself in control. Bitterly he stood and took off his robe and hair shirt. His naked body shivered in the icy rain. He stripped the dead man, putting on his clothes. If he was compelled to reenter the world, he couldn't expect to survive by attracting attention in a habit. He had to take precautions. This man had not been alone; others were out there, waiting to kill him. Why? He didn't know. But a new understanding had come to him. His motive had passed beyond

41

the need to avenge his fellow monks. A base emotion, necessarily dismissed. For now that he'd killed again, he'd put his immortal soul in jeopardy, and whoever was responsible had better have a damned good reason.

24

His enemy's clothes fit Drew badly, everything too loose. He had to pull his own socks over the dead man's in order for the hiking boots to feel firm. The jeans sagged as if he'd been on a diet, which in fact he had. If not for the padded vest on top of the heavy outdoor shirt, Drew might have looked as if his chest had caved in. He put the handkerchief that contained Stuart Little into a pocket of the vest and tied the skipping rope around his waist. He retrieved the photographs from his robe and slipped them into the other pocket of the vest. Then he stalked up the slope toward the tripod, rifle, and infrared scope.

Rain drenched him. Glancing around, he focused on the knapsack that his opponent had wedged in the crook of a tree. He opened it . . .

A Mauser pistol. He checked it, making sure that it was fully loaded, and shoved it behind his jacket, beneath the belt at the base of his spine.

Two magazines filled with ammunition. He put these in the pocket with Stuart Little.

A large plastic bag containing chocolate bars, peanuts, and dehydrated fruit. Starting with the peanuts, wanting their salt, he chewed them slowly, hungrily.

No time. What else could he scavenge before he left? He forced himself to think. What else would he need to confront the world? What had he formerly taken for granted but learned to live without?

One item occurred to him, and he reached for the hip on the jeans he wore, removing the dead man's wallet. He opened it, squinting to protect his eyes as lightning flashed, and saw several twenties and fives. All right, then, he had what amounted to another weapon. In a compartment of the wallet, he felt several plastic cards, which he assumed would be a driver's license and credit cards. All the statistics on them would be fake, of course. A professional would never go into an operation with bona fide I.D., the purpose of the documents merely to avert suspicion if the man were inadvertently involved in a traffic incident or forced to spend a night in a motel. But the fake identity would survive offhanded scrutiny, and Drew could temporarily use it.

What else? As he glanced around, debating, he suddenly heard a voice behind him. He crouched, spinning, his palms raised to defend himself. Despite the shrieking wind, he heard the voice again – ahead, to his left, strangely muffled, loud yet distant.

'George?'

Drew frowned, suspicious, scanning the woods.

'George, where are you?' The voice sounded amplified, vaguely metallic. Static crackled. 'George, what the hell are you doing, taking a leak? You're supposed to check in.' More static.

42

Drew relaxed, feeling the urgency drain from his muscles. He approached the sound of the voice. The walkie-talkie hung near the knapsack on the
tree, formerly sheltered by the nylon sheet but now exposed to the rain.

'For Christ's sake, George. Check in.'

Drew almost pressed the send button, strongly tempted to answer – not
to pretend to be George, however, for Drew had no idea of whether
George's voice was high or low, whether George had a distinctive accent or
even a cold. It was highly unlikely that the man on the other end would be
deceived. But Drew nonetheless wanted to answer, to imagine the shock
that the man would feel if an unfamiliar voice came over the walkie-talkie
and suddenly announced, 'I'm sorry. George can't come to the phone
right now. He's dead. But can I take a message?'

Get control, Drew thought. When you start imagining jokes like that,
you're close to the edge.

He restrained the impulse. But already he knew more than he had a
minute ago. The spotter had not been out here alone. Somewhere close,
the spotter had a partner.

He assessed the possibilities. This hill above the monastery was the best
spot from which to study all the exits from the compound. But was it
practical to put two men up here? Did it make more sense for the men to
work in shifts, taking turns so that they each had a chance to get out of the
cold and sleep?

Sleep where? Did the surveillance team have a vehicle in the area? As
much as Drew wanted answers, he also needed transportation, but he
didn't have much time to look for it.

'George, what the hell's going on?' the crackling voice demanded from
the walkie-talkie. 'Quit fooling around! Are you okay?'

Before the man on the other end became sufficiently disturbed to search
for his partner or else drive away from the area, Drew had to find him. And
if Drew's logic was valid, he had a good chance by searching along the
road.

He left the trees, pushed by the rain, descending the gloomy slope. But
coming to the dead man, he stopped abruptly. He'd asked himself what
else he would need to survive in the world. An object on the naked corpse
the only thing that Drew hadn't thought to remove, attracted his attention.
Totally artificial, completely unnecessary for the past six years, it suddenly
seemed essential.

He knelt in the rain and took the wristwatch from the body.

Buckling it on, he felt a change come over him. Yes, he thought with
immense sorrow, tears again flowing. He'd rejoined the world now.

Time had begun again.

25

At the bottom of the slope, Drew angled right, shifting quickly through
another stretch of forest till he came to a section of the high chain-link
fence that enclosed the land around the monastery. The noise of the storm
persisted, hiding the jangle that the fence made as he climbed it. The

moment he dropped to the mud on the other side, he assumed an instinctive defensive crouch. He'd crossed yet another threshold. Like the watch on his wrist, the fence was one more shift from the peace of the monastery toward the turmoil of the world.

But he couldn't allow his regrets to disturb him. He had to reach the Church, specifically Father Hafer, his contact, his protector. He had to accept the conditions that had been forced upon him, to go where necessity took him. The answers, the dead monks in the monastery, *they* were what mattered. Not his reluctance.

He proceeded through the storm down the next wooded slope until he reached the road. A flash of lightning revealed that, as he'd remembered, it was paved. Rain glistened off it. After the difficult landscape through which he'd struggled, the smooth, unobstructed surface invited him. But he didn't dare show himself; he'd have to creep through the undergrowth along its border.

He paused to assess his location. The monastery was now to his left. Farther to his left, several miles away along corkscrew winding turns, was the nearest town, Quentin. He tried to imagine the strategy of the death team. If he was one of two men they'd left behind to check the monastery – he wouldn't want to be camping in the woods. Too damp and cold. He'd want a dry, warm place in which to sleep and change clothes and get something to eat while his partner took his turn on the hill. But he'd also want mobility, the chance to leave the area in a hurry if he had to. That combination of requirements suggested a vehicle large enough to hold equipment and a bed – a camper-truck, for example, or a van. And he certainly wouldn't park it where the authorities might drive by. Its probable hiding place would not be along the portion of the road that led toward Quentin. Instead, it would be on the opposite side of the monastery. On Drew's right. Where the road led toward the maple syrup factory, and after that, scenery, little else.

He found a van fifteen minutes later. On the far shoulder of the road, just before a curve would have made it impossible for an occupant to see the entrance to the lane up to the monastery. The position was logical, Drew thought. The only sure sign that I escaped would be a lot of vehicles arriving at the monastery – ambulances, cops, the coroner. Who else could have warned the authorities except a survivor of the killings? As soon as the team felt confident that I wasn't in the area, their back-up pair could pull out. Conversely, the longer the authorities failed to arrive, the more suspicious the team would be that I hadn't escaped.

But he had to verify that the van wasn't parked here simply because of a breakdown or an innocent sleepy driver. He crawled farther through the undergrowth along the road until he faced the rear of the van – no windows along the side but a bubblelike window in back. Ducking to keep from being spotted through that window, he sprinted across the pavement to crouch beside the rear right tire. The convex back window could have been designed to deflect the heat of the sun; on the other hand, it could have been designed to keep an outsider from getting an undistorted view of the interior. Perhaps the window worked only from inside to out; or perhaps it had a pull-down blind. The glass might even be bullet-proof, the body as well reinforced against attack. These possibilities were hypothetical, of course, unverifiable except by assault.

Nonetheless, there was one easy test to find out if a seemingly ordinary vehicle had been designed to go into combat. All Drew needed to do was sink to the pavement and peer beneath the chassis. In the dark, he had to wait for lightning to reflect its gleam off the asphalt, but even with the brief illumination, he saw what he needed. The van had no visible gas tank.

The conclusion was obvious. Mounted inside the back compartment of the van, the fuel tank would be as protected as the vehicle's occupants. There wasn't any question now. He had to believe that the van was armored. To get into it, he'd need a weapon considerably more powerful than a Mauser pistol.

But even Goliath could be defeated. A reinforced vehicle was designed to survive an attack while it was moving. Stopped, it became more vulnerable, especially if the enemy got close to it. He knelt to feel the right rear tire, concluding without surprise that the rubber was extra thick and no doubt layered with metal. A bullet from the Mauser would do little damage, not enough to prevent the driver from speeding away.

The trick was to convince the occupant – already distressed because he couldn't raise his partner on the walkie-talkie – that he had another and more immediate problem: the rain's long-term effect on the gravel shoulder of the road. Even a bullet-resistant tire had to be inflated, or to use that logic in the reverse, it could also be deflated. True, by letting air from the tire, Drew wouldn't be able to drive the van away, but this well-equipped vehicle would surely have a spare.

Feeling along the gravel shoulder, he found what he needed. The van's designer had not anticipated that an attacker could get this close. The caps on the air valves didn't have a lock. Drew hurriedly unscrewed the one on the right rear tire, jammed a chunk of wood inside it, and heard a hiss of air.

The van began to list in Drew's direction, slowly sinking onto the rain-soaked gravel shoulder. He yanked the Mauser from behind his belt at his spine and scurried back to position himself with a good view of the rear door and both doors in front. His tactic was based on the assumption that as the occupant felt the van tilt beneath him, he'd conclude the rain had weakened the road's shoulder to such an extent that the van was sinking into the mud, listing toward the forest.

Would the driver come out to check?

A door banged open.

Drew rolled to the ditch and lay in frigid muddy water, waiting for the driver to check the listing side of the van.

But the driver did something else. Already nervous because he couldn't contact his partner, he bolted. Drew heard footsteps charge across the pavement toward the forest on the other side, and lunged to the top of the ditch. On his stomach, unable to reach the man, he fired the Mauser through the space beneath the van and the road, shifting his aim toward the sound of the rushing footsteps, clustering his bullets.

He heard a groan, a body toppling onto the asphalt. He scrambled to his feet and veered past the van toward the road. He hadn't shot to kill; instead, he'd chosen the legs as a target, needing to subdue the man and get some answers. Who'd ordered the hit? Why had they tried to kill him?

The man crawled awkwardly ahead of him.

45

A cracking flash from a handgun made Drew dart left. A second shot missed even farther. The man stopped shooting, pivoted forward again, and scuttled farther toward the trees beyond the road. He reached the edge of the pavement. In a moment, he'd be into the ditch and gain the cover of bushes from which to defend himself. Drew had to stop him now.

He sprinted at the man from the side. With no other choice, he kicked the man's forehead and stomped the hand that held the weapon. The man wailed, slumping off the pavement onto gravel, landing hard on his battered forehead. Drew yanked the weapon from his hand and kicked him again. The man groaned, rolling onto the leg that he'd been dragging, where a liquid darker than rain soaked the calf of his jeans. The resulting shriek was louder than that of the wind. The shriek broke, losing its pitch, descending to a moan, then silence.

The man lay still. As much as Drew could tell, he'd passed out from pain and shock. Even so, the next step was risky, for now Drew had to stoop to touch him. If the man was faking unconsciousness, if he had a knife . . .

Drew bound the arms with the skipping rope from around his waist. Next, he searched the man, not finding any other weapons. Then he grabbed his collar and dragged him across the pavement toward the van, tilting him slightly so that the wounded leg took a lot of stress. He needed to keep applying pain, to make sure the man stayed unconscious. He paused at the driver's door, which the wind had shut (or had it?), and studied the darkness beyond the window. Suppose he was wrong? His calculations had been based on the assumption that two men – and only two – had been left behind by the death team. After all, the fewer the members of the surveillance team, the less chance of drawing attention if the authorities arrived, and two was the minimum for the job. But suppose there was a third man who'd stayed inside, ready to shoot as Drew opened the door.

Standing out of the line of fire, pressed against the side of the van, Drew pointed his Mauser and slowly pulled the driver's door open. As he expected, the interior light did not come on. In the old days, he himself had always unscrewed the interior light of any vehicle he drove, anticipating a night when he might not want to show himself as he got out. But the corollary was that he'd always left a flashlight under the seat where he could get to it in a hurry if he needed it. So many habits of his former profession (*former?* he asked himself; what do you think you're doing *now?*) were common practice for everyone in it. That was one advantage when dealing with experts. You worked within a set of rules. The anxiety of the unpredictable came only when you dealt with amateurs.

The flashlight was under the seat where he himself would have left it, rubber-coated, a long, high-powered, four-battery model. Drew pressed the switch and sent its beam toward the back of the van.

No one.

The air inside smelled stale. He saw two sleeping bags on top of two mattresses. One wall held a bank of sophisticated two-way radio equipment. Against the other wall were two open knapsacks with clothes poking out of them, a partly empty pack of Cokes, a naphtha-fueled Primus stove, several cans of Hormel chili, Heinz spaghetti and meatballs, and Armor corned-beef hash. Drew's mouth tasted rancid. Didn't these guys eat anything that didn't contain meat? Beneath the edge of one sleeping bag, the tips of two rifles protruded. There's no place like home.

He leaned back from the van and glanced down through the rain toward the man at his feet. Nudging the wounded leg and getting no response, he confirmed that the man was still unconscious. Only then did he stoop and grab the man's armpits from behind, lifting him to shove him into the back.

He froze when he saw headlights in the distance, two specks getting larger, approaching from the direction of Quentin, passing the lane up to the monastery, continuing this way.

Take it easy, he thought. The lights might pose no danger. Just a late-night motorist trying to stay on the road in this storm.

But what would the motorist think when he or she passed and saw one man pushing the motionless body of another into the van?

Drew shut off his flashlight. Breathing quickly, he tilted the driver's seat forward, shoving the body through the gap between the seat and the door frame. As soon as the man lay in back, he covered him with a sleeping bag, even his head, then leaned in to shift the knapsacks on top, anything to increase the impression of clutter, to disguise the fact that a body lay underneath.

Pivoting, he glanced along the road. The headlights magnified, growing brighter, closer. There wasn't time to scramble inside without looking furtive and arousing suspicion. He didn't want the driver to stop or, worse, become concerned enough to stop in the next town and call the police.

Or what if the car belonged to the people who were after him? If he climbed inside the van, he'd be trapped. He couldn't even drive away since he hadn't changed the deflated tire and he didn't know yet where the key was.

You'd better watch yourself, he thought. It's just a car. Six years out of action have made you paranoid. All the same, in the old days, he remembered, he'd respected the small details.

Needing an acceptable reason to be standing out here, he shut the van door and walked around the hood to face the ditch, then pulled down the fly on his pants. Glancing toward the headlights that were now blinding him, so large they seemed like searchlights, he turned with apparent indifference toward the forest and pretended to urinate. If this car did belong to the death team, he'd have a chance to reach the trees.

The approaching vehicle began to reduce its speed, its headlights gleaming. Drew watched in dismay. It slowed even more. He squinted through the rain and shivered when he saw a rack on the roof of the car. On the rack were two domes.

Oh, swell, he thought. Wonderful.

The police. It was hardly a reprieve. Drew couldn't risk telling them what had happened at the monastery. The first thing a cop would do would be to take him to the station, and after that, the police band on the C.B. radio would be filled with talk. He had to assume that the death team was monitoring transmissions from the area. They'd learn where he was, come for him, and sooner or later they'd get past the cops.

The cruiser stopped beside the van. A spotlight came on, aimed at Drew.

Okay, Drew thought. I've just spent six years in the strictest order of the Catholic Church. I've just survived a multiple hit. I stalked and killed a man. I wounded another man. I tied him up and managed to throw him in the back of this van before the cop arrived. Now let's see if I can do something really hard.

Like urinate.

Increasing pressure on his bladder, he squinted behind his shoulder toward the spotlight, vaguely able to read the words along the cruiser's door: VERMONT STATE POLICE. He contracted his muscles and sighed with mental relief as the liquid flowed.

'You couldn't wait?' a gruff male voice said behind the spotlight.

Drew shook himself and pulled up his fly. Turning, he grinned with feigned embarrassment toward the unseen presence behind the spotlight.

He opened his mouth to speak, but no words came. Except for mandatory choir and required responses at daily mass, he hadn't spoken to another human being for the past six years. His only conversation, one-sided, had been with a mouse.

'Couldn't wait? I asked you.' The policeman was impatient.

Drew continued to grin with feigned embarrassment. Words formed in his mind, but his vocal cords resisted. Come on, you know you can talk. Pretend you're responding at mass. His lips and tongue felt thick. 'Well – sure – I – hey, when you've got to go, you've got to go.'

Amen. His voice sounded hoarse and gravelly.

'Something wrong with your throat?'

Drew shook his head but pretended to cough. 'It's just a cold.' The words came easier.

'You sound like you'd better see a doctor. Where you headed, into Quentin?'

Drew pretended to be puzzled. 'Where?'

'Next town. Twelve miles south. The direction I came from.'

'If I'd known a town was that close, I'd have tried to wait to take a leak. This isn't exactly cozy.' Drew held out the palm of his hand, collecting rain.

'It's damp all right.' The policeman was silent for a moment, unseen behind the spotlight. 'You'd better get inside.'

Drew coughed again. 'Right.' But as he turned toward the driver's door on the van, he suddenly wondered if the cop had meant for him to get inside the cruiser. He reached for the latch on the driver's door.

'You didn't tell me where you were headed,' the cop said.

'Massachusetts. Down to Boston.' Drew waited tensely.

'You're driving late.'

Apparently he'd answered acceptably. 'They need me back at the office. I took a fall vacation, hunting up in Canada.'

'You get anything?'

'Yeah. This cold.'

The policeman laughed. 'Well, next time don't stop with your lights off. In this storm, somebody might have come around this bend behind you and –'

'Whacked into me. It's true. I wasn't thinking.' Drew coughed. 'I guess I just didn't want to advertise what I was doing.'

The policeman shut off the spotlight. Drew's eyes relaxed. From the lights on the cruiser's dashboard, he could make out the face – younger and thinner than the husky voice had suggested. 'Stay awake, huh?' the cop said. 'Keep your eyes on the road.'

'You can count on it.'

Raising his thumb, the policeman drove away. Drew watched the red specks of his taillights disappear around the bend in the road. He exhaled, leaning against the van. If the man in back had woken up and started making noises . . .

But what if he'd woken up anyhow and used the time to slip out of the rope, and now he's waiting for me? Drew yanked the door open. Turning on the flashlight, he saw that the heap beneath the sleeping bags wasn't moving. *Dead? Had he suffocated?*

Drew scrambled in, tugging off the sleeping bags, and relaxed when he heard faint breathing. But the wounded leg was pumping blood. The sleeping bag was soaked with it. He had to hurry. After making sure that the rope still bound the man's arms, he used the man's belt to apply a tourniquet above the bullet wound in the calf of the leg. The blood slowed.

Drew pulled him forward, easing him into the passenger seat, where he propped him into what appeared to be a comfortable position, then secured him across the waist and chest with the safety belt. He didn't want his enemy out of sight behind him, and this way, to a casual observer, the man seemed just a passenger fallen asleep.

Drew searched him, found a ring of keys, and got out in the rain to open the back of the van, looking for a spare tire. In an under-the-floor compartment, he did find a tire, but even better, he found an emergency air pump with a foot pedal and a pressure gauge. Five minutes later, he'd reinflated the back right tire. Then, getting behind the steering wheel, he tested several keys until one at last fit the ignition slot. He turned it; the engine started smoothly. But he frowned at the unfamiliar dashboard, the confusing levers and knobs on the steering column, many more than he was used to. The last time he'd driven was in 1979. He had no way of knowing what design changes had been introduced since then. Had the technology altered so much that he might not be able to control the van?

At least the transmission was automatic; he shouldn't have any trouble merely pressing the throttle and steering. But as he put the floor-shift into drive, he realized that he couldn't see through the rain on the windshield, and it took him thirty seconds to figure out that one of the knobs on the turn-signal lever controlled the wipers. A knob on another lever worked the headlights.

Get moving, he thought. That cop might come back this way. He had to head into Quentin. He didn't want to; there was still a risk that other members of the team were watching for him there. But he couldn't afford to go in the opposite direction, where he might run into the cop again.

At least Quentin lay south, and south was where he needed to go, to Boston, to his contact in his new network. To his confessor, Father Hafer. The Church would protect him.

But as he proceeded along the road through the storm, obeying the speed limit – was it still fifty-five? – he was filled with misgivings. He glanced to his left toward the murky gate and the narrow lane that wound up through the concealing forest toward the monastery. He imagined the peak of the lodge poking up above the fir trees at the top of the hill. He imagined the silence of the dead in their cells. His jaw muscles hardened.

Then the lane was behind him, and when he glanced toward his rear-view mirror, all he saw was darkness. His heart sank, heavy with sorrow, hating to leave.

What strange new world lay ahead of him? he wondered. What answers? For six years, he'd lived in suspended time. But the world had moved on. About to confront what for him was an alien future, he knew that what he also would have to confront was his past, for the answers lay somewhere behind him. Who had attacked the monastery? Why? Was it Scalpel, his previous network? But Scalpel believed that he was dead. Again he thought about Arlene, his former lover, and about her brother, Jake, his friend. Jake, the only person, apart from Father Hafer, who knew that Drew wasn't dead. All right then, he thought. First I talk to Father Hafer; then I'll go to Jake. Despite his confusion, this much was sure. During his former life, he'd made many enemies, not just Scalpel. In stalking the sins of his past, he'd also be stalking himself.

PART TWO
PILGRIMAGE

STRANGE NEW WORLD

1

Ahead, Drew saw streetlights muted by the rain. He entered the outskirts of Quentin and veered from the main road, using side streets, avoiding the straight route through town where a hostile observer would be most likely to expect him to pass. At the far end of Quentin, he returned to the main road and continued south.

The clock on the dashboard was different from the type he'd been used to in cars in 1979. Instead of a circular face with arrows, this had a row of green glowing digits and letters, which made him feel as if he faced the cockpit of an aircraft. Another change he'd have to adjust to. 5:09 A.M. Dawn would come soon, he thought, anxious to get as far from Quentin as he could before it was light.

The man secured in the passenger seat began to groan. Drew glanced at him with concern, not yet prepared for him to wake up. Then the reason for the groan became obvious – the tourniquet had been on too long. He had to stop at the side of the road and loosen the belt, allowing the leg to get some circulation. Blood flowed from the wound and trickled onto the floor. The van was filled with a sick-sweet coppery odor.

He opened his window and drove ten minutes longer, peering through the rain on the windshield, then stopped again to refasten the tourniquet and once more proceeded. It occurred to him that this road was as likely a place for the team to be watching for him as the central route through Quentin, so as a further precaution, he turned left at the next intersection. A narrower road took him through several mountain valleys, winding past storm-shrouded peaks, climbing, dipping. He passed a few small towns, seeing their once familiar New England quaintness as if through the freshness of foreign eyes. A white peaked church aroused associations with the great New England preachers, Cotton Mather, Edward Taylor, Jonathon Edwards, though they of course had not achieved their greatness in Vermont. Edwards reminded him of the famous sermon 'Sinners in the Hands of an Angry God', and he discovered that he'd begun to pray out loud.

'Forgive us our trespasses as we forgive those who trespass against us, and lead us not into temptation, but deliver us from evil.'

Forgiveness, though, was not the issue. Survival was. Atonement was. Temptation? Yes. And evil.

At dawn, the road he was on intersected with another, and turning right, he proceeded south again, always south, toward Boston and Father Hafer. As the storm eased off, becoming a mist, a road sign told him that his route had taken him across a river into New Hampshire. That was all right. To get to Boston, it was quicker to cut through the bottom of New Hampshire anyhow. But now as he entered towns, he began to see sporadic traffic, occasional people on the streets, the world waking up to go about its business. He'd have to perform his errands before too many witnesses had a look at him. Though he hadn't slept since the previous night, the sensory bombardment of seeing the world again kept him fully awake. Soon the sun was high enough to burn off the mist that remained from the storm, and he noticed a sign for a picnic area up ahead. This early – 8:14, the clock said – the place wouldn't be occupied, and he needed to stop again to loosen the wounded man's tourniquet.

The picnic area was small but attractive. A dense line of woods concealed it from the road. Five redwood tables were dispersed amid a grove of chestnut trees their leaves turned autumn brown. A white-stone path led to a narrow log bridge that went across a stream toward a seesaw and swing.

He stopped beside the first table and admired the glinting stream – no doubt unexceptional to jaded eyes but to Drew, it was sensational – and then got to work. This time, he sensed a change in his prisoner.

Drew's defensive instincts took charge. He aimed the Mauser, staring at his prisoner's face. The man's eyelids came open; not completely, somewhat listlessly, but nonetheless open.

'Don't move,' Drew said. 'I'm not sure how awake you are, but in case you feel lucky, you ought to know we're alone here. I'll shoot if you force me to.'

The warning got no response.

'You hear me?' Drew asked.

No answer.

'Do you understand?'

No reply.

There was one way to find out how groggy the man truly was. Drew waved his free hand in front of his prisoner's face, then abruptly touched his index finger against the tip of the prisoner's nose. This technique was favored by referees in boxing matches. If a boxer was fully conscious, his eyes would automatically follow the movement of the finger.

That happened now.

'You're awake all right,' Drew said. Words came easier the more he talked. 'Pay attention. I have to loosen the belt on your leg. It's in your best interest not to try kicking me while I do it. I'd only have to give your wound a punch to calm you down.'

The prisoner studied him harshly. 'Go ahead. Loosen the belt.'

Drew did.

The prisoner squinted out the window toward the picnic tables. 'Where's this? We still in Vermont?'

'New Hampshire.'

'Ah.' The man licked his cracked lips.

'What's wrong?'

'If we're all the way to New Hampshire, I guess I can't expect . . .'

54

'Your friends to find you? No, I wouldn't count on it.'

The man stared down at his leg. 'How bad?'

Drew shrugged. 'The bullet went straight through. It missed the bone.'

'That's something to be thankful for, isn't it? I've got a first aid kit in the back. If you wouldn't mind.'

Drew thought about it. 'Sure. Why not?'

The man seemed surprised.

'And you'll be thirsty from loss of blood. I'll open one of those Cokes. Too bad they're not cold.'

Drew cleaned the wound, disinfected and bandaged it. He swabbed crusted blood off the man's forehead, then tilted an opened Coke can against his lips. 'Don't swallow too much at once. I don't want you sick.'

The man blinked, incredulous.

Thirsty, Drew opened a Coke for himself. After six years of nothing to drink but water, milk, and fruit juice, the carbonated beverage was cloyingly sweet. 'How bad's your pain?'

'I've had it worse.'

'No doubt.'

'If I need to' – he sounded indignant – 'believe me, I can take more.'

'Of course, but even so . . .' Drew opened two small sealed packs of aspirin from the medical kit and pushed four pills between the man's lips.

'Why all the help?'

'Let's just say I'm a good samaritan.'

'Tell me another one. You wouldn't have brought me along unless you wanted to question me. You think you've invented some new technique? I'm supposed to crack up from all this kindness?'

Drew sighed. 'Okay, if you insist, let's get down to it. What you're thinking now is that as long as I need information, I'll keep you alive. So you're weighing your life against the pain I'd give you to make you talk. Under those conditions, you're prepared to suffer the maximum. Or maybe you're planning to tell me whatever lies you think I might be dumb enough to accept. But then again, maybe the lies aren't such a good idea. After all, if I believed them and decided that I didn't have any further use for you, I might just finish you off. Are you with me so far?'

The man stayed silent.

Drew spread his hands. 'If I had chemicals – sodium amytal, for instance – I could make you tell me whatever I wanted. But when it comes to torture, your survival depends on keeping your mouth shut. So here's the point. I don't intend to torture you, and I don't intend to kill you.'

'What kind of –?'

'As far as I'm concerned, you're a hired hand. You were just doing your job. The person who hired you is the one responsible, not you.'

'I don't know what the hell –'

'All right, I'll make it simple. When you hit the monastery, did you know who I was? Were you told about my background?'

'I get it.' The man scowled. 'This whole thing's a trick to get me to tell you who –'

Drew shook his head. 'I did my best to explain. Then settle for this. In case you haven't guessed, I'm not just a monk. I'm not an amateur. Whatever I do with you, I want you to know it'll be professional. And I expect your standards to be the same. No panic, no stupid moves, no sloppiness. All right?'

The man looked baffled.

'For instance,' Drew said, 'I'm going to fasten the tourniquet again. Then I'm going to cover you with a sleeping bag up to your shoulders. You'll pretend to be asleep. We're going to drive till we find a service station. I won't leave the van. I'll talk to the attendant from my window. I need to buy something from him. And you'll keep pretending to be asleep. Otherwise, if you make a commotion, in all good conscience I'll have to stop you.'

'Aside from that? You said no killing, no torture.'

'You've got my word.'

'But you still figure you can make me talk?'

'That's right.'

'This I have to see.'

Drew smiled.

As he drove from the picnic area, he felt assaulted by the noise and commotion of increased traffic. The cars seemed even smaller than he remembered them, a legacy from the gas crisis in the mid-seventies. But then two enormous motorhomes went by, and he recalled predictions from 1979 that fuel-squandering vehicles would be a thing of the past.

Apparently not. The motorhomes were followed by a luxury car, the style and name of which he didn't recognize (had the gas crisis ended? Had a new cheap plentiful fuel been developed?), and then by a big convertible. He didn't understand – convertibles had been discontinued before he entered the monastery. What had happened to cause the turnaround?

He reached a series of fast-food drive-ins. Offensive to him in the seventies, he'd nonetheless been used to them, familiarity rendering them invisible. But now, to his unaccustomed perspective, their ugliness was overwhelming. A sign advertised a special on something called a taco pizza. And what on earth were Chicken McNuggets?

He found a service station. Gas was a dollar twenty per gallon, fifty cents higher than the outrageous price he remembered from 1979, and yet cars still crowded the road.

'I feel like I've come here from Mars.'

The man beside him said, 'What?'

Or maybe this was Mars.

Drew parked the van near the service station pumps. 'Close your eyes and keep quiet. Someone's coming.'

Drew bought a radiator hose from a young attendant using cash from the wallet that he'd taken from the man on the hill. As he drove past the pumps toward the street, he tossed the hose onto his prisoner's lap. 'Here. Got a present for you.'

Despite the restraining safety belts, the man almost jumped. 'What the hell is this for?'

'Why are you upset? Don't you like surprises?'

'I said, what's it *for*?'

'Take a guess.'

'It's used to beat somebody and not leave marks! But you said you wouldn't –'

'Right. No beating. Wrong guess. But keep on trying. It'll help pass the time.'

'And aren't we going back the way we just came?'

'To that picnic area.'

'I get it now.'

'Get what?'

The man squirmed. 'Holy God, you're crazy!'

Drew stared at him. 'I wish you wouldn't take the name of the Lord in vain.'

2

They reached the deserted picnic grounds. Concealed from traffic by the wooded stretch along the road, Drew backed the van until it was almost against a chestnut tree. He shut off the engine and stepped out, smiling. 'Be right back,' he promised, and cheerfully waved the radiator hose.

He shoved one end of the hose on top of the van's exhaust pipe, opened the rear door, and bent the hose until its opposite end was inside the van. Restarting the engine, he backed toward the chestnut tree so the rear door was secure against the hose. He left the engine running. The van began to fill with dense blue acrid exhaust.

The man became hysterical. 'Christ, I was right! You are, you're fucking nuts!'

'Get too excited,' Drew said coldly, 'and you won't be able to hold your breath.'

The man's eyes widened. Surrounded by haze, he started coughing.

Drew used the sleeping bags to seal the cracks around the back door. He made sure the windows were rolled up tightly. As a parting thought, he switched on the radio. 'How would you like some music?'

He'd expected something more strident than heavy-metal rock. But what he heard instead was: 'Linda Ronstadt and the Nelson Riddle Orchestra,' an announcer said.

Against a lush arrangement typical of Frank Sinatra's Capitol recordings from the Fifties, Ronstadt (whose raw-throated versions of 'When Will I Be Loved?' and 'Back in the U.S.A.' Drew vividly remembered) began to sing a standard from the Forties. He felt his sanity tilt.

His prisoner's coughing snapped him back to normal. The exhaust was thicker inside the van.

'Can't breathe,' the man said. 'Don't . . .'

Drew closed the door. He walked in front of the van, along the white-stone path to a log bridge spanning a stream, where he dropped a few pebbles into the water. The air smelled cool and sweet.

With apparent indifference, he glanced back toward the van. The interior was obscured by haze, but he could nonetheless see the man writhing in the passenger seat. More important, the man could see him. Drew stretched his arms and leaned against the railing on the bridge. From the van, he heard screaming.

Shortly, when the screams began to subside, Drew left the bridge to stroll back along the white-stone path. He opened the driver's door and shut off the engine. 'How are you doing?'

The man's face was faintly blue. His eyelids were three-quarters closed. As a breeze helped the exhaust to drift from the van, Drew gently tapped his cheeks. 'Don't go to sleep on me. I'd hate to think I was boring you. I asked you, how are you doing?'

The man retched, dry-heaving 'You son of a bitch.'

'That well, huh?'

The man coughed again, hacking desperately to clear his lungs. 'You bastard, you gave me your word.'

'About what?'

'You promised. No killing, no torture.'

'I'm keeping my promise. You're the one to blame if it's torture. Asphyxiation's supposed to be peaceful. Like going to sleep. Relax and drift with the flow. Make it easy on yourself.'

The man wheezed, his eyes red, watering. 'And this is what you call not trying to kill me?'

Drew looked insulted. 'I meant it. I haven't the slightest intention of letting you die.'

The man squinted. 'Then?'

'I've got questions. If you don't answer them, I'll give you another dose of exhaust. And *another* if I have to. The monoxide's bound to have an effect. Only you can judge to what extent, though there's always the risk that your mind will become too weak for you to realize when you shouldn't stay quiet any longer.'

'You think I'm afraid of dying?'

'I keep telling you, death's not at issue here. You'll survive.'

'Then why the hell should I talk?'

'Because you're facing something worse than death. What's in your future, if you don't talk' – Drew scratched his beard stubble – 'is brain damage. Permanent.'

The man turned pale.

'You'll be a vegetable.'

'They should have told me.'

'Told you what?'

'How good you are. Since the moment I woke up, you haven't stopped screwing with my mind. You've played a half-dozen personalities. You've kept me off-balance all the time. Crazy? Hell, you're as sane as they come.'

Drew turned on the engine again and shut the door.

3

Two sessions later, the man started answering questions. It took a while. He was semicoherent by then, and his statements were frequently garbled. But though forced to be patient, Drew at least felt confident that the man was telling the truth, for the carbon monoxide made him so groggy that it destroyed his inhibitions and in that respect was somewhat like sodium amytal. Two hours later, Drew had learned about as much as he figured he could expect.

But he wasn't encouraged. The hit had been purchased in as professional a manner as it had been carried out. For obvious reasons, the rule was that the client was never directly involved with the operation. If something went wrong, if a member of the team was captured or decided to try to blackmail his employer, there wasn't any direct trail back to whoever had paid the bill. Instead, the client got in touch with a broker, who contacted a sub-broker, who hired the necessary talent and made sure that the job was done. Except for the team itself, none of the principals met face to face. Arrangements among the client, broker, and sub-broker were conducted by intermediaries, using neutral phones. Nothing was ever communicated on paper. Fees were transferred through anonymous Swiss or Bahamian bank accounts.

As much as Drew could determine from what his prisoner told him, that procedure had been followed in this instance. The man convinced Drew that he'd been hired by what amounted to his agent, whose name he'd never learned. The agent knew where to get in touch with his talent, though his talent didn't know how to get in touch with him, and of course, the agent hadn't told his talent who was paying for the hit or why. A job was a job. Bizarre in this case, granted. However, the down payment had been generous.

Drew had frequently needed to rouse the man from his stupor, using smelling salts from the medical kit. Now he let him drift off to sleep, making sure that he had ventilation.

He brooded, discouraged. He'd desperately hoped to find the answers easily, but God had determined otherwise. His ordeal was to be prolonged. Yet another penance.

All right, he'd tried but failed here. Still, the failure wasn't his fault; if he hadn't tried, he'd have been foolish. But now he'd stayed too long. He had to get moving. Boston. His contact, Father Hafer. He had to tell his sponsor what had happened. To warn the Church and be given sanctuary.

He took the radiator hose off the end of the exhaust pipe, removed the sleeping bags from the back door and closed it. As the man slept sickly beside him, Drew steered the van from the picnic grounds and continued through New Hampshire, heading southeast now, toward Massachusetts.

4

It was twilight when he came to Boston. He took his prisoner's wallet, then left the van and its unconscious occupant on the nearly empty top level of a parking ramp at Logan Airport. He had to do something with his prisoner, after all, and he had made promises. But that didn't mean he couldn't cause trouble.

Dusk had turned to dark when he found a pay phone near a bus stop in front of the airport, and called airport security, telling them where the van was parked (he'd taken care to wipe off his fingerprints) and what they'd find inside.

'He's a terrorist. I'm telling you, it's twisted, sick, perverted. You just ask him. He's got all these guns and – hey, he bragged about how he planned to hijack an overseas plane, make it fly to Florida, and crash on Disneyworld. Sick. So what could I do? Just put yourself in my place. I had to shoot him.'

Drew hung up. Smiling inwardly, he got on a downtown bus, paid the driver, and took a seat to himself in back. The other passengers stared with disapproval at his stubble and grimy clothes. They'd remember him, he thought, and imagined the activity back at Logan.

Airport security's equipment would be sophisticated enough to trace even his twenty-second call, because a jamming device would keep the line open as if he'd never hung up. By now, a security team would have found the van, and another would be rushing toward that pay phone in front of the airport. They'd question people near it. Someone was bound to remember a disheveled, grungy-looking man in jeans and a padded outdoor vest coming out of the phone booth – and possibly even remember that the unshaven man had boarded a bus.

He was leaving a trail. If he intended to disappear, he'd have to get off the bus and do something about his appearance, change it, improve it. Soon. Only then could he go to Father Hafer.

He glanced out the back toward traffic in the Boston night. No flashing lights of pursuit cars sped this way. Not yet at least. But how long . . . ?

The stores were closed; he'd have to wait till morning to get unobtrusive clothes. Meanwhile? Assessing his options, he rejected a hotel, even a sleazy one. Not the way he looked. All hotel clerks had memories. Right now, he needed camouflage.

He amused himself by imagining the questions that his prisoner would have to answer when the security officials found him. What kind of story would the man invent to explain the bullet-proof van, the weapons, the radio equipment? Whatever the story, Drew thought, the one thing the man didn't dare refer to was the monastery.

He recalled the exhilaration he'd felt when talking to his prisoner, when making his speech to airport security. After six years of relative silence, talking had made him feel strangely good. His mood changed abruptly as he asked himself why he'd bothered to leave his prisoner in the van.

Well, I couldn't very well have taken him with me.

No, of course not. But . . .

I had an option.

Yes, but you didn't take it.

In the old days . . .

True. When you fought for your life on the hill, you killed your opponent. (*Mea culpa.*) But here you had a choice.

At once the implication struck him. In the old days, he wouldn't have allowed the man to live.

5

Despite the changes in the world while he'd been away, one aspect at least remained the same. Or possibly it too was worse. Boston's Combat Zone.

After leaving the bus, he headed toward downtown Boston, walking through streetlight-haloed darkness along the city's weirdly angled streets (the legacy of the haphazard 1600s, a city planner's nightmare), passing chrome-and-glass structures next to historic brick-and-board facades, their interiors no doubt stripped and varnished, filled with hanging plants and Oriental rugs.

But as he ventured farther into the city's labyrinth, the buildings became oppressive. Pride gave way to neglect. He reached the jungle of the predators. The scavengers. The Combat Zone.

Prostitutes, twenty feet apart, lined both sides of the streets. Despite the cold October night, some wore tight skirts, often leather, hitched above their knees, or slashed long dresses that bared the skin up to a buttock.

As Drew walked past, they squinted at him, assessing.

'Hey, sweet thing.'

'How'd you like your string pulled, love?'

Drew studied them as they studied him, scanning their faces, searching for a faint suggestion that this or that woman could be of use to him.

A garish yellow car screeched to a stop beside him. Drew pivoted on guard, gripping the Mauser beneath his padded vest. He blinked, startled, as a woman in the passenger seat exposed her breasts, the nipples encircled by lipstick, and raised her eyebrows in question.

Drew felt an unfamiliar tingle in his groin. He shook his head fiercely. She laughed and turned to the man beside her, who raised a beer can to his mouth and stomped on the gas pedal, roaring away.

He struggled to subdue the perverse swelling. His sex drive had disappeared effortlessly in the monastery; now, within hours of returning to the world, it was back. He forced himself to continue walking, searching, but Arlene's face came vividly to his memory.

A young black woman attracted his attention. Her thick dark hair was cropped close, like a boy's. Her breasts swelled beneath a Celtics sweatshirt; above it, she wore an open plastic coat. But what attracted him was that she kept pinching in distress at what appeared to be a rip in the calf of her panty hose. The gesture evoked his sympathy.

As he approached, her eyes flickered. She straightened, jutting out her breasts.

'Have you got a place?' Drew asked.

'What for?'

'It has to have a bed.'

'*What for?*'

Drew frowned. He couldn't believe that he'd made a mistake about her.

'Be specific,' she added. 'What are you asking me?'

He understood. 'Entrapment? You're afraid I might be a cop?'

She blinked her long eyelashes. 'Now why would a cop want to bother me?'

'It's been so long I forgot. I'm supposed to ask how much. If I'm the one who mentions the money, you can't be charged for soliciting.'

'How much for what?'

'To spend the night.'

'And what do you want to *do* for the night?'

She wouldn't believe the truth, he realized, so he made a proposition.

'Oh.' She relaxed. 'Is that all? For a minute, I thought you looked kinky. All I can say is you must have a high opinion of yourself if you think you can do *that* all night. Fifty bucks.'

Even six years ago, that price would have been low. 'For all night?'

'Hon, one thing at a time. Maybe. We'll see.' She tapped him gently on his stubbled cheek. 'But we'll have to do something about that sandpaper.'

'That's part of the idea.'

The glint returned to her eyes. 'Just follow me.'

6

She led him two blocks over, to a dingy apartment building with grime on the bricks and dust on the windows. The concrete front steps were spotted white with bird droppings.

At the door, she paused. 'Now, love, what you have to know is my boyfriend lives in the apartment next door. So in case you're the kind who enjoys the rough stuff . . .'

'He and two pals with baseball bats pay us a visit.'

'There you go. I knew you'd understand.'

They entered a musty vestibule and went up two creaky flights of stairs, the bannister wobbly. She unlocked a door to a small apartment and spread out her arm in a gesture of welcome. 'Home is where the heart is. The den of inequity.'

Noticing the pun, Drew suddenly realized that she was intelligent beyond being street smart. 'You've been to college?'

'Yeah, the school of hard knocks. But if it's loving you want to learn about, I'll teach you tonight.' She grinned and shut the door. The room was small but neat and attractive. 'You'll notice I didn't lock us in, just in case my boyfriend has to pay us a visit. There's booze in the cabinet. Scotch, rye, bourbon. Beer in the fridge. It all costs extra. I've even got a place to send out for sandwiches, but that costs extra too.'

'I bet,' Drew said. 'No booze. But I'm starving. Anything that doesn't have meat. Tomato and lettuce sandwiches. Three, no make it four. Milk.' He scanned the room, his stomach rumbling, as she used the phone to order the food. A small Zenith television, a Sony stereo, a sofa, a director's chair.

'Is that the bedroom?' he asked, pointing toward a door.

She laughed. 'You think you're in the Ritz? That's the closet. Over there's the john. Excuse the expression. The sofa's the bed. Just lift the cushions and pull that sucker out.'

He did so. At once he heard the rustle of cloth behind him. Alarmed, he turned. Too late. With practiced efficiency, she'd dropped her plastic raincoat, tugged off her Celtics sweatshirt, and was now yanking down her leather skirt.

He raised a hand. 'No. What I said I wanted to do – I lied.'

She froze in an awkward crouch, her skirt down around her knees, wearing only panty hose, her pubic hair showing darkly through them. Her eyes blazed. Stooped as she was, her breasts dangled, making her look vulnerable. 'What?' Furious, she straightened. '*What?*'

Her breasts and hips showed creamy stretchmarks against the smooth chocolate skin, evidence that she'd once had a child.

'It's not what I had in mind. I wanted to explain on the street, but I didn't think you'd –'

'Hey, I told you. Any rough stuff, anything kinky and –' She raised a fist to slam it against the wall of the room.

'No! Stop!' Drew held up his arms. He knew that the walls were so thin that shouts would be as disastrous as her pounding.

He strained to speak softly. 'Please, don't do it. Look, I'm backing away. I'm nowhere close. You've got nothing to be afraid of.'

'What the hell?'

'I meant exactly what I said on the street. I want to spend the night. That's all. To have a bath. To use your razor and make myself presentable. And go to bed. And sleep.'

Her eyebrows arched. 'You're into baths? I'm supposed to wash you, is that it?'

'Not at all.' Though he tried not to look at her pubic hair, his body betrayed him. After all, he hadn't seen a woman, let alone a naked woman, since 1979, and he couldn't help feeling attracted to her. But he *had* to resist, and struggled to focus on her dark boyish face ignoring her breasts. 'Please, I wish you'd put some clothes on.'

'Now that,' she said, but her voice was no longer angry, 'is kinky for sure. You mean to tell me' – she posed suggestively, her eyes amused, sticking out one hip – 'you don't like what you see?'

'If it helps you to understand, I'm . . . or almost was . . . a priest.'

She narrowed her eyes. 'So what? A friend of mine, she does two priests a week. I believe in equal opportunity. I don't discriminate.'

Drew laughed.

'There, that's the idea. Loosen up, huh?'

'Really, how much for the night? But no sex.'

'You're serious?'

He nodded.

'Would I have to leave?'

He shook his head. 'In fact, I'd prefer it if you stayed.'

'If that isn't weird.' She calculated. 'Okay, then, two hundred bucks.' The furtive movement in her eyes suggested that she expected him to argue.

'That's just about what I have.' He pulled out the wallets he'd taken from the man on the hill and the one in the van, tossing money on the pulled-out bed.

'You never heard of a hotel?'

He gestured toward his dirty clothes. 'Like this? I'd be remembered.'

'And you don't want to be remembered?'

'Let's just say I'm shy.'

Her smile became a sober reassessment of him. 'And love, you're also cool. Okay, I read you now. No need to fret. You're safe here. Have your bath.'

'But if it's all the same to you,' Drew said.

She opened the closet, pulling out a housecoat.

'I'd feel better if . . .'

She turned to him, putting it on.

'You were in there with me.'

'Oh?'

'Yeah, I've got some questions for you.'

7

And, he didn't add, he wanted to keep her in sight.

In the bathroom, he took off his grimy vest. She sat on a chair in the corner and lit a joint.

'You sure you don't want a drag?' she asked.

'It goes against my religion.'

'What does, relaxing?'

'Dulling my senses.'

She chuckled. 'We wouldn't want to do that.'

Hot water from the faucet cascaded into the bathtub, raising steam that coated the mirror above the sink.

Drew put his clothes on the shelf behind him, unobtrusively shoving his Mauser beneath the padded vest. The act of stripping in front of her wasn't difficult. Physical shame had never been one of his – what was the slang from the old days? – hang-ups.

'Not bad,' she said, judging his physique, then inhaling sharply, retaining the smoke. 'A little gaunt in the haunches.' She gestured with the joint. 'A little skinny in the ass. If I had your rear end, I'd have to go on welfare. All the same, not bad.'

Drew laughed. 'I owe it all to diet and exercise.'

'Exercise? Hell, you look like one of those guys that runs.'

Drew's chest warmed; he'd been a passionate runner. 'Yeah.' He smiled. 'Jim Fixx, Bill Rodgers.'

'God, I hope not. Fixx is dead.'

Drew felt a jolt. 'You're kidding.'

She sucked on the joint and shook her head. 'Nope. He went out happy. Died on his jog.' She looked at him. 'Where have you been? If you're into that stuff you'd know Fixx is dead. He had an inherited heart condition. All that jogging and –'

Drew tried to recover from his shock. 'I guess there aren't any guarantees.' He turned to step into the bathtub.

Abruptly she leaned forward from her chair. 'Holy shit!'

He swung back, ready to grasp for the gun beneath his pile of clothes. 'What's wrong?'

'What's *wrong*? Good Christ, your back! What happened to you?'

'Keep your voice down.'

64

'Sorry, I forgot. My boyfriend.'

'What about my back?'

'The scars.'

'The *what?*'

'It looks like somebody whipped you.'

Drew felt cold. He'd never realized. The years of penance he'd inflicted upon himself. The skipping rope with which he'd lashed his back. 'Yeah, I was in Nam. Tortured.'

'It must have been awful.'

'I don't like to talk about it. I don't want to think about it anymore.'

Drew kept his back turned away from her and stepped over the side of the bathtub. He shut off the water and slowly sank down, feeling it rise past his groin, then above his waist, the heat relaxing his aching muscles. Indeed, he hadn't had a hot bath since he'd entered the monastery, and the unaccustomed luxury made him feel vaguely guilty. He inhaled the lilac fragrance of the soap. As if he'd never seen one before, he studied a huge sponge that she'd given him to use as a washcloth, then soaked it and squeezed soapy water over his head.

She'd taken another drag off the joint and now exhaled the smoke she'd been holding as long as she could in her lungs. 'Well, I was wrong. About your being shy.'

'It's only a body.'

'Yeah, I learned that quite a while ago. The shampoo's on that plastic shelf near your head. Talk about dirty. Look at the water. You'll have to drain the tub and start all over. What were you doing, rolling in mud?'

The irony amused him. 'You don't know how right you are.'

He scratched his stubble. 'We both agreed that I need a shave.'

'The razor's next to the shampoo on that shelf.'

She didn't have shaving cream, and he had to use hand soap. 'I'm sure this'll sound odd,' he said. 'Who's President?'

She choked on the smoke she'd inhaled. 'You're kidding me.'

'I wish I was.'

'But that's the second time you've . . . When I mentioned Fixx. Don't you watch television, read the papers?'

'Not where I've been.'

'Even in jail, they've got television and newspapers.'

'Then that should tell you something.'

'You weren't in jail? But I had the impression . . .'

'Believe me, don't ask. The less I tell you . . .'

'The better off I am. All right, you claim you're a priest.'

'Almost. What they call a brother.'

'If that's your story, I'll pretend to believe you were in a monastery. Reagan's President.'

Surprised, Drew stopped shaving for a moment. 'So Carter didn't get reelected.'

'Not the way he let those Iranians make fools of us.'

'Iranians?'

'The hostage crisis. Don't you know anything?'

'I guess that's becoming obvious. Tell me.'

Class was in session, and it distressed him. He learned about the Iranian

65

assault on the American Embassy in Teheran in 1979. He learned that in 1980 the Soviets, claiming to be nervous about the violence in Iran, had invaded Afghanistan to make that country a protective buffer. Both of these crises, he realized with a shudder, had occurred because of him, because of something he'd done, or rather *hadn't* done. Ripples. Causes and consequences. If he'd completed his last assignment, if he'd killed the man his network had ordered him to, the sequence would probably never have started. Instead, he'd entered the monastery, and his target had risen to power in Iran.

Was I wrong? Drew thought. How many people have suffered because of me? But how can the decision not to kill be wrong?

The woman continued. Because of Afghanistan, President Carter had refused to allow American athletes to attend the 1980 Moscow Olympics. The Soviets in turn had refused to allow their athletes to attend the 1984 Olympics in Los Angeles.

'The Russians claimed they didn't go to the Olympics because they were worried about terrorists,' the woman said. 'But everybody knew they were just getting even for what Carter did.'

Terrorists. Inwardly, Drew groaned. He'd hoped never to hear that word again.

But there was more, much more. As she smoked another joint, free-associating about the major events of the past six years, the sickness in his soul became worse. He learned that Reagan had nearly been assassinated by a love-struck maniac who wanted to attract the attention of a teenage movie star who'd just begun classes at Yale. The Pope had been wounded during a procession in St Peter's Square by a Turkish religious fanatic supposedly working for the Bulgarian secret police. A South Korean commercial airliner filled with passengers, some American, had intruded on Soviet airspace and been shot down with no survivors, but nothing really had been done about it.

'Why not?' she asked indignantly. 'How come we let them push us around?'

Drew couldn't bring himself to tell her that nothing in such matters was ever what it seemed, that commercial airliners didn't just happen to stray into hostile airspace.

The gist was clear. These disasters seemed commonplace to her, but after his six peaceful years in the monastery, the effect of her list was devastating to him. He tried to avoid concluding that the unacceptable had become ordinary, that the world had gone insane.

'Détente?' he asked.

'What's that?'

'The arms talks. Nuclear treaties.'

'Oh, they keep trying. But do you know what some assholes – they call themselves experts – are claiming? That we can actually win, *survive*, a nuclear war. They say it's predicted in the Bible. That Christians will defeat the Communists.'

Drew moaned. 'Don't tell me any more.' He stood, dripping water, preparing to step from the tub.

She threw him a towel. 'Better cover yourself up, love. Otherwise' – she raised an eyebrow – 'you never know. I might get interested.'

He'd made the right choice, he decided. She was good for him; she made him laugh. He wrapped the towel around his waist, then glanced at his clothes. 'I guess I'd better wash them.'

'I might as well do *something* for what you paid me. Let me help.'

He wasn't able to stop her in time. With a look of disgust, she picked up his grimy clothes. And stared at the Mauser beneath them.

She was motionless. 'You're full of surprises.'

He regarded her intensely. 'So what do we do about this one?'

'I scream. Then my boyfriend comes running.'

'I hope not.'

She studied his eyes.

He didn't want to hurt her. What would he do if she did start to scream?

'All right, I won't.'

He exhaled.

'Half the people I know pack guns, but they don't mind their manners like you do. I'll grant you this. You sure give a girl an interesting time for two hundred dollars.' Still holding the clothes, she wrinkled her nose. 'But what's this bundle in your vest pocket? It smells kind of off.'

'I told you, you'd better not ask.'

He took the vest and set in on top of the shelf. Then he drained the tub and washed the socks, underwear, jeans, and wool shirt in fresh water. He asked her for a plastic bag, and while she phoned to find out what was taking their food so long to be delivered, he put the bloated body of Stuart Little into the plastic bag and tied the end in an airtight knot. Next, he set the bag and the Mauser beneath a towel, along with the photographs he'd brought with him from the monastery, and finally washed the vest.

Later, when she gave him a brown corduroy housecoat to wear, he waited until she wasn't looking and transferred the mouse, the photographs, and the gun to its pockets. She noticed the bulges, but by now she'd learned.

'I know,' she said. 'Don't ask.'

8

The knock made him nervous. Holding the gun in the pocket of the housecoat, he stood on the blind side of the door while she asked, 'Who is it?'

'Speedy's Take-Out. Gina, it's Al.'

She nodded to Drew and opened the door just wide enough to pay with the money Drew had given her and take the food. She closed the door.

'Gina? Is that your name?'

'Sort of. My mother called me Regina. I had to shorten it. In my line of work, I didn't need jokes about being a queen.'

He grinned. 'If you wouldn't mind, Gina, could we lock the door?'

'My boyfriend wants to be able to get in here fast if he has to.'

'But we both know he won't have to.'

She studied him. 'I'm not sure why I'm taking these chances with you.'

But she did what he asked, and at once he felt easier. Famished, he sat at the table and ate his sandwiches quickly. The bread was stale, the lettuce and tomatoes soggy, but after his recent diet of peanuts, chocolate bars, and freeze-dried fruit, he didn't care. Even the lukewarm milk tasted delicious.

The food hit him right away, the sugar making him tired. He hadn't slept in thirty-six hours. His eyes felt raw from the effort of driving all day. He glanced at the bed. 'I hate to do this, but I have to ask one more favor.'

She dipped a french fry into ketchup. 'I haven't turned you down so far.'

'I'd like to go to sleep now.'

'So?' She chewed the french fry, licking a drop of ketchup off her lip. 'Then go to sleep.'

'But I want you with me.'

'What?' Her eyes flashed. 'I wish you'd make up your mind. First you make a big deal about giving me the night off, and now . . .'

'Next to me in bed. That's all. Nothing else.'

'Just lie there?' She frowned. 'Come on. You must want me to do *something*.'

'Go to sleep. The same as me.'

She looked baffled.

He wasn't sure how to explain that he wouldn't be able to sleep if he didn't know where she was and what she was doing. If he told her the truth – that he couldn't trust her with his life while he slept – she might not cooperate. He fidgeted, pretending to be embarrassed. 'It's hard to . . . See . . . Let me put it this way. I . . .'

She tapped her long fingernails on the table.

'. . . need someone to hold.'

Her rigid face relaxed. 'That's got to be the saddest thing I've ever –' She took his hand.

He walked with her to the pulled-out sofa and helped her to put a sheet across it and to cover two pillows that she took from a cupboard.

'It's cold tonight.' She shivered and spread two blankets out, but despite her remark about the cold, she started to take off her housecoat.

'No,' he whispered.

'Force of habit. Sorry.' She grinned and refastened the robe, then turned off the lights.

He crawled beneath the blankets with her. In darkness, holding her, feeling her softness, he ignored the temptation of her breasts, her mound, her hips. He hadn't been in bed with a woman since 1979, and the memory of Arlene aroused him again. In his former profession, he hadn't been close to many women, unable to risk a commitment. Only Arlene had been important to him, a member of his former network, the one woman he'd permitted himself to love. His throat ached. Gina squirmed beside him, getting comfortable, and he distracted himself with the practical matter of making sure that the Mauser was under his leg where she couldn't reach it without waking him.

He snuggled against the mattress – the first he'd lain on since he entered the monastery – and tried to relax.

'Sweet dreams,' she murmured against his ear.

He hoped. And amazingly, it was so.

Or rather he had *no* dreams. Terribly, he slept like the dead.

A flicker of light woke him. He realized that Gina wasn't next to him any longer. Startled, he sat up in the dark, on guard, realizing that the light came from the television set. The images made him think he was still asleep and having a nightmare. He saw wild-eyed young men, their faces as pasty as corpses, dressed as Nazi storm troopers, and – he had to be hallucinating – purple Mohawk hair with rings through their earlobes. Women wearing black leather motorcycle jackets aimed fire hoses at billboards depicting hydrogen bomb-blast mushrooms.

A shadow stirred in front of the television.

He groped for his Mauser. But stopped.

The shadow was Gina. Turning, she took something out of her ear. The insane images persisted in silence.

'Sorry,' she said. 'I didn't think the television would wake you. I figured if I used this earphone . . .'

He pointed toward the screen. 'What is *that*?'

'MTV. It stands for Music Television. These are punkers.'

'What?'

'Hey, I said I'm sorry. I know you wanted me to sleep, but you've got to understand, my hours aren't the same as yours. I'm used to the night shift. Right now I'm wide awake. Unless it's eight o'clock in the morning, after I get a doughnut and coffee with some friends down at the . . .'

'What time is it?'

She squinted at her watch. 'Almost five-thirty.'

'That late?' In the monastery, he'd have been awake and ready for mass by now. He pulled the blankets off and stepped from the bed. Even in Gina's robe, he felt cold. After using the bathroom, he touched the clothes he'd washed where they hung on towel racks. They were still wet. 'Have you got a hair dryer?'

She laughed. 'Now I *know* you weren't in a monastery.'

'For my clothes.'

She laughed again. 'You'd better hope it doesn't make them shrink.'

It didn't, and at breakfast – 'Fruit,' he said. 'Give me any kind of fruit you've got' – he surprised himself by leaning over and kissing her on the cheek.

She too was surprised. 'What was that for?'

'Just saying thanks.'

'You mean half a thanks.'

He didn't resist when she returned his kiss. Not long, not sensual, but intimate. On his lips.

In another life, he thought, his nostrils filling with her sweetness. Again he thought about Arlene. But that other life was denied to him.

Because of my sins.

9

At half-past nine, he used a phone booth in a drug store two blocks west of Boston Common. Despite his tattered outdoor clothes, he was shaved and clean and didn't seem to attract attention from the pharmacist typing a prescription at the counter next to the phone booth.

'Good morning. Holy Eucharist Parish,' an old man's brittle voice said, as dusty as the better sherry sometimes used for mass wine.

'Yes, Father Hafer, please.'

'I'm terribly sorry, but Father Hafer won't be available this morning.'

Drew's heart fell. At the airport last night and several times later at Gina's, he'd called the rectory, but no one had answered, or rather a machine had answered, this same dusty brittle voice, prerecorded, explaining that the priests weren't near the phone right now, requesting the caller to leave a name and message. In Drew's case, that wasn't likely. Not the message *he* was bringing.

Dear God. Clutching the phone, he debated his options.

'Hello?' the brittle voice asked uncertainly on the phone. 'Are you still –?'

Drew swallowed. 'Yes, I'm here. Do you know . . . ? Wait. You said he won't be available this morning? Does that mean you expect him this afternoon?'

'It's difficult to be sure. Perhaps. But he might not want to be available after his treatment.'

'Treatment?' Drew clutched the phone harder.

'If it's a priest you need, I can help you. Or any of the other priests here. Is this an emergency? You sound distressed.'

'It's personal. I have to talk to *him*. I don't understand. What treatment?'

'I'm sorry. I don't feel at liberty to discuss it. But since you know him, no doubt he'd be willing to explain it to you. Why don't you leave your name and number?'

'I'll call back.'

Drew hung up, opened the door, and stepped from the booth. The pharmacist glanced toward him. Trying to hide his distress, Drew looked at his watch, then walked past shelves and counters, exiting onto the noisy street.

This afternoon? And maybe not even then?

Someone had to be told. At Gina's apartment, he'd seen yesterday's *Boston Globe*. There'd been no mention of what had happened at the monastery. Unless the authorities were keeping the story a secret, the bodies had not yet been found. But it was hard to believe that such a story could be contained. As he proceeded along the crowded sidewalk, heading back toward Boston Common, his imagination conjured up the bloated corpses sprawled across the table or on the floor of their cells. Dead. All dead.

Again, reluctantly, he thought about the police. Perhaps if he simply called them. But they wouldn't believe him. They'd ask him to identify himself, to meet with them, and he wasn't prepared to do that, not until he was guaranteed safety. In the meantime, if he managed to convince them that he wasn't a crank they'd alert the authorities in Vermont, where someone would check the monastery. When the bodies were found, it would soon be clear that one monk had escaped. The Boston police would make the connection with the man who'd called them. Who else could have known about the bodies, except a survivor or someone who'd killed them?

Drew shook his head. At worst, the police would suspect he was implicated in the deaths. At best, even if they believed he was innocent, they'd send out an APB for him, in effect helping the hit team to narrow their own search. And he hadn't even considered what would happen when the police looked into his background, first puzzled, then alarmed by the smokescreen of his past. It would be disastrous if their questions led them in that direction.

No. The route he'd first selected remained the best, the safest. Father Hafer. His confessor. Bring me in. As soon as possible. And help me find out who my enemies are!

Alien, he wandered the haphazard maze of Boston's streets. He roamed through shopping centers, introduced to glaring noisy video arcades and the incredible technology that taught adolescents to develop the deadly reflexes of fighter pilots. At every game he examined, the purpose was to attack and destroy. The winner obliterated the enemy. And sometimes nuclear clouds announced survival or defeat.

Adolescent males strode through the shopping centers in fashionable camouflage combat fatigues, while style-conscious older men wore imitation World War II bomber-pilot leather jackets.

Madness. Dear God, he asked himself, what had happened in the six years that he'd been away?

He fought to subdue his concern. Something was more important. Salvation. If the world was determined to destroy itself, very well. But what he needed was peace and seclusion. To die was inevitable. To do so during prayer made death acceptable.

He phoned the rectory several times that afternoon, feeling more lost and impatient when he learned that Father Hafer had still not returned. Time became torturous. The newest edition of *The Boston Globe* still contained nothing about the monastery, though that in itself was not significant. Several explanations for the absence of the story were possible. But he couldn't bear the thought that the corpses had not yet been discovered, a blasphemous secret. At almost half-past four, as he walked through another shopping center, he suddenly faltered, blinking at what confronted him. A crowd shuffled toward him, their eyes red, wiping tears away.

Something horrible must have happened, he thought. He remembered 1963, America's reaction to President Kennedy's assassination, and braced himself for the worst.

He went over to them, alarmed by their grief. 'What's happened? Why are you crying?'

A heavy middle-aged woman sniffled into her handkerchief, shaking her head. 'So sad.'

'What?'

'Seen it eight times. It still makes me cry. She looks so beautiful, dying from cancer.'

'Cancer?'

'Debra Winger.'

'*Who?*'

The woman looked shocked. '*Terms of Endearment*. Where have you been?'

The woman pointed beyond the crowd behind her. A movie theater. The show had just ended, the audience coming out.

In confusion, he found a row of phones next to a Lady Godiva lingerie store, its window filled with panties. A man wearing earrings walked past, then a woman with a heart tattooed on her hand. Drew shoved coins in the phone and hurriedly dialed the number he'd memorized.

'Holy Eucharist Parish.'

'*Please*, is Father Hafer in yet?'

'Ah, it's you again. I told him about your calls. Just a moment. I'll see if he can be disturbed.'

Drew slumped against the wall and waited. When at last he heard a rattle as the phone was picked up, he didn't recognize the strained, out-of-breath voice. 'Yes, hello. This is Father Hafer.'

Drew frowned. He hadn't spoken to Father Hafer in six years. How could he be sure? 'I have to meet with you, Father. Now. Believe me, it's urgent.'

'What? Who *is* this?'

Drew stared at the phone, suspicious. Suppose in their search the hit team had guessed the logical man to whom Drew would go for sanctuary? Suppose this voice, which sounded too hoarse and breathless to be Father Hafer's, belonged to one of the men who was after him? No, Drew had no choice. He had to follow the safeguards of his former profession. He couldn't afford to be careless.

'I asked, who *is* this?' the raspy voice insisted.

Drew's thoughts became frantic. Despite his misgivings, he nonetheless hoped. He needed to believe. A recognition code, some information that only the two of them shared. 'Six years ago, we met in your office. We had an argument. But then we went to the church across the street, and you heard my confession.'

'I've heard a lot of . . . six years ago? There's only one confession I can think of that anyone could be certain I'd remember.'

'We had a discussion about a liqueur.'

'Good God, it can't be! *You*?'

'No, listen. The liqueur. Do you remember its name?'

'Of course.'

Drew scowled. 'It comes to mind so quickly?'

'The Carthusians make it. I chose it deliberately. It's named for the fatherhouse. Chartreuse.'

Drew relaxed. Good. Or at least, it would have to do.

Father Hafer kept talking. 'What in heaven's name is all this mystery about? Where on earth *are* you? Why are you calling me?' The priest was even more out of breath. 'You're obviously not at –'

'No, there's been an emergency. I had to leave. We've got to talk.'

'Emergency? What kind?'

'I can't say on the phone. I have to meet with you. *Now*.'

'Why are you being so evasive? Meet where? And what's wrong with telling me over the phone?' The voice paused abruptly. 'Surely you're not suggesting . . . ?'

'It might be tapped.'

'But that's absurd.'

'Absurd is what it is out here, Father. I'm telling you I don't have time. An emergency. Please listen to me.'

The phone was silent except for the priest's strained breathing.

72

'Father?'

'Yes, all right. We'll meet.'

Drew glanced around the shopping center, keeping his voice low but urgent. 'Get a pad and pencil. I'll tell you the way to do this. You've got to help me, Father. You have to bring me in.'

10

A classic intercept operation. A version of the dead drop. Theoretically. But this time Drew had to make allowance for more than one variable.

His primary fear, after all, was that the hit team had assumed where he'd have to go for help. By definition, not to the police, not with Drew's background. And not with his predictable need to avoid being held in their custody.

The logical alternative? The priest who'd sponsored him as a candidate for the Carthusians. After all, who else would be understanding? But by the same logic the hit team would maintain surveillance on the priest. And when Father Hafer suddenly left the rectory during supper hour, an alert would be issued. He'd be followed.

The extra factor? Suppose the police had become involved, either because the bodies had been discovered or because Father Hafer was sufficiently disturbed by Drew's call to ask them for protection? It was possible that not only the hit team or the police but both would follow the priest. That complication changed an otherwise textbook operation from the equivalent of algebra into calculus. Regardless of how sophisticated the plan became, Drew had to begin with the basics.

Several times during the day, he'd passed Boston Common, scouting it from every angle, calculating its advantages. A large park filled with trees and paths, gardens, ponds, and playground equipment, it was flanked by rows of adjoining buildings, commercial and residential, on every side. He'd chosen a likely vantage point and, by seven o'clock that night, had positioned himself on an apartment building's roof. He crouched behind the cover of a chimney, concealing his silhouette, and peered down toward the Common. In mid-October, the sun had already set; the park was in darkness except for streetlights along the borders and lamps beside the paths.

The advantage of this rooftop location was that Drew could study three of the four streets flanking the Common. The far side was cloaked by the black intersecting branches of leafless trees. But the far side didn't matter; it was too remote for the hit team or the police to rush to this side without exposing themselves and giving Drew a chance to get away. And it was on this side that Drew intended to approach Father Hafer.

But not in person.

He'd been cautious about what he told the priest. If he'd merely instructed Father Hafer to go to the Common and wait for further developments, he'd have risked being found on this roof by either the hit team or the police when they predictably checked the buildings along the Common's perimeter. That way of thinking assumed that the rectory's

73

phone had been tapped or that the priest was cooperating with the authorities. But Drew's survival depended upon assumptions. Even now, after many years, he vividly recalled the Rocky Mountain Industrial College in Colorado, Hank Dalton, and his lectures: 'Paranoia will save your life. In *your* world, boyos, it's crazy *not* to be paranoid. Assume the bastards are against you. All the time. Everywhere.'

So Drew's instructions had been so complicated that he'd told Father Hafer to write them down. No hit team or police force could possibly have so many men that they could cover the complete itinerary with only a few hours' notice. They'd have no specific target area. From their perspective, contact might be established anywhere.

But needing an extra margin of safety, Drew had decided not to make that contact in person. As he scanned the three shadowy but visible streets – below him, and to his right and left – he saw no evidence of surveillance, no loiterers or vehicles that stopped with no one getting out. The streets looked normally occupied, innocent, ordinary.

He'd soon find out. At ten past seven, he saw the priest. Father Hafer wore a long dark overcoat, its top buttons open as instructed, the white of his collar clearly visible in the partly illuminated night. But the way Father Hafer moved caused Drew to frown. The priest didn't walk so much as he shuffled, slightly stooped, with evident fatigue. He came from the corner on Drew's right, beginning to cross the Common. Something was wrong. Drew shifted his gaze toward the street that the priest had left. No one seemed to be following.

Drew darted his eyes back toward the priest, and abruptly his alarm increased. Not because he'd discovered a trap, but because of something far more unexpected, though now that Drew thought about it he'd been given all the clues. He should have realized. Father Hafer was bent over, coughing so hard that fifty yards away Drew was able to hear it. The priest seemed in pain. And thinner than Drew recalled. Even at night his pallor was evident.

The priest was dying.

'Treatment,' the sherry-dusted voice had said from the rectory phone. 'He might not want to be available after his treatment.'

Chemotherapy. Radiation. Father Hafer was dying from cancer. The hoarseness, the lack of breath, how else to account for them? The cancer was in his throat more likely in his lungs. And with terrible sorrow Drew recalled the cigarette after cigarette that Father Hafer had smoked six years ago during the interview. The priest once more bent over, coughing, in evident pain. He used a handkerchief to wipe his mouth and straightened slowly, proceeding with difficulty toward the Common. Drew concentrated on the third bench along the path that the priest had been instructed to walk along.

The first. The second.

As Father Hafer reached the third, a shadow darted from bushes, rushing toward him.

Now, Drew thought. If he's under surveillance, *now*. Instead of watching the lean, jackal-like figure that seemed to be attacking the priest, Drew focused all his attention on the neighboring streets.

But nothing happened, no shouts, no sirens, no sudden eruptions of shadows or gunfire. Nothing. Eerie, the night remained still and, except for nearby traffic, silent.

74

Drew jerked his attention back toward the third bench along the path. His instructions to the lunging shadow had been explicit, based on the location of lamps in the park, allowing Drew an unimpeded view of what would happen. If the priest had been given a microphone and battery pack to hide beneath his clothes, the shadow's hasty frisk would reveal it. The figure would raise his right hand, warning Drew to run.

Of course, the shadow needed incentive to perform the frisk, and earlier Drew had looked for an evident but functional junky in the Combat Zone. He'd given the addict some, but promised him more, of a glassine bag of heroin that Drew had spent part of the afternoon relieving from a second-rate pusher. The bribe had been sufficient to motivate the junky but not enough to moderate his desperation, and not enough for Drew's purpose – or the possible danger – to be questioned.

Drew watched as the darting shadow collided with the priest, frisked him without seeming to, and delivered a note to the palm of Father Hafer's hand. At once, the shadow lunged away, retreating through a dark space between two path lamps, visible again when he scrambled through illuminated playground equipment, rushing as instructed toward the corner of the Common on Drew's left.

My, my, Drew thought. Well, what do you know? Not bad. Really not too shabby. It just goes to show – in a pinch, don't underestimate a junky, as long as he's properly motivated. Drew was delighted not only by the junky's performance but by his survival. The junky had not been killed.

Conclusion: If the hit team was in the area, they'd realized that the shadow down there wasn't Drew but instead a courier. They'd devote their attention to the courier as much as to the priest, in the hope that the courier would lead them back to Drew or at least give them information about what was in the note. The courier would lead them all right – to a cul-de-sac alley three blocks away where Drew had promised to pay the junky the rest of the heroin in the glassine bag.

Drew had left the bag on a window sill, and now, as he watched the junky disappear safely, he began to believe that neither the hit team nor the police had followed Father Hafer. But he still wasn't totally sure. He'd planned yet another diversion, and that was the purpose of the note that the priest now held in his hand.

Drew switched his attention back to the park. Father Hafer stood next to the third bench on the path, clutching one hand to his chest as if to control the startled pounding of his heart. Recovering from the assault, he peered down mystified at the note he held in his other hand, but before he could read it, he suddenly burst into another fit of coughing, pulling out his handkerchief, retching into it.

May God have mercy, Drew thought.

The priest wearily approached a nearby lamp and hunched his shoulders, straining to read the note. Drew knew what he would see.

My apologies for the surprise. I have to be sure that you're not being followed. If there'd been another way . . . But we're almost there. Go back the way you came. Return to the rectory.

The priest jerked his head up from the note, glancing around with what, even at this distance, was evident annoyance. He crammed the note into

75

his overcoat pocket, bent forward again, and coughed painfully into his handkerchief. With energy born from impatience, he turned to shuffle angrily from the Common, back the way he'd come.

If I'd known you were sick, I wouldn't have done it this way, Drew thought. I'd have chosen a shorter, less difficult route. Forgive me, Father, for the suffering I've caused you. I had no choice. I had to make the enemy feel as impatient as you are.

He watched the priest walk with effort away from the Common, then trudge out of sight down the street to Drew's right. He saw no evidence of hastily reorganized surveillance. No vehicle turned to head in the priest's new direction. No figure pivoted, hurrying to keep the priest in sight.

Drew waited twenty seconds longer, and when he still saw nothing unusual, he became as convinced as he was going to be that neither the police nor a hit team were involved.

Still, from his rooftop position, Drew couldn't see the street that the priest had entered. Unless he hurried from this roof and rushed to peer around the corner, he couldn't know if that street was safe. To approach the priest there might be a risk.

He did have another option. If he couldn't go to the priest, the priest could come to him.

11

From the darkness of bushes beside the church, Drew peered across the street toward the rectory. Above him, light from within the church cast a glow through stained-glass windows depicting the Stations of the Cross. Though the windows were closed, Drew heard the prayers of an evening mass, a priest's muffled voice intoning, 'Lamb of God, who takes away the sins of the world, have mercy on us. Lamb of God . . .'

The congregation joined in, 'Give us peace.'

Drew's note had told Father Hafer to retrace the meandering directions he'd been given, returning to the rectory. But Drew had used a direct route to get here sooner. He needed to study various vantages on the rectory, to determine if anyone was watching it. A final precaution. After all, if a hit team had followed Father Hafer, one of its members might nonetheless have been left behind, a final precaution of their own. Only when Drew felt satisfied that the rectory was safe would he risk going forward with the rest of his plan.

But after six years in the monastery, he'd forgotten that during the seventies the Church had relaxed its rules on obligating Catholics to attend Sunday mass – a Saturday-evening mass could take its place.

And this was Saturday evening. With mass in progress, with parishioners' cars parked along the street of this well-to-do neighborhood, others pulling to a stop in front of the rectory, their motors running, their drivers apparently waiting to pick up worshippers when mass was completed, Drew found himself confronted with too many possible trouble spots. A match flared in a car down the street, a silhouette lighting a cigarette. Would a professional reveal his position that blatantly?

Perhaps – if he wanted to seem like just another driver waiting for a passenger.

And what about the woman on the steps leading up to the church? She hugged an infant in a pink knitted cap and soft-looking blanket, patting its back as she paced. Had she left mass early because the infant had begun to cry, disturbing the parishioners, and now she waited for her husband? Then why was the infant no longer crying? And given the frost that escaped from the woman's mouth, why didn't she wait in the vestibule of the church, where she and the infant could be warm?

Too much to worry about.

Worse, he knew that his suspicions would increase when mass ended and the parishioners came out. In the swarm of activity, he'd never be able to determine if the area was safe. His plan had depended upon his being able to reach the rectory before Father Hafer returned. The priest would be coming back any time, and Drew couldn't risk crossing the street.

Unless. The mass, he decided. Instead of ruining his scheme, it might be a blessing. He turned and crept back through the bushes toward the side door of the church. In shadow, the door was thirty feet from the rear, adjacent to a sidewalk that allowed parishioners convenient access from the street behind it. He turned the iron latch, then tugged at the large oak door.

It resisted, and for a moment, his heart pounding, he worried that the door was locked. He tugged it harder; it opened, creaking.

His shoulders became rigid as he peered inside. He faced a concrete landing, its smooth plaster walls painted gleaming white. To his left, seven steps led up to a door behind which the service was being said – the main part of the church. Straight ahead, other steps led down to the church's darkened basement. And to his right, a third set of steps led up to another door.

He climbed the steps to his right, gently trying that door. It wasn't locked; he hadn't expected it to be. The priest who not long ago had gone through here to prepare himself for mass would hardly have expected an intruder while he and his servers were at the altar. Even so, Drew had to be silent.

Behind him, shuffling footsteps beyond the door to the main part of the church suggested that communion was now in progress, the congregation approaching the altar rail to receive the host. At once, from the church he heard the muffled strumming of guitars, a soprano singing the John Lennon–Yoko Ono tune 'Give Peace a Chance', on occasion substituting 'God' for 'peace'. Remembering the liturgical hymns that he and his fellow monks had sung at daily mass, Drew winced at the contrast. But at least the congregation was occupied, though now that he thought about it there were always a few impatient worshippers who left mass early, as soon as communion was nearly finished. Any moment, someone might come through that other door from the church and see Drew sneaking into here. He had to hurry.

He stepped through the opening, closed the door behind him, and studied the chamber that curved around behind the wall in back of the altar. This area was the sacristy, and it was here that the priest put on his vestments – the alb and cincture, chasuble and stole – before saying mass. Closets, cupboards, and shelves contained not only these vestments and others, but also altar cloths, candles, linen towels, incense, bottles of mass wine, and various other objects necessary for the many Catholic rituals.

He'd been concerned that one of the priest's assistants might have come back here in search of some forgotten item, but the sacristy was empty. To his left, he saw the archway that led out to the altar, the twinkling candles that flanked the golden tabernacle into which unused consecrated hosts, contained by a chalice, would be locked. The space in front of the altar was deserted, the priest and his assistants still down at the rail, giving communion to the parishioners. The guitars kept strumming. The soprano must have had the Beatles on her mind – she'd switched to the verse of George Harrison's 'Here Comes the Sun', but now the 'sun' meant 'Son' and was sometimes changed to 'Lord'.

The sacristy was designed so that the congregation could not see into it through the archway. Confident of concealment, Drew opened several cupboards, at last discovering what he needed – a black, ankle-long cassock. He quickly put it on and secured the numerous buttons. Next, he chose a white, linen, hip-long surplice, pulling it over his head and down on top of the cassock. This combination of vestments was commonly used by priests who took the place of altar boys, assisting the celebrant of the mass.

On a counter beside the sink, he found a formal head covering known as a biretta – a black square hat with three symmetrical ridges at the top and a pompom in the middle. On impulse, he also took a prayer book from a stack beside an incense burner. The fragrance of the incense, even unlit, suffused his nostrils.

He stared toward the archway, hearing muffled footsteps cross the carpet toward the altar. He had to get out of here. Quickly returning to the door, closing it behind him, his chest tight, he caught a blurred glimpse of the priest and his servers arriving at the tabernacle now that communion was over. The guitars and the soprano mercifully stopped.

He gently slipped the latch into place, turned to dart down the stairs to the landing, and froze when the door that led to the main part of the church creaked open.

A red-haired man and a freckled woman backed out of the church, glancing inward – to the right, toward the altar – each dipping their right hand in a marble holy-water basin, making the sign of the Cross. They were too preoccupied leaving mass early to notice him, but the instant they closed the door and turned to start down the stairs, they straightened, seeing his vestments, and fidgeted with embarrassment.

Drew lowered the hat to his side, holding the prayer book against the front of his surplice.

'Oh, uh . . . Hello there, Father,' the man whispered.

Drew nodded soberly, his voice low. 'My son. Escaping the benediction, are we?'

'Well, yes, that is, you see, Father, we . . .'

'Quite all right. No need to explain to me.'

The man and woman glanced at each other, relieved.

'But you might explain to the Lord. I'm sure you've heard the parable about the guests who left the banquet early.'

They blushed until the woman's freckles were hidden and the man's face matched the color of his hair. 'I'm sorry, Father.' The man bowed his head.

Beyond the door, Drew heard the priest intoning, 'The mass is ended. Go in peace.'

He gave the man and woman a paternal smile. 'But I'm sure you had what you thought was a valid reason. At least you came to mass in the first place.'

'As often as we're able to, Father.'

The door to the main part of the church came open, the congregation leaving.

Drew raised his right hand in blessing. 'The Lord be with you,' he told the man and woman, then opened the door that led outside and motioned for the couple to go ahead of him.

On the shadowy sidewalk next to the church, he exhaled frost in the chill October night and put on the hat. He started to say good night, but seeing that the man and woman were headed toward the front of the church instead of toward the street in back, he walked with them. Behind him, parishioners left the church, many of them heading in his direction. That was fine with him. The bigger the crowd, the better. He heard them talking about the sermon, about the weather, about Michael Jackson (whoever *he* was).

'You must be new in the parish, Father,' the woman said. 'I haven't seen you before.'

'I'm here for just a few days, visiting.'

They reached the front of the church, where the bulk of the congregation streamed out the main doors, dispersing both ways along the street. Several cars started; traffic became congested. People clustered, talking. Perfect, Drew thought. If anyone was watching the rectory, so much commotion would be a distraction, and the one person who'd most blend with the scene would be a priest.

'Well, good night, Father,' the man said. 'See you in church.' He seemed to think he'd made a grand joke.

When the man took the woman's hand, Drew assumed the proud look of a priest who'd just had the satisfaction of meeting a good church-going Catholic couple.

He didn't change expression when, beyond the crowd and the procession of departing cars, he noticed Father Hafer approaching the rectory on the opposite side. The priest had his handkerchief to his mouth, coughing. With all the activity, Drew couldn't tell if the priest was being followed, but in a way, it no longer mattered. He'd done as much as he could, had taken as many precautions as he could invent. From now on, everything was out of his control, in the hands of God.

No, you don't dare think that way, Drew warned himself. You can't presume to depend on God. The Lord helps those who help themselves.

He crossed the street toward the rectory. For a moment, he had a desperate misgiving about having put on the white surplice over the cassock. In the lamp above the door to the rectory, the surplice would make a perfect target. His spine itched. He clutched the doorknob, turned it, pushed the door open, and stepped inside.

But he wasn't in the rectory. Having been here before, he remembered that the rectory had a vestibule, a short narrow hallway that led to another door, the top half made of frosted glass beyond which pale light outlined the shadows of bulky furniture. A tiny lever projected from the middle of the door, just below the opaque glass, and Drew recalled from the last time that, if he turned the lever, a bell would be set off on the other side, a housekeeper soon arriving to let him in. If he decided not to ring the bell, he could simply open the door and enter, his assumption being that the door wasn't locked.

But he did neither. Instead, he turned and watched the outside door and waited. In winter, this vestibule would prevent wind from penetrating the rectory's interior, though Drew couldn't help concluding that those drafts would be insignificant when compared with the bone-cold winters he'd spent in the monastery, where his only source of heat had been the logs the custodian brothers had brought to his cell for his wood stove. The custodian brothers. The hermits. Dead! All dead! A groan escaped from him. He suddenly realized that Father Hafer was taking too long, that the priest who'd celebrated the mass would soon be coming from the church and discover him here, a stranger pretending to be a priest, and raise an outcry when he recognized the vestments that Drew had stolen from the sacristy.

Drew's pulse quickened as he heard the outside latch. He lunged behind the door as it swung open. A shadow appeared. Drew squeezed himself against the wall, feeling the pressure of the door against his chest. The shadow entered. And as Father Hafer shut the door, coughing, he found himself face to face with Drew.

12

'Father, I can explain.'

Father Hafer's eyes widened, dark, yet bright with anger.

'*You.*'

Drew raised his hands. 'I'm sorry. Honestly. If I'd realized you were sick, I wouldn't have – I'd have found another way –'

'*You!*'

'There isn't time. We have to leave. It isn't safe to talk here.' Drew spoke in a rush, trying to calm the priest, to keep him from such an outburst of indignation that he'd attract concern in the rectory. 'Believe me, I wish I hadn't made you walk so –'

'Isn't time? We have to leave? It isn't safe?' Father Hafer glared. 'What in God's name are you talking about? You've left the monastery. You've forced me to suffer through that charade with the note. Look at the way you're dressed. Have you lost your . . .' At once he halted, his role as a psychiatrist taking precedence over his other role as a priest. He seemed to recognize the mistake he'd made.

'No, Father, not my mind. My soul perhaps.' Drew gestured toward the traffic noises outside the door. 'And if I'm not careful, my life. The monastery was attacked. All the monks are dead. I'm being hunted.'

Father Hafer's gray face turned shockingly pale. He stepped back, either revolted by what Drew had said or afraid to be within Drew's reach. 'Dead? But that's impossible! Do you realize what you're saying?'

'I told you there isn't time. We're both in danger. Whoever killed the others might be coming here. They might be here already.'

Father Hafer stared toward the door. 'But this is madness. I don't. . .'

'Later. I'll explain. But first we've got to leave. Do you know a place where we can talk? A place that's secure.'

Hearing a sudden noise, Drew whirled toward the inside door to the rectory. It opened, a tall, thin priest squinting out with concern.

'Yes, I thought I heard voices.' The priest studied the two of them, focusing on Drew's surplice and cassock, frowning as he became aware of the agitation on their faces. 'Father Hafer? Is everything all right?'

Drew's chest pounded. He kept his eyes on Father Hafer.

Father Hafer seemed to hold his breath. He returned Drew's gaze, intense, debating, then swung toward the priest in the open doorway. 'All right? No, not at all. I've just received the bad news about someone I've been counseling. I'm afraid I'll have to go back out again.'

Drew felt his stomach muscles relax.

The priest at the door considered what he'd heard. 'If you have to. Remember, Father, you're supposed to rest.'

'In time. But this matter can't wait.'

The priest at the door brought his attention back to Drew. 'You must have come in a hurry that you didn't change your vestments after mass. What parish are you . . . ?'

Father Hafer interrupted. 'No, it's better if he doesn't violate a confidence. You wouldn't want to be burdened with troublesome information.'

'Yes, that's true. I understand.'

'But' – distressed, Father Hafer turned to Drew – 'perhaps the vestments *can* be taken off now.'

They stared at each other.

PART THREE
GUARDIAN

RETREAT HOUSE

1

'No. Surely not. *All* of them?' Father Hafer's voice cracked.

Drew sat across from him, assessing. The priest appeared to believe, and yet to fight against believing, as if having first suspected that Drew had lost his sanity, he now was frantic to protect his own by questioning the unacceptable, the unendurable.

'*None* – God help us – survived?'

'I didn't check every cell. There wasn't time. It wasn't safe. But in the ones I did check . . . and in the kitchen where I found the two custodians who'd been shot. See, at first the vespers bell didn't ring. Then it did, but later than it should have. That's how I know that the others are dead.'

'I'm not sure I –'

'Habit. If any monk survived, he couldn't have known that the others were dead. When he felt the summons of the bell, he'd have automatically gone to the chapel.'

'And?' Father Hafer seemed to want to add 'escaped.'

'Been executed. I didn't hear any shots, but the guns would have been equipped with silencers. Then, too, I have to assume that the team had garottes.'

Father Hafer stared at Drew as if the word 'garottes' came from an unintelligible language. With the shock of sudden comprehension, his face contorted. He leaned forward in his chair, buried his face in his hands, and moaned. 'May God have mercy on their souls.'

2

They were in an apartment on the fifteenth floor of a glass-and-chrome building. Father Hafer had parked the rectory's station wagon in an underground garage then taken Drew in an elevator to the private entrance of this unit.

But after the priest had locked the door and turned on the lights, Drew had glanced around in confusion. The living room was well appointed, yet strangely impersonal, reminding Drew of an expensive hotel room.

85

'What *is* this place? Are you sure it's. . . ?'

'"Secure" is the word you used earlier. You needn't worry. No one, or at least very few, have any knowledge of it.'

'But why?' The apartment made Drew nervous. It looked unlived in. 'What's it used for?'

Father Hafer seemed reluctant to answer. 'For matters of discretion. My duties as a psychiatrist aren't limited to advising the Carthusians. I'm often called upon to counsel priests from various orders who – let us say – have special problems. A crisis of faith. An overfondness for a young woman in the parish choir. A preference for alcohol, or drugs, or even another man. I trust I'm not saying anything that shocks you.'

'Temptation's the key to human nature. In my former life, I took for granted that everyone had a weakness. I just had to look till I found it. If people weren't sinners every intelligence network would be out of business.'

Father Hafer nodded sadly. 'The threat of embarrassment, of scandal. In that respect, perhaps our worlds aren't far apart. A priest who finds himself in moral conflict with his sacred vows sometimes becomes so distressed that he –'

'Cracks up?'

'I'd prefer to say has a nervous breakdown. Or perhaps he drinks so much that he jeopardizes the reputation of the Church.'

'So you use this place to calm them down or dry them out.'

'For rest and counseling. Or in an emergency, it's a temporary cloister while arrangements are made to take them to their order's rest home. Then, too, the separation of Church and State isn't always as clear as the constitution demands. Politicians offering incentives to the Church in exchange for the Catholic vote often prefer to meet here rather than be seen arriving at the office of the bishop or the cardinal.'

'In other words, a safe house for priests,' Drew said grimly. 'No, Father, our worlds aren't different at all.'

3

'*May God have mercy on their souls.*'

Drew wasn't sure whose souls Father Hafer meant – those of the monks who'd been killed or the men who'd murdered them.

The moan produced another coughing fit.

Drew watched him, helpless. As sick as Father Hafer had appeared when Drew first saw him from the distant roof at Boston Common, the priest looked even worse up close. His skin, which had always been gray, was now even darker, drabber, making Drew think of lead poisoning.

Or another kind of poisoning. Chemotherapy. The flesh had shrunk on his cheeks and chin, emphasizing his facial bones. At the same time, the flesh seemed unconnected to those bones, about to peel away. His eyes seemed to bulge. His hair – once salt-and-pepper – was now a lusterless white, thin and brittle, sparse.

His body as well had begun to shrink; the black suit and white collar

86

hung on him as if they'd been borrowed from a larger man. Drew couldn't help comparing their oversize fit with the way his own borrowed jeans, shirt, and vest were slightly too large for him. But there was a difference. Drew's lean, lithe body had the healthy glow of asceticism, whereas the priest's seemed to absorb light instead of giving it off – a collapsing black hole.

Of death.

'*Garottes?*' Father Hafer swallowed sickly. 'But you don't know for sure. As far as you can tell, only the two custodian brothers in the kitchen were shot. You saw no evidence of strangulation.'

'That's right. Except for the kitchen staff, the bodies I saw had been poisoned.'

'Then – God help them – there's a chance that they didn't suffer.'

'Oh, more than a chance. They never knew what hit them.'

'*But how can you be sure?*'

'Because of the mouse.'

The priest stared with utter incomprehension.

'That's something I've been waiting to tell you about.' Sighing, Drew showed him the plastic bag containing the body of Stuart Little. 'The poison killed him instantly. If I hadn't tossed him a chunk of bread and paused to say grace, I'd be dead myself.'

Father Hafer reacted with horror. 'You've been carrying that *thing* with you all this time?'

'I had to.'

'*Why?*'

'When I came down from the attic, I didn't know if the corpses had been removed. Later I saw that they were still in their cells. But what if, after I escaped, the team came back and disposed of them? I still had to take the mouse's body with me to find out what poison was used. Some specialists have trademarks. They're fond of particular types. I'm hoping that an autopsy will tell me –'

'Specialists? Trademarks? Autopsy on a mouse? And you've been carrying it in your pocket? I was wrong. May God have mercy on them? No, not on them. May God have mercy on us *all.*'

Father Hafer stood angrily. 'You say that the monastery was attacked four nights ago?'

'That's right.'

'And you escaped two nights later?' The priest's voice became strident. 'Yes.'

'*But instead of going to the police, you wasted all that time coming to me.*'

'I couldn't take the risk that they'd keep me in jail. I'd have been a target.'

'But for Heaven's sake, couldn't you at least have phoned them? Now the trail's gotten colder. It'll be harder for them to investigate.'

'No. There was another reason that I didn't call them. *Couldn't.*'

'I can't imagine why.'

'It wasn't my choice to make. The Church authorities had to know first. They had to decide what to do.'

'Decide? You honestly think they'd have had an option and not have called the police?'

'They probably would have, but not right away.'

'You're not making sense.'

'Perfect sense. Remember who I am. Who I was. *Where* I was.'

As the implications struck him, Father Hafer groaned. 'How I wish that you'd never come to my office.' He paled. 'You say that our worlds aren't different? That's certainly how the Church's enemies will interpret this. Because of *you*. And *me*. Because of my weakness in believing that you wanted salvation despite your shocking sins.'

'But I do!'

Father Hafer dug his fingernails into his palms. 'Because I recommended that the Carthusians accept you. Because your crimes caught up with you and now those holy monks have suffered the punishment intended for you' – he coughed – 'I've jeopardized the reputation not just of the Carthusians, but of the Holy Mother Church herself. I can see the headlines now. Catholic Church Protects an Assassin, Gives Refuge to an International Killer.'

'But I was on the side of . . .'

'Good? Is that what you wanted to say? Good? Killing?'

'I did it for my country. I thought I was right.'

'But then you decided you were wrong?' Father Hafer's voice was filled with scorn. 'And you wanted to be forgiven? Ah. Now those monks are dead. *And you've put the Church in danger.*'

'You'd better get control.'

'*Control?*' He walked to the sofa, grabbed the phone on the table beside it, and pressed a sequence of numbers.

'Wait a minute. Who are you calling? If that's the police . . .' Drew reached for the phone.

With unexpected strength, Father Hafer shoved Drew's hand away.

'This is Father Hafer. Is he in? Well, wake him. I said wake him. It's an emergency.'

With his ear to the phone, Father Hafer cupped a hand across the mouthpiece. 'I'll be dead by the end of the year.' He held up his hand; asking for silence. 'What does it have to do with this? Do you recall our interview six years ago?'

'Of course.'

'We talked about vows. I said I was fearful that if I recommended admitting so young a man as yourself to the rigors of the Carthusians, I'd be responsible for your soul if you found the order's sacred vows too harsh and broke them.'

'I remember.'

'And your response? You said that I'd be responsible anyhow, in a different way, if I refused your application. Because you felt such despair that you were tempted otherwise to kill yourself. If I turned you away, I'd be responsible for your damnation.'

'Yes.'

'It was specious reasoning. Every man's soul is his own responsibility. Your suicide would have been self-willed damnation. But I heard your confession. I thought, a man with your past, what hope did you have for salvation? What possible penance could compensate for your terrible sins?'

'So you recommended that the order accept me?'

'And now, if not for me, those monks would still be striving to save their souls. Because of me, they're dead. This isn't just a scandal. It's not just a controversy about the Church protecting a killer. God damn you. You're responsible. To them, to me. And I to them. Because of you, I've jeopardized my soul. I told you I'm going to die. By Christmas. *I think you've put me in Hell.*'

Drew stared, absorbing the accusation, and now it was his turn to lean forward, to bury his face in his hands. He glanced up abruptly, hearing Father Hafer speak into the phone.

'Your Excellency? I deeply regret disturbing you this late, but something terrible has happened. Catastrophic. It's imperative that I meet with you at once.'

4

The bishop, His Excellency the Most Reverent Peter B. Hanrahan, had a lean, rectangular face. He was in his late forties, and though he'd been wakened less than an hour ago, his short, sandy hair looked freshly washed and blow-dried. It was combed impeccably. His green eyes reminded Drew of porcelain, but their glint, he noted, was that of steel.

The bishop sat behind a large oak desk in a paneled office decorated with testimonial plaques from various charitable organizations – Protestant and Jewish as well as Catholic – along with framed glossy photographs of him in a grinning handshake with various mayors of Boston, governors of Massachusetts, and presidents of the United States. But the pictures of him with several popes took the place of honor on the wall behind his desk.

Perhaps because he'd sensed that this meeting would be both disturbing and lengthy, he'd arrived at his office wearing clothes that looked considerably more comfortable than his bishop's robes or his priest's black suit and white collar. He'd chosen gray loafers, navy, corduroy slacks, a light-blue Oxford button-down, and on top of it a burgundy sweater, the sleeves of which were pushed up slightly, revealing a Rolex watch. Steel, though, not gold.

To Drew, he looked like a politician, an appropriate comparison since at this level a Church official had to be a politician. The smoothness in the voice, the carefully effective choice of words, were probably less the result of Sunday sermonizing than negotiating with local Catholic businessmen for donations to construction projects in the diocese.

His Excellency sat behind his desk, tilting his chair back, eyes firm with concentration, as first Father Hafer and then Drew explained.

Four times, the bishop asked Drew for clarification. He considered the mouse in the plastic bag, nodded, and gestured for Drew to continue.

At last Drew concluded what he automatically thought of as his debriefing, indeed his second of the night. He glanced at his watch. It was seven minutes after one. Though thick beige draperies covered the windows, the muffled roar of a car rushing past outside intruded. Otherwise the room was silent.

The bishop shifted his gaze impassively from Drew to Father Hafer, then back to Drew. He blinked but otherwise stayed motionless. The silence persisted. At once his chair creaked as he leaned forward, placing his elbows on the desk.

His eyes glinted sharply. 'You've certainly endured a most remarkable series of events.' His voice remained resonant, smooth. 'And of course most disturbing.' He debated, then pressed a button on his intercom. 'Paul?'

An equally smooth male voice responded. 'Your Excellency?'

'Ah, good, you haven't gone back to your room.'

'I thought you might need me.'

'I don't know how I'd get along without you. Do you remember Pat Kelley?'

'Vaguely. But I can check his file.'

'No need. He owns a construction equipment business. Last summer he and his wife took a trip to Rome. He asked if I could arrange for His Holiness to give them a blessing.'

'Ah yes, I remember now.' The voice chuckled. 'He framed the certificate of the blessing and hung it on a wall in his office.'

'If memory serves, his firm owns a helicopter. He claims it's for lifting heavy equipment onto high-rises, but I've always suspected that it's merely a toy that he writes off on his income tax. Would you phone him please? Tell him that his Church needs a favor from him, the loan of his helicopter. Explain that I'll be in touch to thank him as soon as I can.'

'Of course, your Excellency. I'll make sure I talk to him before he leaves his home for the office.'

'No, now.'

'You mean wake him?'

'I want that helicopter available by dawn. If he hesitates, hint that the Knights of Columbus might hold a banquet in his honor. Next, check our computer for priests in the diocese who've had experience in hospitals or been in combat. Three will be sufficient, but one of them has to be able to fly the helicopter.'

'Very good, your Excellency. Anything else?'

'Yes, bring us some coffee, maybe some doughnuts. I'm going to be busy for quite a while.'

Bishop Hanrahan took his finger off the intercom and seemed to organize his thoughts. 'Let me ask you something, Brother MacLane. I want to make sure that I understand the situation. After you escaped, your concern – apart for your safety – was for the well-being of the Church? That was your reason for not alerting the authorities but instead coming to your confessor and then to me?'

'That's right.'

'Then may I assume you have some practical suggestions about how I should deal with this information?'

Drew nodded.

'What precisely?'

'Three possibilities.' Drew touched his index fingers together. 'First, as Carthusians those monks had removed themselves from the world. They'd sold whatever property they owned, closed out their bank accounts, quit their jobs. They'd said their final goodbyes to friends and relatives and made clear that no one from their former life could ever be in touch with them again. No visits, no phone calls, no letters. They even notified the government that they'd stop filing tax returns.'

'I'm aware of that. Please make your suggestion.'

'As far as the world is concerned, those men might as well have been dead already. They'd made themselves invisible, and in the normal course of events, when they did die, they should have been equally invisible. As I'm sure you know, the Carthusians don't use a coffin. The fully clothed body is placed on a board, the face covered with a cowl. The robe is nailed to the board. Then the corpse is buried in a private cemetery marked only with a simple white cross. To emphasize humility, there's no inscription.'

'I'm aware of that, too. Just what are you getting at?'

'Follow the procedure.'

'What?'

'Go ahead and bury them.'

'*And not tell anyone?*'

'Who otherwise would know? If they'd died from an epidemic or from accidental food poisoning, would the Church have publicized it? The Church would merely have laid them to rest. They'd have still been invisible. The Church's secret.'

'In other words, you're suggesting that the Church cover up a mass murder?'

'It's one possibility.'

Bishop Hanrahan stared. 'But if the authorities can't investigate, if they can't track down the men responsible, who may I ask is supposed to punish . . . ?'

'God.'

The bishop jerked his head back. 'I seem to have forgotten that you too were a Carthusian. Your faith is remarkable.'

'No, please don't say that. Faith? I believe in Hell.'

'Indeed.' The bishop frowned. 'So to protect the Church's reputation, we consign the murderers to their ultimate judgment and in the meantime pretend that the killings never occurred?'

'I said it's one option. It has to be considered.'

'But would you act upon it?'

'No.'

'Why not?'

'Because there's too great a risk of the story getting out. That kind of operation – the cleanup, the burial – requires a lot of personnel, the probability of gossip. If this were an intelligence assignment, if professionals did the cleanup, I wouldn't be worried. But priests would be doing the work, and what they'd have to deal with would be so shocking that they might not be able to keep their mouths shut afterward.'

The bishop considered. 'Perhaps. But don't forget that priests are used to the vow of secrecy. I could make them swear discretion.'

'Even so, what's the point of doing it the hard way? Why involve a lot of people? The problem isn't that those monks were killed. The problem is . . .'

'You,' Father Hafer said, the first time he'd spoken in quite a while.

Drew nodded somberly. 'Me.'

'And you as well,' the bishop told Father Hafer. 'If not for you, there would have been no massacre.'

'I'm well aware, your Excellency. *Mea culpa.* I'll soon have to make a case for my soul.' Father Hafer tried unsuccessfully to stifle a cough.

The bishop's hard gaze softened. 'Forgive me. I shouldn't speak harshly.' He turned to Drew. 'Your second suggestion?'

'Don't erase the evidence of the murders. Instead, erase the evidence of my presence in the monastery. Take everything out of my cell. Make it look unlived in. Remove my file from the order's records. Then alert the authorities, and when they ask about the empty cell, explain that the order's been having difficulty attracting recruits, that the monastery wasn't fully occupied. Because there'll be no way for the police to find out that a former assassin was given refuge there, the Church avoids the scandal.'

'And do you recommend that second option?'

'It has the merit of being simple. The police can investigate. There's almost no chance that someone'll talk. The only people who'd know are the three of us and whoever cleans out my cell.' He paused. 'There is a third option, of course.'

'Indeed?'

'The simplest of all.'

'And that is?'

'To tell the police the truth.'

The bishop narrowed his eyes.

The intercom buzzed. He pressed a button on it. 'Yes?'

'Your Excellency, I've made arrangements for the helicopter.'

'And the crew?'

'Jesuits. Before they joined the order, they served in Vietnam. One of them flew a gunship.'

'Appropriate. The commandos of the Church. A few other things,' the bishop said. 'I'd like you to make an appointment for me with the cardinal as soon as possible this morning.'

'Do you want me to wake him?'

'Good gracious, no. Wait until seven. Before he says his private daily mass. And Paul, I'm a little confused about who has jurisdiction over the Carthusians in Vermont. Find out.'

'At once, your Excellency.'

The bishop released the button on the intercom. He settled back. 'You must be wondering what I'm doing.'

'Not at all,' Drew said. 'You're planning to send those Jesuits up to the monastery. To make sure I'm telling the truth.'

The bishop blinked.

'And you plan to meet with the cardinal in time to send a message to stop them if he disagrees with you. But you doubt that the cardinal will. The chances are that he'll commend you for acting so quickly. But the hard part, the final decision, you'll leave to him.'

'You have to admit that your story makes one skeptical. A monastery filled with corpses? Really, I'd be foolish to make decisions before I had all the facts.'

'But why would I lie?'

'Perhaps not lie. Perhaps after six years as a hermit, you're mistaken. Confused.'

'Deranged?' Drew felt angry.

'Of course not. *Confused.* At this point, who can say? All I know is that you've been carrying a dead mouse in your pocket for several days. In my place, would you feel that inspires confidence?'

The bishop glanced at the plastic bag on his desk. Too casually, he reached for it.

In a blur, Drew intercepted his hand. The bishop flinched. Drew put the bag back into his pocket.

'Attached to your little friend?'

'Let's say I'm sentimental.'

The bishop's expression hardened. 'Very well. If His Eminence, the cardinal, agrees, the helicopter should arrive at the monastery by midday. And if what you claim is true, we'll decide which of the options you suggest seems wisest.'

'And in the meantime?'

'You'll need a place to stay. Whatever the truth of what you've been through, you're clearly exhausted. And I might suggest that a change of clothing would be appropriate.'

Drew peered down, self-conscious, at his battered woodsman's clothes. 'Then where are you sending me?'

'I don't quite know yet. I'll have to consult with Paul.'

Father Hafer coughed. 'And what about myself? Should I plan to go with him?'

The bishop pursed his lips. 'I think not. We don't want to draw attention to ourselves. Until we know exactly how the situation stands, it's better if we go about our regular routine. There is one thing I suggest, however. Did you hear this man's confession?'

'Of course. Before I recommended that the Carthusians accept him. His life as a hermit was his penance.'

'No, I mean recently. Tonight.'

'Well, no. That is . . .' Father Hafer frowned. 'I never thought . . .'

'Because he claims he killed a man two nights ago. If true, his soul is in danger. He has to be absolved.'

Drew remembered the crucifix that he'd used as a weapon and wondered if absolution was possible.

5

'Wake up. We're there,' the voice said.

Drew lay on the rear seat of the black Cadillac that the bishop had sent for. The driver – a young, trim, athletic-looking man with blue eyes and a brushcut, wearing deck shoes, jeans, and a U. of Mass. sweatshirt – had been introduced to him as Father Logan. 'But you can just call me Hal.' The priest looked as if he belonged on a varsity track team. It took Drew a moment to recognize the double significance of 'Mass' on his sweatshirt.

They'd left the bishop's residence shortly before dawn, and as the Cadillac headed west on Interstate 90 through the sparse lights of traffic out of Boston, Hal had said, 'We'll be driving awhile. You might as well get some sleep.'

93

But there'd been too much to think about, Drew hadn't felt tired. Still, after they'd stopped for breakfast, he'd fallen asleep as soon as he got back in the car. He later wondered if he'd been sedated. But Hal had never been close to Drew's food. Except, Drew thought, when I went to the men's room. But why would the bishop want me sedated?

He thought about it as he lay in back of the Cadillac, pretending to waken slowly after Hal had spoken to him. Sitting up, he rubbed his eyes and squinted at the brilliant morning sunlight, the gorgeous hues of maples on the hills along the road. At once he realized that, even if he hadn't been sedated, the effect was the same. He didn't know where he was.

'We left the Interstate?'

'Quite a while ago. How did you sleep?'

'Like a baby.'

Drew noticed Hal's smile.

The road was a two-lane blacktop with mountains on either side. Drew didn't see any traffic or buildings. The digital clock on the dashboard showed 10:31. 'Are we still in Massachusetts?'

'Yep.'

'What part?'

'Far west.'

'But where exactly?'

'It's a complicated route. It'd take too long to explain.'

'And you said we'd arrived – wherever it is that you're taking me."

'It isn't far ahead. I wanted to give you the chance to wake up before we got there.'

Dissatisfied, Drew studied the terrain, still wondering where he was. They entered a gentle wooded valley and turned down another road. A quarter mile along it they reached a high stone wall on the right and drove through an open iron fence. In the distance, Drew saw a looming white crucifix, haloed by sunlight, on top of a large rectangular building. Smaller buildings flanked it. The grounds were spacious. The lawn, though brown in October, looked recently cut. Shrubs bordered gardens whose flowers had died. As Drew came closer, he noticed a deserted basketball court.

'What *is* this place?' Its apparent peacefulness did not reassure him. He wondered if it might be a sanitarium.

'A couple of things,' Hal said. 'It started as a seminary. But candidates for the priesthood haven't exactly been lining up these past few years. So the Church decided that the empty rooms ought to be put to use. That building to the right is a dormitory. Once a month for a weekend, various Catholic men's clubs come here to have a retreat.'

Drew nodded, sympathetic with the concept. The Church believed that the faithful needed to escape the pressures of the world from time to time. So for forty-eight hours, usually from a Friday to a Sunday night, parishioners had the chance for a nominal fee to go to a 'retreat house', often a seminary, where they immersed themselves in Catholic rituals. A retreat master, usually an eminent priest, gave lectures on matters of dogma and spirituality. Except during discussion groups, conversation was not permitted. Abundant religious literature was available in each dormitory room as an aid to meditation.

'But that's just once a month,' Hal said. 'That building on the left gets the most use. It's a rest home. At the bishop's, I saw you talking to Father Hafer. I guess you know he's a psychiatrist. I wouldn't want his job for anything. He has to counsel priests who can't bear the strain of their vows.'

'Well, people get weak sometimes.'

'Don't I know. It's sad. You'd be surprised how many burned-out cases I've driven out here. From what I'm told, there are three or four other places like this in the country. But this is the only one I've seen. That building to the left of the seminary is where they sleep. They don't have any duties, except of course to say their daily mass. Otherwise, they get medication and therapy from the local staff.'

'How long do they stay?'

'A month or two for most of them. Till they're off the booze or they realize that even saints don't have to work twenty-five hours a day. But a few of them – well, I took an old pastor out here four years ago, and he still swears that the Virgin Mary sings to him every night.

6

They stopped at the large middle building, the one with the crucifix on top. The angle of the sun was such that the cross's shadow fell across the Cadillac, and as Drew got out, he noted that despite the clear bright sky, the air was crisp.

He faced the building, scanning its windows. The bricks looked dingy. The concrete steps were cracked.

'The place seems deserted.'

Hal shrugged. 'It's almost eleven. The seminarians must be in class.'

As if on cue, the voices of young men drifted out from somewhere deep in the building. 'Lord have mercy. Christ have mercy. Lord have mercy. Glory to God in the highest . . .'

'It sounds like the Kyrie and the Gloria,' Hal said. 'They must be practicing the liturgy.'

Drew shook his head. 'Classes on Sunday? I don't think so. And mass would have been first thing this morning. No, something isn't right.'

He started up the cracked concrete steps.

Hal stopped him. 'Sure, but this Sunday was special. Mass was postponed till now.'

Puzzled, Drew turned to him.

'We're supposed to stay away from the seminarians. The bishop told the housemaster you'd be here. But it's understood that you're not to attract attention. You'll be sleeping over there.' Hal pointed toward the building on the right. 'Where they hold the retreats.'

Drew felt uneasy. 'But if they're holding a retreat what's the difference, if *they* see me or the seminarians do?'

'There's no retreat this weekend. We've got that building all to ourselves.'

How much has Hal been told about me? Drew wondered. Why do I feel

I've met his type before? The way he stands at attention. The way he kept checking the Cadillac's rear-view mirror.

In another line of work.

'Yeah, it'll be nice and quiet. Restful,' Hal said.

A slight wind touched Drew's face. Unsettled, he came back down the steps and walked with Hal across the lawn toward the building on the right. Something else bothered him. 'If we're not supposed to be noticed, don't you think you'd better move the car?'

'I will in a couple of minutes. I've got to come back anyway.'

'Oh?'

'To get you some clothes. I don't have much to choose from. These seminarians don't exactly dress for style. Black shoes, black socks, black pants. Depressing. But they like to play sports, so I think I can get you a sweatshirt. Maybe a workshirt. Could be even a windbreaker. Are you hungry?'

'Vegetables. Fresh. A lot.'

Hal laughed. 'Yeah, carrots, huh? What's up, Doc? You want anything to read?'

Drew shook his head. 'I figured I'd exercise.'

'Great! You like basketball? You feel like a little one-on-one? No, wait a minute, that's no good. The court's outside. You're not supposed to show yourself.'

Drew stopped abruptly.

'Something wrong?'

'A question. I'm bursting to ask it.'

'Be my guest.'

'Are you really a priest?'

'Does the Pope hate Polish jokes? Was John a Baptist? You better believe I'm a priest.'

'What else?'

'Beg pardon?'

'What else are – were – you? You've got military intelligence written all over you.' Drew watched him soberly.

'Okay. Yeah, I used to be in military intelligence. The Navy. Like *Magnum, P.I.*'

Drew didn't understand the reference. 'What made you join the priesthood?'

Hal started walking again. 'You've got your choice of rooms. Which one?'

Drew answered quickly, not wanting to change the subject. 'Anything near the stairs on the second floor.'

'Yeah, that's what I'd choose, too. No chance of somebody coming through your window. And the high ground's easier to defend. But it's not like on the third floor, where it takes too long to get outside.'

'I asked you, why did you join the priesthood?'

'And you can keep asking.'

'Then let me ask you this.'

Hal stopped, impatient.

'I'm used to a pattern. Five days ago, I was forced to give it up. And now it's Sunday.'

'So?'

96

'At the bishop's, Father Hafer heard my confession. Five days are too long. I want to receive communion.'

'Hey, now you're talking. Never mind basketball. I haven't said my mass for today. But I don't have a server.'

'Sure, you do. Just show me the way to an altar.'

'There's a chapel in the retreat house.'

'I'll fill the cruets for your water and wine. I'll serve the best mass you ever said.'

'Pal, you've got a deal. What's funny?'

'We sound like two kids getting ready to play.'

7

A board creaked, Drew knelt, praying, in the front pew of the chapel. He raised his head to look past his shoulder toward the shadows behind him.

No one. He turned to the altar and resumed his prayers.

It was after midnight. Though the mass he'd served for Hal had been almost twelve hours earlier, he still remembered the touch of the thin stiff host on his tongue. His spirit had swelled.

The rest of the day had depressed him. He'd tried to keep busy – washed and shaved and put on the clothes that Hal had brought him. He'd paced his room, done pushups and situps, rehearsed the dance steps of martial arts, and wondered where Hal had gone.

By mid-afternoon, he knew that the helicopter would long ago have reached the monastery. The Jesuits would have found the bodies and told the bishop. The bishop would have talked to the cardinal. The cardinal would have talked to Rome. So why hasn't someone talked to me? What decisions were made? *What's happening?*

The irony of his nervous boredom struck him forcibly. For six years, living in solitude, he'd never felt the burden of time. And now, after five days' absence from the monastery, he couldn't keep from looking at his watch, a watch that he'd taken from a man he'd killed. Moaning, he sank to his knees and begged for this burden to be lifted from him. I know that nothing happens without a reason. I'm only an instrument. But please, Lord, pass this cup from my lips. All I want is peace.

All? He touched the bulge in the jacket pocket, remembering the urge he'd felt to seek revenge for the death of the monks. He felt the photographs in another pocket – the man and woman in flames, the young boy screaming – and prayed for his soul.

Near six, Hal entered his room. 'I brought you some milk and vegetables. Raw cauliflower you said you wanted? I can't even stand the stuff cooked.'

'How long am I supposed to stay here?'

'Till they tell us different, I suppose. Hey, if you're bored, they've got just one television here, and that's in the seminary building, but I can get you a radio.'

'What about a phone?'

'Just relax, why don't you? Smell the country air.'

'Indoors?'

'You've got a point. But not to worry. Everything's taken care of.'

'Oh?'

'It's going down to thirty tonight. But I figured out how to get the heat turned on in the building.'

Hal left.

Drew glanced impatiently at his watch again. Its hands were aimed precisely at six – when for years the vespers bell had rung.

He craved the satisfaction that he'd felt today during mass. He wanted to reestablish the blissful pattern of the monastery. Six o'clock. As if he heard the vespers bell start tolling, he obeyed its summons and left his room.

8

The retreat house was silent. A light glowed at the end of the hall, beckoning him to the stairwell. With his hand on the pitted metal railing, he descended, reached the first floor, ignored the half-lit lobby, and continued to the basement. He brushed his hand against a clammy plaster wall and proceeded through darkness toward a door to the right. The chapel where earlier he'd served at mass, where the vespers service ought to occur.

He pushed the door open and entered. Blackness. Recalling a light switch to his left, he felt for it and flicked it on. But the power for the basement must have been on a different circuit from the one for his room on the second floor, because the blackness continued to face him. Earlier, sunlight gleaming through windows high on one wall had been sufficient for him to help at mass. But now . . .

He imagined the hands on his watch moving farther past six. His compulsion increased.

As he groped along the wall to his left, he bumped against a chair. Then he reached another wall and felt his way past the bulky compartment of a confessional. The odor of mildew widened his nostrils. But beneath the mildew was the redolence of incense from years of services. When his waist touched the altar railing, he knew that he was almost home.

Now if only there were matches. He remembered the rows of votive candles that flanked the inside right and left stretch of the altar railing. Yes, when he straddled the altar railing, stepping forward, he felt matches in a metal cup, struck one against the cup, and smiled at the gleam. His smile persisted as one by one he lit the candles, filling the front of the chapel with a shimmering radiance. He knelt in the first pew, silently reciting the vespers prayers.

At midnight, with still no word from the bishop, he again felt compelled by the ritual, coming back to recite the matins prayers.

And heard the creak behind him.

9

The first time he heard it, he told himself that the sound was only wood contracting because of cold.

The second time, he told himself that the tired old building was sagging.

The third time, he pulled his Mauser from beneath his jacket and sank to the floor.

'Okay, pal, relax,' a voice said in back. 'I didn't mean to make you nervous.'

Hal.

Drew stayed out of sight on the floor beneath the pew.

'Come on,' Hal said, concealed by the dark at the rear of the chapel. 'I know where you are. I saw you duck down. But first I saw you pull a gun from under your jacket. So let's be calm, all right? I'm supposed to keep an eye on you, not let you use me for target practice.'

Drew didn't intend to take chances. He glanced ahead of him toward a door on his left beyond the altar railing, remembering from the mass he'd served at noon that it led to the sacristy behind the altar. Beyond it, another door opened on a stairwell. If I have to, I can jump the altar railing and get away.

Another creak, coming closer.

Drew's forehead felt slick with sweat. But the chapel was terribly cold.

'Just loosen up, okay,' Hal asked, 'while I explain? See, I know you came down here at six. I figured you were following the routine you had in the monastery. Vespers service. The next service is matins, at midnight. So I got here earlier. I thought I'd watch you from out of sight so I wouldn't disturb your prayers. I'm only doing my job. How was I to know that the floor back here creaks every time I breathe?'

Drew debated. Hal could be telling the truth. But why didn't he just come down here with me? I wouldn't have cared if he was in the chapel while I prayed. No, something's wrong.

Another creak. Closer.

Drew eased from the pew and began to squirm toward the altar railing. His chest felt chilled by the floor.

'We're in a bind,' Hal said, a little closer. 'You don't want to show yourself till I do. But I don't want to do it first, not with that gun in your hand. Hey, I made a mistake by not letting you know I was here. I admit that. But we've got to end this stand-off. I'm on your side.'

Another creak.

Drew squirmed a half-foot closer to the altar rail. The candles shimmered.

'Think,' Hal said. 'If I wanted to move against you, I could have done it while you slept in the car.'

Good point.

'Or I could have . . .'

Creak. Drew squirmed another half-foot closer to the altar railing.

'. . . shot you while you were praying just now.'

A second good point.

'So, let's call a truce. I'm a victim of circumstance.'

All right, Drew thought. I like to believe I'm open-minded. Instead of crawling the rest of the way to the altar railing, he rolled in the opposite direction, toward the pews on the right side of the chapel.

He aimed, and for the first time, spoke. 'Then all you have to do is tell me why you joined the priesthood.'

At the sound of Drew's voice, the door to the chapel burst open. A man in a priest's black suit and white collar lunged forward, aiming an M-16.

'No!' Hal screamed. He stood, much closer than Drew had expected, raising an arm. It was hard to tell in the shadows. He might have been holding a pistol.

But the priest swung in Hal's direction, squeezing the trigger on the M-16. The muzzle flash lit the shadows in back as the weapon – on automatic – rattled, ejecting empty casings which clinked on the floor. The force of the volley lifted Hal off his feet and threw him back against the wall. Blood spattered. Hal rebounded shuddering, toppling to the floor.

As Drew rose, kneeling, aiming his Mauser, a second priest appeared in the doorway, flanking the first, clutching an Uzi, strafing the chapel. The noise, magnified by the echoing walls, struck Drew's ears. In agony, they started to ring.

He crouched back down below the pew. *Priests? Killers?* His sanity tilted. *Religion? Violence?* The contradiction shocked him.

The priest-assassins had the advantage of darkness back there. He didn't dare show himself in the candlelight to aim and shoot. A Mauser against an M-16 and an Uzi? The odds were against him. As the acrid stench of cordite wafted toward him, he turned, thrust upward from his knees, and vaulted the altar railing. His body arched. He landed hard on the carpeted floor beyond, gasping from the impact against his shoulder, and lunged up, scrambling toward the sacristy door. Bullets tore apart the altar behind him.

At once the staccato reports of a handgun interrupted the rattling gunfire. The unmistakable wallop of a .45 automatic pistol. Again. And again.

Drew grabbed the knob on the sacristy door, twisting it, shoving inward, falling to conceal his body. He glanced back and caught a furtive glimpse of someone else in the chapel. Enough to make him pause where he crouched.

Another priest. But this man was older. Early fifties, average height, but large in the chest. Muscular shoulders. Dark hair. Slavic features, mustache.

In the dark of the sacristy, Drew forced himself to keep staring. The priest had appeared from – Drew shuddered, suddenly realizing – the confessional on the right.

Had he been there all along? When I groped through the dark and bumped against that confessional earlier?

He had stepped out, shooting, when Hal had been killed. Drew still aimed his pistol toward the priests in back, his caution needless. The men lay motionless in the aisle, a pool of blood spreading around them.

The pistol was in the priest's left hand. Drew's perspective gave him a good view of the outside of that hand. A glint of reflected candlelight attracted his attention. Off the middle finger.

100

A ring, and even at this distance, it was compelling. Eerie. It seemed to glow.

A ring with a large red brilliant stone.

The priest, his pistol still raised, swung toward the open door to the sacristy. Though he couldn't possibly see Drew in the darkness back there, Drew had the terrible sense that their gazes met. His jaw set grimly, the priest stalked toward the altar railing.

Drew tightened his finger on the Mauser's trigger. He didn't know whether to shoot the man or to question him. After all, the man had saved his life.

Or had he? Two priests just tried to kill me. Hal's dead. And this guy looks like he'd kick your teeth in for penance if he didn't like what you told him in confession. Why was he hiding in the chapel? What in God's name is going on?

The priest lunged out of sight, ducking for cover beneath the altar railing.

Drew held his breath.

The voice from out there was full-throated, husky, tinged with a Slavic accent. 'I know you're in the sacristy. Listen to what I tell you. Yanus.'

With difficulty, Drew controlled his breathing.

'Yanus,' the Slavic voice repeated. 'We have to talk about Yanus.'

Drew's delicately balanced choices tipped. Hearing sudden footsteps rushing along the corridor outside, louder as they neared the chapel, he bolted.

10

He wasn't the only one. As voices entered the chapel the priest ran too, leaping the altar railing, charging toward the sacristy.

Drew reached the door that led to another hallway and yanked it open. At noon, when he'd helped Hal prepare for mass, he'd glanced beyond the door and seen a stairwell angling up. But now, at night, without the sun streaming through a window, he couldn't see the stairs.

Not that it mattered. He didn't intend to use them. Instead he sprinted straight ahead, toward a tunnel's entrance. He didn't know where it led, but he did know this – the two priests who'd tried to kill him had acted with such professional detachment that they would surely have followed other professional standards and not have moved alone. In case Drew had managed to escape, there'd be other assassins watching the stairs up from this basement. As soon as they heard him approaching, they'd prepare themselves for the kill. If there'd been time, he could have tried to mount the stairs silently. But behind him, the pursuing footsteps of the priest who'd hidden in the confessional forced Drew to take the route he hoped was least expected and one that the hit team possibly didn't even know about. In that case, all he had to deal with was the priest chasing after him.

The footsteps came closer.

Far back, other footsteps charged into the chapel.

Drew hurried through blackness. He walloped against a table, battering his thighs, wincing as the impact scraped the bottom of the table's legs across the concrete floor.

He turned. Though he saw nothing, he heard the subtle crunch of carefully lowered shoes, the brush of stealthy footsteps coming toward him. Drew resisted the urge to shoot. The Mauser's muzzle flash would reveal his position. And what would be the use if he couldn't see his target? True, he could try to judge his opponent's location from the sounds he made. But suppose his opponent made deceptive noises to trick him? If Drew fired, the muzzle flash would doom him. Of course, he could stay where he was, crouching to one side. After all, the dark was his specialty. Hand-to-hand combat with total sightlessness. But that type of combat was painstaking, time-consuming. To do it properly, which meant to survive, required the care of a specialist defusing a bomb.

Drew didn't have the time for care. He had to get out of here. Voices echoed from the sacristy. He thought about the likelihood that other assassins were waiting in the retreat house and listened to the solitary footsteps shifting toward him.

'You don't understand,' the Slavic voice whispered. 'I don't want to hurt you. Yanus. We need to talk about Yanus. I'm here to protect you.'

Disoriented, Drew couldn't afford to believe him. He hurried forward again. His pursuer followed. When Drew stopped, his pursuer stopped.

'You must let me explain,' the Slavic voice hissed.

No way, Drew thought, plunging forward again. I don't know who you are or if you're even a priest. I don't know who the hell tried to kill me in there or why. But I do know this. I tried to do this by the rules. I got in touch with my confessor, my control. I trusted my superiors in the Church (Drew almost substituted 'network'). But someone else isn't playing by the rules. There's been an informer. A leak. Someone's told them where I was.

So now I'll play by my own rules. I'll do this my way.

He charged through spiderwebs, feeling them stick to his face. Water dripped. He smelled fetid dankness and mold. Behind, the footsteps continued after him. As he splashed through a pool of water, feeling it soak his shoes and pants, he heard the echo of voices far back in the tunnel. The group that had entered the chapel now came this way. He hurried on. Too soon, the man behind him splashed through the water. The voices seemed louder behind him. Turning to listen, he slammed the side of his head against a pipe that stretched from one wall to the other. He reeled back, seeing crimson behind his eyes, clutching the lump that began, to swell. Feeling moisture in his hair, he lowered his fingers to his mouth, relieved when he tasted the salt of sweat, not the copper of blood. He scurried forward again.

What was the tunnel used for? Where did it go? He stooped as he rushed, protecting his head from other pipes. But as he bumped past a row of insulated ducts against the left wall, he guessed that it must be a maintenance tunnel. Sure. The water and heating systems must be routed through here, he thought, making it easy for the seminary's work crew to make repairs. If so, the tunnel must lead to the seminary building. With a goal at last in mind, he felt better. But something was wrong. The sounds behind him had stopped.

Why?

Ahead of him, he struck a wall. His nose stung.

He'd been wrong – the tunnel was a trap! And now his pursuer waited back there.

Drew clutched the Mauser, turned, and squinted uselessly toward the pitch-black gauntlet through which he'd have to return. He felt along the wall to his left, inching back the way he'd come. But as his shoes touched a chunk of broken concrete on the floor, the sound of his own footsteps changed. He stopped and frowned. Easing forward again, he heard the scuff of his shoes return to the narrow echo he'd been used to. He tried an experiment, took three steps back, and the echo became more full again.

Understanding, he groped toward the wall across from him, and as he expected, where the wall should have been, his hand touched nothing. His foot struck concrete, though. He raised the foot, and now it, like his hand, touched nothing. A little higher, concrete again. A stairwell! He scurried up.

The stairway turned. He reached a wooden door, turned the knob, and pulled it. Nothing happened, He had a sudden intuition, pushed instead of pulled, and exhaled as the door swung open. In case someone was hiding behind it, he shoved it against a wall, then peered out, facing a dimly lit hall. The tunnel had led him to the seminary building.

Seeing no one, he lunged to the left. He reached a large room: sofas, chairs, tables, a television. Moonlight gleamed through windows, revealing the lawn in front of the building. Beyond the lawn would be the forest and the mountains. Safety.

But he had to leave before a seminarian found him or his pursuers intercepted him. Passing the room, he entered a lobby, seeing a door on his left that led outside. But as he moved in that direction, he heard the rustle of cloth behind him. Pivoting, he aimed the Mauser and froze.

'Oh, Jesus, thank you.'

Drew's scalp tingled.

'I knew you'd come.' From the dark, the voice sounded desperate, ancient, brittle. 'Deliver me. You know how much I've suffered.' The voice began to sob. 'They won't believe that your mother sings to me each night.'

From a shadowy corner, an apparition appeared. An old stooped man. His hair and beard were white. He wore a white nightgown.

Drew's stomach felt chilled. The old man clutched a staff. His feet were bare. His eyes gleamed insanely.

Dear God, Drew thought, I'm not in the seminary building. I passed that staircase. I went farther. I'm in the rest home. This is the old priest that Hal said he'd brought here. This is where they keep –

The old man knelt, pressing his hands together, peering up in rapture. 'But thank you, Jesus.' The old man wept. 'You'll make them understand. You'll tell them I wasn't lying about your blessed mother. I've waited so long for you to deliver me.'

Drew stumbled back in horror. The old man gasped, and Drew thought that he might be having a heart attack. But he was only inhaling, beginning to sing.

'No, please,' Drew said.

The brittle voice cracked in its frenzy. 'Holy Go-od, we praise Thy name. Lord Almighty, we wor-ship, ad-ore Thee.'

Drew rushed toward the door that led outside.

Upstairs, a man's voice scolded. 'Father Lawrence, have you snuck out of your room again? You know you're not supposed to sing at night. You'll wake –'

'A miracle!' the old man yelled. 'A miracle!' He burst into song again. 'In-fi-nite, Thy va-aaa-st domain.'

11

Drew charged outside, breathing the cold air, feeling it sting his nostrils. He raced down concrete steps, sprinting across the lawn through the dark, the frost-hardened grass crunching under his shoes.

To his left, he saw that all the lights were on in the seminary building. The seminarians crowded outside, staring toward the retreat house farther to the left. Some ran toward it; others had already reached it, scrambling inside.

The retreat house itself was dark. But abruptly it began to brighten, first floor, second floor, third floor, every window gleaming in rapid succession.

Why? Drew wondered as he ran. Do they think I'm still in the building, or are they looking for somebody else? The priest who chased me, the rest of the death team?

Shouts filled the night. He sprinted harder as other lights came on, directly behind him, from the rest home. Their sudden blaze stretched far enough for him to see the shadow he cast ahead of him and the thick gasps of frost exploding from his mouth.

Someone yelled, so near that Drew turned. A tall man in a bathrobe stood at the rest home's open door, pointing in Drew's direction. He scrambled down the steps, but his stride was awkward. He lost a slipper, stumbled and fell.

Still, his shouts had attracted attention. A group of seminarians sprinted toward the fallen man in front of the rest home. Another group raced after Drew.

He thought he was seeing things. A chunk of grass erupted ahead of him, but he didn't hear the shot. It might have been muffled by his hoarse rapid breathing and the frantic yells behind him. Or the weapon might have had a silencer. All he knew was that, as he reached the edge of the light coming from the rest home, another chunk flew up ahead of him. He veered, beginning to zigzag.

Now he heard, not the next shot itself, but the *whump!* as another bullet tore up grass. The angle was such that the sniper had to be ahead of him. On the wooded slope.

And I'm in the middle, Drew thought, hearing the seminarians rushing after him. Did they know about the sniper? Would they stop when they realized?

But instead the sniper stopped, and with a final burst of speed, Drew lunged through bushes into the greater darkness of the forest.

His chest felt tight. Bent low, he shifted past trees, through undergrowth, over a fallen trunk. With a disconcerting sense of déjà vu, he recalled his escape from the monastery. But the parallel wasn't exact. Six nights ago, the marksman on the hill hadn't known that Drew was out of the building, stalking him. And Drew had not been chased. Now he couldn't take the time to stalk the sniper without his pursuers catching him; and if he concentrated on eluding his pursuers, he might head into the sniper's sights.

'It's going down to thirty tonight,' Hal had said.

Drew wasn't dressed for that. The lightweight black pants, cotton sweatshirt, and unlined jacket that Hal had brought him were useless against the cold. Already, despite the burning in his lungs, Drew shivered, his sweat absorbing the forest's chill. He could have easily survived in the insulating wool of the robe that he'd worn in the monastery. But what he now wore retained the cold instead of protecting him against it. If he spent all night in the woods, he would risk being overcome by hypothermia. And that took only three hours before it killed.

The Mauser's cold metal numbed his hand. He snuck past a deadfall, creeping deeper into the forest. Behind him, bodies charged through bushes. Branches snapped.

Would the sniper decide that the situation was out of control and back away? But even then, Drew realized, the seminarians won't stop chasing me.

What I need is a car.

The Cadillac that Hal had used to bring him here. It was parked somewhere. From his second-floor retreat house window, Drew had watched Hal drive it around to the back of the seminary building. There had to be a garage in back. Hadn't Hal insisted that the seminarians weren't supposed to see it?

Avoiding the threats behind and ahead, Drew veered to the right. He'd been angling in that direction already but his eventual plan had been to head deeper into the woods. Until now, however, it hadn't occurred to him to move in a semicircle, doubling back toward the seminary. After all, what would have been the point? Crossing the open lawn, he'd again have been a target. And what would have been his goal? He wanted to get away from here, not hide as he'd done at the monastery. But how?

12

He stepped from the trees to the edge of the lawn. Behind, he heard his pursuers thrashing deeper into the forest. Before him, lights continued to gleam in the rest home, seminary, and retreat house. Figures still milled in front of the buildings.

Those figures would see him, of course, if he crossed the lawn from here, so he decided to follow the edge of the forest. The grass was silent, and the dark of the woods behind him hid his silhouette. He moved toward the area behind the buildings, risked exposing himself, and sprinted toward the rear of the seminary.

No one raised an alarm.

His suspicion proved correct. In a section behind the seminary – the lights were much less bright back here – he found a cinderblock structure with five garage doors. The first two he tested were locked. But the third budged when he tugged up on the handle.

He raised it slowly, trying to make as little sound as possible. The glimmer of moonlight showed him the bishop's black Cadillac. Drew assumed that Hal had left this garage door unlocked in case he had to leave quickly. He opened the driver's door, and the inside lights came on. Normally he would have turned them off, afraid of making himself a target. But now he so appreciated the lights that he propped the door open, lying on his back, peering beneath the dashboard, finding the wires he needed. He pressed two together. They bypassed the Cadillac's ignition and started the engine.

It purred. He scrambled behind the steering wheel and slammed the door. Again, as in the van that he'd driven from Vermont, the dashboard confused him. He wasn't sure how to turn on the headlights. Not that it mattered. The last thing he wanted now was headlights. He pressed his foot on the accelerator and rocketed the Cadillac from the garage.

The car gained speed so rapidly that, before he could turn, he left the driveway and jounced over a concrete curb, his head snapping back. He swung the steering wheel and skidded sideways across the grass. A clatter behind him suggested that the impact against the curb had dislodged a hubcap. He kept turning sharply left and felt the Cadillac's wheels gouging furrows in the lawn. Then he straightened the car, came back down off the grass and the curb to the driveway, and drove along the side wall of the seminary. The lane would curve to the left in front of the seminary, he anticipated, take him past the retreat house, and finally curve again, this time to the right, leading him through the woods beyond the lawn, toward the metal gate and the public road.

But he wasn't about to try to pass the figures in front of those buildings. Instead, as he left the side of the seminary, he aimed straight ahead, struck yet another curb, and fishtailed across the grass until the tires gripped, gaining traction, tearing up more lawn.

He sped across it. His window was down. He heard shouts. Figures bolted toward him from the buildings. Ahead, he saw utter blackness. With his headlights off, he didn't know where to steer to reach the continuation of the lane. For all he knew, he'd soon crash into the forest. He tapped his brakes, then realized that his taillights would flash, so that even without headlights, he'd be making himself a target.

Damned if he did, and damned if he didn't.

Why not, then?

He pawed at knobs and levers and, with seconds to spare, turned on the headlights as the forest's black wall loomed before him. Wrenching the steering wheel to the left, he scraped past a tree and heard the Cadillac's right rear fender crunch. Then he saw the road and aimed down its wooden tunnel. For a moment, he felt relieved. But at once his scalp froze – ahead he saw the priest from the chapel, the one with the dark hair, mustache, and Slavic features. The one with the .45 automatic pistol.

The priest stood with his legs apart, facing Drew's onrushing car, blocking the road. The Cadillac's headlights glinted off the priest's white collar. They flashed off the disturbing red ring on his left hand, the hand he used to raise the pistol.

Drew pressed the accelerator, feeling his stomach surge against his spine, aiming the Cadillac toward the priest. The trees pressed narrowly on each side.

Instead of shooting, the priest frantically waved his hands, signaling Drew to stop.

No way, Drew thought. He steadied the steering wheel and pressed even harder on the accelerator.

The priest kept waving his hands, his gestures urgent, his body larger and larger through the windshield.

Two seconds would have made the difference.

But the priest turned sideways, darting back to the left, aiming. Drew's ears were stunned by the .45's roar. Only the priest hadn't shot toward the Cadillac. He had shot above it, beyond the car's roof.

An automatic rifle rattled fiercely from the forest on Drew's right. Bullets smashed against the Cadillac. Windows ruptured, chunks of glass showering Drew.

Desperate, he tried to steer at the same time he shielded his eyes from the flying glass. He sensed the priest falling back toward the woods. The road curved, narrowing. Trees scraped the car. A sudden jolt in the rear suggested that the bumper had snagged on something. As his headlights gleamed down a straightaway, the Cadillac like a rocket again, Drew saw the high stone wall on either side. The metal gate was before him.

But the gate was shut. Another automatic weapon rattled behind him. He strengthened his grip on the steering wheel.

Thirty feet.

Twenty.

Ten.

13

The impact threw him forward against the steering wheel. Groaning from the pain in his ribs, he heard a sharp blat from the horn and rebounded against the seat.

The front of the Cadillac buckled. A headlight shattered. Glass arched, glinting in the glare from the other headlight. The chrome rim around the headlight frisbeed through the air. A chunk of metal starred the Cadillac's windshield. Drew fought to control the broken steering wheel. To his right and left, the metal gate separated. Bent, the sections walloped against the stone wall on either side.

Though he stomped the brakes, the Cadillac shot across the road. A ditch opened up before him, and the car flew across the gap. Dipping, it hit a stretch of grass, skidded ahead, veered sideways, and jerked to a stop. Drew stared. Another ten feet, and the Cadillac would have struck a jumble of trees and rocks. His chest arched, making him wince when he breathed.

He shook his head to clear it. Have to get away. The headlight on the left still gleamed, though the force of hitting the gate had deflected its aim toward the right. Steam hissed from the radiator. The engine still worked, though its purr had become a clatter.

He tried the accelerator. The car responded sluggishly, crossing the stretch of grass. The suspension had been destroyed, jostling him every time he hit a bump. He reached a stream, turned left to avoid it, and found a shallow part of the ditch. A little encouragement, and the car went down, then up to the road. He increased speed.

But the right front wheel had a wobble now. The speedometer – digital like the clock – showed zero. The engine wheezed, and the radiator hissed. He didn't know how far or fast he could go. If the engine overheated, it might be ruined.

That struck him as funny. Ruined? The bishop's Cadillac was a total wreck as it was. He couldn't cause it much more damage.

But the car amazed him. It kept going. And that too struck him as funny. Takes a licking, keeps on ticking.

He glanced toward his rear-view mirror, wanting to check for pursuing headlights. But he couldn't find the mirror. Squinting down, he saw it on the floor.

Nothing was funny after that.

He turned left at the first intersection, then right at the next, five miles farther on, anxious to lose his pursuers in a maze of mountain roads.

His chest tightened, pinching him. The broken steering wheel felt awkward in his hand. When he next turned right, sensing the looming mountains around him, he made out a road sign that told him a town called Lenox was twelve miles in the opposite direction.

Lenox? The name nudged his memory. The little red house. He'd never been there, but he knew that the town and that house were famous.

Hawthorne once had lived there. Hal hadn't lied when he'd said that they'd driven to western Massachusetts. I'm in the Berkshire Hills.

And Pittsfield ought to be close, where Melville had lived. Melville, who'd often ridden down to visit Hawthorne, wanting so much to be Hawthorne's friend that he'd written *Moby Dick* for him.

There were ghosts around him. Drew's reverie ended as the pain in his chest made him cough. The engine was overheating. He heard it straining. The radiator no longer hissed.

Because it was empty.

The car began to slow. A piece of grill fell off, clanging on the road. He chugged past a dark country store, lurched into a sleepy town, and as the engine coughed, dying, he glided to a stop in front of a dingy house whose lawn was badly in need of mowing.

Though the house was dark, a corner streetlight showed motorcycles propped against the side and front of the listing porch. He left the Cadillac and soon discovered that none of the motorcycles was chained to anything.

How trustful. They probably figure that no one would dare to fool with them. Well, I'm in the mood.

He chose the biggest Harley-Davidson and pushed it down the street. Among trees, he emptied the chopper's saddlebags, which were stuffed with tools and an old leather jacket. He exposed the electrical system and hot-wired the bike as he had the Cadillac. To start the engine, he had to straddle the seat and stomp down on the ignition lever. The engine rumbled to life.

He hadn't ridden a motorcycle in almost ten years, since the time he'd used one in an operation that required him to –

No. He shook his head. He didn't want to remember.

The cold October air stung his face as he twisted the throttle lever and roared through the night. He wondered how the bikers would react in the morning. Would they feel so angered by the stolen bike that they'd strip what was left of the Cadillac and sell the parts for revenge? He wiped away the tears that the wind forced from his eyes. The bishop's Cadillac. Four wheels and a board. He knew he shouldn't find that thought amusing. All the same he did, just as he felt exhilarated by the powerful roaring thrust of the Harley under him, taking him back to Boston.

And some answers.

14

'Father Hafer, please.' Drew kept his voice flat, standing in a phone booth next to a service station, just after 8 A.M., struggling to hide his anger. His hands were numb. He shivered from the cold wind that had buffeted him all night. The morning sun, bringing a hint of Indian summer, blessedly warmed the booth.

The male voice who'd answered the phone at Holy Eucharist Rectory didn't reply.

'Can't you hear me?' Despite Drew's effort, he couldn't keep rage from his voice. He wanted explanations. Who screwed up? Why had he been attacked at the seminary? By priests! 'I said I want to speak to Father Hafer.'

He glanced angrily through the dusty glass of the booth toward the road out front, checking for motorcyclists, cops, anybody who showed an interest in him. His plan had been to go all the way into Boston, but he'd gotten too cold and had to stop in Concord, nineteen miles to the west.

The voice on the phone still didn't reply.

Stalling for time? Drew thought. Was the call being traced?

Abruptly the man said, 'Just a moment.'

Drew heard a thump as the phone was set down. Voices murmured in the background.

I'll give him twenty more seconds, Drew thought. Then I'm hanging up.

'Hello?' A different male voice. 'Did you say you wanted to speak with –?'

'*Father Hafer*. What's the problem?'

'Who is this, please?'

Drew became apprehensive. 'A friend of his.'

'Then you obviously haven't heard.'

'Heard *what*?'

'I'm sorry to have to tell you like this. It seems so impersonal over the phone . . . I'm afraid he's dead.'

The booth seemed to tilt.

'But that's . . .' The word 'impossible' stuck in Drew's throat. 'I saw him early yesterday morning.'

'It happened last night.'

109

'*But how?*' Drew's voice was hoarse with shock. 'He was dying. I know that. But he told me the doctors had given him till the end of the year.'

'Yes, but it wasn't his illness that killed him.'

15

Stunned, Drew hung up. He forced himself to move, knowing he had to get out of Concord as soon as possible – in case his call had indeed been traced. He needed a place where he'd feel secure.

To allow himself the luxury of grief.

To try to understand.

The trip to Lexington farther east, eleven miles from Boston, did not register on his brain. He remembered none of it, his eyes – his consciousness – misted with pain. He left the motorcycle on a quiet side street doubting that the report of its theft would have reached the Lexington police this soon.

In brilliant sunshine that mocked his gloom, he wandered through the village green, pretending interest in the spot where America's War for Independence had begun.

His fists clenched, he barely noticed the golden autumn trees, or the smell of woodsmoke, or the rustle of fallen leaves beneath his feet. His mind was too full of sorrow and rage.

Last night, Father Hafer had received a phone call at the rectory. He'd told the other priests that he had to go out. He'd crossed the street to the sidewalk in front of the church, where a car had struck him. On the sidewalk. The force of the impact had thrown him all the way up the steps and against the church's front door.

('He couldn't have suffered.'

'But . . . how do you know?'

'There was so much blood. The driver didn't stop. He must have been drunk. To lose control like that, to veer off the street. The police haven't found him yet but when they do . . . The law isn't strict enough. The poor man had so little time left. To have it stupidly wasted by an irresponsible drunk!')

Drew clenched his fists harder as he walked, oblivious to the crunch of leaves.

Received a phone call? Hit by a car while he stood on the sidewalk? The principal link between my former life and the monastery killed by a drunk?

Like hell.

Drew felt the bulge in his jacket pocket. The plastic bag. The body of Stuart Little. He thought of the dead monks. Now he had something else to make someone pay for.

110

16

'Put me through to the bishop.' Drew's voice was hoarse as he stood in the phone booth, glancing toward his motorcycle on the side street, then toward the tourists on the green.

'I'm terribly sorry . . .'

Drew recognized the resonant voice. It belonged to Paul, the man the bishop had spoken to on his office intercom two nights ago.

'. . . but his Excellency isn't available now. If you'd care to leave your name and number.'

'That's all right. He'll talk to me.'

'And who . . .'

'Just tell him the man with the mouse.'

'Yes, that's correct. He wants to talk with you.'

Drew heard a sudden click. He glanced at his watch and made a bet with himself: fifteen seconds. But the bishop came on the phone even sooner, in twelve.

'Where *are* you? I've been waiting for your call. What happened at the –'

'Seminary? Funny thing. I was hoping you'd tell me.'

'Make sense. My phone's been ringing since five A.M. about this. I asked you what –'

'Two priests tried to kill me, that's what!' Drew felt like slamming a fist through the glass of the booth. 'They did kill Hal. And someone else, another priest, was hiding in the confessional!'

'Have you gone insane?'

Drew froze.

'Two priests tried to kill you? What are you talking about? Hal's dead? I just received a note from him. What I want to know is why you shot at those seminarians. Why did you break into the rest home, scare those priests half to death, and steal my car?'

Drew's heart felt squeezed by ice.

'And something else – this fantasy of yours,' the bishop said.

'*Fantasy?*'

'About the monastery. Thank God, I took the precaution of sending those Jesuits to investigate. If the cardinal and I had decided to alert the police it would have been a disaster. There aren't any bodies in that monastery.'

'*What?*'

'There aren't any monks at all. The place is deserted. I don't understand where they went, but until I learn a *lot* more about this situation, I don't intend to make a fool of the Church.'

Drew's voice shook with rage. 'So you chose the first option, the cover-up. And you're leaving me out here alone.'

'I don't intend to leave you out there. Believe me, I want some answers. Listen carefully. It isn't wise for you to come to my office. I'll tell you where to report.'

'Forget it.'

'Don't speak to me that way. You'll report to the address I'm about to give you.'

111

'No.'

'I'm warning you. Don't compound the trouble you're in. You vowed obedience. Your bishop is giving you an order.'

'I won't obey it. I tried things your way. They didn't work.'

'I'm very displeased by your attitude.'

'Wait till you see your car.' Drew slammed down the phone.

17

Impatient, he straddled the motorcycle. His chest, already in pain from the impact of the steering wheel against it, ached more sharply from grief and rage. He kicked down on the ignition lever. The engine rumbling, he grabbed the throttle.

But where could he go? What should he do?

The Church, it was now clear, could not be considered a refuge. Someone somewhere in the chain of command could not be trusted. The bishop perhaps, though not necessarily – he might very well be sincere, as confused as Drew himself.

Then what about Paul, the bishop's assistant? But the bishop had treated Paul with absolute trust.

Then who? And more important, why?

And what about the Slavic priest with the strange red gleaming ring and the .45, who'd hidden in the chapel's confessional?

All right. Drew bit his lip. The Church no longer mattered. God did. Drew's own survival. To save his soul.

He had to forget that he'd joined the monastery. He had to ignore his retreat from his former life.

Pretend that you're still in the network, he told himself. What would you have done if you couldn't trust it, if you feared an enemy within it?

The answer was obvious. Instinctive. But tainted with pride, for which he begged God's forgiveness. He'd once been the best. He could still be the best. Six years meant nothing.

Yes. He twisted the throttle, roaring away, determined. But not toward Boston now. Not east, but south.

New York. To the only people he could depend on. To his former lover and his former friend, Arlene and Jake.

PART FOUR
RESURRECTION

SATAN'S HORN

1

The brownstone on Twelfth Street, near Washington Square, was familiar
to him from the old days. Of course a stranger might now be living there,
Drew thought, so before he began his surveillance, he took the precaution
of finding a phone booth whose residential directory had miraculously not
been stolen by vandals. His pulse sped as he flipped through the pages for
H, moved his finger down one list, and exhaled, finding Hardesty, Arlene
and Jake.

The same address.

That didn't mean Arlene and Jake were in town. For sure, Drew wasn't
about to put in the effort of watching the house unless he knew it was
occupied. The problem was that he couldn't simply call to find out – the
phone might be tapped, and he didn't want to let his enemies know he was
in the neighborhood. They might have figured he'd try to contact Arlene
and Jake.

He chained the motorcycle to a metal fence near Washington Square
and strolled through the large square park, ignoring the junkies and
dealers who slumped on benches. He passed the playground equipment,
gravitating toward the huge graffiti-covered arch that marked the beginning of Fifth Avenue, the wide majestic thoroughfare stretching north
as far as he could see. The sky was gray, but the temperature was
warm, upper fifties, and the customary crowd of park musicians gathered
beneath the arch, playing mournfully, as if the omen of the dismal sky was
sufficient warning that they wouldn't be using the park much longer.

'You want to earn five dollars?'

The young man he'd chosen sat to the side of the arch, beneath a leafless
tree, replacing a broken string on his guitar. Long blond hair, a beard,
CCNY jacket, a rip in the knee of his jeans, and a toe coming out of one
sneaker. Glancing up, the young man said – his voice surprisingly guttural
– 'Get lost.'

'Don't get me wrong. This isn't an obscene proposition. And it isn't
illegal. All you have to do is make a phone call for me. I tell you what. I'll
even raise the price to ten.'

'Just to make a phone call?'

'I'm feeling generous.'

'It isn't obscene or illegal?'

115

'I guarantee it.'

'Twenty.'

'Done. I'm pressed for time.'

He could have paid the young man even more. Last night, he'd gone hunting, walking dark streets, making himself a target for predators. Three times he'd attracted attention, confronted respectively by a pistol, a knife, and a club. He'd left each mugger with broken kneecaps and elbows ('For your penance. Go in peace and sin no more') and taken whatever money they had. The mugging business was lucrative. His total take was two hundred and twenty-three dollars, enough to buy an earth-tone Thinsulate-padded coat and a pair of wool gloves this morning. But though he could afford to be generous with what was left over, he didn't want to give this young man so much money that common sense would suggest that something was terribly wrong.

As it was, the young man seemed unable to believe his good fortune. He stood, suspicious. 'So where's the money?'

'Half now, half later. The way this works, we find a phone booth. I touch the numbers for you. I give you the phone. If a man answers, ask if he's Jake. Tell him you live down the street, and you're angry about the noise from last night's party. It kept you awake.'

'Did he have a party?'

'Doubt it. Who knows? But stick to your story. Slam the phone back on the hook. If a woman answers, use the same story, but ask if she's Arlene.'

'What's this supposed to prove?'

'Isn't it obvious? That either Jake or Arlene is home.'

Five minutes later, the young man stepped from a nearby phone booth. 'A woman,' he said. 'Arlene.'

2

As usual, Drew started three blocks away from his target, walking with apparent leisure along Twelfth Street, seemingly indifferent to the neighborhood while studying every detail ahead of him. In keeping with so many other skills he'd reactivated, his instinct for surveillance had not been blunted by his years of inactivity. Nor had the pleasure he'd always taken from it. He let his mind luxuriate in the memory of how he'd first learned.

Hong Kong, 1962. When he was twelve. His 'Uncle' Ray had been distressed because Drew was playing hooky from the private school in which most parents at the embassy enrolled their children. Ray's distress had been even greater when he learned what Drew was doing – roaming with Chinese street kids, hanging around the slums and the docks.

'But why?' Ray asked. 'An unattended American boy in some parts of this city – *those* parts – can get himself killed. One morning, the police'll find you floating dead in the harbor.'

'But I'm not alone.'

'You mean those kids you hang around with? They're used to surviving in the streets. And they're Chinese, they fit in.'

116

'That's what I want to learn. To fit in on the streets here, even though I'm American.'

'It's a wonder those kids don't just beat you up instead of accepting you.'

'No. You see, I give them my allowance, food from home, clothes I've grown out of.'

'Good God, why is it so important?' Ray's usually ruddy face had lost its color. 'Because of your parents? Because of what happened to them? Even after two years?'

Drew's tortured eyes said everything.

The next time he played hooky, prowling the streets with the Chinese gang, Ray offered a compromise.

'You can't keep doing this. I mean it, Drew. It's too dangerous. What you think you're learning isn't worth the risk. Don't take me wrong. The way you feel about what happened to your parents, that's your business. Who am I to say you're wrong? But at least do it properly.'

Drew squinted, intrigued.

'To start with, don't settle for fifth-rate teachers. And for heaven's sake, don't ignore the things you can learn at school. They're just as important. Believe me, someone who doesn't understand history, logic, mathematics, and the arts is just as defenseless as someone who doesn't understand the streets.'

Drew's expression changed to puzzlement.

'Oh, I don't expect you to understand what I mean right away. But I think you respect me enough to know that I'm not a fool.'

'Fifth-rate teachers?'

'Promise that you won't miss any more school, that your grades won't be less than Bs. In return . . .' Ray debated with himself.

'In return?'

'I'll arrange for you to have a proper teacher. Someone who really knows the streets, who can give you the discipline that your friends in the gang can't.'

'Who?'

'Remember our bargain?'

'But *who*?'

Thus began one of the most exciting times of Drew's life. After school the next day, Ray escorted him to a restaurant in downtown Hong Kong where the food though Oriental, was not Chinese. And where the owner – amazingly short, round-faced, always grinning, old but with gleaming black hair – was introduced to him as Tommy Limbu.

'Tommy's a Gurkha,' Ray explained. 'Of course, he's retired now.'

'Gurkha? What's a . . .'

Tommy and Ray laughed.

'See, you're learning something already. A Gurkha' – Ray turned with deference to Tommy, almost bowing – 'is the finest mercenary soldier in the world. They come from a town by that name in Nepal, a mountainous state north of India. The region's principal business is export. Soldiers. Mostly for the British and Indian armies. When the job's too tough for any other soldier, they send in the Gurkhas. And the job gets done. You see that curved knife in a scabbard mounted on the wall behind the bar?'

Drew nodded.

'It's called a *kukri*. It's the Gurkhas' trademark. The sight of it will make most otherwise tough men afraid.'

Drew glanced with skepticism toward the short, grinning, seemingly ineffectual Nepalese, then back toward the knife. 'Can I hold it? Can I touch the blade?'

'You wouldn't like the consequences,' Ray said 'The Gurkhas have a rule. If you draw the knife from its sheath, you also have to draw blood. If not your enemy's, then your own.'

Drew's mouth hung open.

Tommy laughed, his eyes glinting. 'Good gracious me.' He surprised Drew not only by his genteel English but by his British accent. 'We mustn't scare the boy. My heavens, no. He'll think I'm an awful terror.'

'Tommy lives in Hong Kong because many Gurkhas are stationed at the British barracks here,' Ray explained. 'Off-duty, they like to come here for a meal. And of course, they remember him from when he belonged to the regiment.'

'You'll be my teacher?' Drew asked, still skeptical about this eager-to-please, jolly man.

'My, my, no.' Tommy's voice was mellifluous, almost as if he were singing. 'Dear me, my bones are too old. I'd never have the energy to keep up with a dervish such as yourself. And I have my business to manage.'

'Then?'

'Another boy, of course.' With gleeful pride, Tommy turned to a child who, unnoticed by Drew, had silently come up beside him. A miniature image of Tommy, even shorter than Drew, though Drew would later learn that the boy was fourteen.

'Ah, there you are,' Tommy proclaimed. 'My grandson.' He chuckled and turned to Drew. 'His father belongs to the local battalion and prefers to have the child stay with me instead of in Nepal. They visit when he's on leave, though in truth that seldom happens. At the moment, he's helping to settle an unsavory but no doubt minor altercation in South Africa.'

As Drew later learned, Tommy Two's last name was the consequence of the British attempt to deal with the confusing similarity of names among a people who referred to themselves by the tribes they belonged to (hence the elder Tommy's last name, Limbu). Because the bureaucracy couldn't distinguish one Tommy Limbu from the other, at least on paper, Two had been chosen instead of Junior.

But Tommy Two was essentially different from his grandfather. He didn't smile. He didn't even say hello. Drew sensed his disinterest and, overcome with misgivings, couldn't help wondering how they would ever get along – or what this sullen boy could possibly teach him.

His misgivings waned within half an hour. Left alone by the adults, they went out onto the narrow busy street, where Tommy Two informed him in perfect English that Drew was going to be taught to pick pockets.

Drew couldn't restrain his surprise. 'But Uncle Ray brought me here because the gang I hung around with was doing that stuff. He doesn't want me . . .'

'No.' Tommy Two held up a finger, like a magician. 'Not just any pocket. Mine.'

Drew's surprise increased.

'But first' – Tommy Two moved his finger back and forth – 'you have to understand how it feels to have someone do it to *you*.'

The sight of this little kid assuming command was startling. 'And you're the one who's going to do it?' Drew asked, raising his eyebrows in disbelief.

Tommy Two didn't answer. Instead, he gestured for Drew to follow him. They turned a corner and went out of sight from the restaurant. Less confident now, Drew found himself facing a still narrower street, cluttered with shoppers, bicyclists, pushcart vendors, and awninged stalls. The babble of voices, the mixture of smells, mostly rancid, were awesome.

'Count to ten,' Tommy Two announced. 'Then walk down this street. By the end of three blocks' – he pointed toward Drew's back pocket – 'I'll have your wallet.'

Drew's confusion changed to fascination. 'Three blocks, huh?' He peered down the chaotic street. Inspired, he removed his wallet from his back pocket and shoved it into a tighter pocket in front, then subdued a smirk. 'Okay, you're on. But it doesn't seem fair. I mean, while I'm counting, don't you want me to hide my eyes? To give you a chance to hide?'

'Why bother?' As glum as ever, Tommy Two walked down the street.

Drew mentally counted. One, two . . . Watched Tommy pass between a moped and a rickshaw. Three, four, five . . .

All at once, he frowned. Tommy Two had vanished. Drew straightened, staring. How had he done that? Like a stone dropped into water, Tommy Two had become absorbed within the swirling mob. By the time Drew adjusted to the trick he'd just witnessed, he realized that the remaining count of five should long ago have been over.

Trick? Sure, that was all it had been, Drew decided. A trick. Bracing his shoulders, mustering confidence, he started down the street. But as he himself became immersed in the crowd, he realized that this was more complicated than he'd first anticipated. There were too many choices. For one thing, should he walk slow or fast, be cautious or hurry? For another, should he keep glancing around, on guard against Tommy Two, or should he look straight ahead, so he'd be able to avoid –

A bicyclist sped by so close that Drew was forced to jump to the right, jarring an elderly Chinese woman carrying a basket of laundry. She barked what must have been unfriendly things at him in Chinese, which he didn't understand. All the kids in the street gang had been better at his language than he was at theirs. Maybe Uncle Ray was right about school having its advantages. Hearing a shout behind him, Drew turned in reflexive alarm, but never did learn its source. He stumbled on a crack in the cobbled road and banged against a pushcart filled with fruit. The elbow of his shirt came away wet with juice. As the vendor shrilled at him, Drew almost stopped to pay the man, then he realized that if he took out his wallet . . .

Tommy Two. Drew swung around, suspicious, feeling his stomach flutter, rushing forward through the crowd. The vendor kept yelling at him. But soon the yells were swallowed by inviting cries from hucksters in stalls that flanked the street. The smells worsened – stale cooking oil, charred meat, rotten vegetables. Drew began to feel sick.

Nonetheless, he hurried. He had to keep his mind on his wallet. Pressing his hand against the satisfying bulge in his front pants pocket, he reached the second block. Now he noticed the attention he attracted, a Caucasian among an even denser throng of Orientals. He darted his eyes in every direction before him, searching for a hint of Tommy Two, and entered the final block.

Walking fast, he felt relieved when he saw the end of the swarming gauntlet before him and a prominent sign, HARRY'S HONG KONG BAR AND GRILL. He used the sign as a beacon, dodged a man without legs who pushed himself on a platform equipped with rollers, and swelled in triumph as he noticed Tommy Two lounging against the wall on the corner beneath the sign. With a grin, he crossed the teeming intersection and stopped.

'So what's so hard about it?' Drew shrugged with disdain. 'I should have made a bet that I could do it.'

'How would you have paid?'

Troubled, Drew reached for the wallet in his front pocket. 'With this, of course.' But even as he touched the wallet, he knew that something was wrong. Pulling it out, he blushed. The wallet was dirty, made of cloth. His had been brand-new polished leather. And this one, when he looked inside, was empty. He opened his mouth, but no words came out.

'Would this be what you're looking for?' Tommy Two pulled a hand from behind his back and held up the trophy. 'I agree with you. We should have made a wager.' But this round-faced boy with gleaming black hair, three inches shorter than Drew though older, showed no satisfaction in his triumph – no grin, no swagger, no ridicule.

'How did you do it?'

'Distraction is always the key. I kept pace with you, out of sight in the crowd. When you mashed the vendor man's fruit, you were too confused to notice that I'd switched wallets with you. All you cared about was that you still felt something in your pocket.'

Drew scowled, angry that he'd been made a fool of. 'So that's all there is to it? It's easy. Now that I know what's up, I'd never get caught that way again.'

Tommy Two shrugged. 'We shall see. You still have thirty minutes remaining in your lesson. Shall we try again?'

Drew was taken aback. Thirty minutes left in the lesson? Briefly he'd assumed that they were playing together. But now he realized that Tommy Two was teaching him for money.

'Try again?' Drew asked, his feelings hurt but responding again to the challenge. 'You're darn right.'

'And this time, would you care to make a wager?'

Drew almost said yes, but suspicion muted his determination. 'Not just yet.'

'As you wish.' Tommy Two straightened. 'I suggest that we use the same three blocks, but this time in the reverse, moving back to our starting point.'

Drew's hands were sweaty. Putting his own wallet back into his pocket, he watched Tommy Two again disappear like magic within the crowd.

And two blocks later when, just to be sure, Drew reached inside his pocket, he knew right away that the wallet he carried was not his own. He cursed.

As before, Tommy Two lounged against a wall at the end of the third block, showing Drew his wallet.

The next afternoon after school, Drew tried it again. The results were the same.

The next afternoon. And the next.

But each time, Tommy Two gave Drew an added piece of advice. 'To avoid an attack, you must not invite one. You have to become invisible.'

'Easy for you to say. You're Oriental. You fit in.'

'Not true. To you, an American, no doubt all Orientals seem alike. But to a Chinese, a Nepalese such as myself attracts as much attention as you. Or should.'

Drew was bewildered. 'Or should. You mean you don't?'

'I move with the rhythm of the street. I don't look at anyone's eyes. I'm never in any spot long enough to be noticed. And I draw myself in.'

'Like this?' Drew tried to squeeze his body tighter, assuming such a grotesque position that Tommy Two permitted himself a rare laugh.

'No. Good gracious me, of course not. What strange ideas you have. I mean that I draw my thoughts in. Mentally I make myself' – he grasped for the words – 'not here.'

Drew shook his head.

'In time, you will learn. But something else. You must never – never – become distracted. Allow nothing to confuse you or to disturb your concentration. Not just here while we practice. Any time. Everywhere.'

This kid's supposed to be fourteen, Drew thought. No way. Just because he's short, he thinks he can lie about his age. He has to be twenty at least. Become invisible. Move with the crowd. Don't let anything distract you. Drew tried again.

And again. Until one afternoon after school, as Drew came through another gauntlet, approaching Tommy Two, who lounged as usual against a wall, he reached in his pocket, disgusted at another failure, only to blink at the wallet he pulled out. His own. 'You let me win.'

Tommy Two soberly shook his head. 'I never let anyone win. You did what I taught you. You didn't react to the beggar who wanted money. You never glanced at the parrots on sale at that stall. Above all, you showed no interest in the cart of vegetables that overturned, but merely stepped around it, not even glancing at the peppers beneath your feet. You made it impossible for me to trick you.'

Drew's heart beat faster with pride. 'Then, I–'

'Did it once. Once is not a pattern. Are you ready to try again?'

The next time, Drew again produced his own wallet.

But Tommy Two did not congratulate him. The young yet ancient Nepalese seemed to take for granted that success was its own reward. 'Now we begin the hard part.'

'Hard?' Drew's spirits sank.

'You've proven that I can't steal your wallet. Is it possible for you to steal mine?'

Drew shifted his feet. 'Let's give it a try.'

Drew snuck through the crowd, coming from behind, seeing his

121

chance, darting forward, reaching. Tommy grabbed his hand. 'I knew where you were every second. You didn't become invisible. Try it again.'

And, 'Let the crowd absorb you.'

And, 'Anticipate what might distract me.'

'*Nothing* distracts you.'

'Then that's a problem for you to solve.'

Three days later, Drew lounged against the wall at the end of the gauntlet. When Tommy Two saw the posture, his eyes flashed with understanding. Reaching into his pocket, he pulled out the wrong wallet.

'When the orange struck my shoulder?' Tommy Two asked.

'I paid a kid to throw it at you.'

'Foolishly, I turned in that direction. Because I was sure you'd thrown it.'

'But I was behind you.'

'Excellent!' Tommy Two laughed. 'Good gracious, my, what a joke!'

'But aren't you forgetting something?'

Tommy Two looked puzzled. At once, he understood and shrugged. 'Of course.' Without a hint of disappointment, he gave Drew an American dollar.

Because this time Drew had decided to bet.

3

Proceeding down Twelfth Street, beginning his surveillance of the brownstone from three blocks away Drew realized he'd begun to think of Tommy Two. He had never seen him after the lessons were over, but Tommy and his lessons had remained vivid in his memory. He knew that Tommy would look glummer than usual – and be more sternly rebuking – if he were somehow here and knew that Drew had allowed himself to be distracted, even for an instant.

Blend with the pattern of the street. Compact your spirit. Make yourself invisible. Concentrate. Drew obeyed the silent genteel British voice and knew that everything would be okay. Composed, he stepped from the first block, crossing the noisy intersection approaching the other two blocks.

But he didn't intend to pass the midpoint of this second block. The tactic he employed required patience, circumnavigating the neighborhood, using several approaches from different directions, always narrowing the area. Confident that he attracted no attention, he crossed the street halfway down the second block and returned the way he'd come. At the intersection he headed south, walked down to Tenth Street, proceeded along it in a direction parallel to the brownstone, and eventually headed north, coming back to Twelfth. Now he was three blocks away from the brownstone again but this time coming from the opposite direction. As before, blending with the rhythms of the street, studying every detail before him, he began his reconnaissance. When he reached the middle of the second block he crossed the street again, returning.

All right, he thought, I've narrowed the perimeter and so far everything looks fine. By definition – because I haven't been attacked. If the house is being watched the spotters are within a block and a half on either side.

He knew exactly what to look for. First, a car. You had to assume that if your target left the surveillance area, he or she would get in a taxi. And that meant you needed a car to keep up. But the city's parking problem was so severe that once you found a spot, you didn't dare give it up. What's more, you had to stay near the car in case your target left quickly. Two men in a parked car would attract attention, so one man usually stayed in the car while the other man found a vantage point in a nearby building.

There were variations on these tactics, and Drew had been watching for all of them: the car whose hood was up while someone made repairs, the van with too many antennas, the man setting up an umbrella stand on the corner.

But already he'd seen what he wanted to know. At the west end of the brownstone's block, a man sat in a dark blue (the rule was never to use a bright-colored) car, more interested in the brownstone than in a platinum blonde in a tight leather suit who passed him, walking a Malamute.

Blend with the rhythm of the street, pal, Drew thought. If the occasion demands, look distracted even though you're not.

Drew wasn't sure where the other spotter was. In fact, he assumed there'd be two more in the area, one to remain near the brownstone, the third to get in the car with the driver and be let out wherever the target decided to go.

But their primary purpose, Drew reminded himself, was not to watch the Hardestys. The brownstone was just the bait. I'm the reason the spotters are here, and they'll follow Arlene and Jake only on the chance that I might try making contact somewhere other than the brownstone.

Fine, he thought. No problem. Having determined the closest safe distance from the brownstone, he hurried back to where he'd left the motorcycle near Washington Square. He unlocked the chain with which he'd secured it to a metal fence and kicked down on the starter lever, heading back to Twelfth Street. He parked between two cars three-quarters of a block behind the spotter in the car, pushed down the kickstand, leaned against the padded seat, and, shielded by the vehicle in front of him, began to wait.

4

Three hours.

Shortly after 4 P.M., as it began to drizzle, he saw a woman step out of the brownstone two blocks down. Even at this distance, her outline so small that Drew felt he was watching her through the reverse end of a telescope, he recognized her.

Arlene. His throat swelled tight till he had trouble breathing. He'd thought he'd prepared himself for the shock of seeing her again, but his pent-up emotions denied for six years, assaulted him. His love for her rushed back with a jolt. Her training as an athlete specifically as a mountain climber, had given her a distinctive sensuous walk, energetic but with no movement wasted, her footsteps springy yet firmly placed. Disciplined gracefulness. He remembered the feel of her body and the sound of her voice, and he longed to touch her and to hear that voice again.

Her clothes revealed her background. She almost never dressed formally; instead, she preferred jogging shoes or hiking boots, jeans, a heavy sweater, a denim jacket. In place of a purse, she carried a small nylon pack slung over a shoulder, walking in the opposite direction down the street, oblivious to the drizzle that fell on her auburn hair.

His throat still swollen, tears suddenly in his eyes, he started the motorcycle but didn't move from between the cars that shielded him. When Arlene had almost reached the far corner of her block, a wino stood from the steps down to a basement door across the street from the brownstone. Skirting an iron railing, he veered toward Drew, crossing the street toward the surveillance car on the corner. The wino scrambled into the back of the car and hadn't closed his door before the driver pulled out onto the street and sped toward the corner where Arlene now turned right.

Drew grinned, his predictions proved accurate. Somewhere in that block, another spotter would have been left behind. In the meantime, the surveillance car would reach that other corner in time to learn if Arlene stayed on the avenue or went inside a store or hailed a taxi.

Drew started driving, but he couldn't continue down Twelfth Street where the remaining spotter might notice him. Instead, he avoided the block by turning right at the intersection before it and headed north, parallel to Arlene. He turned left onto Thirteenth Street and sped toward the next corner of the avenue that Arlene had taken, hoping to catch up to her.

He didn't see her. What he did see was the dark blue surveillance car. Inside, the two men stared forward as they drove past the corner. Whom were they working for, Drew wondered. Scalpel?

When he reached the intersection, Drew glanced up and down the avenue. No Arlene. He restrained his impatience long enough to let several cars go by before he roared out into traffic to follow the surveillance car, which presumably had her in sight.

His assumption was that when she'd reached the avenue, she'd hailed a taxi. If so, her choice surprised him because she almost always walked where she was going, even if her destination was at some distance.

At least he had the surveillance car ahead of him, and that was as good as seeing Arlene. The several cars between the spotters and himself made it improbable that they would notice him if they happened to look back. The drizzle, which had now become a full-fledged rain, provided a shield as well, though the drops streaking cold down his face made it difficult for him to stop blinking.

To control the blinks, he mustered the discipline he'd learned in fencing classes at the Rocky Mountain Industrial School. The object had been to make him so accustomed to the lethal tip of a rapier being jabbed at his unprotected eyes that he learned to subdue the reflexive action of his eyelids. Some students never did develop that skill; they weren't at school much longer.

Through the stronger rain that now had soaked his wool gloves and collected beneath his coat collar, he followed the dark blue car. He entered midtown Manhattan and turned onto Fiftieth Street.

124

He slowed as the surveillance car did. In a moment he understood why. Ahead, near enough to distinguish the sheen in her auburn hair, the glow on her healthy skin, he saw Arlene getting out of a taxi stopped at the curb.

He felt his heart race. She'd never needed makeup; the sun and wind had always given her sufficient color. Her forehead, cheekbones, and chin were perfectly proportioned, her features exquisite. But she was hardly a porcelain doll. Though she had an angular figure her hips, waist, and breasts equal to those of any actress, she was sinewy, not at all soft.

The surveillance car stopped. The man in the grimy clothes of a wino crawled from the back seat into the front, sliding behind the steering wheel. The well-dressed driver got out to follow Arlene. As horns blared, the replacement driver responded, moving the surveillance car ahead. Drew sympathized with his problem. Where could this new driver find a parking space in midtown Manhattan? Unless he double-parked and risked a challenge from a policeman, he'd have to drive around the block, again and again, until his partner reappeared. At once, though, Drew noticed that the executive who followed Arlene had put a set of small earphones over his head. A wire dangled from them to an inside pocket of his suit.

Back in Boston, while walking through the mall, Drew had been puzzled when he saw teenagers and even adults wearing similar earphones. On occasion, he'd heard dim music drifting from them. He'd gone to a stereo store and learned that the earphones belonged to compact radios and tape players, known as Walkmans. The well-dressed man wasn't using a Walkman, though the earphones looked like they belonged to one and didn't attract attention. No, he was maintaining contact with the driver of the surveillance car by means of a small hidden two-way radio. The wino could drive the car around the block for the rest of the afternoon and still know exactly when and where to pick up his partner.

Though the time was now four-thirty, the gloom made the afternoon seem like dusk. Drew straddled his motorcycle at the curb, deciding to risk a ticket. Passing vehicles ignored him. He in turn ignored the chill of the rain and looked fifty yards ahead, past the well-dressed man with the earphones, watching Arlene go into a store.

Drew had already guessed where she was going when he saw her leave the taxi. The store she entered had its windows filled with sporting equipment, most of it for mountain climbers. Coiled, lightweight, twisted-nylon ropes, one hundred and fifty feet long, capable, he knew, of sustaining four thousand pounds of stress, carabiners, pitons and piton hammers, nylon slings, mountain packs, ice axes, climbing boots.

The store sold ordinary sporting goods as well, but because of its specialty, climbers from all over the northeast knew about it. Drew himself had several times been here with Arlene and Jake.

The swinging glass door closed behind her. The well-dressed man with the earphones moved casually along the sidewalk close to the buildings, then found a break in traffic and crossed the street to a spot beneath an awning where he could watch her through the windows in the store without being noticed.

But if he glances this way, Drew thought, he might notice me.

The dark blue car would soon be coming around the block. Drew raised his motorcycle to the sidewalk turned, and walked it back to the intersection. He crossed the avenue and moved the bike far enough back on the sidewalk to ensure that the wino driving the dark blue car wouldn't see him when the car came around the other block. Despite the rain and the distance, he could still see the man who watched the store and be able to notice Arlene when she came out.

Twenty minutes later, she did, carrying three packages.

Her luck was amazing. She hailed a cab right away. But the surveillance team's luck was equal to her own – the dark blue car came around the corner just as her taxi was pulling away. While the executive scrambled into the back, the wino kept moving, continuing their pursuit.

Then Drew's luck failed him.

He pushed the motorcycle across the sidewalk onto the street, kicked down on the starter lever, gripped the throttle, and found himself blocked by traffic, the light against him. By the time red had turned to green, they were out of sight.

5

The man behind the counter looked Swiss – tall, robust, blue-eyed, blond. In his early thirties, Drew guessed and in excellent shape, broad back, muscular arms and chest. With an energetic smile, he turned from placing coiled ropes on a shelf as the swinging glass door hissed shut behind Drew.

His accent was closer to the Bronx than Switzerland. 'Hell of a day, huh? Glad I'm not on a slope in this.' He gestured toward the downpour outside. 'You want a cup of coffee? Your coat's so wet, you look like you'll catch hypothermia.'

Drew returned his smile. 'Coffee? I'm tempted. But it makes me feel like I'm on speed.'

'Decaffeinated?'

Drew wondered what on earth he was talking about. Decaffeinated coffee? What was that? 'No. But thanks just the same. I was in a store across the street, and I happened to notice a woman come in here. Good-looking athletic type, auburn hair, carried an equipment pack instead of a purse? She looked like a friend of mine. Arlene Hardesty.'

'That was her, all right. She and her brother buy a lot of stuff from us.'

'Good old Jake. I figured I'd step in and say hello. But one thing led to another. I see I missed her.'

'Ten minutes ago.'

Drew feigned disappointment. 'That's the way the pitch angles, I guess. I haven't seen her in so long I ought to make sure I call her.'

'Pitch angles?' The clerk's eyes twinkled. 'You're a climber?'

'Lately I don't have much time, but I used to climb a lot. With Jake and Arlene, in fact. Maybe I should ask them if they'd like to go out again soon.'

'Sooner than you think. You'd better get in touch with Arlene right away. That's why she was in here. Replacing worn-out equipment. She's going up tomorrow. The truth is, you'd be doing her a favor if you asked to go along.'

126

'Why a favor?'

'Because she told me she was going up by herself. I don't know how strict you are about the rules, but even with expert climbers, we discourage them from climbing alone. It just isn't right. Oh, sure, she knows what she's doing, but what if there's an accident? And the rock she's climbing isn't any practice slope.'

'Where?'

'Satan's Horn. Over in Pennsylvania.'

'The Poconos.'

'You know it?'

'I've been there with Jake and Arlene a couple of times. Arlene used to say Satan's Horn worked better than aspirin to cure a headache. Whenever she was troubled, she used to climb it as therapy.'

'Well, I've climbed it too, and believe me, what it did was give me a headache. You've been there, so you know it isn't something you try alone. That damned shale. Every time I got a grip on an overhang, I started believing in God again for fear the rock would come loose in my hand.'

Drew grinned. 'In God? I know the feeling.'

'Then talk her out of it, okay? Or failing that, invite yourself along.'

'I'd hate to have her get hurt.' Drew pretended to think about it. 'But what the heck, lately I've been working too hard. Okay, you've convinced me. But if I'm going climbing tomorrow, I'd better get some equipment. The stuff I use is at my summer place.'

The clerk's eyes twinkled even brighter. This near to closing time, he apparently hadn't expected another sale. 'Let's start with boots.'

6

Surrounded by early-morning mist, Drew walked down a damp wooded slope. The saturated leaves and earth were spongy beneath him. Rounding two boulders he reached a stream. The sun eased above the slope behind him, burning off some of the mist, allowing him a better view of the fallen trunks and boughs around him. He selected one – ten feet long and ten inches thick, less rotten than the others – and carried it to the stream dropping it across the bank. With his coiled rope and nylon sling around one shoulder, he walked over it, his arms slightly outstretched for balance, hearing the log beneath him groan.

On the other side, he climbed a slope, his nostrils spreading from the musky odor of pungent loam, and paused at the top. He'd taken a half hour to walk the quarter mile of dense forest to get here. His motorcycle was hidden in bushes off the two-lane road that led to the gravel parking area where hikers and climbers usually began their expeditions. In New York, he'd slept at a shelter, telling the priest in charge that he'd wash dishes in exchange for a meal and a cot. And now, after two hours of driving, he enjoyed the exercise, the relief to his stiff cramped muscles, the stillness in contrast with the vibrating roar of the chopper.

Ahead, through scraggly undergrowth, the mist disappearing as the sun rose higher, he saw his destination, peering up and toward the gray cone called Satan's Horn. On the far side, it was thirty feet from a neighboring cliff, once linked to it by a natural bridge of rock that had crumbled back in the fifties. The fact that the Horn had separated from the cliff was dramatic evidence of how brittle the rocks here were. And judging from the pile of fallen fragments at its circular base, Drew knew that the Horn would one day crumble as the bridge had.

For now, though, it loomed, imposing – inviting? – protected from the erosion of wind at least by the bluffs of this semicircular basin.

He pushed through the undergrowth, crossed a stretch of dead brown ferns and knee-high grass, their tassles having given up their seeds, feeling moisture from them chill his skin through his pantlegs. He carefully placed his boots on the rock shards that angled up toward the Horn, concerned that the shards might shift beneath him and cause him to sprain an ankle.

The stillness of the basin was eerie, the bluffs around him amplifying, emphasizing, the intrusive crunch of his footsteps. Indeed, as he took another cautious step, he heard branches scrape behind him.

He spun alarmed, his Mauser drawn in a blur, aiming . . . Where? The scraping continued, coming closer.

The nearest cover was thirty yards away, back in the forest, and what guarantee did he have that the bushes he chose would not already be occupied?

To his right.

There. Branches parted. Bushes moved.

He blinked.

Three white-tailed deer, two does and a buck, stepped into the stretch of ferns and grass, the buck's antlers resembling the leafless branches behind him. Drew saw the terror in their eyes, a shock that rendered them immobile for an instant, frozen like a photograph.

The instant cracked. At once the deer burst into motion, turning, their white tails up as they charged back into the forest, the sound of their hoofs like a rumbling rockfall. Lessening. Growing fainter.

The silence of the basin descended again.

Inhaling deeply, replacing the Mauser, Drew continued his cautious ascent across the shards.

7

At the base of the Horn, he peered up only once. The rule was, Don't look up, don't look down, just study the surface before you. But he couldn't resist appreciating the magnificence of this uncanny formation.

Securing the coiled rope and the nylon sling around his shoulder, he studied the deceptively easy task. Though the cliff went almost straight up, tapering inward near the top, its surface was so uneven that handholds and footholds would be no problem.

Until you started to climb, that is. And then you realized that the rock could snap as easily as a potato chip. No grip could be taken for granted.

Each time you eased your weight down on a ledge or tensed your fingers around an outcrop, you had to test it – and test it again, slowly adding more pressure, never sure if it would hold. Only the most experienced, confident, and daring of climbers were qualified to attempt the Horn. Would *want* to climb the Horn. Two hundred feet to the top, that was all. But the ascent might last as long as two hours. One hundred and twenty nerves-stretched-to-the-snapping-point minutes. Thousands of stomach-contracting, sweat-dripping-off-your-forehead decisions. He understood why Arlene liked to climb the Horn when she needed to clear her head. You couldn't think of anything *except* the Horn when you climbed it.

But why was she so troubled that she needed the therapy of this cliff?

He shut the thought out. The Horn was a task for an existentialist. No preoccupations. Only instant-by-instant choices. Nothing before and nothing after.

Contrary to the expectations of an amateur, you didn't squeeze close to the cliff. You didn't hug it for support, for reassurance. The proper way to climb, to survive, was to lean out from the rockface. That position gave you a better view of the next hand- and footholds. It also allowed you to extend your arms and legs and thus relax them. Starting up, choosing his supports with suspicious care, Drew recalled the secret to climbing that Arlene had taught him. The secret to a lot of things now that he thought about it. Hang loose.

Nervousness wormed into his stomach. He felt both elated and frightened. Soon he would see her again.

8

The Horn was crowned with scraggly shrubs, barren now, but tangled and dense enough to give Drew cover. After squirming over the lip of the cliff, he forced himself to wait until he had crawled across a five-foot stretch of open rock before he allowed himself to rest in the deepest part of a thicket. The sun was above him, but though it gleamed from a pure blue sky, it gave little warmth. His sweat, formerly heated by exertion, began to turn cold. He shivered, reaching into his coat for sunflower seeds, dried fruit, and a Granola bar.

Chewing slowly, he unhooked a canteen from the belt beneath his coat and swallowed tepid water. Soon his strength returned. The top of the brush-covered Horn was roughly forty feet across, ample room for him to maneuver if he had to. He flexed his rock-abraded hands, relieving their soreness, and concentrated on the only entrance to the basin, the section of trees through which he'd come. Far above tree level, his vantage point made him feel small. He said a prayer of thanks for God's magnificence.

Sprawling flat on his stomach, trying to relax, he waited. In retrospect, the decisions he'd made seemed logical. If he'd stayed in New York, he might have had to wait several days before he saw a chance to get a message to Arlene without alerting the surveillance team. And the more he followed the spotters as they in turn followed Arlene, the more he risked being noticed by them.

But this way, knowing her destination, arriving here before her, he felt safe. After all, though the team would no doubt follow her to the Horn, they wouldn't dare show themselves by climbing up to find out what she was doing at the top. They might of course be tempted to climb to a neighboring bluff and watch from there, but the odds were that they didn't know the terrain and weren't experienced climbers. The main reason he didn't think the team would try to watch from a neighboring bluff was that it would take them too long to get up and down from there. Arlene, in the meantime, would have a chance to elude them.

Drew confirmed his decisions, confident that for a while, at least, he'd have the chance to talk to her alone, unseen, up here. As he pressed his stomach against the rocky earth, he saw Arlene step from the forest. A pulse throbbed in his forehead, and he fought to still the pounding in his heart. Tiny from Drew's perspective, she paused to survey the Horn, then straightened in satisfaction, shifting through the undergrowth, approaching.

She carried a coiled rope as he himself had. In addition, he saw a bulging heavy pack. Her clothes fit her loosely, rugged wool pants and shirt, both blue, and an open khaki jacket well supplied with pockets. Despite the austere shapelessness of those garments, however, she was unmistakably a woman. With her auburn hair tucked beneath a gray knit cap, she showed the sensuous angle of her neck. And even in solid climbing boots, her stride remained athletically graceful. Images of her body filled his brain. Drew shut his eyes to chase them away.

9

A hand appeared first. Abraded like his own, it gripped the lip of the cliff. Then another hand. He saw the gray knitted cap. And her effort-strained face, beaded with sweat, as she inhaled deeply, mustering a final surge of strength.

He watched unseen from the bushes, her features vivid before him. She pulled herself up, raised a knee to the edge of the cliff, and squirmed to the flat stretch of rock, rolling onto her back, her chest heaving.

She stared at the cloudless sky for several moments, swallowed, then reached for the canteen on her belt. As Drew expected, she drank in short measured gulps, taking care not to make herself sick. When the rhythm of her breathing had returned to normal, she wiped the sleeve of her coat across her brow and slowly sat, her back to Drew, peering toward the autumn landscape below.

She took off her cap, shook her head to release her hair, and combed her hands through the sides. Her back was as straight as a fashion model's.

Drew glanced past her down toward the dense forest but still couldn't see the surveillance team. He hoped that she'd stand and relax her legs by pacing through the bushes and thus approach him, but she continued sitting, peering down.

Finally he couldn't waste more time. He took a chance, depending upon her discipline.

'Arlene, it's Drew.'

He whispered, but to her, it was likely a shout.

'No. Don't turn around.'

A ripple of tension and surprise swept across her shoulders. But as he'd anticipated, her training took command. Accustomed to adjusting to instantaneous changes in circumstance, she showed no other reaction, maintaining her gaze toward the woods. A vein throbbed in her neck.

'Don't talk,' he continued. 'I'll explain why I'm here. But not in the open. You've been followed. They're watching from down there.'

She took another sip from her canteen.

Yeah, you're the best, Drew marveled. 'When it seems natural, stand, stretch your arms, get the kinks out. Pace a little. Since you're up here, what the hell, you figure you'll explore. Step into the thicket. But once you're out of sight from down there, sit and we can talk.'

She swallowed more water and put the cap back on the canteen.

'I need your help,' he added. 'I'm in a mess.'

A minute later, she stood, put her hands in her jacket pocket, turned to survey the bluffs at her end of the basin, and casually entered the thicket.

With all his heart, he wanted to hold her again, to feel her breasts, to kiss her opening lips. For Christ's sake Drew agonized, what's the matter with you? You took a sacred vow!

Arlene sank beneath the bushes toward him, her hand in her jacket pocket. Her eyes disturbed him. They showed neither curiosity nor pleasure at seeing him again. Instead, they looked terribly calm. And her smile was fixed.

His pulse sped. As she knelt, she pulled her hand from the pocket.

And at once swung a piton hammer toward his left temple.

One end of it was curved, its underside serrated. Hearing the point cut the air with a whistle, he toppled back, avoiding it, seeing its blur pass before his eyes.

'No.' His voice was tense, hoarse. As she swung the hammer again, he rolled back in the opposite direction. Fear scalded his stomach. She was strong enough, the hammer deadly enough, that it would at least have shattered his jaw.

He rolled again, trying to gain the advantage, to overcome his shock.

'Arlene, *why?*'

Air rushed, the hammer going past.

'For God's sake!'

This time the hammer, misaimed, snicked the shoulder of his coat.

He kicked up as she struck at the spot between his eyes. His boot caught her wrist, deflecting the point. She groaned. He thrust up, grabbing her arm at the wrist and biceps, throwing her flat. His body pressed on hers, his hands restraining both of hers, conscious of his chest on her own. He was five inches away from the anger in her eyes.

Their harsh forceful breathing was indistinguishable. He smelled her.

'*You rotten bastard*,' she said.

He flinched.

She writhed, glaring hate. 'Where the hell is Jake?'

His energy left him. Implications soared through his mind. 'Jake?'

'You heard me, you sonofabitch. Where *is* he? God damn you, if you killed him.'

Arlene thrashed, trying to knee Drew's groin.

He pressed her leg down, squinted deeply into her seething eyes, and, shaking his head in frustration, rolled away from her, staring bleakly past the bushes toward the sky.

The only gesture he could think of to mollify her. To show his innocence. Total exposure – surrender.

She scrambled up, eyes fierce, swinging the hammer. But he made no effort to repel it.

With a gasp, she buried the hammer's tip in the shallow ground beyond Drew's neck, the curved edge conforming to the contour of his throat, the serrated underside stinging his skin.

Neither moved. They glared at each other. On a bluff beyond them, a bird took off, fluttering.

Her chest began to heave, demanding oxygen.

'You . . .'

'Bastard,' he said. 'I know. I got that idea. And God's going to damn me for being a sonofabitch. I got that idea, too. The thing is, tell me why.'

She hesitated. Gulping more air, she slowly sank to the ground beside him. 'I almost . . .'

'Decided not to miss my neck? Yeah, I figured that. But I also figured I had to take the chance.'

'So I'd think you weren't a threat? I'm still not convinced.'

'But at least you know I could have killed you when I was lying on you.'

'And that's the only reason I didn't . . .' She scowled at the hammer pinned against his throat. 'Same old Drew. You didn't even flinch.'

He shrugged, removing the hammer, then sat up, hefted it, and gave it back to her. 'Regrets? You want to try it again?'

Frustrated, she shook her head.

'Then what's this all about?'

Her eyes flared. 'The same goes for you. What are you doing here? How did you know I'd be here?'

'You've been followed.'

'I know.'

He raised his eyebrows. 'You do?'

'Three of them. One in a dark blue car down the street. Another lying on basement steps across the street, pretending to be a wino. The third sells umbrellas at a portable stand on the corner. When it's sunny, he switches to bratwurst and sauerkraut.' She made a face. 'They showed up five days ago.'

Drew tensed. 'On Saturday?'

She studied him. 'Yes, Saturday. In the morning. Why? Is that important?'

Drew rubbed a hand across his mouth. Friday night, he'd arrived in Boston. He'd left his prisoner in the van at the parking ramp in Logan Airport. A few hours later, the death team – and whoever had ordered the attack on the monastery – would have learned that he was out of Vermont.

Jake? Arlene had wanted to know where her brother was. She'd assumed that Drew had something to do with Jake's disppearance. That was why she'd almost killed him.

'It tells me a lot,' Drew said, still wanting to hold her, with difficulty keeping his voice steady. 'What about Jake? You told me he disappeared. Before last Tuesday?'

Arlene's knuckles whitened on the hammer. 'You *do* know something about him!'

'Not at all. Come on, we used to be close, remember? Take it easy. I made a guess at Tuesday because that's when my own troubles started. I'm beginning to think that what happened to Jake has something to do with me.' His mind raced. 'When exactly did he disappear?'

'Friday. Before that Tuesday.'

'And why did you blame me?'

'Because of Janus.'

'*What?*'

'You and Janus.'

'A woman named Janice?'

'No. The name from myth.' She spelled it. 'J-a-n-u-s. You look as if you'd never heard of him. That's your new cryptonym, isn't it?'

Janus? He abruptly remembered the voice of the Slavic priest: 'Yanus! I've got to talk to you about Yanus!' Had the accent distorted the word?

Drew's head began to throb. The ache swelled squeezing the inside of his skull. Janus? The Roman god who looked backward and forward. The two-faced.

Insanity.

'I don't know what you're talking about,' he said.

'But the cryptonym, it's *yours*. The newspaper articles. The photographs.'

As much as he wanted to hold her, madness was added to madness. Nothing made sense. 'Of me?' He feared that his mind would crack. 'But there *can't* be any photographs. It isn't possible.'

She glowered.

'What is it?' he asked.

'There can't be any photographs . . . Not possible . . . That's what Jake kept saying.'

'You bet he said it. He ought to know.'

She slammed the hammer into the dirt. 'Damn you, stop playing games with me!'

'Janus. Who is he? Why is he so important?'

'If you're Janus, you should know.'

'*Tell me.*'

'A free-lance assassin. An international killer. A rogue. He executed twenty people in the last two years.'

Drew felt the blood drain from his face. 'And I'm supposed to be him?'

Her hard gaze became uncertain. 'The more Jake heard about you, the more he became upset. He wouldn't tell me why. Two and a half weeks ago, he finally said he couldn't wait any longer. He had to find out what was going on.'

'And that's when he . . . ?'

'Disappeared. Last Saturday the surveillance team showed up. I couldn't go anywhere without them. It didn't matter what tactic I tried. They outguessed me. That's why I'm here. To try to shake them. I planned to stay on top till dark, rappel down, climb a bluff behind the Horn, and lose them.'

'Not bad.' His chest aching with affection, Drew smiled at her cleverness. 'Then you planned to find out what happened to Jake?'

'Believe it.'

'You've got a partner.' His voice was taut. 'I want answers as much as you do. *To a lot of things.* Look, I'm sorry that I didn't tell you what happened to me.' He studied her, almost touching her. 'But you're wrong about the surveillance team. They're not watching you. They don't want to stop you from finding Jake.'

'Then?'

'Me.'

She narrowed her eyebrows.

'They're watching you in case . . . They're after me,' Drew said. 'A while ago, you wondered why Jake was sure that I couldn't be Janus. Why the newspapers had to be wrong. Why there couldn't be photographs.'

She waited, breathing deeply.

'Because for the past six years, I've been in a monastery. *Because six years ago, Jake killed me.*'

10

'Killed?' Her face lost its color. She jerked her head back as if she'd been struck. 'A monastery? What are you talking about? Jake *killed* you?'

'I don't have time to explain. Not now. You'd have more questions. And other questions after that.'

'But . . .'

'No,' he insisted. 'Those men down there will be getting suspicious. They'll want to know what you're doing. You've been out of sight too long as it is.'

She seemed to debate with herself.

'I promise. Later,' he said.

With a sudden nod, she glanced toward the brush that concealed her from the surveillance team. At once she unbuckled her belt, undoing the button on her pants, pulling down the zipper.

He reacted with shock. 'What are you doing?'

'You said it yourself – they'll want to know what I was up to.'

His shock turned to understanding, then admiration. 'Smart.'

'But you're in this with me? You'll help me to find Jake?'

'I *have* to find Jake. From what you've just told me, I'm sure he knows who's after me. We'll wait till dark then leave together. As soon as we're someplace safe, I'll answer your questions. Between what you know and I do, maybe we can figure out where he is.'

She studied him, smiling, her eyes loving. 'It's been a long time. I always wondered what happened to you.' She took his hand. 'I'm sorry about the hammer.'

'Forget it.' Emotion made him tremble. 'I figured that if you'd really wanted to kill me, you would have.'

'I figured the same. You could have killed *me*.' She squeezed his hand. 'I can't tell you how glad I am to see you again. How I've missed you.'

134

His voice was thick. 'I've missed you, too.' He felt torn apart, his love for her tugging him one way, his vow of celibacy the other. The turmoil increased as she leaned close, kissing him on the lips. He felt her breath on his skin. Badly he wanted to kiss her in return, to hold her, to feel the comfort of her flesh. But his crisis of will passed. What he felt now wasn't lust. He didn't want to make love to her. He wanted to show he cared. How could that be sinful? He held her tight.

'Those men down there,' he said.

'I know.' She grinned. 'We'd better not get distracted.' Sobering, she stood and left the bushes, pulling up the zipper on her pants.

Still feeling the touch of her lips against his own straining to subdue his confusion, he peered unseen from a gap in the thicket, nervous for her. She closed the button at her waist, then buckled her belt, and sat on the flat stretch of rock at the lip of the cliff. Her gestures were convincing, he decided. The impression she'd give the surveillance team was that she'd gone out of sight to relieve herself. In their place, I'd accept the explanation.

He watched her eat some trail food. She drank more water and lay back on the rock as if to rest before her descent. Through the bushes, he saw that she closed her eyes. In a while, except for the rise and fall of her chest, she didn't move. Whether or not she'd actually gone to sleep, the surveillance team would think that she had.

He scanned the forest but couldn't find any sign of the team. Either they're awfully good, or they're not down there. Wouldn't that be a joke? he thought. To go through all this trouble when we didn't have to.

11

After dusk, he chose the best support on the rear side of the Horn – a boulder that his full strength couldn't budge.

Arlene came through the bushes, holding her rope and pack, kneeling beside him. 'You found an anchor?'

'Here.' He put her hand on the barely visible rock.

'You tested it?'

'It'll hold. With luck.'

'Luck? Oh, brother.' But she seemed to know he was joking. 'We'd better get started.' She reached in her pack and pulled out a nylon sling.

'I'll need your extra hardware. All I have is a rope and sling.'

'That isn't like you, not to come fully prepared.' Now *she* was joking.

'Well, I had a slight problem. A temporary shortage of funds.'

As they spoke, keeping their voices low, Drew felt good to be working with her. He tied his nylon sling around the boulder. Arlene hooked a metal carabiner onto the sling, making sure that the carabiner's hinged flap was safely closed. She knotted the ends of her rope and looped its midpoint onto the carabiner. Drew knew that a simpler method would have been to attach the rope directly to the sling, but the rope, like the sling, was made from nylon, and nylon had a dangerously low friction point. If the rope and the sling were allowed to rub against each other, the weight of a climber could easily make them overheat and snap. This way, the metal carabiner acted as a buffer, reducing the heat.

Almost ready. Arlene tied a sling around her legs and waist in a pattern that resembled a diaper. She hooked a carabiner through it, at her crotch. Drew did the same, borrowing equipment from her pack. As night enveloped them, he was nonetheless able to see her shadowy outline, athletic and lithe. His love for her intensified.

She hooked the doubled rope into the carabiner, looped the two strands of rope around her left shoulder, down her back, and around to the right side of her waist. The carabiner at her crotch would thus take the main stress of the rope. Her shoulder and back would absorb the remainder of the stress, and if she needed to, she could use her right hand to press the rope against her waist, applying a brake.

'I'll take the pack and go first,' she whispered. 'There's a ledge sixty feet down. I'll rig another anchor. And another one farther down after that. It takes three separate rappels to reach the bottom.'

'I know.'

'Then you still remember how to do this?' She seemed to grin.

'I had a good teacher.'

'Flattery. My, my.'

She was gone, walking backward off the cliff, gripping the section of the rope above the carabiner, pressing the other section against her waist. He imagined the graceful ease with which she would drop. She'd always enjoyed a free-fall. A piece of cloth tied near the end of her rope would warn her when she would soon run out of rope. Then she would stop and rig yet another anchor.

That would be the dangerous part, searching for a solid spot on this brittle cliff. But after that, all she needed to do was balance herself on the ledge while she unhooked the rope from the sling around her crotch. She'd free the knotted ends of the rope and pull down on one side, tugging the other side up through the anchor at the top of the cliff, then down to her. She'd reposition the rope, this time on the new anchor, and continue her descent.

Anxious, his affection adding to his worry about her safety, he crouched, gently touching the rope, feeling it start to move. Okay. He relaxed temporarily. She would set up the other anchor. Soon, lower, she'd set up the third. When he judged that she'd had sufficient time to reach the bottom, to step back from the cliff and avoid any rocks that he might dislodge when he came down, only then would he begin.

Five minutes – that was all the time he'd need. He wondered what the surveillance team was doing. They must have become suspicious. Professionals, they presumably had an infrared scope that allowed them to see that Arlene had disappeared. They'd approach to investigate. If I don't get there soon . . .

He quit counting, secured his rope, turned his back to the cliff, and as his stomach soared toward his throat, he dropped.

12

He stepped on a loose chunk of rock. It tilted. Lurching sideways, fighting for balance, he heard it clatter in the dark. He froze.

He'd reached the bottom. Behind the Horn, the wall of the neighboring bluff loomed close behind him, creating a thicker dark. The narrow enclosure smothered him. He felt disoriented, defenseless. Where was Arlene?

The snap of a finger told him where she stood. To his left. Across from him, near the other cliff. With as little noise as possible, he started in that direction.

He realized that anyone could have made that noise. In the dark, the surveillance team might have approached the base of the Horn, assumed that Arlene would descend from the back, and waited there for her.

For me as well, he thought. He strained to see a figure in the night. Again he heard fingers snap. He pulled out his Mauser, his muscles hard with tension, stalking forward.

A scream broke the silence. Unnerving, it came from above. Drew felt a rush of air – again from above – and stumbled frantically back as a massive object plummeted past him, walloping on the rocks. Though it seemed to be heavy and solid, it made a sickening plop, like a watermelon dropped from an overpass onto a freeway. Warm liquid spattered his face. He jerked a hand to his cheek.

His surprise became shock. His shock changed to urgency, commanding him. Though he knew what had fallen, he had to find out if this was Arlene. The fear made bile rush into his mouth.

But he felt Arlene suddenly next to him. This close, he recognized her shape, her smell. Then who had . . . ? He lunged forward, crouching with his Mauser in one hand, reaching with the other. His fingers touched bloody hair, a shattered skull, warm and sticky. He traced his hand along the torso. A man. The clothes were grimy, torn, buttons missing, a rope for a belt. The dingy clothes a wino might wear. Or someone disguised as a wino, one of the men who'd followed Arlene from her brownstone.

But how could this have happened?

As Arlene knelt beside him, he tried to think the problem through. The surveillance team must have become impatient. Suspecting that she would try to sneak down from the Horn at night, they'd split up. The wino must have tried to find a way up to the bluff behind the Horn. In turn, his partner, the well-dressed man with the earphones, had waited in case Arlene decided on the easy route and came back through the trees at the entrance to the basin.

So far, it made sense, Drew thought. The wino, hiding on top of the bluff in the dark, must have heard the scrape of our boots on the rocks when we touched down. If he leaned too close to the rim, he could have lost his balance and fallen. Easy enough to do at night.

But the explanation troubled him. It wasn't the kind of mistake you'd expect from a pro. Beside him, Arlene removed her hands from the corpse and slowly stood. He knew that she too would be trying to figure out the sequence. They didn't need – didn't *dare* – to discuss what had happened.

The other member of the team was still in the area. Maybe up on the bluff, in fact. Maybe both men had gone up there, reasoning that the cliff behind the Horn was the logical spot for Arlene to try eluding them.

Too many variables. Too much uncertainty.

But this he did know. The falling wino's scream would have warned his partner. If the well-dressed man was in the woods at the basin's entrance, he might decide to come this way and investigate.

On the other hand, a professional wasn't supposed to allow a scream – even one from his partner – to lure him into what might be a trap.

Arlene touched his shoulder, communicating the same urgent need he felt to get away. They crossed the dark narrow chasm and stopped at the bluff behind the Horn. Behind them, the corpse made a gurgling sound, pressure forcing gas and blood from the torso.

Drew shut out the noise, concentrating on the problem he faced. Though a night climb was always difficult, the cliff behind the Horn offered one compensation. It wasn't as severely vertical as the Horn, and it offered more ledges, more outcrops. Arlene's shadowy form reached up, choosing a handhold, testing it, then raising her boot to fit it into a crack. Drew brooded. If the well-dressed man had gone with the wino up to the top of the bluff, we'll never get over the rim. We'll be pushed down here with his friend.

No, all of this felt wrong. He tugged the back of Arlene's jacket as she raised herself. She stiffened, resisting. He tugged again. She stepped back down, her indistinct face swinging toward him. He gripped her hand and used it to point away from the cliff, past the Horn, toward the entrance to the basin. He touched her hand to his chest, to hers, and again pointed past the Horn. The message, he hoped, was clear. It might be better if we went *that* way. She seemed to think about it. Two taps on his shoulder. Okay.

They crept from the chasm between the Horn and the bluff. If the well-dressed man was out there hidden in the dark of the woods, watching them through a nightscope, they'd be obvious targets caught in the open. But Drew had an intuition, an instinct, that the situation was even more confused than he imagined, that no bullet would pierce his chest, that he and Arlene had a better-than-even chance to get away.

They angled to the right, leaving the bluff on their flank, descending the slope of fragmented rock, entering the narrow exit from the basin. The woods they reached were still and cold but, because of their tangle reassuring.

In keeping with their training, they stayed twenty feet apart, Drew taking the lead, shifting past deadfalls and boulders. Separated, they made less easy targets, and if a sniper shot at one of them, the other would have a chance to see the muzzle flash and return the fire. Drew felt reassured by the pistol that she'd taken from her pack.

This time, when he reached the stream, he didn't waste effort trying to find a log with which to cross, but simply waded, nervous about the inadvertent splashing sounds he made.

Then the stream was behind him, and hearing Arlene follow, he crept farther through the bushes and trees, easing his boots down on leaves that blessedly were still so soaked from yesterday's rain that they didn't crackle. With the stars to guide him, he headed east toward the two-lane road and the motorcycle he'd hidden near it.

His tension eased when he saw the blacktop. The moon had risen, casting a glow across it. The skeletal silhouette of a hydro pylon loomed against the pattern of stars to his right. When he'd arrived that morning, he'd chosen the pylon as a landmark to guide him back to where he'd hidden the chopper, and now heading right, through the bushes that flanked the road, he came to the Harley. He checked the bike; no one had tampered with it.

Still, he didn't want to start the motor and attract attention, so he walked the bike down the road, heading left of the pylon this time, soon reaching the spot where Arlene waited for him.

In the moonlight, he saw her gesture toward an overgrown lane that jutted into the woods. The bushes and saplings had been bent as if a car had gone along it. She motioned for him to follow, and thirty yards down the lane, he found the dark blue car almost indistinguishable from the forest.

It was occupied.

The well-dressed man sat motionless behind the steering wheel. A thin gash encircled the front half of his throat. The gash was deep, the obvious aftermath of powerful hands on a razor-sharp garotte. Moonlight filtered through the trees, revealing the blood that drenched the front of the dead man's overcoat.

Drew spun toward the black of the forest. The wino hadn't fallen from the cliff near the Horn! He'd been pushed! There was someone else in the forest!

Silence no longer mattered. Whoever's out there knows every move we've made.

He straddled the motorcycle, stomping down on the starter. The engine's roar broke the stillness. 'Let's get the hell out of here.'

13

Feeling Arlene's breasts against his back, her arms around his chest, he sped toward the gravel parking area where she'd left her car – a Firebird, the nameplate said, though he didn't recognize its design.

They quickly inspected it, but as with the Harley, no one had meddled. Indeed, it started the instant Arlene turned the ignition key. Its tires throwing up gravel, Arlene raced from the parking area. Drew hurried after her.

But five miles down the road, just after a hairpin turn, he let her taillights disappear while he hid in bushes beside the road, watching for anyone who followed. He waited ten minutes.

No one came. It doesn't make sense, he thought. Whoever killed those men must have seen us leave. Why aren't we being tailed? Frowning, he left his hiding place and met Arlene ten miles farther along.

'There *has* to be someone,' she said.

'I know.' He glanced along the dark road. 'I never thought I'd be bothered because I wasn't being followed.'

'Let's try it one more time. After the next sharp turn, pull off the road again and wait.'

No car followed. Distressed, he hurried to join her.

'That's it then,' she said. 'Let's put some miles behind us. Stay close. I'll use back roads.'

'To where?'

'You said it yourself. We need to find a place that's safe, where you can answer my questions.' She sounded exhausted. 'And tell me what all of this has to do with Jake.'

Troubled, they both glanced behind them. *What had happened in those woods?*

'We've *got* to find Jake,' Arlene said urgently.

14

Heading south through Pennsylvania, they stopped at Bethlehem on the Lehigh River. The motel they chose was off a side street, a line of adjoining units with a parking slot outside each door. Facing a sleepy clerk, they registered as Mr and Mrs Robert Davis, requested the unit that was farthest in back ('So the morning traffic doesn't wake us'), and discovered that at 3 A.M. all the nearby diners were closed. They had to settle for the rest of their trail food along with stale cheese and crackers from a coin dispenser in the motel's lobby.

They parked the Firebird in front of the unit but left the motorcycle around the side out of sight from the street, locked the unit's door behind them, closed the drapes, and only then turned on the lights.

At once, Arlene sank across the bed, her arms outstretched. Against the white spread, she looked as if she were making angels in snow. She closed her eyes and laughed. 'Just like the old days, huh? Reminds me of the time we holed up in Mexico City. You and me and –'

She opened her eyes, no longer relaxed.

'And Jake,' Drew said.

She frowned. 'It's time.'

He didn't answer.

'You promised.'

'Sure. It's just that . . .'

'Jake. You said you were in a monastery. You said six years ago Jake killed you. What does that mean?' Her voice hardened. 'Tell me.'

He'd known this was coming. During the troubled drive here (again the terrible question: *What had happened in those woods? Why hadn't they been followed?*), he'd tried to prepare himself.

But he still wasn't ready.

'I'm afraid it will take a while.'

'Then don't waste time. Get started.' She stood, taking off her khaki jacket, beginning to unbutton her heavy wool shirt.

The intimate gesture surprised him, though clearly she didn't think twice about it, still relating to him as if they were lovers. Again he felt a rush of love for her, a bittersweet nostalgia for their former life.

'And while you're at it' – she opened the door to the bathroom – 'I've got dibs on the shower.' She turned impatiently, oblivious to the corner of one breast that showed through her partly opened shirt. 'Come on, Drew. Talk to me.'

His thoughts were in chaos, his subconscious struggling not to give up the nightmares it had buried. He glanced at the floor.

When he peered up, Arlene was gone. From the bathroom, he heard the scrape of hooks on a shower curtain, the spray of water into a tub.

The curtain scraped again, and he walked in. Her shadow moved behind the yellow-flowered barrier. Her dusty climbing clothes were piled beneath the sink. Steam rose, filling the room. 'Drew?'

'Here. I'm trying to decide where to start.' He bit his lip, closed the lid on the toilet seat, and eased himself down.

'But you said six years ago.'

'No, it starts before then. Unless you know what happened before, the rest of it doesn't make sense.' He stared at the steam that filled the bathroom. Despite their intimacy, he had never told her any of this before. The memories had been too depressing. 'Japan,' he murmured.

'What? I can't hear you. This shower.'

'Japan,' he said louder.

The mist swirled thicker. For a dizzying moment, he had the sensation of falling in.

PART FIVE
VISITATION

THE SINS OF THE PAST

1

Japan, 1960.
On June 10, prior to a planned visit by American President Dwight D. Eisenhower, a raging mob of ten thousand Japanese anti-American demonstrators stormed Tokyo's airport to protest a new Japanese-American defense treaty that permitted the continued presence of American military bases, and worse – considering the A-bombs the United States had dropped on Hiroshima and Nagasaki – the inclusion of nuclear weapons on Japanese soil. The immediate targets of their fury were the American Ambassador to Japan, along with several members of Eisenhower's White House staff. As a warning of worse riots to come if the American President arrived in Japan, the mob surrounded the limousine in which the American contingent had planned to drive to the embassy, so threatening the occupants that a U.S. Marine helicopter made an emergency landing among the protestors and flew the officials to safety.

Six days later, the Japanese government requested a postponement of Eisenhower's visit. However, the massive demonstrations continued.

2

Tokyo, one week later. The recent 'troubles' – Drew had heard his father use the expression often lately – the 'troubles' were to blame for the cancellation of his birthday party. He didn't know what the troubles were (something to do with the mysterious place called the embassy where his father worked!), but he did know that last year when he turned nine there'd been twenty children at his party, and this year, tomorrow, there wouldn't be any.

'With the troubles, it isn't safe for Americans to associate with each other,' his father had said. 'So many cars and parents arriving. They'd attract too much attention. We can't afford further incidents. I'm sure you understand, Drew. Next year, I promise, we'll give you a bigger, better party than the one we planned for this year.'

But Drew didn't understand – not any more than he understood why his

145

father had told his mother at supper last night that they might have to move from their house to the embassy.

'Temporarily.' Sometimes Drew's father used words too big for Drew to grasp. 'Only until the situation has stabilized.'

Whatever 'stabilized' meant. The only sign Drew had of anything wrong was that during the past few weeks, most of their Japanese servants had resigned. And now that Drew thought about it, there'd been one other thing. His best friend in the neighborhood, a Japanese boy, no longer came to play. Drew often phoned him, but his friend's parents always said that the boy wasn't home.

'Hey, never mind the party, sport,' Drew's father said, and playfully mussed his hair. 'Don't look so glum. You'll still have presents. Lots of them. And a big chocolate cake, your favorite. I'll even stay home from work to help you celebrate.'

'You mean you can actually get away?' Drew's mother asked, delighted. 'Won't they be needing you at the embassy?'

'With the hours I've been putting in, I told the ambassador my son's more important than any damned crisis.'

'And he didn't get angry?'

'All he did was laugh and say, "Tell your son Happy Birthday for me."'

3

A long black limousine stopped in front of the house at two the next afternoon. Drew watched, excited, from his bedroom window. The car had a small American flag on a metal post near the driver's side-view mirror. Its license plates were the same kind as on his father's car – from the embassy. A uniformed American got out, took a large red-white-and-blue package from the seat beside him, straightened the bow, and proceeded up the curved front walk, past an ornate Japanese garden, toward the entrance.

He knocked on the door and, while he waited, adjusted his chauffeur's cap, then turned, attracted to the song of an unseen bird in a nearby blossoming cherry tree. An elderly Japanese woman, one of the few local servants who hadn't quit working here, came out and bowed gracefully in her brilliant orange kimono.

The driver bowed slightly in return and then, from American habit, tipped his cap. 'Please tell Mr MacLane that the ambassador sends his compliments.' The driver grinned. 'Or I guess you should tell his son. And give him this birthday present. The ambassador hopes it makes up for the canceled party.'

The driver handed the package to the servant, bowed again, and returned to the limousine.

4

Despite his growing impatience, Drew obeyed instructions and waited in his room while his mother and father made sure that everything was properly arranged.

'It's just the three of us,' his mother had said. 'But we'll have enough fun for twenty.'

Eagerly he paged through the American comic books – Superman and Davy Crockett were his favorites – that his father had arranged to be specially delivered. 'In the diplomatic pouch,' his father had said, though Drew knew he was joking. 'Nothing's too good for my son.'

He lay on his bed, staring anxiously at the ceiling.

'Okay, Drew,' he heard his mother call from the garden at the rear of the house. 'You can come out now.'

He leaped from his bed and scurried out of his room. The quickest way to the garden in back was through his father's study. As he passed his father's desk, he saw through the open sliding door to where his mother and father sat at a circular table piled high with presents, all sizes and colors. Sunlight glinted off the tall, frosted glass that his mother held.

'Why, even the ambassador sent you a present,' she said, excited when she saw him coming, and raised the glass to her mouth.

'He didn't need to. Thinks of everything. Wonder what's in it,' Drew's father said and shook the box.

Drew entered the garden.

The stunning blast deafened him, throwing him back through the open study door, slamming him hard against his father's desk. He must have blacked out for a moment. He didn't remember falling from the desk to the floor. The next thing he knew, he was staggering to his feet. The roar behind his ears made hlm sick. His vision was blurred. As he stumbled toward the indistinct wreckage of the study door, he realized – confused – that his clothes were wet, and peering down, frantic to clear his eyes, he saw that he was drenched with blood. The blood alone should have made him scream. But it didn't. Nor did he scream as he panicked, afraid of how badly he might be hurt, nor as he realized – no! – that the blood wasn't his.

He lurched through the shattered doorway, seeing his mother and father in fragments across the lawn, the grass wet from their blood. The birthday cake, the plates and cups and gaily wrapped presents that had covered the table no longer existed. The table itself had disintegrated. Acrid smoke from the blast swirled thickly around him, making him choke. A nearby bush was in flames.

But still he didn't scream.

Not until he focused on his mother's almost-severed head. The force of the blast had rammed the glass from which she'd been drinking into her mouth. Its circular base propped her lips apart. Inside her mouth, the rest of the glass had shattered. Blossoming shards protruded, dripping blood, from both her mangled cheeks.

Then he did scream.

5

The steam began to clear. Arlene's shadow was motionless behind the curtain. The bathroom was silent. Drew hadn't been aware that she'd turned off the water.

The silence was broken by the rasp of metal hooks on the curtain as she opened it part way, her features taut with sympathy. 'I didn't know.'

'You couldn't have. It's something I don't like to talk about. Even now, it's too painful.' Except, Drew thought, once, in a moment of weakness, he had told Jake. He wiped what might have been steam from around his eyes.

'I'm deeply, terribly sorry.'

'Yeah.' His voice was flat.

'The present from the embassy –'

'With red-white-and-blue wrapping paper.'

'– was booby-trapped?'

Drew nodded.

'But it didn't come from the embassy, and the limousine wasn't an official car, and the government license plates were fake,' she said.

'Of course. And the driver – nobody knew anything about him. The embassy's security staff made me look at photographs. Nothing.'

'Classic.'

'Yeah.' Drew closed his eyes. 'Wasn't it, though?'

6

His mind blank, his body numbed from grief, he faced the ambassador in the large, oppressive office. From his ten-year-old perspective, the ceiling disturbed him; it was so high that it made him insecure, as if he'd suddenly become shorter. The hulking furniture was covered with leather and looked uncomfortable. The walls had somber wood paneling, brooding books on massive shelves, disturbing photographs of important-looking men. The carpet was so thick that he didn't know if he was allowed to stand on it with his shoes.

'Will that be all, sir?' an embassy guard – Drew's eyes had widened at the gun in the holster on his belt – asked the elderly white-haired man behind the desk at the far end of the enormous room.

Drew recognized the man, having met him several times before when his parents had brought Drew to the embassy for Christmas and Fourth of July parties. The man wore a gray pin-striped suit and vest. His closely trimmed mustache was as white as his hair. His lean face looked wrinkled, tired.

'Yes, thank you,' the man told the guard. 'Instruct my secretary to hold all my calls and appointments for the next fifteen minutes.'

'Very good, sir.' The guard stepped backward, leaving the office and shutting the door behind him.

'Hello. It's Andrew, isn't it?' The ambassador studied him, seeming to choose his words. 'Why don't you come over here and sit down?'

Confused, Drew obeyed. The leather chair made a creaking sound as he settled onto it, his feet dangling off the floor.

'I'm glad you're out of the hospital. Did they treat you well?'

Bewildered, Drew only sighed. In the hospital there'd been soldiers with guns that had scared him. There'd been no other children in the ward, and groggy from the injection he'd been given to make him sleepy, he hadn't understood why the nurses were called lieutenants.

'Your doctor tells me that apart from several cuts and bruises – and those flashburns on your eyebrows – there's nothing wrong with you. A miracle, really. He says not to worry, by the way. The hair on your eyebrows will grow back.'

Drew frowned at him, mystified. His eyebrows? What difference did his eyebrows make? His parents – the shards of glass sticking out of his mother's bloody mangled cheeks – *they* were what mattered.

Grief cramped his stomach, rising cold to his aching heart.

The ambassador leaned forward with concern. 'Are you all right, son?'

Drew wanted to sob but controlled the impulse, swallowing thickly, nodding.

The ambassador waited, trying to smile. 'And your room here at the embassy? I'm sure that you miss your home, but under the circumstances, we couldn't very well let you stay there, even with guards. You understand. I trust that you're comfortable now, at least.'

The bedroom Drew had been given reminded him of a hotel room – if he'd had the vocabulary, he'd have called it impersonal – where he and his parents once had stayed during a vacation trip to Hawaii. Again, he forced himself to nod.

'I know my staff's been treating you well,' the ambassador said. 'In fact, I've given orders to the kitchen crew that you can have all the ice cream you want. For the next few days, at any rate. Strawberry is your favorite, I believe.'

The thought of strawberry ice cream, its color and consistency, reminded Drew of his mother's bloody cheeks.

'Is there anything else we can get you? Something you miss from home perhaps?'

My mother and father, Drew wanted to scream. He suffered in silence.

'Nothing at all?'

Aware of the tension, Drew struggled for something, *anything*, to say and murmured the first words that entered his mind.

The ambassador straightened. 'I'm sorry, son. I didn't hear you.'

Don't call me 'son,' Drew inwardly raged. *I'm not your son. I'm not anybody's son. Not anymore.*

But all he said, not caring, was 'My comic books.'

The ambassador looked relieved. 'Of course. Whatever you like. I'll send a man out this afternoon to get them. Have you any preference, any you're especially fond of?'

'Superman.' It made no difference. Drew wanted desperately to get out of the office. 'Davy Crockett.'

'I'll get a boxload for you.' The ambassador pursed his lips. 'Now then.'

He stood, came around to the front of his desk, and leaned his hips against it, bending forward to put his gaze at Drew's eye level. 'I have a few things we have to discuss. This isn't easy, but it has to be done. Your parents' funeral . . .'

Drew winced. Though only ten, he'd been taught by yesterday's horror to have a sudden understanding of death. Certainly, after having seen his parents' fragmented bodies, he knew that they couldn't possibly be put back together.

'. . . will be tomorrow morning. My assistants and myself have had several discussions on the matter. We know how painful this is for you, but we've agreed that you ought to attend it. To lay your nightmares to rest, so to speak. And to make you a symbol . . .'

Drew didn't understand the word.

'. . . of what hate can do. Of what shouldn't be allowed to happen again. I know that this is all terribly confusing for you, but sometimes we have to make good things come out of bad. We want you to sit in the front pew at the funeral. A lot of photographers will take your picture. A lot of people – the world, in fact – will be watching. I'm sorry that you have to grow up so fast. For what it's worth, I feel confident that your mother and father would have wanted you to go.'

At last Drew did cry. No matter how hard he tried, he couldn't stop himself.

The ambassador held him tightly, patting his back. 'That's the stuff. Get it out of you. Let it go. Believe me, it's all right to cry.'

Drew didn't need encouragement. He continued to sob, convulsing so hard that he thought his heart must surely break. Finally his spasms subsided. Wiping his eyes, feeling the sting of the tears on his cheeks, he frowned in pain at the ambassador. 'Why?' His throat was so swollen that the word was a croak.

'I'm sorry, Andrew. I'm not sure I understand. Why what?'

'Who killed them? *Why?*'

The ambassador sighed. 'I wish I knew. These days, America isn't very popular, I'm afraid.' He named several countries, most of which Drew had never heard of – Cuba, Cameroon, Algeria, the Congo. 'It's not just here in Japan that we've had riots against us. Everything's changing. The world's a different place.'

'But isn't there *someone* you can punish?'

'I'm sorry. We just don't know enough. But I promise we're doing everything we can to find out.'

Drew blinked through his tears.

'I hate to do this all at once. There's something else we have to discuss. A while ago I said that I've told the kitchen staff to give you all the ice cream you want for the next few days. The reason for the time limit is that after the funeral, after you've had a chance to rest, you'll be flown back to the States. Someone has to take care of you. I've spoken to your uncle and made arrangements for you to stay with him. You'll have a chance to speak with him on the overseas telephone' – the ambassador glanced at his watch – 'in twenty minutes.'

Confused, Drew tried to remember what his uncle looked like, but all he saw in his mind was his father's face, or rather, an indistinct image of his father's face. It alarmed him that he couldn't recall what his father

150

looked like. Except for the fragments of the body strewn across the blood-soaked lawn.

7

'But who killed your parents?' Arlene sat beside him on the bed, clutching a blanket around her.

'I never knew. At the embassy, I heard a lot of talk. The American who'd dressed as a chauffeur and delivered the bomb was described as a free-lance, a mercenary. That was the first time I'd ever heard the word. The assumption was that he'd been hired by Japanese fanatics, but one man on the embassy's security staff – he'd lived in Japan since the end of the war – insisted that a bomb wasn't the Japanese style. He kept talking about samurai and *bushido* and a lot of other things I didn't understand. The code of the warrior. He said a Japanese worthy of that name was honor-bound to kill his enemy in the open, face to face. Not with a bomb, not even with a gun, but with a sword. Three months later, in fact, a Japanese protestor did just that, shoving his way through a crowd to impale a Japanese politician who favored the new treaty with America. And the security guard also said that a true Japanese wouldn't have tried to kill his enemy's wife and child – only the husband, the father.'

'But if the guard didn't blame the Japanese, who *did* he blame?'

'The Russians. Much of this didn't make sense to me at the time, of course, but I later got the idea of what he meant. The point of the new defense treaty was for America to help protect Japan from an attack by the Soviets. With our bases in Japan, we had our thumb on Southeast Asia and could try to stop communism from spreading. The guard's theory was that, if the Soviets could make it seem that the Japanese had blown up an American diplomat and his family . . .'

'The deaths would be so shocking they'd widen the gap between America and Japan. The treaty would be threatened,' said Arlene.

'That was the guard's idea. But if so, the tactic didn't work. My parents' murders made everybody realize how out of control the situation had become. The Japanese, embarrassed that they were being blamed for the assassinations, began to stop demonstrating. The crisis passed.'

Arlene took his hand. 'But not your nightmares.'

He looked at her with anguish. '*I wanted someone to blame.*'

8

He'd often gone to mass with his parents, but he'd never realized until their funeral how many images of death surrounded him in church. Christ on the Cross, the nails through His hands and feet, His back slashed by whips, His head crowned with thorns, His side split open by a spear. In a prayer book, he found a colorful depiction of the tomb from which Christ had risen. Christ's disciples stood before the rolled-away stone, raising their faces in celebration.

But nothing could bring his parents back, he knew. He'd seen the bloody fragments of their bodies.

The thunderous organ music was scary, the Latin of the mass as meaningless as the English that the priest used to describe 'this terrible tragedy'. In the front pew, Drew felt everybody staring at him. Photographers kept taking his picture. He wanted to scream.

The ambassador had explained that the bodies would be flown to a place called Andrews Air Force Base, where his uncle and 'even the Secretary of State' would be waiting. Whoever the Secretary of State was. It didn't matter. There'd be another service at his father's family plot in Boston, but to Drew, that didn't matter either, though apparently this first service was more important, a symbol – the ambassador had used that word again – of the need for friendship between America and Japan.

Drew noticed many hard-faced men, their suitcoats open, clutching what might have been guns attached to their belts.

And when the service ended, the ambassador took the American flags – one had covered each coffin – folded them, and brought them over for Drew to touch.

He pressed his face against them, soaking them with his tears.

9

'And that's why I couldn't be this free-lance assassin you told me about. This mercenary terrorist.' Drew said the words with disgust. 'Janus. Because a man like Janus killed my parents. And he wasn't alone. The ambassador told me there were many other mercenaries like the one who'd disguised himself as a chauffeur.' Drew bristled. 'Without the honor of a Japanese. Cowards. Sneak thieves, who didn't have the dignity to face their enemies directly. Mothers, fathers, children – it made no difference to them who they hurt, what grief and pain they caused. Each night as I cried myself to sleep, I repeated a vow I made to myself.' He clenched his teeth. 'If I might never have the satisfaction of seeing the man who'd murdered my parents receive the punishment he deserved, I'd punish those who were like him. I'd make it my business to get even with all of them.'

'You were – how old? – ten, you said?' Arlene looked astonished. 'And you made that choice? You stuck to it?'

'There's nothing surprising about it.' Drew swallowed bitterly. 'You see, I *loved* my parents. To this day, I still miss them. I used to visit their graves. A lot.' His voice cracked. 'Ten years old, I thought I could get revenge on my own. I didn't know how. But later, in my teens, I learned that others felt as I did. I went to work for . . .'

'Scalpel.' She breathed the word.

The phone rang harshly, interrupting them.

152

10

Drew swung in surprise toward the bedside table. He glanced sharply at Arlene. Her eyes wide, she seemed as startled as he was. He stared again toward the table where the phone rang a second time.

'Wrong number?' Arlene clearly didn't believe it.

Drew didn't even bother shaking his head. The phone rang a third time.

'The clerk in the office?' Arlene asked. 'Something he forgot to tell us?'

'Like what?'

She couldn't think of anything. The phone rang again.

'Maybe we're talking too loud. Maybe we woke up somebody next to us,' Drew said. 'There's one way to know for sure.' He leaned from the bed to pick up the phone. Despite his tension, he kept his voice calm. 'Hello.'

'Yes. Not to alarm you' – the voice on the other end was male, husky, heavily accented – 'but I have no choice except to call you.'

Regardless of that reassurance, Drew did feel alarmed, nagged by the terrible suspicion that he'd heard the voice before, though he couldn't identify it. Arlene left the chair, putting her head next to Drew's, listening as he held the phone slightly away from his ear.

The voice kept talking. 'It's unfortunate, but even with the best equipment, I'm not able to hear everything you say in your room. The shower, in particular, presented a problem. And you're coming to the part that interests me.'

Drew shivered from a cold spot between his shoulderblades as he remembered, with frightening vividness, where he'd heard the voice before. It belonged to the priest who'd suddenly appeared from the confessional when Drew had been attacked in the chapel at the retreat house in the Berkshire Hills. The priest with the gleaming red ring, the .45, and the Slavic accent. The priest who'd shot the two priest-assailants and chased Drew down the tunnel.

'I realize you need time to adjust to my intrusion,' the voice said. 'I've no doubt surprised you. But please, don't hesitate much longer. Time, as the saying goes, is short.'

Drew gripped his Mauser. 'Where are you?'

'In the unit next to yours. Note how freely I tell you. I put myself in your hands.'

Drew scowled toward the opposite wall. 'How did you find us?'

'Everything in due course. I want permission to enter your room. I'd prefer not to leave the building, however. A locked door separates our units. If you'll unbolt your side, I'll do the same on mine, and then at last we can meet.'

Drew raised his eyebrows in question toward Arlene. She nodded, pointing at herself and then at the bed. Her next gesture told Drew to go to the wall beside the adjoining door.

Drew spoke to the phone. 'If you show a weapon . . .'

'Please,' the voice said, 'I understand the rules. I took a risk by phoning you. Respect my candor. Unbolt the door.'

Arlene nodded firmly again.

'All right,' Drew said.

He set the phone on its cradle. Arlene got onto the bed, propping her back against its pillows. He aimed his Mauser and stepped toward the connecting door.

Hard enough to make an obvious sound, he twisted the bolt on the lock, then stepped toward the wall where he'd be out of sight when the door came open. But as an extra precaution, he shifted toward the corner, in case a bullet burst through the wall.

The lock on the other side was twisted. The door creaked, opening into the room.

On the bed, Arlene – in full view of the open door – separated the folds of the blanket she'd been clutching around her, revealing sleek, inviting breasts, their nipples hardening from the sudden comparative cold, her pubic hair . . .

Drew took advantage of the distraction. An instant was all he needed. He yanked the door completely open so it banged against the wall. Thrusting his Mauser hard against the man's kidney, he quickly, expertly, frisked him.

The priest groaned from the pistol's sharp jab. 'No need, I left my weapon in my room.' Having stooped in pain, he now straightened. 'I told you, I understand the rules. I'm not a threat to you.'

Drew finished his search, even thrusting a hand at the crotch of the priest's black trousers, probing the area around the man's testicles.

'And please,' the man told Arlene, 'kindly wrap the blanket around you again. I'm a priest. But I'm not immune to temptations of the flesh.'

Arlene closed the blanket.

'Thank you.' The man wore a black suitcoat, a black bib, a white collar. He was husky, of medium height, compact, muscular, with gray hairs in his thick dark mustache and hints of silver in his dense black hair. His face was square, craggy, strong-boned, ruggedly European. He seemed in his early fifties, but a deep brooding portion of his eyes, much blacker than his clothes, mustache, and hair, outlined by fierce strong wrinkles, suggested that his experiences had made him infinitely older.

Drew stepped cautiously back. 'How did you find us?'

'At the retreat house, you were given clean clothes. A change of shoes.' The priest waited for Drew to make his own conclusions.

Drew winced in disgust for not having suspected. 'A homing device?'

'In the heel of one shoe. After you fled the seminary, I followed its signal. I found where you left the bishop's car – shockingly devastated, I might add.' The priest allowed himself to chuckle. Drew started to talk, but the priest raised a hand. 'Let me finish. I discovered that you'd switched the ruined Cadillac for a motorcycle. Resourceful of you. I followed you to Concord and Lexington. You made phone calls. From there, I followed you to Greenwich Village in New York and watched your efforts to contact this young lady. You gave me concern when you changed from the shoes with the homing device to those climbing boots at Satan's Horn. But I attached a homing device to your motorcycle. And' – glancing toward Arlene – 'to your car.'

For the first time since the priest had entered the room, she spoke. 'And in the meantime?' She frowned. 'You killed the men who'd been . . .'

'Following you? It was unavoidable, I'm afraid. I couldn't let them do

154

the same to both of you. There were prior obligations. You see how open I'm being with you?'

'You pushed the man disguised as a wino off the cliff?' she asked.

The priest nodded slightly.

'And slit the other man's throat with a garotte?'

'It was necessary. Otherwise, you wouldn't be alive for us to have this talk.'

'A priest who kills?' Drew looked at him in horror.

'I might ask the same of you, though you're not in fact a priest but only a brother. Even so you're not unacquainted with killing. Or am I wrong?'

They stared at each other.

Arlene broke the silence. 'What he says makes sense. With a homing device, he could have stayed far enough back that you didn't see his car when you waited at the side of the road.'

'Quite true,' the priest said. 'I kept a distance. But finally we're together.'

Drew shook his head again. 'Why?'

'Isn't it obvious? The attack on the monastery.'

'The bishop claims it didn't happen.'

'He was told to pretend so. After we'd removed the evidence.'

'*We?*'

'In good time.'

'The bishop also claimed that Hal had *not* been killed at the retreat house. That I wasn't attacked.'

'More instructions he followed. I stayed briefly at the retreat house to arrange the cleanup. The seminarians know only that a guest had a nervous breakdown. Nothing's been compromised.'

Drew slammed his fist against the wall. 'And I can't wait any longer! I want answers!'

'Of course. But, please, there's no need for dramatic gestures. I'm your guardian.'

Drew froze. 'My *what?*'

'The moment you came with Father Hafer to report to the bishop, I was sent for. I've never been far. Twice – at the chapel and at the Horn – I saved your life.'

Drew's scalp prickled. 'Saved my life? *Why?* And why didn't you let me know at the start what you were doing?'

'I didn't tell you at the retreat house because I didn't want to show myself. I wanted to see what would happen if you seemed alone, except for Hal. As I suspected, your apparent vulnerability invited an attack.'

'You used me as bait?' Drew shook with indignation.

'It seemed an expedient way to draw out your enemies.'

'You should have warned me!'

'I disagree. Even a professional such as yourself –'

'A *former* professional.'

'That's the point. I wasn't sure how well you'd adapt to being back in the world. Extremely well, it turned out. But at the time, I wondered if six years of being a hermit would have blunted your skills. Suppose I'd told you I wanted to use you as bait to invite an attack? What if you were no longer capable of behaving naturally under stress? If you'd so much as glanced in my direction, you'd have warned your assailants of a possible

155

trap. The two men who burst into the chapel weren't priests, by the way. They dressed to appear so and avoid attracting attention at the seminary. I want to emphasize, they didn't belong to the Church.'

'Who were they?'

'We haven't been able to learn. They carried no identification, of course. We took photographs and made impressions of their fingerprints. Our contacts are trying to put names to them now, but I suspect we'll merely discover that they were mercenaries, that there's no way to link them to whoever hired them. After the attack at the retreat house, I tried to explain who I was and why I was there, but you ran. This is the first safe opportunity I've had. I should introduce myself.' He held out his hand. 'I'm Father Stanislaw.'

Drew studied the hand, uneasy. 'Stanislaw?'

'The name is Polish. I was born there, and it amused me to take the name of the patron saint of the country of my ancestors.'

Reluctantly, Drew gripped the hand.

The priest's clasp was firm. Drew reached for the priest's other hand. His left. The one with the ring on the middle finger.

Father Stanislaw did not resist.

The ring had a thick gold band and setting. Its stone was large, distinctive, gleaming, red – a ruby with a symbol emblazoned upon it. A sword intersecting with a Maltese cross.

'I don't think I've ever seen this symbol. What order does it represent?'

'Order?' Father Stanislaw shook his head. 'Not quite an order, though we've been in existence much longer than most orders. From the time of the Crusades, to be sure. But we call ourselves a fraternity.'

Drew waited.

'The fraternity of the stone. We'll get to that in time,' Father Stanislaw said. 'But first, we have some catching up to do. If you'll allow me . . .'

The priest went into his room, came back with a briefcase, removed a folder, and handed it to Drew.

Puzzled, opening it, Drew discovered a dossier about himself – details about his youth. 'Wait a minute.' He looked up. 'Where'd you learn all this?'

'It isn't important. What is,' Father Stanislaw said, 'is that you learn to trust me. I'm showing you the dossier to prove that I already know a great deal about you. As a consequence, I'm hoping that you'll tell me things I *don't* know. Think of this as confession. A confidence. A basis for understanding. Perhaps it will save your life. And more important, your soul.'

Arlene leaned forward. Holding the blanket around her with one hand, she impatiently took the folder from Drew, set it down on her lap, and flipped through its contents. 'What *is* this?'

'What happened to me after my parents were killed.' Drew's voice was thick.

'But what does this have to do with Jake? My brother's in trouble. For all I know, he might even be dead !'

'To do with Jake?' Drew repeated. 'Everything. Unless you know all of it, you can't understand.'

156

11

'Here we are, Drew.' His uncle stopped the red Mercury in front of a lawn that sloped up to a ranch house, as he called it. 'We had it built last fall. There aren't many like it yet in Boston. The latest design. I hope you'll be happy here. You're home.'

Drew stared at the building, feeling foreign and strange. Long and low, the house was made of bricks. It had a chimney; a crowded flower garden; a few short trees. It certainly didn't look anything like a ranch, and he couldn't help comparing it to the traditional Japanese house made of wood, with a high sloping roof, where he'd lived in Tokyo for half his life. Bricks? he asked himself. What would happen here in an earthquake?

And why was the garden so crowded?

'Home,' his uncle had said, but it made Drew angry. No. This wasn't his home. His home was back in Japan. Where he'd lived with his parents.

A woman and boy came out of the house. Drew's aunt and cousin. Drew hadn't seen them since his parents had taken him from America when he was five, and he didn't remember them. But this much was clear. The two of them – and his uncle when he made the introductions – were awkward, uneasy. His aunt kept wringing her hands. His cousin kept scowling. And his uncle kept saying that everything was going to work out, you bet, yes, all of them would get along just fine.

'You'll be happy here.'

Drew wondered, though. He had the terrible sense that he'd never be happy again.

The next day, he went to his parents' second funeral.

12

He spent the summer alone watching television or, if someone came into the den, reading comic books behind the closed door of what everybody still called the 'guest room'. Whenever his aunt told his uncle that it wasn't natural for a boy to stay indoors in summer his uncle said, 'Give him time to get adjusted. Remember, he's been through a lot. What's the matter with Billy? Tell Billy to play with him.'

'Billy says he's tried.'

In truth, Billy hadn't, and Drew knew the reason – jealousy about the new kid in the house.

His aunt said, 'Billy thinks he's strange. The way he never talks, and . . .'

'Wouldn't you seem strange?'

'You're at work all day. You don't know what he's like. He sneaks around. I'll be doing the ironing, and I won't even hear him. Suddenly he's right there beside me, staring. He's just like –'

'What? Go on and say it.'

'I'm sure I don't know. A ghost. He makes me nervous.'

'This is hard on all of us. But we'll have to get used to it. After all, he's my brother's son.'

'And Billy's your *own* son, and I don't see why we have to pay more attention to –'

'So where's the kid supposed to go, huh? Tell me that. He didn't ask for somebody to blow up his parents. What the hell do you want me to do?'

'Stop shouting. The neighbors'll hear you.'

'And so can the kid when you talk about him, but that doesn't seem to bother you!'

'I won't let you speak to me like that. I –'

'Never mind. I don't feel like eating supper, okay? Put something in the fridge for me. I'm taking a walk.'

Drew, having listened out of sight in the hall, went back to the guest room, where he closed the door and read another comic book.

Batman now.

13

September was worse. The first day Drew came back from the local grade school, he had bubble gum stuck in his hair.

'How on earth did you manage that?' his aunt asked.

Drew didn't answer.

She tried to pull the gum out, tugging his hair till tears leaked from his eyes. Finally she cut the gum out with scissors, leaving a bald spot on the crown of his head that resembled a buck private's new haircut or a tonsure on a monk.

The next day, Drew returned from school with black indentations all down his left arm.

'My word, what have you been doing to yourself?' Pursing her lips, his aunt examined the indentations, went for the tweezers, and pulled the point of a pencil out of his skin. 'How in heaven's name did that happen?'

The following day, the knee on Drew's new pants was torn, soaked with blood, his skin scraped raw.

'Those pants cost good money, you know.'

The day after that, Drew's aunt made an urgent phone call to her husband at his real estate office.

She could hardly speak. But through her sobs, her husband understood enough. Shocked, he agreed to meet her at Drew's grade school after classes let out.

14

'Now I don't deny that your nephew had provocation.' The principal had a wobbly double chin. 'The Whetman boy is known to be a bully. I assume you're familiar with his parents? His father runs the Cadillac dealership over on Palmer Road.'

Drew's aunt and uncle didn't recognize 'Whetman', but they certainly recognized 'Cadillac'.

'So the situation's this.' The principal mopped his forehead with a handkerchief. 'The Whetman kid is twelve. He's big for his age, and he likes to throw his weight around. The fact is . . . I'll tell you this in confidence. I assume you won't repeat it. The kid takes after his father – pushy. But the father donates a lot of cash to our athletic fund. Anyway, the kid lets everybody know who's boss. So your nephew . . . Well, he didn't buckle under, is what it amounts to. I've got to give him credit. Tough little monkey. Everybody else buckles under. I don't know why your nephew didn't. When school got started, I guess the Whetman kid checked around to see who's new on the block and decided to pick on Andrew as an example. The way I hear it, the Whetman kid put bubble gum in Andrew's hair. And then he stuck pencils into him. And shoved him in the gravel at recess, ripping his pants.'

Drew's uncle asked, 'Why wasn't anything done to stop this?'

'It's only rumors, things I heard from the children. If I believed everything that the students told me . . .'

'Go on.'

'Well, basically . . .' The principal sighed. 'Today, the Whetman kid took a whack at Andrew. A pretty good one. He split Andrew's lip.'

Drew's uncle squinted angrily. 'And?'

'Andrew didn't cry. I'll give him credit for that as well. He sure is a tough little monkey. But the thing is, he should have complained to a teacher in the playground .'

'Would it have mattered?'

The principal scowled. 'I'm sorry. I don't understand.'

'Never mind. Go on.'

'Instead, Andrew lost his temper.'

'I can't imagine why.'

'He hit the Whetman kid in the mouth with a baseball bat.'

Drew's uncle turned pale. 'Oh, shit.'

'Loosened the Whetman kid's front teeth is what he did. Now the kid had some discipline coming, sure. I won't argue that point. But a *baseball bat*? Overreaction wouldn't you think? And Mr Whetman was in here earlier. He's upset, I don't need to tell you. He wants to know what kind of school I'm running. He's threatened to go to the education board and the police. Thank God, I managed to talk him out of it, but the point is, until this problem is settled . . . Well, what I asked you here to talk about is your nephew's suspended. I want him to stay home from school.'

15

'It's a damned good thing for you,' Mr Whetman told Drew's uncle and aunt in their living room that night. 'If my son had lost his teeth, I'd be suing you so fast . . .'

'Mr Whetman, please. I know you've got every reason to be angry.'
Drew's uncle held up his hands. 'Believe me, we're disturbed about this
ourselves. I'll be glad to pay for any doctor or dentist bills. Your boy isn't
disfigured, I hope.'

Whetman fumed. 'No thanks to your nephew. The doctor says that the
stitches won't leave scars, but right now my son's got lips the size of
sausages. I'll be direct. The principal told me about your nephew's
background, about what happened to his parents. Terrible. It's the only
excuse I can think of for his behavior. Obviously your nephew's disturbed. I've decided not to go to the police. On one condition. That the
boy get professional help.'

'I'm not sure what you mean.'

'A psychiatrist, Mr MacLane. The sooner, the better. Oh, yes, and
something else.'

Drew's uncle waited.

'I don't want that boy near my son. Have him transferred to another
school.'

Drew listened behind the partly open door of his room. His eyes stung
bitterly. But he'd made a promise to himself, and he kept it. He didn't cry.

16

On the third day after his transfer, Drew's aunt heard the phone ring as
she carried groceries into the kitchen.

She hurried to set down the bags and answer it.

'Mrs MacLane?'

The officious voice distressed her. 'Speaking.'

'I'm sorry to bother you. This is the principal over at Emerson grade
school.'

She tensed.

'I'm sure this is nothing. You probably, well, just forgot.'

She gripped the cupboard.

'But since we didn't receive any word this morning, I thought I'd better
call to find out if your nephew's sick.'

She herself felt sick. 'No.' She swallowed something sour. 'Not that I
know of. He seemed perfectly well when he got on the bus this morning.
Why? Has he been complaining about a stomach ache?'

'That's just it, Mrs MacLane. No one here has seen him to ask him.'

Inwardly, she groaned.

'I assumed you'd kept him home from school and simply forgot to let
the attendance office know. It happens all the time. But because I'm aware
of your nephew's situation, I thought there wouldn't be any harm in my
asking. Just in case, you understand.'

'In case?'

'Well, I don't think anything's happened to him, though you never can
tell. But he wasn't here yesterday, either.'

17

Standing next to the policeman, Drew stared down at the sidewalk in front of his aunt and uncle's house.

The screen door banged open. He peered up as his uncle stormed out. 'It's after supper, Andrew, you had us worried. Where on earth have you been?'

'The cemetery,' the policeman said.

'*What?*'

'Pleasant View. That's ten miles north of here.'

'Yes, officer, I'm familiar with it.'

'They've had some vandalism recently. Teenagers sneaking in, toppling tombstones, that sort of thing. I can't imagine why anybody would think that's funny. Anyway, the cemetery director asked us to keep a watch, so I've been driving through there on my rounds. Yesterday morning, I saw this youngster staring down at some graves. I didn't think much about it, mostly because I had a radio call about a burglary in progress, and I had to hot-tail it over to a liquor store. But this morning, I was driving through that cemetery again, and there was this youngster again, and I thought, "Now wait a minute," and stopped. He sure doesn't talk much, does he?'

'That's a fact,' Drew's aunt said.

'Even when I walked up to him, he didn't pay me any attention. He just kept staring down at the graves. So I went around behind him and saw that the last names on the tombstones were both the same.'

'MacLane,' Drew's uncle said.

'That's right. A man and a woman.'

'Robert and Susan.'

'Right. So I asked him what he was doing, and the first and last thing he said to me was, "I'm talking to my mom and dad."'

'Dear God.'

'Then he wiped at his eyes, but the funny thing was, I couldn't see any tears. I figured he must have someone with him, but when I looked, there wasn't anyone in sight. And most children, you know, this uniform makes them pay attention. Not him, though. He just kept staring down at those graves. He wouldn't tell me his name or where he lived. All by himself. Why wasn't he in school? So what could I do? I took him down to the station.'

'You did right,' Drew's uncle said.

'I even bought him a chocolate bar, but he still wouldn't talk to me, and his wallet had no I.D., so that's when I started calling all the MacLanes in the book. You say you're his guardians?'

'He was telling the truth,' Drew's uncle said. 'His parents are buried there.'

'I sure feel sorry for him.'

'Yeah,' Drew's uncle said, 'it's a long, sad story. Here, let me pay you for the chocolate bar you bought him.'

'That's okay. My treat. Besides, he's a tough little kid. He never ate it.'

'Right,' Drew's uncle said. 'A tough little kid.'

18

Mrs Cavendish set down the pointer she'd been aiming at multiplication lists on the blackboard.

'Andrew, I asked you a question.'

The children giggled.

'Andrew?' Mrs Cavendish stalked between rows of desks until she reached a seat near the back. Drew was slumped across the desktop, his head on his arms, asleep. She towered over him, glaring, her voice loud. 'Andrew?'

He murmured in his sleep.

She nudged his shoulder. Nudged it again. 'Andrew?' she barked.

He sat up bolt-straight, blinking.

'I asked you a question.'

'I'm sorry, Mrs Cavendish.' Drew shook his head to clear it. 'I guess I wasn't listening.'

'Of course not. How could you? *When you were asleep.*'

The children had turned around in their desks to watch the excitement. Now as Mrs Cavendish shot an angry glance their way, they swiveled to peer ahead, their flushed necks the only sign of the laughter they struggled to contain.

'This isn't the first time. Do I bore you so much that I put you to sleep?'

'No, Mrs Cavendish.'

'Then it must be mathematics that makes you sleepy.'

'No, Mrs Cavendish.'

'What is it then?'

Drew didn't answer.

'Well, young man, you can sleep on somebody else's time. From now on, you sit in the desk right in front of me. Stand up.'

She marched him to the front and made him switch places with another student.

'And now, young man, the next time you're tempted to show me how boring I am by falling asleep, I won't have to reach far' – she picked up her pointer and whacked it hard against the front of the desk – 'to wake you up.'

Of all the children, only Drew didn't flinch.

19

Four A.M. A chilly October wind nipped Drew's cheeks as he stood with the policeman in front of the house.

'I hate to wake you up this late,' the policeman said, 'but I figured you must be frantic with worry.'

Light spilled from the open front door. Drew's aunt clutched the front of her housecoat. Beside her silhouetted in the doorway, Drew's uncle glanced nervously at the darkened houses along the street as if he hoped that the neighbors wouldn't notice the police car parked in front. 'You'd better come in.'

'I understand.' The policeman guided Drew in and shut the door. 'I'm sure you weren't expecting company. I'll just stand here in the hall.'

'*But where did you find him?*'

The policeman hesitated. 'The cemetery.'

Drew's uncle blinked. 'We didn't even know he was gone.'

Drew's aunt raised a trembling hand to her hairnet. 'I put him to bed right after supper. I checked him before we went to sleep.'

'It seems he snuck out after. I've got his bicycle in the trunk of the car,' the policeman said.

'He biked ten miles?' Drew's uncle slumped against the wall. 'In the night, in this cold? He must be –'

'Exhausted,' Drew's aunt said. She looked at her husband. 'Dear Lord, do you suppose?' She shivered and stared at Drew. 'Is that what you've been doing? Is that why you're so tired at school?'

'This time around, I managed to get him to talk to me,' the policeman said. 'Not a lot, but enough to get the idea. I gather that he's been biking over there at night and . . . maybe it's better if he tells you himself. Go on, Drew. Why have you been biking over there? I don't mean just to visit your parents. You can do that in daylight. Why at night?'

Drew glanced from the policeman to his aunt and uncle. He peered at the door.

'Go on, Drew.' The policeman crouched. 'Tell them what you told me.'

Drew's aunt and uncle waited sternly.

'Vandals,' Drew said.

His aunt and uncle looked shocked. 'Vandals?'

Drew nodded.

'The cat has his tongue again,' the policeman said, 'so let me fill in the blanks. When I brought him home before, he heard me talk about the teenagers who've been vandalizing the cemetery.'

'I remember,' Drew's uncle said.

'Well, apparently that got him thinking. For starters, he didn't know what "vandals" meant, so he says he looked it up in the dictionary. I don't know what he read, but it sure upset him.'

'That still doesn't explain why he's been sneaking out at night to go to the cemetery,' Drew's aunt said.

'It does if you think about it. What he's been doing is –' Drew fidgeted, self-conscious; they stared at him '– protecting his parents' graves.'

20

Saturday morning, bright and cold. As a group of neighborhood children played football in the distance, Drew sat alone on a swing at the far end of the lot.

A shadow loomed across him. From in back.

Drew turned. At first, with the sun angled toward his eyes, he couldn't make out the face of the tall man in the overcoat.

But as his vision got used to the glare of the sun, he suddenly grinned excitedly and rushed to the man.

'Uncle Ray!'

In truth, the man was not related to Drew, but from years of habit, that was what Drew had always called him.

'Uncle Ray!'

Drew threw his arms around the man's waist, feeling the soft brown cloth of the overcoat.

The man laughed, picked Drew up, and swung him around. 'It's good to see you, sport. How's the world been treating you?'

Drew was too delighted to pay attention to the question. As the man continued laughing, Drew laughed as well, enjoying the wonderful dizziness of being swung around.

The man set him down and, smiling, crouched to face him. 'Surprised?'

'Boy, I'll say!'

'I happened to be in Boston on business, and I thought, "What the heck, as long as I'm here, I might as well visit my old friend Drew."' Uncle Ray mussed Drew's hair. 'A good thing I did, huh? When I saw you on that swing, you looked pretty glum.'

Drew shrugged, remembering how he'd felt, returning to his somber mood.

'Got troubles, sport?'

'Yeah, I guess so.'

'Any you'd like to tell me about?'

Drew scuffed his running shoes in the dead brown grass. 'Just stuff.'

'Well, it might be I know a few of them already. I stopped at the house. Your aunt told me where you'd gone.' Ray paused. 'She also told me what's been happening. Your problems at school.' He bit his lip. 'The other things. And I hear you've been getting in fights with your cousin.'

'He doesn't like me.'

'Oh? You're sure of that?'

'He's mad because I live there. He's always playing practical jokes on me or hiding my homework or blaming me for things I didn't do.'

'I can see how that might happen. So you decked him, huh?'

Drew grinned, holding up his right hand. 'Bruised my knuckles.'

'It could be an even trade. At the house, I saw his black eye.'

The man was as old as Drew's father had been. For some reason, 'thirty-five' stuck in Drew's mind. He had neatly trimmed sandy hair, expressive blue eyes and a narrow, handsome face, his jaw strongly outlined. Drew loved the sweet smell of his aftershave.

'Yeah, a lot of commotion,' Ray said. 'The question is, what are we going to do about it? You feel like taking a walk, sport?'

21

Puzzled, his heart thumping, Drew listened out of sight in the hall as the grown-ups talked about him in the living room.

'As you're aware, Drew's father and I were very close,' Ray said. His smooth voice carried down the hall. 'I knew him for years. We went to Yale together. We received our State Department training together. We were both stationed in Japan.'

Drew's uncle said, 'Then you were at the embassy when his parents were killed?'

'No, by the time the demonstrations started, I'd already been transferred to Hong Kong. When I heard what had happened, well, I couldn't believe that anybody would do such a horrible thing. I was involved in a diplomatic emergency at the time, and I couldn't leave Hong Kong even to go to the funeral. In fact, my assignment was serious enough that I wasn't free to get away till just last week. I'm sure you'll understand that I can't be specific about what I was doing. But as soon as I could, I wanted to come here to Boston – to pay my respects, to at least see their graves. It's hard to put this into words. Of course, he was your brother, Mr MacLane, so I hope you don't take this wrong if I say that I felt . . . well, like a brother to him also. As I said, we were very close.'

'I understand,' Drew's uncle said. 'The fact is, you probably knew him better than I did. I hadn't seen him in the past five years, and even before then, we didn't get together much.'

'What about the boy?'

'I don't believe I saw him more than three or four times. Ever. My brother and I were the only children in our family. Our parents died several years ago. So naturally, when my brother called me to say that he was having a new will made out and would I take custody of Drew if anything happened to Susan and himself . . .'

'Yes, naturally you agreed.'

'There wasn't anybody else he could ask, you see. But I never dreamed that I'd have to make good on my promise.'

'What I want to talk to you about is this. I've always been fond of Andrew. I guess I feel like an uncle to him. Again, I don't mean any offense. I'm not trying to be presumptuous. But my wife and I don't have any children. It seems we're not able to. At any rate, given the difficulties you've been having with him . . .'

'Difficulties. That's putting it mildly.'

'I wondered if you'd let my wife and me have custody of him.'

'Have custody! Are you serious?'

'It could be the answer to several problems. The grief I feel for my friend. My fondness for the boy. My wife and I had already considered going to an adoption agency. Add to that the problems you've been having with Drew.'

Drew's uncle sounded suspicious. 'What makes *you* think you can do any better with him?'

'I'm not sure I can. But I'd like to try.'

'And if it didn't work out?'

'I wouldn't bring him back to your doorstep, if that's what you mean. I'd abide by our agreement. If you're hesitant, though, if you think you'd want him back, we could arrange a compromise. Perhaps the boy could spend a month or so with my wife and myself, and after that, we all could talk about it again. This way, you'd have a chance to get your household back the way it used to be.'

'I don't know. Where would you take him?'

'Hong Kong. For half of his life, he lived in the Orient. Hong Kong isn't Japan, of course. But perhaps he'd feel more at home if he went back to the Far East.'

Drew's uncle sighed. 'This is hard to . . . Your offer's certainly tempting. I confess I've been at my wits' end. But there might be a problem. Suppose the boy doesn't want to go?'

'We can always ask him.'

Hiding in the hall, his heart swelling, Drew silently shouted, *Yes!*

22

The bitter wind brought tears to his eyes, though he might have been crying for a different reason as he stared down at his parents' graves.

Uncle Ray pulled up the collar on his overcoat and shoved his gloved hands into its pockets. 'I miss them too, sport.' His sandy hair was blown by the wind.

'Maybe I . . .'

'Yes? Go on.' Ray put an arm around him.

'. . . should have brought the flowers anyhow.'

'On a raw day like this? They wouldn't have lasted long. No, it's better that we let them live a while longer back at the flower shop.'

Drew understood. There wasn't any reason why the flowers should die as well. Only the people who'd killed his parents ought to die.

'So what do you think?' Ray asked. 'I know you want to stay, but we've been here almost an hour. We have to catch that plane at five o'clock. It's not forever you know. Someday, you'll be back.'

'Sure. It's just . . .'

'Hard to leave them? You bet. But we've got photographs. You can still remember them while you're away. I mean, a guy can't very well camp here in the cemetery, can he?'

'No.' Drew's eyes stung, misty, this time definitely not from the wind. He had trouble breathing. 'I guess not.'

23

Reading the dossier's objective summary, Drew recalled – and reexperienced – the emotions of his youth. As if a child again, he walked with Ray toward the car that would take them to the airport. In his painful memory, he glanced back, his throat tight, toward his parents' graves.

He knew that the priest's intention was to get him to talk about those days, and he did so freely, not caring if he gave the priest his wish. He needed to vent his sadness. 'In later years, whenever I was in Boston, I used to go back to that cemetery. I went there before I became a Carthusian. Last week, though, I never had the chance to visit them.'

'It was prudent of you not to,' Father Stanislaw said. 'Whoever wanted you dead would have put a surveillance team near those graves, just as Arlene was being watched in case you showed up.' The priest retrieved the dossier. 'Just a few more items. In Hong Kong, you began to run with a Chinese street gang. The man you called Uncle Ray understood your motive – to acquire the skills you thought you'd need to go after your parents' killer. To ensure your safety, he arranged for the grandson of a Gurkha to teach you street sense. Tommy Limbuk was the child's name.'

'Limbu,' Drew said. 'Known as Tommy Two.'

Father Stanislaw wrote a correction in the dossier. 'And after that, wherever Uncle Ray was stationed – France, Greece, Korea – he arranged for you to learn the martial skills of the local population. Foot boxing, wrestling, judo, karate. When you were seventeen, your need for revenge had still not abated. During your stay in various countries, you'd learned an impressive number of languages – and acquired a remarkable liberal arts education, I might add. Uncle Ray, aware of your life's ambition, knowing you couldn't be dissuaded, approached you with a suggestion. The United States, nervous about growing anti-American sentiment in the world, had decided to form a counterterrorist unit, designed to confront the very enemies you yourself had chosen. So you agreed to his suggestion and enlisted in the Rocky Mountain Industrial School in Colorado, a cover for military-intelligence instruction, a training facility much more secret than the farm in Virginia that the CIA used for its operatives.'

'Scalpel,' Arlene said.

Father Stanislaw glanced surprised at her. 'You know about it?'

'I belonged to it. So did Jake. That's where we met Drew.'

The priest leaned back in his chair. 'Thank God. I was starting to think you still didn't trust me. I wondered if you'd ever volunteer information.'

'You didn't ask the right questions. I'll tell you anything I can,' she said, 'if it helps me find Jake.'

'Then tell me,' Father Stanislaw said, 'about Scalpel.'

24

'Nineteen sixty-six: the year international terrorism became organized. In an effort to unite the struggles of Communist groups in Africa, Asia, and Latin America, Fidel Castro invited revolutionists from eighty-two countries to come to Cuba for an intensive training session, known as the Tricontinental Conference. A school for urban guerrilla warfare resulted, where members from almost every later infamous terrorist group received instruction. The IRA, the Red Brigades, The Baader-Meinhof Gang. The principles of terrorism worked out at that school became a Devil's bible. Qaddafi followed Castro's lead and organized training schools of his own in Libya. With Libya's enormous oil wealth, Qaddafi was able to accomplish more than Castro, not merely providing instruction to terrorists but also financing their operations. Random assassination; embassy takeovers; the slaughter of the Israeli athletes at the 1972 Munich Olympics. The kidnapping of the OPEC oil ministers in Vienna in '75. Commercial airliners destroyed by bombs. School buses blown apart. On and on. The list of horrors grew longer each year but they all dated back to 1966, Castro, and Cuba. Even the fanatical Muslim sects from the time of the Crusades were not as barbarous.'

(At the mention of the Crusades, Father Stanislaw touched the ruby ring on his left hand, tracing the symbol of the intersecting sword and Maltese cross. Arlene continued.)

'In 1968, the U.S. State Department, warned by intelligence sources about Castro's school for terrorists financed its own school for counterterrorists. The State Department could, of course, have gone to the CIA for that kind of service. But given the notoriety that the CIA had acquired since the Bay of Pigs, the State Department chose instead to sponsor its own clandestine unit. *A truly* clandestine unit, spared exposure in *The New York Times* and *The Washington Post*. Only a few insiders knew about it.'

As Arlene paused, Father Stanislaw nodded. 'Scalpel.' He glanced at Drew. 'The unit into which your Uncle Ray recruited you.'

'Now wait a minute,' Drew said. 'He didn't recruit me into anything.'

'Then let's say he made a discreet suggestion,' Father Stanislaw said. 'We can play with words all you want. The end result is what matters. He approached you about it, and you joined. Why was Scalpel chosen as the code name for the unit?'

Drew tried to mute his anger. 'Precise surgical removal.'

'Ah, yes, of course. The terrorists were like cancer. As a consequence, their excision was morally permissible. An ingenious choice of name. It symbolized its justification.'

'You find something wrong with the concept?' Arlene asked.

Father Stanislaw kept his eyes on Drew. 'Obviously *you* did, or you wouldn't have resigned.'

'Not wrong with the concept. Wrong with me.'

'Ah,' Father Stanislaw said. 'In that case, we should perhaps have met earlier.'

'Why?'

'To refresh your memory of St Augustine. The concept that killing is necessary if a war is just.'

'War?'

'Not nation fighting nation, not a conventional war. All the same, a war. The oldest, most basic one of all: good against evil. Terrorists, by definition, turn their backs on civilized standards. Their weapon is outrageous attack – to so disrupt the lives of average citizens that those citizens rebel against their government. But no end can justify such hellish means.'

'You believe that?' Drew glared.

'Apparently you don't.'

'There was a time when I would have.'

'But?' Father Stanislaw asked.

Drew didn't answer.

'At last,' Father Stanislaw said, 'We're there. *The part I don't know about.*' He sighed. 'After graduating from the Rocky Mountain Industrial School – a remarkable facility, I'm informed – you worked for Scalpel. From sixty-nine to early seventy-nine, you engaged in retaliatory strikes against whatever terrorists attracted your director's wrath. Sometimes, too, the strikes weren't after but *before* the fact. Preemptive. Made necessary by reliable intelligence reports. Terrorist activities were nipped in the bud, so to speak. Your urge to avenge your parents should have made you even more zealous. *What happened?* Why did you suddenly enter the monastery?'

Drew glanced toward the floor.

'No. Answer him,' Arlene said. 'I want to know as much as he does.' She turned Drew's face, making him look at her. 'What about Jake? *Is he involved?*'

Drew saw the anguish in her eyes. He hated what he had to tell her. 'Eventually.'

PART SIX
CHARTREUSE

MIRROR IMAGE, DOUBLE EXPOSURE

1

'The assignment was complicated.'

'When?' Father Stanislaw asked. 'Be specific.'

'In January of seventy-nine. In fact, I remember feeling puzzled – because I'd never been sent on a mission quite like it before.'

Father Stanislaw prompted him. 'What made it unusual? Its hazards?'

'No. The timing. You see, I hadn't been given one job, but two, and they had to be completed within forty-eight hours. They were both in France, so that didn't pose a problem, getting from one location to the next within the time limit. The difficulty was the method I was told to use. The same in each case. And in the first job, the geography was troublesome.'

Drew paused, distressed, sorting through information, trying to organize it. Arlene and Father Stanislaw watched him intently. At last he continued.

'The other thing that made the assignment unusual was that I didn't get a briefing on my targets. Usually, I was told what the criminal was being punished for. How many innocent people he'd killed. What maniac he was working for. I learned all about his habits, his vices. And that made it easier. It's not hard to kill vermin.'

Drew paused again, then resumed. 'Sometimes the method of execution was left up to me. Long-range sniping. A car-bomb in imitation of the bombs the terrorists so enjoyed setting off. Poison. Lethal viruses. The method was usually appropriate to the crime. But in this case, the mission had to be accomplished in a certain way. And as I said, there were in fact *two* missions. With a deadline. Quite unusual.'

'That didn't bother you?'

'In Colorado, I was trained not to question orders. And after you've killed as many times as I have, when you think you're justified, you're bothered by nothing. Except . . .'

Arlene leaned forward. 'Tell him everything. How you received your orders.'

'I needed a cover that allowed me to disappear at any time for as long as a week without attracting attention. A job was out of the question, too restricting, too many people to account to. But I had to do *something*. So I lived in a college town and became a student. The cover was easy. I was

171

always good at school. I've always enjoyed taking classes. Liberal arts. Literature mostly. I got a B.A. from one institution, then moved to another and got a second B.A. By then, I was too old to be an undergraduate, so I moved to a third school and got a master's degree. In fact, I have two of them, and I was working on the third when . . .'

'I still don't see the advantage of that cover,' Father Stanislaw said.

'A student can be anonymous. But you have to pick a school that's large. The Big Ten was my preference. A college town, the type where the students outnumber the local population. The students are transient, so if I came to town and stayed for a year or two, then transferred to another school, and then another, well, a lot of students did that – I wasn't unusual. I took only large lecture courses, and I never chose the same seat, so if the lecturer didn't keep attendance records – and I made sure he wasn't the type who did – I wouldn't draw attention when I disappeared for a couple of days. I've always been a loner, so it wasn't hard for me to resist making friends with other students. The friends I did have, professionals like Arlene and Jake' – he smiled at her – 'were all I needed. Between semesters or at term breaks, I went to visit them. At school, I was invisible. The only risk to my anonymity was, I went to a local gym every morning, to make sure I stayed in shape to be able to handle my assignments, and I went to a crowded diner every day at one, a bookstore at four, and a neighborhood grocery at seven.'

'Why take the risk? Why those particular places and times?'

'I had to. The times were chosen arbitrarily. The places themselves didn't matter. I could have substituted a movie theater for the bookstore, and a desk at the library for the grocery. What did matter was the routine. So a courier would have several chances to contact me easily and, more important, inconspicuously. At the diner, someone might sit next to me and leave a Canadian quarter as a tip for the waitress. Or at the grocery, a woman might ask for Mexican beer. That would be my signal to go to my apartment as soon as I could. If a dish towel was over the sink, I'd know to look beneath my bed, and in my suitcase, I'd find everything I needed to get to where I was going. Plane tickets, a passport, identification under another name. Cash in various currencies. An address in a foreign city.'

'Weapons?' Father Stanislaw asked.

'No,' Drew said emphatically. 'Never weapons. They were always made available to me from my contact at the foreign address. While I was gone, a lookalike would take my place and keep to my routine. It wasn't hard to make the switch. No one really knew me. Sure, they saw me. Mostly from a distance, though. I was merely part of the scene. The students and the locals didn't *know* me. That way, with someone doubling for me, a blur at the edge of the crowd, I had an alibi if something went wrong.'

Father Stanislaw gasped.

'What's wrong?' Drew asked.

'Don't stop. You're telling me more than you think.'

Drew glanced at Arlene. 'What does he mean?'

'The pieces are coming together.' Her voice was low. 'I agree. Keep going. What about the assignment?'

He breathed deeply. 'I received instructions to go to France but to do so indirectly, through London, where my double took my place. He went on a tour of literary landmarks – Stratford, Canterbury, that sort of thing, what a graduate student in English would find amusing. I'd been to those sites already, so if I had to account for my stay in England, I could do so easily. But while my alibi was being established, I flew to Paris, using another name, and received my instructions. Above Grenoble in the Alps of France, I learned that there was a monastery.'

'Of course!' the priest said. 'The Carthusian charterhouse, La Grande Chartreuse.'

'A man was scheduled to visit it, I'd been told. His car was described to me. Even the number on his license plate. I was to kill him.' Drew bit his lip. 'Have you ever been to La Grande Chartreuse?'

Father Stanislaw shook his head.

'It's extremely remote. In the Middle Ages, the founding monks selected its location carefully. They thought that the world was going to hell, which it always seems to be doing. They wanted to get away from the corruption of society, so they marched from the lowlands of France up into the Alps, where they built a primitive monastery. The Pope objected. After all, in the Middle Ages, what was the point of being a priest if you lived in deprivation?

'God seemed to side with the Pope by sending an avalanche onto the monastery, destroying it. But you've got to give the monks credit. They simply moved the monastery a safe distance lower, protected from snow-slides but still secluded from the world. And over the centuries, they built a magnificent cloister. It reminded me of a medieval castle. A mighty fortress for God.

'When the order spread to England, the monks were martyred by Henry the Eighth. Because he wanted a divorce and the Pope refused, Henry formed his own church, made himself its leader, and decreed that the divorce he craved was divinely sanctioned. When the Carthusian monks in England objected, Henry put them to death in the cruelest manner he could devise. They were hanged, cut down near death, disemboweled but left sufficiently alive for them to see their guts being eaten by dogs. Molten metal was poured into their body cavities. Their corpses were drawn and quartered, boiled, then thrown into ditches.'

'You describe it vividly,' Father Stanislaw said, his voice calm. 'What happened at La Grande Chartreuse?'

Drew began to sweat. He could not fight down his emotion. 'My assignment was to plant explosives at the side of a winding road that sloped up toward the monastery. The location was carefully chosen. A cliff on the far side. A steep drop on the near side – toward me, where I was waiting on the opposite slope. After I planted the explosives at night, it took me half the next day to climb out of sight through gorges until I reached the opposite bluff. The mountains were thick with snow. A few miles either way, I could have been skiing. If only I had been.' Drew shook his head. 'But I crouched behind bushes, my boots in the snow, my parka not really warm enough for the weather, and as I watched my breath drift up before my eyes, I studied that winding road. Because soon, my target car wound up toward the monastery. The occupant was sightseeing, you understand. Taking in the local attractions. Of course, he could never have gone inside the cloister itself, never have seen the hermit monks. But he could tour the perimeter and walk through the central court and perhaps provide a generous donation in exchange for a sample of the famous Chartreuse liqueur.' Drew felt the cold even now; he heard the squeak of the snow beneath his boots and recalled the stillness in those terrible claustrophobic mountains.

Blinking, he abruptly returned to the motel room, Arlene, and the priest. 'I'd planted the explosives on the far side of the road. Against the cliff. The thrust of the blast would send the car toward me, toward the cliff on the side that faced me. And the car, in flames, would fall. But this is the clever part. Someone at Scalpel must have thought long and hard about it. I'd been given a camera. Through its telephoto lens, I was to study the bend in the road that led up through the mountains. And when the car I was looking for came around the bend, when I made doubly sure it was the right car by verifying the number from the front license plate, I was to start taking pictures.'

'That's all? Just take pictures?' Father Stanislaw stood and began to pace the room.

'Not quite all. You see, the trigger mechanism on the camera was also the trigger for the explosive. The camera had a motor-driven shutter, designed for rapidly repeating exposures as long as I kept the button pressed down. Click, click, click. The bomb went off. The car veered sideways, toward me. Its gas tank burst into flames. And remember, the shutter kept clicking. I saw a telephoto image of everything. Just as the car began to topple over the cliff, a door in back flew open . . .'

'And?' Arlene watched him anxiously.

Drew's voice rose. 'God showed me a sign. He sent me a message.'

'*What?*' Father Stanislaw roared the word. 'You can't be serious?'

'But He did.' Drew's voice was suddenly calm. 'You believe in the bolt of light that toppled Saul from his horse on the road to Damascus, don't you? Saul, the sinner, who understood at once that God was telling him something, who changed his life that instant to follow the way of the Lord. Well, this was my bolt of light. My sign from God. I'd call it a miracle, except a miracle's supposed to make you feel good and this . . . A kid fell out. A boy. I've studied the photographs often. The boy was . . .'

'What?' Again the voice was Arlene's.

'. . . identical to me.'

She stared at him. 'You mean you noticed a resemblance. The same coloring perhaps. And size. Boys at the same age tend to look alike.'

'No, it was *more* than that. I'm telling you the resemblance was uncanny. When he grew up, he could have been my double back at the college. While I went out and killed.'

'Executed. Punished. Stopped them from doing it again.' Father Stanislaw's tone was harsh. 'Speak precisely. Don't exaggerate. You were under stress. You have to make allowance for . . .'

'The circumstances? For the moment? Listen, the moment is all I think about. That kid . . . *me* . . . tumbling from the car. Horror in his eyes.'

Drew fumbled in his pants pocket, yanking out the four wrinkled photographs he'd taken with him from the monastery. He thrust them at Father Stanislaw. Arlene leaned quickly toward the priest to see them.

Drew's face was tormented. 'They're all I kept from my former life. Before I joined the Carthusians, I went to every place I'd hidden money, passports, weapons. I got rid of them. I canceled everything about my former existence, erased myself, even to the point of making it seem as if I was dead.'

Shuddering, Drew glanced at the photographs. He knew the images by heart. 'The one on top is me. In Japan in 1960. It was taken in the garden behind my parents' house. Three days before they were murdered.'

Father Stanislaw set it aside.

'The next one,' Drew said, 'is my parents. Again, the same location, three days before they were killed. The others I took in seventy-nine below La Grande Chartreuse. After I detonated the explosives and the boy fell from the car. I had a section of the boy's photograph enlarged, to show his face. The picture's grainy, sure. And the smoke from the explosion was drifting in front of him, and snow had started to fall. But I think you get my point.'

The priest peered up from the photograph, staring toward Drew. His hands quivered. 'At first, I thought this third photograph was a poor reproduction of the first. I thought it was –'

'Me. But it isn't. If you look closely, really closely, you'll see it isn't. I tried to tell myself that the resemblance was coincidental. As Arlene said, kids often tend to look alike. But this is more than just a vague similarity. This is . . .'

'Unnerving.'

'I'm just getting started. Look at the last photograph. I took it after the car had toppled from the cliff. But the car didn't drop all the way down the gorge. It snagged on an outcrop, its front end angling down, and by then, flames from the gas tank were streaking across the snow. That's when the two front doors burst open, and two adults leaped out. My instructions had been specific. Take as many photographs as you can. So despite my shock at seeing the boy, I stared through the viewfinder, aiming the telephoto lens, pressing the button, and then I realized God was still giving signs.' His voice broke. 'The man and woman looked like my parents. *Were* my parents.'

'But they're in flames,' Father Stanislaw said.

'Look closely!' Drew urged.

'I am!'

'They *are* my parents. I know they aren't, but they *are*. I couldn't get a focus on their faces when they leaped from the car. But before they burst into flames, their faces were quite distinct. On the cliff, on that freezing bluff, I was sure they were my mother and my father.'

The room became silent.

'Of course – I don't mean any offense – we don't have any way to verify the comparison,' Father Stanislaw said. 'I grant that the boy from the car, even with the distortion of the smoke and the falling snow, could be your counterpart. At first, indeed, I thought it was you. But allowing for the coincidence, isn't it possible that your imagination carried you away? Could you have made the logical leap from the boy who looked like you, to the man and woman who, well, you *imagined* looked like your parents?'

'I know what I saw.' Drew's voice was hoarse. 'Finally I couldn't keep my finger pressed on the shutter button any longer. I lowered the camera. Across the gorge from me, the flames reached their faces. The gas tank exploded. My mother and father disintegrated. Just as in 1960. Only this time, I was the man who'd killed them.'

'The circumstances were different.'

'*Were they?* What we call a mercenary on their side is an operative on ours. I was the same as the man I'd been hunting. I was my enemy. Pieces of their bodies tumbled down the gorge, their clothes and flesh in flames. I *smelled* them. And on the top of the cliff, silhouetted against the snow, I saw the grieving face of the boy – I wasn't looking through the telephoto lens anymore, but I seemed to see his tears in close-up. *My* tears. After nineteen years, my need for revenge had caught up with me. And nothing mattered anymore. Except to beg God's forgiveness; to save my soul.'

Arlene touched his shoulder. He flinched, then gratefully accepted her comfort.

'To save your soul?' Father Stanislaw said, his voice raised in astonishment. 'All the time you were an operative, you felt *religious?*'

'I had my own religion. The justice of the Old Testament's angry God. But God had a different idea. I'm more honored than Saul on the road to Damascus thrown from his horse by a bolt of light. God sent me not one but *two* signs. He's certainly generous. Everything I've described happened in maybe ten seconds, though it seemed to take forever. The blast rumbled through the mountains, and as its echo dwindled, I heard something else – the shriek of the boy across the gorge from me, raising his hands to his face, trying to shut out what he'd just seen, his parents in flames. He screamed through his fingers. And after that? God's *third* sign to me. It wasn't enough that I'd recognized myself, that I'd come full circle and killed the parents I'd set out to avenge. As the rumble of the blast diminished, as the boy choked on his own screams, as the silence returned, I heard a chant.

'Later, I understood why. It was January sixth. The Feast of the Epiphany – when the Magi saw Christ and saved His life. Because the Wise Men, having seen the baby Jesus, having seen a light of their own, refused to go back to Herod and reveal where Christ could be found, though they'd promised Herod they'd do so. *That*, it seems to me, is why the Church decided that the Epiphany should be a major feast. Not because the Wise Men saw the baby Jesus, but because in a way they were double agents, who finally made a choice about which side to believe in. Just as I made a choice that day.

'The monks, in honor of the Magi and that crucial day in Christ's continuing existence, must have scheduled a special convocation. Above me, from the chapel in the cloister in the mountains, I heard their chant. Their hymn in honor of that anniversary. It drifted down through the chasms, past the peaks, obscuring the echo of the explosions and the screams. The hymn praised God's will, His infinite foresight, His all-encompassing plan. But the words weren't nearly as powerful as the sound of those eerie voices, those hermits who'd divorced themselves from the falsehoods of the world.

'My knees bent. I found myself kneeling, staring toward that boy across the gorge from me. He tried to scramble down the cliff to find his parents. I wanted to stand up from the bushes that hid me and shout to tell him not to, that he'd fall and kill himself. Grow up! I wanted to shout. Hunt the man who murdered your parents! Who murdered my own! Come after me! And that's when I became religious. It was either that . . . or kill myself.' He paused, exhausted.

176

Arlene studied his anguished face. Lovingly, she put an arm around him.

'And after that?' Father Stanislaw asked.

'I wandered for three days through those mountains. The length of time had appropriate religious overtones, don't you think? Of course, I didn't realize what I was doing. Later, it amazed me that I'd never dropped the camera. I don't know how I lived or where I slept or what I ate.

'It snowed while I wandered. I'm sure the authorities must have searched the area. But the storm hid my footprints. Was that a lucky coincidence, or another sign from God? I don't remember where or how I went. The next clear image I have is a village low in the mountains, smoke drifting up from chimneys, children skating on an icy pond, horse-drawn sleighs jingling down a road. Postcard stuff. And I later found out that I'd somehow walked a hundred kilometers, which is why the local police never linked me with the murders below La Grande Chartreuse. I collapsed in front of a chalet. An old woman there took me in. She fed me soup and bread and the sweetest pastries I've ever tasted.'

'Three days?' Arlene asked. 'That's how long you wandered through the mountains? But . . .'

Father Stanislaw completed her thought. 'Your assignment had been two missions in forty-eight hours. The deadline for the second mission had passed.'

'At the start, I didn't think about the implications. I was alive, and that in itself amazed me. Not to mention the vision I'd had. The sight of my parents – *myself* – the circle closing, vengeance leading to . . . That boy, when he grew up, would hunt for me. When I was well enough to travel, I went to Paris to reach my contact. On the way, I checked back issues of newspapers to find out who my victims had been. The man, it turned out, was an American businessman, an oil executive, who'd brought his wife and son to France for a long-postponed vacation. The papers described the killings as senseless. I agreed. Of course, what you read in the papers isn't always true. But what if . . . ? I had the feeling that something was terribly wrong. What would an oil executive and his family have to do with terrorism? What motive could possibly justify those killings? I needed answers. I wanted to go to ground. To reach a safehouse. To rest. I guess God's messages hadn't quite come through. I still had some worldliness, and self-centeredness, left in me. That ended soon.'

Father Stanislaw pursed his lips. 'Because you'd screwed up. And now you were suspect.'

2

In Paris, Drew left the train station, blending with the crowd. He walked to the next arrondissement, making sure that he wasn't followed, and only then used a public phone. Perhaps a needless added precaution, but under the circumstances advisable.

He called the number he'd been given when he'd first arrived in France – a week, a lifetime ago. He let it ring four times, then broke the connection and called that number again. The husky male voice that answered in French announced the name of a dress designer shop.

Drew responded in French as well. 'My name is Johnson. I bought two dresses for my wife a week ago. One fit, the other didn't. I want a second appointment.'

The proprietor gushed, 'But yes, we later suspected that something was wrong with the second fit. We tried to contact you, but you weren't available. All we could do was hope that you'd call. We value your business. Can you possibly see us as soon as possible? We'd like to study the dress and find what went wrong.'

'I'm free this afternoon.'

'As you may remember, we're in the process of moving. Our new location . . .'

Drew memorized the directions. 'Within an hour,' he said.

The old house was made of stone and covered with vines. It was two storeys high, with smoke swirling from the chimney. A fallow vegetable garden stretched to the left, two barren apple trees to the right. And beyond, the frigid, ice-covered Seine. Despite the ice on the water, Drew heard the subtle hiss of the river's current. He smelled dead fish and sulphurous smoke from factories upriver.

His breath coming out in vapor, he strolled around to the back as if he belonged here. The door creaking, he stepped inside a narrow hallway, smelling French bread, warm and fresh. His mouth watering, he opened a second door that took him into a shadowy kitchen.

He saw steam rise from a kettle on a large iron stove and felt a hand shove him forward while another hand twisted a pistol against his kidney. A third hand grabbed his hair from behind, touching a knife to his Adam's apple.

'*You'd better have a fucking good explanation, boyo.*'

He flinched and tried to turn to see them, but they restrained him. Nor could he speak, his breath knocked out of his lungs as they threw him hard across the kitchen table, frisking him roughly.

He didn't have a weapon. The assignment hadn't called for one, and there'd been no need to go to his cache in Paris. Not that it would have mattered if he had.

'Why are –'

He didn't have the chance to finish his sentence. They dragged him off the table, held him in the air, and let him go. He struck the floor with his face. At once, they jerked him to his feet, thrusting him through an open doorway into a living room. He toppled onto a dusty, threadbare sofa. It smelled of mildew.

The room was brighter than the kitchen. Logs blazed in a fireplace. The dingy drapes were closed. A well-worn carpet covered the middle of the floor. The only other furniture was a rocking chair, a stand-up lamp with no shade, a battered coffee table with circular water stains, and an empty bookshelf. Rectangular marks on the wall, rimmed by grime and dust, showed where pictures once had hung.

He straightened on the sofa, facing his assailants. 'You don't understand.' His heart pounded. 'I was told to come here. I wasn't breaking in.'

The tall one hissed. He wore a woodsman's sweater and hiking boots, gesturing with his knife. 'No, boyo, *you* don't understand. We know you're supposed to be here. What we *don't* know is why the fuck you didn't finish your assignment.'

The second man – he had a mustache, massive shoulders, and a brown-checkered sport coat straining against his muscles – held a .22 Hi-Standard pistol with a silencer attached to it. An executioner's weapon. 'How much did they pay you not to do it?'

'How did they contact you?' the third man said. In contrast with the others, he sounded genteel. He was thin and wore a business suit. His delicate hands opened a satchel, taking out a hypodermic and a vial of liquid, setting them carefully on the coffee table.

Their questions came so fast that, as soon as Drew opened his mouth to answer the first, he was interrupted by the second and third.

'Did you compromise the network?' the first man demanded.

'How many operatives are in danger? How much did you tell them?' the second man snapped.

'Tell *who*?'

'If you insist.' The third man filled the hypodermic. He pressed the plunger, freeing air bubbles. 'Take off your coat. Roll up your sleeve.'

'This is crazy.' Drew's stomach burned. He shook his head. 'All you had to do was simply ask. You don't need all this . . .'

'His feelings are hurt,' the second man said. 'He wants us to be polite. He thinks we're here for coffee and croissants.' The man flicked the switch on the stand-up lamp. The sudden stark light emphasized the anger on his face. 'Just in case you still don't get the message, I want you to see this coming.' His clenched fist was suddenly magnified.

Drew's head jolted back against the sofa. His blood tasted coppery. Stunned, he jerked his hands to his mouth. He touched the sticky warmth of his blood feeling his lips ache and swell.

'Is that polite enough for you? Maybe not.' The second man kicked Drew's left shin. Groaning, Drew dropped his hands in pain to massage the leg, and the man punched his mangled lips again. Drew's head snapped back.

'You were given questions to answer,' the third man said, his voice reedy, approaching with the full hypodermic. 'I'd prefer that we didn't waste time waiting for the amytal to take effect. Please, save me the trouble. Why didn't you finish the job?'

Drew's speech was distorted by his puffy lips. 'After I blew up the car, I was seen!'

'By the child who survived?'

'He fell from the car before it went over the cliff. No one could have guessed that would happen. But that's not who saw me!' Drew swallowed blood.

He took advantage of his injury, prolonging a coughing spell, needing time to think. It was obvious now that if he told these men what had really happened in those mountains, they'd think he'd lost his mind. They'd decide that he was even more undependable than they'd first suspected.

'It was someone else,' Drew said, gagging. 'When I ran up the opposite slope, a car came around the bend in the road.' He coughed again. 'It was headed down from the monastery. A man got out. I turned. He saw me. The car had a two-way radio antenna.' Drew's breath whistled stridently through his mangled lips. 'I knew the police would be alerted. I didn't dare go to the rented car I'd parked in a village down the road, so I went the other way – up – through the mountains. A blizzard set in. I got lost. I nearly died. It's taken me this long to get back to Paris.'

The first man shook his head. 'You must think we're pretty stupid. You're supposed to be an expert when it comes to survival in the mountains. That's why you were chosen to do the job. The child you saw. Is that why you sold us out? Because you lost your nerve?'

'I didn't lose my nerve! I told you the truth!'

'Oh, sure. But let's see if your story's the same when the amytal takes effect. For your information, the hit was necessary. The stakes were enormous.'

Drew's mouth filled with blood; he spat it into a handkerchief. 'Nobody explained a thing.'

'Iran,' the second man said.

('Hold on,' Father Stanislaw said. 'You don't mean they told you the purpose of the mission?'

'Everything.'

'Dear God.'

'Yeah, that's what I thought. I was hearing things I shouldn't know.'

'They never meant for you to leave that house alive.'

'It certainly looked that way. Till then, I'd thought I had a fifty-fifty chance of surviving. If I could bluff my way through. But when they started volunteering information . . .')

'Iran,' the second man said. 'The people are rioting. The Shah's about to be deposed. So the question is, who gets to take his place? The man you killed in the mountains' – and his wife, and almost his son, Drew thought – 'pretended he was in France on vacation. Actually, he'd come to represent American oil interests, to negotiate for business-as-usual with the future ruler of Iran. You know who I'm talking about.'

Drew shook his head, puzzled. 'How the hell would I?'

'Quit it. Of course you know who he is. *Since you sold out to him.* An exiled Muslim fanatic. The Ayatollah Khomeini. He's living right here in Paris. And he's worse than the Shah. At least the Shah's pro-American. The Ayatollah isn't. So what are we to do? Let Iran – and all that oil – go someplace else?'

The first man interrupted. 'Your job was to kill that executive, and then the Ayatollah. To take them out with explosives. And to make sure you came back with photographs. Because we wanted it to look as if the same nasty folks had done both hits. The photographs would be sent to the major newspapers, along with a bragging note from the Iran People's Movement.'

'I've never heard of it,' Drew said.

'Of course not. It doesn't exist. We made it up. What difference does that make? The note would have said that the Ayatollah – and the American oil executive – had been executed because they'd made a bargain to replace the Shah with the same old repressive government. And when Iran's indignation reached its peak, the next popular choice to rule the country, a man just behind the Ayatollah, would have taken over. But he'd have done what the Ayatollah should have. He'd have cooperated with the Western oil companies.'

(Father Stanislaw nodded. 'And because an American and his family had been killed, no one would have suspected that American interests were to blame. It might have worked.'

'Except . . .'

'Indeed, except for you.'

'And because of me, the Iranian hostage crisis occurred, the Soviets invaded Afghanistan, Reagan defeated Carter . . .')

'It could have worked!' the first man shouted at Drew, his face distorted with anger. 'But, boyo, just one problem. It all depended on a timetable. Forty-eight hours from one hit to the next, *but you didn't stay on schedule*! On those two days, we knew for sure you could get at *both* the oil executive and the Ayatollah. We'd learned their itinerary. We'd found the spots where they'd be most exposed!'

Drew tried to shift the blame. 'You should have allowed for contingencies. If the timing was so important, why wasn't another operative given the second assignment?'

'Because, you stupid bastard, the same man had to do both hits! *Because of the camera*! Both hits had to be recorded on the same roll of film. When we sent the photographs and the negatives to the press, we wanted the pictures to be in the same numbered sequence – to prove to Iran that whoever had killed the oil executive had also killed the Ayatollah. The Iranians had to be convinced that one of their own groups was responsible.'

'Why blame me? You've got the camera. Reschedule the second assignment.'

The first man sighed and looked at his companions. 'You hear what he's saying? How simple he thinks it is to make things right again. Boyo, we *can't* reschedule! It's too fucking late! The Ayatollah's tightened security around him. We can't get near him anymore. Not close enough to use that camera. That first hit's worthless now! You did it for nothing!'

Drew heard the young boy's screams of grief

'But the second hit – or rather, the one you didn't do,' the aristocratic man said, 'your failure earned you something, didn't it. How much did the Ayatollah pay for you to get conveniently lost in the mountains? You went to him, right?'

'That isn't true.'

'I said quit it!' The first man stepped behind the sofa, yanking Drew's head back, pressing the knife against his throat again.

The third man continued. 'Be reasonable. We want an excuse that makes sense. Later, after I give you the amytal, if your story's the same, we'll know you're not lying. And if we can sympathize with your reasons we'll call it an honest mistake. We'll set you free. Of course, you wouldn't ever be hired again. But I don't think you'll object.'

Drew's throat was stretched so taut that he couldn't speak. The man behind him seemed to understand; he removed the knife.

Drew coughed and swallowed. He had no more to invent. 'All right.' He massaged his throat. 'I lied.'

'Now there, that's better. At last, we're making progress,' the third man said.

'But I didn't sell out. It's not what you think. Something – I don't know how else to say it – happened to me in the mountains.'

'What?' The first man came from behind the sofa.

181

Drew told them. He'd anticipated their reaction correctly; they looked at him as if he'd gone mad.

'Boyo, not hire you again is right. Something happened to you for sure. You lost your nerve.'

'There's one way to know,' the third man said and gestured with the full hypodermic. 'As I asked you earlier, please take off your coat. Roll up your sleeve.'

Drew stared at the hypodermic, his spine feeling cold. They'd brought too much. His interrogators had enough amytal to kill him, as soon as they'd verified his story. He was being invited to participate in his own execution.

'Under amytal, I'll say the same thing,' he insisted. 'Because it's the truth.' Standing, he took off his coat.

He threw it to his left, toward the man with the knife, obscuring his face. He had to reach the pistol. Lunging, he twisted the second man's wrist, tilting the silencer on the barrel toward the gunman's face. He pulled the trigger. The gun made a noise like the muffled impact of a fist against a pillow. The bullet went through the man's right eye, spewing blood and brain.

The man with the knife yanked the coat from his face. Drew shoved the sagging corpse at him. As they toppled, he pivoted toward the third man, jerked the hypodermic out of his delicate hand, and rammed the needle into the side of his neck. Blood flew, crimson spurting from a high-pressure hose, as he shoved the plunger all the way in. The genteel man collapsed.

Drew swung toward the upright lamp, clutched it like a staff, and parried the knife that the first man, freed from the coat and the body, lunged at him. The cord on the lamp broke, extinguishing the bulb. Flickering light from the fireplace silhouetted their movements. Drew whipped the base of the lamp toward his enemy's shoulder, reversed his attack, and thrust the bulb-end of the lamp against the knife hand. He jumped back, using the skills he'd been taught in Colorado, struck his assailant in the crotch with the base of the lamp, and slammed the knife from his hand with the other end.

He grabbed the knife off the floor, ramming it up beneath his enemy's chin, through the tongue, through the roof of the mouth, into the brain.

Drew continued to hold the knife, feeling warm blood cascade down its blade and over his fingers on the handle. He kept the man standing up for a moment, feeling him tremble, scowling at his dying eyes.

Then he released his grip. The man fell backward, his head cracking sharply on the bricks in front of the fireplace.

Drew grabbed his boots and dragged him back from the flames, unable to bear the stench of burning hair. He shuddered, staring at the blood, the bodies around him. The odor of urine, of excrement, filled the room.

Though hardly innocent of the smell, he wanted to vomit. Not from fear but from revulsion. Death. Too much. For too many years.

3

'And then?' Arlene asked. She had taken his hand as he talked, giving him at least some comfort.

'I'd left the pistol in the house. No time to get it, though I'd made time to grab the camera. I'm sure a psychiatrist would find the choice interesting. But I did have a handgun in my emergency cache in Paris, along with money and a passport under another name. I rented a car and drove to Spain. I got rid of the handgun, of course, in case I was searched when I crossed the border.'

'Why Spain?' Father Stanislaw asked.

'Why not? I figured they'd be looking for me everywhere. At least' – Drew shrugged – 'Spain was warmer. I left the car with the rental company and hired a private plane to fly me to Portugal. There, in Lisbon, I had another alias on a passport. And after that? Ireland. America. Three times, they almost got me. Once, at a service station, I had to set a car on fire. But at least I didn't have to kill anymore. And finally I was home. In America. I knew exactly where I was going. I didn't care about shahs and ayatollahs and oil and terrorists. None of it was important. I'd killed the equivalent of my parents. I'd caused a boy to suffer for the rest of his life as I had. The world was a madhouse. By comparison, those Carthusian monks lived in paradise. They had their priorities straight. They set their sights toward the long view. Toward eternity. Since I was ten, I've been a wanderer. But after I fled from that house on the Seine, faced with the prospect of wandering still more, I finally had a direction. I saw a goal. I wanted peace.

'A priest named Father Hafer was my sponsor. He arranged for me to go into the monastery. But before I entered the Carthusians, I had to get rid of all my possessions. Except these photographs, of course. But when I thought I'd finished, when I wondered if I'd canceled myself, I realized that there was one last thing I had to do. A sentimental weakness. A final breaking of the ties.'

4

In darkness, Drew crouched behind bushes and jumped up with all his strength, his fingers clutching the concrete rim of the wall he'd been hiding against. It was March. His bare hands swelled from the aching cold as he scraped the soles of his shoes against the wall, struggling to climb.

He reached the top, sprawled flat upon it, breathing hard, then squirmed down the other side, supporting himself by his numbed fingertips.

He landed on frozen earth, his knees buckling, and surged up defensively, his only weapons his hands. He could have brought a pistol, of course, but he'd vowed that he wouldn't kill again. Subdue an enemy with his hands, that he could justify. But kill again? His soul recoiled from the possibility. If he in turn were killed tonight, it would be God's will. But no one challenged him.

He scanned the dark. After the glare of streetlights on the far side of the wall, his eyes would normally have needed a second or two to adjust to the deeper gloom. But he'd shut his eyes as he dropped from the wall. And now that he'd opened them, his irises were already wide.

He saw murky trees and bushes, a few waist-high upright pipes with taps, watering cans beside them. And tombstones. Rows and rows of them, their shadows stretching off until the night concealed them.

Pleasant View Cemetery, Boston.

He crept through shadows, passing trees and bushes, crouching by gravestones, sprinting stooped across gravel lanes, exhaling with relief as he reached silent grass again. Pressing his back for cover against the wall of a cold mausoleum, he studied the gloom. The darkness was eerily silent. The only disturbance was the lonely far-off drone of a car.

And at last, as he crept farther, he saw them, never confused for a moment as to where they would be.

The headstones, the graves, of his parents.

But he came at them indirectly, circling, checking every likely hiding place, remembering the vandals he'd protected his parents against so many years ago.

Finally he stood before them, staring down at the headstones where the names would be if he could have seen them.

But even at night, he knew that this place was theirs. He traced his fingers lovingly across their names, the dates of their births, their deaths; then stepped back, brooding down at them for an instant that became a minute, two, then three, and said at last, 'If only you hadn't died.'

A voice made him stiffen.

'Drew.'

He swung.

The voice was male. It was far away, hushed.

'Why did you have to do it?' The voice was ghostly.

Drew strained his eyes but couldn't penetrate the blackness . . . over there, to his right.

He didn't feel threatened. Not yet, at least. Because he knew that the man could easily have shot him while he stood in front of his parents' graves.

Which meant that the man felt the need to talk.

He recognized the voice.

Jake's.

'Do you realize the shit you've caused?' Jake asked from the dark.

Drew almost smiled. A rush of friendship overcame him.

'Or how many men they've got hunting you?' Jake's voice was low.

'And what about you?' Drew asked. 'Were you told to hunt me, too? You're a long way from New York. You're not here because you like cemeteries at three A.M. Are you going to kill me?'

'That's what I'm supposed to do.' Jake's voice was resonant, mournful.

'Then go ahead.' Exhausted, empty, Drew suddenly didn't care any longer. 'I'm dead already. I might as well fall down and be still.'

'But *why*?'

'Because you've got your orders,' Drew said.

'No, that isn't what I mean. I want to know why you sold the network out.'

'I didn't.'

'They say you did.'

'And I can say I'm the Pope. That doesn't make it true. Besides, you didn't believe them. Otherwise, you'd never have given me the chance to talk. You'd have shot me while I stood here. How did you find me?'

'Desperation.'

'That's what I always liked about you. Your knack for long explanations.'

'They sent a team to watch where you lived, just in case, but I knew you wouldn't go back there. In fact, the more I thought about it, the more I realized you wouldn't go back to *any* place that the network associates with you. My best guess was you'd holed up somewhere in the mountains. You know enough to survive there for months, years, even in winter. So that was that, I figured. The race was over. You'd won.'

'That doesn't explain . . .'

'I'm coming to it. See, something kept nagging at me. A speck of a memory. There had to be *some* place that irresistibly tugged you. Even people like us are human. Where, though? What made you what you are? And then I remembered what you'd told me once – when a snowstorm forced us to camp for the night on a peak, the wind chill so bad we had to keep talking to each other to make sure we didn't fall asleep and die. Remember?'

Drew did. With fondness. 'In the Andes.'

'Right.' Jake's voice came out of the dark. 'And when you couldn't think of anything else, you told me what had happened to your parents and how you lived with your uncle and aunt in Boston.'

'My uncle's dead now.'

'Yes, but your aunt's still alive, though the way you'd described her I knew you'd never get in touch with her for help. But Boston reminded me of your story about how you protected your parents' graves. How you used to sneak into the cemetery every night. How even as an adult, you still went to visit them whenever you could. It wasn't hard for me to learn which cemetery your parents were buried in or to find their graves. But I kept asking myself, before you went to ground, before you shut yourself off from the world, would you say your final goodbyes, would you still obey the old impulse? Or had you done so already and I'd missed you?'

'A long shot.'

'Sure. But the only shot I had.'

Drew squinted toward the dark. 'I've been on the run since January. You've been watching these graves every night since then?'

'I told you. Desperation. But I gave myself till the end of this month.' Jake laughed. 'Imagine my surprise when you suddenly came out of the shadows. For a second, I thought I was seeing things.'

'It's a good place for ghosts. And reunions. And executions. The undertaker might just as well skip the funeral and plant me where I fall. But you still haven't shot me. Why?'

185

In the darkness, Jake sighed. 'Because I want to know what really happened.'

Drew told him.

For a moment, Jake didn't react. 'It makes a good story.'

'It's more than a story!'

'But don't you see. It doesn't matter. *What they believe is what matters.* They came to me. "You're his friend," they said. "You know his habits. You know what he'll do. He's dangerous. There's no telling who he might sell us out to next."'

'I told you already. I didn't sell them out!'

'And they also said, "We'll give you a hundred thousand dollars if you find him . . . and you kill him."'

Drew lost his patience. He stepped ahead, stretching out his arms. 'Then do it! What are you waiting for? Earn the bounty!'

'Don't rely on our friendship,' Jake warned from the darkness. 'Don't come any closer, and don't try to run.'

'Run? I'm *sick* of running. Kill me, or let me go.'

'If I let you go, you'd still be running.'

'No. Tomorrow I'm supposed to enter a monastery.'

'*What?*'

'That's right. I'm becoming a Carthusian.'

'You mean you really did get religion? A Carthusian? Wait a minute. Aren't they the ones who live alone in a cell and pray all day? That's fucking weird. It's like crawling into a grave.'

'The opposite. Like being resurrected. I'm in a grave already. And not because of the gun you're aiming at me. Think what you want. From your point of view, by joining the Carthusians I'd be dead already, wouldn't I? You wouldn't have to kill me.'

'You were always good with words,' Jake said from the darkness.

'I won't insult our friendship by thinking that you're tempted by the hundred thousand dollars they offer you to kill me. I won't insult you either by trying to tempt you with a larger amount if you let me go. The fact is, I don't have that kind of money anymore. I gave everything away.'

'Weirder and weirder.'

'What I *am* doing is counting on our friendship. I saved your life once. On that same climb in the Andes. Remember?'

'Oh, I remember all right.'

'Nobody knows you found me. Return the favor. Save my life. Let me walk away.'

'If only things could be that simple. See, there's something else I haven't told you. And more at stake here than just the hundred thousand. That's just the carrot on the end of the stick. But that stick has another end, a sharp end, and it's being jabbed right into my back. You really made them angry, Drew. A failed assignment. A *major* one. And those three operatives you killed. The network's sure you've become a free-lance, a rogue.'

'They're wrong!'

'But that's what they *think*. They're sure you sold out. The things you know, you could do a lot of damage to the network. So they're falling on you hard. They won't ever stop looking. And the angrier they get, the more they start falling hard on other people, too. Like me. It's like because I know you, because we're friends, they figure I should be able to find you. And if I don't, then I must be a rogue. Next month, I expect them to put the boots to me. So you see my point? I can't let you go.'

Drew heard the sorrow in Jake's tone. 'But do you *want* to kill me?'

'Christ, no! Why do you think I'm stalling?'

'Then maybe there's a better way.'

'If there is, I don't know it.'

'Go back and tell them you found me and killed me.'

'What the hell good would that do? They wouldn't just take my word. I'd have to bring them proof!'

'So what's the problem? *Give* them that proof!'

'Make sense.'

'Tell them you rigged a car-bomb and blew me up.' Drew remembered the method of execution he'd been told to use in the Alps. 'Take photographs. They like photographs.'

'Of what? A bombed-out car won't . . .'

'No, of me getting in the car and driving away. Of the car blowing up, toppling into a river. Under the circumstances, if you tell them you couldn't get me except with a bomb, what more proof could they want? But I won't be in the car.'

'You stop the car and get out before it blows?'

'That's right. Tomorrow, I'm supposed to report to the monastery. It's up in Vermont. But I can wait till morning to help you take the pictures.'

Drew started forward, toward Jake's voice in the darkness.

'*Stay where you are, Drew.*'

'I can't wait any longer. I have to know. It's time to put our friendship on the line. Shoot me, or help me. There's no other choice.' He stretched his arms out again. A gesture of openness.

'I'm warning you, Drew.' Jake sounded panicked. 'Don't make me do it. Don't come any closer.'

'Sorry, buddy. I've been running too long. I'm tired. And I want to see your face.'

'For Christ's sake!'

'Yes, that's right!' Drew came within ten feet from the clump of bushes where Jake was hidden. Five. And stopped. He stared at the darkness. 'So what's it going to be? Do you want to help me prove to them that you killed me? So you can get me off the hook, and I can spend the rest of my life in peace? Or do you want to kill me for real?'

He waited. Silence closed in.

The bushes rustled.

Drew tensed, fearing he'd miscalculated, imagining Jake raise his weapon.

A figure emerged from the darkness.

Jake approached, his arms outstretched as Drew's were. 'God love you, pal.'

They embraced.

5

'In seventy-nine?' Arlene scanned Drew's face, her voice as taut with emotion as Drew's had been.

'In March. In Boston. The day before I entered the monastery.'

She slumped back into her chair. 'You're right. I had to hear all of it before I could understand. It's like . . .'

Drew watched her struggle to find the words. 'I came to think of it as a spiderweb,' he said. 'Everything interlocked, interwoven, coming full circle. For a terrible purpose. Because the ultimate spider's waiting.'

She studied him. 'And Jake did what you asked? He helped you?'

'We staged the photographs. I don't know what he told Scalpel. But he must have been convincing. From what you've said, there weren't any repercussions. In fact, until two weeks ago, you didn't notice anything unusual.'

'That's right.' She brooded. 'But then he became nervous.'

'And shortly after Jake disappeared, the monastery was attacked,' Father Stanislaw said.

The room seemed to narrow with tension.

'Are the two events related?' The priest turned to Drew. 'Did someone decide that Jake knew more than he was telling? Was he forced to admit that you were still alive, to reveal where you were?'

'But why the six-year delay?' Drew asked. 'If Scalpel was suspicious about his story, why did they wait so long to question him?'

'Scalpel?' Arlene looked incredulous. 'You're assuming *they're* responsible? That they caused Jake's disappearance and attacked the monastery?'

'I have to. Everything points to them.'

'But –' She became more agitated.

'What's wrong? I thought you took that for granted the same as I did.'

'No, you don't understand. It's impossible.'

'But everything fits.'

'It can't! Scalpel doesn't exist anymore!'

Drew's stomach dropped. '*What?*'

'The network was disbanded, in 1980. When you were in the monastery.'

Drew flinched.

'She's right,' Father Stanislaw said. 'My sources are very firm about its cancellation. As you discovered, the program had gotten out of control. Far exceeding its mandate, it wasn't just counterattacking terrorists but had taken the potentially catastrophic step of interfering in foreign governments and plotting assassinations of heads of state. If the Ayatollah had learned that Americans were trying to kill him, he might have executed the hostages instead of merely holding them for ransom. For sure, he would have used the assassination attempt as proof that everything he said against America and its degeneracy was true. That's no doubt why Scalpel wanted you killed. Your failure to accomplish the hit and, worse, their suspicion that you'd become unstable enough to give away their secrets must have terrified them.'

'But then they thought I was dead.'

188

'And probably got their first good night's sleep since your failed assignment,' Father Stanislaw said. 'My sources feel that Scalpel decided it had come too close to disaster. A few even feel that someone in Scalpel was worried enough to let the State Department know how politically dangerous the program had become. Remember what happened to the CIA when the Senate's Church Committee uncovered the agency's assassination plots? Against Castro, Lumumba, Sukarno, the Diem brothers?'

'The CIA was almost disbanded,' Drew said. 'As a compromise, its powers were severely restricted. And seven hundred members of the covert operations branch were fired.'

'Obviously Scalpel didn't want the same scandal. Protecting their careers, its administrators carefully and quietly dismantled the anti-terrorist network. The dismantling took a year from your failed attempt against the Ayatollah.'

'Then who the hell tried to kill me? And why?' Drew asked.

'*And what made Jake so nervous?*' Arlene stared at them.

'Maybe the poison will give us a clue,' Drew said. 'If we knew the type used to attack the monastery.'

Father Stanislaw considered him. 'Yes. The bishop told me you'd kept the corpse of the mouse that saved your life. Your pet.'

'Stuart Little.' Drew had trouble breathing. 'I figured the last thing he could do for me was to help me find the answers. With an autopsy, if the poison was distinctive, I might have the information that would lead me to whoever had ordered the attack.'

'I wonder. Would you mind? May I see the body?'

'It isn't pretty.'

'I expect that by now you know I'm not innocent.'

Drew glanced at the eerie red ring, the intersecting sword and Maltese cross. 'I got that impression. The fraternity of the stone?'

'That's right.'

'You'll have to tell me about it.'

'When the time is suitable. And in the meanwhile?'

Drew went to his coat. Remarkably, when he pulled out the plastic bag, the tiny cadaver seemed unusually preserved. It was dry and shrunken, like a mummy.

Father Stanislaw accepted it with reverence. 'From tiny creatures . . .' He glanced from the mouse to Drew. 'I've explained that I had the corpses removed from the monastery. Your concern was well founded, the fear of scandal you expressed to the bishop. If the authorities had learned about the attack, their investigation would have led them to discover that *one* monk had survived. And when they'd dug more deeply, they'd have learned about your background. The Church protecting an international assassin? It wouldn't do. So after our own investigation, we erased the evidence. The corpses were buried in keeping with Carthusian custom. Respectfully, but humbly, without a headstone to identify them. We maintained the privacy that the monks had always wanted. But autopsies *were* performed. The poison *is* distinctive. And under the circumstances appropriate.'

Drew waited.

'Monk's hood.'

The play on words was blasphemous. 'If I ever get my hands on . . .'

'Patience,' Father Stanislaw said. He set the plastic bag on the dresser and touched his priest's white collar. 'I should have put on my vestments.'

'For what?'

'Your confession, for that's what this has been. A difficult problem of canon law. I wonder if my oversight makes your confession invalid.'

Drew's voice broke. 'I don't think so.'

'I don't, either. God understands. Is that the end of it? Have you told me everything you think is pertinent? Everything that leads up to the attack on the monastery?'

'Everything I can think of.'

'Then bow your head, and complete the ritual.'

'Father, I'm heartily sorry for these sins and the sins of all my life.'

Father Stanislaw raised his right hand, making the sign of the Cross. The priest prayed in Latin. Drew recognized the petition to God for forgiveness.

Father Stanislaw paused. 'To kill another human being is one of the ultimate crimes. Only suicide is greater. But the circumstances moderate your culpability. As does your lifelong ordeal. Make a good act of contrition.'

Drew did so.

The priest said, 'Go in peace.' Then added, his voice suddenly harsh, 'But stay right where you are.'

Drew glanced up, startled.

'It's time to talk about Yanus.'

Drew frowned. 'You said that in the chapel at the retreat house. It took me a while to figure it out. Your accent. You mean *Janus*?'

'The assassin,' Arlene interrupted.

Father Stanislaw nodded. 'The two-headed god. Who's supposed to be Drew.'

PART SEVEN
JANUS

THE SINS OF THE PRESENT

1

In Ancient Rome, when an imperial army marched off to war, complex rituals had to be obeyed, lest ill fortune fall upon the venture. One of the most important of these rituals required that the army pass through a ceremonial archway while the favor of the gods – and one in particular, the god of good beginnings – was invoked. There were many such archways throughout the city, and most were not connected to walls or buildings but rather stood freely, as if their lack of practical purpose would emphasize their symbolic function. Likewise, small buildings were sometimes constructed for no other purpose than to provide a suitable setting for a priest or politician to walk into and out from.

The most respected of these buildings was a shrine to the north of the Forum. Simple, rectangular, it had double bronze doors on its east and west side, facing the rising and setting sun, as if to signify that, while the good beginning of a venture was hoped for, so too was a successful end. Like the archway through which Rome's mighty armies marched on their way to battle, this temple too was associated with war. Indeed, so frequently did the empire's generals pass into and out of the double doors facing east and west that by custom the doors were left open. Only when Rome was at peace were the doors closed, an event that happened rarely – during the first seven hundred years of the city's greatness, from the reign of Numa to that of Augustus, only three times.

The god to whom this shrine was dedicated was not, as might be expected, Mars. Instead, the statue that priests, politicians, and generals meditated upon as they passed from one set of doors to the next was that of a greater deity, Janus, whose likeness could easily be distinguished from those of all other gods because he had two faces, one in front, the other in back, peering toward each set of doors, the east and the west, the start and the finish.

When petitioned for success at the start of a day, he was known as Matutinus, from which comes matins, the Roman Catholic Church's word for the first canonical service of the day, just after midnight. But Janus was also petitioned at the start of each week and each month and, in particular, at the start of each year. Appropriately, the first month of the Roman calendar was named in his honor: January.

Janus, the two-faced, staring eternally forward and backward.
Toward the beginning. And the end.

2

'At the start,' Father Stanislaw said, 'what we had were mostly rumors. Almost a year ago.'

'We?' Drew squinted. 'Who's we?' He gestured toward Father Stanislaw's ring, the magnificent ruby, the intersecting sword and cross. 'The fraternity?'

'Is it necessary to be explicit? A man with your experience . . .' Father Stanislaw considered him. 'It shouldn't surprise you. The Church with its seven hundred million followers is virtually a nation unto itself. Indeed, in the Middle Ages it was a nation, composed of all of Europe, during the Holy Roman Empire. It needs to watch over its interests. Just as all major nations do, it needs an intelligence network.'

'Intelligence network?' Drew's voice hardened. 'I'm beginning to understand.'

'At least, you think you understand. But one stage of explanation at a time. The principal sources of our intelligence are various members of an ambiguous religious order that has come into prominence since you entered the monastery. The order is known as Opus Dei, the great work of God. I describe the order as ambiguous because its members – mostly successful middle-class professionals, doctors, lawyers, business people – continue to pursue their lay vocation despite their vows of poverty, chastity, and obedience. They dress according to the fashions of society, though many retreat at night to cloisters, and all bequeath their possessions to the Church. Their views are conservative. They're fiercely loyal to the Pope. Their membership in Opus Dei is kept a strict secret.'

'In other words, an invisible order.'

'Correct. The theory is that they can spread the Church's influence by using its doctrines in their daily business practice. A kind of Catholic fifth column, if you like. Imagine the effect if members of Opus Dei were elected to Congress, or if one became a member of the U.S. Supreme Court. But they aren't merely in America. Opus Dei exists in strength in over eighty countries. One hundred thousand professionals, using their ambition, striving to gain as much secular power as they can, for the sake of the Catholic Church. *They* are the basis for the Church's intelligence network. And it was from rumors they began to pick up that I first heard about . . .'

3

A free-lance mercenary, who as if from nowhere appeared abruptly on the European scene and was reputed to be responsible for five assassinations in rapid sequence, all involving Catholic priests. In each case, the priests – politically active, influential, and fiercely opposed to Communist factions in their country's government – had died in ways that at first seemed merely unfortunate. A car accident, for example, a heart attack, a fire.

Widely separated, the deaths would not have attracted notice, but so many in quick succession, and most in Italy, prompted Opus Dei eyebrows to be raised. Powerful members of the order used their influence to make sure that investigations became more thorough. Soon, various factors in each death began to seem suspicious, though not conclusively incriminating. In the case of the car accident, the brakes had failed, and yet the brakes had recently been serviced. In the case of the heart attack, an autopsy on the victim revealed no weakness in his cardiovascular system. In the case of the fire, no one could recall the priest, who'd always been compulsively neat, ever allowing oily rags to accumulate in the rectory's basement.

At the same time, in Geneva, a young woman deeply in love made a frightening discovery. The man with whom she'd been having an affair, a pleasure-giving American, had recently installed a set of bookshelves in her apartment. One of the brackets that held the shelves to the wall had pulled from the plaster, causing the shelves to lean out alarmingly. Because the boyfriend, Thomas McIntyre, was out of the city on business (what kind of business she didn't know, something to do with imports and exports), she telephoned her brother to come to her apartment and advise her about the shelves.

When the two of them chanced to peer behind the shelves, they noticed a hole in the wall that had not been there before. And exploring further, they discovered a cavity filled with plastic explosives, detonators, automatic weapons, ammunition, and a metal container from which they extracted the equivalent of a hundred thousand dollars in various European currencies, along with three passports for Michael McQuane, Robert Malone, and Terence Mulligan. Despite the difference in names, the photographs on each of the passports was identical. It portrayed the face of the woman's boyfriend, Thomas McIntyre.

After a long, intense, and violent argument, in which the woman defended her lover, threatening never to speak to her brother again if her lover wasn't given the chance to explain, the brother phoned the authorities. Three policemen arrived within the hour. They examined the objects concealed behind the bookshelves and proceeded at once to the apartment of the boyfriend, who – it turned out – had come back from his business trip early and, without informing his lover, was having a party. After the policemen knocked on the door and were with reluctance admitted by one of the guests, they faced a group of drunken revelers in the midst of which a man who resembled the photograph in the various passports agreed to answer questions in the bedroom. Once inside, however, the American pulled a pistol, shot the three policemen, and fled down a fire escape.

One policeman lived to tell the story. Further investigation revealed that the metal container concealed in the wall behind the girlfriend's bookshelves also held a notebook in which addresses in various cities and countries turned out to be those of the five priests who had died.

4

'Reactions so far?' Father Stanislaw asked

Drew thought about it, troubled. 'If this McIntyre's an assassin, he needs a few lessons in tradecraft. That rickety bookshelf. Panicking in front of the police.' He shook his head. 'An amateur.'

'So it seemed to me. Unless . . .'

'I don't understand.'

'Unless he was putting on an act.'

'You think he *wanted* to expose himself?' Arlene asked, surprised.

'But why?' Drew added.

'To announce himself. To gain a reputation quickly,' Father Stanislaw said. 'And once he'd been exposed, no doubt deliberately on his part, he suddenly became professional. The authorities did everything possible but couldn't find him, and in rapid succession, three other politically active priests were killed. Then Opus Dei members themselves began to be killed. Corporation executives, publishers, but mostly politicians. And it now was clear, this Thomas McIntyre, and his various other similar names on other bogus passports, was engaged in systematic terrorism against –'

'– the Catholic Church.' Sickened, Drew turned to Arlene. 'You told me he'd been killing politicians, but you didn't tell me –'

'– they were in Opus Dei? How could I have known?'

'You couldn't have,' Father Stanislaw said. 'How could anyone outside the intelligence network of the Church have known? That's the whole point. The members of Opus Dei are a secret.'

'Not anymore,' Drew said.

'And now we come to you.' Father Stanislaw sat down next to Drew. 'As the authorities investigated, spurred on by powerful members of Opus Dei anxious to find the man who was stalking them, other rumors began to surface. A man with the code name Janus was buying weapons and explosives on the European black market and at the same time hiring free-lance investigators to document scandals involving the Catholic Church. These scandals ranged from mistresses whom various Church officials maintained, to homosexual affections, to rich estates that no priest, given the vow of poverty, ought to have the resources to own. Alcoholism. Drug addiction. Deadly sins. If a priest or a member of Opus Dei had a vice, Janus wanted to know about it. And be given the proof. Sometimes he merely sent the documentation, including photographs, to the news-papers. Other times, he killed the priest or the Opus Dei member and *then* sent the documents, apparently to justify the assassinations.'

'Janus,' Drew said.

'The connection was obvious. Thomas McIntyre, the assassin with the same ambition? Could *he* be Janus? Indeed, when the authorities tracked down one of Janus's contacts and made him talk, the man identified the passport photograph of Thomas McIntyre as his employer.'

'Identified?' Drew stiffened. 'You're telling me that this Janus – this McIntyre – actually let his contacts see him? He didn't even have the sense to use a safe phone? Something's wrong. The tradecraft's so clumsy it almost seems . . .'

'Intentional?' Father Stanislaw asked. 'Almost as if he *wants* to be caught? Indeed. The same pattern. And yet, despite the efforts of the most powerful members of Opus Dei, and their considerable influence on Interpol and MI-6, no one's been able to find him.'

'But *you* thought I was Janus,' Drew told Arlene. 'Or at least you did till I made you give me the benefit of the doubt. Why were you tempted to make the connection in the first place?'

'Because of the photograph in all those passports,' Father Stanislaw answered for her. 'It took some time, but finally the American authorities managed to find the same face in its files. Part of the difficulty was that your own legal passport had now expired. But as they searched their previous records . . . Younger. Thinner, though not as thin as you are now. Nonetheless an obvious likeness. Andrew MacLane. The similarity of your last name with Janus's many last names attracted immediate attention. McIntyre, McQuane, Malone, Mulligan. Granted, an odd blend of Irish and Scot. But nonetheless the parallel could not be ignored. Janus, the authorities decided, had to be you.

'Your choice of code name seemed puzzling for a time. But intelligence officials soon understood. You'd worked for a now defunct American anti-terrorist network, though what you did for that network was naturally never revealed. In seventy-nine, you'd sold out to Iran. You'd dropped out of sight for several years, but now you were back, ignoring your former loyalties, working for whoever paid you the most. Janus. The code name then seemed perfectly apt. The Roman god who stared forward and backward.'

'Janus, the two-faced,' Drew said bitterly.

'When the story went public,' Arlene said, 'Jake and I were stunned. How could you be an assassin attacking the Catholic Church? It didn't make sense. But the proof was overwhelming. Jake got more and more upset. He began to act strangely. And disappeared.' She clenched her fists. '*Why didn't he tell me what was going on?*'

'He couldn't,' Drew said. 'Not until he was sure it was me. After all, Jake knew I was supposed to be dead. He was the man who claimed to have killed me, and Scalpel had accepted his proof. But as far as Jake could tell, I was in a Carthusian monastery up in Vermont. So how could I be killing priests and politicians in Europe?'

'Unless you'd left the monastery,' Father Stanislaw said. 'Unless you'd simply used him. So you think he went to the monastery to find out?'

'I never saw him there. But my guess is he didn't.'

'What then?'

'Let me put it this way. Whoever Janus is, he's taken a lot of effort to make the authorities think –'

'– that he and you are the same,' Arlene completed his thought.

Drew struggled to concentrate. '*Why* would he do that? Why would he be so determined to blame the killings on me? If the authorities found me, I could prove that I hadn't done them.'

'True,' Father Stanislaw said. 'If you were in a monastery, your alibi would be perfect.'

Drew's scalp tingled. 'But Janus couldn't have known I was in that monastery. And yet he was sure I'd never be able to prove I wasn't Janus. Why?'

197

Arlene spoke, her voice somber. 'He thought you were dead.'

The three of them stared at each other.

'If the authorities were hunting a dead man, Janus wouldn't have to worry. I'd be a perfect distraction for them. While they went after a ghost, he could . . .'

'Be invisible and do what he wanted.' Arlene stood, distressed. 'Then did Jake investigate his former superiors in Scalpel?' Her voice shook. 'Because he believed that one of them was using the fact that you were dead – or *supposed* to be dead – as a cover for Janus?'

Drew nodded.

'And whoever invented Janus found out what Jake was doing?' She shuddered. 'I hate to think it, let alone say it. Did someone kill Jake to prevent him from finding out who was masquerading as you?'

'Arlene, we don't know that.'

'But is that what you suspect?'

Drew looked at her with pain. 'I'm sorry.'

Her face went pale. Her eyes became frightening. 'Whoever did it will be even sorrier.'

'But the sequence didn't stop there. Whoever invented Janus must have forced Jake to admit why he was investigating them,' Drew said. 'If they found out I was still alive, in the monastery, they'd have had to kill me as well. To protect their cover for Janus. And that presented a problem. Because the Carthusian monks are anonymous, the entire monastery had to be taken out to make sure I was really dead this time. And then, I assume, my body would have disappeared.'

Father Stanislaw's mouth tightened. 'And the Church, when it investigated, would have wondered why. Which brings us back to the concern you expressed to the bishop. No one could know that the Church inadvertently was sheltering an assassin, albeit one whose motives could be justified. The controversy would have been intolerable, undermining the authority of the Church.'

Drew's voice was guttural with rage. 'Like a spiderweb. Everything interconnected. Janus must have found it amusing. Thinking I was dead, he used me as an alias to attack the Church. Then, realizing I was alive, he decided he could kill me without the authorities ever finding out. Because the Church, to protect itself, would have to cover up the mass murder. The Church in effect would be helping him. Clever to the point of genius. And if I have my way, I'll see that he suffers in a clever part of Hell.

'*My double*,' Drew suddenly added. The rush of understanding made him shiver.

Father Stanislaw squinted, rubbing the sword and cross on his gleaming ring. 'So he occurred to you as well?'

Arlene nodded forcibly. 'When you mentioned him earlier, I started to wonder.'

Drew shivered again.

A turncoat assassin . . . assuming Drew's identity, resembling Drew's passport photograph, sufficiently similar to convince those who met him that he was Drew.

'Dear God,' Drew said. 'It sounds like the double I used when I was in Scalpel. My alibi when I went on a mission. They disbanded Scalpel. But they must have contacted some of its former members and created another network like it. Under another name, Scalpel still exists!'

'But what network?' Father Stanislaw studied Arlene. 'Were you and your brother asked to join another intelligence unit?'

Arlene shook her head. 'These days, I'm a civilian. I teach outdoor survival and climbing techniques.'

'What about your brother?'

'He worked for another network. That much I know. But he never told me which one, and I followed protocol by never asking. He wouldn't have told me if I had. I wouldn't have expected him to.'

'Janus,' Drew said with disgust. 'Like monk's hood, the poison used at the monastery, Janus is another God-damned pun. The two-faced. The hypocrite. Sure. But *literally* Janus is a man with two lookalike faces. And the only person I can think of to tell us who's behind this is my double.'

'Do you know where to find him?' Father Stanislaw asked.

5

The bond that Drew and his classmates had shared at Scalpel's training school in Colorado had been too strong to be dissolved by their dispersal after graduation. He, Arlene, and Jake had kept in touch with each other, for example, maintaining their friendship; eventually Drew and Arlene became lovers.

But Scalpel had forbidden Drew ever to associate with Mike, his double, lest their remarkable resemblance attract attention and jeopardize assignments. It hadn't been a burden for Drew to accept this separation, for among all his classmates at the training school, the only one he'd never gotten along with was Mike. Their similarity had produced a rivalry, particularly on the part of Mike, that prevented them from ever feeling close to each other. Drew had nonetheless remained curious about the man upon whom he depended for his life, and whenever he'd had the chance, he'd asked former classmates what his lookalike was doing. In '78, Drew had learned that Mike was taking courses at the University of Minnesota. American Lit. The same kind of master's program that Drew had been taking at Iowa. It figured. He and his double didn't just look alike; they thought alike. They preferred the same cover as literature students in college towns.

'One of the few differences between us was that I liked classical American authors, and he liked the moderns,' Drew said. 'I heard that after he finished his degree at Minnesota, he planned to go to the University of Virginia to work on Faulkner. After Faulkner, he wanted to become an expert in Fitzgerald, then in Hemingway. Figure two years for each master's degree. If the timing's right, he should be working on Hemingway now.'

'Assuming he kept to that schedule. Even if he did, it won't help us find him,' Father Stanislaw said. 'Every university in the country teaches Hemingway.'

'No, the two top specialists on Hemingway are Carlos Baker and Philip

Young. Baker's at Princeton; Young's at Penn State. Their approaches are so different that someone determined to be an expert in Hemingway would have to work with either or even both of them. Believe me, I've got enough advanced degrees to know what I'm talking about.'

Princeton or Penn State? But how to be certain? How, among tens of thousands of students, to find the quarry? The literature department would be the focus of the search. So would the local gyms. Because Drew's double had to keep himself in shape for his missions, he had to work out every day. But he'd want to be invisible, so he'd go to the gym as early as possible when hardly anyone was around. Drew knew – he was sure – because he himself had followed that schedule.

Father Stanislaw made phone calls to his Opus Dei contacts. Seven hours later, the priest received a call from the Penn State campus about a man who matched Drew's age and description, who was taking graduate courses in American Lit, who worked with Philip Young on Hemingway, and went to a local gym every morning at six.

The man was a loner.

A half-hour later, Drew, Arlene, and Father Stanislaw were on the road.

6

A cold wind nipped Drew's cheek as he crouched with reverence at the side of a meadow halfway up a slope where he was concealed by thick leafless trees. He, Arlene, and Father Stanislaw had traveled together in the priest's black Oldsmobile, leaving Arlene's Firebird at a parking garage that offered long-term rates, paying several weeks' rent in advance. Drew had driven the motorcycle to the sleaziest bar he could find, making sure that no one saw him take off the license plates when he left the chopper next to the garbage cans in back. The police would eventually find it, but without the plates, they'd be slow to link the Harley with one stolen in Massachusetts. And because he'd wiped off his fingerprints, no one could link it to him.

While Arlene slept, Drew sat next to Father Stanislaw, still smelling the acrid smoke from Bethlehem's steel plants. He peered toward the Appalachian slopes before him. 'I guess this place will do.' He pointed toward a wooded ridge that loomed ahead on his right. 'As good as any.'

'Do you think you'll be long?' Father Stanislaw asked.

'We've got a schedule to keep. Not long. Leave the motor running.'

Father Stanislaw parked on the gravel shoulder, and though the sky was clear and blue Drew felt a stinging wind as he got out. His eyes narrowed, he climbed the dead grassy slope. For all a passing motorist might guess, he was headed toward the trees above to relieve himself.

But when he reached the trees, he continued through them, pausing only when he came to the edge of this upper meadow. He glanced around, seeing game trails through the grass, smelling autumn's sagelike fragrance. Yes, this place would do.

With a sturdy branch, he dug a tiny trough in the grass, two inches wide, ten inches down. The semi-frozen earth resisted. The tip of the branch broke. Finally, though, he was finished. Crouching, he reached in his coat and pulled out the plastic bag that contained the body of Stuart Little. Strange that the mouse hadn't rotted. Was that a sign? he wondered. A message of approval from God? He dismissed the thought, unable to allow himself to pretend to know God's mood.

Untying the plastic bag, he gently dropped Stuart's body into the bottom of the trough, then used his hands to fill in the dirt, covering it with a clump of grass. To complete the ritual, he gingerly stepped on the grass, tamping down the earth, making everything smooth. The edge of the meadow now looked undisturbed.

He stared down, for a distressing instant reminded of his parents' graves.

'Well,' he said, 'you saved my life. The fact is, you brought me *back* to life. I'm grateful.' He almost turned before he thought of something else. 'And I'll get even for you, pal.'

He left the trees, grimly descended the windy grassy slope, and got in the car.

'Drew?' Arlene was awake now, frowning with concern.

He shrugged.

'Are you okay?'

'Fine.'

'You're sure?'

'You were up there twenty minutes,' Father Stanislaw said. 'We almost went looking for you.'

'Well, now I'm back,' Drew said. 'I made a promise up there. So let's put some miles behind us. I want to see this damned thing finished. I want to make sure I keep my promise.'

'The look in your eyes,' Father Stanislaw said. 'God help the people we're after.'

'No, that's wrong.'

'I'm not sure what you mean.'

'God help us all.'

7

One range blended with another, then another. By mid-afternoon, they reached the Alleghenies, following the twists and turns of roads that led past barren strip-mined slopes and dying towns. Massive oil pumps were sometimes visible among skeletal trees, their metallic beaks rising and falling, rising and falling, their relentless thump oppressive even through the car's closed windows.

In contrast with their long intense discussions back at the motel room, neither Drew, Arlene, nor Father Stanislaw spoke much now, each brooding privately.

They reached their destination, zigzagging down a road that took them into a circular valley, located at almost the exact mid-point of Pennsylvania. And there, in the middle of the valley, they came to State College.

It was one of those towns that Drew had said was best for cover. The sprawling campus was large, with majestic vine-covered buildings and rows of towering trees. Because the town had no other major business, the local population had been forced to adjust to the vagaries of the more than twenty thousand students upon whom they depended for their livelihood. Typical of any large college town, half the population was constantly in flux, students coming and going, enrolling and graduating. An operative who liked to fill his time between assignments by reading and going to classes could have a satisfying life here and, more important, could have a cover that no one questioned. As long as he didn't need a social life, he'd be invisible. He could disappear.

8

Father Stanislaw used a pay phone in a supermarket on the outskirts of town, getting directions to the local Catholic church. The church had a modern design, low, long, made of concrete, with an iron statue of Christ on the Cross in front. They parked the car and entered the front door.

A tall, balding man in a business suit sat on a chair beside the holy water fountain in the vestibule, reading a prayer book. He glanced up as they came in.

'God be with you,' he said.

'And with your spirit,' Father Stanislaw added.

'*Deo gratias.*'

'Amen,' the priest responded. 'I must say it's good to hear Latin spoken in a church.'

Drew stood with Arlene in the background, watching with interest.

'Is the suspect still being followed?' Father Stanislaw asked.

Nodding, the businessman set down the prayer book and stood. 'He doesn't seem aware of it. As you suggested, we're keeping a cautious distance and tailing him – is that the right word? – in shifts.' He permitted a smile. 'It's almost like taking turns for forty-hours devotion.'

'You know where he lives?'

The businessman nodded again. 'It was difficult to learn. The university sends his mail, grades and such, to a postal box. He isn't listed in the phone book. But our source at the phone company discovered that he did indeed have a phone, unlisted. The computer's billing file had his address.' The businessman reached into his suitcoat and pulled out a folded piece of paper, giving it to Father Stanislaw.

'It's a section of town where a lot of students live,' the businessman continued. 'I've marked it on this map. Years ago, the landlord owned a rundown mansion that he divided into as many single-room apartments as he could. He made so much money that he couldn't resist adding onto the mansion. Sections on the sides, in back, in front, each with tiny rooms. After a while, you couldn't see the mansion for all the additions. And still not satisfied, he started buying houses along the block and in back. He built additions onto those as well until all the additions came together and you couldn't tell one house from another. It's as if the block imploded.

Only God knows how many apartments he's got there. The place is crammed with intersecting hallways and alleys so the students can get to the inner apartments. It's a maze. You can get lost in there.'

Father Stanislaw glanced at the paper. 'Number eighty-five?'

'The sequence isn't always in a continuous line. You'll have to do your best and then ask directions.'

'But he's not at home right now?'

'Not that I know of. There's a pay phone here in the basement. I've been getting reports every hour. The last I heard, he'd finished a class in Depression novelists and gone to the library.'

'Is there anything else I should know about where he lives?'

'Only that the students don't take well to strangers. They realize how unusual the place looks, and they get tired of sightseers.'

'Perhaps they won't object to a priest. You did good work. All of you. Your Church is grateful. Tell the others.'

'We're the ones who are grateful. As long as it was necessary to preserve the faith.'

'Believe me, it was.'

'For the honor and glory of God.'

'And the protection of His Church.'

Father Stanislaw raised his right hand in blessing. 'Please continue to receive your reports. Periodically I'll phone in case you have any change in the target's status.'

The businessman bowed his head. 'God's will be done, Father.'

'Indeed it will. And thank you again.'

Father Stanislaw turned, gesturing for Drew and Arlene to leave the church with him.

The heavy door thumped behind them.

Outside, the air was nippy, the dark sky bright with stars. A car drove by, its muffler streaming frosty exhaust.

'Opus Dei?' Drew asked.

Father Stanislaw didn't answer.

9

Drew stood in shadows across the street from the complex. Filling an entire block, it was situated at the level top of a gentle slope, bordered by shrubs. These shrubs and the night made it almost impossible to tell where one house ended and the next began.

But this much was sure, there were many houses. Twenty? Drew wondered. Thirty? The houses had been expanded with no consideration for consistency of style or materials. A plain cinderblock structure abutted an ornate wooden chalet attached to a modernistic glass-brick tower, and these all protruded from a Victorian mansion with gables and dormer windows. The mansion in turn adjoined a two-story log cabin, and then something that resembled a castle.

Jammed together, the entire hodgepodge seemed the work of an architect gone insane from the wondrous possibility of choice, though the prosaic truth was probably that the owner had simply built each new addition in whatever style was necessitated by the cheapest materials he could get his hands on from year to year.

Drew scanned the lit windows in the jumbled levels across from him. He stepped deeper into the shadows, watching silhouettes disappear among the crazily contrasting buildings.

Nervous, he turned from the eerie glow of gaslamps up there to frown at Arlene. 'Father Stanislaw should have been back by now.'

She shrugged. 'He might have had trouble finding his way.'

'Or else . . . Another five minutes. Then we'd better find out what happened to him.'

'We?'

'Okay' – he allowed himself to grin – 'I mean you.'

She grinned back.

They both understood. Because of Drew's resemblance to the man they were looking for, he couldn't risk attracting attention by wandering the complex.

Five minutes lengthened to ten.

'That's it. Now I'm worried, too,' she said. 'I'm going in there. He should have . . .'

A shadow emerged from the bushy slope across the street. Drew relaxed as he recognized Father Stanislaw.

The priest approached, exhaling frost. 'I found it. *Finally*. That place is like a rabbit warren. It's astonishing how easy it is to get lost up there.'

'The apartment?'

'In a narrow alley. It's got an outside entrance, with no doors on either side, and it faces a cinderblock wall.'

'So the neighbors can't see him going in and out. And if he disappeared for a couple of days, no one would notice.'

'Or probably care. These people aren't what you'd call friendly. Twice, I needed to ask directions; not to his apartment, of course, just near it. They treated me as if I'd demanded their youngest child. By the way, his apartment has an opaque glass window with its curtain closed, but I could tell that the lights were on.'

'Timers, probably,' Arlene said. 'The last we heard, he was still downtown.'

'An hour ago,' Father Stanislaw warned. 'Be careful.'

'How do I get there?' Drew asked.

'At the top of the slope, you'll face three alleys. Take the middle one. You'll come to a tree carved into a totem pole.'

'Totem pole?'

'Turn left till you reach a statue that looks like twisted airplane propellors. Then turn right.' Father Stanislaw sighed. 'I think I'd better draw you a map.'

10

A gaslamp hissed, barely dispelling the gloom. When Drew passed the statue, he had to stoop beneath an arch and found himself in one of the buildings. To his right, along a musty hall with pale bare bulbs dangling from the ceiling, he saw doors. To his left, a rickety wooden stairwell led down to an earthen floor. And down there, beyond in the shadows, he saw other doors. Father Stanislaw had called this place a rabbit warren. Drew's own impression was that of an anthill, except that ants didn't play rock music or cook onions.

He left the building and entered a courtyard where another gaslamp revealed a One Way Only traffic sign that stood in front of three tunnels. The map that Father Stanislaw had drawn told Drew to angle left. The tunnel led him through a further building to a courtyard that housed a chicken coop. He heard fowl clucking in there. And later in another courtyard, he saw a goat in a pen. Glancing down, he found that the long stone slabs he was walking on were tombstones. Madness. The deeper he followed the zigzagging corridors into the chaos, the more he accepted the bizarre.

His double had chosen his lodging well. In this environment, a man who stayed to himself would hardly be noticed. Indeed, everyone here seemed to want to be alone, as if convinced that the rest of the tenants were crazy. Drew realized why Father Stanislaw had encountered suspicion when he knocked on doors to ask for directions. Here, a priest would be inappropriate.

Several times, tenants stared suspiciously at Drew. But he didn't give them a chance to see his face, and as he moved purposefully forward, appearing to belong here, they relaxed.

As soon as he was out of their sight, he checked his map again, and at last he came to his destination. The narrow alley. The cinderblock wall to the right. The single door on the left, and the opaque window with the curtain behind it, the faint projection of light from inside.

He paused, his cheeks cold. From an apartment somewhere behind him, he heard muffled voices arguing about Plato and Aristotle.

Read St Augustine, Drew thought, as he shifted toward the end of the narrow alley. He stood in the dark at the corner farthest along, shifting behind a head-tall stack of boards, leaning against the crook in the wall, his insulated coat protecting his back from the chill of the cinderblocks.

He waited.

11

Just before midnight, a shadow came around the opposite end of the alley. The timing was right. Drew had often followed this schedule himself. Don't head home till the neighbors have settled down. In the meantime, go to a movie. Maybe one of those retrospectives of Truffaut at the

Student Union or, for a laugh, the latest James Bond movie downtown. In a college community, there were many other distractions: a lecture by this year's notable literary critic, a touring company's version of *Measure for Measure*, the music department's Mozart concert. If you wanted soothing diversion, especially in Drew's former line of work, a university was perfect. The next best thing to becoming a priest.

All the same, this approaching shadow might just be a student using the alley to reach an apartment farther back. But as the figure moved closer to the door across from the cinderblock wall, Drew became certain. The man approaching him was himself!

Drew held his breath; the figure stopped. He had Drew's proportions – the same build, the same height. The facial resemblance was uncanny, making Drew shiver. I wonder if he's been told I'm not dead, Drew thought. Or if he knows about the monastery. Then wouldn't he have gone into hiding?

The shadow reached into his coat, pulling out a key. Drew hadn't known quite how to act, but now he followed his instincts, deciding to play it casual. Good buddy time.

'Hey, Mike.' His voice echoed.

The shadow turned, on guard, toward this dark corner.

'What?'

'Hey, don't get panicky,' Drew said heartily. 'It's your old classmate. Drew. I've been waiting to talk to you. Man, I'm in trouble. Please, you've got to listen. I need your help.'

Mike stiffened, staring toward the darkness. 'Drew?'

'Remember those Colorado jack rabbits Hank Dalton made us use for target practice at the school? How Hank's dog used to eat them?'

'No. It can't be you.' There was fear in Mike's voice.

'How about that coffin Hank used to keep our guns in?'

'Christ, it *is*!'

'Good to see you, man.'

'But how did you find me?'

'I'll tell you later. Right now, you've gotta help me. Find me a place that's safe. Man, I'm in shit.'

'Oh, sure, I'll help. The thing is, who else is with you?'

'With me? Why would – I just told you. Who'd be with me when I'm in trouble?'

'Yeah?' The shadow glanced around nervously.

'How many years has it been?' Drew asked. 'Enough to make us wonder where our youth went, huh?' He took a chance and stepped from the darkness, holding out his hand in greeting. 'For God's sake, will you help me out?'

'You're sure nobody's with you?'

As Drew came closer, Mike's likeness to him became more unsettling. 'With me? What makes you keep asking that?'

'Because, good buddy' – Mike held out his hand and grinned – 'it's been so long that –'

'Yeah?'

'– I heard you were dead.'

Mike lunged in Drew's direction. Heart thumping, Drew crouched protectively. Boards suddenly clattered behind him, from the end of the alley where he'd been hiding. Startled, sensing a trap, Drew pivoted sideways, ready to defend himself not only from Mike but from men who'd been guarding Mike in case Drew showed up. I walked right into it! Drew thought in alarm.

But no one lunged from the end of the alley.

Instead, Mike seemed as startled as Drew. Freezing in mid-attack, staring toward the clattering boards, he seemed convinced that Drew had lied about being alone. Jerking back, on guard against unseen assailants, he cursed and swung around sharply, racing toward the opposite end of the alley, unaware of the Irish setter that emerged from the dark to nose at something beneath the boards it had toppled.

12

Drew scrambled in pursuit. He had to keep Mike in view. His lungs burned, but he knew that in this maze of alleys, courtyards, and tunnels, Mike needed only seconds to make Drew lose him. Mike knew all the twists and turns. He'd no doubt scouted the place for dozens of emergency places in which to hide.

Mike ducked around the alley's corner. Wary, Drew pulled out his Mauser. Mike might continue running away – or he might stop abruptly, taking Drew by surprise as Drew charged around the corner after him. Drew had to reduce his speed, cautiously rounding the corner, using up precious seconds. He didn't think Mike would have a handgun on him. Why would Mike take the risk of destroying his cover if someone happened to bump against a gun beneath Mike's coat in a throng of students leaving class?

But a knife? Mike could easily carry one. A stiletto in his boot, or a pocket knife. No one would question that. For that matter, Mike didn't need any weapon except his hands. Like Drew, the man could kill with one sharp blow to the chest or the larynx.

But Mike didn't attack as Drew crept around the corner. Instead, Drew saw him racing down the continuation of the alley. His chest heaving, Drew rushed after him. Even in the shadows, he had a sufficient target to shoot at. But he didn't dare. Not only because of the noise, the commotion it would cause, a crowd, the police. But because he might kill Mike instead of wounding him. And Mike had to be kept alive to answer Drew's questions.

Mike charged around another corner; Drew followed. Beyond a courtyard, its gaslamp hissing, he saw Mike veer past a greenhouse made from storm windows, then sprint inside an imitation English manor. Now Drew could rush ahead again. As he entered the building, he bumped past a man coming through a door to the left. The man toppled back inside his apartment, sprawling hard on the cracked linoleum floor. 'Watch where the hell you're –!'

Drew didn't hear the rest. He was already through the building's central hallway and banging out the exit door, not worried that Mike might be lurking behind it because before the door had swung shut he'd seen his double charging ahead across another lamplit courtyard. This one had a sandbox and swing set.

The building beyond it was a barn. But instead of darting into it, Mike swung to the right, rushed down another alley, leaped over a bicycle, raced left past a wishing well, and, with a furtive glance behind him scurried down wooden steps to the basement entrance of a looming Victorian house.

The door creaked as Drew stalked into the basement. He wasn't surprised when he faced another corridor. The floor was earthen, like the one he'd seen earlier. Doors lined the hallway. Only half the dangling bare bulbs were illuminated.

At the far end, Mike lunged through another door. Rushing after him, Drew heard the crunch of broken glass beneath his shoes. He frowned. The earth floor should have absorbed his weight. The fragments of glass should have been squeezed down into the earth instead of cracking now.

The detail troubled him, but he couldn't become distracted. There was too much else to think about. He was gaining on Mike, and in the alley outside this house or in the next courtyard, he had a good chance of catching him. Drew neared the door through which Mike had disappeared.

He aimed the Mauser, pushed the door open, and faced a brick wall directly in front of him. A hurried glance showed another wall on his left, behind the door. He darted right. The door swung shut. His bowels contracted as absolute darkness smothered him. Oh, Jesus, he prayed. Spiders scuttled inside his stomach. Total darkness.

Frantic, he pressed his back against the wall, and though his lungs ached after his urgent chase, he struggled not to breathe. Because the rasp of his breath could now get him killed. Oh, Jesus and Mary. He was trapped inside a black room.

The broken glass on the earth floor of the hallway outside made sense now. Most of the dim bare bulbs in the ceiling out there hadn't been illuminated. Mike, in rushing along the hallway, had hit at the bulbs, smashing them. That accounted for the broken glass Drew had heard beneath his shoes.

The extinguished bulbs had been at this end of the hallway – the approach to the door through which Drew had entered this black room. If the entire hallway had been lit, Drew might have been able to see inside this room and notice where the light switch was and turn it on to find where Mike was hiding. Or maybe Mike wasn't even here. He might have ducked out a now-unseeable door and left Drew to think he was trapped in here with an equally unseeable opponent. Mike might be racing out of the complex by now while Drew tried to guess if he was in danger.

But Drew had to assume that Mike was here. The implications made his heart contract. A completely black room. He knew the situation well – from the black room in the airplane hangar at the Rocky Mountain Industrial School. Fighting in the dark had been their chief instructor's specialty. And Hank Dalton had mercilessly drilled his students in the principles of that unnerving form of combat. But Mike had been trained just as thoroughly. Drew was fighting someone just as good. He was fighting himself.

13

In Colorado, Drew and the other students – including Mike and Jake –
had gone to the gym as usual for their first class at 8 A.M. They'd studied
the double doors through which Hank Dalton always pushed the gleaming
copper coffin. Though proud of their eighteen-year-old maturity, they
nonetheless felt the anticipation of children about to play with toys. Soon
Hank would open the coffin and give them their weapons, urging them to
see who could take apart and reassemble them in the shortest time. Jake
was always fast. But Drew and Mike were faster, rivals in this as in
everything else, their physical similarities seeming to make them want to
test their resemblance in other ways.

That morning, they waited for the class to begin. Fifteen minutes later
than usual, Hank Dalton came through the double doors. But without the
coffin.

'Outside on the double!'

The sharp edge in his voice made the students think that Hank was
angry at them. Anxious not to make him angrier, conditioned to be
obedient, they snapped to attention and ran through the double doors,
down a corridor, and outside, where they squinted from the morning sun
toward an unmarked bus parked in front of the obstacle course. The
motor was rumbling.

'What are you gawking at?' Hank barked. 'You never seen a bus
before?' At once he grinned and scratched his leathery cheek. 'It's time for
a little field trip. Hustle aboard.'

Relieved that Hank wasn't angry, everybody scrambled in, and with
Hank himself driving, they left the chain-link fence of the compound,
following a dirt road into the mountains.

Two hours later, after a seemingly aimless route, with nothing but pine
trees and sagebrush to look at, Hank drove through the open gate of
another chain-link fence and parked in front of a corrugated-metal
airplane hangar. There were no other buildings. In the distance, a small
dirt airstrip cut through the scrubgrass of this small valley.

Not that the students had a chance to study the place. Hank hustled
them into the hangar, and that was the last they saw of the sun for what
they later learned was twenty-five days.

He shut the door and marched the students forward. They bumped
against each other in the dark.

'Having problems with your eyes?' Hank asked. 'Well, we'll fix that.
You'll soon think the dark is home.' He laughed good-naturedly.

Indeed, as their eyes adjusted to the dark, the students glanced around
with interest. Helped by hints of light that showed through the cracks in
the metal walls, they noticed something large in the middle of the building
– so large that it might have been a one-story house without windows.

'Wonder what *that* is,' someone murmured.

'All in good time,' Hank answered, directing them toward a shadowy
area to the right of the structure. Here they found a row of bunkbeds, each
with two dark sheets and one dark blanket, and on top of each blanket, the
top and bottom of a plain black garment.

'Pajamas?'

'More or less.' Hank's voice drifted out of the shadows. 'Strip and put them on. They'll be your uniform.'

More puzzled, the students obeyed. Their eyes adjusted further to the shadows, allowing them to see that Hank had changed from his usual cowboy boots, faded jeans, denim shirt, and battered stetson to the loose black pajamas.

'You'd better get some rest now. 'Cause from here on in we'll train at night.'

Rest? In the middle of the day? Drew didn't feel tired, and yet he yawned as soon as he stretched out on his bunk.

Abruptly he wakened to Hank's voice echoing from a loudspeaker somewhere in the hangar.

'Rise and shine.'

At night?

'He sounds like God,' someone said.

Supper – or was it breakfast? – consisted of rice and fish in something that tasted like oyster sauce. It was followed by tea.

The training began immediately. Hank led them to the back of the hangar, where, by feel, they learned that sandbags had been stacked against the wall. Drew heard Hank move, leaning toward something beside the bags, and at once, a pale yellow light came on behind them from the opposite side of the hangar. It struggled through the otherwise absolute darkness toward the sandbags.

Hank shrugged, looking Oriental in his black pajamas. 'Even the night has stars. And a moon, though of varying brightness. Unless there are clouds. And then you believe in demons.'

Drew's eyes strained, fighting to admit as much as possible of the pale yellow light on the other side of the hangar. He was amazed at how much better he began to see the sandbags against the wall; his imagination learned to add the dimensions concealed by the shadows.

Hank instructed them on the proper way to hold a throwing knife. For hours, he made them hurl the knives against the sandbags. He made them hurl straight razors, Japanese throwing stars, even sticks, ashtrays, and rocks.

The exercise didn't seem to be a rehearsal for killing, though often Drew felt confident that his opponent would have been felled by the deep blow of his knife. Rather, as Hank clapped his hands, the purpose seemed to be the speed with which they hurled the object on command and the accuracy with which the object struck.

'Because you can't know in the dark if your target's dead,' Hank barked. 'The instant you hear your weapon hit, you've got to assume your enemy's been distracted and –'

But the 'and' was apparently for the next day – or night, given the reversal of their normal schedule – because Hank interrupted himself to correct the throwing stance of one student.

He made them turn their backs to the sandbags. Now, when he clapped his hands, the group had to pivot in order to throw.

He shouted commands about their balance, the need to keep their feet spread – not too much, just the width of the hips. And to keep their legs bent, so their knees – in that flexible position – could act as a better pivoting mechanism. They learned to hunch slightly forward, so their hips could help the body twist better.

Often the sharp objects they threw at the sandbags fell clattering to the concrete floor.

That too had its value, Hank insisted. 'Because you can't allow yourself to pay attention to any noise you can anticipate. By the end of your stay here, I plan to make you familiar with the sound of any weapon you can imagine as it falls on any surface you can imagine. Not just this concrete floor. But sand and carpet and grass and shale.'

Drew crawled exhausted into his bunk that morning, seeing the glow of the rising sun creep through the cracks in the hangar's metal walls.

But the difference in time didn't matter, he thought, as Hank turned off the pale yellow light and Drew snuggled naked between the dark sheets, beneath the dark blanket. What mattered was sleep. In his dreams, he threw Coca-Cola cans at sandbags.

The next night, Hank continued the throwing exercises. They became so repetitious that Drew no longer flinched from the sound of the various objects as they fell on the floor in the darkness.

In nights to come, Hank added refinements. The students now had to lunge at their target, holding a felt-tipped pen as if it were a knife, attacking the sandbag in the shadows and slashing upward.

After each assault, Hank would inspect the sandbag, using a shielded penlight, commenting on the accuracy of the thrust. His command was always the same. Use what little light you have, and learn to judge the rest of the target from the part you see.

Next, Hank had the students throwing fragile objects at each other in the almost total dark, then lunging with felt-tipped pens to slash at the opponent's pillow-buffered chest.

And each time, Hank used the shielded penlight to assess the theoretical damage.

Eventually the students weren't allowed the advantage of pillows. If a felt-tipped pen bruised your stomach, well, you should have been more careful. Imagine if the blow had come from a knife.

In these and many similar ways, Hank trained his students to develop reflexes in the dark.

They were taught to move with a knife as if it were an extension of the hand. In turn, to make the hand an extension of the arm. To sweep the arm, to make the hand follow it. And thus the knife to follow the hand. Fluidity.

How to crouch while shifting sideways, never extending the feet beyond the width of the hips. Always slowly, *gradually*, shifting weight. Never to the rear, and never forward. Silently.

They learned the parts of the body: spleen, epiglottis, testicles, sphenoid, maxilla, thyroid, transverse sinus, septum, carotid, humorus, orbital. And lunged through the dark at the sandbags or at each other with felt-tipped pens, and later with the palms of their hands or the tips of their elbows.

As their training became more intense, they had the sense that Hank was preparing them for an ultimate test. Night followed night – how many, it became impossible to know. They couldn't help glancing more often toward the single-story structure that waited for them in the middle of the hangar's darkness.

211

At last, after they'd successfully demonstrated their skill in stalking an opponent through the darkness across various surfaces that resembled a sand shore, a thick carpet, a slick waxed floor; after they'd learned how to step silently around and over shadowy obstacles with the same grace that they'd developed in their ballet classes back at the school, Hank said, 'Okay, it's time. You're ready to find out what's in the compartment.'

Eager, they followed him through the shadows to its door. Hank opened it, but neither Drew nor anyone else was able to see inside.

Hank pointed to Jake. 'After I go in and shut the door, give me fifteen seconds. Then you come in and shut the door.'

Jake hesitated. 'And?'

'You never played hide-and-seek? Try to find me. Just one thing, though. I'm supposed to be your enemy. If you give me a chance, if you're not careful and you let me hear you or sense you, well, in real life, I'd be able to kill you. For now, we'll play the game this way – whoever surprises the other first, with a touch, is the winner. Simple enough?'

'Sure.'

Hank went inside. Fifteen seconds later, Jake followed, closing the door behind him. In thirty seconds the door opened again, and Jake stepped out. Drew saw the frustration on his face.

'What happened in there?' someone asked.

'I'm not supposed to talk about it. He wants you all to line up, and one by one to go in.'

Drew felt uneasy. Standing near the end of the line, he watched each of the others go in. None lasted any longer than Jake had.

Mike took his turn, and he too came out almost at once. Drew sensed his humiliation. Always competitive, Mike seemed to challenge Drew to do any better.

Then it was Drew's turn.

He opened the door, concentrated to heighten his reflexes, stepped inside, and nervously closed the door behind him. Almost at once he felt stifled, as if the air was thicker in there, squeezing him.

And the darkness. He'd thought that the hangar was dark. But now he understood what darkness really was.

In here, it was absolute, compressing him. The silence made his eardrums hiss; he debated what to do. Stepping forward in search of Hank, he bumped against a table. Its legs screeched on the concrete floor, and at once Hank grasped his right elbow.

'You just got killed.' Hank whispered so close that his breath tickled Drew's ear.

Leaving the black room, trying not to look embarrassed, Drew noticed Mike's satisfied expression, his delight that Drew had been no more successful than himself.

Hank called the group together and asked them to assess what had happened. He made them repeat the exercise, debriefed them again, and gradually instilled in them the principles of this type of confrontation.

'All of you tried to find me too soon. You didn't let yourselves *feel* the stillness. Your anxiousness betrayed you. Take your time. It might be the last time you ever have, so why not prolong it? Sense it fully.'

Hank taught them patterns with which to search the room instead of merely moving blindly forward. He encouraged them to use the skills which they'd already developed in attacking the sandbags and avoiding obstacles in the hangar.

'But this is different,' someone said.

'How?'

'In the hangar, we had plenty of room. And the darkness wasn't total. Besides, you were in there first. You had the advantage of being able to hide.'

'Imagine that. And if you're up against an enemy, I suppose you'll complain to him that he isn't playing fair if he too has an advantage. In this game, you have to make your own advantage,' Hank said. 'By being better than your opponent. The most important thing you have to remember – apart from the pattern I told you to follow once you're in the room – the most important thing is to move so slowly that you're barely moving at all.'

They tried the exercise again and yet again, and each time they lasted a little longer before Hank touched them. Five seconds longer perhaps. Then ten. But that slight extension of their endurance was, by comparison, a major accomplishment. And the first time Drew survived for a *minute*, he had the exhausted but giddy sense afterward of having been in the room much longer.

'You're still not moving slowly enough,' Hank insisted. 'You're still not feeling the dark. Did you ever watch the way a blind man knows an obstacle's in front of him, even if he doesn't have his cane? It's because he's so used to living in the dark that he can feel the air bounce off his surroundings. He can sense things around him, almost as if they give off vibrations. And that's what *you've* got to learn to do. Compensate for your lack of sight by heightening all your other senses. Jake, you moved silently, I have to give you credit. But you're a smoker. I smelled stale cigarettes on you and knew your exact location, even though I couldn't see or hear you. From now on, nobody on this team is allowed to smoke. And I don't mean just while we're here. *Ever*. Mike, you use deodorant. I smelled you coming too. Get rid of it.'

'But we can't help giving off some kind of odor,' Mike said. 'Sweat, for instance. That's natural under stress.'

'No. The kind of stress we're dealing with makes your sweat glands dry up. They stop functioning. Oh, maybe one or two of you aren't typical, and your glands won't quit. We'll soon find out. And you'll be out of the school.'

Soon the students were able to survive the exercise for an even longer time. Two minutes lengthened to five. And then to ten.

Drew gradually learned about the objects in the room. Proceeding slowly, methodically, he discovered that the layout resembled that of a living room: chairs, a sofa, a coffee table, a television set, a lamp, a bookshelf. But one night, the furniture had been rearranged, and instead of a concrete floor, there now was a rug. Another night the set-up had been transformed into a bedroom. Yet another night, the room was filled with crates at random, as if in a warehouse.

'You can't assume anything,' Hank warned.

At last, each member of the class was able to stalk Hank for an hour without being touched. Then Hank changed the exercise. 'From now on, you stalk each other. One of you goes in, then someone else goes after you. After that, you'll do it in reverse, the second man going in first, so the hunter becomes the hunted. And you'll keep changing partners. Everybody gets a chance to go against everybody else.'

Drew glanced at Mike, who returned his look, clearly anxious for the chance to test his skills against Drew. They weren't paired right away. Only after four other partners did they find themselves in the room together. Drew, the hunted, won the first time. But when Mike became the hunted, he won. And later when they were paired again, their score again was tied. The final time, after they stayed in the room for three hours, neither winning, Hank broke up the game.

14

Now, after sixteen years, they were paired again. But their weapons would not be felt-tipped markers, and Hank wasn't here to stop the exercise. Their rivalry had reached the ultimate. There'd be no question about who was better. And no rematch.

Drew didn't *want* to kill. He had to keep Mike alive, to make him talk about Janus. But his reluctance to kill was a liability. Because Mike for sure wouldn't hesitate.

The instant Drew realized the terrifying implications of this pitch-dark basement room into which Mike had lured him, he automatically bent his knees, assuming the crouch Hank had made second nature for him. He spread his feet apart, the width of his hips, and stretched his arms before him, also spread apart, the width of his shoulders, testing the dark with his hands. He spread his arms farther apart, feeling the emptiness to his right and left. At once, he changed his location, shifting to the left, not far, just a body's width, and stopped.

These initial tactics had one purpose only – to move from where he'd been as he came into the room, lest Mike take advantage of the inadvertent sounds Drew made and attack while he was still unprepared. But now Drew was one with the dark, just as Mike was. The stalk would begin.

Drew was even more sure that Mike had not been carrying a gun; there'd been too many chances for him to use one. Certainly as Drew came into this room, an instant before the door swung shut, cloaking him with total darkness, Mike would have had a reliable target.

Even so, Mike might have a knife. Drew considered that risk and decided that Mike would have thrown it when Drew first entered the room. The moment Mike heard the knife hit Drew, he would have attacked, taking advantage of the blow's distraction to kill Drew with his hands if the knife hadn't done the job. Hank Dalton had drilled that tactic into them. Second nature.

So there had to be a reason for Mike to hang back. The only explanation Drew could think of was that Mike didn't have a weapon, that he was depending on his skill in hand-to-hand combat. Which meant that Mike would wait for Drew to come close and then take him by surprise.

Drew did have a weapon, the Mauser he clutched, but in the dark it was useless – even a liability, because it limited the right hand with which he held it. Under the circumstances, Drew would have preferred to have his

214

right hand nimble, so it could better sense the feel of the stillness, the subtle vibrations of the dark. But he didn't dare risk the sound of putting the gun in his pocket.

He waited, crouching, on guard, for five minutes, listening intensely. This room was apparently so deep within the ground, its walls so thick, that no outside sound intruded. He strained to hear subtle breathing. Or the brush of a footstep. But he heard nothing except the pounding of blood behind his ears.

Inhaling slowly, he assessed the smells in the room, separating and identifying them. A turpentine odor. Paint. Something like varnish. A vague whiff of gasoline.

A storeroom? he wondered. The more he judged the odors, the more his conclusion seemed correct. Maintenance supplies. Maybe even a lawn-mower. Maybe tools.

He'd soon find out. Because he had to begin the hunt, just as, he assumed, Mike had started to hunt for him.

'Never head directly into the room,' Hank Dalton had insisted. 'Avoid the middle. Check the perimeter first. Which means you've got two choices. Right or left. Keep your back against the wall. The layout of the room – its obstacles – will determine which direction seems better.'

In the present case, neither right nor left seemed to offer any advantage. True, he'd moved to the left when he entered and recognized the trap. Mike might assume that Drew would continue toward the left. The way to fool him, then, would be to shift in the direction Mike didn't expect, to the right.

But guessing, and second-guessing, and triple-guessing, were part of the hunt. Mike might anticipate Drew's logic. He might assume that Drew, having started toward the left, as a feint, would then switch direction. Eventually, no matter what logic either opponent used, there was no way for one or the other to anticipate in which direction the hunt would begin. To think about it too long would lead to paralysis.

Arbitrarily, Drew decided to keep going left. With agonizing slowness. Shifting his arms, his hands, testing the darkness. Gently moving his feet.

The floor, like the hallway outside, was earth. But at least the dirt was packed solid, absorbing his weight as he slowly eased his foot down. No crunch communicated his position.

He paused again, listened, smelled, sensed. Again he tested the dark-ness with his hands and slowly crept a few inches farther to his left.

Gingerly moving his feet, he stiffened as the edge of his left shoe touched an object. Almost imperceptible pressure against his left leg and hip warned him that the object was large, but when he moved his left hand in its direction, he felt nothing. Whatever it was, the object rose no higher than his waist. When he lowered his hand to that level, he felt wood, gouged and battered, heavily grained, somewhat oily.

A workbench. Silently exploring with his hand, he felt a metal vice clamped onto the side of the bench. A pockmarked pair of pliers. A gritty oil can with a spout.

From now on, the complications multiplied. For all he knew, Mike was waiting on the other side of the workbench, ready to attack as Drew inched around the bench to return to the wall. Or maybe Mike was directly across from him, against the *opposite* wall, and as soon as he sensed that Drew's attention was fully occupied with the problem of getting around the bench . . .

Second-guessing, triple-checking. As Drew began to ease around the table, he imagined Mike's thoughts.

Hey, Drew, it's just like back in Colorado, when we were rivals. Sure, we looked so much alike everybody wondered which of us was better, didn't they? But we never settled the issue. Not to my satisfaction. Of course, the higher-ups had their own stupid idea that you were better than me. Otherwise, they wouldn't have chosen me to act as a double for you instead of the other way around. You were the star; I was the stand-in. Shit. But I outlasted you. You're supposed to be dead. I got to take your place. I *became* you, and I like it that way just fine. I won't switch places again. I won't go back to being second-best. This time, I plan to make damned sure you *stay* dead.

His muscles aching from tension, Drew inched through the darkness around the bench. But to check out the corner between the bench and the wall, he'd have to leave himself partly vulnerable to an attack from across the pitch-black room. He sharpened his senses, on guard against the slightest sound or shift in the dense, still air.

Subtly, silently, he waved his left hand in front of him, toward the continuation of the wall. He wanted to cause a gentle waft of air that might make Mike think Drew was closer than he was, that might prompt Mike to attack prematurely from the corner of the wall and the bench.

But no attack came, and as Drew eased around the other side of the workbench, coming closer to the wall, he aimed his Mauser toward it. If Mike indeed were hiding there, if he attacked, Drew would shoot as soon as he felt Mike's body.

But nothing happened. And with a mental exhalation of relief, Drew reached the wall, pressing his back against it again. He waited in the darkness, mustering energy, concentrating.

'Discipline,' Hank had told them. 'Patience. Those are the secrets to winning this game. One thoughtless move. One careless gesture. That's all it takes, and you're dead. You have to ignore the future. You can't let yourself imagine how good it'll feel to win and leave the room and relax. Because *now* is what counts, and if your enemy's concentrating on now while you're in the future, well, pal, you'll never see the future. You'll be history.'

Drew continued to shift along the wall to his left. As before, he used his feet, the side of his leg and hip, to test for obstacles. Aiming the Mauser with his right hand, he moved his left hand before him, almost caressing the dark. His silent foot touched an object to his left; indeed, he sensed that the object was there even before his shoe touched it. The object was wood. It projected sixteen inches into the room. He felt it with his left hand. The object rose all the way to the ceiling. And when he eased his fingers around its side, he touched cold circular metal. Paper, wrapped around it, was partly peeled away. Here, the odor of turpentine was stronger. A paint can? Yes, he decided. Ceiling-high shelves of paint cans. Keeping his back against the shelves as if they were the wall, he continued to his left.

He'd progressed no more than ten or twelve feet and had been in here for possibly forty minutes, maybe longer. It was hard to know. In a black room, time was distorted by the agonizing slowness of movement. Every second seemed eternal. Terribly full.

Breath held, he came to the end of the shelves, felt around them toward the wall, but touched another wall instead. It extended to his left. He tested that corner.

With alarming abruptness, something hit the shelves to his right. The object clattered down, thumping onto the floor.

Drew flinched. He couldn't help it. His heart expanding as if it would burst, he fought not to gasp. In fact, he made no sound at all. Instead, as his training spurred him, he crouched reflexively – so low that his hips touched the back of his legs. With his back wedged into the corner, he raised his hands, his Mauser aimed.

The reaction was so instantaneous that even before the object had finished thumping onto the floor he was ready.

Mike might be attacking. That had been one of Hank Dalton's tactics. Startle your opponent. Throw something. The moment it clatters, take the advantage. Go for him.

But as silence again filled the room, as the stillness once more gelled, Drew felt no impact, no body charging into him. He waited, his stomach contracting, his nerves stretched taut.

Nothing happened.

He tried to calculate the direction from which the object had been thrown. Couldn't. But at least he knew that Mike was in here, that his look-alike had not ducked out an unseen exit before Drew entered this room.

Most surely now, this was to the death.

But something else bothered him. Why hadn't Mike attacked? Drew debated, tense, deciding.

Because Mike hasn't figured out where I am. In the dark, if he rushes me but misjudges my location, he knows I can kill him. He threw something toward where he thought I might be and hoped that I'd lose control, that I'd make a sound. But because he missed, he'll throw something else. If he hits me, as soon as he hears the impact against my body, he'll assume I'm distracted, and he'll attack.

Another Hank Dalton strategy.

As Drew crouched with his back to the corner, facing the dark of the room, a second object struck the shelves on his right. The clatter was nearer, sending a vibration against Drew's shoulder.

But this time Drew had expected the noise. He took advantage of the object's fall to shift toward the left along this new wall.

Sure, Mike decided I moved in this direction. He's trying to box me in. The moment he hits me, he'll rush.

A third object whacked against the corner where Drew had been crouching. Again he took advantage of the sound to shift a little farther along this new wall.

And now he had more information. The deflecting angle of the various objects, the direction of their sound when they hit the earthen floor, told him that Mike was on the far side of the room, probably in the corner opposite to the one in which he himself had just been crouching.

Or at least Mike had probably been there a moment ago. For all Drew could tell, his double had taken advantage of the clatter to shift position as Drew had.

In which direction would Mike have shifted, though? Toward the wall Drew was following – to meet Drew head on? Or toward the wall Drew first had crept along – to come at him from behind?

Drew wondered if he should reverse his direction. A flip of a coin. A fifty-fifty chance. They could go on like this, double- and triple-guessing, all night. He imagined them circling the room forever.

A fourth object clattered. But this time, it rebounded off the wall Drew first had crept along, thumping onto the floor.

Does Mike think I've doubled back? Or is he trying to trick me into thinking that's what *he* thinks?

As Hank Dalton had repeatedly stressed, that was the point of the exercise. To confuse your opponent until his mind was tired, off-balance. And then to kill him.

'The rules. Trust them. Depend on them,' Hank had demanded. 'It took me almost twenty-five years to discover them. And they're one reason I'm still alive.'

But as Hank had pointed out, few other warriors knew those rules. In actual combat, one of Hank's students shouldn't need to exhaust himself, stalking an opponent. Because Hank's system of fighting in the dark wasn't standard training anywhere else. 'Remember,' he'd said, 'you've got the advantage. Don't be overconfident. But don't feel overwhelmed. Because, if you follow the rules, you've got a better-than-even chance of winning.'

Sure, Drew thought. Just follow the rules. But listen, Hank, tell me this. What do you do when your opponent also knows the rules? Back in Colorado, I had an awful lot of stalemates with him. He not only looks like me. He's been *trained* like me. What's to prevent another stalemate? Except that this time the stalemate must be broken. And exhaustion will probably do it. Since the monastery, I've been running too long. If stamina's the deciding factor, I'll probably lose.

He didn't panic. Instead, as his spine tingled, he had a sudden inspiration. What do you do when you're up against someone who also knows the rules?

Do the completely unexpected. *Break* the rules. Go back to the way you behaved when you first entered that black room in the hangar in Colorado. Circle the room, follow its wall, the way Hank insisted? No. Go straight across. Crouch in the middle and wait for Mike to throw again.

And then, when you sense exactly where he is, go after him.

His shoes seemed not to touch the earthen floor as he crept silently toward the middle of the room. He maintained his slow careful pace, shifting his left hand before him while he aimed the Mauser with his right, testing the dark.

And when he judged that he'd reached the middle of the room, he hunkered down, resting as comfortably as possible on his haunches while he waited for Mike's next move.

He felt the shift of air from the object as it hurtled past him, only inches above his head, cracking against the wall he'd been following. There. In the opposite corner. Drew inched closer.

Another object whipped air past his head, whacking the wall behind him.

Drew inched even closer.

It happened with startling suddenness. Drew sensed an obstacle abruptly in front of him. He didn't touch it. No, as Hank Dalton had insisted, he didn't need to touch it. If he was alert enough, he'd actually be able to feel the vibrations coming off it.

The obstacle was a man.

Mike, who looked like Drew, who'd been trained the same as Drew, also *thought* like Drew. Mike, as well, had debated how to stalk an opponent who had the same advantage of Hank Dalton's training, who could anticipate.

Because of the rules. So break the rules.

And with unexpected abruptness, Drew found himself grappling chest-to-chest, face-to-face, with his double.

The shock was sickening. As they stumbled one way, then the other, Drew no longer feared making noise. Instead, he breathed stridently, desperately needing oxygen, pushing, straining against the man he held and who held him.

He groaned from a knee that struck his thigh, barely missing his testicles.

He winced as he lurched back against the sharp edge of the workbench, hitting his kidneys.

'Mike . . .'

He rammed the heel of his left palm into his attacker's solar plexus.

Mike groaned.

'For God's sake, listen . . .'

Drew gasped from a crushing blow to the side of his neck.

'We have to talk!'

But when the blunt edge of a screwdriver tore – shockingly, oh, blessed Jesus – into Drew's left shoulder, his coat buffering the damage, he understood that Mike was determined to win.

What choice did Drew have?

He shoved Mike away and squeezed his finger on the Mauser's trigger.

Shot.

And shot.

He emptied the magazine, his ears stunned by the repeated blasts, his eyes offended by the muzzle flashes.

Yet despite the various injuries to his body, he spread his bullets skillfully. And when he heard a bullet hit home, he narrowed his aim, his nostrils flaring from the acrid stench of cordite and flashburns, scorched fabric and flesh.

He blew his lookalike to Hell.

As blood pelted onto the earthen floor, as it splattered warm and salty across his lips, he felt Mike lunge against him once more, still determined to keep up the battle. But Mike shuddered in death. The two men embraced each other, almost as lovers.

Mike sank toward the floor, his flaccid jaw sagging past Drew's chest, stomach, groin, and knees.

'Why didn't you listen?' Drew whispered, though he wanted to shriek. Damnable discipline kept him in control. '*You should have listened.* All you had to do was tell me who you were working for. You stupid . . . You'd still be alive. Maybe finally, we could have been friends instead of . . .'

Rivals? Doubles?

Janus. He'd killed Janus, but the man behind Janus was still alive!

Enraged at the pointlessness of the death, Drew wanted to kick Mike's corpse, to smash its teeth, to crush its nose.

You stupid . . .

Instead he sank to his knees in the dark.

With tears streaking down his cheeks, he prayed for Mike's soul.

And his own.

15

Time had been so distorted in the black room that, when Drew left the building, he blinked in surprise. The night had passed. A cold October sun was rising. Now, all the gaslamps were extinguished, the apartments silent, though chickens clucked eerily from somewhere. Obviously the people who lived here had not heard the shots or else had deliberately ignored them, not wanting to get involved. He followed the zigzagging hallways, passages, and tunnels back to the narrow alley with a cinderblock wall on the right, where an eternity ago he'd stepped from the stack of sheltering boards and confronted his double.

He'd used a handkerchief to wipe Mike's blood from his face and hands. He'd used the same handkerchief to staunch the flow of blood from his shoulder where Mike had struck it with a screwdriver. Then he'd taken off his coat and carried it folded across his shoulder to hide both the wound and the bloodstains on the coat. The precaution was needless. This early, he encountered no one.

Cold, his shoulder throbbing, sick at heart, he used a key that he'd taken from Mike as he searched the body, and unlocked the door to Mike's room. He had no fear of boobytraps or anti-intruder alarms. Earlier, Mike had taken no precautions as he pulled out this same key and aimed it toward the lock. So Drew's assumption was that the apartment was unprotected. And if it wasn't?

Drained, he didn't care. He had killed again, and nothing else mattered.

Nothing. Except the continuation of his quest. The need to avenge the monks in the monastery. To discover who Mike had been working for.

He turned the knob and opened the door, frowning when he saw no light in the room. His instincts quickened in alarm. Last night, there'd been a glow beyond the closed drapes and the opaque window. Who'd been in here to turn off the light? As his chest tightened, he scanned the room. Even with the light off, it wasn't pitch-dark. The rising sun illuminated the open doorway, dispersing the shadows.

Despite his uneasiness, he made two assumptions. The first was that the room was deserted. After all, anyone hiding here had already been given ample opportunity to attack him.

The second was the consequence of the first. The lights were off because, as Arlene had suspected last night, they were on a timer.

Stepping farther in, he saw brick-and-board bookshelves, a desk with a typewriter, a sofa-bed, a dinette table, a television and stereo.

Nothing fancy. The furnishings a graduate student would have. The same sort of furnishings Drew had once had, though he – like Mike – could have afforded much better.

The apartment was all in one room; a stove and fridge were set off by a counter.

Something moved near the sofa. Drew bent his knees, raising his hands, preparing to defend himself. Then his scowl changed into a grin, which broadened as he remembered Stuart Little. For now he was crouched defensively against a cat.

It meowed, approaching. Not a kitten, but not full-grown either. Orange with white spots. Another cat appeared from beneath the desk, and another from behind the counter, one totally black, the other a Siamese, its blue eyes distinctive even in the shadows. He almost laughed but stopped himself, his injured shoulder throbbing, again reminded of the parallel between Mike and himself.

In the old days, before the monastery, Drew had enjoyed keeping cats. They'd been his luxury; his social life. And later, when not a cat but a mouse had entered his cell in the monastery, he'd once again felt alive. Because, despite the Carthusian insistence on effacing oneself from the world, the one thing he'd missed was the chance to share his existence with another creature.

'Cats, I bet you wonder why no one came home last night,' he said, with a sudden vision of Mike dead in that black room. Shuddering, he tried to stifle his terrible emotion. His voice sounded hoarse. 'I bet you're awful hungry.'

He closed the door behind him, locked it, noticed a murky light switch on the wall, and flicked it up.

Two lamps came on, one beside the sofa, the other on the desk. He flinched, stumbling back. A door came open to his left. And across from him, a figure rose from behind the counter. He braced himself.

Father Stanislaw appeared from the door. Beyond it, Drew saw a closet. He swung toward the counter where Arlene stood all the way up.

She came to him. He wanted desperately to hold her.

'Thank God, you're alive.' She hugged him longingly. 'When you didn't come back to the car . . .'

He felt her arms around him, her breasts pressed against his chest. Reflexively, he leaned to kiss her.

Father Stanislaw cleared his throat. 'If I can interrupt.'

Drew glanced at him in confusion.

'We waited till just before dawn,' Father Stanislaw said.

Arlene stepped back slightly, still keeping her arms around him. But Drew's chest retained the sensation of her breasts. He remembered the way he'd held her, lovingly, so often in the old days. To camp and go climbing. And hold her, as she held him, in the sleeping bag they shared.

'By then we didn't know what else to do,' she added. 'We *had* to come in and find you.'

'From the outside, the apartment was quiet.' Father Stanislaw stepped closer. 'Everything seemed peaceful. But we reasoned that, if there'd been trouble, your counterpart would have fled instead of staying here. The risk seemed acceptable. But we even knocked on the door before . . .'

'You picked the lock?'

221

Arlene still had her arms around him as he glanced toward the priest. Seeing a nod, Drew shook his head. 'You keep surprising me.'

'Well' – Father Stanislaw shrugged – 'the Lord is with me.'

'And with your lockpicks.'

The priest grinned.

'When you stepped through that door,' Arlene said, 'I almost thought you were . . .'

'My double?'

'You were carrying your coat instead of wearing it. For a moment, I thought he'd taken it off you.'

'No.' Drew swallowed. 'He's dead.' He slid his coat off his shoulder, revealing his bloody shirt and the bulge beneath it where he'd stuffed the handkerchief.

'Drew!'

'He stabbed me with a screwdriver. My coat helped to ease the blow.'

Before he could argue with her, Arlene had unbuttoned his shirt. The intimacy made him feel weak. Gently, she took out the bloody handkerchief, peering beneath the torn cloth.

'It could have been worse,' Drew said. 'At least, the bleeding stopped. I don't think it needs stitches.'

'But it sure needs disinfecting. Take off your shirt. I'll get a washcloth and soapy water.'

'It can wait.'

'No, it can't.' Again he didn't have the chance to argue. '*Hold still.*'

It made him feel oddly good to accept her orders. While she cleaned the wound, using a first-aid kit from the bathroom to dress it, he told them what had happened.

Father Stanislaw raised his right hand and gave Drew absolution. 'I'm sure you're forgiven. You had to defend yourself.'

'But his death was so pointless.' Drew's throat constricted, only partly because of the swelling from the fist Mike had struck against it. 'What did it accomplish?'

'Your life,' Arlene insisted.

'Insignificant. The answers. *They* were what mattered.'

'We've been looking for them,' she said.

He listened intently.

'We went through his papers. Receipts. Canceled checks. Bills.'

'What did you find?'

'Exactly what you'd expect,' Father Stanislaw said. 'The man was a professional. Nothing.'

'Nothing?' Drew thought about it. 'Maybe. At least, that's how it seemed.'

'I don't understand.'

'From what you just said, you saw it, all right. But you didn't know what you were seeing. What to look for.'

'I still don't know what you mean.'

'Receipts, you said. Canceled checks, bills?'

'That's right.'

Drew glanced tenderly toward Arlene. 'You couldn't have understood. Because you' – he turned toward Father Stanislaw – 'and *you* didn't have my cover. The way the system worked, I used a post office box for my

222

mail. Anonymous. As long as I made sure I wasn't being watched when I picked up my magazines, tuition bills, whatever. But I had another post office box in the nearest town. And *that* was where I picked up the stuff that mattered . . . Like my pay.'

He let it sink in.

'Of course.' Arlene got it first. 'Scalpel was part of the government.'

'A buried branch of it. The government itself never knew what was going on.'

'But records had to be kept,' she said. 'And payrolls justified. Because the network had a budget, no matter how buried. The ledger had to be balanced.'

Father Stanislaw understood now. 'The same way the CIA or any other intelligence network has to keep accounts. But not directly. Its budget might be channeled through the Department of Agriculture or the Interior.'

'However it's channeled, the money has to come from somewhere,' Drew said. 'If the funds belong to the system, there's a paper trail. There has to be.'

'But if Scalpel's defunct' – puzzled, Arlene glanced from Drew to the priest – 'if the network was canceled but someone reactivated it, someone not in the government, then the money comes from the private sector.'

'All the more reason to need ledgers, explanations for where the money went,' Drew said. 'The IRS is ruthless. It demands an accounting.'

'So?'

'We follow the paper trail,' Drew said. 'Canceled checks. You told me you'd found them. What's the name of the local bank? And' – Drew turned toward Father Stanislaw – 'who's the most powerful Opus Dei contact here? The one in banking and business?'

'Ah,' the priest said, understanding.

'Yes,' Drew told him.

Father Stanislaw glanced at his watch. 'It's only seven in the morning. We'll have to wait till –'

'Fine,' Drew said. 'I've got something almost as important to keep me busy.'

16

He found an opener in a drawer beside the sink and took the lids off every container of cat food in the apartment. Ten, all told. Some were chicken, others liver and fish, and one, Gourmet Delight, seemed to be a combination of everything.

He found two bags of dry food underneath the sink and opened them as well, then carried all of it to the alley outside and in the cold morning air spread the goodies along the cinderblock wall.

The cats ate voraciously.

'Enjoy,' he said. 'That's all there is. There won't be any more.'

He felt an ache in his chest.

Because your master's dead. I killed him.

17

At five after nine, as Drew and Arlene watched, Father Stanislaw used the phone in the apartment to reach his contact. He explained what he needed, hung up, and ten minutes later received a call from someone else.

Again he listened. He nodded and thanked whoever was calling. At once, he phoned someone else, received more information, and called yet another number.

The process took fifty minutes. And when for the final time he set down the phone, he leaned back exhausted on the sofa.

'Well?' Drew asked.

'When you cash a check, the bank keeps microfilm records of the transaction. Mike's inheritance – sometimes it's called a scholarship; never mind, let's say his checks – came from the Fairgate Institute. So what's the Fairgate Institute? I charged long distance to this number. I didn't think the occupant would mind. According to my contacts in New York and Washington, the Fairgate Institute is part of the Golden Ring Foundation. A non-profit help-to-the-needy, et cetera, et cetera. And the Golden Ring Foundation . . . remember the IRS insists on these records . . . God bless bureaucracy . . . the Golden Ring Foundation is part of . . . well, the bottom line is, when layer after layer is peeled away, the Risk Analysis Corporation. In Boston.'

Drew shook his head. 'Am I supposed to make a connection?'

'No. At least, not on the face of it. You won't like this,' Father Stanislaw said. 'My contact in Boston found out the name of the man who runs this Risk Analysis Corporation.'

'And I know him?'

'Oh, indeed,' Father Stanislaw said. 'The coincidence is too shocking to be dismissed. I think it proves that Risk Analysis is Scalpel, and that this man ran it as well.'

'*Who?*'

When Father Stanislaw told him, Drew ignored everything – Arlene's hand on his shoulder, the meow of the cats outside, the memory of Mike's blood dribbling salty past his lips.

The name.

Oh, yes, the name.

It and nothing else mattered.

His world came together.

The name was the secret to his life.

PART EIGHT
JUDGMENT

THE FRATERNITY OF THE STONE

1

The woman's voice was prim, professional, precise. 'Good morning. Risk Analysis Corporation.'

In a phone booth on Boylston Street, just down from Boston's public library, Drew managed to subdue his anger, to force himself to sound equally businesslike. 'Mr Rutherford, please.'

'I'm sorry. He's in a meeting right now. But if you'd care to speak to his executive assistant.'

'No. It has to be Mr Rutherford. I can't do business with anyone else.'
Drew let her think about it. The phone booth muffled the roar of 10 A.M. traffic.

'Of course,' the receptionist said. 'I understand. In that case, why don't you give me your name and phone number? Mr Rutherford will . . .'

'I'm afraid that isn't possible. My schedule's rather uncertain at the moment, and I'm not sure where I'll be. It's better if I call him.'

As he expected, the receptionist for the Risk Analysis Corporation didn't think his evasion was unusual. Her voice became more alert. 'By all means. If you have the chance, phone back at eleven-fifteen. He should be available then.'

'I hope so.'

'And your name?'

He gave her credit for trying again. 'Just tell him the matter's urgent.'

He hung up. Outside the phone booth, he stared at the clear cold October sky, then lowered his gaze toward the traffic on Boylston Street.

His eyes narrowed. Soon now, he thought. He shoved his hands in his new coat and started down the street. Yes, everything was coming together. He felt it. In his soul. Even his return to this city seemed appropriate. Boston, the graves of his parents, the start of everything. And now the end. Soon. Very soon.

Yesterday, he, Arlene, and Father Stanislaw had driven here from Pennsylvania, each taking a turn at the wheel while the others had a chance to sleep. Or in Drew's case, *tried* to sleep. His throbbing shoulder, his troubling thoughts, had kept him awake. When the others had been alert, he'd explained what he wanted to do. His plan had made them uneasy.

A minute ago, he'd told the receptionist, 'My schedule's uncertain. I'm not sure where I'll be.' He'd lied. His schedule was quite precise. And so were those of Arlene and Father Stanislaw. As he'd instructed, at this moment Arlene would be approaching an office building across the Charles River in Cambridge. Father Stanislaw would be leaving the northern limits of the city, about to reconnoiter a mansion on the Bay. Yes, soon. His anger accumulating, Drew stalked down Boylston Street. It would all come together soon.

2

Intelligence officials seldom leave their profession willingly. True, a few become disillusioned and walk away, but most are forced to retire or asked to resign. Outside their network, they feel lost. Addicted to secrets and the intrigue of high-risk gambles, they look for ways to satisfy their craving. Their choices, as a rule, come down to three.

First, to accept an offer from an international corporation anxious to have an intelligence expert on its board of directors. Such an expert, the corporation feels, can be of critical value in solving business crises that occur in troublesome, but lucrative, countries. This tactic was especially useful, for example, when in the early seventies Salvador Allende, the Marxist president of Chile, attempted to nationalize American business holdings there. Dissidents, rumored to be funded by American corporations with advice from former CIA officials, began a coup. Allende eventually 'committed suicide'.

The second option is to accept an offer from a wargames think-tank, where a top intelligence officer's knowledge of global intrigue adds data to the computer's calculations of which major power, under which circumstances, will use which tactic to blow the others to hell.

The third option is to refuse such offers and go into business for oneself. Specifically, to organize a company in which the former intelligence official creates a network of his own. But this time, the network isn't affiliated with his government. It belongs in the private sector, and its purpose – like the former intelligence official's on the board of directors for an international corporation – is to advise major companies, to encourage or else to warn them about the ever-shifting global situation. Should a company drill a testwell for oil in X? Or build a smelter for copper in Y? A factory for potash in Z? Will anti-American factions sabotage those operations? What about the banana pickers here, the dockworkers there? Do they plan to go on strike? Is there any basis to rumors about a coup? What about the bad health of this bought-off dictator? How long will he last? Who's likely to take his place?

The private intelligence network, extremely lucrative, funded by global companies, even foreign nations, was typified by the Risk Analysis Corporation.

Here in Boston. Owned by Mr Rutherford, though Drew had called him by another name.

Again he thought of Janus.

228

3

'Mr Rutherford, please.'

At 11:15, as instructed, Drew clutched the phone in another booth, this one on Falmouth Street, down from the Prudential Center. He imagined what Arlene and Father Stanislaw were doing – at the office building in Cambridge, at the estate on Massachusetts Bay.

Yes, soon now, he thought, and waited.

The receptionist spoke. 'Sir, are you the same party who called at ten?'

'That's right. To discuss an urgent matter.'

'One moment, please. Mr Rutherford's been waiting for you to phone back. I'll put him on the line.'

Drew heard a click.

'Yes? Hello?'

The resonant voice was so familiar, so friendly, so formerly reassuring, that Drew's stomach dropped, making him sick.

'This is Mr Rutherford.'

Drew had to muster all his discipline, to force himself to sound equally friendly. 'Long time no see. How are you?'

'What? Excuse me? I'm not sure who this is.'

'Come on. You don't mean to tell me you don't recognize my voice?'

'No. That is, not exactly.'

'I'm really disappointed. A long-lost relative, and . . .'

'Long-lost . . . ?'

'How are you, Uncle? It's good to talk to you again.'

'Uncle?' The voice sounded more and more puzzled. 'I don't have any nephews.'

'Well, that's true, I'm not exactly your nephew. I mean, we're not related by blood. But I think of you as a relative. And that's what I used to call you. Uncle Ray.'

The man on the other end breathed sharply. 'My God, it's . . . No, it can't be. Drew? Is this *Drew*?'

'Yep, me. None other. The one and only.'

Ray burst out laughing. 'I can't believe it! Drew! Why didn't you tell me right away?'

'A practical joke.' Drew chuckled. 'I just felt like putting you on. Remember how you rescued me from my *real* uncle and his family? How you took me to Hong Kong?'

'Remember? Christ, sport, how could I ever forget?' Ray laughed again. 'But it's been *years* since we talked. What happened to you? Where have you been keeping yourself?'

'Well, that's the problem.'

'What?'

'It's the reason I'm calling.' Drew swallowed hard.

'Go on. Say it, Drew. What's the matter? Is something wrong?'

'I really hate to get you involved in this, but I don't know who else to ask. Uncle Ray, I'm in trouble. I need your help.'

'Trouble?'

'The worst. Some people are trying to kill me.'

'Wait a second. You'd better not say any more. I'm using one of our open phones. We get tapped a lot, and if this is as serious as you believe, we don't want to take any chances. I'll switch to a phone that's secure.'

'Good idea. I'll call you right back. Hold on. I'll get out my pen and pad. What's the number?'

'It's . . .' Ray started to dictate the number and stopped. 'No, that won't work. It's better if I call you. I've got a client coming in at eleven-thirty. I can't put him off. But I'll deal with him fast. Half an hour, and I'll get back to you.'

'Noon?'

'Even earlier if I can. Stay close to your phone. What's the number?' Drew told him.

'Fine. Now just relax. I'll call as soon as I can. But, sport, you shouldn't have worried about asking me to get involved. Believe me, I'm glad to help.'

Drew swallowed again. 'I knew I could count on you.'

'Well, I'm your uncle, aren't I?'

'Hey, you bet.'

'Don't worry.'

'Uncle Ray, I mean it. Thanks.'

'Come on, we go back a long way. You don't need to thank me.'

4

From his hidden vantage point near the Prudential Center, Drew studied a pizza store down the street, and the phone booth outside, the phone whose number Drew had given to Uncle Ray.

At ten to twelve, amid the chaos of traffic and the swarm of pedestrians, he spotted the surveillance teams. As he'd anticipated, he didn't have any difficulty. Just before noon, with everybody in a rush, those who weren't hurrying were bound to attract attention. It wasn't their fault. To watch the phone booth, they had no choice except to stay motionless. After all, they'd been given short notice. There wasn't time for anything skillfully complicated. A woman on one corner glanced too often down the street toward the booth. A man on the opposite corner kept peering down at his watch as if a friend was late to meet him, but the phone booth was apparently more important to him than his friend or his watch. A taxi, double-parked, waited for a never-arriving fare. A van with several antennas circled the block. A pizza delivery boy didn't seem to care that his boxes were getting cold.

No doubt there were more. Drew had to give them credit for mobilizing this well in such a hurry. But not well enough.

The message was obvious. The surveillance team was waiting for Drew to appear from his hiding place at noon and answer his 'uncle's' call. After that, Drew thought, the team would converge while I was distracted by Uncle Ray on the phone. I'd be killed on the street.

Or better, from a tradecraft point of view, I'd be dragged inside the van and killed out of sight by the kid with the pizzas. At night, a fishing boat would take me far out into the Bay.

Drew clenched his fists as he left his hidden vantage point beside the Prudential Center, heading west on Belvidere Street, away from the pizza store.

5

'Mr Rutherford, please.' Despite his disciplined, calm tone, Drew shook from the rage in his chest.

'I'm terribly sorry,' the receptionist said. 'Mr Rutherford isn't . . .'

'No, listen carefully. I called at ten. And again at eleven-fifteen. Believe me, Mr Rutherford wants to talk to me again. Just tell him I asked for Uncle Ray.'

The receptionist paused. 'I must have been mistaken. Mr Rutherford *is* available.'

Almost at once, the familiar reassuring voice was on the line. 'Drew, where the hell *are* you? I called the number you gave me, but no one answered. I got worried! Did something happen?'

'You could say that. Imagine my surprise when a hit team showed up.'

'A *hit* team. How –'

'Because you traced the location of the number I gave you. Look, Ray, I'll save us a lot of time. When everything started to point in your direction, I told myself, "It can't be Ray. He's my friend. I lived with him from the time I was ten till I was seventeen. He took me in when no one else really wanted me." You took me in, all right.'

'I don't know what you're talking about. I've always felt close to you.'

'Save it. I'm not impressed. So I figured I'd better not jump to conclusions. But I didn't want to be stupid, either. I decided to test you. A phone call; a plea for help to someone I'd once depended on. A chance for you to prove your loyalty. And Uncle Ray, guess what? You failed.'

'Now wait a minute.'

'No. *You* wait. You've had your chance. I want an explanation. For Christ's sake, *why?* I know you used what happened to my parents to recruit me for Scalpel.'

'Drew, stop. Don't say any more!'

But furious, Drew kept on. 'At the time, that was what I wanted, though. A chance to get even for what happened to my parents. I can almost forgive you. But why did you hit the monastery?'

'I told you to stop! We're still on an unsecured phone! I can't discuss it on . . .'

'Okay, I'll call you back, and then, by God, you'd better have a phone that's safe. Give me the number.'

Ray did. Drew made him repeat it, writing it down.

'There's just one other thing,' Drew said. 'After you hang up, I want you to leave your office, go past the receptionist, and look in the hall.'

'What will *that* prove?'

'You'll understand. After you've looked in the hall, I think you ought to phone home. The mansion north of the city? The estate by the Bay?'

'How did you know about that?'

231

'I've got contacts, too. Just do what I told you. I know you're trying to trace this call, so I'll hang up now. I'll phone back in fifteen minutes. On another line.'

'No, wait!'

Drew broke the connection. He made another call, this one to Arlene, who was at a phone booth across the Charles River in Cambridge. The phone booth was near an office building, the fifth floor of which was rented in part by the Risk Analysis Corporation.

Early that morning, Father Stanislaw had driven Drew and Arlene past the building. They'd chosen the phone booth and written down its number. Since 10 A.M., Arlene had been waiting there for Drew to report to her. He'd done so periodically, and now, as before, she answered quickly.

'Is everything ready?'

'No problem,' she said.

'Then press the button.'

He left the phone booth. Heading north toward Commonwealth Avenue, he smiled with angry satisfaction, imagining what was now taking place. The button he'd told Arlene to press was on a radio transmitter that sent a signal to a detonator in a shopping bag she'd left in the fifth-floor hall of the office building, outside the suite rented by the Risk Analysis Corporation.

Uncle Ray – curious why Drew had told him to look outside in the hall – should have seen the bag by now. With luck, he would even see it explode.

But the blast would be small. Drew didn't want people hurt, though they'd certainly be alarmed and inconvenienced. The minuscule blast would fill the hallway with smoke, and the smoke would have such a horrible odor that the entire floor, perhaps the entire building, would have to be evacuated.

To add to the confusion, Arlene would by now have phoned the fire department, the police, the 911 line, the bomb squad. The street outside the building would soon be in chaos as police cars and fire engines converged, lights flashing, sirens wailing; they'd snarl traffic during rush hour. Drew's satisfaction swelled. It would be a mess, all right. A wonderful mess.

But there was more. As soon as Arlene completed her calls to the authorities, she'd make yet another – this one to Father Stanislaw, who'd earlier checked in by phone with her, just as Drew had been doing, and who had told her the number where he could be reached. In the village near Uncle Ray's country estate.

6

Halfway through the first ring, Ray picked up the phone. 'You son of a bitch! What the hell do you think you're doing?'

'Watch your temper.'

'Temper? I'm just getting started. For Christ's sake, the stench of that smoke, I swear to God it's in the walls – in the carpet, the *furniture*! I'll never get rid of it. I might have to move the fucking office!'

'Such language. Did you call home?'

'That's something else, you bastard. Somebody set a bomb off in my front yard! I don't mean a stink bomb like the one in the hall. I mean a *bomb*!'

'It must have been local vandals,' Drew said, his heart cold.

'Local, my ass! Just what do you think you're –?'

'Uncle Ray, don't disappoint me. I thought the message was perfectly clear. I'm angry. You betrayed me. Not just with that hit team you sent. I sort of expected that. But you used me from the start. You took advantage of what happened to my parents to recruit me for Scalpel. The thing is, I guess it slipped your mind at the time, huh? You forgot to tell me that you organized Scalpel, that you were in charge of it.'

'I won't apologize. I *loved* your parents. Your father was the closest friend I had! You and I, both of us wanted revenge.'

'But you reached too far. You weren't satisfied with fighting back at mercenaries and terrorists.'

'The same type of scum who killed your parents. Remember that!'

'I never disagreed. I did my share of killing. For the sake of my parents. But you weren't satisfied with exterminating rabid dogs. You had to start predicting the future, judging which leaders fit your standards. In Iran, the Shah had his terror squads and his torture chambers. But you didn't hit him. Instead, you had to try to assassinate the man who replaced him.'

'The Ayatollah's insane.'

'In hindsight. But you didn't know that at the time. You were playing God. The trouble is, I screwed up the hit. *And so did you.* Because you made the mistake of sending me to kill that American family first, that oil executive who was trying to grease the wheels with the Ayatollah. I have to give you the credit. The alibi for Scalpel would have been perfect. After the Ayatollah was killed in the same way that American family was – after a non-existent radical sect of Iranians claimed both hits – no one would have suspected that an American network was actually responsible. Brilliant in its own twisted way. But you screwed it up. You should have sent someone else to do the job. When I saw the parents I'd killed, and the boy who survived like me, who now has to suffer the nightmares I did . . .'

'You're not making sense!'

'*Perfect* sense. I'd turned into the maniacs I was hunting. Worse, I'd got religion. I wasn't dependable any longer. I might have even talked about Scalpel. So I had to be terminated. To protect your glorious plan.'

'Drew, listen, you've got it wrong. This is all a misunderstanding.'

'You bet it is. And you're the one who doesn't understand!' Drew fought to get control of himself.

'Believe me, Drew, you don't realize how important–'

'You're right. I *don't* realize. After you thought I was dead, why did you use my double to pretend he was me? Why did you create Janus to attack the Church?'

Uncle Ray didn't answer.

'I asked you a question!' Drew screamed.

'No.' Ray swallowed. 'Even on a safe phone. I won't answer that.'

'Oh, you will.' Drew raged. 'Believe me. That stink bomb at your office . . . The explosion at your home. You wondered why? *To get your*

233

attention. Because the shopping bag in the hall outside your office could have been a *real* bomb. It could have blown you and your staff to hell. And the explosion at your home? It could have been bigger. It could have blasted your whole damned mansion apart – when *you* were in it! Next time, maybe that'll happen. Count your blessings. Count the seconds. I'm about to give you a taste of your enemy, Uncle Ray. You're about to get a crash course in terrorism. From the victim's side.'

'No, listen!'

'I'll be in touch.'

7

Arlene was puzzled. 'But . . .'

'What's wrong?' Drew asked. 'What is it?'

Father Stanislaw waited, curious.

They'd rendezvoused across from Boston Common at the Park Street Church; from there, they'd driven to Beacon Hill, where they sat now at a gleaming glass-and-metal kitchen table in an oak-paneled townhouse. One of Father Stanislaw's Opus Dei contacts had arranged to have it lent to them for the next few days.

'I don't understand,' Arlene said. 'If you told Ray you planned to blow up his home and his office, he'll have them guarded. He'll stay away from them.'

Drew nodded. 'That would be my guess.'

'But doesn't that make it harder for us?'

'Maybe easier.' Drew shrugged. 'I hope. What I'm trying to do is skip a few steps. We knew from the start that we couldn't just make a grab for him. Since the monastery, he's been hunting me. He'd be a fool if he hadn't increased protection around himself, in case I figured out who was after me and decided to start hunting *him*. Believe me, I know him well. He isn't stupid.'

'All right.' Arlene raised her hands. 'I see that. I agree. As soon as we tried to grab him, we'd have been killed. But why did you warn him there'd be other bombs?'

'I want to weaken his defenses, to surround him with distractions. The guards he orders to watch his home and his office will mean he has less guards to protect himself. You're right. He'll be so nervous he'll stay away from those places. But that's to the good. We've restricted his movements. We've gained the same effect as if we did blow them up. What I want to do now is escalate our attacks. Make each one more serious than the last. Strike where we're least expected. Do it more often. Use the basic principles of terrorism.'

'But *why*?' She seemed distressed by his evident joy in terrorizing Ray.

He avoided her searching eyes. 'I'm not sure what you mean.'

'But I do,' Father Stanislaw said. 'I think she wants to know where all of this is leading. Is your ultimate purpose to kill him?'

Drew tensed, evading the question. 'We have to get our hands on him. We need more answers.'

'To learn about Jake. To find out what happened to him,' Arlene said quickly.

'But in the end?' Father Stanislaw asked.

They stared at Drew.

'In honesty?' the priest asked.

They waited.

Drew sighed. 'I wish I knew.' He frowned at his grim reflection off the shiny glass table. 'For so many years, I fought back at substitutes for the bastards who killed my parents. I let them know how terror feels on the receiving end. But then I walked away in disgust. I made a sacred vow that I was through. And now, here I am, right back doing it again. The truth? I hate to admit this. Today, it felt as good as it used to.' Drew stared toward Father Stanislaw. His eyes felt hot and moist.

'Even God gets angry sometimes,' the priest said. 'If the cause is just. And make no mistake, *this* cause – to protect the Church, to stop the attacks against it, to find out what happened to Jake – this cause is just. God will forgive your righteous anger.'

'But will I forgive myself?'

The phone rang, startling them. As Drew and Arlene glanced uneasily at one another, Father Stanislaw crossed the kitchen toward the phone on an oaken wall. 'Hello?' He listened. 'And with your spirit. *Deo gratias*.' He reached for a pad and pencil. 'Good.' He finished writing. 'Your Church is pleased.'

Hanging up, he turned toward Drew and Arlene. 'My contacts apparently aren't as well placed as Uncle Ray's. He needed only twenty minutes to trace the number you gave him, the phone booth on Falmouth Street. But we needed several hours to trace the number of the safe phone he gave you.'

'You've got the location?' Drew asked.

Father Stanislaw nodded. 'As you suspected, the phone isn't in the Risk Analysis office. Instead, it's two blocks down the street. A florist shop. But not the business phone. A private number, unlisted.'

'Is he there now?'

The priest shook his head. 'But he's been calling there, checking in with his surveillance team. It seems they're still checking the area in case you're around. We managed to trace one call he made to that number.' Father Stanislaw set the slip of paper on the glass table. 'As close as we can tell, this is where Uncle Ray is.'

Drew studied the address.

8

In the night, Drew walked yet again around the block. An expensive residential section of Cambridge, it was near the target area, yet far enough away that he wouldn't be noticed by Uncle Ray's guards. For the same reason – to avoid attracting attention – he'd decided not to stand in one place and wait but rather to appear to be taking a late-night stroll.

The exercise helped to dispel the cold. Passing streetlights, he noticed puffs of frosty breath coming out of his mouth. With a shiver, he pulled the hood of his coat up over his head and kept his gloved hands inside his pockets.

It was after midnight. He noticed few cars or pedestrians, though he did see occasional activity beyond glowing windows in magnificent homes. The trees were leafless, their branches scraped by the wind.

He heard a car and, glancing behind him, saw headlights turn a corner, coming his way. In the glow of a streetlight, he saw that the car was black, an Oldsmobile. He recognized Father Stanislaw's profile behind the steering wheel and quickly got in when the car stopped beside him.

The heater was on. Drew took off his gloves and warmed his hands.

'The house we want is on a corner,' Father Stanislaw said. 'It's surrounded by walls. It belongs to a friend of his.'

'Any lights on the grounds?'

'None at all. The house has all its lights on, though.'

'Sure. A flame for the moth. In case I found out where he was. Any guards?'

'I didn't see any. Mind you, I didn't have much chance. I had to keep driving by. But the entrance to the driveway has a large metal gate. It's closed. Beyond the gate, I saw several cars.'

'So the guards must be waiting out of sight in case the shadows look tempting and someone comes over the wall. That's when the grounds get lit up.'

'So I suspect,' Father Stanislaw said. He drove around the corner and stopped at the darkest part of the block.

A sports car – Drew didn't recognize the model – pulled up behind them. A figure emerged, approached the Oldsmobile, and opened the door.

Arlene got in back. 'I checked the house the same as you did,' she told the priest. 'I didn't see any guards.'

'So what do you think? Should we risk it?' Drew asked.

Their gazes were steady.

'It's time.' Drew turned toward a wooden case of soft-drink bottles on the back seat. But the bottles contained something stronger than soda pop.

9

Gasoline mixed with liquid detergent, each bottle's mouth stuffed with a tampon. Homemade napalm. The burning gasoline would cling to whatever surface it struck.

They divided the bottles evenly, each putting eight in a knapsack. Leaving the Oldsmobile, they walked to the corner. Father Stanislaw went straight across the street and continued down the block, while Drew and Arlene turned right and proceeded down the adjacent street. When the two of them reached the next corner, they faced each other.

'Be careful,' Drew said, a wave of sadness rushing through him. What was he forcing her to do?

'When this is over . . .'

He waited, uncertain if he wanted her to continue.

'You and I have a lot to talk about,' she said. A streetlight reflected off her intensely probing eyes.

He knew what she meant, but as his sadness deepened, he didn't know what to tell her. He hadn't given himself time to decide.

'I never stopped missing you,' she said.

He still didn't know what to say. But he didn't resist when she kissed him. Indeed, not allowing himself to think, he returned the kiss, holding her close.

'All right. When this is over' – he breathed painfully – 'we'll talk.'

10

Cautious, holding his knapsack, he walked along the murky street in back of the target area. He passed two darkened houses and left the sidewalk to creep between them, using hedges and bushes for cover. In a moment, his eyes adjusting quickly to the greater blackness, he saw the lane that ran parallel to the street he'd just left. And beyond the lane, he saw the ten-foot-high brick wall that separated him from the back of the house.

From this perspective, with the wall partly shielding it, he saw only the upper levels, but as Father Stanislaw had said, lights were on inside. To protect his night vision, Drew didn't look at them. He scanned the lane – it was gravel, he saw now – and studied the sheltered spots where someone might hide. There was always the risk that Ray had posted sentries outside the walls, though Drew doubted that he had done so. For one thing, a neighbor might notice the sentries and call the police to complain about prowlers. For another, with Ray's forces now dispersed – some at the office, some at his estate on the Bay – he'd probably want to concentrate his remaining men on the inside of the property, spacing them effectively, so they could make sure that no one came over the wall.

All the same, no harm in being careful, Drew thought. Besides, as he cupped a hand over the luminous dial of his watch, he saw that he still had a minute to wait while Arlene and Father Stanislaw got in position. So he might as well use that minute to double-check the darkness of the lane.

A light came on in the house behind him.

He squirmed beneath the spreading boughs of a fir tree. Smelling its resin, he squinted through needles toward the light. It was on the second floor of the house. The curtain was drawn. He saw a silhouette stand sideways, motionless for several seconds. Then the silhouette reached down, pressed something, and walked out of sight. The light went off.

A bathroom? Drew wondered. A man relieving himself? Whatever, the silhouette hadn't peered outside. There seemed no cause for alarm.

But as he returned his attention toward the wall, a whoosh of flame erupted on the other side of the wall, toward the front of the house. Another fiery roar. Then another.

While he'd been studying the light in the window, concerned that he'd been spotted, the others had reached their positions on either side at the front of the house. The minute had passed. They'd started lighting and throwing their napalm-filled bottles. The grounds at the front – and to the right and left – exploded with flames.

They'd calculated that for each of them to light and throw eight bottles would take thirty seconds. Possibly less; an adrenaline rush could make a person move awfully fast. Then they had to scramble out of the area. Because after thirty seconds the element of surprise would have dissipated. Ray's guards would come charging out of the compound, guns ready, searching.

Drew had to get started. But as he braced himself to surge from beneath the branches, he froze.

Someone else was out here. A shadow detached itself from the blackest section of the wall. A man with a gun, a silencer projecting from it. He turned to stare toward the top of the wall, toward the reflection of flames off the house.

Their roar grew louder, fiercer. Sixteen bottles thrown evenly around the front and sides of the house. And the bottles didn't have to shatter when they landed. The heat of the burning tampon would ignite the napalm inside, causing the glass to explode, scattering the fiery gasoline-and-detergent mixture. The house would be surrounded by flames.

At least, the house was *supposed* to be surrounded by flames if Drew accomplished his part of the mission. He stared at the man with the gun who'd appeared from the blackness of the wall.

Drew's approach had been such that bushes concealed him. But if it hadn't been for the sudden light in the house behind him, he would have crept a little closer and been seen, been shot.

Distraught, the man abruptly raced down the lane, around the corner, toward the front of the house.

Drew's instincts told him to use this chance and get away. But he couldn't let himself. The plan depended upon the full effect of all the explosions. If Uncle Ray were inside, he had to be made to feel totally trapped, completely vulnerable. Taking several deep breaths, an athlete preparing himself, Drew lunged from beneath the fir tree, pulled the bottles from the knapsack, and hurriedly lit them, then frantically threw one, two, desperate to make the bottles land as far inside the compound as possible.

Three, four.

Heaving them as hard as he could, he kept darting his eyes toward the corner of the lane.

The bottles exploded.

Five, six.

Flames roared, cresting the wall. On the other side, men shouted.

Seven.

His heart pounding, he lit the eighth. Lights came on in several houses behind him. Their manifold gleam, added to the glare of the flames, made him feel exposed as if in daylight.

Attracted by the explosions at the rear of the house, the man with the gun came running back around the corner of the wall. Sprinting along the lane, he skittered to a stop when he saw Drew, and raised his gun.

Drew had no chance to reach for his own. He realized that the only weapon he had available was the bottle, its tampon burning closer to the napalm.

The man aimed. Drew flung the bottle toward him, diving for the cover of the fir tree. The man, distracted by the flame on the bottle streaking toward him, shot at Drew but missed.

The bottle struck the gravel in front of the man. Drew had thrown with such force that the glass broke on impact against the stones, and a wall of flames erupted, blocking the lane.

The man stumbled back, his hands up, protecting his face. But he lost his balance and fell as the blaze streaked toward him. He rolled to avoid the splatter of the fire. Swatting at specks of flaming detergent that clung to his coat, he screamed.

Drew lunged to his feet. As he raced between the houses, a man in pajamas burst out the side door.

'What the hell's going on?'

Drew jolted against the man, toppling him against the house, and continued racing toward the street. Behind him, he heard the increasing roar of the fires in the compound. Screams. Shots, though he didn't know if they were aimed at him. He saw the reflection of the blaze off clouds in the sky.

His lungs in agony from exertion, he ran across the street, between more houses, across another street. His shirt was drenched with sweat beneath his insulated coat. He vaulted a fence, turned right at the next street, and sprinted along the sidewalk. He ducked left down a lane, glanced behind him, banged his hip against an unseen barrel, but ignored the ache in his muscle, and ran.

In the distance, sirens shrieked.

11

Limping from fatigue, at last he reached the rendezvous point. He'd been forced to approach it in a roundabout fashion, using precious time to hide every time he saw headlights or thought he saw someone searching the street. But finally he was here, a parking lot near MIT. Their fall-back position. After the attack on the house, Arlene and Father Stanislaw were supposed to have hurried to their cars, making sure they weren't followed. Drew, on foot, was supposed to have joined them at this parking lot an hour ago.

But the only two cars in the shadowy lot were neither an Oldsmobile nor a sports car.

He paused, exhausted. Had Arlene and Father Stanislaw been caught? Or, like him had they been forced to flee at random till they couldn't get back to their cars or couldn't reach the rendezvous point in time?

Or perhaps they had reached this parking lot on schedule, waited, and finally decided that prudence required them to leave before the authorities widened their search.

In that case, he had to cross one of the two near bridges to get to the townhouse in Beacon Hill on the other side of the river. If the townhouse was safe anymore. What if Arlene and Father Stanislaw had been caught? What if . . . ?

No, he thought, angry at himself. Neither Arlene nor Father Stanislaw, if they were caught, would talk. Unless chemicals were used.

Soaked with sweat, he shivered. Headlights caught him in their glare. From the side of a building to his left. He stiffened, debating whether to trust that this was Arlene, or whether to run.

The headlights came toward him.

In case this was a cop, he decided that he'd better keep walking – straight ahead, away from the approaching headlights. He tried to look natural, as if one of the two cars in the lot belonged to him.

The headlights veered to follow. His reflexes quickened. He turned to look.

And sighed, recognizing Arlene in the sports car.

She stopped and he got in, his body welcoming the heat, the chance to relax.

'Some date *you* are.' She put the car in neutral. 'I was beginning to think you'd stood me up.' But despite the joke, her voice didn't hide her concern, and she leaned over, touching him.

'Sorry. I had this marathon to run first,' he said.

'Excuses, excuses.'

He couldn't help it; he returned her embrace. 'But I'm here now. Are you okay?'

'It's a good thing I've got long legs. They came in handy running tonight,' she said. 'But I missed the rendezvous time. In fact, I didn't get here till twenty minutes ago. I thought maybe something had happened to you. Or you'd been here already, got afraid of waiting, and left. I kept expecting a police car to check out the lot.'

'That's what I thought you were.' He studied her face. 'Thanks. For taking the risk. For waiting for me.'

'Shut up. You want to thank me? Monk or not, hold still for this.'

She kissed him on the lips, a gentle kiss, soft and full of love.

In this night of surprises, his body responded. At once, self-conscious, he leaned back. 'It's been a long time.' He shook his head in torment. 'Too much has happened. I vowed to be celibate.'

'That means not marry. I'm not proposing. I'll give you all the time you want.'

He stared at her. 'I can't promise anything.'

'I know it.'

'Fair enough,' he said.

She put the car in gear, and drove from the lot.

'Where's Father Stanislaw? Did he go ahead to the townhouse?'

'He was shot.' Her voice became professional.

'Dear God.'

'He's alive. Bleeding heavily. But it looked to me like the bullet passed through his shoulder. I don't think anything vital was hit. He's one of the reasons I was late. I had to take him for help.'

'A hospital? The police will . . .'

'No, he made a phone call to one of his contacts. They gave him the address of a doctor we can trust. And they sent someone to get the Oldsmobile.'

'Father Stanislaw and his contacts.' Drew's voice was filled with admiration.

'Their motivation's powerful.'

'To save their souls.'

She turned a corner. Ahead, Drew saw the bridge that would take them to Beacon Hill.

'What if the police have a roadblock?'

'Then we'll just tell them the truth,' she said.

He didn't understand.

'We were back in that parking lot necking,' she said. Her eyes crinkled. 'Well, sort of necking, anyhow.'

12

The woman's voice was the same – prim, precise, professional. 'Good morning. Risk Analysis Corporation.'

'Mr Rutherford, please,' Drew said in a Charlestown phone booth down the street from the Bunker Hill Monument.

'I'm sorry. Mr Rutherford won't be coming into the office today.'

'I had a hunch he wouldn't be. But I wonder if you can get a message to him.'

'I'm not sure if . . .'

'To Uncle Ray? Could you tell him his nephew would like to speak with him?'

The woman's voice became alert. 'He did mention he hoped you'd be calling. He left a phone number where you could reach him.'

'Good. I look forward to talking to him.'

She read the number to him; he wrote it down.

'If you speak to him in the next few minutes, tell him I'll phone that number as soon as –'

The receptionist interrupted. 'Mr Rutherford asked me to tell you that his schedule is extremely crowded today. The only time he'll be at that number is four o'clock this afternoon. He said if you called any earlier or later, you wouldn't be able to reach him.'

Drew's head ached as he hung up.

Arlene stood next to him. In the background, tourists surveyed the Bunker Hill Monument.

'So?' she asked.

Drew explained what he'd been told, then showed her the number he'd written down.

'Four o'clock. Okay, what's the matter? How come you're frowning?'

'I'm not quite sure yet. Something. I don't know – call it a premonition. I feel like I'm being manipulated.'

'We have to expect he'll want to get back at you.'

'That's the point,' Drew said. 'Why would he let me have all day to learn the address of this new number?' He studied the tourists on Bunker Hill. 'Maybe I'm overly cautious, but we'd better not hang around this phone booth.'

They started down Monument Avenue.

'If it makes you nervous, don't call him,' she said.

'I have to.'

'Why?'

'To say I want to meet with him.'

She turned, surprised. '*Meet* with him? He'll set up a trap.'

'Of course. But I won't show up. I'll make an excuse and arrange another meeting. But I won't arrive for that one, either. In the meantime, we can think of other ways to put pressure on him. I want to keep aggravating him, make him nervous. Or better yet, maybe we could plan a meeting in such a way that we could turn his trap around.' Drew couldn't quell his uneasiness. 'That new number he gave me. To call at four o'clock. What's he up to?'

'You're right – he has to assume you'll learn its location.'

Drew stopped abruptly and studied her face. 'Is *that* it? He's trying to trick me into going to that location? He wants me to try to grab him while he's making the call?'

'And his men would kill you instead.'

He shook his head. 'No. He gave us too much time to anticipate the trap. Whatever he's got in mind, it isn't that. His tactic's working, though. He's got us confused. He's put us on the defensive. I told you. He isn't stupid.'

13

At noon, a van arrived outside the Beacon Hill house. Two men helped Father Stanislaw get out. The priest was pale, his arm in a sling. Supported by his escorts, wincing from the strain, he mounted the steps of the townhouse; but once inside, with the door closed, he crumpled into their arms. Gently, they lowered him onto a sofa.

A middle-aged woman came in behind him. Handsome rather than pretty, with a conservative haircut and no makeup, she wore a blue London Fog overcoat and a gray wool suit. As the two men left, never saying a word, shutting the door again, she explained that she was there to take care of the priest. His wound wasn't critical, but he'd soon be needing another sedative, she said, and there was always the danger of infection. She carried a medical bag. Drew noticed that she didn't volunteer her name, and neither he nor Arlene asked for it.

They helped Father Stanislaw up the stairs to a bedroom, made him as comfortable as they could, and let him sleep.

'His constitution's remarkable,' the woman said when they returned to the living room. 'Polish, I believe. Hardy Slavic stock. He barely has a fever.'

'We have to wake him up soon.'

The woman spoke sharply. 'I'm afraid I can't allow that.'

'We wouldn't do it if we had a choice.'

'I'll be the judge of that.' She stood with her back to the stairs, as though to bar Drew from going up again. 'What did you wish to speak with him about?'

He had a sudden intuition. Remembering how Father Stanislaw had addressed the businessman in the church in Pennsylvania, he said, 'The Lord be with you.'

'And with your spirit.'

'*Deo gratias.*'

The woman relaxed. 'Then you're one of us.'

'Not exactly. Close enough. For six years, I was a Carthusian.'

'In New Hampshire.'

Drew sensed he was being tested. 'No. In Vermont.'

She smiled. 'The Carthusians are saints on earth.'

'Not this one, I'm afraid. I'm a sinner.'

'Aren't we all? But God understands human weakness.'

'I hope so. We have to talk to Father Stanislaw so we can get in touch with his contact at the telephone company. We need to find the location of a number we've been given.'

The woman reached out her hand. 'Give the number to me.'

'But . . .'

'If that's the only information you want, there's no need to wake Father Stanislaw. I'll take care of it myself.'

Drew blinked.

'Surely you don't think I'd have been allowed to attend him if I weren't responsible,' the woman said. 'Please, give me that number.'

Drew did.

She walked to a phone, dialed, and, in a soft voice, gave instructions. She hung up, and they waited.

At two o'clock, the phone rang. The woman answered, listened, said, '*Deo Gratias.*' And hanging up, she turned to Drew.

'A pay phone near the Paul Revere statue and Old North Church.'

'A pay phone?'

'In North End,' the woman said.

'But . . .'

Arlene leaned forward from a canvas director's chair. 'What's wrong?'

'A pay phone? Near the Paul Revere statue – a tourist area?' Drew's stomach felt packed with ice. 'And Uncle Ray gave us the day to find where it was? That doesn't make sense. He wouldn't *dare* to use that phone. It's too exposed. If we staked out that location, we could tell right away if Ray was setting up a trap. He'll *never* go there. But he'll spread men through the neighborhood in case *we* do.'

'Which means we won't,' Arlene said.

'Right. But Ray expects that, too. He wants to use that phone for another reason. Someone, not Ray, will answer my call. And give me another number. That pay phone's just a relay. We'd better get moving.'

'No,' Arlene insisted. 'I'm staying right here till you tell me what's going on.'

'It's a setup, all right. For sure, a trap. But not the one we expected. This is algebra turned into trigonometry. He's skipped a dozen steps. But I know what he's doing. I learned from the same set of rules. I used the same trick in . . .' He shuddered at the memory.

'If you don't explain what's going on.'

'When we get in the car. Hurry.' He swung toward the woman with the medical bag. 'We need a room with a door that has a window. I have to be

243

able to stand outside and look through the window into the room. An isolated location. And the room has to have a phone.'

The woman considered. 'I don't . . . No, wait a minute. There's a local parish hall with a kitchen in the basement. The kitchen has a swinging door with a window so people coming in and out can see and not bump the door against each other. The kitchen has a phone.'

'What's the address?'

The woman told him.

Drew wrote it down. 'Call and make sure no one's there.' He glanced at his watch. 'We don't have much time till four o'clock.'

'For what?' Arlene asked.

'To buy a tape recorder. And, God help me, a mouse.'

14

It was white – unlike Stuart Little, who'd been gray. Drew bought it with a cage. He paid the petshop owner. 'Have you got any mouse treats?'

'Mouse treats?' The overweight man with thinning hair and a bird-dung-stained apron raised his eyebrows.

A parrot squawked in the background.

'Sure. Whatever a mouse likes to eat the best. Something he'd really love. Gourmet.'

'Gourmet?' The man looked at Drew as if he were crazy. 'Hey, listen, I could cheat you, but I want my customers happy. There's no reason to spend a lot of money on mouse food. This stuff over here, it's cheap, it's filling, they don't know the difference. I mean, a mouse, what the hell does a mouse know?'

'He's only the one who's eating it, right?'

'Yeah, except this particular mouse is female.'

'Then *she*. I want the best for her. I want her to stuff herself with the best meal she ever had. And I don't care about the cost.'

The man sighed. 'Whatever you say. It's your wallet. Step right this way. What I've got here on this shelf, it's what you might call the Rolls Royce of mouse food.'

Drew paid another ten dollars and left the petshop, a five-pound bag of food in one hand, the mouse in the cage in the other.

At the curb, Arlene sat waiting in the sports car, its motor rumbling. 'Cute,' she said. 'Personally, mice never bothered me. Have you given it a name?'

His voice was grim. 'Stuart Little the second.'

She suddenly understood. 'Oh, shit.' Her look was consoling. 'I'm sorry I tried to be funny.'

Drew shut the door, clutching the cage. 'No problem. It's Ray who has to be sorry.'

15

Even at half-past three, the basement of the parish hall was shadowy. As the autumn sun drooped low, the church on that side of the hall blocked out its descending brilliance. The windows at the top of the basement's western hall were shrouded with gloom.

The place was damp. Drew felt the chill as he came down concrete stairs, pausing while the echo of his footsteps diminished.

Silence.

He squinted at rows of long plastic-topped tables that smelled from years of church socials, beans and hot dogs, potato salad, coleslaw.

Arlene descended quickly behind him, holding a box that contained a tape recorder.

'Is anyone here?' Drew called. His voice echoed. Silence. 'Good.'

The mouse skittered in her cage.

Scanning the shadows, Drew pointed toward a door with a window halfway along the wall to his right. 'That must be the kitchen. Now if only our friend remembered correctly and there's a phone.'

There was. As Drew pushed open the swinging door and flicked on a light switch, he saw a phone on a counter between a stove and a humming refrigerator. 'Let's make sure.' He picked up the phone, exhaling when he heard a dial tone.

He set down the scrambling mouse in her cage and again glanced at his watch. 'Less than twenty-five minutes. The tape recorder worked in the store. It had better work now.'

Indeed, when he took the box from Arlene, unpacked and plugged in the recorder, it functioned perfectly. He dictated into the microphone and played the tape back.

'Does that sound like me?' he asked with concern. The recorded tone of his voice didn't seem like the tone inside his head.

Arlene said, 'Lower the bass.'

He did and played the tape again.

'That's you,' she said. 'It certainly ought to be. That machine's worth a fortune.'

Drew rewound the tape. 'Fifteen minutes. Time to feed our friend.'

He opened the bag of mouse treats and sprinkled the tiny chunks through the top bars of the cage. The mouse became frantic with ecstasy.

'Good,' Drew said. 'Enjoy.' He rubbed his forehead. 'What else? I'd better rig the remote control.' He pulled an electrical cord from the cardboard box, plugged it into the tape recorder, and led it across the kitchen floor, through the swinging door, and into the murky hall. The space beneath the kitchen door was sufficient for Drew to be able to close the door over the cord. The last thing he did was attach a remote control hand switch to his end of the wire.

In the light that came from the kitchen through the door's window, he studied the buttons on the hand switch. 'On. Off. Pause. Play. Record.' He nodded. 'Ten minutes. Have we forgotten anything?'

Arlene thought about it. 'Just in case, you'd better test that hand switch.'

He did. It worked. 'Then I guess there's just one thing left to do.'
She didn't need to ask what he meant.
'Pray.'

16

At four o'clock, Drew picked up the phone in the kitchen. A fist seemed to squeeze his heart. He'd know soon If he'd misjudged. Everything depended upon the logical assumptions he'd been making

But what if Ray had anticipated those assumptions?

Drew stared at the phone. It was black, with an old-fashioned rotary dial. As his apprehension strengthened, he dialed the number that the Risk Analysis secretary had given him. The digits clicked ominously. He glanced at Arlene, reached out, and held her hand.

Relays connected. Drew heard a buzz as the phone at the other end – near the Paul Revere statue in North End – began to ring.

Someone answered it almost at once. In the background, Drew heard sounds of traffic. A gruff voice said, 'Hello?'

'Mr Rutherford, please.'

'Who?'

'Uncle Ray. It's his nephew calling.'

'Why didn't you say so? He isn't here.'

'But' – Drew made himself sound puzzled' – 'I was told to call at four o'clock.'

'He had an unexpected appointment. You can get in touch with him at . . .' The husky voice dictated a number. 'You got it?'

Drew read the number back.

'Perfect,' the voice said. 'That housewarming you gave us last night? Cute, pal.'

The man hung up.

Drew slumped against the counter.

'We were right?' Arlene asked.

He nodded. 'Ray never intended to go near that phone. It was only a relay. I'm supposed to call another number.'

'As you expected. But you could be wrong about the next call. It might not mean what you think. Suppose Ray was only being careful. Suppose he took for granted that we'd learn the location of the number you were given this morning. This way, by using that phone booth as a relay, he was simply protecting himself. He knows you can't possibly find the location of this new number before he finishes the call and leaves.'

Drew's shoulders ached from nervousness. 'Possibly. But I don't think that's what's going on here. In sixty-eight, a man named Hank Dalton taught me a procedure. I used it once on a mission. Against a hit man for the Red Brigades. And Uncle Ray was Hank Dalton's boss. I have to suspect Ray'll try it on me.' He paused. 'Let's put it this way. If I'm wrong, we've lost nothing.'

'But if you're right . . .' She nodded soberly.

'There's no more time,' Drew said. 'Ray's expecting my call. I don't dare let him wait.'

Drew set the tape recorder next to the phone. His hand trembled as he set the cage beside the tape recorder. Inside the cage, the white mouse kept eating greedily, its sides bulging, mouth full, chewing ecstatically.

'I hope you're as happy as you look,' Drew said. He turned to Arlene. 'You'd better go out to the hall.'

She went through the swinging door.

He stared at the slip of paper, put his index finger into the first digit's slot, and dialed.

He waited, hearing the phone ring at the other end. Ray was playing this cool, not answering right away. But after the fourth ring, Drew wondered if anyone was going to answer at all.

Halfway through the fifth ring, the phone was picked up. 'Hello?' a voice said.

Drew didn't reply.

'Hello? Drew? Come on, sport, talk to me. I've been waiting for you to call.'

No question now. The voice belonged to Uncle Ray.

As gently as possible, he set the phone down onto the counter, making no sound. The speaking end was next to the tape recorder, the opposite end next to the mouse.

Faintly from the receiver, he heard Ray's voice. 'I'm anxious to talk, Drew. To get this settled.'

But Drew left the kitchen. Outside in the murky hall where Arlene waited, he picked up the tape recorder's remote control and pressed the play button.

The door was solid enough that he barely heard his recorded voice. No matter. It would be sufficiently loud against the phone.

'Uncle Ray, I want to arrange a meeting,' the recorder said. *'I could blow up everything you own, but that won't get me the answers I want. I need . . .'*

Staring through the window in the kitchen door, Drew didn't concentrate on the tape recorder. Or on the phone.

He focused all of his attention on the mouse.

'. . . to see your face, you bastard,' Drew's recorded voice said, *'to watch those damned lying eyes of yours when you try to justify –'*

With frantic speed Drew pressed the stop button, cutting off his recorded voice. Because a jet of blood had burst from the mouse's ears. The mouse toppled, trembling, the white fur around its neck turning crimson.

Drew stooped, tugging at the cord that led from the remote control to the tape recorder. He pulled the cord, feeling pressure against it now. 'Come on,' he whispered urgently. 'Come on.'

He slumped in satisfaction as he heard a clatter from inside the kitchen.

'Did it fall?' he asked Arlene.

Peering through the window in the kitchen door, she nodded.

His knees felt weak as he stood. Through the window, he saw where the tape recorder had been pulled off the counter to crash on the floor.

'That's it, then,' he murmured. 'We did it. When that recorder fell, Ray must have heard it.'

'And now he hears nothing,' she said, her voice low.

'He thinks I'm dead.' His tone matched hers. 'The clatter of the tape recorder falling – he'll figure it was me when I fell, still clutching the phone.'

The tactic that Hank Dalton had taught Drew in Colorado in 1968 was a way to kill a man remotely, using the phone. If the target was sufficiently distracted, if the arrangements were properly made, the man would never suspect the means of assassination.

Dalton had called it a supersonic bullet. With sophisticated electronics equipment, a super-high-pitched tone could be transmitted through the phone line, rupturing the victim's eardrum, piercing his brain, and killing him instantly.

As the mouse had been killed, its cage against the receiving end of the phone.

Customarily, the assassin would then hang up. But Drew suspected that Uncle Ray planned to add a variation to this tactic. He imagined Ray hearing the sudden interruption of Drew's voice, the clatter as Drew in theory collapsed, still holding the phone.

But what would Ray do after that?

Keep listening, Drew guessed. If I had someone with me, Ray knows he ought to hear shouts, cries for help.

But if there *weren't* any shouts? If Ray heard only silence on this end of the line?

Drew concentrated. He'll have to assume that I was alone when I made the call.

And in his place, I'd want to make doubly sure that my hunter, my enemy, was really dead.

Drew brooded about the final step. For the past two hours, he'd been analyzing the conclusion he'd reached, testing it for flaws. But it still made sense. Excitement jolted him.

If my end of the line stays open, Ray can trace my call. He can find out where I was phoning from. Provided he doesn't hear any sounds from this end of the phone, he'll think it's safe to send a team here to verify that I'm dead.

And just as important, to get my body.

The authorities think I'm Janus. If he wants to continue using Janus as a cover for his other assassinations, he can't let my corpse be found.

With painstaking care, Drew opened the swinging door, making sure it didn't creak. Gently, he stepped toward the phone.

'It's been five minutes. Any sounds yet?' Drew recognized Ray's voice.

'Nothing.'

'Okay, keep listening, just in case. But I think it's worth a try. Start the trace.'

Drew silently left the kitchen. In the murky hall, he gestured for Arlene to follow him. They walked a safe distance, stopping at the stairs.

'Here's the slip of paper with the second number I called. Find a pay phone outside and call the townhouse. Tell Father Stanislaw's contacts to learn where this number's located.'

She took the paper. 'And you?'

'I think I'd better stay here. In case Ray's people arrive sooner than we expect.'

'If they do?'

248

'I'm not quite sure how to play it. For starters, I want to take a look around this hall and find a good hiding place. As soon as you get the address, come back. But be careful. And make sure Father Stanislaw's contacts go to that address.'

Her eyes were frightened. 'Drew.'

'I know,' he said. 'From here on in, it gets dicey.'

He didn't reconsider his impulse but simply obeyed it. He kissed her.

In the gloom, they held each other for a moment.

Her voice sounded thick. 'I'd better get going.'

He felt hollow. 'See you.'

'God, I hope so.'

She paused once halfway up the concrete stairs, looking back at him. Then she went up the rest of the way and out the door. In a moment, the hall again was silent.

To his amazement, what he experienced now was disturbingly unfamiliar. Loneliness. Inexplicably, his eyes felt warm. *What if he never saw her again?*

17

Just before six, the autumn sun now almost completely gone, the basement hall in deeper gloom, Drew heard the door at the top of the stairs creak open. From where he hid, between rows of stacked chairs against the middle of the left wall at the bottom of the stairs, his first thought was that Arlene had returned, and he felt a wave of joy. But as the door snicked shut, whoever had entered didn't come down.

Drew waited. Still, no one descended.

Arlene would be careful when she came back, he knew. She might be taking the time to sense if something was wrong. Or she might be waiting for Drew to call her. But he couldn't allow himself to do so.

When sufficient time had passed that the memory of the sound of the door seemed a fantasy, Drew heard another sound. Softly – so softly that it too might have been imagined – a shoe touched a concrete step.

And stopped.

Drew's position between the stacks of metal chairs was comfortable. Hank Dalton had always insisted that his students should take that precaution. 'You don't know how long you might have to wait. So make sure you like where you're hiding. Otherwise someone might hear you stretch your leg to relieve a cramp.'

Yet despite Drew's comfortable position, tension had made his body stiff. He strained to keep silent as he listened for yet another soft footstep on the stairs to his right. He breathed imperceptibly.

Yes! A sound. But not from the stairs, as he'd anticipated. Instead, the sound came from the opposite end of the hall, from the darkness across from him on the left. It could have been anything, the brush of wind against a window at the top of the wall over there, or the settling of a joist in the ceiling.

But he heard it again and now identified it – the subtle easing down of a sole on the concrete floor.

Not one, but two intruders were down here. Earlier, after Arlene had gone and he'd scouted this basement, he'd found a set of stairs in that other corner. Unlike the stairs that he and Arlene had used, to his right, those other stairs didn't have a door at the top, so he'd felt secure. Now he realized, his pulse hammering, that he should have followed the stairs where they turned to go up to ground level. He should have checked the main floor. Because it was clear that the second intruder had entered through an upstairs door Drew had not discovered. While Drew had been distracted by the door at the top of the stairs to his right, the other intruder had crept down the stairs on the far side of the room.

Two of them, Drew thought. Okay, as long as I know where they are, I can deal with them. He directed his attention back to the stairs on his right, seeing a shadow reach the bottom.

He understood. This first intruder's a decoy. He's supposed to attract attention. If somebody moves against him, his partner's across the room, ready to protect him.

The light through the kitchen door's window beckoned the shadow. Across the hall, the subtle sounds of the second intruder stopped. Drew watched from the dark between the stacks of metal chairs as the shadow on his right crept toward the window. A man, he saw now. Holding a pistol with a silencer on the barrel, the shadow paused at the side of the swinging door.

Before Drew had chosen his hiding place, he'd returned to the kitchen, and silently, terribly conscious of the telephone receiver lying on the counter, he'd picked up the dead mouse in its cage and hidden it outside in the hall. He'd done the same with the tape recorder. As a final precaution, he'd set the open tape recorder box over the telephone.

Now, when the intruder went into the kitchen, he wouldn't see anything to alarm him. He'd decide that the phone – and the body – had to be somewhere else down here. He and his partner would continue searching.

But I don't dare try anything, Drew thought, clutching his Mauser, unless I've got them both together.

The shadow next to the kitchen door risked a furtive glance through its lighted window. He ducked back. Ten seconds later, he risked another glance.

On the opposite side of the hall, the other shadow moved, creeping forward to join his partner beside the kitchen door. This second shadow, too, had a pistol with a silencer. They flanked each side of the door. One man charged in, the second lunging directly after him. Before the door swung shut, Drew saw them standing back to back, their pistols aimed at opposite sections of the kitchen.

Now!

He shifted from his shelter between the stacks of metal chairs. Mauser ready, he braced himself, crouching in the darkness. As he'd expected, he didn't hear any conversation. Until the men were confident of their safety, they'd remain as silent as they could.

I'll have to shoot them both, Drew thought. While I've got them together.

But not to kill. I need them alive. I need them to tell me where Ray is. When I'm through with them, they'll talk. They'll *beg* me to ask them more questions.

The kitchen door swung open; the two men slipped out, silhouetted by the glow through the kitchen window. Facing the hall, one gestured to the other to check the left side while he took the right.

'Don't move!' Drew shouted. Prepared to fire, he meant to order them to drop their guns. He didn't get the chance.

A shot filled the darkness. But not from the men. Deafening, it came from the opposite end of the hall. Drew dove to the floor, the concrete jolting his chest. A second roar walloped his ears. He fired, but not toward the sniper across the room, rather toward the targets he could see – the two men in front of the kitchen door. As they darted for cover, still exposed by the light through the window, he shot again and again. Screaming, both went down.

He rolled, afraid that the muzzle flashes from his Mauser would attract the sniper's aim. Sprawling on his stomach, he glanced back and forth from the shadows of the two men he'd shot toward the unseen gunman on the other side of the hall.

He blinked, his eyes in pain, as the overhead lights blazed. Blinded, he firmly closed his lids as he'd been trained to do, then barely opened them, allowing his corneas to adjust to the sudden illumination, opening his lids a little more now, desperate, aiming.

He found himself peering beneath rows of tables toward the body of a man on the floor near the opposite stairs. The man wasn't moving. Blood poured from his chest. A pistol lay near his hand.

But how the hell –?

His spine cold, Drew glanced toward the two men on the floor outside the kitchen. One lay still. The other clutched his stomach, moaning.

Drew stared back toward the man on the floor across the room. Two shots had come from that direction. But who had killed the sniper?

He heard footsteps scrape on the concrete stairs over there. The sounds were unsteady, slow. He grimaced, aiming, unable to see who was coming down.

A shoe appeared. Then another. He steadied the Mauser. Dark trouser legs came into view. Drew squinted down the Mauser's sights. The footsteps paused.

A man spoke. His voice, though husky, was weak. 'Drew? Are you all right?'

The Slavic accent was unmistakable. Father Stanislaw.

'All right?' Drew exhaled with nervous relief. 'I suppose so.'

The priest coughed. With painful slowness, he came down the rest of the stairs. His left arm was in a sling. His right hand clutched a pistol. Wavering, the priest leaned back against a wall and took several deep breaths.

'But *you* don't look all right.' Drew stood.

'How do they say it on television. It's only a superficial wound? Don't believe the "only" part.' Father Stanislaw winced. 'Even with sedatives, it hurts.'

Drew had to grin. 'I thought you Poles were supposed to be tough.'

Father Stanislaw forced himself to stand straight. 'Believe me, we are. If you've ever eaten *pierogies*, you know how tough I mean.'

Drew's grin broadened.

But he didn't let his growing affection for this man distract him from being practical. He glanced toward the men he'd shot. One lay as still as before. The other continued to clutch his stomach, groaning. He searched them and took their guns. Then it seemed all right to cross the room and help the priest.

But Father Stanislaw mustered his strength and approached Drew's side of the hall, motioning to Drew to stay where he was. 'I made it this far on my own. I don't need any help.'

'How did you get here?'

'Arlene called the townhouse. With another phone number and instructions to find its location.'

'I know. I asked her to.'

'I was awake when she called. I insisted on talking to her. She told me what had happened while I was asleep. Then I insisted on coming back here with her. My friend, you tried to accomplish too much by yourself.'

'I had no choice.'

'Perhaps. But recent events' – Father Stanislaw gestured toward the men on the floor – 'prove that I was right.'

'Arlene.' Drew whispered her name. 'Where is she?'

'Outside, watching in case these three weren't alone. When we got here, we realized that we couldn't enter the building without alarming you. So we decided to act as your surveillance team. We saw three men enter, one on the side, two upstairs through two different doors. It seemed obvious that they were planning to use the first man as a decoy and the other two as backups.'

'So you followed the two men who'd entered upstairs.'

'My instincts were right.' Father Stanislaw gripped a table for support. 'Of the two men I followed, one made himself a further decoy and eventually joined his confederate at the kitchen. But the third man remained behind, to protect his associates if they were surprised. As they were. He shot at you. But I shot him.' The priest closed his eyes, swallowing hard.

'You're sure you're okay?'

'Quite the contrary. I'm *not* okay.' Father Stanislaw's face was the color of chalk. 'It occurs to me that this is the third time I've saved your life. Back at the retreat house when I hid in the chapel's confessional. At Satan's Horn. Now here.'

'I'm in your debt,' Drew said.

'Three times,' the priest reminded him.

'Yes.' Drew looked at his friend. 'No matter the cost, even my life, I promise to return the favor.'

'In kind.'

'I don't understand.'

'In kind,' the priest insisted.

'All right. Whatever that means. In kind.'

'Make sure you remember that promise. Because' – Father Stanislaw breathed painfully again, his face white – 'when we finish this, I intend to demand . . . on your honor . . . that you fulfill your word.' He coughed. 'Right now, we have business to attend to.'

Drew understood. He stalked toward the men he'd shot. Grabbing the one who was still alive, he shook him hard. 'Where's your boss?'

The man groaned.

'You think you hurt now?' Drew said. 'You don't know what "hurt" can mean.' He reached back his hand, preparing to strike him.

'No!' Father Stanislaw said.

Drew barely heard him. *'Where's your boss, you bastard? You'll tell me or –'*

'No!' The priest grabbed Drew's hand.

Drew glared at him. 'I get it now. You don't mind the killing. But you don't like seeing your victims suffer. What's the matter? You're not prepared to go the limit for your faith? You'd better watch out. You've got a soft spot, Father.'

'No.' Despite his pain, the priest straightened fully. 'For my faith, I've gone what you call "the limit". Many times. More than you can imagine.' His ruby ring – its sword and cross intersecting – glinted. 'But never unless it was necessary. Torture? Certainly. Unless there were chemicals available. But *only* when it was necessary to make someone talk. I know where Ray is. The location of the final number you were given. Now put that man down!'

Drew stared at the man he was holding, feeling his heart contract in disgust at what he'd almost been forced to do, reminded again of how far he'd come from the monastery. Gently, almost with reverence, he set the man down. 'All right. We'll call your people and get him medical help. He's just a drone. He deserves the chance to live. But I have to say, that's a chance the bastard wouldn't give *me*.'

'Of course,' Father Stanislaw said. 'And that's what distinguishes us from them. Our motives aren't based on money. Or the need for power. Or political theories, which by definition are fleeting and shallow. No, our motives are ultimate. And our mercy, if suitable, is that of the Lord.'

Drew felt a sudden rush of sorrow. 'Too much, too long,' he said. 'I'm tired of running. I want this to end.'

'And it will. Tonight, if God wills it.' Wincing, Father Stanislaw reached in his suit pocket. 'I have the address. I can take you to Uncle Ray.'

18

But despite his anxiousness, Drew had something to do first. Like the ancient Greek paradox that to travel a mile you first had to travel a half mile and after that a quarter mile and after that an eighth of a mile, and thus by subdividing your journey you could never reach its end, so Drew felt there was always something more to do, yet another interruption, always another risk. Perhaps his ordeal would never end. Perhaps he was dead, and this was Hell.

He turned to the wounded man. 'Can you hear me?'

The man nodded.

'If you want a doctor, you'll do what I tell you.'

The man peered up, helpless.

'But I've told you we already have the address,' Father Stanislaw said. 'There's no need to –'

'Isn't there?' Drew's voice was urgent. 'We've forgotten something.' He explained what had to be done.

The priest looked distressed. 'You're right. And he has to be made to do it soon.'

Drew knelt beside the wounded man, giving him orders. 'You understand?'

The man nodded, sweating, in pain.

'And then we'll get you a doctor. All you have to do is show us how tough you are. There's nothing to it.' Drew dragged him toward the kitchen. 'To stay alive, just talk without groaning.'

In the kitchen, Drew sat him on the floor against a cupboard and lifted the cardboard box off the unhooked phone. Crouching, he held the receiver near the wounded man's face, leaning close so that he himself could hear what was said on the other end of the line.

He pointed his Mauser toward the wounded man's temple, silently ordering him to talk. The man's eyes glazed, out of focus. For a moment, Drew was afraid he would faint.

'We've got him.' The man sounded hoarse as he spoke to the phone.

'Just a moment,' a gruff voice replied.

In fifteen seconds, Uncle Ray's voice came on the line. 'Is he dead?'

'That's right'

'What took you so long? You had me worried.'

'We couldn't find him at first.'

'He's alone?'

'Yes.'

'Bring the body back here. I want to make sure it's disposed of.'

'We're on our way.' The wounded man's eyes flickered. He sagged toward the floor.

Drew set the phone down onto its receiver, breaking the connection, then eased the man flat on the floor. 'You chose the wrong profession, my friend. You should have been an actor.'

'You promised.' The man groaned.

'I'll keep it. How did you get here? What kind of car?'

'A dark blue van. A Ford.' The man's lips looked parched. 'It's in the parking lot behind this hall.'

Turning, Drew saw Father Stanislaw watching from the open kitchen door. 'You can use this phone to get him a doctor now. And you'd better tell your people to remove the bodies.' He searched the wounded man, finding what he wanted – the keys to the van. 'By the way,' he told the priest, 'I'll need some help when we get there. Did Arlene explain?'

'I'll make the arrangements.'

'And while you're doing that, I'd better let Arlene know we're okay. She'll have heard the shots. She'll be worried.'

'She's beside the church.' The priest picked up the phone. 'I'll hurry.'

'Please. There's a lot to be done.'

Drew rushed from the kitchen. As he ran up the stairs, he remembered the powerful, unfamiliar emotion he'd felt when Arlene had gone up these same stairs two hours ago, his unexpected loneliness when she'd left and shut the door. Again he ached with longing. It seemed a betrayal of his years in the monastery that he wanted so badly to see her again, to hold her. And yet if it *was* a betrayal, he no longer cared. He stepped outside, saw her waiting near the church, and started toward her. Despite the dark, her eyes shone, relieved that he was safe, eager. In a moment, she was in his arms.

254

Fighting the impulse to press his foot harder onto the van's accelerator, knowing he'd be foolish to risk being stopped for speeding, he drove steadily north out of Boston. The city's glow filled his rear-view mirror; his headlights blazed toward night-cloaked trees and fields.

Knuckles stiff from the pressure of his grip on the steering wheel, Drew followed Father Stanislaw's instructions. At first, he hadn't recognized the address on the slip of paper the priest had given him. Then, with growing excitement, he had, no longer surprised that the priest knew how to get there. Because the priest had been at that address before – two days ago. It was Uncle Ray's country estate, north of Boston, on the Bay.

Drew had to admire his enemy's cleverness. Ray, appearing to have fled his estate on the Bay because of Drew's threat, had now reversed his tactic and gone back, apparently assuming that the estate was the last place Drew would look. But in gaining the advantage of the unexpected, Ray had chosen a site that was difficult to defend. Father Stanislaw had described the estate as remote and sprawling, too large, with too much cover to be adequately protected. 'Getting onto the grounds will be easy,' the priest had said. 'Getting into the house, though, that's another matter. He'll concentrate his men there. To go in and grab him, you'd need a small army.'

That won't be necessary, Drew thought, as he headed relentlessly toward the Bay. All we need is the three men I asked for.

And three untraceable cars.

Shortly after seven, he reached the Bay, its white-tipped waves distinct in the dark. Rolling down his window, he smelled a cold sea breeze and stopped at the side of the road where his headlights revealed a historical marker about the Revolutionary War.

He waited. Five minutes later, headlights appeared in his rear-view mirror, stopping behind him. The headlights at once went out. He stepped from the van, noting with fondness Arlene's silhouette behind the steering wheel of the Oldsmobile, the priest slumped beside her as if asleep.

He saw three other pairs of headlights coming toward him. They slowed and stopped in a row behind the Oldsmobile. They too went dark. Three men got out of the cars. As Arlene left the Oldsmobile, Drew joined them on the gravel road.

'The Lord be with you,' he said to the men.

'And with your spirit,' they answered as one.

'*Deo Gratias.*' He studied the men. They were in their middle thirties. Their outdoor clothes were dark, their haircuts conservative, almost military, their eyes direct, disturbingly serene. 'I appreciate your help. Father Stanislaw says you've had experience.'

They nodded.

'For what it's worth, if everything goes as planned, if there aren't any accidents, I don't think your lives are in danger.'

'It doesn't matter,' one said. 'Our lives don't matter. The Church does.'

The Oldsmobile's passenger door came open. Father Stanislaw stepped from the car. 'The equipment's in the trunk.'

Arlene had the key. When she opened it, a light went on. Drew blinked in surprise at automatic weapons, magazines filled with ammunition, grenades, even a miniature rocket launcher.

'You've had this stuff in the trunk all the time?' Drew asked, astonished. 'You could start a war.'

'We *are* at war.' Father Stanislaw's face was as pale as the sling supporting his arm.

They reached inside the trunk, taking up assault rifles, inspecting and loading them. The light inside the trunk glinted off a large red ring on the middle finger of each left hand. The rings had the same insignia – an intersecting sword and cross.

The fraternity of the stone.

Drew felt a chill.

'What do you want us to do?' the first man asked holding the barrel of his weapon toward the dark sky.

Hiding his increasing astonishment, Drew matched their professional tone. 'Adjust the carburetor on each car.' He turned to Father Stanislaw. 'How far is the estate?'

'A mile down the road.'

'Good enough. The timing shouldn't be a problem.'

He finished explaining. They thought about it.

'Could be,' one said. 'As long as he does what you expect.'

'I know him. Besides, does he have a choice?' Drew asked.

'If you're wrong . . .'

'Yes?'

'Nothing. Our part's easy. You're the one taking the risk.'

20

The van approached the estate's closed metal gate. Two armed sentries stood beyond it, one on each side, but when the headlights came close enough for the guards to recognize the van, they snapped into motion and opened the gate. '*Bring the body back here. I want to make sure it's disposed of,*' Uncle Ray had told his man on the phone. As Drew had anticipated, these sentries were under orders to expect the retrieval team and to let the van through at once. Not stopping, the driver waved in thanks and drove quickly through the opening in the wall, proceeding down a blacktop lane past shadowy trees and bushes toward the large three-story Tudor house in the distance.

The carburetor on the van had been adjusted, its idling mechanism turned up so high that the engine would race even if the accelerator weren't pressed. Because the van had an automatic transmission, a driver could leave the gear shift in drive, leap out of the van, and know that the van would follow the direction in which it had been aimed: in this case, down the lane toward the mansion.

As the driver, clutching a weapon, tumbled smoothly onto the lawn, disappearing into the dark, the van continued surging forward. It bumped up onto a sidewalk and jolted to a stop halfway up the mansion's front steps. The driver had lit a fuse before leaping out, a fuse that blazed back to the van's open gas tank. Now the vehicle abruptly, stunningly, exploded. Its massive roaring fireball, chunks of metal flying, ripped apart the mansion's entrance.

The guards at the gate had not yet fully closed it. Spinning, startled, toward the deafening roar, they raised their weapons, rushing toward the blaze in front of the house. At that moment, three other vehicles, their headlights extinguished, crashed through the partly closed gate. Each of these vehicles too had an automatic transmission, each carburetor adjusted to give the engines maximum idle, so that when these drivers too lit fuses and leaped from their vehicles, the cars continued on course, one to the left and two to the right of the blazing van on the steps of the mansion.

In rapid sequence, the vehicles struck the building's facade, erupting in a fiery wallop. Windows shattered. Flames roared up the front of the building.

As the drivers scurried back to shadowy cover, they fired their automatic weapons, strafing the blaze that obscured the house. They riddled parked cars, rupturing tires, shattering the grill of a Rolls Royce and a Mercedes. Tracer bullets made gas tanks explode. Burning gasoline spewed across the pavement. The assailants threw grenades at the guards who raced down the lane from the gate. The guards flew backward, landing motionless on the road. More grenades followed, this time aimed at the mansion.

Arlene, who'd leaped from one of the vehicles used a portable rocket launcher. The model, an RPG-7, was a favorite of terrorists because it was only slightly longer than a yardstick; and because it weighed only fifteen pounds, she could carry it easily when she'd leaped from her moving vehicle. Its projectiles were 3.3 inches wide, capable of piercing 12-inch-thick metal armor. One by one, they blasted impressively into the mansion, blowing out one entire corner.

Now guards raced from the building, some of them flailing, screaming in horror, at their fiery clothes. The reflection of the blaze off night clouds could be seen, it was later reported, fifteen miles away. The powerful blasts rattled windows in the nearby town. The entire front of the mansion began to sag. Defensive automatic weapons rattled from adjacent buildings to which the guards had raced. Throughout, the attackers kept shifting their position, firing, reloading, shooting, throwing grenades, making the assault force seem huge, gradually pulling back.

Two minutes had passed.

21

Drew wasn't with them. On foot, he stalked toward the estate through the dark, along the rocky shore of the Bay. Two days ago, Father Stanislaw had studied the perimeter of the grounds, noting the yacht moored at a dock. As soon as the fireballs erupted from the house at the top of the slope, the three guards who patrolled the beach swung toward the startling brilliance and charged up the wooden steps toward the rattle of gunfire. His dark clothes indistinct against the black water, Drew raced along the rocks of the shore. He rushed down the dock and onto the yacht.

There he hunched below deck. Thirty seconds later, he saw figures scurry down the wooden steps from the house. Waves lapped the hull of the yacht. It tilted slightly, starboard, then port.

Though he hadn't seen Uncle Ray for six years, he recognized the elegant, well-dressed silhouette hurrying down the steps. He also recognized the silhouette of a second man, distinctive because he wore a cowboy hat. And *that* man Drew hadn't seen since 1968. My, my, Drew thought. You must be in your sixties, Hank Dalton. I've got to give you credit. You ought to be retired by now. But I guess it's in your blood. You can't give up the game.

Ray and Hank reached the beach before the others. They paused on the dock. 'All right,' Ray told the guards who'd come with him, sounding as smooth as ever. 'You know where to go. Use the dark and disappear. Don't try to fight them. They've won. But our turn will come. Just remember, I appreciate your loyalty. Good luck to each of you.'

The guards spun toward the automatic gunfire at the burning mansion on the hill. They hesitated only a moment before they separated, disappearing into the dark. Ray and Hank rushed down the dock, their footsteps rumbling hollowly, and hurriedly cast off the mooring lines, climbing down into the yacht. Behind them, on the bluff, another explosion shook the night. Ray darted forward to start the engines. The stern sank slightly as the screws gained traction. Then the yacht evened out, gaining speed, cutting through waves, roaring toward the dark of the Bay.

Standing at the rear of the yacht, surveying the battle zone, Hank braced his hands on his hips, his cowboy hat profiled against the rising flames on the hill. 'Shitfire. Who'd have figured?' he muttered. 'I taught him too good.'

In all the years since '68, Drew had thought of Hank as eternal. This sudden realization of how students could one day outmatch their teachers was shocking. Is that what it means to get old? There's always someone better coming along, because that person is younger?

And it felt so easy. All Drew did was creep forward from the below-deck hatch and nudge Hank. That's all. Nudge him. A gentle tap on Hank's shoulder, and Drew discovered that his former master . . .

(In those days, I thought you were God. I went to sleep in fear of you. I trembled when you spoke.)

. . . was only human. Hank tumbled gracefully into the Bay. His cowboy hat floated. Splashing, coughing he came up.

'I never asked you, Hank! Can you swim?'

'You son of a bitch!' Hank sputtered

At the wheel, Ray spun in alarm. Drew pointed the Mauser at him. 'Be very careful, Uncle. Keep your hands on that wheel. I wouldn't want to have to kill you. We still need to talk.'

In the churning water, Hank kept sputtering, yelling obscenities.

'That's the stuff, Hank. Keep up your spirits. You're close enough to shore – you can make it. Remember what you taught us? Get a fire going – find dry clothes. You don't want to die from hypothermia!'

As Hank's wave-tossed body receded in the distance, Drew – his Mauser steady – never took his eyes from Ray.

'That's right, Uncle, keep your hands where they are. On that wheel. Because, believe me, I'm out of patience. For a moment there, I almost hoped you'd give me an excuse to shoot. But you didn't. So. What I think' – Drew stalked angrily forward – 'is, *now we talk*.'

At the house on top of the bluff, one last explosion shook the night, its flames reflecting eerily off the clouds. The rattle of automatic weapons dwindled as the yacht continued into the dark of the bay. A few seconds later, the rumble of the engine obscured the shots completely. But the shots would soon be stopping anyhow, Drew thought. Arlene and the three men would be pulling back. They'd forced Ray out of the house, and now they'd have to disappear before the police arrived.

Ray glanced from Drew toward the burning mansion on the bluff, its aura receding into the distance. Night enveloped the yacht.

Drew reached inside his coat and pulled out a packet of C-4 explosive, holding its Play-Dough shape in front of the control panel's lights so Ray could see it. 'I assume you recognize my incentive for conversation.'

Ray's pupils widened.

Drew set the plastique on top of the control panel, removed a timer and detonator from his coat, and attached them to the explosive. He twisted the crank on the timer. Eight minutes. It began to tick.

'So,' Drew said, 'that ought to give us plenty of time for a chat. If not . . ' He shrugged.

'You'd be blowing yourself up, too.'

'At the moment, as tired as I am, as sick of running' – Drew exhaled – 'I don't really care.'

'I don't believe you.'

Drew studied Ray – tall and slender, with a lean, handsome face and deep blue eyes that glinted from the control lights. He'd be in his late fifties now, but he looked fit and youthful. His short, sandy hair had hints of silver through it, but these only made him seem more distinguished. Beneath his open topcoat, he wore an impeccably tailored gray suit, an immaculate white shirt, a striped club tie. His shoes were custom-made Italian. His topcoat, Drew realized with anger, was brown camel's hair, the same type of coat that Ray had worn the Saturday morning in October in 1960 when he had come to the playground in Boston where Drew had mourned for his parents, for his ruined life.

Now it was October again. Boston again.

Drew's jaw muscles hardened.

'Oh, I believe you'd kill me,' Ray said. 'What you did to my house – or what your *friends* did to my house – is thoroughly convincing. You'd shoot me, yes. But blow us both up? Take your life with mine?'

Drew's voice was thick. 'You still don't understand.' The timer kept ticking. Drew glanced at it. Less than seven minutes. 'You have to ask yourself *why* I would want to live. Give me a reason.'

Ray frowned, unsettled. 'Well, that's obvious. Everybody wants to live.'

'For what? Why do you think I entered that monastery? From the time I was ten, I've hated my life. The last happy moment I knew was the second before I saw my parents blown to pieces. Everything after that was desperation.'

259

'But you got even for what happened to them. I *helped* you get revenge!'

'It sure as Hell didn't bring me peace. There was always another terrorist to kill, another fanatic to punish. But others showed up to take their place. There'd never be an end. And what did I accomplish?'

Ray looked baffled. The timer kept clicking. He swallowed.

'I thought I was right to get even for my parents. The terrorists think *they're* right to attack governments they feel are corrupt. How many rights can there be, Ray? In the name of what I thought was right, I did the same thing I condemned them for. I murdered innocent people. I became the enemy I was hunting.'

'The timer,' Ray said.

'We'll come to that. Relax. For now, I want to explain about the monastery. I'm sure you're anxious to know about it. As soon as I realized what I'd become, I wanted to leave the world and its horrors, to let the madness go on without me. Let the world blow itself to Hell for all I cared. The monastery gave me refuge. But you destroyed it. You forced me back to the horrors. And for that, I can't forgive you.'

Six minutes.

'What I am Ray is a sinner. But you're a sinner, too. You made me what I am.'

'Now just a second. Nobody forced you. You *wanted* my help!'

'You manipulated me into joining Scalpel. You know what I think? Sometimes, in the blackest part of my mind, I think it was *you* who ordered the death of my parents.'

'I loved your parents!'

'So you say. But isn't it interesting how many different motives there might have been for killing them? A fanatical Japanese might have decided to blow up my parents in revenge for the atomic bombs we dropped on Japan, as a way of showing us how much we weren't wanted there. Or the Soviets might have killed my parents to increase the tension between Japan and America, to jeopardize the new defense treaty and keep America away from Southeast Asia. Or maybe someone like you had the bright idea to blow up my parents and blame it on the Japanese, as a way of shaming the Japanese into stopping their demonstrations.'

'That isn't true! I never —'

'Someone, for one of those twisted motives, did! Maybe it wasn't you. But you were ready enough to have me kill that boy and his parents in France. To me, you're no different than the self-righteous bastard who did kill my parents. If I'm a sinner, *you're* a sinner. And I think it's time we atoned for our sins, don't you?'

Ray stared again at the time. Less than five minutes now.

'Drew. For Christ's sake . . .'

'Yes, that's right. Now you're getting it. For Christ's sake.'

Suddenly exhausted, he felt himself tremble. The yacht rumbled farther into the blackness of the Bay. Behind, the blaze of the house had diminished to a glow.

'You don't think I'd blow myself up with you?' Drew asked. 'The way I feel right now, I can't think of a reason not to.'

'No.' Ray's eyes flickered with sudden hope. 'You can't. You don't dare. It's suicide. You'd automatically damn your soul to Hell.'

'Of course. But I deserve to go to Hell. Certainly *you* do. Because

260

of the hit on the monastery. Because of Janus and the attacks on the Church.'

'But wait a minute, Drew. There isn't *really* a Hell. What are you talking about?'

Drew's exhaustion intensified. He could hardly listen.

'There's no God, Drew. You've got your mind confused by superstition. Shut off that timer. Please. Let's talk.'

'We *are* talking. No God? No Hell? Do you feel like gambling, Ray? What do you say we find out?'

'*No!*'

'That's too bad. Because I'm in a gambling mood. I have to be honest, though. You're right. I don't intend to to commit suicide.'

'Then you'll shut off the timer?'

'No. I've got something else in mind. A test. Just before the yacht explodes, you and I are going over the side.'

'We're miles from shore! That water's freezing! We'd never be able to swim to –'

'Maybe. That's what I mean by gambling. There was a time, back in the Middle Ages, when they tested to see if someone was a sinner by throwing that person into freezing water and forcing him to stay there for hours. He passed the test if God allowed him to live. What I'm thinking is, if we die in the water, God wasn't happy with us. But it wouldn't be suicide. Because God's in control now. If He allows us to survive, if He lets us make our way to shore, it'll be a sign that He isn't angry. He'll be giving us the chance to save our souls.'

Ray trembled. 'You've gone crazy.' He stared at the cold, dark water. At the timer. Almost three minutes. 'What do you want to know? Just turn off the –!'

Aiming the Mauser, Drew shook his head. 'It depends on what you've got to say. I'll even be generous and help you get started. Scalpel, Ray. In 1980, because you'd exceeded your authority, because the program was dangerously out of control, you were forced to resign from the government. Scalpel was disbanded. So you founded the Risk Analysis Corporation.'

'How did you learn –?' Ray stared at the timer. 'All right, yes, a private intelligence service.'

Drew blazed. 'A private *assassination* service.'

'We work for major corporations. Sometimes for other intelligence networks. We helped organize the rebels in Nicaragua, for example. That way, there's less criticism about the U.S. interfering with foreign governments. Because the Agency isn't officially involved, it keeps Congress from complaining but still fights the Communists in –'

'I don't *care* about Nicaragua! Janus, get to Janus!'

Ray took a hand off the wheel to gesture impatiently. 'Give me time! I'm –!'

Drew tensed his finger on the Mauser's trigger. 'Put your hand back on that wheel or you won't be alive when that bomb explodes.'

Ray grasped the wheel again. His eyes darted toward the clicking timer. Two minutes, forty-five seconds.

'Janus!' Drew said again. '*Why?*'

Ray's chest heaved. 'We have another contract. In Iran. To take out the Ayatollah.'

261

'Yes.' Drew bitterly smiled. 'Our old friend, the Ayatollah. Isn't it amazing how things keep leading back to him? Who gave you the contract against him?'

'I was never told. A free-lance negotiator came to us with the offer. But I always assumed it was Iraq.' Ray became more agitated as the timer clicked. 'What difference does it make who hired us? I gladly accepted the contract. The Ayatollah's a maniac. Something has to be done about him.'

Two minutes, twenty seconds.

'You'd better hurry, Ray.'

'We haven't been able to get near him. Five attempts. Whatever we do, he seems to know about it. So we tried another tactic. Oh, please, shut off . . . We wanted to force the West to decide he was so insane he had to be stopped. Something so outrageous that the U.S. and Europe would side with Iraq against him.'

'Janus. What about Janus?'

The timer kept clicking.

'You'd bungled a hit against the Ayatollah. It looked as if you'd become a rogue – that you'd sold out to him. Even if you hadn't, you'd become too unstable to be trusted with what you knew. I hated to do it.'

'But you tried to have me killed.'

'*Tried?* I was *sure* you were dead. Later, after Risk Analysis was formed, after we had the contract against the Ayatollah, I realized a way to use you even in death.'

One minute, forty seconds.

Ray shuddered. 'I invented Janus. The two-faced. You. The turncoat, working for the Ayatollah. Since you didn't exist anymore, the authorities would be chasing a ghost. To keep them on the trail, I used Mike to make an appearance once in a while. Not for anything dangerous. A blurred photograph taken near the site of a job. A conversation with a hotel clerk who'd remember him later when the authorities asked about strangers in the area. Once we'd established Janus, Mike went to ground. He put on a little weight. Changed his haircut. Kept to himself, but maintained a regular schedule. He had alibis. No one could link him with Janus. Then my people did the actual jobs. Drew, *the timer.*'

'Jobs against the Catholic Church?' Drew burned with such outrage he wanted to crash the butt of his pistol across his uncle's face. '*You killed priests to create a smokescreen?*'

'A holy war. We wanted it to look as if the Ayatollah was fighting a *jihad* against the heathen, against the Church. He's fanatical enough to do that. A new crusade. But in the reverse. This time not in the Mideast but in Europe.'

Fifty-five seconds.

'Shut it off!'

Drew touched the knob on the dial. 'Then you'd publish proof of what the Ayatollah was supposed to be doing. The West would react with outrage and crush him. When the dust settled, Iraq would have gained what it wanted.'

'The *world* would have gained! I don't care about the money. What I did was necessary!'

Drew repeated the word, almost spitting it out with contempt. '*Necessary?*'

'Yes! Now shut it off!'

Instead, Drew shrugged and let the timer click off its final seconds. He smiled. 'Goodbye, Uncle Ray.'

Ray gasped. 'No! Wait! You're really going to do it?'

'You'd better start believing in God. If I were you, I'd make an Act of Contrition. Remember how it goes? "Oh, my God, I am heartily sorry . . .'''

With a scream, Ray lunged toward the stern. A wave buffeted the yacht, adding force to his dive. He went over, plunging into blackness.

The timer stopped. A cold wind stung Drew's face. Waves, splashing the yacht, sent an icy mist over him. He shut off the engine. The night became silent – except for the hiss of the wind and the whump of waves against the hull. He grabbed a rubber flashlight off the control panel and walked to the stern, peering toward Ray, who was struggling to keep afloat in the churning water.

Panicked, Ray squinted at the flashlight's glare.

'I'd take that overcoat off, if I were you,' Drew said. 'It'll drag you down.'

'The bomb.' Ray thrashed in the water.

'An oversight. I forgot to attach the timer to the detonator. As I said, I didn't intend to commit suicide.'

'You son of a bitch!'

'Here. Take this life preserver.' Drew tossed it to him .

Ray clutched it, spitting water. 'Cold.' His voice shook. 'So cold. You can't imagine.'

Drew studied him.

'Please. Pull me in.'

'Sorry. I gave you the life preserver so you wouldn't drown. That doesn't mean I won't let you die from exposure. Drowning's too quick, and they say it's even pleasant. But this way . . .'

'You bastard, I did what you asked! I told you what you wanted to know!' Ray's face was shockingly white. His teeth chattered. *'Please!'*

'But you didn't tell me everything. Those priests Janus murdered. How could you bring yourself to order it? How could you think that good could ever come out of the murder of innocent priests?'

His voice quivering, Ray thrashed in the water. 'If those priests were strong in their faith, they went to Heaven. They were martyrs. They gave up their lives to stop the Ayatollah. *Anything's* justified to stop him.'

'You claim those priests went to Heaven? But a while ago, you said you didn't believe in an afterlife. You'll say anything, *do* anything, for what you think is right.' Drew paused; certainty filled his soul. 'You did kill my parents. For the sake of a principle.' Bile rose bitterly in his throat. He was afraid he was going to be sick.

'But I didn't! Please . . . so cold. Get me out of here!'

'We'll see. It all depends on how you answer my next few questions. Then I'll decide what to do with you. The monastery. I need to know about the hit on the monastery. How did you find out I wasn't dead? How did you learn where I was?' Though Drew suspected the answer, close to vomiting because of it, he needed to know for sure.

'Jake.' A wave struck Ray's open mouth, making him gag.

'What about him? What happened to him?'

His teeth chattering, face turning blue, Ray struggled in the cold, black water. 'I caught him investigating Janus. My men picked him up. Under amytal, he confessed he hadn't killed you. He told me about the monastery.'

'You had him killed?'

'He knew too much. He couldn't be trusted. It had to be done.'

'No!' Drew shivered in revulsion. He screamed out his grief.

How could he tell Arlene?

'My arms.' Ray sank, then struggled to the surface. 'Cramps. Help me. Cold . . . In the name of . . . Please! So cold!'

Jake was dead? All along, Drew had realized that possibility. He thought he'd prepared himself to accept it. Now he felt so stunned that he almost didn't hear Ray beg. But a wave sloshed across the yacht, stinging Drew's face, shocking him into awareness.

Again Ray sank beneath the water.

Vengeance insisted. It would feel so good to let Ray die. And yet Ray's death wouldn't bring Jake back.

Ray didn't come up. Tensing, Drew understood. God was testing him. And the consequence would be ultimate. I can't hope for God to show mercy if I don't show mercy to someone else.

Drew pulled the rope on the life preserver frantically. But when he tugged Ray to the surface, the body was motionless, mouth hanging open, draining water.

No!

Drew strained on the line. Desperate, he dragged Ray over the side, slumping with him onto the deck.

Ray moaned. Alive!

I have to make him warm!

In search of blankets, hot tea, dry clothes, Drew scrambled toward the hatch that led below deck. No! he realized, appalled. *I should take him with me. It's too cold up here. The mist from the waves will make the blankets wet!*

He spun, rushing back toward Ray.

And dove to the deck as his uncle fired.

Ray's hand shook from the icy water he'd been in. His bullet missed Drew, walloping into the cabin. Ray gripped the gun with both hands, cursing as he steadied his aim.

Drew shot him three times in the face.

And screamed. In rage, in frustration, almost in despair. Too much death. Everywhere. But this time, he'd tried to prevent it.

Pointless. Useless.

And the worst part was, he knew what was coming. He'd have to tell Arlene her brother was dead. He knew what Father Stanislaw would ask of him now. His ordeal wasn't over yet.

Waves crashed icy mist across his face. The dark closed in.

22

The god of beginnings.

Drew stood in the cemetery in Boston, once more staring down at the graves of his parents, a ritual he hadn't been able to obey since leaving the monastery. Robert and Susan MacLane. Their birth dates were different, the date of death the same. June 25, 1960. With a flinch, he remembered the segments of his father's body strewn across the Japanese garden. And the shards of broken glass projecting from his mother's bloody cheeks.

In my beginning is my end.

It was one day after Uncle Ray's death. Saying prayers for the dead, Drew had dumped the body overboard and guided the yacht south along the coastline, finding a private dock where after removing his fingerprints, he left the yacht unmoored, letting it drift back out to the Bay. In the dark, he headed into Boston.

Now the sun was setting again. As twilight gathered around him, he continued to stare at the gradually dimming names on the gravestones. A cold breeze ruffled his hair.

A figure approached, making no effort at stealth. In the thickening shadows, Drew wasn't sure who it was, but because the figure was taking care to be obvious, Drew subdued his alarm. He saw a swath of white against a black overcoat. A sling for an injured arm. Father Stanislaw.

The priest came up beside him, his voice respectful. 'Am I intruding? If so, I can wait for you at my car.'

'No. Stay if you like. I don't mind the company. But how did you know I'd be here?'

'I suppose I could pretend to understand you well enough to predict your patterns. The truth is, at the townhouse when you woke up this afternoon, you told Arlene where you'd be. I hope you don't think she violated your confidence by telling me.'

'Not at all. I trust her judgment.'

'It's peaceful here.'

'Yes. Peaceful.' Drew waited for the priest to say what was on his mind.

'When we first met' – Father Stanislaw's voice was resonant – 'you asked me about my ring. I told you, one day when we knew each other, I'd explain.'

'About the fraternity of the stone?' Drew's interest quickened.

'Yes.'

Even in shadow, the ruby was so rich that a subtle fire seemed to glow within it. Father Stanislaw rubbed its insignia. The intersecting sword and cross. 'This is a copy of a ring that dates back to the time of the Crusades. It represents history. Are you a student of history?'

'You have my attention, if that's what you mean.'

Father Stanislaw chuckled. 'Palestine,' he said. 'Eleven ninety-two. The Third Crusade. With the blessing of the Pope, armies from France and England invaded the Holy Land to capture it from the Muslims, the heathen. But at the victorious siege of Acre, a rift developed between the French and English forces. You see, the English claimed considerable territory in France, and the French king, Philip, grasping the chance to gain an advantage, decided to take his forces and leave the Holy Land, to go home. His purpose was to ensure control of those contested regions in France while the English king, Richard, and his army remained in the Holy Land, continuing the Crusade.'

'Politics,' Drew said with contempt.

'But shrewd. And good came out of it. Before the French returned to Europe, their intelligence officers met with their English equivalents. As a gesture of professional brotherhood, despite their political differences, the French proposed a solution to a growing dangerous problem that the English would now have to deal with alone. The assassins.'

'Yes. The first of their kind. They originated terrorism,' Drew said.

'The crusaders were certainly terrorized. As knights, they were used to a noble code of battle, in the open face to face. They had no experience with an enemy who considered it equally noble to attack under cover of night, to enter an opponent's tent and kill him while he was helpless, unarmed, asleep. The assassins took particular delight in cutting off the head of a crusader and setting it on the altar where mass would take place the next morning. Such barbarism made the crusaders feel that the world had become unhinged.'

'The purpose of terrorism.'

'Precisely. To kill so as to demoralize. But the French intelligence officers, before they left the Holy Land, proposed a solution. Fight fire with fire. Use assassins to fight assassins. Demoralize as they themselves had been demoralized. This proposal met with serious objections from the English. "Descend to the level of our enemy? Never." But in the end, the English agreed. Because the Christian assassin would not be one of themselves but, instead, a former Muslim. A Palestinian who'd converted to the one true faith, Catholicism. A monk at the Benedictine monastery in Monte Cassino, Italy.

'This monk, because of his heritage, knew the traditions of the assassins. And because he was of their race he could pass easily among them. An assassin attacking assassins, he would fight terror with terror. But *this* terror would be different. With the blessing of the Pope, this crusading assassin would be killing for God. His terror would be holy.'

Drew listened with growing distress, the darkness seeming to smother him.

'The monk's Christian name was Father Jerome. His Muslim name has never been verified, though legend has it that he was called Hassan ibn al-Sabbah, by divine coincidence the same name as the founder of the original Muslim assassins. I take this to be apocryphal. But of his achievements, there is no doubt. He did strike terror into the terrorists, and at the close of his service for God, when the Third Crusade was over, he returned to the monastery at Monte Cassino, where he was given the honor and rewards he deserved.'

'By "rewards" you mean the ring?'

'No, that came later. In fact, it was first given to someone else, though in time it was also given to Father Jerome.'

The cold night air stung Drew's face. 'If you expect me to play Twenty Questions . . .'

'Forgive me for being cryptic. The history is complicated. At the end of the Third Crusade, the English king, Richard – he was known as the

Lion-Hearted – set out to return to England. Part of his motive for discontinuing the Crusade was his realization of the mistake he'd made in allowing the French to return before him. The French king, Philip, had negotiated a treasonous bargain with Richard's temporary replacement. Indeed, the acting head of state was Richard's brother, John. The bargain was intended to settle the dispute about the English lands in France. John agreed to give up England's claim to the lands in France. Philip in turn agreed to support John's claim to the English throne – against the rightful claim of Richard.'

'So Richard decided he'd better head home,' Drew said.

'But he was stopped. On his way through Europe from the Holy Land, he was captured by the Austrians and held for ransom. The problem was, how to pay it. Richard's brother, John, didn't want his brother released. John did everything possible to prevent the ransom from being paid. He sent agents pretending to be from Richard and had them collect valuables intended to be part of the ransom. But those valuables went into John's own treasury. Meanwhile Richard rotted in prison. At last, in desperation, Richard found a way to guarantee that his subjects would know which ransom collectors were truly from him and not from John.'

'The ring? Am I right?'

'Yes. The ring. Almost identical to the one I wear.' Father Stanislaw rubbed its insignia again. 'Richard gave his ring to a trusted assistant. His subjects had learned to identify the ring with him. By showing it, the assistant could prove that the valuables he collected would help get Richard out of prison and not go into John's treasury.'

Drew shook his head.

'You see a problem with that tactic?' Father Stanislaw asked.

'To stop his brother, all John had to do was order a jeweler to make a copy of the ring.'

'John had mental limitations. He never thought of it. If he had, he might have gained the throne. Instead, with the aid of the ring, Richard's assistant collected the ransom, and Richard was released. He returned to England and crushed his brother. *Because of his ring*. With a slight distinction, *this* ring. It had importance. It was a password. It possessed a power.'

Drew became more uneasy; he sensed a disturbing undertone to the story.

Father Stanislaw continued. 'Richard refused to abide by John's agreement with the French. He took his army to the mainland and reclaimed his territories. But there, one of his new subjects, a French peasant, saw him walking outside the walls of a castle one day and shot him with an arrow. The wound was in the shoulder. It should not have been fatal, but unskilled treatment made it mortal. Dying, Richard insisted that his attacker be brought before him. "Why did you kill me?" Richard asked. The peasant answered, "Because you would have raped my wife and starved my children." Richard objected, "My subjects love me. All I wanted was the land. I would have let you live in peace." But the peasant answered, "No, your brother would have let us live in peace." And Richard, understanding how this simple man had been used by his enemies, said "God help you. You know not what you've done. I forgive you. Let this man go away unhurt." It is said that the priest who was present at Richard's

267

deathbed exhorted him to repentance and restitution for his sins, but Richard drove the priest away and died without benefit of the sacraments.'

'And the peasant?' Drew asked. 'Was he allowed to go away unharmed?'

Father Stanislaw stepped closer to Drew in the darkness. 'That's the point of my story. After Richard died, his angry associates debated what to do about their lord's final wish. They wanted to question the peasant to learn if anyone else had been involved in the assassination. But before they did, a priest went to hear the peasant's confession. The peasant died shortly after his confessor left. It seems he committed suicide by swallowing poison, though no one discovered how he got the poison.'

'From the priest?' Drew asked.

'Would it help if I said that the priest who heard the peasant's confession was also the priest whose medical treatment failed to save Richard's life?'

Drew's spine tingled. 'The priest was Father Jerome?'

'No. His Mideastern features would have betrayed him. But the priest was *trained* by Father Jerome.'

'And why did he kill . . .'

'To keep the peasant from revealing that King Philip had hired him. Only a priest would not be suspected of silencing Richard's assassin. In this way, a Franco-English war was averted.'

'That's not what I meant. Why a priest? Why did Father Jerome let himself become involved?'

'In exchange for his service – and his assistant's service – Father Jerome gained some of England's land in France for the Church to which he'd converted.'

Drew felt sick. 'And the Church went along with it?'

'The Church, the Pope and his associates, never knew. They have *never* known. The fraternity of the stone is an order located on the Atlantic coast of France in one of the regions once claimed by England. Its symbol is this ring. The intersecting sword and cross.'

'Religion and violence?' Drew was appalled.

'The symbol of a warrior for God. Holy terror. Through the years, using the example of Father Jerome, the fraternity has intervened for the Church whenever the profane world has threatened it. Soldiers for Christ. Church militant. We fight Satan with Satan's tactics. In Richard's time. And even more today.'

As he'd felt last night when Uncle Ray had died, Drew wanted to vomit. The revelation put him on guard. The priest was telling him things Drew shouldn't know.

'The three men who helped you last night – you noticed their rings – are members of the fraternity,' Father Stanislaw said. 'I emphasize that our order is distinct from the members of Opus Dei who've been assisting us. Opus Dei is the intelligence branch of the Church. We are –'

'The Church's assassins.' Drew was outraged. 'Except the Church doesn't know about it.'

'Though we do have the Church's sanction.'

'That doesn't make sense. Sanction? How? If the Church doesn't know.'

'By tradition. Just as each Pope inherits the mandate given by Christ to Peter, so we inherit the absolution given to Father Jerome by the Pope at the time of the Third Crusade. A Pope is infallible. If it was justifiable to kill for the Church at *that* time, it must be equally justifiable to kill for the Church at other times.'

'I don't want to hear any more.'

'But I thought you'd find it interesting.' Father Stanislaw rubbed his ring. 'After all, you did ask for an explanation of the stone. Given your reaction, you realize now why I waited.'

'Till we knew each other better.'

'Yes.'

The cemetery was silent in the deepening night. Drew sensed what was coming.

'Join us,' Father Stanislaw said.

In spite of his premonition, Drew wasn't able to prepare himself. He reacted automatically – with disgust. 'Become an assassin for God?'

'To some degree, you already are. Since you left the monastery, you've killed several men. To protect the Church.'

'I had a different motive.'

'What, to stay alive? To get even with those who'd attacked you? You're a complex man. Those reasons aren't sufficient. A Carthusian, who once was a killer but for the wrong reasons, you could use your skills now for the *right* reasons. To safeguard the Holy See. To defend Christ's mission on earth.'

'To defend Christ's mission?' Drew couldn't contain his anger any longer. 'Maybe I read a different New Testament than you did. Didn't Christ say something about turning the other cheek, about the *peaceful* inheriting the earth?'

'But that was before his Crucifixion. The world, my friend, is a desperate place. Without the fraternity, the Church would long ago have failed. History, which is the record of God's will, has justified our cause.'

'I pass,' Drew said.

'But you can't.'

'Killing? I want nothing more to do with it. What I want is peace.'

'But in *this* world, peace isn't possible. Only a long hard fight. Till Judgment Day.'

'You're wrong. But I'll pray for your soul.'

Father Stanislaw inhaled sharply. 'Three times I saved your life.'

'I know that. I promised I'd do anything to save your life in return.'

'You aren't remembering correctly. Last night, you promised you'd return the favors in kind. Remember how I phrased the demand? Return the favors *in kind*! And now I'm asking you to fulfill your promise. To keep your word. Join us. Not to save my life – to save the life of the Church. Use your talents for the good of the Lord.'

'I wonder,' Drew said bitterly. 'Which Lord is that?'

'God. I'm asking you to serve God!'

'But how many Gods can there be? The Ayatollah thinks his God is the one and only. The Hindus think theirs is. The Buddhists. The Jews. The Muslims. The Catholics. The Protestants. The aborigines who pray to the moon. God sure gets around. And He sure seems to want a lot of killing. How many millions have died for Him? You say history's the record of God's will? To me, it's an uninterrupted sequence of holy wars. And each side was absolutely certain it was right! Totally confident that if they died for their faith they saved their souls! Well, how many true causes can there be? How many heavens? Last night, Uncle Ray told me that to stop the Ayatollah, he considered it justifiable to make the Ayatollah seem to be attacking the Catholic Church. The priests who died, he said, would achieve salvation because of their unknowing sacrifice. Ray didn't even believe in God, yet he used religion to defend his actions. Madness. Religion? Save us from the sins we commit in the name of religion.'

Father Stanislaw shuddered. 'Then you vindicate the Ayatollah?'

'No more than I vindicate you. Or Ray. To kill in self-defense I can understand. I've done it myself in the last two weeks. But to kill for the sake of a principle? That's inexcusable.'

'Then we don't disagree.'

Drew felt his heart pounding. 'How can you say that?'

'Because we protect the Church,' Father Stanislaw said, 'it *is* self-defense.'

'The Church shouldn't need protecting. If God stands behind it – or any other religion – He'll make sure it survives. Without violence. He sent you a test. You failed. I told you, I'll pray for your soul.'

Drew walked away.

'I'm not finished yet!' Father Stanislaw said.

Drew kept walking.

Father Stanislaw followed. 'You can't refuse my offer!'

'I did.' In the shadows, gravestone led to gravestone.

Father Stanislaw kept after him. 'There's something I haven't told you.'

'It won't make a difference.'

'Remember, I said this ring was *almost* identical to Richard's? The ruby's the same. The gold band and setting. The insignia. The intersecting sword and cross.'

Drew passed a mausoleum.

'But there's a crucial difference.' Father Stanislaw walked close behind him. 'The stone tilts up. And beneath the stone, there's a tiny compartment. Within there's a capsule. The poison is instantaneous. Because if one of the order should ever be captured, he must guarantee that no outsider can threaten us. Our secret must be kept. I can think of no other instance in which suicide would be justified. Surely you understand what I'm telling you. If we're prepared to kill ourselves to protect the order's secret, we're prepared to go to other extremes.'

Drew continued through the dark.

'My friend, if you don't stop right now and agree to join us, I'll be forced to kill you. No outsider can ever know about us.'

Drew didn't turn. 'You want me to make it easy for you? I'm supposed to try to fight? So you'll feel justified? Like hell. In the back – that's how you'll have to kill me. And you'll be doing me a favor. Because if I die refusing you, I'll have a good chance of saving my soul.'

'Don't force me to do this,' Father Stanislaw said. 'I've grown to like you. Even to admire you.'

Drew didn't stop.

'Your choice is final?'

Walking, Drew studied murky tombstones.

'Very well then.' Father Stanislaw sighed.

'You know I'm not a threat to you. I'd never tell.'

'Oh, certainly, I have no doubt. You'll never tell.'

Drew felt an icy tickle between his shoulderblades where the knife or the bullet would strike. Self-defense, he thought. It's not a sin if I protect myself.

The spit of a silenced pistol was terribly close behind him. He dove to the right, scrambling around a marble angel of death, drawing his Mauser.

Instead of another spit, he heard a groan. He reversed his direction, spinning the opposite way around the angel, risking exposure to fire.

The risk was needless.

Father Stanislaw sagged toward the grassy mound of a grave. His silenced pistol went off. With a muffled report, it tore up grass on top of the grave. He fell across the grass, his head toward the gravestone. Trembled. And lay still.

Drew tensed, scanning the darkness.

A shadow moved. He held his breath, crouching.

The shadow emerged, coming closer.

Jake.

EPILOGUE
'AND FOR YOUR PENANCE . . .'

THE WANDERERS

1

An hour later, Drew entered the townhouse in Beacon Hill. 'We'd better get going,' he told Arlene.

She seemed surprised. 'Right now?'

'Our business is finished. It's safer not to stay in town.'

The woman who'd taken care of Father Stanislaw asked if the priest would be returning.

'No. He's been called away on an urgent matter. He asked me to thank you for all your kindness. He thanks your friends and the man who lent us this house. I've put the sports car in the garage.' Drew gave her the keys to the car and the house. 'May God be with you.'

'And with your spirit.'

'*Deo gratias.*'

2

'What's going on?' Arlene demanded. 'Why the rush?'

In the night, Drew walked with her around the corner.

She stopped, confused, when she saw where the Oldsmobile was parked. 'But you said Father Stanislaw had been called away.'

'In an ultimate sense, he was. He's dead.'

'He's *what*?'

'Someone shot him.' Drew gestured toward the Oldsmobile's trunk. 'The body's in there.'

'Shot him?'

'Saved my life.'

'But *who*?'

Drew opened the passenger door.

Jake grinned. 'Sis, how about a hug?'

She burst into tears.

3

Jake had changed little. His mustache was still as red as ever, his hair thick, crinkly, and red, his forehead high, handsome. He wore outdoor clothes. Hiking boots. A nylon pack sat beside him.

'They wanted my death to look like an accident – to keep you from asking questions, Sis. I was supposed to take a fall while I was climbing. They forgot how good I am.' Jake grinned. 'I made the idiots with me take the fall and got my ass away from there.'

'I wish you'd told me. You could have sent a message to me somehow and let me know where you were, so I wouldn't worry.'

'But suppose they questioned *you*? If they gave you amytal, even though you're my sister, you'd have had to tell them where I was the same as they used amytal to make me tell them Drew was still alive and in the monastery. I couldn't risk contacting you. I kept checking for news about a hit on the monastery. Nothing in the papers or on television. I started to wonder. Had something gone wrong with the hit? Had Drew survived? I couldn't go to you, Sis, but I knew there was one place Drew would go if he was out. Maybe not right away, but eventually. The same place I found him in seventy-nine.'

'My parents' graves.'

'And now we're together,' she said.

But for how long? Drew wondered.

4

Leaving Boston, they drove the Oldsmobile back to Pennsylvania, to Bethlehem, to Arlene's Firebird where they'd left it at a long-term parking garage. The journey, three hundred miles, took most of the night. Along the way they stopped near the grave of Stuart Little to bury Father Stanislaw in the dark on a cold, high, wooded slope.

Before they covered the body, they removed his priest's clothes, a St Christopher medal around his neck, and his ring. As Drew had done when he'd lowered Uncle Ray's body into the Bay, he silently recited the prayers for the dead. Maybe God is truly forgiving, he thought. Maybe He makes allowance for those who worship Him too fervently. As a gentle rain began to fall – possibly in blessing – Drew turned away.

In Bethlehem, at 4 A.M., Arlene roused a sleepy garage attendant, redeemed her Firebird, and followed Drew and Jake in the Oldsmobile to a secluded bank of the Lehigh River. In the rain and dark, they pushed the priest's car and its weapons down a steep embankment into a deep part of the river. With its windows open the car sank quickly.

Drew pulled Father Stanislaw's ring from his pocket traced his finger along the intersecting cross and sword on the ruby, and hurled it far out into the river. In the gloom, he never saw where it disappeared.

The rain fell harder, obscuring dawn. They headed east, crossing the

Delaware River into New Jersey where finally exhaustion forced them to pull in at a roadside rest area. Drew slept fitfully, squirming from nightmares, until the blaring horn of a passing semitruck startled the three of them fully awake, upright, just after 11 A.M. Weary, anxious, they continued eastward.

Throughout the afternoon, the news on the radio repeated the details about the attack on Uncle Ray's mansion, and his mysterious disappearance. A former intelligence official, committed to fighting terrorism, he was rumored to have been kidnapped, killed by terrorists in reprisal for his lifelong vendetta.

A separate story from State College, Pennsylvania, announced that the body of a man found four days ago in the cellar of a student rental complex resembled photographs of an international assassin known as Janus. Preliminary reports revealed that this mercenary had been using various cover identities, including that of Andrew MacLane, a member of a disbanded government anti-terrorist group, who'd disappeared in 1979. MacLane, it was theorized, had been killed by Janus because their coincidental resemblance allowed Janus to assume MacLane's identity. Hunting MacLane, a dead man, the authorities would thus be misled from the actual target of their search.

Taking turns driving, Drew, Arlene, and Jake reached New York and waited until night before scouting Twelfth Street. The brownstone was not being watched. Drew wasn't surprised; with Uncle Ray gone, Risk Analysis destroyed, and Janus exposed, there'd be no reason for anyone to stake out the house. Neither Drew nor Arlene had given their names to Opus Dei. The fraternity didn't know that Father Stanislaw was dead. Arlene could not be linked to Risk Analysis. Nor to Drew. Nor Drew to her. Going in seemed safe.

But cautious by nature, they entered the brownstone through a building on Eleventh Street, leaving that building's rear, crossing a narrow garden in a walkway where Arlene had once tried unsuccessfully to grow flowers.

The kitchen smelled musty. Arlene opened windows, checked the refrigerator – she'd thrown out anything that would spoil before she'd left to go to Satan's Horn, at the start of her search for Jake – and opened several cans of tuna that she kept in the cupboard.

'You still won't eat meat, huh?' she kidded Drew.

He didn't smile at the tease. 'It's the last habit I kept from the monastery.'

Not quite.

Jake seemed to understand. 'I'd better leave you two alone.'

5

Drew glanced across the table toward Arlene.

'What's wrong?' she asked.

He didn't answer.

'Do I make you nervous?' she asked.

'How could you possibly make me nervous?' He smiled and took her hand.

'Because I made you promise when this was over we'd talk.'

He remembered the promise and sobered. 'Yes, we'd talk.'

'About the future. Us. I don't want you to feel any pressure,' she said. 'I know you have to make a lot of adjustments. After six years in a monastery. But there's something we used to have. To share. It was special. Maybe one day we can have it again.'

'One day,' he echoed dismally.

'Do you want to go back to the monastery? Is that what you're trying to tell me?'

'No. I won't go back. I can't.'

'Can't?'

He couldn't bring himself to explain. He'd promised when this was over they'd talk. But he couldn't subdue his apprehension that this wasn't over. Explain? Ruin what might be their last peaceful moments together? Instead, he walked over, embracing her.

Without a word, they went upstairs to her bedroom.

And at last made love.

He felt no guilt. What Arlene had once said was true: His vow was really one of celibacy, not chastity. Given the Church's attitude toward communal property, a member of a religious order wasn't so much forbidden to have sex as not to marry. The restriction was legal, not moral, to prevent a wife from wanting to share what her husband worked for, the Church's assets.

Otherwise, the restriction was only one of self-denial. And at the moment, weary, heartsick, Drew didn't care about self-denial. It occurred to him that two human beings who chose to give comfort to each other, to ease each other's pain, couldn't possibly be committing wrong.

Naked, his body against hers, feeling her warmth, her lean, lithe, muscular response to his thrusts, her breasts and pelvis returning his thrusts, hard yet soft, demanding yet giving, he felt a completeness in himself.

The feeling was sensual, yes. Erotic, yes. But it was more. For beyond the physical pleasure, this sharing of each other cast away his loneliness, his anguish, his sense of imminent doom. In this long eternal instant, he no longer felt damned.

But eternity was shattered. The present cruelly insisted as Drew heard the phone ring.

He pivoted from Arlene's body, staring toward the phone on the bedside table.

No, not yet! I had things I wanted to say! I wanted to –!

The phone rang again. He felt Arlene's body stiffen next to him.

But I'm not ready! Couldn't they have given us a few more hours together?

The phone rang a third time. Its jangle seemed extra harsh in the gathering silence.

'I'd better answer it,' she said. 'Maybe a neighbor saw the lights and decided to make sure I'm back. We don't want the cops to show up looking for a burglar.'

He nodded in agony.

She picked up the phone. 'Hello?' Her eyes darkened. 'Who? I'm sorry. I don't know anyone with that name . . . Oh, yes, I see. I understand. Since you put it that way.' She pressed a hand across the mouthpiece.

Drew didn't need to ask who it was.

'A man wants to speak to you. I don't understand how he knew you were here. He says he offers you a choice. The easy way, or –'

'I get the point.' Straining to quell his apprehension, Drew took the phone. 'Hello?'

'Brother MacLane' – the voice was deep but smooth; Drew imagined it intoning a mass – 'we'd like to know what happened to Father Stanislaw. He didn't check in with us as scheduled. We know he went to recruit you. We want you to tell us what you did with him. *And with his ring.*'

The room seemed to tilt. 'I can't discuss this over the phone.'

'Of course. Shall we meet in fifteen minutes? At the arch in Washington Square? It's just a few blocks away.'

'I'll be there.'

'We know you will. We're sure you're as anxious as we are to settle any misunderstanding.'

'That's what it is. A misunderstanding.' Swallowing, Drew hung up.

He reached for his clothes.

'Who *was* that?' Arlene asked.

He put on his shirt and pants.

'*Who?*'

'The fraternity.'

She shivered.

'They want to know what happened to Father Stanislaw. They want me to meet them. In Washington Square.'

'But you can't take the risk!'

'I know.' He hugged her, long and hard, feeling her naked body against him. 'If I let them get their hands on me, no matter how I resist, I'll be forced to tell them who killed Father Stanislaw. Jake, not me. And after they've finished with me, they'll come after Jake, maybe even after you. I can't let that happen. Christ, I love you.'

She held him so tightly his injured shoulder throbbed. 'But where will you go?'

'I don't dare answer. In case they use drugs to question you.'

'I'll go with you.'

'And prove you're involved?' Drew shook his head. 'They'd kill you.'

'I don't care!'

'But I do!'

'I'd go *anywhere* for you.'

'To Hell? I'm giving you your life. Next to your soul, that's the greatest gift. Please take it.'

She kissed him, sobbing. 'But when will . . . ?'

Drew understood. 'We see each other again? One day during Lent.'

'What year?'

He didn't know. As a drowning man clutches his saviour, he clung to her.

Then released his grip.

And was gone.

EXILE

Egypt. South of Cairo, west of the Nile.

He wandered into the Nitrian desert, where in A.D. 381 the first Christian hermits, fleeing Rome, had begun monasticism. It hadn't been easy for him to reach this wilderness. Without money or a passport, pursued by the fraternity, he'd needed every trick and wile, every ounce of strength and scrap of determination. His torturous journey had lasted six months, and now as he walked across the sun-parched sand, squinting toward the rocky bluff in the distance where he meant to establish his cell, he felt a great relief, a burden falling away from him. Safe now, away from people, the horrors of civilization, he no longer had to fear for Arlene's safety. All he had to fear for was his soul.

Finding a cave among the rocks, a tiny waterhole nearby, a village a day's walk away where he could buy provisions, he reestablished his routine from the monastery, silently reciting the vespers prayers, recalling the matins service, providing responses to an imaginary celebrant of mass. He meditated.

Rarely he saw another person passing by in the distance. He always hid. But every six weeks – he waited as long as possible – he had to encounter the world when he went to the village for more provisions. On those traumatic occasions, he spoke only as much as was necessary to conduct his business, and the tradesmen, normally fond of haggling, didn't invite conversation. This tall, lean, sunburned man with haunted eyes, his hair grown past his shoulders, his beard hanging down his chest, his robe in rags, was obviously a holy one. They gave him distance and respect.

His days were filled with solitude. But not with peace. As hard as he meditated, he still was often struck by thoughts of Arlene. One day in Lent, he'd vowed, I'll go back to her.

He thought about Jake. And Uncle Ray. And Father Stanislaw. The fraternity. Would they ever stop hunting him? Or was that part of that penance, constantly to be hunted?

Sometimes he remembered his parents. Their deaths. Their graves. Beginnings and ends.

He gazed to the west toward Libya, the madman who ruled it, the terrorists being trained there.

He gazed to the east toward Iraq and Iran, toward Israel and its enemies, toward the Holy Land and the birthplace of assassins and terrorism.

His heart filled with gall.

He had much to think about.

THE LEAGUE OF NIGHT AND FOG

To Paul Seydor
a friend for all seasons

New evils require new remedies . . .
new sanctions to defend and vindicate
the eternal principles of right
and wrong.

The Times (LONDON)
ON THE NUREMBERG TRIALS

Contents

PROLOGUE

FOUR SHADES
OF NIGHT

The Night of
the Long Knives

A phrase invented by the Nazis, the Night of the Long Knives, refers to the events of the night of June 30, 1934, in Austria and Germany. Hitler, having achieved the titles of chancellor and dictator, still needed to gain the remaining position that would give him absolute power over Germany – the presidency. Determined to remove all obstacles, he flew secretly to Munich . . . where, accompanied by his personal bodyguards, he arrested at gunpoint his main rival and former friend, Ernst Röhm. Röhm, the chief of the so-called Brownshirts – a terrorist paramilitary unit of the Nazi party, officially known as *Sturmabteilung* . . . or Storm Troopers, SA for short – had sought to merge his four-hundred-thousand-member force with the German army and consequently (so Hitler alleged) take over Germany. Hitler, anxious not to lose the support of the army, even more anxious to rid himself of competitors, executed Röhm and several ambitious Brownshirt officers.

Not satisfied with half-measures, the Führer decided to eliminate other threats as well. While Röhm and his staff were being shot in Munich, Hitler's close associates Himmler and Göring conducted a similar purge in Berlin. Among those executed were the former chancellor of Germany, unfriendly police and state officials, and dissident executives of the Nazi party. Hitler later claimed that seventy-seven traitors had been killed in order to prevent an overthrow of the German government. Survivors of the purge insisted that the actual number was over four hundred. A postwar trial in Munich raised the total even higher – beyond one thousand.

The significance of the Night of the Long Knives is two-fold. As a consequence of the terror that Hitler created, he did gain the final crucial title of president and, as absolute ruler of Germany, steered his nation toward the obscenities of the Second World War. Beyond that, his use of bodyguards in executing his rivals raised that group to a stature that equaled and eventually surpassed the power of Röhm's paramilitary terrorists. In time, the guards numbered more than a million. Just as Röhm's Brownshirts, *Sturmabteilung* . . . or Storm Troopers, were known as SA, so Hitler's Blackshirts, *Schutzstaffel* . . . or elite guard, were known by their unit's initials. But unlike SA, initials remembered today by few, the initials of the Blackshirts remain synonymous with depravity. The hiss of a snake. The rasp of evil.
SS.

The Night of
Broken Glass

Also known as *Kristallnacht* or Crystal Night, the Night of Broken Glass refers to events on November 9, 1938, throughout Germany. Two days earlier, Herschel Grynszpan, a Polish Jew, assassinated Ernst von Rath, a minor diplomat at the German embassy in Paris, in retaliation for the deportation of Grynszpan's family and 23,000 other Jews from Germany to Poland. Grynszpan's intended target had been the German ambassador to Paris, but von Rath attempted to intervene and was shot instead. Ironically, von Rath had openly criticized Nazi anti-Semitic attitudes and was scheduled for disciplinary action by the Gestapo. No matter – a Jew had killed a German official, and Hitler took advantage of the incident. Publicly claiming that the assassination had prompted anti-Semitic riots throughout Germany, he privately gave orders for the as yet nonexistent riots to occur.

These 'spontaneous demonstrations' were organized by Reinhard Heydrich, second in command of the SS. After Nazi mobs enthusiastically completed their work on the night of November 9, Heydrich was able to give a preliminary report to Hitler that 815 Jewish shops, 171 Jewish homes, and 119 synagogues had been set on fire or otherwise destroyed; twenty-thousand Jews were arrested and sent to concentration camps; thirty-six were killed, another thirty-six critically injured. These figures turned out to be drastically underestimated. So widespread was the destruction that everywhere streets were littered with fragments from shattered windows, hence the expression 'the Night of Broken Glass.'

Concluding his report, Heydrich recommended that

the best course to follow would be for the insurance companies to settle the Jews' claims in full and then confiscate the money and return it to the insurers. My information is that claims for broken glass alone will amount to some five million marks . . . As for the practical matter of cleaning up the destruction, this is being arranged by releasing Jews in gangs from the concentration camps and having them clean up their own messes under supervision. The courts will impose upon them a fine of a billion marks, and this will be paid out of the proceeds of their confiscated property. Heil Hitler!

The Night of Broken Glass represents the start of Germany's undis-

4

guised state-directed pogrom against the Jews. Though many foreign governments – and even some executives within the Nazi party – objected to the atrocities committed on *Kristallnacht*, no one did anything to stop them or to ensure that they weren't repeated and in much worse degree.

The Night
and Fog

The *Nacht und Nebel Erlass* . . . or Night and Fog Decree, one of Hitler's personal edicts, was issued on December 7, 1941, the same day Japan attacked America's naval base at Pearl Harbor. Directed against 'persons endangering German security' and specifically against members of resistance groups in German-occupied territories, it proposed that execution was not itself a sufficient deterrent against anti-German threats. Psychological as well as physical force was necessary. Thus, not all agitators would be killed upon discovery; many instead would be transported to an unknown location, their destiny never to be learned by outsiders. Friends and family members would forever be kept in suspense. As the edict stipulated, 'The intimidating effect of these measures lies (a) in the disappearance without trace of the guilty person, (b) in the fact that no kind of information must be given about the person's whereabouts and his fate.' Those tempted to participate in anti-German activity would fear that they, like their loved ones, would disappear within the night and the fog.

An example of how this decree was carried out occurred in 1942: the fate of the village of Lidice, in Czechoslovakia. In reprisal for the assassination of Reinhard Heydrich, Nazi soldiers surrounded the village and shot every male within it, ten at a time. It took all day before the executions ended. The women of the village were transported to the concentration camp at Ravensbrück in Germany, where they died from weakness or were gassed. But the children of the village, ninety of them, simply vanished into the night and fog. Relatives in other villages could not find a trace of them.

The Dark Night
of the Soul

On January 20, 1942, six weeks after the Night and Fog Decree, Hitler ordered his senior SS officers to attend a special conference in Berlin for the purpose of organizing the Final Solution to what the Führer called 'the Jewish question.' Anti-Semitic riots and laws, intended to force the Jews to leave German territory of their own accord, had been only partially successful – most Jews had been reluctant to leave their homes and businesses. Massive deportations too had been only partially successful – the process took too much time and was too expensive. But now the ultimate extension of Crystal Night was set in motion. Extermination.

Mass executions by firing squad were uneconomical due to the cost of ammunition. A cheaper method, that of cramming victims into trucks and killing them with engine exhaust, was judged unsatisfactory because not enough victims could be asphyxiated at one time. But asphyxiation itself was not at fault. The problem was how to do it efficiently. In the spring of 1942, the death camps began.

These were not the same as concentration camps, where huge numbers of people were squeezed together into squalid barracks from which they were marched each day to factories to work for the German war effort. As a consequence of brutal workloads, insufficient food, and unsanitary conditions, most occupants of the concentration camps did indeed die, but death was not the primary purpose for which prisoners had been sent to these work camps. Slavery was.

The death camps, however, had no other function than to kill with the utmost speed and efficiency. There were killing centers at some concentration camps, Auschwitz and Maidanek for example, but the exclusive death camps numbered only four. All were situated in Poland: Sobibor, Belzec, Chelmno, and Treblinka.

As Treblinka's commandant, Franz Stangl, confessed,

it was Dante's Inferno. The smell was indescribable. The hundreds, no, the thousands of bodies everywhere, decomposing, putrefying. All around the perimeter of the camp, there were tents and open fires with groups of Ukrainian guards and girls – whores, I found out later, from all over the countryside – weaving drunk, dancing, singing, playing music.

In the fifteen months of its existence, from July of 1942 to September

7

of 1943, the camp at Treblinka exterminated one million Jews – a sixth of all Jews murdered in the Holocaust. When the camp was at its most efficient, twenty thousand people were killed each day, a statistic that becomes even more horrible when one realizes that all of these executions occurred in the morning. The rest of the day was devoted to disposing of the bodies by burning them in huge open pits. At night, the flames were allowed to die out, the nauseating smoke to drift away, so the next morning's victims would not be alarmed by the unmistakable stench of incinerated corpses.

2

The victims tumbled from overcrowded cattle cars, relieved to be off the train that had brought them from the Jewish ghetto in Warsaw. Some with whom they'd traveled had smothered or been crushed to death. The survivors tried not to look at the bodies. Instead they squinted at the painful but renewing sunlight, finally able to free their lungs of the poisonous fumes of vomit and excrement.

Signs said TREBLINKA, CASHIER, and TRANSFER HERE FOR EASTBOUND TRAINS. Fear was offset by hope: *this wasn't a camp.* The SS soldiers, with their twin lightning-bolt insignia, were to be expected – though another insignia, a death's head on their caps, aroused apprehension. The clock on the station had hands that were painted on and didn't move. Soldiers blurted commands to enter the railway station, to strip, to proceed to the showers. A shower would be welcome, but the victims wondered why such a luxury was being granted. A guard seemed to read their thoughts: 'We can't stand your filthy stench!'

Herded into the station, they took off their clothes and surrendered their valuables. 'To protect your keepsakes while you're in the shower,' they were told. They were given haircuts, down to the scalp, and this too made them fearful. Guards burst into the station, lashing their victims with whips, chasing them out the back . . . where naked they were urged along a path, which the SS had nicknamed 'the Road to Heaven.' Other guards struck them with clubs. 'Faster! Run *faster!*'

The victims stumbled over fallen companions. At the end of the path, there was only one direction in which to go – to the right, up five concrete steps, through a huge open door. When the last of the group of five hundred had been squeezed inside the chamber, the door was slammed shut and locked. Instead of shower nozzles, there were vents. Outside, an engine roared. Exhaust filled the room. As the victims struggled not to inhale, they didn't realize that they'd been chased so that their lungs would rebel against the attempt not to breathe. They didn't realize that their clothes and valuables would help the Germans fight the war, that their hair would be stuffed inside military mattresses and pillows, that the gold fillings in their teeth would be extracted to pay for guns and ammunition. All they knew was that they couldn't hold their breath any longer. They died standing up.

8

In the pit of brutality, the human spirit managed to triumph. During August of 1943, Jews who'd been forced to do work at Treblinka that even the SS and their Ukrainian assistants couldn't endure – dragging corpses from the gas chambers, arranging them on railway ties in trenches, and setting fire to them – revolted. Using makeshift weapons, they killed their guards and raced toward the nearby forest. Many were strafed by machine guns, but others, possibly as many as fifty, reached the cover of the trees and escaped.

The Nazis abandoned the camp. With the Russians approaching from the east and most of the Jews in Poland already exterminated, the SS hurriedly destroyed the evidence of their obscenities. Treblinka's phony railway station, its Road to Heaven, its gas chambers and incineration pits were all plowed beneath the earth.

A farmer and his cattle were positioned over them. But despite the flames that had charred one million corpses, the victims insisted on bearing witness even in death. The gases from so much decay made the earth heave five feet into the air. The gases dispersed. The earth settled – five feet below its former level. More gases heaved the earth. Again it sank. And rose again.

The cattle fled. So did the farmer.

BOOK ONE

SUMMONS

Icicle

CARDINAL'S DISAPPEARANCE
REMAINS A MYSTERY

ROME, ITALY, February 28 (AP) – Vatican officials and Rome
police remain baffled five days after the disappearance of Cardinal
Krunoslav Pavelic, influential member of the Roman Catholic
Church's administration group, the Curia.

Pavelic, seventy-two, was last seen by close associates after
celebrating a private mass in the chapel of his Vatican living
quarters Sunday evening. On Monday, he had been scheduled
to give the keynote address to a widely publicized conference of
Catholic bishops on the subject of the Church's political relations
with Eastern European communist regimes.

Authorities at first suspected right-wing terrorists of abducting
Cardinal Pavelic to protest a rumoured softening of the Vatican's
attitude toward any communist regime willing to ease restrictions on
Church activities. However, no extremist group has so far claimed
responsibility for Pavelic's disappearance.

2

St Paul, Minnesota. March. For the second time that night, the cards
Frank Miller held became a blur. Though red and black were distinct,
he couldn't tell the difference between a heart and a diamond or a
spade and a club. Trying to subdue his concern, he took off his glasses,
rubbed his eyes, and massaged his aching forehead.

'Something the matter?' Sid Henderson asked across the table from
him. Like Miller, Henderson was in his seventies. Indeed all the bridge
players in this room in the St Paul community service center were
either that old or just slightly younger.

Miller strained to focus on his cards. 'The matter? Nothing.'

'You sure? You look kinda sick.'

'It's too hot in here. They've turned up the thermostat too high.
Somebody ought to open some windows.'

'And give us all pneumonia?' Iris Glickman asked to Miller's right.
She *claimed* she was only sixty-seven. 'It's freezing outside. If you're
hot, take off your suitcoat.'

But Miller had already loosened his tie. He couldn't allow himself to ignore decorum completely and play cards in his shirt-sleeves.

'Maybe you should go home,' Harvey Ginsberg said on the left. 'You're awful pale.'

Miller dabbed his sweaty brow with a handkerchief; his stomach felt queasy. 'You need four players. I'd ruin the game for everybody.'

'Screw the game,' Harvey said.

As usual, Iris pursed her lips in pretended shock at Harvey's vulgar language.

Miller's forehead throbbed. 'You won't think I'm a poor sport?'

'What I'll think, Frank, is you're a damned fool if you're sick and you don't go home.'

Miller smiled. 'Such good friends.'

'I'll call you tomorrow and make sure you're feeling better,' Harvey said.

3

The instant Miller stepped from the hall, an icy wind stung his face. Shocking snow pelted him as he trudged toward the parking lot across the street, clutching his overcoat. At least he didn't feel ill anymore. The gusts revived him, affirming his suspicion that his headache and nausea had been caused by excessive heat inside the hall. He fondly remembered the winters of his youth. Toboggan rides and ice-skate races. My mind's still spry, he thought. It's this damned body that's let me down.

The street was deserted; the arc lamps in the parking lot were shrouded by falling snow. He reached his car – an Audi, a gift from his son – unlocked the driver's door, and heard a voice behind him.

Frowning, he turned, straining to see through the swirling snow. The voice had been muffled by the shriek of the wind. A *man's* voice, he thought, but when he didn't hear it again, he began to wonder if his ears were playing a trick on him.

He shrugged and gripped the latch on his car door. But again he heard the voice behind him, closer, though still not distinct. It seemed to be saying a single word, a first name, *his* first name.

Once more, he turned. 'Is someone there?'

No answer.

He opened the Audi's door.

A hand grasped his shoulder, preventing him from getting in. Another hand slammed the door shut. A third hand spun him with such force that he almost lost his glasses. Three men. The snow obscured their faces.

'Please. I'm old. Take my wallet. But just don't hurt me.'

'Wallet?' One of them laughed.

The snow lessened. When he saw their faces and understood what they really wanted, he despaired.

14

4

Sounds we don't hear can sometimes wake us. So it was that William Miller, unconsciously aware of the silence outside his bedroom windows, began to squirm in his sleep. Like a father whose rest is not complete until his teenage son or daughter comes home from a date that shouldn't have lasted past midnight, he felt uneasy because no car had entered the driveway, no automatic garage door had rattled as it opened and shut. But he wasn't a father who waited for his son. The opposite – a son, who waited for his father. His mental alarm went off. He opened his eyes and blinked at the digital clock beside his bed.

2:38 a.m.

Taking care not to wake his wife, he eased from bed and peered out a window toward the driveway below. A distant streetlight glinted off falling snow. Fir trees were cloaked with white. There weren't any tire tracks in the driveway.

'What's the matter, hon?'

He turned to his wife. 'Sorry. I tried to be quiet.'

'I couldn't sleep either. What are you looking at?'

'It's what I'm *not* looking at that bothers me.'

Miller explained.

'No tire tracks?' She slipped from bed and put on a robe. 'Maybe it snowed after he got in.'

'Yeah . . . maybe.'

He left the bedroom, passed his children's rooms, and reached his father's room at the opposite end of the hallway. When he didn't see a form on the bed, he flicked on the light. The room was empty.

His wife appeared beside him. 'Let's think a minute. This might not mean anything. He might be downstairs asleep in front of the television.'

'Maybe.'

They went downstairs but couldn't find him.

'Car trouble?'

'He'd have phoned,' Miller said.

'Unless he's with a friend.'

'This late? He hardly ever stays out past midnight.'

'I said with a *friend*. He might have decided to spend the night.'

'With a *woman?*'

She smiled. 'Why not?'

'It doesn't make a difference. He'd still have phoned.'

'Unless he felt embarrassed.'

'*What?*'

'You know, with your mother dead a year now and . . .'

'Hey, I loved my mother, and I'm sorry she's gone. But if he's still interested in women at his age, more power to him.'

'Maybe he doesn't know that's how you feel. Have you ever talked about sex with him?'

'With my seventy-three-year-old father? Give me a break.' He

15

studied the kitchen clock. 'It's close to three. If he isn't home by three-thirty, I'm calling the cops.'

But his father *wasn't* home by three-thirty, and Miller did call the cops. No auto accidents involving an Audi had been reported. No old men had been admitted to the local hospitals after midnight, and none of those admitted earlier had been Miller's father. The Audi, covered with snow, was discovered in a parking lot across the street from the community service hall. The keys had been dropped and somehow kicked beneath the car.

But Miller's father was never found.

5

Mexico City. April. Martin Rosenberg, seventy-two, stepped out of the synagogue, tucked his yarmulka into his suitcoat pocket, and surveyed the cobbled street. From two blocks away, the drone of traffic along the Paseo de la Reforma disturbed his sense of tranquillity. To his right, the lights of the ancient castle on Chapultepec hill gleamed against the darkened sky.

He exchanged shaloms with a group of young people coming out of the synagogue and turned left toward a corner. His son's home was five blocks away, one of the historic Spanish mansions interspersed with high-rise apartments in this affluent section of Mexico City. As usual, his son had offered to have him driven to and from the synagogue, but Rosenberg had insisted that walks were essential to his health, and besides, the scenery throughout this district never failed to give him pleasure.

He rounded the corner, proceeding toward the well-lit broad avenue that connected Chapultepec hill with government buildings.

6

'I don't care how old he is!' Aaron Rosenberg said. 'It's never taken him more than an hour to walk back home!' He paced in front of the arched windows that took up one wall of his living room. 'But it's been more than *two* hours, not one!'

With his pencil-thin mustache, aquiline nose, and dark burning eyes, Rosenberg looked more Spanish than Jewish. He seldom went to the synagogue anymore, but he donated generously to it and knew the rabbi, whom he'd telephoned forty-five minutes ago, learning that his father had left the synagogue at dusk.

'Perhaps he stopped to visit with someone,' his wife said. Her face was deeply tanned. Thirty-eight, lithe from daily tennis workouts, she wore a solid-gold watch, a turquoise necklace, and a bright red designer version of a peasant skirt and blouse.

'Who? And surely not for two hours.'

16

He saw the headlights of a Mercedes sedan pulling up at the curb. 'Esteban's come back. Perhaps he's found him.'

But Esteban reported that he'd driven along every route that the father would have used to return from the synagogue. Then he had widened his search to every street within a twenty-block grid. Other servants, having searched on foot, came back with the same disturbing report.

'Go back out again! Keep looking!'

Rosenberg called every hospital in Mexico City. Nothing. At midnight, when the servants again returned without his father, he sacrificed a cardinal rule of his import-export business – never deal with the police except to bribe them – and phoned a captain whose home on Lake Chalco, eight miles south of the city, had recently been renovated thanks to Rosenberg.

One month later, his father had still not been found.

7

Toronto. May. From the window of his first-class seat in the Air Canada 727, Joseph Kessler peered down at the glinting expanse of Lake Ontario. Even at twenty thousand feet, he could see the distinctive length of a Great Lakes freighter. Ahead, close to shore, he saw the smaller outlines of barges, the gleam of wind-swollen sails. Despite the brilliance of the day, Kessler knew that the water would be numbingly cold. The crews of the sailboats down there had to be fanatical about their sport.

He nodded with approval. Because of his own ability to harness his obsessions, he'd developed a small Providence electronics firm into a thriving corporation that had made him a millionaire by the age of forty. But at the moment, his obsession was not related to business. It was personal, fueled by rage.

He didn't allow himself to show it. Throughout the flight, he'd maintained composure, studying business documents while inwardly he seethed. Patience, he told himself. Success depends on patience. Keep control.

For now.

Below, he saw the sprawl of Toronto, its flat residential subdivisions stretching along the lake shore, its skyscrapers projecting from the heart of the city. He felt a change in pressure as the jet began to descend. Six minutes later, it landed at Toronto's international airport.

He went through customs. 'Nothing to declare. I'm here on business.' His briefcase and carry-on bag were not inspected. He proceeded through a sliding glass door into the noisy concourse, scanned the crowd, and approached a muscular man who wore the same blue-and-red striped tie that Kessler did.

'How much did you pay for that tie?' Kessler asked.

'How much did *you* pay?'

'Someone gave it to me.'

'I found mine.' The code completed, the muscular man added, 'Have you got any luggage?'

'Just what I'm carrying.'

'Then let's get out of here.' The man's Canadian accent made 'out' sound like 'oot.'

From the terminal, they entered a parking lot, got into a station wagon, and soon reached a divided four-lane highway, heading west on Highway 401.

Kessler looked behind him toward the receding skyline of Toronto. 'How soon till we get there?'

'An hour.'

'Everyone showed up?'

'You're the last,' the man said.

'Good.' Kessler felt his fury blossom. To distract himself, he pointed toward the farm fields and stands of timber at the sides of the highway. 'Something's missing.'

'What?'

'No billboards.'

'Right. They're against the law.'

'Three cheers for Canada.'

Kessler put on his sunglasses and stared straight ahead. The small talk was over.

8

Eighty kilometers farther, they reached the exit ramp for Kitchener. Instead of entering the city, the driver used side roads to head deep into farm country, finally turning up a zigzag gravel driveway toward a mansion on a bluff above a river.

Kessler stepped from the station wagon and studied the estate – surrounding wooded hills, a nine-hole golf course, a tennis court, a television satellite receiver, a swimming pool. He turned toward the five-car garage, then toward the mansion. With its dormer windows, towers, and gables, it looked like it belonged in New England more than in Ontario.

'Mr Halloway knows how to live well,' the driver said. 'Of course, he owes it all to—'

One of the double doors at the mansion's entrance came open. A lithe man of medium height, wearing a perfectly fitted exercise suit and expensive jogging shoes, stepped out. He was in his early forties, had thick wavy hair, and beamed with health. 'Thank you, John. We won't be needing you for the rest of the day. If you like, you can use that new set of exercise machines in the gym. Have a steam bath. A drink. Relax.'

'I appreciate it, Mr Halloway.'

The driver got in the station wagon. Halloway came down the granite front steps and held out his hand. 'Joe? Or is it . . . ?'

'Joseph.' Kessler shook hands with him.

'We've been a long time meeting. With so much in common, it's a pity we had to wait for misfortune to bring us together.'

'Misfortune's not exactly what I'd call it.'

'What then?'

'Fucking insanity.'

'The nature of the world. That's why I prefer to live out here. Away from the madness.' Grimacing, Halloway gestured toward the road hidden beyond the wooded hills. 'Come. The others feels as distressed as ourselves. They're waiting.'

9

The mansion's foyer was shadowy; its slate floor emphasized the click of their footsteps. Still needing to calm himself, Kessler paused to examine a colorful landscape painting. The artist's signature was Halloway.

'My father's,' Halloway said. 'His acrylic period.'

The reference to Halloway's father rekindled Kessler's indignation. Down the hall, he heard angry voices and, preceded by Halloway, entered a large oak-paneled room where eight men interrupted their fierce discussion to look at him.

Kessler studied them in return. They were of different heights, weights, and facial structures, but they shared one physical characteristic: their ages fit within the same narrow range, late thirties, early forties.

'It's about time,' one said.

Two others spoke in rapid succession.

'I've been here since yesterday.'

'This meeting was supposed to be urgent!'

'My flight got delayed,' Kessler told them. 'I came as soon as I could.'

The three men who'd spoken had accents – Spanish, Swedish, and American midwestern. Coming down the hall, Kessler had heard other accents – French, British, Italian, Egyptian, and American southern.

'Gentlemen, please,' Halloway said. 'If we start to argue among ourselves, we help the enemy achieve the second half of his purpose.'

'*Second* half?' The Frenchman frowned.

'And what do you mean "his"?' the Texan asked. '*One* man couldn't have done this!'

'Of course,' Halloway said. 'But no matter how many, they're organized, and they share a common goal. That's why I think of them as one and why *we* have to act as one.'

'It's true,' the Italian said. 'We can't allow ourselves to be distracted by our frustrations. We mustn't be divided. Isn't that why we got in touch with each other so many years ago and why we *stayed* in touch?

19

Because as a group we're stronger than each of us is alone. We can better protect ourselves.'

'But we're not the ones who need protecting!' the Spaniard said.

'Not physically perhaps,' Halloway said. 'At least not yet. But in our hearts? And suppose they're not satisfied? Suppose they decide to come for *us* now, our wives, our children?'

The others straightened.

'That's what I meant by the second half of our enemy's purpose. It's to torture us with uncertainty, to make us suffer from constant dread.'

'Dear God.' The Egyptian paled.

'You understand?'

'It's the Night and Fog all over again.'

Kessler couldn't restrain himself. 'What's the matter with all of you?'

They stared at him.

'Before you pat yourselves on the back about how smart you were to stay in touch with each other, why don't you admit you've been your own worst enemy?'

'What are you talking about?'

'How do you think they found us? All they had to do was track down just one and follow the trail to the rest.'

'We took precautions.'

'Obviously not well enough. And look at us now. All together.'

The American midwesterner stepped forward, his features twisted with resentment. 'My father would never have told.'

'Under torture? Come on,' Kessler said. 'How much pain can an old man stand? Or what if chemicals were used? I was late because I almost didn't come at all. The reason I did was to warn you. You're as much to blame as whoever did this. Don't stay in touch with each other. I don't want to know anything more about you, and I don't want you to know anything more about me.'

'That won't solve the problem,' Halloway said. 'We'd still be in danger, and it doesn't bring our fathers back.'

'I've already accepted the fact – mine's dead.'

'I don't give up as easily as you,' Halloway said. 'But what if you're right? What if your father and mine and everybody else's are dead? Do you intend to let the matter end?'

'Oh, believe me, I want the bastards to pay.'

'In that case, we have plans to discuss.'

Kessler stepped quickly forward. 'You have something specific?'

'Indeed. It may be you didn't notice. You weren't the only member of the group who had second thoughts about coming. Two of us in fact declined. In many respects, the most important members.'

Kessler glanced at the group in confusion and suddenly understood.

'Given what I intend to propose, their participation is crucial,' Halloway said.

Kessler nodded.

Seth and Icicle.

Sydney, Australia. June. St Andrew's Cathedral, the foundation of
which had been set in 1819, was as impressive as the guidebook
maintained. Kessler roamed the shadows of its echoing interior,
studied its vaulted ceiling, admired its stained-glass windows, and
strolled outside. Squinting in the painfully brilliant sunlight, he
descended a wide tier of steps to the sidewalk. Next to the cathedral here on George Street, he reached the town hall, used for
concerts and assembly meetings, his guidebook explained. After
lingering as long as seemed appropriate, he strolled to the corner, hailed a taxi, and proceeded to one of the many Oriental
restaurants that Sydney was famous for. He'd arranged to meet
his business connection there, but he arrived deliberately early,
went to a phone booth, and dialed the number Halloway had
given him.

A male voice answered. 'Bondi Beach Surf and Dive Shop.'

'Mr Pendleton, please.'

'The son or the father?'

'It doesn't matter.'

'I'm the son.'

'Mr Pendleton, do you have icicles in Australia?'

For a moment, the silence was so intense that Kessler thought the
phone had gone dead. 'Mr Pendleton?'

'Who *is* this?'

'A friend.'

'I've got customers waiting. I rent and sell surfboards. I sell and fill
scuba tanks. Icicles I don't need. Or people with stupid questions.'

'Wait. Perhaps if I mentioned a name. Thomas Conrad. Post office
box four thirty-eight.'

Again the line was silent. When Pendleton finally spoke, his voice
sounded muffled, as if he'd cupped a hand to his mouth. 'What do
you want?'

'A meeting. It's obvious if I meant you harm, I didn't need to call.
I wouldn't have put you on guard.'

'You're from *them*, aren't you?'

'My name is Kessler.'

'Christ, I made it clear. I want nothing to do with—'

'Things have happened. Circumstances have forced me to come
here.'

'You're in *Sydney*? Mother of God!'

'I'm using a pay phone in a restaurant. I've never been here before.
This call can't possibly be overheard or traced.'

'But you know my name, where to reach me! If you're picked
up . . . !'

'I was careful not to be followed.'

'Careful?' Pendleton's voice was contemptuous. 'If you're so sure you weren't followed, you wouldn't have called me. You'd have come here.'

'I didn't want to risk surprising you in person. If I seemed a threat, I might not have had the chance to explain.'

Pendleton swore.

'I've tried to show good faith,' Kessler said. 'Please, we need to meet. The sooner we talk, the sooner I'm out of the country.'

'Not here.'

'Not at the shop? Of course. I wouldn't want to put you in danger.'

'Don't write this down,' Pendleton said. 'At four this afternoon . . .'

11

The instructions completed, Pendleton set down the phone. He'd kept his voice low. His assistant, waiting on a customer at the front of the store, could not have heard. Even so, he felt threatened. To be contacted so directly broke one of the most sacred rules he'd ever learned. God save me from amateurs. He stepped from his office, passed a row of scuba tanks, and pretended an interest in his assistant's customer.

'That wetsuit's the top of the line. You shouldn't have trouble keeping warm in it,' Pendleton told the customer. 'Any problems, if the fit seems wrong, make sure you come back and tell us. We'll make it right.' Though he and his father had come to Australia almost ten years ago, Pendleton still retained American patterns of speech. The local beach hogs thought him quaint; he liked it that way. Invisibility was sometimes better achieved by standing out. As a local character, he created the illusion of being ever-present, except for occasional diving expeditions, his absences easily explained.

He waved goodbye to the customer, patted his assistant on the back – 'Nice big sale' – and returned to his office, stepping out the back door. Even in the off-season, Bondi Beach was surprisingly crowded. Tourists. A few diehard surfers. Some muscle-bound gays on the make. In his terrycloth pullover, faded jeans, and canvas deck shoes (no belt, no shoelaces, no socks), Pendleton looked like a beach hog himself. Overaged, granted. But even at forty, with his sun-bleached windblown hair, his deeply tanned face, and his iron-hard shoulders and chest, he could give the beach hogs competition if he wanted to. Not that he'd ever show off his full skills.

He scanned the activity on the beach and saw his father waxing a surfboard, talking to teenagers gathered around him, holding court.

Pendleton's eyes crinkled with affection. He stepped from the deck at the back of the dive shop, crossed the sand, and reached his father.

Waves lapped the shore. The cool wind smelled salty. Pendleton waited respectfully while his father described to his audience an astonishing series of waves five years ago. His father – as tall as

Pendleton, as muscular, and, even at seventy-two, wrinkled by age and ten years of sun, almost as ruggedly handsome – glanced at him.

'A minor problem's come up, Dad. I need to talk to you.'

His father sighed in mock frustration. 'If it's really necessary.'

'I'm afraid it is.'

'I'll be back, lads.'

Pendleton walked with his father toward the shop. 'A contact from your former friends just phoned me. He's here in town.'

His father's sigh was genuine now. 'I told those fools to stay away from me. I never approved of maintaining contact. If it weren't for the priest. I should have anticipated the problem and solved it years ago.'

'The contact wanted a meeting. It sounded like an emergency.'

'It must have been for someone to come all this way. The planet isn't big enough to hide in.'

'The letter they sent last month . . .'

'Demanding a meeting in Canada.' Pendleton's father scoffed. 'Do they think I'm a fool?'

'It seems that they're the fools. But I have no choice now. To keep him from coming to the shop, I have to meet with him somewhere else.'

'For the first and last time. Make sure he understands that.'

'What I wanted to tell you . . . While I'm gone, be careful.'

'Icicle's always careful.'

'I know.' Pendleton smiled and hugged him.

12

Entering Sydney's Botanic Gardens precisely at four as instructed, Kessler felt nervous. He suspected he hadn't been convincing when he'd used sudden illness as his motive for leaving his business meeting in the middle of delicate negotiations. Though business was hardly the reason he'd come to Australia, it was what he believed was called his 'cover.' Of the group that had met in Canada, he had the best excuse for traveling to Sydney without attracting attention. But now, by interrupting negotiations for a long-sought merger between his electronics firm and one in Sydney, he'd attracted the attention he'd hoped to avoid. In retrospect, he wished that he'd insisted to Pendleton that their meeting take place later, but on the other hand, Pendleton had been so reluctant to meet that Kessler was in no position to make demands.

As he proceeded along a path rimmed by exotic plants, Kessler worried that, despite his precautions in coming here, he'd been followed. Not just to these gardens but all the way from America. I'm a businessman, not an expert in intrigue, he thought. Perhaps my father would know – he almost changed the tense to 'would have known' but tried to be hopeful – would know how to conduct himself in this sort of situation, but I was never trained for it.

Still, he didn't think he could go wrong if he used his common sense. Don't look around to see if you're being watched. The recent disappearances had demonstrated that the enemy was remarkably organized and skillful. A 'tail' – he allowed himself what he believed was the correct melodramatic expression – surely wouldn't be careless enough to let him know he was being followed. He'd made sure to bring his guidebook along. Though the nape of his neck itched from the strain of resisting the impulse to look back down the path, he forced himself to peer at the guidebook and then at the abundant plants before him. The path led upward. He reached a bench flanked by shrubs and paused, facing west, apparently to survey a building that his book explained was Government House, the home of the governor for New South Wales. His actual motive for pausing, though, was to obey the instructions Pendleton had given him.

Pendleton was another reason Kessler felt nervous. In his prime, Pendleton's father, Icicle, had been one of the most feared men in Europe. Though Icicle would now be in his seventies, there wasn't any reason to assume he wasn't still dangerous. Rumor had it – Halloway was the source – that Icicle's son was equally to be respected, trained by his father. This meeting, exposed, in a public place obviously chosen for its cover and its many escapes routes, could pose a danger from Icicle's son as much as from the enemy.

As instructed, Kessler sat on the bench. From the far side of shrubs where the path curved around and continued, he heard the voice of the man he'd spoken to on the phone.

'All right, so you've got your meeting. Make it quick.'

Kessler's instinct was to turn toward the bushes, but the voice anticipated him.

'Look straight ahead. Keep staring toward Government House. If anybody comes along, shut up. And this better be important.'

Kessler swallowed. He started explaining.

13

On the bench on the opposite side of the bushes, wearing jogging clothes, wiping his sweaty forehead as if exhausted and needing a rest, Pendleton peered north toward the State Conservatorium of Music. Its design dated back to 1819, and Pendleton wished that he lived in that simpler time. No instant satellite communications. No computer files. No jets that made Australia no longer a hard-to-reach outpost. 'The planet isn't big enough to hide in,' his father had said. Of course, the obverse was that without those modern conveniences of communication and travel, he and his father would not have been able to practice their trade.

His face hardened as Kessler, unseen behind the bushes, explained. '*What? All of them? Disappeared?* For God's sake, why didn't the message you sent make that clear?'

'I didn't draft the message,' Kessler said. 'It seemed obscure to me as well, but I understood the need for caution. Since my own father had disappeared, the reference to "recent losses" made me realize the implications.'

'Implications?' Pendleton's voice, though low, had the force of a shout. 'We thought the message meant that some of my father's old acquaintances had died! We thought we were being invited to a wake! We didn't come all the way to Australia to risk exposing ourselves by going to Canada for toasts and tears!'

'Then your father's all right?'

'No thanks to you! Coming all this way! Maybe letting our hunters follow you!'

'The risk seemed necessary.'

'*Why?*'

'Just a moment. Someone's coming.'

Pendleton debated whether to stay or disappear.

'Two kids and a dog. They went up a fork in the path. It's fine,' Kessler said.

'Answer me. *Why did you come?* We made it clear we want nothing to do with the rest of you.'

'Halloway told me that's what you'd say. I'm aware, Icicle was never known for being sociable. But the group insisted.'

'Despite our wishes? At the risk of endangering . . . ?'

'With a proposition,' Kessler said. 'If Icicle feels no nostalgia for his former friends, no sense of kinship in mutual adversity, then maybe he – or you – can be swayed by a different motive.'

'I can't imagine . . .'

'Money. The group's been financially successful. We have resources. You and your father – we know what you are, what you do. We're willing to pay you handsomely to find out what happened to our fathers. And if' – Kessler's voice become hoarse – 'God help me for thinking it let alone saying it, if they're dead, we want you to be our revenge.'

'*That's* what this is all about? You came all this way to *hire* me?'

'We don't know what else to do.'

'No, it's impossible. I can't.'

'The fee . . .'

'You don't understand. You could offer a fortune, it wouldn't matter. It's too risky.'

'But under the circumstances . . . old friends . . .'

'And lead the enemy to us, as you maybe have? I'm leaving.' Pendleton stood. 'Tell them no.'

'I'm at the Captain Cook Lodge! Think about it! Change your mind!'

'I won't.' Pendleton started to walk away.

'Listen to me!' Kessler said. 'There's something else you should know!'

Pendleton hesitated.

'Cardinal Pavelic!' Kessler said.

'What about him?'

'He disappeared as well.'

25

His chest aching, Pendleton rushed down a sandy slope toward Bondi Beach. It was half past five. His jogging suit clung to him. He'd switched taxis several times to elude possible surveillance. When the final taxi had been caught in a traffic jam near the beach, he'd paid the driver and run ahead.

He had much to fear. Not just the risk that Kessler's arrival had posed. Or the disturbing information that the priest had disappeared. What truly bothered him was that his own father might vanish as the others had. Icicle had to be warned.

But when he'd called from a phone booth near the gardens, he'd received no answer either at the dive shop or at the ocean-bluff home he shared with his father. He told himself that his assistant must have closed the shop early, though that had never happened before. He tried to convince himself that his father had not yet returned home from the beach, though his father never failed to get home in time to watch the five o'clock news. Closer to Bondi Beach, he'd phoned the shop again; this time his call had been interrupted by a recorded announcement telling him that line was out of order. His stomach felt as if it were crammed with jagged glass.

He reached the bottom of the sandy slope and blinked through sweat-blurred vision toward a line of buildings that flanked the ocean. Normally, he'd have had no trouble identifying his dive shop among the quick-food, tank-top, and souvenir stores, but chaotic activity now obscured it. Police cars, a milling crowd, fire engines, swirling smoke.

His pulse roaring behind his ears, he pushed through the crowd toward the charred ruin of his shop. Attendants wheeled a sheet-covered body toward an ambulance. Ducking past a policeman who shouted for him to stop, Pendleton yanked the sheet from the corpse's face. The ravaged features were a grotesque combination of what looked like melted wax and scorched hamburger.

A policeman tried to pull him away, but Pendleton twisted angrily free, groping for the corpse's left hand. Though the fingers had been seared together, it was clear that the corpse was not wearing a ring. Pendleton's assistant had not been married. But Pendleton's father, though a widower, always wore his wedding ring.

He no longer resisted the hands that tugged him from the stretcher. 'I thought it was my father.'

'You belong here?' a policeman asked.

'I own the place. My *father*. Where's—?'

'We found only one victim. If he's not your father—'

Pendleton broke away, running through the crowd. He had to get to the house! Inhaling acrid smoke, he darted past a police car, veered between buildings, and charged up a sandy slope. The stench of scorched flesh cleared from his nostrils. The taste of copper spurted into his mouth.

The home was on a bluff a quarter-mile away, a modernistic sprawl of glass and redwood. Wind-ravaged trees surrounded it. Only as he raced closer did he realize the danger he himself might be in.

He didn't care. Bursting through the back door, he listened for voices from the television in the kitchen where his father always watched while drinking wine and preparing supper. The kitchen was silent, the stove turned off.

He yelled for his father, received no answer, searched the house, but found no sign of him.

He grabbed the phone book in his father's bedroom, quickly paged to the listing for the Captain Cook Lodge, and hurriedly dialed. 'Put me through to Mr Kessler's room.'

'One moment . . . I'm sorry, sir. Mr Kessler checked out.'

'But he couldn't have! *When?*'

'Let me see, sir. Four o'clock this afternoon.'

Shuddering, Pendleton set down the phone. His meeting with Kessler had been at four, so how could Kessler have checked out then?

Had Kessler been involved in his father's disappearance? No. It didn't make sense. If Kessler were involved, he wouldn't have announced his presence; he wouldn't have asked for a meeting. Unless . . .

The suspicion grew stronger.

Kessler might have been a decoy, to separate father and son, to make it easier to grab Icicle.

Of course, there was an alternate explanation, but Pendleton didn't feel reassured. Someone else could have checked Kessler out, the checkout permanent. To spread the reign of terror. In that case, Pendleton thought, the next logical victim ought to be . . .

Me.

Professional habits took over. He withdrew his father's pistol from a drawer, made sure it was loaded, then went to his own room and grabbed another pistol. He searched the house again, this time more thoroughly, every alcove, not for his father now but for an intruder.

The phone rang. He swung toward it, apprehensive; hoping it was his father, he picked it up. The caller broke the connection.

His muscles became like concrete. Wrong number? An enemy trying to find out if I'm home?

He had to assume the worst. Quickly he took off his jogging suit and put on warm woolen outdoor clothes. Dusk cast shadows. Creeping from the house, he reached a nearby bluff from which he could watch every approach to the building.

Timer lights flicked on. The phone rang again; he could hear it faintly. After two rings, it stopped. Before he'd left the house, he'd turned on his answering machine, which now would instruct the caller to leave a message. Though desperate to know if the call was from his father, he couldn't risk going back to the house to listen to the tape. He'd anticipated this problem, however, and brought a cordless phone

27

with him, leaving it turned off so that it wouldn't ring and reveal his position on this bluff. But now he switched the phone on. As if he'd picked up an extension within the house, he heard the end of the machine's request for a name and number. But as before, the caller simply hung up.

A police car arrived, presumably because of the fire at the shop, though maybe this wasn't a real police car. An officer knocked on the door and tried to open it, but Pendleton had left it locked. The officer went around to the back door, knocked and tested it as well, then drove away. No one else approached the house.

His father had disappeared! Just like all the other fathers. But unlike the sons of those fathers, Pendleton wasn't typically second-generation, wasn't an amateur. Icicle had trained him well. *One day, the enemy will return,* his father had warned.

Indeed it had. And taken his father.

So now it's my turn! Pendleton inwardly shouted. He'd refused the job the other sons had offered him because he had to avoid attracting attention to his father. But avoiding attention no longer mattered. I'll do it! he thought. But this isn't business! This is personal!

If my father isn't back by tomorrow, after forty years you bastards will finally get what's coming to you!

For Icicle!

For me!

The Return of
the Warrior

North of Beersheeba. Israel. Hearing a sudden rattle of gunfire, Saul threw his shovel to the ground, grabbed his rifle, and scrambled from the irrigation ditch. He'd been working in this field since dawn, sweating beneath the blaze of the sun as he extended the drainage system he'd constructed when he first came to this settlement almost three years ago. His wife, Erika, had been pregnant then, and both of them had been anxious to escape the madness of the world, to find a sanctuary where the futility of their former profession seemed far away. Of course, they'd realized that the world would not let them ever escape, but the illusion of escape was what mattered. In this isolated village where even the conflict between Jews and Arabs was remote, they'd made a home for themselves and the baby – Christopher Eliot Bernstein-Grisman – who'd been born soon after.

The villagers had commented on the boy's unusual name. 'Part Christian, part Jewish? And why the hyphen at the end?'

Bernstein was Erika's last name, Grisman Saul's. Christopher had been his foster brother, an Irish-Catholic with whom he'd been raised in an orphanage in Philadelphia. Eliot had been their foster father, the sad-eyed gray-faced man who always wore a black suit with a rose in his lapel, who'd befriended Chris and Saul, been the only person to show them kindness, and recruited them for intelligence work, specifically to be assassins. In the end, their foster father had turned against them, Chris had been killed, and Saul had killed Eliot.

The bitterness Saul still felt over what had happened – the grief, disgust, and regret – had been his main motive for wanting to escape from the world. But love for his foster brother and indeed, despite everything, for Eliot had prompted him to want to name the baby after the two most important men in his life. Erika, understanding, had agreed. Generous, wonderful Erika. As graceful as an Olympic gymnast. As beautiful as a fashion model – tall, trim, and elegant with high strong cheeks and long dark hair. As deadly as himself.

The sound of gunfire scorched his stomach. Racing frantically toward the village, his first thought was that he had to protect his son. His second was that Erika could protect the boy as well as he could. His third was that, if anything happened to either of them, he'd never rest till their killers paid.

Though he hadn't been in action since he'd come to Israel, old instincts revived. Some things apparently could never be forgotten.

29

He leapt a stone wall and neared the stark outline of the village, making sure that dust hadn't clogged the firing mechanism or the barrel of his rifle. Though he always kept it loaded, he inspected the magazine just to be certain. Hearing screams, he chambered a round and dove behind a pile of rocks.

The shots became louder, more frequent. He stared at outlying cinder-block buildings and saw strangers wearing Arab combat gear who fired from protected vantage points toward the homes at the center of the village. Women dragged children down alleys or into doorways. And old man lurched to the ground and rolled from repeated impacts as he tried to reach a young girl frozen with fright in the middle of the street. The girl's head blew apart. An invader tossed a grenade through an open window. The blast spewed smoke and wreckage. A woman shrieked.

Sons of bitches! Saul aimed from behind a pile of rocks. He counted six targets, but the volume of gunfire told him that at least six other invaders were on the opposite side of the village. The shots increased, other rifles joining the fight. But the sound of these weapons was different from the characteristic stutter of the Kalashnikovs that the invaders were using and that he himself used, preferring a weapon whose report would blend with that of the type Israel's enemies favored. No, the rifles that now joined the fight had the distinctive crackle of M-16s, the available weapon that Saul had taught the teenagers of the village to shoot.

An invader fell, blood pouring from his back. The five remaining terrorists on Saul's side of the village directed their aim toward a corrugated-metal shed from which the volley had come. The shed quivered, dozens of holes appearing along its side. The M-16 became silent.

But others, from different buildings, sought vengeance. Another invader spurted blood, falling. Saul eased his finger onto the trigger, smoothly absorbed the recoil, and disintegrated an invader's spine. He switched his aim, hit another target, this time in the skull, and scrambled from the pile of rocks, firing as he ran.

Another enemy fell. Caught in a crossfire, the remaining Arab glanced backward and forward, sprinted toward a low stone wall, and halted in astonishment as Saul's favorite student popped up, firing at point-blank range, blowing his enemy's face apart. A mist of blood hovered over the falling body.

Using the cover of ditches and walls that he and his students had constructed to provide defensive positions, Saul charged toward the opposite side of the village. At the corners of his vision, he noticed his students spreading out and heard the crackle of other M-16s, the answering stutter of more Kalashnikovs. A second grenade exploded within the building already partially destroyed by the first. This time, as a wall erupted, Saul heard no shrieks. With doubled fury, he completed the semicircle that brought him to the other group of invaders. He emptied his magazine, reloaded, emptied the new magazine, grabbed a Kalashnikov that a retreating Arab had dropped, emptied it, picked up an M-16 that his second-favorite student had dropped when dying, emptied it, and outraced a terrorist whose hand-to-hand combat skills were no match for the killer-instinct training that Saul had received twenty years ago. Using the palm of one hand, then the other, lunging with all his force, he drove the enemy's rib cage into his heart and lungs.

The gunfire stopped. Saul squinted toward the enemy at his feet. His students, excited by victory, gathered around him.

'No! Don't form a crowd! Split up! Take cover! We don't know if we got them all!'

He followed his own directive and dove toward a ditch. But he cursed himself for being so right. He told himself that his soul was doomed for being professional. He tried to remind himself that the good of the village came first. In a culture barely hanging on, individuals had to come second. Here, sacrifice was the norm. But he desperately wanted to know about Erika and his son.

Forced to set a good example, he divided his students into groups and methodically scoured the village. Cautiously, he approached and checked every enemy corpse. Despising himself for being irresponsible, he supervised the search of intact buildings, verifying that no invader hid within them. He organized assessment teams – ten villagers dead, fifteen wounded.

'Where's the medic squad? Communications, did you radio an SOS to the base at Beersheeba?'

Only when every emergency procedure had been followed, when every precaution had been taken, did he allow his humanity to assert itself. And knew again that he was doomed. His former life had intruded, controlling him. Responding to the rote with which he'd been trained, he'd behaved correctly. And from another perspective, completely, absolutely, the correctness was wrong. He'd allowed his public duties to overwhelm his private needs.

The building that had received the most gunfire, that had erupted from two grenade blasts, was his own. As villagers and students surrounded him, in awe of his control, deeply respectful, he finally absolved himself of his public function. Tears streaking down his cheeks, he stalked toward the ruined building, the refuge of his wife and child. The right wall had toppled outward. On that side, the roof had collapsed, its angle bizarre.

When the first grenade had exploded, he'd heard a woman shriek. Apprehensive, he peered through what had been the window but was now just a wide jagged hole. The curtains were blackened and tattered. To his left, he saw the remnants of a toy wooden truck he'd made for his son. Next to it lay shattered plates, fallen from a shelf that no longer existed. The ruins of a table almost covered them. He smelled burnt wood, scorched cloth, and melted plastic. The fallen roof obscured his view of the central part of the kitchen.

He reached the door, which came off its hinges as he touched it, and swallowing sickly, stepped inside. He moved slowly, suddenly fearful of what he might step on, afraid of desecrating twisted limbs

31

and – he hated to think about it – dismembered portions of bodies. He shoved away a sheet of metal, lifted a wooden beam, stepped over what used to be a chair, but he saw no blood, and hope made his heart beat faster.

He tugged at a section of roof, throwing it out the open doorway, stooping, hefting more rubble. Still he found no blood. He heaved against the section of roof that leaned down into the kitchen, budged it far enough to expose the only part of the room that he hadn't been able to see, and squinted at shadows.

He saw no bodies. The well-disguised trapdoor broke two of his fingernails as he clawed at it. Fingers bloody, hefting the trapdoor against a wall, he stared into the murky chamber below him.

'Erika!'

The pit absorbed his voice, giving off no echo.

'Erika! It's Saul!'

Too impatient to wait for an answer, he squirmed down, his shoes touching earth four feet below him. 'It's over.'

He strained his eyes to penetrate the darkness. For a desperate instant, he suspected he was wrong, then suddenly realized he hadn't given the all-clear signal. An enemy might try to mimic his voice. In this darkness, the trick might work. 'Baby Ruth and roses.'

'Lover, it's about time you said that. You had me worried. I was trying to decide if I should shoot you.' Erika's deep sensual voice came reassuringly from the rear of the chamber. 'I hope you gave them hell.'

He couldn't help it; he laughed. 'Jews aren't supposed to believe in hell.'

'But under certain conditions, it's a wonderful concept. For attacking this village, *our home*, I hope the bastards roast.'

In the dark, his son asked, 'Daddy?'

'It's me, son. You don't need to worry. But, Erika, watch your language in front of the boy, huh?'

'You'll hear a lot worse if you don't tell me what took you so long.'

He tried to interpret her tone; his best guess was that she was joking.

'The shooting stopped a while ago,' she said. 'What did you do, stop off for a drink?'

Because Erika knew that Eliot had conditioned him to abstain from alcohol, Saul was sure now that she was joking, and slumping with relief, not only because she and the boy were safe but because she wasn't angry with him for being so inhumanly professional, he couldn't subdue his tears.

Shoes scraped against dirt. Bodies squirmed along the earthen tunnel.

'Saul?' Erika's voice was close and resonant, concerned, against his ear.

'Daddy?'

'Son, I'm fine. I just . . .' Sorrow cramped his throat, choking his voice.

32

Erika's strong arm hugged him. 'What's wrong, Saul?'

'I . . .' Wiping his eyes, he struggled to explain. 'We killed them all. But if . . .' He mustered his strength. 'If I'd run here right away, if I'd looked out only for us, for you and Chris, then everything I tried to teach those kids in the village . . . every principle about the group being more important than the individual . . . would have seemed a lie. The next time we were attacked, they'd have looked out for themselves instead of . . .'

In the dark, Chris nuzzled against him.

Erika hugged him tighter. 'You're a dope.'

Surprised, he stifled his tears. 'What?'

'We're professionals. Or used to be. We both know what combat means. Personal needs are a luxury. If the group doesn't defend itself, no family has a chance. The minute the shooting started, I grabbed Chris with one hand and this Uzi with the other. I told myself that if you were still alive, you'd do what the rules required – and so would I. Which in my case meant hiding our son and protecting him. And which in *your* case meant doing your best to protect the village. There's no need for tears. I dearly love you. *My* job was to guard the family, *yours* to defend the group. I've got no complaints. If anything, I'm proud of you. We did it right.'

Saul had trouble breathing. 'I love you.'

'After the village calms down, when we organize a sentry schedule and it gets dark and we put Chris to bed, I'd be glad for you to show me how much.'

2

Twenty minutes later, an Israeli combat helicopter circled the rocky fields around the village, checking for other invaders. Two trucks filled with soldiers jounced along a potholed road and stopped at the outskirts. Their eyes reminding Saul of hawks, the soldiers scrambled down, scanned the devastation, and snapped to attention while a captain gave them orders. Well-trained, strongly disciplined, they established defensive positions in case of another attack. A squad searched the pockets of the enemy corpses.

A hot wind blew dust.

The captain, his face like a shale slope furrowed with gulleys, came over to Saul. 'Your radio team said the attack had been subdued.' He gestured toward the bodies. 'Isn't "crushed" more accurate?'

'Well' – Saul shrugged – 'they pissed off.'

'Apparently.' The captain lit a cigarette. 'The way I hear it, the last thing anyone should want to do is piss you off. It's Grisman, right? Saul Grisman? American? Former CIA?'

'That gives you a problem?'

'Not after what just happened. This must be Erika.'

Saul turned. He hadn't heard Erika come up behind him.

'Christopher's next door,' she said. 'He's still afraid, but he promised

33

he'd close his eyes and try to sleep. He's being watched.' She faced the captain.

'You were with the Mossad,' the captain said to her. 'I'm surprised this village isn't boring for you.'

'Today it certainly hasn't been.'

The captain cocked his head toward the teenagers holding M-16s. 'Where are the men?'

'In the military,' she said. 'Or Jerusalem, or Tel Aviv. This is a village of widows, orphans, and deserted wives. It was barely hanging on when we got here.'

'But that's what we wanted,' Saul said. 'A place on the edge of the world. So we decided to improve the civil defense.'

'You're telling me these *kids*, with some help from you, took care of this team?'

'All they needed was a little encouragement.' Grinning, Saul hugged the two nearest teenagers.

'My source says that *you*,' the captain told Saul, 'had a reason for wanting to get away from it all.'

'Did he say what my reason was?'

The captain shook his head.

'Allergies.'

'Sure. My source also said that *you*,' he told Erika, 'could have stayed in Israeli intelligence. Your record was clean. So you didn't have to come here.'

'Wrong,' she said. 'I had the best reason possible.'

'What?'

'To be with him.' She gestured toward Saul.

The captain drew on his cigarette. 'Fine. What happened here – I have a few problems about it.'

'I know,' Saul answered. 'So do I.'

'For starters, this team wasn't just a bunch of amateurs. They're well armed. Soviet weapons. It wasn't impromptu – they'd planned the attack, six approaching this side of the village, the other six the other. That number of men, it isn't easy, it takes a lot of determination, and a damned good reason, to try to sneak past our border defenses. A village in contested territory, I could see them trying for it. A strategic target – let's say an air base, a munitions site – a risky surprise attack would make sense. But a village of widows, orphans, and deserted wives? Fifty miles from the border? *What's going on?*'

'Don't think it hasn't worried me,' Saul said.

3

At sunset, a dusty sedan arrived. Outside the ruin of what had been home, facing a small fire fueled by the wreckage he'd carried out, Saul heard the engine as he ate rehydrated chicken noodle soup and watched Erika spoon the broth to Christopher's mouth.

Glancing up, he saw soldiers step from cover and gesture for the driver to stop at the edge of the village. The car was too far away, its windshield too dusty, for Saul to see who sat behind the steering wheel. The soldiers spoke to someone inside, examined the documents they were handed, and turned toward the village, pointing the driver in Saul's direction. The car approached.

Saul stood. 'Do you recognize it?'

Erika peered at the car and shook her head. 'Do you?'

'This village is getting too crowded.'

The car stopped twenty feet away. Villagers watched suspiciously from open doors. The driver shut off the engine. Something wheezed beneath the hood. A man got out.

He was six feet tall, thin, his shoulders bent slightly forward. He wore a rumpled suit, the top button of his shirt open, his tie hanging loose. He had a mustache, a receding hairline. Saul guessed that he was in his late thirties, and sensed that his thinness was due to enormous energy held in check, constantly burning calories even when sitting at a desk, a position suggested by the stoop of his shoulders.

Grinning, the man approached. Saul had never seen him before, but the delight in the stranger's eyes made it clear that the stranger knew *him*.

In a moment, Saul realized his mistake.

It isn't me he knows.

It's Erika.

Her eyes glinted with the same delight as the stranger's. She smiled broadly, ecstatically, her voice an incredulous whisper. 'Misha?'

'Erika.'

She rushed forward, hugging him. 'Misha!' she whooped.

Saul relaxed when he heard the name. If his guess was right, the last name would be Pletz. He'd never met the man, but he remained grateful for favors that Misha – at Erika's request – had done for his foster brother and himself three years ago.

He waited respectfully until Erika stopped hugging Misha. Then stepping forward, holding Christopher in his left arm, he extended his right. 'Welcome. Are you hungry? Would you like some soup?'

Misha's grip was strong. 'No, thanks. I ate two bagels in the car. They gave me heartburn.'

'I often wondered what you look like.'

'As I did you. About your brother – I'm sorry.'

Saul nodded, retreating from painful emotion.

'Misha, why aren't you in Washington?' Erika asked.

'Two years ago, I was transferred back to Tel Aviv. To be honest, I wanted it. I missed my homeland, my parents. And the transfer involved a promotion. I can't complain.'

'What's your assignment now?' she asked.

Misha reached for Christopher's hand. 'How are you, boy?'

Christopher giggled.

But Misha's avoidance of Erika's question made Saul uneasy.

'He's a fine-looking child.' Misha surveyed the ruined building behind the small fire. 'Renovations?'

35

'The interior decorators came today,' she said.

'So I heard.'

'Their work wasn't to our liking. They had to be fired.'

'I heard that as well.'

'Is that why you're here?' Saul asked.

Misha studied him. 'Maybe I'll have some soup, after all.'

They sat around the fire. Now that the sun was almost gone, the desert had cooled. The fire's heat was soothing.

Misha ate only three spoonfuls of soup. 'Even while I was in Washington,' he told Erika, 'I knew that you'd come here. When I went back to Tel Aviv, I kept up with what you were doing.'

'So you're the source of the rumors the captain heard,' Saul said. He pointed toward the officer who stood at a sentry post on the outskirts of the village, talking to a soldier.

'I thought it was prudent to tell him he could depend on both of you. I said he should leave you alone, but if you got in touch with him, to pay attention to what you said. I wasn't trying to interfere.'

Saul watched him steadily.

'After what happened here today,' Misha said, 'it was natural for him to get back to me, especially since the raid had its troubling aspects. Not just the pointlessness of attacking a village so far from the border, one with no military or geographic value.'

Saul anticipated. 'You mean their fingernails.'

Misha raised his eyebrows. 'Then you noticed? Why didn't you mention it to the captain?'

'Before I decided how much to depend on him, I wanted to see how good he was.'

'Well, he's *very* good,' Misha said. 'Dependable enough to share his suspicions only with me until I decided how to deal with this.'

'We might as well stop talking around it,' Saul said. 'The men who attacked this village weren't typical guerrillas. Never mind that their rifles still had traces of grease from the packing crate, or that their clothes were tattered but their boots were brand-new. I could explain all that by pretending to believe they'd recently been reequipped. But their fingernails. They'd smeared dirt over their hands. The trouble is, it hadn't gotten under their nails. Stupid pride. Did they figure none of them would be killed? Did they think we wouldn't notice their twenty-dollar manicures? They weren't terrorists. They were assassins. Imported. Chosen because they were Arabs. But their usual territory isn't the desert. It's Athens, Rome, Paris, or London.'

Misha nodded. 'Three years out here, and you haven't lost your skills.'

Saul pointed toward the ruined building behind him. 'And it's pretty obvious, the attack wasn't directed against the whole village. Our home took most of the damage. The objective was *us*.'

Erika stood, walked behind Misha, and put her hands on his shoulders. 'Old friend, why are you here?'

Misha peered up sadly.

'What is it? What's wrong?' she asked.

'Erika, your father's disappeared.'

36

4

The stability of the past three years had now been destroyed. The sense of peace seemed irretrievable. The constants of his former life had replaced it – tension, suspicion, guardedness. Escape was apparently impossible. Even here, the world intruded, and attitudes he'd been desperate to smother returned as strong as ever.

In the night, with Christopher asleep at a neighbor's house and Misha asleep in his car, Saul sat with Erika by the fire outside the ruin of their home.

'If we were the target,' he said, 'and I don't think there's any doubt that we were, we have to assume other teams will come for us.'

Erika repeatedly jabbed a stick at the fire.

'It wouldn't be fair to allow our presence to threaten the village,' he added.

'So what do we do? Put up a sign – the people you want don't live here anymore?' The blaze of the fire reflected off her eyes.

'They'll find out we've gone the same way they found out we were here.'

'But why did they come at all?'

Saul shook his head. 'Three years is a long time for the past to catch up to us. And my understanding with the Agency was if I stayed out of sight they'd pretend I didn't exist.'

'That's one thing we did, all right,' she said bitterly. 'We stayed out of sight.'

'So I don't think this has anything to do with the past.'

'Then whatever the reason for the attack, it's new.'

'That still doesn't tell us why.'

'You think it's coincidence?'

The reference was vague, but he knew what she meant. 'Your father's disappearance?'

'Yesterday.'

'And today the attack?'

'Bad news always seems to come in twos and threes,' she said, 'but . . .'

'I don't believe in coincidence. The obvious shouldn't be ignored. If a pattern stares you in the face, don't turn away from it.'

'So let's not turn away,' she said.

'You know what it means.'

She poked the stick harder at the fire. 'It's another reason to abandon our home. What's *left* of our home.'

Saul thought about the irrigation ditches he'd worked three years to construct and improve. 'It makes me angry.'

'Good. This wasn't worth having if we give it up easily.'

'And we don't have a chance against whoever we'll be hunting if we go after them indifferently.'

37

'I'm not indifferent about my father. One of the sacrifices of living out here was not seeing him.'

The fire crackled. Erika suddenly stood. 'We'd better get ready. The men who attacked us did us a backhanded favor. What's left of our possessions we can literally carry.'

'To find out what happened to your father.'

'And pay back whoever drove us from our home.'

'It's been three years.' Saul hesitated. 'Regardless of Misha's compliments, are we still good enough?'

'Good enough? Hey, for the past three years, I've just been resting. The people who took my father will wish to God they'd never messed with us when they find out exactly how good we are.'

The Penitent

South of Cairo, west of the Nile. The Nitrian Desert. Egypt. It wasn't a mouse this time but a lizard he was watching, and it didn't do tricks as Stuart Little had. It didn't tug Drew out of his self-denying shell. It didn't make him miss the company of others – his friends, or even strangers. All it did was crawl from its hole beneath a rock and bask in the sun for a few hours just after dawn. At dusk, it stretched out on a slab, absorbing radiant heat. Between-times, during the full destructive blaze of the day, it hid. A foot-long, squat, wrinkled, yellow, unblinking, tongue-flicking testament to God's perverse creative whims.

Slumping in the dark at the back of the cave, Drew watched the monster assume its regular morning position at the tunnel's entrance. He hated the thing and for that reason tolerated it, because he knew that God was testing him. The lizard was part of his penance. As the sun rose higher, sending rays into the cave, Drew surveyed the rocky contours of his cell, comparing their bleak austerity to the relative luxury he'd known for six peaceful years in his simple quarters in the Carthusian monastery in Vermont. Again he compared the lizard, which he alternately called Lucifer and Quasimodo, to Stuart Little, the mouse that had been his companion for the last two years of his stay at the monastery. But the mouse had been killed, assassins had attacked the monastery to get at Drew, and he'd been forced to leave his haven, a sinner confronting a sinful world. The resulting events – his war with Scalpel, his reunion with Arlene, his encounter with the Fraternity of the Stone – had paradoxically redeemed him and yet damned him again, compelling him to seek out this hole in the rock in the desert where Christian monasticism had first begun, here to strive once more for purity through penance and the worship of God.

He'd done so for a year now. With no change in seasons, each day tediously the same as the one before, time seemed strangely extended and yet compressed. The year could have been an eternity or a month or a week. His only ways of measuring how long he'd been here were checking the growth of his hair and beard and watching his food supply, which gradually dwindled until he had to trek across the desert to the nearest village, a day away, and replenish his simple provisions. The villagers seeing this tall, lean, sunburned man with haunted eyes, his robes in rags, gave him distance and respect, conferring upon him the status of a holy one, though he refused to consider himself as such.

39

Apart from that interruption, his routine was constant – exercise, meditation, and prayer. Lately, however, he'd felt too weak to exercise and lay at the back of the cave, intoning responses to imaginary masses. He wondered what the lizard thought of the Latin that sometimes made it cock its ugly unblinking head toward him. Or was its reaction due to nothing more than stimulus-response? If so, what purpose did this monstrous creation serve? A rock, though unthinking, had a beauty to be appreciated. But the lizard could not appreciate the rock, except for the heat its ugly yellow skin absorbed. And no conscious being could appreciate the obscenity of the lizard.

That was the test, Drew thought. If I can appreciate the lizard, I can save myself. I can show that I've opened myself to every aspect of God.

But bodily needs disturbed his meditation. He had to drink. A spring – one reason he'd chosen this spot – was not far away. As usual, he'd postponed slaking his thirst, partly to increase his penance, partly to increase his satisfaction when he did at last drink. This balancing of pain and pleasure caused him great mental stress. He finally resolved it by concluding that the pleasure of drinking had been intended by God as a survival mechanism. If he denied himself that pleasure, if he didn't drink, he would die. But that would be suicide, and suicide was the worst sin of all.

In his weakened state, his thoughts began to free associate. Pleasure, pain. Arlene, and being separated from her. If things had been different, he could imagine nothing more rewarding than to have stayed with Arlene for the rest of his life. But the Fraternity of the Stone had made that impossible. To save Drew's life, Arlene's brother had killed a member of the Fraternity, and to save his savior, Drew had made himself appear to be the guilty one, running and hiding. Craving love, Drew had sacrificed himself for love of a different type.

He tried to move, to get to the spring, but couldn't. His lips were blistered from thirst. His body was ravaged by his failure to eat. His mind began to swirl. The lizard raised itself, repelled by the heat of the day. It scuttled beneath its rock. Time became even more fleeting. A shadow hovered over the entrance to the cave. Was it sundown already?

Or am I hallucinating? Drew wondered. For the shadow became the silhouette of a human being, the first such silhouette Drew had seen here since he'd occupied this cell. It couldn't be.

But the shadow, growing longer, did indeed become the silhouette of a person.

And the person impossibly was—

2

When she saw the lizard scuttle from the mouth of the cave, Arlene muttered, 'Shit.' More forcibly, she felt a stab of suspicion that she'd been given wrong directions. After all, would the lizard have chosen that vulnerable spot in which to soak up heat if the cave were occupied? The way the squat ugly reptile had jerked its head toward the clatter of the rock she'd dislodged as she climbed the slope, the way it had tensed and fled as her shadow fell over it told her unmistakably that the lizard had been frightened by her alone, not someone in the cave. Did the corollary follow, that the cave was deserted?

She paused, discouraged, but the heat of the sun on her back thrust her forward. Exhausted, so dehydrated that she'd stopped sweating, she needed to get to shelter. She plodded the rest of the way up the slope, her shadow stretching toward the cave, and strained to see within the darkness. The silence from inside reinforced her suspicion that she'd been misdirected.

The question was, had the misdirection been an honest mistake or a deliberate deception? Yesterday morning, two hours after she'd left the nearest village, her rented car had stopped, its engine coughing into silence. An experienced mechanic, she'd lifted the hood and tried to diagnose the problem, but she couldn't find what was wrong. She'd debated returning to the village, but the distance she'd traveled by car was a half day's walk, almost the same amount of time it would take to continue forward and reach her destination. She'd filled her canteen before she left the village. Familiar with desert survival, she knew that if she conserved her body's moisture by resting in shadow during the heat of midday, hiking at dusk and through the night, she'd have enough water to reach this cave in the morning, with enough left over to return. Provided she rationed her intake.

But when she'd made camp just before noon, anchoring a thin canvas sheet across the space between two boulders, crawling under to shield herself from the worst of the sun, she'd heard the faint crunch of footsteps – from behind her and to her right. Their stealthy approach had told her everything. She'd been unwilling to risk using her handgun, the reports from which would have carried for miles across the otherwise silent desert and perhaps have attracted other predators. So she'd pretended to be alarmed and defenseless when the two Arabs, each wearing a sun-bleached cotton headscarf and robe, confronted her with pistols, gesturing for her to take off her clothes. Distracting them with a glimpse of her breasts, she'd pivoted, kicking, disarmed the nearer gunman by breaking his wrist, continued spinning with the blur of a dervish, kicked the second assailant's gunhand, again snapping bone, and killed them in a rapid succession with fists to the throat, cracking their windpipes. It happened so quickly that they died still leering. She hid their bodies among rocks where the scavengers of the desert would dispose of them. Proceeding to another campsite, again erecting the thin canvas sheet, she wondered whether the men had found her by accident or whether they'd followed her from the village where she'd asked directions. If the men who'd tried to assault her were indeed from that village, if they'd sabotaged her car, it wasn't surprising that this cave was abandoned – she'd been given false information simply to lead her deeper into the wilderness.

Again she despaired. Having come all the way from New York City,

41

only to find that her search was not yet over, she wanted to raise her fists and curse at the sky. But she needed to escape from the sun. The thought of rinsing her dry swollen mouth with tepid water from her canteen compelled her. A tall, limber, green-eyed, auburn-haired, sensuous woman, in her mid-thirties, wearing a wide-brimmed canvas hat, a knapsack, khaki shirt and pants, and hiking boots, she aimed her handgun against unseen dangers and entered the cave.

3

It smelled vinegary, like carbon dioxide. Beneath that odor was another – a musky animal smell that made her conclude that the cave had recently been used for a den. Standing just inside the entrance, blocking out the sunlight, she stared toward the darkness. Though the cave was by no means cool, it was much less hot than the outside inferno. Handgun ready, she held her breath, straining to listen for sounds.

'Drew?' Her voice was tentative, uneasy. After all, if he were here, he'd have spoken to her by now. Unless, like the lizard, he'd noticed her coming and scuttled to a hiding place. In which case, her quest had been useless, her hope that he'd welcome her a cruel tease.

The echo of her voice died down. Again she held her breath, listening. Something – intuition – told her that the cave was occupied. She heard – or *thought* she heard – a subtle brush of cloth, a slight exhale of air, a faint scrape of flesh against stone. The almost imperceptible sounds came from far in the back. She crouched and shifted to the right, away from the mouth of the cave, simultaneously hiding her silhouette and allowing sunlight to enter the cave.

Now that her eyes were accustomed to the dark, the added illumination was sufficient for her to see the worn sandals on the dusty feet of the scabrous legs of a man sprawled against the rear wall. His tattered robe was tugged above his fleshless knees. The hands stretched out against each thigh looked skeletal.

'Dear God.' The echo of the cave amplified her anguished whisper. 'Drew,' she said louder.

She rushed to him, tugging him toward the sunlight, shocked by his matted waist-long beard and hair, by his gaunt ravaged face. 'Oh, Jesus, Drew.'

Through eyes that were slits, he studied her. His blistered mouth quivered.

She hurried to unhitch the canteen from her belt, twisting its cap off. 'Don't try to talk.'

But he persisted, his voice so weak she could barely hear it. The sound reminded her of a footstep on dry crusted mud. 'Ar . . .' He made a desperate effort to try again. 'Ar . . . lene?' The tone communicated surprise, disbelief. And something else. Something akin to the awe one would feel when having a vision.

'It's me. I'm here, Drew. I'm real. But stop trying to talk.'

She raised the canteen to his blistered lips, pouring just a few drops of water between them. Like a sponge, his flesh seemed to absorb the water. She gripped his wrist, his pulse so weak she could barely feel it. She ran her hands along his body, startled by how much weight he'd lost.

'You finally got what you wanted,' she said. 'You fucked yourself up. If you weren't so weak' – she poured a few more drops of water between his parched lips – 'I'd be furious instead of sorry for you.'

Amazingly his eyes crinkled. They glowed faintly with . . .

What? Amusement? Love? He inhaled as if to . . .

'Laugh,' she said, 'and I'll hit you over the head with this canteen.'

But somehow he did have strength to laugh, just a short stubborn 'hah,' and of course she did not make good on her threat. She simply poured another few drops of water into his mouth, knowing she wouldn't be able to give him more for a while, lest he become sick to his stomach, but reassured because his attempt at a laugh was a life sign. She'd gotten here in time. His spirit hadn't failed. He was going to be all right.

4

But when she let him have another sip of water, she stiffened with doubt. Despite the heat, apprehension chilled her. There wasn't enough water for both of them to walk out of here.

Her swollen tongue stuck to the roof of her mouth. She had to drink. The tepid water tasted bitter. Even so, she swallowed, felt less lightheaded, took another sip, then poured a few more drops between Drew's lips.

Gradually his pulse strengthened. He breathed easier, deeper.

But his voice remained a croak. 'Misjudged . . .' He grinned with embarrassment, like a child who'd been naughty.

She shook her head, not understanding.

'Should have drunk sooner . . .' He coughed.

Again she shook her head.

'Should have gone for food sooner . . . Didn't realize . . . how weak I was . . . Couldn't reach the spring.'

'*What* spring?'

His eyes drooped.

'Damn it, Drew, what spring?'

'Outside . . . down the slope . . . to the right.'

'How far?'

'A hundred yards . . . around the curve of the hill . . . a cluster of rocks.'

She gave him one more sip of water and stood. 'I'll be back.'

She took off her knapsack, left the dark of the cave, and at once felt

43

the hammer force of the blinding sun. Wincing from a pain behind her eyes, she clambered down the dusty slope and followed the curve of the hill.

But after what she judged was a hundred yards, she still hadn't found a cluster of rocks at the base of the slope. Panic slithered within her. Had Drew been delirious? Had he only imagined there was a spring?

No, there *had* to be a spring. Otherwise how could he have survived here? If she didn't find it, if Drew didn't become more lucid before the canteen was emptied, there was every chance both of them would die.

She walked twenty-five yards farther, felt her knees weaken, and knew that she couldn't risk continuing. For as far as she could see along the slope of this hill, no mound of rocks provided a goal. Discouragement weighed upon her. Mustering strength, licking her parched lips, she turned to go back to the cave. Instead of swinging to the right toward the contour of the hill, she pivoted left toward the broad expanse of the desert. And tingled when she saw the mound.

She stumbled toward it. As far as they went, Drew's instructions had been accurate. But he'd left out a crucial detail. The cluster of rocks was a hundred yards around the curve of the hill, all right. But *out* from the hill, not against it. And if you looked that way, the cluster was so obvious, so tall and wide, so clear a landmark, that you couldn't fail to notice it.

She made her feet move faster. The rocks became larger. Climbing over them, down to a hollow, she found a stagnant pool protected from wind, skimmed dust to the side, glanced around to make sure no skeletons of animals warned against trusting the water, and dipped her mouth beneath the surface. Hot, the water did not refresh her. Nonetheless, she felt her body absorb it.

Quickly she filled the canteen. Ten minutes later, she stooped to enter the dark of the cave.

Drew was flat on his back. Eyes slitted, he shrugged and tried to grin. 'Forgot to tell you . . .'

'I *know* what you forgot to tell me, friend. I found it just the same.'

She raised the canteen to his lips. He swallowed gratefully. She drank as well.

That still left the problem of food. In her knapsack, she'd carried enough provisions for an emergency – peanuts and beef jerky, along with dried fruit. But after she searched the cave and found nothing to eat, she had to conclude that what she'd brought was not sufficient for both of them to cross the desert.

She gave Drew more water, took some herself, and became more hopeful as his energy returned.

'Why are you here?' he asked.

'Isn't it obvious?'

He shook his head.

'Because I love you,' she said.

He breathed deeply, overcome with powerful emotion, 'Love . . . Yes.' It was hard for him to continue. 'But how did you find me?'

'Persistence.'

'I don't understand.' He gathered strength. 'I thought I'd hidden my trail.'

She nodded.

'Then how . . . ?'

'The Fraternity.'

Drew shuddered.

5

'You ran from them,' she said, 'to save my brother's life. Because he saved yours. You thought you'd eluded them. You haven't.'

She reached in her knapsack and pulled out a bag of peanuts. Chewing, she savored their salt.

He reached for one.

'Promise not to swallow it right away.'

He nodded.

She pressed one between his lips. 'If you weren't so grungy, I'd kiss you.'

'Threats'll get you nowhere.' He slumped. 'The Fraternity?'

'They followed you from the moment you left my brownstone in New York,' she said. 'The reason you thought you'd gotten away was they never made a move against you. After England, Italy, and Morocco, you felt it was safe to come to Egypt. But they followed you here as well. They've been keeping track of you.'

'You know this . . . ?'

'Because two weeks ago, one of them came to see me.'

Drew groaned. 'Then all of this has been for nothing?'

'No, it saved your life. The way the priest explained it to me,' she said, 'the Fraternity decided your exile here was worse than any punishment they could have thought of. From the looks of you, they were right.'

His pitiful appearance dismayed her – his gaunt torso, his haggard face, his matted waist-long hair and beard. 'We have to get some strength back into you. Do you think your stomach could hold down another peanut?'

'It better. I need the salt.'

She gave him one and nibbled on a piece of beef jerky. 'The priest told me the Fraternity's decided you've suffered enough for the death of their operative.'

Drew stared at her.

'You'd return to me sometime in Lent – that's what you promised.' She tenderly kissed his forehead. 'Each day before Easter, I waited, hoping. When you didn't come this first year, I worried that you'd never come.'

'No matter how hard I tried, I couldn't stop thinking of you,' he said.

'I love you.'

With a tremble, he touched her arm. 'And now my exile's over? They've pardoned me?'

She hesitated.

'What's wrong?'

'Not pardoned,' she said. 'You're being summoned. "To pursue your calling" is how the priest described it.'

He frowned. 'What do you mean?'

'There's something they want you to do for them.' Troubled, she glanced away. 'It's the only condition under which they'll let you leave. When the priest told me where you were, I grabbed at the chance to see you again, just to be with you. Since you ran away that night, I've never felt so empty. Losing you the first time, and then . . .' She kissed him again.

He returned her embrace. 'Arlene?'

She waited.

'What do they want?'

'That's the problem. The priest wouldn't tell me. He sent me here. To talk to you. To convince you. To bring you to him.'

6

At sunset, she helped him squirm from the cave. The evening's lower temperature made the heat that radiated from the rocks feel soothing. In the last light of day, she unsheathed her survival knife and snicked its edges across his hair and beard. When she'd finished, he looked like, in her words, 'a sexy ascetic by El Greco.'

She stripped off his robe and sloshed water from her canteen all over his body, washing him thoroughly. She dressed him and cautiously fed him. Before the sun completely faded, she went down the slope toward the cluster of rocks around the spring, refilled the canteen, and returned to the cave.

By then, night cloaked them. In his cell, she lay huddled next to him, her pelvis against his hips, spoonlike, giving him warmth.

'Water's not a problem,' she said.

'But food is.'

'Right. There's enough for me, but not enough for you to regain your strength. How are we going to manage to cross the desert?'

'I've got an idea,' he said.

7

At dawn, she waited, poised with her knife. When the lizard crawled from beneath its rock, she stabbed it, skinned it, and cut it into strips. The lizard, after all, did have a purpose. The strips of its flesh, spread out in front of the cave, baked in the sun. She brought them inside to Drew, who bit off a piece and chewed until it was like gruel and would not offend his stomach.

'I used to hate the thing,' he said.

'And now?'

'I'm sorry it died for me. It's a part of me. I love it.'

8

They left at night. He'd gained sufficient strength to stay on his feet, provided he leaned against Arlene. Taking their direction from stars, they plodded across the desert. He shivered against her. With her arm around his back, she felt him sweating. But as long as he was sweating, she didn't worry. Sweat meant his body fluid had been replenished.

They rested frequently, eating the last of their food, trying not to fall asleep. At dawn, they reached a pass between low hills. She exhaled in distress. The pass was near where her car had failed, halfway between Drew's cave and the village. They hadn't walked far enough. In a couple of hours, the heat would be so intense they'd have to stop and put up the canvas sheet. They wouldn't be able to proceed again until late afternoon. At the earliest, they wouldn't reach the village till tomorrow morning, provided they maintained the pace they'd set throughout the night. But now that their food was gone, Drew's strength would diminish rapidly. Already she could feel him leaning more heavily against her. If they didn't reach the village by the morning, they'd have to stop and rest again throughout the next day, and by then Drew might be so weak that she'd never be able to get him to the village.

I might have to leave him, she thought. To go for help.

But what if he becomes delirious and wanders? What if I can't find him?

A bullet struck a boulder on her right. A splinter of rock sliced the back of her hand. The report from the rifle followed at once, its echo filling the pass. Ignoring the blood that dripped from her hand, she dove with Drew behind the boulder.

In the same motion, she unholstered her pistol. As she squinted from the edge of the boulder, scanning the rocky slope on the right, searching for a target, she flinched from the impact of a second bullet spewing rock shards behind her.

She realized sickly that the second bullet had come from the left, from the opposite side of the pass. She and Drew were trapped in a crossfire.

'Leave me,' Drew told her weakly.

'No.'

'Listen.' He breathed with effort. 'You can't fight them and take care of me. I'll get both of us killed.'

'I told you no.'

Almost simultaneously, two bullets spewed rock shards – from behind them and from in front – so close her ears rang.

'Their argument's better than yours,' Drew said.

'I didn't come all this way to get separated again.' She scanned one slope, then the other.

'Listen to me.'

She was shocked to see blood streaming from his knees where they'd landed on jagged stones.

'Our friends up there,' he said, 'they could've killed both of us before we knew it. They're either lousy shots, or they missed on purpose.'

'So?'

A bullet from the left sprayed pebbles over Arlene's boots. A bullet from the opposite slope *carammed* off the boulder.

'They've got something else in mind,' Drew said. 'Don't give them a chance to keep pinning us down.' He struggled to a crouch. 'Leave. Go after them. Until they get what they want, they won't kill you unless they have to.'

'But what about you?'

'I'll take my chances. I'd only hold you back. This way, *you* at least have a chance.'

She shook her head, aiming anxiously one way, then the other, toward the rocky slopes.

'Okay,' Drew said. 'I'll make the choice for you.'

As weak as he was, he hefted himself to his feet and staggered from behind the boulder, knees buckling, rolling into a ravine.

'You bullheaded . . .'

Gunshots echoed.

She charged toward the slope on the right, diving below a mound.

But he'd judged correctly. The bullets that sprayed stones before and behind her seemed calculated to box her in, not kill her.

Okay, then, she thought. Let's dance.

9

Drew winced from the jolt as he tumbled off the rim and down the ravine. He landed hard, losing his breath. The morning sun was still so low its rays didn't penetrate to the bottom. In shadow, he mustered the little strength he had, took care to keep his head down, and wavered along the bottom of the ravine.

To a certain extent, what happened next was predetermined, he knew. The snipers, having seen Arlene support him and realizing how weak he was, would fear him less than they did her. Granted, in Arab culture, women were not held in high regard, but the snipers would still have to give her credit for being brave enough, having knowledge enough, to travel through the desert unprotected, and after all, she was an American, an incalculable factor. When she started shooting at them, they'd definitely give her their respect.

So, for the sake of efficiency, they'd eliminate the easy target first. One sniper would distract Arlene while the other went after Drew. Once he was taken care of, they could devote all their attention to her. But not kill her. No. He remained convinced that the snipers could have hit them both if that had been their intention. The purpose of the shots was to play with the quarry, to restrict, to corner, to trap without killing. At least not kill just yet.

He was too weak to fight, but even if all he did was keep moving, he'd still be helping Arlene. Divide and conquer – that's what the snipers were hoping to do. But that tactic could work the other way around.

10

As Arlene lunged up the rocky slope, dodging from boulder to boulder, the sniper shot at her again. Diving behind cover, she suddenly recognized where she was. This cluster of jagged stone was where she'd hidden the bodies of the two men who'd attacked her. She glanced around, startled.

But this *couldn't* be the place. There wasn't any sign of the bodies. Even allowing for the efficiency of the desert scavengers, the corpses wouldn't have disappeared completely yet. There ought to be something – bits of flesh, bone, and cloth – crumbs, as it were.

All the same, she was positive that she recognized this spot.

Then how . . . ?

A bullet ricocheted off shale. She peered upward through a chink between boulders, pistol ready, eager for a target. The shot made her wonder if this ambush in the same spot where she'd been attacked earlier was more than coincidence. Had the bodies been found and carried away? Were these snipers avenging friends who'd been killed? If so, the ambush made sense, as did the way the snipers seemed deliberately to have avoided killing her. Before that eventuality, they meant to do to her what their friends had intended to do. Her chest heaving, she stared harder through the gap in the boulders, straining to see the target.

But when she did distinguish a blur of movement – a scarved, robed Arab scurrying down the slope, over boulders, across a ridge, and down the continuation of the slope – she became confused again. Because the Arab took cover and aimed a rifle, but not toward her. Instead he aimed toward the ravine at the bottom of this slope. *The ravine into which Drew had tumbled.*

Swinging her gaze in that direction, she saw the second sniper: another Arab, his scarf flapping behind him as he ran down the opposite slope, converging on the ravine.

A welter of possibilities occurred to her. Perhaps the snipers had not been convinced that Drew was as weak as he appeared. Or else these Arabs felt so superior to women that even an obviously weakened man seemed more of a threat to them than an able armed woman.

49

But yet another possibility insisted, its implications so disturbing it had to be considered before the others. Now that she thought about it, it was the most obvious explanation but so outrageous that she must have subconsciously rejected it.

She wasn't the target. Drew was!

11

Drew flinched from a bullet that grazed the right edge of the ravine, continued its downward trajectory, and walloped shale below him to his left. Dizzy, he lunged toward an indentation in the wall to his right, the direction from which the bullet had come.

But in that instant, a bullet from the left cracked against that indentation. Avoiding the crossfire, he toppled backward. Through a swirl of weakness, he fought to reason out his dilemma. He'd been convinced that Arlene was the primary target, that one of the gunmen would grudgingly take the time to kill him, then join his partner to assault Arlene. But both were now attacking him! It didn't make sense!

He rubbed his aching jaw where his teeth had smacked together from the force of his fall. Hearing rifle shots from his right and left, he shielded his eyes from shale spewing off both rims of the ravine. He heard another shot, this one less powerful, from a handgun, not a rifle. Arlene.

But another sound, subtle, like a breeze or a deflating tire, was more obtrusive. Down here in the muffled ravine, it had paradoxically deafening force.

An angry cobra rose to strike at him.

12

Arlene ignored the risk of breaking an ankle and continued to charge down the rocky slope. She cursed herself for letting her judgment be clouded by sexual arrogance. Admit you took for granted that the biological accident of your being female makes you an irresistible target for lust. You were so self-absorbed you didn't understand what was going on. You helped them without knowing it.

Scrambling lower, she shifted her gaze from one Arab to the other as they flanked the ravine below her. Her handgun wasn't accurate at this range. They shot again into the ravine. She stopped and fired, hoping that the bullet would at least distract them.

It didn't.

The Arab on the left dropped into the ravine. The Arab on the right moved parallel to it, glancing warily toward her, making sure she wasn't close enough to be a threat, then darting his eyes toward the depression his partner had entered.

'Look out, Drew!'

The echo of her scream merged with another scream.

The Arab who'd entered the ravine staggered halfway up its steep slope, his face in agony. Raising his eyes toward the sky as if in prayer, he shuddered and fell back out of sight.

The second Arab froze in astonishment. His paralysis lasted just long enough for Drew to crawl to the top of the ravine, aim a rifle, and shoot him in the face.

The rifle's echo subsided. Drew collapsed back into the ravine.

By now, the sun was high enough to scorch her. Despite the brutal strain on her body, she ran even harder. Scrambling into the ravine, she found him.

His voice was guttural. 'Be careful. There's a cobra down here.'

She whirled.

The snake lay coiled on the sand fifteen feet away from her. Unblinking, it assessed her.

'It's going to strike!' She aimed her pistol.

'Wait,' Drew said.

'But . . . !'

'Give it a chance to live.'

The cobra poised itself. Just as Arlene decided she couldn't afford to delay, the snake sank its head to the ground again, flicked its tongue, and slithered away. It seemed contemptuous, dismissive.

'I froze when I saw it,' Drew said. 'The gunman jumped down here. The sudden motion diverted the snake's attention.'

'And it bit the gunman instead of you?'

'With a little help.'

She shook her head, not understanding.

'The snake was only an arm's length away from me. When it turned toward the gunman, I grabbed it behind the head and threw it. It flopped across his shoulder.'

Arlene felt sick.

'It bit his stomach. When he screamed and dropped the rifle to shove the thing off him, I yanked the gun off the ground. He tried to crawl to the top of the ravine. The snake bit him again. By then, I was over here, out of its reach.'

'And while the gunman's partner was distracted by the screaming, you shot him.' She studied him with admiration.

'I was lucky.'

'No, you made your luck. As weak as you are, when you had to, you thought and moved fast. Instinct. Reflex.'

'I'm not sure that's a compliment.'

He stood with effort. She steadied him and helped him from the ravine. After its shadow, the sun stabbed her eyes.

'The snake reminded me of the lizard,' he said. 'I hated it. Now I love it.'

'As long as we don't have to eat it. There's a sure test to learn if you're a mystic. Can you bring yourself to love the men who tried to kill you?'

'No.' Drew stared at the body of the Arab he'd shot in the face. 'God help me, I can't.'

They searched the corpse. Inside a packet attached to the gunman's waist, they found dates and figs.

'That solves our food problem.'

'Extra bullets for the rifle. No papers. No identification.' Drew turned to her. 'It's clear they were after me, not you. Why?'

Arlene shook her head in puzzlement. 'I do know this. In case they're from the nearest village, we'd better avoid it.'

'Sure. But they weren't from the village.'

She followed his gaze toward the gunman's mouth and tingled when she realized what he meant.

The bullet's impact had parted the gunman's jaws, exposing teeth. Even those in back were clearly visible. They glinted from the rays of the sun, amazingly perfect, stunningly white.

'No fillings,' Drew said.

'But *everybody* has fillings.'

'In America maybe, if you've got the money to go to a dentist. Out here, though?'

'There might not be fillings. But there'd be cavities.'

'If you still had teeth. But this guy doesn't just have all his teeth. He's got *perfect* teeth. It's been a while since I went to a dentist, so I don't know what the going rate is. But my guess is . . . since when do Arabs from outlying villages have a mouthful of three-hundred-dollar crowns?'

She nodded in outrage. 'Professionals.'

BOOK TWO
COMPULSION

Between an Anteater
and a Dog

Icicle: that was how Pendleton now thought of himself. Angry, determined, identifying with his lost father, he drove his rented car along the narrow blacktop road that fronted his destination. He saw the gravel lane that led up through trees toward a sloping lawn and a mansion on a bluff above the river. Instead of turning up the lane, however, he continued along the blacktop, rounded a bend, crossed a metal bridge above the river, and five kilometers later turned left at the next intersection. Fields of knee-high corn surrounded him. Turning left twice more, completing a square, he came back to the road along which he'd first driven. This time he stopped two kilometers away from his destination, hid the car on a weed-grown lane among trees off the blacktop, and hiked overland, through woods, toward the mansion on the hill.

He wore brown outdoor clothes and woodsman's boots, purchased in a town called Milton that was along Highway 401 halfway between Toronto's airport and this lush farming area near Kitchener. He hadn't risked bringing a handgun through Canadian customs, nor had he attempted to buy even a rifle at a sporting goods store – Canada's laws controlling the sale of every type of firearm were extremely strict. If this had been a country in Europe, Africa, or South America, he could have easily retrieved a weapon from one of his many hiding places or have purchased one from a black-market contact. But he'd worked in southern Ontario only once, seven years ago, within a rigid time limit that had prevented him from establishing caches and contacts.

Still, to find his father, Icicle had to take this present risk. He shifted with greater resolution through the forest. Thick leaves shut out the sun; the pungent loamy ground absorbed his weight, making his cautious footsteps soundless. He reached the edge of the trees and stooped, concealing himself among dense bushes. Ahead, he saw a waist-high wire fence. Beyond, a well-maintained lawn led up to a tennis court and a swimming pool next to the mansion on top of the hill.

The sun was behind the mansion, descending toward the opposite side of the hill. Dusk would thicken in just a few hours. He scanned the top of the hill but saw no one. Earlier, though, when he'd driven past the entrance to the estate, he'd noticed two cars in front of the mansion, so he had to conclude that the house was not deserted. He'd also noticed that the estate was not equipped with an obvious security system. There weren't any closed-circuit television cameras in the trees near the lane, for example, or guards, or roaming attack dogs. For that matter, there wasn't even a decent high solid fence around the property, only a flimsy wire one, and the front gate had been left open.

But despite the apparent innocence of the place, Icicle had no doubt he'd found his target. Before leaving Australia, he'd gone to the safe-deposit box he and his father kept for emergencies. He'd hoped that his father, on the run perhaps, had reached the box not long before him and left a message, explaining his sudden disappearance. He'd found the weapons, money, and documents he and his father had stored there, but heart-sinkingly, there hadn't been a message. Nonetheless, as he'd sorted through the documents, he *had* found the sheet of directions his father had been sent for what they'd assumed was a wake, but what was actually an emergency meeting, here in Canada. The directions had been specific, complete with the name of the exit ramp from 401, the number of a side road, and a note about the silhouette of a greyhound on the mailbox outside the estate. Icicle nodded. This was the place, all right, but as he studied the grounds, he became more puzzled by the lack of obvious security.

He stared at the waist-high fence ahead of him. There were no glass insulators on the posts. The wires were rusty. If the fence was electrified, how could the current be conducted? Whatever security there might be, it didn't depend on the fence.

Were there pressure-detecting grids beneath the grass *beyond* the fence? he wondered. He focused on the grass. Faint depressions from tires were evident. Tracks from a power mower, a big one, the kind a groundskeeper rode. But that kind of mower weighed more than a human would. Every time the lawn was trimmed the alarm would have to be shut off, and that made the system worthless. All an intruder would have to do would be to enter the grounds while the caretaker was on duty. No, he decided, the only place to bury pressure-detecting wires was in a forest, and the forest would have to be within the fence, where hikers and large roaming animals wouldn't press down on the soil with a weight sufficient to activate the system. But there wasn't even a small band of woods within the fence. If there *were* sophisticated detectors, they hadn't been placed down here but instead on top of the hill, around the mansion.

He would soon find out. The sun had now descended behind the hill. Dusk would deepen to night, and the night was his friend.

2

Lights glowed inside the house. Two spotlights came on, at the front and side of the house. Again Icicle felt puzzled. If the house had an adequate security system, there ought to be more outside lights. On the other hand, perhaps the few outside lights were intended to deceive, to make it seem as if the mansion were unprotected.

Six of one, half a dozen of the other. He stood, emerged from the bushes, and prepared to climb the fence. But he froze when headlights blazed on the hill. A car engine droned. The headlights veered down the gravel lane toward the blacktop in front of the estate, disappearing into the night. The noise of the engine dwindled until the only sound was the screech of crickets.

But there'd been *two* cars parked at the top of the hill. He couldn't afford to assume that the estate was now unoccupied. He climbed the fence, dropped onto the lawn, and knelt, not moving, straining to detect a threat.

He waited five minutes before creeping upward, periodically inter-rupting his cautious ascent to study the night. A hundred yards and thirty minutes later, he reached the edge of a tennis court on top of the hill. Wary of triggering alarms, he snuck toward a swimming pool, its placid water reflecting light from the mansion. A small structure next to the pool seemed to be a changing room. He ducked behind it, peering past a corner toward the five-stalled garage to his right, its doors all closed. He shifted his position and stared left toward the car, a dark Cadillac, in front of the mansion. Then he studied the mansion itself.

It was peaked, with chimneys and gables. On this side, a flagstone patio led to closed French doors; beyond the windows, lamps glowed in a room lined with paintings and books. He tensed as a man walked past the windows. The brief glimpse showed the man was well-built and middle-aged, dressed in a blue exercise suit – he seemed to be alone.

Icicle studied the windows in the other rooms. Most were dark. The few with lights didn't seem occupied. Not seeing any guards, he sprinted from behind the small building near the pool, crossed the driveway, and dove below the cover of a concrete balustrade that flanked the patio, then studied the area before him. At once he realized that the patio, which went all along this side of the mansion and presumably along the other sides as well, held the only alarm system the mansion needed. An intruder couldn't get inside unless he crossed the flagstones, but they weren't joined by concrete. The light from the room beyond the French doors made clear that each flagstone was rimmed by sand. The sand was sloppy, grains of it speckling the patio. But why would the owner of a million-dollar property cut costs on so minor a detail? Why this inconsistency in an otherwise carefully maintained estate? The answer was obvious. Because each stone, independent, rested upon a pressure detector. The moment an intruder stepped upon *any* stone in the patio, an alarm would sound.

He glanced to the right and left, hoping for a tree whose branches would allow him to climb through an upper window. Seeing none, he decided to look for an equipment shed where a ladder might have been stored. By setting one end of the ladder on top of the patio's balustrade and easing the other end of the ladder onto the sill of a window in a darkened room farther along, he'd have what amounted to a bridge he could use to crawl across above the flagstones.

He began to creep backward.

'So you guessed,' a voice said.

Icicle spun.

'About the patio.' The voice was flat, thin, emotionless. It came from his left, from an open window of the Cadillac parked in front of the mansion. 'I'd hoped you would. I wouldn't want your reputation to exceed your ability.'

Icicle braced himself to run.

'I'm not your enemy.' The Cadillac's passenger door came open. A tall gangly man stepped out. 'You see. I willingly show myself. I mean you no harm.' The man stepped into the full blaze of the spotlight in front of the mansion. He held his arms out, away from his gray suit. His face was narrow, his nose and lips thin, his eyebrows so sparse they were almost nonexistent. His red hair contrasted with his pallid skin.

The patio doors burst open. 'Is he here? Pendleton, is that you?' The man in the exercise suit reached toward the inner wall and flicked what seemed to be a switch, deactivating an alarm, before he stepped out onto the patio. '*Pendleton? Icicle?*'

For an instant, Icicle almost lunged toward the darkness beyond the swimming pool. Already he imagined his rush down the slope toward the fence and the trees and . . .

Instead he straightened. 'No. Not Icicle. I'm his son.'

'Yes, his son!' the man on the patio said. 'And this man' – pointing toward the Cadillac – 'is Seth, or rather Seth's son! And I'm known as Halloway, but I'm the *Painter's* son!'

The cryptonym 'Painter' had force, but 'Seth' made Icicle wince as if he'd been shot. He stared at the lanky, pale, impassive man beside the Cadillac. Seth's gray suit matched his eyes, which even in the spotlit night were vividly unexpressive, bleak.

But Seth didn't matter, nor did Halloway. Only one thing had importance.

Icicle swung toward Halloway on the patio. 'Where's my father?'

'Not just *your* father,' Halloway said. 'Where's *mine*?'

'And mine,' Seth said.

'That's why we've been waiting for you.'

'*What?*'

'For you to come here – to help us find *all* our fathers,' Halloway said. 'We'd almost despaired that you'd ever show up.' He gestured toward the mansion. 'Come in. We've a great deal to talk about.'

3

When they entered the study, Halloway closed the patio doors, pulled the draperies shut, and activated the alarm switch on the wall. Next to the switch, Icicle noticed a landscape painting.

'My father's,' Halloway said.

Similar colorful paintings hung on the other walls.

Icicle nodded. 'I'd heard he was talented. I've never seen his work.'

'Of course not. His early paintings were either stolen or destroyed. For precaution's sake, even though no one saw his later work outside this house, he changed from water-color to acrylic, and just as important, he altered his style.' Halloway's tone changed from reverence to dismay. 'What did you plan to do? Attack me?'

'I had to make sure I could trust you,' Icicle said.

'Trust me? Right now, Seth and I are the only ones you *can* trust.'

'I had to find out about Kessler.'

'He went to see you in Australia.'

'I *know* that! I met him there!' Icicle said. 'But after I saw him, he disappeared. So did my father. Did Kessler set me up? Was Kessler a way to separate my father and me, to make it easier for someone to grab him?'

Halloway spread his hands. 'He never returned from Australia. He was reliable. If you'd been here at the meeting, you'd have realized that once he committed himself to a purpose, he wouldn't back out. So when he didn't return . . . when he disappeared . . .'

'You assume he's dead?'

'Yes.' Halloway thought about it. 'In all probability, yes.'

'So either your meeting was bugged or one of the group betrayed you.'

'No. I took precautions,' Halloway insisted. 'Believe me, this house has never been bugged. And I can't imagine why one of us would betray his own best interests. But there are other considerations.'

Icicle raised his eyebrows.

'At the time of the meeting, your father and Seth's were the only members of the original group who hadn't yet disappeared,' Halloway said. 'We sent messengers to each – to emphasize the danger, to convince them . . . and yourselves . . . to join us. Unfortunately, Seth's father disappeared before the messenger could reach him. That left only *your* father.'

Icicle stared. 'Go on.'

'If our enemies were in place to attack your father, if they discovered Kessler in the area, they might have given in to temptation and taken Kessler as well, hoping he hadn't yet warned your father and yourself.'

Icicle shook his head. 'But Kessler disappeared at almost exactly the same time my father did. If they wanted to stop him from warning my father, they'd have taken Kessler first and only then have set up the trap for my father. No, they must have had another reason for picking up Kessler.'

'Several explanations occur to me. They may have wanted to make you suspect – as you did – that Kessler was responsible for your father's disappearance. To turn you against *us*. Or they may have wanted to make you realize that no one, not even the children of the fathers, was safe. To instill fear in *you*. For *yourself*.'

59

'We think they're bringing back the Night and Fog,' Seth said.

Barbed wire seemed to bind Icicle's chest.

'Yes, the ultimate terror,' Halloway said. 'Not only to punish the heads of each family but to imply a threat to us, their children, and to torture our imaginations because we don't know what was done to them and what might be done to ourselves.'

'From one generation to the next.' Icicle grimaced. 'It never ends.'

'Oh, but it will,' Seth said. 'I guarantee it.' Despite the anger in his words, his voice remained flat.

The contrast made Icicle tingle. He stared at Seth's red hair, his pale, gaunt, expressionless face, the effect so hypnotic he had to force himself to turn toward Halloway. 'What made you sure I'd come, so sure that you waited for me?'

'We felt you had no other choice. When Kessler didn't return, it was obvious his mission had gone terribly wrong. Neither he nor you responded to our further messages. We concluded, reluctantly, that your father too had vanished. Perhaps you'd been taken as well. But if you were free, we knew you wouldn't stop until you found your father. Your logical destination? Here. To the site of the meeting you didn't attend, to the group who sent Kessler to find you. What other lead did you have?'

'I hope,' Seth added, his voice dry and inflectionless, 'you don't mind working with me.'

No explanation was necessary. Icicle knew very well what he meant.

Seth's father and Icicle's father had once been two of the most feared men in Europe. Though linked by a common purpose, they'd nonetheless been rivals, as close to enemies as cohorts could be. What one achieved, the other fought to surpass, for the rewards of success, the advantages of being favored by their leader, were considerable. Both men had loved the same woman, and when Icicle's father had been chosen instead of Seth's, professional differences became personal. Jealousy – at least on Seth's father's part – turned to hate. Their conflict worsened after the failure of the cause to which they'd pledged their lives. As subsequent freelance specialists, they often found themselves on opposite sides, an extra incentive for Seth's father. Eventually retired, they'd put the world between them, one living in Australia, the other in South America. At Bondi Beach in Sydney, Icicle's father had always worn a T-shirt, to hide the two bullet scars on his chest. From his rival.

4

Now Icicle faced the son of his father's lifelong enemy. The sight of the lean, pale, severe-faced man in the gray suit made his stomach swarm with spiders. Even the cryptonym 'Seth' implied the unnatural. Seth, the Egyptian god of the desert, of barrenness, drought, and chaos, of darkness and destruction. The red god, red like this man's hair. When depicted in human guise, Seth was always pale, as this man's skin was pale. But most often, the god was a monstrous animal, its body that of a greyhound, its snout an anteater's, its ears square, its tail inexplicably forked.

The god of death.

Seth. The perfect cryptonym for an assassin.

And what about *my* cryptonym? Icicle?

Seth reached out his hand. 'My father loved your mother very much.'

Icicle nodded. 'My father always regretted that he and *your* father couldn't be friends.'

'But you and I can be friends. Or if not friends, then allies. Joined by a common purpose.'

Icicle sensed that Seth could never be a friend to anyone. It didn't matter. No conflict existed between them directly, and they had the best of reasons to join forces. The combination of their considerable talents couldn't be matched by their opponents. They would triumph, either finding their fathers or gaining revenge.

Icicle shook his dry, cold hand. He turned again to Halloway. 'Where do you suggest we start?'

'Go after the common denominator. Our fathers never associated with each other. True, they kept in touch, so they could help each other if they sensed danger, but they carefully separated their past lives from their present ones. They lived thousands of miles away from each other. Yet their enemies found out where they were.'

'It's not surprising,' Icicle said. 'All the enemy had to do was locate *one* of our fathers. Under chemicals, he'd have told how to find the rest. My father always felt uncomfortable about that flaw in the pact.'

'But the pact had a limitation,' Halloway said. 'Precisely to guard against that danger, each member of the group knew the location of only one other member. Your father and Seth's remained ignorant of each other, for example. If the enemy tracked down one father and made him tell what he knew, the enemy would then have to go to the next man, and the next, in sequence, till all of the group had been discovered.'

'But it didn't happen like that,' Seth said.

Halloway resumed. 'Some members of the group disappeared simultaneously. Besides, that still leaves the question, how did the enemy find the *first* man who disappeared? No.' Halloway's voice became hoarse. 'Our fathers didn't unwillingly betray each other. The information about them came from outside the group.'

'*How?*'

'I told you – the common denominator. The one man who knew about all of them. A different kind of father. A priest. Cardinal Pavelic.'

Icicle suddenly remembered the last thing Kessler had said to him in Sydney. 'Cardinal Pavelic! He disappeared as well.'

'Find out what happened to the cardinal, and you'll find out what happened to my father,' Halloway said, 'and yours and—'

'Mine,' Seth said. 'And everyone else's.'

'The Horror,
the Horror'

Vienna. Saul stood respectfully in the background, holding Christopher's hand, as Erika morosely surveyed her father's living room. It occupied the second level of a three-story rowhouse on a quiet tree-lined street three blocks from the Danube. Outside, a heavy rain made the day so drab, the room so glum, that even in early afternoon Misha Pletz had been forced to turn on the lights when they entered.

The room was simply furnished, a rocking chair, a sofa, a coffee table, a plain dark rug, a hutch with photographs of Erika, Christopher, and Saul. No radio or television, Saul noticed, but he did see a crammed bookshelf – mostly histories and biographies – and several reading lamps. From studying the austere room, a stranger would not have guessed that Erika's father, retired from the Mossad, received an adequate pension from Israel. With supplementary dividends from a few modest investments, her father could have surrounded himself with more belongings and better ones. But after disposing of his wife's possessions when she died five years ago, Joseph Bernstein had preferred to live ascetically. The sole luxuries he allowed himself were morning and evening cups of hot chocolate at a small café that bordered the Danube. A pipe tobacco, the fragrance of which permeated the furniture and walls of the apartment. Saul himself had never smoked – another legacy from Eliot. But the sweet lingering odor pleasantly widened his nostrils.

Though he didn't see any photographs of Erika's father, Saul remembered him as a tall stocky man in his late sixties, slightly stooped, with thick white hair that never stayed in place, dense white eyebrows, and a thin inch-long scar along the right ridge of his narrow jaw. On his own initiative, the man had never commented on the scar, and when asked, he'd never explained what had caused it. 'The past,' was the most he'd ever allowed himself to murmur, and the expression in his gray eyes, behind his glasses, would grow sad.

Occasionally rubbing his son's back to reassure him, Saul watched Erika turn her gaze slowly around the room.

'Tell me again,' she said to Misha.

'Four days ago' – Misha sighed – 'Joseph didn't come to the café for his morning cup of hot chocolate. The owner didn't think much about it till your father failed to show up that evening as well. Even if your father wasn't feeling well, if he had a cold for example, he *always* went twice daily to that café.'

63

'And my father seldom even had a cold.'

'A strong constitution.'

'A man of habit,' Saul interrupted.

Misha studied him.

'I'm assuming the café owner is one of you,' Saul said. 'Mossad.'

Misha didn't respond.

'Joseph's visits to the café weren't just for hot chocolate, were they?' Saul asked. 'Despite his retirement, he still kept a schedule, a customary routine that made it easy for a contact to reach him without attracting attention.'

Misha stayed silent.

'Not that his skills would probably ever be needed,' Saul said. 'But who can tell? Sometimes a knowledgeable old man, no longer officially a member of his network, to all appearances divorced from intelligence work, is exactly what a mission requires. And this way, it made Joseph feel he still had a purpose, was being held in reserve as it were. Even if you didn't have a use for him, you were kind enough to make him feel he hadn't been discarded.'

Misha raised his eyebrows slightly, either a question or a shrug.

'Plus . . . and this was probably your network's principal motive . . . his schedule, dropping in twice a day, was a subtle way for you to make sure he was doing all right, wasn't helpless at home, hadn't suffered a stroke or a heart attack, for example. You also made sure he wasn't being victimized by an old enemy. In a way that didn't jeopardize his pride, you protected him.'

Erika stepped close to Misha. 'Is that true?'

'You married a good man.'

'I knew that already,' she said. 'Is Saul right?'

'What harm was done? We took care of our own and made him feel he had worth.'

'No harm at all,' she said. 'Unless . . .'

'He wasn't working on anything for us, if that's what you mean,' Misha said. 'Though I'd have welcomed him on an assignment. Nothing violent, of course. But for stakeouts or routine intelligence gathering, he was still a first-rate operative. You have to remember, Erika. Your father's retirement was *his* choice, not ours.'

'What?'

'You mean you didn't know?'

She shook her head.

'Despite his age, I could have bent some rules and kept him,' Misha said. 'We're not so rich with talent we can afford to throw away a seasoned specialist. But he *asked* for retirement. He *demanded* it.'

'I don't understand,' she said. 'His work meant everything to him. He loved it.'

'No question. He loved his work and his country.'

'But if he loved his country so much,' Saul asked, 'why did he choose to live here? In Vienna? Why not in Tel Aviv or Jerusalem or . . . ?'

Erika agreed. 'That bothered us. Saul's arrangement with his network was if he stayed out of sight they'd leave him alone, and the other networks would leave him alone as well. In exchange for the information he gave them, they agreed to ignore the rules he'd broken. As long as he lived where we did, in a village on the edge of the world. But my father didn't have to live here. Repeatedly we asked him to join us, to add to our family, to watch his grandson grow up. And he repeatedly refused. It didn't make sense to me. The comforts of civilization weren't important to him. As long as he had hot chocolate and tobacco, he'd have been content anywhere.'

'Perhaps,' Misha said.

Erika watched his eyes. 'Is there something you haven't told us?'

'You asked me to explain it again, so I will. After your father missed his morning schedule and didn't complete the evening rendezvous, the café owner – Saul's right, he *is* one of ours – sent an operative who works for him to bring some sandwiches and hot chocolate as if your father had ordered them over the phone. The operative knocked on the door. No answer. He knocked again. He tested the doorknob. The lock had not been secured. When the operative unholstered his weapon and entered, he found the apartment deserted. The sheets' – Misha pointed toward the door to the bedroom – 'were tucked in, stretched taut, in military fashion.'

'The way my father always makes his bed,' Erika said. 'He's addicted to order. He tucks in the sheets as soon as he wakes up.'

'Correct,' Misha said. 'Which meant that whatever had happened, your father either didn't go to bed the night before, when he came back from the café, or else he made his bed the morning of his disappearance and for some reason didn't go to the café again as he normally would have.'

'So the time frame is twenty-four hours,' Saul said.

'And Joseph wasn't sick at home. The operative briefly concluded that something had happened to Joseph while he was coming to or from his apartment. A traffic accident, let's imagine. But the police and the hospitals had no information about him.'

'A moment ago, you used the word "briefly,"' Saul said.

Misha squinted.

'You said, the operative *briefly* suspected Joseph had left the apartment and something happened to him. What made the operative change his mind?'

Misha grimaced, as if in pain. He reached in a jacket pocket and pulled out two objects. 'The operative found these on the coffee table.'

Erika moaned.

Saul turned, alarmed by her sudden pallor.

'My father's two favorite pipes,' Erika said. 'He never went anywhere without at least one of them.'

'So whatever happened, it happened here,' Misha said.

'And he didn't leave willingly.'

65

2

The room became silent. The rain lashed harder against the window.

'Our people are searching for him,' Misha said. 'We're about to ask friendly networks to help us. It's difficult to focus our efforts. We don't know who'd want to take him or why. If the motive was revenge for something Joseph did while he still worked for us, why didn't the enemy merely kill him?'

'Unless the enemy wanted' – Erika swallowed – 'to torture him.'

'As a means of revenge? But that would make it personal not professional,' Misha said. 'In my twenty years of intelligence work, I've never heard of an operative allowing his emotions to control him so much he violated protocol and used torture to get even with someone. Assassination? Of course – on occasion. But sadism?' Misha shook his head. 'If other operatives found out, the violator would be shunned, despised, forever mistrusted, judged undependable. Even you, Saul, with all the reason you have to hate Eliot, you killed him but didn't torture him.'

The memory filled Saul with bitterness. 'But we all know there's one circumstance in which torture *is* acceptable.'

'Yes, for information,' Misha said, 'though chemicals are more effective. But that brings us back to my earlier questions. What network would want him? What would they want to know? We're searching for him. That's the best I can tell you for now . . . Of course, as soon as our local people understood how serious the situation was, they contacted our headquarters. Because of my relationship with Joseph and you – remember, he was one of my teachers – I decided to take charge of the assignment rather than delegate it. I also decided to bring you the bad news in person, rather than give it to you coldly in a message. But I would have come to you anyhow, as soon as I heard about the raid on your village. The coincidence can't be ignored. I don't like my premonition.'

'That the two events are connected? That *we're* targets as much as my father was? The thought occurred to us,' Erika said. 'But why would *we* be targets?'

'I don't know any more than I know why your father disappeared. But wouldn't it be wiser if you and your family stayed out of sight while we investigate? If you *are* a target, you won't be able to move as freely as we can.'

'*You think I'd be satisfied doing nothing, waiting, while my father's in danger?*'

Misha exhaled. 'In conscience, I had to suggest the prudent course of action. But before you commit yourself, there's one thing I still haven't told you.'

Saul waited uneasily.

'What we found in the basement,' Misha said.

For an instant, no one moved. At once Saul reached for the doorknob, about to go out to the stairs in the hallway, when Misha's voice stopped him.

'No, through there.' Misha pointed toward the bedroom door.

'You said the basement.'

'The part I'm talking about can't be reached from downstairs. In the bedroom, in the far right corner, there's a door.'

'I remember,' Erika said. 'The first time I came here to visit, I thought the door led into a closet. I tried to open it and found it was locked. I asked my father why. He claimed he'd lost the key. But you know my father never lost anything. So I asked him what was in there. He said, "Nothing important enough to call a locksmith." '

'Then why did he lock the door?' Saul asked.

'Exactly my question,' she said. 'His answer was he didn't remember.'

Misha opened the door to the bedroom – the shadows beckoned.

'When our investigators searched the apartment, looking for anything that might explain your father's disappearance, they came to that door, and obviously they had to know what was behind it, so they picked the lock and . . . well, with a little research, they learned that this house has a history. They checked old city directories. They located the architectural firm that built the house. They managed to find a few former neighbors, quite old by now. In the thirties, a doctor owned this building. His name was Bund. Well-to-do. Large family. Seven children. They lived on the second and third stories of the building. Bund had his offices on the first floor. He kept his records and supplies in the basement.'

Misha's shoulders sagged as he continued.

'The war started. And in 1942 – the Holocaust. From files our investigators found, carefully hidden beneath the basement floor, they learned that many of the doctor's patients were Jewish. Beyond that – and this reaffirms my belief in humanity, a belief sorely tested from time to time – the records made clear that even after the war began, after the *Holocaust* began, he continued to treat his Jewish patients. It's astonishing. He truly believed in his Hippocratic oath. Our good doctor continued to care for his Jewish patients till the day the SS came to take him and his family away to the concentration camp at Mauthausen.'

Saul felt a chill.

'But Dr Bund did more than administer medicine to his Jewish patients,' Misha said. 'He actually *hid* the sickest ones, those whose weakened condition would have meant automatic execution instead of forced labor. Bund' – Misha glanced toward the ceiling – 'the unnameable loves you.'

'Hid them?' Erika whispered.

'In the basement. The way the house was set up, Bund had a stairway down from his bedroom to his clinic on the first floor. He never had to pass his patients in the waiting room as he entered his office. He merely admitted them to his sanctum. But as long as he had the stairway through a door in back, from his office to his apartment, why not continue the stairs all the way to the basement? He wouldn't have to go through the waiting room to reach his records and his medications below him. Efficient, direct, simple.'

'And' – Erika shook her head – 'in the end, it killed him.'

'At the height of the pogrom, conscience-torn between his need to survive and his oath to heal, he built a partition across his basement. The front half, reached from an alternate and obvious door at the bottom of the outside stairs, was cluttered with boxes of records and supplies. Bund knew that the SS, prigs at heart, wouldn't dirty their uniforms to wade through the boxes, finally reach the partition, and test it. How could the so-called Elite Guard have strutted in front of the populace with dust stains on their shirts? For a time, that logic saved the doctor's life. Meanwhile, after dinner every evening, the doctor went down to the *back* half of his basement where, hidden by the partition, he took care of his Jewish patients. I don't know what medical horrors faced him, or how the SS learned his secret, but I *do* know he saved at least a dozen Jewish lives, men and women who somehow found ways to leave Europe, before he and his family were arrested. That's the point. Not only Bund. But also his family. His wife and children. They *all* accepted the risk. They chose to reject the obscenity of their nation's politics. They sacrificed themselves for us.'

'But how do you know?'

'Because our investigators were able to find two Jews in Israel, now elderly, who in those days were hidden downstairs. To use Christian terminology, the doctor was a saint.'

'Then maybe there's hope,' Saul said.

'Or maybe not. After all, he was killed,' Misha said.

'My point exactly. He died for *us*,' Saul said. 'So there *is* hope.'

His eyes sad, Misha nodded. 'We don't know if Joseph chose to live here because of the house's association with the Jewish cause or if he selected this apartment at random. If it *was* at random, there's no way to tell how he learned about that stairway behind his bedroom – because the SS sealed both that entrance and the one from the office down on the first floor. They removed the doors and put in new sections of wall. We asked the landlord about this upper floor. He claimed the door wasn't here six years ago when he bought the building. We asked several former tenants about it. The door wasn't here when they rented the apartment.'

'So my father must have been the one who unsealed the opening and put the door in,' Erika said.

'But then he locked it,' Saul said. 'I don't understand. What was he protecting?'

'You'll have to find out for yourselves. Experience this the same way I did – with no expectation, no prejudgment. Maybe you'll understand what I still haven't.'

'And whatever we find, you think it's connected with my father's disappearance?' Erika asked.

'I haven't made up my mind. If the people who took your father were looking for something, they surely would have been suspicious about the locked door. They'd have investigated. The door shows no sign of having been forced open. So if they did go through it, they must have picked the lock as we did, or possibly they made your father tell them where the key was. When they finished searching, they locked the door again, leaving the apartment exactly as they found it. But I assume if they'd discovered what your father was hiding and it *was* what they wanted, they'd have taken it or else destroyed it. By the way, you might as well leave your son up here with me. He looks like he needs a nap.'

'You mean, it's better if he doesn't see what's down there.'

'No one should.'

4

Saul glanced toward Erika. Apprehensive, they entered the bedroom. It too, smelled of pipe smoke. The covers on the bed were tucked in neatly. A handkerchief and a comb were on the otherwise bare dresser.

Saul allowed himself only a moment to register these details. The door alone occupied his attention. Already Erika was testing the knob. She pulled, and the door swung open, its hinges silent. Darkness faced them. She groped along the inside wall but didn't find a lightswitch. Her shoe touched an object on the floor. She picked it up. A flashlight. When she turned it on, its beam revealed steps descending to the left. The walls were unpainted, stained by mildew. Cobwebs hung from the ceiling; dust covered each side of the steps, the middle section brushed clean by footsteps.

The bitter smell of dust made the inside of Saul's nostrils itchy. He stifled the impulse to sneeze. Peering down, he saw a landing. As Misha had described, the former entrance to the first floor had been sealed by a section of wall. Even the dust and mildew couldn't disguise the contrast between the dark original and the later light wood. In the apartment on the other side, wallpaper or paint would have hidden the renovation. But on this side, no attempt had been made to conceal where a door had been.

Saul went down. The wood of the landing's middle wall was the same type the SS had used to seal the door on the left. Despite its layer of dust, the pallor of pine was evident. Saul shoved at the middle wall – it felt solid. He drew his index finger along it and discovered two barely detectable seams, a shoulder-width apart. Opening a pocketknife, he inserted its blade within one seam, used the knife as a lever, and nudged the handle sideways. A section of the wall creaked loose. He pulled it

69

toward him, setting it to his right. Erika aimed the flashlight through the opening to reveal the continuation of the stairs.

They stepped through, descending. Below, the gleam of the flashlight showed the concrete floor of the basement. A stronger musty smell, accentuated by dampness, attacked Saul's nostrils. Reaching the bottom, he turned left as Erika swung the beam of the flashlight.

He gasped.

The narrow range of the flashlight emphasized the horror. Each object, isolated by the beam, surrounded by darkness, seemed to have greater force alone than it would have had as part of a group. While Erika shifted the light across the room, one terrible image gave way to another, and another, the series becoming more and more unbearable. The blackness toward which the flashlight headed seemed to intensify with the threat of what it hid. Saul's shoulder blades tightened. 'Dear God.'

Erika stopped pivoting the flashlight. Though she hadn't yet scanned the full length of the basement, she seemed unable to tolerate seeing yet another obscene affront. She lowered the beam and revealed a battered table upon which stood a lamp.

A box of matches lay beside the lamp. Saul approached the table, struck one of the matches, and lit the wick. A flame grew, casting shadows. He set the glass chimney on top of the lamp. The flame became brighter.

He forced himself to look again, only to discover that his initial impression had been wrong. The darkness hadn't made each image worse alone than it would have been if seen in a group.

He was staring at photographs: large and small, black-and-white and color, glossy and grainy, from newspapers and magazines, books and archives. Thumbtacks attached them to the wall, which, unlike the other three walls, wasn't made from concrete but was wooden, the partition Dr Bund had built across the basement so he could hide his sick Jewish patients in the rear compartment down here. The partition was thirty feet wide and ten feet tall; every inch of it was crammed with photographs.

Of concentration camps. Gaunt-cheeked prisoners. Gas chambers. Corpses. Ovens. Pits filled with ashes. Trucks crammed with clothing, shoes, jewelry, human hair, and teeth. In a snapshot, SS officers, their lightning-bolt and death's-head insignia prominent on pristine black uniforms, stood in a line, their arms around each other, grinning at the camera while in the background bodies formed a disheveled pyramid so large it stunned the mind.

Saul slumped on a rickety chair beside a table. He reached for Erika's hand, squeezing it.

'What was my father *doing* down here?' Erika asked. 'He never mentioned . . . I never knew he was obsessed by . . . This wasn't sudden. All along he had this room down here.'

'Madness confronting madness.' Saul scanned the rest of the room. It was cluttered with stacks of cardboard boxes. Drawn as if toward a vortex, he approached a stack, pried open the flaps on a box, and found documents.

Some were originals. Others were carbons, photostats, Xeroxes. Brittle yellow pages alternated with smooth white ones. The language varied – English, French, German, Hebrew. Saul's French and German were good, and Erika's Hebrew was perfect. Between them, they managed to translate enough of the documents to understand the common theme.

Concentration camp records kept by German commandants. Lists of SS officers, of Jewish prisoners. Military dossiers. Progress reports on how many inmates were executed at which camp on which day, week, month, and year. Lists of the comparatively few Jews who'd survived the death camps, of the correspondingly few Nazis who'd been punished after the war for their participation in the Holocaust.

Saul's eyes ached from translating faded typescript and cramped handwriting. He turned to Erika. 'I met your father only once, when we were married. I never had a chance to get to know him. Was he in one of the camps?'

'My father and mother almost never talked about what had happened to them during the war. When I was young, though, I once overheard them mention it to each other. I didn't understand, so I pestered them with questions. It was the only time they discussed the war in my presence. Other times, they were willing to talk about the pogroms, the persecutions. They wanted me to know about the Holocaust, in detail, as history. But their own experience . . . They were both in the Jewish ghetto in Warsaw when the Nazis laid siege to it.'

Saul grimaced, understanding. In 1943, Nazi soldiers had surrounded the Warsaw ghetto. Jews were forced into it, but no one was allowed to leave – except in groups being transported to concentration camps. The 380,000 Jews there were reduced to 70,000. Those that remained revolted against the Nazis. In a massive retaliation that lasted four weeks, the Nazis crushed the rebellion and razed the ghetto. Of the Jewish survivors, 7,000 were executed on the spot. Twenty-seven thousand were sent to labor camps.

'My father and mother were part of the group the Nazis sent to Treblinka.'

Saul shuddered. Treblinka hadn't been a labor camp but rather a death camp, the worst of the worst. Arriving prisoners lived less than one hour.

'But how did your mother and father survive?'

'They were young and strong. They agreed to do the work – removing the corpses from the gas chambers and burning them – that even the SS couldn't stomach. That's why my parents didn't talk about the war. They survived at the expense of other Jews.'

'*What other choice did they have?* As long as they didn't collaborate with the Nazis, as long as they didn't participate in the killing, they had to do what they could to stay alive.'

'The first and last time my father talked to me about it, he said

71

he could justify what he did in his mind – but not in his soul. I always thought that's why he joined the Mossad and dedicated his life to Israel. To try to make amends.'

'But even helping to dispose of the bodies would have given your parents just a temporary reprieve. The Nazis fed slave laborers almost nothing. Eventually your parents would have been too weak to work. The SS would have killed them and forced other Jews to dispose of the bodies.'

'Treblinka,' she said. 'Remember where this happened.'

He suddenly realized what she meant. The prisoners at Treblinka had revolted against their guards. Using shovels and clubs as weapons, more than fifty had subdued their captors and managed to escape.

'Your parents took part in the revolt?'

'First in Warsaw, then at Treblinka.' She smiled wanly. 'You've got to give them credit for persistence.'

Saul felt her pride and shared it, squeezing her hand again. He scanned the wall. 'An obsession. A lifetime's worth. And you never suspected.'

'No one else did either. He couldn't have kept his position in the Mossad if they'd known what was festering in his mind. They don't trust fanatics.' She seemed startled by a thought.

'What's wrong?'

'My mother died five years ago. That's when he asked to retire from the Mossad, moved from Israel to here, and in secret began setting up this room.'

'You're saying, your mother was the controlling influence?'

'Subduing his obsession. And when she died . . .'

'His obsession took over.' Saul imagined ghosts around him. 'God help him.'

'If he's still alive.'

'This room . . . Have we found the reason he disappeared?'

'And if we have, was he taken?' Erika asked. 'Or did he run?'

'From what?'

'His past.'

As Erika's expression became more grim, he spoke before he realized. 'You don't mean . . . suicide?'

'An hour ago, if anyone had suggested it, I'd have said my father was too strong to give up, too brave to destroy himself. But now I'm not sure. This room . . . His guilt must have been intolerable.'

'Or his hatred for those who'd made him feel guilty.'

On the counter, an open book – spread with its pages flat, straining the spine – attracted Saul's attention. He picked it up and read the title. *The Order of the Death's Head: The Story of Hitler's SS*. The author was Heinze Höhne, the text in German, its publication date 1966. Where the pages had been spread open, a passage was underlined in black. Saul mentally translated.

The sensational fact, the really horrifying feature, of the annihilation of the Jews was that thousands of respectable fathers of families

72

made murder their official business and yet, when off duty, still regarded themselves as ordinary law-abiding citizens who were incapable even of thinking of straying from the strict path of virtue. Sadism was only one facet of mass extermination and one disapproved of by SS Headquarters. Himmler's maxim was that mass extermination must be carried out coolly and cleanly; even while obeying the official order to commit murder, the SS man must remain 'decent.'

'Decent?' Saul murmured with disgust.

In the margin beside the passage, a cramped hand holding a black-inked pen had scribbled several words in Hebrew – two groups of them.

'My father's handwriting,' Erika said.

'You're the expert in Hebrew.'

'They're quotations. From Conrad's *Heart of Darkness*, I think. The first group says, "The horror, the horror."'

'And the second group?'

She hesitated.

'What's the matter?'

She didn't answer.

'You're having trouble translating?'

'No, I can translate.'

'Then?'

'They're from *Heart of Darkness* as well . . . "Exterminate the brutes."'

5

An hour of searching brought them back to the confusion with which they'd started. In that shadowy room, Saul finally couldn't bear it any longer. He had to get away.

Erika closed a box of documents. 'How could my father have come back repeatedly to pin those photographs to the wall and go through these records? The persistent exposure *must* have affected him.'

'There's still no proof he committed suicide.'

'There's no proof he didn't either,' Erika responded grimly.

They extinguished the lamp and started up the stairs. In the darkness, Saul suddenly remembered something. He gripped Erika's shoulder.

'There's one place we didn't look.' He guided her back down the stairs, scanning the flashlight along the floor.

'What are you . . . ?'

'Misha wouldn't tell us what we'd find down here. He didn't want us to have preconceptions. But inadvertently he did tell us something about this room. During the war, the doctor hid his sickest Jewish patients down here. And also hid their files.'

73

'He said that, yes. But how does . . . ?' Erika's voice dropped.
'Oh.'

'Yes, "oh." The doctor hid the files beneath the floor, Misha said.
There must be a trapdoor.'

Saul scanned the flashlight across the floor. In a corner, behind a
stack of boxes, he found a layer of dust that seemed contrived. He
felt a niche where fingers could grab and lifted a small section of
concrete.

A narrow compartment. The stark gleam from the flashlight
revealed a dusty notebook.

Saul flipped it open. Though the words were written in Hebrew,
Saul couldn't fail to recognize a list.

Of names.

Ten of them.

All Jewish.

6

The rain persisted. Christopher slept on the sofa. Beside him, Misha
stared toward the open bedroom door.

Saul stepped through, gesturing angrily with the notebook.

'So you found it,' Misha said.

Erika entered, even more angry. 'We almost didn't. That makes me
wonder if you *meant* for us to find it.'

'I wasn't sure.'

'Whether you *wanted* us to find it, or whether we would?'

'Does it matter? You did.'

'For the first time, I'm beginning not to trust you,' she said.

'If you hadn't found it and you'd still insisted on wanting to hunt
for your father, I'd have resisted,' Misha said.

Christopher squirmed in his sleep.

'Think about it,' Misha said. 'From my point of view. How do I
know how soft you got in the desert?'

'You should try it some time,' Erika said.

'I'm allergic to sand.'

'And to telling the truth?'

'I didn't lie. I merely tested you.'

'Friends don't need to test each other.'

'Professionals do. If you don't understand, you did get soft in the
desert.'

'Fine. So now we've found it.' Saul's grip tightened around the
notebook. 'Tell us the rest. What does the list of names mean?'

'They're not the names of Jewish patients the doctor hid in the
war,' Erika said. 'This notebook's dusty, yes, but the paper's new.
My father's name is included. The handwriting isn't his.'

'Correct. The notebook belongs to me.'

'What do the names on the list have to do with what happened to
my father?'

74

'I have no idea.'

'I don't believe that. You wouldn't have made the list if there isn't a connection among them.'

'Did I say there isn't a connection? We know their backgrounds, their addresses, their habits, their former occupations.'

'Former?'

'*These men are all ex-Mossad, all retired*. But you asked how they related to what happened to your father, and that puzzle I haven't been able to solve yet.'

'They claim they don't know my father? They won't answer your questions? What's the problem?'

'I haven't been able to ask them *anything*.'

'You're doing it again. Evading,' Erika said.

'*I'm not*. These men share two other factors. They survived the Nazi death camps . . .'

'And?'

'They've all disappeared.'

Church Militant

Despite the worsening heat of the desert, excitement overcame exhaustion, making Drew and Arlene stumble quickly toward the tire tracks in the sand at the far end of the pass.

After their encounter with the two Arab assassins, they'd taken the small canvas sheet from Arlene's knapsack and anchored it across a space between two rocks where, protected from the sun, they'd sipped water sparingly, then eaten some of the dates and figs the killers had carried with them. But the killers hadn't brought enough food to sustain them long out here.

'What about their water supply?' Drew had wondered. 'We searched the slopes from where they shot at us.' He held up two canteens and shook them. Water sloshed hollowly. 'Not enough here for them to walk any distance. So how did they hope to get back?'

With a sudden thrill of understanding, they got to their feet, ignoring the hammer force of the sun. Reaching the end of the pass, they veered to the right, followed the indentations in the sand, and came to a clump of boulders behind which a jeep had been hidden.

'Outsiders, for sure,' Drew said. 'No local villager has a jeep, let alone a new one. It even has air-conditioning. Those killers were used to traveling first-class.'

The jeep had a metal top. The angle of the sun cast a shadow over the driver's side. Arlene welcomed the slight relief from the scorching blaze as she peered through the open driver's window. 'Small problem.'

'What?' he asked.

'No ignition key.'

'But we searched both bodies and didn't find it on them.'

'So logically they must have left it in the jeep.'

But fifteen minutes later, they still hadn't found the key.

'In that case . . .' Drew climbed inside.

'What are you doing?' she asked.

'Waiting.'

'For what?'

'You to hotwire the ignition.'

She laughed and leaned beneath the dashboard.

But after she started the engine, as they jolted across the bumpy desert, he lapsed into sober silence. He had many questions. Though he didn't want to, he had to talk to the priest.

76

2

Cairo. The next afternoon. Sitting on the bed in the Western-style hotel room, Arlene listened to the spray of water from the bathroom as Drew took a shower. But her attention was focused on the telephone.

She didn't know what to do. When the priest had contacted her in New York, directing her to go after Drew, he'd given her a Cairo telephone number. 'Call me as soon as you bring him out of the desert.' At the time, she'd been so grateful to be told where Drew was, to have the chance to be with him again, that she'd readily agreed to the priest's condition. But now that she and Drew were together, she hesitated. Whatever the Fraternity wanted from Drew, it would surely not be a dispensation. No, by definition, a summons from the Fraternity meant trouble. She'd lost Drew once when he entered the monastery. She'd lost him again when he fled to the desert. She didn't intend to lose him a third time.

But what if the Fraternity's punishment for disobedience was . . . ?

To kill Drew, whom they'd spared till now, and instead of killing her as well, leave her to grieve for the rest of her life.

She decided to make the call. But her hand felt so heavy she couldn't raise it toward the phone on the bedside table.

In the bathroom, the water stopped flowing. The door came open, and Drew stepped out, naked, drying himself with a large plush towel. She had to smile. After his six years in the monastery, after his monk's vow of celibacy, he had sexual inhibitions, true. But modesty? He was more comfortable with his body, naked or clothed, than any man she'd ever met.

He grinned as he toweled himself. 'Once a year, whether I need it or not.'

She touched her still damp hair. 'I know. I feel like I lost a ton of sand.'

Drew had used her Egyptian money to buy shampoo, scissors, shaving soap, and a razor. His beard was gone now. He'd trimmed his hair. Tucked back behind his ears, it made his gaunt cheeks look even thinner. But the effect was attractive.

He set down the towel. 'I've had a lot of time . . . too much . . . to think,' he said.

'About . . . ?'

'Some laws are God-made, others are human-made.'

She laughed. 'What are you talking about?'

'My vow of chastity. If Adam and Eve weren't allowed to have sex, God wouldn't have made them man and woman.'

'Is this your way of telling me sex is natural? I knew that already.'

'But as you've probably noticed, I've been confused.'

'Oh, *that* I've definitely noticed.'

'So I've decided . . .'

'Yes?'

'If you wouldn't mind . . .'

'Yes?'

'Choosing nature over artificial laws . . .'

'Yes?'

'I'd enjoy making love to you.'

'Drew . . .'

It was his turn now to ask, 'Yes?'

'Come over here.'

3

In the late afternoon, with the draperies closed and the room in cool shadows, they held each other on the bed after making love. Naked, relaxed, enjoying the touch of each other's skin, neither spoke for quite a while. But preoccupations intruded.

'The priest,' Drew said.

'I know. I wish we didn't have to.'

'But the problem won't go away.'

Brooding, he reached for his clothes.

'There's something I'm curious about,' Arlene said.

He stopped buttoning his shirt. 'Curious?'

'Before, when you had to leave the monastery, you couldn't stop asking questions. About how the culture had changed in the six years you'd been away and who was president and what had happened in the world. But this time, after a year in the desert, you haven't asked me anything.'

His cheek muscles rippled. 'Yes. Because the last time, I didn't like what I learned.'

'Then why call the priest? Why don't we disappear? Retreat. Together.'

'Because I no longer believe I *can* retreat. I want this settled. So I don't have to worry about the Fraternity. Or anyone else interfering with us. *Ever again.*'

4

Cairo was heat, noise, crowds, and traffic jams. Automobile exhaust fought to destroy the fragrance of Arabian food and spices sold at bazaars. The complex directions they'd been given over the telephone led Drew and Arlene through a maze of narrow streets. They reached a door to a restaurant whose Egyptian sign Drew translated as 'The Needle's Eye.' He glanced both ways along the lane, seeing no sudden reaction from anyone, no interruption of the natural rhythm of the crowd. Of course, the absence of unusual activity didn't prove they weren't being followed; a professional tail wasn't likely to give himself away so easily. On the other hand, at least they hadn't proved they *were* being followed, and for the moment, that consolation would have to do.

78

They entered the restaurant's murky interior. Drew's first impression, apart from shadows, was one of smell. Pungent tobacco smoke. Strong coffee aroma. Next came touch – the gritty feel of the stone floor beneath his shoes. In a moment, his eyes adjusted to the layout of the restaurant – wooden tables and chairs, no tablecloths, but several ornate Arabian rugs on the walls, except in back, where behind a counter, colorful bottles and polished brass containers were stacked on shelves below a mirror. Here and there along the walls, intricately carved wooden partitions surrounded the tables. Apart from a white-aproned waiter behind the counter and two men dressed in dark suits and red fezzes sitting at the far left corner table, the place was deserted.

Drew and Arlene chose a table on the right. The table was equidistant between the entrance and what Drew assumed would be a rear exit through the kitchen behind the counter. They sat with their back to the wall.

'What time did he say he'd meet us?' Drew asked.

'He didn't exactly. All he said was, he'd be here before sundown.'

Drew tapped his fingers on the table. 'You want some coffee?'

'*Egyptian* coffee? That stuff's so strong I might as well put a gun to my head and blow my brains out *that* way.'

Drew started to laugh but stopped when he heard a chair scrape behind a wooden partition to his left. A man in a white suit appeared from behind the partition and paused at the table.

The man was solidly built, olive-complexioned, with a thick dark mustache that emphasized his smile. The smile was one of amusement as much as friendliness. 'Ms Hardesty, I spoke to you earlier on the phone.'

'You're not the priest who came to me in New York,' Arlene said.

Drew braced himself to stand.

'No,' the man said agreeably. 'You're right, I'm not. The priest you spoke to – Father Victor – was called away on an urgent assignment.' The man continued to smile. 'My name is Father Sebastian. I hope the shift in personnel is acceptable. But of course, you'll want credentials.'

The man held out his left hand, palm down, revealing a ring on his middle finger.

The ring had a large perfect ruby that glinted even in shadow. Its band and setting were thick gleaming gold. On the tip of the ruby, an insignia showed an intersecting sword and cross. Religion and violence. The symbol of the Fraternity of the Stone. Drew shuddered.

'I see you're familiar with it.' Father Sebastian kept smiling.

'*Anybody* can wear a ring.'

'Not *this* ring.'

'Perhaps,' Drew said. 'May the Lord be with you.'

Father Sebastian's smile faded. 'Ah.'

'That's right.' Drew's tone became gruff. 'The code. Go on and finish it. The Fraternity's greeting. "May the Lord be with you."'

'And with your spirit.'

'The rest of it?'

'*Deo gratias*. Are you satisfied?'

'Just getting started. *Dominus vobiscum.*'

'*Et cum spiritu tuo.*'

'*Hoc est enim . . .*'

'*Corpus meum.*'

'*Pater Noster . . .*'

'*Qui est in coeli.*'

Arlene interrupted, 'What are you two talking about?'

'We're exchanging the responses of a traditional mass,' Drew said. 'The Fraternity's conservative. In the mid-sixties, it never shifted Catholic ritual from Latin into the vernacular. And you' – Drew studied the swarthy, Egyptian-looking man with the ring who'd said his name was Father Sebastian – 'are younger than I am. Thirty? Unless you belonged to the Fraternity, you wouldn't have seen a *real* mass in so long you couldn't remember the Latin responses. Who founded the Fraternity?'

'Father Jerome.'

'When?'

'The Third Crusade. Eleven ninety-two.'

'His real name?'

'Hassan ibn al-Sabbah. Coincidentally the same name as the Arab originator of terrorism a hundred years earlier. Though a monk, Father Jerome was recruited as an assassin by the crusaders because he was an Arab and hence could mix freely with the heathen. But in contrast with Arab terror, Father Jerome's was *holy* terror. And since that time, we've' – Father Sebastian shrugged – 'done whatever was necessary to protect the Church. Now are you satisfied?'

Drew nodded.

The priest sat at the table. 'And *your* credentials?'

'You had plenty of chance to study me through that partition. You must have a photograph.'

'Plastic surgery can work wonders.'

'Your ring has a poison capsule inside. Your monastery is on the western coast of France, across from England, in the territory contested by France and England during the Third Crusade. Only someone who'd been approached, to be recruited, by the Fraternity would know these things.'

'True. Approached. And now we approach you again.'

Drew felt suddenly tired. It was all coming back. There was no escape. His voice shook. 'What do you want? If you knew where I was hiding, why did you force me to spend a year . . . ?'

'In a cave in the desert? You had to do penance for your sins. For your soul. To purify you. We kept you in reserve. You refused to join us, but we found a way to encourage you to help us if we needed it.'

'Help?'

'Find.'

'What?'

'A priest.'
The room exploded.

5

The concussion struck Drew a millisecond before he heard the actual
sound of the blast. The room became bright, then smotheringly dark
as he flew back against the wall. The back of his head struck stone.
He rebounded toward the table. It collapsed from his weight and
the force of the explosion. The impact of his chest against the floor
took his breath away. As he squirmed in pain, the room burst into
flames.

The counter, now obliterated, must have been where the bomb
had been hidden. The waiter behind it and the two men near it
never screamed, presumably torn apart by the detonation. But this
understanding came much later.

He did hear screaming. Not his own. A woman's. Arlene's. And his
urgent loving need to save her brought him back to the flames and the
devastated room.

Smoke made him gag convulsively. Crawling toward Arlene's
anguished screams, he felt someone grab him. He struggled and
cursed but couldn't stop himself from being lifted and dragged away.
Outside in the hot, dusky, narrow street, encircled by a crowd, he
couldn't hear Arlene screaming any longer. He made a final frantic
effort to free himself from the arms that encircled his chest, to lunge
back into the ruined building.

Instead he collapsed. Through swirling vision, he peered up,
convinced he was hallucinating, for the face above him . . . belonged
to Arlene.

6

'I was afraid you were dead.'

'The feeling was mutual,' Arlene said.

He squeezed her hand.

They sat on metal chairs in a sandy courtyard enclosed by a high
stone wall. Beyond the walls, the din of Cairo intruded on the
peacefulness of one of the few churches in this Arab city. A Greek
Orthodox church, its bulbous spires in contrast with the slender
minarets of a mosque.

It was early the following morning. Shadows filled one side of the
courtyard. The heat was not yet oppressive.

'When the fire started, I heard you screaming.' He continued to
squeeze her hand.

'I *was* screaming. Your name.'

'But you sounded so far away.'

'I sounded far away to me as well. But after the blast, I wasn't hearing *anything* that didn't sound far away. Even my breath seemed to come from outside. All I knew was, I could move better than you could. And both of us had to get out of there.'

He laughed. The laugh made his ribs hurt, but he didn't care. It felt too good to know that Arlene was alive. 'How did we escape?'

'Father Sebastian had a backup team.'

'Professional.'

'They got us away from the restaurant before the police arrived,' she said. 'I don't remember a lot after we reached the street, but I do remember both of us being carried through the crowd and lifted into the back of a truck. After that, things got fuzzy. The next thing I recall is waking up in our room in the rectory of this church.'

'Where's Father Sebastian?'

'Very much alive,' a voice said.

Drew turned. Father Sebastian, looking more Italian than Egyptian now that he wore a priest's black suit and white collar, stood in the open doorway. He held a handkerchief to his nose. When he stepped from the rectory's shadows into the sunlit courtyard, the handkerchief showed spots of blood, a consequence of the explosion, Drew assumed.

The priest brought over a metal chair and sat down. 'I apologize for not joining you earlier, but I was celebrating morning mass.'

'I could have served for you and taken communion,' Drew said.

'You were still asleep when I looked in on you. At the time, your bodily needs seemed more important than your spiritual ones.'

'Right now, my psychological needs are even *more* important.'

'And those are?'

'I get miserable as hell when someone tries to blow me up. Under other circumstances, I might believe we simply happened to be where terrorists decided to set off a bomb. In Israel, say. In Paris or Rome. But in Cairo? It's not on their itinerary.'

'That isn't true any longer. While you were away in the desert, Cairo too became a target of terrorists.'

'But in an unimportant restaurant, in an out-of-the-way part of the city? What political purpose would the explosion have served? That bomb wasn't placed at random. We didn't just happen to be there when the blast went off. We were the targets.'

'For the second time in two days,' Arlene added.

Father Sebastian straightened his chair.

'That's right. For the *second* time,' Drew said. 'While Arlene and I were crossing the desert . . .'

He told the priest about the two Arab gunmen in the pass. Arlene elaborated.

'You don't think they were simply marauders?' Father Sebastian glanced toward Arlene. 'You mentioned an earlier attack by two would-be rapists. In that same pass. Possibly the second pair . . . They could have been relatives out to avenge . . .'

'The first two were amateurs,' Arlene insisted. 'But the second pair . . .'

'If not for the grace of God and a cobra, we'd have been killed,' Drew said. 'Those men were fully equipped. They were pros.'

'Someone knew I'd been sent to get Drew. But I told no one,' Arlene said.

'So the leak could have come only from within your organization,' Drew said.

Father Sebastian rubbed his forehead.

'You don't seem surprised. You mean you'd already suspected—?'

'That the order had been compromised, that someone in the Fraternity was using his position to gain his own ends?' Father Sebastian nodded.

'How long have you—'

'*Merely* suspected? Almost a year. Became virtually certain? Two months. Too many of our missions have ended badly. Twice, members of the order have been killed. If not for our backup teams, the bodies of our fallen brethren would have been found by the authorities.'

'And their rings,' Drew said.

'Yes. And their rings. Other missions were aborted before such disasters could occur. Our enemies had been warned they were in danger and changed their schedules, increased their security. All of us in the Fraternity fear we're in danger of being exposed.'

Arlene's eyes blazed with resentment. 'So that's why you sent me to bring back Drew. You wanted an outside operative, someone not associated with you but nonetheless *controlled* by you.'

Father Sebastian shrugged. 'What's the gambler's expression? An ace in the hole. And indeed,' he told Drew, 'apart from your skills and reputation, you do seem to have a gambler's luck.'

'We all do,' Drew said. 'For sure, we didn't survive that blast because of skill, but only because the bomb was placed in the only likely hiding spot, away from us, behind the counter in back.'

'Two customers and a waiter died in the explosion,' Arlene said. 'If you hadn't sent us there . . .'

Father Sebastian sighed. 'Their deaths were regrettable – but unimportant compared to protecting the Fraternity.'

'What's important to me is survival,' Drew said, 'the chance for Arlene and me to live in peace, some place where you and your colleagues can't get to us.'

'Are you certain there *is* such a place? Your cave wasn't it.'

'I want the chance to keep looking. I asked you yesterday. What do I have to do to stop being threatened by you? You mentioned a priest. You wanted me to—'

'Find him. His name is Krunoslav Pavelic. He's not just a priest. He's a cardinal. Extremely influential. A member of the Vatican's Curia. Seventy-two years old. On the twenty-third of February, a Sunday evening, after celebrating a private mass in the Papal city, he disappeared. Given his important position within the Curia, we consider his abduction to be a serious assault upon the Church. If

83

Cardinal Pavelic wasn't safe, no other member of the Curia is. We believe it's the start of an ultimate attack. But because the Fraternity seems threatened from within, we need your help. An outsider, an independent but motivated operative.'

'What if he can't be found? What if he's dead?' Drew asked.

'Then punish those who took him.'

Drew flinched inwardly. He'd vowed to himself – *and to God* – that he'd never kill again. He concealed his abhorrence. Though determined to keep his vow, he negotiated.

'What do I get in exchange?'

'You and Ms Hardesty are relieved of your obligation to us, your need to atone for your part in the death of one of our members. I consider this condition to be generous.'

'That's not the word I'd have used.' Drew glanced toward Arlene, who nodded. With a silent crucial qualification, he continued. 'But you've got a deal.'

Father Sebastian leaned back. 'Good.'

'There's just one thing. Break your word, and you'd better keep praying an Act of Contrition. Because, believe me, Father, when you least expect it, I'll come for you.'

'If I broke my word, you'd have every right. But as far as an Act of Contrition is concerned, my soul is always prepared.'

'Then we understand each other.' Drew stood. 'Arlene and I could use some breakfast. A fresh change of clothes. Travel money.'

'You'll both be given an adequate amount to start with. In addition, a numbered bank account will be opened for you in Zurich, along with a safe-deposit box. The Fraternity will have a key for it. We'll use the box as a way to send messages between us.'

'What about travel documents? Since the enemy knows we're involved, it isn't smart for us to use our own.'

'To leave Egypt, you'll be given Vatican passports, under different names, for a nun and a priest.'

'We'll attract attention in an airport filled with Arabs.'

'Not if you leave with other nuns and priests who've been in Egypt on tour. You'll fly to Rome, where a priest and a nun will attract no attention at all. If you choose to switch to lay identities, other passports, American, several, under various names, will be placed in the Zurich safe-deposit box.'

'Weapons?'

'Before you leave Egypt, you'll give me the ones you have. When you reach Rome, others will be supplied to you. Weapons will also be left in the Zurich safe-deposit box.'

'Fair enough. As an added precaution . . .'

Father Sebastian waited.

'I don't want to test my luck a third time. Our weapons, our passports – make sure they're supplied by an outside contractor, not someone in your network. Open our Zurich bank account yourself.'

'Agreed. The leak in my network makes me as nervous as it does you.'

'One thing you haven't told us.'

Father Sebastian anticipated. 'Where do you start to look? The same place your predecessor narrowed his search and failed.'

'Predecessor?'

'The priest who contacted Ms Hardesty in New York and sent her to find you. Father Victor. I said he'd been called away on an urgent assignment. He was. To his Maker. He was killed in Rome, two days ago. Take up the hunt where he left off. He must have been very close.'

7

In the room where they'd slept in the rectory, Drew and Arlene put on the religious costumes the priest had supplied. Except for Drew's black bib and white collar, he looked as natural as if he'd put on a dark business suit. But he'd been concerned that Arlene, with her athletic grace, would seem awkward in a nun's robe. Quite the contrary. The black garment flowed in rhythm with her figure. The white cowl that hid her auburn hair and framed her green eyes turned worldly beauty into innocent loveliness.

'Astonishing,' Drew said. 'You look like you've found your vocation.'

'And *you* could be a confessor.'

'Well, let's just hope no one asks us for religious counseling.'

'The best advice is "go in peace and sin no more."'

'But what about us?' Drew asked. 'What *we're* about to do – for the second time I'd hoped I wouldn't have to face the decision – will *we* sin no more?'

She kissed him.

'Just one more assignment,' she said. 'We'll watch over each other and do our best.'

'And if our best is good enough . . .' he said.

'We'll be free.'

They held each other.

BOOK THREE
PINCER MOVEMENT

Death's
Head

Halloway stood on the granite steps before his mansion, watching Icicle and Seth get into the Cadillac. The three of them had spent the night and morning making plans. Now at last, in midafternoon, the plans were ready to be activated. Seth would drive Icicle to the rented car he'd hidden down the road the night before. Icicle would follow Seth to Toronto's international airport. This evening, the two assassins would fly from Canada to Europe. Soon – *yes, soon*, Halloway thought – normality would be reestablished.

But as he squinted from the bright June sunlight, watching Icicle and Seth drive away, Halloway wondered if his life could in fact ever again be normal. His father had disappeared seven weeks ago, abducted while sketching a river gorge at a nearby painter's community called Elora. The assailants had left his father's materials – sketch pad, charcoal, and equipment case – on a picnic table a hundred yards from his father's car. With no word about him since then, Halloway was forced to suspect, with grim reluctance, that his father was dead.

He watched from the steps of his mansion till the Cadillac disappeared among the trees on the road below him. Turning toward the large double doors of the mansion, he reconsidered the thought. His father dead? He paused, exhaled, then continued morosely up the steps. All he could do was hope. At least he'd done what he could to protect his family and himself, to stop the madness. If his father indeed had been killed, this much consoled him – Icicle and Seth were perfect weapons. The enemy would pay.

He entered the mansion, proceeded along the shadowy hallway, and reached the telephone in his study. Though he didn't want to think about it, other decisions, other arrangements had to be made. Four months ago, before the Night and Fog had been reinstituted, he'd made a business commitment that no amount of personal pressure could allow him to ignore. He'd demanded a fortune, guaranteeing delivery of merchandise the deadly nature of which was exceeded only by the homicidal tendencies of his clients. To fail to abide by his agreement would be fatal. With no alternative, Halloway drew on resources ingrained in him by his father and picked up the phone.

★ ★ ★

89

Mexico City. For the third time since he'd started making love to his wife, Aaron Rosenberg's erection failed him. He attempted to arouse himself, but his wife restrained his hand. At first, he suspected she'd become impatient with his repeated failure and intended to ask him to give up. Instead she kissed his chest, then his stomach, murmured 'Let me do the driving,' and shifted lower.

Sunlight gleamed through the parted drapes of the bedroom windows. A breeze cooled the sweat on his body. Closing his eyes, feeling his wife's hair dangle over his groin, he barely heard the roar of traffic outside on the Paseo de la Reforma.

His inability to perform had many causes: concern about his missing father, fears for his family and himself. Despite bodyguards, he felt apprehensive every time he went out and as a consequence left the house less often than was good for his business. Ironically, he'd stayed home today precisely *because of* business. Since early this morning, he'd been waiting for a phone call about such sensitive information he didn't dare receive it at his office. For that matter, even the phone in his house and indeed the house itself, both of which were tested daily for eavesdropping devices, couldn't be fully trusted.

As his wife continued, his penis responded. He made a determined effort to ignore yet another reason for his earlier impotence. For the past two months, he was certain, she'd been having an affair with her bodyguard, Esteban. Glances between them couldn't be ignored, nor could her newly expanded catalogue of sexual techniques, one of which was her sudden fondness for 'doing the driving.' At least he had one thing to be thankful for – the affair was discreet. Otherwise, to maintain respect among the police and his business contacts in this city of Spanish values, Rosenberg would never have been able to pretend to be unaware of his wife's infidelity.

He admitted he was partly to blame for her actions. Since his recent troubles, his sex drive had virtually disappeared, and even before then, his business had kept him away from home so much that she spent more time with Esteban than she did with him. All the same, he thought with a brief flare of anger, if his business required her to be lonely, didn't she have the compensating reward of luxury? Her solid-gold watch, her imported French-designed clothes, her $100,000 Italian sports car.

His penis began to fail once more. She moaned in what seemed genuine disappointment. She'd been the one to suggest making love this afternoon; he wondered if there was still a chance to salvage his marriage.

The phone call, Rosenberg thought. When would that damned call come through? The truth was, if it weren't for his wife's expensive needs, if it weren't for his own need to impress her, he would never have allowed himself to become involved in the terrible risk that the call represented.

But what was the alternative? To confront his wife about her affair? If the scandal became public, honor would require him to divorce her, which he did not want to do. His wife was stunning, a descendant from Indian royalty. Apart from his pride in being married to her, she added to his attempt to look Mexican – his hair dyed black and combed straight back, his skin cosmetically treated to look swarthy, his eyes fitted with non-corrective contact lenses to make them look dark. He needed her to help him be a chameleon. And as for Esteban, the giant was too formidable a bodyguard for Rosenberg to feel safe without him during the present emergency.

His penis began to respond again.

The phone rang. He pulled away from his wife and lunged toward the bedside table. '*Hello?*'

The male voice wasn't Halloway's, but it did have a southern Ontario accent, a vague Scottish burr. Rosenberg realized the sequence he was part of. Halloway had made an untraceable local call to a conduit, who in turn had used a secure phone to relay the message. 'Maple trees.'

'Chaparral.'

'Be ready to talk in forty minutes.' A click concluded the call.

Rosenberg shut his eyes with a mixture of relief and nervousness. 'I have to leave.'

His wife nuzzled him. 'Right now?'

'I need to be somewhere in forty minutes.'

'How long will it take you to get there?'

'Twenty-five minutes.'

'Ten minutes to wash yourself and get dressed. That still leaves . . .'

Five minutes. They were enough.

3

Rosenberg told his three bodyguards to wait outside in the car, entered a dilapidated building, hurried up its creaky stairs, and unlocked a room on the second floor.

The room was little more than a closet with a window. Except for a phone on the floor and an ashtray on the windowsill, it was empty. He rented it and paid the phone bill under the name of José Fernandez. The arrangement existed for one reason only – to provide a secure location where he could make and receive delicate long-distance phone calls without fear of leaving a trail.

In southern Ontario, he knew, Halloway had a similar safe phone in a similar office. As soon as Halloway had instructed his conduit to warn Rosenberg about the impending call, Halloway would have set out toward that office, just as Rosenberg had set out toward his. Rosenberg knew this because, if Halloway had been in place, he wouldn't have needed a conduit; he'd have made the call directly. So circumstances had now changed sufficiently that Halloway refused to waste time calling Rosenberg from the safe phone, then waiting for Rosenberg to get to his. By using the conduit, Halloway was signaling that even the forty minutes it took him to reach his own safe phone were critical.

He opened his briefcase and removed an electronic device the size of a portable radio. He plugged it into a wall socket, checked its dial, and scanned it around the room. The device emitted a hum. If a microphone had been hidden in the room, the device would not only send but receive the hum that the microphone was relaying. The resultant feedback would register on the dial. But the dial remained constant. No hidden microphones.

Not satisfied, Rosenberg removed a second electronic device from his briefcase and used a clip to attach it to an eighth-inch section of exposed wires on the telephone cord. The device monitored the strength of electrical current in the telephone line. Because a tap would drain power, the strength of the current would automatically increase to compensate for the drain. The dial Rosenberg watched indicated no such increase in power. The phone wasn't tapped.

He hastily lit a cigarette – a Gauloise; he hated Mexican tobacco – then checked his watch, the mate to his wife's. The call should come through in the next two minutes. If it didn't, if he or Halloway had been detained, the agreement was to wait another thirty minutes and, if necessary, another thirty minutes after that.

He inhaled and stared at the telephone. When it finally rang, he grabbed it. 'Aztec.'

'Eskimo.'

'I expected your call this morning. What took you so long to get in touch with me?'

'I had to wait till they left,' Halloway said, his acquired Canadian accent convincing. 'It's started. They'll get there tomorrow morning.'

'Europe?'

'Rome. Everything points to Cardinal Pavelic. If they find out why he disappeared—'

'How long will it take them?' Rosenberg interrupted.

'How long? They're the best. Their fathers were the best. It's impossible to predict. The most I can say is they won't take longer than necessary.'

'The *least* I can say is if we fail to honor our business agreement . . .'

'You don't need to tell me,' Halloway said. 'As if the Night and Fog isn't bad enough, we have to worry about our clients.'

'Who *insist* upon delivery.'

'Our guarantees remain valid,' Halloway's voice said. 'I have confidence in Seth alone. But now that Icicle's joined him, *nothing* can stop them.'

'I hope, for everyone's sake, that you're right.'

'If I'm wrong, we'll face two different kinds of enemies. Call our contact in Brazil. Tell him to arrange for delivery. Our clients are desperate enough to ignore the delay, provided we can assure them it's safe to accept delivery, and I think we can do that now. If the enemy knew what we were doing, they'd have used that knowledge as a weapon against us weeks ago.'

92

'Or maybe the Night and Fog operatives are waiting for us to trap ourselves.'

'Soon the Night and Fog won't exist.'

'I want to believe that,' Rosenberg said.

'We *have* to believe it. If Icicle and Seth can't stop them, no one can – and in that case, we're as damned if we go ahead with the shipment as if we don't. So do it. Give the order. Send the merchandise.'

4

Rome. The bored American, his back sore from slumping too many hours on an unpadded chair, gagged on a mouthful of bread, salami, and cheese when he realized what he'd just seen on the monitor. 'Holy . . . !'

He dropped the remnant of his sandwich beside the can of diet Coke on the metal table before him and leaned abruptly ahead to stop the videotape machine.

'Come here! You've gotta see this!'

Two operatives, a man and a woman, turned in his direction, their features haggard from too many hours of watching their own monitors.

'See what?' the man asked. 'All I've been doing is seeing—'

'Nothing,' the woman said. 'These damned faces all blur together till they're just dots on the screen, and then they're—'

'Hey, I'm telling you. Come here and see this.'

The man and woman crossed the spartan office and flanked him.

'Show us,' the woman said.

The first man rewound thirty seconds of videotape and pressed the play button.

Dots on the screen became images.

'Faces,' the woman sighed. 'More damned faces.'

'Just watch,' the first man said. He pointed toward airline passengers coming out of an exit tunnel into Rome's airport. 'There.' He pressed the pause button.

Minuscule lines furrowed over the face and chest of a man suspended in midstride about to enter the concourse. The man wore a loose-fitting sports coat, an open-collared shirt, but his muscular chest and shoulders were nonetheless evident. His face was square and tanned, his eyes intelligent, his hair bleached by the sun.

'I wouldn't kick him out of my sleeping bag,' the woman said.

'But would you still be alive after he'd screwed you?' the first man asked.

'What?'

'Just watch.' The first man released the pause button on the tape machine and pushed the play button. Other faces moved past the camera. Italy's intelligence service had installed the system at every exit ramp in Rome's airport, an attempt to improve security, specifically to guard against terrorists. After Italian specialists had watched, the tapes

93

were released to other networks of various sorts, civilian, military, and political.

'Okay, who else should I notice?' the second male operative asked.

'Him. *Right here*,' the first man said and again pressed the pause button.

Another exiting male passenger froze in place, lines across his face and chest. Tall, thin, pale, red-haired, bleak eyes.

'Holy . . . !' the woman said.

'What a coincidence. Exactly what I said.' The first man straightened, his pulse speeding. 'If you'll check the mug shots of—'

'That guy's—!'

'Cryptonym Seth,' the first man said. 'As assassins go, they don't get more scary. Except for . . .' He stopped the tape, rewound, and expertly stopped it again. 'Take another look at . . .' Excited, he pressed play.

Again the blond muscular man stepped out of the passenger tunnel toward the camera.

'Yes . . . !' the second man breathed.

'It's Icicle,' the first man said. 'Fans, what we've got here is—'

'A reminder to pay attention,' the second man admitted. 'Those bastards do show up, even if we get too bored to expect them.'

'And not just that,' the woman said. 'We watch for days and days. Now suddenly we get *two* of them, *together*, trying to appear as if they're traveling separately.'

'Or maybe each didn't know the other was on the plane,' the second man said.

'Give me a break,' the woman said. 'These guys are state of the art.'

'Okay, all right, I grant the point.'

'Which raises the question,' the first man said. 'Did they know beforehand, or did they find out after the plane took off?'

'What's the city of origin for the flight?' the woman said.

'Toronto,' the first man said. 'So what went down in Toronto?'

'Nothing recently, so far as we know. Not even a rumor,' the woman said.

'So if they weren't on a job there—'

'They must have met there, been sent from there.'

'Unless they both just happened to catch the same flight,' the second man said.

'With those guys, nothing's accidental.'

'Maybe they're working for opposite sides,' the second man said. 'No, that's no good. They didn't look nervous getting off the plane.'

'Of course not. They're professionals,' the woman said. 'Unlike some of us.' She glanced at the second man, then turned to the first. 'But the feeling I get—'

'Is they're traveling together,' the first man said. 'They're being discreet, but they didn't try to disguise themselves; they don't care if we notice. Something big's going down, and they're giving us a signal. It isn't business.'

'Personal?' the woman asked.

'My guess is, *extremely* personal. They're telling us, 'we're here, we're playing it open, we're cool, so *you* be cool, this doesn't concern you.'

'Maybe,' the woman said. 'But if you're right, God help the target they're after.'

5

St Paul, Minnesota. William Miller stomped the accelerator of the Audi that had been left behind when his father disappeared four months ago. Despite his polarized glasses, the afternoon sun stabbed his eyes. His head throbbed, but not from the sun. He skidded around a corner, raced along his tree-lined street, and veered up his driveway, stopping so abruptly he jolted against his seat belt.

As he scrambled out, his wife ran frantically from the house and across the lawn.

'I had to meet with the city engineer,' he said. 'When I checked in with my secretary . . .' Anger strained his voice. 'Where is the damned thing?'

'The swimming pool.'

'*What?*'

'I didn't see it when I had coffee on the patio this morning. Whoever did this must have waited till I left to play tennis this afternoon.'

She followed as Miller hurried past the flower beds at the side of the house. He reached the back and stood at the edge of the swimming pool, staring apprehensively down.

The swimming pool was empty. He'd been planning to have one of his construction crews come over this weekend and reline it before he filled it for the summer.

At the bottom, someone had used black paint, drawing a grotesque symbol whose borders stretched from end to end, from side to side of the pool.

His throat felt sandy. He swallowed before he could talk. 'They wanted to give us time to think they'd gone away, to make us believe they were satisfied just to have taken my father.'

He made a choking sound as he stared at the symbol – large, black, obscene.

A death's head.

'What the hell do they want?' his wife said.

He answered with a more insistent question. '*And what the hell are we going to do?*'

Shadow
Game

Vienna. Again it was raining, though compared to yesterday's storm this was only a drizzle. Saul had to remind himself that this was June and not March as he put his hands in his overcoat pockets and continued along a concrete walkway next to the Danube.

But then, he admitted, it wasn't hard to feel chilled after having been used to the heat of Israel's desert. He remembered the irrigation ditches he'd worked so hard to complete. These two days of Austrian rain would have turned his meager cropland into an oasis. Imagining that wondrous possibility, he ached to go back home but wondered if he'd have the chance to do so.

Barges chugged along the river, hazy in the drizzle. He passed beneath dripping trees, entered a wooded park, and reached a gloomy covered bandstand. Its wooden floor rumbled hollowly as he crossed it.

A man sat with one hip on the railing, angled sideways, smoking a cigarette, peering out toward the rain. He wore a pale brown nylon slicker, its metal fasteners open, a darker brown suit beneath it. In profile, his chin protruded. His cheeks showed sporadic pockmarks. As he exhaled smoke from his cigarette, he seemed unaware of Saul's footsteps coming toward him.

For his part, Saul was aware of another man in an identical brown nylon slicker who waited beneath a nearby chestnut tree and looked with unusual interest at birds huddling in the branches above him.

Saul stopped at a careful distance from the man on the railing. The drizzle on the bandstand's roof seeped through a few cracks and pattered next to him.

'So, Romulus,' the pockmarked man said, then turned, 'how are you?'

'Obviously out of bounds.'

'No kidding. You were spotted as soon as you showed up at the airport. We've been watching you ever since.'

'I didn't try to sneak in. The first thing I did was go to a phone and contact the bakery. This meeting was my idea, remember?'

'And *that*, my friend, is the only reason you're walking around.' The pockmarked man threw his cigarette into the rain. 'You've got a bad habit of breaking rules.'

'My foster brother's the one who broke the rules.'

'Sure. But you helped him escape instead of turning him in.'

'I guess you don't have any brothers.'

'Three of them.'

'In my place, would you have helped them or sided against them?'

The man with the pockmarks didn't reply.

'Besides, my foster brother was eventually killed.' Saul's voice became thick. After almost three years, his grief for Chris still hurt him terribly.

'We're here to talk about you, not him.'

'I admit I made a bargain with Langley. Exile. To stay in the desert. But things have happened.'

'What things?'

'The settlement where I live was attacked. My wife and son were nearly killed.'

'In Israel' – the man shrugged – 'attacks can happen.'

'But this was personal! My son, my wife, and I were the targets!'

The man's eyes narrowed.

'A day before that, my wife's father disappeared! Here in Vienna! That's why I left Israel – to find out what was—!'

'Okay, I get your point. Take it easy.' The man with the pockmarks gave a reassuring gesture to his partner beneath the nearby chestnut tree, who'd started approaching when he heard Saul shout.

'What you're saying' – the pockmarked man studied Saul – 'is you're not back in business? You haven't signed on with another firm?'

'Business? You think that's why I'm here? *Business?* It makes me want to throw up.'

'Graphic, Romulus, but evasive. When I give my report, my superiors will want direct statements.'

'You're giving your report right now. I assume you're wired. That blue van at the entrance to the park is recording every word we say. Am I right?'

The man with the pockmarks didn't bother turning toward the van.

'All right, for the record,' Saul said, 'I'm not on anybody's payroll. This is a family matter. I'm asking for a dispensation from the bargain I made. Temporary. Till I settle my problem. The minute I do, I'll be on a plane back to Israel.'

The pockmarked man's gaze became calculating. 'My superiors will want to know why they should make the dispensation.'

'As a favor.'

'Oh?'

'In exchange, I'll do *them* a favor.'

The man slowly stood from the railing. 'Let's be clear. A favor? You want to put it on that formal a basis? You're invoking a professional courtesy?'

'A favor for a favor. I don't have any other choice.'

'You'll do anything they ask?'

'With reservations.'

'Ah, then your offer isn't serious.'

'Wrong. It's *very* serious. But I'd need to know the assignment.

97

The risk factor's not as important as the ultimate objective. It can't be suicidal. But it *mustn't* be morally repugnant.'

'*Morals?* Don't tell me you've acquired morals, Romulus.'

'The desert can do that to you. In case your superiors haven't thought of this, I remind them that an operative publicly exiled from the network but secretly affiliated with it can have great value. I wouldn't be linked with it.'

The pockmarked man's gaze became more calculating. 'You're that determined to find out what happened to your father-in-law?'

'And protect my family from another attack. *I told you this isn't business – it's personal.*'

The pockmarked man shrugged. 'My superiors will have to assess the tape of our conversation.'

'Of course.'

'We'll get back to you.' The man crossed the bandstand, his footsteps echoing.

'I'm staying at my father-in-law's apartment. I'd give you the address and phone number, but I assume you already know them.'

The man turned, studied Saul, and nodded. His nod was ambiguous, either in farewell or out of respect.

2

In a bookstore across the street from the park, Erika watched the van pull away. She waited until it disappeared around a corner, then turned her attention back toward the park. In the rain, the bandstand was barely visible. She and Saul had assumed that his contact would have a backup. As a consequence, she had come here earlier, prepared to act as backup for Saul.

She stepped from the bookstore, pulled up the hood on her nylon jacket, and hurried through the downpour.

Saul was waiting for her at the bandstand.

'Do you think they'll agree?' she asked.

'If they feel there's something in it for them. I had to promise a favor for a favor.'

Her voice sank in despair. 'I'm sorry. I know how much you'd hate going back to work for them.'

'But what's the alternative? Do nothing to find your father and protect ourselves? I'd hate that even more. Only one thing matters. Doing what's necessary to keep our family safe.'

'The more I know you, the more I love you.'

'Step closer when you say that.' He pulled down the hood on her jacket, joined his hands at the back of her neck beneath her long dark hair, and gently drew her toward him, kissing raindrops off her cheeks.

But she sensed his nervousness. 'What if they don't give permission?'

'I'll have to go ahead anyhow.'

'No,' she said. '*We* will.' She hugged him. 'And God help whoever tries to stand in our way.'

3

'*I'm staying at my father-in-law's apartment. I'd give you the address and phone number, but I assume you already know them.*'

Exhaling cigarette smoke, the pockmarked man leaned forward from a leather-covered chair and shut off the tape machine positioned on the conference table. He turned to the CIA's chief of station for Austria. 'You want to hear it again?'

Fluorescent lights hummed. Three other men in the oak-paneled room sat motionless, showing no reaction as the station chief tapped his fingers on the table.

His name was Gallagher. A short wiry man in a blue pinstriped suit, he stopped drumming his fingers and splayed them firmly across the edge of the table. 'No, the third time was sufficient. I'm clear about what he told you. But you were there. I wasn't. You saw the expression in his eyes. Did Romulus *mean* what he told you?'

'A gut reaction?' The pockmarked man stubbed out his cigarette. 'Yes.'

'Provided Romulus feels the mission isn't suicidal, provided he doesn't object to the mission's objective, he'll do *anything* for us?'

'Again a gut reaction? Yes.'

'My, my.'

A balding man decided to risk a comment. 'It's a major shift in his position. The original agreement was – he promised to remain in exile, but *we* had to promise to leave him alone.'

'A man of his talents,' Gallagher said, 'he could be useful if he rejoined the game and no one knew he was working for us. A master operative. A world-class assassin. And he's throwing himself on our mercy.'

'But only once,' the pockmarked man reminded him.

Gallagher lifted his calloused fingers, the product of his black-belt karate training, and massaged his temples. 'Well, then, if he wants to pursue a personal vendetta, let him do it. Something bothers me, though.'

The men in the room waited to hear what it was.

'This personal vendetta might have professional consequences. We don't know who's responsible for the attack on Romulus and his family, after all. Or who's responsible for the disappearance of his wife's father. We have to make sure he remains independent, unaffiliated.'

'I don't understand,' the pockmarked man said.

'You will. Romulus must be impatient to hear from us. It's time I got clearance from Langley.'

The rain had stopped. Streetlights reflected off wet grass and puddles. The night air smelled sweet. Scanning the shadows of the park, Saul left the walkway beside the Danube and once again approached the bandstand.

Again the pockmarked man sat on the railing, waiting for him.

'Romulus' – grinning, the man spread his arms in welcome – 'it's your lucky day. I've been authorized by Control to agree to your proposal.'

Saul breathed out. 'All right.' He steadied himself. 'When I've settled my family concerns, I'll wait to be contacted – so the network can have its half of the bargain.'

'Oh, believe me, you'll be contacted.'

Saul turned to leave.

'There's just one problem, Romulus.'

'Problem?' Saul tensed, looking back.

'Well, maybe not exactly a problem. Let's call it a condition. A stipulation.'

'What are you talking about?'

'You can't have any help from your Israeli friends.'

'*What?*'

'The way my superiors look at it, you're valuable to them only if you're perceived to remain a freelance.'

'Perceived to . . . ? Damn it, say what you mean!'

'What you're about to do has to stay on a personal basis. If you accept help from Israeli intelligence, it'll look as if you're cooperating with them, working for them.'

'My father-in-law used to be in their network, for God's sake! Of course, I'm cooperating with them! *They* want to find out what happened as much as I do!'

'Then I'll say it again. You can't accept Israeli help. Or any other network's help, for that matter. Our plans for you require an absolute detachment from every organization. You have to be totally disaffected. Otherwise, if the mission we send you on is compromised, if *you're* compromised, the enemy could blame the Israelis, and the Israelis would blame *us*, and we'd be in the same shit as if you were still on our payroll. You said this matter was personal. Keep it that way. No outside help. If you don't agree to this condition, we'll be forced to punish you for breaking your original bargain with us.'

'Bastards. I should have known better than to—'

'Negotiate with us? Romulus, for what it's worth, you had no other option. Otherwise you'd be dead.'

'And how am I supposed to—?'

'Use the talents you're famous for. I'm sure Israeli intelligence has already compiled information that gives you leads. By all means, take advantage of it. The professional community wouldn't be surprised if Mossad got in touch with you about your wife's father, one of their former operatives. But from here on, reject them. You're on your own.'

'And who's supposed to believe this?'

'I don't know what you mean.'

'This park. This bandstand. We meet here twice in one day. No attempt at concealment. Other networks *must* be watching us by now.'

'That would be my assumption. I certainly hope so.'

Furious, Saul raised his hands.

'Excellent, Romulus. It's time to put on a show.'

Bewilderment made Saul lower his fists.

'You're supposed to try to attack me,' the pockmarked man said. 'My backup's supposed to try to shoot you. To demonstrate your disaffection. To prove to the other networks you're still divorced from us. Here, let me make it easy for you.'

The pockmarked man stood from the railing and punched Saul – hard – in the stomach.

Unprepared, Saul doubled over, gasping.

The pockmarked man braced himself, drawing back a fist to punch Saul's face.

Instinct overcame surprise and pain. In a blur, pivoting angrily to avoid the blow, Saul thrust the palm of his hand against his assailant's shoulder. Cartilage cracked.

The man fell, groaning, his shoulder dislocated.

'You stupid son of a bitch!' Saul said. 'I could have killed you!'

A gunshot shattered the silence of the park. A bullet slammed against a post that supported the roof of the bandstand. Saul dove to the floor.

The pockmarked man lay near him, holding his shoulder, in agony. Through gritted teeth, he murmured, 'Welcome back to the shadow game, Romulus. Get out of here.'

'*That sniper's one of you?*' Saul demanded in disgust.

'I said get out of here!'

A bullet splintered the bandstand's railing. Saul scrambled across the floor. A third shot walloped the bannister on the steps leading down from the bandstand. He lunged toward the railing on the opposite side of the bandstand and vaulted it, landing on rain-softened grass. With the bandstand between him and the supposedly serious sniper, he raced through darkness toward a carousel. The way he'd been manipulated enraged him. His contact's readiness to suffer if his network ordered him to suffer was sickening. 'Welcome back to the shadow game,' the pockmarked man had said. *Exactly. Shadows. Illusions*, Saul thought with revulsion. In the night, the sniper – no matter how skilled – could easily have made a mistake and not have missed.

A shot roared behind him, blowing off the nose of a spotted horse on the carousel. That's enough! Saul mentally shouted. You've made your point!

A murky figure appeared ahead of him, from behind the carousel. For an instant, Saul thought it was Erika, who, not understanding the show the network had choreographed, was coming to help him. The figure raised a handgun.

It's not Erika! I'm the target!

Misha Pletz had given him a Beretta. He yanked it from his dark windbreaker, but instead of firing toward the enemy ahead of him, he darted toward the right, hoping to blend with trees and bushes. A gunshot, much closer, made his ears ring. A bullet slashed the leaves of a bush beside him. He dove behind a concrete bench and spun to fire at the figure near the carousel.

But the figure was gone. Behind him, urgent footsteps ran along a sidewalk, from the direction of the bandstand. Ahead, he saw a shadow step from behind a tree and aim. Saul fired.

But the figure ducked behind the tree.

A bullet cracked against the bench, chunks of concrete making Saul flinch. The bullet had come from a *third* sniper in the park! Not from behind him or ahead! But to his right! He charged past a fountain. Someone shouted. Sirens wailed. His lungs burning, he surged from the park. The trees ended. The walkway beside the Danube appeared before him. He spun to the right. Fifty yards away, a figure raced out of bushes. He spun to the left. Another figure! Gripping the metal guardrail, his lungs protesting, he heaved himself over.

Cold water enveloped him. He couldn't be sure, but swimming under the surface, resisting the weight of his sodden clothes, struggling toward the middle of the river, he thought he heard a bullet strike the water.

5

Erika hid among shadows on the street side of the park, watching the murky bandstand. She stiffened when she saw Saul's contact punch him in the stomach. Rushing forward, handgun drawn, determined to protect her husband, she noticed Saul pivot to avoid another blow and knock the man to the bandstand's floor. A shot. Saul scrambled off the bandstand. Chaos. First one, then two, then *three* gunmen raced through the shadowy park. More shots. Sirens wailed in the distance. Erika's only thought was to get to Saul, to help him. But the chaos intensified as Saul charged through the darkness, burst through bushes at the edge of the park, and vaulted the guardrail next to the Danube. A gunman shot at the water, turned, and saw other figures racing toward him. Firing repeatedly toward the shadows, not aiming so much as providing distraction, the gunman hurried along the walkway, vanishing into the night. The sirens wailed louder. Figures darted in separate directions out of the park.

She was one of them. She couldn't guess where Saul would surface along the river. Knowing he'd do everything possible to save himself, she had her own obligation. Indeed she took for granted that Saul would *expect* her to do what she now intended. Retreating from the park in the direction from which she'd arrived, she raced across the street and into an alley, reaching its far end just as police cars stopped at the park. She sprinted across another street and into a farther alley, her mind repeating the same frantic thought. Yes, Saul would understand she couldn't find him; he had to try to save himself on his own. *She* had to save . . .

A restaurant glowed before her. Lunging into its lobby, barely registering the smell of sauerkraut, she shoved coins into a pay phone.

She dialed her father's apartment. One buzz. Two. But nobody answered. Three.

She shuddered with relief when she heard a familiar, reassuring voice say, 'Hello.'

'Misha, it's Erika! I don't have time to explain!' She struggled to catch her breath. 'It's bad! Wake Christopher! Don't even bother dressing him! Get out of there!'

No response.

'Misha!'

'Where shall I meet you?'

'Where my father was supposed to go but didn't!' she said. 'You understand? Every morning and evening.'

'Yes,' Misha said. 'I'll wake the boy at once. He'll be safe.'

'I pray to God.'

'Just make sure *you* remain safe.'

'Get moving!'

She hung up the phone and turned to see startled patrons of the restaurant staring at her in the lobby. She rushed past them, leaving the restaurant.

But what about Saul? she worried as she ran along the street. Would *he* remain alive to reach the rendezvous they'd agreed upon?

6

Gallagher's voice had the force of a shout. *'Were they ours?'*

The pockmarked man winced, adjusting the sling on his dislocated arm. 'Not unless you assigned another team to cover this. They sure as hell weren't on *my* team.'

'Jesus.' Gallagher sat rigidly at the head of the conference table. Two other men waited in nervous silence. Gallagher drummed his fingers. *'Three* of them?'

'In addition to our own man, yes,' the pockmarked man said. 'We played it exactly as you wanted. I punched him. He defended himself. Our marksman opened fire, pretending to want to kill him.'

'I want to know about the others,' Gallagher said.

'The first was hidden behind a carousel. The other two seemed to come out of nowhere. They tried to catch Romulus in a pincer movement.'

'And they weren't pretending? You're certain they meant to kill him?'

'Romulus surely believed it – he returned their fire. Before the police could arrive, the intruders fled. Of course, so did we.'

Gallagher's lips tightened. 'If only Romulus had managed to kill one. Then at least we'd have a body. We'd be able to find out who else was in the game. Damn it, your team should have kept closer watch on the park!'

'We couldn't. You said you wanted witnesses from other networks. The point of the demonstration was to convince every organization that Romulus was still an outcast. We had to back off, to let our audience take position.'

'Great. The operation worked so well it failed.'

'Maybe it didn't fail,' the pockmarked man said.

Gallagher raised his eyebrows in question.

'If anything, since Romulus almost *was* executed, the other networks will be even more convinced he's not involved with us,' the pockmarked man said. 'Nothing's changed. He can still pursue his vendetta. He still has to give us the favor he promised.'

'Does he? *Will* he? What if Romulus believes the intruders belonged to us? Suppose he decides the mission went out of control and your men did try to kill him? He won't repay any favor. What he might do is turn against us. What a mess! To keep him on our side, to use him later, we might be forced to help him.'

'On the other hand,' the pockmarked man said, 'we don't even know if he survived.'

7

Chilled and exhausted, Saul waded from the murky Danube. It had taken him fifteen minutes to swim out of range down current and then across the river. The lights along this opposite shore glinted coldly. He plodded from mud to a concrete ramp, passed a boathouse, and finally reached a narrow street beyond a warehouse. No one had pursued him across the river. For the moment, he felt safe. But questions tortured his mind. Who'd tried to kill him? Had his former network decided to punish him after all? He shook his head, not believing it. The pockmarked man wouldn't have put himself in the line of fire. Then had the mock-assassination become too realistic? Or had his as-yet-unknown enemies been waiting for an opportunity to make another attempt against him? If he'd been killed back there in the park, his former employers would have seemed responsible. They'd never convince other networks of their innocence. And the actual assailants would go undetected.

Shivering, Saul mustered strength from an even more distressing concern. Erika and Christopher. His wife, having seen the attack against him, realizing she was powerless to help, would have gone to protect their son. He *counted* on her doing so, that reassuring thought his only consolation. Erika's mandatory first step would have been to contact Misha Pletz and warn him to rush Christopher to safety. He trudged ahead with greater determination. For a moment, a single goal obsessed him – the fall-back site he and Erika had agreed upon. He had to get there.

8

Christopher's eyes still ached from his abrupt awakening. His blue pajamas were covered by a sweater that the stoop-shouldered man named Misha Pletz had made him put on. His nostrils felt pinched by thick clouds of tobacco smoke, but his mouth watered from the sweet cocoa smell in this room of many tables and red-cheeked, laughing men. He recalled the urgency with which Misha had carried him down the stairs. The rush of the taxi ride. The scurry into this 'coffee house,' as Misha called it. His mother suddenly appearing, her eyes red with tears as she hugged him. All bewildering.

He sat on a bench against a wall, his mother on one side, Misha on the other. Their conversation confused him.

'If he isn't here in fifteen minutes,' his mother said, 'we can't risk staying any longer.'

A hefty man wearing a white apron leaned his head down toward his mother. 'Come into the kitchen. We've just received a rare form of coffee.'

More confusion. His mother carrying him through a swinging door, Misha leading them. Glinting metal counters. Steaming pots. His father, clothes wet, stepping out of a room. Misha laughing. His mother sobbing, embracing his father. 'Thank God.'

9

'Quickly. We have to go,' Misha said.

'Where?' Saul asked.

'Back to Israel.'

'No,' Erika said. 'Not us.'

'I don't understand.'

'Just you and Christopher. Take him with you. Protect him.'

'But what about *you*?' Misha asked.

'Christopher won't be safe till Saul and I are. If something happens to us, put Christopher in a kibbutz. Give him a new identity.'

'I don't believe the Agency tried to kill me,' Saul said. 'It was someone else. The people we're after.'

'Even so, can you trust your former network?'

'I have to. But I had to make a deal with them. In exchange for their letting me come back from exile, I promised I wouldn't take help. We have to do this on our own.'

'But . . .'

'No. We have the information you gave us. We've got to accept the risk. But if we fail, take over for us. Don't let the bastards win.'

'You're sure there's no other way?'

105

'For us to survive?' Saul shook his head. 'To get back to Christopher? No.'

10

His father kissed him. Why was his father crying?

'Goodbye, son. Misha, take care of him.'

'Always remember, Christopher . . .'

Why was his *mother* crying too? More kisses. Her tears wet on his cheek.

'We love you.'

Shouts from beyond the swinging doors. 'You can't go back there!'

'They've found you! Hurry!' Misha said.

A rush toward another door, this time into darkness, an alley, neverending, into the night. But when he looked in terror behind him, he saw that he and Misha had gone one way, his parents another. Eyes brimming with tears, he couldn't see them any longer.

Eternal
City

Dressed as a priest and a nun among many actual priests and
nuns, Drew and Arlene walked along Rome's crowded Via della
Conciliazione. Though the street wasn't narrow, it seemed constricted
when compared with the vista ahead of them. The eastern edge of
Vatican City . . . St Peter's Piazza . . . Like the head of a funnel, the
street opened out to the right and left, melding with the four curved
rows of Doric columns that flanked the piazza's right and left side.

'I've heard this called St Peter's Square,' Arlene said. 'But it isn't
square. It's oval.'

They reached the piazza's center. An Egyptian obelisk stood
between two widely spaced fountains. Though impressive in themselves, the obelisk, fountains, and surrounding columns seemed
dwarfed by the majesty of St Peter's Basilica, which rose beyond the
piazza, its massive dome haloed with radiance from the midafternoon
sun. Renaissance buildings stretched to the right and left of the basilica
and the huge tiers of steps leading up to it.

'I didn't realize how big this place is,' Arlene said.

'It all depends on your perspective,' Drew said. 'The piazza, the
basilica, and everything else in Vatican City would fill less than a
seventh of New York's Central Park.'

She turned to him in disbelief.

'It's true,' he said. 'The whole thing's only a fifth of a square
mile.'

'Now I know why they call this the world's smallest city-state.'

'And it hasn't even been a city-state very long,' Drew said. 'It
wasn't until 1929 – believe it or not, thanks to Mussolini, who
wanted the Church to give him political support – that Vatican City
was established and granted independence as a state.'

'I thought you told me you hadn't been here before.'

'I haven't.'

'Then how come you know so much about it?'

'While you were asleep on the plane from Cairo, I read a guidebook.'

'Devious,' she said as he grinned. 'Since you're such an expert, how
do we get to the rendezvous?'

'Just follow me, Sister.'

He guided her to the left, along a walkway next to the steps leading
toward the basilica. Showing Vatican passports, they walked by

107

Swiss guards, the Pope's traditional bodyguards, whose long-handled battle-axes and striped uniforms with billowy sleeves looked more theatrical than threatening, and proceeded beneath the Arch of the Bells, finally within the capital of the Catholic Church. Though the Vatican's permanent population was only slightly more than one thousand, the crowd of clergy and tourists was considerable. Guides supervised the laity.

They crossed a small rectangular open area, the Piazza of the First Roman Martyrs. On its right, the basilica loomed. But on the left, at the end of a narrow street, cypresses canopied a tiny cemetery.

'Important sponsors of the Church used to have the honor of being buried here,' Drew said. 'To add to the honor, the Vatican brought in dirt from the hill in Jerusalem where Christ was crucified.'

They passed beneath two further arches, reached the Vatican courthouse, rounded the back of St Peter's Basilica, and followed a maze of wooded lanes till they came to their destination, the Vatican gardens. Fountains and hedges, ponds and flowers surrounded them, creating a sense of peace. One of the fountains was shaped like a Spanish galleon. Cannons on each side spouted water, as did the horn in the mouth of a child on the bow.

'I thought you'd appreciate these gardens,' a voice said behind them. 'They make Rome – and indeed the world – seem far away.'

Though sudden, the voice wasn't startling. Drew had been expecting contact soon. He turned toward Father Sebastian. 'Is this where he died?'

'Father Victor?' The priest wore a white collar, black bib, and suit. His eyes were bleak. 'At two o'clock in the morning. Over there, by that lily pond. Beside that marble angel. Shot twice in the head.'

Drew frowned. 'What was he doing here so late?'

'Meeting someone. Father Victor was thorough. He kept an appointment book, which he submitted to us before his daily activities. The record indicates he didn't know whom he'd be meeting here at such an hour. But his notation makes clear, the meeting concerned Cardinal Pavelic's disappearance.'

Drew peered past the trees of the gardens toward the towering basilica and the other buildings within the Vatican. 'Do we assume that whoever met him lived in one of the Vatican's apartments? That would explain why the gardens were chosen as the meeting place.' Drew shook his head. 'On the other hand, maybe that's what we're supposed to think. Maybe someone from outside chose the gardens just to make it seem as if he lived in the Vatican.'

'Or maybe the person who was scheduled to meet Father Victor didn't show up, or someone else came along after the meeting,' Arlene said. 'An unidentified contact, a meeting place that might be intended to mislead us. We don't know anything.'

'Except for the nature of Father Victor's wounds,' Father Sebastian said.

Drew's interest quickened. 'What about them?'

108

'Both were full in the face. The powder burns indicate extremely close range. You understand?'

'Yes. Anything's possible in the night. But from what you've said about Father Victor, he was a professional. Even granting that a professional is capable of being fooled, the powder burns suggest the killer was probably someone he knew, someone he trusted enough to come up close to him.'

Father Sebastian's dark eyes blazed. 'Conceivably a member of my order.'

Drew glanced toward the ring on Father Sebastian's left hand, middle finger. Gold setting. Magnificent ruby. Its insignia an interesting cross and sword. Again he felt chilled by the symbol of religion and violence, by his enforced involvement with the Fraternity of the Stone.

'Perhaps the same member of my order who twice tried to stop you from cooperating with us,' Father Sebastian continued. 'To keep you from finding out why Cardinal Pavelic disappeared. Be careful, Brother MacLane. Coming to this rendezvous, I made triply sure I wasn't followed. But after this, it isn't wise for us to meet again. Use the safe-deposit box in Zurich to pass on messages.'

'We don't have the key for it, or the number of the bank account, or—'

'The records Father Victor kept that led him to be summoned to these Vatican gardens at two A.M. You'll also want the weapons I promised.'

'Those in particular.'

'After I leave, stroll over to the marble angel beside that lily pond. The site of Father Victor's death. Behind the angel, a metal plate covers a niche in the marble. Raise the metal plate. Beside the tap that controls the flow of water for the fountain, you'll find a package. It contains everything you need.'

2

The package – ten inches long and wide, four inches thick, wrapped in coarse brown paper, addressed to an illegible name and stamped as if had gone through the Vatican's postal system – was heavy out of proportion to its shape. Drew held it with deceptive casualness while he and Arlene left the Vatican, crossing St Peter's Square. So far, their cover as a priest and a nun had allowed them to seem invisible, but now he anticipated what they'd have to do next, and the disadvantage of their disguise quickly became apparent.

Arlene said what he was thinking. 'If we keep hanging around together dressed like this, we *will* attract attention. We'll cause a damned scandal.'

'Sister, such language. I'm shocked.'

She made a face at him. 'Where are we going to study the documents? Not in public. And a nun and a priest can't rent a room together. I can't even visit you if we rent rooms separately. What about tonight? It isn't safe to sleep apart.'

'Safe? Your sense of romance touches me deeply.'

She grinned. 'Not to disillusion you, but . . .'

'Yes?'

'Your body isn't high on my list of priorities right now.'

'Commendable, Sister. Subdue carnal thoughts.' Drew glanced at the shops along the Via della Conciliazione. 'But a change of wardrobe might not be a bad idea.'

'Where do we put on the clothes? We'll raise a lot of eyebrows if we do it in the stores.'

'We'll find a place. How hard can it be?'

3

How hard? Drew mentally repeated after fifteen minutes of washing his hands in the train station's men's room, waiting for it to be empty. *How hard?* It seemed an unwritten law that every patron of this rest room had to pass the time of day with the padre with whom they shared such intimate facilities. 'Yes, my son. Very good, my son,' Drew answered in Italian, continuing to wash his hands.

At last the men's room was empty. Ducking into a stall, he quickly changed from his priest's black suit and white collar into gray slacks, a blue shirt, and a navy blazer. He stuffed the priest's suit into the paper bag from which he'd taken his purchases, then carried both the bag and the small heavy package of weapons and documents from the stall just as a security guard walked into the rest room. Drew restrained himself from saying 'Good day, my son,' and went out into the train station.

The noise of the crowd was awesome, reverberating within the cathedral-like structure. From habit, he scanned the surge of bodies, looking for anyone who didn't fit the pattern of hurried travelers. Satisfied, he made his way to a pillar, behind which Arlene – wearing beige slacks, a matching jacket, and an emerald blouse that emphasized the green of her eyes – was waiting.

'What took you so long?' she said. 'I was starting to think I'd have to come in after you.'

'Talking to my flock. See these hands. The cleanest in the city.'

4

The draperies were closed. Beyond them, the roar of evening traffic intensified. The husk of the opened package lay on the hotel bed, next to a safe-deposit box key, Italian money, two Mausers, and the sheaf of documents.

Drew divided the documents between Arlene and himself. All were photocopies. Of newspaper clippings, Father Victor's appointment book, transcripted telephone conversations, reports from informants, files compiled by the lay investigators assigned to the case.

Arlene looked up, impressed. 'Father Victor's sources were excellent. He had access to everything Interpol and the local police knew.'

'And a lot they *didn't* know, thanks to his contacts within the Church. Look at this. He even had sources in all the major intelligence networks, including the KGB.'

It took them three hours before they felt they'd studied the documents sufficiently. Drew slumped on the sofa. 'Looks like the Fraternity went through a lot of wasted trouble bringing us into this. I don't see anything that gives us a lead.'

Arlene rubbed her tired eyes. 'Father Victor did everything I'd have done. He covered every angle – religious, political, criminal.'

'And apparently came up with nothing. Yet someone killed him. Why?'

'It could have been an unrelated matter. Nothing to do with the cardinal's disappearance,' she said.

'Could be. But his appointment book suggests the meeting at the Vatican gardens involved this case. And something else bothers me. The Fraternity's one of the best networks I've ever seen. With all its resources, what are *we* supposed to do that it can't?'

'Just what Father Sebastian explained,' she said. 'A member of the Fraternity wants to sabotage the order. Two motivated outsiders have a better chance of learning why Cardinal Pavelic disappeared.'

'Because the traitor within the network won't know what we're doing and can't interfere.' Drew stood and paced. 'Does that make sense? Why doesn't Father Sebastian detach himself from his order and rely on his own devices to do what he expects *us* to do? What's the difference? Why *me*? Why *us*?'

'You think we're being set up?'

'Sure looks that way. The ambush in the desert. The bomb in Cairo. The traitor obviously knows you were sent to bring me to Father Sebastian. Maybe Father Sebastian chose us because as outsiders we're expendable. Instead of risking his life or someone else's in the Fraternity, he lets us take the risk and hopes the traitor will make a mistake when he comes after us.'

'But wouldn't *any* outsider have served his purpose?' Arlene asked. 'For sufficient money, Father Sebastian could have had his pick among any number of independent contractors.' She hesitated. Her green eyes flared. 'Except, no amount of money would have kept an independent contractor on the job after two attempts against him. *We* were chosen because we had a better motivation. If we don't cooperate, the Fraternity will kill us.'

'Life does seem very sweet right now.' Drew smiled and squeezed her hand. 'We've got the greatest reason in the world to want to keep living.' His voice became hoarse. 'So we weigh a certain death against a less certain death. And here we are. We know we're being manipulated, but we have to permit it.'

'Then let's get the job done.'

111

'And get on with our lives.' He picked up a photostat of a newspaper story.

CARDINAL'S DISAPPEARANCE REMAINS A MYSTERY

ROME, ITALY, February 28 (AP) – Vatican officials and Rome police remain baffled five days after the disappearance of Cardinal Krunoslav Pavelic, influential member of the Roman Catholic Church's central administration group, the Curia.

Pavelic, seventy-two, was last seen by close associates after celebrating a private mass in the chapel of his Vatican living quarters Sunday evening. On Monday, he had been scheduled to give the keynote address to a widely publicized conference of Catholic bishops on the subject of the Church's political relations with Eastern European communist regimes.

Authorities at first suspected right-wing terrorists of abducting Cardinal Pavelic to protest a rumored softening of the Vatican's attitude toward any communist regime willing to ease restrictions on Church activities. However, no extremist group has so far claimed responsibility for Pavelic's disappearance.

Drew finished reading. He turned to Arlene, who'd leaned forward to read past his shoulder.

'What can a newspaper story tell you that isn't better substantiated in the primary documents Father Victor had?' she asked.

'Right now, I'm interested in what *isn't* in those other documents.' Drew's hand tightened on the photostat of the newspaper story. 'You said Father Victor had covered every angle – religious, political, criminal? But one angle's missing.'

'Missing?'

'It might be the reason Father Sebastian wanted us. Wanted *me*.' He had trouble speaking. 'It used to be my specialty.' Again, unbearably, he suffered through the memory of the explosion that had dismembered his parents before his eyes, the rage that had turned him into an instrument of vengeance and had ultimately driven him to the penance of the monastery.

'Terrorists.' The word made bile rise to his mouth. 'The newspaper story mentions the possibility that Cardinal Pavelic was abducted by them. But where in these other documents has that possibility been investigated and dismissed? Is *that* our direction?'

5

The morning sun fought through a veil of smog. Escaping the blare of traffic, Drew entered a pay phone near the Colosseum and dialed a number he hadn't used in almost eight years. He felt an unnerving sense of déjà vu.

A man, whose raspy voice Drew didn't recognize, answered in Italian. 'Forum Dry Cleaners.'

Drew replied in Italian, 'Mr Carelli, please.'

'No Carelli here.'

'But can you relay a message to him?'

'*I told you no Carelli. I never heard of him.*' The man hung up.

Drew replaced the phone on its hook and leaned against the glass wall of the booth.

Arlene stood just outside. 'From the look on your face, I gather you didn't make contact.'

'Apparently some changes have been made.'

'Eight years. It isn't surprising. Relays are changed as often as every week.'

'I guess I'd hoped we could do this easily.'

'Who *is* Carelli?'

'A pseudonym for a man called Gatto. In the old days, when I was an operative, he was a middleman. Sometimes we used him as a backup, in case a mission went sour. More often, we bought information from him.'

The look in her eyes made clear she understood. Terrorists usually operated in small groups independent of one another. This tactic gave them the advantage of secrecy, but it also meant they had no network to depend upon for weapons, information, and safety routes. After all, an assassination required careful planning. Unless a terrorist group was engaged in a suicidal mission, they needed 'clean' weapons, never before used, untraceable to them. As soon as a mission was completed, these weapons would be disassembled and either destroyed or discarded in widely separated areas, preferably at sea. Such virgin weapons were expensive. But even before an operation, the victims had to be located, their daily schedules determined, their moments of exposure discovered. This information was costly to acquire. After the mission, of course, the terrorists would need to go to ground. Alibis, escape procedures, safe houses – these too were expensive. A first-class mission, one which by definition meant that the terrorists would survive unapprehended and be able to kill again, had a minimum price tag of $150,000. The money was supplied to terrorists by various governments committed to causing chaos, and the terrorists in turn paid the money to middlemen, sometimes called brokers, who provided the weapons, information, and safe houses, no questions asked. As far as the middleman was concerned, what his clients did with the services he made available was none of his business. Carelli, a.k.a. Gatto, had been one of these middlemen.

'He had professional ethics,' Drew said.

'You mean he was careful.'

'Exactly. The information he gave us never exposed his clients,' Drew continued. 'But he had no qualms about accepting money in exchange for what he knew about terrorists imprudent enough not to have hired him.'

'Sounds like a charming fellow.'

'To tell the truth, if you could forget what he did for a living, he was.'

'And of course you hated him.'

'Him and the hate he fed off. But if anyone might know if terrorists abducted Cardinal Pavelic, it's Gatto.'

'Or it would have been Gatto eight years ago. Either he's changed his conduit system since then, or he's left the business,' Arlene said. 'Of course, there's a third possibility. Maybe he knew too much and became a liability to his clients. Do business with the Devil . . .'

'And the Devil destroys you. In this case – I never thought I'd say it – I hope the Devil held off.'

'It looks like you'll never know.'

Drew shook his head. 'There were alternate methods to get in touch with him. Different phone numbers, different intermediaries.'

He stepped back into the booth. His next three attempts resulted in similar 'no Carelli' answers. Glancing with discouragement toward Arlene, he made his final call.

A nasal female voice said, 'Pontine Medical Supplies.'

'Can you get a message to Mr Carelli?' Drew asked.

The woman didn't answer.

'Carelli,' Drew repeated. 'Can you . . . ?'

'I haven't heard that name in almost six months.'

'It's been even longer since I spoke with him,' Drew said.

'If I *can* get in touch with him, who . . . ?'

'Mr Haverford,' Drew told her, supplying the pseudonym he'd always used when dealing with Gatto.

'I'll ask around. Please call again in thirty minutes.'

Drew walked with Arlene toward the Colosseum, back toward the phone booth, back toward the Colosseum. Precisely thirty minutes later, he redialed the number.

'I phoned earlier about Mr Carelli.'

'Write down these directions.'

6

Filled with misgivings, Drew urged the rented Fiat up a zigzag wooded road. Never, in his many discussions with Gatto, had they met at a residence. The rule was to use a one-time-only public meeting place, a restaurant or a park, a location that could never be traced to Gatto's organization. You didn't do business at anyone's home. For Gatto to jeopardize the safety of whoever lived here, he must have had an extremely good reason.

The moment Drew entered the lavish drawing room in the heavily guarded villa, he knew the reason – Gatto was too sick to leave the premises. The villa was ten miles north of the outskirts of Rome, situated on a bluff with a view for miles around. Every luxury surrounded him. But the once-robust man, formerly engorged on the fees he earned from terrorist killings, was now a shell, his facial skin hanging loose, his complexion liver-spotted, his loss of hair disguised by a wide-brimmed hat. He slumped on a sofa.

'Ah, Haverford.' Gatto wheezed. 'It's been too long. And such an attractive companion you bring with you.'

'Mr Carelli.' Smiling, Arlene grasped the bony fingers he extended. Her smile didn't waver when he pressed his shrunken lips to the back of her hand.

Two bodyguards stood at the narrow ends of the room.

'Yes, it's been a while,' Drew said. 'I had a change of heart . . . I might say a change of soul . . . I retreated from the profession.'

Gatto coughed. 'As did I. Refreshment? Wine?'

'You know I never indulged.'

'I remember. But with your permission . . .'

'Of course.'

Gatto poured purple liquid into a glass. He had trouble swallowing it. The room smelled of medication. 'Now that we've honored the amenities, Haverford, how may I help you?' His grin was a rictus.

'In former times, you used to provide me with information about those foolish enough not to be your clients.'

Gatto's sagging clothes shook as he laughed. 'Those foolish enough.' He chortled. 'Haverford, have you seen my new Matisse?' He gestured toward one wall.

Drew turned, assessing it. 'Impressive.'

'A million dollars, Haverford. What I sometimes earned on one assignment. How many people died, do you suppose, for Matisse to paint that picture?'

'None . . . except a part of Matisse.'

Gatto coughed again. 'And even if I sold it for the magnificent profit due to me, it wouldn't save my life. Come closer, my dear. Sit next to me.'

With a smile, Arlene complied.

'So tell me, Haverford, in my place what would *you* do?'

'In your place?'

'If you were dying.'

'I see. In *that* case, I'd confess.'

'Oh?'

'To a priest.'

'Oh?'

'And do my best to save my soul.'

'You've got religion, Haverford?'

'Late. But finally.'

'And is it comforting?'

Drew thought about it. 'No. In fact, it's quite a burden. But it's powerful.'

'Power, I understand.'

'And it helps me to adjust to thoughts of death.'

'*That*, my friend, is priceless,' Gatto said.

'So let me make an offer. A minister of God has disappeared. Can you help me find out why?'

'A minister?'

'Actually a cardinal. Krunoslav Pavelic.'

Gatto nodded, recognizing the name.

'We think some of your former associates might be responsible for his disappearance. If you help me find him, I'd consider it a favor. No doubt, the Lord too would consider it a favor. And of course I would pay you.'

'Pay me? In this regard, Haverford, I don't *care* to be paid.'

'Then . . . ?'

'I want revenge!'

'Against?'

'Those who abandoned me in my infirmity!'

Drew spread his hand. 'You know what they're like. You can't blame them. They're survivors.'

'Survivors? Not if I can help it!' The effort of his outburst made Gatto close his eyes in pain. 'The bastards dispense death readily enough, but they can't bear to do business with someone on the *verge* of death.'

'You're that offended because they won't do business with you?'

'Business gave my life meaning.'

'Then maybe it's time to find another meaning.'

'Religion?' Gatto's spasm of pain subsided. He opened his eyes into slits. 'Very good, Haverford. Help you find the cardinal, and in the process save my soul?'

'*Try* to save it anyhow.'

'If it isn't too late.'

'The greatest sin is despair.'

'I meant if it isn't too late to find the cardinal. He disappeared months ago. From rumors I've heard, I gather the fullest efforts were made to find out what happened to him. Now that the trail has gone cold . . .'

'I'm interested in other kinds of rumors,' Drew said.

'About my former clients?' Gatto's eyelids trembled as he fought back his pain. 'If they were responsible for taking the cardinal, don't you think they'd have bragged about it? Letters to newspapers, phone calls to Interpol?'

'Since they didn't, I'm wondering if they bragged among themselves.'

'The truth?'

'It's always refreshing.'

'You won't like it. The truth is, I don't know. My disease was diagnosed in January. Word traveled fast. I haven't heard insider news since February. I always enjoyed discussing world events with you, Haverford, so for old times' sake, I agreed to see you. But your trip here, I'm afraid, has been wasted. I'm not the man to ask.' Gatto winced and held his breath. When he exhaled, it sounded like a tire deflating.

Drew stood. 'I'm sorry. We've stayed too long. We've exhausted you.'

116

'But I do know who you *should* ask.'

Drew kept himself perfectly still. 'Who?'

'The maggot who replaced me. The vermin who took my clients, who *would* have insider news. His name is Bonato.'

'His pseudonym?'

'Medici.'

'Political intrigue. Chaos. Appropriate. Can you arrange an introduction with him?'

'From me? Impossible, Haverford. When he gained the favor of my clients, I became dispensable. I exist by his sufferance, because I'm close to death already. If I told him I was sending you to meet with him, such an introduction would cost you your life. I'll tell you how to get in touch with him. The rest is up to you. Be cautious. Ask him questions at your peril.'

'Believe me, I intend to be careful. Tell me about him. Everything.'

'Perhaps you're right, Haverford. Perhaps God will look with favor upon me if I show concern for His cardinal.'

7

Dressed in black, Drew stood with Arlene in the shadows of an alley, watching the cars in a parking lot next to a restaurant across the street. The time was shortly after 8 P.M. They'd waited here for fifteen minutes, and if Gatto's information was correct, the broker with the pseudonym of Medici would arrive at the restaurant within the next five minutes. *The restaurant is considered off-limits*, Gatto had said. *Neutral ground. No business is ever conducted there. Medici favors its menu and its wine list. He always arrives at five minutes after eight, eats heartily, tips generously, and at precisely ten o'clock returns to his mansion, where a whore – different each night – attends to his pleasure. His home, of course, is superbly guarded. But his weak spot is that restaurant. Mind you, under usual circumstances, his routine presents no risks. Terrorist groups have no reason to harm him. And the authorities realize that, if they moved against him, all terrorist groups who'd commissioned services from him would automatically revise their plans.*

Then if we move against him, Drew had said, *won't that alert whatever terrorist group might have taken Cardinal Pavelic?*

The cardinal is ancient history. Who'd suspect that the motive for grabbing Medici was to learn about an operation from several months ago? Haverford, you needn't worry.

Drew did, however – about whether what he and Arlene planned was possible. This kind of mission normally required a well-rehearsed team of at least ten people. Two could do the essentials, yes, but what about contingencies? What if the unpredictable happened and backup was needed, for defense and for distractions to implement escape?

In the shadowy alley, Drew put his hand on Arlene's shoulder, pressing it gently, providing reassurance.

117

She raised a hand, lovingly touching his in return; she spoke as if she knew what he'd been thinking. 'We don't go in unless it looks good. Only two of us, there's a good chance we won't attract attention as even the best of teams can. And Medici certainly won't be expecting us.'

Drew agreed. The alternative was to give up this potential source of information. And then what? With no other leads, they'd be forced to hide and bide their time until the Fraternity found them and punished them for their failure. As he and Arlene had decided the previous night, an uncertain death was better than a certain one. To gain his freedom to be with her, he would face – eagerly – the calculated risk awaiting him.

To his left, a limousine swung into the nearest intersection, coming his way. He took his hand off Arlene's shoulder. They stepped back farther into the alley. As the limousine came closer, Drew saw a chauffeur. A shadowy partition separated the driver from whoever was in back. Drew studied the passenger window on his side, but its smoke-colored, reflective, and presumably bulletproof glass concealed the rear seat. Not that Drew needed to see inside. The license plate was identical to the one Gatto had mentioned. The limousine belonged to Medici.

It pulled into the restaurant's driveway and stopped. The chauffeur got out, a handgun in a shoulder holster bulging his jacket. He opened a rear door, allowing another man to step out. This second man wore a suit instead of a uniform, but his jacket too bulged from a handgun. Next came a short weasely-faced man in a tuxedo; he matched Gatto's description of Medici.

The plan was to subdue the chauffeur while he waited for Medici to eat dinner. When Medici came out at ten, Drew and Arlene would cancel the bodyguard in the suit and escape with Medici in the limousine. The plan had the merits of simplicity and practicality. From the information Drew had been given, he gathered that Medici would be too difficult to grab from his home. But here? Regardless of his armed escorts, Medici clearly felt unassailable.

The death merchant walked ahead of his bodyguard toward the restaurant. The chauffeur turned toward the limousine. Drew took a deep breath, preparing himself to attack the chauffeur as soon as he parked the car in the lot beside the restaurant.

But Arlene suddenly murmured, 'Something's *happening*.'

It didn't take long. Twenty seconds at most. But the length of time was difficult to determine. Too much occurred. The driver of a small red car stopped behind the limousine and got out, shouting obscenities at the chauffeur. The man wore a peaked cap that almost concealed his red hair. His face, though contorted with fury, was extremely pale. He was taller than the chauffeur but thin, almost emaciated. He shook his fists at the chauffeur, screaming insults at him for having blocked the driveway. The chauffeur strode indignantly to meet him.

At once another man appeared from the shadows of the parking lot. He wore a black knitted cap that didn't completely conceal his blond hair. He was square-faced, tanned, and muscular. He pulled a

118

cannister from his windbreaker and sprayed its contents at the face of
the bodyguard, who fell, unmoving, as if he'd been clubbed. Bracing
himself like a boxer, the blond man punched Medici's chin and, even
as the death merchant toppled, shoved him into the limousine.

The red-haired man confronting the chauffeur easily dodged the
punch directed at him and chopped the chauffeur's larynx with a
force great enough to break it. The chauffeur fell. The red-haired
man jumped into the limousine with the blond-haired man and Medici.
The red-haired man backed the limousine onto the street, ran over the
chauffeur, and sped away.

It had happened so swiftly, so smoothly that only when the limousine
disappeared down the street did a crowd gather, staring down at the
bodies. Almost as an afterthought, someone screamed.

8

Drew pressed his foot harder on the rented Fiat's accelerator. Tires
squealed up the winding road.

'"Professional" doesn't begin to describe it. Those guys were *artists*,'
he said.

Arlene gripped the dashboard, bracing herself against the car's
sudden swerves. 'They had the same plan as we did. But instead of
waiting for Medici to come outside after dinner, they moved in as soon
as he arrived. Who *are* they? And why did they want Medici?'

'Let's hope we soon find out.' Drew braked. His headlights gleamed
toward Gatto's estate. For the second time today, they were coming
here for information.

The gate to Gatto's villa was disturbingly open. Two guards lay dead
beyond them, chests dark with blood. Drew sped up the lane to the
Romanesque house. He rejected caution, suspecting that whoever had
killed the guards had departed quite a while ago. The absence of lights
in the villa confirmed his suspicion. The attack had occurred during
daylight.

He stopped before the huge front door of the villa and raced from
the Fiat, Arlene running beside him. Three guards lay dead on the
steps. He charged through the open door, found a light switch and
flicked it, staring in momentary paralysis at yet more bodies, then
scurried from room to room. *Death. Everywhere death.*

Gatto lay on a lounge beside his swimming pool, his throat slit, his
cotton robe soaked with his blood.

'The two men at the restaurant. The blond and the redhead,' Arlene
said. 'They must have come here.'

Drew nodded.

'It's the only explanation I can think of,' Arlene continued. 'They
made Gatto talk. About Medici. They realized the perfect time to grab
him, the same as we did.'

Dismay made Drew's throat ache. 'Coincidence? I don't believe in
it. What happened here and what happened at the restaurant are

related.' He stared at Gatto's corpse. 'I wonder. What do you do to a man who's dying from cancer? How do you add to his misery so much that his cancer can't compare to the pain you inflict upon him? How do you convince him to reveal what he doesn't want to when death is a foregone conclusion?'

Drew tugged open Gatto's robe, revealing the obscene mutilation inflicted upon him.

His mouth soured. 'Yeah, those guys are geniuses, all right.'

'But Gatto didn't tell them about us,' Arlene said. 'Otherwise they'd have tried to take us out before they moved against Medici.'

Again Drew nodded. 'I hope the Lord did look with mercy upon you, Gatto. In the end, you did damned fine.'

'The blond and the redhead,' Arlene said. 'What did they want with Medici?'

'Maybe their motive was the same as ours.'

'To find the cardinal?'

'I wish to God I knew. Are those two guys moving parallel to us? Or are they behind us?'

'Drew, they're just skilled enough, they might be *ahead* of us.'

BOOK FOUR
COLLISION COURSE

Grave
Images

Mexico City. Using the phone in the backseat of his Mercedes sedan, Aaron Rosenberg called ahead to warn his bodyguards to double-check for suspicious strangers outside his home. Nothing had happened to persuade him an attack was imminent, but now that he and Halloway had decided to honor their business commitment, he'd become increasingly uneasy. The abduction of his father had filled him with foreboding. His wife's affair with her bodyguard had further destroyed his peace of mind. Now, in spite of Halloway's assurances that Seth and Icicle would root out the source of the Night and Fog, no reports of success had arrived. Yet Halloway's prediction of their success had been the major reason Rosenberg had agreed to the danger of going ahead with delivery of the Devil's merchandise. If the Night and Fog learned about the shipment, or if the Devil learned that the Night and Fog might be able to expose the nature of the shipment and who had ordered it, we'd face two enemies, Rosenberg thought. And both would attack, for different reasons.

The Mercedes was trapped in a line of stalled traffic. At the head of the line, steam gushed from beneath the hood of an open truck filled with crates of chickens. Bystanders gesticulated around it. What the hell am I doing in this country? Rosenberg thought. For a nostalgic instant, he had a vision of mountains, streams, and forests. He jerked his head toward the bodyguard on his left, then with equal abruptness toward the bodyguard next to the driver. Madness, he thought. Before he realized what he was doing, he slid open the hatch on the bar built into the seat ahead of him, took out a bottle of tequila, filled a tumbler, and swallowed its oily contents in one gulp. As it jolted into his stomach, the Mercedes moved ahead, the stalled truck having been pushed to the side of the street.

But the air conditioning in the Mercedes had been strained. Tepid, recycled air drifted over him. Combined with the tequila in his stomach, it made him want to gag. He raised his fist to his mouth as if to stifle a cough and kept his dignity, anxious to reach the sanctuary of his home.

Perhaps Maria would be in the mood to do more 'driving,' he fantasized. Anything to distract him from his troubles. She owed it to him, he concluded. Didn't he heap upon her the bounty of his labor? Hadn't he held off confronting her about her infidelity?

His driver managed to turn onto the spacious Paseo de la Reforma,

123

gaining speed along the avenue, reaching the Spanish mansion squeezed between high-rise apartment buildings. Rosenberg's bodyguards scrambled from the Mercedes, assessing potential dangers.

Nonexistent ones apparently. One of the bodyguards nodded to Rosenberg. The mansion's security force stepped from the entrance. Rosenberg darted from the car, up the stone steps, and into the vestibule of his home, where he slumped against a wall. Admittedly his arrival hadn't been dignified, but death wasn't dignified either, no matter what form it took. His security force might joke among themselves about his fear, but he paid them well, and they could joke all they wanted as long as they did their job.

He straightened from the wall when he noticed his maid standing beside the curved staircase, surveying him in confusion.

'It's quite all right,' he said in Spanish. 'The heat overcame me briefly. Is your mistress upstairs?'

'No, Señor Rosenberg,' the servant said. 'Your wife has gone out for the afternoon.'

'Gone out?' Rosenberg scowled. 'Where?'

'She did not tell me, Señor.'

'With Esteban?'

'But of course, with her bodyguard.'

Her bodyguard? Rosenberg thought. Her body *violator* would be more accurate!

He charged up the stairs. Damn it, they fuck all day while I take the risks!

At the top of the stairs, he stopped abruptly, hearing voices from Esteban's room at the end of the hallway. The voices were too muted for Rosenberg to identify them, but they belonged to a man and a woman, and Rosenberg had the keen suspicion that the maid had been either mistaken or instructed to lie. He was powerless to solve his other problems, but by God, he could settle *this* one right now.

He stormed toward Esteban's room, and even when he'd gone sufficiently far along the hall to realize that the voices in fact came from the maid's room – a television soap opera she'd forgotten to turn off – even then he was too committed to stop himself. He rammed Esteban's door open, bursting in, fully expecting to find his wife and her bodyguard embracing on the bed.

They weren't. The room was deserted, but what he saw on the bed was so much more shocking than the tryst he'd imagined that his knees wavered. He gripped Esteban's bureau to steady himself and, as soon as the spasms in his legs subsided, lunged for the bedspread, clutching it to his chest. An iron band seemed to tighten around his rib cage. He spun, staring furtively behind him, apprehensive lest the maid might have followed him upstairs and seen what was on the bedspread. She still might come up and wonder about his actions. He had to get the bedspread out of sight.

He compacted the bedspread and shifted it from his chest to his right side where the maid might not notice it as he hurried along the hallway, toward the master bedroom. He'd already entered the bedroom, closed

124

the door, and rushed toward the dresser to hide the spread when he saw the reflection of his own bed in the dresser's mirror – and what was *on* the bedspread.

It was identical to what he'd found on the spread in Esteban's room. Huge, black, grotesque, so unnerving that after Rosenberg crumpled this spread too and shoved it into a drawer with the other, he didn't consider driving to the secret office he maintained. He quite simply, absolutely panicked and lurched toward the bedside phone.

2

Halloway was appalled by Rosenberg's stupidity in using an unsecured phone. That lapse in procedure, combined with Rosenberg's babbling, made clear that the man had obviously lost all control. 'Slow down, for Christ's sake,' Halloway urged. 'What are you talking about? You found *what?*'

'A skull! A fucking death's head! Painted in black on my bedspread! My wife's bodyguard had one on *his* bed too!'

'Take it easy. This might not mean what you think. It might be just a death threat. There's no reason to assume—'

'If we're dealing with the Night and Fog, I *have* to assume! It's more than just a death threat! You know what else the symbol means! Whoever painted those skulls wants to remind us they know all about us!'

Halloway kept his voice low, not wanting to attract the attention of his bodyguards outside in the corridor. 'All right, suppose they *are* reminding us, what difference does it make? It doesn't change things. We already *knew* they'd found us out.'

'It changes everything!' Rosenberg's voice verged on hysteria. 'It proves they weren't content to take our fathers! Now they want *us!* The sins of the fathers! The next generation has to suffer! And they can do it! They managed to sneak inside my home despite every possible security precaution!'

'We can't keep talking about this on an unprotected phone,' Halloway warned. 'Hang up. Call me an hour from now at . . .'

Rosenberg rushed on. 'And that's not all! Why *two* skulls? Why on my *bed?* Why on the bed of my *wife's bodyguard?*'

'I assume to double effect. To . . .'

'Damn it, you don't understand! My wife and her bodyguard are having an affair! I thought no one knew! I've been trying to pretend I don't suspect! But the Night and Fog know! That's why they painted the skulls on both beds! They're telling me they know everything about me, including who's screwing my wife! They're bragging they know all my secrets! All *our* secrets, Halloway! The merchandise! The shipment! If they've learned about . . . !'

'You're jumping to conclusions.'

'Jumping to conclusions?' Rosenberg moaned. 'Dear God, why did

125

I ever go into business with you? You're so damned self-confident you won't admit . . . !'

'Seth and Icicle will take care of—'

'*Will* take care of? *Will?* But they haven't done it yet, have they? And that's all I care about! While those two chase shadows, I've got a situation here! I'm canceling our arrangement right now!'

'What are you—?'

'Either that, or you let me stop the shipment! I don't need *two* enemies, Halloway! If our clients find out we went ahead without warning them the Night and Fog might know about the shipment, they'll come for us! They'll make the Night and Fog seem a minor nuisance!'

'But I'm telling you . . .'

'No, I'm telling *you!* The moment I hang up, I'm calling Rio! I'll do what I should have done in the first place! I'll tell him "no"! And then I'll hope to God your two maniacs find a way to stop the Night and Fog!'

Halloway's mouth felt parched. He had no doubt that Rosenberg meant what he said. A balance had tipped. Events were now out of control.

He tried to moisten his dry mouth. 'All right,' he murmured. 'If that's what you think is best.'

3

Halloway set down the phone. The truth was – and he would never have dared tell Rosenberg – he'd received three other calls from members of their group, all about death's heads. Miller in St Paul, Minnesota, had found one painted on the bottom of his drained swimming pool. Culloden in Bristol, England, had found one painted on a billiard table in his games room. Svenson in Göteborg, Sweden, had found one painted on the floor of his kitchen.

The parallels had disturbing implications. In each case, the symbol had been left at the victim's home, as if to say 'We can get close to you anyplace, even where you feel most protected. But if we'd wanted, we could have painted the death's head where others could see it, at your workplace perhaps or in full view of your neighbors. We want you to realize – we can expose you at any time, humiliate your wife and children, embarrass your business contacts. And after that? Do you hope we'll be satisfied? Or will we come after you as we did your father? Will you have to pay the ultimate penalty? As our own loved ones had to pay. As *we* had to pay.'

Halloway shuddered, disturbed by one other parallel. After Miller, Culloden, Svenson, and now Rosenberg had discovered the death's head, they all had ignored safe procedure and phoned him directly instead of through intermediaries. The Night and Fog was achieving its purpose, eroding discipline, promoting panic. How many others of the group would soon call him? When would *he* discover a death's

126

head? He'd instructed his guards to double security on the safe house in Kitchener where his family was being sequestered. He'd also hired as many extra guards as he needed to protect this estate. But perhaps the time had come to abandon the estate, to give up the exquisite surroundings his father had provided for him.

He shook his head. No! As long as Seth and Icicle were on the hunt, there was every reason to believe in eventual victory. The Night and Fog would be destroyed.

And in the meantime? Determination was everything.

I won't be defeated! Halloway thought. The vermin won't control me!

But again he wondered, When will it be my turn to find a death's head?

He struggled against his misgivings. He'd asked the wrong question, he realized. The proper question was, When will Seth and Icicle be victorious for us all?

4

Rio de Janeiro. From his glass-walled penthouse, the businessman had a perfect view of the throngs of bathers on the sensuous curve of Copacabana Beach. If he'd cared to, he could have walked to the opposite glass wall and peered up toward the faroff massive statue of Christ the Redeemer on top of Corcovado mountain, but he seldom chose that option. Situated between the Spirit and the Flesh, he almost always found himself drawn toward the telescope on his beach-side window and its view of the most arousing women in the world. His wealth guaranteed a temptation few of them could resist.

But at the moment, all he felt was anger. He pressed a portable phone against his ear. 'Rosenberg, you think I've got nothing better to do than make deals and then tell the clients it was all a mistake? Never mind that this is a hundred-million-dollar deal and I get fifteen percent down-payment from them, and the money's gaining interest in a Zurich bank. Let's forget all that for a second. Friend to friend, a deal's a deal. In the first place, my clients become severely unpleasant if a contract's canceled. In the second place, the contracts *can't* be canceled because the shipment's on its way, and I always take care not to have any connection with it. I don't even know what ship it's on. I use so many intermediaries I wouldn't know how to stop it. You should have thought of this earlier.'

Rosenberg started to babble.

The businessman interrupted. 'If you've got cold feet, you shouldn't step into the water. Or is it *more* than cold feet? Do you know a security reason that I don't know for not delivering the merchandise? If you do, my friend, and you didn't warn us, you'll find out how truly unpleasant the clients can be. So what's with the second thoughts? What problem's on your mind?'

'Nothing . . .' Rosenberg whispered.

127

'What? I can barely hear you.'

'It's all right. No problem.'

'Then why the hell did you call me?'

'Nerves . . . I . . .'

'*Nerves?*' The businessman frowned. 'Friend, this conversation's starting to bore me.'

'There's so much money at stake . . .'

'You bet there is, and fifteen percent of it is mine.'

'So many risks. The merchandise scares me. The *clients* scare me. My stomach's been giving me problems.'

'Try Maalox. You're right about the clients. Any bunch who wants a hundred million dollars worth of black-market weapons is *definitely* scary. Incidentally, don't call me again. I won't do business with you anymore. You're interfering with my peace of mind.'

5

Rosenberg set down the phone and stared at his trembling hands. He'd never believed in fate, but he was quickly beginning to wonder if something very like it was taking charge of him. He couldn't recall when he'd felt this helpless, and he found himself mentally grasping for the only chance of salvation now afforded him – Icicle and Seth, their pursuit of the Night and Fog.

His spirit felt buoyed for less than five seconds. About to go downstairs from his secret office, he suddenly stopped, his palm pressed so hard against the doorknob that he felt its cutglass pattern indent his flesh. If the Night and Fog knew enough about his past to use a death's head symbol to terrorize him, if they knew enough about his present to paint the symbol not only on his bed but on the bed of the bodyguard who was screwing his wife, wasn't it also possible that they knew about *other* secrets in his life?

Such as this office?

With a tremor, he realized that he'd been in such a hurry he hadn't checked for a tap on the phone before he called his contact in Rio. Trying to prevent the Night and Fog from learning about the shipment, had he inadvertently let them find out? Furious at himself, he slammed the door and locked it, hurrying down the stairs.

6

A windowpane absorbs vibrations from a voice in a room.

Across the street from Rosenberg's office, a fan stood in the open window of a second-story hotel room. The fan was actually a microwave transmitter, which bounced waves off Rosenberg's window and received, along with them, the vibrations from Rosenberg's conversation. A decoder translated the waves into words and relayed them to a tape recorder. The tape was picked up every evening.

128

Rosenberg's home was also under microwave surveillance, as was Halloway's and that of every other member of the group. It didn't matter if they checked for bugs and phone taps. Everything they said was overheard. *They had no secrets.*

7

William Miller stared at the large manila envelope his secretary brought into his office.

'It came special delivery,' she said. 'I started to open it with the other mail, but you see it's marked "personal," underlined, with an exclamation mark, so I thought I'd better let you open it yourself.'

Miller studied the envelope. It was eight-by-twelve, crammed till it seemed that not one more sheet of paper could be squeezed inside. A hot pressure made him squirm. 'Thanks, Marge. It's probably just a new advertising scheme. Or maybe some young architect who wants to join the firm, trying to overwhelm me with his designs.'

'Sure, it could be anything,' Marge said, eyes mischievous. 'But for a second there, I wondered if you'd subscribed to some pornographic magazine you didn't want your wife to know about.'

He forced a laugh. 'Whatever's in the package, I didn't send for it.'

'Aren't you going to open it?'

'In a while. Right now, I've got this proposal to finish. The city council needs convincing on this low-rent renewal project.'

He lowered his gaze to the cold print before him and pretended to concentrate on the cost-projection figures.

'Anything I can do to help, Mr Miller, just buzz me on the intercom.' She left, closing the door behind her.

The envelope – bold black ink emphasizing its PERSONAL! caution – lay on his desk. The postage cost, including the special delivery fee, had been nine dollars and fifteen cents. No return address.

So why am I nervous? he thought. It's just an envelope.

He glanced back down at the cost-projection figures but found himself compelled to glance again at the envelope. Couldn't turn his eyes away.

Well, maybe if I didn't open it at all. Maybe if I threw it in the trash.

No, Marge might find it there and open it.

Then I could take it with me when I left the office and get rid of it on the way home. And anyway, so what if Marge saw what was in it? What difference would that make?

Because it's marked PERSONAL!, and after what you found at the bottom of your swimming pool, you'd better pay attention when your psychic alarm bells start going off. You might not want to open it, but you'd damned well better.

Even so, he sat motionless, staring at the envelope.

At last, he exhaled and inched his fingers across the desk. The envelope felt heavy, dense. He started to tear open its flap and froze, tasting something sour.

This might be a letter bomb, he thought. His impulse was to drop it back on the desk and hurry from the office, but he hesitated, compelled by a stonger impulse to pinch it gently and trace a finger along its edges. The contents felt solid – no give in the middle where cardboard might cover a hollow filled with explosives. Cautiously, he tore open the flap and peered inside.

At a thick stack of photographs. He stared at the image on top. It was black-and-white, a reproduction of what evidently had been a picture taken years ago.

The horror of it made him gasp. Filled with disgust, he leafed through the stack, finding other horrors, each more revolting than the one before, obscenity heaped upon obscenity. His lungs didn't want to draw in air.

Corpses. The top photograph – and the countless others beneath it – showed corpses, stacks and stacks of corpses, thrown together on top of each other, arms and legs protruding in grotesque angles, rib cages clearly outlined beneath starved flesh. Gaunt cheeks, sunken eyes, some of which were open, accusing even in death. Scalps shaved bare. Lips drawn inward over toothless gums. Features contorted with permanent grimaces of fright and pain. Old men. Women. Children.

So many. He almost screamed.

8

'It's true! You have to believe me! I don't know!' Medici insisted. 'Please!'

Again Seth slapped him across the mouth. The slap, though it produced less pain than a punch, resulted in paradoxically greater terror, as if assaulting Medici's dignity was the key to breaking him.

'The priest!' Seth demanded. 'Cardinal Pavelic! I'm losing my patience! Who abducted the priest?'

'If I knew, I'd tell you!'

This time Seth used the back of his hand, slapping Medici's head to the side, leaving angry red welts on Medici's cheek. Seth's own cheeks were as red as his hair, his usually nonexpressive eyes bright with what might have been pleasure.

Icicle stood in a corner of the kitchen in the isolated farmhouse they'd rented, watching with interest.

His interest had two causes: Seth's interrogation technique and Medici's response to it. Seth had tied Medici to a chair, bound the prisoner's wrists behind the back of the chair, and looped a noose around the prisoner's neck, the tail of the noose attached to the rope that bound his wrists. Every time Medici's head jerked from a slap, the noose tugged into his throat and the resultant pressure yanked Medici's wrists up toward his shoulder blades.

Ingenious, Icicle decided. A minimum force produces a maximum effect. The prisoner realizes he's inflicting most of the agony upon himself. He struggles to resist the impact of the slap, but the way he's been tied, he *can't* resist. His body becomes his enemy. His self-confidence, his *dignity*, becomes offended. You'll crack any time now, Medici, he decided. The tears streaming down Medici's face confirmed his conclusion.

'One more time,' Seth demanded. 'Who abducted the cardinal?'

Medici squinted, calculating his answer. Pain had unclouded his mind. He understood his situation now. None of his men realized where he was. No one was going to rescue him. Pain wasn't his problem so much as how to survive. 'Listen first. *Why don't you listen before you slap me again?*'

Seth shrugged. 'The problem is, I need something to listen to.'

Medici tried to swallow, but the tight noose constricted his throat. 'I'm just a middleman. Clients come to me. They want weapons, information, surveillance teams, safe houses. I supply these services. They don't tell me *why* they want these services. I don't ask.'

Seth turned to Icicle, pretending to yawn. 'I ask him about the cardinal, he gives me the story of his life.'

'You're not letting me explain!' Medici said.

'I will when you *say* something!'

Medici hurried on. 'My clients don't tell me their plans, but I do keep my ears to the ground.'

'Now he gives me grotesque images,' Seth told Icicle.

'I have to keep up with the ins and outs of the profession, don't I? To keep on top of things?'

'He has a problem with prepositions,' Seth told Icicle.

'But I haven't heard any rumors, *not a whisper*, about terrorists going after the cardinal. Believe me, I would have heard.' Medici squirmed, causing the noose to bind his neck tighter. He made a gagging sound. 'Whoever took the cardinal they weren't radicals, they weren't . . .'

'Terrorists. Scum,' Seth said. 'Your clients have no style. They're indiscriminate and clumsy. Bombs on buses.' Seth pursed his lips in disgust. 'Dismembered children.'

For an instant, Icicle wondered if Seth had dimensions of character he hadn't recognized. But then he realized that Seth's objections were aesthetic, not moral. If Seth were paid enough, and if the plan required children to be killed as a distraction from the central purpose of executing a diplomat, this man would do it.

On the other hand, Icicle thought and firmly believed, I'd never agree to killing children. Not under any circumstances. *Never.*

Medici continued. 'Terrorists might attack the Church as an institution they believed was corrupt, abduct a cardinal whose politics disagreed with their own. They went after the Pope a few years ago, didn't they? But what I'm telling you is I haven't heard about anyone going after the cardinal. I don't believe you're on the right trail.'

'In that case,' Seth said and spread his hands magnanimously, 'as one professional to another' – his words implied respect, but his tone was mocking – 'what course do you suggest we follow?'

Medici's eyes became furtive. 'Have you thought about the Church itself? Someone *in* the Church?'

Seth turned to Icicle.

'A possibility.' Icicle shrugged.

'I'm not convinced,' Seth said.

'That the cardinal might be a victim of the Church?'

'That this predator is telling the truth.'

'I *am!*' Medici insisted.

'We'll soon find out.' Seth turned to Icicle. 'We'll do it your way now.'

'Thanks for the belated confidence.'

'It's a matter of using every method. Force by itself can lead to convincing lies. Chemicals can elicit programmed responses. But the two together make up for each other's liabilities.'

'In that case, I'll fill a hypodermic with Sodium Amytal. Stand back. As you say, it's *my* turn now.'

9

With the noose removed from his neck but his body still tied to the chair, Medici slumped, semiconscious. In theory, the Sodium Amytal had eliminated his mental censors, making it possible to elicit information that Medici otherwise, even in pain, might not reveal. The trick was not to inject so much Amytal that Medici's responses became incoherent or that he sank fully into unconsciousness.

Now it was Icicle's turn to stand before the prisoner. Holding the almost empty hypodermic in one hand, he asked the key question that had brought him from Australia to Canada and finally to Italy. 'Does the expression Night and Fog mean anything to you?'

Medici responded slowly. His tongue seemed stuck in his mouth. 'Yes . . . from the war.'

'That's right. The Second World War. The Nazis used it as a terrorist tactic. Anyone disloyal to the Third Reich risked vanishing without a trace, disappearing into the Night and Fog.' Icicle spoke slowly, distinctly, letting the words sink in. 'Has the Night and Fog come back? Have you heard rumors about its being reactivated?'

Medici shook his head. 'No rumors. No Night and Fog.'

'Try to remember. Did terrorists or a group pretending to be terrorists approach you? Did anyone ask for information about Cardinal Pavelic? Did anyone hire you to put surveillance on the cardinal?'

'No surveillance on the cardinal,' Medici whispered. 'No one asked me about him.'

'Who do you think abducted the cardinal?'

'Don't know.'

'*Why* would he have been abducted?'

'Don't know.'

'Could someone within the Church be responsible?'

'Don't know.'

Seth stepped forward. 'That last answer's interesting. He doesn't know whether someone in the Church was responsible.'

Icicle understood what Seth meant. Forty minutes ago, Medici had insisted that they direct their attention toward the Church. 'Before, he was grasping for any way he could imagine to distract us. He doesn't know anything.'

'But the more I think about it, his suggestion is worth exploring.'

'The Church? Why not? We have to eliminate the possibilities. It's conceivable that someone within the Church discovered what the cardinal knew and passed it on to the Night and Fog.'

'Or that someone in the Church *is* the Night and Fog.'

'Pavelic.' Icicle's voice was fraught with hate. 'For forty years, the bastard kept his hooks in our fathers. The records he kept. God knows how much money he demanded in exchange for keeping those records a secret. Pavelic was the only outsider who had the information that linked all our fathers. The Night and Fog couldn't have organized its terror against them without knowing what was in the cardinal's files.'

'Logical,' Seth said, 'but not necessarily the case. There could be an explanation we've overlooked.'

'Such as?'

'That's the problem. We don't know enough,' Seth said. 'But this man doesn't either. I suggest we investigate the cardinal's private life.'

'"Private"?' Icicle laughed. 'I didn't know priests were allowed to have "private" lives.' He hesitated. 'And what about . . . ?' He gestured toward Medici.

'Kill him, of course. He's useless to us, even a danger. Another injection of Amytal should be sufficient. Painless.' Seth raised his shoulders. 'Perhaps even pleasureful.'

'That still leaves the man and the woman in the alley across from where we grabbed him. You noticed them as I did. They weren't hiding there by coincidence. They had the same interest in Medici that *we* did.'

'If we see them again, we'll kill them.' The blaze in Seth's eyes suggested that too would be a pleasure.

Nightmares Then
and Now

As the mountain road curved higher, the rented Volkswagen's engine began to sputter. The car refused to gain speed to compensate for the incline. A half-kilometer later, Saul smelled gasoline and veered toward an observation point at a bend in the road. He shut the ignition off.

Beside him, Erika squirmed and wakened. When she peered toward the valley below them, the bright morning sun made her squint. The sky was turquoise, the farm fields emerald. Yawning, she glanced at her watch. 'Ten forty-six?' Concern made her fully alert. 'You've been driving since dawn. You must be exhausted. I'll change places with you.'

'I can manage. We've only got fifteen kilometers to go.'

'Fifteen kilometers? If that's all, why did you stop?'

'We almost had a fire.'

Her nostrils widened. 'I smell it now. Gasoline.'

'I think it's the carburetor.' He opened the driver's door, approached the front of the car, and lifted the hood. A film of liquid covered the engine. Vapor rose. Erika appeared beside him and studied the engine.

'Hand me your pocketknife,' she said.

She opened its blade and adjusted a screw on the carburetor's stem. Saul knew what she was doing. The car, which they'd rented in Vienna, must have been tuned for lowland city driving. Now after struggling against the thin air of the mountains, the carburetor hadn't been able to mix sufficient oxygen with gasoline to allow the fuel to be detonated by the spark plugs. The engine had flooded. The excess fuel had backed up into the carburetor, which had overflowed. The simple adjustment to the carburetor would remedy the problem.

'Another five minutes, and we'd have been walking,' Saul said.

'Running's more like it.' She laughed self-critically. 'Before the gas tank blew up. We've been living in the desert too long. We forgot the problems altitude can cause.' Her long dark hair glinted in the morning sun. Her beige jacket emphasized the deep brown of her eyes.

Saul had never loved her more. 'I hope that's all we forgot. I'd hate to think we've just been lucky so far, and now, out of practice for years, we're making mistakes.'

'Keep thinking that way. It'll stop us from being over-confident.'

'That's one thing I'm not.'

Eager to get moving, they subdued their frustration and waited for

134

the gasoline to evaporate from the engine. The surrounding slopes, above and below, were lush with evergreens. The thin air of six thousand feet made breathing difficult. Snow-capped mountains towered in the distance. Under other circumstances, these dramatic conditions – the Swiss Alps, south of Zurich – would have been mesmerizing.

Saul shut the car's hood. 'It's probably safe to drive now. According to the map, the road'll take us down to the neighboring valley. But Misha investigated the names on the list he made. His agents must have already been where we're going. If they'd learned anything important, we'd have been told about it. Let's be prepared for disappointment.'

'We have to start *somewhere*.'

Saul's voice thickened. 'Right. And if the answer isn't here, it's somewhere else . . . We'll keep searching till we finish this.'

2

The village was Weissendorf: a cluster of perhaps a hundred buildings perched upon a small plateau with a gently sloping pasture above and below. A road ran through it. The buildings were narrow, often four stories tall, the upper levels projecting an arm's-length out from the bottom one so that they seemed like awnings designed to keep pedestrians dry when it rained. With their peaked roofs that curved slightly up at the eaves, the buildings reminded Saul of fir trees. At the same time, elaborately carved designs on railings, windowsills, and doors reminded him of gingerbread houses.

He parked the Volkswagen outside an inn. An oversized ale tankard with a handle and hinged lid hung above the entrance. He turned to Erika. 'Which one of us should ask directions to where Ephraim Avidan lives?'

She realized the problem. Switzerland had no language of its own. Its citizens spoke the language of the nearest bordering country. 'Your German's better than mine,' she said. 'But this is *southern* Switzerland. Our French is about the same, but my Italian's—'

'Better. Besides – excuse a sexist remark – they might be more receptive to a female stranger. You want to give it a try?'

With a grin that didn't disguise her troubled mood, she opened the passenger door and entered the inn.

Saul waited uneasily. Before promising his former network that he wouldn't accept help from any intelligence agency, he'd already received a great deal of help from Misha Pletz and the Mossad. He didn't think he could be accused of reneging on his agreement if he took advantage of that prepromise help. For one thing, Misha had supplied them with Israeli passports using cover names and fictitious backgrounds that, if questioned by the authorities, would be endorsed by Israeli civilians and businesses secretly affiliated with the Mossad. For another, Misha had given them sufficient money to conduct their search. He'd also provided them with weapons, though Saul and Erika had hidden these before leaving Austria, not wanting to risk crossing the border with them.

But at the moment, the most important of Misha's contributions was a photocopy of his notebook – the list of names he'd made and the information about them. The first name on the list was Ephraim Avidan.

'*What do the names on the list have to do with what happened to my father?*' Erika had asked.

'*I have no idea,*' Misha had answered.

'*I don't believe that. You wouldn't have made the list if there isn't a connection among them.*'

'*Did I say there isn't a connection? We know their backgrounds, their addresses, their habits, their former occupations.*'

'*Former?*'

'*These men are all ex-Mossad, all retired. But you asked how they related to what happened to your father, and that puzzle I haven't been able to solve yet.*'

'*They claim they don't know my father? They won't answer your questions? What's the problem?*'

'*I haven't been able to ask them anything.*'

'*You're doing it again. Evading.*'

'*I'm not. These men share two other factors. They survived the Nazi death camps . . .*'

'*And?*'

'*They've all disappeared.*'

As Erika's father had disappeared.

The inn door swung open. Saul couldn't interpret the expression on Erika's face when she got in the car.

'Anything?' he asked.

'They didn't exactly gush with information. I gather we're not the only strangers who've asked about Avidan, and these people don't take well to strangers, male *or* female, who aren't here just to spend money as tourists.'

Saul thought about it. 'Whoever came before us must have belonged to Misha.'

'Maybe. Let's find out. I managed to get directions.'

Saul started the car and drove along the narrow street. 'Tell me when to turn.'

'It's outside town. The third farmhouse on the left.'

He increased speed.

The house was old, with white stucco walls, on a level section of the upper grassy slope. Though wider than the buildings in town, it did have a high peaked roof, its silhouette conforming with a mountain beyond it. Saul turned and drove up a rutted dirt lane, hearing cowbells from the pasture as he stopped outside the house. The sun made the valley even more brilliant. He didn't pay attention to the scenery, his thoughts completely preoccupied with the list they'd discovered.

And the first name on the list.

They stepped from the car.

A woman with handsome, almost mannish features came out of the house. She was in her early thirties, with short sun-bleached hair and ruddy cheeks. Muscular, she wore sturdy ankle-high shoes, woolen kneesocks, leather shorts, and a blue-checked shirt with its sleeves rolled up. Her shoes thunked on a wooden porch, then on stairs leading down to the car. When she stopped, her eyes flashed with suspicion.

Saul took for granted that Erika would do most of the talking, just as he would have if this had been a man. Erika used Italian. 'We're sorry to bother you, but we're told that Ephraim Avidan used to live here.'

The woman spoke in English. 'Your accent. American?'

Erika replied in kind. 'No, I'm Israeli, but I lived in the United States for many years. In fact, I'm more comfortable with English than I am with my native language. Would you prefer . . . ?'

'To speak in English?' The woman shook her head and switched to Italian. 'I could use the practice, but not when discussing Ephraim Avidan. He used to live here, but he's gone.' She seemed sullen. 'Are you with the others who came to ask about him?'

'Others?'

'Two men. Five days ago. They claimed to be old friends of Avidan. But they were thirty years younger. Like Avidan and yourself, they said they were Israeli. They claimed they owed Avidan money. Such conscientious debtors, don't you think? They wanted to know where he'd gone.'

'And what did you tell them?'

'The same thing I tell you. I don't know where. He left abruptly. In February. One evening he was here, the next morning he wasn't. As far as I could tell, he took nothing with him. After several days, I notified our policeman in town. A search was organized, but we didn't find a body.' She gestured toward the mountains. 'We didn't expect to. No one goes hiking in the woods at night during winter. Suicide was a possibility. He'd been moody. But without a body . . . Our policeman notified the authorities in Bern. The matter passed out of our hands. But we treated him fairly, the same as if he'd been one of us. And he treated *me* fairly. Before he disappeared, he paid his rent. I never had trouble with him.'

'Of course.'

The woman tightened her arms across her chest. 'And what about yourselves? Are you also "old" friends who owe him money?' She directed her question toward Saul.

'We didn't know him at all.'

The woman smiled, apparently not having expected a candid response.

Saul nodded toward Erika. 'My wife's father was a friend of Ephraim Avidan, though.' He paused for effect. 'And her father has also disappeared.'

The woman seemed caught between surprise and skepticism. 'On

137

the other hand, your explanation might merely be more inventive than that of old friends owing money to someone.'

'Why are you so suspicious?' Erika asked. 'All we want is information.'

'Suspicious? If your husband had left you . . . If you had the responsibility of managing . . .' Her voice trailed off. She stared toward swollen-uddered cattle in the pasture. 'I probably wouldn't be suspicious if not for the priest.'

Saul's pulse quickened. 'Priest?'

'Not that he said he was a priest. He was rugged, handsome. A hiker, so he claimed. He arrived two weeks before the Israelis did. He had blue eyes and straw-colored hair. He chopped wood for his supper. He was muscular. His chest was strong. But what I noticed most were his hands.'

'What about them?'

'He took extreme care of them. I didn't think it unusual when he wore gloves to chop wood. A precaution against slivers and blisters. But later, after he'd taken off the gloves and washed his hands, when I ate supper with him, I couldn't help noticing how soft and smooth his hands were in comparison with his muscles. He was tanned, but on his left hand . . . here at the base of his middle finger . . . he had a white rim of skin where he'd recently taken off a ring. I still don't understand why he'd have done that. Who knows? Perhaps he'd merely lost it. But his right hand . . . here . . . the thumb, the first and second finger . . . those he was especially self-conscious about. He didn't want food to touch those fingers, and later, when he helped me wash dishes, he kept a towel around his right hand, using his left to pick up the plates. Do you see the significance?'

'I'm sorry,' Erika said. 'I'm afraid I don't.'

'As an Israeli, you wouldn't, I suppose. I myself am a Lutheran, but I know that for a Roman Catholic priest the thumb, first, and second fingers of his right hand are the most important parts of his body. They're blessed. They're what he uses to hold the wafer of bread that he consecrates and changes into what Catholics believe is the spiritual presence of Jesus Christ. If a priest's right thumb and first two fingers were amputated, he couldn't be a priest any longer, not totally. He couldn't say mass. He couldn't perform the ritual of consecrating the host and giving out Communion. And because those fingers have been blessed, he has to protect them not only from physical harm but also from indignities.'

Erika was puzzled. 'But couldn't he merely have been left-handed, and that's why he seemed to favor his right?'

'After supper, he put his gloves back on and offered to go to the barn, to do a few more chores. I needed help, so I promised him breakfast and agreed.' She pointed toward the barn, a corner of which projected from behind the house. 'He worked longer than I expected. When I went to see if anything was wrong, I caught him by surprise. He shoved a small black book into his knapsack. Then I knew for certain.'

'I don't follow you,' Erika said.

But Saul did. He remembered what his foster brother, Chris, an Irish-Catholic, had taught him about the Church. 'The small black book was probably a breviary,' he explained. 'The collection of prayers a priest has to read every day.' He faced the woman. 'But you said you knew "for certain." Forgive me, it still seems like supposition.'

'No,' the woman said. 'In the night, I went to his room in the barn and searched through his knapsack. The small black book *was* a breviary.'

'Searched through his . . . ?'

'You think I was bold? How could he rebuke me when he was as bold as I was, when he'd snuck from his room and gone up the hill to search *Avidan's* room?' Her face flushed with indignation. 'I'd left the cabin as Avidan had left it. There was always the chance Avidan would return, and since no one else had asked to rent it, I didn't care to waste my time by moving his possessions. Where would I have put them anyhow? When I crept up the hill, I heard the priest in the cabin. I heard drawers being opened and shut. I saw the waver of a flashlight beam through cracks in the window shades.'

'What did you do about it?'

'What would you expect? A woman alone? An apparently innocent guest who turns out to be a prowler? I returned to the house and did nothing. In the morning, I pretended not to know he'd gone to Avidan's cabin, and he – if he'd guessed I'd searched his knapsack – pretended not to have noticed. He ate the breakfast I prepared, asked if there were other chores he could do, and, when I declined, continued the hiking vacation he claimed to be on. For the next few nights, I kept a close watch on the cabin. So far as I know, the priest never came back.'

'And what would be the significance of the ring he took off?' Erika asked.

'It could have been the insignia of his order,' Saul said. 'A few religious groups wear them.'

'I didn't find a ring in his knapsack,' the woman said.

'Maybe he considered it so valuable he kept it in a pocket.'

'Perhaps. Then, two weeks later, the Israeli pair arrived. They asked if they could see Avidan's cabin in case something in it might tell them where he'd gone – you understand, so they could repay the fabulous debt they said they owed him.'

'Did you let them?'

'Yes. I had the sense that, if I refused, they'd return in the night and search it anyhow. Or search the cabin right then, despite my objections. I didn't want trouble. I hoped that, if I agreed, I'd see the end of it. Besides, what did I have to hide?'

'Or what did Avidan have to hide?' Saul said.

'Now *you* arrive, and you ask why I'm suspicious. Who *was* this Avidan? Why are you and those others interested in him?'

'I can't speak for the priest,' Saul said. 'He's as puzzling to me as he is to you. But the two Israelis were probably intelligence operatives.

139

Mossad. Avidan used to belong to their organization. When one of them – even one who's retired from them – disappears, they want to know why, especially if his disappearance seems linked to the disappearance of yet another ex-Mossad operative. My wife's father.'

The woman inhaled sharply. 'Politics? I don't want anything to do with politics.'

'We're not sure it's politics. It could be a personal matter from years ago. Honestly, we don't know. For us, it's definitely personal, though.'

'Are *you* Mossad?'

Erika hesitated. 'I used to be.'

'Politics.'

'I said I *used* to be. Look, please, we've told you a lot more than we should have. How can we make you trust us?'

'How? Tell me a way to keep strangers from coming around here asking about Avidan.'

'If you help us, maybe we'll be able to find out what happened to him. Then the strangers will stop coming around.'

The woman studied them.

'May we see Avidan's cabin?' Saul asked.

The woman remained motionless. Saul held his breath.

The woman nodded.

3

The cabin was past the house and the barn, up the continuation of the sloping pasture. Behind it, dense forest rose to rocky bluffs. The Alpine air smelled pure and sweet, tinged with the fragrance of evergreens.

The cabin was small, single-story, made from logs whose bark had long ago disintegrated. A rusty stovepipe projected from a roof that needed reshingling. Saul turned to survey the view: the lush lower part of the valley, a faroff small lake, the towers of the town, partly obscured by intervening fir trees, a kilometer to his right.

Why would Avidan choose such primitive, secluded lodgings? Saul wondered.

'How long did Avidan live here?' he asked the woman.

'He came last fall. In October.'

'He planned to spend all winter here?'

'He said he was a writer. He needed solitude and privacy to finish a novel.'

A retired Mossad operative a novelist? Saul thought. It was possible. Anything was possible. But probable? Once the winter storms started blowing . . . Solitude and privacy? Avidan had certainly gone to an extreme for those conditions. What had made him choose this place?

They entered the cabin. It was divided into a bedroom and a kitchen. In the absence of a fireplace, a large black wood-burning stove served for heating the cabin as well as preparing food. The rooms were spartan. Plain pine boards covered the walls. A slab of wood on trestles was the kitchen table, a bench beside it. There were austere cupboards, a rocking chair, another bench along one wall. The bed was a top-and-bottom bunk, its mattresses packed with straw. A cracked mirror hung above a battered bureau, the drawers of which were lined with yellowed newspapers from 1975. The drawers contained a few items of clothing. Books, mostly histories related to Israel, filled a shelf beside the bureau. Photographs of Israel's desert, along with images of crowded downtown Tel Aviv, were tacked here and there on the walls. In the kitchen, Erika found plastic cups and plates in a cupboard, along with cans of food. Dish detergent was in a compartment beneath the sink.

A man could go crazy spending a winter up here, Saul thought.

He turned to the woman. 'You said you didn't remove Avidan's possessions because you thought he might come back. It doesn't look like he had all that much to pack up.'

'And if he was working on a novel,' Erika said, 'he must have taken it with him. I don't see a typewriter. I can't find a manuscript.'

The woman stood silhouetted by sunlight at the open doorway. 'From October to February, I almost never saw him. From my house, sometimes I couldn't see the cabin for the gusting snow. Sometimes I thought the snow would *smother* the cabin. But on clear days, as long as I saw smoke from the stovepipe, I didn't worry. And the first of every month, he waded down through drifts to pay his rent.'

Saul remembered that the woman had said she'd been deserted by her husband. Avidan's monthly rent must have been sufficient comfort for her to ignore her tenant's eccentricities.

'Something was wrong,' the woman said. 'I knew that. And when he disappeared, in case the police reopened the investigation, I was determined not to touch *anything*.'

'But so far as you know, you don't think the priest and the two Israeli men learned anything from their search,' Saul said. 'We could sort through the pages of these books. We could sift through the packages of food. We could test for loose floorboards. My guess is we'd be wasting our time. Avidan was a professional.'

'The priest and the two Israeli men assumed they could take advantage of me, trick me, dominate me,' the woman said angrily. 'They never offered money.'

Saul's skin tingled. 'But if *we* offered money . . . ?'

'It's difficult to manage this farm alone.'

'Of course,' Erika said. 'We want to help you. Our resources are limited. We recently had to leave our home in Israel. But we're willing to make a contribution.'

The woman moved her head from side to side, calculating, and named an amount. It was high, almost half of what Misha Pletz had given to Saul and Erika. But it was insignificant if the woman's information was as important as her rigid features suggested.

141

'Done,' Saul said. 'Provided you don't merely show us an out-of-date address book or . . .'

'A diary,' the woman said. 'The dates are from October of last year until he disappeared. It's about this cabin. It's about *him*. There are photographs. They made me sick.'

Saul's chest contracted.

Erika stepped forward. 'How did you get them?'

'I found where they were hidden.'

'Yes, but *how?*'

'After the priest searched this cabin, I wondered what he was looking for. When I felt he was really gone, I came up here and searched as well. I tested the floor. The walls. The ceiling. I even budged the stove and pried up the firebricks beneath it.'

'And?'

'I found nothing. But the priest wasn't thorough,' the woman said. 'He didn't identify with Avidan's routine. He didn't put himself in Avidan's mind. There's another building.'

Saul knew. 'The outhouse.'

'I found the diary and the photographs attached beneath the platform of the hole above the pit. Each day when he came and went along the path he dug through the snow, he must have taken them with him, possibly even concealed them beneath his clothes.'

'And they're worth the sum you asked?'

'The worth is your concern. The sum you know.'

Erika reached into a pocket. 'The money's Austrian.'

'It could be Japanese for all I care. This is Switzerland. Every currency is welcome here.' The woman counted the bills.

'Where's what we paid for?'

'Come down to the house.'

4

They sat at a table in a rustic kitchen. As the woman made coffee, Saul opened the plastic-wrapped packet she'd given them. He winced when he saw the photographs. Erika's hands shook sorting through them.

Nazi concentration camps. SS soldiers aiming sub-machine-guns at refugees being shoved from trucks and railway cattle cars. Gaunt-faced prisoners staring with haunted eyes through barbed-wire fences. Endless trenches, quicklime-covered corpses, bulldozers poised to fill in dirt. Gas chambers, naked people – mostly children, old men and women – so squeezed together they'd died standing up. Open doors of massive ovens. Unimaginable quantities of ashes and bones.

Saul studied them all, every obscene one, and when he'd finished, he'd learned what he already knew – that the human ability to invent new methods of brutality was boundless.

He stacked the photographs and turned them face down on the table. 'The examined life isn't worth living,' he said, his voice trailing off. He stared at the diary. 'God knows what else is in . . .'

142

'The night I looked through that packet, no matter how many logs I put on the fire, I was still cold,' the woman said. 'I paced until dawn. I knew about such atrocities, but to see them, to read about them . . .'

'Read about . . . ?' Erika looked at the diary, reached for it, hesitated, and drew her hands back as if from vomit.

'Yes, the diary,' the woman said. 'Avidan, his parents, his sister, and two brothers lived in Munich. In 1942, when the Holocaust was set into motion, the SS arrested them and trucked them to the concentration camp at Dachau. It was only twenty kilometers away from their home. A work camp, not a death camp, though the way he describes it, there wasn't much difference. With the other prisoners, he and his family were used as slave labor at an ammunition factory. They received a minimum of food. They were given little time to rest or sleep. Sanitary facilities were inadequate. Toilets were nothing more than open trenches. Drinking water was contaminated. Their barracks leaked. There were rats. For two years, Avidan and his family slaved for Hitler's war. And one by one, they died. Avidan's mother went first – she collapsed in the factory and died from exhaustion. When Avidan's father couldn't get off the barracks' floor one morning, the SS dragged him outside and shot him in front of the other prisoners. His corpse was left in the assembly area for three days before prisoners were ordered to put the body on a cart and push it to a burial pit outside the camp. Next, Avidan's ten-year-old sister coughed herself to death. His older brother didn't move fast enough to suit a guard and had his head split open with a club. His remaining brother went insane and gashed his wrists with a splinter of wood. Avidan himself became determined to survive. In small unnoticeable ways, he rested while he worked, conserving his strength. He devoured spiders, flies, worms, anything he could find in camp. And he *succeeded*. In 1944, in September, he was part of a work force trucked from the camp to pick up liquor and food from town for an SS party that night. The truck blew a tire. In the confusion, prisoners fled. The SS soldiers recovered quickly and shot three of the four escaping prisoners. The fourth was Avidan. The thrill of freedom was so overwhelming he pushed himself to limits he didn't know he had. He stole food from storage bins. He slept in haystacks. He kept moving. Dachau is a hundred kilometers from Switzerland. In his diary, he doesn't say how he passed the Bodensee, but he arrived at neutral territory, and still kept going, still not sure he'd reach sanctuary, till he finally came to rest here. My former husband and I bought this farm in 1978. I have no idea who owned it during the war. But whoever lived here found Avidan cowering in the barn one night. They understood his circumstances, took pity, and let him stay in the cabin. They supplied him with food. He remained from October of 'forty-four till the end of the war the following May, when he went to Palestine.'

The woman stopped. The room became eerily silent. Saul had listened so raptly that it took a moment before a reference at the end of her words tugged at his memory.

143

'He reached the cabin in October of 'forty-four?' Heat rushed into Saul's stomach. 'But didn't you say he came back last year . . . ?'

'In October,' the woman said. 'Given what he wrote in his diary, about his ordeal in the war, I doubt the parallel of the months was coincidental. The past was on his mind. Something must have driven him to return. His diary's so vivid it's as if he did more than recall his terrors – he *relived* them.'

'To be that obsessed . . .' Erika shuddered.

'As obsessed as your father was,' Saul said. In the presence of their hostess, he didn't mention the photographs in the basement of the Vienna apartment building.

'But you said that in 1945 Avidan left here in May, at the end of the war,' Erika said. '*This* year, though, he left in February. The pattern isn't exact.'

'Unless he intended to leave in May,' the woman said, 'and something forced him to leave early, just as something had forced him to come back here. He left without warning. He took almost nothing with him. His decision must have been abrupt.'

'Or someone abruptly made the decision for him,' Erika said, 'just as I suspect someone did for my father.'

'Abducted him?' the woman asked.

'It's possible.' Erika exhaled. 'We still don't know enough.'

Through open windows, Saul heard the drone of a car coming along the road. The drone became louder. All at once it stopped.

His shoulder blades contracted. He left the kitchen and, careful to stand to the side of the big front window, peered out past the porch. A black Renault stood in the open gate of the rutted lane that led from the road toward the house. He saw the silhouettes of three men inside.

Erika came into the living room. 'What's the matter?' The woman followed her.

Saul turned to the woman. 'Do you recognize that car?'

The woman stepped toward the window.

'Don't show yourself,' Saul warned.

The woman obeyed, moving to the side of the window as Saul had. 'I've never seen it before.'

The three men got out of the car. They were tall and well-built, in their mid-thirties. Each wore thick-soled casual shoes, dark slacks, and a zipped-up windbreaker. The jackets were slightly too large.

In June? Saul thought. On a warm day like this? Why zipped-up windbreakers?

As the men walked up the lane, each pulled down the zipper on his jacket.

Saul felt Erika close behind him.

'They could have driven all the way up to the house,' she said.

'But instead they blocked the gate. Until they move their car, we can't drive out.'

The men walked abreast of each other. Though their expressions were blank, their eyes kept shifting, scanning the Volkswagen, the house, the pasture on either side, the woods and mountains beyond.

Each had his left hand raised toward his belt. They were halfway up the lane now, close enough for Saul to notice the bright red ring each wore on the middle finger of his raised left hand.

He spun toward the woman. 'Have you got a gun in the house?'

The woman stepped back, repelled by the force of his question. But her voice was steady. 'Of course. This is Switzerland.'

She didn't need to explain. Switzerland, though a neutral country, believed in military preparedness. Every male from the age of twenty to fifty was obligated to undergo military training. Every family had to keep a weapon in the house.

'Get it. Quickly,' Saul said. 'Make sure it's loaded. We have to leave here *now*.'

'But why would. . . ?'

'Now!'

Eyes widening, the woman rushed to a closet, removing a Swiss-made *Sturmgewehr*, or storm rifle. Saul knew it well. The length of a carbine, it was chambered for NATO's 7.62-mm caliber bullets. It had a fold-down tripod beneath the barrel and a rubber-coated stock that helped to lessen the force of the recoil.

The woman groped for two magazines on the shelf above her. Erika took them, checking to make sure they were full to their twenty-round capacity. She inserted one into the rifle, switched off the safety, set the weapon for semiautomatic firing, and pulled back the arming bolt to chamber a round. She shoved the remaining magazine under her belt.

The woman blinked in dismay. 'Those men surely wouldn't . . .'

'We don't have time to talk about it! Get out of here!' Saul lunged for the diary and the photographs on the kitchen table and crammed them into their cardboard packet. With the rifle in one hand, Erika yanked open the rear door to the kitchen. Saul grabbed the woman's arm, tugging her with him, and charged out after Erika.

They raced across a small grassy area, through the barn, and up the slope toward Avidan's cabin.

Saul heard a shout behind him. Legs pounding, he pressed the cardboard packet against his chest and risked stumbling to glance backward. Two of the men darted around the left side of the barn while the other man appeared at the right, pointing upward. The third man yelled in French. '*Ici!*'

Each pulled a pistol from beneath his windbreaker.

'Erika!' Saul shouted.

She looked back, saw the three men aiming, and spun. In a fluid motion, she dropped to one knee, propped an elbow on her upraised other knee, and sighted along the rifle. Before the three men could fire, she pulled the trigger, then shot again. And again. The range was fifty meters. She was a skilled sharpshooter, but with no time to steady her muscles, the barrel wavered. She grazed one man's shoulder, the other bullets slamming against the barn.

The injured man grabbed his arm and darted back behind the barn. His companions ducked out of sight inside it. If she hadn't killed them, at least she'd distracted them, and she rose, sprinting after Saul, and the woman, who'd already reached the top of the slope. A bullet tore splinters off a log on Avidan's cabin as she took cover behind the building.

Saul and the woman waited for her, breathing deeply. Erika took a chance and showed herself to shoot twice more down the slope at the men scrambling after them.

The men sprawled flat.

'You know these woods,' Saul told the woman. 'Take us into the mountains.'

'But where will we . . . ?'

'Hurry. *Move!*'

5

The woman squeezed through a line of bushes and came to a narrow path that veered up a wooded slope, her muscular bare legs taking long forceful strides toward the summit. Saul and Erika followed, struggling to adjust to the unaccustomed altitude. At the top, the path changed direction, angling to the left, then descending between two chest-high boulders. Dense trees shut out the sun. Saul sensed their pine resin fragrance, their fallen needles soft beneath the impact of his shoes, but what occupied his attention was the crack of branches behind him, the muffled echo of angry voices.

The woman led them down the path to a shallow stream. Saul splashed across it, ignoring the cold wetness of his pants clinging to his legs, and forced himself into the shadowy continuation of the forest. He heard Erika's feet plunge through the stream behind him.

The woman led them up another slope, but this slope was steeper, the trail almost indiscernible. Saul zigzagged past deadfalls, thickets, and clumps of boulders. Finally at the top, his lungs on fire, he pivoted to stare past Erika down toward the hollow. The men weren't in sight, but he could hear footsteps splashing through the stream.

The woman had brought them to a grassy plateau. A hundred meters away, another stretch of dense forest angled up, it seemed forever. They raced ahead. High grass tugged at Saul's shoes. His back itched as he imagined the three men suddenly appearing at the top of the slope behind him, but no bullet punched through his spine. He threw himself to the ground behind bushes at the opposite edge of the clearing. Erika dropped beside him, aiming the rifle. The woman rushed farther, stopped when she realized her protectors weren't racing to follow, then sank to her knees behind a tree.

In contrast with her obvious terror, Saul felt almost joyous. We made it! he thought. We crossed before they saw us! They didn't catch us in the open! Now it's our turn!

Beside him, Erika calmed her breathing, pulled down the tripod attached to the rifle's barrel, steadied her aim, and became rock-still.

146

Not long now, Saul thought. Not long. He wiped sweat from his eyes and concentrated on the opposite edge of the clearing. Any moment, the bushes over there would part. The men would show themselves.

Five seconds became ten. Fifteen. Thirty. After what seemed two minutes, Erika scrambled backward, and Saul knew exactly why. The situation was wrong. The men should have reached the top of the slope by now. *They should have shown themselves.*

He followed Erika, scurrying toward the woman. When the woman opened her mouth to speak, he clamped a hand across her lips and gestured forcibly toward the continuation of the forest. She reacted to the desperation in his eyes and ran, leading them upward through the trees.

He could think of only one reason the men hadn't shown themselves. They'd approached the clearing, sensed the trap, and separated, following the rim of trees on either side, trying to get ahead of their quarry. It was possible they'd already done so.

The crack of a gunshot parallel to Saul, on his left, spurred him faster up the wooded slope. The bullet shredded leaves beside him. He heard it – *felt it* – zip past him.

But was the shot meant to force them toward a sniper waiting at the top of this slope? Or was it intended to make them stop and take cover while the three men encircled them?

Instincts assumed control. Motion – *escape* – was everything. Saul understood why Erika didn't bother returning fire. She didn't have a target, and even if she did, the trees would interfere with her aim. He knew they couldn't even hope that the gunshots would attract help from the village. In Switzerland, mandatory military training required farmers to practice their marksmanship on a regular basis. Gunshots in the Alps were as ordinary as the tinkle of cowbells. No one would pay attention.

The air had cooled. Clouds had covered the sky. Drops of moisture pelted his shirtsleeves. He pressed the cardboard packet of photographs and Avidan's diary harder against his chest, grateful for its plastic wrapping. The rain increased, drenching him. He shivered. Black clouds scudded over the mountains, making him realize how dangerous the weather had become. The strain of racing ever higher in unaccustomed altitude could lead to delirium from oxygen privation. Add to that a cold extended rain, and conditions were perfect for hypothermia, a rapid drain of strength and body heat, death from exposure.

Three hours, Saul thought. That's the maximum time hypothermia takes to kill. That's how long we've got now. His only consolation was to imagine the similar apprehension of his hunters.

Trembling from cold, he reached the top of this farther hill, only to wince when he saw yet another wooded ridge above, obscured by darker clouds and worsening rain. The downpour muffled a shot from his right. The bullet slammed against a tree behind him.

Propelled by fear, the woman raced ahead. Saul had trouble keeping up with her. She guided them through a maze of obstacles. Higher.

Steeper. We must be at eight thousand feet by now, Saul thought. The thin air threw him off-balance. No matter how quickly and deeply he breathed, he couldn't satisfy his lungs. His thoughts began to swirl. Movement became automatic, a reflexive struggle. Twice he fell, helped up by Erika. Then Erika fell, and he helped *her* up. His head throbbed. But the woman, as agile as a mountain goat, scrambled ever higher.

He wasn't sure when the trees became less dense, when pine needle-covered ground gave way to more and more rocks and open space, but suddenly his thoughts and vision cleared sufficiently for him to realize that he'd passed the treeline, that only granite and snow-covered peaks rose above him.

We're trapped, he thought. We can't go much higher. We'll faint.

Or freeze to death. The rain, which had chilled him to his core, had changed to snow. Above the timberline, a June blizzard wasn't unusual; experienced mountaineers took that danger into account and carried woolen clothes in their knapsacks. But Saul hadn't expected to be up here; he was dressed for summer conditions. Far below him, in the untouched village, this sudden faroff storm would have been merely picturesque, but up here, it was life-threatening. Already the snow had accumulated on his scalp. His shoulders were covered, his hands numb.

We're going to die up here, he thought. We've gone so far, even if we turned around and tried to get back to the woman's farm, we wouldn't make it there before we fainted from exposure and froze to death. And somewhere along the way we'd be ambushed by our hunters.

The snow obscured the gray of the granite slopes above. But despite the freezing wind, the woman persisted, climbing higher. She's crazy, Saul thought. She's so afraid of those men she'll scramble up till she collapses, and in the meantime, the men'll realize the danger we're heading into. They'll hang back. They'll stay below the treeline, take shelter beneath a deadfall, and stalk us when the storm is over. They'll find us frozen where we fell and simply leave us there. In July, after the snow melts, hikers will come upon us and report another mountain accident.

The thought made Saul angry enough to keep following the woman. The flakes cleared sporadically, allowing him to see that the three of them had reached another plateau, this one completely barren. The woman pushed onward.

But not toward the next even steeper slope, instead toward a wooden door set into a granite wall.

The door had been placed here precisely for conditions such as this – a common Swiss precaution against unexpected storms. The snow gained such volume that he couldn't any longer see the door, let alone the granite slopes beyond it. There wasn't a choice. He and Erika had to follow.

But when the woman opened the door, revealing a murky cave beyond, he balked.

'The door's two inches thick!' the woman insisted. 'Bullets can't go through it! Those men will die if they try to wait us out!'

Saul understood her logic. From years of living next to the mountains, she was conditioned to think of this cave as a refuge. But his own years of training rebelled against enclosing himself. A refuge could also be a trap. What if the storm let up? What if the men decided not to linger beneath a deadfall at the treeline and instead followed their tracks through the snow and besieged the cave? What if the men had carried more than pistols beneath their slightly too large windbreakers?

Explosives, for instance.

No! He had to fight the enemy on open gound, free to maneuver. But he couldn't leave Erika unable to defend herself. Tempted to reach for the rifle she carried, he forced his arms to remain by his sides. 'I'll be back. If you don't recognize my voice, shoot anyone who tries to open the door.'

Snow clung to Erika's face. The falling temperature had blanched her skin. She squeezed his arm. 'I love you.'

The snow fell harder.

'If I knew another way . . .' he said. 'But there isn't.'

She opened her mouth to say something else.

He echoed her 'I love you' and, knowing she'd understand, shoved her toward the cave. She acquiesced, darting inside after the woman. Darkness cloaked her. The door slammed shut with a thud that was almost inaudible in the wind.

6

He spun toward the slope below him. With his back turned toward the gusts, he saw more clearly now. Boulders that had been invisible loomed murkily in the storm. Going down, he'd have a slight advantage against his hunters. They'd be blinded by the snow squalling at their eyes, just as he'd been blinded when he came up. Perhaps that advantage would compensate for his lack of a weapon. *They* had the advantage of three against one. The equalizer was the numbing cold.

He didn't dare analyze – he had to act. Snow stung him harder. It covered the ground, preventing him from judging where he could safely place his feet. He knew that a sprained ankle would be disastrous, but he couldn't worry about it. He had to keep scrambling down the slope, to reach cover before his hunters arrived.

He stayed well away from the trail that he, Erika, and the woman had made in the snow. Though the storm was quickly filling in the tracks, they were still apparent enough to provide a direction for his hunters. Of course, the men wouldn't stay in a group. Down in the forest, shots had come from the left and right as the men spread out, trying to outflank their quarry. Obstacles might force them to converge, but wherever possible, they'd keep far away from one another. Saul would have to maintain a considerable distance from the tracks he'd made coming up. His plan was to descend well away from his hunters, get below them, turn, and stalk them from behind, taking them out, widely separated, one at a time.

If he could control his shivering. His shirt and pants were shockingly cold, the wind excruciating. His hands stiffened, his fingers losing sensation. He slipped on a snow-slick slab and tumbled, bumping his arms, his legs, and his back over rocks, jolting to a halt against the trunk of a pine tree at the bottom of the slope. Branches drooped over him, protecting him from the streaking snow. He lay on his back, exhausted, struggling to catch his breath. His vision grew fuzzy. With agonizing effort, he forced his eyes to focus, his body to respond. He sat painfully up, pushing at the pine limbs, about to stand . . .

And halted when he saw motion, a dark figure creeping upward past scattered storm-obscured trees.

The figure – a man, his dark windbreaker and trousers evident now – stopped often, aiming his handgun from side to side before him, then glancing right, toward what must have been another member of his team, though Saul couldn't see the other man. The cold metal of his handgun must be painful in his grip, Saul thought. His fingers might not respond if he tries to shoot.

But with an inward groan, Saul changed his mind. The snowgusts lessened briefly, just long enough for him to see that the man wore gloves. He remembered the woman's description of the hiker-priest. That man's left hand had shown a pale circle on the middle finger where a ring had recently been removed. Saul began to wonder if that ring would have matched the bright red ring he'd seen on the left hand, middle finger, of each of these men as they'd stalked up the lane toward the farmhouse.

He remembered something else the woman had said – that the hiker had shown unusual caution about his hands, wearing gloves whenever possible. Just as *these* men had taken care, even in summer, to carry gloves in their windbreakers. Were these men associated with that hiker? Were they *priests*, just as the woman suspected the hiker had been?

Priests who carried guns? Who stalked him like professionals? Who were obviously prepared to kill? It didn't seem possible! The woman must have been mistaken! What would priests have to do with the disappearance of Erika's father and of Avidan? Religion and violence? They were incompatible.

The wind changed direction, lancing through the pine boughs, stinging his eyes. He shivered, envying his hunters for the jackets and gloves they wore. The repeated impacts of his tumble down the slope had numbed his joints. He felt caked with ice. No time. Don't analyze! Just do!

His hunter crept closer. Saul eased behind the tree trunk. Pressed against the ground, he saw his hunter's shoes and trouser legs pass next to the tree. He imagined the man scanning right and left, then up the slope.

But the shoes paused. They turned as if the man were looking at this tree. Saul clenched his teeth in dread, expecting to see the man peer beneath these boughs and fire.

Instead the shoes shifted forward again, the man proceeding upward. Saul wriggled after him. The gusts increased with such intensity that the man became obscured.

It had to be now! Saul rose to a crouch and lunged. The force of his attack jolted the man to the rocky slope. Saul landed with a knee on his target's spine, grabbed the man's head, and jerked up with all his might. His hunter's spine snapped just before his larynx gave. Despite the shrieking wind, Saul heard the sickening double cracks. His hunter trembled, whistled through his teeth, and suddenly stilled.

In a rush, desperate not to be seen, Saul dragged the body down beneath the cover of the pine boughs. He fumbled to peel off the corpse's leather gloves. His own fingers – swollen and numb – didn't seem to belong to him. Putting the gloves on his hands was even more difficult. He had to cram his fingers beneath his armpits, trying to warm them into flexibility. But his armpits too were achingly cold, and he knew he was close to the danger point. If his temperature dropped any lower, he'd lose consciousness.

For a disorienting instant, he fantasized about the heat of Israel's desert. He reveled beneath an imaginary blazing sun. Abruptly he became aware again of the terrible wind, of the snow-shrouded slope. Appalled by the symptoms of altitude sickness and hypothermia, he compelled himself to strip the corpse of its windbreaker and put it on. The jacket's protection was minimal, but compared to his thin shirt, the added layer was luxurious.

He scurried to the edge of the pine boughs, glanced to his right, toward where the remaining two men would probably be creeping upward, and darted forward, reaching the spot where he'd attacked. He pawed through the snow and gripped the pistol his victim had dropped. But his first finger refused to obey his mind's command, wouldn't squeeze into the trigger guard. He slapped one gloved hand against the other, trying to make them pliant, his efforts useless. From the wrist down, he had no sensation.

He shoved the pistol beneath his belt and retreated down the slope, stopping when he reached a dense line of trees. Using them for cover, he stalked toward his right, toward the other men, trying to get behind them. Soon they'd notice that the man on their left flank was missing. They'd investigate. In his weakened condition, without the advantage of surprise, he'd have little chance of subduing both of them together. He had to confront them singly, before they realized they were being hunted.

Flakes streaked harder. After what he judged was fifty meters, he came to fresh footprints in the snow. They led upward. He followed, emerging from the trees, suddenly unprotected. Above, amid a squall, he saw the back of another dark figure. Mustering strength, he lunged. By now, the gloves had returned some warmth to his hands, making them flexible enough that he could grip the pistol, though his fingers

151

still weren't agile enough to fire it. He slammed its barrel savagely against the crown of the figure's head. The tip gouged deeply into bone. Hot blood pelted his face. The figure moaned. Saul struck again, with greater force. The figure toppled, shuddering. Saul struck again. And again! He couldn't stop himself. He struck, pulping bone until in a crimson drift the man lay quiet.

Saul pivoted toward his right, straining to see the third man. He rushed along the slope, squinting through gusts, desperate for a glimpse of dark slacks and a windbreaker. But fifty meters farther, he still hadn't found his quarry.

Has he already gone up the slope? Did I pass below him?

Saul glanced toward the crest, unable to see it in the storm. If he's above me, I'd have passed his tracks! No, he has to be farther along this hill!

But twenty meters farther, still failing to glimpse the man or his tracks, he came to a sudden stop. A terrible suspicion filled him with panic.

They wouldn't have stayed this far apart. I made a mistake. The first man I killed – he wasn't on their left flank! *He was in the middle!* Somewhere behind me along this slope, the third man, the one who was really on the left flank, must have noticed he's alone! He'll find the marks in the snow where I killed his partner! He'll find the body! He'll search for me!

Saul whirled to stare behind him, appalled by the unavoidable trail he'd left in the snow. All the third man had to do was follow the footprints till they led him to . . . ! A handgun cracked, a bullet nipping Saul's sleeve. He dove to the snow and rolled down the slope, ignoring the impact of rocks beneath him. The handgun cracked again, it's bullet kicking up snow. Saul reached the bottom of the slope and scrambled to his feet, hearing a third crack from the handgun. He didn't dare stop, didn't dare let the man pin him down. With his frozen hands, he wouldn't be able to return fire. The man would merely circle till he had a clear aim and shoot Saul from a safe distance.

Saul raced on. Exertion in this unaccustomed altitude made him afraid he'd vomit. The trees became more frequent, less far apart. He charged down a farther slope. The man wouldn't follow directly along Saul's tracks but instead would stay to the side, to avoid a trap. Counting on that strategy, Saul veered away from the man, scrambling through a gap between boulders. He saw a dead branch projecting from a drift and yanked it free. He ran back up the slope, in the direction from which he'd come, hoping a line of bushes would conceal him. At the top of the slope, he angled back toward the man. His intention was to make a wide circle, get behind the man, find his tracks, and stalk him. In a moment, he crossed his own tracks and entered the enemy's territory. The falling snow transformed afternoon into dusk. Objects as near as ten meters were indistinct. He crept from tree to tree and suddenly found his pursuer's tracks.

He calculated his next moves. By now, the man would have reached Saul's own trail, would have seen where Saul stopped descending and doubled back. The man would realize the likelihood that Saul intended to circle behind him. The man would hurry back this way to intercept him.

Clutching the jagged branch he'd picked up, Saul glanced along his pursuer's downward trail. He saw a clump of boulders the man had passed and approached them, staying within the tracks his enemy had made. When he came to the boulders, he leapt as far as he could, hoping the new imprints would be sufficiently spaced from the trail he'd just left that his hunter wouldn't see them in time to realize that Saul was hiding among the boulders.

Braced in a cleft, he imagined the sequence he willed to occur. His hunter, coming back this way, would ignore his own tracks and keep staring ahead in search of Saul's. By the time he came abreast of these boulders, he'd be able to see where Saul's tracks intersected with his own farther up the slope. Briefly distracted, the man wouldn't be prepared for an immediate attack.

So Saul hoped. There were many variables he couldn't control. Suppose the man didn't retrace his tracks exactly but instead moved *beside* them, passing these boulders on the left instead of the right. It was difficult enough for Saul to concentrate in one direction, let alone both. Or suppose the man followed Saul's tracks where they circled back up the slope. In that case, the man would approach these boulders from ahead, not behind, and Saul would be in full view.

I should have kept running, Saul thought.

But to where? The farmhouse is too far away. In the storm, I'll lose my way. And what about Erika and the woman? I can't abandon them.

But I wouldn't be abandoning them. They've got shelter, a rifle. All I've got is a handgun my stiffened fingers can't shoot.

And a branch.

The weapon seemed ludicrous now. He shivered, fearful he'd freeze to death before his hunter ever searched in this direction. He felt weak, dizzy, nauseous.

I can't believe I've done this.

At once it occurred to him that the man must be shivering too. *His* judgment has to be weakened, the same as mine. It could be we're even.

Tense seconds passed, accumulating into minutes. Snow gathered around him. *On* him. His joints felt immobilized. He wasn't sure he'd be able to move now, even if his hunter did creep into the trap.

The forest darkened. Soon he'd be completely disoriented, unable to fight his adversary or find his way back to the cave. Not that he'd ever have to contend with either problem. If he stayed immobile like this, the cold seeping deeper into his core, he'd be dead long before nightfall.

Snow half-filled his enemy's tracks. If the man couldn't see them, there'd be little chance of his passing these boulders. Already so much time had elapsed that Saul suspected the man must have chosen another direction. Or perhaps he couldn't bear the cold anymore and retreated, trying to get back to the farmhouse.

I have to move, make my muscles work, get my circulation flowing!

His patience snapped. He stepped from the cleft between two boulders, turned to the right . . .

And found himself face-to-face with his hunter. The man had just come abreast of the boulders, looking carefully up the slope. Shock paralyzed them; cold retarded their reflexes. Saul swung the branch as the man pivoted, aiming his pistol. The branch had a finger-long projecting barb. It impaled the hunter's right eye. Gel spurted, followed at once by blood. The man screamed, a soul-rending wail of outrage and violation. The force of Saul's blow had thrust the barb all the way through the eye socket, cracking the crust of bone behind the orb, lancing the brain. The man's arms flapped as if he tried to fly. His scream, now only a motor reflex, persisted, then stopped. His mouth remained open. He dropped his pistol and gripped the branch. In quick succession, he stood on tiptoes, dropped his hands to his sides, peered at Saul with his remaining eye, and fell.

The branch projected sideways, obscenely, from his face. Horror, fear, exhaustion, cold, and the altitude all had their effect. Saul vomited. It seemed impossible that the contents of his frigid stomach would steam so. He staggered back against the boulders he'd hidden among. He clutched his midsection, doubled over, and heaved yet again, collapsing to his knees. The snowy forest floor tilted one way, then the other.

I'm going to die, he thought. *I've won, but I'm going to die.*

His disgust at what he'd just been forced to do shifted suddenly into anger: at himself, the circumstance, the weather, his weakness! He raised his face and roared in rebellion.

No! If I'm going to die, it won't be because I gave up!

He staggered to his feet, pushed himself away from the boulders, and lurched through snowdrifts up the slope. A mental vision of Erika's face swirled before him. It changed to that of his son. He wanted desperately to live. But not for himself.

For his family.

His shoulders felt like blocks of wood, his legs like posts, but he persisted, reached the top of this slope, and staggered up another. Snow struck his eyes. He lost his balance and fell, squirmed upright, fell again . . .

And crawled.

Higher.

Farther.

Though his consciousness was clouded, he sensed that the stronger bite of the wind meant he'd left the shelter of the treeline, had reached the rocky slope up to the open plateau.

But the plateau seemed to go on forever. The harder he worked, the less ground he seemed to cover. On his hands and knees, he struck his head against a rock, struggled to crawl over it, couldn't, and realized that the rock was a wall.

The wall on the far side of the plateau.

The door. If his memory wasn't tricking him, the door had to be against the wall. *But which way? Right or left?* His survival depended upon an instantaneous decision. Completely disoriented, he chose left.

And almost passed the door before he understood what it was. Exhaustion negated excitement. Stupefied, he pawed at the door, scraping his fingernails against it. 'Erika, it's Saul. For God's sake, Erika.'

The snow became a warm blanket. It covered him. He sank, toppling forward as the door swung open.

He landed hard on a rocky floor.

And heard Erika scream.

7

His first impression was that Erika's horrified face swirling above him was but another vision of her face that had acted as a beacon, drawing him onward through the storm. A dim part of his remaining consciousness jabbed him, however, rousing him into the realization that he'd reached the door and been granted admission into the cave.

His second impression was of a faroff hissing light. A naphtha-fueled lantern. Its almost mystical glow revealed shelves of canned food and bottled water, a white plastic box with a red cross stenciled on it, coats, shirts, socks, and pants, a two-way radio.

His third impression, and the most important, was of warmth. It pained him. He squirmed, groaning as Erika dragged him toward the lantern. He realized that a kerosene-fueled heater stood next to the lamp, that a tube in the ceiling was venting the heater's gases. The tingle of warmth upon his skin made him cringe. Erika's urgent embrace was excruciating. He tried to protest but was powerless.

The Swiss woman slammed the cave door shut, blocking out the wind and snow. She ran to touch Saul's forehead. 'His temperature's too low. His body can't warm itself.'

Saul understood. The core of heat in his body was like a furnace. If the furnace stopped working, outside heat wouldn't help him. The heat had to come from within. The furnace had to be made to start generating again.

'He'll die if . . .'

'Blankets,' Erika said.

'They won't be enough.'

'We'll heat up some cocoa.'

The woman shook her head. 'Hot cocoa won't be enough either. Besides, he doesn't have the strength to swallow it.'

'What then? How can I save my husband?'

'Your body heat.'

'What? I don't understand!'

'Use your body heat! Save him!'

Erika understood. She tugged off Saul's wet clothes. He shivered, clutching his arms across his chest. She grabbed a sleeping bag from a shelf, unrolled it beside him, and opened its zipper. She laid him into it and tugged it shut.

The sleeping bag was thick and soft.

But cold. 'So cold,' he murmured.

In the glow from the lamp, he saw Erika take off her own clothes. She threw everything – jacket, blouse, slacks, shoes, socks, bra, panties – into a corner and scurried into the sleeping bag with him.

She squeezed down beside him, put her arms around him, and pressed her breasts, stomach and thighs against him. The sleeping bag was almost too small for both their bodies. Though her embrace was painful, he felt the down of the sleeping bag trap her warmth. Heat radiated from her onto him. She wedged a knee between his legs, her thigh between his own. She kissed his cheeks, his neck, his shoulders. She breathed deeply, repeatedly against his chest, anything to smother him with warmth.

The embrace was the most intimate he'd ever experienced. Her urgent attempt to enfold his skin with her own, to thrust her heat into him, to meld her body with his, was a more complete union than he'd ever imagined was possible. Their bodies became the most sensitive organs each possessed, a totality of their separate senses. Saul didn't know how long she pressed herself fully against him, skin to skin, soul to soul, but he gradually felt heat seeping into him, sinking toward his core. His stomach warmed first, then his lungs, his heart. When the nerves in his spine tingled with heat, he realized that his power to generate his own warmth had been revitalized.

Breathing became easier. His chest expanded. He stopped shivering, smiled at Erika, touched her beautiful face, saw it blur before him, and drifted into unconsciousness.

8

When he woke, he was still in the sleeping bag, but he was fully dressed now in dry garments. He felt weak and yet amazingly rested. He stretched his legs against the soft interior of the bag, drew his hands out, rubbed his eyes, and in the glow from the lamp saw Erika and the woman leaning against the cave wall, studying him. Erika too was dressed now.

'How long have I—'

'It's ten A.M.,' she said. 'Rise and shine.' She opened the cave door.

He jerked a hand to his eyes and turned away. Outside, the sun was searing. 'Rise and shine?' He groaned. 'That isn't the sun. It's a laser beam.'

'You can't sleep your life away.'

He groaned again. Water dripped in front of the cave door. Sunlight reflected blindingly off the snow. He pulled a corner of the sleeping bag over his face.

'If you insist,' she said.

When he peered up from beneath the corner of the sleeping bag, he saw the gleam of humor in her eyes. She eased the door almost shut. A few inches of daylight intruded, adding to the glow of the lantern.

'You sure know how to put a guy to sleep,' he said.

'My pleasure.'

Saul shuddered, this time not from cold but emotion. 'I love you.'

The Swiss woman looked embarrassed by their intimacy and coughed. 'Are you hungry? We made some freezedried soup.'

'I'm starved.'

He was strong enough to spoon the liquid to his mouth.

'What happened out there?' Erika finally asked.

'I killed them.'

The Swiss woman paled. Erika merely nodded.

He left out the details. 'There's a lot to be done.' He crawled from the sleeping bag, felt an ache in his back, and waited until his equilibrium became balanced and steady.

Erika collected Saul's wet clothes and gave him the packet that contained Avidan's diary and the photographs. She picked up the rifle. After making sure that the heater, lantern, and stove were shut off, they stepped outside.

The woman closed the door. 'I'll have to replace what we used.'

'We'll pay,' Saul said.

'No. You've paid me well enough. Not just with money. You saved my life.'

'But you wouldn't have needed to be saved if we hadn't come to your house. We're still in your debt.'

They stepped through melting drifts down the slope, sunlight stinging their eyes. Distressed, Saul sensed they were near the first man he'd been forced to kill.

I don't want to do this, he thought.

But it has to be done.

'You'd better wait here.'

He continued downward toward a fir tree while Erika stayed behind to distract the woman. He reached the drooping pine boughs and stood reluctantly beneath them to study the man whose spine he'd broken. Breath held, with difficulty he removed the ring on the middle finger of the corpse's stiff left hand.

The ring had a brilliant gold band, capped by a large gleaming ruby. An insignia upon the stone showed an intersecting sword and cross.

He searched the corpse thoroughly, finding only a passport and a wallet. The passport was French, made out for Jean Lapierre, a neutral name that was probably a pseudonym. He checked the passport's inside pages, finding immigration stamps for Austria and Switzerland. The same route *we've* been following, Saul thought. Are these the men who attacked me in the park in Vienna?

157

He examined the wallet, finding the equivalent of a thousand American dollars in various European currencies. Two credit cards and a French driver's license had the same signature that was on the passport. The address was in Paris. A photograph of an attractive woman and a bright-eyed young daughter provided the proper personal touch to what Saul assumed was an expertly forged set of documents.

It took him forty minutes, but he finally found the other bodies, removed the ring from each, and examined their wallets and passports. Neutral names. A Marseilles address. A Lyon address. Family photographs. The documents looked perfectly in order and, like the first set, were no doubt perfectly forged.

He returned to Erika and the woman where they sat on a sun-dried rock. 'The question is, do we hide the bodies or leave them where they are?'

The woman reacted with alarm. 'Hide them? but why would—?'

'For *your* sake,' Saul answered. 'To keep you from being implicated. In good weather, how far are we from your farm? An hour? The cave we stayed in suggests hikers like to come up this way. They'll find the bodies. The authorities will question you. Can you convince them you don't know anything about what happened here?'

'If I have to . . . I can do anything.'

'You've proven that. But think about what I've said. Make sure before we leave these bodies.'

The woman trembled. 'There's a ravine above us. Hikers avoid it. Most of the year, it's filled with snow. Hide them.'

'You don't have to help.'

The woman didn't make even a token effort to object. She merely stared toward the valley.

Saul glanced toward Erika, who stood. After ninety minutes and three unnerving trips to the ravine, they returned to the woman.

Saul's voice was taut. 'It's done.'

The woman hadn't changed her position. She continued to stare toward the valley. As if coming out of a trance, she blinked at them. 'My husband and I used to come up here. It once was my favorite spot.'

They went down toward the valley.

9

At the sun-bathed farmhouse, cows bellowed in pain, needing to be milked. The woman ran to them. Saul sensed that her eagerness to get away was based only partly on her concern for her animals. We're pariahs, he thought. He peered toward the mountains from which they'd descended. The snow-covered peaks were massive gravestones. He walked with Erika toward the Volkswagen they'd driven here.

He showed her an ignition key he'd taken from one of the corpses. 'Follow me. I'll drive their Renault. We'll go to Zurich. That's far enough that no one will link the bodies – if they're discovered – to the car. Give me a couple of minutes, though. I assume it's a rented car, but I still haven't found the receipt from the agency. It's probably in the glove compartment. I want to check the trunk, then copy the license number and the serial number that's on the motor block. No matter how many buffers they used, someone had to pay for using that car, and I want to find out who.'

'But we don't have access to a network for that kind of information. Remember your bargain.'

'To do this on our own? Sure. But I think I've found a way to make the Agency cooperate, to make them agree I've done them a favor. At the same time, I'll get their help.'

'I don't see how.'

'*This* is how.' Saul pulled one of the ruby rings from his pocket. 'I wanted to be away from the woman before I showed you. It would only have confused her.'

Erika examined the ring. 'I've never seen anything like it. A gold band. A perfect ruby with an inset sword and cross. The design's medieval, right?'

'But the surfaces are smooth. The manufacture's recent.'

'Sword and cross.'

'Religion and violence. All three of the men had rings like this. It's obviously a symbol for a group. A recognition device for those who understand. It's probably the ring the hiker took off before he came to this farm.'

Saul tugged at the gleaming ruby on the ring. With a snick, the ruby swung up on a hidden swivel, revealing a compartment.

In the compartment, Erika saw a capsule. It was yellow. She raised it to her nostrils.

'Cyanide.'

'Or something even quicker.' Saul pressed the ruby cap down on the poison. 'My guess is, if those men had lived they'd have swallowed the poison before I could question them. I think we're dealing with a death cult. Very old, and very skilled. Between us, you and I have almost thirty years of experience in the profession. But neither of us has seen this ring or this insignia. Another network exists, one we don't know about and I'm betting no one else does either.'

'But how could that be possible?'

'I don't know how they stayed secret so long or why they'd risk exposing themselves. But clearly they exist. And clearly they're expert. So wouldn't you think, if I offered this information to the Agency, they'd cancel my obligation to do them a favor?'

'As long as I find out what happened to my father and see my son again.'

'*Our* son.' Saul's voice rose; he thought of bloody snow. 'And if they accept my offer, maybe I won't ever have to kill again.'

159

Unnatural
Conjunction

Zurich. In his former profession, Drew had often sought refuge here; it was one of his favorite cities. But on this warm clear morning, as he walked with Arlene along the river that divided the city, he barely noticed the quays and pleasure boats or the gardens and guildhouses on the opposite shore. Instead, in his memory, he saw the dead security men at the villa outside Rome and Gatto's tortured corpse sprawled on a lounge beside his swimming pool. After discovering the massacre site the night before, Drew and Arlene had at once made arrangements to leave Rome, flying to Zurich as soon as possible. Now they left the sidewalk beside the river and, without a word, proceeded along a street of imposing buildings, approaching the Swiss Zurichsee Bank. It was here that Father Sebastian had said he'd open a safe-deposit box for them. In a trouser pocket, Drew had the key – in his memory, the code words 'Mother of God' – that would give them access to the box.

As they reached the entrance to the bank, Arlene's green eyes flashed with apprehension. 'Suppose the code words don't work. Or the key. Suppose Father Sebastian didn't plan to back us up as he said he would.'

'So far he's kept his word. He met us at the Vatican gardens. He supplied us with weapons, passports, money, and Father Victor's research about Cardinal Pavelic's disappearance. There's something terribly wrong for sure, but I don't think Father Sebastian's to blame.'

'We'll know soon enough.'

They entered the bank. Its marble floor, massive pillars, and high curved ceiling reminded Drew of a church. Echoing voices had the awe of parishioners responding at mass. They passed guards and clerks, desks and counters, found a sign in German, French, Italian, and English that directed them toward safe-deposit boxes in the basement, and descended as if to a crypt.

'Mother of God,' Drew said in German to a severe-faced woman, the guardian of the sanctum, and showed her the number on his key.

She examined a list of box numbers and code words, then directed her narrow gaze toward Drew. 'Very good, sir.'

Drew suppressed his tension while the woman escorted him into a vault of safe-deposit boxes and used Drew's key, along with her own, to open a metal slot. She pulled out an enclosed tray and, with the reverence of a priestess conferring a sacrament, handed it to him.

Three minutes later, he and Arlene were alone behind the closed door of a cubicle. Drew opened the lid, finding two pistols, two passports, and an envelope that, as Father Sebastian had promised, contained money.

'He kept his bargain,' Drew said. 'It's good to know a priest who belongs to the Fraternity can be trusted.'

'So far,' Arlene said.

They concealed the weapons behind their jackets. Before they'd passed through the metal detectors in Rome's airport, they'd rented a locker and hidden the handguns Father Sebastian had earlier given to them. Oppressed by the weight of the pistol against his spine, Drew pocketed the money and passports, then pulled out a pen and piece of paper, printing boldly IMPERATIVE WE MEET WITH YOU SOONEST POSSIBLE. LEAVE INSTRUCTIONS FOR TIME AND PLACE. THE PENITENT.

He set the note in the tray, closed the lid, and opened the cubicle door. The guardian came to attention as if about to receive a holy relic. The tray safely locked away, the key in his pocket, Drew followed Arlene from the temple of the money changers. He scanned the busy street, found no indication that he and Arlene were under surveillance, and walked back toward the river.

'So now we wait,' Drew said. 'We'll come back this afternoon and tomorrow morning and however many other mornings and afternoons it takes. Maybe a miracle will happen, and we'll *never* be contacted. This isn't our fight. We were forced into it. We've done our part for now. After this, it's up to Father Sebastian, and if he doesn't get in touch, we can't be blamed. I could gladly wait here forever with you.'

'But you know it won't happen that way,' she said.

In despair, Drew nodded. 'The Fraternity never lets up. Until we accomplish what they want, we won't be free of them. I hate the things I was trained to do, but I'll use those skills to finish this. So we can start our lives together.'

Arlene held his hand. 'We already *have* started our lives together. All we can count on is now.'

2

At four o'clock that afternoon, Drew opened the safe-deposit box for the second time that day. Instead of the note he'd left, he found a different one, its printing more forceful than his own. The instructions were clear, professional, precise. Below them, in a melted drop of wax, an insignia had been indented, a sword intersecting with a cross.

This time, he'd entered the bank alone. He left, walked in the opposite direction from the river, and reached the Bahnhofstrasse, Zurich's main business district, where he paused to peer at flowers in a window. A moment later, Arlene stood beside him. He saw her reflection in the window. She'd been following him since he'd left the bank.

'No one showed any interest,' she said.

That didn't prove they weren't being watched. Nonetheless, they'd have been foolish not to take the precaution. They joined the stream of shoppers along the street.

'We got a message,' Drew said. He didn't show it to her. Couldn't. In the cubicle at the bank, he'd torn the note into minuscule pieces and kept them in a pocket of his trousers. While he'd walked to the Bahnhofstrasse, he'd surreptitiously dropped the bits here and there along the sidewalk.

'Assuming the message was actually from Father Sebastian,' Drew said, 'he gave us a time and place for a meeting tonight. He also gave us two fallback times and places for tomorrow in case we didn't get his message today.'

'Thorough.'

'No more than I'd expect from a member of the Fraternity.'

Again her eyes flashed with apprehension. 'Where do we meet him?'

3

At 1 A.M., they emerged from the darkness of an alley, crossed the narrow stone expanse of the Rathausbrucke, and reached an ornate fountain. Mist from the river drifted toward them.

'I can think of better places for a meeting,' Arlene said.

'One less exposed?' Drew asked. 'On the other hand, anyone following us would have to cross the bridge. This late at night, hardly anyone else around, we'd be sure to notice him.'

The instructions had been to reach the fountain at five minutes after one, but they knew that the rendezvous might not occur until as long as a half-hour later. Father Sebastian would want to satisfy himself that they hadn't been followed before he showed himself.

But a half-hour later, the priest had still not arrived.

'I don't like what I'm feeling. We'll try the fallback time and place tomorrow morning,' Drew said. 'We'd better get out of here.'

Arlene didn't need encouragement. She walked from the fountain, but not back toward the bridge, instead toward the street along this side of the river. Drew followed.

The mist thinned. Reaching a murky side street, they passed a restaurant, its windows dark. Ahead, a young man drove a motorcycle through an intersection, the noise so loud that for a moment Drew didn't hear the car behind him. He spun toward its headlights. The car raced toward them. Drew pressed Arlene back toward a doorway and reached for his pistol. The car was already stopping.

Through an open window, Father Sebastian said, 'Get in. Quickly.'

They did. Drew barely had a chance to close the door before Father Sebastian stepped on the throttle and urged the car down the street.

'What took you so long?' Drew said. 'Why didn't you meet us?'

Father Sebastian sped around a corner. 'I've been watching you from a block away. In case you'd been followed, I wanted to make it seem the meeting had been aborted and you'd given up. I waited till contact was least expected, with little chance of anyone catching up to us.'

The priest wore dark slacks, a dark zipped-up windbreaker, and dark driving gloves. The ring on the middle finger of his left hand made a bulge in the glove.

'I'm surprised you got our message as soon as you did. We left it at the bank only this morning,' Drew said. 'Are you staying here in Zurich?'

'No. In Rome.'

'Then how . . . ?'

'From the moment I gave you the safe-deposit box key and the code words, my most-trusted assistant has been assigned to a cloister here in Zurich. He checks the box daily. When he found your message, he phoned me in Rome. I told him to arrange for several possible meetings and left at once for Zurich. My flight arrived this evening.'

'But if your assistant knew about your plans . . .'

'Exactly. As much as I trust him, prudence required me to add my own variation. By such precautions, the Fraternity has kept itself secret all these centuries. And we mustn't forget – I recruited you, an outsider who had no choice except to help me, precisely because I have reason to believe there is an enemy within the order.' The priest sped around another corner and checked his rearview mirror. 'No one behind us. It seems we've accomplished our purpose. Would you care to do some late-night sightseeing?'

The priest sped north, toward the wooden hills outside the city.

4

'Your request for a meeting was unexpected. Indeed, from a security point of view, most distressing.' Father Sebastian continued driving. 'What do you want?'

'Information,' Drew said.

'You couldn't have put your questions in writing and left them at the bank?'

'So your assistant could learn what I needed before *you* did? What precautions could you have taken after that?'

'I grant your point.'

'Besides, a great deal's happened since we met you at the Vatican.'

'I hope that means you've made progress.'

'It means there are other players in the game.'

Father Sebastian turned sharply toward him. '*Who?*'

'If I knew, I wouldn't have had to risk asking for this meeting. I need your resources, your network, to help me find out.'

The priest concentrated on the road. 'Explain.'

Drew began with his decision to investigate the possibility that terrorists were responsible for Cardinal Pavelic's disappearance. 'Terrorists used to be my speciality, after all,' he said bitterly. 'But Father Victor's research seemed to indicate he hadn't explored that possibility.'

'Cardinal Pavelic's disappearance might have been the first stage of a terrorist attack against the Church? My compliments. It hadn't occurred to me.'

'I'm not sure I'm right. But two other men had the same suspicion.' Drew explained about his conversation with Gatto and how the arms merchant, no longer privy to confidential information, had directed him to Medici. 'But when Arlene and I were set to grab Medici, two men took him first. And when we returned to Gatto to ask what he knew about these men, we found his villa had been attacked. His bodyguards were dead. He'd been tortured. His throat had been slit.'

Father Sebastian gripped the steering wheel. 'Then you assume the two men forced Gatto to reveal what he'd already told you?'

'Yes. I believe those two men tortured Gatto to learn if terrorists were involved in the cardinal's disappearance. I think they have the same purpose I do. And I want to know who they are.'

'Describe them.'

Drew remembered his view from the alley as the two men subdued Medici's bodyguard and chauffeur, then shoved Medici into his limousine. The confrontation and abduction had been amazingly quick – no longer than twenty seconds – but Drew's expert memory envisioned it again as if he were watching a filmstrip.

'They were in their early forties,' he said. 'They both wore caps. Even so, I could see hair at the back of their heads and along their ears. One man was a blond, the other a redhead. The blond was six feet tall, tanned, well-built, as if he lifted weights, big shoulders and chest, wide forehead and jaw. The redhead was taller, maybe six foot-two, extremely thin and pale. His cheeks were gaunt. His face seemed squeezed together.'

'A charming couple,' Father Sebastian said. 'But without more information, I don't see how my sources can identify them. A muscular blond and a pasty redhead. Did you get any sense of their nationality?'

'Only in a negative sense. I had the impression they weren't French, Spanish, or Italian. Still, we do have other information.'

'Oh?'

'Those men were professionals. I don't mean just that they knew what they were doing. I mean world-class. I've seen few men better, and in my former life, I dealt with a lot of experts. They can't be that good and not have a reputation. My guess is the color of their hair is part of their trademark. Ask your sources about top-of-the-line assassins. Find out if two of them are a blond and a redhead. And something else – assuming they're not Italian, they had to come through immigration. Check with your Opus Dei people in Italian security, Interpol, the CIA. Maybe our two friends entered Italy recently. Maybe somebody spotted them.'

'It still isn't much of a lead.'

'It's all we've got,' Drew said. 'All *you've* got. I'm handing the case over to you for now.'

'For now? Or is this your attempt to bow out completely? You haven't forgotten your bargain, I hope. If you cooperate, we'll pardon your sins against us.'

'I haven't forgotten. All I want is the chance to be with Arlene. I know if I betray you I'll never get the chance. *But how can I cooperate if I don't get the information I've asked for?*'

Father Sebastian debated. 'As you say, it's in my hands for now. Check the safe-deposit box every morning at ten, every afternoon at three.'

Exhausted by the discussion, Drew leaned back. Next to him, in the rear of the shadowy car, he felt Arlene gazing at him searingly.

'I'll try to have an answer for you soon,' the priest said.

5

The Langenberg Wildlife Park, off a scenic road southwest of Zurich, allowed its visitors an intimate glimpse of chamois, marmot, deer, and boar. Drew and Arlene drove from the park's two acres of rocky forested hills and proceeded farther south along a series of rising switchbacks until they stopped at the top of Albis Pass. From its 2,600 feet, they had a view of rolling countryside. More important, their position gave Father Sebastian a chance to see if they'd been followed from the park.

Ten minutes later, Father Sebastian pulled up beside them. After Drew and Arlene got in, the priest sped down the road from the pass. He soon turned onto a wooded side road and checked his rearview mirror. It was the afternoon after their late-night meeting. The sky was cloudy, with a threat of rain.

'Icicle and Seth.'

Drew didn't understand. 'Icicle and . . . ?'

'Seth,' the priest repeated. 'Those are their cryptonyms. I confess I didn't think I'd learn anything about them. But as soon as I mentioned a blond and a redhead, I got an immediate reaction from my Opus Dei contacts in Interpol. I'm embarrassed I hadn't heard about these two men before. The only excuse I can think of for my ignorance is they haven't made a move against anything that involves the Church. They're not terrorists; you wouldn't have known about them either.'

'What about them?' Drew asked.

'They're extremely expensive, extremely skilled, extremely deadly. They don't work often, but when they do, it's a major job. They're experts at hiding. No one knows where they live.'

165

'By definition,' Drew said. 'Otherwise there'd have been reprisals against them.'

'One Interpol theory is that they use a major proportion of their income to buy protection. But even so, they've made a few mistakes. Along the line some security cameras took photographs of them. Only a couple. The images are blurred. But these days, computers can do wonders to add high-resolution to murky photographs. And those enhanced photographs were used to identify two men who came through Rome's airport two days ago from Canada. Each man alone might not have triggered interest. But both of them on one plane . . .'

'Sure. They attracted attention to each other. The watcher was bound to notice.'

'That's part of the reason they were spotted,' Father Sebastian said. 'But there's a stronger reason for both of them on one plane to be unusual. I told you their code names are Icicle and Seth. Both are appropriate to killing.'

'Death is an iceman. Seth is the red-haired Egyptian god of the underworld.'

'And forty years ago, the men with those code names were mortal enemies,' Father Sebastian said.

'That's impossible! Forty years ago, the men I saw would have been infants!'

'I'm talking about their fathers whose code names the sons inherited. In the Second World War, Icicle and Seth were Hitler's personal principal assassins. Each tried to outdo the other's body count – to gain approval from the Führer. And after the Third Reich collapsed, the favored assassins continued to challenge each other. On several occasions, they tried to kill each other. Because of a woman, some sources say. Do the sons of old enemies consort with each other? Travel on the same plane? Cooperate to kidnap an informant? *That's* what attracted Interpol's attention. Whatever's happening is more disturbing than I feared. Icicle and Seth – the conjunction's unnatural.'

6

The sky became grayer. A light rain started falling as Father Sebastian let them off at the top of Albis Pass. 'And now the case is yours again,' the priest said. 'I don't know how you can use the information I've given you. But I recruited you precisely because I didn't want to risk involving the Fraternity in the investigation. If you need me to do your work for you, why should I have bargained with you? I'm becoming impatient.' With an angry glare, the priest sped away.

Drew watched him disappear down the pass. The rain was like a heavy mist. It drifted across his face. Despondent, he and Arlene got into their car.

'What now?' Arlene asked. 'Even with what he told us, I feel helpless. Where do we go?'

'I think back to Rome.' He tried to sound confident. 'Where Cardinal Pavelic disappeared, where Father Victor was shot, where Seth and Icicle went after Gatto and Medici.'

Her gaze became hopeful. 'But what's the connection?'

'Between the sons of Hitler's private assassins and the disappearance of Cardinal Pavelic? I'm not sure there *is* a connection, not a direct one anyhow. Seth and Icicle didn't abduct the cardinal – otherwise they wouldn't be looking for him. They want answers the same as we do. Why, though? Why are they so interested? What would make the sons of Nazi executioners – and remember their fathers were enemies – want to join forces to find a missing cardinal? From the start, we overlooked the obvious. The cardinal's the key to this. But we were thinking of him only as a figurehead, a Church luminary, not as a man. Who *was* he? We hardly know anything about him.'

Drew turned the ignition key and steered toward the road. At once he saw a Renault go by, driven by a man speeding down the pass toward Zurich. Behind the Renault, another car, a Volkswagen Golf, followed closely. In it, a woman stared at the car ahead with intensity, as if the worst thing that could happen would be for her to lose sight of the Renault. Drew was positive he'd never seen them before, yet he felt a puzzling kinship. He pulled onto the road and drove behind them down the pass, but wherever they were headed, he and Arlene were going toward Zurich's airport and the next flight back to Rome.

7

Saul found a space in a crowded parking lot near Zurich's railway station. The skin of his face felt taut from exhaustion. I tried to do too much, he thought. I should have rested longer at the cave. Mustering strength, he stepped from the Renault and locked it. The drizzle persisted. He glanced at the Renault's closed trunk, which he'd discovered contained automatic weapons and plastic explosives as well as three sets of passports, credit cards, and drivers' licenses providing alternate identities for the men who'd used this car.

They wouldn't have risked bringing that stuff through Swiss customs, Saul thought. They got everything after they entered the country. Which means they weren't alone; they had contacts, an organization to back them up. They must have thought we wouldn't be suspicious and run. Otherwise they'd have come after us sooner.

Their mistake.

Erika pulled up in the Volkswagen. He got in beside her.

'A couple of times, you wavered on the road,' she said. 'Your eyes look dull. Your skin's pale. Are you sick?'

His raw throat made him cough. 'Let's not worry about it till I make a phone call.'

'After that, this Jewish lady's going to pamper you.'

'I'll hold you to that promise.' Saul smiled. 'Drive toward the lake.'

He could have used a telephone in the train station, but by habit, he avoided all phones in public transport terminals – security agencies frequently tapped them. Halfway along the Bahnhofstrasse, he pointed toward a phone booth. 'It's as safe as any, I suppose.'

Erika stopped at the curb.

'Keep circling the block,' he said, then darted from the Volkswagen. He picked up the receiver, inserting Swiss coins.

A gruff voice answered in German. 'Zurich Flower Shop.'

'This is a priority order. Put me through to your international dispatcher?'

'Have you dealt with us before? To expedite delivery, I'll need an account number.'

'My account was listed under a name.'

'What is it?'

'Romulus.'

The German voice hesitated only briefly. 'I'll check your invoice file and see if the dispatcher's available.'

'Tell him I've found a flower shop I don't think he knows about.'

'I'm sure he'll be interested – if I can reach him.'

'I'm sure you can.'

Saul studied his watch. Forty seconds later, another voice – speaking English – came on the line.

'What kind of flowers did you wish to send?'

'Roses. I'm calling from a Zurich phone booth. I want to send the order to the Black Bread Bakery in Vienna. My friend there was nicknamed Pockmark. This is the number in the booth.' Saul dictated it. 'I don't have an alternate phone. Tell Pockmark to call as soon as possible. Tell him I want to discuss the favor he wanted.'

'This might take a while.'

Saul knew they would use the number he'd given them to locate this phone and verify by sight that he was who he claimed to be. 'I understand. Just make sure Pockmark calls me.'

Saul hung up and glanced out the rain-streaked window of the booth. He saw Erika drive the Volkswagen past him and gestured reassuringly to her.

He waited. Through the phone booth's window, now misted by his breath, he saw Erika drive past several more times.

Ten minutes later, the phone rang. He grabbed for it.

A German voice again, but this one sounded as if its accent had been learned in New England. 'I'm calling about some flowers you want to send to me.'

'Your accent's terrible, Pockmark.'

'And you're as discourteous as ever. You agreed not to get in touch with us.'

'I want to discuss my near-accident in Vienna.'

Pockmark spoke quickly. 'We had nothing to do with that.'

168

'I know. I found out who was involved. You'll be surprised. Do we talk about it now or switch to another phone?'

The line became silent.

'Romulus?'

'I'm listening.'

'You're sure I'll be surprised?'

'Utterly fascinated.'

'How would you like to rent a hotel room? Our treat.'

'Which hotel?'

'By now, the flower shop should have found the booth you're using.'

'A man's been standing outside for the past five minutes. He looks cold in the rain.'

'I'll try to get back to you by tonight.'

The phone went dead. Saul stepped from the booth. A gray-haired man stood close to a building, trying to avoid the rain.

'You like flowers?' Saul asked.

'Roses.'

'Know any good hotels?'

'Oh, indeed!' the man said.

Erika drove around the corner.

8

'Ouch! It's too hot!'

'We have to sweat the cold out of you.'

'I liked it better the way you got me warm last night.'

'How'd you guess my backup plan? Now take off the rest of your clothes and get in the tub.'

He stripped and sank slowly into the steaming water. She scrubbed his back. He couldn't help smiling when she toweled him dry. 'Now about that backup plan of yours.'

She shook her head. 'We'll have company soon.'

He made a face.

'Besides, you need your strength,' she said. 'You have to eat.'

It was evening. They'd already called for room service. By the time Saul dressed – there'd been clothes in various sizes in the hotel room's closet – they heard a knock on the door. Saul confirmed that the knock was from room service. He opened the door. The waiter who wheeled a cart into the room had a pockmarked face.

'I hope you don't mind,' Pockmark said and closed the door. 'I ordered for three. I haven't had anything since breakfast.'

'It's all on the company's tab,' Saul said.

'Exactly. And all of us hope what you're offering is worth our hospitality.'

'I wouldn't have called if I didn't think it was worth more than that.'

Five minutes earlier, Saul had been hungry. Now he barely glanced at the dishes on the cart.

'And this must be Erika,' Pockmark said. 'I've never had the pleasure.' He shook hands with her and poured three cups of coffee. Neither Saul nor Erika picked theirs up.

Pockmark tasted his. 'So. Let's review the situation. Rules were established. We ignored your violation of the exile we agreed upon. In exchange, you promised us a favor. But to get the maximum effect from your favor, we wanted you to keep a distance from us . . . and from every other network. You had to appear to be disaffiliated. Would you say that your call this afternoon was in keeping with that promise? We constantly monitor our communication system, on guard against eavesdroppers. But no safeguards are foolproof. It's possible other networks know about your call. You identified yourself by your cryptonym. There's a chance . . . slim but of concern . . . that unfriendly ears overheard. You've jeopardized the nature of the favor we wanted from you.'

'I think I've already *done* you the favor.'

Pockmark sipped again. 'That's hard to imagine.'

'By gaining information you don't have.'

'So you said on the phone. Be specific. What *kind* of information?'

'Are you wired?'

'Our conversation is completely one-to-one.'

'Of course. *But are you wired?*'

Pockmark shrugged. 'I suppose the next think you'll search me.' He pulled a small tape recorder from a pocket of his white jacket and set it on a bedside table. Even from a distance, Saul could see the tiny reels turning.

'That's the whole of it?' Saul asked. 'No radio transmitter?' He stepped toward the cart.

'All right,' Pockmark said. 'Just leave it alone. You'll screw up the transmission.' He gently lifted the white linens on the cart, revealing a microphone and a power unit on a shelf underneath. 'Happy now?'

'I want this official. I want your directors to know. I want to avoid misunderstandings.'

'More than anything, believe me, we want to understand.'

'Three men tried to kill me.'

'Yes. In Vienna. I was there, remember.'

'Not just in Vienna.'

Pockmark lowered his cup in surprise.

'Here in Switzerland,' Saul said. 'In the mountains. South of Zurich. I assume the same three men. This time I discouraged them.'

'Too bad for them.'

'I've got their rings.'

'*Say that again?*'

'Rings. You can have them if we reach an agreement. They're my favor to the network. In exchange for fulfillment of our bargain.'

Pockmark blinked. 'Wait just a second. Let me understand this. You're saying you'll show us some rings, and that fulfills your obligation?'

170

'Along with automatic weapons, plastic explosives, and bogus IDs. You're going to love it. There's a network no one knows about.'

Pockmark laughed. 'Don't be absurd.'

'Fine. Then shut off your tape recorder, wheel your cart out, and give us five minutes to get away.'

'Five minutes? You'd never make it. But just because I said "absurd" doesn't mean I won't listen.'

'More than that, you have to agree. I give you the rings. I tell you where to find the car the men drove. Maybe you find this other network, maybe you don't. *But our agreement has to be fulfilled. I don't want shadows behind me.*'

Pockmark hesitated. 'I'll need to discuss this with . . .'

The phone rang.

Saul had expected the call, but Pockmark jerked in surprise.

'That'll be our faithful listeners,' Saul said. 'Let's find out what our ratings are.'

Pockmark picked up the phone. He listened, nodding as if eager to please. 'Yes, sir. Of course. If that's what you want, sir.' He set down the phone. 'All right then, Romulus, damn you. Tell us what you have. If it checks out, if it's as new as you claim, you've done your favor. I emphasize the *if*. Don't try to jerk us around. And remember, we could have used chemicals to get the same information.'

'But chemicals only get answers from questions, and you don't know what questions to ask.' Saul was aware of Erika sitting on the bed, one of the gunmen's pistols beneath a blanket on her lap. 'Besides, I've got too much to lose.'

'The rings.' Pockmark thrust out his hand.

Saul took them from his pocket and dropped them into Pockmark's hand.

'A sword and cross?'

'Religion and violence,' Saul said. 'There's a clasp on the side of each ring. Tilt the ruby up.'

Pockmark lifted the stone. His eyes narrowed when he saw the yellow capsule. 'Poison?'

'Ever seen a ring like that?'

'Sure, every day.'

'Like hell. The men who wore these rings were extremely well trained killers.'

Pockmark shook his head. 'But that's not enough to fulfill your obligation. It still doesn't prove they belonged to a new network.'

'Did I say it was new? Look at the design on those rings. Medieval. I think the network's very old.'

'But nobody's ever heard of it? Ridiculous.'

'I'll give you the chance to find out.' Saul wrote down the license number he'd memorized and handed the note to Pockmark. 'Their car's a black Renault. Last year's model. It's at the parking lot near the railway station. You'll find the automatic weapons, plastic

171

explosives, and bogus IDs. And maybe fingerprints, though I doubt it. These men were fond of gloves. But to rent a car, they had to leave a paper trail.'

'With bogus IDs, the paper trail won't take us far.'

Saul hadn't expected to lose control. 'Quit being deliberately stupid. To rent a car, they had to use a credit card. Even if the card's made out to an alias, somebody has to pay the bill. The money has to come from somewhere.'

'Take it easy.'

'I didn't promise answers! I told you what I said I would! Do we have a deal or not? Is our bargain finished? Tell your bosses to make a decision! Put it on the record! Abide by it! *I want to find Erika's father and see my son again!*'

9

One floor down, in a room directly under Saul's, Gallagher sat at a long narrow table, watching the reels turn on a tape recorder connected to a radio receiver. The Agency station chief for Austria, he glanced down the table toward his counterpart, a short man with soft pale manicured hands, the station chief for Switzerland.

Gallagher's suit was rumpled from his hurried flight with Pockmark from Vienna. Strictly speaking, he didn't have authority here. But Romulus had insisted on dealing with the Vienna bakery, not the Zurich Flower Shop, and the bargain for a favor from Romulus had been made in Vienna, so that involved Gallagher regardless of whether his counterpart objected to his being here, though Zurich in fact didn't seem to mind at all.

'What do you think?' Gallagher asked, pretending deference to his host.

Zurich assumed a look of grave deliberation. 'It's out of our power really. Langley will have to make the decision.'

'Based partly on our recommendation,' Gallagher said. *'What do you think?'*

'I'd like to see those rings and look at the car.'

'That's not the deal Romulus offered. He wants a decision *before* you check out the car.'

'He hardly has much say in the matter, does he? What recourse does he have if his information leads us nowhere and we tell him he still owes us the favor?'

Gallagher grimaced, appalled by Zurich's attitude. 'You've never worked with Romulus, have you?'

'No. But so what? I know all I have to about him. He's a troublemaker.'

'He's a man of character. In Vienna, he made his bargain with us in good faith. I fully expect he'd have done us the favor.'

'Would have? Past tense?' Zurich looked puzzled.

172

'Because now he expects good faith from us, and if we jerk him around, he'll refuse to cooperate.'

Zurich spread his hands. 'Then we punish him and use him as an example of what happens to troublemakers. Honestly, I don't see the problem.'

Gallagher wanted to slam his hands on the table. Instead he managed to keep his voice calm. 'Let me explain. I *have* worked with Romulus, and I know how he thinks. He's shrewd. I take for granted he hasn't told us everything. He'll have kept some important detail in reserve, as a further negotiation tactic.'

'So we pretend to agree until he tells us everything.'

'And what happens when word gets out that we didn't show good faith? The repercussions would be disastrous. Freelance operatives wouldn't deal with us. We have to say yes or no to Romulus. Maybe isn't good enough. Besides, we need him.'

'To gain the extra information you think he hasn't told us?' Zurich asked. 'Unlike you, I doubt that information exists.'

Again Gallagher mustered patience. 'Listen. Romulus got into this because his wife's father is missing. They want to find out what happened to him. Now they claim they found a network no one's heard of. Assuming the network does exist, it's related to what happened to the missing father. Everything Romulus knows about the one is pertinent to what we want to know about the other. We have to encourage him, not fight with him. As long as he keeps searching for his wife's father, he'll be doing the favor we wanted from him.'

Zurich surprised Gallagher. He agreed. 'Yes, the search for the father is by extension a search for the unknown network. I see that now, and it does make sense to encourage Romulus. But there's a further implication. We want him to do a favor for us. But if we investigate the possibility of this other network, if this other network has something to do with the missing father, we'll be helping Romulus in his search. We'll be doing a favor for *him*.' Zurich's eyes twinkled. 'He's as shrewd as you said he was. He's found a way to turn the situation around, to manipulate us into backing him up.'

As Zurich started to make his phone call to Langley, Gallagher picked up another phone and dialed the number in the room directly above.

'Put Romulus on . . . This is Gallagher. I'm in the hotel. I've been listening with interest. We're asking Langley to accept the bargain you're offering. Understand, all we can do is recommend. Langley has the final say.'

'Of course.'

'But this is a good-faith gesture,' Gallagher said. 'I promise I'll do everything I can to back you up. I need something more from you, though. You haven't told us everything. I'm sure of it. Give me something extra, something to help tilt the balance with Langley.'

'Good faith?'

'You have my word. I might have manipulated you, Romulus. But I never lied to you. Tell me something more.'

'The three men who wore the rings.' Romulus hesitated. 'The men I killed.'

'What about them?'

'I think they were priests.'

BOOK FIVE

IMPACT

Medusa

Washington, DC. Though it was only 9:16 A.M. and the kosher restaurant had not yet opened its doors to the public, eight elderly men sat at a banquet table in a private room in the rear. The room was usually rented for Bar Mitzvah parties and wedding feasts, but the present occasion was not a celebration. Memories of death and despair pinched each face, though solemnity did not preclude grim satisfaction as each man raised a glass of wine and drank ceremoniously. To retribution. To vindication.

Their first names were Abraham, Daniel, Ephraim, Joseph, Jacob, Moshe, Nathan, and Simon. Each man was in his late sixties or early seventies, and each had a number tattooed on a forearm.

'Has everything been arranged?' Ephraim asked.

He studied his comrades. They nodded.

'The mechanisms are in place,' Nathan said. 'All that remains is to set the final process in motion. A week from today will see the end of it.'

'Thank the Lord,' Abraham said.

'Yes, that justice will finally be achieved,' Jacob said.

'No, that our part in achieving justice will have been concluded,' Abraham answered. 'What we've done is distressing enough. But now we go farther.'

'What we do is necessary,' Moshe objected.

'After all these years, what good is served?'

'It doesn't matter how much time has gone by. If justice had value back then, it must have value now,' Simon insisted. 'Or do you question the value of justice itself?'

'Do you urge passivity and forgiveness?' Joseph asked.

Abraham answered with force. 'Passivity? Of course not. To be passive is to risk extinction.' He paused. 'But forgiveness is a virtue. And justice is sometimes merely a word used to hide the ugliness of revenge. God's chosen people must defend themselves, but do we remain His chosen people if we become obsessed by ignoble motives?'

'If you don't approve of what we're doing, why don't you leave?' Jacob asked.

'No,' Joseph said. 'Abraham is right to raise these issues. If we act without moral certainty, we do become ignoble.'

'I confess to hatred, yes,' Ephraim said. 'Even now, I can see the

177

corpses of my parents, of my brothers and sister. What I want – what I crave – is to punish.'

'I have as much reason as you to hate,' Abraham said. 'But I resist the emotion. Only feelings that nourish have worth.'

'And we respect your opinion,' Ephraim said. 'But it's possible for each of us to do the same thing for different reasons. Let me ask you two simple questions.'

Abraham waited.

'Do you believe that those who profited from our suffering should be allowed to retain those profits, to enjoy them?'

'No. That isn't justice.'

'So I believe as well. Do you believe that the sins of the fathers should be allowed to be repeated by the children?'

'No, evil must not be permitted to thrive. Weeds must be destroyed before they can reproduce.'

'But in this case, they *have* reproduced, and once again our people are threatened. We must act, don't you see that? Whether some of us do so for revenge doesn't matter. The end is what matters, and this end is good.'

The room became silent.

'Are we all agreed?' Joseph asked.

They nodded, Abraham reluctantly.

'Then let us eat together,' Ephraim said. 'To symbolize our united resolve, the beginning of a too-long-postponed end.'

2

Mexico City. Aaron Rosenberg sat between two bodyguards in the backseat of his bulletproof Mercedes sedan, staring past the driver and the bodyguard in the front seat toward the Oldsmobile filled with more security personnel ahead of him. He turned to peer through the rear window toward the Chrysler van behind him filled with yet another team of guards. His imagination was tortured by images of what his wife and her bodyguard were probably doing with each other now that he'd left the house. At the same time, he dreaded whatever other threats the Night and Fog might leave at his home while he was gone. He'd tripled his security precautions, both at home and while away. He now refused to go anywhere unless his Mercedes was flanked front and back by protective vehicles. Nonetheless, he would never have left the house today if it hadn't been absolutely necessary, if he hadn't been summoned by one of the growing number of men he couldn't refuse. There's no question about it, Rosenberg thought. My life's out of my control.

The caravan proceeded along the Paseo de la Reforma, maintaining a constant moderate speed, keeping a close formation. Soon the group drove south, leaving the sweltering city, heading toward the cool air of the estates at Lake Chalco. The compound through which

178

his Mercedes passed was familiar to him. The red tiled roof on the sprawling main house had been reconstructed at Rosenberg's expense. The large swimming pool in back, with its stunning view of the lake, had been Rosenberg's gift to the occupant. The many gardeners and servants no doubt received their salaries through the special bank account into which Rosenberg deposited a considerable sum the first of every month.

The cost in doing business, Rosenberg thought, again reminded him of how much his life was out of control. Depressed, he stepped from the car and approached the house.

A high-ranking member of Mexico City's police force stepped outside to greet him. His last name was Chavez. He wore sandals, shorts, and a bright red shirt open to his pudgy stomach. When he smiled, his pencil-thin mustache somehow maintained its straight horizontal line.

'Señor Rosenberg, how good of you to come.'

'It's always a pleasure, Captain.'

Rosenberg followed the captain from the shadow of the house into the glaring sunshine beside the pool. He considered it significant that he hadn't been offered a drink and began to feel apprehensive.

'Wait here, please,' the captain said. He went through a sliding glass door at the back of the house and returned with a slender packet. 'I've received information of importance to you.'

'A problem of some sort?'

'You tell me.' The captain opened the packet and withdrew a large black-and-white photograph. He handed it to Rosenberg.

Fear squeezed Rosenberg's heart. 'I don't understand.' He raised his eyes toward Chavez. 'Why would you show me a photograph of a German soldier from World War Two?'

'Not just a soldier, an officer. I'm told the rank . . . excuse my poor German accent . . . was *Oberführer*, or senior colonel. He belonged to the *Totenkopfverbande*, the so-called Death's Head formation. You can see the silver medallion of a death's head on his military cap. You can also see the twin lightning bolts on the sleeve of his jacket – the symbol for the SS. The photograph is so detailed you can even see the unit's personal pledge to the Führer on his belt buckle – 'My loyalty is my honor.' Note carefully in the background – the mounds of corpses. The Death's Head division was in charge of exterminating the Jews.'

'You don't need to tell me about the Holocaust.' Rosenberg bristled. 'Why are you showing me this photograph?'

'You don't recognize the officer?'

'Of course not. Why should I?'

'Because he bears a striking resemblance to your father, whose photograph you gave me when you asked me to investigate his disappearance a few months ago.'

'That man is not my father.'

'Don't lie to me!' Chavez snapped. 'I've compared the photographs in detail! Add facial wrinkles! Take away some hair! Add gray to

179

the rest! Allow for minor reconstructive surgery! That man *is* your father!'

'*How could a Jew be an SS officer?*'

'Your father wasn't a Jew, and you're not either! Your real family name is Rodenbach! Your father's first name was Otto! Yours is Karl!' Chavez took documents from the packet. 'That officer's picture appeared on SS identification records and on immigration forms when he came to Mexico. The face is the same, though the name is different. Government authorities will soon be told who he really is! The United States authorities will also be told, and as both of us know, the United States bolsters its relations with Israel by pretending indignation toward Nazi war criminals!'

Rosenberg couldn't move. 'Who told you these things?'

'You don't expect me to reveal my sources.' Chavez spread his arms in a gesture of goodwill. 'But I wonder, how much are you willing to pay for me to neutralize my informants, to assure the authorities there's been a mistake?'

Rosenberg wanted to vomit. Blackmail never ended. It only bought time. But time was in limited supply. It would last only as long as his money did. He thought of the cargo in the ship headed toward the Mediterranean and what he assumed now was certain disaster.

'How much do you want?' he asked.

The glint in the captain's coal-black eyes didn't reassure him.

3

St Paul, Minnesota. William Miller feigned a polite smile of greeting as he crossed the cocktail lounge and approached the man in the left rear booth.

On the phone, the man had said his name was Sloane. He was with the Associated Press, he claimed, and wanted to talk about Miller's father.

Now Sloane imitated Miller's smile of greeting, stood, and extended his hand.

They surveyed each other.

'Somebody sent you what?' Sloane asked. 'On the phone, you said something about filth.'

'You're really a reporter?'

'Cross my heart.'

'Shit.' Miller swallowed, disgusted at himself. 'I'm sorry I lost my temper when you called. I thought for your . . .'

'That's why we're here. To talk about it.' Sloane gestured toward the booth.

They sat across from each other. Sloane was in his mid-thirties, short, heavy-chested, with dark thin hair and intelligent eyes. 'What do you mean by filth?' he asked.

'Photographs.'

'Of?'

'Nazi concentration camps. Corpses. Ashes.' Miller massaged his forehead. 'God. My father disappeared. Then somebody painted a death's head on the bottom of my swimming pool.'

'Death's head?'

'Now you show up . . .'

'And you assumed . . .'

'Well, wouldn't *you* assume? My wife doesn't know about the photographs.'

'Slow down,' Sloane said. 'What you're telling me connects with what I came for. I'll give you my side, and we'll see what we come up with.'

'Credentials.'

'What?'

'You're an AP reporter. Prove it.'

Sloane sighed and pulled out his press card.

'Anybody can have a card printed up,' Miller said.

'There's a phone number. The AP central office.'

'And anybody can hire a voice to claim he's in the AP office.'

'Right. And I bet you've got all kinds of fascinating theories about the JFK assassination. The UN's controlled by drug dealers. Satan's responsible for heavy-metal rock.'

Reluctantly, Miller laughed.

'Good,' Sloane said. 'As long as you can laugh at yourself, you're in control.'

'Sometimes I wonder. You said you wanted to talk about my father. Why?'

'I have contacts in the Justice Department. It's what you might call a symbiotic relationship. I do them a favor, write stories that bolster their public image. They do me a favor, let me know when they're working on something I can use.'

'I still don't understand. What does the Justice Department have to do with my father?'

'Someone sent them documents that made them decide to investigate him.'

Miller clutched his drink so hard he feared the glass would break. 'This gets more and more insane.'

'And since your father disappeared—'

'You already knew that?'

'I figured the only other person to talk to was you.'

'Okay,' Miller said wearily. 'Give it to me all at once. Worst case. Bottom line.'

'Your father's name is Frank Miller. The theory is he's really Franz Müller, a German officer in World War Two. He's supposed to have been an *Obersturmbannführer*.' Sloane spoke the German haltingly. 'In English, that means lieutenant-colonel. During World War Two, Franz Müller commanded a unit in an SS formation known as *Einsatzgruppen*. They were a special military task force that followed regular Nazi soldiers into newly invaded German territory – Czechoslovakia, Poland, and Russia, for example – where they executed

181

every Jew they could find, shot them where they stood or herded them into pits to make it easy to bury them after the firing squad was finished. Their body count in Russia alone was a half million.'

'And you're telling me the Justice Department suspects my father was part of that insanity? *A Nazi mass murderer?*'

'They more than suspect. They're convinced of it. They claim they've got proof. And they think your father disappeared because he'd been warned about their investigation. As far as they're concerned, your father *ran* from them. Are you all right? You just turned pale.'

'My whole fucking world's falling apart, and you ask me if I'm all right? Jesus, I . . . Look, somebody has to stop this craziness. Just because my father's name is similar to Franz Müller . . .'

'No, there's more than that. The Justice Department wouldn't base an investigation on something that tenuous. Your father emigrated here from Germany. You knew that?'

'Sure. After the war. A lot of Germans did. There wasn't anything illegal about it.'

'But did you also know he changed his name?'

A muscle twitched in Miller's cheek.

'My God, you *did* know,' Sloane realized.

'Let me explain. I knew. But not the specifics. All he told me was he'd Americanized his name to avoid anti-German feelings here after the war.'

'Did he tell you he'd been a German soldier?'

'I don't have to listen to this crap.' Miller stood.

Sloane reached out, careful not to touch him. 'For sure you'll have to listen when an investigator from the Justice Department comes around. If I were you, I'd think of this as a dress rehearsal, and while I was at it, I'd think about *this*. It would do your family a lot of good to be treated sympathetically by the press.'

Miller hesitated. 'Sympathetically?'

'The past comes back to haunt a family that didn't even know about the past. I can build an effective human interest story out of that. A story in your favor. Assuming, of course, that you're telling the truth about your father.'

'I meant what I said.' Miller sat down. 'I can't believe anybody would accuse my father of—'

'Accusing him's one thing. Whether you knew anything about his past is another. You truly believe he's innocent?'

'Damn it, yes!'

'Then answer my questions. Did he tell you he'd been a German soldier?'

Miller thought about it. 'Sometimes, as he got older, he talked about the war. He said, toward the end every male he knew, even kids, had been conscripted. Despite his inexperience, he was made a sergeant and ordered to defend a bridge. When the Allies invaded, he hid till the worst was over and then surrendered.'

'You didn't think it strange that a German soldier was allowed to come to America? That was hardly standard procedure.'

'He explained about that too. German soldiers were placed on POW camps. The Allies didn't exactly take kindly to them, and none of the German soldiers knew how long the imprisonment would last. So the trick was, before the Allies picked you up, you had to find a civilian corpse and exchange clothes and identity papers with it. My father managed to get himself placed in a refugee camp, not a POW camp. He lived there for more than a year before some administrator paid attention to his repeated applications and allowed him to emigrate to America. If what you've told me is true, is sounds like it was my father's bad luck that the dead civilian whose papers he exchanged with his own was named Franz Müller. I mean, Franz Müller's a common German name. There must have been hundreds, maybe thousands of Franz Müllers. But only one of them was this SS hit-squad leader.'

Sloane drew his finger through a circle of moisture his glass had made. 'The Justice Department has photographs of the SS officer we're talking about. It also has a photograph from your father's immigration file. The face is the same. Why did he disappear?'

'I don't know! Christ, he's seventy-three years old. Where would he run? The Justice Department's absolutely wrong about him!'

'Good. You stick with that attitude, and when the Justice Department decides to go public, you can count on a story that makes you look sympathetic. Even if the Justice Department proves its case, you'll still be presented as an innocent bystander, a loving but misinformed son. On the other hand – I warn you – if you've held back, if you're lying, I'll turn the story around. You and your family will be part of the conspiracy.'

'I haven't lied.'

'Keep it that way. This isn't just another story to me. I'm supposed to be objective. What I am is furious. Nazi war criminals are all over this fucking country. I could give you dozens of names and addresses right now. There's no mystery about them. The Justice Department knows about them. Most are in their late sixties or early seventies. They keep their lawns mowed. They tip the paperboy. They have the neighbors over for barbecues. I could accuse them in front of their friends. It wouldn't matter. No one would care. Because they don't make trouble. How could that nice man down the street have done all those terrible things? And anyway all of that was a long time ago. Why dredge up unpleasant memories?'

'You're exaggerating.'

'If anything, the reverse.' Sloane pulled a sheet of paper from his jacket pocket. 'Here's a list from my contacts in the Justice Department. Twenty mass murderers. Jack the Ripper, Son of Sam, and John Wayne Gacy are bush-league compared to this bunch.'

'*And every one of them's a war criminal?*'

'There are plenty of others. This is just the tip of the slime heap.'

'But if the Justice Department knows who these Nazis are . . . ?'

'Why haven't they been prosecuted? Because after the war American intelligence made a bargain with them. Help us take over your Nazi spy networks and use them against the Russians. In exchange, we'll give

183

you immunity. Or if you don't have a bargain of immunity, we still won't prosecute because your crimes were committed in Europe. To save a lot of diplomatic hassle, we'd just as soon deport you. On the other hand, if we revoke your citizenship, no other country will accept you, so we're stuck with you. Let's forget the whole mess. These Nazis will die soon anyhow. At least that was the theory until a few years ago. A group of idealistic lawyers in the Justice Department decided to do something about the government's lassitude. In 1979, the Office of Special Investigations was formed.'

'Then something *is* being done about the men on that list.'

'Yes, but not enough. There's no way to be certain about the numbers, but an educated guess is that as many as *ten thousand* Nazi war criminals came to this country. So far the Justice Department has prosecuted *forty* of them. Punishment takes the form of denaturalization and deportation.'

'Against mass murderers?'

'The murders didn't take place in the United States. In effect, the only crime they're charged with is lying about their true identity on their immigration forms.'

'If the public knew, they'd be outraged.'

'Would they? In the cases that have gone to trial, the friends and neighbors of the men who were charged wanted to leave the past alone.'

'Is that the point of your story?'

'I want to help the Justice Department. If I can rouse the public, maybe the Office of Special Investigations will get more government funding. These bastards – I don't care how old they are – should all be made to feel the same terror their victims felt.'

'Including my father?'

'If he's guilty,' Sloane said, 'yes.'

Miller snatched Sloane's angry gaze. 'I've trusted and respected my father all my life. If impossibly the Justice Department is right about him . . . If he's what this so-called proof says he is . . .'

'You agree he ought to be punished?'

'Even my father . . .' Miller felt sick. 'Provided he's guilty, even my father can't be absolved.

4

Despite the five o'clock traffic, Miller managed to reduce a twenty-minute drive to slightly more than ten. The elevator to the fifth floor seemed to take forever. When he opened the door to MILLER AND ASSOCIATES, ARCHITECTS, he saw that his secretary had not yet gone home.

'How was your meeting, Mr Miller? Did you get the assignment?'

'It's too soon to tell. I want to make some notes, Marge. If anybody calls. I'm not here. No interruptions.'

'Will you be needing me for dictation?'

184

'No, thanks. Go home when you finish what you're typing.'

'Whatever you say.'

He went into his office, shut the door, and leaned against it. *How is it possible to know if someone you love is a monster?*

Sweat trickled past his eyes. An eternal five minutes later, the tapping on the keyboard mercifully stopped. He heard the click of switches on the computer, the indistinct rustle of a dustcloth being positioned over the monitor.

'Good night, Mr Miller.'

'Good night,' he said through the door.

The tap of high-heeled footsteps. The click of a latch. The snap of the outside door.

Silence.

Miller exhaled, relieving the pressure in his lungs, and stared at the combination safe in the corner to his right, where he stored his plans-in-progress. Two days ago, when he'd received the hideous photographs of corpses and ashes, he'd wanted to destroy them. But an intuition had warned him to move cautiously. The photographs were obviously not just a prank. If he destroyed them, he might lose information he'd need later, clues about why he'd been sent the photographs at all.

Now he wished he hadn't saved them – for fear of the truth he might find. He knelt, dialed the combination on the safe, and removed the packet of photographs. One by one, he studied the black-and-white sheets.

Death. Terrible death.

He'd lied to Sloane, but only in response to one question – and only a part of that response had been a lie. But the lie, even partial, had been out of proportion to all the rest of the truth.

Yes, he'd answered honestly, I knew that my father came from Germany. I knew he'd changed his name. I knew he'd been a German soldier.

Yes, a soldier. But Miller was aware that his father hadn't been an innocent participant in the war, an inexperienced young draftee promoted absurdly to the rank of sergeant. Not at all. His father had been a colonel in the SS.

As Miller's father had aged, he'd been drawn increasingly back to the past. On a handful of days that had unexplained personal significance for him – January 30, April 20, November 8 – he'd become more and more sentimental. On those occasions, his father had made and received mysterious phone calls. Then late one night, his father had confessed to his son what he did in the war.

'Yes, I was SS. I followed the Führer's orders. I believed in the master race. And yes, I believed in *lebensraum*, the space we needed to expand and flourish. But I didn't believe in racial extermination. Since we were superior, why couldn't we exist in tolerant harmony with inferior races? Why couldn't we allow them to serve us? I wasn't Death's Head. I wasn't one of the exterminators. Instead I was *Waffen-SS*, the legitimate military branch of the *Schutzstaffel*.

185

I was a decent soldier. I served my country with dignity. That country lost. So be it. History decides morality. Now I live in America. Its citizens call it the greatest nation in the world. So be it. My conscience is clear, and if I had to, I would fight to defend America with the same determination I gave to Germany.'

Miller had been convinced. War by its nature blurred judgments and clouded values. Yet surely *some* values remained constant, he hoped.

His father and other *Waffen-SS* commanders had managed to escape the aftermath of Germany's defeat. They'd exchanged identity papers with dead civilians and fled to Bolivia, Mexico, America, Canada, England, Sweden. But they'd remained in touch, phoning each other to remember their heritage, to assure themselves that no matter how severely history had proved them wrong, they were still a part of their country's elite.

Just as the *sons* of the elite had kept in contact. Miller had eventually been drawn into his father's circle of former friends. He and the sons of those other fathers had pledged to help one another in case their fathers came under attack. On the first of each year, there'd been dues to be paid, twenty thousand dollars per family, a bribe to the one outsider who knew their secret, an insurance premium of sorts, blackmail that guaranteed his silence.

Now those bribes had proved useless. The pledge among the sons – to stand as one and defend the group – had turned out to be ineffectual. Despite precautions, their fathers *had* been attacked. They themselves, the sons of the fathers, were also under attack.

Insanity.

Let the past rest, Miller thought. The present and the future are what matter. Our fathers aren't what you think they were. Bring them back. Leave us alone. You've made a mistake. The Night and Fog has to end.

Yet the handsome young SS officer who gazed proudly from a photograph that Miller couldn't set down reminded him uncannily of his father. No! My father wouldn't have lied to me!

But would he have dared reveal this sanity-threatening truth?

I have to be wrong, Miller thought. I looked at this same SS officer two days ago. It never occurred to me he might be my father.

Or maybe I didn't *want* the thought to occur to me.

But the thought insisted now. Miller's vision focused more narrowly onto the photograph, more intensely toward the SS officer's forehead, just below the peak of the ornate military cap.

He tried to believe that what he saw on that forehead was an imperfection in the photograph itself, a scratch on the negative, but he couldn't convince himself. The scar was identical to the one on his father's forehead, the consequence of a near fatal car accident when he'd been ten.

How is it possible to love a monster?

But how is it possible to know if someone you love *is* a monster?

Before he realized what he was doing, Miller had picked up the phone.

'*The US Justice Department? Who told you this?*' Halloway pressed the phone harder against his ear.

'An Associated Press reporter.'

'Jesus Christ.'

'He said my father was a Nazi war criminal,' Miller said. 'The commander of a goddamned SS extermination team.'

'But that's absurd!'

'Is it? I'm beginning to wonder. Some of the things he told me—'

'You mean you actually believe him? He's a *reporter!* He'll tell you anything!'

'But I took another look at those photographs and—'

'You were supposed to destroy the damned things!'

'One shows my father in a Death's Head SS uniform! In front of civilian corpses!'

'A photograph from World War Two? How do you know what your father even looked like back then? That photograph proves nothing!'

'My father had a scar on the top right corner of his forehead! So does this SS officer!'

'Coincidence!'

'That's not a good enough explanation!' Miller's voice rose. 'I have to know! *Was* my father in charge of a Nazi extermination squad? What about all the other fathers! Were *they* mass murderers too?'

'If you're suggesting *my* father . . . ? That's ridiculous! It's insulting! I don't have to listen to—!'

'Stop evading the question, Halloway! Answer it!'

'I won't dignify—!'

'*Were they Nazi war criminals?*'

'Of course not! They were SS, yes! *Waffen-SS!* Legitimate soldiers! Not the Death's Head-SS who killed the Jews! But outsiders don't understand that distinction! Civilians think *all* SS were war criminals. So our fathers had to lie. The Night and Fog made the same mistake we feared the immigration authorities would make, the same mistake the US Justice Department and the Associated Press reporter are making.'

'You're trying to tell me the Justice Department can't tell the difference between *Waffen-SS* and Death's Head-SS? Bullshit!'

'Then how did they make this mistake!'

'My father, your father, and the other members of the group used to phone each other on days that were special to them. April twentieth. November eighth. January thirtieth. Do those dates mean anything to you?'

'Of course,' Halloway said. 'They were birthdays for some of the members of the group.'

'You bastard,' Miller screamed, 'if only you hadn't lied!'

'Lied? About what?'

'April twentieth was someone's birthday, all right. In 1889. *Hitler's* birthday. November eighth is the anniversary of the so-called beer-hall rebellion. Hitler's first attempt to take over the German government. That was in 1923. The rebellion failed. But ten years later he did gain control. On January thirtieth. Those are the three most sacred dates in Nazi tradition. And the three dates on which our fathers, despite the risk, couldn't resist getting in touch with each other.'

'All right,' Halloway said, 'so I didn't realize the significance of those dates.'

'I don't believe you. You know what those dates mean. I can hear it in your voice.'

'Obviously you're determined to believe what you want. But I assure you—'

'I've got another question,' Miller interrupted. 'Our fathers were all senior officers. That means they didn't serve together. They commanded separate units. When the war ended, they'd have been widely divided. What's the basis of their bond? What makes them a group?'

'My father said they trained together,' Halloway answered.

'But the Nazi army was spread all over. The eastern front, the western front, the North African front. Russia, France, Italy, Egypt. If our fathers trained together, they probably never saw each other again throughout the war. You bastard, you lied again. The bond had nothing to do with their having trained together. Why, out of all the German soldiers who tried to conceal their war records, did this group get in touch with each other? They hid all over the world. But they stayed in touch. Goddamn it, *why?*'

Halloway didn't answer.

'Who were they paying blackmail to?' Miller demanded. 'Why?'

Silence on the other end of the line.

'I think the reporter was right,' Miller said. 'I think there's a hell of a lot my father didn't tell me and you didn't tell me either. But you will. I'm coming up there, Halloway. I'm coming to Canada to choke the answers out of you.'

'No! That's crazy! You can't come here! If the Justice Department is watching you, you'll draw their attention to me and—!'

Halloway didn't finish his sentence. Miller had slammed down the phone.

6

Halloway slowly set down his own phone. For several seconds, he wasn't able to move. With effort, he turned toward his father's acrylic landscapes, which he'd been nostalgically studying when the phone rang. The row of paintings was broken periodically by patio windows through which he saw his guards patrolling the grounds.

As a rule, he would never have accepted Miller's call at this number; instead he would have gone to the secure phone in the nearby city,

Kitchener. But he didn't feel it was wise to risk leaving the estate, not even to visit his family at the safe house in the city. Achingly, longingly, he missed his wife and children, but he didn't dare endanger them by bringing them back here.

Earlier, Rosenberg – dangerously out of control – had called from Mexico City, babbling that the authorities there had discovered the truth about his father. Similar frightened calls had reached him from the sons of the other fathers in the group. The past was being peeled away. The Night and Fog had managed its reprisal well, twisting its vengeance ever tighter and deeper.

But Halloway had a foreboding that the screw had not yet been fully turned, that another more forceful twist was yet to come. The ship, he kept thinking. By now, it would have passed through the Strait of Gibraltar and entered the Mediterranean Sea. Halloway wished he'd paid attention to Rosenberg's second thoughts about that ship. He wished he'd acquiesced to Rosenberg's fears and ordered the ship to return. Too late now. Even if Halloway tried, he wouldn't be able to get through the complex system of contacts to warn the ship in time.

Whatever would happen now was out of his control. But if the Night and Fog knew about that ship just as they knew about everything else, if the truth about that ship were revealed, we'll face two enemies, the Night and Fog and our clients, Halloway thought, and I'm not sure which is worse.

7

The cargo ship *Medusa* had a registry as tangled as the snarl of snakes associated with her legendary namesake. Her ostensible owner was Transoceanic Enterprises, a Bolivian corporation. But a close examination of Transoceanic Enterprises' incorporation papers would have revealed that the company whose office address was a post office box, was owned by Atlantis Shipping, a Liberian corporation, and in Liberia the company's office was as difficult to find as the mythical continent after which Atlantis Shipping was named.

This company was in turn owned by Mediterranean Transport, a Swiss concern owned by a Mexican concern owned by a Canadian concern. Many of the officers did not exist. Those who did were paid to provide no other service than that of allowing their signatures to be used on legal documents. Of the handful of actual directors, one was Aaron Rosenberg of Mexico City Imports; another was Richard Halloway of Ontario Shipping.

Medusa regularly crisscrossed the Atlantic, carrying textiles, machinery, and food to and from Greece, Italy, France, Spain, England, Canada, Mexico, and Brazil. But the profit from these shipments was minimal, and if not for another cargo that was often hidden among the textiles, machinery, and food, neither Aaron Rosenberg nor Richard Halloway would have been able to maintain his luxurious life-style.

That cargo was aboard the *Medusa* as she proceeded toward her rendezvous with a freighter whose registration was equally tangled and whose owner had an opulent estate on the Libyan coast. Tomorrow night, off the coast of northern Africa, crates would be transferred. *Medusa* would continue toward Naples to deliver Brazilian coffee, her waterline higher now that she no longer carried plastic explosives, fragmentation grenades, antipersonnel mines, automatic pistols, assault rifles, machine guns, portable rocket launchers, and heat-seeking missiles.

Under usual circumstances, these weapons would have been smuggled out of Belgium, the principal European supplier of black-market arms, and transported under various disguises to Marseilles. There, *Medusa* would have picked up 'medical supplies' and distributed them to various terrorist groups along the southern European coast.

But recent antiterrorist surveillance, the result of increased terrorist bombings, made Marseilles and other European ports too dangerous for arms smuggling. The alternative was to bring the arms from South America, where various civil wars had resulted in ample stockpiles of Soviet and American munitions, most of which were readily for sale. Thus *Medusa* had brought Brazilian coffee piled on top of Contra weapons supplied by the CIA across the Atlantic to meet a Libyan freighter in the Mediterranean thirty-six hours from now. Whatever Libya chose to do with the arms was not Transoceanic's concern. The hundred-million-dollar fee was all Rosenberg and Halloway cared about.

8

Tel Aviv, Israel. The instant the helicopter touched down, Misha Pletz scrambled out. He ran toward the smallest of several corrugated-metal buildings at the south corner of the airport. A burly man in a short-sleeved white shirt waited for him.

'Did you bring it with you?' Misha shouted.

The burly man gestured toward a briefcase in his hand. 'Do you want to read it in the car or—?'

'No right here,' Misha said.

They entered the air-conditioned building.

'We received the message forty minutes ago,' the man said, pulling a document from his briefcase. 'When I saw the code name, I contacted you at once.'

Misha took the paper. He'd been at a kibbutz twenty miles outside the city, fulfilling his promise to Erika and Saul to ensure that their son was protected. Leaving Christopher with Mossad-affiliated guardians had been one of the most difficult things he'd ever been required to do. 'Your parents love you, and they'll be back soon,' Misha had said. 'I love you, too.' He'd kissed the boy, and unsure if Erika and Saul were even alive, afraid his emotion would distress their son, he'd hurried toward the waiting helicopter.

Flying back toward Tel Aviv, the pilot had told Misha to put on his earphones – headquarters wanted him. Though the helicopter's radio was equipped with a scrambler, Misha's assistant had refused to reveal the nature of the urgent message they'd received, but he *had* revealed its source. The Coat of Many Colors.

The code name had the force of a blow. It belonged to Erika's missing father, Joseph Bernstein.

His eyes accustomed to the shadows of the building, Misha studied the document. 'How did this come in? Which station, which country?'

'Our embassy in Washington,' the assistant said. 'One of our people there was trained by Joseph ten years ago. So our man's in a coffee shop this morning. He looks next to him at the counter and guess who's sitting there?'

Misha tingled. 'Is our man positive? There's no possibility of doubt?'

'None. It was Joseph for sure. That's probably why Joseph chose him for a relay – because they knew each other well. Apparently Joseph wanted to guarantee that the source of the message wasn't suspicious to us. Contact lasted no longer than a minute. Joseph told our man we weren't to worry about him. He was taking care of unfinished business, he said. The end was near.'

'And what was *that* supposed to mean?'

'Our man asked. Joseph refused to elaborate. Instead he passed a note to our man. It was solid information, he said. He wanted you to know about it. He expected you to act upon it. The next thing, he was gone.'

'Just like that? Didn't our man try to follow him?'

'"Try" is the word. Joseph knows every trick there is. He lost our man within two blocks.'

'Did he say how Joseph looked?'

'Terrible. Pale. Thin. Shaky hands. The eyes were the worst, he said.'

'What about them?'

'They seemed – and I quote – our man lapsed into subjectivity here – tormented.'

'By what?'

The assistant shrugged.

Misha shook his head. 'We've been searching for Joseph everywhere, and all of a sudden he shows up in a coffee shop in Washington.'

'At least we know he's still alive.'

'For that I'm grateful, believe me. But what's he been doing all this time? Why was he in Washington?' He tapped on the document. 'How did he get this information?'

'You always said he was one of the best. I emphasize he told our man in Washington it was solid information.'

191

Misha reread the message. 'A cargo ship, the *Medusa*, will rendezvous tomorrow night with a Libyan freighter for the transfer of munitions intended for terrorist attacks against Israel.' The message provided the scheduled time of delivery, the coordinates for the rendezvous in the Mediterranean Sea, and the codes each ship would use to identify itself to the other.

'How did he get this information?' Misha asked again.

'The more important question is, what do you intend to do about it?'

'Misha felt paralyzed. Despite Joseph's assurances about the validity of the message, there was still a chance he'd made a mistake. Standard procedure required other sources to corroborate the information before countermeasures could be considered. But there wasn't sufficient time to confirm what Joseph claimed. If the weapons existed and if something wasn't done by tomorrow night, the transfer would occur. The munitions would be distributed. The attacks against Israel would take place. On the other hand, if the weapons did *not* exist and Israeli planes destroyed the ship . . .

Misha didn't want to imagine the international consequences.

'What do you want to do?' his assistant asked.

'Drive me back to headquarters.'

'And?'

'I'll tell you when we get there.'

The truth was, Misha still didn't know. As they left the building, he distracted himself with the wish that he could contact Erika and Saul.

Erika, your father's alive, Misha wanted to tell her. *He was seen in Washington. I'm not sure what he's up to, but from what I've learned, it's important and I can't decide what to do about it. Find him. Help me. I need to know what's going on.*

Saul, you're not in this alone now. Your former network can't stop you from getting our help. We insist on helping. We're invoking professional protocol. Our national security's at stake. Your search is our search in a way we never imagined. We'll back you up.

Misha got into his assistant's car. He registered almost nothing of the drive toward Mossad headquarters in Tel Aviv. But just before they arrived, he made his decision.

Do you trust Joseph?

Yes.

Do you believe his message is true?

On balance? Yes.

Are you going to order an air strike?

No. Not an air strike. I've got a better idea. It solves a lot of problems. It avoids an international incident. Besides, what's the point of blowing up those weapons? We've got better uses for them than the Libyans do.

He must have been speaking out loud. His assistant turned to him, frowning. 'What did you say?'

'I always wanted to be a pirate.'

192

With growing dislike for the son of his father's enemy, Icicle sat in a Rome hotel room, watching Seth read what he called his reviews.

The red-haired assassin had bought a copy of every major European, English, and American newspaper he could find. His versatility in languages was considerable, and for the few in which he wasn't fluent he'd asked Icicle's help.

'I knew we'd make the Italian papers,' Seth said. 'Paris and London, I expected. Athens and West Berlin. But Madrid even picked it up. So did New York and Washington.'

Icicle didn't bother hiding his mixture of boredom and disgust.

'I admit it isn't front page,' Seth said. 'I didn't expect it to be.'

The newspaper stories were basically similar. The body of an Italian underworld figure known as Medici had been discovered outside Rome, floating in the Tiber River. Medici, who reputedly had ties to international terrorist organizations, had been killed with what authorities suspected was a lethal drug overdose. The results of an autopsy were not yet available. Rome police theorized that Medici's criminal associates had turned against him for reasons still to be determined.

As such, the story would not have had sufficient scope to merit being reported on an international scale. But investigators had raised the question of whether the discovery of Medici's corpse was related to the much more sensational discovery of nine bodies in a villa outside Rome. Eight of the victims, all shot to death, had been identified as security personnel. The ninth victim, an Italian underworld figure known as Gatto, had been tortured prior to having his throat slit. Gatto, reputed to have ties with international terrorism, had recently retired from criminal activities for reasons of poor health. Reliable but unnamed sources alleged that Medici had taken Gatto's place as a black-market arms dealer. The murders of both men caused authorities to speculate that a gang war was in progress, with obvious international implications.

'As far as the police are concerned, we did them a favor,' Seth said. 'Better than that, they suspect the wrong people. We can't complain.'

'But what happens when the blood tests on Medici show he died from an overdose of Sodium Amytal?' Icicle asked. 'The police will compare that to the knife marks on Gatto and decide both men were interrogated.'

'So what? They'll never guess it was us or what kind of information we wanted.'

Icicle was amazed at how much color his companion's face now had. It was almost as if Seth gained life by administering death, and that made Icicle nervous. For him assassination was a profession, while for Seth it seemed a need. Icicle had never killed anyone he didn't feel morally certain deserved to be eliminated – dictators, drug lords, communist double agents. Seth, on the other hand, gave the impression of not caring who it was he killed as long as the fee was sufficient. If Seth's father had been anything like his son, Icicle didn't wonder why his own father had hated the man.

Granted, both fathers had been Hitler's primary assassins. But Seth's father had specialized in stalking leaders of underground organizations that protected Jews, while Icicle's father had gone after Allied intelligence infiltrators and on more than one occasion had begged for the chance to try for Churchill. The difference was important. Racial extermination was heinous under any circumstances. Political assassination was justifiable if your country's survival depended upon it.

But what if your country was wrong? Icicle asked himself. What if your nation's policy was based on racial hatred? Did patriotism require you to defend an immoral country? Or was national defense merely understandable *self*-defense?

Was my father self-deluded?

Icicle continued to watch the man he loathed. His eyes, Icicle thought. The more Seth killed, the brighter they became.

'Something troubles you?' Seth asked.

'We've got a great body count. Otherwise we haven't accomplished a thing.'

'Not true.' Seth lowered a newspaper. 'We've narrowed possibilities. We've determined that terrorism and the cardinal's disappearance aren't related.'

'I never believed they were.'

'But the possibility had to be considered. Given Halloway's involvement in black-market arms to terrorists—'

'For Christ's sake, *what?*'

'You didn't know? That's how Halloway makes his living. Munitions.'

'*You're telling me this is all about illegal weapons?*'

'And the cardinal's insistence on a yearly blackmail payment. Surely you knew about *that*.'

'I didn't object. I thought of it less as blackmail, more as an extended payment for services rendered.'

'Well, some of us thought about killing the priest. Account paid in full.'

'He did our fathers a favor.'

'Yes, one that was in his own interest. Or his *Church's* best interest. After more than forty years, the payments amount to a fortune. Eight million dollars.'

'If you want my opinion,' Icicle said, 'the price was cheap, given the atrocities they committed.'

'Including your father?' Seth asked.

Icicle stood. 'Not my father! He divorced himself from the others!'

'Really? sorry to disillusion you, but your father killed as many Jew-savers as my own father did. Their argument wasn't about Jews but about a woman, about your mother! She chose your father over mine! I could have been you! And *you* would not have existed!'

194

Icicle realized how deep their hatred was. He raised his hands in surrender. 'It's a stupid argument. There are too many problems we have to face.'

Seth's eyes dulled. 'Of course. And we still haven't found our fathers.' With effort, he reverted to professional control. 'In that case' – he breathed – 'in my opinion' – he breathed again – 'the situation is as follows.'

Icicle waited.

'We've eliminated the theory that what Halloway calls the Night and Fog is a terrorist group that discovered what the cardinal knew, abducted him, and wants to take over Halloway's munitions network.'

'I agree,' Icicle said. 'The theory isn't valid.'

'But the cardinal's disappearance is related to the disappearance of our fathers,' Seth continued. 'The Night and Fog couldn't have found our fathers if not for the cardinal.'

'Again I agree.'

'So if the purpose of abducting them wasn't to hold them hostage for money, that leaves the possibility that the Night and Fog are doing this for *personal* reasons. That the Night and Fog are Israelis. But to suspect the cardinal, to have discovered what he knew, the Jews would have had to infiltrate the security system of the Catholic Church.'

'I doubt that.'

'I do as well. And it makes me wonder.'

'Wonder what?'

'Eliminate the possibilities. Could someone . . . or some group . . . *within* the Church be the Night and Fog?'

Black
Jesuits

Eight blocks to the east of Zurich's Limmat River, Saul and Erika passed an Agency guard in an alley, opened a door, and entered a garage.

The room was large, its overhead lights brighter than the morning sunlight they'd just left, its concrete floor immaculate. There was only one car, the Renault the three assassins had used. An Agency team had picked it up where Saul told them he'd left it – at the parking lot near Zurich's train station. Overnight, a crew had been working on it, checking for fingerprints, dismantling and searching it. It was now a mechanical skeleton.

'These guys were ready for World War Three,' a gravelly voice said.

It belonged to Gallagher. Saul turned as the burly station chief came over, holding an RPG-7 rocket launcher. He nodded toward the munitions laid out on the floor. Plastic explosives, grenades, Uzis, AK-47s.

'Did you find any fingerprints?'

'All kinds,' Gallagher said. 'But this is a rental car – we can't tell which belongs to your friends and which belong to whoever used the car before them.'

'You know where we hid the bodies. You could send a team to get their prints.'

'I already have. My men should be back by tonight. Aside from the weapons, we didn't find anything unusual in the car. But it was rented in Austria. They wouldn't have risked bringing a trunkful of weapons through Swiss customs. They had to get the stuff in Switzerland.'

'Right. And since they were following us, they wouldn't have had much time to pick up the weapons without losing us,' Saul said. 'Their contacts must be excellent.'

'A network we don't know about?' Gallagher said. 'Maybe. I can buy that a lot more than I do your suspicion these men were priests. Just because of the rings they wore.'

'An intersecting cross and sword.'

'That still doesn't make them priests.' Gallagher set the rocket launcher down beside the AK-47s. 'Religion and violence aren't exactly compatible with the meek inheriting the earth. When I spoke to Langley, I didn't tell them about the religious angle. I'm waiting on that till I'm sure. Right now, our people are checking on the French

IDs you took from the men. The passports and drivers' licenses are probably fake. Our contacts in French intelligence will let us know soon enough.'

'But the credit cards,' Saul said. 'They're the key.'

'No question. My guess is we'll find the cards have a perfect rating. And I'm damned curious about who pays the bills.'

A phone rang. Saul glanced at Erika as Gallagher went over to answer it. They couldn't hear what he said. Mostly Gallagher listened, and when he came back, he looked excited.

'The men whose names are on those passports died years ago. The addresses are rooming houses for transients. But the credit cards are three months old, and the bills were paid as quickly as they were received.'

'Who paid them?'

'Each man had a different card. Each bill was paid through a different bank. But each bank has photocopies of the checks paid through each account, and the signature on the checks wasn't the bogus name of each man you killed. No, the man who wrote the checks was an accountant. Unusual – don't you think? – for someone whose address is a transient's rooming house to have a need for an accountant. Even more unusual for *three* transients with *separate* addresses to have the *same* accountant. But it gets better. The accountant doesn't exist either. His checks are good. But he's in a graveyard in Marseilles. And he has a post office box instead of an office. So we go past the bogus accountant, and what do we find? You were right, Romulus. I'm sorry I ever doubted you.'

'Tell me.'

'The Catholic Church. The bills were paid through Rome. Through the Vatican office of a cardinal whose name is Krunoslav Pavelic. And here's the kicker. The cardinal disappeared several months ago. So what does a missing cardinal have to do with three assassins who might be priests and the disappearance of—?'

'My father,' Erika said. 'A Jew, not a Catholic.'

'But if the cardinal disappeared, who paid the bills?' Saul asked.

'The cardinal's assistant,' Gallagher said. 'Father Jean Dusseault.'

2

Hunched over a wooden table in the muffled silence of a reading room in Rome's Vallicelliana Library, Drew and Arlene examined the books a librarian had given to them. The half-dozen titles, all in Italian, were dictionaries of religious biographies, the equivalent of *Who's Who* in the Vatican, the Curia, the Roman Catholic Church. They found the information they wanted and glanced at each other with dissatisfaction, returned the books, and stepped from the library's vestibule to face the brilliance and noise of Rome.

'Well, at least it was worth a try,' Drew said.

Arlene's response surprised him. 'As far as I'm concerned, we learned a lot.'

'I don't see what. The biographical references in those books were little more than public relations for the cardinal.'

'He doesn't lack ego, that's for sure,' Arlene said. 'Most *Who's Whos* base their citations on information supplied by the people listed in them. The cardinal apparently views himself as a saint on earth. He has medals and testimonials from dozens of religious groups. He even has a papal decoration. But a list of honors isn't a biography. The cardinal didn't supply many details about his life. Either he thinks his biography is boring, which I doubt given his willingness to let everybody know his various titles and honors, or else—'

'He's got something to hide?'

'Let's put it this way,' Arlene said. 'We know he was born in 1914 and raised in Yugoslavia. We know he felt an early calling to the Faith and entered the Church when he was eighteen. We knew he received his religious training here in Rome. For a time, he served as the Church's liaison with the Red Cross. He moved rapidly up through the ranks of the Church. At thirty-five, he was one of the youngest men to be admitted into the Curia. As a controller of the Church's finances, he holds one of the most powerful positions in the Vatican.'

'He must have had talent, all right,' Drew said. 'The question is at what? There's nothing in his biography to indicate why he was promoted so rapidly. If you're right, if he's hiding something, it won't be in any official biography. I doubt we'd find it even if we checked the Vatican archives. A member of the Curia has the power to make sure his past is sanitized.'

'How do we get the *un*official version of Pavelic's life?' Arlene asked.

'I think it's time to have an intimate conversation with the cardinal's close associates,' Drew said. 'In the newspaper accounts of his disappearance, I remember a reference to Pavelic's personal assistant. Father Jean Dusseault, I believe the name was.'

'French.'

'We can narrow the range of our discussion with him. What I'm interested in—'

'Is World War Two,' Arlene said, 'and why the assassin sons of *Nazi* assassins would be determined to find our missing cardinal. Let's go back to the Vatican.'

3

Father Jean Dusseault had an apartment in one of the many Renaissance palaces within the Vatican. The simplest way to contact him, of course, would have been to phone him and schedule an appointment at his office. But the subsequent conversation was unlikely to prove productive. Saul imagined the stony response to the questions he wanted to ask. 'Do you know anything about a connection between Cardinal Pavelic and checks written out of your office to assassins who might be priests? Have you ever heard about a secret intelligence network within the Catholic Church? Absurd? Of course. I'm sorry I troubled you.' No, Saul thought as he waited in an alcove across from Father Dusseault's apartment building. An interview in his office wouldn't do. A private approach, an intimate – if necessary, forced – conversation: those were the only practical options.

Saul had agreed with Gallagher that, despite the Agency's new willingness to help, it was best for Saul and Erika to go in alone. They had no present affiliations with any network. If they were caught, the worst accusation would be that a man and woman who happened to be Jews had too energetically questioned a Catholic priest about the woman's missing father.

Besides, Saul thought, this really is still a personal matter. Erika's father is all I care about. Gallagher gave me information I didn't have – about the Vatican connection with the men who stalked me. In return, *he* learned about the possibility of a network, the existence of which no one suspected. It's a fair exchange.

Lights flicked off in several apartments. The night became blacker. The Vatican was closed to tourists after 7 P.M., but Saul and Erika had hidden in a basement of one of the office buildings, creeping out after sunset. From his vantage point, Saul glanced down the narrow street toward where Erika waited in a similar alcove. They had flanked the entrance to Father Dusseault's apartment building. As soon as the light went off in his apartment, they'd go up. Or if he came out, they were ready to follow.

As it was, he came out. Saul recognized the robust young Frenchman, with his thick dark hair and his slightly weak chin, from a late-afternoon visit he'd made to Father Dusseault's office, pretending to be a journalist inquiring if there were developments in the search for the cardinal. The priest had been aloof, abrupt, dismissive. Saul wasn't going to regret demanding answers from him.

The priest paused beneath a light above the entrance to the palace, then headed toward Saul's right, in Erika's direction. His dark suit blended with the shadows; his white collar remained visible, however.

Saul shifted from his hiding place, having given Erika a chance to go after the priest before he himself did. He concentrated on a dim light at the end of the street, waiting to see which direction Father Dusseault would take.

The priest went straight ahead. His apartment building was to the right of St Peter's Square, near the so-called downtown area of the Vatican, where its supermarket, pharmacy, and post office were located. His route led Saul and Erika between the Sistine Chapel and St Peter's Basilica, past the Pontifical Academy of Science, and deep within the Vatican woods and gardens, the darkness of which was only partially dispelled by periodic lamps. Twice Saul had to stop and hide – once when two priests walked past him from one building to another, again while a Swiss guard patrolled a street. As soon as he entered the cover of shrubs and trees, he felt less uneasy. But he was troubled by two gestures the priest made. One was to remove his white collar and tuck it into his suitcoat pocket. The other was to push his right hand along the middle finger of his left hand as if he put on a ring.

With an intersecting cross and sword?

Is Father Dusseault connected with the three men who tried to kill me? Is that why their bills were paid through the cardinal's office?

The priest's movements, formerly casual, now became wary. A man of the cloth on a late-night stroll became an operative on guard against danger. He skirted the pale glow of a garden lamp. Without the white collar, his black suit blended perfectly with the darkness of shrubs.

He disappeared.

Somewhere ahead, among trees and bushes, Erika would be watching, Saul knew. Perhaps she was close enough to see where the priest went. But as she stalked him, would the priest be stalking her as well? Had Father Dusseault suspected he was being followed?

Saul was sure of *this*. He and Erika thought so much alike, the same suspicion would have occurred to her. She'd take extra care. Silently he crept forward, past fountains, hedges, and statues. Marble angels had always reminded him of death. The scent of the plants was cloying, as in an undertaker's parlor. He sank to the ground, squirming forward through a gap between shrubs, pausing when he saw a clearing before him. A large fountain in the shape of a Spanish galleon loomed ahead.

At first he thought the priest with his back to the fountain was Father Dusseault. Then the emergence of a quarter moon made him realize that *this* priest wore a white collar. The man was taller than Father Dusseault. His strong-chinned profile made Saul tingle. In these gardens that reminded him of a cemetery, he had the eerie sensation he was seeing a ghost. For an instant, he would have sworn he was looking at his dead foster brother, Chris.

Saul stared in shock. Had Chris somehow survived? Saul had never seen Chris's body; he'd only been told about the knife attack that had killed him. But despite the longing in Saul's heart, he knew in his soul that his hope was groundless. This priest, no matter the resemblance, was not in fact Chris.

A subtle movement at the side of the fountain attracted Saul's attention. Was it Erika trying to gain a better vantage point on this unexpected second priest?

No, he decided. She was too professional to let curiosity force her into the risk of revealing herself.

The movement beside the fountain became more evident. A shadow detached itself from darker shadows. A man stepped forward. In a priest's black suit but without the white collar. A man with a ring on the middle finger of his left hand.

Father Dusseault.

The other priest had apparently been aware of Father Dusseault's approach. Calmly, he turned to his visitor and raised his hands in a gesture of peace. Or so it seemed. The gesture was identical to an operative's invitation to search him, a signal that he wasn't armed.

4

To protect his night vision, Drew had taken care not to glance up at the moon or toward a lamp down a nearby path. Instead he'd concentrated on the darkest group of shrubs before him, keeping his back protected against the fountain. Though Father Dusseault should have arrived by now, he assumed that the priest was being cautious, approaching slowly, on guard against a trap. When he heard soft movement behind the fountain and turned with exaggerated calm, raising his arms in a gesture of nonaggression, he was grateful that Father Dusseault had chosen the darkest approach to this clearing, inadvertently helping Drew to preserve his sight.

Of course, the priest might not be Father Dusseault at all. Drew had never met the man. That afternoon, he'd phoned the priest at his Vatican office and asked for an appointment.

'What did you wish to speak with me about?' a smooth voice with a slight French accent had asked.

'Cardinal Pavelic,' Drew had said.

'You'll have to be more specific. If this is about the cardinal's disappearance, I've already had one reporter here today, and I told him what I'm telling you. We have no information. Talk to the police.'

'I'm not a reporter,' Drew had said. 'And I don't think you should tell me to see the police. I might make trouble for you.'

'I haven't the faintest idea what you're—'

'You asked for something specific. Try this. Two assassins are looking for the cardinal. The sons of Nazi SS men from World War Two. Their fathers reported directly to Hitler. Does that spark your interest?'

The line had been silent for a moment. 'Ridiculous,' Father Dusseault had said. 'What would make you imagine—?'

'Not on the phone. I told you I want an appointment. In private. As soon as possible. Tonight.'

'Who *is* this?'

'Sorry,' Drew had answered.

'*You expect me to trust an anonymous voice on the phone? To meet you in secret and talk about assassins?*'

Father Dusseault's outburst had seemed more calculated than spontaneous. Drew had decided to test him. 'If you want a character reference, I can direct you to a Fraternity.'

Again the line had been silent.

Encouraged, Drew had tested him further, beginning the Fraternity's recognition code. '*Dominus vobiscum.*'

'I don't understand why you told me that.'

'Surely, Father, you recognize a quotation from the Latin mass.'

'Of course. "The Lord be with you." '

201

'And do you remember the response?'

'*Et cum spiritu tuo.*'

'That's right. "And with your spirit." *Deo gratias.*' Drew had held his breath, waiting for the last part of the Fraternity's recognition code.

'"Thanks be to God." Amen.'

Drew had exhaled silently. The code had been completed. 'There's a Spanish-galleon fountain in the Vatican gardens.'

The reference to the fountain was also a test. Several days ago, when Drew and Arlene had disguised themselves as a priest and a nun to meet Father Sebastian at the Vatican gardens, that fountain had been their rendezvous. It was where Father Victor, the member of the Fraternity who'd sent Arlene to find Drew in Egypt, had been shot.

Any citizen of the Vatican would immediately link the meeting place Drew suggested with the recent murder there. Any indignant but innocent Vatican bureaucrat would call attention to the morbid choice of site. But Father Dusseault, pausing briefly, had merely said, 'I'll meet you there at one A.M.'

5

Now, fifteen minutes late for the appointment, Father Dusseault stepped from the darkness behind the fountain. He didn't seem surprised that Drew was dressed as a priest. It was understandable, Drew thought. After all, a voice who gave the Fraternity's recognition code would logically, in the Vatican, be expected to wear the appropriate uniform. Where else could a Catholic chameleon safely show his true colors?

Drew couldn't help noticing that Father Dusseault wasn't showing all of *his* colors, though – the priest had taken off his white collar to help him blend with the night. The tactic reinforced Drew's suspicion that the priest's training had not been entirely religious.

But Father Dusseault apparently hadn't discovered Arlene, who like Drew had once again entered the Vatican wearing the costume of a religious order. She'd arrived in the gardens well before the 1 A.M. meeting time, had taken off the white trim from her nun's habit, and had spread herself flat on the ground, merging her black clothing with the darkest group of bushes in the area, the same bushes Drew had been looking at when Father Dusseault arrived.

In the glow from the moon, Drew studied the ring on the middle finger of Father Dusseault's left hand: a ruby ring with the insignia of an intersecting cross and sword. It was obvious that Father Dusseault had worn the ring to verify his membership in the Fraternity – and equally obvious that the absence of an identical ring on Drew's finger put him under suspicion.

Indeed Father Dusseault pointed at Drew's naked finger. 'I assumed you were one of us.'

Drew recognized the resonant voice he'd heard on the phone. 'No.'

Alarmed, the priest and the nun swung toward him.

'This is the biggest risk I've ever taken,' Saul said. He raised his hands. 'I'm not alone, so stay as you are. I trust you. Please don't make a move against me.'

The priest seemed paralyzed between conflicting motives, whether to run or to attack. The nun pulled a pistol from beneath her robe.

Saul raised his hands even higher, stepping closer. 'You didn't know I was out there watching, so assume I could have killed you if I'd wanted to. Assume we've got mutual concerns.'

'Mutual concerns?' the priest asked.

Saul felt another eerie tingle. The voice was Chris's. It couldn't be. But it was.

Or am I going crazy?

'What you did is what *we* wanted to do,' Saul said.

'Which is?' The nun continued to aim the pistol.

'Get our hands on Father Dusseault and make him tell us what he knows about . . .'

The priest cocked his head. 'About?'

Saul hesitated, unsure how much to reveal, and abruptly committed himself. 'About my wife's missing father and why three men – I think they were priests – tried to kill my wife and myself.'

'You say you think they were *priests?*'

'Yes, like the man who just attacked you. He wears the same kind of ring they wore. A ruby with the insignia of an intersecting sword and cross.'

10

Drew stared in surprise. 'You know about the Fraternity?'

The stranger was in his late thirties, tall and muscular, dark-haired, square-jawed, swarthy.

Drew felt a momentary déjà vu, thinking he'd seen him before, though he couldn't imagine where. He disregarded the unnerving sensation and waited for the man to answer.

'The Fraternity?' The stranger frowned. 'Is that what they call themselves? No, I don't know about them, but I'd sure like to learn.' The man stepped closer. 'I do know this – the ring has a poison capsule hidden under the stone.'

'Yes, the stone,' Drew said. 'The Fraternity of the Stone. They're supposed to swallow the poison if there's a danger they'll be captured and forced to reveal the secrets of their order.'

'*Order?*' The stranger spoke quickly. 'Then I was right? They're all priests?'

Drew nodded. Reminded of the poison, he crouched beside Father Dusseault and took the precaution of slipping the ring off the priest's finger.

'You didn't kill him, I hope,' the stranger said.

'I tried my best not to. He'll wake up sore.'

'As long as he wakes up. I've got questions to ask him. On the other hand, since you seem to know about the Fraternity, maybe you can save me the effort. You don't wear one of their rings. I assume you're not a member. Something tells me you're not a priest either, any more than your friend's a nun.'

'I *have* seen you before,' Drew said.

11

Saul felt as if he'd been jolted.

'Yesterday. In Switzerland,' the priest said. 'At the crest of the Abliss Pass.'

'I drove over it yesterday. Heading toward Zurich.'

'In a Renault.'

'How the hell—?'

'A woman was in a car behind you,' the priest said. 'She drove a Volkswagen Golf.'

'She's my wife. But how did you—?'

'She looked so intense, so tired, and yet so determined to concentrate on you driving ahead of her. I can't explain why, but when both of you drove past. I identified with you.'

Saul felt a second jolt. He wanted to tell the priest about Chris, about his own eerie sense of identification.

But his attention was drawn toward Father Dusseault.

'We have to get him out of here,' the priest said.

'Before a guard comes along,' Saul agreed and glanced behind him toward the darkness. 'My wife'll be wondering what we're talking about. I'd better let her know it's safe to show herself.' He turned toward a clump of bushes and waved for her to come out. 'You didn't tell me your names. Unless you're still suspicious of me.'

The man and the woman looked uncertainly at each other.

'Drew.'

'Arlene.'

'Saul. My wife's name is Erika. You'll like her.' He waved his arm again for Erika to come out.

Waited.

Waved a third time.

And suddenly realized that she wouldn't be emerging from cover, that the world had gone terribly wrong, that his life was on the verge of destruction.

12

Saul raced toward the edge of the murky gardens and stared toward the massive dome of St Peter's haloed by the night lights of Rome. He'd searched one half of the grounds while the man who called himself Drew checked the other half. Now, seeing a guard near a palace across from him, he knew he had reached the point where he didn't dare go any farther. If Erika wasn't in the gardens, he certainly couldn't hope to find her in the maze of Vatican buildings. Again he wondered what had happened to her. He struggled to analyze the possibilities and concluded that only two made sense. She'd been forced to run, or else she'd been caught. But forced to run or caught by whom? Guards? Someone else in the Fraternity?

More than the agreed-upon twenty minutes had elapsed since he'd begun to search. By now, Drew would have returned to the fountain. *Maybe Drew had found Erika.*

Saul rushed through the night, charging into the clearing next to the fountain, stunned to see it deserted.

He clenched his fists in outrage but heard a footstep to his right and recognized Drew coming out from cover.

'We hid in case a guard came along,' Drew said. 'You're late.'

'Did you find her?'

'No . . . I'm sorry.'

Saul felt as if razor blades slashed his heart.

'I'm afraid we have to leave,' Drew said.

'I understand.'

'Will you be coming with us, or do you plan to go on searching?'

Saul turned toward the dark expanse of the gardens. He felt grievously tempted. 'No.' He had trouble speaking. 'If she were here, she'd have shown herself or we'd have found her. I'll keep looking. Somewhere else.' His voice broke. 'But I can't imagine where.'

'We've still got the problem of where to go with the priest.'

Saul studied the gardens one last time. It took all his discipline to rouse himself. If he were discovered here, he told himself, it wouldn't help Erika. On the other hand, Father Dusseault might know why she'd disappeared.

He struggled to concentrate. 'You'd better follow me.'

They had limited options, he realized. They could try to take Father Dusseault back to his apartment, but the odds were too great that a guard would notice and raise an alarm. And if they did somehow manage to reach the apartment, what would they do after that? Question him there? In the morning, someone on his staff might be puzzled by his absence and come to look for him. No, they had to get Father Dusseault out of the Vatican. But how? They'd certainly be stopped if they attempted to carry him through the Vatican's guarded gates at 2 A.M. They might be able to find a hiding place and stay there till morning, but what then? Walk the priest through the checkpoints while the guards were distracted by the usual throng of tourists? But how would they prevent Father Dusseault's battered face from being noticed, and what if the priest caused a commotion at the gate? Only one solution seemed practical. To leave the Vatican now, but not past the guardposts.

Before coming here yesterday, Saul and Erika had scouted the Vatican's perimeter. The city-state was enclosed by a high stone wall.

An invader couldn't climb over it unassisted, and anyone trying to scale it with a rope or a ladder would surely attract police intervention.

But invasion was not the intention now. Escape was, and climbing over the Vatican wall from the inside wasn't as difficult as doing so from the outside. Yesterday, Saul had noticed several places where trees on the inside grew close to the wall.

While Drew and Arlene carried the unconscious priest, Saul preceded them, hoping he'd find Erika. They reached the rear wall of the Vatican and searched along till they came to a sturdy tree whose branches they could climb to the top of the wall.

Hoisting the priest up through the branches wouldn't be difficult. Getting the priest down the other side would be less easy, requiring two people to stand at the bottom while someone on top held the priest's hands and lowered him as far as possible before letting him drop into waiting arms. As soon as they had him down, they had to assume they'd attract police attention. It was imperative that they leave the area at once.

'I'll go over first,' Saul said. 'Erika and I left a rented car nearby. Give me twenty minutes to get back here with it. Then start climbing. Lift the priest to the top of the wall. Who knows? Maybe Erika'll be at the car.'

'What happens if it isn't where you left it?' Drew asked.

'I'll steal one. No matter what, I'll be back.'

13

Drew sank to the ground, his back to the wall, shivering from the dampness. Arlene slid down beside him. He worried that Father Dusseault might waken, feign unconsciousness, and attack when least expected. He tested the injured priest's pulse. It was steady but weak, definitely not the heartbeat of an assassin mustering his reflexes.

Arlene leaned close to his ear. 'Do you trust him?'

'Saul? Yes. I have no idea why, but I do.'

Reassured, she eased against his shoulder. 'What did you say to Father Dusseault to make him attack you?'

'I'm not certain.' He had conflicting theories about the attack and needed time to think.

Perhaps Father Dusseault had come to the late-night rendezvous with the same intention as Drew, to force answers.

Or else the priest had reacted impulsively, suddenly threatened by Drew's questions about the cardinal and the Nazis.

But as Drew recalled the incident, he realized that Father Dusseault's seemingly spontaneous attack had actually been quite calculated. The priest hadn't thrust his knife toward vital organs, the throat for example, where the kill would be quick and sure, but instead had concentrated on wounding the chest and stomach, where death would take longer and in fact might not occur at all. He wanted to question me, Drew thought. To find out who I was and why I was so curious about the cardinal. After that, he'd have finished me off.

I think I've found the man who killed Father Victor beside that fountain.

But why would one member of the Fraternity want to kill another? Are Father Sebastian's suspicions correct about someone in the Fraternity trying to destroy it? Is Father Dusseault the traitor?

The answers would come soon enough, he thought. After Saul got back with the car.

But what had Saul said? His wife's father was missing? The disappearance had something to do with three priests, members of the Fraternity, who tried to kill Saul's wife and himself?

And now Saul's wife too was missing. Drew began to suspect that Saul's quest and his own were somehow related, that the answers to Saul's questions would help to answer his own.

He glanced at his watch. Twenty minutes had elapsed.

Arlene anticipated him. 'It's time.'

She went up the tree, bracing herself among branches, reaching down while Drew lifted Father Dusseault to her.

14

A Peugeot pulled up below them, its headlights gleaming. For a tense moment, Drew wondered if the car might belong to the police or the Fraternity. But Saul stepped out, and Drew relaxed. Arlene edged over the wall, landing smoothly. Drew lowered the priest to them, then went down as well. Seconds later, they were in the car.

To Saul's dismay, Erika had not been waiting at the car. 'My wife and I rented a hotel room,' he said as he drove. 'If she's all right, if she had to run from somebody, the hotel's where she'll know she can get in touch with me.' He glanced toward Drew and Arlene in the back, the priest out of sight on the floor. 'I suggest we take him there.'

Saul exhaled with relief when he heard Drew answer, 'Under the circumstances, it's the only choice.'

The layout of the hotel had been the reason for choosing it, Saul explained. Both the elevator and the fire stairs were down a corridor invisible from the lobby. A rear entrance, near the hotel's parking garage, led into that corridor.

At 3 A.M., no one paid attention to a priest helping another priest into the building, or to a nun who entered a few minutes later, or to the tall swarthy man who'd gone in ahead of them, carrying a suitcase.

The suitcase contained the street clothes Drew and Arlene had worn before they dressed as a priest and nun. On the way to the hotel, Drew had retrieved it from a locker at the train station. They encountered no one in the elevator or along the corridor that led to Saul's hotel room. Once inside, Drew and Arlene took turns using the bathroom to change back into their street clothes while Saul examined the unconscious priest where he lay on the bed.

'His nose is broken.'

'That was my intention,' Drew said. 'The way he came at me, I tried my damnedest to discourage him. What about his jaw?'

'The bones seem secure. He'll be able to talk.'

'But he's awfully slow waking up,' Arlene said.

'Yes, that worries me,' Saul said. 'I checked his eyes. They respond to light. His reflexes work. We might want to put some ice on his nose.'

'I'd prefer he stay in pain. He'll answer questions more readily,' Drew said.

'You don't have chemicals to make him talk?'

'No,' Drew said. 'We were given IDs, weapons, and money. That's all.'

'What do you mean "given"? By whom?'

'Someone in the Fraternity forced us to help him.'

Saul's eyes widened.

'It's a debt we're paying off,' Drew said.

'Believe us,' Arlene said, 'we don't feel loyal to them.'

Saul studied them, reluctantly committing himself further. 'All right. I've trusted you so far. Since you're being honest, I'll do the same. There's a group I owe a favor as well.'

'Who?'

'I used to work for them. I don't want anything more to do with them, but they manipulated me into cooperating.'

'I asked you—'

'The CIA.'

'Dear God!'

'I'd like to call them now,' Saul said. 'We can kid ourselves about the priest's condition, but the fact is he needs medical attention or he won't be alert enough to respond to questions. You put him down good. For all we know, he's got a concussion. We need a team with the proper facilities to bring him back up.'

The room became silent.

Arlene turned to Drew. 'He's got a point. By the time Father Dusseault's fully conscious, we'll have lost too much time.'

'But the *CIA*,' Drew said. 'You know how I feel about—'

'The way you handle yourself,' Saul said, 'I would have figured you were with them.'

'Not with the Agency. With the State Department's version of it. I want nothing to do with either.'

'But you agreed to cooperate with the Fraternity,' Saul said.

'There wasn't a choice.'

'Listen carefully. *My wife is missing.* That's all I care about right now. But I think if I get some answers from this priest, I stand a good chance of finding out where she is. I can get an expert team over here to help. I can do my best to guarantee the Agency doesn't know about you. I'm asking you to let me make the call.'

Drew stared at the floor.

Arlene said, 'If it helps to end this, Drew, tell him it's okay.'

Drew raised his eyes. 'We're getting in deeper.'

'Tell him.'

'All right' – Drew sighed – 'make the call.'

Saul grabbed the phone and dialed.

A husky voice answered, repeating the number Saul had used.

'This is Romulus. Tell Gallagher I have a reluctant source of information. I need a medical interrogation team. Now.'

'What address?' the voice asked.

'He knows where I'm staying.'

Saul set the phone back onto its cradle.

'Where the fuck is my wife?'

15

A half hour later, Saul heard a knock on the door. He glanced through its peephole, expecting the man with the pockmarked face, surprised to see Gallagher himself out there. He made a warning gesture to Drew and Arlene, who took their suitcase and shut themselves into the bathroom. Then he opened the hallway door.

Gallagher stepped in, his eyes puffy from lack of sleep. '"A reluctant source of information"?'

Saul shut the door and locked it.

Gallagher kept talking. 'Strictly speaking, I belong back in Austria. Our Zurich people didn't object to my entering their jurisdiction. But our Rome people like to run their show themselves. If you'd just agree to let another station chief be your control . . .'

'You wanted this relationship. Now you're stuck with it,' Saul said. 'I won't risk trusting anyone else.'

'It's so nice to be popular. What have you got?'

Saul led him down a short hallway into the bedroom.

Gallagher blanched when he saw who was on the bed. 'Good God, I don't believe it! You kidnapped a priest! How the hell can I put this into a report? And look at his face! What did you do, run over him with a truck?'

'He's not just a priest. He's a personal assistant to a cardinal in the Vatican's Curia.'

Gallagher's mouth hung open. 'I'll get even with you for this! You've just made my life—!'

'Before you start worrying about your job, take a look at this.' Saul showed him the ring Drew had taken from Father Dusseault.

Gallagher studied it in surprise.

'The details are starting to fit together. You already proved that the men who tried to kill me were funded through an office in the Vatican.' Saul pointed toward Father Dusseault. 'Through *his* office. His boss is the cardinal who's missing.' Saul raised the priest's right arm and rolled up the coat sleeve, revealing the spring-loaded sheath. He handed Gallagher the knife Father Dusseault had used. 'Just your basic standard equipment for a priest. Believe me, he knew how to use it.'

'Keep going. You're convincing me.'

'Not only is there a network we never heard of, but I was right – it's

211

composed of priests,' Saul said. 'They call themselves after the ruby on their ring. The Fraternity of the Stone.'

Gallagher chuckled. 'Romulus, you're as good as you ever were. You've learned a lot.'

'But not enough. I told your man on the phone. I want a medical interrogation team.'

'They won't know all the right questions to ask.'

'But I do. As soon as he's ready, I want to be alerted. I'll do the questioning. I intend to squeeze this priest for everything he knows.'

'What's wrong? Has something happened to you? Your voice sounds—'

'My wife's disappeared.'

'*What?*'

'She was with me when we staked out the priest's apartment. He left the building. We followed him separately, to avoid attracting attention.' Conscious of Drew and Arlene in the bathroom, Saul omitted their part in the night's events. 'After I got my hands on him, I looked for Erika.' His throat squeezed shut; he had difficulty continuing. 'She vanished. I searched *everywhere*. She's gone. If this priest knows anything about why she disappeared, by God he's going to tell me. If anything's happened to her, whoever did it is going to die.'

Gallagher stepped backward.

The phone rang. Saul lunged for it. 'Erika?'

But a man's voice said, 'Put Gallagher on.'

Saul closed his eyes, trying to control his disappointment. He handed the phone to Gallagher.

'Yes, come up,' Gallagher said into the phone and set it back on its cradle. He turned to Saul. 'That was the team. They're down the block. I didn't want to send them here till I understood what was happening.'

'And now you're satisfied?'

'Take it easy. Remember, I'm on your side.'

'Are you? Fair warning, Gallagher. Just tell your team to prep the priest. Then he's mine.'

'Under other circumstances' – Gallagher squinted – 'I wouldn't put up with your tone.' His glare diminished. 'But I guess you're entitled. Get some sleep. You'd better eat something. You look awful.'

'Sleep? Eat? How the hell, when Erika's—?'

'Do it, Romulus. You're no good to her or anyone else if you fuck yourself up.'

Saul suddenly realized how close to the edge he was. He took a deep breath. 'You're right . . . I'm sorry.'

'For what? In your place, I'd be climbing the walls. Count on me. I'll do everything I can to help.'

Saul smiled in gratitude.

Five minutes later, three men arrived. One was slight and wore glasses. He pursed his lips when he saw the priest's battered face. He checked the priest's vital signs, then turned to Gallagher. 'It's safe to move him.'

212

Gallagher nodded.

The two other men stepped forward. Both were well built. 'Where do we take him? Back to the shop or—?'

'Can you do it here?' Gallagher asked. 'In another room in the hotel?'

'Sooner or later we'll have to take a skull X-ray, but I didn't see any swelling behind his eyes, so I'm probably being overcautious. His blood pressure checks out. Yes, I guess I can do it here in the hotel.'

'I already phoned down for a reservation. They had a room at the end of this floor.' Gallagher motioned to one of the well-built men. 'Go down and check in. Bring the key.'

Ten minutes later, the team was ready to leave with the priest.

'I'll need some equipment from the van,' the man who wore glasses said.

'Whatever you want,' Gallagher said, 'you get.'

They checked the hallway outside. It was empty. The well-built men braced the priest between them. Holding his arms around their necks, they walked him down the hall. The man who wore glasses followed. No one saw them.

Gallagher turned from where he'd been watching at Saul's open doorway. 'Remember, get some rest. I'll phone when he's ready.'

Saul leaned against a wall, his knees weak from exhaustion. 'I'll be waiting.' He locked the door.

16

The bathroom door came open.

'You,' Arlene told Saul, 'are going to take Gallagher's advice. I'm calling for room service.'

'She thinks she's Florence Nightingale. She gets mean when her patients don't let her help,' Drew said.

Saul smiled. Fatigue made him slump toward a chair.

Arlene picked up the phone. 'My friend here seldom eats meat,' she told Saul. 'How about scrambled eggs, rolls, and coffee?'

'I'm too tense already,' Saul said. 'No coffee.'

'Milk,' Drew said, 'and fruit. Lots of fruit.'

Arlene made the call to room service. Saul watched her. She was tall and lithe, reminding him of Erika. But there the similarity ended. Arlene's hair wasn't as dark and long. Her face, though beautiful, was more oval. Her skin, though tanned, wasn't naturally swarthy as Erika's was. The big difference was in the eyes. Arlene's were green while Erika's were brown.

Erika.

To distract himself, he shifted his attention toward Drew and again was reminded of Chris. 'You still haven't told me whether you're really a priest.'

'No.' Drew sounded wistful. 'I was once a brother, though.'

The reference caught Saul by surprise. 'Brother? You mean like—?'

'I'm a Roman Catholic. I used to be a monk.'

Saul strained to sound casual. 'I had an extremely close friend, a foster brother you might say, who was Roman Catholic. Irish.'

'I'm Scottish.'

'My friend joined a Cistercian monastery and stayed there for six years,' Saul said.

'Really? That's quite a coincidence.'

'Oh?' Saul's nerves quivered. 'How's that?'

'I was in the monastery almost as long. But I was a Carthusian.'

'Yes, my friend told me about the Carthusians. He said his own order, the Cistercians, were tough. They didn't speak. They believed in hard physical labor. But the Carthusians – they each lived alone in a cell, hermits for life, totally solitary – he said the Carthusians were the toughest.'

'I enjoyed the peace. What was your friend's name?'

'Chris.'

'Why did he leave the order?'

'He had nightmares about things he'd been forced to do before he joined the order. In fact, those things were what made him join the order in the first place.'

'Things?'

'He was manipulated into being an assassin.'

Drew flinched. His shock was palpable.

'You can't understand unless you know that Chris and I were orphans. The institution where we lived was modeled after the military. From when we were kids, we were taught to be warriors. A man officially adopted us. His name was Eliot. He took us on trips. He gave us candy. He made us love him.'

Saul had difficulty continuing. 'It turned out he worked for the government, and his motive for becoming our foster father was to recruit us into intelligence work. After we went through extensive training, he sent us out on missions. The US doesn't officially condone assassination, of course, but that's what we did just the same. We thought our missions were government-sanctioned, supposedly for a just cause. As it happened, we weren't working for the government but for Eliot himself. We loved him so much we'd do anything for him. So he told us to kill. For his own reasons. Chris broke down from the stress of what we were doing. To atone for the things he'd done, he entered the monastery. But his nightmares kept haunting him, and he retreated even more from the world. He lapsed into trances. The condition's called catatonic schizophrenia. Meditative paralysis. The Cistercians insisted on each monk contributing equally to the labor of the monastery, but Chris's trances kept him from working. The order had to ask him to leave.'

'He must have felt torn apart.'

'Oh, believe me, he did. But he's at peace now.'

'How?'

'He was killed,' Saul said.

214

Drew's eyes narrowed.

'Stabbed to death – because Eliot eventually turned against us. To protect his secrets, he betrayed us. I evened the score for Chris, though.'

'How?'

'I killed Eliot . . . And you?'

'I'm not sure what you mean,' Drew said.

'Why did you leave the Carthusians?'

'A hit team took out the monastery.'

Saul blinked in amazement.

17

Beside him, Drew felt Arlene tense in astonishment at his candor.

'Took out the monastery?' Saul asked.

'I'm an orphan, too. My parents were killed when I was ten,' Drew said. 'In Tokyo. My father worked for the US State Department there. In 1960, he and my mother were blown up by terrorists. The authorities never found whoever was responsible. I was only ten, but I made a vow that one day I'd track them down or, if I couldn't find them, I'd punish whoever was *like* the people who'd murdered my parents. I was sent to America to live with my uncle.' Bitterness distorted his voice. 'That didn't work out too well. So my father's best friend adopted me. His name was Ray. He worked for the State Department, the same as my father had, and he took me all over the world on his assignments. Wherever we went, he made sure I learned the martial art of that country. I still intended to keep the vow I'd made – to revenge my parents – so Ray recruited me into a secret State Department antiterrorist group called Scalpel. I was trained to be an assassin. For ten years I killed.'

'Ten years? What made you stop? Why did you enter the monastery?'

'The same reason as your friend. I had nightmares. In 1979, I was sent on a mission that ended with the death of an innocent man and woman. I blew them up, just as *my* parents had been blown up. Their son saw it happen just as *I'd* seen it happen to mine.'

'This man and woman, you say they were innocent? You made a mistake?'

'No. Scalpel *wanted* them killed for political reasons. But I couldn't justify what I'd done. I'd become a version of the people who'd murdered my parents. I'd turned into the scum I was hunting. I was my enemy. I had a . . . breakdown, I guess you'd call it. I was so desperate to redeem myself, to punish myself for my sins, that I became a Carthusian. For almost six years, through penance and prayer, I achieved a measure of peace.'

'And that's when the hit team took out the monastery?'

'Nineteen monks were poisoned. Two others were shot. I was the primary target, but I escaped. I vowed to find out who'd killed my

215

fellow monks and threatened my chance for redemption. In the end, I discovered that the man who'd ordered the hit was Ray. He feared that one day, because of my breakdown, I'd reveal secrets about him. He'd been searching for me all those years, and when he finally learned where I'd gone to ground . . . Well, as you said about the man who ordered your foster brother's death, I found Ray, and I killed him.'

18

Saul listened, deeply moved. The parallels between his story and Drew's were unnerving.

But Chris had been killed.

And Drew had survived, resembling Chris, with his fair hair, fiery eyes, hint of freckles, and strong-boned rectangular face. Saul had the sense that a niche had been filled in his life, that a ghost had come back.

'You didn't say if you had any brothers,' Saul said.

'No brothers. I'm an only child.'

Saul smiled. 'If you want a brother, you've got one now. You wouldn't have told me your background if you didn't recognize the similarities between . . . It's uncanny.'

'I noticed the parallels,' Drew said, 'and I can't explain them either.'

'Running into each other. How could—? I can't believe it's just a coincidence.'

'The question is,' Arlene interrupted, 'how many other similarities are there?'

19

The two men turned to her.

Arlene had listened with growing distress as Saul and Drew talked to each other. It was startling enough that two men who'd never met before should quickly become so open with each other. Even more startling were the parallels between Drew and Saul's dead foster brother. What Saul had said just now was true – it was uncanny. And the most disturbing part was that she didn't think the surprises were over.

'Other similarities?' Saul asked.

'You showed up in the Vatican gardens at the same time we did – to force information from Father Dusseault,' she said. 'Doesn't that make you wonder? You've got to be curious what we were doing there. I'm sure curious to know what *you* were doing there. In different ways, did we come there for the same reason?'

'Your wife's father was missing – isn't that what you said?' Drew asked. 'And three men tried to kill you? Men who wore a ring identical to Father Dusseault's?'

Saul didn't answer for a moment. Then he shuddered, and it seemed to Arlene that he did so to force his attention back to this conversation. Because, if she guessed correctly, the disappearance of his wife was related to everything they were discussing.

'Right,' Saul said. 'And we traced those three men to Father Dusseault. To what you called the Fraternity of the Stone. All priests. What *is* the Fraternity?'

'Soldiers of God,' Drew said. 'Church militants.'

'Explain.'

'The order dates back to the twelfth century, the Third Crusade,' Drew said. 'They follow a tradition established by an Arab who converted to Catholicism, became a priest, and used his knowledge of Arab ways to help the crusaders try to liberate the Holy Land from the Muslims.'

'Help the crusaders? How?'

'As an assassin. Since he was an Arab, he could easily infiltrate the enemy. His mandate was to execute Muslim leaders in the same brutal way that *their* assassins had executed leaders of the Crusade. Specifically, he came upon his targets while they slept and cut off their heads.'

'Graphic,' Saul said drily. 'And no doubt dramatically effective.'

'The theory was to fight terror with terror. Of course, the crusaders felt that *their* terror was holy.'

'And the Church condoned this?'

'At the time,' Drew said. 'You have to remember the religious fervor that motivated the Third Crusade. The Pope gave a dispensation for any sins committed during what was supposed to be a divinely inspired war against the heathens.'

'Times change, though.'

'Yes, but the order founded by that assassin-priest didn't. Unknown to the Church, the Fraternity of the Stone continued to practice holy terror throughout the centuries – whenever they considered it necessary to defend the Faith.'

'And the ring?'

'A way for them to identify each other. It's a replica of the ring King Richard wore during the Third Crusade. A ruby that signifies the blood of Christ.'

'But why would they want to stop me and Erika from finding her father?' Saul asked. 'Are they involved in *Erika's* disappearance?'

'Maybe Father Dusseault will tell us when we question him,' Arlene said. 'The reason *we* came to the gardens to meet him involved a disappearance as well. A cardinal named Krunoslav Pavelic. Father Dusseault is his assistant.'

'I've heard about the disappearance. But why are you looking for him?'

'To pay off a debt,' Drew said. 'A priest who belonged to the

217

Fraternity tried to recruit me into the order. When I refused, he tried to kill me to protect the order's secrets. Arlene's brother shot him to save my life.'

'The Fraternity thought *Drew* had killed the priest,' Arlene said. 'To protect my brother, to thank him for saving his life, Drew fled as if he were guilty. For the past year, he's been living in Egypt. Three weeks ago, a member of the Fraternity came to me in New York. He said the order had learned where Drew was hiding. He asked me to go to Drew and convince him to provide a service to the Fraternity. In exchange, the order would consider the debt paid in full for the death of the priest.'

'What was the service they wanted?'

'Drew had to find the missing cardinal.'

'Why couldn't they handle the job themselves?'

'That's what we wondered, too,' Drew said. 'A Fraternity priest we met in Cairo told us that someone in the order was trying to destroy it, that the key to finding whoever was responsible had something to do with Pavelic's disappearance. If Arlene and I wanted to live in peace, we had to find the cardinal and in so doing find whoever was trying to sabotage the Fraternity. I have a suspicion that Father Dusseault is involved in the betrayal, so some things are starting to come together. But what puzzles me is that two *other* people are looking for the cardinal. Two assassins, the sons of Nazi assassins.'

'*The sons of Nazi assassins?*'

'Their code names are Icicle and Seth.'

Saul stood in distress. 'A blond and a redhead?'

'You *know* about them?'

'When I was in the Agency, I heard rumors. About Seth in particular. He's supposed to be crazy. *What the hell is going on?*'

'And is there a connection? Among what you want, we want, and *they* want?' Arlene asked.

'Disappearances – my wife and her father,' Saul said. 'And priest-assassins.'

'A cardinal's disappearance,' Drew said. 'And the sons of Nazi assassins.'

20

In darkness, Icicle sat on a damp concrete floor in the basement of a palace near the Sistine Chapel. He couldn't see the unconscious woman sprawled beside him, but he could feel her body heat and, if he leaned close, hear her faint breathing. Of course, he couldn't see Seth on the other side of her either, but it bothered him that he could *hear* Seth – the faint brush of Seth's hand along her body. Icicle tried to hold his disgust in check.

Yesterday afternoon, determined to force information from the missing cardinal's assistant, Father Dusseault, they'd entered the

Vatican among a group of tourists. A guide had escorted the group through St Peter's Basilica; Icicle and Seth had hung back, looking for a place where they could hide until nightfall. The door to this murky basement had been unlocked. At midnight, they'd left the palace basement and walked toward Father Dusseault's apartment. Experts at becoming one with the night, they were never noticed.

Their plan was to enter the priest's apartment while he slept, so subdue him, and to question him throughout the night. When they reached the corner of the street that ran along the entrance to the priest's apartment building, they paused to study the approach before moving in. But just as Seth stepped forward, Icicle tugged him back behind cover and pointed toward an alcove a third way down the street, on the opposite side. That recess, deep and dark, had been one of Icicle's intended hiding places.

But someone else had the same idea. A shadow moved within the alcove. A man leaned forward, gazed up toward a window of the apartment building across from him, then stepped back into the dark. He showed himself for only a moment, but it was enough for Icicle to see that the man did not wear the black suit of a priest – he was an outsider, the same as Icicle and Seth.

They watched the man watch the building. In a while, the man peered down the street, then moved back in. He didn't do so conspicuously. He was obviously experienced. The way he peered down the street suggested that he wasn't alone, that he was waiting to give or receive a signal.

A priest stepped out of the apartment building, glanced both ways along the street and headed to his left, away from Icicle and Seth, away from the man who watched the building. The man remained in place, but farther down the street, after the priest had passed a doorway, a *woman* eased into view and followed. Icicle's muscles tightened. A man and a woman? He and Seth had crossed paths with a man and a woman before. During the abduction of Medici.

But the man shifted out to follow the priest as well, and when Icicle got a good look at him, he decided that this couple was definitely not the couple he'd seen before. The man was more husky, the woman had longer hair.

Despite the differences, the fact that again a man and woman were staking out sites where Icicle and Seth were engaged in a mission made Icicle nervous. Were they, too, after Father Dusseault? Indeed, was the priest he'd just seen Father Dusseault? He'd never met the man or seen a photograph of him. The best thing to do, Icicle decided, was to follow. Icicle motioned to Seth and stepped out into the street.

Their wary pursuit led them deep within the Vatican gardens where, staying carefully back from the man and woman, they had a distant view of a Spanish-galleon fountain in a clearing. Moonlight revealed a priest standing before the fountain. Icicle sank to his stomach. With Seth beside him, he crawled nearer, wanting a better view of the priest, anxious to see if he was the same priest who'd left the apartment building.

219

No. He wasn't. But with a shock, Icicle realized that this *was* the same man he'd seen in the alley during Medici's abduction. Baffled, he glanced at Seth, who had also recognized the man and shook his head in confusion. A second priest – the one who'd left the apartment building, whom Icicle suspected was Father Dusseault – stepped into the clearing. They spoke to one another. Surprisingly, Father Dusseault lunged with a knife. Just as amazingly, the other priest defended himself superbly. Though Father Dusseault was good, the other priest was better, taking the advantage, striking Father Dusseault repeatedly, knocking him senseless to the ground.

Icicle watched in awe. He'd never heard of priests who handled themselves like warriors. A nun rushed into the clearing – the same woman Icicle had seen the other night in the alley with this man. Icicle wanted more desperately to know what was going on. He and Seth could have used their silenced handguns to disable them and make them explain. But he was aware that he and Seth weren't alone out here. The other couple, the strangers, were hidden somewhere, watching. The man they'd followed stepped into the clearing, his hands raised. Icicle was tempted to risk crawling even closer in the hopes of hearing what they said to one another.

But Seth distracted him. The assassin pulled a flat leather case from a jacket pocket, removed a hypodermic, and crawled not forward but toward the right, as if he meant to circle the clearing. Puzzled, Icicle went after him, and as Seth stopped, scanned dark bushes, and crawled farther, Icicle realized that Seth was stalking the woman they'd noticed outside the apartment building. She hadn't yet shown herself in the gardens; she must have decided to wait to see what would happen in the clearing.

Her shadow rose behind a tree twenty yards to Icicle's left. From the clearing, she could not have been seen, but from Icicle's vantage point behind her, she was distinct. Seth inched toward her, poised himself, and lunged to sweep a hand across her mouth at the same time that he plunged the needle into her arm. She struggled for less than five seconds.

Seth eased her silently backward, away from the clearing. Icicle joined him, reaching to help him carry her, but Seth shoved his arm away. The red-haired man's eyes gleamed fiercely, signaling *she's mine*. Icicle shuddered, realizing that Seth was sicker than he'd imagined. Seth shuddered also, with sexual pleasure, lifting the woman so her stomach was over his shoulder, her breasts pressed against his back.

They returned to this dark palace basement . . . where, the unconscious woman next to him and Seth on the other side of her, Icicle struggled to contain his revulsion, hearing Seth's hand brush along her body. The night had been long. He pressed a button on his digital watch: 7:23. He imagined the daylight outside. He didn't know how he'd be able to bear sitting in this dark musty room, waiting for nine o'clock, when tourists would be allowed to enter the

Vatican and they could leave, pretending the woman had suddenly fainted.

21

'Too much wine, too little sleep,' Icicle said in Italian to a solicitous desk clerk when he and Seth reached their hotel. They stood with the woman held up between them while they waited for the elevator doors to open. 'Jet lag and all-night partying don't go together, I'm sorry to say.' He tipped the clerk in appreciation for his concern. 'Tonight, she'll probably want to go dancing.'

The clerk smiled knowingly and told them if they needed anything . . .

'We'll phone the front desk and ask specifically for you,' Icicle said.

The elevator opened. They stepped inside and went up to their room.

While Icicle locked the door, Seth carried the woman to the bed. 'Is she all right?'

Seth checked her eyes. 'She's coming around. We'll soon be able to question her.' He took off her shoes and massaged her feet.

Icicle tasted bile. It took all his effort to keep from telling Seth to stop touching her. 'Did you recognize the man and woman dressed as a priest and nun?'

'From when we grabbed Medici. They wore street clothes then. It makes me wonder if tonight they were in disguise. And now *another* man and woman are involved. The one couple didn't seem to know the other.' Seth brooded. 'What was their interest in Father Dusseault? Did each couple have a different motive or the same? Are their motives *ours*?'

'To learn what the priest knows about the disappearance of our fathers?' Sickened, Icicle averted his gaze from where Seth now touched the woman. 'No. They're not part of our group. They don't have a reason to look for our fathers.'

'But they might have a reason to look for the missing cardinal,' Seth said. To Icicle's relief, he took his hands away from the woman. 'And there might be a connection between this woman and our missing fathers. She's almost certainly Jewish.'

'That could be coincidental.'

'Possibly,' Seth said, 'but not probably.'

'We'll soon find out.' Seth undid her belt, opened the button on the waist of her slacks, and tugged her zipper down, revealing a glimpse of peach-colored panties.

Icicle couldn't restrain his disgust any longer. 'No.'

Seth glanced at him, frowning. His voice was hard. 'I beg your pardon?'

'What you've got in mind to do to her before she wakes up, forget it.'

221

'Do to her?' Seth smiled coldly. 'My indignant friend, what exactly do you think I intend to do to her?'

'I'm telling you to forget it.'

'What I intend to do is remove her slacks – to make her more comfortable during the interrogation. As well, her bodily functions are overdue. She'll need to use the bathroom.' Seth pulled off the woman's slacks, exposing her legs.

The woman murmured, drawing her knees toward her stomach as if she were cold.

'Come along now.' Seth raised her to a sitting position, put her arm around his neck, and helped her to stand. With a challenging look toward Icicle, he started into the bathroom with her.

'I'll go with you,' Icicle said.

'No need. I can manage her myself.'

'The two of us can manage her better.'

Seth squinted. 'One moment you're afraid I'll assault her – the next you want to watch her go to the bathroom. Your values are confused.'

Refusing to be taunted, Icicle took the woman's other arm and escorted her and Seth into the bathroom. Embarrassed, he watched Seth take off her panties and sit her on the toilet. Her head flopped one way, then the other.

'Try to relieve yourself,' Seth said. 'We don't want any accidents, do we?'

Icicle almost slapped Seth's hand away when he pressed her abdomen.

No! My father! I have to find my father! Nothing must interfere! I can deal with Seth later, but right now . . . !

To Icicle's relief, the woman urinated.

They carried her back to the bed. Again she drew her knees toward her stomach.

'*What are you doing?*' Seth barked at Icicle.

'Putting her underwear back on.'

'She doesn't need them!'

They stared at each other. The room compacted with tension.

Icicle reached for a corner of the bedspread, about to drape it over her.

'No,' Seth's eyes blazed in warning. 'The drug works better if she's chilly.'

Icicle realized they were at the danger point. If he didn't back off, in all probability there'd be a fight. His father had to take priority. 'Whatever you say.'

'That's exactly correct. Whatever I say. I wouldn't want our friendship to be strained.' Seth's tone was mocking. '*Get on with it. Question her.*'

While you concentrate on her nakedness, Icicle thought angrily.

He stepped to the bureau, opened a drawer, and removed a vial of Sodium-Amytal powder. In a larger vial, he mixed five hundred milligrams of the powder with twenty milliliters of distilled water. He filled a hypodermic.

222

'Can you hear me?'

The woman didn't answer.

Icicle leaned close and repeated the question.

The woman nodded, her voice weak. 'Hear you . . .'

'Good. You mustn't worry. You're safe. You have nothing to fear. You're with friends.'

'Friends . . .'

'That's right. Now tell me your name.'

'Erika . . .'

'And your last name?'

'Bernstein-Grisman.'

The last name left no doubt, Icicle thought. The woman was Jewish, as Seth had suspected.

Icicle's tone was gentle. 'Why did you follow Father Dusseault to the Vatican gardens?'

'Three men tried to kill us . . .'

The nonsequitur made Icicle close his eyes in frustration. But he persisted with his gentle tone. 'You can tell us about the three men later, Erika. What about Father Dusseault?'

Another nonsequitur. 'My father disappeared.'

The problem, Icicle decided, was whether to keep her talking about Father Dusseault or whether to follow her random associations. What Erika knew might be so complicated that he'd fail to learn vital information if he kept his questions within too narrow a range. Certainly her statement about her father, though seemingly irrelevant, was disturbing enough to merit inquiry. 'Disappeared? When?'

'Two weeks ago.'

'Where?'

'Vienna.'

'Why did he disappear?'

'Don't know . . .'

Even in a stupor, the woman became so agitated that Icicle chose nonthreatening questions – to make her feel at ease, to accustom her to talking freely. 'Tell us about your father.'

She didn't answer.

Icicle made his questions more specific. 'How old is he?'

'Seventy . . .'

'Does he still have a job?'

'Retired . . .'

'From what?' Already Icicle felt bored by the unimportant questions with which he attempted to calm her. 'How did he earn his living?'

'Mossad . . .'

The unexpected response cramped Icicle's heart. He pivoted toward Seth, who jerked his surprised gaze up from the woman's legs.

Icicle turned again to the woman. 'Your father was once an operative for the Mossad?'

'Yes.'

'Do *you* work for the Mossad?'

'No.'

The pressure around Icicle's heart eased.

'Resigned . . .'

'Why?'

'Wanted to be with my husband . . .'

'The man who was with you in the Vatican gardens? Does *he* work for the Mossad?'

'No.'

'Did he ever?'

'No.'

'What's your husband's profession?'

'Farmer.'

'Where?'

'In Israel.'

'Why did the two of you leave there?'

'To look for my father.' Her voice increased in strength. Her eyelids fluttered.

Icicle walked to the bureau, filled a second syringe with the Sodium-Amytal solution he'd prepared earlier, and injected a small amount into her femoral artery. The drug worked almost instantaneously. Her body relaxed.

'When you and your husband left Israel to search for your father, where did you go?'

'Vienna.'

'Where he disappeared. Of course. And where did you go after that?'

'Switzerland.'

The answer surprised him. 'What?'

'The Alps south of Zurich.'

Icicle hesitated. 'Why did you go there?'

'To look for a friend of my father.'

'Did you find him?'

'No . . . Disappeared.'

For a second time, an unexpected answer.

'A diary . . .'

'I don't understand.'

'Found a diary . . .'

'What was in it?'

'Nazi concentration camp . . .'

Oh, Jesus, Icicle thought.

'Your father's friend wrote a diary about the camp?'

'Yes.'

'Was your father ever in a camp?'

'Yes.'

Icicle had the terrible sense that a pattern was forming.

But she suddenly shifted topics. 'Three men tried to kill us.'

Icicle let her lead him. 'Yes, you mentioned them earlier. Where did this happen?'

'The Alps.'

'Who were they?'

'Think they were priests . . .'

She was talking nonsense. Had the drug distorted her memory?

She began to tremble, agitated by the semiconscious memory of the . . .

'Priests?' Icicle asked. 'Why would priests want to kill you?'

Her trembling increased. 'Father Dusseault.'

Icicle's pulse sped. They were back to the question with which he'd started.

'What about Father Dusseault? Why did you follow him? Is he connected with the priests who tried to kill you?'

'Paid through the cardinal's office.'

'Cardinal *Pavelic's* office? The one who disappeared? *Do you know where the cardinal is?*'

'No.'

'Are you looking for him?'

'No.'

Icicle's excitement changed to frustration. She had led him in a meaningless circle.

23

It took two hours. Icicle guided her back through what she'd told him, prompting her for more details. As before, she became agitated when she talked about her missing father, about the three priests who'd tried to kill her husband and herself. At last, he turned from the woman and paced toward the far end of the room. He'd asked every question he could think of and learned too little. What bothered him were the questions he *hadn't* been able to think of, the unimaginable information she might have volunteered if only he knew what to ask for.

Seth continued to stare at the woman's nakedness.

'What do you make of the rings she described?' Icicle asked.

'Assassin-priests?' Seth turned from her. 'I've practiced my trade for twenty years, and I've never heard of such a group.'

'Nor have I. That doesn't mean she's mistaken. The group might be extremely cautious. And what about her father's disappearance? Is it related to the disappearance of our own fathers? To the disappearance of the cardinal?'

'The common element seems to be Father Dusseault,' Seth said. 'For different reasons, our search and this woman's led us to him.'

'Let's not forget the other man and woman we saw in the gardens, the ones dressed as a priest and a nun. What reason did *they* have to go after Father Dusseault? Why were they interested in Medici, just as we were? I'm sure it's all connected. Father Dusseault has the answers, but we've lost the chance to question him.'

'Perhaps,' Seth said.

Icicle frowned. 'What are you thinking of?'

'The notion isn't fully formed yet. I'll tell you when I'm sure it'll work.' Staring at the woman, Seth took off his sportscoat and began to unbutton his shirt.

Icicle stepped protectively toward her. 'Why are you undressing?'

'Relax. For the moment, this woman's body no longer interests me. I need to shave and shower. I'm going out. You'll have to stay here and keep her sedated.' Seth walked toward the bathroom.

'Going out?' Icicle's stomach squirmed with suspicion. 'Why?' He quickly followed Seth into the bathroom. 'What do you—? Of course,' he realized. 'It's time we reported to Halloway. You'll want to use a safe phone to call him.'

'Report to Halloway?' Seth said with contempt. 'Not at all. We don't have anything conclusive to tell him. I make a habit of announcing success, not failure.' Seth turned on the shower. 'But with luck, if my errand proves successful, we will have positive news for him. Very soon.'

24

Saul awoke from a nightmare in which, surrounded by darkness, he heard Erika scream. He bolted up, heard his wife scream again, and scrambled from bed to get to her before he realized that the screams were really the ringing of the telephone. Fully clothed, he found himself in the middle of the Rome hotel room. He had slept on a couch, Drew and Arlene on the double bed. Sunlight glowed beyond closed draperies.

Saul picked up the phone, praying he'd hear Erika's voice. Instead he heard Gallagher's, raspy, tired.

'Romulus, the priest is ready for you to hear his confession. Come down to the room.'

'I'm on my way.' Saul looked at his watch. The time was shortly after 10 A.M. He'd gotten six hours sleep, but his nightmares had tortured him. He felt as exhausted as when he'd lain down.

Drew and Arlene had awoken.

'Who was that?' Drew asked.

'Gallagher. It's quiz time.' Saul went into the bathroom, splashed cold water on his face, then returned to Drew and Arlene. 'Are you still determined not to get involved with the Agency?'

'I've got trouble enough with the Fraternity. I don't want to complicate my troubles by dealing with another network. After Scalpel, I've had my fill of networks,' Drew said. 'The Agency would want to know everything about me. They'd try to recruit me, and failing that, they'd keep me under surveillance. They're like Krazy Glue. Once they touch you, you're stuck. Arlene and I just want to be left alone.'

'Then we've got a problem,' Saul said. 'I have to go to Gallagher and the priest, but I don't know what questions to ask. *You're* here to find the cardinal and whoever's trying to destroy the Fraternity. *I'm* here to find Erika and her father. I'm sure your search and mine have something to do with each other. I think the answers to your questions might help me answer my own. But if you won't let the Agency know you're involved, how can we both question the priest?'

25

Saul knocked on Gallagher's door. He heard the scrape of a lock being freed. In a moment, the door was opened, and he stepped inside, his nostrils feeling pinched from the smell of medication. He approached Father Dusseault, who was lying on the bed. The priest looked pasty. His broken nose had swelled. So had the bruised skin along his eyebrows. His jaw was puffy. The priest's black suitcoat had been removed, his shirt opened, his sleeves rolled up. Sensors attached to his chest and arms transmitted signals to portable heart and blood-pressure monitors that sat on a bureau shifted close to the bed.

Saul surveyed the rest of the room. The bathroom door was open. The doctor and his assistant were gone.

'Where—?'

'I sent them out to eat breakfast,' Gallagher said. 'What they don't hear won't burden them with something else to forget. I can have them paged in the restaurant if we have an emergency. They'll phone in an hour to find out when it's time to come back.'

Saul turned again toward Father Dusseault, studying the IV that controlled the flow of Sodium Amytal into the priest's arm.

'He's still asleep,' Saul said. 'Does that mean he had a concussion?'

'No. In fact, he came around two hours ago. The doctor had to sedate him.'

'But he can answer questions?'

'The monitors show he's at an ideal semiconscious level. He's primed to tell you anything you want to know.'

'Good. Now I've got a favor to ask.'

Gallagher shifted his weight. 'You've had plenty of favors as it is. In case you've forgotten, this started with your promising to do *us* a favor if we let you come out of exile. But little by little, you've maneuvered us so we keep giving *you* favors. It's getting tiresome.'

'One more. What's the harm?'

'I'll know when you tell me what you want.'

'To be alone when I question the priest.'

Gallagher stopped moving. 'Jesus, you've got more nerve than—!'

'It's for your own benefit. If something goes wrong, if he *dies*, do you really want to be present when it happens? Do you want the Agency implicated in the death of a Vatican official?'

'Bullshit, Romulus. If he died, who'd know except you and me?'

'That's the point. Both of us would be one too many. You'd worry if you could trust me with what I knew if the priest didn't survive the

227

interrogation. Maybe you'd decide I'm too dangerous a liability. I'm not anxious to sell my soul to the Agency again or have an unexpected accident. So do yourself a favor and join the team for breakfast. Do *me* a favor by letting me take as many risks as I have to when I question the priest. I'll tell you everything I learn.'

'How can I be sure of that?'

'Because I need you. I wouldn't have been able to come this far without your help. And with more help from you, I hope to go a lot farther. It's for sure he'll tell me things I can't follow up without the resources of the Agency. You have my word. You'll be told everything I learn about the Fraternity. All I want to know is what happened to my wife and her father.'

Gallagher pursed his lips. 'I know I'll be sorry for this. Your word?'

Saul nodded.

'You always played straight,' Gallagher said. 'It's one of the reasons I went along with you this far. I hope you haven't changed – because in that case you *will* have an accident. Two hours. After that, no matter what excuses you make, I'm coming back.'

'You've got a deal.'

Gallagher left. Saul waited long enough for Gallagher to have gone downstairs, then picked up the phone. He dialed as silently as possible, let the other end ring once, then hung up. He swung toward Father Dusseault. Two hours. He had to cram as much as he could into them. In a rush, he disconnected the sensors from the priest's chest and arms. He buttoned the priest's shirt but lifted the IV tube in his arm. Raising the priest off the bed, Saul grabbed the bottle of Sodium-Amytal solution and supported the priest toward the door. He managed to free the lock. Someone opened the door from the other side – Drew, who'd been alerted to hurry from Saul's room down to this one as soon as he heard a single ring on the phone. Wordlessly, Drew helped Saul bring Father Dusseault into the hallway, then gently shut the door behind them.

Silence was mandatory. It wasn't sufficient for Gallagher to have left the room so that Saul could protect Drew and Arlene from the Agency, because Saul was certain the room had electronic eavesdropping monitors. Gallagher was thorough. He'd want a record of the interrogation, a tape to listen to while he sifted through the information the priest supplied. In fact, Saul had counted on the microphones in the room to give Gallagher a rationalization for going downstairs. After all, from Gallagher's point of view, what difference did it make if he wasn't in the room during the interrogation as long as he had a recording of what was said? But if the interrogation had taken place in the room, Drew and Arlene would have had their voices on the tape, and Gallagher would next have interrogated *them*.

Saul felt exposed in the corridor, worrying that a guest or a member of the hotel staff would appear and notice Drew and himself supporting Father Dusseault. There wasn't any way to eliminate that danger. Saul heard the elevator rising and muffled voices behind a door. A lock scraped open behind him. He and Drew got the priest to his own door, opened it, and stepped inside just as a door came open down the hall and someone stepped out.

But by then Arlene was already closing his own door, locking it while he and Drew carried Father Dusseault to the bed. They set him down gently, placing a pillow beneath his head and stretching out his legs.

'Gallagher gave me only two hours.'

'It's not enough time,' Drew said.

'It'll *have* to be enough.'

'What if Gallagher has a team listening to the microphones you think are planted in the other room?' Arlene asked. 'When all they hear is silence, they'll know you're not questioning the priest. They'll warn Gallagher that something's wrong.'

'I don't think there *is* a team,' Saul said. 'When Gallagher found out I'd kidnapped a Vatican official, he started worrying about his involvement with me. If this goes wrong, he knows he could lose his job. He's already concerned about the doctor and his assistants learning too much. He told them to leave before he sent for me. My guess is he doesn't have anyone listening to the microphones. The recording he hoped to get from the interrogation would have been for his ears only.'

'Then at least we can count on the two hours we've got.'

'Less than that now,' Saul said. 'We'd better get started.'

Drew held up the bottle of Sodium-Amytal solution. Arlene inserted the needle from its tube into the valve mechanism of the tube leading into Father Dusseault's arm. Saul leaned close to the priest.

'We're your friends. You're safe. You don't have anything to worry about. Relax.'

'Relax . . .' Father Dusseault's voice was faint, scratchy, as if his throat were dry.

'You feel at peace. Tell us everything we ask for. Hold nothing back. You can trust us.'

'Trust you . . .'

Saul hesitated, trying to decide what his first question should be. There were many to choose from, but if he asked them at random, it would take too long to fit the priest's disparate responses together. He needed to construct a sequence in which the questions would lead logically from one to another.

But Drew intervened, going directly to the core of his own problem. 'Do you know what happened to Cardinal Pavelic?'

'I killed him . . . cremated his body.'

In shock, Drew glanced at Arlene and Saul.

'*Why?*'

'He found out what I'd done.'

'What was *that?*'

'Told the Jews.'

Saul stiffened. 'Jews?'

Arlene asked, 'What did you tell them?'

229

'About the Nazis.'

The room became silent. Saul had the sense that a log was about to be overturned, a monstrosity revealed.

26

The revelation came slowly.

In 1941, as the result of an anti-Nazi coup that overthrew the pro-German government of Yugoslavia, Hitler determined to punish Yugoslavia so severely that no other nation would be similarly tempted to try to secede from the Third Reich. Its capital, Belgrade, was destroyed by massive aerial bombardment. The German army invaded, crushing all further rebellion. The country was subdivided, chunks of it annexed into Bulgaria, Albania, Hungary, and Italy. The greater portion became a separate Nazi puppet-state called Croatia.

Hell was in season. The newly installed Croatian government instigated a policy of racial and religious purification so brutal that even seasoned SS officers were appalled. A fanatical group of Croatians, called the Ustashi, became the government's instrument of purgation, hunting down Serbs, Jews, and gypsies. Victims were prodded to death in ponds; were made to kneel, their hands on the ground, while their heads were sawn off; had sharp sticks shoved down their throats; had drills thrust up their rectums; were disemboweled, set on fire, sledgehammered, trucked to mountaintops and thrown off cliffs, then blown apart by grenades. Those not killed where they were discovered endured the agony of concentration camps, dying slowly from starvation, dysentery, and exposure. The lucky ones were merely shot. At least six hundred thousand persons were slaughtered, perhaps as many as one and a quarter million.

Father Krunoslav Pavelic – born and raised in Yugoslavia – supported the Ustashi and their Nazi masters. Part of his motive was practical: to ally himself with the winning side. But part of his motive was also ideological: he firmly believed he was doing God's work. Racial matters aside, he applauded the elimination of all religions except Roman Catholicism. The Jews and the gypsies were heathen as far as he was concerned, and the Serbs – primarily Greek Orthodox Catholic – needed to be eliminated because of their break from the one true Faith. Not only did Father Pavelic support the Ustashi: he banded with them; he led them.

Church officials were unaware of Pavelic's personal holy war. But the inner circle did know about the massive Greek Orthodox murders in Croatia and knew as well about the even more massive Nazi slaughter of the Jews. With some exceptions, Church officials did nothing to try to stop the slaughter. Their rationalization was that, to protect its existence, the Church had to remain neutral. If Hitler won the war and if he'd perceived the Church as his enemy, he would destroy it just as he had Yugoslavia. 'Pray and wait' became the Church's motto. 'Survive these desperate times as best we can.'

Following Hitler's defeat in 1945, one of the Church's methods of compensation was to assist refugees, particularly through the Red Cross. By then, Father Pavelic had been transferred from Croatia to Rome, where he arranged to be assigned to the Red Cross refugee program. From there, he secretly passed word through his contacts in the Ustashi that he would help defeated followers of what he still believed to be a just cause to escape retribution for what the Allies were calling war crimes.

He would do this for a fee – to assist the Church in its good works. The fee was the equivalent of the then considerable sum of two thousand dollars per fugitive. Only high-ranking Nazi officials were able to plunder enough to afford such a price. As a consequence, Father Pavelic's clients were among the most-hunted of war criminals, some of those directly responsible for the organization and perpetration of the Holocaust. Using Red Cross passports, Father Pavelic provided them with new identities and arranged for their safe passage to hiding places in South America, Mexico, the United States, Canada, and the Middle East. On occasion, he disguised his clients as priests, sequestered them in monasteries, waited until their hunters had lost the trail, and then used Vatican passports to expedite their escape.

But if his clients thought they'd heard the last of him when they reached safety, they were soon surprised to learn that he'd kept track of them – where they'd finally settled, how they earned their living – and demanded a yearly bonus payment from them in exchange for his silence. Failing that, he threatened he would expose them. He took a risk, he knew. If his clients refused to pay and he had to inform against them, those he'd betrayed would no doubt implicate him in their escape. But it never came to that; his clients were too afraid of being punished to refuse his demands. He took another risk as well – that his clients would try to kill him rather than pay their yearly tribute. To protect himself, he made sure they understood that the documents about them were carefully hidden. If he were killed, a trusted associate would receive instructions about where the papers were, with orders to relay them to the authorities.

His clients acquiesced. At first, their yearly payment was the same as what they'd paid initially – two thousand dollars. But as they prospered, Father Pavelic increased the amount. In total, he'd received millions. The money was not for his own use. He wasn't venal. Every penny was given to the Church, to support the Faith. With the power that the money gave him, and with his talent for bureaucratic intrigue, he managed to attract supporters within the Vatican. Other Curia members, who'd discovered the nature of his activities during and after the war, found that they too had to support him, for unless he was promoted, he threatened to embarrass the Church by implicating it in his rescue of Nazi war criminals. Here, too, he took a risk – his loyalty to the Church was such that he would never have created a scandal about it. But his enemies weren't aware of his scruples, and along with his supporters, they did promote him. By the age of thirty-five, he was both a cardinal and a junior member of the Church's

231

governing body. Five years after that, he became a senior member, one of those responsible for administering the Church's finances.

Saul, Drew, and Arlene learned all this from Father Dusseault. The priest's explanation wasn't coherent. They had to assemble the puzzle on their own. But when this portion of the interrogation was completed, they knew that Father Dusseault, a member of the Fraternity assigned to the Vatican, using the cover of Cardinal Pavelic's assistant, had become suspicious about the source of some of the funds the cardinal was contributing to the Church. Through resources available to him as a member of the Fraternity, Father Dusseault discovered the cardinal's secret. Outraged by the cardinal's participation in the Holocaust and his manipulation of the Church, Father Dusseault determined to see justice finally done.

27

Saul leaned even closer to Father Dusseault. Drew and Arlene had been told much of what they needed to know. Now it was his turn. *Where was Erika and her father?* The priest's story about Nazis and Jews made him more convinced than ever that he was close to the truth.

'What did you do about what you learned? How did you seek justice?'

'By telling the Jews.'

'What Jews? Who did you tell?'

'Mossad.'

'*Who* in the Mossad?'

'Ephraim Avidan.'

Saul's stunned reaction must have shown. Drew and Arlene looked at him in wonder.

Of course, he thought. They don't know about the cabin in the Alps that Erika and I visited. They don't know about the diary Avidan kept.

'Why did you choose him?' Saul asked.

'He'd been in a camp . . . Wanted someone who'd act.'

Saul understood. In recent years, Israel had been much less assiduous in tracking down war criminals, preferring instead to create an image of restraint and balance, of being superior to the methods of its enemies. Vengeance had been replaced by politics and the due process of law. Impatient, Father Dusseault had used the resources of the Fraternity to find a Mossad operative who hated the Nazis for persecuting his family and himself as well as his race, whose background guaranteed direct reprisal in place of bureaucratic paralysis.

'But Cardinal Pavelic discovered what you'd done?' Arlene asked.

'Threatened me. Had to shoot him.'

The cardinal's body had been cremated just as many of his victims had been, a prudent and appropriate method of disposing of the cardinal's remains. An investigation into the cardinal's disappearance

232

was less dangerous for Father Dusseault than an investigation into his murder.

'Did you kill Father Victor?' Drew asked.

Saul started to ask who Father Victor was, but Drew stopped him with a gesture.

'Yes.'

'Because he suspected you'd murdered the cardinal?' Drew asked.

'No.'

'Then why did you kill Father Victor?' Drew asked.

'Discovered my attempts to destroy the Fraternity.'

A further layer was revealed. The priest had come to despise the militant philosophy of the order to which be belonged, convinced that God wanted peacemakers, not warriors. As he'd felt obligated to cleanse the Church of Cardinal Pavelic's corruption, so he'd set out to excise the cancer of the Fraternity from the Church, sabotaging its operations whenever he could. When Father Victor, an investigator for the Fraternity, had become too suspicious, his quarry had been forced to shoot him during a late-night meeting in the Vatican gardens. The pistol had been equipped with a silencer. Nonetheless, its muffled noise had been heard by a guard who raised an alarm. Father Dusseault had to escape before he could dispose of the body as he had Cardinal Pavelic's. That explained why he'd chosen the greater silence of a knife when he'd gone after Drew in the gardens.

Saul was impatient. The priest had veered from what he needed to know. 'Does the name Joseph Bernstein mean anything to you?'

'No.'

'My wife followed you into the gardens. Did you have someone there with you, as a backup? Do you know why she would have disappeared?'

'No.'

Saul rubbed his temples. He stared at his watch. 'We've only got twenty minutes before Gallagher comes back to the other room,' he told Drew and Arlene. 'It's not enough time. How am I going to find out—?'

The phone rang, harsh. Saul flinched in surprise. 'If that's Gallagher . . .'

'He might have called his own room,' Arlene said. 'When he didn't get an answer, he called here.'

'Maybe,' Saul said. 'But I don't think Gallagher would have used the phone. He'd have come right up. Besides, it isn't time for him to check in. He promised me a full two hours.'

'It could be he had misgivings and changed his mind,' Drew said.

The phone kept ringing.

'Maybe it isn't Gallagher,' Saul said. 'Maybe it's—' He didn't say Erika, but her name screamed through his mind as he reached for the phone. 'Hello.'

'Saul Grisman?' The voice belonged to a man. It was thin, with a faint metallic edge like a knife being sharpened on a whetstone.

'Yes.'

'You must be distressed about your wife. No need to wonder any longer. We have her.'

'*We?* Who the hell—?'

Drew and Arlene stood rigidly straight.

'You surely don't expect us to reveal our names,' the voice said. 'All you need to know is that we have her and she's safe.'

'*How do I know that?*' Saul demanded. '*Let me talk to her.*'

'Unfortunately, that isn't possible. She isn't with me at the moment, and even if she were, she's been sedated. But you can see her.'

'*How?*'

'In fact,' the voice said, 'you can have her returned to you. If certain conditions are met. We'd like to arrange a trade. Your wife for the priest. You *do* have the priest, I hope. Otherwise there's no point to this conversation.'

'Yes. I have the priest.'

'We'd want to be sure of that. It wouldn't do to base your transaction on dishonesty. It would go very hard on your wife if you weren't completely honest.'

'I told you I've got him!' Saul said.

'At six o'clock this evening, bring him to the Colosseum. In the last hours before sunset, the ruins will still be crowded with tourists. Blend with them. Sit the priest down in the middle of the terraces on the northern side. I'll use binoculars from the opposite side to identify him. Make sure he's reasonably alert. I want to satisfy myself that he's capable of walking under his own power. But I don't want him so conscious that he'll make trouble. As soon as I'm sure you've brought the priest, I'll arrange for your wife to be placed across from you, on the southern terraces of the Colosseum. Bring binoculars, and assure yourself that she too is in satisfactory condition. When each of us sees what he wants, a man who appears to be a tourist will set a blue travel bag beside her and walk away. That will be the signal for us to make the trade. Approach your wife by circling to the right of the arena. I in turn will circle to your left. In this way, we'll never pass each other, and there won't be a risk of an unfortunate confrontation. Wait five minutes before leaving the Colosseum with your wife. I'd prefer not to rush getting the priest out of there.'

Saul gripped the phone so tightly he thought its plastic would crack. 'Agreed. At six o'clock.'

'There *is* one further condition.'

Saul began to sweat.

'In questioning your wife,' the voice said, 'I learned that she used to be an operative for the Mossad. Are they involved in this?'

'No.'

'You'd say that, no matter what. I have to be sure. It's imperative – your wife's safety depends upon it – that you don't bring help with you when the transfer is made. No associates of any kind. That includes the man and the woman who were dressed as a priest and a nun in the Vatican gardens last night. We know what they look like. If we see them, if we suspect any sign of surveillance, any attempt to interfere with the transaction, your wife will be killed. When I leave with the priest, if I sense I'm being followed, I can still arrange for her to die.'

Saul imagined a sniper hidden somewhere in the Colosseum, in two-way radio contact with the man he now spoke to. But he wasn't prepared for the tactic the voice described.

'A packet of explosive will be attached to your wife's back. I'll hide it under her jacket. The bomb will have a radio-controlled detonator whose electronic trigger will be in my pocket. As long as I'm within a mile of her, I'll be able to set the bomb off if I feel threatened. Don't fool yourself into thinking that all you have to do is remove the bomb from her and then betray me. The explosives will be held in place by a locked metal belt that's been wired in such a way that any attempt to remove it – by using metal clippers, for example – will blow her apart. Only when I'm out of radio range will the detonator be deactivated. Only then can the belt be safely cut off.'

Saul felt as if insects had invaded his chest. 'You seem to have thought of everything.'

'That's why I've stayed alive so long. Six o'clock. Don't try to be clever. Just do what you've been told.' With a click, the line was disconnected.

Saul set down the phone. He tried to keep his voice from shaking while he explained to Drew and Arlene.

Drew was briefly silent, assessing the information. At once he spoke with resolve. 'It's twenty after twelve. We've just got five minutes to take Father Dusseault back down to the other room before Gallagher shows up. You can question the priest for a while after that. But if he's supposed to be able to walk from the Colosseum, you'll have to stop giving him Sodium Amytal and let the drug wear off.'

'That's assuming Gallagher agrees to surrender the priest,' said Saul.

Arlene looked surprised. 'You think he might not?'

'Gallagher wants to learn everything he can about the Fraternity. He won't be happy about the deal I made. Suppose he thinks he can infiltrate a surveillance team into the Colosseum? Suppose he decides the threat about the bomb is a lie and figures he can get the priest back after the exchange? I won't bet Erika's life on someone else's tradecraft. And something else – I'm not supposed to have moved the priest. How am I going to explain to Gallagher where I got the phone call? I'd have to tell him I brought the priest here so the two of you could help question him. He'd learn about you.'

Drew glanced at Arlene. She nodded.

'Tell Gallagher,' Drew said. 'Your wife is more important than hiding us from Gallagher.'

Saul felt a surge of warmth. His voice was choked with feeling. 'I know how much your privacy means to you. I appreciate your gesture. Truly. More than I can say.'

'It's not just a gesture,' Drew said.

'But even if I did let Gallagher know about you, it wouldn't solve the problem. I still couldn't count on his keeping the bargain I made. I don't want his men at the Colosseum, and the only way I can guarantee they won't be there . . .'

'Is not to tell him?' Drew asked.

'We're going to have to steal the priest.'

Drew committed himself immediately, reacting as if he and Saul had been working together for years. 'Arlene, check the hallway. Make sure Gallagher isn't out there. Saul and I will carry Father Dusseault down the fire stairs. Get the car. Have it waiting for us outside.'

'But you'll be seen taking the priest from the hotel!'

'We'll pretend it's an emergency. We'll leave so fast no one'll have time to question us.'

28

When Icicle heard a knock on the door, he stood abruptly. He'd been staring at the unconscious woman on the bed, brooding about Seth's behavior. To kill as an automatic choice, without sufficient reason, was a sign of lack of control. It wasn't professional. It wasn't . . . He *likes* it, Icicle thought. That's what bothers me. The gleam he gets in his eyes. It's as if he's having . . .

Sex? That realization made Icicle remember the near fight he'd had with Seth to keep him from abusing the woman. Employing drugs or force to interrogate a prisoner was justified. But abusing this woman merely for the sake of self-gratification insulted Icicle's sense of dignity. Victims had a right not to be caused needless pain, not to be treated as objects.

Keep thinking about your father, he told himself. Nothing else . . . not the woman, not your principles . . . matter.

But he couldn't help noting that the conflict between Seth and himself was a replication of the lifelong enmity between their fathers. Was it happening all over again?

He checked the peephole, identified Seth, and freed the lock on the door. He felt uneasy about the packages Seth carried and the gleam in his eyes.

The gleam abruptly diminished when Seth glanced toward the bed. 'You dressed her.'

'She was shivering.'

'Shivering?' Seth's gleam returned. 'Since you feel so protective about her, I'm sure you'll be relieved to know that she'll be leaving us.'

'What do you mean?'

'When you interrogated her, she told us her husband's name and where they were staying in Rome,' Seth said.

Icicle nodded.

Seth put the packages on the bureau. 'I phoned her husband.'

'You *what?*'

'I've made arrangements to exchange her for the priest.' Seth opened the packages, revealing a fist-sized clump of plastic explosive

236

along with a radio-controlled detonator and transmitter. There were batteries, wires, a metal belt welded to a metal box, a lock.

'Where the hell did you get—?'

'One of my contacts here in Rome.' As Seth placed the explosive and the detonator in the metal box, he explained what he'd told the woman's husband.

Icicle's lips parted in astonishment. No wonder Seth didn't want to reveal why he was going out, he thought. I would never have agreed to the plan. 'It's too risky. Despite what the husband promised, there's bound to be a surveillance team.'

'With this bomb attached to her? If the husband loves her, he'll follow orders.' Seth removed a blasting cap from his lapel pocket, inserted it into the explosive and wired it to a post on the detonator. He took the remaining wire, attached one end to a contact on the metal belt and the other to a second post on the detonator. 'Once I put the batteries into the detonator and lock the belt, I've got a continuous electrical circuit. I'll close the metal box and wire the lid to the detonator. It's foolproof. If anyone opens the box to get at the detonator, the circuit will be broken. A switch on the detonator will engage another set of batteries that automatically triggers the bomb. The same thing will happen if someone unlocks the belt or snips it apart. Of course, the other way to detonate the bomb is by using this.' He held up the radio-controlled transmitter.

Icicle watched him with loathing, troubled by a discrepancy between Seth's explanation and what he claimed to have told the husband. 'Once you're out of radio range, the bomb can be dismantled?'

'No way.'

'But you told the husband . . .'

'I lied.' Seth slid the belt around the woman's waist and locked it. He inserted two sets of batteries into the detonator, closed the metal box's lid on the bare end of a wire attached to the detonator, and locked the lid. He smiled. 'The only way to get this thing off her now is to blow the bitch up. How, my friend, do you feel about *that*?'

Critical
Mass

Toronto, Canada. 6:30 A.M. The sun had just risen. Exhausted, Joseph Bernstein told the taxi driver to let him off at the next corner. He'd directed the driver to one of the few decaying sections of the city. Soon to be purged by urban renewal, ill-maintained two-story houses lined the street. Bernstein paid the driver and gave him a tip neither so large nor so small that the driver would remember. The moment the taxi was out of sight, Bernstein tested his weary body's resources by walking one block south and two blocks east. He felt the way the worst houses looked. Lights were on in some of them, but he passed no one on the street, only a stray dog tearing apart a bulging plastic garbage bag. In the middle of the final block, he turned onto a cracked concrete sidewalk that led to a listing front porch. All the windows in the house were dark. An empty beer can lay on its side to the right of the top of the steps – the signal that everything was as it should be. He knocked three times on the front door, waited while a curtain was pushed aside, then stepped in when the door was opened.

Ephraim Avidan quickly closed the door and locked it, only then placing the Beretta he held into a shoulder holster beneath his rumpled suitcoat. 'You had no problems?'

'Everything's on schedule. What about the others?'

'Upstairs asleep. We take turns, two at a time standing guard.'

'No, I meant the *others*,' Bernstein said. 'Have you had any problems with them?'

'They take orders well.' Avidan's mouth showed a trace of a bitter smile. 'The sedatives in their food help.'

'I want to see them.'

'Your stomach must be stronger than mine. I despise them so much I try to see them as little as possible.'

'I want to remind myself.'

'As you wish.' Avidan led him down a narrow corridor into a shadowy kitchen whose linoleum tile was peeling at the edges. He knocked three times on a warped plywood door, unlocked and opened it, then stepped back.

Bernstein peered down musty steps toward a concrete floor the color of a bullet. A pale light at the bottom revealed a tall, bearded man of about seventy who wore a thick pullover sweater and stared up anxiously, holding a Beretta as Avidan had. Seeing Bernstein, the man lowered his pistol.

When Bernstein reached the bottom, he put his arms around the man. David Gehmer was one of the most dependable, long-suffering members of the team. For the past four months, he – along with Gideon Levine – had endured without complaint the tedious, disagreeable task of acting as jailer. One by one, captives had been brought here from around the world – all told, eleven of them by now – imprisoned in the basement of this dilapidated house in Toronto. Yesterday, the other members of the team, having completed their tasks, had converged here as well and were asleep now in the upper floors of the house.

Bernstein scanned the large cellar. Its windows had been boarded over. Spaced equally apart, three bare lights dangled from the ceiling. White slabs of plastic insulation had been attached to the walls to minimize dampness. Nonetheless, the room felt cold and clammy. Bernstein understood why, even in June, David Gehmer wore a sweater.

The walls were lined with cots, eleven of them, upon each of which an old man lay covered with a woolen blanket. Some were awake, their eyes dazed by the lingering effects of the sedation in last night's supper. Most were deeply asleep. All were pale from lack of exposure to the sun. All were handcuffed. A chain led from each cuff to a ring bolted into the wall.

A few books and magazines lay next to each cot. Against a narrow wall at the far end of the room, shelves of plates and tinned food stood next to a small gas stove near an unshielded toilet.

'It's quite an assembly line,' Bernstein said drily. 'All the comforts of home.'

'By comparison with Auschwitz, this is the promised land,' Gehmer said. 'I shave each of them every other day. I cook all their meals. I make them take turns, cuffed to the sink, doing the cleanup. They're only allowed to use plastic spoons. I count the spoons after every meal. When they have to go to the toilet, I let them go one at a time, chained to the sink again. That's when they're allowed to wash up.'

'Yes, you've organized them remarkably.'

'They inspired me. These monsters had a special talent for organization, after all. Sometimes I remember so vividly I think I'm back in the camp. I want to . . .' Gehmer raised his pistol and aimed it at the nearest prisoner.

Bernstein touched Gehmer's hand. 'Patience, my friend. We both have nightmares. But we won't have to endure them much longer. Soon justice will be served.'

'*Soon?*' Gehmer spoke quickly. '*When?*'

'Tomorrow.'

2

'Joseph surfaced again.'

Misha Pletz, intent upon rechecking the plans for tonight's

Operation Salvage, needed a moment before he realized what his assistant had said to him. 'Surfaced?'

'Two hours ago.'

'Where? Still in Washington?'

'No. Toronto this time.'

'*Toronto?*'

'He contacted another of our operatives,' the assistant said. 'The same as before. He chose one of his former students. It was four-thirty in the morning there. Joseph showed up at the man's apartment, woke him, and gave him a message to relay to you. The operative had it coded and radioed here to Tel Aviv.'

Misha held out his hand for the piece of paper his assistant clutched, but when he read it, he was baffled. 'Two names?'

'Aaron Rosenberg. Richard Halloway.' The assistant handed Misha a second piece of paper. 'This is the operative's summary of the verbal instructions Joseph gave him. They're related to his previous message – the arms shipment he warned us was being sent to the Libyans to be used against us. Joseph says when you stop the shipment tonight he wants you to leak those names to the Libyans but not in a way that'll make them suspect it's a leak. He wants you to make it seem as if the two men accepted money from us in exchange for information about the shipment.'

'But if the Libyans believe the leak, they'll want revenge.' Misha stared at the paper in bewilderment. 'We'd be setting them up to be killed. Why does Joseph want—?'

'Rosenberg and Halloway are the arms dealers responsible for the shipment.'

'He wants to make it look as if they accepted money from and then doublecrossed the Libyans? He wants Rosenberg and Halloway punished by the people they were working for? Some crazy sense of justice? Why didn't Joseph give us these names in his first message? Why did he wait until—?' Misha paused; an explanation occurred to him. 'Because he didn't want to give us time to check on them before we stopped the shipment? Is there another time limit we don't know about, another schedule Joseph is following?'

The assistant pointed toward the last paragraph of the report. 'He made it a point of honor. The price for Joseph telling us about the shipment is we have to leak the names to the Libyans.'

3

Saul waited anxiously with Father Dusseault in a recess of one of the middle terraces at the northern side of the Colosseum. The priest was able to walk, but he was still groggy enough to be passive, easily guided. He'd made no trouble when Saul had brought him here and sat him down. The many tourists paid no attention to the infirm priest.

Saul had arrived fifteen minutes early for the six o'clock appointment, and now it was ten minutes after. He used his binoculars to scan the opposite side of the Colosseum, worried that the exchange would not take place. As instructed, he'd come here alone with Father Dusseault. But terribly conscious of the sun setting lower, he cursed himself for disobeying one condition of the exchange by allowing Drew and Arlene to watch the Colosseum from the gardens of the Esquiline across the street. The Esquiline, one of the seven hills of Rome, was dominated by Nero's palace, the so-called Golden House, and the sightseers swarming through both it and the surrounding park made the chances of an enemy spotting Drew and Arlene highly unlikely. It had seemed prudent to take the slight risk.

But now he wished he hadn't permitted the violation. Because by twenty after six he was sure that something was wrong. The number of tourists began to dwindle. A woman with blue-tinted hair stepped in front of Saul, obscuring his gaze through the binoculars. Her overweight husband joined her, listening to her complain about the high-heeled shoes he shouldn't have let her wear.

Saul stepped to the right, to reestablish his view of the opposite terraces. Scanning them, he suddenly froze the binoculars on a woman sitting on a walkway, her back against a wall. Saul had trouble steadying his hands on the binoculars. Erika? Even magnified, the woman wasn't distinct, her head drooping toward her chest. But her hair was long and dark like Erika's, and she seemed to be the same age, to have the same long legs and lithe body. What confused him was that this woman wore a green nylon jacket, which Erika did not possess.

Abruptly he remembered the voice on the phone telling him that Erika would wear a jacket to hide the bomb secured to her. When a man strolled over to her and set down a blue travel bag, Saul realized that the exchange was about to take place. With his binoculars, he tracked the tall pale man who'd left the travel bag and was moving to Saul's left. At once, the man stopped and raised his own binoculars, aiming them at Saul.

He's waiting for me to start circling in the other direction, Saul thought. He won't move until I do.

Saul didn't need encouragement. He left the priest sitting in the recess of the terrace and walked rapidly to the right. It took all his self-control not to run. For a moment, though, he almost faltered as the significance of something about the man occurred to him.

The color of his hair. *It was red.*

Dear God, had the voice on the phone belonged to *Seth*? The assassin, the son of a *Nazi* assassin, whom Drew and Arlene had described? If so, would his partner, the blond-haired Icicle, be in the Colosseum with him?

Saul didn't dare turn to scan the crowd. The gesture might disturb Seth into blowing Erika up as he'd threatened. Besides, at the moment Seth didn't matter. Nor did Icicle. Only Erika did. Rounding the curve of the Colosseum, approaching its southern side, he quickened his steps, his gaze focused anxiously on Erika. She continued to sit with her head drooped toward her chest. He hadn't seen her shift position. Had Seth reneged on his bargain? Was *Erika dead*?

He zigzagged through clusters of tourists, ignoring their angry objections, too distraught to murmur apologies. He was thirty yards from Erika now, and she still hadn't moved. He started running. Twenty yards. No sign of life. He reached her. When he raised her face and saw her eyelids flutter, he sank to his knees, almost weeping with relief.

'Erika, it's me. It's Saul.' He put his arms around her.

And froze when he felt the metal box under the back of the rainjacket. Moving his hands to her waist, he touched the metal belt that secured the box to her. Seth hadn't been bluffing.

Saul swung to stare toward the opposite side of the Colosseum. Seth had reached the priest, had lifted him to his feet, and was guiding him along a walkway toward an exit. The priest moved groggily. A few tourists glanced at him, but most were preoccupied with their cameras and the sunset-tinted ruins. At the exit, Seth turned toward Saul, raised his right arm, almost in an ancient Roman salute, his gesture ironic. Then Seth and Father Dusseault were gone.

Wait five minues before leaving, Seth had instructed.

Five minutes it would be.

He turned to Erika, hugging her again. 'It's Saul,' he repeated. 'You're safe.' He kissed her. 'I love you. We've got nothing to worry about.'

4

Among shadows caused by sunset, Drew and Arlene watched from the Oppian Park to the east of Nero's palace. Their view of the Colosseum was impeded by the busy traffic on the Via Labicana, but even the frustration of an obstructed view was better than the greater frustration they'd have felt if they'd stayed away.

With only the northern and eastern curves of the Colosseum available to them, they probably would not see Father Dusseault and his captor, Drew realized. Still, the Via Labicana was the most likely escape route, and for that reason, he concentrated less on the Colosseum and more on the street leading away from it.

He checked his watch. Twenty-five minutes after six. The exchange was scheduled to have occurred on the hour. Unless something had gone wrong, a no-show for example, they'd probably missed seeing Father Dusseault being led away.

All the same, Drew kept staring toward the opposite side of the street. If he still didn't spot the priest by seven o'clock, he and Arlene would go to a nearby phone booth where, by prearrangement, Saul would call to report.

He felt Arlene grip his arm. On the other side of the street, a priest – *Father Dusseault* – was being guided through a crowd of tourists emerging from the Colosseum. A gray Citroën veered from traffic and

242

stopped at the curb. The priest was pushed inside onto the backseat, his abductor following. The Citroën sped away.

The pickup had taken no more than ten seconds, but even with the distraction of tourists and traffic, Drew had seen enough. There was no mistaking the red-haired man guiding the priest or the blond man driving the Citroën. *Seth and Icicle.* He bolted from Arlene's grasp, charging toward the street. Arlene ran after him. There was still a risk that Seth and Icicle had posted a surveillance team to watch for any attempt to follow the Citroën. In that case, if they noticed Drew and Arlene in pursuit, all the team had to do was contact the Citroën via two-way radio, and Seth or Icicle might make good on their threat to blow up Erika. But Drew was convinced that there wasn't a surveillance team. After all, Seth and Icicle hadn't arranged for help when they grabbed Medici, and the efficiency of that operation made Drew strongly suspect they trusted no one but themselves.

The Citroën was far enough down the street that he couldn't see it. That meant Seth and Icicle couldn't see Drew either as he darted through speeding traffic. He gestured frantically to a passing taxi. Arlene raced across the street to him, reaching the curb as the taxi responded to Drew's waving arms. They scrambled inside.

Drew blurted instructions to the driver. If only we don't get caught in traffic, he worried. If only Seth and Icicle don't take a side street before I see where they turn. He wondered whether Saul had gotten Erika back and fervently prayed that his friend's wife was safe.

5

'What took you so long?' Driving, Icicle glanced quickly toward the backseat. 'Did something go wrong?'

'I scouted the ruins before I showed myself. The husband followed instructions exactly. I couldn't be more pleased.'

'Well, *I* won't be pleased till we get out of here. What if the other man and woman are hanging around?'

'Even if they are,' Seth said, 'they'll keep their distance. They know I can still use this.' He held up the detonator. 'All that remains is to question the priest. They wouldn't have abducted him unless they were certain he had vital information.'

'But perhaps not the information we want.'

'What reason would they have to question the priest, except to learn about the cardinal? He's the only outsider who knew where our fathers were. Once we find out why he disappeared, we'll know how the Night and Fog discovered our fathers.' Seth grinned. 'Yes, all that remains is to question him. But on second thought, perhaps not all. Pull over.'

'We have to get away from here. Why do you—?'

'*Do it. Stop.*'

Icicle obeyed, halting at the curb. 'Tell me why—'

'I can't resist the temptation.' Seth peered through the Citroën's rear window toward the Colosseum. 'Of course, I won't be able to see the explosion, but I'll hear it.' He shrugged. 'The commotion among the tourists should be interesting.' He flicked a switch to activate the radio-controlled detonator. A red light glowed.

'No,' Icicle said.

Seth turned. 'You still feel protective about her?' His eyes gleamed.

He's doing this to taunt me, Icicle realized. Not to punish the woman but *me*.

'What's the point? You told me you'd lied to the husband. In a while, when we're out of radio range, he'll think it's safe to disconnect the bomb without setting it off. Since she'll die soon anyhow, why kill her now?'

'Do I sense you hoping that the husband will find a way to remove the bomb without setting it off?'

'What would be the harm if he did? The drug kept her from seeing us. She can't identify—'

'The harm,' Seth said, 'is to my pleasure. Why should this woman, a stranger, matter to you?'

'Why should she matter to *you*? She isn't a threat to us. She doesn't have to die.'

'But she does, my friend. To teach you a lesson. *Never interfere with me again.*' Seth aimed a finger toward the detonator.

Even then, Icicle might not have acted if it hadn't been for the cruel look Seth gave him. Rage broke Icicle's control. Like a tightly wound spring suddenly released, he flicked the switch to deactivate the detonator and yanked it out of Seth's hand. His movement was so forceful he ripped a flap of skin from one of Seth's fingers.

Seth's face contorted when he saw his own blood. 'Give the detonator back.'

'We've got too much at risk for you to delay. We'll settle this later when we get away from here.'

'*We'll settle it now.*'

In a blur, Seth drew a pistol. It had a silencer on the barrel, but even so, the confines of the Citroën made the muffled shot feel as if hands had slammed Icicle's ears. The moment he saw the weapon, he twisted away and took the bullet intended for his chest through the flesh of his upper left arm. The projectile exited from his arm and slammed against the dashboard. Icicle ignored the shock of pain and lunged again, deflecting the pistol's aim before Seth could fire a second time. They struggled for possession of the gun.

Blood dripped from Icicle's arm. Despite his force of will, his weakened biceps were no match for Seth. Inexorably the pistol's barrel shifted toward Icicle's face.

Seth's lips curled. 'I should have killed you before. The same as I did your father.'

Icicle's eyes widened. '*Killed my father?*' Perhaps Seth had hoped that the statement would distract him, make him falter sufficiently for Seth to move the pistol the last few inches toward Icicle's face. If so, Seth miscalculated. Instead of faltering, Icicle screamed insanely and, with a savage burst of strength, he rammed the pistol back toward

244

Seth's face, cracking the silencer against Seth's forehead. Seth's eyes lost focus.

Icicle scrambled over the seat, punching Seth's mouth. 'You bastard, what do you mean you killed my father?' He punched Seth's lips a second time, mangling them. 'Tell me!' he shouted, yanking the pistol out of Seth's hand. Just as he twisted it around to put his finger on the trigger, a taxi stopped behind the Citroën, its doors flying open. Icicle saw the man and the woman who'd been dressed as a priest and a nun in the Vatican gardens.

Seth struck Icicle in the stomach. Doubling over, Icicle felt Seth grab for the pistol, but Seth didn't get a firm hold, and the gun thumped onto the floor. Outside, the man and the woman were running toward the Citroën. With no time to do anything but obey his instincts, Icicle pivoted, grabbed the detonator off the front seat, shoved open the curbside door, and raced into the crowd. His wounded arm hurt terribly. He heard a muffled shot. A window shattered. Pedestrians scattered, screaming.

6

When Drew saw the gray Citroën stopped ahead at the side of the street, he yelled for the taxi driver to pull over. Through the rear window of the Citroën, he saw two men struggling with each other. For an instant, he thought one of them was Father Dusseault, now sufficiently alert to put up a fight. But then he saw the blond and red hair of the two men grappling for what appeared to be a gun and realized that Icicle and Seth were trying to kill each other.

Their struggle was so intense, their distraction so great, Drew realized they wouldn't notice until he and Arlene were in position to overpower them. The taxi stopped. Drew darted out, followed by Arlene, racing toward the Citroën.

But Icicle's rugged face turned abruptly in their direction. His look of shocked comprehension was replaced by one of pain as Seth punched him in the stomach. In quick succession, Icicle grabbed something from the Citroën's front seat and lunged from the car just as Seth picked up an object from the rear floor, gaped at Drew and Arlene, who were about to reach the Citroën, and raised a pistol, firing.

The rear window shattered. Pedestrians screamed. Drew and Arlene dove to the street. Drew hadn't wanted to alarm the taxi driver by showing his handgun earlier, but now he pulled it out, prepared to return fire. The detonator, he kept thinking. Have to get the detonator. But he now identified the object that Icicle had grabbed from the front seat before rushing out of the Citroën. He could see the small rectangular control in Icicle's right hand as the blond assassin surged through the scattering crowd. At the same time, he noticed the stream of blood on Icicle's left arm.

Flat on the street, Drew shifted his attention back toward the Citroën, aiming at the shattered rear window. The moment Seth

245

showed himself, Drew was prepared to pull the trigger. But Seth stayed low, charging out the open curbside door and racing into the crowd. Powerless, Drew couldn't shoot without hitting bystanders. He watched Seth escaping.

Or *was* he escaping? Seth didn't seem to want to get away so much as to chase after Icicle. The blond man ran along the Via Labicana and veered to the right, disappearing around a corner. Holding his pistol, the red-haired assassin sprinted after him.

What had happened to turn them into enemies? Drew wondered.

He stared into the Citroën. The priest was slumped across the backseat. 'Arlene, get him out of here. Make sure you're not followed. Take him back to the hotel.'

'But what about—?'

Drew shouted as he ran. 'I'm going after them!'

7

The son of a bitch is coming after me! Icicle thought. Even when he's almost cornered, he still wants to kill me!

Icicle hadn't even been aware that he'd grabbed the detonator as he ran from the Citroën. The gesture had been reflexive. Only when he reached for the pistol wedged behind his belt beneath the back of his jacket did he realize that he was holding something in his right hand. The detonator. He switched it to his blood-smeared left hand, pulled out his pistol, and darted right off the Via Labicana.

He expected Seth to shoot at him, but not to kill, at least not right away. Seth would want to bring him down, disarm him, and make him watch the detonator being pushed. A few blocks away from the Colosseum, they would be able to hear the blast. Only then, having gained the maximum pleasure from his victory, would Seth kill Icicle and still have time to escape.

It didn't have to be this way! Icicle raged. *If it hadn't been for the woman, we wouldn't have argued! Seth wouldn't have told me he'd murdered my father! We'd be safely out of here! The woman means nothing to me! Why did I protect her from him?*

Another thought was equally distressing. Seth's arrogance, his pride and hate, had such control of him that, in taunting Icicle, he'd lost the chance to question the priest and find his father.

He's more insane than I imagined.

Racing down the side street, Icicle felt an excruciating jolt against the back of his right shoulder. The impact threw him off balance, twisting him to the right, almost shoving him to the pavement. Blood sprayed ahead of him. The muscles along his right arm refused to obey his mental commands; his hand opened involuntarily. His pistol clattered onto the sidewalk. Still able to make his wounded other arm respond, he clutched the detonator to his chest and ran with greater determination. But his loss of blood had weakened him. His vision blurred. His legs became wobbly. He hadn't heard the spit of Seth's

246

silenced weapon. He didn't expect to hear it the next time either, but he had no doubt that Seth would aim toward one of his legs.

I'm too easy a target. Have to get off this side street. Find a place to hide.

Ahead, to his right, Icicle saw a structure that took up half the block and whose shadow filled the street. An ancient church! He rushed unevenly toward it. At that moment, Seth fired, his bullet missing Icicle's leg, smacking against concrete twenty feet ahead.

Arms throbbing, Icicle realized he was too exposed, too likely to be shot if he went up the steps to the huge main entrance to the church. He hurried forward, his face dripping sweat. In pain, he came to an intersection and veered toward the right once more.

But along this further street, he saw a side entrance to the church. A sign said St Clement's Basilica. Seth rounded the corner, about to aim. With no other possibility of escape, Icicle lurched toward the church's small side door, mustering strength to shove it open.

Inside, he slammed the door and tried to lock it, but there wasn't a bolt to slide into place, only a slot for a key. Whirling, he raced onward, finding himself in a massive chamber that stretched to his right and left. Frescoes of Christ and the apostles lined the walls. Two aisles were broken up by towering columns. A guide appeared, telling him that the basilica was closed to tourists after six-thirty. Icicle scurried past him, sensing rather than seeing the altar far to his left.

His impulse was to hide in what appeared to be the sacristy across from him, but the tour guide kept objecting to his presence, and when he heard the side door bang open, he knew that the guide would attract Seth to him.

I've got to find somewhere else to hide.

To the right of the sacristy, stairs descended. He started down them just as the side door slammed shut and Seth's footsteps echoed urgently after him. It was possible that Seth hadn't seen him, but he couldn't fail to see the trail of blood.

He came to a landing, turned right to descend another tier of stairs, and groaned not only from pain but also from desperation when he saw that he'd entered a long empty corridor. He heard Seth's footsteps coming nearer and rushed lower toward a door along the right side of the corridor. He entered yet another basilica.

The must of fourteen hundred centuries swelled his nostrils. Pale lights fought to dispel the darkness. But the ancient shadows couldn't hide him, not with the blood from his arms dripping across the floor. He staggered past faded frescoes depicting a Roman nobleman and his servants, all of whom had apparently been blinded by the aura of a holy man, and heard Seth's footsteps charging down the stairwell.

He stared toward the left of the altar toward an exit. *If I can get through it before Seth takes another shot at me, maybe I can find a way to surprise him. He's so confident, he might not expect me to attack.*

Quit kidding yourself. You don't have the strength. You've lost your pistol.

But I've got a knife.

He flinched as a bullet spattered pieces of fresco from a wall. Seth's footsteps rushed closer. But at once the tour guide entered this lower basilica, shouting at them. Seth shot the man. Hearing the body fall, Icicle could barely breathe.

By the time Seth aimed again toward the front of the church, Icicle had reached the exit to the left of the altar. He rushed through, hearing a bullet crack against a wall behind him, and saw only more stairs. Even older than the lower church that he'd just left, these stairs led down as well. There was no other choice – he had to follow them.

A landing. A turn to the right. He passed a sign that said Mithraeum and stumbled into an eerie underground structure that might have dated back to the birth of the Catholic Church. Directly below the altar of the lower basilica, the remnants of two Roman houses had been joined to form a temple, but the temple was, astonishingly, not Christian but pagan. Beyond two parallel stone benches that reminded Icicle of pews, there stood a statue of the Roman god Mithras. The center of the temple was taken up by an altar upon which another statue of the god – clean-shaven, resplendently handsome – performed some kind of sacred rite by slicing open the throat of a bull. A dog, a scorpion, and a serpent were trying to kill the bull before Mithras could complete the sacrifice.

In the time it took him to scan the temple, he realized he was trapped. He heard Seth scramble down the lower stairs and chose the only possible hiding place: behind the altar. His blood pooled on the ancient stone floor almost as if blood from the bull's slit throat were streaming off the altar down to him. Putting the detonator into a pocket, he used his more mobile left hand to withdraw a knife from a sheath strapped above his right ankle. He held his breath, wiped sweat from his face, quivered with pain, and waited.

Seth stalked into the temple. 'Blood hides no secrets. I know where you are.' His shoes scraped on the ancient stone floor. His shadow loomed over the altar.

Icicle peered up toward the red-haired man, whose punched lips were swollen, crusted with blood. Seth's eyes had never been brighter.

'The detonator.' Seth held out his hand.

'I hid it before I came down here.'

'Then you won't mind if I search you.' Seth stepped closer.

Icicle squirmed backward.

'Give it to me,' Seth said, 'and maybe I won't kill you.'

'You'll kill me, all right. But not until after you force me to watch you press the button.'

'Our few days together have been like a long-term marriage, I see. You've learned to understand me.' Seth stepped even closer. 'Give me the detonator.'

Icicle continued backward. 'You'll have to take it.'

Seth shook his head. 'What I'll do is shoot you again, in the stomach this time, before I come closer. You'd live to see me press the button, but you wouldn't have the strength to attack.' Seth raised his pistol.

Icicle's mind raced, desperate to think of a way to distract his opponent. 'Did you mean what you said in the car?'

Seth hesitated.

'Did you really kill my father?' Icicle asked.

'Would I lie when the truth is so satisfying? Of course, I killed him.'

'*Why?*'

'It was Halloway's idea to bring you into this. I told him I didn't need help, but Halloway insisted. The trouble was, your father hadn't disappeared. Mind you, he might have been next on the list, but I didn't want to use up valuable time waiting for it to happen. So I got my hands on him myself.' Seth's mangled lips formed a smile. 'I did it at your dive shop in Australia. Used a silencer. Shot your father and your salesclerk while you were meeting with Halloway's emissary. I wrapped your father's body in a tarpaulin and loaded him into the trunk of my car. Did it in plain sight of everyone on the beach. No one paid attention. Does anyone *ever* pay attention? Went back to the shop and set fire to it. Drove away. I might as well have been invisible.'

Icicle wanted to vomit. 'What did you do with the body?'

'Rented a boat. Took it out to sea. Let the sharks have a feast.'

Icicle made a choking sound.

'The body had to disappear,' Seth said, 'to make it seem as if the Night and Fog was responsible. So you'd join us and help look for the rest of our fathers.'

'What about Halloway's emissary? Why did *he* disappear?'

'I waited for him at his hotel. Identified myself. Took him for a drive. Shot him. Fed him to the sharks the same as I did your father. The theory was that if he too disappeared you'd think Halloway had something to do with the disappearances. I wanted to force you to seek out Halloway . . .'

'And when I did, like a fool I let both of you convince me you were innocent. I joined you.'

'And proved of some help, I admit, when it came to grabbing Medici. But really,' Seth said, 'Halloway was wrong – I didn't need you. We could never have gotten along. Your father stole the woman my father loved. Your mother could have been *my* mother. *You* would never have been born. If my father's still alive, if I can manage to find him, I'm sure he'll be overjoyed to learn that I killed both his enemy and the *son* of his enemy. It's ironic, don't you think? Like our fathers, we fell out over a woman. Give me the detonator. I promise your death will be quick after you watch me push the button.'

Loss of blood made Icicle sleepy. *Concentrate*, he told himself. *Don't let the bastard win.* 'Your word?' he asked. 'You'll kill me cleanly?' He raised his almost useless right arm to point toward the soft spot behind his right ear.

'You have my promise.'

With the same arm, Icicle reached in his pocket and took out the detonator, holding it out to his enemy.

'Set it on the floor. Slide it over to me,' Seth said.

'Too weak.'

'I don't think so.'

His heart sinking in despair, Icicle did what he was told, hearing the detonator scrape across the stone floor.

'Excellent.' Seth stooped to pick up the detonator. He shifted his gaze from Icicle only for a second.

That second would be the only chance Icicle got. He whipped his agonized left arm from behind his back and threw the knife with all his remaining strength.

Seth jerked his head up. With a curse, his eyes fierce, he aimed. Not soon enough. The knife struck his throat, the blade entering his Adam's apple, splitting it. The tip made an obscene scraping sound against his neckbone. The handle's guard stopped against fractured cartilage.

Seth stumbled backward, his face twisting in shock, his skin almost chalk white in contrast with the crimson spewing from his throat. The massive trauma to his Adam's apple would cause swelling that would shut off the passage of air to his lungs, Icicle knew. He'd die from asphyxiation before he bled to death. But he wouldn't die instantly.

Icicle watched horrified as Seth squinted at him. You think you've won, his eyes seemed to say. But you haven't. I still have the strength to shoot you again. We'll *both* die. But not before you watch me do *this*.

Seth grasped the detonator and flicked the activation switch.

Icicle screamed, scrambling to stop him, but slipped and fell in the pool of his blood.

Seth staggered back out of reach and lowered a finger toward a button.

A shadow lunged from the stairwell, the man who'd been dressed as a priest in the Vatican gardens. The stranger yanked the detonator from Seth's grasp at the same time that he twisted the pistol away from him.

Seth turned toward his sudden assailant. Wheezing, he tries to remove the knife from his throat, but the stranger rammed the butt of the knife so the blade reentered Seth's throat. The impact made the knife twist sideways, widening the gap in Seth's Adam's apple. Crimson gushed. Spastic, Seth lurched from the force of the blow. He fell against the statues on the altar, turned to grab them for support, slid down, and collapsed unmoving upon the floor. His blood trickled over the knife Mithras held to the throat of the bull.

Icicle had not yet adjusted to the sudden arrival of the stranger, who now flicked off the switch of the detonator and stalked toward him, aiming Seth's pistol. The stranger's expression was a combination of disgust and fury.

'Get me out of here,' Icicle said, 'before the authorities arrive. We don't have much time. If you help me, *I'll* help you.' Delirium made his thoughts drift. He fought to steady them. 'I'll tell you anything you want to know. My father's dead. This isn't my fight any longer. Halloway has to be punished.'

250

'Halloway? Who's Halloway?'

'For God's sake, get me out of here. The woman we kidnapped from the gardens. Seth rigged explosives to her.'

'I know that.'

'But her husband thinks he can safely remove the bomb if we're out of radio range. Seth lied. The bomb'll go off if the husband tries to disconnect the wires.'

The stranger spoke urgently. 'Can you walk?'

'I think so.' Icicle almost fainted from pain when the stranger helped him up.

The stranger put his jacket over Icicle's shoulders. 'It'll hide the blood.'

Icicle leaned against the stranger and, through a haze, stumbled from the temple. The next thing he knew, he was in the subterranean basilica. He didn't remember going up the final group of stairs or crossing the upper basilica. He only knew that he was outside, that the last rays of sunset were blinding, that a police siren's wail was approaching.

'Walk faster,' the stranger said, supporting him.

They reached a corner and turned in the direction opposite to the siren.

At another corner, they turned again.

And again. Disoriented, Icicle had the sense of wandering through a maze. 'I don't think I can stand up much longer.'

'We're almost there.'

A park to the south of the Arch of Constantine, Icicle saw. In the dimming blaze of sunset, tourists milled through the area, admiring the carvings on the monument. The stranger set him on the ground against a tree. Given the emergency, the cover was perfect, Icicle realized. As long as I don't bleed through the jacket he slipped over my shoulders, I won't attract attention.

'Stay here. I'll be back,' the stranger said.

'Tell the woman's husband not to try to remove the bomb.'

But the stranger had already disappeared through the crowd.

8

'Damn it, Romulus, I warned you not to jerk me around. Where the hell's the priest? I promised you two hours alone with him. I come back, and the room's deserted. Nothing's on the fucking tape recorder.' Gallagher pounded a fist into his hand.

The station chief had been pacing angrily in the hotel room when Saul brought Erika back there. Saul had hoped to see Drew and Arlene, not Gallagher. He'd waited outside the Colosseum, expecting his friends to emerge from the park across from the ruins. When they hadn't come, he'd tried to call them where they should have been waiting at the prearranged contact site, a pay phone. But the first time no one had answered, and the second time a strident woman had asked if he was Luigi and why was he keeping her waiting. By then, it was after 7 P.M., the deadline for contact. Filled with misgivings, he'd decided that the hotel room was the only other place where Drew and Arlene would know they could get in touch with him. Besides, the hotel room would give him the privacy he needed to remove the explosives from Erika's back. Guiding her, he'd hailed a taxi and returned to the hotel as quickly as possible.

But now, in addition to his other pressures, he had to deal with Gallagher.

'The priest doesn't matter,' Saul said. 'I've got my wife back. That's all I care about.'

'You're telling me the priest is gone because you traded him?'

'Yes! And I'd do it again! I questioned him, don't worry! I'll keep my bargain! I've got plenty to tell you! But not before I deal with this!' Saul slipped the rainjacket off Erika, showing Gallagher the metal box attached to the belt at her spine.

Gallagher started. 'Jesus Christ, it's a bomb.'

Erika murmured something unintelligible; gradually the effects of the drug were lessening. Saul sat her on the bed and studied the apparatus secured to her. 'I'll have to break the lock or cut the belt. But the belt's wired to the box. The whole thing – lock, belt and box – forms a continuous electrical circuit.'

'Then the bomb might be rigged to go off if the circuit's broken.'

'Seth told me it was safe to take it off as soon as he was out of radio range.'

'Seth? Who the hell is Seth?'

'I'll explain later. First I have to—' Saul reached toward the wires, stiffening when he heard a knock on the door. He swung his troubled gaze toward the sound.

Gallagher went to answer it.

'No! Wait!' Saul said. He suspected Drew and Arlene were in the corridor, and he didn't want Gallagher to see them.

'What's the problem, Romulus? Another secret?'

Gallagher opened the door; Saul's suspicion had been half-correct. Arlene stood out there, supporting the groggy priest.

'Who the hell are *you*?' Gallagher demanded.

Saul slumped into a chair.

Arlene held back for a moment, then acquiesced when Gallagher tugged her and Father Dusseault into the room.

'Romulus, who *is* this woman?' Gallagher insisted, locking the door.

'A friend.'

'That's not a good enough explanation.'

'It's all you need to know. You've got the priest back. That's what you wanted, isn't it? Thank her. Don't ask questions about who she is.'

Arlene brought the priest to the bed and laid him down on the side away from Erika.

'The priest back?' Gallagher said. 'No, that *isn't* what I wanted.'

'I wish you'd make up your mind.'

'I don't want *him*. I want what he *knows*. After I learn about the Fraternity, the sooner I'm rid of him the better.'

'He killed Cardinal Pavelic. He's been trying to sabotage the Fraternity. What's more, he can tell you where to find a dozen or more Nazi war criminals.'

Gallagher's mouth opened in surprise.

Saul turned to Arlene. 'I'm glad to see you again. When I couldn't make contact . . . How did you get the priest back? Drew? Where's Drew?'

'He went after Seth and Icicle,' she said.

'Icicle?' Gallagher looked even more mystified. 'Drew?'

Saul and Arlene ignored him.

'Your wife?' Arlene asked. 'Is she all right?'

'Still groggy from being drugged. It doesn't seem as if they hurt her.'

'She's beautiful.'

'Yes.' Saul felt tears in his eyes. 'And smart and funny and kind. Strong, maybe stronger than I am – in all sorts of ways. I don't know what I'd do without her.'

'Would somebody please tell me what's going on?' Gallagher said.

'After World War Two, Cardinal Pavelic helped Nazi war criminals escape from the Allies,' Arlene said. 'Over the years, he kept track of them. He blackmailed them in exchange for his silence. His assistant' – Arlene gestured toward Father Dusseault – 'found out what the cardinal was doing. Father Dusseault belongs to the Fraternity, but he hates what the order stands for. He used his position in the order to try to sabotage it. He saw the cardinal as a further example of corruption within the Church. Not only did he kill the cardinal – he decided to punish the war criminals the cardinal had been protecting.'

'Punish them? How?'

Saul added to Arlene's explanation. 'Father Dusseault gave the information to a Mossad operative whose family had been killed and who himself had nearly been killed in Dachau. The theory was that someone with so terrible a grievance, particularly someone with his training and resources, would be a more reliable instrument of punishment than trials that might take years.'

'Punishment? Do you mean vengeance?' Gallagher asked. 'Did Father Dusseault hope the Mossad operative would kill the Nazis?'

Saul nodded. 'I'm less sure about the rest of it, but my guess is that the Mossad agent – his name was Ephraim Avidan by the way – decided he needed help. I think he went to other Mossad operatives who'd been in concentration camps and organized a team. These operatives were old enough to be retired. Many of them were widowers. They had the freedom, both politically and personally, to do what they wanted. In Vienna, Erika and I were given a list of men's names by our contact with the Mossad. The men on that list matched the profile I just described. During the past few months, they all disappeared. I think

253

they were dropping out of the limited society they still had, preparing for their mission.'

'Disappearing?' Gallagher asked. 'It sounds like . . .'

'My wife's father,' Saul said. 'I think he's one of the team.'

The room seemed to shrink.

'What about the two men you mentioned – Seth and Icicle?'

'Assassins. Sons of Nazi assassins. I think their fathers are two of the war criminals the cardinal protected. If Avidan's team moved against their fathers, Seth and Icicle would want to know who was doing it and why. They seem to have decided that the cardinal was the key to the puzzle. If they found out why the cardinal disappeared, they'd find out why those war criminals became targets after so many years.'

Gallagher gestured toward Arlene. 'So how do *you* fit into this? Who's Drew?'

'No more questions,' Saul said. 'Erika's all that matters. *I have to get this damned thing off her.*'

That afternoon, he'd asked Arlene to buy the metal clippers Seth had claimed he'd need to get the belt off Erika once Seth was out of radio range. Now Arlene reached in her purse and gave them to Saul.

He pressed them against the metal belt and hesitated. 'Arlene, maybe you, Gallagher, and the priest ought to get out of here. In case this thing blows up.'

'If you think it's that risky, don't do anything.'

Saul shook his head. 'Suppose Seth isn't out of radio range. You said Drew was chasing him. Seth might press the detonator.'

'Maybe we should all get out of here,' Gallagher said. 'I'll phone for an Agency explosive expert.'

'By the time he got here, it might be too late.' Saul studied the wires attached to the metal belt and box. 'Unless . . . maybe. *Yes, it just might work.*' He hurried to unplug a lamp on a bureau. With sweat-slippery hands, he used the metal clippers to snip the cord from the base of the lamp and cut the electrical plug from the opposite end of the cord.

'What are you doing?' Gallagher asked.

Saul was concentrating too hard to answer. Gently, he pressed the clippers against the rubber insulation on the cord, nicked it two inches from each end, then peeled off the strips of insulation, exposing the wires. He went back to Erika and secured one end of the cord to a bare wire leading from the metal box to the belt. He attached the other end of the cord to a second bare wire leading from the box to the belt. He'd been afraid that the bomb would go off if he cut the belt and interrupted an electrical circuit. But now the lamp cord provided the same function that the belt did. In theory, he could now cut the belt, and the circuit wouldn't be damaged.

In theory.

'I think,' Saul said, 'that this would be a good time for all of you to leave.'

Unprotesting, Arlene raised the priest from the bed. 'Gallagher, let's take a stroll to the end of the hall.'

254

'Romulus?'

Saul waited.

'Good luck.'

'Thanks.'

Gallagher grinned. 'You're something else.'

Ten seconds later, Saul was alone with Erika.

Aching with love, he pressed the clippers to the front of the belt and snipped it.

The phone rang precisely when he'd anticipated the explosion. The harsh sound jolted his nerves; his heart lurched.

'Shit!'

The phone rang again.

He tried to regain control, working with as much speed as caution would allow, removing the belt and the bomb from Erika's waist. Careful not to disturb the wires he'd attached to it, he set the apparatus on a chair.

The phone kept ringing.

He grabbed it.

'It's Drew! For God's sake, don't try to take that bomb off your wife! Seth lied! The bomb's rigged to explode if the belt's opened!'

Saul sank onto the bed and began to laugh. '*Now* you tell me?'

'What are—?'

Saul roared. He knew he sounded hysterical, but the release felt too good for him to care. 'Everything's fine. The bomb's not on her anymore.'

'How, sweet Jesus, did you manage *that*?'

Saul's laugh became one of affection toward his friend. Drew was the only person he knew who could make an expletive sound like a prayer. 'With some help from a lamp cord. I'll tell you about it when I see you. But are *you* okay? Arlene said you'd gone after Seth and Icicle.'

'Yes . . . Seth's dead. Icicle killed him.'

'*What?*'

'Icicle's been wounded. If we help him, he promises to tell us anything we want to know.'

At once Saul stood. 'Where should I meet you?'

'The park south of Constantine's Arch. That's where I left Icicle. We'll be waiting along the Via di San Gregorio.'

'Are you sure we can trust him?'

'Yes. He was the one who told me not to try taking the bomb off your wife. He didn't have to warn us. He didn't have to help Erika. When we talk to him, I think we'll get the last of our questions answered.'

'I'll be there in twenty minutes.' Saul set the phone back onto its receiver and hurried from the room toward Arlene, Gallagher, and the priest in the corridor. 'Arlene, please stay with Erika. Take care of her.' He ran toward the elevator.

'Just wait a damned minute,' Gallagher said. 'I'm not through with you. Where do you think you're going?'

'To meet a friend and bring back an Icicle. Tell your medical team

255

we're going to need them again.' When the elevator took too long to arrive, Saul rushed down the fire stairs.

9

Dusk and the chaos of headlights made Saul despair of noticing Drew and Icicle as he sped past Constantine's Arch, driving his rented car down the Via di San Gregorio. Pedestrians thronged the adjacent sidewalks. *I should have asked Drew which side of the street he'd be on.*

But Drew was suddenly ahead of him, his arm around Icicle as if holding up someone who'd drunk too much. Saul steered in their direction, hearing angry car horns behind him, and skidded to a stop at the curb. The instant Drew helped Icicle into the back of the car and shut the door, Saul sped away.

Icicle wore the jacket that Drew had been wearing this afternoon. The blond assassin's face was as pale as his hair. Blood soaked through the arms of the jacket.

'How badly is he hurt?' Saul asked.

'Shot in both shoulders. One of the bullets passed through. As much as I can tell, the other's still in him. He's delirious.'

'Halloway,' Icicle murmured.

'Who's Halloway?' Saul glanced back toward Drew.

'I haven't found out yet. Whoever he is, Icicle sure doesn't like him.'

'Pay the son of a bitch back,' Icicle mumbled.

'Why?' Drew asked.

'Sent Seth to kill my father,' Icicle said.

'Why would Halloway . . . ? Is he an Israeli?'

Icicle laughed. 'No.'

'It doesn't make sense.' Saul steered around a corner. 'If Halloway isn't an Israeli, why would he be involved with the team that went after the Nazis?'

'Night and Fog,' Icicle whispered.

'And how does *that* fit in?' Saul asked. 'The Night and Fog was a Nazi terror tactic during World War Two.'

'I wonder if . . . Could it be he just explained the Israeli team's method of revenge?' Drew asked.

Saul shuddered as he steered around another corner. 'Using Nazi tactics against their enemies? Abducting war criminals and making their families suffer as Jewish families suffered during the Holocaust. *Erika's father is involved in this insanity?*'

'A passion for revenge,' Drew said. 'Because of the murder of my parents, I know all about hate. I *was* hate for many years. And I know when you borrow the tactics of your enemy you become your enemy. You learn to hate yourself.'

Saul remembered the hate with which he'd stalked and killed his foster father to avenge his foster brother's death. But getting even for

256

Chris hadn't brought satisfaction, only a terrible hollowness. 'I've got to find Erika's father. I've got to stop him.'

'Halloway,' Icicle murmured.

'Who *is* he?' Drew asked. 'If he isn't Jewish—'

'The Painter's son.'

'Oh, my God,' Saul said. 'The Painter was the nickname for the assistant SS commandant at the Maidanek death camp. Day after day, he processed – that was *his* word, that was how he thought of it, a system, a *dis*assembly line – thousands of prisoners through the gas chambers and the ovens. At night, he painted idyllic scenes of forests and meadows.'

'Was Halloway's father the assistant commandant at Maidanek?' Drew asked Icicle.

'Yes.'

'Why did Halloway want Seth to kill your father?'

'To force me to join them. To make me think the Night and Fog had kidnapped my father.'

'Where is Halloway now?'

Icicle didn't answer.

'If that bullet isn't removed, if he doesn't get a transfusion,' Drew said, 'we'll never get an answer.'

'You're right. He'll die. And his jacket's soaked with blood now. We'll never be able to sneak him into the hotel. We need a safe house. Gallagher has to tell us where to meet his medical team.' Saul stopped at the curb and scrambled from the car toward a phone booth.

But not before he heard Drew ask Icicle again, 'Where is Halloway?'

'Kitchener. Near Toronto. In Canada.'

10

Despite the sourness in his stomach, Misha Pletz swallowed yet another mouthful of scalding coffee and restrained his impulse to hurry down to the communications room in the basement of Mossad headquarters in Tel Aviv. It was only 11 P.M., he reminded himself. Operation Salvage wouldn't occur for another hour, and in the meantime its team was under orders to obey radio silence. Besides, I'd only get in the way down there, he thought. I've done my job. The plan's been checked repeatedly.

Nonetheless, he worried that the information Joseph had given him might be incorrect. Verification of the contraband, the time and place of delivery, and the identification codes had been impossible. With an informant other than Joseph, with a threat less critical to Israel's existence, Misha would not have risked acting. But under the circumstances, to do nothing was a worse risk. His superiors had reluctantly agreed with him.

The door to his office came open. Misha's assistant hurried in, his exhausted features flushed with excitement. 'Romulus just made contact.'

257

Misha's shoulders straightened. 'I've been hoping. Where is he?'

'Rome.'

'How did he get in touch with us?'

'Through the CIA.' The assistant gave Misha a piece of paper with a number written on it. 'He wants you to phone him as soon as possible.'

The message was puzzling. When Misha had last seen Saul, the Agency had possibly been involved in an assassination attempt against him, and even if the Agency *hadn't* been involved, it had made Saul promise to stay away from them. Then why was Saul now using one of their contacts? Was Saul in trouble with them? Was this message a hoax?

But though puzzling, the message was also a double blessing. Not only was he anxious to talk with Saul and Erika, but he felt grateful to be distracted from waiting for news about Operation Salvage. He picked up his safe phone and dialed the number. Trans-Mediterranean static crackled. At the other end, the phone rang only once before Saul's distinctively resonant husky voice said, 'Hello.'

'This is Sand Viper. Can you talk freely where you are?'

'I'm in an Agency safe house. They tell me the phone's secure.'

'Are you in trouble?'

'With the Agency? No, they're cooperating. It'd take too long to explain.' Saul's voice hurried on. 'I've learned some disturbing things about Erika's father.'

'So have I,' Misha said. 'Twice in the last two days he sent messages to me. I've had visual confirmation – he's alive. Tell Erika. Her father's alive, and he isn't being held captive. He wants to stay out of sight, though. He eluded two attempts to follow him. The messages he sent me—'

'About the Nazis?' Saul sounded surprised. 'He actually told you?'

'Nazis?' Misha pressed the phone hard against his ear. *'What are you talking about?'*

'War criminals. That's why Joseph disappeared. He and Ephraim Avidan and the other former operatives whose names were on the list you gave us – they learned where war criminals were hiding. They formed a team and went after them.'

Misha felt too astonished to speak.

Saul's voice became more urgent. 'If Joseph didn't tell you, what was in his messages?'

'Even on a phone as secure as this, I can't risk telling you. He had information vital to Israel. That's all I can say. By noon tomorrow, I'll be free to explain.'

'But tomorrow could make all the difference. Joseph might already have done things that'll haunt him for the rest of his life. For his sake, for *Erika's* sake, I've got to stop him. You said he disappeared again. Haven't you any idea where he is?'

'He keeps moving. His messages came from different countries. First the United States, then Canada.'

'Did you say *Canada?*'

258

'Is that important?'

'*Where in Canada?*' Saul demanded. '*What city?*'

'Toronto.'

'I thought so!'

'What's wrong?' Misha asked. 'Do you know why Joseph would have gone there?'

'The son of one of the Nazis lives near there. The father was the Painter, the assistant commandant at Maidanek. The son's name is Halloway.'

The name made Misha inhale as if he'd been struck. He wanted to tell Saul that Halloway was one of the arms merchants Joseph had revealed in his message. But he didn't dare discuss it until Operation Salvage had been brought to a close. When the team was safely back home, he'd leak information that would make the Libyans think Halloway was implicated in the mission, and then he'd be free – but only under guaranteed secure conditions – to explain to Saul.

'I have to hang up,' Misha said. 'I'll call you again at noon tomorrow. This is important. Don't do anything further. Just wait for my call. I have information for you.'

Misha broke the connection.

11

A dial tone. Distraught, Saul set down the phone and turned toward the modest living room of this safe house, a farm on the outskirts of Rome. It had been converted into an emergency medical facility. Icicle, his skin almost the literal color of ice, lay on a foldout bed, a bottle of plasma suspended above a tube leading into his arm. The same doctor who'd attended to Father Dusseault had disinfected and now was suturing the wound in Icicle's left arm. He applied a dressing and bandaged it.

'Now comes the hard part,' the doctor said. He assessed the readings on portable monitors. 'His heartbeat's arrhythmic. His blood pressure's low. His respiration's . . . Keep giving him oxygen,' he told an assistant.

'You think he might die?' Saul asked.

'With two bullet wounds, he tried for a record in the hundred-yard dash. Every move pumped more blood out of him. Die? It's a miracle if he doesn't. And he still has to go through the trauma of my probing for the bullet in his other arm.'

'He can't die!'

'Everybody dies.'

'But I still need information from him!'

'Then this is the time to ask him. Before I put him under. In fifteen minutes, even if he lives, he won't say anything till tomorrow night.'

Conscious of the doctor and his two assistants, of Gallagher hovering tensely behind them, of Drew standing uneasily in an open doorway behind which Arlene watched Erika and Father Dusseault, Saul leaned over Icicle. He used a cloth to wipe sweat from Icicle's pain-ravaged face.

'Can you hear me?'

Icicle nodded weakly.

'They say you might die. But if you hang on, I guarantee once you're well they'll let you go.'

'For Christ's sake,' Gallagher said, 'that promise isn't yours to make.'

Saul pivoted toward Gallagher. 'I'll promise anything if it gets me the answers I want. From the start, I told you this was personal. But it isn't just about my wife's father any longer. It's also about my wife. When she learns what her father's up to, she'll never forgive me if I don't do everything I can to stop him. Try to stop *me* and I'll . . .'

'What would you do to me? And what would that make *you*? Another version of her father?' Gallagher asked.

Saul hesitated, aware of the truth in what Gallagher said. But his devotion to Erika made him press on. 'No, there's a difference. This isn't hate. It's love.'

'Maybe that makes it worse.'

'Look, I'm sorry. I didn't mean to threaten you. But you've got to understand.' Saul leaned over Icicle again. 'Tell me what I need to know. Use all the strength you can manage. Live. And you'll go free. Or I'll die trying to protect you.'

'A hell of a promise,' Icicle murmured.

'Count on it.'

Icicle licked his dry lips. 'What . . . do you need to know?'

'In the car, as we drove here, you told me Halloway lived near Toronto. A place called Kitchener. Concentrate. How do I get to Halloway? *Where is* . . . ?'

'Kitchener?' Icicle's voice was faint, like the rustle of dead dry leaves. 'He lives' – a painful swallow – 'just outside it. Highway four-oh-one . . . west of Toronto . . . eighty kilometers . . . exit number . . .'

Saul strained to remember every word.

12

Midnight. The Mediterranean. South of Crete, north of Libya. The captain of the cargo ship *Medusa* felt uneasy about the signal light flashing from the darkness off his starboard bow. His rendezvous with the Libyan pickup ship wasn't due until 3 A.M. It was three hours early, and he hadn't been alerted about a change in schedule. Since 11 P.M. he'd been maintaining radio silence, just as the Libyans were supposed to, lest enemies learn about the delivery. So if there *had* been a change in schedule, he wouldn't have been told. The important thing was that the signal being flashed to him was the agreed-upon code. He gave orders for the confirmation code to be flashed, waited, and relaxed when the Libyans flashed a further confirmation code. The sooner he got rid of his cargo, the better.

The smokestack of a ship loomed out of the darkness and stopped a close but safe distance from where *Medusa* lay still in the water. Boats disembarked from the opposite ship, their engines roaring. The captain told his men to lower rope ladders and ready the ship's crane to unload the cargo.

The pickup boats pulled up against *Medusa*. Men scurried up the rope ladders. The captain's welcoming smile dissolved when he saw that they wore masks, that they held automatic weapons, that they were subduing *Medusa*'s crew, forcing them into lifeboats. A pistol barrel was rammed against his head. He screamed.

Adrift in a lifeboat, he watched *Medusa* gain speed, disappearing into the night with her one-hundred-million-dollars worth of machine pistols, assault rifles, plastic explosive, grenades, ammunition, portable rocket launchers, and heat-seeking missiles. Two members of the assault force followed *Medusa* in the long-distance speedboats that had brought them here. What he'd mistaken for the Libyan ship was actually a canvas silhouette of a smokestack that the marauders had hoisted above one of the boats. He suspected that a similar silhouette would be raised above *Medusa*'s deck to change her profile and make it difficult for pursuers to identify her. A new name would probably be painted over her own. By tomorrow morning, the pirates could reach a safe harbor. The captain touched his head where the pistol barrel had been rammed against it. He asked himself how in hell he was going to explain to the Libyans when they arrived, and blurted orders for his crew to row as fast as they could. To where? What difference did it make? As long as it was away from here. Away from the Libyans, who weren't renowned for their understanding and certainly not for their mercy.

13

Fully conscious now, Erika tried to overcome her confusion to assimilate everything Saul told her: how he, Drew, and Arlene had joined forces, and what had happened after she'd been abducted. Bewilderment turned into shock as she listened to what they'd learned.

'A hit team? My father and Avidan and the rest . . . seventy-year-old men . . . disappeared because they're out for revenge against Nazi war criminals?'

'That might not be all they're doing.'

'*Worse?*'

Drew helped Saul explain. 'In the car, Icicle mentioned the Night and Fog. He didn't mean the Nazi Night and Fog. He meant . . . We think your father and his team weren't satisfied with punishing the war criminals they learned about. We think they decided to terrorize the *children* of the Nazis. To pay the fathers back in kind.'

Sudden understanding gave Erika strength to stand from the bed. 'But don't you see? If the point was to torture the fathers by terrorizing the children, the fathers must still be alive. Otherwise the vengeance isn't complete. The Nazis have to *know* their children are being terrorized. They have to suffer by realizing their loved ones are suffering. There's still a chance to stop my father's team before they kill.'

Drew smiled. 'Saul was right about how smart you are.'

'If I'm so smart, why aren't I cheering my father on?' Erika asked. 'Part of me *wants* him to get even.'

'Part of me feels that way, too,' Saul said. 'Maybe that's why I'm so angry about trying to protect them.'

'That's just the point,' Drew said. 'Part of you wants vengeance. But *only* part of you. I feel like an outsider – without a right to an opinion. *My* relatives weren't killed in the Holocaust. *My* race wasn't hunted and almost exterminated. But when I think about the SS, I feel so outraged I want to . . .' He sighed. 'Some of them weren't even crazy enough to believe in what they were doing. They just complied with the craziness around them. To earn a living. To feed their families. If enough of the hypocrites had objected with sufficient force . . .'

'But the world isn't like that,' Erika said.

'We are,' Drew said. 'That's why we refuse to condone Nazi methods being used against Nazis. Because we refuse to *become* like Nazis. Isn't that what the Nuremberg trials were about? Not vengeance but reason and law. Believe me, I want to see these war criminals punished. I don't care how old they are. They *must* be punished. Death in my opinion. An absolute crime requires absolute penance. But not by individuals, not on the basis of anger alone, not without the sanction of society.'

'But how . . . ?' Erika faltered, reaching for the bed.

'Are you all right?' Saul hurried over and put his arm around her. She nodded, anxious to ask her question. 'How are we going to stop my father?'

'Toronto,' Saul said. 'Halloway lives nearby. Your father was last seen there. Do you feel strong enough to travel?'

'Even if I didn't, I'd say I did. For my father's sake.'

'But *do* you?'

'Yes. Get two tickets on the first plane you can.'

'Four,' Drew said.

Erika glanced up quickly at him in surprise.

Arlene, who'd listened in silence, stepped forward. 'I agree with Drew. Four tickets. We're coming along.'

'But you don't . . .'

'Have to? Is that what you wanted to say?'

'It's not your problem.' Erika gestured in frustration. 'That sounds rude. I don't mean it that way. But he's not your father.'

'Right,' Drew said. 'We're not obligated. All the same, we're coming along.'

'You don't even know me.'

'We will.'

262

14

Joseph Bernstein sat alone in the dark living room of the house-turned-into-a-prison in Toronto. He tried to relax before the tension of tomorrow. A few minutes' quiet.

I'm seventy, he thought. Other old men . . . my comrades – sleep upstairs. Equally old men – my enemies – are our prisoners. Tomorrow, after more than forty years, I fulfill a vow I made in my youth. To avenge my family. To punish monsters as they punished me.

15

The Air Canada DC-10 landed in Toronto shortly after 2 P.M. Saul's body was still set for Rome time, where the sun would be setting, not blazing above him. He'd slept little the night before and felt exhausted. His legs ached from lack of exercise.

Arlene and Drew said they felt as he did. But Erika had an excess of energy. Concern about her father prompted her to take charge as soon as they passed through immigration and customs. She found a car-rental booth and twenty minutes later drove the group out of the airport complex, merging with Highway 401.

Traffic was considerable, most drivers ignoring the hundred-kilometer-an-hour speed limit. But Erika didn't want trouble with the police and, despite her impatience, maintained the legal maximum. The afternoon sun was oppressive. She switched on the sedan's air conditioner and stared straight ahead, oblivious to the farm fields that flanked the highway.

Saul watched the exit numbers and, fifty minutes later, pointed. 'Here. Take this one.'

He regretted that he hadn't been able to wait for Misha Pletz's phone call in Rome. Misha had insisted he had something important to say, and Saul had suspected the information was related to Halloway. But when it came to a choice between waiting in Rome or catching the earliest plane to Toronto, speed had dictated which decision to make.

'Turn here. To the left,' Saul said.

Erika drove along a country road. Five kilometers farther, Saul told her to turn left again. The sun-bathed countryside was gentle hills, woods alternating with corn and pasture.

'We ought to be close now,' Saul said. The blacktop road curved. He pointed to the right toward a gravel lane that led up through trees toward a sloping lawn and a mansion on a bluff. 'I think this is it. The layout's the same as Icicle's description. There should be a . . . Yes, see the silhouette of a greyhound on the mailbox at the side of the road.'

'Lots of people put decorations on their mailbox, and lots of those decorations are silhouettes of dogs,' Drew cautioned.

'Icicle said there'd be a metal bridge around a bend past the mansion.'

A minute later, Erika drove across such a bridge. 'I'm convinced. It's almost three-thirty. Let's not waste daylight.' She turned the car around and drove back across the bridge, stopping at the side of the blacktop. 'Near the river, the abandoned car won't look suspicious. It'll seem as if somebody stopped to go fishing.'

'I wish we'd been able to bring our weapons,' Saul said.

'Through airport security? We'd still be back in Rome. In jail,' Drew said.

'It's just a wish. But I'm going to feel severely underdressed when we get to that mansion.'

'You never know. Weapons might not be necessary,' Arlene said. 'Halloway could be nothing more than a businessman.'

'Don't forget his connection with Seth and Icicle. It's better if we anticipate trouble.'

They got out of the car. On the opposite side of the road, woods obscured them from the mansion.

16

The woods were dense. Only on occasion did sunbeams pierce the canopy of leaves. Smelling fragrant loam, Drew followed a zigzagging game trail, stepped over a fallen trunk, and started up a more densely wooded slope. He glanced back toward Arlene, admiring her graceful movements, her obvious feeling of being at home in difficult terrain. We'll have to go rock-climbing, he thought. Just the two of us in a wilderness for a couple of weeks.

When this is over.

He concentrated only on the present and climbed higher through the trees. At the top, he waited for Arlene to join him and touched her shoulder lovingly. Beyond the clearing, a break in a line of trees revealed the mansion to the right on the continuation of this bluff. Saul and Erika were ahead of them, crouched among bushes.

Even at a hundred yards, Drew could see a half-dozen armed guards in front of the mansion. Their attention was directed toward the entrance to the estate. Ten cars of different types were parked beside them. A man in a blue exercise suit strode out of the mansion's front door and stopped abruptly, appalled by what he saw. A truck arrived, raising dust as it sped up the gravel lane.

17

The previous evening, Halloway had felt so nervous about the impending munitions delivery that he'd decided to risk visiting his wife and children at the safe house in Kitchener. Three A.M. in Libya was 9 P.M. in Ontario, and allowing for the time required to transfer the arms from *Medusa* to the Libyan freighter and for the further time the Libyan freighter would need to get back to home port, he didn't expect to receive word about the transaction until the next morning.

Though he wasn't religious, he prayed that the mission would be a success, for he now shared Rosenberg's tense misgivings about the Night and Fog's possible discovery of the shipment. The enemy had learned so much with which to terrorize them that perhaps they'd learned about *Medusa* too. But Halloway couldn't warn the Libyans about the potential information leak. Assured of maximum punishment for sending a shipment that might have been compromised, he took the gamble of not alerting his clients and hoped that nothing would go wrong.

His hope was manifested by a toast at dinner. He raised a glass of wine and feigned a smile toward his wife and children. 'I know you're confused about what's going on. The past few months have been a strain. You wish you were home. The bodyguards make you nervous. But sometimes international finance creates enemies. If it helps, I believe we'll soon see the end of the crisis. In the meantime, your patience and understanding have been remarkable.' He sipped his wine and silently proposed another toast. To *Medusa*. To the satisfactory conclusion of a hundred-million-dollar agreement.

He noted that it was precisely 9 P.M., the time for the Mediterranean delivery. A bodyguard came into the dining room and handed him a telegram.

Halloway ripped open the side of the envelope and pulled out the message. He had to read it several times before he absorbed the impact of the words.

ALL PROBLEMS SOLVED. YOUR FATHER SAFE. RETURNING HIM TOMORROW. YOUR TIME THREE P.M. YOUR ESTATE. ICICLE. SETH.

Halloway exhaled, overcome with relief. For the first time in several months, he felt buoyant, liberated. True, he wondered why Seth and Icicle had sent a telegram instead of phoning, and why they'd sent the telegram here, to the safe house he'd told them about, instead of to the estate outside town. But after he phoned a guard at the estate and learned that a telegram had just arrived there as well, he felt reassured that Seth and Icicle had tried to contact him at both of the places where he'd probably be. They must have worried that a phone call, for whatever reason, would have endangered them. He instructed the security force at his estate to expect company tomorrow.

'Your grandfather's coming home,' he told his children. With a beaming smile toward his wife, he departed from his usual abstemiousness and poured himself a second glass of wine.

By noon the next day, he felt so nervous he couldn't keep still. Protected by bodyguards, he drove out to his estate. A car had already arrived. Overjoyed, he rushed toward it.

But instead of his father, Rosenberg stepped out of the car.

Halloway froze in astonishment. 'What are *you* doing here?'

'Your telegram.'

'*Telegram?*'

'You didn't send one?'

'For Christ's sake, no!'

'But it's got your name on it.' Rosenberg took the telegram from his suitcoat pocket.

Halloway yanked it away from him. His heart shrank as he read it.

PHONE CAN'T BE TRUSTED. ALL PROBLEMS SOLVED. OUR FATHERS SAFE.
ARRIVE TOMORROW. MY TIME THREE P.M. MY ESTATE. HALLOWAY.

'And you *believed* this?' Halloway crushed the paper.

'What was I supposed to do? Phone when you told me I shouldn't? Stay in Mexico when I hoped my father was here in Canada?'

'You stupid bastard, I received a telegram as well! The message was almost the same! *My* father was supposed to be here.'

'Then you're as stupid as you think I am!'

'*They* did this!' Halloway pivoted toward the entrance to his estate. 'They set us up!'

'*They?*' Rosenberg's knees bent. 'The Night and Fog?'

'Who else would . . . ? They must be watching us right now!'

Halloway and Rosenberg retreated toward the mansion.

But Halloway pivoted again, hearing a car roar up the gravel lane. As guards rushed toward it, Halloway recognized Miller behind the steering wheel. 'I told you not to come here!'

Miller's car crunched to a halt on the gravel. The angry architect surged from his car. 'And I told you I was coming! You *knew* what my father was! You knew what *all* the fathers were! I tried to convince myself I'd only be sinking to your level if I came here and strangled you. But God help me, even knowing my father's crime, I wanted him back! And then you sent me this telegram! My father! You said he'd be here! *Where is he?*'

Halloway grabbed the piece of paper with which Miller gestured in fury. The message was the same that Rosenberg had received. 'They're out there,' Halloway cried. 'I know it. I'm sure of it. They're out there.'

'Out there?' Miller's anger rose. 'What are you—? Out there? Who?'

'We've got to take cover. Quickly. Inside.' Halloway scurried toward the front steps. He shouted orders to the captain of his guards. 'Pull your men in from the perimeter! Protect the house!'

But at once he spun again, hearing a car roar up the lane. Oh, Jesus, he thought. Not another one.

18

It went on like that for the next two hours, cars rushing up to the mansion, men scrambling out, each clutching a telegram. From around the world, they'd been summoned. From Mexico, America, England,

France, Sweden, Egypt, and Italy, they'd rushed to be reunited with
their fathers, only to learn of the trick that had brought them to
Halloway's estate. Sheltered in his study while guards watched the
mansion, they raised frightened angry voices. They shouted, accused,
complained.

'I'm getting out of here!'

'But it isn't safe to leave!'

'It isn't safe to stay!'

'What's supposed to happen at three o'clock?'

'Why was that time specified in the telegram?'

'What if our fathers *will* be returned?'

'What if we'll be *attacked*?'

The appointed time passed. Halloway heard another vehicle enter
the lane. He rushed outside, hoping he was wrong about the Night
and Fog, praying this was Icicle and Seth.

But instead of a car, he saw a truck. With wooden slats along its
sides, a tarpaulin covering the top. It looked like . . .

Halloway shivered.

. . . a cattle truck.

God have mercy, he thought, filled with a sickening premonition.
The threat was all the more horrifying because it was vague. But of
this he was certain – the end had begun.

19

'What's happening down there?' Saul asked. Crouched beside Erika,
Drew, and Arlene, he watched from the bluff as the truck approached
the nine cars parked in front of the mansion. The man in the blue
exercise suit gestured frantically to his guards, who raised their rifles
toward the truck.

Drew's voice was strained. 'We have to get closer.'

'Now. While the guards are distracted,' Erika said.

Beyond the bushes in which they hid, a waist-high barbed wire
fence separated them from the lawn of the estate. Erika hurried
toward it. There were no glass insulators on the posts; the wires
weren't electrified. She didn't see any closed-circuit cameras. There
might be hidden sound and pressure detectors, but need made her take
the risk. She climbed a post, tumbled to the lawn, and crawled.

To her right, a hundred yards away, she saw the man in the blue
exercise suit shouting orders to his guards, who aimed toward the cattle
truck. It reached the top of the lane, approaching the cars parked in
front of the mansion.

Impelled by a horrible foreboding, Erika crawled faster. She turned
toward Saul, who was squirming through the grass in her direction.
Drew and Arlene were farther to her left, spreading out so there'd be
less chance of anyone seeing them.

With the sun on her back, she hurried toward a garden plot filled with tall orange snapdragons that would give her more concealment on the way to the mansion.

Abruptly she stopped. Two guards at the back of the mansion had scrambled toward the commotion in front. They joined their counterparts and aimed at the cattle truck, which had turned so that its hatch was pointed toward the group in front of the mansion.

She took advantage of the guards' preoccupation and hurried closer to the mansion. But on her left she saw a sentry. She crouched behind a shrub. The sentry, rifle at the ready, approached a shed, only to lurch back as if struck. He plucked at something on the side of his neck and suddenly collapsed. Baffled, Erika watched two elderly men emerge from behind the shed. One of them held a gun whose distinctive shape she recognized – it was used to shoot tranquilizer darts. Despite their advanced age, the men worked with surprising speed, dragging the sentry into the shed. One shut the door while the other grabbed the sentry's rifle. They hurried toward the back of the mansion and disappeared.

Erika's bewilderment increased when she looked to her right, toward the front of the mansion, and saw an elderly man get out of the passenger door of the truck. The man walked toward the truck's back hatch and joined another old man, who'd gotten out on the driver's side and unseen by Erika had walked to the back. They braced themselves in front of the guards' rifles. With a mixture of fear and dismay, Erika crawled faster. Her heart pounded. Her premonition worsened. The elderly man who'd just appeared from the blind side of the truck was her father.

20

Rage had made him incapable of fear. Joseph Bernstein stopped at point-blank range from the rifles and turned toward Halloway. 'Is this any way to welcome visitors?'

'Who *are* you?'

'I think you already know,' Ephraim Avidan said. Standing next to Joseph, he lifted his hand toward the tarpaulin that covered the truck's back hatch. 'Tell your guards to lower their guns.' Ephraim yanked the tarpaulin to the side of the truck. The back hatch slammed down.

A bearded elderly man sat in the truck, aiming a machine gun. 'Since munitions are your business, you're no doubt aware I've pulled back the cocking bolt on this weapon,' he said. 'You also know the devastation rapid-feed thirty-caliber bullets can accomplish. Even if someone shot me right now, my nervous reflex would pull the trigger. I'm aiming directly at your chest. Please do what my associate requested and order your guards to lower their rifles.'

'If you need further incentive, look deeper into the truck,' Joseph said.

Lips parted with apprehension, Halloway squinted toward the interior.

'Step closer. We want you to see every detail,' Ephraim said.

Halloway took two nervous steps forward and paled when he saw what was in there.

Drugged, ashen, hollow-cheeked, the fathers were chained together, eleven of them slumped on the floor of the truck. An elderly man guarded the prisoners, pressing an Uzi against the forehead of Halloway's father.

'Dear God.' Halloway clutched his stomach, as if he might vomit.

'Tell your guards to put down their rifles or we'll shoot the prisoners,' Joseph said. He pulled a Beretta from a windbreaker pocket.

'Do it,' Halloway said:

The guards set their rifles on the lane. Joseph searched them, found several handguns, and told the guards to lie facedown on the gravel.

'*Why are you doing this?*' Halloway asked. '*What do you want?*'

'Isn't it obvious by now?' Ephraim said. 'We're here to discuss Nazi racial theories.'

The large front door to the mansion came open. One by one, the other members of Halloway's group stepped out, their hands raised, their faces pinched with fear. Two elderly men holding Uzis followed them.

'Ah,' Ephraim said, 'the rest of our audience has consented to join us.'

'I don't know what you think you're doing,' one of Halloway's group shouted, 'but—!'

'Mr Miller,' Joseph said, 'please shut your mouth.'

'You can't keep something like this a secret! You can't—'

Joseph struck him across the head with the Beretta.

Miller fell to the gravel. He moaned, clutching his bleeding scalp.

'Would anyone else like to say something?' Joseph asked.

The group stared appalled at the blood streaming down Miller's face.

'Very good,' Joseph said.

Other old men, aiming Uzis, appeared from each side of the house.

'Did you restrain the rest of the guards?' Ephraim asked.

'The perimeter's been secured. We searched every room in the house.'

'In that case, it's time to begin.' Ephraim stepped toward the truck.

'Whatever you plan to do, it's wrong,' a Mexican-looking man said.

'Rosenberg, don't presume to tell *me* about what's wrong. You and Halloway are perfect proof that the vices of the fathers are inherited by the sons.'

'What are you talking about?'

'The weapons you sold to Libya to be used against Israel.'

'You *know* about—?'

'The weapons are now in Israeli hands.'

Rosenberg gasped.

'It's only fitting that, even if you didn't intend to do so, you helped protect my race, the race your father tried so hard to destroy,' Ephraim said. He reached into the truck and threw shovels onto the gravel. 'Pick them up. All of you.' He threw out more shovels. 'We brought enough for everyone. We mustn't take all day about this. Efficiency is something your fathers always recommended. Teamwork. Organization.'

'Shovels?' Halloway blanched. 'What do you—'

'Dig a hole, of course. A large deep hole.'

'You're insane!'

'Were your fathers insane when they forced Jews to dig pits for the bodies of other Jews? Or is killing Jews a perfectly rational thing to do? Is it only insane when the executioners are executed? *Pick up the shovels.*'

Prodded by Uzis, the group stumbled forward.

'We'll dig the pit behind the house, out of sight from the road down there,' Ephraim said. 'I'm sure you're all wondering what we intend to do with *you* when the hole is ready. Will we force you to watch the death of your fathers and then shoot you just as your fathers shot those they ordered to dig burial pits? We offer you the same temptation your fathers offered their victims. Cooperate with us, and we'll let you go. Dig the pit – we'll be understanding. How much do you love your fathers? Many Jews were faced with that question during the war. If your father's going to die, is it a useless sacrifice to resist and die along with him? Or does it make more sense to cooperate with your persecutors and take the chance that you'll be spared? An interesting dilemma. If you refuse to dig the pit, we'll kill you. If you obey . . . ?' Ephraim raised his hands, expressing a quandary. 'Who knows? Experience what we did. It'll be an education for you.'

21

Erika crouched behind a gazebo and surveyed the back of the mansion. The two old men who'd dragged the guard into a shed weren't in view anymore, presumably having entered a rear door of the mansion. But on the far side of the house, two other old men dragged a guard behind what appeared to be a long garage. They came back into sight, holding Uzis, and ran toward the rear of the mansion.

She looked toward Saul crawling behind her, held up a palm to warn him, and pointed toward the rear of the house. She couldn't see Drew and Arlene, assumed they were trying to circle the grounds, and hoped they would realize there were other strangers on the property.

At the rear of the mansion, the two old men had been joined by two others. They hurried inside the building. Erika forced herself to wait, to watch for an opportunity.

She was glad she had. The four men came back outside, aimed their Uzis toward the grounds as if making sure that the perimeter had been secured, then separated, two men running along each side of the house to join the group in front.

Now! She sprinted toward the rear of the house, pressed herself against the back wall, and peered through a screen door toward shadows and silence. The instant Saul joined her, she opened the screen door and stepped inside.

She saw stairs on her right leading down to a basement. Ahead, three steps led up to a short corridor. While Saul checked the basement, she followed the corridor, smelling pot roast and freshly baked bread. The corridor opened into a large gleaming kitchen where two men, wearing servants' uniforms, lay motionless on the floor, a tranquilizer dart protruding from each neck.

She felt a chill on her own neck. When Saul returned from the basement, she proceeded through a swinging door toward another corridor, this one wider and longer, with landscape paintings on the walls. Though the paintings were beautiful, with a mystical quality of light, they filled her with horror because of the monster, Halloway's father, the assistant commandant of Maidanek, who'd probably created them.

On her right, she saw a dining room, on her left a large study where full ashtrays and empty liquor glasses showed that a large group had recently gathered here. But her attention was directed from the study toward the end of the corridor. The front door had been left open. Male voices – some angry, others pleading, a few disturbingly calm – drifted in from outside. *One of the voices belonged to her father*. Pulse pounding behind her ears, she eased along the corridor and hid against the wall next to the open door. Through a slight gap between the door and jamb, she squinted toward the sunlit front steps where old men held middle-aged men at gunpoint.

Again she heard her father. The flood of excitement she felt at being close to him suddenly drained from her. Despair made her hollow. The conversation she heard was grotesque, as was the crunch of shovels being thrown onto gravel and the command to dig a pit behind the house. Restraining the reflex to be sick, she put a hand on Saul's shoulder.

22

As Ephraim described the pit that the sons would dig for the fathers, Joseph vividly remembered the pits that he and his wife had been forced to dig at Treblinka. In the absence of ovens, the SS had burned corpses in those pits, promising a reprieve to the Jews who shoveled the earth as long as their strength held out. Cooperate and live. Refuse out of loyalty to your fellow Jews and die in the gas chamber you could have escaped, be burned in the pit you refused to dig.

That terrible choice had threatened his sanity – the choice to live by disposing of the remains of his fellow human beings. Guilt had so consumed him, rage had so festered within him that to vent his agony he'd been prepared to do *anything*. Now that the moment had come, he didn't only remember Treblinka. He felt as if he were truly back there, the smoke of smoldering corpses swirling around him, the stench of charred flesh making him double over. But he had to force himself upright, had to keep working as the SS ordered more wood to be put on the corpses, more sacks of quicklime to be opened, more bodies to be carted from the gas chambers. Tears came to his eyes.

'Out!' he heard the SS scream. 'All of you! Hurry! Faster! Jump, goddamn you! Out of the truck!'

Truck? But there *weren't* any trucks at Treblinka. The Nazis brought the prisoners in stockcars on trains. Why would a truck be at—?

He snapped from the nightmare of then to now, from Treblinka to Halloway's estate, and saw Ephraim's eyes bulging with hate.

'Out!' Ephraim shouted at the aged SS officers and whipped them with a rope, urging them faster from the truck. Chained together, the prisoners lost their balance as they did their best to descend in a hurry, falling on top of each other, chains rattling, frail bodies crunching on gravel. Jumbled together, they whimpered, squirming.

'No,' Joseph said.

But Ephraim's shouts made his objection a whisper. Ephraim whipped the old men harder. 'On your feet, vermin! Hurry! No time! Müller, you're an expert in what happens next! After the pit's been dug, we'll place a plank across it and make you stand in the middle! So when we shoot you, we'll know for sure you'll fall into the pit! We wouldn't want to waste time having to kick your body down if you fell on the rim! Efficiency, Müller! Wasn't that the motto? Organization! We mustn't waste time!'

'No,' Joseph said again.

But again, amid Ephraim's shouts, no one heard him.

The sons were pale with shock.

'Aren't you going to try to stop us?' Ephraim asked. 'Halloway? Rosenberg? Try to stop us! No? Are you beginning to understand how fear can rob you of your will? The SS used to say that the Jews deserved to die because they didn't resist being marched to the gas chamber! Well, now it's your turn! Resist! Show us how superior you are!' He whipped their fathers again. 'On your feet! Damn you, hurry!'

Joseph watched Ephraim's hate-contorted face and felt sickened. It wasn't supposed to be like this. He'd expected to feel satisfaction, not disgust. Relief, not nausea.

Ephraim whipped the old men faster. 'Soon you'll learn how it feels to see your sons dig your graves, to watch your sons being forced to watch you getting shot! You'll feel afraid, humiliated, debased!' Ephraim glared toward the sons. 'And soon *you'll* learn how it feels to see your father killed, to stand helplessly back after you participated in his execution by digging his grave! Soon you'll learn how it feels to wonder if the obscene bargain you made will be honored, if you'll be killed or spared!'

The old men were being herded toward the back of the house, their sons prodded with Uzis, forced to carry shovels for the pit.

'Try to escape!' Ephraim shouted. 'That's what *we* were tempted to do! We knew we'd be shot, and yet we kept hoping that something, *anything*, would stop the efficiency, stop the—!'

Joseph opened his mouth to shout again, 'No!' But the word froze in his throat.

Because someone else, a woman, shouted it first.

23

Joseph swung toward the open front door of the mansion. The others spun with their Uzis, Ephraim drew his Beretta.

With dizzying astonishment, Joseph watched the woman step out of the mansion.

No! he thought. This can't be happening! I'm imagining it!

But he knew he wasn't. As the gravel beneath him seemed to tilt, he recognized beyond a doubt.

The woman was Erika.

Her face was flushed with anger. 'No! You can't! This is wrong! It's *worse* than wrong! If you do to them what they did to you, to *us*, to our people, you make yourselves them! You destroy yourselves! This has to stop!'

'Erika . . .' Joseph murmured.

'You *know* this woman?' Ephraim asked.

'My daughter.'

'*What?*'

A man and woman rushed from the right side of the house, grappled with two members of Ephraim's team, and grabbed their Uzis. Almost at once, a man lunged through the mansion's open door, held a member of Ephraim's team in a stranglehold, and took his weapon.

Joseph felt a further disorienting sense of unreality. *The man at the open door was Erika's husband.*

'Saul?' he asked, bewildered. 'But how did—?'

'It's finished!' Erika shouted. 'There'll be no execution! We're leaving these old men with their sons! We're getting out of here!'

But Ephraim continued to aim his pistol at her. 'No, *you're* going to leave! I've waited too long for this! I've suffered too much! Before I die, before *they* die, they'll be punished!'

'And it'll happen!' Erika rushed down the steps. 'In the courts! Let the law take care of this!'

Ephraim scowled with contempt. 'The law? Where was the law in Nazi Germany? I know what the law will do! Waste time! It'll give them rights their victims never dreamed of! The trials will take forever! And in the end, instead of being executed, they'll die peacefully at home.'

'If you won't respond morally . . . !'

'*Did the SS?*'

'Then think about this! Kill them, and you'll be hunted for the rest of your life! You'll be caught and die in prison!'

'You're proving my point! The law would punish me more than them! And as for my life, it ended more than forty years ago!'

'Then you're a fool!'

Ephraim stiffened so abruptly Joseph feared he'd pull the trigger on his pistol.

'Yes, a fool!' Erika said. 'By a miracle, you survived! But instead of giving thanks to God, instead of savoring life, you savored death! God granted you a gift, and you threw it away!'

Ephraim aimed toward Halloway's father.

'No!' Joseph yelled.

Erika ran to her father. 'Tell him! Convince him! If you love me, make him stop!' She grabbed his shoulders. 'Do it! For me! I'm begging you! Tell him these monsters aren't worth destroying your lives! You've got a grandson you've seldom seen! You could watch him grow up! You could learn about innocence and maybe even regain your own! You could be young again!' Tears streamed down her face. 'For God's sake, do it! If you love me!'

Joseph felt a tightness in his chest that took his breath away. It was overpowering, frighteningly different from the pressure that had brought him here. Produced by love, not hate.

'Ephraim . . .' It was difficult to speak. 'She's right.' He sounded raspy, in pain, though the feeling was quite the opposite. 'Let's get out of here.'

Ephraim squinted down the barrel of his pistol toward Halloway's father. 'It would be so easy to squeeze the trigger. It would be so satisfying.'

'You didn't see yourself when you whipped them. You reminded me of the commandant of the work force at Treblinka.'

'Don't compare me with—!'

'You aren't relieving my nightmares. You're bringing my nightmares back. I'm ashamed that my daughter saw us doing this. Ephraim, please, I know now what I want. To forget.'

'*And let them go?*'

'What difference will it make? Killing them won't bring our loved ones back. It won't stop hate. But if you kill them, you'll be a part of hate.'

Like Erika, Ephraim had tears running down his face. 'But what's to become of me?'

Joseph took his gun away and held him. 'With luck . . . both of us . . . we'll learn to live.'

24

There were five of them now in the rented car. Drew and Arlene in front. Saul, Erika, and Joseph in back. As they drove from Halloway's estate, followed by the truck in which Ephraim brought away the rest of the team, Saul said, 'Halloway won't dare call the police. He and the others have too much to hide.'

Joseph nodded solemnly and turned to Erika. 'How did you find me?'

'I'll need the flight back to Europe to explain.'

'I'm afraid I won't be going back with you.'

She paled. 'But I assumed . . .'

'I wished I could.' Joseph held her. 'But there's much to be done. The operation has to be dismantled. Our escape procedures have to be canceled. Besides' – Joseph glanced sadly toward Ephraim in the cab of the truck behind them – 'my friends and I have a lot to talk about. To adjust to. It won't be easy. For Ephraim. For any of us.'

'Then you have to promise you'll come to visit us, to see your grandson,' Erika said.

'Of course.'

'When?' she asked quickly.

'Two weeks.'

'Thank God we got to you in time,' Drew said.

'I wonder.' Joseph brooded. 'Ephraim was right about one thing. They'll die peacefully before they're punished.'

'No. We'll contact Misha,' Erika said. 'We'll tell him what you found out. He'll force extradition. They *will* be punished.'

'I want to believe that. But on the other hand . . .' Joseph smiled at something outside the car.

'What do you mean "on the other hand"? Why are you smiling?'

'No reason.'

He'd just seen a car go past. A big car. Heading toward Halloway's estate. It was filled with Arabs. Libyans, he was sure. Angry Libyans. About to demand an explanation from Halloway and Rosenberg about the hijacked munitions shipment.

Yes, Joseph thought and hugged Erika again, justice feels satisfying.

25

They caught a night flight back to Rome. Saul slept most of the way, but an hour before landing, he felt a hand grip his shoulder. Waking, he saw that Drew had just passed him and was motioning for him to follow. Careful not to wake Erika, noticing that Arlene was still asleep as well, Saul unbuckled his seat belt and joined Drew where he waited out of sight in a narrow corridor between two rows of rest rooms.

'Before we landed,' Drew said, 'I wanted to talk with you.'

'I figured we could do that in Rome.'

'We won't have time. Arlene and I have to report to the Fraternity. We fulfilled our bargain with them. We learned why the cardinal disappeared and who was trying to sabotage the order. We're anxious to arrange for our freedom.'

'Are you sure they'll stick by their agreement?'

'They'd better. What I wanted to tell you is I'm glad everything worked out for you and your wife. The way she stepped out of that

275

mansion to face those Uzis – she's remarkable. Good luck to both of you.'

'Erika and I couldn't have solved our problems without your help.'

'And Arlene and I couldn't have made it without you and Erika. We're grateful.'

'This is difficult for me to say.'

Drew waited.

'At the start,' Saul said, 'I felt an instinctive friendship for you. Because of my dead foster brother. You don't only have the same background that Chris did. You even look like him.'

'What do you mean "at the start"? What's changed?'

'Resemblance to someone is a poor basis for a friendship. I want to be friends with you – because of what *you* are.'

Drew smiled. 'Fair enough.'

They clasped each other's shoulders.

'There's something I want you to do for me,' Drew said.

'Name it.'

'Convince Gallagher not to look for us. Tell him we've had our fill of networks. We don't want to be recruited. All we want to do is drop out of sight. To live in peace.'

'He'll get the message.'

'And something else,' Drew said. 'We can't report to the Fraternity as long as the Agency has Father Dusseault.'

Saul understood. If the Fraternity discovered that the priest was a CIA prisoner, the order would blame Drew and Arlene for jeopardizing its secrecy. Instead of gaining their freedom, Drew and Arlene would be killed.

'The last time I saw him, the priest was drugged,' Drew said. 'He doesn't know anything that happened since the night in the Vatican gardens. He doesn't know about you or that he's been questioned by the Agency. Tell Gallagher to learn what he needs to and then leave the priest near the Vatican. Father Dusseault will seek protection from the Fraternity, but after my report to them, they'll punish him for killing the cardinal and sending Avidan's group after the Nazis.'

'And in time the Agency will go after the Fraternity. It shouldn't be hard to arrange,' Saul said. 'Gallagher's already nervous about keeping the priest. He's afraid of having exceeded his authority. What he wants is information without controversy about how he got it.' Saul paused. 'Will you keep in touch?'

'As soon as Arlene and I are free.'

'Where do you plan to settle?'

'We're not sure yet. Maybe the Pyrenees.'

'How about the desert? We'd like you to stay with us in Israel.'

'I spent a year in the desert. It didn't agree with me.'

Saul grinned. 'Sure. I understand.' His grin faltered. 'It's just . . .'

'Tell me.'

'I have a favor of my own to ask.'

'Name it.'

276

'Two weeks ago, when all of this started, our village was attacked. To get at *us*. We thought it had something to do with Joseph's disappearance. Maybe someone trying to stop us from finding out why he disappeared. The problem is, none of what we've learned is related to that attack. I'm worried that someone else is out there, someone with a different reason to want to kill Erika and me. I think they'll try it again.'

Drew touched his new friend's arm. His eyes were hard with determination, yet bright with love. 'We'll be there as soon as possible. After that . . .' he sounded so much like Chris. 'I'd like to see the bastards try. Against the four of us? Let them come.'